THE COMPLETE NOVELS OF MARK TWAIN

Also by Charles Neider:

THE WHITE CITADEL, a novel

THE AUTHENTIC DEATH OF HENDRY JONES, a novel

FAMILY ALBUM, a novel

THE FROZEN SEA, a study of Franz Kafka

Charles Neider has also edited:

THE COMPETE SHORT STORIES OF MARK TWAIN

THE COMPLETE HUMOROUS SKETCHES AND TALES OF MARK TWAIN

THE COMPLETE ESSAYS OF MARK TWAIN

MARK TWAIN: LIFE AS I FIND IT

THE AUTOBIOGRAPHY OF MARK TWAIN

THE TRAVELS OF MARK TWAIN

The Complete Novels of MARK TWAIN

Edited with an introduction by

Charles Neider

Volume Two

DOUBLEDAY & COMPANY, INC.
Garden City, New York

Library of Congress Catalog Card Number 64–19239

Printed in the United States of America

CONTENTS

Volume Two

THE COMPLETE NOVELS OF MARK TWAIN

A Connecticut Yankee

in

King Arthur's Court

CONTENTS

PREFACE

The ungentle laws and customs touched upon in this tale are historical, and the episodes which are used to illustrate them are also historical. It is not pretended that these laws and customs existed in England in the sixth century; no, it is only pretended that inasmuch as they existed in the English and other civilizations of far later times, it is safe to consider that it is no libel upon the sixth century to suppose them to have been in practice in that day also. One is quite justified in inferring that wherever one of these laws or customs was lacking in that remote time, its place was competently filled by a worse one.

The question as to whether there is such a thing as divine right of kings is not settled in this book. It was found too difficult. That the executive head of a nation should be a person of lofty character and extraordinary ability, was manifest and indisputable; that none but the Deity could select that head unerringly, was also manifest and indisputable; that the Deity ought to make that selection, then, was likewise manifest and indisputable; consequently, that He does make it, as claimed, was an unavoidable deduction. I mean, until the author of this book encountered the Pompadour, and Lady Castlemaine and some other executive heads of that kind; these were found so difficult to work into the scheme, that it was judged better to take the other tack in this book, (which must be issued this fall,) and then go into training and settle the question in another book. It is of course a thing which ought to be settled, and I am not going to have anything particular to do next winter anyway.

MARK TWAIN

Hartford, July 21, 1889

A WORD OF EXPLANATION

It was in Warwick Castle that I came across the curious stranger whom I am going to talk about. He attracted me by three things: his candid simplicity, his marvelous familiarity with ancient armor, and the restfulness of his company—for he did all the talking. We fell together, as modest people will, in the tail of the herd that was being shown through, and he at once began to say things which interested me. As he talked along, softly, pleasantly, flowingly, he seemed to drift away imperceptibly out of this world and time, and into some remote era and old forgotten country; and so he gradually wove such a spell about me that I seemed to move among the spectres and shadows and dust and mold of a gray antiquity, holding speech with a relic of it! Exactly as I would speak of my nearest personal friends or enemies, or my most familiar neighbors, he spoke of Sir Bedivere, Sir Bors de Ganis, Sir Launcelot of the Lake, Sir Galahad, and all the other great names of the Table Round—and how old, old, unspeakably old and faded and dry and musty and ancient he came to look as he went on! Presently he turned to me and said, just as one might speak of the weather, or any other common matter—

"You know about transmigration of souls; do you know about transposition of epochs—and bodies?"

I said I had not heard of it. He was so little interested—just as when people speak of the weather—that he did not notice whether I made him any answer or not. There was half a moment of silence, immediately interrupted by the droning voice of the salaried cicerone:

"Ancient hauberk, date of the sixth century, time of King Arthur and the Round Table; said to have belonged to the knight Sir Sagramore le Desirous; observe the round hole through the chain-mail in the left breast; can't be accounted for; supposed to have been done with a bullet since invention of firearms—perhaps maliciously by Cromwell's soldiers."

My acquaintance smiled—not a modern smile, but one that must have gone out of general use many, many centuries ago—and muttered apparently to himself:

"Wit ye well, *I saw it done.*" Then, after a pause, added: "I did it myself."

By the time I had recovered from the electric surprise of this remark, he was gone.

All that evening I sat by my fire at the Warwick Arms, steeped in a dream of the olden time, while the rain beat upon the windows, and the wind roared about the eaves and corners. From time to time I dipped into old Sir Thomas Malory's enchanting book, and fed at its rich feast of prodigies and adventures, breathed-in the fragrance of its obsolete names, and dreamed again. Midnight being come at length, I read another tale, for a night-cap—this which here follows, to-wit:

HOW SIR LAUNCELOT SLEW TWO GIANTS, AND MADE A CASTLE FREE.

Anon withal came there upon him two great giants, well armed, all save the heads, with two horrible clubs in their hands. Sir Launcelot put his shield afore him, and put the stroke away of the one giant, and with his sword he clave his head asunder. When his fellow saw that, he ran away as he were wood,* for fear of the horrible strokes, and Sir Launcelot after him with all his might, and smote him on the shoulder, and clave him to the middle. Then Sir Launcelot went into the hall, and there came afore him three score ladies and damsels, and all kneeled unto him, and thanked God and him of their deliverance. For, sir, said they, the most part of us have been here this seven year their prisoners, and we have worked all manner of silk works for our meat, and we are all great gentlewomen born, and blessed be the time, knight, that ever thou wert born; for thou hast done the most worship that ever did knight in the world, that will we bear record, and we all pray you to tell us your name, that we may tell our friends who delivered us out of prison. Fair damsels, he said, my name is Sir Launcelot du Lake. And so he departed from them and betaught them unto God. And then he mounted upon his horse, and rode into many strange and wild countries, and through many waters and valleys, and evil was he lodged. And at the last by fortune him happened against a night to come to a fair courtelage, and therein he found an old gentlewoman that lodged him with a good will, and there he had good cheer for him and his horse. And when time was, his host brought him into a fair garret over the gate to his bed. There Sir Launcelot unarmed him, and set his harness by him, and went to bed, and anon he fell on sleep. So, soon after there came one on horseback, and knocked at the gate in great haste. And when Sir Launcelot heard this he arose up, and looked out at the window, and saw by the moon-light three knights come riding after that one man, and all three lashed on him at once with swords, and that one knight turned on them knightly again and defended him. Truly, said Sir Launcelot, yonder one knight shall I help, for it were shame for me to see three knights on one, and if he be slain I am partner of his

* Demented.—M. T.

death. And therewith he took his harness and went out at a window by a sheet down to the four knights, and then Sir Launcelot said on high, Turn you knights unto me, and leave your fighting with that knight. And then they all three left Sir Kay, and turned unto Sir Launcelot, and there began great battle, for they alight all three, and strake many strokes at Sir Launcelot, and assailed him on every side. Then Sir Kay dressed him for to have holpen Sir Launcelot. Nay, sir, said he, I will none of your help, therefore as ye will have my help let me alone with them. Sir Kay for the pleasure of the knight suffered him for to do his will, and so stood aside. And then anon within six strokes Sir Launcelot had stricken them to the earth.

And then they all three cried, Sir knight, we yield us unto you as man of might matchless. As to that, said Sir Launcelot, I will not take your yielding unto me, but so that ye yield you unto Sir Kay the seneschal, on that covenant I will save your lives and else not. Fair knight, said they, that were we loth to do; for as for Sir Kay we chased him hither, and had overcome him had ye not been; therefore, to yield us unto him it were no reason. Well, as to that, said Sir Launcelot, advise you well, for ye may choose whether ye will die or live, for an ye be yielden, it shall be unto Sir Kay. Fair knight, then they said, in saving our lives we will do as thou commandest us. Then shall ye, said Sir Launcelot, on Whitsunday next coming go unto the court of King Arthur, and there shall ye yield you unto Queen Guenever, and put you all three in her grace and mercy, and say that Sir Kay sent you thither to be her prisoners. On the morn Sir Launcelot arose early, and left Sir Kay sleeping: and Sir Launcelot took Sir Kay's armour and his shield and armed him, and so he went to the stable and took his horse, and took his leave of his host, and so he departed. Then soon after arose Sir Kay and missed Sir Launcelot: and then he espied that he had his armour and his horse. Now by my faith I know well that he will grieve some of the court of King Arthur: for on him knights will be bold, and deem that it is I, and that will beguile them; and because of his armour and shield I am sure I shall ride in peace. And then soon after departed Sir Kay, and thanked his host.

As I laid the book down there was a knock at the door, and my stranger came in. I gave him a pipe and a chair, and made him welcome. I also comforted him with a hot Scotch whiskey; gave him another one; then still another—hoping always for his story. After a fourth persuader, he drifted into it himself, in a quite simple and natural way:

THE STRANGER'S HISTORY

I am an American. I was born and reared in Hartford, in the State of Connecticut—anyway, just over the river, in the country. So I am a Yankee of the Yankees—and practical; yes, and nearly barren of sentiment, I suppose—or poetry, in other words. My father was a blacksmith, my uncle was a horse doctor, and I was both, along at first. Then I went over to the great arms factory and learned my real trade; learned all there was to it; learned to make everything; guns, revolvers, cannon, boilers, engines, all sorts of labor-saving machinery. Why, I could make anything a body wanted—anything in the world, it didn't make any difference what; and if there wasn't any quick new-fangled way to make a thing, I could invent one—and do it as easy as rolling off a log. I became head superintendent; had a couple of thousand men under me.

Well, a man like that is a man that is full of fight—that goes without saying. With a couple of thousand rough men under one, one has plenty of that sort of amusement. I had, anyway. At last I met my match, and I got my dose. It was during a misunderstanding conducted with crowbars with a fellow we used to call Hercules. He laid me out with a crusher alongside the head that made everything crack, and seemed to spring every joint in my skull and make it overlap its neighbor. Then the world went out in darkness, and I didn't feel anything more, and didn't know anything at all—at least for a while.

When I came to again, I was sitting under an oak tree, on the grass, with a whole beautiful and broad country landscape all to myself—nearly. Not entirely; for there was a fellow on a horse, looking down at me—a fellow fresh out of a picture-book. He was in old-time iron armor from head to heel, with a helmet on his head the shape of a nail-keg with slits in it; and he had a shield, and a sword, and a prodigious spear; and his horse had armor on, too, and a steel horn projecting from his forehead, and gorgeous red and green silk trappings that hung down all around him like a bed-quilt, nearly to the ground.

"Fair, sir, will ye just?" said this fellow.

"Will I which?"

"Will ye try a passage of arms for land or lady or for—"

"What are you giving me?" I said. "Get along back to your circus, or I'll report you."

Now what does this man do but fall back a couple of hundred yards and then come rushing at me as hard as he could tear, with his nail-keg bent down nearly to his horse's neck and his long spear pointed straight ahead. I saw he meant business, so I was up the tree when he arrived.

He allowed that I was his property, the captive of his spear. There was argument on his side—and the bulk of the advantage—so I judged it best to humor him. We fixed up an agreement whereby I was to go with him and he was not to hurt me. I came down, and we started away, I walking by the side of his horse. We marched comfortably along, through glades and over brooks which I could not remember to have seen before—which puzzled me and made me wonder—and yet we did not come to any circus or sign of a circus. So I gave up the idea of a circus, and concluded he was from an asylum. But we never came to any asylum—so I was up a stump, as you may say. I asked him how far we were from Hartford. He said he had never heard of the place; which I took to be a lie, but allowed it to go at that. At the end of an hour we saw a far-away town sleeping in a valley by a winding river; and beyond it on a hill, a vast gray fortress, with towers and turrets, the first I had ever seen out of a picture.

"Bridgeport?" said I, pointing.

"Camelot," said he.

My stranger had been showing signs of sleepiness. He caught himself nodding, now, and smiled one of those pathetic, obsolete smiles of his, and said:

"I find I can't go on; but come with me, I've got it all written out, and you can read it if you like."

In his chamber, he said: "First, I kept a journal; then by and by, after years, I took the journal and turned it into a book. How long ago that was!"

He handed me his manuscript, and pointed out the place where I should begin:

"Begin here—I've already told you what goes before." He was steeped in drowsiness by this time. As I went out at his door I heard him murmur sleepily: "Give you good den, fair sir."

I sat down by my fire and examined my treasure. The first part of it—the great bulk of it—was parchment, and yellow with age. I scanned a leaf particularly and saw that it was a palimpsest. Under the old dim writing of the Yankee historian appeared traces of a penmanship which was older and dimmer still—Latin words and sentences: fragments from old monkish legends, evidently. I turned to the place indicated by my stranger and began to read—as follows.

THE TALE OF THE LOST LAND

CHAPTER 1

CAMELOT

"Camelot—Camelot," said I to myself. "I don't seem to remember hearing of it before. Name of the asylum, likely."

It was a soft, reposeful summer landscape, as lovely as a dream, and as lonesome as Sunday. The air was full of the smell of flowers, and the buzzing of insects, and the twittering of birds, and there were no people, no wagons, there was no stir of life, nothing going on. The road was mainly a winding path with hoofprints in it, and now and then a faint trace of wheels on either side in the grass—wheels that apparently had a tire as broad as one's hand.

Presently a fair slip of a girl, about ten years old, with a cataract of golden hair streaming down over her shoulders, came along. Around her head she wore a hoop of flame-red poppies. It was as sweet an outfit as ever I saw, what there was of it. She walked indolently along, with a mind at rest, its peace reflected in her innocent face. The circus man paid no attention to her; didn't even seem to see her. And she—she was no more startled at his fantastic make-up than if she was used to his like every day of her life. She was going by as indifferently as she might have gone by a couple of cows; but when she happened to notice me, *then* there was a change! Up went her hands, and she was turned to stone; her mouth dropped open, her eyes stared wide and timorously, she was the picture of astonished curiosity touched with fear. And there she stood gazing, in a sort of stupefied fascination, till we turned a corner of the wood and were lost to her view. That she should be startled at me instead of at the other man, was too many for me; I couldn't make head or tail of it. And that she should seem to consider me a spectacle, and totally overlook her own merits in that respect, was another puzzling thing, and a display of magnanimity, too, that was surprising in one so young. There was food for thought here. I moved along as one in a dream.

As we approached the town, signs of life began to appear. At intervals we passed a wretched cabin, with a thatched roof, and about it small fields and garden patches in an indifferent state of cultivation. There were people, too; brawny men, with long, coarse, uncombed hair that hung down over their faces and made them look like animals. They and the women, as a rule, wore a coarse tow-linen robe that came well below the knee, and a rude sort of sandals, and many wore an iron collar. The small boys and girls were always naked; but nobody seemed to know it. All of these people stared at me, talked about me, ran into the huts and fetched out their families to gape at me; but nobody ever noticed that other fellow, except to make him humble salutation and get no response for their pains.

In the town were some substantial windowless houses of stone scattered among a wilderness of thatched cabins; the streets were mere crooked alleys, and unpaved; troops of dogs and nude children played in the sun and made life and noise; hogs roamed and rooted contentedly about, and one of them lay in a reeking wallow in the middle of the main thoroughfare and suckled her family. Presently there was a distant blare of military music; it came nearer, still nearer, and soon a noble cavalcade wound into view, glorious with plumed helmets and flashing mail and flaunting banners and rich doublets and horse-cloths and gilded spear heads; and through the muck and swine, and naked brats, and joyous dogs, and shabby huts it took its gallant way, and in its wake we followed. Followed through one winding alley and then another,—and climbing, always climbing—till at last we gained the breezy height where the huge castle stood. There was an exchange of bugle blasts; then a parley from the walls, where men-at-arms, in hauberk and morion marched back and forth with halberd at shoulder under flapping banners with the rude figure of a dragon displayed upon them; and then the great gates were flung open, the drawbridge was lowered, and the head of the cavalcade swept forward under the frowning arches; and we, following, soon found ourselves in a great paved court, with towers and turrets stretching up into the blue air on all the four sides; and all about us the dismount was going on, and much greeting and ceremony, and running to and fro, and a gay display of moving and intermingling colors, and an altogether pleasant stir and noise and confusion.

CHAPTER 2

KING ARTHUR'S COURT

The moment I got a chance I slipped aside privately and touched an ancient common looking man on the shoulder and said, in an insinuating, confidential way—

"Friend, do me a kindness. Do you belong to the asylum, or are you just here on a visit or something like that?"

He looked me over stupidly, and said—

"Marry, fair sir, me seemeth—"

"That will do," I said; "I reckon you are a patient."

I moved away, cogitating, and at the same time keeping an eye out for any chance passenger in his right mind that might come along and give me some light. I judged I had found one, presently; so I drew him aside and said in his ear—

"If I could see the head keeper a minute—only just a minute—"

"Prithee do not let me."

"Let you *what?*"

"*Hinder* me, then, if the word please thee better." Then he went on to say he was an under-cook and could not stop to gossip, though he would like it another time; for it would comfort his very liver to know where I got my clothes. As he started away he pointed and said yonder was one who was idle enough for my purpose, and was seeking me besides, no doubt. This was an airy slim boy in shrimp-colored tights that made him look like a forked carrot; the rest of his gear was blue silk and dainty laces and ruffles; and he had long yellow curls, and wore a plumed pink satin cap tilted complacently over his ear. By his look, he was good-natured; by his gait, he was satisfied with himself. He was pretty enough to frame. He arrived, looked me over with a smiling and impudent curiosity; said he had come for me, and informed me that he was a page.

"Go 'long," I said; "you ain't more than a paragraph."

It was pretty severe, but I was nettled. However, it never phazed him; he didn't appear to know he was hurt. He began to talk and laugh, in happy, thoughtless, boyish fashion, as we walked along, and made himself old friends with me at once; asked me all sorts of questions about myself and about my clothes, but never waited for an answer—always chattered straight ahead, as if he didn't know he had asked a question and wasn't expecting any reply, until at last he happened to mention that he was born in the beginning of the year 513.

It made the cold chills creep over me! I stopped, and said, a little faintly:

"Maybe I didn't hear you just right. Say it again—and say it slow. What year was it?"

"513."

"513! You don't look it! Come, my boy, I am a stranger and friendless: be honest and honorable with me. Are you in your right mind?"

He said he was.

"Are these other people in their right minds?"

He said they were.

"And this isn't an asylum? I mean, it isn't a place where they cure crazy people?"

He said it wasn't.

"Well, then," I said, "either I am a lunatic, or something just as awful has happened. Now tell me, honest and true, where am I?"

"In King Arthur's Court."

I waited a minute, to let that idea shudder its way home, and then said:

"And according to your notions, what year is it now?"

"528—nineteenth of June."

I felt a mournful sinking at the heart, and muttered: "I shall never see my friends again—never, never again. They will not be born for more than thirteen hundred years yet."

I seemed to believe the boy, I didn't know why. *Something* in me seemed to believe him—my consciousness, as you may say; but my reason didn't. My reason straightway began to clamor; that was natural. I didn't know how to go about satisfying it, because I knew that the testimony of men wouldn't serve—my reason would say they were lunatics, and throw out their evidence. But all of a sudden I stumbled on the very thing, just by luck. I knew that the only total eclipse of the sun in the first half of the sixth century occurred on the 21st of June, A. D. 528, O. S., and began at 3 minutes after 12 noon. I also knew that no total eclipse of the sun was due in what to *me* was the present year—*i. e.*, 1879. So, if I could keep my anxiety and curiosity from eating the heart out of me for forty-eight hours, I should then find out for certain whether this boy was telling me the truth or not.

Wherefore, being a practical Connecticut man, I now shoved this whole problem clear out of my mind till its appointed day and hour should come, in order that I might turn all my attention to the circumstances of the present moment, and be alert and ready to make the most out of them that could be made. One thing at a time, is my motto —and just play that thing for all it is worth, even if it's only two pair and a jack. I made up my mind to two things; if it was still the nineteenth century and I was among lunatics and couldn't get away, I would presently boss that asylum or know the reason why; and if on the other hand it was really the sixth century, all right, I didn't want any softer thing: I would boss the whole country inside of three months; for I judged I would have the start of the best-educated man in the kingdom by a matter of thirteen hundred years and upwards. I'm not a man to waste time after my mind's made up and there's work on hand; so I said to the page—

"Now, Clarence, my boy—if that might happen to be your name—I'll get you to post me up a little if you don't mind. What is the name of that apparition that brought me here?"

"My master and thine? That is the good knight and great lord Sir Kay the Seneschal, foster brother to our liege the king."

"Very good; go on, tell me everything."

He made a long story of it; but the part that had immediate interest for me was this. He said I was Sir Kay's prisoner, and that in the due course of custom I would be flung into a dungeon and left there on scant commons until my friends ransomed me—unless I chanced to rot, first. I saw that the last chance had the best show, but I didn't waste any bother about that; time was too precious. The page said, further, that dinner was about ended in the great hall by this time, and that as soon as the sociability and the heavy drinking should begin, Sir Kay would have me in and exhibit me before King Arthur and his illustrious knights seated at the Table Round, and would brag about his exploit in capturing me, and would probably exaggerate the facts a little, but it wouldn't be good form for me to correct him, and not over safe, either; and when I was done being exhibited, then ho for the dungeon; but he, Clarence, would find a way to come and see me every now and then, and cheer me up, and help me get word to my friends.

Get word to my friends! I thanked him; I couldn't do less; and about this time a lackey came to say I was wanted; so Clarence led me in and took me off to one side and sat down by me.

Well, it was a curious kind of spectacle, and interesting. It was an immense place, and rather naked—yes, and full of loud contrasts. It was very, very lofty; so lofty that the banners depending from the arched beams and girders away up there floated in a sort of twilight; there was a stone-railed gallery at each end, high up, with musicians in the one, and women, clothed in stunning colors, in the other. The floor was of big stone flags laid in black and white squares, rather battered by age and use, and needing repair. As to ornament, there wasn't any, strictly speaking; though on the walls hung some huge tapestries which were probably taxed as works of art; battle-pieces, they were, with horses shaped like those which children cut out of paper or create in gingerbread; with men on them in scale armor whose scales are represented by round holes—so that the man's coat looks as if it had been done with a biscuit-punch. There was a fireplace big enough to camp in; and its projecting sides and hood, of carved and pillared stone-work, had the look of a cathedral door. Along the walls stood men-at-arms, in breastplate and morion, with halberds for their only weapon—rigid as statues; and that is what they looked like.

In the middle of this groined and vaulted public square was an oaken table which they called the Table Round. It was as large as a circus ring; and around it sat a great company of men dressed in such various and splendid colors that it hurt one's eyes to look at them. They wore their plumed hats, right along, except that whenever one addressed himself directly to the king, he lifted his hat a trifle just as he was beginning his remark.

Mainly they were drinking—from entire ox horns; but a few were still munching bread or gnawing beef bones. There was about an average of two dogs to one man; and these sat in expectant attitudes till a spent bone was flung to them, and then they went for it by brigades and divisions, with a rush, and there ensued a fight which filled the prospect with a tumultuous chaos of plunging heads and bodies and flashing tails, and the storm of howlings and barkings deafened all speech for the time; but that was no matter, for the dog-fight was always a bigger interest anyway; the men rose, sometimes, to observe it the better and bet on it, and the ladies and the musicians stretched themselves out over their balusters with the same object; and all broke into delighted ejaculations from time to time. In the end, the winning dog stretched himself out comfortably with his bone between his paws, and proceeded to growl over it, and gnaw it, and grease the floor with it, just as fifty others were already doing; and the rest of the court resumed their previous industries and entertainments.

As a rule the speech and behavior of these people were gracious and courtly; and I noticd that they were good and serious listeners when anybody was telling anything—I mean in a dog-fightless interval. And plainly, too, they were a childlike and innocent lot; telling lies of the stateliest pattern with a most gentle and winning naivety, and ready and willing to listen to anybody else's lie, and believe it, too. It was hard to associate them with anything cruel or dreadful; and yet they dealt in tales of blood and suffering with a guileless relish that made me almost forget to shudder.

I was not the only prisoner present. There were twenty or more. Poor devils, many of them were maimed, hacked, carved, in a frightful way; and their hair, their faces, their clothing, were caked with black and stiffened drenchings of blood. They were suffering sharp physical pain, of course; and weariness, and hunger and thirst, no doubt; and at least none had given them the comfort of a wash, or even the poor charity of a lotion for their wounds; yet you never heard them utter a moan or a groan, or saw them show any sign of restlessness, or any disposition to complain. The thought was forced upon me: "The rascals—*they* have served other people so in their day; it being their own turn, now, they were not expecting any better treatment than this; so their philosophical bearing is not an outcome of mental training, intellectual fortitude, reasoning; it is mere animal training; they are white Indians."

CHAPTER 3

KNIGHTS OF THE TABLE ROUND

Mainly the Round Table talk was monologues—narrative accounts of the adventures in which these prisoners were captured and their friends and backers killed and stripped of their steeds and armor. As a general thing—as far as I could make out—these murderous adventures were not forays undertaken to avenge injuries, nor to settle old disputes or sudden fallings out; no, as a rule they were simply duels between strangers—duels between people who had never even been introduced to each other, and between whom existed no cause of offense whatever. Many a time I had seen a couple of boys, strangers, meet by chance, and say simultaneously, "I can lick you," and go at it on the spot; but I had always imagined until now, that that sort of thing belonged to children only, and was a sign and mark of childhood; but here were these big boobies sticking to it and taking pride in it clear up into full age and beyond. Yet there was something very engaging about these great simple-hearted creatures, something attractive and lovable. There did not seem to be brains enough in the entire nursery, so to speak, to bait a fish-hook with; but you didn't seem to mind that, after a little, because you soon saw that brains were not needed in a society like that, and, indeed would have marred it, hindered it, spoiled its symmetry—perhaps rendered its existence impossible.

There was a fine manliness observable in almost every face; and in some a certain loftiness and sweetness that rebuked your belittling criticisms and stilled them. A most noble benignity and purity reposed in the countenance of him they called Sir Galahad, and likewise in the king's also; and there was majesty and greatness in the giant frame and high bearing of Sir Launcelot of the Lake.

There was presently an incident which centred the general interest upon this Sir Launcelot. At a sign from a sort of master of ceremonies, six or eight of the prisoners rose and came forward in a body and knelt on the floor and lifted up their hands toward the ladies' gallery and begged the grace of a word with the queen. The most conspicuously situated lady in that massed flower-bed of feminine show and finery inclined her head by way of assent, and then the spokesman of the prisoners delivered himself and his fellows into her hands for free pardon, ransom, captivity or death, as she in her good pleasure might elect; and this, as he said, he was doing by command of Sir Kay the Seneschal, whose prisoners they were, he having vanquished them by his single might and prowess in sturdy conflict in the field.

Surprise and astonishment flashed from face to face all over the house; the queen's gratified smile faded out at the name of Sir Kay, and she looked disappointed; and the page whispered in my ear with an accent and manner expressive of extravagant derision—

"Sir *Kay*, forsooth! Oh, call me pet names, dearest, call me a marine! In twice a thousand years shall the unholy invention of man labor at odds to beget the fellow to this majestic lie!"

Every eye was fastened with severe inquiry upon Sir Kay. But he was equal to the occasion. He got up and played his hand like a major —and took every trick. He said he would state the case, exactly according to the facts; he would tell the simple straightforward tale, without comment of his own; "and then," said he, "if ye find glory and honor due, ye will give it unto him who is the mightiest man of his hands that ever bare shield or strake with sword in the ranks of Christian battle—even him that sitteth there!" and he pointed to Sir Launcelot. Ah, he fetched them; it was a rattling good stroke. Then he went on and told how Sir Launcelot, seeking adventures, some brief time gone by, 22 killed seven giants at one sweep of his sword, and set a hundred and forty-two captive maidens free; and then went further, still seeking adventures, and found him (Sir Kay) fighting a desperate fight against nine foreign knights, and straightway took the battle solely into his own hands, and conquered the nine; and that night Sir Launcelot rose quietly, and dressed him in Sir Kay's armor and took Sir Kay's horse and gat him away into distant lands, and vanquished sixteen knights in one pitched battle and thirty-four in another; and all these and the former nine he made to swear that about Whitsuntide they would ride to Arthur's court and yield them to Queen Guenever's hands as captives of Sir Kay the Seneschal, spoil of his knightly prowess; and now here were these half dozen, and the rest would be along as soon as they might be healed of their desperate wounds.

Well, it was touching to see the queen blush and smile, and look embarrassed and happy, and fling furtive glances at Sir Launcelot that would have got him shot in Arkansas, to a dead certainty.

Everybody praised the valor and magnanimity of Sir Launcelot; and as for me, I was perfectly amazed, that one man, all by himself, should have been able to beat down and capture such battalions of practiced fighters. I said as much to Clarence; but this mocking featherhead only said—

"An Sir Kay had had time to get another skin of sour wine into him, ye had seen the accompt doubled."

I looked at the boy in sorrow; and as I looked I saw the cloud of a deep despondency settle upon his countenance. I followed the direction of his eye, and saw that a very old and white-bearded man, clothed in a flowing black gown, had risen and was standing at the table upon unsteady legs, and feebly swaying his ancient head and surveying the company with his watery and wandering eye. The same suffering look that was in the page's face was observable in all the faces around—the look of dumb creatures who know that they must endure and make no moan.

"Marry, we shall have it again," sighed the boy; "that same old weary tale that he hath told a thousand times in the same words, and that he *will* tell till he dieth, every time he hath gotten his barrel full and feeleth his exaggeration-mill a-working. Would God I had died or I saw this day!"

"Who is it?"

"Merlin, the mighty liar and magician, perdition singe him for the weariness he worketh with his one tale! But that men fear him for that he hath the storms and the lightnings and all the devils that be in hell at his beck and call, they would have dug his entrails out these many years ago to get at that tale and squelch it. He telleth it always in the third person, making believe he is too modest to glorify himself—maledictions light upon him, misfortune be his dole! Good friend, prithee call me for evensong."

The boy nestled himself upon my shoulder and pretended to go to sleep. The old man began his tale; and presently the lad was asleep in reality; so also were the dogs, and the court, the lackeys, and the files of men-at-arms. The droning voice droned on; a soft snoring arose on all sides and supported it like a deep and subdued accompaniment of wind instruments. Some heads were bowed upon folded arms, some lay back with open mouths that issued unconscious music; the flies buzzed and bit, unmolested, the rats swarmed softly out from a hundred holes, and pattered about, and made themselves at home everywhere; and one of them sat up like a squirrel on the king's head and held a bit of cheese in its hands and nibbled it, and dribbled the crumbs in the king's face with naïve and impudent irreverence. It was a tranquil scene, and restful to the weary eye and the jaded spirit.

This was the old man's tale. He said:

"Right so the king and Merlin departed, and went until an hermit that was a good man and a great leech. So the hermit searched all his wounds and gave him good salves; so the king was there three days, and then were his wounds well amended that he might ride and go, and so departed. And as they rode, Arthur said, I have no sword. No force,* said Merlin, hereby is a sword that shall be yours and I may. So they rode till they came to a lake, the which was a fair water and broad, and in the midst of the lake Arthur was ware of an arm clothed in white samite, that held a fair sword in that hand. Lo, said Merlin, yonder is that sword that I spake of. With that they saw a damsel going upon the lake. What damsel is that? said Arthur. That is the Lady of the lake, said Merlin; and within that lake is a rock, and therein is as fair a place as any on earth, and richly beseen, and this damsel will come to you anon, and then speak ye fair to her that she will give you that sword. Anon withal came the damsel unto Arthur and saluted him, and he her again. Damsel, said Arthur, what sword is that, that yonder the arm holdeth above the water? I would it were mine, for I have no sword. Sir Arthur King, said the damsel, that sword is mine, and if ye will give me a gift when I ask it you, ye shall have it. By my faith, said Arthur, I will give you what gift ye will ask. Well, said the damsel,

* No matter.—M. T.

go ye into yonder barge and row yourself to the sword, and take it and the scabbard with you, and I will ask my gift when I see my time. So Sir Arthur and Merlin alight, and tied their horses to two trees, and so they went into the ship, and when they came to the sword that the hand held, Sir Arthur took it up by the handles, and took it with him. And the arm and the hand went under the water; and so they came unto the land and rode forth. And then Sir Arthur saw a rich pavilion. What signifieth yonder pavilion? It is the knight's pavilion, said Merlin, that ye fought with last, Sir Pellinore, but he is out, he is not there; he hath ado with a knight of yours, that hight Egglame, and they have fought together, but at the last Egglame fled, and else he had been dead, and he hath chased him even to Carlion, and we shall meet with him anon in the highway. That is well said, said Arthur, now have I a sword, now will I wage battle with him, and be avenged on him. Sir, ye shall not so, said Merlin, for the knight is weary of fighting and chasing, so that ye shall have no worship to have ado with him; also, he will not lightly be matched of one knight living; and therefore it is my counsel, let him pass, for he shall do you good service in short time, and his sons, after his days. Also ye shall see that day in short space ye shall be right glad to give him your sister to wed. When I see him, I will do as ye advise me, said Arthur. Then Sir Arthur looked on the sword, and liked it passing well. Whether liketh you better, said Merlin, the sword or the scabbard? Me liketh better the sword, said Arthur. Ye are more unwise, said Merlin, for the scabbard is worth ten of the sword, for while ye have the scabbard upon you ye shall never lose no blood, be ye never so sore wounded; therefore, keep well the scabbard always with you. So they rode unto Carlion, and by the way they met with Sir Pellinore; but Merlin had done such a craft that Pellinore saw not Arthur, and he passed by without any words. I marvel, said Arthur, that the knight would not speak. Sir, said Merlin, he saw you not; for and he had seen you ye had not lightly departed. So they came unto Carlion, whereof his knights were passing glad. And when they heard of his adventures they marveled that he would jeopard his person so alone. But all men of worship said it was merry to be under such a chieftain that would put his person in adventure as other poor knights did."

CHAPTER 4

SIR DINADAN THE HUMORIST

It seemed to me that this quaint lie was most simply and beautifully told; but then I had heard it only once, and that makes a difference; it was pleasant to the others when it was fresh, no doubt.

Sir Dinadan the Humorist was the first to awake, and he soon roused the rest with a practical joke of a sufficiently poor quality. He tied some metal mugs to a dog's tail and turned him loose, and he tore around and around the place in a frenzy of fright, with all the other dogs bellowing after him and battering and crashing against everything that came in their way and making altogether a chaos of confusion and a most deafening din and turmoil; at which every man and woman of the multitude laughed till the tears flowed, and some fell out of their chairs and wallowed on the floor in ecstasy. It was just like so many children. Sir Dinadan was so proud of his exploit that he could not keep from telling over and over again, to weariness, how the immortal idea happened to occur to him; and as is the way with humorists of his breed, he was still laughing at it after everybody else had got through. He was so set up that he concluded to make a speech—of course a humorous speech. I think I never heard so many old played-out jokes strung together in my life. He was worse than the minstrels, worse than the clown in the circus. It seemed peculiarly sad to sit here, thirteen hundred years before I was born and listen again to poor, flat, worm-eaten jokes that had given me the dry gripes when I was a boy thirteen hundred years afterwards. It about convinced me that there isn't any such thing as a new joke possible. Everybody laughed at these antiquities—but then they always do; I had noticed that, centuries later. However, of course the scoffer didn't laugh—I mean the boy. No, he scoffed; there wasn't anything he wouldn't scoff at. He said the most of Sir Dinadan's jokes were rotten and the rest were petrified. I said "petrified" was good; as I believed, myself, that the only right way to classify the majestic ages of some of those jokes was by geologic periods. But that neat idea hit the boy in a blank place, for geology hadn't been invented yet. However, I made a note of the remark, and calculated to educate the commonwealth up to it if I pulled through. It is no use to throw a good thing away merely because the market isn't ripe yet.

Now Sir Kay arose and began to fire up on his history-mill, with me for fuel. It was time for me to feel serious, and I did. Sir Kay told how he had encountered me in a far land of barbarians, who all wore the same ridiculous garb that I did—a garb that was a work of enchantment, and intended to make the wearer secure from hurt by human hands. However, he had nullified the force of the enchantment by prayer, and had killed my thirteen knights in a three-hours' battle, and taken me prisoner, sparing my life in order that so strange a curiosity as I was might be exhibited to the wonder and admiration of the king and the court. He spoke of me all the time, in the blandest way, as "this prodigious giant," and "this horrible sky-towering monster," and "this tusked and taloned man-devouring ogre;" and everybody took in all this bosh in the naïvest way, and never smiled or seemed to notice that there was any discrepancy between these watered statistics and me. He said that in trying to escape from him I sprang into the top of a tree two hundred cubits high at a single bound, but he dislodged me with a stone the size of a cow, which "all-to brast" the most of my bones, and then swore me to appear at Arthur's court for sentence. He ended by condemning me to die at noon on the 21st; and was so little concerned about it that he stopped to yawn before he named the date.

I was in a dismal state by this time; indeed, I was hardly enough in my right mind to keep the run of a dispute that sprung up as to how I had better be killed, the possibility of the killing being doubted by some, because of the enchantment in my clothes. And yet it was nothing but an ordinary suit of fifteen-dollar slop-shops. Still, I was sane enough to notice this detail, to-wit: many of the terms used in the most matter-of-fact way by this great assemblage of the first ladies and gentlemen in the land would have made a Comanche blush. Indelicacy is too mild a term to convey the idea. However, I had read "Tom Jones," and "Roderick Random," and other books of that kind, and knew that the highest and first ladies and gentlemen in England had remained little or no cleaner in their talk, and in the morals and conduct which such talk implies, clear up to a hundred years ago; in fact clear into our own nineteenth century—in which century, broadly speaking, the earliest samples of the real lady and real gentleman discoverable in English history—or in European history, for that matter—may be said to have made their appearance. Suppose Sir Walter, instead of putting the conversations into the mouths of his characters, had allowed the characters to speak for themselves? We should have had talk from Rachel and Ivanhoe and the soft lady Rowena which would embarrass a tramp in our day. However, to the unconsciously indelicate all things are delicate. King Arthur's people were not aware that they were indecent, and I had presence of mind enough not to mention it.

They were so troubled about my enchanted clothes that they were mightily relieved, at last, when old Merlin swept the difficulty away for them with a common-sense hint. He asked them why they were so dull—why didn't it occur to them to strip me. In half a minute I was as naked as a pair of tongs! And dear, dear, to think of it: I was the only embarrassed person there. Everybody discussed me; and did it as unconcernedly as if I had been a cabbage. Queen Guenever was as naïvely interested as the rest, and said she had never seen anybody with legs just like mine before. It was the only compliment I got—if it was a compliment.

Finally I was carried off in one direction, and my perilous clothes in another. I was shoved into a dark and narrow cell in a dungeon, with some scant remnants for dinner, some moldy straw for a bed, and no end of rats for company.

CHAPTER 5

AN INSPIRATION

I was so tired that even my fears were not able to keep me awake long.

When I next came to myself, I seemed to have been asleep a very long time. My first thought was, "Well, what an astonishing dream I've had! I reckon I've waked only just in time to keep from being hanged or drowned or burned, or something. . . . I'll nap again till the whistle blows, and then I'll go down to the arms factory and have it out with Hercules."

But just then I heard the harsh music of rusty chains and bolts, a light flashed in my eyes, and that butterfly, Clarence, stood before me! I gasped with surprise; my breath almost got away from me.

"What!" I said, "you here yet? Go along with the rest of the dream! scatter!"

But he only laughed, in his light-hearted way, and fell to making fun of my sorry plight.

"All right," I said resignedly, "let the dream go on; I'm in no hurry."

"Prithee what dream?"

"What dream? Why, the dream that I am in Arthur's court—a person who never existed; and that I am talking to you, who are nothing but a work of the imagination."

"Oh, la, indeed! and is it a dream that you're to be burned tomorrow? Ho-ho—answer me that!"

The shock that went through me was distressing. I now began to reason that my situation was in the last degree serious, dream or no dream; for I knew by past experience of the life-like intensity of dreams, that to be burned to death, even in a dream, would be very far from being a jest, and was a thing to be avoided, by any means, fair or foul, that I could contrive. So I said beseechingly:

"Ah, Clarence, good boy, only friend I've got,—for you *are* my friend, aren't you?—don't fail me; help me to devise some way of escaping from this place!"

"Now do but hear thyself! Escape? Why, man, the corridors are in guard and keep of men-at-arms."

"No doubt, no doubt. But how many, Clarence? Not many, I hope?"

"Full a score. One may not hope to escape." After a pause—hesitatingly: "and there be other reasons—and weightier."

"Other ones? What are they?"

"Well, they say—oh, but I daren't, indeed I daren't!"

"Why, poor lad, what is the matter? Why do you blench? Why do you tremble so?"

"Oh, in sooth, there is need! I do want to tell you, but—"

"Come, come, be brave, be a man—speak out, there's a good lad!"

He hesitated, pulled one way by desire, the other way by fear; then he stole to the door and peeped out, listening; and finally crept close to me and put his mouth to my ear and told me his fearful news in a whisper, and with all the cowering apprehension of one who was venturing upon awful ground and speaking of things whose very mention might be freighted with death.

"Merlin, in his malice, has woven a spell about this dungeon, and there bides not the man in these kingdoms that would be desperate enough to essay to cross its lines with you! Now God pity me, I have told it! Ah, be kind to me, be merciful to a poor boy who means thee well; for an thou betray me I am lost!"

I laughed the only really refreshing laugh I had had for some time; and shouted—

"Merlin has wrought a spell! *Merlin*, forsooth! That cheap old humbug, that maundering old ass? Bosh, pure bosh, the silliest bosh in the world! Why, it does seem to me that of all the childish, idiotic, chuckle-headed, chicken-livered superstitions that ev—oh, damn Merlin!"

But Clarence had slumped to his knees before I had half finished, and he was like to go out of his mind with fright.

"Oh, beware! These are awful words! Any moment these walls may crumble upon us if you say such things. Oh call them back before it is too late!"

Now this strange exhibition gave me a good idea and set me to thinking. If everybody about here was so honestly and sincerely afraid of Merlin's pretended magic as Clarence was, certainly a superior man like me ought to be shrewd enough to contrive some way to take advantage of such a state of things. I went on thinking, and worked out a plan. Then I said:

"Get up. Pull yourself together; look me in the eye. Do you know why I laughed?"

"No—but for our blessed Lady's sake, do it no more."

"Well, I'll tell you why I laughed. Because I'm a magician myself."

"Thou!" The boy recoiled a step, and caught his breath, for the thing hit him rather sudden; but the aspect which he took on was very, very respectful. I took quick note of that; it indicated that a humbug didn't need to have a reputation in this asylum; people stood ready to take him at his word, without that. I resumed:

"I've known Merlin seven hundred years, and he—"

"Seven hun—"

"Don't interrupt me. He has died and come alive again thirteen times, and traveled under a new name every time: Smith, Jones, Robinson, Jackson, Peters, Haskins, Merlin—a new alias every time he turns up. I knew him in Egypt three hundred years ago; I knew him in India five hundred years ago—he is always blethering around in my way, everywhere I go; he makes me tired. He don't amount to shucks, as a magician; knows some of the old common tricks, but has never got beyond the rudiments, and never will. He is well enough for the provinces—one-night stands and that sort of thing, you know—but dear me, *he* oughtn't to set up for an expert—anyway not where there's a real artist. Now look here, Clarence, I am going to stand your friend, right along, and in return you must be mine. I want you to do me a favor. I want you to get word to the king that I am a magician myself—and the Supreme Grand High-yu-Muckamuck and head of the tribe, at that; and I want him to be made to understand that I am just quietly arranging a little calamity here that will make the fur fly in these realms if Sir Kay's project is carried out and any harm comes to me. Will you get that to the king for me?"

The poor boy was in such a state that he could hardly answer me. It was pitiful to see a creature so terrified, so unnerved, so demoralized. But he promised everything; and on my side he made me promise over and over again that I would remain his friend, and never turn against him or cast any enchantments upon him. Then he worked his way out, staying himself with his hand along the wall, like a sick person.

Presently this thought occurred to me: how heedless I have been! When the boy gets calm, he will wonder why a great magician like me should have begged a boy like him to help me get out of this place; he will put this and that together, and will see that I am a humbug.

I worried over that heedless blunder for an hour, and called myself a great many hard names, meantime. But finally it occurred to me all of a sudden that these animals didn't reason; that *they* never put this and that together; that all their talk showed that they didn't know a discrepancy when they saw it. I was at rest, then.

But as soon as one is at rest, in this world, off he goes on something else to worry about. It occurred to me that I had made another blunder: I had sent the boy off to alarm his betters with a threat—I intending to invent a calamity at my leisure; now the people who are the readiest and eagerest and willingest to swallow miracles are the very ones who are the hungriest to see you perform them; suppose I should be called on for a sample? Suppose I should be asked to name my calamity? Yes, I had made a blunder; I ought to have invented my calamity first. "What shall I do? what can I say, to gain a little time?" I was in trouble again; in the deepest kind of trouble: . . . "There's a footstep!—they're coming. If I had only just a moment to think. . . . . Good, I've got it. I'm all right."

You see, it was the eclipse. It came into my mind, in the nick of time, how Columbus, or Cortez, or one of those people, played an eclipse as a saving trump once, on some savages, and I saw my chance. I could play it myself, now; and it wouldn't be any plagiarism, either, because I should get it in nearly a thousand years ahead of those parties.

Clarence came in, subdued, distressed, and said:

"I hasted the message to our liege the king, and straightway he had me to his presence. He was frighted even to the marrow, and was minded to give order for your instant enlargement, and that you be clothed in fine raiment and lodged as befitted one so great; but then came Merlin and spoiled all; for he persuaded the king that you are mad, and know not whereof you speak; and said your threat is but foolishness and idle vaporing. They disputed long, but in the end, Merlin, scoffing, said, 'Wherefore hath he not *named* his brave calamity? Verily it is because he cannot.' This thrust did in a most sudden sort close the king's mouth, and he could offer naught to turn the argument; and so, reluctant, and full loth to do you the discourtesy, he yet prayeth you to consider his perplexed case, as noting how the matter stands, and name the calamity—if so be you have determined the nature of it and the time of its coming. Oh, prithee delay not; to delay at such a time were to double and treble the perils that already compass thee about. Oh, be thou wise—name the calamity!"

I allowed silence to accumulate while I got my impressiveness together, and then said:

"How long have I been shut up in this hole?"

"Ye were shut up when yesterday was well spent. It is 9 of the morning now."

"No! Then I have slept well, sure enough. Nine in the morning now! And yet it is the very complexion of midnight, to a shade. This is the 20th, then?"

"The 20th—yes."

"And I am to be burned alive to-morrow." The boy shuddered.

"At what hour?"

"At high noon."

"Now then, I will tell you what to say." I paused, and stood over that cowering lad a whole minute in awful silence; then in a voice deep, measured, charged with doom, I began, and rose by dramatically graded stages to my colossal climax, which I delivered in as sublime and noble a way as ever I did such a thing in my life: "Go back and tell the king that at that hour I will smother the whole world in the dead blackness of midnight; I will blot out the sun, and he shall never shine again; the fruits of the earth shall rot for lack of light and warmth, and the peoples of the earth shall famish and die, to the last man!"

I had to carry the boy out myself, he sunk into such a collapse. I handed him over to the soldiers, and went back.

CHAPTER 6

THE ECLIPSE

In the stillness and the darkness, realization soon began to supplement knowledge. The mere knowledge of a fact is pale; but when you come to *realize* your fact, it takes on color. It is all the difference between hearing of a man being stabbed to the heart, and seeing it done. In the stillness and the darkness, the knowledge that I was in deadly danger took to itself deeper and deeper meaning all the time; a something which was realization crept inch by inch through my veins and turned me cold.

But it is a blessed provision of nature that at times like these, as soon as a man's mercury has got down to a certain point there comes a revulsion, and he rallies. Hope springs up, and cheerfulness along with it, and then he is in good shape to do something for himself, if anything can be done. When my rally came, it came with a bound. I said to myself that my eclipse would be sure to save me, and make me the greatest man in the kingdom besides; and straightway my mercury went up to the top of the tube, and my solicitudes all vanished. I was as happy a man as there was in the world. I was even impatient for to-morrow to come, I so wanted to gather-in that great triumph and be the centre of all the nation's wonder and reverence. Besides, in a business way it would be the making of me; I knew that.

Meantime there was one thing which had got pushed into the background of my mind. That was the half-conviction that when the nature of my proposed calamity should be reported to those superstitious people, it would have such an effect that they would want to compromise. So, by and by when I heard footsteps coming, that thought was recalled to me, and I said to myself, "As sure as anything, it's the compromise. Well, if it is good, all right, I will accept; but if it isn't, I mean to stand my ground and play my hand for all it is worth."

The door opened, and some men-at-arms appeared. The leader said—

"The stake is ready. Come!"

The stake! The strength went out of me, and I almost fell down. It is hard to get one's breath at such a time, such lumps come into one's throat, and such gaspings; but as soon as I could speak, I said:

"But this is a mistake—the execution is to-morrow."

"Order changed; been set forward a day. Haste thee!"

I was lost. There was no help for me. I was dazed, stupefied; I had no command over myself; I only wandered purposelessly about, like one out of his mind; so the soldiers took hold of me, and pulled me along with them, out of the cell and along the maze of underground corridors, and finally into the fierce glare of daylight and the upper world. As we stepped into the vast inclosed court of the castle I got a shock; for the first thing I saw was the stake, standing in the centre, and near it the piled fagots and a monk. On all four sides of the court the seated multitudes rose rank above rank, forming sloping terraces that were rich with color. The king and the queen sat in their thrones, the most conspicuous figures there, of course.

To note all this, occupied but a second. The next second Clarence had slipped from some place of concealment and was pouring news into my ear, his eyes beaming with triumph and gladness. He said:

"'Tis through *me* the change was wrought! And main hard have I worked to do it, too. But when I revealed to them the calamity in store, and saw how mighty was the terror it did engender, then saw I also that this was the time to strike! Wherefore I diligently pretended, unto this and that and the other one, that your power against the sun could not reach its full until the morrow; and so if any would save the sun and the world, you must be slain to-day, whilst your enchantments are but in the weaving and lack potency. Odsbodikins, it was but a dull lie, a most indifferent invention, but you should have seen them seize it and swallow it, in the frenzy of their fright, as it were salvation sent from heaven; and all the while was I laughing in my sleeve the one moment, to see them so cheaply deceived, and glorifying God the next, that He was content to let the meanest of His creatures be His instrument to the saving of thy life. Ah, how happy has the matter sped! You will not need to do the sun a *real* hurt—ah, forget not that, on your soul forget it not! Only make a little darkness—only the littlest little darkness, mind, and cease with that. It will be sufficient. They will see that I spoke falsely,—being ignorant, as they will fancy—and with the falling of the first shadow of that darkness you shall see them go mad with fear; and they will set you free and make you great! Go to thy triumph, now! But remember—ah, good friend, I implore thee remember my supplication, and do the blessed sun no hurt. For *my* sake, thy true friend."

I choked out some words through my grief and misery; as much as to say I would spare the sun; for which the lad's eyes paid me back with such deep and loving gratitude that I had not the heart to tell him his good-hearted foolishness had ruined me and sent me to my death.

As the soldiers assisted me across the court the stillness was so profound that if I had been blindfold I should have supposed I was in a solitude instead of walled in by four thousand people. There was not a movement perceptible in those masses of humanity; they were as rigid as stone images, and as pale; and dread sat upon every countenance. This hush continued while I was being chained to the stake; it still continued while the fagots were carefully and tediously piled about my ankles, my knees, my thighs, my body. Then there was a pause, and a deeper hush, if possible, and a man knelt down at my feet with a blazing torch; the multitude strained forward, gazing, and parting slightly from their seats without knowing it; the monk raised his hands above my head, and his eyes toward the blue sky, and began some words in Latin; in this attitude he droned on and on, a little while, and then stopped. I waited two or three moments: then looked up; he was standing there petrified. With a common impulse the multitude rose slowly up and stared into the sky. I followed their eyes; as sure as guns, there was my eclipse beginning! The life went boiling through my veins; I was a new man! The rim of black spread slowly into the sun's disk, my heart beat higher and higher, and still the assemblage and the priest stared into the sky, motionless. I knew that this gaze would be turned upon me, next. When it was, I was ready. I was in one of the most grand attitudes I ever struck, with my arm stretched up pointing to the sun. It was a noble effect. You could *see* the shudder sweep the mass like a wave. Two shouts rang out, one close upon the heels of the other:

"Apply the torch!"

"I forbid it!"

The one was from Merlin, the other from the king. Merlin started from his place—to apply the torch himself, I judged. I said:

"Stay where you are. If any man moves—even the king—before I give him leave, I will blast him with thunder, I will consume him with lightnings!"

The multitude sank meekly into their seats, and I was just expecting they would. Merlin hesitated a moment or two, and I was on pins and needles during that little while. Then he sat down, and I took a good breath; for I knew I was master of the situation now. The king said:

"Be merciful, fair sir, and essay no further in this perilous matter, lest disaster follow. It was reported to us that your powers could not attain unto their full strength until the morrow; but—

"Your Majesty thinks the report may have been a lie? It *was* a lie."

That made an immense effect; up went appealing hands everywhere, and the king was assailed with a storm of supplications that I might be bought off at any price, and the calamity stayed. The king was eager to comply. He said:

"Name any terms, reverend sir, even to the halving of my kingdom; but banish this calamity, spare the sun!"

My fortune was made. I would have taken him up in a minute, but *I* couldn't stop an eclipse; the thing was out of the question. So I asked time to consider. The king said—

"How long—ah, how long, good sir? Be merciful; look, it groweth darker, moment by moment. Prithee how long?"

"Not long. Half an hour—maybe an hour."

There were a thousand pathetic protests, but I couldn't shorten up any, for I couldn't remember how long a total eclipse lasts. I was in a puzzled condition, anyway, and wanted to think. Something was wrong about that eclipse, and the fact was very unsettling. If this wasn't the one I was after, how was I to tell whether this was the sixth century, or nothing but a dream? Dear me, if I could only prove it was the latter! Here was a glad new hope. If the boy was right about the date, and this was surely the 20th, it *wasn't* the sixth century. I reached for the monk's sleeve, in considerable excitement, and asked him what day of the month it was.

Hang him, he said it was the *twenty-first!* It made me turn cold to hear him. I begged him not to make any mistake about it; but he was sure; he knew it was the 21st. So, that feather-headed boy had botched things again! The time of the day was right for the eclipse; I had seen that for myself, in the beginning, by the dial that was near by. Yes, I *was* in King Arthur's court, and I might as well make the most out of it I could.

The darkness was steadily growing, the people becoming more and more distressed. I now said:

"I have reflected, Sir King. For a lesson, I will let this darkness proceed, and spread night in the world; but whether I blot out the sun for good, or restore it, shall rest with you. These are the terms, to wit: You shall remain king over all your dominions, and receive all the glories and honors that belong to the kingship; but you shall appoint me your perpetual minister and executive, and give me for my services one per cent of such actual increase of revenue over and above its present amount as I may succeed in creating for the state. If I can't live on that, I sha'n't ask anybody to give me a lift. Is it satisfactory?"

There was a prodigious roar of applause, and out of the midst of it the king's voice rose, saying:

"Away with his bonds, and set him free! and do him homage, high and low, rich and poor, for he is become the king's right hand, is clothed with power and authority, and his seat is upon the highest step of the throne! Now sweep away this creeping night, and bring the light and cheer again, that all the world may bless thee."

But I said:

"That a common man should be shamed before the world, is nothing; but it were dishonor to the *king* if any that saw his minister naked should not also see him delivered from his shame. If I might ask that my clothes be brought again—"

"They are not meet," the king broke in. "Fetch raiment of another sort; clothe him like a prince!"

My idea worked. I wanted to keep things as they were till the eclipse was total, otherwise they would be trying again to get me to dismiss the darkness, and of course I couldn't do it. Sending for the clothes gained some delay, but not enough. So I had to make another excuse. I said it would be but natural if the king should change his mind and repent to some extent of what he had done under excitement; therefore I would let the darkness grow a while, and if at the end of a reasonable time the king had kept his mind the same, the darkness should be dismissed. Neither the king nor anybody else was satisfied with that arrangement, but I had to stick to my point.

It grew darker and darker and blacker and blacker, while I struggled with those awkward sixth-century clothes. It got to be pitch dark, at last, and the multitude groaned with horror to feel the cold uncanny night breezes fan through the place and see the stars come out and twinkle in the sky. At last the eclipse was total, and I was very glad of it, but everybody else was in misery; which was quite natural. I said:

"The king, by his silence, still stands to the terms." Then I lifted up my hands—stood just so a moment—then I said, with the most awful solemnity: "Let the enchantment dissolve and pass harmless away!"

There was no response, for a moment, in that deep darkness and that graveyard hush. But when the silver rim of the sun pushed itself out, a moment or two later, the assemblage broke loose with a vast shout and came pouring down like a deluge to smother me with blessings and gratitude; and Clarence was not the last of the wash, be sure.

CHAPTER 7

MERLIN'S TOWER

Inasmuch as I was now the second personage in the Kingdom, as far as political power and authority were concerned, much was made of me. My raiment was of silks and velvets and cloth of gold, and by consequence was very showy, also uncomfortable. But habit would soon reconcile me to my clothes; I was aware of that. I was given the choicest suite of apartments in the castle, after the king's. They were aglow with loud-colored silken hangings, but the stone floors had nothing but rushes on them for a carpet, and they were misfit rushes at that, being not all of one breed. As for conveniences, properly speaking, there weren't any. I mean *little* conveniences; it is the little conveniences that make the real comfort of life. The big oaken chairs, graced with rude carvings, were well enough, but that was the stopping-place. There was no soap, no matches, no looking-glass—except a metal one, about as powerful as a pail of water. And not a chromo. I had been used to chromos for years, and I saw now that without my suspecting it a passion for art had got worked into the fabric of my being, and was become a part of me. It made me homesick to look around over this proud and gaudy but heartless barrenness and remember that in our house in East Hartford, all unpretending as it was, you couldn't go into a room but you would find an insurance-chromo, or at least a three-color God-Bless-Our-Home over the door; and in the parlor we had nine. But here, even in my grand room of state, there wasn't anything in the nature of a picture except a thing the size of a bed-quilt, which was either woven or knitted, (it had darned places in it,) and nothing in it was the right color or the right shape; and as for proportions, even Raphael himself couldn't have botched them more formidably, after all his practice on those nightmares they call his "celebrated Hampton Court cartoons." Raphael was a bird. We had several of his chromos; one was his "Miraculous Draught of Fishes," where he puts in a miracle of his own—puts three men into a canoe which wouldn't have held a dog without upsetting. I always admired to study R.'s art, it was so fresh and unconventional.

There wasn't even a bell or a speaking-tube in the castle. I had a great many servants, and those that were on duty lolled in the anteroom; and when I wanted one of them I had to go and call for him.

There was no gas, there were no candles; a bronze dish half full of boarding-house butter with a blazing rag floating in it was the thing that produced what was regarded as light. A lot of these hung along the walls and modified the dark, just toned it down enough to make it dismal. If you went out at night, your servants carried torches. There were no books, pens, paper, or ink, and no glass in the openings they believed to be windows. It is a little thing—glass is—until it is absent, then it becomes a big thing. But perhaps the worst of all was, that there wasn't any sugar, coffee, tea or tobacco. I saw that I was just another Robinson Crusoe cast away on an uninhabited island, with no society but some more or less tame animals, and if I wanted to make life bearable I must do as he did—invent, contrive, create, reorganize things; set brain and hand to work, and keep them busy. Well, that was in my line.

One thing troubled me along at first—the immense interest which people took in me. Apparently the whole nation wanted a look at me. It soon transpired that the eclipse had scared the British world almost to death: that while it lasted the whole country, from one end to the other, was in a pitiable state of panic, and the churches, hermitages, and monkeries overflowed with praying and weeping poor creatures who thought the end of the world was come. Then had followed the news that the producer of this awful event was a stranger, a mighty magician at Arthur's court; that he could have blown out the sun like a candle, and was just going to do it when his mercy was purchased, and he then dissolved his enchantments, and was now recognized and honored as the man who had by his unaided might saved the globe from destruction and its peoples from extinction. Now if you consider that everybody believed that, and not only believed it but never even dreamed of doubting it, you will easily understand that there was not a person in all Britain that would not have walked fifty miles to get a sight of me. Of course I was all the talk—all other subjects were dropped; even the king became suddenly a person of minor interest and notoriety. Within twenty-four hours the delegations began to arrive, and from that time onward for a fortnight they kept coming. The village was crowded, and all the countryside. I had to go out a dozen times a day and show myself to these reverent and awe-stricken multitudes. It came to be a great burden, as to time and trouble, but of course it was at the same time compensatingly agreeable to be so celebrated and such a centre of homage. It turned Brer Merlin green with envy and spite, which was a great satisfaction to me. But there was one thing I couldn't understand; nobody had asked for an autograph. I spoke to Clarence about it. By George, I had to explain to him what it was. Then he said nobody in the country could read or write but a few dozen priests. Land! think of that.

There was another thing that troubled me a little. Those multitudes presently began to agitate for another miracle. That was natural. To be able to carry back to their far homes the boast that they had seen the man who could command the sun, riding in the heavens, and be obeyed, would make them great in the eyes of their neighbors, and envied by them all; but to be able to also say they had seen him work a miracle themselves—why, people would come a distance to see *them.* The pressure got to be pretty strong. There was going to be an eclipse of the moon, and I knew the date and hour, but it was too far away. Two years. I would have given a good deal for license to hurry it up and use it now when there was a big market for it. It seemed a great pity to have it wasted, so, and come lagging along at a time when a body wouldn't have any use for it as like as not. If it had been booked for only a month away, I could have sold it short; but as matters stood, I couldn't seem to cipher out any way to make it do me any good, so I gave up trying. Next, Clarence found that old Merlin was making himself busy on the sly among those people. He was spreading a report that I was a humbug, and that the reason I didn't accommodate the people with a miracle was because I couldn't. I saw that I must do something. I presently thought out a plan.

By my authority as executive I threw Merlin into prison—the same cell I had occupied myself. Then I gave public notice by herald and trumpet that I should be busy with affairs of state for a fortnight, but about the end of that time I would take a moment's leisure and blow up Merlin's stone tower by fires from heaven; in the meantime, whoso listened to evil reports about me, let him beware. Furthermore, I would perform but this one miracle at this time, and no more; if it failed to satisfy and any murmured, I would turn the murmurers into horses, and make them useful. Quiet ensued.

I took Clarence into my confidence, to a certain degree, and we went to work privately. I told him that this was a sort of miracle that required a trifle of preparation; and that it would be sudden death to ever talk about these preparations to anybody. That made his mouth safe enough. Clandestinely we made a few bushels of first-rate blasting-powder, and I superintended my armorers while they constructed a lightning rod and some wires. This old stone tower was very massive—and rather ruinous, too, for it was Roman, and four hundred years old. Yes, and handsome, after a rude fashion, and clothed with ivy from base to summit, as with a shirt of scale mail. It stood on a lonely eminence, in good view from the castle, and about half a mile away.

Working by night, we stowed the powder in the tower—dug stones out, on the inside, and buried the powder in the walls themselves, which were fifteen feet thick at the base. We put in a peck at a time, in a dozen places. We could have blown up the Tower of London with these charges. When the thirteenth night was come we put up our lightning rod, bedded it in one of the batches of powder, and ran wires from it to the other batches. Everybody had shunned that locality from the day of my proclamation, but on the morning of the fourteenth I thought best to warn the people, through the heralds, to keep clear away—a quarter of a mile away. Then added, by command, that at some time during the twenty-four hours I would consummate the miracle, but would first give a brief notice; by flags on the castle towers, if in the day-time, by torch-baskets in the same places if at night.

Thunder-showers had been tolerably frequent, of late, and I was not much afraid of a failure; still, I shouldn't have cared for a delay of a day or two; I should have explained that I was busy with affairs of state, yet, and the people must wait.

Of course we had a blazing sunny day—almost the first one without a cloud for three weeks; things always happen so. I kept secluded, and watched the weather. Clarence dropped in from time to time and said the public excitement was growing and growing all the time, and the whole country filling up with human masses as far as one could see from the battlements. At last the wind sprang up and a cloud appeared —in the right quarter, too, and just at nightfall. For a little while I watched that distant cloud spread and blacken, then I judged it was time for me to appear. I ordered the torch-baskets to be lit, and Merlin liberated and sent to me. A quarter of an hour later I ascended the parapet and there found the king and the court assembled and gazing off in the darkness toward Merlin's tower. Already the darkness was so heavy that one could not see far; these people, and the old turrets, being partly in deep shadow and partly in the red glow from the great torch-baskets overhead, made a good deal of a picture.

Merlin arrived in a gloomy mood. I said:

"You wanted to burn me alive when I had not done you any harm, and latterly you have been trying to injure my professional reputation. Therefore I am going to call down fire and blow up your tower, but it is only fair to give you a chance; now if you think you can break my enchantments and ward off the fires, step to the bat, it's your innings."

"I can, fair sir, and I will. Doubt it not."

He drew an imaginary circle on the stones of the roof, and burnt a pinch of powder in it which sent up a small cloud of aromatic smoke, whereat everybody fell back, and began to cross themselves and get uncomfortable. Then he began to mutter and make passes in the air with his hands. He worked himself up slowly and gradually into a sort of frenzy, and got to thrashing around with his arms like the sails of a windmill. By this time the storm had about reached us; the gusts of wind were flaring the torches and making the shadows swash about, the first heavy drops of rain were falling, the world abroad was black as pitch, the lightning began to wink fitfully. Of course my rod would be loading itself now. In fact, things were imminent. So I said:

"You have had time enough. I have given you every advantage, and not interfered. It is plain your magic is weak. It is only fair that I begin now."

I made about three passes in the air, and then there was an awful crash and that old tower leaped into the sky in chunks, along with a vast volcanic fountain of fire that turned night to noonday, and showed a thousand acres of human beings groveling on the ground in a general collapse of consternation. Well, it rained mortar and masonry the rest of the week. This was the report; but probably the facts would have modified it.

It was an effective miracle. The great bothersome temporary population vanished. There were a good many thousand tracks in the mud the next morning, but they were all outward bound. If I had advertised another miracle I couldn't have raised an audience with a sheriff.

Merlin's stock was flat. The king wanted to stop his wages; he even wanted to banish him, but I interfered. I said he would be useful to work the weather, and attend to small matters like that, and I would give him a lift now and then when his poor little parlor-magic soured on him. There wasn't a rag of his tower left, but I had the government rebuild it for him, and advised him to take boarders; but he was too high-toned for that. And as for being grateful, he never even said thank-you. He was a rather hard lot, take him how you might; but then you couldn't fairly expect a man to be sweet that had been set back so.

CHAPTER 8

THE BOSS

To be vested with enormous authority is a fine thing; but to have the on-looking world consent to it is a finer. The tower episode solidified my power, and made it impregnable. If any were perchance disposed to be jealous and critical before that, they experienced a change of heart, now. There was not any one in the kingdom who would have considered it good judgment to meddle with my matters.

I was fast getting adjusted to my situation and circumstances. For a time, I used to wake up, mornings, and smile at my "dream," and listen for the Colt's factory whistle; but that sort of thing played itself out, gradually, and at last I was fully able to realize that I was actually living in the sixth century, and in Arthur's court, not a lunatic asylum. After that, I was just as much at home in that century as I could have been in any other; and as for preference, I wouldn't have traded it for the twentieth. Look at the opportunities here for a man of knowledge, brains, pluck and enterprise to sail in and grow up with the country. The grandest field that ever was; and all my own; not a competitor; not a man who wasn't a baby to me in acquirements and capacities; whereas, what would I amount to in the twentieth century? I should be foreman of a factory, that is about all; and could drag a seine downstreet any day and catch a hundred better men than myself.

What a jump I had made! I couldn't keep from thinking about it, and contemplating it, just as one does who has struck oil. There was nothing back of me that could approach it, unless it might be Joseph's case; and Joseph's only approached it, it didn't equal it, quite. For it stands to reason that as Joseph's splendid financial ingenuities advantaged nobody but the king, the general public must have regarded him with a good deal of disfavor, whereas I had done my entire public a kindness in sparing the sun, and was popular by reason of it.

I was no shadow of a king; I was the substance; the king himself was the shadow. My power was colossal; and it was not a mere name, as such things have generally been, it was the genuine article. I stood here, at the very spring and source of the second great period of the world's history; and could see the trickling stream of that history gather, and deepen and broaden, and roll its mighty tides down the far centuries; and I could note the upspringing of adventurers like myself in the shelter of its long array of thrones: De Montforts, Gavestons, Mortimers, Villierses; the war-making, campaign-directing wantons of France, and Charles the Second's sceptre-wielding drabs; but nowhere in the procession was my full-sized fellow visible. I was a Unique; and glad to know that that fact could not be dislodged or challenged for thirteen centuries and a half, for sure.

Yes, in power I was equal to the king. At the same time there was another power that was a trifle stronger than both of us put together. That was the Church. I do not wish to disguise that fact. I couldn't, if I wanted to. But never mind about that, now; it will show up, in its proper place, later on. It didn't cause me any trouble in the beginning—at least any of consequence.

Well, it was a curious country, and full of interest. And the people! They were the quaintest and simplest and trustingest race; why, they were nothing but rabbits. It was pitiful for a person born in a wholesome free atmosphere to listen to their humble and hearty outpourings of loyalty toward their king and Church and nobility; as if they had any more occasion to love and honor king and Church and noble than a slave has to love and honor the lash, or a dog has to love and honor the stranger that kicks him! Why, dear me, *any* kind of royalty, howsoever modified, *any* kind of aristocracy, howsoever pruned, is rightly an insult; but if you are born and brought up under that sort of arrangement you probably never find it out for yourself, and don't believe it when somebody else tells you. It is enough to make a body ashamed of his race to think of the sort of froth that has always occupied its thrones without shadow of right or reason, and the seventh-rate people that have always figured as its aristocracies—a company of monarchs and nobles who, as a rule, would have achieved only poverty and obscurity if left, like their betters, to their own exertions.

The most of King Arthur's British nation were slaves, pure and simple, and bore that name, and wore the iron collar on their necks; and the rest were slaves in fact, but without the name; they imagined themselves men and freemen, and called themselves so. The truth was, the nation as a body was in the world for one object, and one only: to grovel before king and Church and noble; to slave for them, sweat blood for them, starve that they might be fed, work that they might play, drink misery to the dregs that they might be happy, go naked that they might wear silks and jewels, pay taxes that they might be spared from paying them, be familiar all their lives with the degrading language and postures of adulation that they might walk in pride and think themselves the gods of this world. And for all this, the thanks they got were cuffs and contempt; and so poor-spirited were they that they took even this sort of attention as an honor.

Inherited ideas are a curious thing, and interesting to observe and examine. I had mine, the king and his people had theirs. In both cases they flowed in ruts worn deep by time and habit, and the man who should have proposed to divert them by reason and argument would have had a long contract on his hands. For instance, those people had inherited the idea that all men without title and a long pedigree, whether they had great natural gifts and acquirements or hadn't, were creatures of no more consideration than so many animals, bugs, insects; whereas I had inherited the idea that human daws who can consent to masquerade in the peacock-shams of inherited dignities and unearned titles, are of no good but to be laughed at. The way I was looked upon was odd, but it was natural. You know how the keeper and the public regard the elephant in the menagerie: well, that is the idea. They are full of admiration of his vast bulk and his prodigious strength; they speak with pride of the fact that he can do a hundred marvels which are far and away beyond their own powers; and they speak with the same pride of the fact that in his wrath he is able to drive a thousand men before him. But does that make him one of *them?* No; the raggedest tramp in the pit would smile at the idea. He couldn't comprehend it; couldn't take it in; couldn't in any remote way conceive of it. Well, to the king, the nobles, and all the nation, down to the very slaves and tramps, I was just that kind of an elephant, and nothing more. I was admired, also feared; but it was as an animal is admired and feared. The animal is not reverenced, neither was I; I was not even respected. I had no pedigree, no inherited title; so in the king's and nobles' eyes I was mere dirt; the people regarded me with wonder and awe, but there was no reverence mixed with it; through the force of inherited ideas they were not able to conceive of anything being entitled to that except pedigree and lordship. There you see the hand of that awful power, the Roman Catholic Church. In two or three little centuries it had converted a nation of men to a nation of worms. Before the day of the Church's supremacy in the world, men were men, and held their heads up, and had a man's pride and spirit and independence; and what of greatness and position a person got, he got mainly by achievement, not by birth. But then the Church came to the front, with an axe to grind; and she was wise, subtle, and knew more than one way to skin a cat—or a nation; she invented "divine right of kings," and propped it all around, brick by brick, with the Beatitudes—wrenching them from their good purpose to make them fortify an evil one; she preached (to the commoner,) humility, obedience to superiors, the beauty of self-sacrifice; she preached (to the commoner,) meekness under insult; preached (still to the commoner, always to the commoner,) patience, meanness of spirit, non-resistance under oppression; and she introduced heritable ranks and aristocracies, and taught all the Christian populations of the earth to bow down to them and worship them. Even down to my birth-century that poison was still in the blood of Christendom, and the best of English commoners was still content to see his inferiors impudently continuing to hold a number of positions, such as lordships and the throne, to which the grotesque laws of his country did not allow him to aspire; in fact he was not merely contented with this strange condition of things, he was even able to persuade himself that he was proud of it. It seems to show that there isn't anything you can't stand, if you are only born and bred to it. Of course that taint, that reverence for rank and title, had been in our American blood, too—I know that; but when I left America it had disappeared—at least to all intents and purposes. The remnant of it was restricted to the dudes and dudesses. When a disease has worked its way down to that level, it may fairly be said to be out of the system.

But to return to my anomalous position in King Arthur's kingdom. Here I was, a giant among pigmies, a man among children, a master intelligence among intellectual moles: by all rational measurement the one and only actually great man in that whole British world; and yet there and then, just as in the remote England of my birth-time, the sheep-witted earl who could claim long descent from a king's leman, acquired at second-hand from the slums of London, was a better man than I was. Such a personage was fawned upon in Arthur's realm and reverently looked up to by everybody, even though his dispositions were as mean as his intelligence, and his morals as base as his lineage. There were times when *he* could sit down in the king's presence, but I couldn't. I could have got a title easily enough, and that would have raised me a large step in everybody's eyes; even in the king's, the giver of it. But I didn't ask for it; and I declined it when it was offered. I couldn't have enjoyed such a thing with my notions; and it wouldn't have been fair, anyway, because as far back as I could go, our tribe had always been short of the bar sinister. I couldn't have felt really and satisfactorily fine and proud and set-up over any title except one that should come from the nation itself, the only legitimate source; and such an one I hoped to win; and in the course of years of honest and honorable endeavor, I did win it and did wear it with a high and clean pride. This title fell casually from the lips of a blacksmith, one day, in a village, was caught up as a happy thought and tossed from mouth to mouth with a laugh and an affirmative vote; in ten days it had swept the kingdom, and was become as familiar as the king's name. I was never known by any other designation afterwards, whether in the nation's talk or in grave debate upon matters of state at the council-board of the sovereign. This title, translated into modern speech, would be THE BOSS. Elected by the nation. That suited me. And it was a pretty high title. There were very few THE's, and I was one of them. If you spoke of the duke, or the earl, or the bishop, how could anybody tell which one you meant? But if you spoke of The King or The Queen or The Boss, it was different.

Well, I liked the king, and *as* king I respected him—respected the office; at least respected it as much as I was capable of respecting any unearned supremacy; but as *men* I looked down upon him and his nobles—privately. And he and they liked me, and respected my office; but as an animal, without birth or sham title, they looked down upon me—and were not particularly private about it, either. I didn't charge for my opinion about them, and they didn't charge for their opinion about me: the account was square, the books balanced, everybody was satisfied.

CHAPTER 9

THE TOURNAMENT

They were always having grand tournaments there at Camelot; and very stirring and picturesque and ridiculous human bull-fights they were, too, but just a little wearisome to the practical mind. However, I was generally on hand—for two reasons: a man must not hold himself aloof from the things which his friends and his community have at heart if he would be liked—especially as a statesman; and both as business man and statesman I wanted to study the tournament and see if I couldn't invent an improvement on it. That reminds me to remark, in passing, that the very first official thing I did, in my administration —and it was on the very first day of it, too—was to start a patent office; for I knew that a country without a patent office and good patent laws was just a crab, and couldn't travel any way but sideways or backwards.

Things ran along, a tournament nearly every week; and now and then the boys used to want me to take a hand—I mean Sir Launcelot and the rest—but I said I would by and by; no hurry yet, and too much government machinery to oil up and set to rights and start a-going.

We had one tournament which was continued from day to day during more than a week, and as many as five hundred knights took part in it, from first to last. They were weeks gathering. They came on horseback from everywhere; from the very ends of the country, and even from beyond the sea; and many brought ladies and all brought squires, and troops of servants. It was a most gaudy and gorgeous crowd, as to costumery, and very characteristic of the country and the time, in the way of high animal spirits, innocent indecencies of language, and happy-hearted indifference to morals. It was fight or look on, all day and every day; and sing, gamble, dance, carouse, half the night every night. They had a most noble good time. You never saw such people. Those banks of beautiful ladies, shining in their barbaric splendors, would see a knight sprawl from his horse in the lists with a lance-shaft the thickness of your ankle clean through him and the blood spouting, and instead of fainting they would clap their hands and crowd each other for a better view; only sometimes one would dive into her handkerchief, and look ostentatiously broken-hearted, and then you could lay two to one that there was a scandal there somewhere and she was afraid the public hadn't found it out.

The noise at night would have been annoying to me ordinarily, but I didn't mind it in the present circumstances, because it kept me from hearing the quacks detaching legs and arms from the day's cripples. They ruined an uncommon good old cross-cut saw for me, and broke the saw-buck, too, but I let it pass. And as for my axe—well, I made up my mind that the next time I lent an axe to a surgeon I would pick my century.

I not only watched this tournament from day to day, but detailed an intelligent priest from my Department of Public Morals and Agriculture, and ordered him to report it; for it was my purpose by and by, when I should have gotten the people along far enough, to start a newspaper. The first thing you want in a new country, is a patent office; then work up your school system; and after that, out with your paper. A newspaper has its faults, and plenty of them, but no matter, it's hark from the tomb for a dead nation, and don't you forget it. You can't resurrect a dead nation without it; there isn't any way. So I wanted to sample things, and be finding out what sort of reporter-material I might be able to rake together out of the sixth century when I should come to need it.

Well, the priest did very well, considering. He got in all the details, and that is a good thing in a local item: you see he had kept books for the undertaker-department of his church when he was younger, and there, you know, the money's in the details; the more details, the more swag: bearers, mutes, candles, prayers,—everything counts; and if the bereaved don't buy prayers enough you mark up your candles with a forked pencil, and your bill shows up all right. And he had a good knack at getting in the complimentary thing here and there about a knight that was likely to advertise—no, I mean a knight that had influence; and he also had a neat gift of exaggeration, for in his time he had kept door for a pious hermit who lived in a sty and worked miracles.

Of course this novice's report lacked whoop and crash and lurid description, and therefore wanted the true ring; but its antique wording was quaint and sweet and simple, and full of the fragrances and flavors of the time, and these little merits made up in a measure for its more important lacks. Here is an extract from it:

Then Sir Brian de les Isles and Grummore Grummorsum, knights of the castle, encountered with Sir Aglovale and Sir Tor, and Sir Tor smote down Sir Grummore Grummorsum to the earth. Then came in Sir Carados of the dolorous tower, and Sir Turquine, knights of the castle, and there encountered with them Sir Percivale de Galis and Sir Lamorak de Galis, that were two brethren, and there encountered Sir Percivale with Sir Carados, and either brake their spears unto their hands, and then Sir Turquine with Sir Lamorak, and either of them smote down other, horse and all, to the earth, and either parties rescued other and horsed them again. And Sir Arnold, and Sir Gauter, knights of the castle, encountered with Sir Brandiles and Sir Kay, and these four knights encountered mightily, and brake their spears to their hands. Then came Sir Pertolope from the castle, and there encountered with him Sir Lionel, and there Sir Pertolope the green knight smote down Sir Lionel, brother to Sir Launcelot. All this was marked by noble heralds, who bare him best, and their names. Then Sir Bleobaris brake his spear upon Sir Gareth, but of that stroke Sir Bleobaris fell to the earth. When Sir Galihodin saw that, he bad Sir Gareth keep him, and Sir Gareth smote him to the earth. Then Sir Galihud gat a spear to avenge his brother, and in the same wise Sir Gareth served him, and Sir Dinadan and his brother La Cote Male Taile, and Sir Sagramor le Desirous, and Sir Dodinas le Savage; all these he bare down with one spear. When King Agwisance of Ireland saw Sir Gareth fare so he marvelled what he might be, that one time seemed green, and another time, at his again coming, he seemed blue. And thus at every course that he rode to and fro he changed his color, so that there might neither king nor knight have ready cognizance of him. Then Sir Agwisance the King of Ireland encountered with Sir Gareth, and there Sir Gareth smote him from his horse, saddle and all. And then came King Carados of Scotland, and Sir Gareth smote him down horse and man. And in the same wise he served King Uriens of the land of Gore. And then there came in Sir Bagdemagus, and Sir Gareth smote him down horse and man to the earth. And Bagdemagus's son Meliganus brake a spear upon Sir Gareth mightily and knightly. And then Sir Galahault the noble prince cried on high, Knight with the many colors, well hast thou justed; now make thee ready that I may just with thee. Sir Gareth heard him, and he gat a great spear, and so they encountered together, and there the prince brake his spear; but Sir Gareth smote him upon the left side of the helm, that he reeled here and there, and he had fallen down had not his men recovered him. Truly said King Arthur, that knight with the many colors is a good knight. Wherefore the king called unto him Sir Launcelot, and prayed him to encounter with that knight. Sir, said Launcelot, I may as well find in my heart for to forbear him at this time, for he hath had travail enough this day, and when a good knight doth so well upon some day, it is no good knight's part to let him of his worship, and, namely, when he seeth a knight hath done so great labour: for peradventure, said Sir Launcelot, his quarrel is here this day, and peradventure he is best beloved with this lady of all that be here, for I see well he paineth himself and enforceth him to do great deeds, and therefore, said Sir Launcelot, as for me, this day he shall have the honour; though it lay in my power to put him from it, I would not.

There was an unpleasant little episode that day, which for reasons of state I struck out of my priest's report. You will have noticed that Garry was doing some great fighting in the engagement. When I say Garry I mean Sir Gareth. Garry was my private pet name for him; it suggests that I had a deep affection for him, and that was the case. But it was a private pet name only, and never spoken aloud to any one, much less to him; being a noble, he would not have endured a familiarity like that from me. Well, to proceed: I sat in the private box set apart for me as the king's minister. While Sir Dinadan was waiting for his turn to enter the lists, he came in there and sat down and began to talk; for he was always making up to me, because I was a stranger and he liked to have a fresh market for his jokes, the most of them having reached that stage of wear where the teller has to do the laughing himself while the other person looks sick. I had always responded to his efforts as well as I could, and felt a very deep and real kindness for him, too, for the reason that if by malice of fate he knew the one particular anecdote which I had heard oftenest and had most hated and most loathed all my life, he had at least spared it me. It was one which I had heard attributed to every humorous person who had ever stood on American soil, from Columbus down to Artemus Ward. It was about a humorous lecturer who flooded an ignorant audience with the killingest jokes for an hour and never got a laugh; and then when he was leaving, some gray simpletons wrung him gratefully by the hand and said it had been the funniest thing they had ever heard, and "it was all they could do to keep from laughin' right out in meetin'." That anecdote never saw the day that it was worth the telling; and yet I had sat under the telling of it hundreds and thousands and millions and billions of times, and cried and cursed all the way through. Then who can hope to know what my feelings were, to hear this armor-plated ass start in on it again, in the murky twilight of tradition, before the dawn of history, while even Lactantius might be referred to as "the late Lactantius," and the Crusades wouldn't be born for five hundred years yet? Just as he finished, the call-boy came; so, haw-hawing like a demon, he went rattling and clanking out like a crate of loose castings, and I knew nothing more. It was some minutes before I came to, and then I opened my eyes just in time to see Sir Gareth fetch him an awful welt, and I unconsciously out with the prayer, "I hope to gracious he's killed!" But by ill-luck, before I had got half through with the words, Sir Gareth crashed into Sir Sagramor le Desirous and sent him thundering over his horse's crupper, and Sir Sagramor caught my remark and thought I meant it for *him*.

Well, whenever one of those people got a thing into his head, there was no getting it out again. I knew that, so I saved my breath, and offered no explanations. As soon as Sir Sagramor got well, he notified me that there was a little account to settle between us, and he named a day three or four years in the future; place of settlement, the lists where the offense had been given. I said I would be ready when he got back. You see, he was going for the Holy Grail. The boys all took a flier at the Holy Grail now and then. It was a several years' cruise. They always put in the long absence snooping around, in the most conscientious way, though none of them had any idea where the Holy Grail really was, and I don't think any of them actually expected to find it, or would have known what to do with it if he *had* run across it. You see, it was just the Northwest Passage of that day, as you may say; that was all. Every year expeditions went out holy grailing, and next year relief expeditions went out to hunt for *them*. There was worlds of reputation in it, but no money. Why, they actually wanted *me* to put in! Well, I should smile.

CHAPTER 10

BEGINNINGS OF CIVILIZATION

The Round Table soon heard of the challenge, and of course it was a good deal discussed, for such things interested the boys. The king thought I ought now to set forth in quest of adventures, so that I might gain renown and be the more worthy to meet Sir Sagramor when the several years should have rolled away. I excused myself for the present; I said it would take me three or four years yet to get things well fixed up and going smoothly; then I should be ready; all the chances were that at the end of that time Sir Sagramor would still be out grailing, so no valuable time would be lost by the postponement; I should then have been in office six or seven years, and I believed my system and machinery would be so well developed that I could take a holiday without its working any harm.

I was pretty well satisfied with what I had already accomplished. In various quiet nooks and corners I had the beginnings of all sorts of industries under way—nuclei of future vast factories, the iron and steel missionaries of my future civilization. In these were gathered together the brightest young minds I could find, and I kept agents out raking the country for more, all the time. I was training a crowd of ignorant folk into experts—experts in every sort of handiwork and scientific calling. These nurseries of mine went smoothly and privately along undisturbed in their obscure country retreats, for nobody was allowed to come into their precincts without a special permit—for I was afraid of the Church.

I had started a teacher-factory and a lot of Sunday-schools the first thing; as a result, I now had an admirable system of graded schools in full blast in those places, and also a complete variety of Protestant congregations all in a prosperous and growing condition. Everybody could be any kind of a Christian he wanted to; there was perfect freedom in that matter. But I confined public religious teaching to the churches and the Sunday-schools, permitting nothing of it in my other educational buildings. I could have given my own sect the preference and made everybody a Presbyterian without any trouble, but that would have been to affront a law of human nature: spiritual wants and instincts are as various in the human family as are physical appetites, complexions, and features, and a man is only at his best, morally, when he is equipped with the religious garment whose color and shape and size most nicely accommodate themselves to the spiritual complexion, angularities, and stature of the individual who wears it; and besides I was afraid of a united Church; it makes a mighty power, the mightiest conceivable, and then when it by and by gets into selfish hands, as it is always bound to do, it means death to human liberty, and paralysis to human thought.

All mines were royal property, and there were a good many of them. They had formerly been worked as savages always work mines—holes grubbed in the earth and the mineral brought up in sacks of hide by hand, at the rate of a ton a day; but I had begun to put the mining on a scientific basis as early as I could.

Yes, I had made pretty handsome progress when Sir Sagramor's challenge struck me.

Four years rolled by—and then! Well, you would never imagine it in the world. Unlimited power *is* the ideal thing when it is in safe hands. The despotism of heaven is the one absolutely perfect government. An earthly despotism would be the absolutely perfect earthly government, if the conditions were the same, namely, the despot the perfectest individual of the human race, and his lease of life perpetual. But as a perishable perfect man must die, and leave his despotism in the hands of an imperfect successor, an earthly despotism is not merely a bad form of government, it is the worst form that is possible.

My works showed what a despot could do with the resources of a kingdom at his command. Unsuspected by this dark land, I had the civilization of the nineteenth century booming under its very nose! It was fenced away from the public view, but there it was, a gigantic and unassailable fact—and to be heard from, yet, if I lived and had luck. There it was, as sure a fact, and as substantial a fact as any serene volcano, standing innocent with its smokeless summit in the blue sky and giving no sign of the rising hell in its bowels. My schools and churches were children four years before; they were grown-up, now; my shops of that day were vast factories, now; where I had a dozen trained men then, I had a thousand, now; where I had one brilliant expert then, I had fifty now. I stood with my hand on the cock, so to speak, ready to turn it on and flood the midnight world with light at any moment. But I was not going to do the thing in that sudden way. It was not my policy. The people could not have stood it; and moreover I should have had the Established Roman Catholic Church on my back in a minute.

No, I had been going cautiously all the while. I had had confidential agents trickling through the country some time, whose office was to undermine knighthood by imperceptible degrees, and to gnaw a little at this and that and the other superstition, and so prepare the way gradually for a better order of things. I was turning on my light one-candle-power at a time, and meant to continue to do so.

I had scattered some branch schools secretly about the kingdom, and they were doing very well. I meant to work this racket more and more, as time wore on, if nothing occurred to frighten me. One of my deepest secrets was my West Point—my military academy. I kept that most jealously out of sight; and I did the same with my naval academy which I had established at a remote seaport. Both were prospering to my satisfaction.

Clarence was twenty-two now, and was my head executive, my right hand. He was a darling; he was equal to anything; there wasn't anything he couldn't turn his hand to. Of late I had been training him for journalism, for the time seemed about right for a start in the newspaper line; nothing big, but just a small weekly for experimental circulation in my civilization-nurseries. He took to it like a duck; there was an editor concealed in him, sure. Already he had doubled himself in one way; he talked sixth century and wrote nineteenth. His journalistic style was climbing, steadily; it was already up to the back settlement Alabama mark, and couldn't be told from the editorial output of that region either by matter or flavor.

We had another large departure on hand, too. This was a telegraph and a telephone; our first venture in this line. These wires were for private service only, as yet, and must be kept private until a riper day should come. We had a gang of men on the road, working mainly by night. They were stringing ground wires; we were afraid to put up poles, for they would attract too much inquiry. Ground wires were good enough, in both instances, for my wires were protected by an insulation of my own invention which was perfect. My men had orders to strike across country, avoiding roads, and establishing connection with any considerable towns whose lights betrayed their presence, and leaving experts in charge. Nobody could tell you how to find any place in the kingdom, for nobody ever went intentionally to any place, but only struck it by accident in his wanderings, and then generally left it without thinking to inquire what its name was. At one time and another we had sent out topographical expeditions to survey and map the kingdom, but the priests had always interfered and raised trouble.

So we had given the thing up, for the present; it would be poor wisdom to antagonize the Church.

As for the general condition of the country, it was as it had been when I arrived in it, to all intents and purposes I had made changes, but they were necessarily slight, and they were not noticeable. Thus far, I had not even meddled with taxation, outside of the taxes which provided the royal revenues. I had systematized those, and put the service on an effective and righteous basis. As a result, these revenues were already quadrupled, and yet the burden was so much more equably distributed than before, that all the kingdom felt a sense of relief, and the praises of my administration were hearty and general.

Personally, I struck an interruption, now, but I did not mind it, it could not have happened at a better time. Earlier it could have annoyed me, but now everything was in good hands and swimming right along. The king had reminded me several times, of late, that the postponement I had asked for, four years before, had about run out, now. It was a hint that I ought to be starting out to seek adventures and get up a reputation of a size to make me worthy of the honor of breaking a lance with Sir Sagramor, who was still out grailing, but was being hunted for by various relief expeditions, and might be found any year, now. So you see I was expecting this interruption; it did not take me by surprise.

CHAPTER 11

THE YANKEE IN SEARCH OF ADVENTURES

There never was such a country for wandering liars; and they were of both sexes. Hardly a month went by without one of these tramps arriving; and generally loaded with a tale about some princess or other wanting help to get her out of some far-away castle where she was held in captivity by a lawless scoundrel, usually a giant. Now you would think that the first thing the king would do after listening to such a novelette from an entire stranger, would be to ask for credentials—yes, and a pointer or two as to locality of castle, best route to it, and so on. But nobody ever thought of so simple and common-sense a thing as that. No, everybody swallowed these people's lies whole, and never asked a question of any sort or about anything. Well, one day when I was not around, one of these people came along—it was a she one, this time—and told a tale of the usual pattern. Her mistress was a captive in a vast and gloomy castle, along with forty-four other young and beautiful girls, pretty much all of them princesses; they had been languishing in that cruel captivity for twenty-six years; the masters of the castle were three stupendous brothers, each with four arms and one eye—the eye in the centre of the forehead, and as big as a fruit. Sort of fruit not mentioned; their usual slovenliness in statistics.

Would you believe it? The king and the whole Round Table were in raptures over this preposterous opportunity for adventure. Every knight of the Table jumped for the chance, and begged for it; but to their vexation and chagrin the king conferred it upon me, who had not asked for it at all.

By an effort, I contained my joy when Clarence brought me the news. But he—he could not contain his. His mouth gushed delight and gratitude in a steady discharge—delight in my good fortune, gratitude to the king for this splendid mark of his favor for me. He could keep neither his legs nor his body still, but pirouetted about the place in an airy ecstasy of happiness.

On my side, I could have cursed the kindness that conferred upon me this benefaction, but I kept my vexation under the surface for policy's sake, and did what I could to let on to be glad. Indeed, I *said* I was glad. And in a way it was true; I was as glad as a person is when he is scalped.

Well, one must make the best of things, and not waste time with useless fretting, but get down to business and see what can be done. In all lies there is wheat among the chaff; I must get at the wheat in this case: so I sent for the girl and she came. She was a comely enough creature, and soft and modest, but if signs went for anything, she didn't know as much a lady's watch. I said—

"My dear, have you been questioned as to particulars?"

She said she hadn't.

"Well, I didn't expect you had, but I thought I would ask to make sure; it's the way I've been raised. Now you mustn't take it unkindly if I remind you that as we don't know you, we must go a little slow. You may be all right, of course, and we'll hope that you are; but to take it for granted isn't business. *You* understand that. I'm obliged to ask you a few questions; just answer up fair and square, and don't be afraid. Where do you live, when you are at home?"

"In the land of Moder, fair sir."

"Land of Moder. I don't remember hearing of it before. Parents living?"

"As to that, I know not if they be yet on live, sith it is many years that I have lain shut up in the castle."

"Your name, please?"

"I hight the Demoiselle Alisande la Carteloise, an it please you."

"Do you know anybody here who can identify you?"

"That were not likely, fair lord, I being come hither now for the first time."

"Have you brought any letters—any documents—any proofs that you are trustworthy and truthful?"

"Of a surety, no; and wherefore should I? Have I not a tongue, and cannot I say all that myself?"

"But *your* saying it, you know, and somebody else's saying it, is different."

"Different? How might that be? I fear me I do not understand."

"Don't *understand?* Land of—why, you see—you see—why, great Scott, can't you understand a little thing like that? Can't you understand the difference between your—*why* do you look so innocent and idiotic!"

"I? In truth I know not, but an it were the will of God."

"Yes, yes, I reckon that's about the size of it. Don't mind my seeming excited; I'm not. Let us change the subject. Now as to this castle, with forty-five princesses in it, and three ogres at the head of it, tell me—where is this harem?"

"Harem?"

"The *castle,* you understand; where is the castle?"

"Oh, as to that, it is great, and strong, and well beseen, and lieth in a far country. Yes, it is many leagues."

"*How* many?"

"Ah, fair sir, it were woundily hard to tell, they are so many, and do so lap the one upon the other, and being made all in the same image and tincted with the same color, one may not know the one league from its fellow, nor how to count them except they be taken apart, and ye wit well it were God's work to do that, being not within man's capacity; for ye will note—"

"Hold on, hold on, never mind about the distance; *whereabouts* does the castle lie? What's the direction from here?"

"Ah, please you sir, it hath no direction from here; by reason that the road lieth not straight, but turneth evermore; wherefore the direction of its place abideth not, but is sometime under the one sky and anon under another, whereso if ye be minded that it is in the east, and wend thitherward, ye shall observe that the way of the road doth yet again turn upon itself by the space of half a circle, and this marvel happing again and yet again and still again, it will grieve you that you had thought by vanities of the mind to thwart and bring to naught the will of Him that giveth not a castle a direction from a place except it pleaseth Him, and if it please Him not, will the rather that even all castles and all directions thereunto vanish out of the earth, leaving the places wherein they tarried desolate and vacant, so warning His creatures that where He will He will, and where He will not He—"

"Oh, that's all right, that's all right, give us a rest; never mind about the direction, *hang* the direction—I beg pardon, I beg a thousand pardons, I am not well to-day; pay no attention when I soliloquize, it is an old habit, an old, bad habit, and hard to get rid of when one's digestion is all disordered with eating food that was raised forever and ever before he was born; good land! a man can't keep his functions regular on spring chickens thirteen hundred years old. But come—never mind about that; let's—have you got such a thing as a map of that region about you? Now a good map—"

"Is it peradventure that manner of thing which of late the unbelievers have brought from over the great seas, which, being boiled in oil, and an onion and salt added thereto, doth—"

"What, a map? What are you talking about? Don't you know what a map is? There, there, never mind, don't explain, I hate explanations; they fog a thing up so that you can't tell anything about it. Run along, dear; good-day; show her the way, Clarence."

Oh, well, it was reasonably plain, now, why these donkeys didn't prospect these liars for details. It may be that this girl had a fact in her somewhere, but I don't believe you could have sluiced it out with a hydraulic; nor got it with the earlier forms of blasting, even; it was a case for dynamite. Why, she was a perfect ass; and yet the king and his knights had listened to her as if she had been a leaf out of the gospel. It kind of sizes up the whole party. And think of the simple ways of this court: this wandering wench hadn't any more trouble to get access to the king in his palace than she would have had to get into the poor-house in my day and country. In fact he was glad to see her, glad to hear her tale; with that adventure of hers to offer, she was as welcome as a corpse is to a coroner.

Just as I was ending-up these reflections, Clarence came back. I remarked upon the barren result of my efforts with the girl; hadn't got hold of a single point that could help me to find the castle. The youth looked a little surprised, or puzzled, or something, and intimated that he had been wondering to himself what I had wanted to ask the girl all those questions for.

"Why, great guns," I said, "don't I want to find the castle? And how else would I go about it?"

"La, sweet your worship, one may lightly answer that, I ween. She will go with thee. They always do. She will ride with thee."

"Ride with me? Nonsense!"

"But of a truth she will. She will ride with thee. Thou shalt see."

"What? She browse around the hills and scour the woods with me—alone—and I as good as engaged to be married? Why, it's scandalous. Think how it would look."

My, the dear face that rose before me! The boy was eager to know all about this tender matter. I swore him to secrecy and then whispered her name—"Puss Flanagan." He looked disappointed, and said he didn't remember the countess. How natural it was for the little courtier to give her a rank. He asked me where she lived.

"In East Har—" I came to myself and stopped, a little confused; then I said, "Never mind, now; I'll tell you sometime."

And might he see her? Would I let him see her some day?

It was but a little thing to promise—thirteen hundred years or so—and he so eager; so I said Yes. But I sighed; I couldn't help it. And yet there was no sense in sighing, for she wasn't born yet. But that is the way we are made: we don't reason, where we feel; we just feel.

My expedition was all the talk that day and that night, and the boys were very good to me, and made much of me, and seemed to have forgotten their vexation and disappointment, and come to be as anxious for me to hive those ogres and set those ripe old virgins loose as if it were themselves that had the contract. Well, they *were* good children—but just children, that is all. And they gave me no end of points about how to scout for giants, and how to scoop them in; and they told me all sorts of charms against enchantments, and gave me salves and other rubbish to put on my wounds. But it never occurred to one of them to reflect that if I was such a wonderful necromancer as I was pretending to be, I ought not to need salves or instructions, or charms against enchantments, and least of all, arms and armor, on a foray of any kind—even against fire-spouting dragons, and devils hot from perdition, let alone such poor adversaries as these I was after, these commonplace ogres of the back settlements.

I was to have an early breakfast, and start at dawn, for that was the usual way; but I had the demon's own time with my armor, and this delayed me a little. It is troublesome to get into, and there is so much detail. First you wrap a layer or two of blanket around your body, for a sort of cushion and to keep off the cold iron; then you put on your sleeves and shirt of chain-mail—these are made of small steel links woven together, and they form a fabric so flexible that if you toss your shirt onto the floor, it slumps into a pile like a peck of wet fish-net; it is very heavy and is nearly the uncomfortablest material in the world for a night-shirt, yet plenty used it for that—tax collectors, and reformers, and one-horse kings with a defective title, and those sorts of people; then you put on your shoes—flat-boats roofed over with interleaving bands of steel—and screw your clumsy spurs into the heels. Next you buckle your greaves on your legs, and your cuisses on your thighs; then come your backplate and your breastplate, and you begin to feel crowded; then you hitch onto the breastplate the half-petticoat of broad overlapping bands of steel which hangs down in front but is scolloped out behind so you can sit down, and isn't any real improvement on an inverted coal scuttle, either for looks or for wear, or to wipe your hands on; next you belt on your sword; then you put your stove-pipe joints onto your arms, your iron gauntlets onto your hands, your iron rat-trap onto your head, with a rag of steel web hitched onto it to hang over the back of your neck—and there you are, snug as a candle in a candle-mould. This is no time to dance. Well, a man that is packed away like that, is a nut that isn't worth the cracking, there is so little of the meat, when you get down to it, by comparison with the shell.

The boys helped me, or I never could have got in. Just as we finished, Sir Bedivere happened in, and I saw that as like as not I hadn't chosen the most convenient outfit for a long trip. How stately he looked; and tall and broad and grand. He had on his head a conical steel casque that only came down to his ears, and for visor had only a narrow steel bar that extended down to his upper lip and protected his nose; and all the rest of him, from neck to heel, was flexible chain-mail, trowsers and all. But pretty much all of him was hidden under his outside garment, which of course was of chain-mail, as I said, and hung straight from his shoulders to his ancles; and from his middle to the bottom, both before and behind, was divided, so that he could ride and let the skirts hang down on each side. He was going grailing, and it was just the outfit for it, too. I would have given a good deal for that ulster, but it was too late now to be fooling around. The sun was just up, the king and the court were all on hand to see me off and wish me luck; so it wouldn't be etiquette for me to tarry. You don't get on your horse yourself; no, if you tried it you would get disappointed. They carry you out, just as they carry a sun-struck man to the drug store, and put you on, and help get you to rights, and fix your feet in the stirrups; and all the while you do feel so strange and stuffy and like somebody else—like somebody that has been married on a sudden, or struck by lightning, or something like that, and hasn't quite fetched around, yet, and is sort of numb, and can't just get his bearings. Then they stood up the mast they called a spear, in its socket by my left foot, and I gripped it with my hand; lastly they hung my shield around my neck, and I was all complete and ready to up anchor and get to sea. Everybody was as good to me as they could be, and a maid of honor gave me the stirrup-cup her own self. There was nothing more to do, now, but for that damsel to get up behind me on a pillion, which she did, and put an arm or so around me to hold on.

And so we started; and everybody gave us a good-bye and waved their handkerchiefs or helmets. And everybody we met, going down the hill and through the village was respectful to us, except some shabby little boys on the outskirts. They said—

"Oh, what a guy!" And hove clods at us.

In my experience boys are the same in all ages. They don't respect anything, they don't care for anything or anybody. They say "Go up, baldhead" to the prophet going his unoffending way in the gray of antiquity; they sass me in the holy gloom of the Middle Ages; and I had seen them act the same way in Buchanan's administration; I remember, because I was there and helped. The prophet had his bears and settled with his boys; and I wanted to get down and settle with mine, but it wouldn't answer, because I couldn't have got up again. I hate a country without a derrick.

CHAPTER 12

SLOW TORTURE

Straight off, we were in the country. It was most lovely and pleasant in those sylvan solitudes in the early cool morning in the first freshness of autumn. From hilltops we saw fair green valleys lying spread out below, with streams winding through them, and island-groves of trees here and there, and huge lonely oaks scattered about and casting black blots of shade; and beyond the valleys we saw the ranges of hills, blue with haze, stretching away in billowy perspective to the horizon, with at wide intervals a dim fleck of white or gray on a wave-summit, which we knew was a castle. We crossed broad natural lawns sparkling with dew, and we moved like spirits, the cushioned turf giving out no sound of foot-fall; we dreamed along through glades in a mist of green light that got its tint from the sun-drenched roof of leaves overhead, and by our feet the clearest and coldest of runlets went frisking and gossiping over its reefs and making a sort of whispering music comfortable to hear; and at times we left the world behind and entered into the solemn great deeps and rich gloom of the forest, where furtive wild things whisked and scurried by and were gone before you could even get your eye on the place where the noise was; and where only the earliest birds were turning out and getting to business with a song here and a quarrel yonder and a mysterious far-off hammering and drumming for worms on a tree-trunk away somewhere in the impenetrable remotenesses of the woods. And by and by out we would swing again into the glare.

About the third or fourth or fifth time that we swung out into the glare—it was along there somewhere, a couple of hours or so after sun-up—it wasn't as pleasant as it had been. It was beginning to get hot. This was quite noticeable. We had a very long pull, after that, without any shade. Now it is curious how progressively little frets grow and multiply after they once get a start. Things which I didn't mind at all, at first, I began to mind now—and more and more, too, all the time. The first ten or fifteen times I wanted my handkerchief I didn't seem to care; I got along, and said never mind, it isn't any matter, and dropped it out of my mind. But now it was different; I wanted it all the time; it was nag, nag, nag, right along, and no rest; I couldn't get it out of my mind; and so at last I lost my temper and said hang a man that would make a suit of armor without any pockets in it. You see I had my handkerchief in my helmet; and some other things; but it was that kind of a helmet that you can't take off by yourself. That hadn't occurred to me when I put it there; and in fact I didn't know it. I supposed it would be particularly convenient there. And so now, the thought of its being there, so handy and close by, and yet not get-at-able, made it all the worse and the harder to bear. Yes, the thing that you can't get is the thing that you want, mainly; everyone has noticed that. Well, it took my mind off from everything else; took it clear off, and centred it in my helmet; and mile after mile, there it staid, imagining the handkerchief, picturing the handkerchief; and it was bitter and aggravating to have the salt sweat keep trickling down into my eyes, and I couldn't get at it. It seems like a little thing, on paper, but it was not a little thing at all; it was the most real kind of misery. I would not say it if it was not so. I made up my mind that I would carry along a reticule next time, let it look how it might, and people say what they would. Of course these iron dudes of the Round Table would think it was scandalous, and maybe raise Sheol about it, but as for me, give me comfort first, and style afterwards. So we jogged along, and now and then we struck a stretch of dust, and it would tumble up in clouds and get into my nose and make me sneeze and cry; and of course I said things I oughtn't to have said, I don't deny that. I am not better than others. We couldn't seem to meet anybody in this lonesome Britain, not even an ogre; and in the mood I was in then, it was well for the ogre; that is, an ogre with a handkerchief. Most knights would have thought of nothing but getting his armor; but so I got his bandanna, he could keep his hardware, for all me.

Meantime it was getting hotter and hotter in there. You see, the sun was beating down and warming up the iron more and more all the time. Well, when you are hot, that way, every little thing irritates you. When I trotted, I rattled like a crate of dishes, and that annoyed me; and moreover I couldn't seem to stand that shield slatting and banging, now about my breast, now around my back; and if I dropped into a walk my joints creaked and screeched in that wearisome way that a wheelbarrow does, and as we didn't create any breeze at that gait, I was like to get fried in that stove; and besides, the quieter you went the heavier the iron settled down on you and the more and more tons you seemed to weigh every minute. And you had to be always changing hands, and passing your spear over to the other foot, it got so irksome for one hand to hold it long at a time.

Well, you know, when you perspire that way, in rivers, there comes a time when you—when you—well, when you itch. You are inside, your hands are outside; so there you are; nothing but iron between. It is not a light thing, let it sound as it may. First it is one place; then another; then some more; and it goes on spreading and spreading, and at last the territory is all occupied, and nobody can imagine what you feel like, nor how unpleasant it is. And when it had got to the worst, and it seemed to me that I could not stand anything more, a fly got in through the bars and settled on my nose, and the bars were stuck and wouldn't work, and I couldn't get the visor up; and I could only shake my head, which was baking hot by this time, and the fly—well, you know how a fly acts when he has got a certainty—he only minded the shaking enough to change from nose to lip, and lip to ear, and buzz and buzz all around in there, and keep on lighting and biting, in a way that a person already so distressed as I was, simply could not stand. So I gave in, and got Alisande to unship the helmet and relieve me of it. Then she emptied the conveniences out of it and fetched it full of water, and I drank and then stood up and she poured the rest down inside the armor. One cannot think how refreshing it was. She continued to fetch and pour until I was well soaked and thoroughly comfortable.

It was good to have a rest—and peace. But nothing is quite perfect in this life, at any time. I had made a pipe a while back, and also some pretty fair tobacco; not the real thing, but what some of the Indians use: the inside bark of the willow, dried. These comforts had been in the helmet, and now I had them again, but no matches.

Gradually, as the time wore along, one annoying fact was borne in upon my understanding—that we were weather-bound. An armed novice cannot mount his horse without help and plenty of it. Sandy was not enough; not enough for me, anyway. We had to wait until somebody should come along. Waiting, in silence, would have been agreeable enough, for I was full of matter for reflection, and wanted to give it a chance to work. I wanted to try and think out how it was that rational or even half-rational men could ever have learned to wear armor, considering its inconveniences; and how they had managed to keep up such a fashion for generations when it was plain that what I had suffered to-day they had had to suffer all the days of their lives. I wanted to think that out; and moreover I wanted to think out some way to reform this evil and persuade the people to let the foolish fashion die out; but thinking was out of the question in the circumstances. You couldn't think, where Sandy was. She was a quite biddable creature and good-hearted, but she had a flow of talk that was as steady as a mill, and made your head sore like the drays and wagons in a city. If she had had a cork she would have been a comfort. But you can't cork that kind; they would die. Her clack was going all day, and you would think something would surely happen to her works, by and by; but no, they never got out of order; and she never had to slack up for words. She could grind, and pump, and churn and buzz by the week, and never stop to oil up or blow out. And yet the result was just nothing but wind. She never had any ideas, any more than a fog has. She was a perfect blatherskite; I mean for jaw, jaw, jaw, talk, talk, talk, jabber, jabber, jabber; but just as good as she could be. I hadn't minded her mill that morning, on account of having that hornet's nest of other troubles; but more than once in the afternoon I had to say—

"Take a rest, child; the way you are using up all the domestic air, the kingdom will have to go to importing it by to-morrow, and it's a low enough treasury without that."

CHAPTER 13

FREEMEN!

Yes, it is strange how little a while at a time a person can be contented. Only a little while back, when I was riding and suffering, what a heaven this peace, this rest, this sweet serenity in this secluded shady nook by this purling stream would have seemed, where I could keep perfectly comfortable all the time by pouring a dipper of water into my armor now and then; yet already I was getting dissatisfied; partly because I could not light my pipe—for although I had long ago started a match factory, I had forgotten to bring matches with me—and partly because we had nothing to eat. Here was another illustration of the childlike improvidence of this age and people. A man in armor always trusted to chance for his food on a journey, and would have been scandalized at the idea of hanging a basket of sandwiches on his spear. There was probably not a knight of all the Round Table combination who would not rather have died than been caught carrying such a thing as that on his flagstaff. And yet there could not be anything more sensible. It had been my intention to smuggle a couple of sandwiches into my helmet, but I was interrupted in the act, and had to make an excuse and lay them aside, and a dog got them.

Night approached, and with it a storm. The darkness came on fast. We must camp, of course. I found a good shelter for the demoiselle under a rock, and went off and found another for myself. But I was obliged to remain in my armor, because I could not get it off by myself and yet could not allow Alisande to help, because it would have seemed so like undressing before folk. It would not have amounted to that in reality, because I had clothes on underneath; but the prejudices of one's breeding are not gotten rid of just at a jump, and I knew that when it came to stripping off that bob-tailed iron petticoat I should be embarrassed.

With the storm came a change of weather; and the stronger the wind blew, and the wilder the rain lashed around, the colder and colder it got. Pretty soon, various kinds of bugs and ants and worms and things began to flock in out of the wet and crawl down inside my armor to get warm; and while some of them behaved well enough, and snuggled up amongst my clothes and got quiet, the majority were of a restless, uncomfortable sort, and never stayed still, but went on prowling and hunting for they did not know what; especially the ants, which went tickling along in wearisome procession from one end of me to the other by the hour, and are a kind of creatures which I never wish to sleep with again. It would be my advice to persons situated in this way, to not roll or thrash around, because this excites the interest of all the different sorts of animals and makes every last one of them want to turn out and see what is going on, and this makes things worse than they were before, and of course makes you objurgate harder, too, if you can. Still, if one did not roll and thrash around he would die; so perhaps it is as well to do one way as the other, there is no real choice. Even after I was frozen solid I could still distinguish that tickling, just as a corpse does when he is taking electric treatment. I said I would never wear armor after this trip.

All those trying hours whilst I was frozen and yet was in a living fire, as you may say, on account of that swarm of crawlers, that same unanswerable question kept circling and circling through my tired head: How do people stand this miserable armor? How have they managed to stand it all these generations? How can they sleep at night for dreading the tortures of next day?

When the morning came at last, I was in a bad enough plight: seedy, drowsy, fagged, from want of sleep; weary from thrashing around, famished from long fasting; pining for a bath, and to get rid of the animals; and crippled with rheumatism. And how had it fared with the nobly born, the titled aristocrat, the Demoiselle Alisande la Carteloise? Why, she was as fresh as a squirrel; she had slept like the dead; and as for a bath, probably neither she nor any other noble in the land had ever had one, and so she was not missing it. Measured by modern standards, they were merely modified savages, those people. This noble lady showed no impatience to get to breakfast—and that smacks of the savage, too. On their journeys those Britons were used to long fasts, and knew how to bear them; and also how to freight up against probable fasts before starting, after the style of the Indian and the anaconda. As like as not, Sandy was loaded for a three-day stretch.

We were off before sunrise, Sandy riding and I limping along behind. In half an hour we came upon a group of ragged poor creatures who had assembled to mend the thing which was regarded as a road. They were as humble as animals to me; and when I proposed to breakfast with them, they were so flattered, so overwhelmed by this extraordinary condescension of mine that at first they were not able to believe that I was in earnest. My lady put up her scornful lip and withdrew to one side; she said in their hearing that she would as soon think of eating with the other cattle—a remark which embarrassed these poor devils merely because it referred to them, and not because it insulted or offended them, for it didn't. And yet they were not slaves, not chattels. By a sarcasm of law and phrase they were freemen. Seven-tenths of the free population of the country were of just their class and degree: small "independent" farmers, artisans, etc.; which is to say, they were the nation, the actual Nation; they were about all of it that was useful, or worth saving, or really respectworthy; and to subtract them would have been to subtract the Nation and leave behind some dregs, some refuse, in the shape of a king, nobility and gentry, idle, unproductive, acquainted mainly with the arts of wasting and destroying, and of no sort of use or value in any rationally constructed world. And yet, by ingenious contrivance, this gilded minority, instead of being in the tail of the procession where it belonged, was marching head up and banners flying, at the other end of it; had elected itself to be the Nation, and these innumerable clams had permitted it so long that they had come at last to accept it as a truth; and not only that, but to believe it right and as it should be. The priests had told their fathers and themselves that this ironical state of things was ordained of God; and so, not reflecting upon how unlike God it would be to amuse himself with sarcasms, and especially such poor transparent ones as this, they had dropped the matter there and become respectfully quiet.

The talk of these meek people had a strange enough sound in a formerly American ear. They were freemen, but they could not leave the estates of their lord or their bishop without his permission; they could not prepare their own bread, but must have their corn ground and their bread baked at his mill and his bakery, and pay roundly for the same; they could not sell a piece of their own property without paying him a handsome percentage of the proceeds, nor buy a piece of somebody else's without remembering him in cash for the privilege; they had to harvest his grain for him gratis, and be ready to come at a moment's notice, leaving their own crop to destruction by the threatened storm; they had to let him plant fruit trees in their fields, and then keep their indignation to themselves when his heedless fruit gatherers trampled the grain around the trees; they had to smother their anger when his hunting parties galloped through their fields laying waste the result of their patient toil; they were not allowed to keep doves themselves, and when the swarms from my lord's dovecote settled on their crops they must not lose their temper and kill a bird, for awful would the penalty be; when the harvest was at last gathered, then came the procession of robbers to levy their blackmail upon it: first the Church carted off its fat tenth, then the king's commissioner took his twentieth, then my lord's people made a mighty inroad upon the remainder; after which, the skinned freeman had liberty to bestow the remnant in his barn, in case it was worth the trouble; there were taxes, and taxes, and taxes, and more taxes, and taxes again, and yet other taxes—upon this free and independent pauper, but none upon his lord the baron or the bishop, none upon the wasteful nobility or the all-devouring Church; if the baron would sleep unvexed, the freeman must sit up all night after his day's work and whip the ponds to keep the frogs quiet; if the freeman's daughter—but no, that last infamy of monarchical government is unprintable; and finally, if the freeman, grown desperate with his tortures, found his life unendurable under such conditions, and sacrificed it and fled to death for mercy and refuge, the gentle Church condemned him to eternal fire, the gentle law buried him at midnight at the cross-roads with a stake through his back, and his master the baron or the bishop confiscated all his property and turned his widow and his orphans out of doors.

And here were these freemen assembled in the early morning to work on their lord the bishop's road three days each—gratis; every head of a family, and every son of a family, three days each, gratis, and a day or so added for their servants. Why, it was like reading about France and the French, before the ever-memorable and blessed Revolution, which swept a thousand years of such villany away in one swift tidal-wave of blood—one: a settlement of that hoary debt in the proportion of half a drop of blood for each hogshead of it that had been pressed by slow tortures out of that people in the weary stretch of ten centuries of wrong and shame and misery the like of which was not to be mated but in hell. There were two "Reigns of Terror," if we would but remember it and consider it; the one wrought murder in hot passion, the other in heartless cold blood; the one lasted mere months, the other had lasted a thousand years; the one inflicted death upon ten thousand persons, the other upon a hundred millions; but our shudders are all for the "horrors" of the minor Terror, the momentary Terror, so to speak; whereas, what is the horror of swift death by the axe, compared with life-long death from hunger, cold, insult, cruelty and heart-break? What is swift death by lightning compared with death by slow fire at the stake? A city cemetery could contain the coffins filled by that brief Terror which we have all been so diligently taught to shiver at and mourn over; but all France could hardly contain the coffins filled by that older and real Terror—that unspeakably bitter and awful Terror which none of us has been taught to see in its vastness or pity as it deserves.

These poor ostensible freemen who were sharing their breakfast and their talk with me, were as full of humble reverence for their king and Church and nobility as their worst enemy could desire. There was something pitifully ludicrous about it. I asked them if they supposed a nation of people ever existed, who, with a free vote in every man's hand, would elect that a single family and its descendants should reign over it forever, whether gifted or boobies, to the exclusion of all other families—including the voter's; and would also elect that a certain hundred families should be raised to dizzy summits of rank, and clothed-on with offensive transmissible glories and privileges to the exclusion of the rest of the nation's families—*including his own.*

They all looked unhit, and said they didn't know; that they had never thought about it before, and it hadn't ever occurred to them that a nation could be so situated that every man *could* have a say in the government. I said I had seen one—and that it would last until it had an Established Church. Again they were all unhit—at first. But presently one man looked up and asked me to state that proposition again; and state it slowly, so it could soak into his understanding. I did it; and after a little he had the idea, and he brought his fist down and said *he* didn't believe a nation where every man had a vote would voluntarily get down in the mud and dirt in any such way; and that to steal from a nation its will and preference must be a crime and the first of all crimes.

I said to myself:

"This one's a man. If I were backed by enough of his sort, I would make a strike for the welfare of this country, and try to prove myself its loyalest citizen by making a wholesome change in its system of government."

You see my kind of loyalty was loyalty to one's country, not to its institutions or its office-holders. The country is the real thing, the substantial thing, the eternal thing; it is the thing to watch over, and care for, and be loyal to; institutions are extraneous, they are its mere clothing, and clothing can wear out, become ragged, cease to be comfortable, cease to protect the body from winter, disease, and death. To be loyal to rags, to shout for rags, to worship rags, to die for rags—that is a loyalty of unreason, it is pure animal; it belongs to monarchy, was invented by monarchy; let monarchy keep it. I was from Connecticut, whose Constitution declares "that all political power is inherent in the people, and all free governments are founded on their authority and instituted for their benefit; and that they have *at all times* an undeniable and indefeasible right to *alter their form of government* in such a manner as they may think expedient."

Under that gospel, the citizen who thinks he sees that the commonwealth's political clothes are worn out, and yet holds his peace and does not agitate for a new suit, is disloyal; he is a traitor. That he may be the only one who thinks he sees this decay, does not excuse him; it is his duty to agitate any way, and it is the duty of the others to vote him down if they do not see the matter as he does.

And now here I was, in a country where a right to say how the country should be governed was restricted to six persons in each thousand of its population. For the nine hundred and ninety-four to express dissatisfaction with the regnant system and propose to change it, would have made the whole six shudder as one man, it would have been so disloyal, so dishonorable, such putrid black treason. So to speak, I was become a stockholder in a corporation where nine hundred and ninety-four of the members furnished all the money and did all the work, and the other six elected themselves a permanent board of direction and took all the dividends. It seemed to me that what the nine hundred and ninety-four dupes needed was a new deal. The thing that would have best suited the circus side of my nature would have been to resign the Boss-ship and get up an insurrection and turn it into a revolution; but I knew that the Jack Cade or the Wat Tyler who tries such a thing without first educating his materials up to revolution-grade is almost absolutely certain to get left. I had never been accustomed to getting left, even if I do say it myself. Wherefore, the "deal" which had been for some time working into shape in my mind was of a quite different pattern from the Cade-Tyler sort.

So I did not talk blood and insurrection to that man there who sat munching black bread with that abused and mistaught herd of human sheep, but took him aside and talked matter of another sort to him. After I had finished, I got him to lend me a little ink from his veins; and with this and a sliver I wrote on a piece of bark—

Put him in the Man-Factory—

and gave it to him, and said—

"Take it to the palace at Camelot and give it into the hands of Amyas le Poulet, whom I call Clarence, and he will understand."

"He is a priest, then," said the man, and some of the enthusiasm went out of his face.

"How—a priest? Didn't I tell you that no chattel of the Church, no bond-slave of pope or bishop can enter my Man-Factory? Didn't I tell you that *you* couldn't enter unless your religion, whatever it might be, was your own free property?"

"Marry, it is so, and for that I was glad; wherefore it liked me not, and bred in me a cold doubt, to hear of this priest being there."

"But he isn't a priest, I tell you."

The man looked far from satisfied. He said:

"He is not a priest, and yet can read?"

"He is not a priest and yet can read—yes, and write, too, for that matter. I taught him myself." The man's face cleared. "And it is the first thing that you yourself will be taught in that Factory—"

"I? I would give blood out of my heart to know that art. Why, I will be your slave, your—"

"No you won't, you won't be anybody's slave. Take your family and go along. Your lord the bishop will confiscate your small property, but no matter, Clarence will fix you all right."

CHAPTER 14

"DEFEND THEE, LORD!"

I paid three pennies for my breakfast, and a most extravagant price it was, too, seeing that one could have breakfasted a dozen persons for that money; but I was feeling good by this time, and I had always been a kind of spendthrift any way; and then these people had wanted to give me the food for nothing, scant as their provision was, and so it was a grateful pleasure to emphasize my appreciation and sincere thankfulness with a good big financial lift where the money would do so much more good than it would in my helmet, where, these pennies being made of iron and not stinted in weight, my half dollar's worth was a good deal of a burden to me. I spent money rather too freely in those days, it is true; but one reason for it was that I hadn't got the proportions of things entirely adjusted, even yet, after so long a sojourn in Britain—hadn't got along to where I was able to absolutely realize that a penny in Arthur's land and a couple of dollars in Connecticut were about one and the same thing: just twins, as you may say, in purchasing power. If my start from Camelot could have been delayed a very few days I could have paid these people in beautiful new coins from our own mint, and that would have pleased me; and them, too, not less. I had adopted the American values exclusively. In a week or two now, cents, nickels, dimes, quarters and half dollars, and also a trifle of gold, would be trickling in thin but steady streams all through the commercial veins of the kingdom, and I looked to see this new blood freshen up its life.

The farmers were bound to throw in something, to sort of offset my liberality, whether I would or no; so I let them give me a flint and steel; and as soon as they had comfortably bestowed Sandy and me on our horse, I lit my pipe. When the first blast of smoke shot out through the bars of my helmet, all those people broke for the woods, and Sandy went over backwards and struck the ground with a dull thud. They thought I was one of those fire-belching dragons they had heard so much about from knights and other professional liars. I had infinite trouble to persuade those people to venture back within explaining distance. Then I told them that this was only a bit of enchantment which would work harm to none but my enemies. And I promised, with my hand on my heart, that if all who felt no enmity toward me would come forward and pass before me they should see that only those who remained behind would be struck dead. The procession moved with a good deal of promptness. There were no casualties to report, for nobody had curiosity enough to remain behind to see what would happen.

I lost some time, now, for these big children, their fears gone, became so ravished with wonder over my awe-compelling fireworks that I had to stay there and smoke a couple of pipes out before they would let me go. Still the delay was not wholly unproductive, for it took all that time to get Sandy thoroughly wonted to the new thing, she being so close to it, you know. It plugged up her conversation-mill, too, for a considerable while, and that was a gain. But above all other benefits accruing, I had learned something. I was ready for any giant or any ogre that might come along, now.

We tarried with a holy hermit, that night, and my opportunity came about the middle of the next afternoon. We were crossing a vast meadow by way of short-cut, and I was musing absently, hearing nothing, seeing nothing, when Sandy suddenly interrupted a remark which she had begun that morning, with the cry—

"Defend thee, lord!—peril of life is toward!"

And she slipped down from the horse and ran a little way and stood. I looked up and saw, far off in the shade of a tree, half a dozen armed knights and their squires; and straightway there was bustle among them and tightening of saddle-girths for the mount. My pipe was ready and would have been lit, if I had not been lost in thinking about how to banish oppression from this land and restore to all its people their stolen rights and manhood without disobliging anybody. I lit up at once, and by the time I had got a good head of reserved steam on, here they came. All together, too; none of those chivalrous magnanimities which one reads so much about—one courtly rascal at a time, and the rest standing by to see fair play. No, they came in a body, they came with a whirr and a rush, they came like a volley from a battery; came with heads low down, plumes streaming out behind, lances advanced at a level. It was a handsome sight, a beautiful sight—for a man up a tree. I laid my lance in rest and waited, with my heart beating, till the iron wave was just ready to break over me, then spouted a column of white smoke through the bars of my helmet. You should have seen the wave go to pieces and scatter! This was a finer sight than the other one.

But these people stopped, two or three hundred yards away, and this troubled me. My satisfaction collapsed, and fear came; I judged I was a lost man. But Sandy was radiant; and was going to be eloquent, but I stopped her, and told her my magic had miscarried, somehow or other, and she must mount, with all dispatch, and we must ride for life. No, she wouldn't. She said that my enchantment had disabled those knights; they were not riding on, because they couldn't; wait, they would drop out of their saddles presently, and we would get their horses and harness. I could not deceive such trusting simplicity, so I said it was a mistake; that when my fireworks killed at all, they killed instantly; no, the men would not die, there was something wrong about my apparatus, I couldn't tell what; but we must hurry and get away, for those people would attack us again, in a minute. Sandy laughed, and said—

"Lack-a-day, sir, they be not of that breed! Sir Launcelot will give battle to dragons, and will abide by them, and will assail them again, and yet again, and still again, until he do conquer and destroy them; and so likewise will Sir Pellinore and Sir Aglovale and Sir Carados, and mayhap others, but there be none else that will venture it, let the idle say what the idle will. And, la, as to yonder base rufflers, think ye they have not their fill, but yet desire more?"

"Well, then, what are they waiting, for? Why don't they leave? Nobody's hindering. Good land, I'm willing to let bygones be bygones, I'm sure."

"Leave, is it? Oh, give thyself easement as to that. They dream not of it, no, not they. They wait to yield them."

"Come—really, is that 'sooth'—as you people say? If they want to, why don't they?"

"It would like them much; but an ye wot how dragons are esteemed, ye would not hold them blamable. They fear to come."

"Well, then, suppose I go to them instead, and——"

"Ah, wit ye well they would not abide your coming. I will go."

And she did. She was a handy person to have along on a raid. I would have considered this a doubtful errand, myself. I presently saw the knights riding away, and Sandy coming back. That was a relief. I judged she had somehow failed to get the first innings—I mean in the conversation; otherwise the interview wouldn't have been so short. But it turned out that she had managed the business well; in fact admirably. She said that when she told those people I was The Boss, it hit them where they lived: "smote them sore with fear and dread" was her word; and then they were ready to put up with anything she might require. So she swore them to appear at Arthur's court within two days and yield them, with horse and harness, and be my knights henceforth, and subject to my command. How much better she managed that thing than I should have done it myself! She was a daisy.

CHAPTER 15

SANDY'S TALE

"And so I'm proprietor of some knights," said I, as we rode off. "Who would ever have supposed that I should live to list up assets of that sort. I shan't know what to do with them; unless I raffle them off. How many of them are there, Sandy?"

"Seven, please you, sir, and their squires."

"It is a good haul. Who are they? Where do they hang out?"

"Where do they hang out?"

"Yes, where do they live?"

"Ah, I understood thee not. That will I tell thee eftsoons." Then she said musingly, and softly, turning the words daintily over her tongue: "Hang they out—hang they out—where hang—where do they hang out; eh, right so; where do they hang out. Of a truth the phrase hath a fair and winsome grace, and is prettily worded withal. I will repeat it anon and anon in mine idlesse, whereby I may peradventure learn it. Where do they hang out. Even so! already it falleth trippingly from my tongue, and forasmuch as—"

"Don't forget the cow-boys, Sandy."

"Cow-boys?"

"Yes; the knights, you know: You were going to tell me about them. A while back, you remember. Figuratively speaking, game's called."

"Game—"

"Yes, yes, yes! Go to the bat. I mean, get to work on your statistics, and don't burn so much kindling getting your fire started. Tell me about the knights."

"I will well, and lightly will begin. So they two departed and rode into a great forest. And—"

"Great Scott!"

You see, I recognized my mistake at once. I had set her works agoing; it was my own fault; she would be thirty days getting down to those facts. And she generally began without a preface and finished without a result. If you interrupted her she would either go right along without noticing, or answer with a couple of words, and go back and say the sentence over again. So, interruptions only did harm; and yet I had to interrupt, and interrupt pretty frequently, too, in order to save my life; a person would die if he let her monotony drip on him right along all day.

"Great Scott!" I said in my distress. She went right back and began over again:

"So they two departed and rode into a great forest. And——"

"*Which* two?"

"Sir Gawaine and Sir Uwaine. And so they came to an abbey of monks, and there were well lodged. So on the morn they heard their masses in the abbey, and so they rode forth till they came to a great forest; then was Sir Gawaine ware in a valley by a turret, of twelve fair damsels, and two knights armed on great horses, and the damsels went to and fro by a tree. And then was Sir Gawaine ware how there hung a white shield on that tree, and ever as the damsels came by it they spit upon it, and some threw mire upon the shield—"

"Now, if I hadn't seen the like myself in this country, Sandy, I wouldn't believe it. But I've seen it, and I can just see those creatures now, parading before that shield and acting like that. The women here do certainly act like all possessed. Yes, and I mean your best, too, society's very choicest brands. The humblest hello-girl along ten thousand miles of wire could teach gentleness, patience, modesty, manners, to the highest duchess in Arthur's land."

"Hello-girl?"

"Yes, but don't you ask me to explain; it's a new kind of girl; they don't have them here; one often speaks sharply to them when they are not the least in fault, and he can't get over feeling sorry for it and ashamed of himself in thirteen hundred years, it's such shabby mean conduct and so unprovoked; the fact is, no gentleman ever does it—though I—well, I myself, if I've got to confess—"

"Peradventure she—"

"Never mind her; never mind her; I tell you I couldn't ever explain her so you would understand."

"Even so be it, sith ye are so minded. Then Sir Gawaine and Sir Uwaine went and saluted them, and asked them why they did that despite to the shield. Sirs, said the damsels, we shall tell you. There is a knight in this country that owneth this white shield, and he is a passing good man of his hands, but he hateth all ladies and gentlewomen, and therefore we do all this despite to the shield. I will say you, said Sir Gawaine, it beseemeth evil a good knight to despise all ladies and gentlewomen, and peradventure though he hate you he hath some cause, and peradventure he loveth in some other places ladies and gentlewomen, and to be loved again, and he such a man of prowess as ye speak of—"

"Man of prowess—yes, that is the man to please them, Sandy. Man of brains—that is a thing they never think of. Tom Sayers—John Heenan—John L. Sullivan—pity but you could be here. You would have your legs under the Round Table and a "Sir" in front of your names within the twenty-four hours; and you could bring about a new distribution of the married princesses and duchesses of the Court in another twenty-four. The fact is, it is just a sort of polished-up court of Comanches, and there isn't a squaw in it who doesn't stand ready at the dropping of a hat to desert to the buck with the biggest string of scalps at his belt."

"——and he be such a man of prowess as ye speak of, said Sir Gawaine. Now what is his name? Sir, said they, his name is Marhaus the king's son of Ireland."

"Son of the king of Ireland, you mean; the other form doesn't mean anything. And look out and hold on tight, now, we must jump this gully. . . . There, we are all right now. This horse belongs in the circus; he is born before his time."

"I know him well, said Sir Uwaine, he is a passing good knight as any is on live."

"*On live.* If you've got a fault in the world, Sandy, it is that you are a shade too archaic. But it isn't any matter."

"—for I saw him once proved at a justs where many knights were gathered, and that time there might no man withstand him. Ah, said Sir Gawaine, damsels, methinketh ye are to blame, for it is to suppose he that hung that shield there will not be long therefrom, and then may those knights match him on horseback, and that is more your worship than thus; for I will abide no longer to see a knight's shield dishonored. And therewith Sir Uwaine and Sir Gawaine departed a little from them, and then were they ware where Sir Marhaus came riding on a great horse straight toward them. And when the twelve damsels saw Sir Marhaus they fled into the turret as they were wild, so that some of them fell by the way. Then the one of the knights of the tower dressed his shield, and said on high, Sir Marhaus defend thee. And so they ran together that the knight brake his spear on Marhaus, and Sir Marhaus smote him so hard that he brake his neck and the horse's back—"

"Well, that is just the trouble about this state of things, it ruins so many horses."

"That saw the other knight of the turret, and dressed him toward Marhaus, and they went so eagerly together, that the knight of the turret was soon smitten down, horse and man, stark dead—"

"*Another* horse gone; I tell you it is a custom that ought to be broken up. I don't see how people with any feeling can applaud and support it."

"So these two knights came together with great random—"

I saw that I had been asleep and missed a chapter, but I didn't say anything. I judged that the Irish knight was in trouble with the visitors by this time, and this turned out to be the case.

"—that Sir Uwaine smote Sir Marhaus that his spear brast in pieces on the shield, and Sir Marhaus smote him so sore that horse and man he bare to the earth, and hurt Sir Uwaine on the left side—"

"The truth is, Alisande, these archaics are a little *too* simple; the vocabulary is too limited, and so, by consequence, descriptions suffer in the matter of variety; they run too much to level Saharas of fact, and not enough to picturesque detail; this throws about them a certain air of the monotonous; in fact the fights are all alike: a couple of people come together with great random—random is a good word, and so is exegesis, for that matter, and so is holocaust, and defalcation, and usufruct and a hundred others, but land! a body ought to discriminate—they come together with great random, and a spear is brast, and one party brake his shield and the other one goes down, horse and man, over his horse-tail and brake his neck, and then the next candidate comes randoming in, and brast *his* spear, and the other man brast his shield, and down *he* goes, horse and man, over his horse-tail, and brake *his* neck, and then there's another elected, and another and another and still another, till the material is all used up; and when you come to figure up results, you can't tell one fight from another, nor who whipped; and as a *picture*, of living, raging, roaring battle, sho! why, its pale and noiseless—just ghosts scuffling in a fog. Dear me, what would this barren vocabulary get out of the mightiest spectacle?—the burning of Rome in Nero's time, for instance? Why, it would merely say, 'Town burned down; no insurance; boy brast a window, fireman brake his neck!' Why, *that* ain't a picture!"

It was a good deal of a lecture, I thought, but it didn't disturb Sandy, didn't turn a feather; her steam soared steadily up again, the minute I took off the lid:

"Then Sir Marhaus turned his horse and rode toward Gawaine with his spear. And when Sir Gawaine saw that, he dressed his shield, and they aventred their spears, and they came together with all the might of their horses, that either knight smote other so hard in the midst of their shields, but Sir Gawaine's spear brake—"

"I knew it would."

—"but Sir Marhaus's spear held; and therewith Sir Gawaine and his horse rushed down to the earth—"

"Just so—and brake his back."

—"and lightly Sir Gawaine rose upon his feet and pulled out his sword, and dressed him toward Sir Marhaus on foot, and therewith either came unto other eagerly, and smote together with their swords, that their shields flew in cantels, and they bruised their helms and their hauberks, and wounded either other. But Sir Gawaine, fro it passed nine of the clock, waxed by the space of three hours ever stronger and stronger, and thrice his might was increased. All this espied Sir Marhaus, and had great wonder how his might increased, and so they wounded other passing sore; and then when it was come noon—"

The pelting sing-song of it carried me forward to scenes and sounds of my boyhood days:

"N-e-e-ew Haven! ten minutes for refreshments—knductr 'll strike the gong-bell two minutes before train leaves—passengers for the Shore-line please take seats in the rear k'yar, this k'yar don't go no furder—*ahh*-pls, *aw*-rnjz, b'*nan*ners, *s-a-n-d*'ches, p—*op*-corn!"

—"and waxed past noon and drew towards evensong. Sir Gawaine's strength feebled and waxed passing faint, that unnethes he might dure any longer, and Sir Marhaus was then bigger and bigger—"

"Which strained his armor, of course; and yet little would one of these people mind a small thing like that."

—"and so, Sir Knight, said Sir Marhaus, I have well felt that ye are a passing good knight, and a marvelous man of might as ever I felt any, while it lasteth, and our quarrels are not great, and therefore it were a pity to do you hurt, for I feel you are passing feeble. Ah, said Sir Gawaine, gentle knight, ye say the word that I should say. And there-with they took off their helms and either kissed other, and there they swore together either to love other as brethren—"

But I lost the thread there, and dozed off to slumber, thinking about what a pity it was that men with such superb strength—strength enabling them to stand up cased in cruelly burdensome iron and drenched with perspiration, and hack and batter and bang each other for six hours on a stretch—should not have been born at a time when they could put it to some useful purpose. Take a jackass, for instance: a jackass has that kind of strength, and puts it to a useful purpose, and is valuable to this world because he *is* a jackass; but a nobleman is not valuable because he is a jackass. It is a mixture that is always ineffectual, and should never have been attempted in the first place. And yet, once you start a mistake, the trouble is done and you never know what is going to come of it.

When I came to myself again and began to listen, I perceived that I had lost another chapter, and that Alisande had wandered a long way off with her people.

"And so they rode and came into a deep valley full of stones, and thereby they saw a fair stream of water; above thereby was the head of the stream, a fair fountain, and three damsels sitting thereby. In this country, said Sir Marhaus, came never knight since it was christened, but he found strange adventures—"

"This is not good form, Alisande. Sir Marhaus the king's son of Ireland talks like all the rest; you ought to give him a brogue, or at least a characteristic expletive; by this means one would recognize him as soon as he spoke, without his ever being named. It is a common literary device with the great authors. You should make him say, 'In this country, be jabers, came never knight since it was christened, but he found strange adventures, be jabers.' You see how much better that sounds."

—"came never knight but he found strange adventures, be jabers. Of a truth it doth indeed, fair lord, albeit 'tis passing hard to say, though peradventure that will not tarry but better speed with usage. And then they rode to the damsels, and either saluted other, and the eldest had a garland of gold about her head, and she was threescore winter of age or more—"

"The *damsel* was?"

"Even so, dear lord—and her hair was white under the garland—"

"Celluloid teeth, nine dollars a set, as like as not—the loose-fit kind, that go up and down like a portcullis when you eat, and fall out when you laugh."

"The second damsel was of thirty winter of age, with a circlet of gold about her head. The third damsel was but fifteen year of age—"

Billows of thought came rolling over my soul, and the voice faded out of my hearing!

Fifteen! Break—my heart! oh, my lost darling! Just her age who was so gentle, and lovely, and all the world to me, and whom I shall never see again! How the thought of her carries me back over wide seas of memory to a vague dim time, a happy time, so many, many centuries hence, when I used to wake in the soft summer mornings, out of sweet dreams of her, and say "Hello, Central!" just to hear her dear voice come melting back to me with a "Hello, Hank!" that was music of the spheres to my enchanted ear. She got three dollars a week, but she was worth it.

I could not follow Alisande's further explanation of who our captured knights were, now—I mean in case she should ever get to explaining who they were. My interest was gone, my thoughts were far away, and sad. By fitful glimpses of the drifting tale, caught here and there and now and then, I merely noted in a vague way that each of these three knights took one of these three damsels up behind him on his horse, and one rode north, another east, the other south, to seek adventures, and meet again and lie, after year and day. Year and day —and without baggage. It was of a piece with the general simplicity of the country.

The sun was now setting. It was about three in the afternoon when Alisande had begun to tell me who the cow-boys were; so she had made pretty good progress with it—for her. She would arrive some time or other, no doubt, but she was not a person who could be hurried.

We were approaching a castle which stood on high ground; a huge, strong, venerable structure, whose gray towers and battlements were charmingly draped with ivy, and whose whole majestic mass was drenched with splendors flung from the sinking sun. It was the largest castle we had seen, and so I thought it might be the one we were after, but Sandy said no. She did not know who owned it; she said she had passed it without calling, when she went down to Camelot.

CHAPTER 16

MORGAN LE FAY

If knights errant were to be believed, not all castles were desirable places to seek hospitality in. As a matter of fact, knights errant were *not* persons to be believed—that is, measured by modern standards of veracity; yet, measured by the standards of their own time, and scaled accordingly, you got the truth. It was very simple: you discounted a statement ninety-seven percent; the rest was fact. Now after making this allowance, the truth remained that if I could find out something about a castle before ringing the door-bell—I mean hailing the warders—it was the sensible thing to do. So I was pleased when I saw in the distance a horseman making the bottom turn of the road that wound down from this castle.

As we approached each other, I saw that he wore a plumed helmet, and seemed to be otherwise clothed in steel, but bore a curious addition also—a stiff square garment like a herald's tabard. However, I had to smile at my own forgetfulness when I got nearer and read this sign on his tabard:

"Persimmons's Soap—All the Prime-Donne Use It."

That was a little idea of my own, and had several wholesome purposes in view toward the civilizing and uplifting of this nation. In the first place, it was a furtive, underhand blow at this nonsense of knight errantry, though nobody suspected that but me. I had started a number of these people out—the bravest knights I could get—each sandwiched between bulletin-boards bearing one device or another, and I judged that by and by when they got to be numerous enough they would begin to look ridiculous; and then, even the steel-clad ass that *hadn't* any board would himself begin to look ridiculous because he was out of the fashion.

Secondly, these missionaries would gradually, and without creating suspicion or exciting alarm, introduce a rudimentary cleanliness among the nobility, and from them it would work down to the people, if the priests could be kept quiet. This would undermine the Church. I mean would be a step toward that. Next, education—next, freedom—and then she would begin to crumble. It being my conviction that any Established Church is an established crime, an established slave-pen, I had no scruples, but was willing to assail it in any way or with any weapon that promised to hurt it. Why, in my own former day—in remote centuries not yet stirring in the womb of time—there were old Englishmen who imagined that they had been born in a free country: a "free" country with the Corporation Act and the Test still in force in it—timbers propped against men's liberties and dishonored consciences to shore up an Established Anachronism with.

My missionaries were taught to spell out the gilt signs on their tabards—the showy gilding was a neat idea, I could have got the king to wear a bulletin-board for the sake of that barbaric splendor—they were to spell out these signs and then explain to the lords and ladies what soap was; and if the lords and ladies were afraid of it, get them to try it on a dog. The missionary's next move was to get the family together and try it on himself; he was to stop at no experiment, however desperate, that could convince the nobility that soap was harmless; if any final doubt remained, he must catch a hermit—the woods were full of them; saints they called themselves, and saints they were believed to be. They were unspeakably holy, and worked miracles, and everybody stood in awe of them. If a hermit could survive a wash, and that failed to convince a duke, give him up, let him alone.

Whenever my missionaries overcame a knight errant on the road they washed him, and when he got well they swore him to go and get a bulletin-board and disseminate soap and civilization the rest of his days. As a consequence the workers in the field were increasing by degrees, and the reform was steadily spreading. My soap factory felt the strain early. At first I had only two hands; but before I had left home I was already employing fifteen, and running night and day; and the atmospheric result was getting so pronounced that the king went sort of fainting and gasping around and said he did not believe he could stand it much longer, and Sir Launcelot got so that he did hardly anything but walk up and down the roof and swear, although I told him it was worse up there than anywhere else, but he said he wanted plenty of air; and he was always complaining that a palace was no place for a soap factory, anyway, and said if a man was to start one in his house he would be damned if he wouldn't strangle him. There were ladies present, too, but much these people ever cared for that; they would swear before children, if the wind was their way when the factory was going.

This missionary knight's name was La Cote Male Taile, and he said that this castle was the abode of Morgan le Fay, sister of King Arthur, and wife of King Uriens, monarch of a realm about as big as the District of Columbia—you could stand in the middle of it and throw bricks into the next kingdom. "Kings" and "Kingdoms" were as thick in Britain as they had been in little Palestine in Joshua's time, when people had to sleep with their knees pulled up because they couldn't stretch out without a passport.

La Cote was much depressed, for he had scored here the worst failure of his campaign. He had not worked off a cake; yet he had tried all the tricks of the trade, even to the washing of a hermit; but the hermit died. This was indeed a bad failure, for this animal would now be dubbed a martyr, and would take his place among the saints of the Roman calendar. Thus made he his moan, this poor Sir La Cote Male Taile, and sorrowed passing sore. And so my heart bled for him, and I was moved to comfort and stay him. Wherefore I said—

"Forbear to grieve, fair knight, for this is not a defeat. We have brains, you and I; and for such as have brains there are no defeats, but only victories. Observe how we will turn this seeming disaster into an advertisement; an advertisement for our soap; and the biggest one, to draw, that was ever thought of; an advertisement that will transform that Mount Washington defeat into a Matterhorn victory. We will put on your bulletin-board, '*Patronized by the Elect.*' How does that strike you?"

"Verily, it is wonderly bethought!"

"Well, a body is bound to admit that for just a modest little one-line ad., it's a corker."

So the poor colporteur's griefs vanished away. He was a brave fellow, and had done mighty feats of arms in his time. His chief celebrity rested upon the events of an excursion like this one of mine, which he had once made with a damsel named Maledisant, who was as handy with her tongue as was Sandy, though in a different way, for her tongue churned forth only railings and insult, whereas Sandy's music was of a kindlier sort. I knew his story well, and so I knew how to interpret the compassion that was in his face when he bade me farewell. He supposed I was having a bitter hard time of it.

Sandy and I discussed his story, as we rode along, and she said that La Cote's bad luck had begun with the very beginning of that trip; for the king's fool had overthrown him on the first day, and in such cases it was customary for the girl to desert to the conqueror, but Maledisant didn't do it; and also persisted afterward in sticking to him, after all his defeats. But, said I, suppose the victor should decline to accept his spoil? She said that that wouldn't answer—he must. He couldn't decline; it wouldn't be regular. I made a note of that. If Sandy's music got to be too burdensome, some time, I would let a knight defeat me, on the chance that she would desert to him.

In due time we were challenged by the warders, from the castle walls, and after a parley admitted. I have nothing pleasant to tell about that visit. But it was not a disappointment, for I knew Mrs. le Fay by reputation, and was not expecting anything pleasant. She was held in awe by the whole realm, for she had made everybody believe she was a great sorceress. All her ways were wicked, all her instincts devilish. She was loaded to the eye-lids with cold malice. All her history was black with crime; and among her crimes murder was common. I was most curious to see her; as curious as I could have been to see Satan. To my surprise she was beautiful; black thoughts had failed to make her expression repulsive, age had failed to wrinkle her satin skin or mar its bloomy freshness. She could have passed for old Uriens's grand-daughter, she could have been mistaken for sister to her own son.

As soon as we were fairly within the castle gates we were ordered into her presence. King Uriens was there, a kind-faced old man with a subdued look; and also the son, Sir Uwaine le Blanchemains, in whom I was of course interested on account of the tradition that he had once done battle with thirty knights, and also on account of his trip with Sir Gawaine and Sir Marhaus, which Sandy had been aging me with. But Morgan was the main attraction, the conspicuous personality here; she was head chief of this household, that was plain. She caused us to be seated, and then she began, with all manner of pretty graces and graciousnesses, to ask me questions. Dear me, it was like a bird or a flute, or something, talking. I felt persuaded that this woman must have been misrepresented, lied about. She trilled along, and trilled along, and presently a handsome young page, clothed like the rainbow, and as easy and undulatory of movement as a wave, came with something on a golden salver, and kneeling to present it to her, overdid his graces and lost his balance, and so fell lightly against her knee. She slipped a dirk into him in as matter-of-course a way as another person would have harpooned a rat!

Poor child, he slumped to the floor, twisted his silken limbs in one great straining contortion of pain, and was dead. Out of the old king was wrung an involuntary "O-h!" of compassion. The look he got, made him cut it suddenly short and not put any more hyphens in it. Sir Uwaine, at a sign from his mother, went to the ante-room and called some servants, and meanwhile madame went rippling sweetly along with her talk.

I saw that she was a good housekeeper, for while she talked she kept a corner of her eye on the servants to see that they made no balks in handling the body and getting it out; when they came with fresh clean towels, she sent back for the other kind; and when they had finished wiping the floor and were going, she indicated a crimson fleck the size of a tear which their duller eyes had overlooked. It was plain to me that La Cote Male Taile had failed to see the mistress of the house. Often, how louder and clearer than any tongue, does dumb circumstantial evidence speak.

Morgan le Fay rippled along as musically as ever. Marvelous woman. And what a glance she had: when it fell in reproof upon those servants, they shrunk and quailed as timid people do when the lightning flashes out of a cloud. I could have got the habit myself. It was the same with that poor old Brer Uriens; he was always on the ragged edge of apprehension; she could not even turn towards him but he winced.

In the midst of the talk I let drop a complimentary word about King Arthur, forgetting for the moment how this woman hated her brother. That one little compliment was enough. She clouded up like a storm; she called for her guards, and said—

"Hale me these varlets to the dungeons!"

That struck cold on my ears, for her dungeons had a reputation. Nothing occurred to me to say—or do. But not so with Sandy. As the guard laid a hand upon me, she piped up with the tranquilest confidence, and said—

"God's wownds, dost thou covet destruction, thou maniac? It is The Boss!"

Now what a happy idea that was!—and so simple; yet it would never have occurred to me. I was born modest; not all over, but in spots; and this was one of the spots.

The effect upon madame was electrical. It cleared her countenance and brought back her smiles and all her persuasive graces and blandishments; but nevertheless she was not able to entirely cover up with them the fact that she was in a ghastly fright. She said:

"La, but do list to thine handmaid! as if one gifted with powers like to mine might say the thing which I have said unto one who has vanquished Merlin, and not be jesting. By mine enchantments I foresaw your coming, and by them I knew you when you entered here. I did but play this little jest with hope to surprise you into some display of your art, as not doubting you would blast the guards with occult fires, consuming them to ashes on the spot, a marvel much beyond mine own ability, yet one which I have long been childishly curious to see."

The guards were less curious, and got out as soon as they got permission.

CHAPTER 17

A ROYAL BANQUET

Madame seeing me pacific and unresentful, no doubt judged that I was deceived by her excuse; for her fright dissolved away, and she was soon so importunate to have me give an exhibition and kill somebody, that the thing grew to be embarrassing. However, to my relief she was presently interrupted by the call to prayers. I will say this much for the nobility: that, tyrannical, murderous, rapacious and morally rotten as they were, they were deeply and enthusiastically religious. Nothing could divert them from the regular and faithful performance of the pieties enjoined by the Church. More than once I had seen a noble who had gotten his enemy at a disadvantage, stop to pray before cutting his throat; more than once I had seen a noble, after ambushing and dispatching his enemy, retire to the nearest wayside shrine and humbly give thanks, without even waiting to rob the body. There was to be nothing finer or sweeter in the life of even Benvenuto Cellini, that rough-hewn saint, ten centuries later. All the nobles of Britain, with their families, attended divine service morning and night daily, in their private chapels, and even the worst of them had family worship five or six times a day besides. The credit of this belonged entirely to the Church. Although I was no friend to that Catholic Church, I was obliged to admit this. And often, in spite of me, I found myself saying, "What would this country be without the Church?"

After prayers we had dinner in a great banqueting hall which was lighted by hundreds of grease-jets, and everything was as fine and lavish and rudely splendid as might become the royal degree of the hosts. At the head of the hall, on a dais, was the table of the king, queen, and their son, Prince Uwaine. Stretching down the hall from this, was the general table, on the floor. At this, above the salt, sat the visiting nobles and the grown members of their families, of both sexes, —the resident Court, in effect,—sixty-one persons; below the salt sat minor officers of the household, with their principal subordinates: altogether a hundred and eighteen persons sitting, and about as many liveried servants standing behind their chairs, or serving in one capacity or another. It was a very fine show. In a gallery a band with cymbals, horns, harps and other horrors, opened the proceedings with what seemed to be the crude first-draft or original agony of the wail known to later centuries as "In the Sweet Bye and Bye." It was new, and ought to have been rehearsed a little more. For some reason or other the queen had the composer hanged, after dinner.

After this music, the priest who stood behind the royal table said a noble long grace in ostensible Latin. Then the battalion of waiters broke away from their posts, and darted, rushed, flew, fetched and carried, and the mighty feeding began; no words anywhere, but absorbing attention to business. The rows of chops opened and shut in vast unison, and the sound of it was like to the muffled burr of subterranean machinery.

The havoc continued an hour and a half, and unimaginable was the destruction of substantials. Of the chief feature of the feast—the huge wild boar that lay stretched out so portly and imposing at the start—nothing was left but the semblance of a hoop-skirt; and he was but the type and symbol of what had happened to all the other dishes.

With the pastries and so-on, the heavy drinking began—and the talk. Gallon after gallon of wine and mead disappeared, and everybody got comfortable, then happy, then sparklingly joyous—both sexes,—and bye and bye pretty noisy. Men told anecdotes that were terrific to hear, but nobody blushed; and when the nub was sprung, the assemblage let go with a horse-laugh that shook the fortress. Ladies answered back with historiettes that would almost have made Queen Margaret of Navarre or even the great Elizabeth of England hide behind a handkerchief, but nobody hid here, but only laughed—howled, you may say. In pretty much all of these dreadful stories, ecclesiastics were the hardy heroes, but that didn't worry the chaplain any, he had his laugh with the rest; more than that, upon invitation he roared out a song which was of as daring a sort as any that was sung that night.

By midnight everybody was fagged out, and sore with laughing; and as a rule, drunk: some weepingly, some affectionately, some hilariously, some quarrelsomely, some dead and under the table. Of the ladies, the worst spectacle was a lovely young duchess, whose wedding-eve this was; and indeed she was a spectacle, sure enough. Just as she was she could have sat in advance for the portrait of the young daughter of the Regent d'Orleans, at the famous dinner whence she was carried, foul-mouthed, intoxicated and helpless, to her bed, in the lost and lamented days of the Ancient Regime.

Suddenly, even while the priest was lifting his hands, and all conscious heads were bowed in reverent expectation of the coming blessing, there appeared under the arch of the far-off door at the bottom of the hall, an old and bent and white-haired lady, leaning upon a crutch-stick; and she lifted the stick and pointed it toward the queen and cried out—

"The wrath and curse of God fall upon you, woman without pity, who have slain mine innocent grandchild and made desolate this old heart that had nor chick nor friend nor stay nor comfort in all this world but him!"

Everybody crossed himself in a grisly fright, for a curse was an awful thing to those people; but the queen rose up majestic, with the death-light in her eye, and flung back this ruthless command:

"Lay hands on her! To the stake with her!"

The guards left their posts to obey. It was a shame; it was a cruel thing to see. What could be done? Sandy gave me a look; I knew she had another inspiration. I said—

"Do what you choose."

She was up and facing toward the queen in a moment. She indicated me, and said:

"Madame, *he* saith this may not be. Recal the commandment, or he will dissolve the castle and it shall vanish away like the instable fabric of a dream!"

Confound it, what a crazy contract to pledge a person to! What if the queen—

But my consternation subsided there, and my panic passed off; for the queen, all in a collapse, made no show of resistance but gave a countermanding sign and sunk into her seat. When she reached it she was sober. So were many of the others. The assemblage rose, whiffed ceremony to the winds, and rushed for the door like a mob; overturning chairs, smashing crockery, tugging, struggling, shouldering, crowding—anything to get out before I should change my mind and puff the castle into the measureless dim vacancies of space. Well, well, well, they *were* a superstitious lot. It is all a body can do to conceive of it.

The poor queen was so scared and humbled that she was even afraid to hang the composer without first consulting me. I was very sorry for her—indeed any one would have been, for she was really suffering; so I was willing to do anything that was reasonable, and had no desire to carry things to wanton extremities. I therefore considered the matter thoughtfully, and ended by having the musicians ordered into our presence to play that Sweet Bye and Bye again, which they did. Then I saw that she was right, and gave her permission to hang the whole band. This little relaxation of sternness had a good effect upon the queen. A statesman gains little by the arbitrary exercise of ironclad authority upon all occasions that offer, for this wounds the just pride of his subordinates, and thus tends to undermine his strength. A little concession, now and then, where it can do no harm, is the wiser policy.

Now that the queen was at ease in her mind once more, and measurably happy, her wine naturally began to assert itself again, and it got a little the start of her. I mean it set her music going—her silver bell of a tongue. Dear me, she was a master talker. It would not become me to suggest that it was pretty late and that I was a tired man and very sleepy. I wished I had gone off to bed when I had the chance. Now I must stick it out; there was no other way. So she tinkled along and along, in the otherwise profound and ghostly hush of the sleeping castle, until bye and bye there came, as if from deep down under us, a far-away sound, as of a muffled shriek—with an expression of agony about it that made my flesh crawl. The queen stopped, and her eyes lighted with pleasure; she tilted her graceful head as a bird does when it listens. The sound bored its way up through the stillness again.

"What is it?" I said.

"It is truly a stubborn soul, and endureth long. It is many hours now."

"Endureth what?"

"The rack. Come—ye shall see a blithe sight. An he yield not his secret now, ye shall see him torn asunder."

What a silky smooth hellion she was; and so composed and serene, when the cords all down my legs were hurting in sympathy with that man's pain. Conducted by mailed guards bearing flaring torches, we tramped along echoing corridors, and down stone stairways dank and dripping, and smelling of mould and ages of imprisoned night—a chill, uncanny journey and a long one, and not made the shorter or the cheerier by the sorceress's talk, which was about this sufferer and his crime. He had been accused by an anonymous informer, of having killed a stag in the royal preserves. I said—

"Anonymous testimony isn't just the right thing, your Highness. It were fairer to confront the accused with the accuser."

"I had not thought of that, it being but of small consequence. But an I would, I could not, for that the accuser came masked by night, and told the forester, and straightway got him hence again, and so the forester knoweth him not."

"Then is this Unknown the only person who saw the stag killed?"

"Marry, *no* man *saw* the killing, but this Unknown saw this hardy wretch near to the spot where the stag lay, and came with right loyal zeal and betrayed him to the forester."

"So the Unknown was near the dead stag, too? Isn't it just possible that he did the killing himself? His loyal zeal—in a mask—looks just a shade suspicious. But what is your Highness's idea for racking the prisoner? Where is the profit?"

"He will not confess, else; and then were his soul lost. For his crime his life is forfeited by the law—and of a surety will I see that he payeth it!—but it were peril to my own soul to let him die unconfessed and unabsolved. Nay, I were a fool to fling me into hell for *his* accommodation."

"But, your Highness, suppose he has nothing to confess?"

"As to that, we shall see, anon. An I rack him to death and he confess not, it will peradventure show that he had indeed naught to confess—ye will grant that that is sooth? Then shall I not be damned for an unconfessed man that had naught to confess—wherefore, I shall be safe."

It was the stubborn unreasoning of the time. It was useless to argue with her. Arguments have no chance against petrified training; they wear it as little as the waves wear a cliff. And her training was everybody's. The brightest intellect in the land would not have been able to see that her position was defective.

As we entered the rack-cell I caught a picture that will not go from me; I wish it would. A native young giant of thirty or thereabouts, lay stretched upon the frame on his back, with his wrists and ancles tied to ropes which led over windlasses at either end. There was no color in him; his features were contorted and set, and sweat-drops stood upon his forehead. A priest bent over him on each side; the executioner stood by; guards were on duty; smoking torches stood in sockets along the walls; in a corner crouched a poor young creature, her face drawn with anguish, a half-wild and hunted look in her eyes, and in her lap lay a little child asleep. Just as we stepped across the threshold the executioner gave his machine a slight turn, which wrung a cry from both the prisoner and the woman; but I shouted and the executioner released the strain without waiting to see who spoke. I could not let this horror go on; it would have killed me to see it. I asked the queen to let me clear the place and speak to the prisoner privately; and when she was going to object I spoke in a low voice and said I did not want to make a scene before her servants, but I must have my way; for I was King Arthur's representative, and was speaking in his name. She saw she had to yield. I asked her to endorse me to these people, and then leave me. It was not pleasant for her, but she took the pill; and even went further than I was meaning to require. I only wanted the backing of her own authority; but she said—

"Ye will do in all things as this lord shall command. It is The Boss."

It was certainly a good word to conjure with: you could see it by the squirming of these rats. The queen's guards fell into line, and she and they marched away, with their torch-bearers, and woke the echoes of the cavernous tunnels with the measured beat of their retreating footfalls. I had the prisoner taken from the rack and placed upon his bed, and medicaments applied to his hurts, and wine given him to drink. The woman crept near and looked on, eagerly, lovingly, but timorously,—like one who fears a repulse; indeed, she tried furtively to touch the man's forehead, and jumped back, the picture of fright, when I turned unconsciously toward her. It was pitiful to see.

"Lord," I said, "stroke him, lass, if you want to. Do anything you're a mind to; don't mind me."

Why, her eyes were as grateful as an animal's, when you do it a kindness that it understands. The baby was out of her way and she had her cheek against the man's in a minute, and her hands fondling his hair, and her happy tears running down. The man revived, and caressed his wife with his eyes, which was all he could do. I judged I might clear the den, now, and I did; cleared it of all but the family and myself. Then I said—

"Now my friend, tell me your side of this matter; I know the other side."

The man moved his head in sign of refusal. But the woman looked pleased—as it seemed to me—pleased with my suggestion. I went on:

"You know of me?"

"Yes. All do, in Arthur's realms."

"If my reputation has come to you right and straight, you should not be afraid to speak."

The woman broke in, eagerly:

"Ah, fair my lord, do thou persuade him! Thou canst an thou wilt. Ah, he suffereth so; and it is for me—for *me!* And how can I bear it? I would I might see him die—a sweet, swift death; oh, my Hugo, I cannot bear this one!"

And she fell to sobbing and groveling about my feet, and still imploring. Imploring what? The man's death? I could not quite get the bearings of the thing. But Hugo interrupted her and said—

"Peace! Ye wit not what ye ask. Shall I starve whom I love, to win a gentle death? I wend thou knewest me better."

"Well," I said, "I can't quite make this out. It is a puzzle. Now—"

"Ah, dear my lord, an ye will but persuade him! Consider how these his tortures wound me! Oh, and he will not speak!—whereas, the healing, the solace that lie in a blessed swift death—"

"What *are* you maundering about? He's going out from here a free man and whole—he's not going to die."

The man's white face lit up, and the woman flung herself at me in a most surprising explosion of joy, and cried out—

"He is saved!—for it is the King's word by the mouth of the king's servant—Arthur, the king whose word is gold!"

"Well, then you do believe I can be trusted, after all. Why didn't you before?"

"Who doubted? Not I, indeed; and not she."

"Well, why wouldn't you tell me your story, then?"

"Ye had made no promise; else had it been otherwise."

"I see, I see. . . . And yet I believe I don't quite see, after all. You stood the torture and refused to confess; which shows plain enough to even the dullest understanding that you had nothing to confess—"

"*I*, my lord? How so? It was I that killed the deer!"

"You *did*? Oh, dear, this is the most mixed-up business that ever—"

"Dear lord, I begged him on my knees to confess, but—"

"You *did!* It gets thicker and thicker. What did you want him to do that for?"

"Sith it would bring him a quick death and save him all this cruel pain."

"Well—yes, there is reason in that. But *he* didn't want the quick death."

"He? Why, of a surety he *did.*"

"Well, then, why in the world *didn't* he confess?"

"Ah, sweet sir, and leave my wife and chick without bread and shelter?"

"Oh, heart of gold, now I see it! The bitter law takes the convicted man's estate and beggars his widow and his orphans. They could torture you to death, but without conviction or confession they could not rob your wife and baby. You stood by them like a man; and *you*—true wife and true woman that you are—you would have bought him release from torture at cost to yourself of slow starvation and death—well, it humbles a body to think what your sex can do when it comes to self-sacrifice. I'll book you both for my colony; you'll like it there; it's a Factory where I'm going to turn groping and grubbing automata into *men*."

CHAPTER 18

IN THE QUEEN'S DUNGEONS

Well, I arranged all that; and I had the man sent to his home. I had a great desire to rack the executioner; not because he was a good, pains-taking and pain-giving official,—for surely it was not to his discredit that he performed his functions well—but to pay him back for wantonly cuffing and otherwise distressing that young woman. The priests told me about this, and were generously hot to have him punished. Something of this disagreeable sort was turning up every now and then. I mean, episodes that showed that not all priests were frauds and self-seekers, but that many, even the great majority, of these that were down on the ground among the common people, were sincere and right-hearted, and devoted to the alleviation of human troubles and sufferings. Well, it was a thing which could not be helped, so I seldom fretted about it, and never many minutes at a time; it has never been my way to bother much about things which you can't cure. But I did not like it, for it was just the sort of thing to keep people reconciled to an Established Church. We *must* have a religion—it goes without saying—but my idea is, to have it cut up into forty free sects, so that they will police each other, as had been the case in the United States in my time. Concentration of power in a political machine is bad; and an Established Church is only a political machine; it was invented for that; it is nursed, cradled, preserved for that; it is an enemy to human liberty, and does no good which it could not better do in a split-up and scattered condition. That wasn't law; it wasn't gospel: it was only an opinion—my opinion, and I was only a man, one man: so it wasn't worth any more than the Pope's—or any less, for that matter.

Well, I couldn't rack the executioner, neither would I overlook the just complaint of the priests. The man must be punished some how or other, so I degraded him from his office and made him leader of the band—the new one that was to be started. He begged hard, and said he couldn't play—a plausible excuse, but too thin; there wasn't a musician in the country that could.

The queen was a good deal outraged, next morning, when she found she was going to have neither Hugo's life nor his property. But I told her she must bear this cross; that while by law and custom she certainly was entitled to both the man's life and his property, there were extenuating circumstances, and so in Arthur the king's name I had pardoned him. The deer was ravaging the man's fields, and he had killed it in sudden passion, and not for gain; and he had carried it into the royal forest in the hope that that might make detection of the misdoer impossible. Confound her, I couldn't make her see that sudden passion is an extenuating circumstance in the killing of venison—or of a person—so I gave it up and let her sulk it out. I *did* think I was going to make her see it by remarking that her own sudden passion in the case of the page modified that crime.

"Crime!" she exclaimed. "How thou talkest! Crime, forsooth! Man, I am going to *pay* for him!"

Oh, it was no use to waste sense on her. Training—training is everything; training is all there is *to* a person. We speak of nature; it is folly; there is no such thing as nature; what we call by that misleading name is merely heredity and training. We have no thoughts of our own, no opinions of our own; they are transmitted to us, trained into us. All that is original in us, and therefore fairly creditable or discreditable to us, can be covered up and hidden by the point of a cambric needle, all the rest being atoms contributed by, and inherited from, a procession of ancestors that stretches back a billion years to the Adam-clam or grasshopper or monkey from whom our race has been so tediously and ostentatiously and unprofitably developed. And as for me, all that I think about in this plodding sad pilgrimage, this pathetic drift between the eternities, is to look out and humbly live a pure and high and blameless life, and save that one microscopic atom in me that is truly *me:* the rest may land in Sheol and welcome for all I care.

No, confound her, her intellect was good, she had brains enough, but her training made her an ass—that is, from a many-centuries-later point of view. To kill the page was no crime—it was her right; and upon her right she stood, serenely and unconscious of offense. She was a result of generations of training in the unexamined and unassailed belief that the law which permitted her to kill a subject when she chose was a perfectly right and righteous one.

Well, we must give even Satan his due. She deserved a compliment for one thing; and I tried to pay it, but the words stuck in my throat. She had a right to kill the boy, but she was in no wise obliged to pay for him. That was law for some other people, but not for her. She knew quite well that she was doing a large and generous thing to pay for that lad, and that I ought in common fairness to come out with something handsome about it, but I couldn't—my mouth refused. I couldn't help seeing, in my fancy, that poor old grandam with the broken heart, and that fair young creature lying butchered, his little silken pomps and vanities laced with his golden blood. How could she *pay* for him? *Whom* could she pay? And so, well knowing that this woman, trained as she had been, deserved praise, even adulation, I was yet not able to utter it, trained as *I* had been. The best I could do was to fish up a compliment from outside, so to speak—and the pity of it was, that it was true:

"Madame, your people will adore you for this."

Quite true, but I meant to hang her for it some day, if I lived. Some of those laws were too bad, altogether too bad. A master might kill his slave for nothing: for mere spite, malice, or to pass the time—just as we have seen that the crowned head could do it with *his* slave, that is to say, anybody. A gentleman could kill a free commoner, and pay for him—cash or garden-truck. A noble could kill a noble without expense, as far as the law was concerned, but reprisals in kind were to be expected. *Any*body could kill *some*body, except the commoner and the slave; these had no privileges. If they killed, it was murder, and the law wouldn't stand murder. It made short work of the experimenter—and of his family too, if he murdered somebody who belonged up among the ornamental ranks. If a commoner gave a noble even so much as a Damiens-scratch which didn't kill or even hurt, he got Damiens's dose for it just the same; they pulled him to rags and tatters with horses, and all the world came to see the show, and crack jokes, and have a good time; and some of the performances of the best people present were as tough, and as properly unprintable, as any that have been printed by the pleasant Casanova in his chapter about the dismemberment of Louis XV's poor awkward enemy.

I had had enough of this grisly place by this time, and wanted to leave, but I couldn't, because I had something on my mind that my conscience kept prodding me about, and wouldn't let me forget. If I had the remaking of man, he wouldn't have any conscience. It is one of the most disagreeable things connected with a person; and although it certainly does a great deal of good, it cannot be said to pay, in the long run; it would be much better to have less good and more comfort. Still, this is only my opinion, and I am only one man; others, with less experience, may think differently. They have a right to their view. I only stand to this: I have noticed my conscience for many years, and I know it is more trouble and bother to me than anything else I started with. I suppose that in the beginning I prized it, because we prize anything that is ours; and yet how foolish it was to think so. If we look at it in another way, we see how absurd it is: if I had an anvil in me would I prize it? Of course not. And yet when you come to think, there is no real difference between a conscience and an anvil—I mean for comfort. I have noticed it a thousand times. And you could dissolve an anvil with acids, when you couldn't stand it any longer; but there isn't any way that you can work off a conscience—at least so it will stay worked off; not that I know of, anyway.

There was something I wanted to do before leaving, but it was a disagreeable matter, and I hated to go at it. Well, it bothered me all the morning. I could have mentioned it to the old king, but what would be the use?—he was but an extinct volcano; he had been active in his time, but his fire was out, this good while, he was only a stately ash-pile, now; gentle enough, and kindly enough for my purpose, without doubt, but not usable. He was nothing, this so-called king: the queen was the only power there. And she was a Vesuvius. As a favor, she might consent to warm a flock of sparrows for you, but then she might take that very opportunity to turn herself loose and bury a city. However, I reflected that as often as any other way, when you are expecting the worst, you get something that is not so bad, after all.

So I braced up and placed my matter before her royal Highness. I said I had been having a general jail-delivery at Camelot and among neighboring castles, and with her permission I would like to examine her collection, her bric-a-brac—that is to say, her prisoners. She resisted; but I was expecting that. But she finally consented. I was expecting that, too, but not so soon. That about ended my discomfort. She called her guards and torches, and we went down into the dungeons. These were down under the castle's foundations, and mainly were small cells hollowed out of the living rock. Some of these cells had no light at all. In one of them was a woman, in foul rags, who sat on the ground, and would not answer a question, or speak a word, but only looked up at us once or twice, through a cobweb of tangled hair, as if to see what casual thing it might be that was disturbing with sound and light the meaningless dull dream that was become her life; after that, she sat bowed, with her dirt-caked fingers idly interlocked in her lap, and gave no further sign. This poor rack of bones was a woman of middle age, apparently; but only apparently; she had been there nine years, and was eighteen when she entered. She was a commoner, and had been sent here on her bridal night by Sir Breuse Sance Pité, a neighboring lord whose vassal her father was, and to which said lord she had refused what has since been called *le droit du Seigneur;* and moreover, had opposed violence to violence and spilt half a gill of his almost sacred blood. The young husband had interfered at that point, believing the bride's life in danger, and had flung the noble out into the midst of the humble and trembling wedding guests, in the parlor, and left him there astonished at this strange treatment, and implacably embittered against both bride and groom. The said lord being cramped for dungeon-room had asked the queen to accommodate his two criminals, and here in her bastile they had been ever since; hither indeed, they had come before their crime was an hour old, and had never seen each other since. Here they were, kerneled like toads in the same rock; they had passed nine pitch dark years within fifty feet of each other, yet neither knew whether the other was alive or not. All the first years, their only question had been—asked with beseeching and tears that might have moved stones, in time, perhaps, but hearts are not stones: "Is he alive?" "Is she alive?" But they had never got an answer; and at last that question was not asked any more—or any other.

I wanted to see the man, after hearing all this. He was thirty-four years old, and looked sixty. He sat upon a squared block of stone, with his head bent down, his forearms resting on his knees, his long hair hanging like a fringe before his face, and he was muttering to himself. He raised his chin and looked us slowly over, in a listless dull way, blinking with the distress of the torch-light, then dropped his head and fell to muttering again and took no further notice of us. There were some pathetically suggestive dumb witnesses present. On his wrists and ancles were cicatrices, old smooth scars, and fastened to the stone on which he sat was a chain with manacles and fetters attached; but this apparatus lay idle on the ground, and was thick with rust. Chains cease to be needed after the spirit has gone out of a prisoner.

I could not rouse the man; so I said we would take him to her, and see—to the bride who was the fairest thing in the earth to him, once—roses, pearls and dew made flesh, for him; a wonder-work, the master-work of nature: with eyes like no other eyes, and voice like no other voice, and a freshness, and lithe young grace, and beauty, that belonged properly to the creatures of dreams—as he thought—and to no other. The sight of her would set his stagnant blood leaping; the sight of her—

But it was a disappointment. They sat together on the ground and looked dimly wondering into each other's faces a while, with a sort of weak animal curiosity; then forgot each other's presence, and dropped their eyes, and you saw that they were away again and wandering in some far land of dreams and shadows that we know nothing about.

I had them taken out and sent to their friends. The queen did not like it much. Not that she felt any personal interest in the matter, but she thought it disrespectful to Sir Breuse Sance Pité. However, I assured her that if he found he couldn't stand it I would fix him so that he could.

I set forty-seven prisoners loose out of those awful rat-holes, and left only one in captivity. He was a lord, and had killed another lord, a sort of kinsman of the queen. That other lord had ambushed him to assassinate him, but this fellow had got the best of him and cut his throat. However, it was not for that that I left him jailed, but for maliciously destroying the only public well in one of his wretched villages. The queen was bound to hang him for killing her kinsman, but I would not allow it: it was no crime to kill an assassin. But I said I was willing to let her hang him for destroying the well; so she concluded to put up with that, as it was better than nothing.

Dear me, for what trifling offenses the most of those forty-seven men and women were shut up there! Indeed some were there for no distinct offense at all, but only to gratify somebody's spite; and not always the queen's by any means, but a friend's. The newest prisoner's crime was a mere remark which he had made. He said he believed that men were about all alike, and one man as good as another, barring clothes. He said he believed that if you were to strip the nation naked and send a stranger through the crowd, he couldn't tell the king from a quack doctor, nor a duke from a hotel clerk. Apparently here was a man whose brains had not been reduced to an ineffectual mush by idiotic training. I set him loose and sent him to the Factory.

Some of the cells carved in the living rock were just behind the face of the precipice, and in each of these an arrow-slit had been pierced outward to the daylight, and so the captive had a thin ray from the blessed sun for his comfort. The case of one of these poor fellows was particularly hard. From his dusky swallow's hole high up in that vast wall of native rock he could peer out through the arrow-slit and see his own home off yonder in the valley; and for twenty-two years he had watched it, with heart-ache and longing, through that crack. He could see the lights shine there at night, and in the daytime he could see figures go in and come out—his wife and children, some of them, no doubt, though he could not make out, at that distance. In the course of years he noted festivities there, and tried to rejoice, and wondered if they were weddings or what they might be. And he noted funerals; and they wrung his heart. He could make out the coffin, but he could not determine its size, and so could not tell whether it was wife or child. He could see the procession form, with priests and mourners, and move solemnly away, bearing the secret with them. He had left behind him five children and a wife; and in nineteen years he had seen five funerals issue, and none of them humble enough in pomp to denote a servant. So he had lost five of his treasures; there must still be one remaining—one now infinitely, unspeakably precious,—but *which* one? wife, or child? That was the question that tortured him, by night and by day, asleep and awake. Well, to have an interest, of some sort, and half a ray of light, when you are in a dungeon, is a great support to the body and preserver of the intellect. This man was in pretty good condition yet. By the time he had finished telling me his distressful tale, I was in the same state of mind that you would have been in yourself, if you have got average human curiosity: that is to say, I was as burning up as he was, to find out which member of the family it was that was left. So I took him over home myself; and an amazing kind of a surprise party it was, too—typhoons and cyclones of frantic joy, and whole Niagaras of happy tears; and by George we found the aforetime young matron graying toward the imminent verge of her half century, and the babies all men and women, and some of them married and experimenting family-wise themselves—for not a soul of the tribe was dead! Conceive of the ingenious devilishness of that queen: she had a special hatred for this prisoner, and she had *invented* all those funerals herself, to scorch his heart with; and the sublimest stroke of genius of the whole thing was leaving the family-invoice a funeral *short*, so as to let him wear his poor old soul out guessing.

But for me, he never would have got out. Morgan le Fay hated him with her whole heart, and she never would have softened toward him. And yet his crime was committed more in thoughtlessness than deliberate depravity. He had said she had red hair. Well, she had; but that was no way to speak of it. When red-headed people are above a certain social grade, their hair is auburn.

Consider it: among these forty-seven captives, there were five whose names, offences and dates of incarceration were no longer known! One woman and four men—all bent, and wrinkled, and mind-extinguished patriarchs. They themselves had long ago forgotten these details; at any rate they had mere vague theories about them, nothing definite and nothing that they repeated twice in the same way. The succession of priests whose office it had been to pray daily with the captives and remind them that God had put them there, for some wise purpose or other, and teach them that patience, humbleness, and submission to oppression was what He loved to see in parties of a subordinate rank, had traditions about these poor old human ruins, but nothing more. These traditions went but little way, for they concerned the length of the incarceration only, and not the names or the offences. And even by the help of tradition the only thing that could be proven was that none of the five had seen daylight for thirty-five years: how much longer this privation had lasted was not guessable. The king and the queen knew nothing about these poor creatures, except that they were heirlooms, assets inherited, along with the throne, from the former firm. Nothing of their history had been transmitted with their persons, and so the inheriting owners had considered them of no value, and had felt no interest in them. I said to the queen—

"Then why in the world didn't you set them free?"

The question was a puzzler. She didn't know *why* she hadn't; the thing had never come up in her mind. So here she was, forecasting the veritable history of future prisoners of the castle d'If, without knowing it. It seemed plain to me now, that with her training, those inherited prisoners were merely property—nothing more, nothing less. Well, when we inherit property, it does not occur to us to throw it away, even when we do not value it.

When I brought my procession of human bats up into the open world and the glare of the afternoon sun—previously blind-folding them, in charity for eyes so long untortured by light—they were a spectacle to look at. Skeletons, scarecrows, goblins, pathetic frights, every one: legitimatest possible children of Monarchy by the Grace of God and the Established Church. I muttered absently—

"I *wish* I could photograph them!"

You have seen that kind of people who will never let on that they don't know the meaning of a new big word. The more ignorant they are, the more pitifully certain they are to pretend you haven't shot over their heads. The queen was just one of that sort, and was always making the stupidest blunders by reason of it. She hesitated a moment; then her face brightened up with sudden comprehension, and she said she would do it for me.

I thought to myself: She? why what can she know about photography? But it was a poor time to be thinking. When I looked around, she was moving on the procession with an axe!

Well, she certainly was a curious one, was Morgan le Fay. I have seen a good many kinds of women in my time, but she laid over them all, for variety. And how sharply characteristic of her this episode was. She had no more idea than a horse, of how to photograph a procession; but being in doubt, it was just like her to try to do it with an axe.

CHAPTER 19

KNIGHT ERRANTRY AS A TRADE

Sandy and I were on the road again, next morning, bright and early. It was *so* good to open up one's lungs and take in whole luscious barrels-full of the blessed God's untainted, dew-freshened, woodland-scented air once more, after suffocating body and mind for two days and nights in the moral and physical stenches of that intolerable old buzzard-roost! I mean, for me: of course the place was all right and agreeable enough for Sandy, for she had been used to high life all her days.

Poor girl, her jaws had had a wearisome rest, now for a while, and I was expecting to get the consequences. I was right; but she had stood by me most helpfully in the castle, and had mightily supported and reinforced me with gigantic foolishnesses which were worth more for the occasion than wisdoms double their size; so I thought she had earned a right to work her mill for a while, if she wanted to, and I felt not a pang when she started it up:

"Now turn we unto Sir Marhaus that rode with the damsel of thirty winter of age southward–"

"Are you going to see if you can work up another half-stretch on the trail of the cowboys, Sandy?"

"Even so, fair my lord."

"Go ahead, then. I won't interrupt this time, if I can help it. Begin over again; start fair, and shake out all your reefs, and I will load my pipe and give good attention."

"Now turn we unto Sir Marhaus that rode with the damsel of thirty winter of age southward. And so they came into a deep forest, and by fortune they were nighted, and rode along in a deep way, and at the last they came into a courtelage where abode the duke of South Marches, and there they asked harbour. And on the morn the duke sent unto Sir Marhaus, and bad him make him ready. And so Sir Marhaus arose and armed him, and there was a mass sung afore him, and he brake his fast, and so mounted on horseback in the court of the castle, there they should do the battle. So there was the duke already on horseback, clean armed, and his six sons by him, and every each had a spear in his hand, and so they encountered, whereas the duke and his two sons brake their spears upon him, but Sir Marhaus held up his spear and touched none of them. Then came the four sons by couples, and two of them brake their spears, and so did the other two. And all this while Sir Marhaus touched them not. Then Sir Marhaus ran to the duke, and smote him with his spear that horse and man fell to the earth. And so he served his sons. And then Sir Marhaus alight down, and bad the duke yield him or else he would slay him. And then some of his sons recovered, and would have set upon Sir Marhaus. Then Sir Marhaus said to the duke, Cease thy sons, or else I will do the uttermost to you all. When the duke saw he might not escape the death, he cried to his sons, and charged them to yield them to Sir Marhaus. And they kneeled all down and put the pommels of their swords to the knight, and so he received them. And then they holp up their father, and so by their common assent promised unto Sir Marhaus never to be foes unto King Arthur, and thereupon at Whitsuntide after, to come he and his sons, and put them in the king's grace.*

"Even so standeth the history, fair Sir Boss. Now ye shall wit that that very duke and his six sons are they whom but few days past you also did overcome and send to Arthur's court!"

"Why, Sandy, you can't mean it!"

* The story is borrowed, language and all, from the *Morte d'Arthur*.–M. T.

"An I speak not sooth, let it be the worse for me."

"Well, well, well,—now who would ever have thought it? One whole duke and six dukelets; why, Sandy, it was an elegant haul. Knight-errantry is a most chuckle-headed trade, and it is tedious hard work, too, but I begin to see that there *is* money in it, after all, if you have luck. Not that I would ever engage in it as a business; for I wouldn't. No sound and legitimate business can be established on a basis of speculation. A successful whirl in the knight-errantry line—now what is it when you blow away the nonsense and come down to the cold facts? It's just a corner in pork, that's all, and you can't make anything else out of it. You're rich—yes,—suddenly rich—for about a day, maybe a week: then somebody corners the market on *you,* and down goes your bucket-shop; ain't that so, Sandy?"

"Whethersoever it be that my mind miscarrieth, bewraying simple language in such sort that the words do seem to come endlong and overthwart—"

"There's no use in beating about the bush and trying to get around it that way, Sandy, it's *so,* just as I say. I *know* it's so. And, moreover, when you come right down to the bed-rock, knight-errantry is *worse* than pork; for whatever happens, the pork's left, and so somebody's benefited, anyway; but when the market breaks, in a knight-errantry whirl, and every knight in the pool passes in his checks, what have you got for assets? Just a rubbish-pile of battered corpses and a barrel or two of busted hardware. Can you call *those* assets? Give me pork, every time. Am I right?"

"Ah, peradventure my head being distraught by the manifold matters whereunto the confusions of these but late adventured haps and fortunings whereby not I alone nor you alone, but every each of us, meseemeth—"

"No, it's not your head, Sandy. Your head's all right, as far as it goes, but you don't know business; that's where the trouble is. It unfits you to argue about business, and you're wrong to be always trying. However, that aside, it was a good haul, anyway, and will breed a handsome crop of reputation in Arthur's court. And speaking of the cow-boys, what a curious country this is for women and men that never get old. Now there's Morgan le Fay, as fresh and young as a Vassar pullet, to all appearances, and here is this old duke of the South Marches still slashing away with sword and lance at his time of life, after raising such a family as he has raised. As I understand it, Sir Gawaine killed seven of his sons, and still he had six left for Sir Marhaus and me to take into camp. And then there was that damsel of sixty winter of age still excursioning around in her frosty bloom—How old are you, Sandy?"

It was the first time I ever struck a still place in her. The mill had shut down for repairs, or something.

CHAPTER 20

THE OGRE'S CASTLE

Between six and nine we made ten miles, which was plenty for a horse carrying triple—man, woman, and armor; then we stopped for a long nooning, under some trees by a limpid brook.

Right so came bye and bye a knight riding; and as he drew near he made dolorous moan, and by the words of it I perceived that he was cursing and swearing; yet nevertheless was I glad of his coming, for that I saw he bore a bulletin-board whereon in letters all of shining gold was writ—

"USE PETERSON'S PROPHYLACTIC TOOTH-BRUSH
—ALL THE GO."

I was glad of his coming, for even by this token I knew him for knight of mine. It was Sir Madok de la Montaine, a burly great fellow whose chief distinction was that he had come within an ace of sending Sir Launcelot down over his horse-tail once. He was never long in a stranger's presence without finding some pretext or other to let out that great fact. But there was another fact of nearly the same size, which he never pushed upon anybody unasked, and yet never withheld when asked: that was, that the reason he didn't quite succeed was, that he was interrupted and sent down over horse-tail himself. This innocent vast lubber did not see any particular difference between the two facts. I liked him, for he was earnest in his work, and very valuable. And he was so fine to look at, with his broad mailed shoulders, and the grand leonine set of his plumed head, and his big shield with its quaint device of a gauntleted hand clutching a prophylactic tooth-brush, with motto: *"Try Noyoudont."* This was a toothwash that I was introducing.

He was aweary, he said, and indeed he looked it; but he would not alight. He said he was after the stove-polish man; and with this he broke out cursing and swearing anew. The bulletin-boarder referred to was Sir Ossaise of Surluse, a brave knight, and of considerable celebrity on account of his having tried conclusions in a tournament, once, with no less a Mogul than Sir Gaheris himself—although not successfully. He was of a light and laughing disposition, and to him nothing in this world was serious. It was for this reason that I had chosen him to work up a stove-polish sentiment. There were no stoves yet, and so there could be nothing serious about stove-polish. All that the agent needed to do was to deftly and by degrees prepare the public for the great change, and have them established in predilections toward neatness against the time when the stove should appear upon the stage.

Sir Madok was very bitter, and brake out anew with cursings. He said he had cursed his soul to rags; and yet he would not get down from his horse, neither would he take any rest, or listen to any comfort, until he should have found Sir Ossaise and settled this account. It appeared, by what I could piece together of the unprofane fragments of his statement, that he had chanced upon Sir Ossaise at dawn of the morning, and been told that if he would make a short cut across the fields and swamps and broken hills and glades, he could head off a company of travelers who would be rare customers for prophylactics and tooth-wash. With characteristic zeal Sir Madok had plunged away at once upon this quest, and after three hours of awful crosslot riding had overhauled his game. And behold, it was the five patriarchs that had been released from the dungeons the evening before! Poor old creatures, it was all of twenty years since any one of them had known what it was to be equipped with any remaining snag or remnant of a tooth.

"Blank-blank-blank him," said Sir Madok, "an I do not stove-polish him an I may find him, leave it to me; for never no knight that hight Ossaise or aught else may do me this disservice and bide on live, an I may find him, the which I have thereunto sworn a great oath this day."

And with these words, and others, he lightly took his spear and gat him thence. In the middle of the afternoon we came upon one of those very patriarchs ourselves, in the edge of a poor village. He was basking in the love of relatives and friends whom he had not seen for fifty years; and about him and caressing him were also descendants of his own body whom he had never seen at all till now; but to him these were all strangers, his memory was gone, his mind was stagnant. It seemed incredible that a man could outlast half a century shut up in a dark hole like a rat, but here were his old wife and some old comrades to testify to it. They could remember him as he was in the freshness and strength of his young manhood, when he kissed his child and delivered it to its mother's hands and went away into that long oblivion. The people at the castle could not tell within half a generation the length of time the man had been shut up there for his unrecorded and forgotten offence; but this old wife knew; and so did her old child, who stood there among her married sons and daughters trying to realize a father who had been to her a name, a thought, a formless image, a tradition, all her life, and now was suddenly concreted into actual flesh and blood and set before her face.

It was a curious situation; yet it is not on that account that I have made room for it here, but on account of a thing which seemed to me still more curious. To-wit, that this dreadful matter brought from these down-trodden people no outburst of rage against their oppressors. They had been heritors and subjects of cruelty and outrage so long that nothing could have startled them but a kindness. Yes, here was a curious revelation indeed, of the depth to which this people had been sunk in slavery. Their entire being was reduced to a monotonous dead level of patience, resignation, dumb uncomplaining acceptance of whatever might befal them in this life. Their very imagination was dead. When you can say that of a man, he has struck bottom, I reckon; there is no lower deep for him.

I rather wished I had gone some other road. This was not the sort of experience for a statesman to encounter who was planning out a peaceful revolution in his mind. For it could not help bringing up the un-get-aroundable fact that, all gentle cant and philosophising to the contrary notwithstanding, no people in the world ever did achieve their freedom by goody-goody talk and moral suasion: it being immutable law that all revolutions that will succeed, must *begin* in blood, whatever may answer afterward. If history teaches anything, it teaches that. What this folk needed, then, was a Reign of Terror and a guillotine, and I was the wrong man for them.

Two days later, toward noon, Sandy began to show signs of excitement and feverish expectancy. She said we were approaching the ogre's castle. I was surprised into an uncomfortable shock. The object of our quest had gradually dropped out of my mind; this sudden resurrection of it made it seem quite a real and startling thing, for a moment, and roused up in me a smart interest. Sandy's excitement increased every moment; and so did mine, for that sort of thing is catching. My heart got to thumping. You can't reason with your heart; it has its own laws, and thumps about things which the intellect scorns. Presently, when Sandy slid from the horse, motioned me to stop, and went creeping stealthily, with her head bent nearly to her knees, toward a row of bushes that bordered a declivity, the thumpings grew stronger and quicker. And they kept it up while she was gaining her ambush and getting her glimpse over the declivity; and also while I was creeping to her side on my knees. Her eyes were burning, now, as she pointed with her finger, and said in a panting whisper—

"The castle! The castle! Lo, where it looms!"

What a welcome disappointment I experienced! I said—

"Castle? It is nothing but a pig-sty; a pig-sty with a wattled fence around it."

She looked surprised and distressed. The animation faded out of her face; and during many monents she was lost in thought and silent. Then—

"It was not enchanted aforetime," she said in a musing fashion, as if to herself. "And how strange is this marvel, and how awful—that to the one perception it is enchanted and dight in a base and shameful aspect; yet to the perception of the other it is not enchanted, hath suffered no change, but stands firm and stately still, girt with its moat and waving its banners in the blue air from its towers. And God shield us, how it pricks the heart to see again these gracious captives, and the sorrow deepened in their sweet faces. We have tarried long, and are to blame."

I saw my cue. The castle was enchanted to *me*, not to her. It would be wasted time to try to argue her out of her delusion, it couldn't be done, I must just humor it. So I said—

"This is a common case—the enchanting of a thing to one eye and leaving it in its proper form to another. You have heard of it before, Sandy, though you haven't happened to experience it. But no harm is done. In fact it is lucky the way it is. If these ladies were hogs to everybody and to themselves, it would be necessary to break the enchantment, and that might be impossible if one failed to find out the particular process of the enchantment. And hazardous, too; for in attempting a disenchantment without the true key, you are liable to err, and turn your hogs into dogs, and the dogs into cats, the cats into rats, and so on, and end by reducing your materials to nothing, finally, or to an odorless gas which you can't follow—which of course amounts to the same things. But here, by good luck, no one's eyes but mine are under the enchantment and so it is of no consequence to dissolve it. These ladies remain ladies to you, and to themselves, and to everybody else; and at the same time they will suffer in no way from my delusion, for when I know that an ostensible hog is a lady, that is enough for me, I know how to treat her."

"Thanks, oh sweet my lord, thou talkest like an angel. And I know that thou wilt deliver them, for that thou art minded to great deeds and art as strong a knight of your hands and as brave to will and to do, as any that is on live."

"I will not leave a princess in the sty, Sandy. Are those three yonder that to my disordered eyes are starveling swineherds—"

"The ogres? Are *they* changed also? It is most wonderful. Now am I fearful; for how canst thou strike with sure aim when five of their nine cubits of stature are to thee invisible? Ah, go warily, fair sir; this is a mightier emprise than I wend."

"You be easy, Sandy. All I need to know is, how *much* of an ogre is invisible; then I know how to locate his vitals. Don't you be afraid, I will make short work of these bunco-steerers. Stay where you are."

I left Sandy kneeling there, corpse-faced but plucky and hopeful, and rode down to the pig-sty, and struck up a trade with the swineherds. I won their gratitude by buying out all the hogs at the lump sum of sixteen pennies, which was rather above latest quotations. I was just in time; for the Church, the lord of the manor, and the rest of the tax gatherers would have been along next day and swept off pretty much all the stock, leaving the swineherds very short of hogs and Sandy out of princesses. But now the tax people could be paid in cash, and there would be a stake left besides. One of the men had ten children; and he said that last year when a priest came and of his ten pigs took the fattest one for tithes, the wife burst out upon him, and offered him a child and said—

"Thou beast without bowels of mercy, why leave me my child, yet rob me of the wherewithal to feed it?"

How curious. The same thing had happened in the Wales of my day, under this same old Established Church, which was supposed by many to have changed its nature when it changed its disguise.

I sent the three men away, and then opened the sty gate and beckoned Sandy to come—which she did; and not leisurely, but with the rush of a prairie-fire. And when I saw her fling herself upon those hogs, with tears of joy running down her cheeks, and strain them to her heart, and kiss them, and caress them, and call them reverently by grand princely names, I was ashamed of her, ashamed of the human race.

We had to drive those hogs home—ten miles; and no ladies were ever more fickle-minded or contrary. They would stay in no road, no path; they broke out through the brush on all sides, and flowed away in all directions, over rocks, and hills, and the roughest places they could find. And they must not be struck, or roughly accosted; Sandy could not bear to see them treated in ways unbecoming their rank. The troublesomest old sow of the lot had to be called my Lady, and your Highness, like the rest. It is annoying and difficult to scour around after hogs, in armor. There was one small countess, with an iron ring in her snout and hardly any hair on her back, that was the devil for perversity. She gave me a race of an hour, over all sorts of country, and then we were right where we had started from, having made not a rod of real progress. I seized her at last by the tail, and brought her along, squealing. When I overtook Sandy, she was horrified, and said it was in the last degree indelicate to drag a countess by her train.

We got the hogs home just at dark—most of them. The princess Nerovens de Morganore was missing, and two of her ladies in waiting: namely, Miss Angela Bohun, and the Demoiselle Elaine Courtemains, the former of these two being a young black sow with a white star in her forehead, and the latter a brown one with thin legs and a slight limp in the forward shank on the starboard side—a couple of the tryingest blisters to drive, that I ever saw. Also among the missing were several mere baronesses—and I wanted them to stay missing; but no, all that sausage-meat had to be found; so, servants were sent out with torches to scour the woods and hills to that end.

Of course the whole drove was housed in the house, and great guns! —well, I never saw anything like it. Nor ever heard anything like it. And never smelt anything like it. It was like an insurrection in a gasometer.

CHAPTER 21

THE PILGRIMS

When I did get to bed at last I was unspeakably tired; the stretching out, and the relaxing of the long-tense muscles, how luxurious, how delicious! but that was as far as I could get—sleep was out of the question, for the present. The ripping and tearing and squealing of the nobility up and down the halls and corridors was pandemonium come again, and kept me broad awake. Being awake, my thoughts were busy, of course; and mainly they busied themselves with Sandy's curious delusion. Here she was, as sane a person as the kingdom could produce; and yet, from my point of view she was acting like a crazy woman. My land, the power of training! of influence! of education! It can bring a body up to believe anything. I had to put myself in Sandy's place to realize that she was not a lunatic. Yes, and put her in mine, to demonstrate how easy it is to seem a lunatic to a person who has not been taught as you have been taught. If I had told Sandy I had seen a wagon, uninfluenced by enchantment, spin along fifty miles an hour; had seen a man, unequipped with magic powers, get into a basket and soar out of sight among the clouds; and had listened, without any necromancer's help, to the conversation of a person who was several hundred miles away, Sandy would not merely have supposed me to be crazy, she would have thought she knew it. Everybody around her believed in enchantments; nobody had any doubts; to doubt that a castle could be turned into a sty, and its occupants into hogs, would have been the same as my doubting, among Connecticut people, the actuality of the telephone and its wonders,—and in both cases would be absolute proof of a diseased mind, an unsettled reason. Yes, Sandy was sane; that must be admitted. If I also would be sane—to Sandy—I must keep my superstitions about unenchanted and unmiraculous locomotives, balloons and telephones, to myself. Also, I believed that the world was not flat, and hadn't pillars under it to support it, nor a canopy over it to turn off a universe of water that occupied all space above: but as I was the only person in the kingdom afflicted with such impious and criminal opinions, I recognized that it would be good wisdom to keep quiet about this matter, too, if I did not wish to be suddenly shunned and forsaken by everybody as a madman.

The next morning Sandy assembled the swine in the dining room and gave them their breakfast, waiting upon them personally and manifesting in every way the deep reverence which the natives of her island, ancient and modern, have always felt for rank, let its outward casket and the mental and moral contents be what they may. I could have eaten with the hogs if I had had birth approaching my lofty official rank; but I hadn't, and so accepted the unavoidable slight and made no complaint. Sandy and I had our breakfast at the second table. The family were not at home. I said:

"How many are in the family, Sandy, and where do they keep themselves?"

"Family?"

"Yes."

"Which family, good my lord?"

"Why, this family; your own family."

"Sooth to say, I understand you not. I have no family."

"No family? Why, Sandy, isn't this your home?"

"Now how indeed might that be? I have no home."

"Well, then, whose house is this?"

"Ah, wit you well I would tell you an I knew myself."

"Come—you don't even know these people? Then who invited us here?"

"None invited us. We but came; that is all."

"Why, woman, this is a most extraordinary performance. The effrontery of it is beyond admiration. We blandly march into a man's house, and cram it full of the only really valuable nobility the sun has yet discovered in the earth, and then it turns out that we don't even know the man's name. How did you ever venture to take this extravagant liberty? I supposed, of course, it was your home. What will the man say?"

"What will he say? Forsooth what can he say but give thanks?"

"Thanks for what?"

Her face was filled with a puzzled surprise:

"Verily, thou troublest mine understanding with strange words. Do ye dream that one of his estate is like to have the honor twice in his life to entertain company such as we have brought to grace his house withal?"

"Well, no—when you come to that. No, it's an even bet that this is the first time he has had a treat like this."

"Then let him be thankful, and manifest the same by grateful speech and due humility; he were a dog, else, and the heir and ancestor of dogs."

To my mind, the situation was uncomfortable. It might become more so. It might be a good idea to muster the hogs and move on. So I said:

"The day is wasting, Sandy. It is time to get the nobility together and be moving."

"Wherefore, fair sir and Boss?"

"We want to take them to their home, don't we?"

"La, but list to him! They be of all the regions of the earth! Each must hie to her own home; wend you we might do all these journeys in one so brief life as He hath appointed that created life, and thereto death likewise with help of Adam, who by sin done through persuasion of his helpmeet, she being wrought upon and bewrayed by the beguilements of the great enemy of man, that serpent hight Satan, aforetime consecrated and set apart unto that evil work by overmastering spite and envy begotten in his heart through fell ambitions that did blight and mildew a nature erst so white and pure whenso it hove with the shining multitudes its brethren-born in glade and shade of that fair heaven wherein all such as native be to that rich estate and——"

"Great Scott!"

"My lord?"

"Well, you know we havn't got time for this sort of thing. Don't you see, we could distribute these people around the earth in less time than it is going to take you to explain that we can't. We mustn't talk now, we must act. You want to be careful; you mustn't let your mill get the start of you that way, at a time like this. To business, now—and sharp's the word. Who is to take the aristocracy home?"

"Even their friends. These will come for them from the far parts of the earth."

This was lightning from a clear sky, for unexpectedness; and the relief of it was like pardon to a prisoner. She would remain to deliver the goods, of course.

"Well, then, Sandy, as our enterprise is handsomely and successfully ended, I will go home and report; and if ever another one—"

"I also am ready; I will go with thee."

This was recalling the pardon.

"How? You will go with me? Why should you?"

"Will I be traitor to my knight, dost think? That were dishonor. I may not part from thee until in knightly encounter in the field some overmatching champion shall fairly win and fairly wear me. I were to blame an I thought that that might ever hap."

"Elected for the long term," I sighed to myself. "I may as well make the best of it." So then I spoke up and said:

"All right; let us make a start."

While she was gone to cry her farewells over the pork, I gave that whole peerage away to the servants. And I asked them to take a duster and dust around a little where the nobilities had mainly lodged and promenaded, but they considered that that would be hardly worth while, and would moreover be a rather grave departure from custom, and therefore likely to make talk. A departure from custom—that settled it; it was a nation capable of committing any crime but that. The servants said they would follow the fashion, a fashion grown sacred through immemorial observance: they would scatter fresh rushes in all the rooms and halls, and then the evidence of the aristocratic visitation would be no longer visible. It was a kind of satire on Nature; it was the scientific method, the geologic method; it deposited the history of the family in a stratified record; and the antiquary could dig through it and tell by the remains of each period what changes of diet the family had introduced successively for a hundred years.

The first thing we struck that day was a procession of pilgrims. It was not going our way, but we joined it nevertheless; for it was hourly being borne in upon me, now, that if I would govern this country wisely, I must be posted in the details of its life, and not at second hand but by personal observation and scrutiny.

This company of pilgrims resembled Chaucer's in this: that it had in it a sample of about all the upper occupations and professions the country could show, and a corresponding variety of costume. There were young men and old men, young women and old women, lively folk and grave folk. They rode upon mules and horses, and there was not a side-saddle in the party; for this specialty was to remain unknown in England for nine hundred years yet.

It was a pleasant, friendly, sociable herd; pious, happy, merry, and full of unconscious coarsenesses and innocent indecencies. What they regarded as the merry tale went the continual round and caused no more embarrassment than it would have caused in the best English society twelve centuries later. Practical jokes worthy of the English wits of the first quarter of the far-off nineteenth century were sprung here and there and yonder along the line, and compelled the delightedest applause; and sometimes when a bright remark was made at one end of the procession and started on its travels toward the other, you could note its progress all the way by the sparkling spray of laughter it threw off from its bows as it plowed along; and also by the blushes of the mules in its wake.

Sandy knew the goal and purpose of this pilgrimage and she posted me. She said:

"They journey to the Valley of Holiness, for to be blessed of the godly hermits and drink of the miraculous waters and be cleansed from sin."

"Where is this watering place?"

"It lieth a two day journey hence, by the borders of the land that hight the Cuckoo Kingdom."

"Tell me about it. Is it a celebrated place?"

"Oh, of a truth, yes. There be none more so. Of old time there lived there an abbot and his monks. Belike were none in the world more holy than these; for they gave themselves to study of pious books, and spoke not the one to the other, or indeed to any, and ate decayed herbs and naught thereto, and slept hard, and prayed much, and washed never; also they wore the same garment until it fell from their bodies through age and decay. Right so came they to be known of all the world by reason of these holy austerities, and visited by rich and poor, and reverenced."

"Proceed."

"But always there was lack of water there. Whereas, upon a time, the holy abbot prayed, and for answer a great stream of clear water burst forth by miracle in a desert place. Now were the fickle monks tempted of the Fiend, and they wrought with their abbot unceasingly by beggings and beseechings that he would construct a bath; and when he was become aweary and might not resist more, he said have ye your will, then, and granted that they asked. Now mark thou what 'tis to forsake the ways of purity the which He loveth, and wanton with such as be worldly and an offense. These monks did enter into the bath and come thence washed as white as snow; and lo, in that moment His sign appeared, in miraculous rebuke! for His insulted waters ceased to flow, and utterly vanished away."

"They fared mildly, Sandy, considering how that kind of crime is regarded in this country."

"Belike; but it was their first sin; and they had been of perfect life for long, and differing in naught from the angels. Prayers, tears, torturings of the flesh, all was vain to beguile that water to flow again. Even processions; even burnt offerings; even votive candles to the Virgin, did fail every each of them; and all in the land did marvel."

"How odd to find that even this industry has its financial panics, and at times sees its assignats and greenbacks languish to zero, and everything come to a standstill. Go on, Sandy."

"And so upon a time, after year and day, the good abbot made humble surrender and destroyed the bath. And behold, His anger was in that moment appeased, and the waters gushed richly forth again, and even unto this day they have not ceased to flow in that generous measure."

"Then I take it nobody has washed since."

"He that would essay it could have his halter free; yea, and swiftly would he need it, too."

"The community has prospered since?"

"Even from that very day. The fame of the miracle went abroad into all lands. From every land came monks to join; they came even as the fishes come, in shoals; and the monastery added building to building, and yet others to these, and so spread wide its arms and took them in. And nuns came, also; and more again, and yet more; and built over against the monastery on the yon side of the vale, and added building to building, until mighty was that nunnery. And these were friendly unto those, and they joined their loving labors together, and together they built a fair great foundling asylum midway of the valley between."

"You spoke of some hermits, Sandy."

"These have gathered there from the ends of the earth. A hermit thriveth best where there be multitudes of pilgrims. Ye shall not find no hermit of no sort wanting. If any shall mention a hermit of a kind he thinketh new and not to be found but in some far strange land, let him but scratch among the holes and caves and swamps that line that Valley of Holiness, and whatsoever be his breed, it skills not, he shall find a sample of it there."

I closed up alongside of a burly fellow with a fat good-humored face, purposing to make myself agreeable and pick up some further crumbs of fact; but I had hardly more than scraped acquaintance with him when he began eagerly and awkwardly to lead up, in the immemorial way, to that same old anecdote—the one Sir Dinadan told me, what time I got into trouble with Sir Sagramore and was challenged of him on account of it. I excused myself and dropped to the rear of the procession, sad at heart, willing to go hence from this troubled life, this vale of tears, this brief day of broken rest, of cloud and storm, of weary struggle and monotonous defeat; and yet shrinking from the change, as remembering how long eternity is, and how many have wended thither who know that anecdote.

Early in the afternoon we overtook another procession of pilgrims; but in this one was no merriment, no jokes, no laughter, no playful ways, nor any happy giddiness, whether of youth or age. Yet both were here, both age and youth; gray old men and women, strong men and women of middle age, young husbands, young wives, little boys and girls, and three babies at the breast. Even the children were smileless; there was not a face among all these half a hundred people but was cast down, and bore that set expression of hopelessness which is bred of long and hard trials and old acquaintance with despair. They were slaves. Chains led from their fettered feet and their manacled hands to a sole-leather belt about their waists; and all except the children were also linked together in a file, six feet apart, by a single chain which led from collar to collar all down the line. They were on foot, and had tramped three hundred miles in eighteen days, upon the cheapest odds and ends of food, and stingy rations of that. They had slept in these chains every night, bundled together like swine. They had upon their bodies some poor rags, but they could not be said to be clothed. Their irons had chafed the skin from their ankles and made sores which were ulcerated and wormy. Their naked feet were torn, and none walked without a limp. Originally there had been a hundred of these unfortunates, but about half had been sold on the trip. The trader in charge of them rode a horse and carried a whip with a short handle and a long heavy lash divided into several knotted tails at the end. With this whip he cut the shoulders of any that tottered from weariness and pain, and straitened them up. He did not speak; the whip conveyed his desire without that. None of these poor creatures looked up as we rode along by; they showed no consciousness of our presence. And they made no sound but one; that was the dull and awful clank of their chains from end to end of the long file, as forty-three burdened feet rose and fell in unison. The file moved in a cloud of its own making.

All these faces were gray with a coating of dust. One has seen the like of this coating upon furniture in unoccupied houses, and has written his idle thought in it with his finger. I was reminded of this when I noticed the faces of some of those women, young mothers carrying babes that were near to death and freedom, how a something in their hearts was written in the dust upon their faces, plain to see, and lord how plain to read! for it was the track of tears. One of these young mothers was but a girl, and it hurt me to the heart to read that writing, and reflect that it was come up out of the breast of such a child, a breast that ought not to know trouble yet, but only the gladness of the morning of life; and no doubt—

She reeled just then, giddy with fatigue, and down came the lash and flicked a flake of skin from her naked shoulder. It stung me as if I had been hit instead. The master halted the file and jumped from his horse. He stormed and swore at this girl, and said she had made annoyance enough with her laziness, and as this was the last chance he should have, he would settle the account now. She dropped on her knees and put up her hands and began to beg and cry and implore, in a passion of terror, but the master gave no attention. He snatched the child from her, and then made the men-slaves who were chained before and behind her throw her on the ground and hold her there and expose her body; and then he laid on with his lash like a madman till her back was flayed, she shrieking and struggling the while, piteously. One of the men who was holding her turned away his face, and for this humanity he was reviled and flogged.

All our pilgrims looked on and commented—on the expert way in which the whip was handled. They were too much hardened by life-long every-day familiarity with slavery to notice that there was anything else in the exhibition that invited comment. This was what slavery could do, in the way of ossifying what one may call the superior lobe of human feeling; for these pilgrims were kindhearted people, and they would not have allowed that man to treat a horse like that.

I wanted to stop the whole thing and set the slaves free, but that would not do. I must not interfere too much and get myself a name for riding over the country's laws and the citizen's rights roughshod. If I lived and prospered I would be the death of slavery, that I was resolved upon; but I would try to fix it so that when I became its executioner it should be by command of the nation.

Just here was the wayside shop of a smith; and now arrived a landed proprietor who had bought this girl a few miles back, deliverable here where her irons could be taken off. They were removed; then there was a squabble between the gentleman and the dealer as to which should pay the blacksmith. The moment the girl was delivered from her irons, she flung herself, all tears and frantic sobbings, into the arms of the slave who had turned away his face when she was whipped. He strained her to his breast, and smothered her face and the child's with kisses, and washed them with the rain of his tears. I suspected. I inquired. Yes, I was right: it was husband and wife. They had to be torn apart by force; the girl had to be dragged away, and she struggled and fought and shrieked like one gone mad till a turn of the road hid her from sight; and even after that, we could still make out the fading plaint of those receding shrieks. And the husband and father, with his wife and child gone, never to be seen by him again in life?—well, the look of him one might not bear at all, and so I turned away; but I knew I should never get his picture out of my mind again, and there it is to this day, to wring my heart-strings whenever I think of it.

We put up at the inn in a village just at nightfall, and when I rose next morning and looked abroad, I was ware where a knight came riding in the golden glory of the new day, and recognized him for knight of mine—Sir Ozana le Cure Hardy. He was in the gentlemen's furnishing line, and his missionarying specialty was plug hats. He was clothed all in steel, in the beautifulest armor of the time—up to where his helmet ought to have been; but he hadn't any helmet, he wore a shiny stove-pipe hat, and was as ridiculous a spectacle as one might want to see. It was another of my surreptitious schemes for extinguishing knighthood by making it grotesque and absurd. Sir Ozana's saddle was hung about with leather hat-boxes, and every time he overcame a wandering knight he swore him into my service and fitted him with a plug and made him wear it. I dressed and ran down to welcome Sir Ozana and get his news.

"How is trade?" I asked.

"Ye will note that I have but these four left; yet were they sixteen whenas I got me from Camelot."

"Why, you have certainly done nobly, Sir Ozana. Where have you been foraging of late?"

"I am but now come from the Valley of Holiness, please you sir."

"I am pointed for that place myself. Is there anything stirring in the monkery, more than common?"

"By the mass ye may not question it! . . . Give him good feed, boy, and stint it not, an thou valuest thy crown; so get ye lightly to the stable and do even as I bid. . . . . . Sir, it is parlous news I bring, and —be these pilgrims? Then ye may not do better, good folk, than gather and hear the tale I have to tell, sith it concerneth you, forasmuch as ye go to find that ye will not find, and seek that ye will seek in vain, my life being hostage for my word, and my word and message being these, namely: That a hap has happened whereof the like has not been seen no more but once this two hundred years, which was the first and last time that that said misfortune strake the holy valley in that form by commandment of the Most High whereto by reasons just and causes thereunto contributing, wherein the matter—"

"The miraculous fount hath ceased to flow!" This shout burst from twenty pilgrim mouths at once.

"Ye say well, good people. I was verging to it, even when ye spake."

"Has somebody been washing again?"

"Nay, it is suspected, but none believe it. It is thought to be some other sin, but none wit what."

"How are they feeling about the calamity?"

"None may describe it in words. The fount is these nine days dry. The prayers that did begin then, and the lamentations in sackcloth and ashes, and the holy processions, none of these have ceased nor night nor day; and so the monks and the nuns and the foundlings be all exhausted, and do hang up prayers writ upon parchment, sith that no strength is left in man to lift up voice. And at last they sent for thee, Sir Boss, to try magic and enchantment; and if you could not come, then was the messenger to fetch Merlin, and he is there these three days, now, and saith he will fetch that water though he burst the globe and wreck its kingdoms to accomplish it; and right bravely doth he work his magic and call upon his hellions to hie them hither and help, but not a whiff of moisture hath he started yet, even so much as might qualify as mist upon a copper mirror an ye count not the barrel of sweat he sweateth betwixt sun and sun over the dire labors of his task; and if ye—"

Breakfast was ready. As soon as it was over I showed to Sir Ozana these words which I had written on the inside of his hat: *"Chemical Department, Laboratory extension, Section G. Pxxp. Send two of first size, two of No. 3, and six of No. 4, together with the proper complementary details–and two of my trained assistants."* And I said:

"Now get you to Camelot as fast as you can fly, brave knight, and show the writing to Clarence, and tell him to have these required matters in the Valley of Holiness with all possible dispatch."

"I will well, Sir Boss," and he was off.

CHAPTER 22

THE HOLY FOUNTAIN

The pilgrims were human beings. Otherwise they would have acted differently. They had come a long and difficult journey, and now when the journey was nearly finished, and they learned that the main thing they had come for had ceased to exist, they didn't do as horses or cats or angle-worms would probably have done–turn back and get at something profitable–no, anxious as they had before been to see the miraculous fountain, they were as much as forty times as anxious now to see the place where it had used to be. There is no accounting for human beings.

We made good time; and a couple of hours before sunset we stood upon the high confines of the Valley of Holiness and our eyes swept it from end to end and noted its features. That is, its large features. These were the three masses of buildings. They were distant and isolated temporalities shrunken to toy constructions in the lonely waste of what seemed a desert–and was. Such a scene is always mournful, it is so impressively still, and looks so steeped in death. But there was a sound here which interrupted the stillness only to add to its mournfulness; this was the faint far sound of tolling bells which floated fitfully to us on the passing breeze, and so faintly, so softly, that we hardly knew whether we heard it with our ears or with our spirits.

We reached the monastery before dark, and there the males were given lodging, but the women were sent over to the nunnery. The bells were close at hand, now, and their solemn booming smote upon the ear like a message of doom. A superstitious despair possessed the heart of every monk and published itself in his ghastly face. Everywhere, these black-robed, soft-sandled, tallow-visaged spectres appeared, flitted about and disappeared, noiseless as the creatures of a troubled dream, and as uncanny.

The old abbot's joy to see me was pathetic. Even to tears; but he did the shedding himself. He said:

"Delay not, son, but get to thy saving work. An we bring not the water back again, and soon, we are ruined, and the good work of two hundred years must end. And see thou do it with enchantments that be holy, for the Church will not endure that work in her cause be done by devil's magic."

"When I work, Father, be sure there will be no devil's work connected with it. I shall use no arts that come of the devil, and no elements not created by the hand of God. But is Merlin working strictly on pious lines?"

"Ah, he said he would, my son, he said he would, and took oath to make his promise good."

"Well, in that case, let him proceed."

"But surely you will not sit idle by, but help?"

"It will not answer to mix methods, Father; neither would it be professional courtesy. Two of a trade must not under-bid each other. We might as well cut rates and be done with it; it would arrive at that in the end. Merlin has the contract; no other magician can touch it till he throws it up."

"But I will take it from him; it is a terrible emergency and the act is thereby justified. And if it were not so, who will give law to the Church? The Church giveth law to all; and what she wills to do, that she may do, hurt whom it may. I will take it from him; you shall begin upon the moment."

"It may not be, Father. No doubt, as you say, where power is supreme, one can do as one likes and suffer no injury; but we poor magicians are not so situated. Merlin is a very good magician in a small way, and has quite a neat provincial reputation. He is struggling along, doing the best he can, and it would not be etiquette for me to take his job until he himself abandons it."

The abbot's face lighted.

"Ah, that is simple. There are ways to persuade him to abandon it."

"No-no, Father, it skills not, as these people say. If he were persuaded against his will, he would load that well with a malicious enchantment which would balk me until I found out its secret. It might take a month. I could set up a little enchantment of mine which I call the telephone, and he could not find out its secret in a hundred years. Yes, you perceive, he might block me for a month. Would you like to risk a month in a dry time like this?"

"A month! The mere thought of it maketh me to shudder. Have it thy way, my son. But my heart is heavy with this disappointment. Leave me, and let me wear my spirit with weariness and waiting, even as I have done these ten long days, counterfeiting thus the thing that is called rest, the prone body making outward sign of repose where inwardly is none."

Of course it would have been best, all round, for Merlin to waive etiquette and quit and call it half a day, since he would never be able to start that water, for he was a true magician of the time: which is to say, the big miracles, the ones that gave him his reputation, always had the luck to be performed when nobody but Merlin was present; he couldn't start this well with all this crowd around to see; a crowd was as bad for a magician's miracle in that day as it was for a spiritualist's miracle in mine: there was sure to be some skeptic on hand to turn up the gas at the crucial moment and spoil everything. But I did not want Merlin to retire from the job until I was ready to take hold of it effectively myself; and I could not do that until I got my things from Camelot, and that would take two or three days.

My presence gave the monks hope, and cheered them up a good deal; insomuch that they ate a square meal that night for the first time in ten days. As soon as their stomachs had been properly reinforced with food, their spirits began to rise fast; when the mead began to go round they rose faster. By the time everybody was half-seas over, the holy community was in good shape to make a night of it; so we stayed by the board and put it through on that line. Matters got to be very jolly. Good old questionable stories were told that made the tears run down and cavernous mouths stand wide and the round bellies shake with laughter; and questionable songs were bellowed out in a mighty chorus that drowned the boom of the tolling bells.

At last I ventured a story myself; and vast was the success of it. Not right off, of course, for the native of those islands does not as a rule dissolve upon the early applications of a humorous thing; but the fifth time I told it, they began to crack, in places; the eighth time I told it, they began to crumble; at the twelfth repetition they fell apart in chunks; and at the fifteenth they disintegrated, and I got a broom and swept them up. This language is figurative. Those islanders—well, they are slow pay, at first, in the matter of return for your investment of effort, but in the end they make the pay of all other nations poor and small by contrast.

I was at the well next day betimes. Merlin was there, enchanting away like a beaver, but not raising the moisture. He was not in a pleasant humor; and every time I hinted that perhaps this contract was a shade too hefty for a novice he unlimbered his tongue and cursed like a bishop—French bishop of the Regency days, I mean.

Matters were about as I expected to find them. The "fountain" was an ordinary well, it had been dug in the ordinary way, and stoned up in the ordinary way. There was no miracle about it. Even the lie that had created its reputation was not miraculous; I could have told it myself, with one hand tied behind me. The well was in a dark chamber which stood in the centre of a cut-stone chapel, whose walls were hung with pious pictures of a workmanship that would have made a chromo feel good; pictures historically commemorative of curative miracles which had been achieved by the waters when nobody was looking. That is, nobody but angels: they are always on deck when there is a miracle to the fore—so as to get put in the picture, perhaps. Angels are as fond of that as a fire company; look at the old masters.

The well-chamber was dimly lighted by lamps; the water was drawn with a windlass and chain, by monks, and poured into troughs which delivered it into stone reservoirs outside, in the chapel—when there was water to draw, I mean—and none but monks could enter the well-chamber. I entered it, for I had temporary authority to do so, by courtesy of my professional brother and subordinate. But he hadn't entered it himself. He did everything by incantations; he never worked his intellect. If he had stepped in there and used his eyes, instead of his disordered mind, he could have cured the well by natural means, and then turned it into a miracle in the customary way; but no, he was an old numskull, a magician who believed in his own magic; and no magician can thrive who is handicapped with a superstition like that.

I had an idea that the well had sprung a leak; that some of the wall stones near the bottom had fallen and exposed fissures that allowed the water to escape. I measured the chain—98 feet. Then I called in a couple of monks, locked the door, took a candle, and made them lower me in the bucket. When the chain was all paid out, the candle confirmed my suspicion; a considerable section of the wall was gone, exposing a good big fissure.

I almost regretted that my theory about the well's trouble was correct, because I had another one that had a showy point or two about it for a miracle. I remembered that in America, many centuries later, when an oil well ceased to flow, they used to blast it out with a dynamite torpedo. If I should find this well dry, and no explanation of it, I could astonish these people most nobly by having a person of no especial value drop a dynamite bomb into it. It was my idea to appoint Merlin. However, it was plain that there was no occasion for the bomb. One cannot have everything the way he would like it. A man has no business to be depressed by a disappointment, anyway; he ought to make up his mind to get even. That is what I did. I said to myself, I am in no hurry, I can wait; that bomb will come good, yet. And it did, too.

When I was above ground again, I turned out the monks, and let down a fish-line: the well was a hundred and fifty feet deep, and there was forty-one feet of water in it! I called in a monk and asked:

"How deep is the well?"

"That, sir, I wit not, having never been told."

"How does the water usually stand in it?"

"Near to the top, these two centuries, as the testimony goeth, brought down to us through our predecessors."

It was true—as to recent times at least—for there was witness to it, and better witness than a monk: only about twenty or thirty feet of the chain showed wear and use, the rest of it was unworn and rusty. What had happened when the well gave out that other time? Without doubt some practical person had come along and mended the leak, and then had come up and told the abbot he had discovered by divination that if the sinful bath were destroyed the well would flow again. The leak had befallen again, now, and these children would have prayed, and processioned, and tolled their bells for heavenly succor till they all dried up and blew away, and no innocent of them all would ever have thought to drop a fish-line into the well or go down in it and find out what was really the matter. Old habit of mind is one of the toughest things to get away from in the world. It transmits itself like physical form and feature; and for a man, in those days, to have had an idea that his ancestors hadn't had, would have brought him under suspicion of being illegitimate. I said to the monk:

"It is a difficult miracle to restore water in a dry well, but we will try, if my brother Merlin fails. Brother Merlin is a very passable artist, but only in the parlor-magic line, and he may not succeed; in fact is not likely to succeed. But that should be nothing to his discredit; the man that can do *this* kind of miracle knows enough to keep hotel."

"Hotel? I mind not to have heard——"

"Of hotel? It's what you call hostel. The man that can do this miracle can keep hostel. I can do this miracle; I shall do this miracle; yet I do not try to conceal from you that it is a miracle to tax the occult powers to the last strain."

"None knoweth that truth better than the brotherhood, indeed; for it is of record that aforetime it was parlous difficult and took a year. Natheless, God send you good success, and to that end will we pray."

As a matter of business it was a good idea to get the notion around that the thing was difficult. Many a small thing has been made large by the right kind of advertising. That monk was filled up with the difficulty of this enterprise; he would fill up the others. In two days the solicitude would be booming.

On my way home at noon, I met Sandy. She had been sampling the hermits. I said:

"I would like to do that, myself. This is Wednesday. Is there a matinèe?"

"A which, please you, sir?"

"Matinèe. Do they keep open, afternoons?"

"Who?"

"The hermits, of course."

"Keep open?"

"Yes, keep open. Isn't that plain enough? Do they knock off at noon."

"Knock off?"

"Knock off?—yes, knock off. What is the matter with knock off? I never saw such a dunderhead; can't you understand anything at all? In plain terms, do they shut up shop, draw the game, bank the fires—"

"Shut up shop, draw—"

"There, never mind, let it go; You make me tired. You can't seem to understand the simplest thing."

"I would I might please thee, sir, and it is to me dole and sorrow that I fail, albeit sith I am but a simple damsel and taught of none, being from the cradle unbaptised in those deep waters of learning that do anoint with a sovereignty him that partaketh of that most noble sacrament, investing him with reverend state to the mental eye of the humble mortal who, by bar and lack of that great consecration seeth in his own unlearned estate but a symbol of that other sort of lack and loss which men do publish to the pitying eye with sackcloth trappings whereon the ashes of grief do lie bepowdered and bestrewn, and so, when such shall in the darkness of his mind encounter these golden phrases of high mystery, these shut-up-shops, and draw-the-game, and bank-the-fires, it is but by the grace of God that he burst not for envy of the mind that can beget, and tongue that can deliver so great and mellow-sounding miracles of speech, and if there do ensue confusion in that humbler mind, and failure to divine the meanings of these wonders, then if so be this miscomprehension is not vain but sooth and true, wit ye well it is the very substance of worshipful dear homage and may not lightly be misprized, nor had been, an ye had noted this complexion of my mood and mind and understood that that I would I could not, and that I could not I might not, nor yet nor might *nor* could, nor might-not nor could-not, might be by advantage turned to the desired *would,* and so I pray you mercy of my fault, and that ye will of your kindness and your charity forgive it, good my master and most dear lord."

I couldn't make it all out—that is, the details—but I got the general idea; and enough of it, too, to be ashamed. It was not fair to spring those nineteenth century technicalities upon the untutored infant of the sixth and then rail at her because she couldn't get their drift; and when she was making the honest best drive at it she could, too, and no fault of hers that she couldn't fetch the home-plate; and so I apologized. Then we meandered pleasantly away toward the hermit-holes in sociable converse together, and better friends than ever.

I was gradually coming to have a mysterious and shuddery reverence for this girl; for nowadays whenever she pulled out from the station and got her train fairly started on one of those horizonless transcontinental sentences of hers, it was borne in upon me that I was standing in the awful presence of the Mother of the German Language. I was so impressed with this, that sometimes when she began to empty one of these sentences on me I unconsciously took the very attitude of reverence, and stood uncovered; and if words had been water, I had been drowned, sure. She had exactly the German way: whatever was in her mind to be delivered, whether a mere remark, or a sermon, or a cyclopedia, or the history of a war, she would get it into a single sentence or die. Whenever the literary German dives into a sentence, that is the last you are going to see of him till he emerges on the other side of his Atlantic with his verb in his mouth.

We drifted from hermit to hermit all the afternoon. It was a most strange menagerie. The chief emulation among them seemed to be, to see which could manage to be the uncleanest and most prosperous with vermin. Their manner and attitudes were the last expression of complacent self-righteousness. It was one anchorite's pride to lie naked in the mud and let the insects bite him and blister him unmolested; it was another's to lean against a rock, all day long, conspicuous to the admiration of the throng of pilgrims, and pray; it was another's to go naked, and crawl around on all fours; it was another's to drag about with him, year in and year out, eighty pounds of iron; it was another's to never lie down when he slept, but to stand among the thorn-bushes and snore when there were pilgrims around to look; a woman, who had the white hair of age, and no other apparel, was black from crown to heel with forty-seven years of holy abstinence from water. Groups of gazing pilgrims stood around all and every of these strange objects, lost in reverent wonder, and envious of the fleckless sanctity which these pious austerities had won for them from an exacting heaven.

By and by we went to see one of the supremely great ones. He was a mighty celebrity; his fame had penetrated all Christendom; the noble and the renowned journeyed from the remotest lands on the globe to pay him reverence. His stand was in the centre of the widest part of the valley; and it took all that space to hold his crowds.

His stand was a pillar sixty feet high, with a broad platform on the top of it. He was now doing what he had been doing every day for twenty years up there—bowing his body ceaselessly and rapidly almost to his feet. It was his way of praying. I timed him with a stop-watch, and he made 1244 revolutions in 24 minutes and 46 seconds. It seemed a pity to have all this power going to waste. It was one of the most useful motions in mechanics, the pedal-movement; so I made a note in my memorandum book, purposing some day to apply a system of elastic cords to him and run a sewing-machine with it. I afterwards carried out that scheme, and got five years' good service out of him; in which time he turned out upwards of eighteen thousand first-rate tow-linen shirts, which was ten a day. I worked him Sundays and all; he was going, Sundays, the same as week-days, and it was no use to waste the power. These shirts cost me nothing but just the mere trifle for the materials—I furnished those myself, it would not have been right to make him do that—and they sold like smoke to pilgrims at a dollar and a half apiece, which was the price of fifty cows or a blooded race-horse in Arthurdom. They were regarded as a perfect protection against sin, and advertised as such by my knights everywhere, with the paint-pot and stencil-plate; insomuch that there was not a cliff or a boulder or a dead-wall in England but you could read on it at a mile distance:

"Buy the only genuine St. Stylite; patronized by the Nobility. Patent applied for."

There was more money in the business than one knew what to do with. As it extended, I brought out a line of goods suitable for kings, and a nobby thing for duchesses and that sort, with ruffles down the fore-hatch and the running-gear clewed up with a feather-stitch to leeward and then hauled aft with a back-stay and triced up with a half-turn in the standing rigging forward of the weather-gaskets. Yes, it was a daisy.

But about that time I noticed that the motive power had taken to standing on one leg, and I found that there was something the matter with the other one; so I stocked the business and unloaded, taking Sir Bors de Ganis into camp financially along with certain of his friends: for the works stopped within a year, and the good saint got him to his rest. But he had earned it. I can say that for him.

When I saw him that first time—however, his personal condition will not quite bear description here. You can read it in the Lives of the Saints.*

CHAPTER 23

RESTORATION OF THE FOUNTAIN

Saturday noon I went to the well and looked on a while. Merlin was still burning smoke-powders, and pawing the air, and muttering gibberish as hard as ever, but looking pretty down-hearted, for of course he had not started even a perspiration in that well yet. Finally I said:

"How does the thing promise by this time, partner?"

"Behold, I am even now busied with trial of the powerfulest enchantment known to the princes of the occult arts in the lands of the East; an it fail me, naught can avail. Peace, until I finish."

He raised a smoke this time that darkened all the region, and must have made matters uncomfortable for the hermits, for the wind was their way, and it rolled down over their dens in a dense and billowy fog. He poured out volumes of speech to match, and contorted his body and sawed the air with his hands in a most extraordinary way. At

* All the details concerning the hermits, in this chapter, are from Lecky—but greatly modified. This book not being a history but only a tale, the majority of the historian's frank details were too strong for reproduction in it.—EDITOR.

the end of twenty minutes he dropped down panting, and about exhausted. Now arrived the abbot and several hundred monks and nuns, and behind them a multitude of pilgrims and a couple of acres of foundlings, all drawn by the prodigious smoke, and all in a grand state of excitement. The abbot enquired anxiously for results. Merlin said:

"If any labor of mortal might break the spell that binds these waters, this which I have but just essayed had done it. It has failed; whereby I do now know that that which I had feared is a truth established: the sign of this failure is, that the most potent spirit known to the magicians of the East, and whose name none may utter and live, has laid his spell upon this well. The mortal does not breathe, nor ever will, who can penetrate the secret of that spell, and without that secret none can break it. The water will flow no more forever, good Father. I have done what man could. Suffer me to go."

Of course this threw the abbot into a good deal of a consternation. He turned to me with the signs of it in his face, and said:

"Ye have heard him. Is it true?"

"Part of it is."

"Not all, then, not all! What part is true?"

"That that spirit with the Russian name has put his spell upon the well."

"God's wownds, then are we ruined!"

"Possibly."

"But not certainly? Ye mean, not certainly?"

"That is it."

"Wherefore, ye also mean that when he saith none can break the spell—"

"Yes, when he says that, he says what isn't necessarily true. There are conditions under which an effort to break it may have some chance —that is, some small, some trifling chance—of success."

"The conditions—"

"Oh, they are nothing difficult. Only these: I want the well and the surroundings for the space of half a mile, entirely to myself from sunset to-day until I remove the ban—and nobody allowed to cross the ground but by my authority."

"Are these all?"

"Yes."

"And you have no fear to try?"

"Oh, none. One may fail, of course; and one may also succeed. One can try, and I am ready to chance it. I have my conditions?"

"These and all others ye may name. I will issue commandment to that effect."

"Wait," said Merlin, with an evil smile. "Ye wit that he that would break this spell must know that spirit's name?"

"Yes, I know his name."

"And wit you also that to know it skills not of itself, but ye must likewise pronounce it? Ha-ha! Knew ye that?"

"Yes, I knew that, too."

"You had that knowledge! Art a fool? Are ye minded to utter that name and die?"

"Utter it? Why certainly. I would utter it if it was Welsh."

"Ye are even a dead man, then; and I go to tell Arthur."

"That's all right. Take your gripsack and get along. The thing for *you* to do is to go home and work the weather, John W. Merlin."

It was a home shot, and it made him wince; for he was the worst weather-failure in the kingdom. Whenever he ordered up the danger-signals along the coast there was a week's dead calm, sure, and every time he prophecied fair weather it rained brick-bats. But I kept him in the weather bureau right along, to undermine his reputation. However, that shot raised his bile, and instead of starting home to report my death, he said he would remain and enjoy it.

My two experts arrived in the evening, and pretty well fagged, for they had traveled double tides. They had pack-mules along, and had brought everything I needed—tools, pump, lead pipe, Greek fire, sheaves of big rockets, roman candles, colored-fire sprays, electric apparatus, and a lot of sundries—everything necessary for the stateliest kind of a miracle. They got their supper and a nap, and about midnight we sallied out through a solitude so wholly vacant and complete that it quite overpassed the required conditions. We took possession of the well and its surroundings. My boys were experts in all sorts of things, from the stoning up of a well to the constructing of a mathematical instrument. An hour before sunrise we had that leak mended in shipshape fashion, and the water began to rise. Then we stowed our fireworks in the chapel, locked up the place, and went home to bed.

Before the noon mass was over, we were at the well again; for there was a deal to do, yet, and I was determined to spring the miracle before midnight, for business reasons: for whereas a miracle worked for the Church on a week-day is worth a good deal, it is worth six times as much if you get it in on a Sunday. In nine hours the water had risen to its customary level; that is to say, it was within twenty-three feet of the top. We put in a little iron pump, one of the first turned out by my works near the capital; we bored into a stone reservoir which stood against the outer wall of the well-chamber and inserted a section of lead pipe that was long enough to reach to the door of the chapel and project beyond the threshold, where the gushing water would be visible to the two hundred and fifty acres of people I was intending should be present on the flat plain in front of this little holy hillock at the proper time.

We knocked the head out of an empty hogshead and hoisted this hogshead to the flat roof of the chapel, where we clamped it down fast, poured in gunpowder till it lay loosely an inch deep on the bottom, then we stood up rockets in the hogshead as thick as they could loosely stand, all the different breeds of rockets there are; and they made a portly and imposing sheaf, I can tell you. We grounded the wire of a pocket electrical battery in that powder, we placed a whole magazine of Greek fire on each corner of the roof—blue on one corner, green on another, red on another, and purple on the last, and grounded a wire in each.

Abut two hundred yards off, in the flat, we built a pen of scantlings, about four feet high, and laid planks on it, and so made a platform. We covered it with swell tapestries borrowed for the occasion, and topped it off with the abbot's own throne. When you are going to do a miracle for an ignorant race, you want to get in every detail that will count; you want to make all the properties impressive to the public eye; you want to make matters comfortable for your head guest; then you can turn yourself loose and play your effects for all they are worth. I know the value of these things, for I know human nature. You can't throw too much style into a miracle. It costs trouble, and work, and sometimes money; but it pays in the end. Well, we brought the wires to the ground at the chapel, and then brought them under the ground to the platform, and hid the batteries there. We put a rope fence a hundred feet square around the platform to keep off the common multitude, and that finished the work. My idea was, doors open at 10.30, performance to begin at 11.25 sharp. I wished I could charge admission, but of course that wouldn't answer. I instructed my boys to be in the chapel as early as 10, before anybody was around, and be ready to man the pumps at the proper time, and make the fur fly. Then we went home to supper.

The news of the disaster to the well had traveled far, by this time; and now for two or three days a steady avalanche of people had been pouring into the valley. The lower end of the valley was become one huge camp; we should have a good house, no question about that. Criers went the rounds early in the evening and announced the coming attempt, which put every pulse up to fever-heat. They gave notice that the abbot and his official suite would move in state and occupy the platform at 10.30, up to which time all the region which was under my ban must be clear; the bells would then cease from tolling, and this sign should be permission to the multitudes to close in and take their places.

I was at the platform and all ready to do the honors when the abbot's solemn procession hove in sight—which it did not do till it was nearly to the rope fence, because it was a starless black night and no torches permitted. With it came Merlin, and took a front seat on the platform; he was as good as his word, for once. One could not see the multitudes banked together beyond the ban, but they were there, just the same. The moment the bells stopped, those banked masses broke and poured over the line like a vast black wave, and for as much as a half hour it continued to flow, and then it solidified itself, and you could have walked upon a pavement of human heads to—well, miles.

We had a solemn stage-wait, now, for about twenty minutes—a thing I had counted on for effect; it is always good to let your audience have a chance to work up its expectancy. At length, out of the silence a noble Latin chant—men's voices—broke and swelled up and rolled away into the night, a majestic tide of melody. I had put that up, too, and it was one of the best effects I ever invented. When it was finished I stood up on the platform and extended my hands abroad, for two minutes, with my face uplifted—that always produces a dead hush—and then slowly pronounced this ghastly word with a kind of awfulness which caused hundreds to tremble, and many women to faint:

"Constantinopolitanischerdudelsackspfeifenmachersgesellschafft!"

Just as I was moaning out the closing hunks of that word, I touched off one of my electric connections, and all that murky world of people stood revealed in a hideous blue glare! It was immense—that effect! Lots of people shrieked, women curled up and quit in every direction, foundlings collapsed by platoons. The abbot and the monks crossed themselves nimbly and their lips fluttered with agitated prayers. Merlin held his grip, but he was astonished clear down to his corns; he had never seen anything to begin with that, before. Now was the time to pile in the effects. I lifted my hands and groaned out this word—as it were in agony—

"Nihilistendynamittheaterkaestchenssprengungsattentaetsversuchungen!"

—and turned on the red fire! You should have heard that Atlantic of people moan and howl when that crimson hell joined the blue! After sixty seconds I shouted—

"Transvaaltruppentropentransporttrampelthiertreibertrauungsthraenentragoedie!"

—and lit up the green fire! After waiting only forty seconds, this time, I spread my arms abroad and thundered out the devastating syllables of this word of words—

"Mekkamuselmannenmassenmenchenmoerdermohrenmuttermarmormonumentenmacher!"

—and whirled on the purple glare! There they were, all going at once, red, blue, green, purple!—four furious volcanoes pouring vast clouds of radiant smoke aloft, and spreading a blinding rainbowed noonday to the furthest confines of that valley. In the distance one could see that fellow on the pillar standing rigid against the background of sky, his see-saw stopped for the first time in twenty years. I knew the boys were at the pump, now, and ready. So I said to the abbot:

"The time is come, Father. I am about to pronounce the dread name and command the spell to dissolve. You want to brace up, and take hold of something." Then I shouted to the people: "Behold, in another minute the spell will be broken, or no mortal can break it. If it break, all will know it, for you will see the sacred water gush from the chapel door!"

I stood a few moments, to let the hearers have a chance to spread my announcement to those who couldn't hear, and so convey it to the furthest ranks, then I made a grand exhibition of extra posturing and gesturing, and shouted:

"Lo, I command the fell spirit that possesses the holy fountain to now disgorge into the skies all the infernal fires that still remain in him, and straightway dissolve his spell and flee hence to the pit, there to lie bound a thousand years. By his own dread name I command it —BGWJJILLIGKKK!"

Then I touched off the hogshead of rockets, and a vast fountain of dazzling lances of fire vomited itself toward the zenith with a hissing rush, and burst in mid-sky into a storm of flashing jewels! One mighty groan of terror started up from the massed people—then suddenly broke into a wild hosannah of joy—for there, fair and plain in the uncanny glare, they saw the freed water leaping forth! The old abbot could not speak a word, for tears and the chokings in his throat; without utterance of any sort, he folded me in his arms and mashed me. It was more eloquent than speech. And harder to get over, too, in a country where there were really no doctors that were worth a damaged nickel.

You should have seen those acres of people throw themselves down in that water and kiss it; kiss it, and pet it, and fondle it, and talk to it as if it were alive, and welcome it back with the dear names they gave their darlings, just as if it had been a friend who was long gone away and lost, and was come home again. Yes, it was pretty to see, and made me think more of them than I had done before.

I sent Merlin home on a shutter. He had caved in and gone down like a landslide when I pronounced that fearful name, and had never come to since. He never had heard that name before,—neither had I—but to him it was the right one; any jumble would have been the right one. He admitted, afterward, that that spirit's own mother could not have pronounced that name better than I did. He never could understand how I survived it, and I didn't tell him. It is only young magicians that give away a secret like that. Merlin spent three months working enchantments to try to find out the deep trick of how to pronounce that name and outlive it. But he didn't arrive.

When I started to the chapel, the populace uncovered and fell back reverently to make a wide way for me, as if I had been some kind of a superior being—and I was. I was aware of that. I took along a night-shift of monks, and taught them the mystery of the pump, and set them to work, for it was plain that a good part of the people out there were going to sit up with the water all night, consequently it was but right that they should have all they wanted of it. To those monks that pump was a good deal of a miracle itself, and they were full of wonder over it; and of admiration, too, of the exceeding effectiveness of its performance.

It was a great night, an immense night. There was reputation in it. I could hardly get to sleep for glorying over it.

CHAPTER 24

A RIVAL MAGICIAN

My influence in the Valley of Holiness was something prodigious now. It seemed worth while to try to turn it to some valuable account. The thought came to me the next morning, and was suggested by my seeing one of my knights who was in the soap line come riding in. According to history, the monks of this place two centuries before, had been worldly minded enough to want to wash. It might be that there was a leaven of this unrighteousness still remaining. So I sounded a Brother: "Wouldn't you like a bath?" He shuddered at the thought—the thought of the peril of it to the well—but he said with feeling—

"One needs not to ask that of a poor body who has not known that blessed refreshment sith that he was a boy. Would God I might wash me! but it may not be, fair sir, tempt me not; it is forbidden."

And then he sighed in such a sorrowful way that I was resolved he should have at least one layer of his real estate removed, if it sized up my whole influence and bankrupted the pile. So I went to the abbot and asked for a permit for this Brother. He blenched at the idea—I don't mean that you could see him blench, for of course you couldn't see it without you scraped him, and I didn't care enough about it to scrape him, but I knew the blench was there, just the same, and within a book-cover's thickness of the surface, too—blenched, and trembled. He said:

"Ah, son, ask aught else thou wilt, and it is thine, and freely granted out of a grateful heart—but this, oh, this! Would you drive away the blessed water again?"

"No, Father, I will not drive it away. I have mysterious knowledge which teaches me that there was an error that other time when it was thought the institution of the bath banished the fountain." A large interest began to show up in the old man's face. "My knowledge informs me that the bath was innocent of that misfortune, which was caused by quite another sort of sin."

"These are brave words—but—but right welcome, if they be true."

"They are true, indeed. Let me build the bath again, Father. Let me build it again, and the fountain shall flow forever."

"You promise this?—you promise it? Say the word—say you promise it!"

"I do promise it."

"Then will I have the first bath myself! Go—get ye to your work. Tarry not, tarry not, but go."

I and my boys were at work, straight off. The ruins of the old bath were there yet, in the basement of the monastery, not a stone missing. They had been left just so, all these lifetimes, and avoided with a pious fear, as things accursed. In two days we had it all done and the water in—a spacious pool of clear pure water that a body could swim in. It was running water, too. It came in, and went out, through the ancient pipes. The old abbot kept his word and was the first to try it. He went down black and shaky, leaving the whole black community above troubled and worried and full of bodings; but he came back white and joyful, and the game was made! another triumph scored.

It was a good campaign that we made in that Valley of Holiness, and I was very well satisfied, and ready to move on, now, but I struck a disappointment. I caught a heavy cold, and it started up an old lurking rheumatism of mine. Of course the rheumatism hunted up my weakest place and located itself there. This was the place where the abbot put his arms about me and mashed me, what time he was moved to testify his gratitude to me with an embrace.

When at last I got out, I was a shadow. But everybody was full of attentions and kindnesses, and these brought cheer back into my life and were the right medicine to help a convalescent swiftly up toward health and strength again; so I gained fast.

Sandy was worn out with nursing, so I made up my mind to turn out and go a cruise alone, leaving her at the nunnery to rest up. My idea was to disguise myself as a freeman of peasant degree and wander through the country a week or two on foot. This would give me a chance to eat and lodge with the lowliest and poorest class of free citizens on equal terms. There was no other way to inform myself perfectly of their every-day life and the operation of the laws upon it. If I went among them as a gentleman, there would be restraints and conventionalities which would shut me out from their private joys and troubles, and I should get no further than the outside shell.

One morning I was out on a long walk to get up muscle for my trip and had climbed the ridge which bordered the northern extremity of the valley, when I came upon an artificial opening in the face of a low precipice, and recognized it by its location as a hermitage which had often been pointed out to me from a distance, as the den of a hermit of high renown for dirt and austerity. I knew he had lately been offered a situation in the Great Sahara, where lions and sandflies made the hermit-life peculiarly attractive and difficult, and had gone to Africa to take possession, so I thought I would look in and see how the atmosphere of this den agreed with its reputation.

My surprise was great: the place was newly swept and scoured. Then there was another surprise. Back in the gloom of the cavern I heard the clink of a little bell, and then this exclamation:

"*Hello, Central! Is this you, Camelot?* —Behold, thou mayst glad thy heart an thou hast faith to believe the wonderful when that it cometh in unexpected guise and maketh itself manifest in impossible places—here standeth in the flesh his mightiness The Boss, and with thine own ears shall ye hear him speak!"

Now what a radical reversal of things this was; what a jumbling together of extravagant incongruities; what a fantastic conjunction of opposites and irreconcilables—the home of the bogus miracle become the home of a real one, the den of a medieval hermit turned into a telephone office!

The telephone clerk stepped into the light, and I recognized one of my young fellows. I said:

"How long has this office been established here, Ulfius?"

"But since midnight, fair Sir Boss, an it please you. We saw many lights in the valley, and so judged it well to make a station, for that where so many lights be needs must they indicate a town of goodly size."

"Quite right. It isn't a town in the customary sense, but it's a good stand, anyway. Do you know where you are?"

"Of that I have had no time to make inquiry; for whenas my comradeship moved hence upon their labors, leaving me in charge, I got me to needed rest, purposing to inquire when I waked, and report the place's name to Camelot for record."

"Well, this is the Valley of Holiness."

It didn't take; I mean, he didn't start at the name, as I had supposed he would. He merely said—

"I will so report it."

"Why, the surrounding regions are filled with the noise of late wonders that have happened here! You didn't hear of them?"

"Ah, ye will remember we move by night, and avoid speech with all. We learn naught but that we get by the telephone from Camelot."

"Why *they* know all about this thing. Haven't they told you anything about the great miracle of the restoration of a holy fountain?"

"Oh, *that*? Indeed yes. But the name of *this* valley doth woundily differ from the name of *that* one; indeed to differ wider were not pos—"

"What was that name, then?"

"The Valley of Hellishness."

"*That* explains it. Confound a telephone, anyway. It is the very demon for conveying similarities of sound that are miracles of divergence from similarity of sense. But no matter, you know the name of the place now. Call up Camelot."

He did it, and had Clarence sent for. It was good to hear my boy's voice again. It was like being home. After some affectionate interchanges, and some account of my late illness, I said:

"What is new?"

"The king and queen and many of the court do start even in this hour, to go to your Valley to pay pious homage to the waters ye have restored, and cleanse themselves of sin, and see the place where the infernal spirit spouted true hell-flames to the clouds—an ye listen sharply ye may hear me wink and hear me likewise smile a smile, sith 'twas I that made selection of those flames from out our stock and sent them by your order."

"Does the king know the way to this place?"

"The king?—no, nor to any other in his realms, mayhap; but the lads that holp you with your miracle will be his guide and lead the way, and appoint the places for rests at noons and sleeps at night."

"This will bring them here—when?"

"Mid-afternoon, or later, the third day."

"Anything else in the way of news?"

"The king hath begun the raising of the standing army ye suggested to him; one regiment is complete and officered."

"The mischief! I wanted a main hand in that, myself. There is only one body of men in the kingdom that are fitted to officer a regular army."

"Yes—and now ye will marvel to know there's not so much as one West Pointer in that regiment."

"What are you talking about? Are you in earnest?"

"It is truly as I have said."

"Why, this makes me uneasy. Who were chosen, and what was the method? Competitive examination?"

"Indeed I know naught of the method. I but know this—these officers be all of noble family, and are born—what is it you call it?—chuckle-heads."

"There's something wrong, Clarence."

"Comfort yourself, then; for two candidates for a lieutenancy do travel hence with the king—young nobles both—and if you but wait where you are you will hear them questioned."

"That is news to the purpose. I will get one West Pointer in, anyway. Mount a man and send him to that school with a message; let him kill horses, if necessary, but he must be there before sunset to-night and say—"

"There is no need. I have laid a ground wire to the school. Prithee let me connect you with it."

It sounded good! In this atmosphere of telephones and lightning communication with distant regions, I was breathing the breath of life again after long suffocation. I realized, then, what a creepy, dull, inanimate horror this land had been to me all these years, and how I had been in such a stifled condition of mind as to have grown used to it almost beyond the power to notice it.

I gave my order to the superintendent of the Academy personally. I also asked him to bring me some paper and a fountain pen and a box or so of safety matches. I was getting tired of doing without these conveniences. I could have them, now, as I wasn't going to wear armor any more at present, and therefore could get at my pockets.

When I got back to the monastery, I found a thing of interest going on. The abbot and his monks were assembled in the great hall, observing with childish wonder and faith the performances of a new magician, a fresh arrival. His dress was the extreme of the fantastic; as showy and foolish as the sort of thing an Indian medicine-man wears. He was mowing, and mumbling, and gesticulating, and drawing mystical figures in the air and on the floor,—the regular thing, you know. He was a celebrity from Asia—so he said, and that was enough. That sort of evidence was as good as gold, and passed current everywhere.

How easy and cheap it was to be a great magician on this fellow's terms. His specialty was to tell you what any individual on the face of the globe was doing at the moment; and what he had done at any time in the past, and what he would do at any time in the future. He asked if any would like to know what the Emperor of the East was doing now? The sparkling eyes and the delighted rubbing of hands made eloquent answer—this reverend crowd *would* like to know what that monarch was at, just at this moment. The fraud went through some more mummery, and then made grave announcement:

"The high and mighty Emperor of the East doth at this moment put money in the palm of a holy begging friar—one, two, three pieces, and they be all of silver."

A buzz of admiring exclamations broke out, all around:

"It is marvelous!" "Wonderful!" "What study, what labor, to have acquired a so amazing power as this!"

Would they like to know what the Supreme Lord of Inde was doing? Yes. He told them what the Supreme Lord of Inde was doing. Then he told them what the Sultan of Egypt was at; also what the King of the Remote Seas was about. And so on and so on; and with each new marvel the astonishment at his accuracy rose higher and higher. They thought he must surely strike an uncertain place sometime; but no, he never had to hesitate, he always knew, and always with unerring precision. I saw that if this thing went on I should lose my supremacy, this fellow would capture my following, I should be left out in the cold. I must put a cog in his wheel, and do it right away, too. I said:

"If I might ask, I should very greatly like to know what a certain person is doing."

"Speak, and freely. I will tell you."

"It will be difficult—perhaps impossible."

"My art knoweth not that word. The more difficult it is, the more certainly will I reveal it to you."

You see, I was working up the interest. It was getting pretty high, too; you could see that by the craning necks all around, and the half suspended breathing. So now I climaxed it:

"If you make no mistake—if you tell me truly what I want to know—I will give you two hundred silver pennies."

"The fortune is mine! I will tell you what you would know."

"Then tell me what I am doing with my right hand."

"Ah-h!" There was a general gasp of surprise. It had not occurred to anybody in the crowd—that simple trick of inquiring about somebody who wasn't ten thousand miles away. The magician was hit hard; it was an emergency that had never happened in his experience before, and it corked him; he didn't know how to meet it. He looked stunned, confused; he couldn't say a word. "Come," I said, "what are you waiting for? Is it possible you can answer up, right off, and tell what anybody on the other side of the earth is doing, and yet can't tell what a person is doing who isn't three yards from you? Persons behind me know what I am doing with my right hand—they will endorse you if you tell correctly." He was still dumb. "Very well, I'll tell you why you don't speak up and tell; it is because you don't know. *You* a magician! Good friends, this tramp is a mere fraud and liar."

This distressed the monks and terrified them. They were not used to hearing these awful beings called names, and they did not know what might be the consequence. There was a dead silence, now; superstitious bodings were in every mind. The magician began to pull his wits together, and when he presently smiled an easy, nonchalant smile, it spread a mighty relief around; for it indicated that his mood was not destructive. He said:

"It hath struck me speechless, the frivolity of this person's speech. Let all know, if perchance there be any who know it not, that enchanters of my degree deign not to concern themselves with the doings of any but Kings, Princes, Emperors, them that be born in the purple and them only. Had ye asked me what Arthur the great king is doing, it were another matter, and I had told ye; but the doings of a subject interest me not."

"Oh, I misunderstood you. I thought you said 'anybody,' and so I supposed 'anybody' included—well, anybody; that is, everybody."

"It doth—anybody that is of lofty birth; and the better if he be royal."

"That, it meseemeth, might well be," said the abbot, who saw his opportunity to smooth things and avert disaster, "for it were not likely that so wonderful a gift as this would be conferred for the revelation of the concerns of lesser beings than such as be born near to the summits of greatness. Our Arthur the king—"

"Would you know of him?" broke in the enchanter.

"Most gladly, yea, and gratefully."

Everybody was full of awe and interest again, right away, the incorrigible idiots. They watched the incantations absorbingly, and looked at me with a "There, now, what can you say to that?" air, when the announcement came:

"The king is weary with the chase, and lieth in his palace these two hours sleeping a dreamless sleep."

"God's benison upon him!" said the abbot, and crossed himself; "may that sleep be to the refreshment of his body and his soul."

"And so it might be, if he were sleeping," I said, "but the king is not sleeping, the king rides."

Here was trouble again—a conflict of authority. Nobody knew which of us to believe; I still had some reputation left. The magician's scorn was stirred, and he said:

"Lo, I have seen many wonderful soothsayers and prophets and magicians in my life-days, but none before that could sit idle and see to the heart of things with never an incantation to help."

"You have lived in the woods, and lost much by it. I use incantations myself, as this good brotherhood are aware—but only on occasions of moment."

When it comes to sarcasaming, I reckon I know how to keep my end up. That jab made this fellow squirm. The abbot inquired after the queen and the court, and got this information:

"They be all on sleep, being overcome by fatigue, like as to the king."

I said:

"That is merely another lie. Half of them are about their amusements, the queen and the other half are not sleeping, they ride. Now perhaps you can spread yourself a little, and tell us where the king and queen and all that are this moment riding with them are going?"

"They sleep now, as I said; but on the morrow they will ride, for they go a journey toward the sea."

"And where will they be the day after to-morrow at vespers?"

"Far to the north of Camelot, and half their journey will be done."

"That is another lie, by the space of a hundred and fifty miles. Their journey will not be merely half done, it will be all done, and they will be *here,* in this valley."

That was a noble shot! It set the abbot and the monks in a whirl of excitement, and it rocked the enchanter to his base. I followed the thing right up:

"If the king does not arrive, I will have myself ridden on a rail; if he does I will ride you on a rail instead."

Next day I went up to the telephone office and found that the king had passed through two towns that were on the line. I spotted his progress on the succeeding day in the same way. I kept these matters to myself. The third day's reports showed that if he kept up his gait he would arrive by four in the afternoon. There was still no sign anywhere of interest in his coming; there seemed to be no preparations making to receive him in state; a strange thing, truly. Only one thing could explain this: that other magician had been cutting under me, sure. This was true. I asked a friend of mine, a monk, about it, and he said, yes, the magician had tried some further enchantments and found out that the court had concluded to make no journey at all, but stay at home. Think of that! Observe how much a reputation was worth in such a country. These people had seen me do the very showiest bit of magic in history, and the only one within their memory that had a positive value, and yet here they were, ready to take up with an adventurer who could offer no evidence of his powers but his mere unproven word.

However, it was not good politics to let the king come without any fuss and feathers at all, so I went down and drummed up a procession of pilgrims and smoked out a batch of hermits and started them out at two o'clock to meet him. And that was the sort of state he arrived in. The abbot was helpless with rage and humiliation when I brought him out on a balcony and showed him the head of the state marching in and never a monk on hand to offer him welcome, and no stir of life or clang of joy-bell to glad his spirit. He took one look and then flew to rouse out his forces. The next minute the bells were dinning furiously, and the various buildings were vomiting monks and nuns, who went swarming in a rush toward the coming procession; and with them went that magician—and he was on a rail, too, by the abbot's order; and his reputation was in the mud, and mine was in the sky again. Yes, a man can keep his trade-mark current in such a country, but he can't sit around and do it; he has got to be on deck and attending to business, right along.

CHAPTER 25

A COMPETITIVE EXAMINATION

When the king traveled for change of air, or made a progress, or visited a distant noble whom he wished to bankrupt with the cost of his keep, part of the administration moved with him. It was a fashion of the time. The Commission charged with the examination of candidates for posts in the army came with the king to the Valley, whereas they could have transacted their business just as well at home. And although this expedition was strictly a holiday excursion for the king, he kept some of his business functions going, just the same. He touched for the evil, as usual; he held court in the gate at sunrise and tried cases, for he was himself Chief Justice of the King's Bench.

He shone very well in this latter office. He was a wise and humane judge, and he clearly did his honest best and fairest,—according to his lights. That is a large reservation. His lights—I mean his rearing—often colored his decisions. Whenever there was a dispute between a noble or gentleman and a person of lower degree, the king's leanings and sympathies were for the former class always, whether he suspected it or not. It was impossible that this should be otherwise. The blunting effects of slavery upon the slaveholder's moral perceptions are known and conceded, the world over; and a privileged class, an aristocracy, is but a band of slaveholders under another name. This has a harsh sound, and yet should not be offensive to any—even to the noble himself—unless the fact itself be an offense: for the statement simply formulates a fact. The repulsive feature of slavery is the *thing*, not its name. One needs but to hear an aristocrat speak of the classes that are below him to recognize—and in but indifferently modified measure—the very air and tone of the actual slaveholder; and behind these are the slaveholder's spirit, the slaveholder's blunted feeling. They are the result of the same cause in both cases: the possessor's old and inbred custom of regarding himself as a superior being. The king's judgments wrought frequent injustices, but it was merely the fault of his training, his natural and unalterable sympathies. He was as unfitted for a judgeship as would be the average mother for the position of milk-distributor to starving children in famine-time; her own children would fare a shade better than the rest.

One very curious case came before the king. A young girl, an orphan, who had a considerable estate, married a fine young fellow who had nothing. The girl's property was within a seignory held by the Church. The bishop of the diocese, an arrogant scion of the great nobility, claimed the girl's estate on the ground that she had married privately, and thus had cheated the Church out of one of its rights as lord of the seignory—the one heretofore referred to as *le droit du seigneur*. The penalty of refusal or avoidance was confiscation. The girl's defence was, that the lordship of the seignory was vested in the bishop, and the particular right here involved was not transferable, but must be exercised by the lord himself or stand vacated; and that an older law, of the Church itself, strictly barred the bishop from exercising it. It was a very odd case, indeed.

It reminded me of something I had read in my youth about the ingenious way in which the aldermen of London raised the money that built the Mansion House. A person who had not taken the Sacrament according to the Anglican rite, could not stand as a candidate for sheriff of London. Thus Dissenters were ineligible; they could not run if asked, they could not serve if elected. The aldermen, who without any question were Yankees in disguise, hit upon this neat device: they passed a by-law imposing a fine of £400 upon any one who should refuse to be a candidate for sheriff, and a fine of £600 upon any person who, after being elected sheriff, refused to serve. Then they went to work and elected a lot of Dissenters, one after another, and kept it up until they had collected £15,000 in fines; and there stands the stately Mansion House to this day, to keep the blushing citizen in mind of a long past and lamented day when a band of Yankees slipped into London and played games of the sort that has given their race a unique and shady reputation among all truly good and holy peoples that be in the earth.

The girl's case seemed strong to me; the bishop's case was just as strong. I did not see how the king was going to get out of this hole. But he got out. I append his decision:

"Truly I find small difficulty here, the matter being even a child's affair for simpleness. An the young bride had conveyed notice, as in duty bound, to her feudal lord and proper master and protector the bishop, she had suffered no loss, for the said bishop could have got a dispensation making him, for temporary conveniency, eligible to the exercise of his said right, and thus would she have kept all she had. Whereas, failing in her first duty, she hath by that failure failed in all; for whoso, clinging to a rope, severeth it above his hands, must fall; it being no defence to claim that the rest of the rope is sound, neither any deliverance from his peril, as he shall find. Pardy, the woman's case is rotten at the source. It is the decree of the Court that she forfeit to the said lord bishop all her goods, even to the last farthing that she doth possess, and be thereto mulcted in the costs. Next!"

Here was a tragic end to a beautiful honeymoon not yet three months old. Poor young creatures! They had lived these three months lapped to the lips in worldly comforts. These clothes and trinkets they were wearing were as fine and dainty as the shrewdest stretch of the sumptuary laws allowed to people of their degree; and in these pretty clothes, she crying on his shoulder, and he trying to comfort her with hopeful words set to the music of despair, they went from the judgment seat out into the world homeless, bedless, breadless; why, the very beggars by the roadsides were not so poor as they.

Well, the king was out of the hole; and on terms satisfactory to the Church and the rest of the aristocracy, no doubt. Men write many fine and plausible arguments in support of monarchy, but the fact remains that where every man in a State has a vote, brutal laws are impossible. Arthur's people were of course poor material for a republic, because they had been debased so long by monarchy; and yet even they would have been intelligent enough to make short work of that law which the king had just been administering if it had been submitted to their full and free vote. There is a phrase which has grown so common in the world's mouth that it has come to seem to have sense and meaning—the sense and meaning implied when it is used: that is the phrase which refers to this or that or the other nation as possibly being "capable of self-government;" and the implied sense of it is, that there has been a nation somewhere, sometime or other which *wasn't* capable of it—wasn't as able to govern itself as some self-appointed specialists were or would be to govern it. The master minds of all nations, in all ages, have sprung in affluent multitude from the mass of the nation, and from the mass of the nation only—not from its privileged classes; and so, no matter what the nation's intellectual grade was, whether high or low, the bulk of its ability was in the long ranks of its nameless and its poor, and so it never saw the day that it had not the material in abundance whereby to govern itself. Which is to assert an always self-proven fact: that even the best governed and most free and most enlightened monarchy is still behind the best condition attainable by its people; and that the same is true of kindred governments of lower grades, all the way down to the lowest.

King Arthur had hurried up the army business altogether beyond my calculations. I had not supposed he would move in the matter while I was away; and so I had not mapped out a scheme for determining the merits of officers; I had only remarked that it would be wise to submit every candidate to a sharp and searching examination; and privately I meant to put together a list of military qualifications that nobody could answer to but my West Pointers. That ought to have been attended to before I left; for the king was so taken with the idea of a standing army that he couldn't wait but must get about it at once, and get up as good a scheme of examination as he could invent out of his own head.

I was impatient to see what this was; and to show, too, how much more admirable was the one which I should display to the Examining Board. I intimated this, gently, to the king, and it fired his curiosity. When the Board was assembled, I followed him in, and behind us came the candidates. One of these candidates was a bright young West Pointer of mine, and with him were a couple of my West Point professors.

When I saw the Board, I did not know whether to cry or to laugh. The head of it was the officer known to later centuries as Norroy King-at-Arms! The two other members were chiefs of bureaux in his department; and all three were priests, of course; all officials who had to know how to read and write were priests.

My candidate was called first, out of courtesy to me, and the head of the Board opened on him with official solemnity:

"Name?"

"Mal-ease."

"Son of?"

"Webster."

"Webster—Webster. Hm—I—my memory faileth to recall the name. Condition?"

"Weaver."

"Weaver!—God keep us!"

The king was staggered, from his summit to his foundations; one clerk fainted, and the others came near it. The chairman pulled himself together, and said indignantly:

"It is sufficient. Get you hence."

But I appealed to the king. I begged that my candidate might be examined. The king was willing, but the Board, who were all well-born folk, implored the king to spare them the indignity of examining the weaver's son. I knew they didn't know enough to examine him anyway, so I joined my prayers to theirs and the king turned the duty over to my professors. I had had a blackboard prepared, and it was put up now, and the circus began. It was beautiful to hear the lad lay out the science of war, and wallow in details of battle and siege, of supply, transportation, mining and countermining, grand tactics, big strategy and little strategy, signal service, infantry, cavalry, artillery, and all about siege guns, field guns, gatling guns, rifled guns, smooth bores, musket practice, revolver practice—and not a solitary word of it all could these catfish make head or tail of, you understand—and it was handsome to see him chalk off mathematical nightmares on the blackboard that would stump the angels themselves, and do it like nothing, too—all about eclipses, and comets, and solstices, and constellations, and mean time, and sidereal time, and dinner time, and bedtime, and every other imaginable thing above the clouds or under them that you could harry or bullyrag an enemy with and make him wish he hadn't come—and when the boy made his military salute and stood aside at last, I was proud enough to hug him, and all those other people were so dazed they looked partly petrified, partly drunk, and wholly caught out and snowed under. I judged that the cake was ours, and by a large majority.

Education is a great thing. This was the same youth who had come to West Point so ignorant that when I asked him, "If a general officer should have a horse shot under him on the field of battle, what ought he to do?" answered up naively and said:

"Get up and brush himself."

One of the young nobles was called up, now. I thought I would question him a little myself. I said:

"Can your lordship read?"

His face flushed indignantly, and he fired this at me:

"Takest me for a clerk? I trow I am not of a blood that—"

"Answer the question!"

He crowded his wrath down and made out to answer "No."

"Can you write?"

He wanted to resent this, too, but I said:

"You will confine yourself to the questions, and make no comments. You are not here to air your blood or your graces, and nothing of the sort will be permitted. Can you write?"

"No."

"Do you know the multiplication table?"

"I wit not what ye refer to."

"How much is 9 times 6?"

"It is a mystery that is hidden from me by reason that the emergency requiring the fathoming of it hath not in my life-days occurred, and so, not having no need to know this thing, I abide barren of the knowledge."

"If A trade a barrel of onions to B, worth 2 pence the bushel, in exchange for a sheep worth 4 pence and a dog worth a penny, and C kill the dog before delivery, because bitten by the same, who mistook him for D, what sum is still due to A from B, and which party pays for the dog, C, or D, and who gets the money? if A, is the penny sufficient, or may he claim consequential damages in the form of additional money to represent the possible profit which might have inured from the dog, and classifiable as earned increment, that is to say, usufruct?"

"Verily, in the all-wise and unknowable providence of God, who moveth in mysterious ways his wonders to perform, have I never heard the fellow to this question for confusion of the mind and congestion of the ducts of thought. Wherefore I beseech you let the dog and the onions and these people of the strange and godless names work out their several salvations from their piteous and wonderful difficulties without help of mine, for indeed their trouble is sufficient as it is, whereas an I tried to help I should but damage their cause the more and yet mayhap not live myself to see the desolation wrought."

"What do you know of the laws of attraction and gravitation?"

"If there be such, mayhap his grace the king did promulgate them whilst that I lay sick about the beginning of the year and thereby failed to hear his proclamation."

"What do you know of the science of optics?"

"I know of governors of places, and seneschals of castles, and sheriffs of counties, and many like small offices and titles of honor, but him you call the Science of Optics I have not heard of before; peradventure it is a new dignity."

"Yes, in this country."

Try to conceive of this mollusk gravely applying for an official position, of any kind under the sun! Why, he had all the ear-marks of a type-writer copyist, if you leave out the disposition to contribute uninvited emendations of your grammar and punctuation. It was unaccountable that he didn't attempt a little help of that sort out of his majestic supply of incapacity for the job. But that didn't prove that he hadn't material in him for the disposition, it only proved that he wasn't a type-writer copyist yet. After nagging him a little more, I let the professors loose on him and they turned him inside out, on the line of scientific war, and found him empty, of course. He knew somewhat about the warfare of the time—bushwacking around for ogres, and bull-fights in the tournament ring, and such things—but otherwise he was empty and useless. Then we took the other young noble in hand, and he was the first one's twin, for ignorance and incapacity. I delivered them into the hands of the chairman of the Board with the comfortable consciousness that their cake was dough. They were examined in the previous order of precedence.

"Name, so please you?"

"Pertipole, son of Sir Pertipole, Baron of Barley Mash."

"Grandfather?"

"Also Sir Pertipole, Baron of Barley Mash."

"Great-grandfather?"

"The same name and title."

"Great-great-grandfather?"

"We had none, worshipful sir, the line failing before it had reached so far back."

"It mattereth not. It is a good four generations, and fulfilleth the requirements of the rule."

"Fulfills what rule?" I asked.

"The rule requiring four generations of nobility or else the candidate is not eligible."

"A man not eligible for a lieutenancy in the army unless he can prove four generations of noble descent?"

"Even so; neither lieutenant nor any other officer may be commissioned without that qualification."

"Oh come, this is an astonishing thing. What good is such a qualification as that?"

"What good? It is a hardy question, fair sir and Boss, since it doth go far to impugn the wisdom of even our holy Mother Church herself."

"As how?"

"For that she hath established the self-same rule regarding saints. By her law none may be canonized until he hath lain dead four generations."

"I see, I see—it is the same thing. It is wonderful. In the one case a man lies dead-alive four generations—mummified in ignorance and sloth—and that qualifies him to command live people, and take their weal and woe into his impotent hands; and in the other case, a man lies bedded with death and worms four generations, and that qualifies him for office in the celestial camp. Does the king's grace approve of this strange law?"

The king said:

"Why, truly I see naught about it that is strange. All places of honor and of profit do belong, by natural right, to them that be of noble blood, and so these dignities in the army are their property and would be so without this or any rule. The rule is but to mark a limit. Its purpose is to keep out too recent blood, which would bring into contempt these offices, and men of lofty lineage would turn their backs and scorn to take them. I were to blame an I permitted this calamity. *You* can permit it an you are minded so to do, for you have the delegated authority, but that the king should do it were a most strange madness and not comprehensible to any."

"I yield. Proceed, sir Chief of the Herald's College."

The chairman resumed as follows:

"By what illustrious achievement for the honor of the Throne and State did the founder of your great line lift himself to the sacred dignity of the British nobility?"

"He built a brewery."

"Sire, the Board finds this candidate perfect in all the requirements and qualifications for military command, and doth hold his case open for decision after due examination of his competitor."

The competitor came forward and proved exactly four generations of nobility himself. So there was a tie in military qualifications that far.

He stood aside, a moment, and Sir Pertipole was questioned further:

"Of what condition was the wife of the founder of your line?"

"She came of the highest landed gentry, yet she was not noble; she was gracious and pure and charitable, of a blameless life and character, insomuch that in these regards was she peer of the best lady in the land."

"That will do. Stand down." He called up the competing lordling again, and asked: "What was the rank and condition of the great-grandmother who conferred British nobility upon your great house?"

"She was a king's leman and did climb to that splendid eminence by her own unholpen merit from the sewer where she was born."

"Ah, this indeed is true nobility, this is the right and perfect intermixture. The lieutenancy is yours, fair lord. Hold it not in contempt; it is the humble step which will lead to grandeurs more worthy of the splendor of an origin like to thine."

I was down in the bottomless pit of humiliation. I had promised myself an easy and zenith-scouring triumph, and this was the outcome!

I was almost ashamed to look my poor disappointed cadet in the face. I told him to go home and be patient, this wasn't the end.

I had a private audience with the king, and made a proposition. I said it was quite right to officer that regiment with nobilities, and he couldn't have done a wiser thing. It would also be a good idea to add five hundred officers to it; in fact, add as many officers as there were nobles and relatives of nobles in the country, even if there should finally be five times as many officers as privates in it; and thus make it the crack regiment, the envied regiment, the King's Own regiment, and entitled to fight on its own hook and in its own way, and go whither it would and come when it pleased, in time of war, and be utterly swell and independent. This would make that regiment the heart's desire of all the nobility, and they would all be satisfied and happy. Then we would make up the rest of the standing army out of commonplace materials, and officer it with nobodies, as was proper—nobodies selected on a basis of mere efficiency—and we would make this regiment toe the line, allow it no aristocratic freedom from restraint, and force it to do all the work and persistent hammering, to the end that whenever the King's Own was tired and wanted to go off for a change and rummage around amongst ogres and have a good time, it could go without uneasiness, knowing that matters were in safe hands behind it, and business going to be continued at the old stand, same as usual. The king was charmed with the idea.

When I noticed that, it gave me a valuable notion. I thought I saw my way out of an old and stubborn difficulty at last. You see, the royalties of the Pendragon stock were a long-lived race and very fruitful. Whenever a child was born to any of these—and it was pretty often—there was wild joy in the nation's mouth, and piteous sorrow in the nation's heart. The joy was questionable, but the grief was honest. Because the event meant another call for a Royal Grant. Long was the list of these royalties, and they were a heavy and steadily increasing burden upon the treasury and a menace to the crown. Yet Arthur could not believe this latter fact, and he would not listen to any of my various projects for substituting something in the place of the royal grants. If I could have persuaded him to now and then provide a support for one of these outlying scions from his own pocket, I could have made a grand to-do over it, and it would have had a good effect with the nation; but no, he wouldn't hear of such a thing. He had something like a religious passion for a royal grant; he seemed to look upon it as a sort of sacred swag, and one could not irritate him in any way so quickly and so surely as by an attack upon that venerable institution. If I ventured to cautiously hint that there was not another respectable family in England that would humble itself to hold out the hat—however, that is as far as I ever got; he always cut me short, there, and peremptorily, too.

But I believed I saw my chance at last. I would form this crack regiment out of officers alone—not a single private. Half of it should consist of nobles, who should fill all the places up to Major General, and serve gratis and pay their own expenses; and they would be glad to do this when they should learn that the rest of the regiment would consist exclusively of princes of the blood. These princes of the blood should range in rank from Lieutenant General up to Field Marshal, and be gorgeously salaried and equipped and fed by the state. Moreover—and this was the master stroke—it should be decreed that these princely grandees should be always addressed by a stunningly gaudy and awe-compelling title, (which I would presently invent,) and they and they only in all England should be so addressed. Finally, all princes of the blood should have free choice: join that regiment, get that great title, and renounce the royal grant, or stay out and receive a grant. Neatest touch of all: unborn but imminent princes of the blood could be *born* into the regiment, and start fair, with good wages and a permanent situation, upon due notice from the parents.

All the boys would join, I was sure of that; so, all existing grants would be relinquished; that the newly born would always join was equally certain. Within sixty days that quaint and bizarre anomaly, the Royal Grant, would cease to be a living fact, and take its place among the curiosities of the past.

CHAPTER 26

THE FIRST NEWSPAPER

When I told the king I was going out disguised as a petty freeman to scour the country and familiarize myself with the humbler life of the people, he was all afire with the novelty of the thing in a minute, and was bound to take a chance in the adventure himself—nothing should stop him—he would drop everything and go along—it was the prettiest idea he had run across for many a day. He wanted to glide out the back way and start at once; but I showed him that that wouldn't answer. You see, he was billed for the king's-evil—to touch for it, I mean —and it wouldn't be right to disappoint the house; and it wouldn't make a delay worth considering, anyway, it was only a one-night stand. And I thought he ought to tell the queen he was going away. He clouded up at that, and looked sad. I was sorry I had spoken, especially when he said mournfully:

"Thou forgettest that Launcelot is here; and where Launcelot is, she noteth not the going forth of the king, nor what day he returneth."

Of course I changed the subject. Yes, Guenever was beautiful, it is true, but take her all around she was pretty slack. I never meddled in these matters, they weren't my affair, but I did hate to see the way things were going on, and I don't mind saying that much. Many's the time she had asked me, "Sir Boss, hast seen Sir Launcelot about?" but if ever she went fretting around for the king I didn't happen to be around at the time.

There was a very good lay-out for the king's-evil business—very tidy and creditable. The king sat under a canopy of state, about him were clustered a large body of the clergy in full canonicals. Conspicuous, both for location and personal outfit, stood Marinel, a hermit of the quack-doctor species, to introduce the sick. All abroad over the spacious floor, and clear down to the doors, in a thick jumble, lay or sat the scrofulous, under a strong light. It was as good as a tableau; in fact it had all the look of being gotten up for that, though it wasn't. There were eight hundred sick people present. The work was slow; it lacked the interest of novelty for me, because I had seen the ceremonies before; the thing soon became tedious, but the proprieties required me to stick it out. The doctor was there for the reason that in all such crowds there were many people who only imagined something was the matter with them, and many who were consciously sound but wanted the immortal honor of fleshly contact with a king, and yet others who pretended to illness in order to get the piece of coin that went with the touch. Up to this time this coin had been a wee little gold piece worth about a third of a dollar. When you consider how much that amount of money would buy, in that age and country, and how usual it was to be scrofulous, when not dead, you will understand that the annual king's-evil appropriation was just the River and Harbor bill of that government for the grip it took on the treasury and the chance it afforded for skinning the surplus. So I had privately concluded to touch the treasury itself for the king's-evil. I covered sixth-sevenths of the appropriation into the treasury a week before starting from Camelot on my adventures, and ordered that the other seventh be inflated into five-cent nickels and delivered into the hands of the head clerk of the King's Evil Department; a nickel to take the place of each gold coin, you see, and do its work for it. It might strain the nickel some, but I judged it could stand it. As a rule, I do not approve of watering stock, but I considered it square enough in this case, for it was just a gift, anyway. Of course you can water a gift as much as you want to; and I generally do.

The old gold and silver coins of the country were of ancient and unknown origin, as a rule, but some of them were Roman; they were ill shapen, and seldom rounder than a moon that is a week past the full; they were hammered, not minted, and they were so worn with use that the devices upon them were as illegible as blisters, and looked like them. I judged that a sharp, bright new nickel, with a first-rate likeness of the king on one side of it and Guenever on the other, and a blooming pious motto, would take the tuck out of scrofula as handy as a nobler coin and please the scrofulous fancy more; and I was right. This batch was the first it was tried on, and it worked to a charm. The saving in expense was a notable economy. You will see that by these figures: We touched a trifle over 700 of the 800 patients; at former rates, this would have cost the government about $240; at the new rate we pulled through for about $35, thus saving upward of $200 at one swoop. To appreciate the full magnitude of this stroke, consider these other figures: the annual expenses of a national government amount to the equivalent of a contribution of three days' average wages of every individual of the population, counting every individual as if he were a man. If you take a nation of 60,000,000 where average wages are $2 per day, three days' wages taken from each individual will provide $360,000,000 and pay the government's expenses. In my day, in my own country, this money was collected from imposts, and the citizen imagined that the foreign importer paid it, and it made him comfortable to think so; whereas, in fact, it was paid by the American people, and was so equally and exactly distributed among them that the annual cost to the 100-millionaire and the annual cost to the sucking child of the day laborer was precisely the same—each paid $6. Nothing could be equaler than that, I reckon. Well, Scotland and Ireland were tributary to Arthur, and the united populations of the British Islands amounted to something less than 1,000,000. A mechanic's average wage was 3 cents a day, when he paid his own keep. By this rule, the national government's expenses were $90,000 a year, or about $250 a day. Thus, by the substitution of nickels for gold on a king's-evil day, I not only injured no one, dissatisfied no one, but pleased all concerned and saved four-fifths of that day's national expense into the bargain—a saving which would have been the equivalent of $800,000 in my day in America. In making this substitution I had drawn upon the wisdom of a very remote source—the wisdom of my boyhood—for the true statesman does not despise any wisdom, howsoever lowly may be its origin: in my boyhood I had always saved my pennies and contributed buttons to the foreign missionary cause. The buttons would answer the ignorant savage as well as the coin, the coin would answer me better than the buttons; all hands were happy and nobody hurt.

Marinel took the patients as they came. He examined the candidate; if he couldn't qualify he was warned off; if he could he was passed along to the king. A priest pronounced the words, "They shall lay their hands on the sick, and they shall recover." Then the king stroked the ulcers, while the reading continued; finally, the patient graduated and got his nickel—the king hanging it around his neck himself—and was dismissed. Would you think that that would cure? It certainly did. Any mummery will cure if the patient's faith is strong in it. Up by Astolat there was a chapel where the Virgin had once appeared to a girl who used to herd geese around there—the girl said so herself—and they built the chapel upon that spot and hung a picture in it representing the occurrence—a picture which you would think it dangerous for a sick person to approach; whereas, on the contrary, thousands of the lame and the sick came and prayed before it every year and went away whole and sound; and even the well could look upon it and live. Of course when I was told these things I did not believe them; but when I went there and saw them I had to succumb. I saw the cures effected myself; and they were real cures and not questionable. I saw cripples whom I had seen around Camelot for years on crutches, arrive and pray before that picture, and put down their crutches and walk off without a limp. There were piles of crutches there which had been left by such people as a testimony.

In other places people operated on a patient's mind, without saying a word to him, and cured him. In others, experts assembled patients in a room and prayed over them, and appealed to their faith, and those patients went away cured. Wherever you find a king who can't cure the king's-evil you can be sure that the most valuable superstition that supports his throne—the subject's belief in the divine appointment of his sovereign—has passed away. In my youth the monarchs of England had ceased to touch for the evil, but there was no occasion for this diffidence: they could have cured it forty-nine times in fifty.

Well, when the priest had been droning for three hours, and the good king polishing the evidences, and the sick were still pressing forward as plenty as ever, I got to feeling intolerably bored. I was sitting by an open window not far from the canopy of state. For the five hundredth time a patient stood forward to have his repulsivenesses stroked; again those words were being droned out: "they shall lay their hands on the sick"—when outside there rang clear as a clarion a note that enchanted my soul and tumbled thirteen worthless centuries about my ears: "Camelot *Weekly Hosannah and Literary Volcano!*—latest irruption—only two cents—all about the big miracle in the Valley of Holiness!" One greater than kings had arrived—the newsboy. But I was the only person in all that throng who knew the meaning of this mighty birth, and what this imperial magician was come into the world to do.

I dropped a nickel out of the window and got my paper; the Adam-newsboy of the world went around the corner to get my change; is around the corner yet. It was delicious to see a newspaper again, yet I was conscious of a secret shock when my eye fell upon the first batch of display head-lines. I had lived in a clammy atmosphere of reverence, respect, deference, so long, that they sent a quivery little cold wave through me:

HIGH TIMES IN THE VALLEY
OF HOLINESS!

THE WATER-WORKS CORKED!

BRER MERLIN WORKS HIS ARTS, BUT GETS
LEFT!

But the Boss scores on his first Innings!

The Miraculous Well Uncorked amid
awful outbursts of
INFERNAL FIRE AND SMOKE
AND THUNDER!

THE BUZZARD-ROOST ASTONISHED!

UNPARALLELED REJOIBINGS!

—and so on, and so on. Yes, it was too loud. Once I could have enjoyed it and seen nothing out of the way about it, but now its note was discordant. It was good Arkansas journalism, but this was not Arkansas. Moreover, the next to the last line was calculated to give offense to the hermits, and perhaps lose us their advertising. Indeed, there was too lightsome a tone of flippancy all through the paper. It was plain I had undergone a considerable change without noticing it. I found myself unpleasantly affected by pert little irreverencies which would have seemed but proper and airy graces of speech at an earlier period of my life. There was an abundance of the following breed of items, and they discomforted me:

Local Smoke and Cinders.

Sir Launcelot met up with old King Agrivance of Ireland unexpectedly last weok over on the moor south of Sir Balmoral le Merveilleuse's hog dasture. The widow has been notified.

Expedition No. 3 will start adout the first of next mgnth on a search f8r Sir Sagramour le Desirous. It is in command of the renowned Knight of the Red Lawns, assissted by Sir Persant of Inde, who is competegt, intelligent, courteous, and in every way a brick, and further assisted by Sir Palamides the Saracen, who is no huckleberry himself. This is no pic-nic, these boys *mean* busineas.

The readers of the Hosannah will regret to learn that the hadndsome and popular Sir Charolais of Gaul, who during his four weeks' stay at the Bull and Halibut, this city, has won every heart by his polished manners and elegant conversation, will pull out to-day for home. Give us another call, Charley!

The bdsiness end of the funeral of the late Sir Dalliance the duke's son of Cornwall, killed in an encounter with the Giant of the Knotted Bludgeon last

> Tuesday on the borders of the Plain of Enchantment was in the hands of the ever affable and efficient [redacted]Mumble, prince of un3ertakers, than whom there exists none by whom it were a more satisfying pleasure to have the last sad offices performed. Give him a trial.
>
> The cordial thanks of the Hosannah office are due, from editor down to devil, to the ever courteous and thoughtful Lord High Stew[redacted]d of the Palace's Thrid Assistant V[redacted]t for several saucc†s of ice cream[redacted] a quality calculated to make the ey[redacted]of the recipients humid with gr[redacted]ude; and it done it. When this [redacted]administration wants to chalk up a desirable name for early promotion, the Hosannah would like a chance to sudgest.
>
> The Demoiselle Irene Dewlap, of South Astolat, is visiting her uncle, the popular host of the Cattlemen's Boarding Ho&se, Liver Lane, this city.
>
> Young Barker the bellows-mender is hoMe again, and looks much improved by his vacation round-up among the out-lying smithies. See his ad.

Of course it was good enough journalism for a beginning; I knew that quite well, and yet it was somehow disappointing. The "Court Circular" pleased me better; indeed its simple and dignified respectfulness was a distinct refreshment to me after all those disgraceful familiarities. But even it could have been improved. Do what one may, there is no getting an air of variety into a court circular, I acknowledge that. There is a profound monotonousness about its facts that baffles and defeats one's sincerest efforts to make them sparkle and enthuse. The best way to manage—in fact, the only sensible way—is to disguise repetitiousness of fact under variety of form: skin your fact each time and lay on a new cuticle of words. It deceives the eye; you think it is a new fact; it gives you the idea that the court is carrying on like everything; this excites you, and you drain the whole column, with a good appetite, and perhaps never notice that it's a barrel of soup made out of a single bean. Clarence's way was good, it was simple, it was dignified, it was direct and business-like; all I say is, it was not the best way:

COURT CIRCULAR.

On Monday, the king rode in the park.
" Tuesday, " " "
" Wendesday " " "
" Thursday " " "
" Friday, " " "
" Saturday " " "
" Sunday, " " "

However, take the paper by and large, I was vastly pleased with it. Little crudities of a mechanical sort were observable here and there, but there were not enough of them to amount to anything, and it was good enough Arkansas proof-reading, anyhow, and better than was needed in Arthur's day and realm. As a rule, the grammar was leaky and the construction more or less lame; but I did not much mind these things. They are common defects of my own, and one mustn't criticise other people on grounds where he can't stand perpendicular himself.

I was hungry enough for literature to want to take down the whole paper at this one meal, but I got only a few bites, and then had to postpone, because the monks around me besieged me so with eager questions: What is this curious thing? What is it for? Is it a handkerchief?—saddle blanket?—part of a shirt? What is it made of? How thin it is, and how dainty and frail; and how it rattles. Will it wear, do you think, and won't the rain injure it? Is it writing that appears on it, or is it only ornamentation? They suspected it was writing, because those among them who knew how to read Latin and had a smattering of Greek, recognized some of the letters, but they could make nothing out of the result as a whole. I put my information in the simplest form I could:

"It is a public journal; I will explain what that is, another time. It is not cloth, it is made of paper; some time I will explain what paper is. The lines on it are reading matter; and not written by hand, but printed; by and by I will explain what printing is. A thousand of these sheets have been made, all exactly like this, in every minute detail—they can't be told apart." Then they all broke out with exclamations of surprise and admiration:

"A thousand! Verily a mighty work—a year's work for many men."

"No—merely a day's work for a man and a boy."

They crossed themselves, and whiffed out a protective prayer or two.

"Ah-h—a miracle, a wonder! Dark work of enchantment."

I let it go at that. Then I read in a low voice, to as many as could crowd their shaven heads within hearing distance, part of the account of the miracle of the restoration of the well, and was accompanied by astonished and reverent ejaculations all through: "Ah-h-h!" "How true!" "Amazing, amazing!" "These be the very haps as they happened, in marvelous exactness!" And might they take this strange thing in their hands, and feel of it and examine it?—they would be very careful. Yes. So they took it, handling it as cautiously and devoutly as if it had been some holy thing come from some supernatural region; and gently felt of its texture, caressed its pleasant smooth surface with lingering touch, and scanned the mysterious characters with fascinated eyes. These grouped bent heads, these charmed faces, these speaking eyes—how beautiful to me! For was not this my darling, and was not all this mute wonder and interest and homage a most eloquent tribute and unforced compliment to it? I knew, then, how a mother feels when women, whether strangers or friends, take her new baby, and close themselves about it with one eager impulse, and bend their heads over it in a tranced adoration that makes all the rest of the universe vanish out of their consciousness and be as if it were not, for that time. I knew how she feels, and that there is no other satisfied ambition, whether of king, conqueror or poet, that ever reaches half way to that serene far summit or yields half so divine a contentment.

During all the rest of the séance my paper traveled from group to group all up and down and about that huge hall, and my happy eye was upon it always, and I sat motionless, steeped in satisfaction, drunk with enjoyment. Yes, this was heaven; I was tasting it once, if I might never taste it more.

CHAPTER 27

THE YANKEE AND THE KING TRAVEL INCOGNITO

About bedtime I took the king to my private quarters to cut his hair and help him get the hang of the lowly raiment he was to wear. The high classes wore their hair banged across the forehead but hanging to the shoulders the rest of the way around, whereas the lowest ranks of commoners were banged fore and aft both; the slaves were bang-less, and allowed their hair free growth. So I inverted a bowl over his head and cut away all the locks that hung below it. I also trimmed his whiskers and moustache until they were only about a half inch long; and tried to do it inartistically, and succeeded. It was a villanous disfigurement. When he got his lubberly sandals on, and his long robe of coarse brown linen cloth, which hung straight from his neck to his ankle-bones, he was no longer the comeliest man in his kingdom, but one of the unhandsomest and most commonplace and unattractive. We were dressed and barbered alike, and could pass for small farmers, or farm bailiffs, or shepherds, or carters; yes, or for village artisans, if we chose, our costume being in effect universal among the poor, because of its strength and cheapness. I don't mean that it was really cheap to a very poor person, but I do mean that it was the cheapest material there was for male attire—manufactured material, you understand.

We slipped away an hour before dawn, and by broad sun-up had made eight or ten miles, and were in the midst of a sparsely settled country. I had a pretty heavy knapsack; it was laden with provisions—provisions for the king to taper down on, till he could take to the coarse fare of the country without damage.

I found a comfortable seat for the king by the roadside, and then gave him a morsel or two to stay his stomach with. Then I said I would find some water for him, and strolled away. Part of my project was to get out of sight and sit down and rest a little myself. It had always been my custom to stand, when in his presence; even at the council board, except upon those rare occasions when the sitting was a very long one, extending over hours; then I had a trifling little backless thing which was like a reversed culvert and was as comfortable as the toothache. I didn't want to break him in suddenly, but do it by degrees. We should have to sit together now when in company, or people would notice; but it would not be good politics for me to be playing equality with him when there was no necessity for it.

I found the water, some three hundred yards away, and had been resting about twenty minutes, when I heard voices. That is all right, I thought—peasants going to work; nobody else likely to be stirring this early. But the next moment these comers jingled into sight around a turn of the road—smartly clad people of quality, with luggage-mules and servants in their train! I was off like a shot, through the bushes, by the shortest cut. For a while it did seem that these people would pass the king before I could get to him; but desperation gives you wings, you know, and I canted my body forward, inflated my breast, and held my breath and flew. I arrived. And in plenty good enough time, too.

"Pardon, my king, but it's no time for ceremony—jump! Jump to your feet—some quality are coming!"

"Is that a marvel? Let them come."

"But my liege! You must not be seen sitting. Rise!—and stand in humble posture while they pass. You are a peasant, you know."

"True—I had forgot it, so lost was I in planning of a huge war with Gaul"—he was up by this time, but a farm could have got up quicker, if there was any kind of a boom in real estate—"and right-so a thought came randoming overthwart this majestic dream the which—"

"A humbler attitude, my lord the king—and quick! Duck your head! —more!—still more!—droop it!"

He did his honest best, but lord it was no great things. He looked as humble as the leaning tower at Pisa. It is the most you could say of it. Indeed it was such a thundering poor success that it raised wondering scowls all along the line, and a gorgeous flunkey at the tail end of it raised his whip; but I jumped in time and was under it when it fell; and under cover of the volley of coarse laughter which followed, I spoke up sharply and warned the king to take no notice. He mastered himself for the moment, but it was a sore tax; he wanted to eat up the procession. I said:

"It would end our adventures at the very start; and we, being without weapons, could do nothing with that armed gang. If we are going to succeed in our emprise, we must not only look the peasant but act the peasant."

"It is wisdom; none can gainsay it. Let us go on, Sir Boss. I will take note and learn, and do the best I may."

He kept his word. He did the best he could, but I've seen better. If you have ever seen an active, heedless, enterprising child going diligently out of one mischief and into another all day long, and an anxious mother at its heels all the while, and just saving it by a hair from drowning itself or breaking its neck with each new experiment, you've seen the king and me.

If I could have foreseen what the thing was going to be like, I should have said, No, if anybody wants to make his living exhibiting a king as a peasant, let him take the layout; I can do better with a menagerie, and last longer. And yet, during the first three days I never allowed him to enter a hut or other dwelling. If he could pass muster anywhere, during his early noviciate, it would be in small inns and on the road; so to these places we confined ourselves. Yes, he certainly did the best he could, but what of that? He didn't improve a bit that I could see.

He was always frightening me, always breaking out with fresh astonishers, in new and unexpected places. Toward evening on the second day, what does he do but blandly fetch out a dirk from inside his robe!

"Great guns, my liege, where did you get that?"

"From a smuggler at the inn, yester eve."

"What in the world possessed you to buy it?"

"We have escaped divers dangers by wit—thy wit—but I have bethought me that it were but prudence if I bore a weapon, too. Thine might fail thee in some pinch."

"But people of our condition are not allowed to carry arms. What would a lord say—yes, or any other person of whatever condition—if he caught an upstart peasant with a dagger on his person?"

It was a lucky thing for us that nobody came along just then. I persuaded him to throw the dirk away; and it was as easy as persuading a child to give up some bright fresh new way of killing itself. We walked along, silent and thinking. Finally the king said:

"When ye know that I meditate a thing inconvenient, or that hath a peril in it, why do you not warn me to cease from that project?"

It was a startling question, and a puzzler. I didn't quite know how to take hold of it, or what to say, and so of course I ended by saying the natural thing:

"But sire, how can *I* know what your thoughts are?"

The king stopped dead in his tracks, and stared at me.

"I believed thou wert greater than Merlin; and truly in magic thou art. But prophecy is greater than magic. Merlin is a prophet."

I saw I had made a blunder. I must get back my lost ground. After deep reflection and careful planning, I said:

"Sire, I have been misunderstood. I will explain. There are two kinds of prophecy. One is the gift to foretell things that are but a little way off, the other is the gift to foretell things that are whole ages and centuries away. Which is the mightier gift, do you think?"

"Oh, the last, most surely!"

"True. Does Merlin possess it?"

"Partly, yes. He foretold mysteries about my birth and future kingship that were twenty years away."

"Has he ever gone beyond that?"

"He would not claim more, I think."

"It is probably his limit. All prophets have their limit. The limit of some of the great prophets has been a hundred years."

"These are few, I ween."

"There have been two still greater ones, whose limit was four hundred and six hundred years, and one whose limit compassed even seven hundred and twenty."

"Gramercy, it is marvelous!"

"But what are these in comparison with me? They are nothing."

"What? Canst thou truly look beyond even so vast a stretch of time as—"

"Seven hundred years? My liege, as clear as the vision of an eagle does my prophetic eye penetrate and lay bare the future of this world for nearly thirteen centuries and a half!"

My land, you should have seen the king's eyes spread slowly open, and lift the earth's entire atmosphere as much as an inch! That settled Brer Merlin. One never had any occasion to prove his facts, with these people; all he had to do was to state them. It never occurred to anybody to doubt the statement.

"Now, then," I continued, "I *could* work both kinds of prophecy—the long and the short—if I chose to take the trouble to keep in practice; but I seldom exercise any but the long kind, because the other is beneath my dignity. It is properer to Merlin's sort—stump-tail prophets, as we call them in the profession. Of course I whet up now and then and flirt out a minor prophecy, but not often—hardly ever, in fact. You will remember that there was great talk, when you reached the Valley of Holiness, about my having prophecied your coming and the very hour of your arrival, two or three days beforehand."

"Indeed, yes, I mind it now."

"Well, I could have done it as much as forty times easier, and piled on a thousand times more detail into the bargain, if it had been five hundred years away instead of two or three days."

"How amazing that it should be so!"

"Yes, a genuine expert can always foretell a thing that is five hundred years away easier than he can a thing that's only five hundred seconds off."

"And yet in reason it should clearly be the other way: it should be five hundred times as easy to foretell the last as the first, for indeed it is so close by that one uninspired might almost see it. In truth the law of prophecy doth contradict the likelihoods, most strangely making the difficult easy, and the easy difficult."

It was a wise head. A peasant's cap was no safe disguise for it; you could know it for a king's, under a diving bell, if you could hear it work its intellect.

I had a new trade, now, and plenty of business in it. The king was as hungry to find out everything that was going to happen during the next thirteen centuries as if he were expecting to live in them. From that time out, I prophecied myself bald-headed trying to supply the demand. I have done some indiscreet things in my day, but this thing of playing myself for a prophet was the worst. Still, it had its ameliorations. A prophet doesn't have to have any brains. They are good to have, of course, for the ordinary exigencies of life, but they are no use in professional work. It is the restfulest vocation there is. When the spirit of prophecy comes upon you, you merely cake your intellect and lay it off in a cool place for a rest, and unship your jaw and leave it alone; it will work itself: the result is prophecy.

Every day a knight errant or so came along, and the sight of them fired the king's martial spirit every time. He would have forgotten himself, sure, and said something to them in a style a suspicious shade or so above his ostensible degree, and so I always got him well out of the road in time. Then he would stand, and look with all his eyes; and a proud light would flash from them, and his nostrils would inflate like a war-horse's, and I knew he was longing for a brush with them. But about noon of the third day I had stopped in the road to take a precaution which had been suggested by the whip-stroke that had fallen to my share two days before; a precaution which I had afterward decided to leave untaken, I was so loath to institute it; but now I had just had a fresh reminder: while striding heedlessly along, with jaw spread and intellect at rest, for I was prophecying, I stubbed my toe and fell sprawling. I was so pale I couldn't think, for a moment; then I got softly and carefully up and unstrapped my knapsack. I had that dynamite bomb in it, done up in wool, in a box. It was a good thing to have along; the time would come when I could do a valuable miracle with it, maybe, but it was a nervous thing to have about me, and I didn't like to ask the king to carry it. Yet I must either throw it away or think up some safe way to get along with its society. I got it out and slipped it into my scrip, and just then, here came a couple of knights. The king stood, stately as a statue, gazing toward them—had forgotten himself again, of course—and before I could get a word of warning out, it was time for him to skip, and well that he did it, too. He supposed they would turn aside. Turn aside to avoid trampling peasant dirt under foot? When had he ever turned aside himself—or ever had the chance to do it, if a peasant saw him or any other noble knight in time to judiciously save him the trouble? The knights paid no attention to the king at all; it was his place to look out himself, and if he hadn't skipped he would have been placidly ridden down, and laughed at besides.

The king was in a flaming fury, and launched out his challenge and epithets with a most royal vigor. The knights were some little distance by, now. They halted, greatly surprised, and turned in their saddles and looked back, as if wondering if it might be worth while to bother with such scum as we. Then they wheeled and started for us. Not a moment must be lost. I started for *them.* I passed them at a rattling gait, and as I went by I flung out a hair-lifting soul-scorching thirteen-jointed insult which made the king's effort poor and cheap by comparison. I got it out of the nineteenth century where they know how. They had such headway that they were nearly to the king before they could check up; then, frantic with rage, they stood up their horses on their hind hoofs and whirled them around, and the next moment here they came, breast to breast. I was seventy yards off, then, and scrambling up a great boulder at the roadside. When they were within thirty yards of me they let their long lances droop to a level, depressed their mailed heads, and so, with their horse-hair plumes streaming straight out behind, most gallant to see, this lightning express came tearing for me! When they were within fifteen yards, I sent that bomb with a sure aim, and it struck the ground just under the horses' noses.

Yes, it was a neat thing, very neat and pretty to see. It resembled a steamboat explosion on the Mississippi; and during the next fifteen minutes we stood under a steady drizzle of microscopic fragments of knights and hardware and horse-flesh. I say we, for the king joined the audience, of course, as soon as he had got his breath again. There was a hole there which would afford steady work for all the people in that region for some years to come—in trying to explain it, I mean; as for filling it up, that service would be comparatively prompt, and would fall to the lot of a select few—peasants of that seignory; and they wouldn't get anything for it, either.

But I explained it to the king myself. I said it was done with a dynamite bomb. This information did him no damage, because it left him as intelligent as he was before. However, it was a noble miracle, in his eyes, and was another settler for Merlin. I thought it well enough to explain that this was a miracle of so rare a sort that it couldn't be done except when the atmospheric conditions were just right. Otherwise he would be encoring it every time we had a good subject, and that would be inconvenient, because I hadn't any more bombs along.

CHAPTER 28

DRILLING THE KING

On the morning of the fourth day, when it was just sunrise, and we had been tramping an hour in the chill dawn, I came to a resolution: the king *must* be drilled; things could not go on so, he must be taken in hand and deliberately and conscientiously drilled, or we couldn't ever venture to enter a dwelling; the very cats would know this masquerader for a humbug and no peasant. So I called a halt and said:

"Sire, as between clothes and countenance, you are all right, there is no discrepancy; but as between your clothes and your bearing, you are all wrong, there is a most noticeable discrepancy. Your soldierly stride, your lordly port—these will not do. You stand too straight, your looks are too high, too confident. The cares of a kingdom do not stoop the shoulders, they do not droop the chin, they do not depress the high level of the eyeglance, they do not put doubt and fear in the heart and hang out the signs of them in slouching body and unsure step. It is the sordid cares of the lowly born that do these things. You must learn the trick; you must imitate the trade-marks of poverty, misery, oppression, insult, and the other several and common inhumanities that sap the manliness out of a man and make him a loyal and proper and approved subject and a satisfaction to his masters, or the very infants will know you for better than your disguise, and we shall go to pieces at the first hut we stop at. Pray try to walk like this."

The king took careful note, and then tried an imitation.

"Pretty fair—pretty fair. Chin a little lower, please—there, very good. Eyes too high; pray don't look at the horizon, look at the ground, ten steps in front of you. Ah—that is better, that is very good. Wait, please; you betray too much vigor, too much decision; you want more of a shamble. Look at me, please—this is what I mean. . . . . . Now you are getting it; that is the idea—at least, it sort of approaches it. . . . . Yes, that is pretty fair. *But!*

"There is a great big something wanting, I don't quite know what it is. Please walk thirty yards, so that I can get a perspective on the thing. . . . Now, then—your head's right, speed's right, shoulders right, eyes right, chin right, gait, carriage, general style right—everything's right! And yet the fact remains, the aggregate's wrong. The account don't balance. Do it again, please . . . . *now* I think I begin to see what it is. Yes, I've struck it. You see, the genuine spiritlessness is wanting; that's what's the trouble. It's all *amateur*—mechanical details all right, almost to a hair; everything about the delusion perfect, except that it don't delude."

"What then, must one do, to prevail?"

"Let me think . . . . . I can't seem to quite get at it. In fact there isn't anything that can right the matter but practice. This is a good place for it: roots and stony ground to break up your stately gait, a region not liable to interruption, only one field and one hut in sight, and they so far away that nobody could see us from there. It will be well to move a little off the road and put in the whole day drilling you, sire."

After the drill had gone on a little while, I said:

"Now, sire, imagine that we are at the door of the hut yonder, and the family are before us. Proceed, please—accost the head of the house."

The king unconsciously straightened up like a monument, and said, with frozen austerity:

"Varlet, bring a seat; and serve to me what cheer ye have."

"Ah, your grace, that is not well done."

"In what lacketh it?"

"These people do not call *each other* varlets."

"Nay, is that true?"

"Yes; only those above them call them so."

"Then must I try again. I will call him villein."

"No-no; for he may be a freeman."

"Ah—so. Then peradventure I should call him goodman."

"That would answer, your grace, but it would be still better if you said friend, or brother."

"Brother!—to dirt like that?"

"Ah, but *we* are pretending to be dirt like that, too."

"It is even true. I will say it. Brother, bring a seat, and thereto what cheer ye have, withal. *Now* 'tis right."

"Not quite, not wholly right. You have asked for one, not *us*—for one, not both; food for one, a seat for one."

The king looked puzzled—he wasn't a very heavy weight, intellectually. His head was an hour-glass; it could stow an idea, but it had to do it a grain at a time, not the whole idea at once.

"Would *you* have a seat also—and sit?"

"If I did not sit, the man would perceive that we were only pretending to be equals—and playing the deception pretty poorly, too."

"It is well and truly said! How wonderful is truth, come it in whatsoever unexpected form it may! Yes, he must bring out seats and food for both, and in serving us present not ewer and napkin with more show of respect to the one than to the other."

"And there is even yet a detail that needs correcting. He must bring nothing outside;—we will go in—in among the dirt, and possibly other repulsive things,—and take the food with the household, and after the fashion of the house, and all on equal terms, except the man be of the serf class; and finally, there will be no ewer and no napkin, whether he be serf or free. Please walk again, my liege. There—it is better—it is the best yet; but not perfect. The shoulders have known no ignobler burden than iron mail, and they will not stoop."

"Give me, then, the bag. I will learn the spirit that goeth with burdens that have not honor. It is the spirit that stoopeth the shoulders, I ween, and not the weight; for armor is heavy, yet it is a proud burden, and a man standeth straight in it. . . . . . Nay, but me no buts, offer me no objections. I will have the thing. Strap it upon my back."

He was complete, now, with that knapsack on, and looked as little like a king as any man I had ever seen. But it was an obstinate pair of shoulders; they could not seem to learn the trick of stooping with any sort of deceptive naturalness. The drill went on, I prompting and correcting:

"Now, make believe you are in debt, and eaten up by relentless creditors; you are out of work—which is horse-shoeing, let us say—and can get none; and your wife is sick, your children are crying because they are hungry—"

And so on, and so on. I drilled him as representing in turn, all sorts of people out of luck and suffering dire privations and misfortunes. But lord it was only just words, words—they meant nothing in the world to him, I might just as well have whistled. Words realize nothing, vivify nothing to you, unless you have suffered in your own person the thing which the words try to describe. There are wise people who talk ever so knowingly and complacently about "the working classes," and satisfy themselves that a day's hard intellectual work is very much harder than a day's hard manual toil, and is righteously entitled to much bigger pay. Why, they really think that, you know, because they know all about the one, but haven't tried the other. But I know all about both; and so far as I am concerned, there isn't money enough in the universe to hire me to swing a pick-axe thirty days, but I will do the hardest kind of intellectual work for just as near nothing as you can cipher it down—and I will be satisfied, too.

Intellectual "work" is misnamed; it is a pleasure, a dissipation, and is its own highest reward. The poorest paid architect, engineer, general, author, sculptor, painter, lecturer, advocate, legislator, actor, preacher, singer, is constructively in heaven when he is at work; and as for the magician with the fiddle-bow in his hand who sits in the midst of a great orchestra with the ebbing and flowing tides of divine sound washing over him—why, certainly, he is at work, if you wish to call it that, but lord, it's a sarcasm just the same. The law of work does seem utterly unfair—but there it is, and nothing can change it: the higher the pay in enjoyment the worker gets out of it, the higher shall be his pay in cash, also. And it's also the very law of those transparent swindles, transmissible nobility and kingship.

CHAPTER 29

THE SMALL-POX HUT

When we arrived at that hut at mid-afternoon, we saw no signs of life about it. The field near by had been denuded of its crop some time before, and had a skinned look, so exhaustively had it been harvested and gleaned. Fences, sheds, everything had a ruined look, and were eloquent of poverty. No animal was around anywhere, no living thing in sight. The stillness was awful, it was like the stillness of death. The cabin was a one-story one, whose thatch was black with age, and ragged from lack of repair.

The door stood a trifle ajar. We approached it stealthily—on tiptoe and at half-breath—for that is the way one's feeling makes him do, at such a time. The king knocked. We waited. No answer. Knocked again. No answer. I pushed the door softly open and looked in. I made out some dim forms, and a woman started up from the ground and stared at me, as one does who is wakened from sleep. Presently she found her voice—

"Have mercy!" she pleaded. "All is taken, nothing is left."

"I have not come to take anything, poor woman."

"You are not a priest?"

"No."

"Nor come not from the lord of the manor?"

"No, I am a stranger."

"Oh, then, for the fear of God, who visits with misery and death such as be harmless, tarry not here, but fly! This place is under his curse—and his Church's."

"Let me come in and help you—you are sick and in trouble."

I was better used to the dim light, now. I could see her hollow eyes fixed upon me. I could see how emaciated she was.

"I tell you the place is under the Church's ban. Save yourself—and go, before some straggler see thee here, and report it."

"Give yourself no trouble about me; I don't care anything for the Church's curse. Let me help you."

"Now all good spirits—if there be any such—bless thee for that word. Would God I had a sup of water!—but hold, hold, forget I said it, and fly; for there is that here that even he that feareth not the Church must fear: this disease whereof we die. Leave us, thou brave, good stranger, and take with thee such whole and sincere blessing as them that be accursed can give."

But before this I had picked up a wooden bowl and was rushing past the king on my way to the brook. It was ten yards away. When I got back and entered, the king was within, and was opening the shutter that closed the window-hole, to let in air and light. The place was full of a foul stench. I put the bowl to the woman's lips, and as she gripped it with her eager talons the shutter came open and a strong light flooded her face. Small-pox!

I sprang to the king, and said in his ear:

"Out of the door on the instant, sire! the woman is dying of that disease that wasted the skirts of Camelot two years ago."

He did not budge.

"Of a truth I shall remain—and likewise help."

I whispered again:

"King, it must not be. You must go."

"Ye mean well, and ye speak not unwisely. But it were shame that a king should know fear, and shame that belted knight should withhold his hand where be such as need succor. Peace, I will not go. It is you who must go. The Church's ban is not upon me, but it forbiddeth you to be here, and she will deal with you with a heavy hand an word come to her of your trespass."

It was a desperate place for him to be in, and might cost him his life, but it was no use to argue with him. If he considered his knightly honor at stake here, that was the end of argument; he would stay, and nothing could prevent it; I was aware of that. And so I dropped the subject. The woman spoke:

"Fair sir, of your kindness will ye climb the ladder there, and bring me news of what ye find? Be not afraid to report, for times can come when even a mother's heart is past breaking—being already broke."

"Abide," said the king, "and give the woman to eat. I will go." And he put down the knapsack.

I turned to start but the king had already started. He halted, and looked down upon a man who lay in a dim light, and had not noticed us, thus far, or spoken.

"Is it your husband?" the king asked.

"Yes."

"Is he asleep?"

"God be thanked for that one charity, yes—these three hours. Where shall I pay to the full, my gratitude! for my heart is bursting with it for that sleep he sleepeth now."

I said:

"We will be careful. We will not wake him."

"Ah, no, that ye will not, for he is dead."

"Dead?"

"Yes, what triumph it is to know it! None can harm him, none insult him more. He is in heaven, now, and happy; or if not there, he bides in hell and is content; for in that place he will find neither abbot nor yet bishop. We were boy and girl together; we were man and wife these five and twenty years, and never separated till this day. Think how long that is, to love and suffer together. This morning was he out of his mind, and in his fancy we were boy and girl again and wandering in the happy fields; and so in that innocent glad converse wandered he far and farther, still lightly gossiping, and entered into those other fields we know not of, and was shut away from mortal sight. And so there was no parting, for in his fancy I went with him; he knew not but I went with him, my hand in his—my young soft hand, not this withered claw. Ah, yes, to go, and know it not; to separate and know it not; how could one go peacefuler than that? It was his reward for a cruel life patiently borne."

There was a slight noise from the direction of the dim corner where the ladder was. It was the king, descending. I could see that he was bearing something in one arm, and assisting himself with the other. He came forward into the light; upon his breast lay a slender girl of fifteen. She was but half conscious; she was dying of small-pox. Here was heroism at its last and loftiest possibility, its utmost summit; this was challenging death in the open field unarmed, with all the odds against the challenger, no reward set upon the contest, and no admiring world in silks and cloth of gold to gaze and applaud; and yet the king's bearing was as serenely brave as it had always been in those cheaper contests where knight meets knight in equal fight and clothed in protecting steel. He was great, now; sublimely great. The rude statues of his ancestors in his palace should have an addition—I would see to that; and it would not be a mailed king killing a giant or a dragon, like the rest, it would be a king in commoner's garb bearing death in his arms that a peasant mother might look her last upon her child and be comforted.

He laid the girl down by her mother, who poured out endearments and caresses from an overflowing heart, and one could detect a flickering faint light of response in the child's eyes, but that was all. The mother hung over her, kissing her, petting her, and imploring her to speak, but the lips only moved and no sound came. I snatched my liquor flask from my knapsack, but the woman forbade me, and said:

"No—she does not suffer; it is better so. It might bring her back to life. None that be so good and kind as ye are, would do her that cruel hurt. For look you—what is left to live for? Her brothers are gone, her father is gone, her mother goeth, the Church's curse is upon her and none may shelter or befriend her even though she lay perishing in the road. She is desolate. I have not asked you, good heart, if her sister be still on live, here overhead; I had no need; ye had gone back, else, and not left the poor thing forsaken—"

"She lieth at peace," interrupted the king, in a subdued voice.

"I would not change it. How rich is this day in happiness! Ah, my Annis, thou shalt join thy sister soon—thou'rt on thy way, and these be merciful friends, that will not hinder."

And so she fell to murmuring and cooing over the girl again, and softly stroking her face and hair, and kissing her and calling her by endearing names; but there was scarcely sign of response, now, in the glazing eyes. I saw tears well from the king's eyes, and trickle down his face. The woman noticed them, too, and said:

"Ah, I know that sign: thou'st a wife at home, poor soul, and you and she have gone hungry to bed, many's the time, that the little ones might have your crust; you know what poverty is, and the daily insults of your betters, and the heavy hand of the Church and the king."

The king winced under this accidental home-shot, but kept still; he was learning his part; and he was playing it well, too, for a pretty dull beginner. I struck up a diversion. I offered the woman food and liquor, but she refused both. She would allow nothing to come between her and the release of death. Then I slipped away and brought the dead child from aloft, and laid it by her. This broke her down again, and there was another scene that was full of heart-break. By and by I made another diversion, and beguiled her to sketch her story.

"Ye know it well, yourselves, having suffered it—for truly none of our condition in Britain escape it. It is the old, weary tale. We fought and struggled and succeeded; meaning by success, that we lived and did not die; more than that is not to be claimed. No troubles came that we could not outlive, till this year brought them; then came they all at once, as one might say, and overwhelmed us. Years ago the lord of the manor planted certain fruit trees on our farm; in the best part of it, too—a grievous wrong and shame—"

"But it was his right," interrupted the king.

"None denieth that, indeed; an the law mean anything, what is the lord's is his, and what is mine is his also. Our farm was ours by lease, therefore 'twas likewise his, to do with it as he would. Some little time ago, three of those trees were found hewn down. Our three grown sons ran frightened to report the crime. Well, in his lordship's dungeon there they lie, who saith there shall they lie and rot till they confess. They have naught to confess, being innocent, wherefore there will they remain until they die. Ye know that right well, I ween. Think how this left us; a man, a woman and two children, to gather a crop that was planted by so much greater force, yes, and protect it night and day from pigeons and prowling animals that be sacred and must not be hurt by any of our sort. When my lord's crop was nearly ready for the harvest, so also was ours; when his bell rang to call us to his fields to harvest his crops for nothing, he would not allow that I and my two girls should count for our three captive sons, but for only two of them; so, for the lacking one were we daily fined. All this time our own crop was perishing through neglect; and so both the priest and his lordship fined us because their shares of it were suffering through damage. In the end the fines ate up our crop—and they took it all; they took it all and made us harvest it for them, without pay or food, and we starving. Then the worst came when I, being out of my mind with hunger and loss of my boys, and grief to see my husband and my little maids in rags and misery and despair, uttered a deep blasphemy—oh! a thousand of them!—against the Church and the Church's ways. It was ten days ago. I had fallen sick with this disease, and it was to the priest I said the words, for he was come to chide me for lack of due humility under the chastening hand of God. He carried my trespass to his betters; I was stubborn; wherefore, presently upon my head and upon all heads that were dear to me, fell the curse of Rome.

"Since that day, we are avoided, shunned with horror. None has come near this hut to know whether we live or not. The rest of us were taken down. Then I roused me and got up, as wife and mother will.

It was little they could have eaten in any case; it was less than little they had to eat. But there was water, and I gave them that. How they craved it! and how they blessed it! But the end came yesterday; my strength broke down. Yesterday was the last time I ever saw my husband and this youngest child alive. I have lain here all these hours—these ages, ye may say—listening, listening, for any sound up there that—"

She gave a sharp quick glance at her eldest daughter, then cried out, "Oh, my darling!" and feebly gathered the stiffening form to her sheltering arms. She had recognized the death rattle.

CHAPTER 30

THE TRAGEDY OF THE MANOR-HOUSE

At midnight all was over, and we sat in the presence of four corpses. We covered them with such rags as we could find, and started away, fastening the door behind us. Their home must be these people's grave, for they could not have Christian burial, or be admitted to consecrated ground. They were as dogs, wild beasts, lepers, and no soul that valued its hope of eternal life would throw it away by meddling in any sort with these rebuked and smitten outcasts.

We had not moved four steps when I caught a sound as of footsteps upon gravel. My heart flew to my throat. We must not be seen coming from that house. I plucked at the king's robe and we drew back and took shelter behind the corner of the cabin.

"Now we are safe," I said, "but it was a close call—so to speak. If the night had been lighter he might have seen us, no doubt, he seemed to be so near."

"Mayhap it is but a beast and not a man at all."

"True. But man or beast, it will be wise to stay here a minute and let it get by and out of the way."

"Hark! It cometh hither."

True again. The step was coming toward us—straight toward the hut. It must be a beast, then, and we might as well have saved our trepidation. I was going to step out, but the king laid his hand upon my arm. There was a moment of silence, then we heard a soft knock on the cabin door. It made me shiver. Presently the knock was repeated, and then we heard these words in a guarded voice:

"Mother! Father! Open—we have got free, and we bring news to pale your cheeks but glad your hearts; and we may not tarry, but must fly! And—but they answer not. Mother! father!——"

I drew the king toward the other end of the hut and whispered:

"Come—now we can get to the road."

The king hesitated, was going to demur; but just then we heard the door give way, and knew that those desolate men were in the presence of their dead.

"Come, my liege! in a moment they will strike a light, and then will follow that which it would break your heart to hear."

He did not hesitate this time. The moment we were in the road, I ran; and after a moment he threw dignity aside and followed. I did not want to think of what was happening in the hut—I couldn't bear it; I wanted to drive it out of my mind; so I struck into the first subject that lay under that one in my mind:

"I have had the disease those people died of, and so have nothing to fear; but if you have not had it also—"

He broke in upon me to say he was in trouble, and it was his conscience that was troubling him:

"These young men have got free, they say—but *how?* It is not likely that their lord hath set them free."

"Oh, no, I make no doubt they escaped."

"That is my trouble; I have a fear that this is so, and your suspicion doth confirm it, you having the same fear."

"I should not call it by that name though. I do suspect that they escaped, but if they did, I am not sorry, certainly."

"I am not sorry, I *think*—but—"

"What is it? What is there for one to be troubled about?"

"*If* they did escape, then are we bound in duty to lay hands upon them and deliver them again to their lord; for it is not seemly that one of his quality should suffer a so insolent and high-handed outrage from persons of their base degree."

There it was, again. He could see only one side of it. He was born so, educated so, his veins were full of ancestral blood that was rotten with this sort of unconscious brutality, brought down by inheritance from a long procession of hearts that had each done its share toward poisoning the stream. To imprison these men without proof, and starve their kindred, was no harm, for they were merely peasants and subject to the will and pleasure of their lord, no matter what fearful form it might take; but for these men to break out of unjust captivity was insult and outrage, and a thing not to be countenanced by any conscientious person who knew his duty to his sacred caste.

I worked more than half an hour before I got him to change the subject—and even then an outside matter did it for me. This was a something which caught our eyes as we struck the summit of a small hill—a red glow, a good way off.

"That's a fire," said I.

Fires interested me considerably, because I was getting a good deal of an insurance business started, and was also training some horses and building some steam fire engines, with an eye to a paid fire department by and by. The priests opposed both my fire and life-insurance, on the ground that it was an insolent attempt to hinder the decrees of God; and if you pointed out that they did not hinder the decrees in the least, but only modified the hard consequences of them if you took out policies and had luck, they retorted that that was gambling against the decrees of God, and was just as bad. So they managed to damage those industries more or less, but I got even on my Accident business. As a rule, a knight is a lummux, and sometimes even a labrick, and hence open to pretty poor arguments when they come glibly from a superstition-monger, but even *he* could see the practical side of a thing once in a while; and so of late you couldn't clean up a tournament and pile the result without finding one of my accident-tickets in every helmet.

We stood there awhile, in the thick darkness and stillness, looking toward the red blur in the distance, and trying to make out the meaning of a far away murmur that rose and fell fitfully on the night. Sometimes it swelled up and for a moment seemed less remote; but when we were hopefully expecting it to betray its cause and nature, it dulled and sank again, carrying its mystery with it. We started down the hill in its direction, and the winding road plunged us at once into almost solid darkness—darkness that was packed and crammed in between two tall forest walls. We groped along down for half a mile, perhaps, that murmur growing more and more distinct all the time, the coming storm threatening more and more, with now and then a little shiver of wind, a faint show of lightning, and dull grumblings of distant thunder. I was in the lead. I ran against something—a soft heavy something which gave, slightly, to the impulse of my weight; at the same moment the lightning glared out, and within a foot of my face was the writhing face of a man who was hanging from the limb of a tree! That is, it seemed to be writhing, but it was not. It was a grewsome sight.

Straightway there was an ear-splitting explosion of thunder, and the bottom of heaven fell out; the rain poured down in a deluge. No matter, we must try to cut this man down, on the chance that there might be life in him yet, mustn't we? The lightning came quick and sharp, now, and the place was alternately noonday and midnight. One moment the man would be hanging before me in an intense light, and the next he was blotted out again in the darkness. I told the king we must cut him down. The king at once objected.

"If he hanged himself, he was willing to lose his property to his lord; so let him be. If others hanged him, belike they had the right—let him hang."

"But—"

"But me no buts, but even leave him as he is. And for yet another reason. When the lightning cometh again—there, look abroad."

Two others hanging, within fifty yards of us!

"It is not weather meet for doing useless courtesies unto dead folk. They are past thanking you. Come—it is unprofitable to tarry here."

There was reason in what he said, so we moved on. Within the next mile we counted six more hanging forms by the blaze of the lightning, and altogether it was a grisly excursion. That murmur was a murmur no longer, it was a roar; a roar of men's voices. A man came flying by, now, dimly through the darkness, and other men chasing him. They disappeared. Presently another case of the kind occurred, and then another and another. Then a sudden turn of the road brought us in sight of that fire—it was a large manor house, and little or nothing was left of it—and everywhere men were flying and other men raging after them in pursuit.

I warned the king that this was not a safe place for strangers. We would better get away from the light, until matters should improve. We stepped back a little, and hid in the edge of the wood. From this hiding place we saw both men and women hunted by the mob. The fearful work went on until nearly dawn. Then, the fire being out and the storm spent, the voices and flying footsteps presently ceased, and darkness and stillness reigned again.

We ventured out, and hurried cautiously away; and although we were worn out and sleepy, we kept on until we had put this place some miles behind us. Then we asked hospitality at the hut of a charcoal burner, and got what was to be had. A woman was up and about, but the man was still asleep, on a straw shake-down, on the clay floor. The woman seemed uneasy until I explained that we were travelers and had lost our way and been wandering in the woods all night. She became talkative, then, and asked if we had heard of the terrible goings-on at the manor house of Abblasoure. Yes, we had heard of them, but what we wanted now, was rest and sleep. The king broke in:

"Sell us the house and take yourselves away, for we be perilous company, being but late come from people that died of the Spotted Death."

It was good of him, but unnecessary. One of the commonest decorations of the nation was the waffle-iron face. I had early noticed that the woman and her husband were both so decorated. She made us entirely welcome, and had no fears; and plainly she was immensely impressed by the king's proposition; for of course it was a good deal of an event in her life to run across a person of the king's humble appearance who was ready to buy a man's house for the sake of a night's lodging. It gave her a large respect for us, and she strained the lean possibilities of her hovel to their utmost to make us comfortable.

We slept till far into the afternoon, and then got up hungry enough to make cotter fare quite palatable to the king, the more particularly as it was scant in quantity. And also in variety; it consisted solely of onions, salt, and the national black bread—made out of horse-feed. The woman told us about the affair of the evening before. At ten or eleven at night, when everybody was in bed, the manor house burst into flames. The countryside swarmed to the rescue, and the family were saved, with one exception, the master. He did not appear. Everybody was frantic over this loss, and two brave yeomen sacrificed their lives in ransacking the burning house seeking that valuable personage. But after a while he was found—what was left of him—which was his corpse. It was in a copse three hundred yards away, bound, gagged, stabbed in a dozen places.

Who had done this? Suspicion fell upon a humble family in the neighborhood who had been lately treated with peculiar harshness by the baron; and from these people the suspicion easily extended itself to their relatives and familiars. A suspicion was enough; my lord's liveried retainers proclaimed an instant crusade against these people, and were promptly joined by the community in general. The woman's husband had been active with the mob, and had not returned home until nearly dawn. He was gone, now, to find out what the general result had been. While we were still talking, he came back from his quest. His report was revolting enough. Eighteen persons hanged or butchered, and two yeomen and thirteen prisoners lost in the fire.

"And how many prisoners were there altogether, in the vaults?"

"Thirteen."

"Then every one of them was lost."

"Yes, all."

"But the people arrived in time to save the family; how is it they could save none of the prisoners?"

The man looked puzzled, and said:

"Would one unlock the vaults at such a time? Marry, some would have escaped."

"Then you mean that nobody *did* unlock them?"

"None went near them, either to lock or unlock. It standeth to reason that the bolts were fast; wherefore it was only needful to establish a watch, so that if any broke the bonds he might not escape, but be taken. None were taken."

"Natheless, three did escape," said the king, "and ye will do well to publish it and set justice upon their track, for these murthered the baron and fired the house."

I was just expecting he would come out with that. For a moment the man and his wife showed an eager interest in this news and an impatience to go out and spread it; then a sudden something else betrayed itself in their faces, and they began to ask questions. I answered the questions myself, and narrowly watched the effects produced. I was soon satisfied that the knowledge of who these three prisoners were, had somehow changed the atmosphere; that our hosts' continued eagerness to go and spread the news was now only pretended and not real. The king did not notice the change, and I was glad of that. I worked the conversation around toward other details of the night's proceedings, and noted that these people were relieved to have it take that direction.

The painful thing observable about all this business was, the alacrity with which this oppressed community had turned their cruel hands against their own class in the interest of the common oppressor. This man and woman seemed to feel that in a quarrel between a person of their own class and his lord, it was the natural and proper and rightful thing for that poor devil's whole caste to side with the master and fight his battle for him, without ever stopping to inquire into the rights or wrongs of the matter. This man had been out helping to hang his neighbors, and had done his work with zeal, and yet was aware that there was nothing against them but a mere suspicion, with nothing back of it describable as evidence, still neither he nor his wife seemed to see anything horrible about it.

This was depressing—to a man with the dream of a republic in his head. It reminded me of a time thirteen centuries away, when the "poor whites" of our South who were always despised and frequently insulted, by the slave-lords around them, and who owed their base condition simply to the presence of slavery in their midst, were yet pusillanimously ready to side with slave-lords in all political moves for the upholding and perpetuating of slavery, and did also finally shoulder their muskets and pour out their lives in an effort to prevent the destruction of that very institution which degraded them. And there was only one redeeming feature connected with that pitiful piece of history; and that was, that secretly the "poor white" did detest the slave-lord, and did feel his own shame. That feeling was not brought to the surface, but the fact that it was there and could have been brought out, under favoring circumstances, was something—in fact it was enough; for it showed that a man is at bottom a man, after all, even if it doesn't show on the outside.

Well, as it turned out, this charcoal burner was just the twin of the Southern "poor white" of the far future. The king presently showed impatience, and said:

"An ye prattle here all the day, justice will miscarry. Think ye the criminals will abide in their father's house? They are fleeing, they are not waiting. You should look to it that a party of horse be set upon their track."

The woman paled slightly, but quite perceptibly, and the man looked flustered and irresolute. I said:

"Come, friend, I will walk a little way with you, and explain which direction I think they would try to take. If they were merely resisters of the gabelle or some kindred absurdity I would try to protect them from capture; but when men murder a person of high degree and likewise burn his house, that is another matter."

The last remark was for the king—to quiet him. On the road the man pulled his resolution together, and began the march with a steady gait, but there was no eagerness in it. By and by I said:

"What relation were these men to you—cousins?"

He turned as white as his layer of charcoal would let him, and stopped, trembling.

"Ah, my God, how knew you that?"

"I didn't know it; it was a chance guess."

"Poor lads, they are lost. And good lads they were, too."

"Were you actually going yonder to tell on them?"

He didn't quite know how to take that; but he said, hesitatingly:

"Ye-s."

"Then I think you are a damned scoundrel!"

It made him as glad as if I had called him an angel.

"Say the good words again, brother! for surely ye mean that ye would not betray me an I failed of my duty."

"Duty? There is no duty in the matter, except the duty to keep still and let those men get away. They've done a righteous deed."

He looked pleased; pleased, and touched with apprehension at the same time. He looked up and down the road to see that no one was coming, and then said in a cautious voice:

"From what land come you, brother, that you speak such perilous words, and seem not to be afraid?"

"They are not perilous words when spoken to one of my own caste, I take it. You would not tell anybody I said them?"

"I? I would be drawn asunder by wild horses first."

"Well, then, let me say my say. I have no fears of your repeating it. I think devil's work has been done last night upon those innocent poor people. That old baron got only what he deserved. If I had my way, all his kind should have the same luck."

Fear and depression vanished from the man's manner, and gratefulness and a brave animation took their place:

"Even though you be a spy, and your words a trap for my undoing, yet are they such refreshment that to hear them again and others like to them, I would go to the gallows happy, as having had one good feast at least in a starved life. And I will say my say, now, and ye may report it if ye be so minded. I helped to hang my neighbors for that it were peril to my own life to show lack of zeal in the master's cause; the others helped for none other reason. All rejoice to-day that he is dead, but all do go about seemingly sorrowing, and shedding the hypocrite's tear, for in that lies safety. I have said the words, I have said the words! the only ones that have ever tasted good in my mouth, and the reward of that taste is sufficient. Lead on, an ye will, be it even to the scaffold, for I am ready."

There it was, you see. A man *is* a man, at bottom. Whole ages of abuse and oppression cannot crush the manhood clear out of him. Whoever thinks it a mistake, is himself mistaken. Yes, there is plenty good enough material for a republic in the most degraded people that ever existed—even the Russians; plenty of manhood in them—even in the Germans—if one could but force it out of its timid and suspicious privacy, to overthrow and trample in the mud any throne that ever was set up and any nobility that ever supported it. We should see certain things yet, let us hope and believe. First, a modified monarchy, till Arthur's days were done, then the destruction of the throne, nobility abolished, every member of it bound out to some useful trade, universal suffrage instituted, and the whole government placed in the hands of the men and women of the nation there to remain. Yes, there was no occasion to give up my dream yet a while.

CHAPTER 31

MARCO

We strolled along in a sufficiently indolent fashion, now, and talked. We must dispose of about the amount of time it ought to take to go to the little hamlet of Abblasoure and put justice on the track of those murderers and get back home again. And meantime I had an auxiliary interest which had never paled yet, never lost its novelty for me, since I had been in Arthur's kingdom: the behavior—born of nice and exact subdivisions of caste—of chance passers-by toward each other. Toward the shaven monk who trudged along with his cowl tilted back and the sweat washing down his fat jowls, the coal burner was deeply reverent; to the gentleman he was abject; with the small farmer and the free mechanic he was cordial and gossipy; and when a slave passed by with a countenance respectfully lowered, this chap's nose was in the air—he couldn't even see him. Well, there are times when one would like to hang the whole human race and finish the farce.

Presently we struck an incident. A small mob of half naked boys and girls came tearing out of the woods, scared and shrieking. The eldest among them were not more than twelve or fourteen years old. They implored help, but they were so beside themselves that we couldn't make out what the matter was. However, we plunged into the wood, they skurrying in the lead, and the trouble was quickly revealed: they had hanged a little fellow with a bark rope, and he was kicking and struggling, in the process of choking to death. We rescued him, and fetched him around. It was some more human nature; the admiring little folk imitating their elders; they were playing mob, and had achieved a success which promised to be a good deal more serious than they had bargained for.

It was not a dull excursion for me. I managed to put in the time very well. I made various acquaintanceships, and in my quality of stranger was able to ask as many questions as I wanted to. A thing which naturally interested me, as a statesman, was the matter of wages. I picked up what I could under that head during the afternoon. A man who hasn't had much experience, and doesn't think, is apt to measure a nation's prosperity or lack of prosperity by the mere size of the prevailing wages: if the wages be high, the nation is prosperous; if low, it isn't. Which is an error. It isn't what sum you get, it's how much you can buy with it that's the important thing; and it's that that tells whether your wages are high in fact or only high in name. I could remember how it was in the time of our great civil war in the nineteenth century. In the North a carpenter got three dollars a day, gold valuation; in the South he got fifty—payable in Confederate shin-plasters worth a dollar a bushel. In the North a suit of over-alls cost three dollars—a day's wages; in the South it cost seventy-five—which was two days' wages. Other things were in proportion. Consequently, wages were twice as high in the North as they were in the South, because the one wage had that much more purchasing power that the other had.

Yes, I made various acquaintances in the hamlet, and a thing that gratified me a good deal was to find our new coins in circulation—lots of milrays, lots of mills, lots of cents, a good many nickels, and some silver; all this among the artisans and commonalty generally; yes, and even some gold—but that was at the bank, that is to say, the goldsmith's. I dropped in there while Marco the son of Marco was haggling with a shopkeeper over a quarter of a pound of salt, and asked for change for a twenty dollar gold piece. They furnished it—that is, after they had chewed the piece, and rung it on the counter, and tried acid on it, and asked me where I got it, and who I was, and where I was from, and where I was going to, and when I expected to get there, and perhaps a couple of hundred more questions; and when they got aground, I went right on and furnished them a lot of information voluntarily: told them I owned a dog, and his name was Watch, and my first wife was a Free Will Baptist, and her grandfather was a Prohibitionist, and I used to know a man who had two thumbs on each hand and a wart on the inside of his upper lip, and died in the hope of a glorious resurrection, and so-on, and so-on, and so-on, till even that hungry village questioner began to look satisfied, and also a shade put out; but he had to respect a man of my financial strength, and so he didn't give me any lip, but I noticed he took it out of his underlings, which was a perfectly natural thing to do. Yes, they changed my twenty, but I judged it strained the bank a little, which was a thing to be expected, for it was the same as walking into a paltry village store in the nineteenth century and requiring the boss of it to change a two-thousand dollar bill for you all of a sudden. He could do it, maybe; but at the same time he would wonder how a small farmer happened to be carrying so much money around in his pocket; which was probably this goldsmith's thought, too; for he followed me to the door and stood there gazing after me with reverent admiration.

Our new money was not only handsomely circulating, but its language was already glibly in use; that is to say, people had dropped the names of the former moneys, and spoke of things as being worth so many dollars or cents or mills or milrays, now. It was very gratifying. We were progressing, that was sure.

I got to know several master mechanics, but about the most interesting fellow among them was the blacksmith, Dowley. He was a live man and a brisk talker, and had two journeymen and three apprentices, and was doing a raging business. In fact, he was getting rich, hand over fist, and was vastly respected. Marco was very proud of having such a man for a friend. He had taken me there ostensibly to let me see the big establishment which bought so much of his charcoal, but really to let me see what easy and almost familiar terms he was on with this great man. Dowley and I fraternized at once; I had had just such picked men, splendid fellows, under me in the Colt Arms Factory. I was bound to see more of him, so I invited him to come out to Marco's, Sunday, and dine with us. Marco was appalled, and held his breath; and when the grandee accepted, he was so grateful that he almost forgot to be astonished at the condescension.

Marco's joy was exhuberant—but only for a moment; then he grew thoughtful, then sad; and when he heard me tell Dowley I should have Dickon the boss mason, and Smug the boss wheelwright out there, too, the coal-dust on his face turned to chalk, and he lost his grip. But I knew what was the matter with him; it was the expense. He saw ruin before him; he judged that his financial days were numbered. However, on our way to invite the others, I said:

"You must allow me to have these friends come; and you must also allow me to pay the costs."

His face cleared, and he said with spirit:

"But not all of it, not all of it. Ye cannot well bear a burden like to this alone."

I stopped him, and said:

"Now let's understand each other on the spot, old friend. I am only a farm bailiff, it is true; but I am not poor, nevertheless. I have been very fortunate this year—you would be astonished to know how I have thriven. I tell you the honest truth when I say I could squander away as many as a dozen feasts like this and never care *that* for the expense!" and I snapped my fingers. I could see myself rise a foot at a time in Marco's estimation, and when I fetched out those last words I was become a very tower, for style and altitude. "So you see, you must let me have my way. You can't contribute a cent to this orgy, that's *settled.*"

"It's grand and good of you—"

"No, it isn't. You've opened your house to Jones and me in the most generous way; Jones was remarking upon it to-day, just before you came back from the village; for although he wouldn't be likely to say such a thing to you,—because Jones isn't a talker, and is diffident in society—he has a good heart and a grateful, and knows how to appreciate it when he is well treated; yes, you and your wife have been very hospitable toward us—"

"Ah, brother, 'tis nothing—*such* hospitality!"

"But it *is* something; the best a man has, freely given, is always something, and is as good as a prince can do, and ranks right along beside it—for even a prince can but do his best. And so we'll shop around and get up this layout, now, and don't you worry about the expense. I'm one of the worst spendthrifts that ever was born. Why, do you know, sometimes in a single week I spend—but never mind about that—you'd never believe it anyway."

And so we went gadding along, dropping in here and there, pricing things, and gossiping with the shopkeepers about the riot, and now and then running across pathetic reminders of it, in the persons of shunned and tearful and houseless remnants of families whose homes had been taken from them and their parents butchered or hanged. The raiment of Marco and his wife was of coarse tow-linen and linsey-woolsey respectively, and resembled township maps, it being made up pretty exclusively of patches which had been added, township by township, in the course of five or six years, until hardly a hand's-breadth of the original garments was surviving and present. Now I wanted to fit these people out with new suits, on account of that swell company, and I didn't know just how to get at it with delicacy, until at last it struck me that as I had already been liberal in inventing wordy gratitude for the king, it would be just the thing to back it up with evidence of a substantial sort; so I said:

"And Marco, there's another thing which you must permit—out of kindness for Jones—because you wouldn't want to offend him. He was very anxious to testify his appreciation in some way, but he is so diffident he couldn't venture it himself, and so he begged me to buy some little things and give them to you and Dame Phyllis and let him pay for them without your ever knowing they came from him—you know how a delicate person feels about that sort of thing—and so I said I would, and we would keep mum. Well, his idea was, a new outfit of clothes for you both—"

"Oh, it is wastefulness! It may not be, brother, it may not be. Consider the vastness of the sum—"

"Hang the vastness of the sum! Try to keep quiet for a moment, and see how it would seem; a body can't get in a word edgeways, you talk so much. You ought to cure that, Marco; it isn't good form, you know, and it will grow on you if you don't check it. Yes, we'll step in here, now, and price this man's stuff—and don't forget to remember to not let on to Jones that you know he had anything to do with it. You can't think how curiously sensitive and proud he is. He's a farmer—pretty fairly well-to-do farmer—and I'm his bailiff; *but*—the imagination of that man! Why, sometimes when he forgets himself and gets to blowing off, you'd think he was one of the swells of the earth; and you might listen to him a hundred years and never take him for a farmer—especially if he talked agriculture. He *thinks* he's a Sheol of a farmer; thinks he's old Grayback from Wayback; but between you and me privately he don't know as much about farming as he does about running a kingdom—still, whatever he talks about, you want to drop your underjaw and listen, the same as if you had never heard such incredible wisdom in all your life before, and were afraid you might die before you got enough of it. That will please Jones."

It tickled Marco to the marrow to hear about such an odd character; but it also prepared him for accidents; and in my experience when you travel with a king who is letting on to be something else and can't remember it more than about half the time, you can't take too many precautions.

This was the best store we had come across yet; it had everything in it, in small quantities, from anvils and dry goods all the way down to fish and pinchbeck jewelry. I concluded I would bunch my whole invoice right here, and not go pricing around any more. So I got rid of Marco, by sending him off to invite the mason and the wheelwright, which left the field free to me. For I never care to do a thing in a quiet way; it's got to be theatrical or I don't take any interest in it. I showed up money enough, in a careless way, to corral the shopkeeper's respect, and then I wrote down a list of the things I wanted, and handed it to him to see if he could read it. He could, and was proud to show that he could. He said he had been educated by a priest, and could read and write both. He ran it through, and remarked with satisfaction that it was a pretty heavy bill. Well, and so it was, for a little concern like that. I was not only providing a swell dinner, but some odds and ends of extras. I ordered that the things be carted out and delivered at the dwelling of Marco the son of Marco by Saturday evening, and send me the bill at dinner-time Sunday. He said I could depend upon his promptness and exactitude, it was the rule of the house. He also observed that he would throw in a couple of miller-guns for the Marcos, gratis—that everybody was using them now. He had a mighty opinion of that clever device. I said:

"And please fill them up to the middle mark, too; and add that to the bill."

He would, with pleasure. He filled them, and I took them with me. I couldn't venture to tell him that the miller-gun was a little invention of my own, and that I had officially ordered that every shopkeeper in the kingdom keep them on hand and sell them at government-price—which was the merest trifle, and the shopkeeper got that, not the government. We furnished them for nothing.

The king had hardly missed us when we got back at night-fall. He had early dropped again into his dream of a grand invasion of Gaul with the whole strength of his kingdom at his back, and the afternoon had slipped away without his ever coming to himself again.

CHAPTER 32

DOWLEY'S HUMILIATION

Well, when that cargo arrived, toward sunset, Saturday afternoon, I had my hands full to keep the Marcos from fainting. They were sure Jones and I were ruined past help, and they blamed themselves as accessories to this bankruptcy. You see, in addition to the dinner-materials, which called for a sufficiently round sum, I had bought a lot of extras for the future comfort of the family: for instance, a big lot of wheat, a delicacy as rare to the tables of their class as was ice-cream to a hermit's; also a sizeable deal dinner table; also two entire pounds of salt, which was another piece of extravagance in those people's eyes; also crockery, stools, the clothes, a small cask of beer, and so on. I instructed the Marcos to keep quiet about this sumptuousness, so as to give me a chance to surprise the guests and show off a little. Concerning the new clothes, the simple couple were like children; they were up and down, all night, to see if it wasn't nearly daylight, so that they could put them on, and they were into them at last as much as an hour before dawn was due. Then their pleasure—not to say delirium—was so fresh and novel and inspiring that the sight of it paid me well for the interruptions which my sleep had suffered. The king had slept just as usual—like the dead. The Marcos could not thank him for their clothes, that being forbidden; but they tried every way they could think of to make him see how grateful they were. Which all went for nothing: he didn't notice any change.

It turned out to be one of those rich and rare fall days which is just a June day toned down to a degree where it is heaven to be out of doors. Toward noon the guests arrived and we assembled under a great tree and were soon as sociable as old acquaintances. Even the king's reserve melted a little, though it was some little trouble to him to adjust himself to the name of Jones along at first. I had asked him to try to not forget that he was a farmer; but I had also considered it prudent to ask him to let the thing stand at that, and not elaborate it any. Because he was just the kind of person you could depend on to spoil a little thing like that if you didn't warn him, his tongue was so handy, and his spirit so willing, and his information so uncertain.

Dowley was in fine feather, and I early got him started, and then adroitly worked him around onto his own history for a text and himself for a hero, and then it was good to sit there and hear him hum. Self-made man, you know. They know how to talk. They do deserve more credit than any other breed of men, yes, that is true; and they are among the very first to find it out, too. He told how he had begun life an orphan lad without money and without friends able to help him; how he had lived as the slaves of the meanest master lived; how his day's work was from sixteen to eighteen hours long, and yielded him only enough black bread to keep him in a half-fed condition; how his faithful endeavors finally attracted the attention of a good blacksmith, who came near knocking him dead with kindness by suddenly offering, when he was totally unprepared, to take him as his bound apprentice for nine years and give him board and clothes and teach him the trade—or "mystery" as Dowley called it. That was his first great rise, his first gorgeous stroke of fortune; and you saw that he couldn't yet speak of it without a sort of eloquent wonder and delight that such a gilded promotion should have fallen to the lot of a common human being. He got no new clothing during his apprenticeship, but on his graduation day his master tricked him out in spang-new tow-linens and made him feel unspeakably rich and fine.

"I remember me of that day!" the wheelwright sang out, with enthusiasm.

"And I likewise!" cried the mason. "I would not believe they were thine own; in faith I could not."

"Nor others!" shouted Dowley, with sparkling eyes. "I was like to lose my character, the neighbors wending I had mayhap been stealing. It was a great day, a great day; one forgetteth not days like that."

Yes, and his master was a fine man, and prosperous, and always had a great feast of meat twice in the year, and with it white bread, true wheaten bread; in fact, lived like a lord, so to speak. And in time Dowley succeeded to the business and married the daughter.

"And now consider what is come to pass," said he, impressively. "Two times in every month there is fresh meat upon my table." He made a pause here, to let that fact sink home, then added—"and eight times, salt meat."

"It is even true," said the wheelwright, with bated breath.

"I know it of mine own knowledge," said the mason, in the same reverent fashion.

"On my table appeareth white bread every Sunday in the year," added the master smith, with solemnity. "I leave it to your own consciences, friends, if this is not also true?"

"By my head, yes!" cried the mason.

"I can testify it—and I do," said the wheelwright.

"And as to furniture, ye shall say yourselves what mine equipment is." He waved his hand in fine gesture of granting frank and unhampered freedom of speech, and added: "Speak as ye are moved; speak as ye would speak an I were not here."

"Ye have five stools, and of the sweetest workmanship at that, albeit your family is but three," said the wheelwright, with deep respect.

"And six wooden goblets, and six platters of wood and two of pewter to eat and drink from withal," said the mason, impressively. "And I say it as knowing God is my judge, and we tarry not here alway, but must answer at the last day for the things said in the body, be they false or be they sooth."

"Now ye know what manner of man I am, brother Jones," said the smith, with a fine and friendly condescension, "and doubtless ye would look to find me a man jealous of his due of respect and but sparing of outgo to strangers till their rating and quality be assured, but trouble yourself not, as concerning that; wit ye well ye shall find me a man that regardeth not these matters but is willing to receive any he as his fellow and equal that carrieth a right heart in his body, be his worldly estate howsoever modest. And in token of it, here is my hand; and I say with my own mouth we are equals—equals"—and he smiled around on the company with the satisfaction of a god who is doing the handsome and gracious thing and is quite well aware of it.

The king took the hand with a poorly disguised reluctance, and let go of it as willingly as a lady lets go of a fish; all of which had a good effect, for it was mistaken for an embarrassment natural to one who was being beamed upon by greatness.

The dame brought out the table, now, and set it under the tree. It caused a visible stir of surprise, it being brand new and a sumptuous article of deal. But the surprise rose higher still, when the dame, with a body oozing easy indifference at every pore, but eyes that gave it all away by absolutely flaming with vanity, slowly unfolded an actual simon-pure tablecloth and spread it. That was a notch above even the blacksmith's domestic grandeurs, and it hit him hard; you could see it. But Marco was in Paradise; you could see that, too. Then the dame brought two fine new stools—whew! that was a sensation; it was visible in the eyes of every guest. Then she brought two more—as calmly as she could. Sensation again—with awed murmurs. Again she brought two—walking on air, she was so proud. The guests were petrified, and the mason muttered:

"There is that about earthly pomps which doth ever move to reverence."

As the dame turned away, Marco couldn't help slapping on the climax while the thing was hot; so he said with what was meant for a languid composure but was a poor imitation of it:

"These suffice; leave the rest."

So there were more yet! It was a fine effect. I couldn't have played the hand better myself.

From this out, the madam piled up the surprises with a rush that fired the general astonishment up to a hundred and fifty in the shade, and at the same time paralyzed expression of it down to gasped "Oh's" and "Ah's", and mute upliftings of hands and eyes. She fetched crockery—new, and plenty of it; new wooden goblets and other table furniture; and beer, fish, chicken, a goose, eggs, roast beef, roast mutton, a ham, a small roast pig, and a wealth of genuine white wheaten bread. Take it by and large, that spread laid everything far and away in the shade that ever that crowd had seen before. And while they sat there just simply stupefied with wonder and awe, I sort of waved my hand as if by accident, and the store-keeper's son emerged from space and said he had come to collect.

"That's all right," I said, indifferently. "What is the amount? give us the items."

Then he read off this bill, while those three amazed men listened, and serene waves of satisfaction rolled over my soul and alternate waves of terror and admiration surged over Marco's:

2 pounds salt	200
8 dozen pints beer, in the wood	800
3 bushels wheat	2,700
2 pounds fish	100
3 hens	400
1 goose	400
3 dozen eggs	150
1 roast of beef	450
1 " " mutton	400
1 ham	800
1 sucking pig	500
2 crockery dinner sets	6,000
2 men's suits and underwear	2,800
1 stuff and 1 linsey-woolsey gown and underwear	1,600
8 wooden goblets	800
Various table furniture	10,000
1 deal table	3,000
8 stools	4,000
2 miller-guns, loaded	3,000

He ceased. There was a pale and awful silence. Not a limb stirred. Not a nostril betrayed the passage of breath.

"Is that all?" I asked, in a voice of the most perfect calmness.

"All, fair sir, save that certain matters of light moment are placed together under a head hight sundries. If it would like you, I will sepa—"

"It is of no consequence," I said, accompanying the words with a gesture of the most utter indifference; "give me the grand total, please."

The clerk leaned against the tree to stay himself, and said:

"Thirty-nine thousand one hundred and fifty milrays!"

The wheelwright fell off his stool, the others grabbed the table to save themselves, and there was a deep and general ejaculation of—

"God be with us in the day of disaster!"

The clerk hastened to say:

"My father chargeth me to say he cannot honorably require you to pay it all at this time, and therefore only prayeth you—"

I paid no more heed than if it were the idle breeze, but with an air of indifference amounting almost to weariness, got out my money and tossed four dollars onto the table. Ah, you should have seen them stare!

The clerk was astonished and charmed. He asked me to retain one of the dollars as security, until he could go to town and—I interrupted:

"What, and fetch back nine cents? Nonsense. Take the whole. Keep the change."

There was an amazed murmur to this effect:

"Verily this being is *made* of money! He throweth it away even as it were dirt."

The blacksmith was a crushed man.

The clerk took his money and reeled away drunk with fortune. I said to Marco and his wife:

"Good folk, here is a little trifle for you"—handing the miller-guns as if it were a matter of no consequence though each of them contained fifteen cents in solid cash; and while the poor creatures went to pieces with astonishment and gratitude, I turned to the others and said as calmly as one would ask the time of day:

"Well, if we are all ready, I judge the dinner is. Come, fall to."

Ah, well, it was immense; yes, it was a daisy. I don't know that I ever put a situation together better, or got happier spectacular effects out of the materials available. The blacksmith—well, he was simply mashed. Land! I wouldn't have felt what that man was feeling, for anything in the world. Here he had been blowing and bragging about his grand meat-feast twice a year, and his fresh meat twice a month, and his salt meat twice a week, and his white bread every Sunday the year round—all for a family of three: the entire cost for the year not above 69.2.6 (sixty-nine cents, two mills and six milrays,) and all of a sudden here comes along a man who slashes out nearly four dollars on a single blow-out; and not only that, but acts as if it made him tired to handle such small sums. Yes, Dowley was a good deal wilted, and shrunk-up and collapsed; he had the aspect of a bladder-balloon that's been stepped on by a cow.

CHAPTER 33

SIXTH CENTURY POLITICAL ECONOMY

However, I made a dead set at him, and before the first third of the dinner was reached, I had him happy again. It was easy to do—in a country of ranks and castes. You see, in a country where they have ranks and castes, a man isn't ever a man, he is only part of a man, he can't ever get his full growth. You prove your superiority over him in station, or rank, or fortune, and that's the end of it—he knuckles down. You can't insult him after that. No, I don't mean quite that; of course you *can* insult him, I only mean it's difficult; and so, unless you've got a lot of useless time on your hands it doesn't pay to try. I had the smith's reverence, now, because I was apparently immensely prosperous and rich; I could have had his adoration if I had had some little gimcrack title of nobility. And not only his, but any commoner's in the land, though he were the mightiest production of all the ages, in intellect, worth, and character, and I bankrupt in all three. This was to remain so, as long as England should exist in the earth. With the spirit of prophecy upon me, I could look into the future and see her erect statues and monuments to her unspeakable Georges and other royal and noble clothes-horses, and leave unhonored the creators of this world—after God—Gutenberg, Watt, Arkwright, Whitney, Morse, Stephenson, Bell.

The king got his cargo aboard, and then, the talk not turning upon battle, conquest, or iron-clad duel, he dulled down to drowsiness and went off to take a nap. Mrs. Marco cleared the table, placed the beer-keg handy, and went away to eat her dinner of leavings in humble privacy, and the rest of us soon drifted into matters near and dear to the hearts of our sort—business and wages, of course. At a first glance, things appeared to be exceeding prosperous in this little tributary kingdom—whose lord was King Bagdemagus—as compared with the state of things in my own region. They had the "protection" system in full force here, whereas we were working along down towards free trade, by easy stages, and were now about half way. Before long, Dowley and I were doing all the talking, the others hungrily listening. Dowley warmed to his work, snuffed an advantage in the air, and began to put questions which he considered pretty awkward ones for me, and they did have something of that look:

"In your country, brother, what is the wage of a master bailiff, master hind, carter, shepherd, swineherd?"

"Twenty-five milrays a day; that is to say, a quarter of a cent."

The smith's face beamed with joy. He said:

"With us they are allowed the double of it! And what may a mechanic get—carpenter, dauber, mason, painter, blacksmith, wheelwright and the like?"

"On the average, fifty milrays; half a cent a day."

"Ho-ho! With us they are allowed a hundred! With us any good mechanic is allowed a cent a day! I count out the tailor, but not the others—they are all allowed a cent a day, and in driving times they get more—yes, up to a hundred and ten and even fifteen milrays a day. I've paid a hundred and fifteen myself, within the week. 'Rah for protection—to Sheol with free-trade!"

And his face shone upon the company like a sunburst. But I didn't scare at all. I rigged up my pile-driver, and allowed myself fifteen minutes to drive him into the earth—drive him *all* in—drive him in till not even the curve of his skull should show above ground. Here is the way I started in on him. I asked:

"What do you pay a pound for salt?"

"A hundred milrays."

"We pay forty. What do you pay for beef and mutton—when you buy it?" That was a neat hit; it made the color come.

"It varieth somewhat, but not much; one may say 75 milrays the pound."

"*We* pay 33. What do you pay for eggs?"

"Fifty milrays the dozen."

"We pay 20. What do you pay for beer?"

"It costeth us 8½ milrays the pint."

"We get it for 4; 25 bottles for a cent. What do you pay for wheat?"

"At the rate of 900 milrays the bushel."

"We pay 400. What do you pay for a man's tow-linen suit?"

"Thirteen cents."

"We pay 6. What do you pay for a stuff gown for the wife of the laborer or the mechanic?"

"We pay 8. 4. 0."

"Well, observe the difference: you pay eight cents and four mills, we pay only four cents." I prepared, now, to sock it to him. I said: "Look here, dear friend, *what's become of your high wages you were bragging so about, a few minutes ago?*"—and I looked around on the company with placid satisfaction, for I had slipped up on him gradually and tied him hand and foot, you see, without his ever noticing that he was being tied at all. "What's become of those noble high wages of yours?—I seem to have knocked the stuffing all out of them, it appears to me."

But if you will believe me, he merely looked surprised, that is all! he didn't grasp the situation at all, didn't know he had walked into a trap, didn't discover that he was *in* a trap. I could have shot him, from sheer vexation. With cloudy eye and a struggling intellect, he fetched this out:

"Marry, I seem not to understand. It is *proved* that our wages be double thine; how then may it be that thou'st knocked therefrom the stuffing?—an I miscall not the wonderly word, this being the first time under grace and providence of God it hath been granted me to hear it."

Well, I was stunned; partly with this unlooked-for stupidity on his part, and partly because his fellows so manifestly sided with him and were of his mind—if you might call it mind. My position was simple enough, plain enough; how could it ever be simplified more? However, I must try:

"Why, look here, brother Dowley, don't you see? Your wages are merely higher than ours in *name*, not in *fact*."

"Hear him! They are the *double*—ye have confessed it yourself."

"Yes-yes, I don't deny that at all. But that's got nothing to do with it; the *amount* of the wages in mere coins, with meaningless names attached to them to know them by, has got nothing to do with it. The thing is, how much can you *buy* with your wages?—that's the idea. While it is true that with you a good mechanic is allowed about three dollars and a half a year, and with us only about a dollar and seventy-five—"

"There—ye're confessing it again, ye're confessing it again!"

"Confound it, I've never denied it I tell you! What I say is this. With us *half* a dollar buys more than a *dollar* buys with you—and *therefore* it stands to reason and the commonest kind of common sense, that our wages are *higher* than yours."

He looked dazed, and said, despairingly:

"Verily, I cannot make it out. Ye've just *said* ours are the higher, and with the same breath ye take it back."

"Oh, great Scott, isn't it possible to get such a simple thing through your head? Now look here—let me illustrate. We pay four cents for a woman's stuff gown, you pay 8. 4. 0. which is 4 mills more than *double*. What do you allow a laboring woman who works on a farm?"

"Two mills a day."

"Very good; we allow but half as much; we pay her only a tenth of a cent a day; and–"

"Again ye're conf–"

"Wait! Now, you see, the thing is very simple; this time you'll understand it. For instance, it takes your woman 42 days to earn her gown, at 2 mills a day–7 weeks' work; but ours earns hers in forty days–two days *short* of 7 weeks. Your woman has a gown, and her whole seven weeks' wages are gone; ours has a gown, and two days' wages left, to buy something else with. There–*now* you understand it!"

He looked–well, he merely looked dubious, it's the most I can say; so did the others. I waited–to let the thing work. Dowley spoke at last–and betrayed the fact that he actually hadn't gotten away from his rooted and grounded superstitions yet. He said, with a trifle of hesitancy:

"But–but–ye cannot fail to grant that two mills a day is better than one."

Shucks! Well, of course I hated to give it up. So I chanced another flyer:

"Let us suppose a case. Suppose one of your journeymen goes out and buys the following articles:

"1 pound of salt;
1 dozen eggs;
1 dozen pints of beer;
1 bushel of wheat;
1 tow-linen suit;
5 pounds of beef;
5 pounds of mutton.

"The lot will cost him 32 cents. It takes him 32 working days to earn the money–5 weeks and 2 days. Let him come to us and work 32 days at *half* the wages; he can buy all those things for a shade under 14½ cents; they will cost him a shade under 29 days' work, and he will have about half a week's wages over. Carry it through the year; he would save nearly a week's wages every two months, *your* man nothing; thus saving five or six weeks' wages in a year, your man not a cent. *Now* I reckon you understand that 'high wages' and 'low wages' are phrases that don't mean anything in the world until you find out which of them will *buy* the most!"

It was a crusher.

But alas, it didn't crush. No, I had to give it up. What those people valued was *high wages;* it didn't seem to be a matter of any consequence to them whether the high wages would buy anything or not. They stood for "protection," and swore by it, which was reasonable enough, because interested parties had gulled them into the notion that it was protection which had created their high wages. I proved to them that in a quarter of a century their wages had advanced but 30 per cent. while the cost of living had gone up 100; and that with us, in a shorter time, wages had advanced 40 per cent. while the cost of living had gone steadily down. But it didn't do any good. Nothing could unseat their strange beliefs.

Well, I was smarting under a sense of defeat. Undeserved defeat, but what of that? That didn't soften the smart any. And to think of the circumstances! the first statesman of the age, the capablest man, the best informed man in the entire world, the loftiest uncrowned head that had moved through the clouds of any political firmament for centuries, sitting here apparently defeated in argument by an ignorant country blacksmith! And I could see that those others were sorry for me!—which made me blush till I could smell my whiskers scorching. Put yourself in my place; feel as mean as I did, as ashamed as I felt —wouldn't *you* have struck below the belt to get even? Yes, you would; it is simply human nature. Well, that is what I did. I am not trying to justify it; I'm only saying that I was mad, and *anybody* would have done it.

Well, when I make up my mind to hit a man, I don't plan out a love-tap; no, that isn't my way; as long as I'm going to hit him at all, I'm going to hit him a lifter. And I don't jump at him all of a sudden, and risk making a blundering half-way business of it; no, I get away off yonder to one side, and work up on him gradually, so that he never suspects that I'm going to hit him at all; and by and by, all in a flash, he's flat of his back, and he can't tell for the life of him how it all happened. That is the way I went for brother Dowley. I started to talking lazy and comfortable, as if I was just talking to pass the time; and the oldest man in the world couldn't have taken the bearings of my starting place and guessed where I was going to fetch up:

"Boys, there's a good many curious things about law, and custom, and usage, and all that sort of thing, when you come to look at it; yes, and about the drift and progress of human opinion and movement, too. There are written laws—they perish; but there are also unwritten laws—*they* are eternal. Take the unwritten law of wages: it says they've got to advance, little by little, straight through the centuries. And notice how it works. We know what wages are now, here and there and yonder; we strike an average, and say that's the wages of to-day. We know what the wages were a hundred years ago, and what they were two hundred years ago; that's as far back as we can get, but it suffices to give us the law of progress, the measure and rate of the periodical augmentation; and so, without a document to help us, we can come pretty close to determining what the wages were three and four and five hundred years ago. Good, so far. Do we stop there? No. We stop looking backward; we face around and apply the law to the future. My friends, I can tell you what people's wages are going to be at any date in the future you want to know, for hundreds and hundreds of years."

"What, goodman, what!"

"Yes. In seven hundred years wages will have risen to six times what they are now, here in your region, and farm hands will be allowed 3 cents a day, and mechanics 6."

"I would I might die now and live then!" interrupted Smug the mason, with a fine avaricious glow in his eye.

"And that isn't all; they'll get their board besides—such as it is: it won't bloat them. Two hundred and fifty years later—pay attention, now—a mechanic's wages will be—mind you, this is law, not guesswork; a mechanic's wages will then be *twenty* cents a day!"

There was a general gasp of awed astonishment. Dickon the wheelwright murmured, with raised eyes and hands:

"More than three weeks pay for one day's work!"

"Riches!—of a truth, yes, riches!" muttered Marco, his breath coming quick and short, with excitement.

"Wages will keep on rising, little by little, little by little, as steadily as a tree grows, and at the end of three hundred and forty years more there'll be at least *one* country where the mechanic's average wage will be *two hundred* cents a day!"

It knocked them absolutely dumb! Not a man of them could get his breath for upwards of two minutes. Then the coalburner said prayerfully:

"Might I but live to see it!"

"It is the income of an earl!" said Smug.

"An earl, say ye?" said Dowley; "ye could say more than that and speak no lie; there's no earl in the realm of Bagdemagus that hath an income like to that. Income of an earl—mf! it's the income of an angel!"

"Now then, that is what is going to happen as regards wages. In that remote day, that man will earn, with *one* week's work, that bill of goods which it takes you upwards of *five* weeks to earn now. Some other pretty surprising things are going to happen, too. Brother Dowley, who is it that determines, every spring, what the particular wage of each kind of mechanic, laborer, and servant shall be for that year?"

"Sometimes the courts, sometimes the town council; but most of all, the magistrate. Ye may say, in general terms, it is the magistrate that fixes the wages."

"Doesn't ask any of those poor devils to *help* him fix their wages for them, does he?"

"Hm! That *were* an idea! The master that's to pay him the money is the one that's rightly concerned in that matter, ye will notice."

"Yes—but I thought the other man might have some little trifle at stake in it, too; and even his wife and children, poor creatures. The masters are these: nobles, rich men, the prosperous generally. These few, who do no work, determine what pay the vast hive shall have who *do* work. You see? They're a 'combine'—a trade union, to coin a new phrase—who band themselves together to force their lowly brother to take what they choose to give. Thirteen hundred years hence—so says the unwritten law—the 'combine' will be the other way, and then how these fine people's posterity will fume and fret and grit their teeth over the insolent tyranny of trade unions! Yes indeed! the magistrate will tranquilly arrange the wages from now clear away down into the nineteenth century; and then all of a sudden the wage-earner will consider that a couple of thousand years or so is enough of this one-sided sort of thing; and he will rise up and take a hand in fixing his wages himself. Ah, he will have a long and bitter account of wrong and humiliation to settle."

"Do ye believe—"

"That he actually will help to fix his own wages? Yes, indeed. And he will be strong and able, then."

"Brave times, brave times, of a truth!" sneered the prosperous smith.

"Oh,—and there's another detail. In that day, a master may hire a man for only just one day, or one week, or one month at a time, if he wants to."

"What?"

"It's true. Moreover, a magistrate won't be able to force a man to work for a master a whole year on a stretch whether the man wants to or not."

"Will there be *no* law or sense in that day?"

"Both of them, Dowley. In that day a man will be his own property, not the property of magistrate and master. And he can leave town whenever he wants to, if the wages don't suit him!—and they can't put him in the pillory for it."

"Perdition catch such an age!" shouted Dowley, in strong indignation. "An age of dogs, an age barren of reverence for superiors and respect for authority! The pillory—"

"Oh, wait, brother; say no good word for that institution. *I* think the pillory ought to be abolished."

"A most strange idea. Why?"

"Well, I'll tell you why. Is a man ever put in the pillory for a capital crime?"

"No."

"Is it right to condemn a man to a slight punishment for a small offense and then kill him?"

There was no answer. I had scored my first point! For the first time, the smith wasn't up and ready. The company noticed it. Good effect.

"You don't answer, brother. You were about to glorify the pillory a while ago, and shed some pity on a future age that isn't going to use it. *I* think the pillory ought to be abolished. What usually happens when a poor fellow is put in the pillory for some little offence that didn't amount to anything in the world? The mob try to have some fun with him, don't they?"

"Yes."

"They begin by clodding him; and they laugh themselves to pieces to see him try to dodge one clod and get hit with another?"

"Yes."

"Then they throw dead cats at him, don't they?"

"Yes."

"Well, then, suppose he has a few personal enemies in that mob—and here and there a man or a woman with a secret grudge against him—and suppose especially, that he is unpopular in the community, for his pride, or his prosperity, or one thing or another—stones and bricks take the place of clods and cats presently, don't they?"

"There is no doubt of it."

"As a rule he is crippled for life, isn't he?—jaws broken, teeth smashed out?—or legs mutilated, gangrened, presently cut off?—or an eye knocked out, maybe both eyes?"

"It is true, God knoweth it."

"And if he is unpopular he can depend on *dying*, right there in the stocks, can't he?"

"He surely can! One may not deny it."

"I take it none of *you* are unpopular—by reason of pride or insolence, or conspicuous prosperity, or any of those things that excite envy and malice among the base scum of a village? *You* wouldn't think it much of a risk to take a chance in the stocks?"

Dowley winced, visibly. I judged he was hit. But he didn't betray it by any spoken word. As for the others, they spoke out plainly, and with strong feeling. They said they had seen enough of the stocks to know what a man's chance in them was, and they would never consent to enter them if they could compromise on a quick death by hanging.

"Well, to change the subject—for I think I've established my point that the stocks ought to be abolished. I think some of our laws are pretty unfair. For instance, if I do a thing which ought to deliver me to the stocks, and you know I did it and yet keep still and don't report me, *you* will get the stocks if anybody informs on you."

"Ah, but that would serve you but right," said Dowley, "for you *must* inform. So saith the law."

The others coincided.

"Well, all right, let it go, since you vote me down. But there's one thing which certainly isn't fair. The magistrate fixes a mechanic's wage at 1 cent a day, for instance. The law says that if any master shall venture even under utmost press of business, to pay anything *over* that cent a day, even for a single day, he shall be both fined and pilloried for it; and whoever knows he did it and doesn't inform, they also shall be fined and pilloried. Now it seems to me unfair, Dowley, and a deadly peril to all of us, that because you thoughtlessly confessed, a while ago, that within a week you have paid a cent and fifteen mil—"

Oh, I tell *you* it was a smasher! You ought to have seen them go to pieces, the whole gang. I had just slipped up on poor smiling and complacent Dowley so nice and easy and softly, that he never suspected anything was going to happen till the blow came crashing down and knocked him all to rags.

A fine effect. In fact as fine as any I ever produced, with so little time to work it up in.

But I saw in a moment that I had overdone the thing a little. I was expecting to scare them, but I wasn't expecting to scare them to death. They were mighty near it, though. You see they had been a whole lifetime learning to appreciate the pillory; and to have that thing staring them in the face, and every one of them distinctly at the mercy of me, a stranger, if I chose to go and report—well, it was awful, and they couldn't seem to recover from the shock, they couldn't seem to pull themselves together. Pale, shaky, dumb, pitiful? Why, they weren't any better than so many dead men. It was very uncomfortable. Of course I thought they would appeal to me to keep mum, and then we would shake hands, and take a drink all round, and laugh it off, and there an end. But no; you see I was an unknown person, among a cruelly oppressed and suspicious people, a people always accustomed to having advantage taken of their helplessness, and never expecting just or kind treatment from any but their own families and very closest intimates. Appeal to *me* to be gentle, to be fair, to be generous? Of course they wanted to, but they couldn't dare.

CHAPTER 34

THE YANKEE AND THE KING SOLD AS SLAVES

Well, what had I better do? Nothing in a hurry, sure. I must get up a diversion; anything to employ me while I could think, and while these poor fellows could have a chance to come to life again. There sat Marco, petrified in the act of trying to get the hang of his miller-gun—turned to stone, just in the attitude he was in when my pile-driver fell, the toy still gripped in his unconscious fingers. So I took it from him and proposed to explain its mystery. Mystery! a simple little thing like that; and yet it was mystery enough, for that race and that age.

I never saw such an awkward people, with machinery; you see, they were totally unused to it. The miller-gun was a little double-barreled tube of toughened glass, with a neat little trick of a spring to it, which upon pressure would let a shot escape. But the shot wouldn't hurt anybody, it would only drop into your hand. In the gun were two sizes—wee mustard-seed shot, and another sort that were several times larger. They were money. The mustard-seed shot represented milrays, the larger ones mills. So the gun was a purse; and very handy, too; you could pay out money in the dark with it, with accuracy; and you could carry it in your mouth; or in your vest pocket, if you had one. I made them of several sizes—one size so large that it would carry the equivalent of a dollar. Using shot for money was a good thing for the government; the metal cost nothing, and the money couldn't be counterfeited, for I was the only person in the kingdom who knew how to manage a shot tower. "Paying the shot" soon came to be a common phrase. Yes, and I knew it would still be passing men's lips, away down in the nineteenth century, yet none would suspect how and when it originated.

The king joined us, about this time, mightily refreshed by his nap, and feeling good. Anything could make me nervous now, I was so uneasy—for our lives were in danger; and so it worried me to detect a complacent something in the king's eye which seemed to indicate that he had been loading himself up for a performance of some kind or other; confound it, why must he go and choose such a time as this?

I was right. He began, straight off, in the most innocently artful, and transparent, and lubberly way, to lead up to the subject of agriculture. The cold sweat broke out all over me. I wanted to whisper in his ear, "Man, we are in awful danger! every moment is worth a principality till we get back these men's confidence; *don't* waste any of this golden time." But of course I couldn't do it. Whisper to him? It would look as if we were conspiring. So I had to sit there and look calm and pleasant while the king stood over that dynamite mine and mooned along about his damned onions and things. At first the tumult of my own thoughts, summoned by the danger-signal and swarming to the rescue from every quarter of my skull, kept up such a hurrah and confusion and fifing and drumming that I couldn't take in a word; but presently when my mob of gathering plans began to crystalize and fall into position and form line of battle, a sort of order and quiet ensued and I caught the boom of the king's batteries, as if out of remote distance:

"—were not the best way, methinks, albeit it is not to be denied that authorities differ as concerning this point, some contending that the onion is but an unwholesome berry when stricken early from the tree—"

The audience showed signs of life, and sought each other's eyes in a surprised and troubled way.

"—whileas others do yet maintain, with much show of reason, that this is not of necessity the case, instancing that plums and other like cereals do be always dug in the unripe state—"

The audience exhibited distinct distress; yes, and also fear.

"—yet are they clearly wholesome, the more especially when one doth assuage the asperities of their nature by admixture of the tranquilizing juice of the wayward cabbage—"

The wild light of terror began to glow in these men's eyes, and one of them muttered, "These be errors, every one—God hath surely smitten the mind of this farmer." I was in miserable apprehension; I sat upon thorns.

"—and further instancing the known truth that in the case of animals, the young, which may be called the green fruit of the creature, is the better, all confessing that when a goat is ripe, his fur doth heat and sore engame his flesh, the which defect, taken in connection with his several rancid habits, and fulsome appetites, and godless attitudes of mind, and bilious quality of morals—"

They rose and went for him! With a fierce shout, "The one would betray us, the other is mad! Kill them! Kill them!" they flung themselves upon us. What joy flamed up in the king's eye! He might be lame in agriculture, but this kind of thing was just in his line. He had been fasting long, he was hungry for a fight. He hit the blacksmith a crack under the jaw that lifted him clear off his feet and stretched him flat of his back. "St. George for Britain!" and he downed the wheelwright. The mason was big, but I laid him out like nothing. The three gathered themselves up and came again; went down again; came again; and kept on repeating this, with native British pluck, until they were battered to jelly, reeling with exhaustion, and so blind that they couldn't tell us from each other; and yet they kept right on, hammering away with what might was left in them. Hammering each other —for we stepped aside and looked on while they rolled, and struggled, and gouged, and pounded, and bit, with the strict and wordless attention to business of so many bulldogs. We looked on without apprehension, for they were fast getting past ability to go for help against us, and the arena was far enough from the public road to be safe from intrusion.

Well, while they were gradually playing out, it suddenly occurred to me to wonder what had become of Marco. I looked around; he was nowhere to be seen. Oh, but this was ominous! I pulled the king's sleeve, and we glided away and rushed for the hut. No Marco there, no Phyllis there! They had gone to the road for help, sure. I told the king to give his heels wings, and I would explain later. We made good time across the open ground, and as we darted into the shelter of the wood I glanced back and saw a mob of excited peasants swarm into view, with Marco and his wife at their head. They were making a world of noise, but that couldn't hurt anybody; the wood was dense, and as soon as we were well into its depths we would take to a tree and let them whistle. Ah, but then came another sound—dogs! Yes, that was quite another matter. It magnified our contract—we must find running water.

We tore along at a good gait, and soon left the sounds far behind and modified to a murmur. We struck a stream and darted into it. We waded swiftly down it, in the dim forest light, for as much as three hundred yards, and then came across an oak with a great bough sticking out over the water. We climbed up on this bough, and began to work our way along it to the body of the tree; now we began to hear those sounds more plainly; so the mob had struck our trail. For a while the sounds approached pretty fast. And then for another while they didn't. No doubt the dogs had found the place where we had entered the stream, and were now waltzing up and down the shores trying to pick up the trail again.

When we were snugly lodged in the tree and curtained with foliage, the king was satisfied, but I was doubtful. I believed we could crawl along a branch and get into the next tree, and I judged it worth while to try. We tried it, and made a success of it, though the king slipped, at the junction, and came near failing to connect. We got comfortable lodgement and satisfactory concealment among the foliage, and then we had nothing to do but listen to the hunt.

Presently we heard it coming—and coming on the jump, too; yes, and down both sides of the stream. Louder—louder—next minute it swelled swiftly up into a roar of shoutings, barkings, tramplings, and swept by like a cyclone.

"I was afraid that the overhanging branch would suggest something to them," said I, "but I don't mind the disappointment. Come, my liege, it were well that we make good use of our time. We've flanked them. Dark is coming on, presently. If we can cross the stream and get a good start, and borrow a couple of horses from somebody's pasture to use for a few hours, we shall be safe enough."

We started down, and got nearly to the lowest limb, when we seemed to hear the hunt returning. We stopped to listen.

"Yes," said I, "they're baffled, they've given it up, they're on their way home. We will climb back to our roost again, and let them go by."

So we climbed back. The king listened a moment and said:

"They still search—I wit the sign. We did best to abide."

He was right. He knew more about hunting than I did. The noise approached steadily, but not with a rush. The king said:

"They reason that we were advantaged by no parlous start of them, and being on foot are as yet no mighty way from where we took the water."

"Yes, sire, that is about it, I am afraid, though I was hoping better things."

The noise drew nearer and nearer, and soon the van was drifting under us, on both sides of the water. A voice called a halt from the other bank, and said:

"An they were so minded, they could get to yon tree by this branch that overhangs, and yet not touch ground. Ye will do well to send a man up it."

"Marry, that will we do!"

I was obliged to admire my cuteness in foreseeing this very thing and swapping trees to beat it. But don't you know, there are some things that can beat smartness and foresight? Awkwardness and stupidity can. The best swordsman in the world doesn't need to fear the second best swordsman in the world; no, the person for him to be afraid of is some ignorant antagonist who has never had a sword in his hand before; he doesn't do the thing he ought to do, and so the expert isn't prepared for him; he does the thing he ought not to do: and often it catches the expert out and ends him on the spot. Well, how could I, with all my gifts, make any valuable preparation against a near-sighted, cross-eyed pudding-headed clown who would aim himself at the wrong tree and hit the right one? And that is what he did. He went for the wrong tree, which was of course the right one by mistake, and up he started.

Matters were serious, now. We remained still, and awaited developments. The peasant toiled his difficult way up. The king raised himself up and stood; he made a leg ready, and when the comer's head arrived in reach of it there was a dull thud, and down went the man floundering to the ground. There was a wild outbreak of anger, below, and the mob swarmed in from all around, and there we were treed, and prisoners. Another man started up; the bridging bough was detected, and a volunteer started up the tree that furnished the bridge. The king ordered me to play Horatius and keep the bridge. For a while the enemy came thick and fast; but no matter, the head man of each procession always got a buffet that dislodged him as soon as he came in reach. The king's spirits rose, his joy was limitless. He said that if nothing occurred to mar the prospect we should have a beautiful night, for on this line of tactics we could hold the tree against the whole countryside.

However, the mob soon came to that conclusion themselves; wherefore they called off the assault and began to debate other plans. They had no weapons, but there were plenty of stones, and stones might answer. We had no objections. A stone might possibly penetrate to us once in a while, but it wasn't very likely; we were well protected by boughs and foliage, and were not visible from any good aiming-point.

If they would but waste half an hour in stone-throwing, the dark would come to our help. We were feeling very well satisfied. We could smile; almost laugh.

But we didn't; which was just as well, for we should have been interrupted. Before the stones had been raging through the leaves and bouncing from the boughs fifteen minutes, we began to notice a smell. A couple of sniffs of it was enough of an explanation: it was smoke! Our game was up at last. We recognized that. When smoke invites you, you have to come. They raised their pile of dry brush and damp weeds higher and higher, and when they saw the thick cloud begin to roll up and smother the tree, they broke out in a storm of joy-clamors. I got enough breath to say:

"Proceed, my liege; after you is manners."

The king gasped:

"Follow me down, and then back thyself against one side of the trunk, and leave me the other. Then will we fight. Let each pile his dead according to his own fashion and taste."

Then he descended barking and coughing, and I followed. I struck the ground an instant after him; we sprang to our appointed places, and began to give and take with all our might. The pow-wow and racket were prodigious; it was a tempest of riot and confusion and thick-falling blows. Suddenly some horsemen tore into the midst of the crowd, and a voice shouted:

"Hold—or ye are dead men!"

How good it sounded! The owner of the voice bore all the marks of a gentleman: picturesque and costly raiment, the aspect of command, a hard countenance, with complexion and features marred by dissipation. The mob fell humbly back, like so many spaniels. The gentleman inspected us critically, then said sharply to the peasants:

"What are ye doing to these people?"

"They be madmen, worshipful sir, that have come wandering we know not whence, and—"

"Ye know not whence? Do ye pretend ye know them not?"

"Most honored sir, we speak but the truth. They are strangers and unknown to any in this region; and they be the most violent and bloodthirsty madmen that ever—"

"Peace! Ye know not what ye say. They are not mad. Who are ye? And whence are ye? Explain."

"We are but peaceful strangers, sir," I said, "and traveling upon our own concerns. We are from a far country, and unacquainted here. We have purposed no harm; and yet but for your brave interference and protection these people would have killed us. As you have divined, sir, we are not mad; neither are we violent or bloodthirsty."

The gentleman turned to his retinue and said calmly:

"Lash me these animals to their kennels!"

The mob vanished in an instant; and after them plunged the horsemen, laying about them with their whips and pitilessly riding down such as were witless enough to keep the road instead of taking to the bush. The shrieks and supplications presently died away in the distance, and soon the horsemen began to straggle back. Meantime the gentleman had been questioning us more closely, but had dug no particulars out of us. We were lavish of recognition of the service he was doing us, but we revealed nothing more than that we were friendless strangers from a far country. When the escort were all returned, the gentleman said to one of his servants:

"Bring the led horses and mount these people."

"Yes, my lord."

We were placed toward the rear, among the servants. We traveled pretty fast, and finally drew rein some time after dark at a roadside inn some ten or twelve miles from the scene of our troubles. My lord went immediately to his room, after ordering his supper, and we saw no more of him. At dawn in the morning we breakfasted and made ready to start.

My lord's chief attendant sauntered forward at that moment with indolent grace, and said:

"Ye have said ye should continue upon this road, which is our direction likewise; wherefore my lord, the earl Grip, hath given commandment that ye retain the horses and ride, and that certain of us ride with ye a twenty mile to a fair town that hight Cambenet, whenso ye shall be out of peril."

We could do nothing less than express our thanks and accept the offer. We jogged along, six in the party, at a moderate and comfortable gait, and in conversation learned that my lord Grip was a very great personage in his own region, which lay a day's journey beyond Cambenet. We loitered to such a degree that it was near the middle of the forenoon when we entered the market square of the town. We dismounted, and left our thanks once more for my lord, and then approached a crowd assembled in the centre of the square, to see what might be the object of interest. It was the remnant of that old peregrinating band of slaves! So they had been dragging their chains about, all this weary time. That poor husband was gone, and also many others; and some few purchases had been added to the gang. The king was not interested, and wanted to move along, but I was absorbed, and full of pity. I could not take my eyes away from these worn and wasted wrecks of humanity. There they sat, grouped upon the ground, silent, uncomplaining, with bowed heads, a pathetic sight. And by hideous contrast, a redundant orator was making a speech to another gathering not thirty steps away, in fulsome laudation of "our glorious British liberties!"

I was boiling. I had forgotten I was a plebeian, I was remembering I was a man. Cost what it might, I would mount that rostrum and—

Click! the king and I were handcuffed together! Our companions, those servants, had done it; my lord Grip stood looking on. The king burst out in a fury, and said:

"What meaneth this ill-mannered jest?"

My lord merely said to his head miscreant, coolly:

"Put up the slaves and sell them!"

Slaves! The word had a new sound—and how unspeakably awful! The king lifted his manacles and brought them down with a deadly force; but my lord was out of the way when they arrived. A dozen of the rascal's servants sprang forward, and in a moment we were helpless, with our hands bound behind us. We so loudly and so earnestly proclaimed ourselves freemen, that we got the interested attention of that liberty-mouthing orator and his patriotic crowd, and they gathered about us and assumed a very determined attitude. The orator said:

"If indeed ye are freemen, ye have nought to fear—the God-given liberties of Britain are about ye for your shield and shelter! (Applause.) Ye shall soon see. Bring forth your proofs."

"What proofs?"

"Proof that ye are freemen."

Ah—I remembered! I came to myself; I said nothing. But the king stormed out:

"Thou'rt insane, man. It were better, and more in reason, that this thief and scoundrel here prove that we are *not* freemen."

You see, he knew his own laws just as other people so often know the laws: by words, not by effects. They take a *meaning,* and get to be very vivid, when you come to apply them to yourself.

All hands shook their heads and looked disappointed; some turned away, no longer interested. The orator said—and this time in the tones of business, not of sentiment:

"An ye do not know your country's laws, it were time ye learned them. Ye are strangers to us; ye will not deny that. Ye may be freemen, we do not deny that; but also ye may be slaves. The law is clear: it doth not require the claimant to prove ye are slaves, it requireth you to prove ye are *not*."

I said:

"Dear sir, give us only time to send to Astolat; or give us only time to send to the Valley of Holiness—"

"Peace, good man, these are extraordinary requests, and you may not hope to have them granted. It would cost much time, and would unwarrantably inconvenience your master—"

"*Master*, idiot!" stormed the king. "I have no master, I myself am the m——"

"Silence, for God's sake!"

I got the words out in time to stop the king. We were in trouble enough already; it could not help us any to give these people the notion that we were lunatics.

There is no use in stringing out the details. The earl put us up and sold us at auction. This same infernal law had existed in our own South in my own time, more than thirteen hundred years later, and under it hundreds of freemen who could not prove that they were freemen had been sold into life-long slavery without the circumstance making any particular impression upon me; but the minute law and the auction block came into my personal experience, a thing which had been merely improper before became suddenly hellish. Well, that's the way we are made.

Yes, we were sold at auction, like swine. In a big town and an active market we should have brought a good price; but this place was utterly stagnant and so we sold at a figure which makes me ashamed, every time I think of it. The King of England brought seven dollars, and his prime minister nine; whereas the king was easily worth twelve dollars and I as easily worth fifteen. But that is the way things always go; if you force a sale on a dull market, I don't care what the property is, you are going to make a poor business of it, and you can make up your mind to it. If the earl had had wit enough to—

However, there is no occasion for my working my sympathies up on his account. Let him go, for the present: I took his number, so to speak.

The slave dealer bought us both, and hitched us onto that long chain of his, and we constituted the rear of his procession. We took up our line of march and passed out of Cambenet at noon; and it seemed to me unaccountably strange and odd that the King of England and his chief minister, marching manacled and fettered and yoked, in a slave convoy, could move by all manner of idle men and women, and under windows where sat the sweet and the lovely, and yet never attract a curious eye, never provoke a single remark. Dear, dear, it only shows that there is nothing diviner about a king than there is about a tramp, after all. He is just a cheap and hollow artificiality when you don't know he is a king. But reveal his quality, and dear me it takes your very breath away to look at him. I reckon we are all fools. Born so, no doubt.

CHAPTER 35

A PITIFUL INCIDENT

It's a world of surprises. The king brooded; this was natural. What would he brood about, should you say? Why, about the prodigious nature of his fall, of course—from the loftiest place in the world to the lowest; from the most illustrious station in the world to the obscurest; from the grandest vocation among men to the basest. No, I take my oath that the thing that graveled him most, to start with, was not this, but the price he had fetched! He couldn't seem to get over that seven dollars. Well, it stunned me so, when I first found it out, that I couldn't believe it; it didn't seem natural. But as soon as my mental sight cleared and I got a right focus on it, I saw I was mistaken: it *was* natural. For this reason: a king is a mere artificiality, and so a king's feelings, like the impulses of an automatic doll, are mere artificialities; but as a man, he is a reality, and his feelings, as a man, are real, not phantoms. It shames the average man to be valued below his own estimate of his worth; and the king certainly wasn't anything more than an average man, if he was up that high.

Confound him, he wearied me with arguments to show that in anything like a fair market he would have fetched twenty-five dollars, sure—a thing which was plainly nonsense, and full of the baldest conceit; I wasn't worth it myself. But it was tender ground for me to argue on. In fact I had to simply shirk argument and do the diplomatic instead. I had to throw conscience aside, and brazenly concede that he ought to have brought twenty-five dollars; whereas I was quite well aware that in all the ages, the world had never seen a king that was worth half the money, and during the next thirteen centuries wouldn't see one that was worth the fourth of it. Yes, he tired me. If he began to talk about the crops; or about the recent weather; or about the condition of politics, or about dogs, or cats, or morals, or theology—no matter what—I sighed, for I knew what was coming: he was going to get out of it a palliation of that tiresome seven-dollar sale. Wherever we halted, where there was a crowd, he would give me a look which said, plainly: "if that thing could be tried over again, now, with this kind of folk, you would see a different result." Well, when he was first sold, it secretly tickled me to see him go for seven dollars; but before he was done with his sweating and worrying I wished he had fetched a hundred. The thing never got a chance to die, for every day, at one place or another, possible purchasers looked us over, and as often as any other way, their comment on the king was something like this:

"Here's a two-dollar-and-a-half chump with a thirty-dollar style. Pity but style was marketable."

At last this sort of remark produced an evil result. Our owner was a practical person and he perceived that this defect must be mended if he hoped to find a purchaser for the king. So he went to work to take the style out of his sacred majesty. I could have given the man some valuable advice, but I didn't; you mustn't volunteer advice to a slave-driver unless you want to damage the cause you are arguing for. I had found it a sufficiently difficult job to reduce the king's style to a peasant's style, even when he was a willing and anxious pupil; now then, to undertake to reduce the king's style to a slave's style—and by force—go to! it was a stately contract. Never mind the details—it will save me trouble to let you imagine them. I will only remark that at the end of a week there was plenty of evidence that lash and club and fist had done their work well; the king's body was a sight to see—and to weep over; but his spirit?—why, it wasn't even phased. Even that dull clod of a slave-driver was able to see that there can be such a thing as a slave who will remain a man till he dies; whose bones you can break, but whose manhood you can't. This man found that from his first effort down to his latest, he couldn't ever come within reach of the king but the king was ready to plunge for him, and did it. So he gave up, at last, and left the king in possession of his style unimpaired. The fact is, the king was a good deal more than a king, he was a man; and when a man is a man, you can't knock it out of him.

We had a rough time for a month, tramping to and fro in the earth, and suffering. And what Englishman was the most interested in the slavery question by that time? His grace the king! Yes; from being the most indifferent, he was become the most interested. He was become the bitterest hater of the institution I had ever heard talk. And so I ventured to ask once more a question which I had asked years before and had gotten such a sharp answer that I had not thought it prudent to meddle in the matter further. Would he abolish slavery?

His answer was as sharp as before, but it was music this time; I shouldn't ever wish to hear pleasanter, though the profanity was not good, being awkwardly put together, and with the crash-word almost in the middle instead of at the end, where of course it ought to have been.

I was ready and willing to get free, now; I hadn't wanted to get free any sooner. No, I cannot quite say that. I had wanted to, but I had not been willing to take desperate chances, and had always dissuaded the king from them. But now—ah, it was a new atmosphere! Liberty would be worth any cost that might be put upon it now. I set about a plan, and was straightway charmed with it. It would require time, yes, and patience, too, a great deal of both. One could invent quicker ways, and fully as sure ones; but none that would be as picturesque as this; none that could be made so dramatic. And so I was not going to give this one up. It might delay us months, but no matter, I would carry it out or break something.

Now and then we had an adventure. One night we were overtaken by a snow-storm while still a mile from the village we were making for. Almost instantly we were shut up as in a fog, the driving snow was so thick. You couldn't see a thing, and we were soon lost. The slave-driver lashed us desperately, for he saw ruin before him, but his lashings only made matters worse, for they drove us further from the road and from likelihood of succor. So we had to stop, at last, and slump down in the snow where we were. The storm continued until toward midnight, then ceased. By this time two of our feebler men and three of our women were dead, and others past moving and threatened with death. Our master was nearly beside himself. He stirred up the living and made us stand, jump, slap ourselves, to restore our circulation, and he helped as well as he could with his whip.

Now came a diversion. We heard shrieks and yells, and soon a woman came running, and crying; and seeing our group, she flung herself into our midst and begged for protection. A mob of people came tearing after her, some with torches, and they said she was a witch who had caused several cows to die by a strange disease, and practiced her arts by help of a devil in the form of a black cat. This poor woman had been stoned until she hardly looked human, she was so battered and bloody. The mob wanted to burn her.

Well, now, what do you suppose our master did? When we closed around this poor creature to shelter her, he saw his chance. He said, burn her here, or they shouldn't have her at all. Imagine that! They were willing. They fastened her to a post; they brought wood and piled it about her; they applied the torch while she shrieked and pleaded and strained her two young daughters to her breast; and our brute, with a heart solely for business, lashed us into position about the stake and warmed us into life and commercial value by the same fire which took away the innocent life of that poor harmless mother. That was the sort of master we had. I took *his* number. That snow-storm cost him nine of his flock; and he was more brutal to us than ever, after that, for many days together, he was so enraged over his loss.

We had adventures, all along. One day we ran into a procession. And such a procession! All the riff-raff of the kingdom seemed to be comprehended in it; and all drunk at that. In the van was a cart with a coffin in it, and on the coffin sat a comely young girl of about eighteen suckling a baby, which she squeezed to her breast in a passion of love every little while, and every little while wiped from its face the tears which her eyes rained down upon it; and always the foolish little thing smiled up at her, happy and content, kneading her breast with its dimpled fat hand, which she patted and fondled right over her breaking heart.

Men and women, boys and girls, trotted along beside or after the cart, hooting, shouting profane and ribald remarks, singing snatches of foul song, skipping, dancing—a very holiday of hellions, a sickening sight. We had struck a suburb of London, outside the walls, and this was a sample of one sort of London society. Our master secured a good place for us near the gallows. A priest was in attendance, and he helped the girl climb up, and said comforting words to her, and made the under-sheriff provide a stool for her. Then he stood there by her on the gallows, and for a moment looked down upon the mass of upturned faces at his feet, then out over the solid pavement of heads that stretched away on every side occupying the vacancies far and near, and then began to tell the story of the case. And there was pity in his voice—how seldom a sound that was in that ignorant and savage land! I remember every detail of what he said, except the words he said it in; and so I change it into my own words:

"Law is intended to mete out justice. Sometimes it fails. This cannot be helped. We can only grieve, and be resigned, and pray for the soul of him who falls unfairly by the arm of the law, and that his fellows may be few. A law sends this poor young thing to death—and it is right. But another law had placed her where she must commit her crime or starve, with her child—and before God that law is responsible for both her crime and her ignominious death!

"A little while ago this young thing, this child of eighteen years, was as happy a wife and mother as any in England; and her lips were blithe with song, which is the native speech of glad and innocent hearts. Her young husband was as happy as she; for he was doing his whole duty, he worked early and late at his handicraft, his bread was honest bread well and fairly earned, he was prospering, he was furnishing shelter and sustenance to his family, he was adding his mite to the wealth of the nation. By consent of a treacherous law, instant destruction fell upon this holy home and swept it away! That young husband was waylaid and impressed, and sent to sea. The wife knew nothing of it. She sought him everywhere, she moved the hardest hearts with the supplications of her tears, the broken eloquence of her despair. Weeks dragged by, she watching, waiting, hoping, her mind going slowly to wreck under the burden of her misery. Little by little all her small possessions went for food. When she could no longer pay her rent, they turned her out of doors. She begged, while she had strength; when she was starving, at last, and her milk failing, she stole a piece of linen cloth of the value of a fourth part of a cent, thinking to sell it and save her child. But she was seen by the owner of the cloth. She was put in jail and brought to trial. The man testified to the facts. A plea was made for her, and her sorrowful story was told in her behalf. She spoke, too, by permission, and said she did steal the cloth, but that her mind was so disordered of late, by trouble, that when she was overborne with hunger all acts, criminal or other, swam meaningless through her brain and she knew nothing rightly, except that she was *so* hungry! For a moment all were touched, and there was disposition to deal mercifully with her, seeing that she was so young and friendless, and her case so piteous, and the law that robbed her of her support to blame as being the first and only cause of her transgression; but the prosecuting officer replied that whereas these things were all true, and most pitiful as well, still there was much small theft in these days, and mistimed mercy here would be a danger to property—Oh, my God, is there no property in ruined homes, and orphaned babes, and broken hearts that British law holds precious!—and so he must require sentence.

"When the judge put on his black cap, the owner of the stolen linen rose trembling up, his lip quivering, his face as gray as ashes; and when the awful words came, he cried out, "Oh, poor child, poor child, I did not know it was death!" and fell as a tree falls. When they lifted him up his reason was gone; before the sun was set, he had taken his own life.

A kindly man; a man whose heart was right, at bottom; add his murder to this that is to be now done here; and charge them both where they belong—to the rulers and the bitter laws of Britain. The time is come, my child; let me pray over thee—not *for* thee, dear abused poor heart and innocent, but for them that be guilty of thy ruin and death, who need it more."

After his prayer they put the noose around the young girl's neck, and they had great trouble to adjust the knot under her ear, because she was devouring the baby all the time, wildly kissing it, and snatching it to her face and her breast, and drenching it with tears, and half moaning half shrieking all the while, and the baby crowing, and laughing, and kicking its feet with delight over what it took for romp and play. Even the hangman couldn't stand it, but turned away. When all was ready the priest gently pulled and tugged and forced the child out of the mother's arms, and stepped quickly out of her reach; but she clasped her hands, and made a wild spring toward him, with a shriek; but the rope—and the under-sheriff—held her short. Then she went on her knees and stretched out her hands and cried:

"One more kiss—Oh, my God, one more, one more,—it is the dying that begs it!"

She got it; she almost smothered the little thing. And when they got it away again, she cried out:

"Oh, my child, my darling, it will die! It has no home, it has no father, no friend, no mother—"

"It has them all!" said that good priest. "All these will I be to it till I die."

You should have seen her face then! Gratitude? Lord, what do you want with words to express that? Words are only painted fire; a look is the fire itself. She gave that look, and carried it away to the treasury of heaven, where all things that are divine belong.

CHAPTER 36

AN ENCOUNTER IN THE DARK

London—to a slave—was a sufficiently interesting place. It was merely a great big village; and mainly mud and thatch. The streets were muddy, crooked, unpaved. The populace was an ever flocking and drifting swarm of rags, and splendors, of nodding plumes and shining armor. The king had a palace there; he saw the outside of it. It made him sigh; yes, and swear a little, in a poor juvenile sixth century way. We saw knights and grandees whom we knew, but they didn't know us in our rags and dirt and raw welts and bruises, and wouldn't have recognized us if we had hailed them, nor stopped to answer, either, it being unlawful to speak with slaves on a chain. Sandy passed within ten yards of me on a mule—hunting for me, I imagined. But the thing which clean broke my heart was something which happened in front of our old barrack in a square, while we were enduring the spectacle of a man being boiled to death in oil for counterfeiting pennies. It was the sight of a newsboy—and I couldn't get at him! Still, I had one comfort; here was proof that Clarence was still alive and banging away. I meant to be with him before long; the thought was full of cheer.

I had one little glimpse of another thing, one day, which gave me a great uplift. It was a wire stretching from housetop to housetop. Telegraph or telephone, sure. I did very much wish I had a little piece of it. It was just what I needed, in order to carry out my project of escape. My idea was, to get loose some night, along with the king, then gag and bind our master, change clothes with him, batter him into the aspect of a stranger, hitch him to the slave-chain, assume possession of the property, march to Camelot, and—

But you get my idea; you see what a stunning dramatic surprise I would wind up with at the palace. It was all feasible, if I could only get hold of a slender piece of iron which I could shape into a lockpick. I could then undo the lumbering padlocks with which our chains were fastened, whenever I might choose. But I never had any luck; no such thing ever happened to fall in my way. However, my chance came at last. A gentleman who had come twice before to dicker for me, without result, or indeed any approach to a result, came again. I was far from expecting ever to belong to him, for the price asked for me from the time I was first enslaved was exorbitant, and always provoked either anger or derision, yet my master stuck stubbornly to it—twenty-two dollars. He wouldn't bate a cent. The king was greatly admired, because of his grand physique, but his kingly style was against him, and he wasn't salable; nobody wanted that kind of a slave. I considered myself safe from parting from him because of my extravagant price. No, I was not expecting to ever belong to this gentleman whom I have spoken of, but he had something which I expected would belong to me eventually, if he would but visit us often enough. It was a steel thing with a long pin to it, with which his long cloth outside garment was fastened together in front. There were three of them. He had disappointed me twice, because he did not come quite close enough to me to make my project entirely safe; but this time I succeeded; I captured the lower clasp of the three, and when he missed it he thought he had lost it on the way.

I had a chance to be glad about a minute, then straightway a chance to be sad again. For when the purchase was about to fail, as usual, the master suddenly spoke up and said what would be worded thus—in modern English:

"I'll tell you what I'll do. I'm tired supporting these two for no good. Give me twenty-two dollars for this one, and I'll throw the other one in."

The king couldn't get his breath, he was in such a fury. He began to choke and gag, and meantime the master and the gentleman moved away, discussing.

"An ye will keep the offer open—"

" 'Tis open till the morrow at this hour."

"Then will I answer you at that time," said the gentleman, and disappeared, the master following him.

I had a time of it to cool the king down, but I managed it. I whispered in his ear, to this effect:

"Your grace *will* go for nothing, but after another fashion. And so shall I. To-night we shall both be free."

"Ah! How is that?"

"With this thing which I have stolen, I will unlock these locks and cast off these chains to-night. When he comes about nine-thirty to inspect us for the night, we will seize him, gag him, batter him, and early in the morning we will march out of this town, proprietors of this caravan of slaves."

That was as far as I went, but the king was charmed and satisfied. That evening we waited patiently for our fellow-slaves to get to sleep and signify it by the usual sign, for you must not take many chances on those poor fellows if you can avoid it. It is best to keep your own secrets. No doubt they fidgeted only about as usual, but it didn't seem so to me. It seemed to me that they were going to be forever getting down to their regular snoring. As the time dragged on I got nervously afraid we shouldn't have enough of it left for our needs; so I made several premature attempts, and merely delayed things by it; for I couldn't seem to touch a padlock, there in the dark, without starting a rattle out of it which interrupted somebody's sleep and made him turn over and wake some more of the gang.

But finally I did get my last iron off, and was a free man once more.

I took a good breath of relief, and reached for the king's irons. Too late! in comes the master, with a light in one hand and his heavy walking-staff in the other. I snuggled close among the wallow of snorers, to conceal as nearly as possible that I was naked of irons; and I kept a sharp lookout and prepared to spring for my man the moment he should bend over me.

But he didn't approach. He stopped, gazed absently toward our dusky mass a minute, evidently thinking about something else; then set down his light, moved musingly toward the door, and before a body could imagine what he was going to do, he was out of the door and had closed it behind him.

"Quick!" said the king. "Fetch him back!"

Of course it was the thing to do, and I was up and out in a moment. But dear me, there were no lamps in those days, and it was a dark night. But I glimpsed a dim figure a few steps away. I darted for it, threw myself upon it, and then there was a state of things and lively! We fought and scuffled and struggled, and drew a crowd in no time. They took an immense interest in the fight and encouraged us all they could, and in fact couldn't have been pleasanter or more cordial if it had been their own fight. Then a tremendous row broke out behind us, and as much as half of our audience left us, with a rush, to invest some sympathy in that. Lanterns began to swing in all directions; it was the watch, gathering from far and near. Presently a halberd fell across my back, as a reminder, and I knew what it meant. I was in custody. So was my adversary. We were marched off toward prison, one on each side of the watchman. Here was disaster, here was a fine scheme gone to sudden destruction! I tried to imagine what would happen when the master should discover that it was I who had been fighting him; and what would happen if they jailed us together in the general apartment for brawlers and petty law breakers, as was the custom; and what might—

Just then my antagonist turned his face around in my direction, the freckled light from the watchman's tin lantern fell on it, and by George he was the wrong man!

CHAPTER 37

AN AWFUL PREDICAMENT

Sleep? It was impossible. It would naturally have been impossible in that noisome cavern of a jail, with its mangy crowd of drunken, quarrelsome and song-singing rapscallions. But the thing that made sleep all the more a thing not to be dreamed of, was my racking impatience to get out of this place and find out the whole size of what might have happened yonder in the slave-quarters in consequence of that intolerable miscarriage of mine.

It was a long night but the morning got around at last. I made a full and frank explanation to the court. I said I was a slave, the property of the great Earl Grip, who had arrived just after dark at the Tabard inn in the village on the other side of the water, and had stopped there over night, by compulsion, he being taken deadly sick with a strange and sudden disorder. I had been ordered to cross to the city in all haste and bring the best physician; I was doing my best; naturally I was running with all my might; the night was dark, I ran against this common person here, who seized me by the throat and began to pummel me, although I told him my errand, and implored him, for the sake of the great earl my master's mortal peril—

The common person interrupted and said it was a lie; and going to explain how I rushed upon him and attacked him without a word—

"Silence, sirrah!" from the court. "Take him hence and give him a few stripes whereby to teach him how to treat the servant of a nobleman after a different fashion another time. Go!"

Then the court begged my pardon, and hoped I would not fail to tell his lordship it was in no wise the court's fault that this high-handed thing had happened. I said I would make it all right, and so took my leave. Took it just in time, too; he was starting to ask me why I didn't fetch out these facts the moment I was arrested. I said I would if I had thought of it—which was true—but that I was so battered by that man that all my wit was knocked out of me—and so forth and so on, and got myself away, still mumbling.

I didn't wait for breakfast. No grass grew under my feet. I was soon at the slave quarters. Empty—everybody gone! That is, everybody except one body—the slave-master's. It lay there all battered to pulp; and all about were the evidences of a terrific fight. There was a rude board coffin on a cart at the door, and workmen, assisted by the police, were thinning a road through the gaping crowd in order that they might bring it in.

I picked out a man humble enough in life to condescend to talk with one so shabby as I, and got his account of the matter.

"There were sixteen slaves here. They rose against their master in the night, and thou seest how it ended."

"Yes. How did it begin?"

"There was no witness but the slaves. They said the slave that was most valuable got free of his bonds and escaped in some strange way—by magic arts 'twas thought, by reason that he had no key, and the locks were neither broke nor in any wise injured. When the master discovered his loss, he was mad with despair, and threw himself upon his people with his heavy stick, who resisted and brake his back and in other and divers ways did give him hurts that brought him swiftly to his end."

"This is dreadful. It will go hard with the slaves, no doubt, upon the trial."

"Marry, the trial is over."

"Over!"

"Would they be a week, think you—and the matter so simple? They were not the half of a quarter of an hour at it."

"Why, I don't see how they could determine which were the guilty ones in so short a time."

"*Which* ones? Indeed they considered not particulars like to that. They condemned them in a body. Wit ye not the law?—which men say the Romans left behind them here when they went—that if one slave killeth his master all the slaves of that man must die for it."

"True. I had forgotten. And when will these die?"

"Belike within a four and twenty hours; albeit some say they will wait a pair of days more, if peradventure they may find the missing one meantime."

The missing one! It made me feel uncomfortable.

"Is it likely they will find him?"

"Before the day is spent—yes. They seek him everywhere. They stand at the gates of the town, with certain of the slaves who will discover him to them if he cometh, and none can pass out but he will be first examined."

"Might one see the place where the rest are confined?"

"The outside of it—yes. The inside of it—but ye will not want to see that."

I took the address of that prison, for future reference, and then sauntered off. At the first second-hand clothing shop I came to, up a back street, I got a rough rig suitable for a common seaman who might be going on a cold voyage, and bound up my face with a liberal bandage, saying I had a toothache. This concealed my worst bruises. It was a transformation. I no longer resembled my former self. Then I struck out for that wire, found it and followed it to its den. It was a little room over a butcher's shop—which meant that business wasn't very brisk in the telegraphic line. The young chap in charge was drowsing at his table. I locked the door and put the vast key in my bosom. This alarmed the young fellow, and he was going to make a noise; but I said:

"Save your wind; if you open your mouth you are dead, sure. Tackle your instrument. Lively, now! Call Camelot."

"This doth amaze me! How should such as you know aught of such matters as—"

"Call Camelot! I am a desperate man. Call Camelot, or get away from the instrument and I will do it myself."

"What—you?"

"Yes—certainly. Stop gabbling. Call the palace." He made the call.

"Now then, call Clarence."

"Clarence *who?*"

"Never mind Clarence who. Say you want Clarence; you'll get an answer."

He did so. We waited five nerve-straining minutes—ten minutes—how long it did seem!—and then came a click that was as familiar to me as a human voice; for Clarence had been my own pupil.

"Now, my lad, vacate! They wouldn't have known *my* touch, maybe, and so your call was surest; but I'm all right, now."

He vacated the place and cocked his ear to listen—but it didn't win. I used a cipher. I didn't waste any time in sociabilities with Clarence, but squared away for business, straight-off—thus:

"The king is here and in danger. We were captured and brought here as slaves. We should not be able to prove our identity—and the fact is, I am not in a position to try. Send a telegram for the palace here which will carry conviction with it."

His answer came straight back:

"They don't know anything about the telegraph; they haven't had any experience yet, the line to London is so new. Better not venture that. They might hang you. Think up something else."

Might hang us! Little he knew how closely he was crowding the facts. I couldn't think up anything for the moment. Then an idea struck me, and I started it along:

"Send five hundred picked knights with Launcelot in the lead; and send them on the jump. Let them enter by the southwest gate, and look out for the man with a white cloth around his right arm."

The answer was prompt:

"They shall start in half an hour."

"All right, Clarence; now tell this lad here that I'm a friend of yours and a dead-head; and that he must be discreet and say nothing about this visit of mine."

The instrument began to talk to the youth and I hurried away. I fell to ciphering. In half an hour it would be nine o'clock. Knights and horses in heavy armor couldn't travel very fast. These would make the best time they could, and now that the ground was in good condition, and no snow or mud, they would probably make a seven-mile gait; they would have to change horses a couple of times; they would arrive about six, or a little after; it would still be plenty light enough; they would see the white cloth which I should tie around my right arm, and I would take command. We would surround that prison and have the king out in no time. It would be showy and picturesque enough, all things considered, though I would have preferred noonday, on account of the more theatrical aspect the thing would have.

Now then, in order to increase the strings to my bow, I thought I would look up some of those people whom I had formerly recognized, and make myself known. That would help us out of our scrape, without the knights. But I must proceed cautiously, for it was a risky business. I must get into sumptuous raiment, and it wouldn't do to run and jump into it. No, I must work up to it by degrees, buying suit after suit of clothes, in shops wide apart, and getting a little finer article with each change, until I should finally reach silk and velvet, and be ready for my project. So I started.

But the scheme fell through like scat! The first corner I turned, I came plump upon one of our slaves, snooping around with a watchman. I coughed, at the moment, and he gave me a sudden look that bit right into my marrow. I judge he thought he had heard that cough before. I turned immediately into a shop and worked along down the counter, pricing things and watching out of the corner of my eye. Those people had stopped, and were talking together and looking in at the door. I made up my mind to get out the back way, if there was a back way, and I asked the shopwoman if I could step out there and look for the escaped slave, who was believed to be in hiding back there somewhere, and said I was an officer in disguise, and my pard was yonder at the door with one of the murderers in charge, and would she be good enough to step there and tell him he needn't wait, but had better go at once to the further end of the back alley and be ready to head him off when I rousted him out.

She was blazing with eagerness to see one of those already celebrated murderers, and she started on the errand at once. I slipped out the back way, locked the door behind me, put the key in my pocket and started off, chuckling to myself and comfortable.

Well, I had gone and spoiled it again, made another mistake. A double one, in fact. There were plenty of ways to get rid of that officer by some simple and plausible device, but no, I must pick out a picturesque one; it is the crying defect of my character. And then, I had ordered my procedure upon what the officer, being human, would *naturally* do; whereas when you are least expecting it, a man will now and then go and do the very thing which it's *not* natural for him to do. The natural thing for the officer to do, in this case, was to follow straight on my heels; he would find a stout oaken door, securely locked, between him and me; before he could break it down, I should be far away and engaged in slipping into a succession of baffling disguises which would soon get me into a sort of raiment which was a surer protection from meddling law-dogs in Britain than any amount of mere innocence and purity of character. But instead of doing the natural thing, the officer took me at my word, and followed my instructions. And so, as I came trotting out of that cul de sac, full of satisfaction with my own cleverness, he turned the corner and I walked right into his handcuffs. If I had known it was a cul de sac—however, there isn't any excusing a blunder like that, let it go. Charge it up to profit and loss.

Of course I was indignant, and swore I had just come ashore from a long voyage, and all that sort of thing—just to see, you know, if it would deceive that slave. But it didn't. He knew me. Then I reproached him for betraying me. He was more surprised than hurt. He stretched his eyes wide, and said:

"What, wouldst have me let thee, of all men, escape and not hang with us, when thou'rt the very *cause* of our hanging? Go to!"

"Go to" was their way of saying "I should smile!" or "I like that!" Queer talkers, those people.

Well, there was a sort of bastard justice in his view of the case, and so I dropped the matter. When you can't cure a disaster by argument, what is the use to argue? It isn't my way. So I only said:

"You're not going to be hanged. None of us are."

Both men laughed, and the slave said:

"Ye have not ranked as a fool—before. You might better keep your reputation, seeing the strain would not be for long."

"It will stand it, I reckon. Before to-morrow we shall be out of prison, and free to go where we will, besides."

The witty officer lifted at his left ear with his thumb, made a rasping noise in his throat, and said:

"Out of prison—yes—ye say true. And free likewise to go where ye will, so ye wander not out of his grace the Devil's sultry realm."

I kept my temper, and said, indifferently:

"Now I suppose you really think we are going to hang within a day or two."

"I thought it not many minutes ago, for so the thing was decided and proclaimed."

"Ah, then you've changed your mind, is that it?"

"Even that. I only *thought*, then; I *know*, now."

I felt sarcastical, so I said:

"Oh, sapient servant of the law, condescend to tell us, then, what you *know*."

"That ye will all be hanged *to-day*, at mid-afternoon! Oho! That shot hit home! Lean upon me."

The fact is I did need to lean upon somebody. My knights couldn't arrive in time. They would be as much as three hours too late. Nothing in the world could save the King of England; nor me, which was more important. More important, not merely to me, but to the nation—the only nation on earth standing ready to blossom into civilization. I was sick. I said no more, there wasn't anything to say. I knew what the man meant; that if the missing slave was found, the postponement would be revoked, the execution take place to-day. Well, the missing slave was found.

CHAPTER 38

SIR LAUNCELOT AND KNIGHTS TO THE RESCUE

Nearing four in the afternoon. The scene was just outside the walls of London. A cool, comfortable, superb day, with a brilliant sun; the kind of day to make one want to live, not die. The multitude was prodigious and far reaching; and yet we fifteen poor devils hadn't a friend in it. There was something painful in that thought, look at it how you might. There we sat, on our tall scaffold, the butt of the hate and mockery of all those enemies. We were being made a holiday spectacle. They had built a sort of grand stand for the nobility and gentry, and these were there in full force, with their ladies. We recognized a good many of them.

The crowd got a brief and unexpected dash of diversion out of the king. The moment we were freed of our bonds he sprang up, in his fantastic rags, with face bruised out of all recognition, and proclaimed himself Arthur, King of Britain, and denounced the awful penalties of treason upon every soul there present if hair of his sacred head were touched. It startled and surprised him to hear them break into a vast roar of laughter. It wounded his dignity, and he locked himself up in silence, then, although the crowd begged him to go on, and tried to provoke him to it by cat-calls, jeers, and shouts of

"Let him speak! The king! The king! his humble subjects hunger and thirst for words of wisdom out of the mouth of their master his Serene and Sacred Raggedness!"

But it went for nothing. He put on all his majesty and sat under this rain of contempt and insult unmoved. He certainly was great in his way. Absently, I had taken off my white bandage and wound it about my right arm. When the crowd noticed this, they began upon me. They said:

"Doubtless this sailor-man is his minister—observe his costly badge of office!"

I let them go on until they got tired, and then I said:

"Yes, I am his minister, The Boss; and to-morrow you will hear that from Camelot which—"

I got no further. They drowned me out with joyous derision. But presently there was silence; for the sheriffs of London, in their official robes, with their subordinates, began to make a stir which indicated that business was about to begin. In the hush which followed, our crime was recited, the death warrant read, then everybody uncovered while a priest uttered a prayer.

Then a slave was blindfolded, the hangman unslung his rope. There lay the smooth road below us, we upon one side of it, the banked multitude walling its other side—a good clear road, and kept free by the police—how good it would be to see my five hundred horsemen come tearing down it! But, no, it was out of the possibilities. I followed its receding thread out into the distance—not a horseman on it, or sign of one.

There was a jerk, and the slave hung dangling; dangling and hideously squirming, for his limbs were not tied.

A second rope was unslung, in a moment another slave was dangling.

In a minute a third slave was struggling in the air. It was dreadful. I turned away my head a moment, and when I turned back I missed the king! They were blindfolding him! I was paralyzed; I couldn't move, I was choking, my tongue was petrified. They finished blindfolding him, they led him under the rope. I couldn't shake off that clinging impotence. But when I saw them put the noose around his neck, then everything let go in me and I made a spring to the rescue —and as I made it I shot one more glance abroad—by George, here they came, a-tilting!—five hundred mailed and belted knights on bicycles!

The grandest sight that ever was seen. Lord, how the plumes streamed, how the sun flamed and flashed from the endless procession of webby wheels!

I waved my right arm as Launcelot swept in—he recognized my rag—I tore away noose and bandage, and shouted:

"On your knees, every rascal of you, and salute the king! Who fails shall sup in hell to-night!"

I always use that high style when I'm climaxing an effect. Well, it was noble to see Launcelot and the boys swarm up onto that scaffold and heave sheriffs and such overboard. And it was fine to see that astonished multitude go down on their knees and beg their lives of the king they had just been deriding and insulting. And as he stood apart, there, receiving this homage in his rags, I thought to myself, well really there *is* something peculiarly grand about the gait and bearing of a king, after all.

I was immensely satisfied. Take the whole situation all around, it was one of the gaudiest effects I ever instigated.

And presently up comes Clarence, his own self! and winks, and says, very modernly:

"Good deal of a surprise, wasn't it? I knew you'd like it. I've had the boys practicing, this long time, privately; and just hungry for a chance to show off."

CHAPTER 39

THE YANKEE'S FIGHT WITH THE KNIGHTS

Home again, at Camelot. A morning or two later I found the paper, damp from the press, by my plate at the breakfast table. I turned to the advertising columns, knowing I should find something of personal interest to me there. It was this:

DE PAR LE ROI.

ʞnow that the great lord and illustrious kni8ht. SIR SAGRAMOUR LE DESIʞOUS having condescended to meet the King's Minister, Hank Morgan, the which is surnamed The Boss, for satisfgction of offencesanciently given, these wilL engage in the lists by Camelot about the fourth hour of the morning of the sixteenth dav of this next succeeding month. The battle will be à l'outrance, sith the said offence was of a deadly sort, admitting of no composition.

DE PAR LE ROI.

Clarence's editorial reference to this affair was to this effect:

ɩhdrew.
wo.ik maintained
there since, soon
listic have witq
oked interest
upon the ea[redacted]
ve been m[redacted]d
oy the ar[redacted]s,
ent out ch[redacted]y by
yterian *B*[redacted], and
c some y[redacted]ng men
of our unde- the
i guidance ot tha
for aid in a known
he great enterprise
of making pure;
esent
movement haa its
origin .a preven-
has ever been a
sions in our
on of Wis-
other one
ospel,
by-
e
The
.ha same
co represent
ized thirty of
needs and hear-
which, years ago!
.oresgn was osgan-
ing, the missions,
sso that both had
to withdraw' and
much to their
grief,

It will be observed, by a gl7nce at our advertising columns. that the community is to be favored with a treat of unusual interest in the tournament line. The names of the artists are warrant of good enterrainment. The box-office will be open at noon of the 13th; admission 3 cents, reserve*d* seats 5; proceeds to go to the hosoital fund The royal pair and all the Court will be present. With these exceptions, and the press and the clergy, the free list is strictly sus'ended. Parties are hereby warned against buying tickets of speculators; thev will not be good at the door. Everybody knows and likes The Boss, everybodv knows ana likes Sir Sag.; come, let us give the lads a good send-off. ReMember, the proceeds go to a great and free chariry, and one whose broad begevolence sttetcnes out its helping hand, warm witn the blood of a loving heart, to all that suger, regardless of race, creed, condition or color—the only charity yet established in the earth which has no politico-religious stopcock on its compassion, but says Here flows the stream let *all* come and drink! Turn out, all hands! fetcn along your dou3hnuts and your gum-drops and have a good time. Pie for sale on the grounds, and rocks to crack it with; also ciRcus-lemonade—three drops of lime juice to a barrel of water.

N. B. *This is the first tournament under the new law, whidh allows each combatant to use any weapon he may prefer.* You want to make a note of that.

our disappointm
prompuly and n·t
two of their felo
erlain, and othe
ers have alread
spoken, yor
furnisned for
their use, i
make and
the kind
letters
oj introc
duction whi
they are un
ing friends to us
ried, and leave the
tho kind words enc
which you, m, joy-
hind; and it is a
home matter of b
it is our durp
direct them tc
now under the
g field*s* as arc
*T*hese youn8 men
are warm-heartec
azurl. regions bel
not to "build
ond,', and the
der instructi
ons of our
another man
founhati's on.
ociety, whlch
They go un-
say tqat "inr
ionaries to mon
say sending miss

Up to the day set, there was no talk in all Britain of anything but this combat. All other topics sank into insignificance and passed out of men's thoughts and interest. It was not because a tournament was a great matter; it was not because Sir Sagramour had found the Holy Grail, for he had not, but had failed; it was not because the second (official) personage in the kingdom was one of the duellists; no, all these features were commonplace. Yet there was abundant reason for the extraordinary interest which this coming fight was creating. It was born of the fact that all the nation knew that this was not to be a duel between mere men, so to speak, but a duel between two mighty magicians; a duel not of muscle but of mind, not of human skill but of superhuman art and craft; a final struggle for supremacy between the two master enchanters of the age. It was realized that the most prodigious achievements of the most renowned knights could not be worthy of comparison with a spectacle like this; they could be but child's play, contrasted with this mysterious and awful battle of the gods. Yes, all the world knew it was going to be in reality a duel between Merlin and me, a measuring of his magic powers against mine. It was known that Merlin had been busy whole days and nights together, imbuing Sir Sagramour's arms and armor with supernal powers of offence and defence, and that he had procured for him from the spirits of the air a fleecy veil which would render the wearer invisible to his antagonist while still visible to other men. Against Sir Sagramour, so weaponed and protected, a thousand knights could accomplish nothing; against him no known enchantments could prevail. These facts were sure; regarding them there was no doubt, no reason for doubt. There was but one question: might there be still other enchantments, *unknown* to Merlin, which could render Sir Sagramour's veil transparent to me, and make his enchanted mail vulnerable to my weapons? This was the one thing to be decided in the lists. Until then the world must remain in suspense.

So the world thought there was a vast matter at stake here, and the world was right, but it was not the one they had in their minds. No, a far vaster one was upon the cast of this die: *the life of knight-errantry.* I was a champion, it was true, but not the champion of the frivolous black arts, I was the champion of hard unsentimental common-sense and reason. I was entering the lists to either destroy knight-errantry or be its victim.

Vast as the show-grounds were, there were no vacant spaces in them outside of the lists, at ten o'clock on the morning of the 16th. The mammoth grand stand was clothed in flags, streamers, and rich tapestries, and packed with several acres of small-fry tributary kings, their suites, and the British aristocracy; with our own royal gang in the chief place, and each and every individual a flashing prism of gaudy silks and velvets—well, I never saw anything to begin with it but a fight between an Upper Mississippi sunset and the aurora borealis. The huge camp of beflagged and gay-colored tents at one end of the lists, with a stiff-standing sentinel at every door and a shining shield hanging by him for challenge, was another fine sight. You see, every knight was there who had any ambition or any caste feeling; for my feeling toward their order was not much of a secret, and so here was their chance. If I won my fight with Sir Sagramour, others would have the right to call me out as long as I might be willing to respond.

Down at our end there were but two tents; one for me, and another for my servants. At the appointed hour the king made a sign, and the heralds, in their tabards, appeared and made proclamation, naming the combatants and stating the cause of quarrel. There was a pause, then a ringing bugle blast, which was the signal for us to come forth. All the multitude caught their breath, and an eager curiosity flashed into every face.

Out from his tent rode great Sir Sagramour, an imposing tower of iron, stately and rigid, his huge spear standing upright in its socket and grasped in his strong hand, his grand horse's face and breast cased in steel, his body clothed in rich trappings that almost dragged the ground—oh, a most noble picture. A great shout went up, of welcome and admiration.

And then out I came. But I didn't get any shout. There was a wondering and eloquent silence, for a moment, then a great wave of laughter began to sweep along that human sea, but a warning bugle-blast cut its career short. I was in the simplest and comfortablest of gymnast costumes—flesh-colored tights from neck to heel, with blue silk puffings about my loins, and bare-headed. My horse was not above medium size, but he was alert, slender-limbed, muscled with watch-springs, and just a greyhound to go. He was a beauty, glossy as silk, and naked as he was when he was born, except for bridle and ranger-saddle.

The iron tower and the gorgeous bed-quilt came cumbrously but gracefully pirouetting down the lists, and we tripped lightly up to meet them. We halted; the tower saluted, I responded; then we wheeled and rode side by side to the grand stand and faced our king and queen, to whom we made obeisance. The queen exclaimed:

"Alack, Sir Boss, wilt fight naked, and without lance or sword or—"

But the king checked her and made her understand, with a polite phrase or two, that this was none of her business. The bugles rang again; and we separated and rode to the ends of the lists, and took position. Now old Merlin stepped into view and cast a dainty web of gossamer threads over Sir Sagramour which turned him into Hamlet's ghost; the king made a sign, the bugles blew, Sir Sagramour laid his great lance in rest, and the next moment here he came thundering down the course with his veil flying out behind, and I went whistling through the air like an arrow to meet him—cocking my ear, the while, as if noting the invisible knight's position and progress by hearing, not sight. A chorus of encouraging shouts burst out for him, and one brave voice flung out a heartening word for me—said:

"Go it, slim Jim!"

It was an even bet that Clarence had procured that favor for me—and furnished the language, too. When that formidable lance-point was within a yard and a half of my breast I twitched my horse aside without an effort and the big knight swept by, scoring a blank. I got plenty of applause that time. We turned, braced up, and down we came again. Another blank for the knight, a roar of applause for me. This same thing was repeated once more; and it fetched such a whirlwind of applause that Sir Sagramour lost his temper, and at once changed his tactics and set himself the task of chasing me down. Why, he hadn't any show in the world at that; it was a game of tag, with all the advantage on my side; I whirled out of his path with ease whenever I chose, and once I slapped him on the back as I went to the rear. Finally I took the chase into my own hands; and after that, turn, or twist, or do what he would, he was never able to get behind me again; he found himself always in front, at the end of his maneuvre. So he gave up that business and retired to his end of the lists. His temper was clear gone, now, and he forgot himself and flung an insult at me which disposed of mine. I slipped my lasso from the horn of my saddle, and grasped the coil in my right hand. This time you should have seen him come!—it was a business trip, sure; by his gait there was blood in his eye. I was sitting my horse at ease, and swinging the great loop of my lasso in wide circles about my head; the moment he was under way, I started for him; when the space between us had narrowed to forty feet, I sent the snaky spirals of the rope a-cleaving through the air, then darted aside and faced about and brought my trained animal to a halt with all his feet braced under him for a surge. The next moment the rope sprang taut and yanked Sir Sagramour out of the saddle! Great Scott, but there was a sensation!

Unquestionably the popular thing in this world is novelty. These people had never seen anything of that cow-boy business before, and it carried them clear off their feet with delight. From all around and everywhere, the shout went up—

"Encore! encore!"

I wondered where they got the word, but there was no time to cipher on philological matters, because the whole knight-errantry hive was just humming, now, and my prospect for trade couldn't have been better. The moment my lasso was released and Sir Sagramour had been assisted to his tent, I hauled in the slack, took my station and began to swing my loop around my head again. I was sure to have use for it as soon as they could elect a successor for Sir Sagramour, and that couldn't take long where there were so many hungry candidates. Indeed, they elected one straight off—Sir Hervis de Revel.

Bzz! Here he came, like a house afire; I dodged; he passed like a flash, with my horse-hair coils settling around his neck; a second or so later, *fst!* his saddle was empty.

I got another encore; and another, and another, and still another. When I had snaked five men out, things began to look serious to the iron-clads, and they stopped and consulted together. As a result, they decided that it was time to waive etiquette and send their greatest and best against me. To the astonishment of that little world, I lassoed Sir Lamorak de Galis, and after him Sir Galahad. So you see there was simply nothing to be done, now, but play their right bower—bring out the superbest of the superb, the mightiest of the mighty, the great Sir Launcelot himself!

A proud moment for me? I should think so. Yonder was Arthur, King of Britain; yonder was Guenever; yes, and whole tribes of little provincial kings and kinglets; and in the tented camp yonder, renowned knights from many lands; and likewise the selectest body known to chivalry, the Knights of the Table Round, the most illustrious in Christendom; and biggest fact of all, the very sun of their shining system was yonder couching his lance, the focal point of forty thousand adoring eyes; and all by myself, here was I laying for him. Across my mind flitted the dear image of a certain hello-girl of West Hartford, and I wished she could see me now. In that moment, down came the Invincible, with the rush of a whirlwind—the courtly world rose to its feet and bent forward—the fateful coils went circling through the air, and before you could wink I was towing Sir Launcelot across the field on his back, and kissing my hand to the storm of waving kerchiefs and the thunder-crash of applause that greeted me!

Said I to myself, as I coiled my lariat and hung it on my saddle-horn, and sat there drunk with glory, "The victory is perfect—no other will venture against me—knight-errantry is dead." Now imagine my astonishment—and everybody else's too—to hear the peculiar bugle-call which announces that another competitor is about to enter the lists! There was a mystery here; I couldn't account for this thing. Next, I noticed Merlin gliding away from me; and then I noticed that my lasso was gone! The old sleight-of-hand expert had stolen it, sure, and slipped it under his robe.

The bugle blew again. I looked, and down came Sagramour riding again, with his dust brushed off and his veil nicely re-arranged. I trotted up to meet him, and pretended to find him by the sound of his horse's hoofs. He said:

"Thou'rt quick of ear, but it will not save thee from this!" and he touched the hilt of his great sword. "An ye are not able to see it, because of the influence of the veil, know that it is no cumbrous lance, but a sword—and I ween ye will not be able to avoid it."

His visor was up; there was death in his smile. I should never be able to dodge his sword, that was plain. Somebody was going to die, this time. If he got the drop on me, I could name the corpse. We rode forward together, and saluted the royalties. This time the king was disturbed. He said:

"Where is thy strange weapon?"

"It is stolen, sire."

"Hast another at hand?"

"No, sire, I brought only the one."

Then Merlin mixed in:

"He brought but the one because there was but the one to bring. There exists none other but that one. It belongeth to the king of the Demons of the Sea. This man is a pretender, and ignorant; else he had known that that weapon can be used in but eight bouts only, and then it vanisheth away to its home under the sea."

"Then is he weaponless," said the king. "Sir Sagramour, ye will grant him leave to borrow."

"And I will lend!" said Sir Launcelot, limping up. "He is as brave a knight of his hands as any that be on live, and he shall have mine."

He put his hand on his sword to draw it, but Sir Sagramour said:

"Stay, it may not be. He shall fight with his own weapons; it was his privilege to choose them and bring them. If he has erred, on his head be it."

"Knight!" said the king. "Thou'rt overwrought with passion; it disorders thy mind. Wouldst kill a naked man?"

"An he do it, he shall answer it to me," said Sir Launcelot.

"I will answer it to any he that desireth!" retorted Sir Sagramour hotly.

Merlin broke in, rubbing his hands and smiling his lowdownest smile of malicious gratification:

"'Tis well said, right well said! And 'tis enough of parleying, let my lord the king deliver the battle signal."

The king had to yield. The bugle made proclamation, and we turned apart and rode to our stations. There we stood, a hundred yards apart, facing each other, rigid and motionless, like horsed statues. And so we remained, in a soundless hush, as much as a full minute, everybody gazing, nobody stirring. It seemed as if the king could not take heart to give the signal. But at last he lifted his hand, the clear note of the bugle followed, Sir Sagramour's long blade described a flashing curve in the air, and it was superb to see him come. I sat still. On he came. I did not move. People got so excited that they shouted to me:

"Fly, fly! Save thyself! This is murther!"

I never budged so much as an inch, till that thundering apparition had got within fifteen paces of me; then I snatched a dragoon revolver out of my holster, there was a flash and a roar, and the revolver was back in the holster before anybody could tell what had happened.

Here was a riderless horse plunging by, and yonder lay Sir Sagramour, stone dead.

The people that ran to him were stricken dumb to find that the life was actually gone out of the man and no reason for it visible, no hurt upon his body, nothing like a wound. There was a hole through the breast of his chain-mail, but they attached no importance to a little thing like that; and as a bullet-wound there produces but little blood, none came in sight because of the clothing and swaddlings under the armor. The body was dragged over to let the king and the swells look down upon it. They were stupefied with astonishment, naturally. I was requested to come and explain the miracle. But I remained in my tracks, like a statue, and said:

"If it is a command, I will come, but my lord the king knows that I am where the laws of combat require me to remain while any desire to come against me."

I waited. Nobody challenged. Then I said:

"If there are any who doubt that this field is well and fairly won, I do not wait for them to challenge me, I challenge them."

"It is a gallant offer," said the king, "and well beseems you. Whom will you name, first?"

"I name none, I challenge all! Here I stand, and dare the chivalry of England to come against me—not by individuals, but in mass!"

"What!" shouted a score of knights.

"You have heard the challenge. Take it, or I proclaim you recreant knights and vanquished, every one!"

It was a "bluff" you know. At such a time it is sound judgment to put on a bold face and play your hand for a hundred times what it is worth; forty-nine times out of fifty nobody dares to "call," and you rake in the chips. But just this once—well, things looked squally! In just no time, five hundred knights were scrambling into their saddles, and before you could wink a widely scattering drove were under way and clattering down upon me. I snatched both revolvers from the holsters and began to measure distances and calculate chances.

Bang! One saddle empty. Bang! another one. Bang—bang! and I bagged two. Well it was nip and tuck with us, and I knew it. If I spent the eleventh shot without convincing these people, the twelfth man would kill me, sure. And so I never did feel so happy as I did when my ninth downed its man and I detected the wavering in the crowd which is premonitory of panic. An instant lost now, could knock out my last chance. But I didn't lose it. I raised both revolvers and pointed them—the halted host stood their ground just about one good square moment, then broke and fled.

The day was mine. Knight-errantry was a doomed institution. The march of civilization was begun. How did I feel? Ah you never could imagine it.

And Brer Merlin? His stock was flat again. Somehow, every time the magic of fol-de-rol tried conclusions with the magic of science, the magic of fol-de-rol got left.

CHAPTER 40

THREE YEARS LATER

When I broke the back of knight-errantry that time, I no longer felt obliged to work in secret. So, the very next day I exposed my hidden schools, my mines, and my vast system of clandestine factories and work-shops to an astonished world. That is to say, I exposed the nineteenth century to the inspection of the sixth.

Well it is always a good plan to follow up an advantage promptly. The knights were temporarily down, but if I would keep them so I must just simply paralyze them—nothing short of that would answer. You see, I was "bluffing" that last time, in the field; it would be natural for them to work around to that conclusion, if I gave them a chance. So I must not give them time: and I didn't.

I renewed my challenge, engraved it on brass, posted it up where any priest could read it to them, and also kept it standing, in the advertising columns of the paper.

I not only renewed it, but added to its proportions. I said, name the day, and I would take fifty assistants and stand up *against the massed chivalry of the whole earth and destroy it.*

I was not bluffing this time. I meant what I said; I could do what I promised. There wasn't any way to misunderstand the language of that challenge. Even the dullest of the chivalry perceived that this was a plain case of "put up, or shut up." They were wise and did the latter. In all the next three years they gave me no trouble worth mentioning.

Consider the three years sped. Now look around on England. A happy and prosperous country, and strangely altered. Schools everywhere, and several colleges; a number of pretty good newspapers. Even authorship was taking a start; Sir Dinadan the Humorist was first in the field, with a volume of gray-headed jokes which I had been familiar with during thirteen centuries. If he had left out that old rancid one about the lecturer I wouldn't have said anything; but I couldn't stand that one. I suppressed the book and hanged the author.

Slavery was dead and gone; all men were equal before the law; taxation had been equalized. The telegraph, the telephone, the phonograph, the type-writer, the sewing machine, and all the thousand willing and handy servants of steam and electricity were working their way into favor. We had a steamboat or two on the Thames, we had steam war-ships, and the beginnings of a steam commercial marine; I was getting ready to send out an expedition to discover America.

We were building several lines of railway, and our line from Camelot to London was already finished and in operation. I was shrewd enough to make all offices connected with the passenger service places of high and distinguished honor. My idea was to attract the chivalry and nobility, and make them useful and keep them out of mischief. The plan worked very well, the competition for the places was hot. The conductor of the 4.33 express was a duke, there wasn't a passenger conductor on the line below the degree of earl. They were good men, every one, but they had two defects which I couldn't cure, and so had to wink at: they wouldn't lay aside their armor, and they would "knock down" fares—I mean rob the company.

There was hardly a knight in all the land who wasn't in some useful employment. They were going from end to end of the country in all manner of useful missionary capacities; their penchant for wandering, and their experience in it, made them altogether the most effective spreaders of civilization we had. They went clothed in steel and equipped with sword and lance and battle axe, and if they couldn't persuade a person to try a sewing machine on the instalment plan, or a melodeon, or a barbed wire fence, or a prohibition journal, or any of the other thousand and one things they canvassed for, they removed him and passed on.

I was very happy. Things were working steadily toward a secretly longed-for point. You see, I had two schemes in my head which were the vastest of all my projects. The one was, to overthrow the Catholic Church and set up the Protestant faith on its ruins—not as an Established Church, but a go-as-you-please one; and the other project was, to get a decree issued by and by, commanding that upon Arthur's death unlimited suffrage should be introduced, and given to men and women alike—at any rate to all men, wise or unwise, and to all mothers who at middle age should be found to know nearly as much as their sons at twenty-one. Arthur was good for thirty years yet, he being about my own age—that is to say, forty—and I believed that in that time I could easily have the active part of the population of that day ready and eager for an event which should be the first of its kind in the history of the world—a rounded and complete governmental revolution without bloodshed. The result to be a republic. Well, I may as well confess, though I do feel ashamed when I think of it: I was beginning to have a base hankering to be its first president myself. Yes, there was more or less human nature in me; I found that out.

Clarence was with me as concerned the revolution, but in a modified way. His idea was a republic, without privileged orders but with a hereditary royal family at the head of it instead of an elective chief magistrate. He believed that no nation that had ever known the joy of worshiping a royal family could ever be robbed of it and not fade away and die of melancholy. I urged that kings were dangerous. He said, then have cats. He was sure that a royal family of cats would answer every purpose. They would be as useful as any other royal family, they would know as much, they would have the same virtues and the same treacheries, the same disposition to get up shindies with other royal cats, they would be laughably vain and absurd and never know it, they would be wholly inexpensive; finally, they would have as sound a divine right as any other royal house, and "Tom VII, or Tom XI, or Tom XIV by the grace of God King," would sound as well as it would when applied to the ordinary royal tomcat with tights on. "And as a rule," said he, in his neat modern English, "the character of these cats would be considerably above the character of the average king, and this would be an immense moral advantage to the nation, for the reason that a nation always models its morals after its monarch's. The worship of royalty being founded in unreason, these graceful and harmless cats would easily become as sacred as any other royalties, and indeed more so, because it would presently be noticed that they hanged nobody, beheaded nobody, imprisoned nobody, inflicted no cruelties or injustices of any sort, and so must be worthy of a deeper love and reverence than the customary human king, and would certainly get it. The eyes of the whole harried world would soon be fixed upon this humane and gentle system, and royal butchers would presently begin to disappear; their subjects would fill the vacancies with catlings from our own royal house; we should become a factory; we should supply the thrones of the world; within forty years all Europe would be governed by cats, and we should furnish the cats. The reign of universal peace would begin then, to end no more forever. . . . . . *Me-e-e-yow-ow-ow-ow—fzt!—wow!*"

Hang him, I supposed he was in earnest, and was beginning to be persuaded by him, until he exploded that cat-howl and startled me almost out of my clothes. But he never could be in earnest. He didn't know what it was. He had pictured a distinct and perfectly rational and feasible improvement upon constitutional monarchy, but he was too feather-headed to know it, or care anything about it, either. I was going to give him a scolding, but Sandy came flying in at that moment, wild with terror, and so choked with sobs that for a minute she could not get her voice. I ran and took her in my arms, and lavished caresses upon her and said, beseechingly:

"Speak, darling, speak! What is it?"

Her head fell limp upon my bosom, and she gasped, almost inaudibly:

"HELLO, CENTRAL!"

"Quick!" I shouted to Clarence; "telephone the king's homeopath to come!"

In two minutes I was kneeling by the child's crib, and Sandy was dispatching servants here, there and everywhere, all over the palace. I took in the situation almost at a glance—membraneous croup! I bent down and whispered:

"Wake up, sweetheart! Hello-Central!"

2 She opened her soft eyes languidly, and made out to say—

"Papa."

That was a comfort. She was far from dead, yet. I sent for preparations of sulphur, I rousted out the croup-kettle myself; for I don't sit down and wait for doctors when Sandy or the child is sick. I knew how to nurse both of them, and had had experience. This little chap had lived in my arms a good part of its small life, and often I could soothe away its troubles and get it to laugh through the tear-dews on its eye-lashes when even its mother couldn't.

Sir Launcelot, in his richest armor, came striding along the great hall, now, on his way to the stock-board; he was president of the stock-board, and occupied the Siege Perilous, which he had bought of Sir Galahad; for the stock-board consisted of the Knights of the Round Table, and they used the Round Table for business purposes, now. Seats at it were worth—well, you would never believe the figure, so it is no use to state it. Sir Launcelot was a bear, and he had put up a corner in one of the new lines, and was just getting ready to squeeze the shorts to-day; but what of that? He was the same old Launcelot, and when he glanced in as he was passing the door and found out that his pet was sick, that was enough for him; bulls and bears might fight it out their own way for all him, he would come right in here and stand by little Hello-Central for all he was worth. And that was what he did. He shied his helmet into the corner, and in half a minute he had a new wick in the alcohol lamp and was firing up on the croup-kettle. By this time Sandy had built a blanket canopy over the crib, and everything was ready.

Sir Launcelot got up steam, he and I loaded up the kettle with unslaked lime and carbolic acid, with a touch of lactic acid added thereto, then filled the thing up with water and inserted the steam-spout under the canopy. Everything was ship-shape, now, and we sat down on either side of the crib to stand our watch. Sandy was so grateful and so comforted that she charged a couple of church-wardens with willow-bark and sumach-tobacco for us, and told us to smoke as much as we pleased, it couldn't get under the canopy, and she was used to smoke, being the first lady in the land who had ever seen a cloud blown. Well, there couldn't be a more contented or comfortable sight than Sir Launcelot in his noble armor sitting in gracious serenity at the end of a yard of snowy church-warden. He was a beautiful man, a lovely man, and was just intended to make a wife and children happy. But of course, Guenever—however, it's no use to cry over what's done and can't be helped.

Well, he stood watch-and-watch with me, right straight through, for three days and nights, till the child was out of danger; then he took her up in his great arms and kissed her, with his plumes falling about her golden head, then laid her softly in Sandy's lap again and took his stately way down the vast hall, between the ranks of admiring men-at-arms and menials, and so disappeared. And no instinct warned me that I should never look upon him again in this world! Lord, what a world of heart-break it is.

The doctors said we must take the child away, if we would coax her back to health and strength again. And she must have sea air. So we took a man-of-war, and a suite of two hundred and sixty persons, and went cruising about, and after a fortnight of this we stepped ashore on the French coast, and the doctors thought it would be a good idea to make something of a stay there. The little king of that region offered us his hospitalities, and we were glad to accept. If he had had as many conveniences as he lacked, we should have been plenty comfortable enough; even as it was, we made out very well, in his queer old castle, by the help of comforts and luxuries from the ship.

At the end of a month I sent the vessel home for fresh supplies, and for news. We expected her back in three or four days. She would bring me, along with other news, the result of a certain experiment which I had been starting. It was a project of mine to replace the tournament with something which might furnish an escape for the extra steam of the chivalry, keep those bucks entertained and out of mischief, and at the same time preserve the best thing in them, which was their hardy spirit of emulation. I had had a choice band of them in private training for some time, and the date was now arriving for their first public effort.

This experiment was base-ball. In order to give the thing vogue from the start, and place it out of the reach of criticism, I chose my nines by rank, not capacity. There wasn't a knight in either team who wasn't a sceptred sovereign. As for material of this sort, there was a glut of it, always, around Arthur. You couldn't throw a brick in any direction and not cripple a king. Of course I couldn't get these people to leave off their armor; they wouldn't do that when they bathed. They consented to differentiate the armor so that a body could tell one team from the other, but that was the most they would do. So, one of the teams wore chain-mail ulsters, and the other wore plate-armor made of my new Bessemer steel. Their practice in the field was the most fantastic thing I ever saw. Being ball-proof, they never skipped out of the way, but stood still and took the result; when a Bessemer was at the bat and a ball hit him, it would bound a hundred and fifty yards, sometimes. And when a man was running, and threw himself on his stomach to slide to his base, it was like an iron-clad coming into port. At first I appointed men of no rank to act as umpires, but I had to discontinue that. These people were no easier to please than other nines. The umpire's first decision was usually his last; they broke him in two with a bat, and his friends toted him home on a shutter. When it was noticed that no umpire ever survived a game, umpiring got to be unpopular. So I was obliged to appoint somebody whose rank and lofty position under the government would protect him.

Here are the names of the nines:

BESSEMERS.	ULSTERS.
King Arthur.	Emperor Lucius.
King Lot of Lothian.	King Logris.
King of Northgalis.	King Marhalt of Ireland.
King Marsil.	King Morganore.
King of Little Britain.	King Mark of Cornwall.
King Labor.	King Nentres of Garlot.
King Pellam of Listengese.	King Meliodas of Liones.
King Bagdemagus.	King of the Lake.
King Tolleme la Feintes.	The Sowdan of Syria.

Umpire—Clarence.

The first public game would certainly draw fifty thousand people; and for solid fun would be worth going around the world to see. Everything would be favorable; it was balmy and beautiful spring weather, now, and Nature was all tailored out in her new clothes.

CHAPTER 41

THE INTERDICT

However, my attention was suddenly snatched from such matters; our child began to lose ground again, and we had to go to sitting up with her, her case became so serious. We couldn't bear to allow anybody to help, in this service, so we two stood watch-and-watch, day in and day out. Ah, Sandy, what a right heart she had, how simple, and genuine, and good she was! She was a flawless wife and mother; and yet I had married her for no particular reason, except that by the customs of chivalry she was my property until some knight should win her from me in the field. She had hunted Britain over for me; had found me at the hanging-bout outside of London, and had straightway resumed her old place at my side in the placidest way and as of right. I was a New Englander, and in my opinion this sort of partnership would compromise her, sooner or later. She couldn't see how, but I cut argument short and we had a wedding.

Now I didn't know I was drawing a prize, yet that was what I did draw. Within the twelvemonth I became her worshiper; and ours was the dearest and perfectest comradeship that ever was. People talk about beautiful friendships between two persons of the same sex. What is the best of that sort, as compared with the friendship of man and wife, where the best impulses and highest ideals of both are the same? There is no place for comparison between the two friendships; the one is earthly, the other divine.

In my dreams, along at first, I still wandered thirteen centuries away, and my unsatisfied spirit went calling and harking all up and down the unreplying vacancies of a vanished world. Many a time Sandy heard that imploring cry come from my lips in my sleep. With a grand magnanimity she saddled that cry of mine upon our child, conceiving it to be the name of some lost darling of mine. It touched me to tears, and it also nearly knocked me off my feet, too, when she smiled up in my face for an earned reward, and played her quaint and pretty surprise upon me:

"The name of one who was dear to thee is here preserved, here made holy, and the music of it will abide alway in our ears. Now thou'lt kiss me, as knowing the name I have given the child."

But I didn't know it, all the same. I hadn't an idea in the world; but it would have been cruel to confess it and spoil her pretty game; so I never let on, but said:

"Yes, I know, sweetheart—how dear and good it is of you, too! But I want to hear these lips of yours, which are also mine, utter it first—then its music will be perfect."

Pleased to the marrow, she murmured—

"HELLO-CENTRAL!"

I didn't laugh—I am always thankful for that—but the strain ruptured every cartilage in me, and for weeks afterward I could hear my bones clack when I walked. She never found out her mistake. The first time she heard that form of salute used at the telephone she was surprised, and not pleased; but I told her I had given order for it: that henceforth and forever the telephone must always be invoked with that reverent formality, in perpetual honor and remembrance of my lost friend and her small namesake. This was not true. But it answered.

Well, during two weeks and a half we watched by the crib, and in our deep solicitude we were unconscious of any world outside of that sick-room. Then our reward came: the centre of the universe turned the corner and began to mend. Grateful? It isn't the term. There *isn't* any term for it. You know that, yourself, if you've watched your child through the Valley of the Shadow and seen it come back to life and sweep night out of the earth with one all-illuminating smile that you could cover with your hand.

Why, we were back in this world in one instant! Then we looked the same startled thought into each other's eyes at the same moment: more than two weeks gone, and that ship not back yet!

In another minute I appeared in the presence of my train. They had been steeped in troubled bodings all this time—their faces showed it. I called an escort and we galloped five miles to a hill-top overlooking the sea. Where was my great commerce that so lately had made these glistering expanses populous and beautiful with its white-winged flocks? Vanished, every one! Not a sail, from verge to verge, not a smoke-bank—just a dead and empty solitude, in place of all that brisk and breezy life.

I went swiftly back, saying not a word to anybody. I told Sandy this ghastly news. We could imagine no explanation that would begin to explain. Had there been an invasion? an earthquake? a pestilence? Had the nation been swept out of existence? But guessing was profitless. I must go—at once. I borrowed the king's navy—a "ship" no bigger than a steam launch—and was soon ready.

The parting—ah, yes, that was hard. As I was devouring the child with last kisses, it brisked up and jabbered out its vocabulary!—the first time in more than two weeks, and it made fools of us for joy. The darling mispronunciations of childhood!—dear me, there's no music that can touch it; and how one grieves when it wastes away and dissolves into correctness, knowing it will never visit his bereaved ear again. Well, how good it was to be able to carry that gracious memory away with me!

I approached England the next morning, with the wide highway of salt water all to myself. There were ships in the harbor, at Dover, but they were naked as to sails, and there was no sign of life about them. It was Sunday; yet at Canterbury the streets were empty; strangest of all, there was not even a priest in sight, and no stroke of a bell fell upon my ear. The mournfulness of death was everywhere. I couldn't understand it. At last, in the further edge of that town I saw a small funeral procession—just a family and a few friends following a coffin—no priest; a funeral without bell, book or candle; there was a church there, close at hand, but they passed it by, weeping, and did not enter it; I glanced up at the belfry, and there hung the bell, shrouded in black, and its tongue tied back. Now I knew! Now I understood the stupendous calamity that had overtaken England. Invasion? Invasion is a triviality to it. It was the INTERDICT!

I asked no questions; I didn't need to ask any. The Church had struck; the thing for me to do was to get into a disguise, and go warily. One of my servants gave me a suit of his clothes, and when we were safe beyond the town I put them on, and from that time I traveled alone; I could not risk the embarrassment of company.

A miserable journey. A desolate silence everywhere. Even in London itself. Traffic had ceased; men did not talk or laugh, or go in groups, or even in couples; they moved aimlessly about, each man by himself, with his head down, and woe and terror at his heart. The Tower showed recent war-scars. Verily, much had been happening.

Of course I meant to take the train for Camelot. Train! Why, the station was as vacant as a cavern. I moved on. The journey to Camelot was a repetition of what I had already seen. The Monday and the Tuesday differed in no way from the Sunday. I arrived, far in the night. From being the best electric-lighted town in the kingdom and the most like a recumbent sun of anything you ever saw, it was become simply a blot—a blot upon darkness—that is to say, it was darker and solider than the rest of the darkness, and so you could see it a little better; it made me feel as if maybe it was symbolical—a sort of sign that the Church was going to *keep* the upper hand, now, and snuff out all my beautiful civilization just like that. I found no life stirring in the sombre streets. I groped my way with a heavy heart. The vast castle loomed black upon the hill-top, not a spark visible about it. The drawbridge was down, the great gate stood wide, I entered without challenge, my own heels making the only sound I heard—and it was sepulchral enough, in those huge vacant courts.

CHAPTER 42

WAR!

I found Clarence, alone in his quarters, drowned in melancholy; and in place of the electric light, he had re-instituted the ancient rag-lamp, and sat there in a grisly twilight with all curtains drawn tight. He sprang up and rushed for me eagerly, saying:

"Oh, it's worth a billion milrays to look upon a live person again!"

He knew me as easily as if I hadn't been disguised at all. Which frightened me; one may easily believe that.

"Quick, now, tell me the meaning of this fearful disaster," I said. "How did it come about?"

"Well, if there hadn't been any queen Guenever, it wouldn't have come so early; but it would have come, anyway. It would have come on your own account, by and by; by luck, it happened to come on the queen's."

"*And* Sir Launcelot's?"

"Just so."

"Give me the details."

"I reckon you will grant that during some years there has been only one pair of eyes in these kingdoms that has not been looking steadily askance at the queen and Sir Launcelot—"

"Yes, King Arthur's."

—"and only one heart that was without suspicion—"

"Yes—the king's; a heart that isn't capable of thinking evil of a friend."

"Well, the king might have gone on, still happy and unsuspecting, to the end of his days, but for one of your modern improvements—the stock-board. When you left, three miles of the London, Canterbury and Dover were ready for the rails, and also ready and ripe for manipulation in the stock market. It was wildcat, and everybody knew it. The stock was for sale at a give-away. What does Sir Launcelot do, but—"

"Yes, I know; he quietly picked up nearly all of it, for a song; then he bought about twice as much more, deliverable upon call; and he was about to call when I left."

"Very well, he did call. The boys couldn't deliver. Oh, he had them —and he just settled his grip and squeezed them. They were laughing in their sleeves over their smartness in selling stock to him at 15 and

16 and along there, that wasn't worth 10. Well, when they had laughed long enough on that side of their mouths, they rested-up that side by shifting the laugh to the other side. That was when they compromised with the Invincible at 283!"

"Good land!"

"He skinned them alive, and they deserved it—anyway, the whole kingdom rejoiced. Well, among the flayed were Sir Agravaine and Sir Mordred, nephews to the king. End of the first act. Act second, scene first, an apartment in Carlisle castle, where the court had gone for a few days' hunting. Persons present, the whole tribe of the king's nephews. Mordred and Agravaine propose to call the guileless Arthur's attention to Guenever and Sir Launcelot. Sir Gawaine, Sir Gareth, and Sir Gaheris will have nothing to do with it. A dispute ensues, with loud talk; in the midst of it, enter the king. Mordred and Agravaine spring their devastating tale upon him. *Tableau.* A trap is laid for Launcelot, by the king's command, and Sir Launcelot walks into it. He made it sufficiently uncomfortable for the ambushed witnesses—to-wit, Mordred, Agravaine, and twelve knights of lesser rank, for he killed every one of them but Mordred; but of course that couldn't straighten matters between Launcelot and the king, and didn't."

"Oh, dear, only one thing could result—I see that. War, and the knights of the realm divided into a king's party and a Sir Launcelot's party."

"Yes—that was the way of it. The king sent the queen to the stake, proposing to purify her with fire. Launcelot and his knights rescued her, and in doing it slew certain good old friends of yours and mine—in fact, some of the best we ever had; to-wit, Sir Belias le Orgulous, Sir Segwarides, Sir Griflet le Fils de Dieu, Sir Brandiles, Sir Aglovale—"

"Oh, you tear out my heartstrings."

"—wait, I'm not done yet—Sir Tor, Sir Gauter, Sir Gillimer—"

"The very best man in my subordinate nine. What a handy right-fielder he was!"

—"Sir Reynold's three brothers, Sir Damus, Sir Priamus, Sir Kay the Stranger—"

"My peerless short-stop! I've seen him catch a daisy-cutter in his teeth. Come, I can't stand this!"

—"Sir Driant, Sir Lambegus, Sir Herminde, Sir Pertilope, Sir Perimones, and—whom do you think?"

"Rush! Go on."

"Sir Gaheris, and Sir Gareth—both!"

"Oh, incredible! Their love for Launcelot was indestructible."

"Well, it was an accident. They were simply on-lookers; they were unarmed, and were merely there to witness the queen's punishment. Sir Launcelot smote down whoever came in the way of his blind fury, and he killed these without noticing who they were. Here is an instantaneous photograph one of our boys got of the battle; it's for sale on every news stand. There—the figures nearest the queen are Sir Launcelot with his sword up, and Sir Gareth gasping his latest breath. You can catch the agony in the queen's face through the curling smoke. It's a rattling battle-picture."

"Indeed it is. We must take good care of it; its historical value is incalculable. Go on."

"Well, the rest of the tale is just war, pure and simple. Launcelot retreated to his town and castle of Joyous Gard, and gathered there a great following of knights. The king, with a great host, went there, and there was desperate fighting during several days, and as a result, all the plain around was paved with corpses and cast iron. Then the Church patched up a peace between Arthur and Launcelot and the queen and everybody—everybody but Sir Gawaine. He was bitter about the slaying of his brothers, Gareth and Gaheris, and would not be appeased. He notified Launcelot to get him thence, and make swift preparation, and look to be soon attacked. So Launcelot sailed to his Duchy of Guienne, with his following, and Gawaine soon followed, with an army, and he beguiled Arthur to go with him. Arthur left the kingdom in Sir Mordred's hands until you should return—"

"Ah—a king's customary wisdom!"

"Yes. Sir Mordred set himself at once to work to make his kingship permanent. He was going to marry Guenever, as a first move; but she fled and shut herself up in the Tower of London. Mordred attacked; the Bishop of Canterbury dropped down on him with the Interdict. The king returned; Mordred fought him at Dover, at Canterbury, and again at Barham Down. Then there was talk of peace and a composition. Terms, Mordred to have Cornwall and Kent during Arthur's life, and the whole kingdom afterward."

"Well, upon my word! My dream of a republic to *be* a dream, and so remain."

"Yes. The two armies lay near Salisbury. Gawaine—Gawaine's head is at Dover Castle, he fell in the fight there—Gawaine appeared to Arthur in a dream, at least his ghost did, and warned him to refrain from conflict for a month, let the delay cost what it might. But battle was precipitated by an accident. Arthur had given order that if a sword was raised during the consultation over the proposed treaty with Mordred, sound the trumpet and fall on! for he had no confidence in Mordred. Mordred had given a similar order to *his* people. Well, by and by an adder bit a knight's heel; the knight forgot all about the order, and made a slash at the adder with his sword. Inside of half a minute those two prodigious hosts came together with a crash! They butchered away all day. Then the king—however, we have started something fresh since you left—our paper has."

"No? What is that?"

"War correspondence!"

"Why, that's good."

"Yes, the paper was booming right along, for the Interdict made no impression, got no grip, while the war lasted. I had war correspondents with both armies. I will finish that battle by reading you what one of the boys says:

Then the king looked about him, and then was he ware of all his host and of all his good knights were left no more on live but two knights, that was Sir Lucan de Butlere, and his brother Sir Bedivere: and they were full sore wounded. Jesu mercy, said the king, where are all my noble knights becomen? Alas that ever I should see this doleful day. For now, said Arthur, I am come to mine end. But would to God that I wist where were that traitor Sir Mordred, that hath caused all this mischief. Then was King Arthur ware where Sir Mordred leaned upon his sword among a great heap of dead men. Now give me my spear, said Arthur unto Sir Lucan, for yonder I have espied the traitor that all this woe hath wrought. Sir, let him be, said Sir Lucan, for he is unhappy; and if ye pass this unhappy day, ye shall be right well revenged upon him. Good lord, remember ye of your night's dream, and what the spirit of Sir Gawaine told you this night, yet God of his great goodness hath preserved you hitherto. Therefore, for God's sake, my lord, leave off by this. For blessed be God ye have won the field: for here we be three on live, and with Sir Mordred is none on live. And if ye leave off now, this wicked day of destiny is past. Tide me death, betide me life, saith the king, now I see him yonder alone, he shall never escape mine hands, for at a better avail shall I never have him. God speed you well, said Sir Bedivere. Then the king gat his spear in both his hands, and ran toward Sir Mordred, crying, Traitor, now is thy death day come. And when Sir Mordred heard Sir Arthur, he ran until him with his sword drawn in his hand. And then King Arthur smote Sir Mordred under the shield, with a foin of his spear throughout the body more than a fathom. And when Sir Mordred felt that he had his death's wound, he thrust himself, with the might that he had, up to the but of King Arthur's spear. And right so he smote his father Arthur with his sword holden in both his hands, on the side of the head, that the sword pierced the helmet and the brain-pan, and therewithal Sir Mordred fell stark dead to the earth. And the noble Arthur fell in a swoon to the earth, and there he swooned oft-times."

"That is a good piece of war correspondence, Clarence; you are a first-rate newspaper man. Well—is the king all right? Did he get well?"

"Poor soul, no. He is dead."

I was utterly stunned; it had not seemed to me that any wound could be mortal to him.

"And the queen, Clarence?"

"She is a nun, in Almesbury."

"What changes! and in such a short while. It is inconceivable. What next, I wonder?"

"I can tell you what next."

"Well?"

"Stake our lives and stand by them!"

"What do you mean by that?"

"The Church is master, now. The Interdict included you with Mordred; it is not to be removed while you remain alive. The clans are gathering. The Church has gathered all the knights that are left alive, and as soon as you are discovered we shall have business on our hands."

"Stuff! With our deadly scientific war-material; with our hosts of trained—"

"Save your breath—we haven't sixty faithful left!"

"What are you saying? Our schools, our colleges, our vast workshops, our—"

"When those knights come, those establishments will empty themselves and go over to the enemy. Did you think you had educated the superstition out of those people?"

"I certainly did think it."

"Well, then, you may unthink it. They stood every strain easily—until the Interdict. Since then, they merely put on a bold outside—at heart they are quaking. Make up your mind to it—when the armies come, the mask will fall."

"It's hard news. We are lost. They will turn our own science against us."

"No they won't."

"Why?"

"Because I and a handful of the faithful have blocked that game. I'll tell you what I've done, and what moved me to it. Smart as you are, the Church was smarter. It was the Church that sent you cruising—through her servants the doctors."

"Clarence!"

"It is the truth. I know it. Every officer of your ship was the Church's picked servant, and so was every man of the crew."

"Oh, come!"

"It is just as I tell you. I did not find out these things at once, but I found them out finally. Did you send me verbal information, by the commander of the ship, to the effect that upon his return to you, with supplies, you were going to leave Cadiz—"

"Cadiz! I haven't been at Cadiz at all!"

—"going to leave Cadiz and cruise in distant seas indefinitely, for the health of your family? Did you send me that word?"

"Of course not. I would have written, wouldn't I?"

"Naturally. I was troubled and suspicious. When the commander sailed again I managed to ship a spy with him. I have never heard of vessel or spy since. I gave myself two weeks to hear from you in. Then I resolved to send a ship to Cadiz. There was a reason why I didn't."

"What was that?"

"Our navy had suddenly and mysteriously disappeared! Also as suddenly and as mysteriously, the railway and telegraph and telephone service ceased, the men all deserted, poles were cut down, the Church laid a ban upon the electric light! I had to be up and doing—and straight off. Your life was safe—nobody in these kingdoms but Merlin would venture to touch such a magician as you without ten thousand men at his back—I had nothing to think of but how to put preparations in the best trim against your coming. I felt safe myself—nobody would be anxious to touch a pet of yours. So this is what I did. From our various works I selected all the men—boys I mean—whose faithfulness under whatsoever pressure I could swear to, and I called them together secretly and gave them their instructions. There are fifty-two of them; none younger than fourteen, and none above seventeen years old."

"Why did you select boys?"

"Because all the others were born in an atmosphere of superstition and reared in it. It is in their blood and bones. We imagined we had educated it out of them; they thought so, too; the Interdict woke them up like a thunderclap! It revealed them to themselves, and it revealed them to me, too. With boys it was different. Such as have been under our training from seven to ten years have had no acquaintance with the Church's terrors, and it was among these that I found my fifty-two. As a next move, I paid a private visit to that old cave of Merlin's—not the small one—the big one—"

"Yes, the one where we secretly established our first great electric plant when I was projecting a miracle."

"Just so. And as that miracle hadn't become necessary then, I thought it might be a good idea to utilize the plant now. I've provisioned the cave for a siege—"

"A good idea, a first rate idea."

"I think so. I placed four of my boys there, as a guard—inside, and out of sight. Nobody was to be hurt—while outside; but any attempt to enter—well, we said just let anybody try it! Then I went out into the hills and uncovered and cut the secret wires which connected your bedroom with the wires that go to the dynamite deposits under all our vast factories, mills, workshops, magazines, etc., and about midnight I and my boys turned out and connected that wire with the cave, and nobody but you and I suspects where the other end of it goes to. We laid it under ground, of course, and it was all finished in a couple of hours or so. We shan't have to leave our fortress, now, when we want to blow up our civilization."

"It was the right move—and the natural one; a military necessity, in the changed condition of things. Well, what changes *have* come! We expected to be besieged in the palace some time or other, but—however, go on."

"Next, we built a wire fence."

"Wire fence?"

"Yes. You dropped the hint of it yourself, two or three years ago."

"Oh, I remember—the time the Church tried her strength against us the first time, and presently thought it wise to wait for a hopefuler season. Well, how have you arranged the fence?"

"I start twelve immensely strong wires—naked, not insulated—from a big dynamo in the cave—dynamo with no brushes except a positive and a negative one—"

"Yes, that's right."

"The wires go out from the cave and fence-in a circle of level ground a hundred yards in diameter; they make twelve independent fences, ten feet apart—that is to say, twelve circles within circles—and their ends come into the cave again."

"Right; go on."

"The fences are fastened to heavy oaken posts only three feet apart, and these posts are sunk five feet in the ground."

"That is good and strong."

"Yes. The wires have no ground-connection outside of the cave. They go out from the positive brush of the dynamo; there is a ground-connection through the negative brush; the other ends of the wire return to the cave, and each is grounded independently."

"No-no, that won't do!"

"Why?"

"It's too expensive—uses up force for nothing. You don't want any ground-connection except the one through the negative brush. The other end of every wire must be brought back into the cave and fastened independently, and *without* any ground-connection. Now, then, observe the economy of it. A cavalry charge hurls itself against the fence; you are using no power, you are spending no money, for there is only one ground-connection till those horses come against the wire; the moment they touch it they form a connection with the negative brush *through the ground,* and drop dead. Don't you see?—you are using no energy until it is needed; your lightning is there, and ready, like the load in a gun; but it isn't costing you a cent till you touch it off. Oh, yes, the single ground-connection—"

"Of course! I don't know how I overlooked that. It's not only cheaper, but it's more effectual than the other way, for if wires break or get tangled, no harm is done."

"No, especially if we have a tell-tale in the cave and disconnect the broken wire. Well, go on. The gatlings?"

"Yes—that's arranged. In the centre of the inner circle, on a spacious platform six feet high, I've grouped a battery of thirteen gatling guns, and provided plenty of ammunition."

"That's it. They command every approach, and when the Church's knights arrive, there's going to be music. The brow of the precipice over the cave—"

"I've got a wire fence there, and a gatling. They won't drop any rocks down on us."

"Well, and the glass-cylinder dynamite torpedoes?"

"That's attended to. It's the prettiest garden that was ever planted. It's a belt forty feet wide, and goes around the outer fence—distance between it and the fence one hundred yards—kind of neutral ground, that space is. There isn't a single square yard of that whole belt but is equipped with a torpedo. We laid them on the surface of the ground, and sprinkled a layer of sand over them. It's an innocent looking garden, but you let a man start in to hoe it once, and you'll see."

"You tested the torpedoes?"

"Well, I was going to, but—"

"But what? Why, it's an immense oversight not to apply a—"

"Test? Yes, I know; but they're all right; I laid a few in the public road beyond our lines and they've been tested."

"Oh, that alters the case. Who did it?"

"A Church committee."

"How kind!"

"Yes. They came to command us to make submission. You see they didn't really come to test the torpedoes; that was merely an incident."

"Did the committee make a report?"

"Yes, they made one. You could have heard it a mile."

"Unanimous?"

"That was the nature of it. After that I put up some signs, for the protection of future committees, and we have had no intruders since."

"Clarence, you've done a world of work, and done it perfectly."

"We had plenty of time for it; there wasn't any occasion for hurry."

We sat silent awhile, thinking. Then my mind was made up, and I said:

"Yes, everything is ready; everything is shipshape, no detail is wanting. I know what to do, now."

"So do I: sit down and wait."

"No, *sir!* rise up and *strike!*"

"Do you mean it?"

"Yes, indeed! The *de*fensive isn't in my line, and the *of*fensive is. That is, when I hold a fair hand—two-thirds as good a hand as the enemy. Oh, yes, we'll rise up and strike; that's our game."

"A hundred to one, you are right. When does the performance begin?"

"*Now!* We'll proclaim the Republic."

"Well, that *will* precipitate things, sure enough!"

"It will make them buzz, *I* tell you! England will be a hornet's nest before noon to-morrow, if the Church's hand hasn't lost its cunning—and we know it hasn't. Now you write and I'll dictate—thus:

PROCLAMATION

BE IT KNOWN UNTO ALL. Whereas the king having died and left no heir, it becomes my duty to continue the executive authority vested in me, until a government shall have been created and set in motion. The monarchy has lapsed, it no longer exists. By consequence, all political power has reverted to its original source, the people of the nation. With the monarchy, its several adjuncts died also; wherefore there is no longer a nobility, no longer a privileged class, no longer an Established Church: all men are become exactly equal, they are upon one common level, and religion is free. *A Republic is hereby proclaimed,* as being the natural estate of a nation when other authority has ceased. It is the duty of the British people to meet together immediately, and by their votes elect representatives and deliver into their hands the government.

I signed it "The Boss," and dated it from Merlin's Cave. Clarence said:

"Why, that tells where we are, and invites them to call right away."

"That is the idea. We *strike*—by the Proclamation—then it's their innings. Now have the thing set up and printed and posted, right off; that is, give the order; then, if you've got a couple of bicycles handy at the foot of the hill, ho for Merlin's Cave!"

"I shall be ready in ten minutes. What a cyclone there is going to be to-morrow when this piece of paper gets to work! . . . . . It's a pleasant old palace, this is; I wonder if we shall ever again—but never mind about that."

CHAPTER 43

THE BATTLE OF THE SAND-BELT

In Merlin's Cave—Clarence and I and fifty-two fresh, bright, well educated, clean-minded young British boys. At dawn I sent an order to the factories and to all our great works to stop operations and remove all life to a safe distance, as everything was going to be blown up by secret mines, "*and no telling at what moment—therefore, vacate at once.*" These people knew me, and had confidence in my word. They would clear out without waiting to part their hair, and I could take my own time about dating the explosion. You couldn't hire one of them to go back during the century, if the explosion was still impending.

We had a week of waiting. It was not dull for me, because I was writing all the time. During the first three days, I finished turning my old diary into this narrative form; it only required a chapter or so to bring it down to date. The rest of the week I took up in writing letters to my wife. It was always my habit to write to Sandy every day, whenever we were separate, and now I kept up the habit for love of it, and of her, though I couldn't do anything with the letters, of course, after I had written them. But it put in the time, you see, and was almost like talking; it was almost as if I was saying, "Sandy, if you and Hello-Central were here in the cave, instead of only your photographs, what good times we could have!" And then, you know, I could imagine the baby goo-gooing something out in reply, with its fists in its mouth and itself stretched across its mother's lap on its back, and she a-laughing and admiring and worshiping, and now and then tickling under the baby's chin to set it cackling, and then maybe throwing in a word of answer to me herself—and so on and so on—well, don't you know, I could sit there in the cave with my pen, and keep it up, that way, by the hour with them. Why, it was almost like having us all together again.

I had spies out, every night, of course, to get news. Every report made things look more and more impressive. The hosts were gathering, gathering; down all the roads and paths of England the knights were riding, and priests rode with them, to hearten these original Crusaders, this being the Church's war. All the nobilities, big and little, were on their way, and all the gentry. This was all as was expected. We should thin out this sort of folk to such a degree that the people would have nothing to do but just step to the front with their republic and——

Ah, what a donkey I was! Toward the end of the week I began to get this large and disenchanting fact through my head: that the mass of the nation had swung their caps and shouted for the republic for about one day, and there an end! The Church, the nobles, and the gentry then turned one grand, all-disapproving frown upon them and shriveled them into sheep! From that moment the sheep had begun to gather to the fold—that is to say, the camps—and offer their valueless lives and their valuable wool to the "righteous cause." Why, even the very men who had lately been slaves were in the "righteous cause," and glorifying it, praying for it, sentimentally slabbering over it, just like all the other commoners. Imagine such human muck as this; conceive of this folly!

Yes, it was now "Death to the Republic!" everywhere—not a dissenting voice. All England was marching against us! Truly this was more than I had bargained for.

I watched my fifty-two boys narrowly; watched their faces, their walk, their unconscious attitudes: for all these are a language—a language given us purposely that it may betray us in times of emergency, when we have secrets which we want to keep. I knew that that thought would keep saying itself over and over again in their minds and hearts, *All England is marching against us!* and evermore strenuously imploring attention with each repetition, ever more sharply realizing itself to their imaginations, until even in their sleep they would find no rest from it, but hear the vague and flitting creatures of their dreams say, *All England*—ALL ENGLAND!—*is marching against you!* I knew all this would happen; I knew that ultimately the pressure would become so great that it would compel utterance; therefore, I must be ready with an answer at that time—an answer well chosen and tranquilizing.

I was right. The time came. They *had* to speak. Poor lads, it was pitiful to see, they were so pale, so worn, so troubled. At first their spokesman could hardly find voice or words; but he presently got both. This is what he said—and he put it in the neat modern English taught him in my schools:

"We have tried to forget what we are—English boys! We have tried to put reason before sentiment, duty before love; our minds approve, but our hearts reproach us. While apparently it was only the nobility, only the gentry, only the twenty-five or thirty thousand knights left alive out of the late wars, we were of one mind, and undisturbed by any troubling doubt; each and every one of these fifty-two lads who stand here before you, said, 'They have chosen—it is their affair.' But think!—the matter is altered—*all England is marching against us!* Oh, sir, consider!—reflect!—these people are our people, they are bone of our bone, flesh of our flesh, we love them—do not ask us to destroy our nation!"

Well, it shows the value of looking ahead, and being ready for a thing when it happens. If I hadn't foreseen this thing and been fixed, that boy would have had me!—I couldn't have said a word. But I *was* fixed. I said:

"My boys, your hearts are in the right place, you have thought the worthy thought, you have done the worthy thing. You are English boys, you will remain English boys, and you will keep that name unsmirched. Give yourselves no further concern, let your minds be at peace. Consider this: while all England *is* marching against us, who is in the van? Who, by the commonest rules of war, will march in the front? Answer me."

"The mounted host of mailed knights."

"True. They are 30,000 strong. Acres deep, they will march. Now, observe: none but *they* will ever strike the sand-belt! Then there will be an episode! Immediately after, the civilian multitude in the rear will retire, to meet business engagements elsewhere. None but nobles and gentry are knights, and *none but these* will remain to dance to our music after that episode. It is absolutely true that we shall have to fight nobody but these thirty thousand knights. Now speak, and it shall be as you decide. Shall we avoid the battle, retire from the field."

"NO ! ! !"

The shout was unanimous and hearty.

"Are you—are you—well, afraid of these thirty thousand knights?"

That joke brought out a good laugh, the boys' troubles vanished away, and they went gaily to their posts. Ah, they were a darling fifty-two! As pretty as girls, too.

I was ready for the enemy, now. Let the approaching big day come along—it would find us on deck.

The big day arrived on time. At dawn the sentry on watch in the corral came into the cave and reported a moving black mass under the horizon, and a faint sound which he thought to be military music. Breakfast was just ready; we sat down and ate it.

This over, I made the boys a little speech, and then sent out a detail to man the battery, with Clarence in command of it.

The sun rose presently and sent its unobstructed splendors over the land, and we saw a prodigious host moving slowly toward us, with the steady drift and aligned front of a wave of the sea. Nearer and nearer it came, and more and more sublimely imposing became its aspect; yes, all England was there, apparently. Soon we could see the innumerable banners fluttering, and then the sun struck the sea of armor and set it all aflash. Yes, it was a fine sight; I hadn't ever seen anything to beat it.

At last we could make out details. All the front ranks, no telling how many acres deep, were horsemen—plumed knights in armor. Suddenly we heard the blare of trumpets; the slow walk burst into a gallop, and then—well, it was wonderful to see! Down swept that vast horse-shoe wave—it approached the sand-belt—my breath stood still; nearer, nearer—the strip of green turf beyond the yellow belt grew narrow—narrower still—became a mere ribbon in front of the horses—then disappeared under their hoofs. Great Scott! Why, the whole front of that host shot into the sky with a thunder-crash, and became a whirling tempest of rags and fragments; and along the ground lay a thick wall of smoke that hid what was left of the multitude from our sight.

Time for the second step in the plan of campaign! I touched a button, and shook the bones of England loose from her spine!

In that explosion all our noble civilization-factories went up in the air and disappeared from the earth. It was a pity, but it was necessary. We could not afford to let the enemy turn our own weapons against us.

Now ensued one of the dullest quarter-hours I had ever endured. We waited in a silent solitude enclosed by our circles of wire, and by a circle of heavy smoke outside of these. We couldn't see over the wall of smoke, and we couldn't see through it. But at last it began to shred away lazily, and by the end of another quarter-hour the land was clear and our curiosity was enabled to satisfy itself. No living creature was in sight! We now perceived that additions had been made to our defences. The dynamite had dug a ditch more than a hundred feet wide, all around us, and cast up an embankment some twenty-five feet high on both borders of it. As to destruction of life, it was amazing. Moreover, it was beyond estimate. Of course we could not *count* the dead, because they did not exist as individuals, but merely as homogeneous protoplasm, with alloys of iron and buttons.

No life was in sight, but necessarily there must have been some wounded in the rear ranks, who were carried off the field under cover of the wall of smoke; there would be sickness among the others—there always is, after an episode like that. But there would be no reinforcements; this was the last stand of the chivalry of England; it was all that was left of the order, after the recent annihilating wars. So I felt quite safe in believing that the utmost force that could for the future be brought against us would be but small; that is, of knights. I therefore issued a congratulatory proclamation to my army in these words:

SOLDIERS, CHAMPIONS OF HUMAN LIBERTY AND EQUALITY: Your General congratulates you! In the pride of his strength and the vanity of his renown, an arrogant enemy came against you. You were ready. The conflict was brief; on your side, glorious. This mighty victory having been achieved utterly without loss, stands without example in history. So long as the planets shall continue to move in their orbits, the BATTLE OF THE SAND-BELT will not perish out of the memories of men.

THE BOSS

I read it well, and the applause I got was very gratifying to me. I then wound up with these remarks:

"The war with the English nation, as a nation, is at an end. The nation has retired from the field and the war. Before it can be persuaded to return, war will have ceased. This campaign is the only one that is going to be fought. It will be brief—the briefest in history. Also the most destructive to life, considered from the standpoint of proportion of casualties to numbers engaged. We are done with the nation; henceforth we deal only with the knights. English knights can be killed, but they cannot be conquered. We know what is before us. While one of these men remains alive, our task is not finished, the war is not ended. We will kill them all." [Loud and long continued applause.]

I picketed the great embankments thrown up around our lines by the dynamite explosion—merely a lookout of a couple of boys to announce the enemy when he should appear again.

Next, I sent an engineer and forty men to a point just beyond our lines on the south, to turn a mountain brook that was there, and bring it within our lines and under our command, arranging it in such a way that I could make instant use of it in an emergency. The forty men were divided into two shifts of twenty each, and were to relieve each other every two hours. In ten hours the work was accomplished.

It was nightfall, now, and I withdrew my pickets. The one who had had the northern outlook reported a camp in sight, but visible with the glass only. He also reported that a few knights had been feeling their way toward us, and had driven some cattle across our lines, but that the knights themselves had not come very near. That was what I had been expecting. They were feeling us, you see; they wanted to know if we were going to play that red terror on them again. They would grow bolder in the night, perhaps. I believed I knew what project they would attempt, because it was plainly the thing I would attempt myself if I were in their places and as ignorant as they were. I mentioned it to Clarence.

"I think you are right," said he; "it is the obvious thing for them to try."

"Well, then," I said, "if they do it they are doomed."

"Certainly."

"They won't have the slightest show in the world."

"Of course they won't."

"It's dreadful, Clarence. It seems an awful pity."

The thing disturbed me so, that I couldn't get any peace of mind for thinking of it and worrying over it. So, at last, to quiet my conscience, I framed this message to the knights:

TO THE HONORABLE THE COMMANDER OF THE INSURGENT CHIVALRY OF ENGLAND: You fight in vain. We know your strength—if one may call it by that name. We know that at the utmost you cannot bring against us above five and twenty thousand knights. Therefore, you have no chance—none whatever. Reflect: we are well equipped, well fortified, we number 54. Fifty-four what? Men? No, *minds*—the capablest in the world; a force against which mere animal might may no more hope to prevail than may the idle waves of the sea hope to prevail against the granite barriers of England. Be advised. We offer you your lives; for the sake of your families, do not reject the gift. We offer you this chance, and it is the last: throw down your arms; surrender unconditionally to the Republic, and all will be forgiven.

(Signed). THE BOSS

I read it to Clarence, and said I proposed to send it by a flag of truce. He laughed the sarcastic laugh he was born with, and said:

"Somehow it seems impossible for you to ever fully realize what these nobilities are. Now let us save a little time and trouble. Consider me the commander of the knights yonder. Now then, you are the flag of truce; approach and deliver me your message, and I will give you your answer."

I humored the idea. I came forward under an imaginary guard of the enemy's soldiers, produced my paper, and read it through. For answer, Clarence struck the paper out of my hand, pursed up a scornful lip and said with lofty disdain—

"Dismember me this animal, and return him in a basket to the base-born knave who sent him; other answer have I none!"

How empty is theory in presence of fact! And this was just fact, and nothing else. It was the thing that would have happened, there was no getting around that. I tore up the paper and granted my mistimed sentimentalities a permanent rest.

Then, to business. I tested the electric signals from the gatling platform to the cave, and made sure that they were all right; I tested and re-tested those which commanded the fences—these were signals whereby I could break and renew the electric current in each fence independently of the others, at will. I placed the brook-connection under the guard and authority of three of my best boys, who would alternate in two-hour watches all night and promptly obey my signal, if I should have occasion to give it—three revolver-shots in quick succession. Sentry-duty was discarded for the night, and the corral left empty of life; I ordered that quiet be maintained in the cave, and the electric lights turned down to a glimmer.

As soon as it was good and dark, I shut off the current from all of the fences, and then groped my way out to the embankment bordering our side of the great dynamite ditch. I crept to the top of it and lay there on the slant of the muck to watch. But it was too dark to see anything. As for sounds, there were none. The stillness was death-like. True, there were the usual night-sounds of the country—the whir of night-birds, the buzzing of insects, the barking of distant dogs, the mellow lowing of far-off kine—but these didn't seem to break the stillness, they only intensified it, and added a grewsome melancholy to it into the bargain.

I presently gave up looking, the night shut down so black, but I kept my ears strained to catch the least suspicious sound, for I judged I had only to wait and I shouldn't be disappointed. However, I had to wait a long time. At last I caught what you may call indistinct glimpses of sound—dulled metallic sound. I pricked up my ears, then, and held my breath, for this was the sort of thing I had been waiting for. This sound thickened, and approached—from toward the north. Presently I heard it at my own level—the ridge-top of the opposite embankment, a hundred feet or more away. Then I seemed to see a row of black dots appear along that ridge—human heads? I couldn't tell; it mightn't be anything at all; you can't depend on your eyes when your imagination is out of focus. However, the question was soon settled. I heard that metallic noise descending into the great ditch. It augmented fast, it spread all along, and it unmistakably furnished me this fact: an armed host was taking up its quarters in the ditch. Yes, these people were arranging a little surprise party for us. We could expect entertainment about dawn, possibly earlier.

I groped my way back to the corral, now; I had seen enough. I went to the platform and signalled to turn the current onto the two inner fences. Then I went into the cave, and found everything satisfactory there—nobody awake but the working-watch. I woke Clarence and told him the great ditch was filling up with men, and that I believed all the knights were coming for us in a body. It was my notion that as soon as dawn approached we could expect the ditch's ambuscaded thousands to swarm up over the embankment and make an assault, and be followed immediately by the rest of their army.

Clarence said:

"They will be wanting to send a scout or two in the dark to make preliminary observations. Why not take the lightning off the outer fences, and give them a chance?"

"I've already done it, Clarence. Did you ever know me to be inhospitable?"

"No, you are a good heart. I want to go and—"

"Be a reception committee? I will go, too."

We crossed the corral and lay down together between the two inside fences. Even the dim light of the cave had disordered our eyesight somewhat, but the focus straightway began to regulate itself and soon it was adjusted for present circumstances. We had had to feel our way before, but we could make out to see the fence posts now. We started a whispered conversation, but suddenly Clarence broke off and said:

"What is that?"

"What is what?"

"That thing yonder?"

"What thing—where?"

"There beyond you a little piece—a dark something—a dull shape of some kind—against the second fence."

I gazed and he gazed. I said:

"Could it be a man, Clarence?"

"No, I think not. If you notice, it looks a lit—why, it *is* a man!—leaning on the fence."

"I certainly believe it is; let's us go and see."

We crept along on our hands and knees until we were pretty close, and then looked up. Yes, it was a man—a dim great figure in armor, standing erect, with both hands on the upper wire—and of course there was a smell of burning flesh. Poor fellow, dead as a door-nail, and never knew what hurt him. He stood there like a statue—no motion about him, except that his plumes swished about a little in the night wind. We rose up and looked in through the bars of his visor, but couldn't make out whether we knew him or not—features too dim and shadowed.

We heard muffled sounds approaching, and we sank down to the ground where we were. We made out another knight vaguely; he was coming very stealthily, and feeling his way. He was near enough, now, for us to see him put out a hand, find an upper wire, then bend and step under it and over the lower one. Now he arrived at the first knight—and started slightly when he discovered him. He stood a moment—no doubt wondering why the other one didn't move on; then he said, in a low voice, "Why dreamest thou here, good Sir Mar—" then he laid his hand on the corpse's shoulder—and just uttered a little soft moan and sunk down dead. Killed by a dead man, you see—killed by a dead friend, in fact. There was something awful about it.

These early birds came scattering along after each other, about one every five minutes in our vicinity, during half an hour. They brought no armor of offence but their swords; as a rule they carried the sword ready in the hand, and put it forward and found the wires with it. We would now and then see a blue spark when the knight that caused it was so far away as to be invisible to us; but we knew what had happened, all the same, poor fellow; he had touched a charged wire with his sword and been elected. We had brief intervals of grim stillness, interrupted with piteous regularity by the clash made by the falling of an iron-clad; and this sort of thing was going on, right along, and was very creepy, there in the dark and lonesomeness.

We concluded to make a tour between the inner fences. We elected to walk upright, for convenience sake; we argued that if discerned, we should be taken for friends rather than enemies, and in any case we should be out of reach of swords, and these gentry did not seem to have any spears along. Well, it was a curious trip. Everywhere dead men were lying outside the second fence—not plainly visible, but still visible; and we counted fifteen of those pathetic statues—dead knights standing with their hands on the upper wire.

One thing seemed to be sufficiently demonstrated: our current was so tremendous that it killed before the victim could cry out. Pretty soon we detected a muffled and heavy sound, and next moment we guessed what it was. It was a surprise in force coming! I whispered Clarence to go and wake the army, and notify it to wait in silence in the cave for further orders. He was soon back, and we stood by the inner fence and watched the silent lightning do its awful work upon that swarming host. One could make out but little of detail; but he could note that a black mass was piling itself up beyond the second fence. That swelling bulk was dead men! Our camp was enclosed with a solid wall of the dead—a bulwark, a breastwork, of corpses, you may say. One terrible thing about this thing was the absence of human voices; there were no cheers, no war cries: being intent upon a surprise, these men moved as noiselessly as they could; and always when the front rank was near enough to their goal to make it proper for them to begin to get a shout ready, of course they struck the fatal line and went down without testifying.

I sent a current through the third fence, now; and almost immediately through the fourth and fifth, so quickly were the gaps filled up. I believed the time was come, now, for my climax; I believed that that whole army was in our trap. Anyway, it was high time to find out. So I touched a button and set fifty electric suns aflame on the top of our precipice.

Land, what a sight! We were enclosed in three walls of dead men! All the other fences were pretty nearly filled with the living, who were stealthily working their way forward through the wires. The sudden glare paralyzed this host, petrified them, you may say, with astonishment; there was just one instant for me to utilize their immobility in, and I didn't lose the chance. You see, in another instant they would have recovered their faculties, then they'd have burst into a cheer and made a rush, and my wires would have gone down before it; but that lost instant lost them their opportunity forever; while even that slight fragment of time was still unspent, I shot the current through all the fences and struck the whole host dead in their tracks! *There* was a groan you could *hear!* It voiced the death-pang of eleven thousand men. It swelled out on the night with awful pathos.

A glance showed that the rest of the enemy—perhaps ten thousand strong—were between us and the encircling ditch, and pressing forward to the assault. Consequently we had them *all!* and had them past help. Time for the last act of the tragedy. I fired the three appointed revolver shots—which meant:

"Turn on the water!"

There was a sudden rush and roar, and in a minute the mountain brook was raging through the big ditch and creating a river a hundred feet wide and twenty-five deep.

"Stand to your guns, men! Open fire!"

The thirteen gatlings began to vomit death into the fated ten thousand. They halted, they stood their ground a moment against that withering deluge of fire, then they broke, faced about and swept toward the ditch like chaff before a gale. A full fourth part of their force never reached the top of the lofty embankment; the three-fourths reached it and plunged over—to death by drowning.

Within ten short minutes after we had opened fire, armed resistance was totally annihilated, the campaign was ended, we fifty-four were masters of England! Twenty-five thousand men lay dead around us.

But how treacherous is fortune! In a little while—say an hour—happened a thing, by my own fault, which—but I have no heart to write that. Let the record end here.

CHAPTER 44

A POSTSCRIPT BY CLARENCE

I Clarence, must write it for him. He proposed that we two go out and see if any help could be afforded the wounded. I was strenuous against the project. I said that if there were many, we could do but little for them; and it would not be wise for us to trust ourselves among them, anyway. But he could seldom be turned from a purpose once formed; so we shut off the electric current from the fences, took an escort along, climbed over the enclosing ramparts of dead knights, and moved out upon the field. The first wounded man who appealed for help, was sitting with his back against a dead comrade. When the Boss bent over him and spoke to him, the man recognized him and stabbed him. That knight was Sir Meliagraunce, as I found out by tearing off his helmet. He will not ask for help any more.

We carried the Boss to the cave and gave his wound, which was not very serious, the best care we could. In this service we had the help of Merlin, though we did not know it. He was disguised as a woman, and appeared to be a simple old peasant goodwife. In this disguise, with brown-stained face and smooth shaven, he had appeared a few days after the Boss was hurt, and offered to cook for us, saying her people had gone off to join certain new camps which the enemy were forming, and that she was starving. The Boss had been getting along very well, and had amused himself with finishing up his record.

We were glad to have this woman, for we were short handed. We were in a trap, you see—a trap of our own making. If we stayed where we were, our dead would kill us; if we moved out of our defences, we should no longer be invincible. We had conquered; in turn we were conquered. The Boss recognized this; we all recognized it. If we could go to one of those new camps and patch up some kind of terms with the enemy—yes, but the Boss could not go, and neither could I, for I was among the first that were made sick by the poisonous air bred by those dead thousands. Others were taken down, and still others. To-morrow—

To-morrow. It is here. And with it the end. About midnight I awoke, and saw that hag making curious passes in the air about the Boss's head and face, and wondered what it meant. Everybody but the dynamo-watch lay steeped in sleep; there was no sound. The woman ceased from her mysterious foolery, and started tip-toeing toward the door. I called out—

"Stop! What have you been doing?"

She halted, and said with an accent of malicious satisfaction:

"Ye were conquerors; ye are conquered! These others are perishing—you also. Ye shall all die in this place—every one—except *him*. He sleepeth, now—and shall sleep thirteen centuries. I am Merlin!"

Then such a delirium of silly laughter overtook him that he reeled about like a drunken man, and presently fetched up against one of our wires. His mouth is spread open yet; apparently he is still laughing. I suppose the face will retain that petrified laugh until the corpse turns to dust.

The Boss has never stirred—sleeps like a stone. If he does not wake to-day we shall understand what kind of a sleep it is, and his body will then be borne to a place in one of the remote recesses of the cave where none will ever find it to desecrate it. As for the rest of us—well, it is agreed that if any one of us ever escapes alive from this place, he will write the fact here, and loyally hide this Manuscript with the Boss, our dear good chief, whose property it is, be he alive or dead.

END OF THE MANUSCRIPT

Final P. S. by M. T.

The dawn was come when I laid the Manuscript aside. The rain had almost ceased, the world was gray and sad, the exhausted storm was sighing and sobbing itself to rest. I went to the stranger's room, and listened at his door, which was slightly ajar. I could hear his voice, and so I knocked. There was no answer, but I still heard the voice. I peeped in. The man lay on his back, in bed, talking brokenly but with spirit, and punctuating with his arms, which he thrashed about, restlessly, as sick people do in delirium. I slipped in softly and bent over him. His mutterings and ejaculations went on. I spoke—merely a word, to call his attention. His glassy eyes and his ashy face were alight in an instant with pleasure, gratitude, gladness, welcome:

"O, Sandy, you are come at last—how I have longed for you! Sit by me—do not leave me—never leave me again, Sandy, never again. Where is your hand?—give it me, dear, let me hold it—there—now all is well, all is peace, and I am happy again—*we* are happy again, isn't it so, Sandy? You are so dim, so vague, you are but a mist, a cloud, but you are *here*, and that is blessedness sufficient; and I have your hand; don't take it away—it is for only a little while, I shall not require it long. . . . . Was that the child? . . . . Hello-Central! . . . She doesn't answer. Asleep, perhaps? Bring her when she wakes, and let me touch her hands, her face, her hair, and tell her good-bye. . . . . . Sandy! . . . . . Yes, you are there. I lost myself a moment, and I thought you were gone . . . . Have I been sick long? It must be so; it seems months to me. And such dreams! such strange and awful dreams, Sandy! Dreams that were as real as reality—delirium, of course, but *so* real! Why, I thought the king was dead, I thought you were in Gaul and couldn't get home, I thought there was a revolution; in the fantastic frenzy of these dreams, I thought that Clarence and I and a handful of my cadets fought and exterminated the whole chivalry of England! But even that was not the strangest. I seemed to be a creature out of a remote unborn age, centuries hence, and even *that* was as real as the rest!

Yes, I seemed to have flown back out of that age into this of ours, and then forward to it again, and was set down, a stranger and forlorn in that strange England, with an abyss of thirteen centuries yawning between me and you! between me and my home and my friends! between me and all that is dear to me, all that could make life worth the living! It was awful—awfuler than you can ever imagine, Sandy. Ah, watch by me, Sandy—stay by me every moment—*don't* let me go out of my mind again; death is nothing, let it come, but not with those dreams, not with the torture of those hideous dreams—I cannot endure *that* again. . . . . Sandy? . . . . ."

He lay muttering incoherently some little time; then for a time he lay silent, and apparently sinking away toward death. Presently his fingers began to pick busily at the coverlet, and by that sign I knew that his end was at hand. With the first suggestion of the death-rattle in his throat he started up slightly, and seemed to listen; then he said:

"A bugle? . . . . . It is the king! The drawbridge, there! Man the battlements!—turn out the—"

He was getting up his last "effect;" but he never finished it.

THE END

The American Claimant

CONTENTS

EXPLANATORY

The Colonel Mulberry Sellers here re-introduced to the public is the same person who appeared as *Eschol* Sellers in the first edition of the tale entitled "The Gilded Age," years ago, and as *Beriah* Sellers in the subsequent editions of the same book, and finally as *Mulberry* Sellers in the drama played afterward by John T. Raymond.

The name was changed from Eschol to Beriah to accommodate an Eschol Sellers who rose up out of the vasty deeps of uncharted space and preferred his request—backed by threat of a libel suit—then went his way appeased, and came no more. In the play Beriah had to be dropped to satisfy another member of the race, and Mulberry was substituted in the hope that the objectors would be tired by that time and let it pass unchallenged. So far it has occupied the field in peace; therefore we chance it again, feeling reasonably safe, this time, under shelter of the statute of limitations.

MARK TWAIN

Hartford, 1891

THE WEATHER IN THIS BOOK

No weather will be found in this book. This is an attempt to pull a book through without weather. It being the first attempt of the kind in fictitious literature, it may prove a failure, but it seemed worth the while of some dare-devil person to try it, and the author was in just the mood.

Many a reader who wanted to read a tale through was not able to do it because of delays on account of the weather. Nothing breaks up an author's progress like having to stop every few pages to fuss-up the weather. Thus it is plain that persistent intrusions of weather are bad for both reader and author.

Of course weather is necessary to a narrative of human experience. That is conceded. But it ought to be put where it will not be in the way; where it will not interrupt the flow of the narrative. And it ought to be the ablest weather that can be had, not ignorant, poor-quality, amateur weather. Weather is a literary specialty, and no untrained hand can turn out a good article of it. The present author can do only a few trifling ordinary kinds of weather, and he cannot do those very good. So it has seemed wisest to borrow such weather as is necessary for the book from qualified and recognized experts—giving credit, of course. This weather will be found over in the back part of the book, out of the way. *See Appendix.* The reader is requested to turn over and help himself from time to time as he goes along.

CHAPTER 1

It is a matchless morning in rural England. On a fair hill we see a majestic pile, the ivied walls and towers of Cholmondeley Castle, huge relic and witness of the baronial grandeurs of the Middle Ages. This is one of the seats of the Earl of Rossmore, K. G., G. C. B., K. C. M. G., etc., etc., etc., etc., etc., who possesses twenty-two thousand acres of English land, owns a parish in London with two thousand houses on its lease-roll, and struggles comfortably along on an income of two hundred thousand pounds a year. The father and founder of this proud old line was William the Conqueror his very self; the mother of it was not inventoried in history by name, she being merely a random episode and inconsequential, like the tanner's daughter of Falaise.

In a breakfast room of the castle on this breezy fine morning there are two persons and the cooling remains of a deserted meal. One of these persons is the old lord, tall, erect, square-shouldered, white-haired, stern-browed, a man who shows character in every feature, attitude, and movement, and carries his seventy years as easily as most men carry fifty. The other person is his only son and heir, a dreamy-eyed young fellow, who looks about twenty-six but is nearer thirty. Candor, kindliness, honesty, sincerity, simplicity, modesty—it is easy to see that these are cardinal traits of his character; and so when you have clothed him in the formidable components of his name, you somehow seem to be contemplating a lamb in armor: his name and style being the Honourable Kirkcudbright Llanover Marjoribanks Sellers Viscount Berkeley, of Cholmondeley Castle, Warwickshire. (Pronounced K'koobry Thlanover Marshbanks Sellers Vycount Barkly, of Chumly Castle, Warrikshr.) He is standing by a great window, in an attitude suggestive of respectful attention to what his father is saying and equally respectful dissent from the positions and arguments offered. The father walks the floor as he talks, and his talk shows that his temper is away up toward summer heat.

"Soft-spirited as you are, Berkeley, I am quite aware that when you have once made up your mind to do a thing which your ideas of honor and justice require you to do, argument and reason are (for the time being,) wasted upon you—yes, and ridicule, persuasion, supplication, and command as well. To my mind—"

"Father, if you will look at it without prejudice, without passion, you must concede that I am not doing a rash thing, a thoughtless, wilful thing, with nothing substantial behind it to justify it. *I* did not create the American claimant to the earldom of Rossmore; I did not hunt for him, did not find him, did not obtrude him upon your notice. He found himself, he injected himself into our lives—"

"And has made mine a purgatory for ten years with his tiresome letters, his wordy reasonings, his acres of tedious evidence,—"

"Which you would never read, would never consent to read. Yet in common fairness he was entitled to a hearing. That hearing would either prove he was the rightful earl—in which case our course would be plain—or it would prove that he wasn't—in which case our course would be equally plain. I have read his evidences, my lord. I have conned them well, studied them patiently and thoroughly. The chain seems to be complete, no important link wanting. I believe he is the rightful earl."

"And I a usurper—a nameless pauper, a tramp! Consider what you are saying, sir."

"Father, *if* he is the rightful earl, would you, could you—that fact being established—consent to keep his titles and his properties from him a day, an hour, a minute?"

"You are talking nonsense—nonsense—lurid idiotcy! Now, listen to me. I will make a confession—if you wish to call it by that name. I did not read those evidences because I had no occasion to—I was made familiar with them in the time of this claimant's father and of my own father forty years ago. This fellow's predecessors have kept mine more or less familiar with them for close upon a hundred and fifty years. The truth is, the rightful heir did go to America, with the Fairfax heir or about the same time—but disappeared somewhere in the wilds of Virginia, got married, and began to breed savages for the Claimant market; wrote no letters home; was supposed to be dead; his younger brother softly took possession; presently the American did die, and straightway his eldest product put in his claim—by letter—letter still in existence—and died before the uncle in possession found time—or maybe inclination—to answer. The infant son of that eldest product grew up—long interval, you see—and *he* took to writing letters and furnishing evidences. Well, successor after successor has done the same, down to the present idiot. It was a succession of paupers; not one of them was ever able to pay his passage to England or institute suit. The Fairfaxes kept their lordship alive, and so they have never lost it to this day, although they live in Maryland; their friend lost his by his own neglect. You perceive now, that the facts in this case bring us to precisely this result: morally the American tramp *is* rightful earl of Rossmore; legally he has no more right than his dog. There now—are you satisfied?"

There was a pause, then the son glanced at the crest carved in the great oaken mantel and said, with a regretful note in his voice:

"Since the introduction of heraldic symbols, the motto of this house has been *Suum cuique*—to every man his own. By your own intrepidly frank confession, my lord, it is become a sarcasm. If Simon Lathers—"

"Keep that exasperating name to yourself! For ten years it has pestered my eye and tortured my ear; till at last my very footfalls time themselves to the brain-racking rhythm of *Simon Lathers!—Simon Lathers!—Simon Lathers!* And now, to make its presence in my soul eternal, immortal, imperishable, you have resolved to—to—what is it you have resolved to do?"

"To go to Simon Lathers, in America, and change places with him."

"What? Deliver the reversion of the earldom into his hands?"

"That is my purpose."

"Make this tremendous surrender without even trying the fantastic case in the Lords?"

"Ye—s—" with hesitation and some embarrassment.

"By all that is amazing, I believe you are insane, my son. See here—have you been training with that ass again—that radical, if you prefer the term, though the words are synonymous—Lord Tanzy, of Tollmache?"

The son did not reply, and the old lord continued:

"Yes, you confess. That puppy, that shame to his birth and caste, who holds all hereditary lordships and privilege to be usurpation, all nobility a tinsel sham, all aristocratic institutions a fraud, all inequalities in rank a legalized crime and an infamy, and no bread honest bread that a man doesn't earn by his own work—*work*, pah!"—and the old patrician brushed imaginary labor-dirt from his white hands. "You have come to hold just those opinions yourself, I suppose," he added with a sneer.

A faint flush in the younger man's cheek told that the shot had hit and hurt, but he answered with dignity—

"I have. I say it without shame—I feel none. And now my reason for resolving to renounce my heirship without resistance is explained. I wish to retire from what to me is a false existence, a false position, and begin my life over again—begin it right—begin it on the level of mere manhood, unassisted by factitious aids, and succeed or fail by pure merit or the want of it. I will go to America, where all men are equal and all have an equal chance; I will live or die, sink or swim, win or lose as just a man—that alone, and not a single helping gaud or fiction back of it."

"Hear, hear!" The two men looked each other steadily in the eye a moment or two, then the elder one added, musingly, "Ab-so-lutely cra-zy—ab-so-lutely!" After another silence, he said, as one who, long troubled by clouds, detects a ray of sunshine, "Well, there will be one satisfaction—Simon Lathers will come here to enter into his own, and I will drown him in the horsepond. That poor devil—always so humble in his letters, so pitiful, so deferential; so steeped in reverence for our great line and lofty station; so anxious to placate us, so prayerful for recognition as a relative, a bearer in his veins of our sacred blood—and withal so poor, so needy, so threadbare and pauper-shod as to raiment, so despised, so laughed at for his silly claimantship by the lewd American scum around him—ach, the vulgar, crawling, insufferable tramp! To read one of his cringing, nauseating letters—well?"

This to a splendid flunkey, all in inflamed plush and buttons and knee-breeches as to his trunk, and a glinting white frost-work of ground-glass paste as to his head, who stood with his heels together and the upper half of him bent forward, a salver in his hands:

"The letters, my lord."

My lord took them, and the servant disappeared.

"Among the rest, an American letter. From the tramp, of course. Jove, but here's a change! No brown paper envelop this time, filched from a shop and carrying the shop's advertisement in the corner. Oh, no, a proper enough envelop—with a most ostentatiously broad mourning border—for his cat, perhaps, since he was a bachelor—and fastened with red wax—a batch of it as big as a half-crown—and—and—our crest for a seal!—motto and all. And the ignorant, sprawling hand is gone; he sports a secretary, evidently—a secretary with a most confident swing and flourish to his pen. Oh indeed, our fortunes are improving over there—our meek tramp has undergone a metamorphosis."

"Read it, my lord, please."

"Yes, this time I will. For the sake of the cat:

14,042 Sixteenth street,
Washington, May 2.

My Lord—

It is my painful duty to announce to you that the head of our illustrious house is no more—The Right Honourable, The Most Noble, The Most Puissant Simon Lathers Lord Rossmore having departed this life ("Gone at last—this is unspeakably precious news, my son,") at his seat in the environs of the hamlet of Duffy's Corners in the grand old State of Arkansas,—and his twin brother with him, both being crushed by a log at a smoke-house-raising, owing to carelessness on the part of all present, referable to over-confidence and gaiety induced by overplus of sour-mash—("Extolled be sour-mash, whatever that may be, eh Berkeley?") five days ago, with no scion of our ancient race present to close his eyes and inter him with the honors due his historic name and lofty rank—in fact, he is on the ice yet, him and his brother—friends took up a collection for it. But I shall take immediate occasion to have their noble remains shipped to you ("Great heavens!") for interment, with due ceremonies and solemnities, in the family vault or mausoleum of our house. Meantime I shall put up a pair of hatchments on my house-front, and you will of course do the same at your several seats.

I have also to remind you that by this sad disaster I as sole heir, inherit and become seized of all the titles, honors, lands, and goods of our lamented relative, and must of necessity, painful as the duty is, shortly require at the bar of the Lords restitution of these dignities and properties, now illegally enjoyed by your titular lordship.

With assurance of my distinguished consideration and warm cousinly regard, I remain

Your titular lordship's
Most obedient servant,
Mulberry Sellers Earl Rossmore.

"Im-mense! Come, this one's interesting. Why, Berkeley, his breezy impudence is—is—why, it's colossal, it's sublime."

"No, this one doesn't seem to cringe much."

"Cringe—why, he doesn't know the meaning of the word. Hatchments! To commemorate that sniveling tramp and his fraternal duplicate. And he is going to send me the remains. The late Claimant was a fool, but plainly this new one's a maniac. What a name! *Mulberry* Sellers—there's music for you. Simon Lathers—Mulberry Sellers—Mulberry Sellers—Simon Lathers. Sounds like machinery working and churning. Simon Lathers, Mulberry Sel— Are you going?"

"If I have your leave, father."

The old gentleman stood musing some time, after his son was gone. This was his thought:

"He is a good boy, and lovable. Let him take his own course—as it would profit nothing to oppose him—make things worse, in fact. My arguments and his aunt's persuasions have failed; let us see what America can do for us. Let us see what equality and hardtimes can effect for the mental health of a brain-sick young British lord. Going to renounce his lordship and be a man! Yas!"

CHAPTER 2

Colonel Mulberry Sellers—this was some days before he wrote his letter to Lord Rossmore—was seated in his "library," which was also his "drawing-room" and was also his "picture gallery" and likewise his "work-shop." Sometimes he called it by one of these names, sometimes by another, according to occasion and circumstance. He was constructing what seemed to be some kind of a frail mechanical toy, and was apparently very much interested in his work. He was a white-headed man, now, but otherwise he was as young, alert, buoyant, visionary and enterprising as ever. His loving old wife sat near by, contentedly knitting and thinking, with a cat asleep in her lap. The room was large, light, and had a comfortable look, in fact a home-like look, though the furniture was of a humble sort and not over abundant, and the knick-knacks and things that go to adorn a living-room not plenty and not costly. But there were natural flowers, and there was an abstract and unclassifiable something about the place which betrayed the presence in the house of somebody with a happy taste and an effective touch.

Even the deadly chromos on the walls were somehow without offence; in fact they seemed to belong there and to add an attraction to the room—a fascination, anyway; for whoever got his eye on one of them was like to gaze and suffer till he died—you have seen that kind of pictures. Some of these terrors were landscapes, some libeled the sea, some were ostensible portraits, all were crimes. All the portraits were recognizable as dead Americans of distinction, and yet, through labeling added by a daring hand, they were all doing duty here as "Earls of Rossmore." The newest one had left the works as Andrew Jackson, but was doing its best now, as "Simon Lathers Lord Rossmore, Present Earl." On one wall was a cheap old railroad map of Warwickshire. This had been newly labeled "The Rossmore Estates." On the opposite wall was another map, and this was the most imposing decoration of the establishment and the first to catch a stranger's attention, because of its great size. It had once borne simply the title SIBERIA; but now the word "FUTURE" had been written in front of that word. There were other additions, in red ink—many cities, with great populations set down, scattered over the vast country at points where neither cities nor populations exist to-day. One of these cities, with population placed at 1,500,000, bore the name "Libertyorloffskoizalinski," and there was a still more populous one, centrally located and marked "Capital," which bore the name "Freedomolovnaivanovich."

The "mansion"—the Colonel's usual name for the house—was a rickety old two-story frame of considerable size, which had been painted, some time or other, but had nearly forgotten it. It was away out in the ragged edge of Washington and had once been somebody's country place. It had a neglected yard around it, with a paling fence that needed straightening up, in places, and a gate that would stay shut. By the door-post were several modest tin signs. "Col. Mulberry Sellers, Attorney at Law and Claim Agent," was the principal one. One learned from the others that the Colonel was a Materializer, a Hypnotizer, a Mind-Cure dabbler, and so on. For he was a man who could always find things to do.

A white-headed negro man, with spectacles and damaged white cotton gloves appeared in the presence, made a stately obeisance and announced—

"Marse Washington Hawkins, suh."

"Great Scott! Show him in, Dan'l, show him in."

The Colonel and his wife were on their feet in a moment, and the next moment were joyfully wringing the hands of a stoutish, discouraged-looking man whose general aspect suggested that he was fifty years old, but whose hair swore to a hundred.

"Well, well, well, Washington, my boy, it *is* good to look at you again. Sit down, sit down, and make yourself at home. There, now—why, you look perfectly natural; aging a little, just a little, but you'd have known him anywhere, wouldn't you, Polly?"

"Oh, yes, Berry, he's *just* like his pa would have looked if he'd lived. Dear, dear, where have you dropped from? Let me see, how long is it since—"

"I should say it's all of fifteen years, Mrs. Sellers."

"Well, well, how time does get away with us. Yes, and oh, the changes that—"

There was a sudden catch of her voice and a trembling of the lip, the men waiting reverently for her to get command of herself and go on; but after a little struggle she turned away, with her apron to her eyes, and softly disappeared.

"Seeing you made her think of the children, poor thing—dear, dear, they're all dead but the youngest. But banish care, it's no time for it now—on with the dance, let joy be unconfined is my motto, whether there's any dance to dance, or any joy to unconfine—you'll be the healthier for it every time,—every time, Washington—it's my experience, and I've seen a good deal of this world. Come—where have you disappeared to all these years, and are you from there, now, or where are you from?"

"I don't quite think you would ever guess, Colonel. Cherokee Strip."

"My land!"

"Sure as you live."

"You can't mean it. Actually *living* out there?"

"Well, yes, if a body may call it that; though it's a pretty strong term for 'dobies and jackass rabbits, boiled beans and slapjacks, depression, withered hopes, poverty in all its varieties—"

"Louise out there?"

"Yes, and the children."

"Out there now?"

"Yes, I couldn't afford to bring them with me."

"Oh, I see,—you had to come—claim against the government. Make yourself perfectly easy—I'll take care of that."

"But it isn't a claim against the government."

"No? Want to be postmaster? *That's* all right. Leave it to me. I'll fix it."

"But it isn't postmaster—you're all astray yet."

"Well, good gracious, Washington, why don't you come out and tell me what it is? What do you want to be so reserved and distrustful with an old friend like me, for? Don't you reckon I can keep a se—"

"There's no secret about it—you merely don't give me a chance to—"

"Now look here, old friend, I know the human race; and I know that when a man comes to Washington, I don't care if it's from heaven, let alone Cherokee Strip, it's because he *wants* something. And I know that as a rule he's not going to get it; that he'll stay and try for another thing and won't get that; the same luck with the next and the next and the next; and keeps on till he strikes bottom, and is too poor and ashamed to go back, even to Cherokee Strip; and at last his heart breaks and they take up a collection and bury him. There—don't interrupt me, I know what I'm talking about. Happy and prosperous in the Far West wasn't I? *You* know that. Principal citizen of Hawkeye, looked up to by everybody, kind of an autocrat, actually a kind of an autocrat, Washington. Well, nothing would do but I must go Minister to St. James, the Governor and everybody insisting, you know, and so at last I consented—no getting out of it, *had* to do it, so here I came. *A day too late*, Washington. Think of that—what little things change the world's history—yes, sir, the place had been filled. Well, there I was, you see. I offered to compromise and go to Paris. The President was very sorry and all that, but *that* place, you see, didn't belong to the West, so there I was again. There was no help for it, so I had to stoop a little—we all reach the day some time or other when we've got to do that, Washington, and it's not a bad thing for us, either, take it by and large and all around—I had to stoop a little and offer to take Constantinople. Washington, consider this—for it's perfectly true—within a month I *asked* for China; within another month I *begged* for Japan; one year later I was away down, down, down, supplicating with tears and anguish for the bottom office in the gift of the government of the United States—Flint-Picker in the cellars of the War Department. And by George I didn't get it."

"Flint-Picker?"

"Yes. Office established in the time of the Revolution, last century. The musket-flints for the military posts were supplied from the capitol. They do it yet; for although the flint-arm has gone out and the forts have tumbled down, the decree hasn't been repealed—been overlooked and forgotten, you see—and so the vacancies where old Ticonderoga and others used to stand, still get their six quarts of gun-flints a year just the same."

Washington said musingly after a pause:

"How strange it seems—to start for Minister to England at twenty thousand a year and fail for flint-picker at—"

"Three dollars a week. It's human life, Washington—just an epitome of human ambition, and struggle, and the outcome: you aim for the palace and get drowned in the sewer."

There was another meditative silence. Then Washington said, with earnest compassion in his voice—

"And so, after coming here, against your inclination, to satisfy your sense of patriotic duty and appease a selfish public clamor, you get absolutely nothing for it."

"Nothing?" The Colonel had to get up and stand, to get room for his amazement to expand. "*Nothing*, Washington? I ask you this: to be a Perpetual Member and the *only* Perpetual Member of a Diplomatic Body accredited to the greatest country on earth—do you call that nothing?"

It was Washington's turn to be amazed. He was stricken dumb; but the wide-eyed wonder, the reverent admiration expressed in his face were more eloquent than any words could have been. The Colonel's wounded spirit was healed and he resumed his seat pleased and content. He leaned forward and said impressively:

"What was due to a man who had become forever conspicuous by an experience without precedent in the history of the world?—a man made permanently and diplomatically sacred, so to speak, by having been connected, temporarily, through solicitation, with every single diplomatic post in the roster of this government, from Envoy Extraordinary and Minister Plenipotentiary to the Court of St. James all the way down to Consul to a guano rock in the Straits of Sunda—salary payable in guano—which disappeared by volcanic convulsion the day before they got down to my name in the list of applicants. Certainly something august enough to be answerable to the size of this unique and memorable experience was my due, and I got it. By the common voice of this community, by acclamation of the people, that mighty utterance which brushes aside laws and legislation, and from whose decrees there is no appeal, I was named Perpetual Member of the Diplomatic Body representing the multifarious sovereignties and civilizations of the globe near the republican court of the United States of America. And they brought me home with a torchlight procession."

"It is wonderful, Colonel, simply wonderful."

"It's the loftiest official position in the whole earth."

"I should think so—and the most commanding."

"You have named the word. Think of it. I frown, and there is war; I smile, and contending nations lay down their arms."

"It is awful. The responsibility, I mean."

"It is nothing. Responsibility is no burden to me; I am used to it; have always been used to it."

"And the work—the work! Do you have to attend all the sittings?"

"Who, I? Does the Emperor of Russia attend the conclaves of the governors of the provinces? He sits at home, and indicates his pleasure."

Washington was silent a moment, then a deep sigh escaped him.

"How proud I was an hour ago; how paltry seems my little promotion now! Colonel, the reason I came to Washington is,—I am Congressional Delegate from Cherokee Strip!"

The Colonel sprang to his feet and broke out with prodigious enthusiasm:

"Give me your hand, my boy—this is immense news! I congratulate you with all my heart. My prophecies stand confirmed. I always said it was in you. I always said you were born for high distinction and would achieve it. You ask Polly if I didn't."

Washington was dazed by this most unexpected demonstration.

"Why, Colonel, there's nothing *to* it. That little narrow, desolate, unpeopled, oblong streak of grass and gravel, lost in the remote wastes of the vast continent—why, it's like representing a billiard table—a discarded one."

"Tut-tut, it's a great, it's a staving preferment, and just opulent with influence here."

"Shucks, Colonel, I haven't even a vote."

"That's nothing; you can make speeches."

"No, I can't. The population's only two hundred—"

"That's all right, that's all right—"

"And they hadn't any right to elect me; we're not even a territory, there's no Organic Act, the government hasn't any official knowledge of us whatever."

"Never mind about that; I'll fix that. I'll rush the thing through, I'll get you organized in no time."

"*Will* you, Colonel?—it's *too* good of you; but it's just your old sterling self, the same old ever-faithful friend," and the grateful tears welled up in Washington's eyes.

"It's just as good as done, my boy, just as good as done. Shake hands. We'll hitch teams together, you and I, and we'll make things hum!"

CHAPTER 3

Mrs. Sellers returned, now, with her composure restored, and began to ask after Hawkins's wife, and about his children, and the number of them, and so on, and her examination of the witness resulted in a circumstantial history of the family's ups and downs and driftings to and fro in the far West during the previous fifteen years. There was a message, now, from out back, and Colonel Sellers went out there in answer to it. Hawkins took this opportunity to ask how the world had been using the Colonel during the past half-generation.

"Oh, it's been using him just the same; it couldn't change its way of using him if it wanted to, for he wouldn't let it."

"I can easily believe that, Mrs. Sellers."

"Yes, you see, he doesn't change, himself—not the least little bit in the world—he's always Mulberry Sellers."

"I can see *that* plain enough."

"Just the same old scheming, generous, good-hearted, moonshiny, hopeful, no-account failure he always was, and still everybody likes him just as well as if he was the shiningest success."

"They always did: and it was natural, because he was so obliging and accommodating, and had something about him that made it kind of easy to ask help of him, or favors—you didn't feel shy, you know, or have that wish-you-didn't-have-to-try feeling that you have with other people."

"It's just so, yet; and a body wonders at it, too, because he's been shamefully treated, many times, by people that had used him for a ladder to climb up by, and then kicked him down when they didn't need him any more. For a time you can see he's hurt, his pride's wounded, because he shrinks away from that thing and don't want to talk about it—and so I used to think *now* he's learned something and he'll be more careful hereafter—but laws! in a couple of weeks he's forgotten all about it, and any selfish tramp out of nobody knows where can come and put up a poor mouth and walk right into his heart with his boots on."

"It must try your patience pretty sharply sometimes."

"Oh, no, I'm used to it; and I'd rather have him so than the other way. When I call him a failure, I mean to the world he's a failure; he isn't to me. I don't know as I want him different—much different, anyway. I have to scold him some, snarl at him, you might even call it, but I reckon I'd do that just the same, if he was different—it's my make. But I'm a good deal less snarly and more contented when he's a failure than I am when he isn't."

"Then he isn't always a failure," said Hawkins, brightening.

"Him? Oh, bless you, no. He makes a strike, as he calls it, from time to time. Then's my time to fret and fuss. For the money just flies—first come first served. Straight off, he loads up the house with cripples and idiots and stray cats and all the different kinds of poor wrecks that other people don't want and he *does,* and then when the poverty comes again I've *got* to clear the most of them out or we'd starve; and that distresses him, and me the same, of course. Here's old Dan'l and old Jinny, that the sheriff sold south one of the times that we got bankrupted before the war—they came wandering back after the peace, worn out and used up on the cotton plantations, helpless, and not another lick of work left in their old hides for the rest of this earthly pilgrimage—and we so pinched, *oh* so pinched for the very crumbs to keep life in us, and he just flung the door wide, and the way he received them you'd have thought they had come straight down from heaven in answer to prayer. I took him one side and said, 'Mulberry we can't have them—we've nothing for ourselves—we can't feed them.' He looked at me kind of hurt, and said, 'Turn them out?—and they've come to me just as confident and trusting as—as—why Polly, I must have *bought* that confidence sometime or other a long time ago, and given my note, so to speak—you don't get such things as a *gift*—and how am I going to go back on a debt like that? And you see, they're so poor, and old, and friendless, and—' But I was ashamed by that time, and shut him off, and somehow felt a new courage in me, and so I said, softly, 'We'll keep them—the Lord will provide.' He was glad, and started to blurt out one of those over-confident speeches of his, but checked himself in time, and said humbly, '*I* will, anyway.' It was years and years and years ago. Well, you see those old wrecks are here yet."

"But don't they do your housework?"

"Laws! The idea. They would if they could, poor old things, and perhaps they think they *do* do some of it. But it's a superstition. Dan'l waits on the front door, and sometimes goes on an errand; and sometimes you'll see one or both of them letting on to dust around in here—but that's because there's something they want to hear about and mix their gabble into. And they're always around at meals, for the same reason. But the fact is, we have to keep a young negro girl just to take care of *them,* and a negro woman to do the housework and *help* take care of them."

"Well, they ought to be tolerably happy, I should think."

"It's no name for it. They quarrel together pretty much all the time —most always about religion, because Dan'l's a Dunker Baptist and Jinny's a shouting Methodist, and Jinny believes in special Providences and Dan'l don't, because he thinks he's a kind of a free-thinker—and they play and sing plantation hymns together, and talk and chatter just eternally and forever, and are sincerely fond of each other and think the world of Mulberry, and he puts up patiently with all their spoiled ways and foolishness, and so—ah, well, they're happy enough if it comes to that. And I don't mind—I've got used to it. I can get used to anything, with Mulberry to help; and the fact is, I don't much care what happens, so long as he's spared to me."

"Well, here's to him, and hoping he'll make another strike soon."

"And rake in the lame, the halt and the blind, and turn the house into a hospital again? It's what he would do. I've seen a plenty of that and more. No, Washington, I want his strikes to be mighty moderate ones the rest of the way down the vale."

"Well, then, big strike or little strike, or no strike at all, here's hoping he'll never lack for friends—and I don't reckon he ever will while there's people around who know enough to—"

"Him lack for friends!" and she tilted her head up with a frank pride

—"why, Washington, you can't name a man that's anybody that isn't fond of him. I'll tell you privately, that I've had Satan's own time to keep them from appointing him to some office or other. They knew he'd no business with an office, just as well as I did, but he's the hardest man to refuse anything to, a body ever saw. Mulberry Sellers with an office! laws goodness, you know what that would be like. Why, they'd come from the ends of the earth to see a circus like that. I'd just as lieves be married to Niagara Falls, and done with it." After a reflective pause she added—having wandered back, in the interval, to the remark that had been her text: "Friends?—oh, indeed, no man ever had more; and *such* friends: Grant, Sherman, Sheridan, Johnston, Longstreet, Lee—many's the time they've sat in that chair you're sitting in—" Hawkins was out of it instantly, and contemplating it with a reverential surprise, and with the awed sense of having trodden shod upon holy ground—

"*They!*" he said.

"Oh, indeed, yes, a many and a many a time."

He continued to gaze at the chair fascinated, magnetized; and for once in his life that continental stretch of dry prairie which stood for his imagination was afire, and across it was marching a slanting flame-front that joined its wide horizons together and smothered the skies with smoke. He was experiencing what one or another drowsing, geographically-ignorant alien experiences every day in the year when he turns a dull and indifferent eye out of the car window and it falls upon a certain station-sign which reads "Stratford-on-Avon!" Mrs. Sellers went gossiping comfortably along:

"Oh, they like to hear him talk, especially if their load is getting rather heavy on one shoulder and they want to shift it. He's all air, you know,—breeze, you may say—and he freshens them up; it's a trip to the country, they say. Many a time he's made General Grant laugh—and that's a tidy job, I can tell you, and as for Sheridan, his eye lights up and he listens to Mulberry Sellers the same as if he was artillery. You see, the charm about Mulberry is, he is so catholic and unprejudiced that he fits in anywhere and everywhere. It makes him powerful good company, and as popular as scandal. You go to the White House when the President's holding a general reception—sometime when Mulberry's there. Why, dear me, *you* can't tell which of them it is that's holding that reception."

"Well, he certainly is a remarkable man—and he always was. Is he religious?"

"Clear to his marrow—does more thinking and reading on that subject than any other except Russia and Siberia: thrashes around over the whole field, too; nothing bigoted about him."

"What is his religion?"

"He—" She stopped, and was lost for a moment or two in thinking, then she said, with simplicity, "I think he was a Mohammedan or something last week."

Washington started down town, now, to bring his trunk, for the hospitable Sellerses would listen to no excuses; their house must be his home during the session. The Colonel returned presently and resumed work upon his plaything. It was finished when Washington got back.

"There it is," said the Colonel, "all finished."

"What is it for, Colonel?"

"Oh, it's just a trifle. Toy to amuse the children."

Washington examined it.

"It seems to be a puzzle."

"Yes, that's what it is. I call it Pigs in the Clover. Put them in—see if you can put them in the pen."

After many failures Washington succeeded, and was as pleased as a child.

"It's wonderfully ingenious, Colonel, it's ever so clever. And interesting—why, I could play with it all day. What are you going to do with it?"

"Oh, nothing. Patent it and throw it aside."

"Don't you do anything of the kind. There's money in that thing."

A compassionate look traveled over the Colonel's countenance, and he said:

"Money—yes; pin money: a couple of hundred thousand, perhaps. Not more."

Washington's eyes blazed.

"A couple of hundred thousand dollars! do you call that pin money?"

The colonel rose and tip-toed his way across the room, closed a door that was slightly ajar, tip-toed his way to his seat again, and said, under his breath—

"You can keep a secret?"

Washington nodded his affirmative, he was too awed to speak.

"You have heard of materialization—materialization of departed spirits?"

Washington had heard of it.

"And probably didn't believe in it; and quite right, too. The thing as practised by ignorant charlatans is unworthy of attention or respect —where there's a dim light and a dark cabinet, and a parcel of sentimental gulls gathered together, with their faith and their shudders and their tears all ready, and one and the same fatty degeneration of protoplasm and humbug comes out and materializes himself into anybody you want, grandmother, grandchild, brother-in-law, Witch of Endor, John Milton, Siamese twins, Peter the Great, and all such frantic nonsense—no, that is all foolish and pitiful. But when a man that is competent brings the vast powers of *science* to bear, it's a different matter, a totally different matter, you see. The spectre that answers *that* call has come to stay. Do you note the commercial value of that detail?"

"Well, I—the—the truth is, that I don't quite know that I do. Do you mean that such, being permanent, not transitory, would give more general satisfaction, and so enhance the price of tickets to the show—"

"Show? Folly—listen to me; and get a good grip on your breath, for you are going to need it. Within three days I shall have completed my method, and then—let the world stand aghast, for it shall see marvels. Washington, within three days—ten at the outside—you shall see me call the dead of any century, and they will arise and walk. Walk?—they shall walk forever, and never die again. Walk with all the muscle and spring of their pristine vigor."

"Colonel! Indeed it does take one's breath away."

"*Now* do you see the money that's in it?"

"I'm—well, I'm—not really sure that I do."

"Great Scott, look here. I shall have a monopoly; they'll all belong to me, won't they? Two thousand policemen in the city of New York. Wages, four dollars a day. I'll replace them with dead ones at half the money."

"Oh, prodigious! I never thought of that. F-o-u-r thousand dollars a day. Now I do begin to see! But will dead policemen answer?"

"Haven't they—up to this time?"

"Well, if you put it that way—"

"Put it any way you want to. Modify it to suit yourself, and my lads shall still be superior. They won't eat, they won't drink—don't need those things; they won't wink for cash at gambling dens and unlicensed rum-holes, they won't spark the scullery maids; and moreover the bands of toughs that ambuscade them on lonely beats, and cowardly shoot and knife them will only damage the uniforms and not live long enough to get more than a momentary satisfaction out of that."

"Why, Colonel, if you can furnish policemen, then of course—"

"Certainly—I can furnish any line of goods that's wanted. Take the army, for instance—now twenty-five thousand men; expense, twenty-two millions a year. I will dig up the Romans, I will resurrect the

Greeks, I will furnish the government, for ten millions a year, ten thousand veterans drawn from the victorious legions of all the ages—soldiers that will chase Indians year in and year out on materialized horses, and cost never a cent for rations or repairs. The armies of Europe cost two billions a year now—I will replace them all for a billion. I will dig up the trained statesmen of all ages and all climes, and furnish this country with a Congress that knows enough to come in out of the rain—a thing that's never happened yet, since the Declaration of Independence, and never will happen till these practically dead people are replaced with the genuine article. I will re-stock the thrones of Europe with the best brains and the best morals that all the royal sepulchres of all the centuries can furnish—which isn't promising very much—and I'll divide the wages and the civil list, fair and square, merely taking my half and—"

"Colonel, if the half of this is true, there's millions in it—millions."

"Billions in it—billions; that's what you mean. Why, look here; the thing is so close at hand, so imminent, so absolutely immediate, that if a man were to come to me now and say, Colonel, I am a little short, and if you could lend me a couple of billion dollars for—come in!"

This in answer to a knock. An energetic looking man bustled in with a big pocket-book in his hand, took a paper from it and presented it, with the curt remark—

"Seventeenth and last call—you want to out with that three dollars and forty cents this time without fail, Colonel Mulberry Sellers."

The Colonel began to slap this pocket and that one, and feel here and there and everywhere, muttering—

"What *have* I done with that wallet?—let me see—um—not here, not there—Oh, I must have left it in the kitchen; I'll just run and—"

"No you won't—you'll stay right where you are. And you're going to disgorge, too—this time."

Washington innocently offered to go and look. When he was gone the Colonel said—

"The fact is, I've got to throw myself on your indulgence just this once more, Suggs; you see the remittances I was expecting—"

"Hang the remittances—it's too stale—it won't answer. Come!"

The Colonel glanced about him in despair. Then his face lighted; he ran to the wall and began to dust off a peculiarly atrocious chromo with his handkerchief. Then he brought it reverently, offered it to the collector, averted his face and said—

"Take it, but don't let me see it go. It's the sole remaining Rembrandt that—"

"Rembrandt be damned, it's a chromo."

"Oh, don't speak of it so, I beg you. It's the only really great original, the only supreme example of that mighty school of art which—"

"Art! It's the sickest looking thing I—"

The colonel was already bringing another horror and tenderly dusting it.

"Take this one too—the gem of my collection—the only genuine Fra Angelico that—"

"Illuminated liver-pad, that's what it is. Give it here—good day—people will think I've robbed a nigger barber-shop."

As he slammed the door behind him the Colonel shouted with an anguished accent—

"Do please cover them up—don't let the damp get at them. The delicate tints in the Angelico—"

But the man was gone.

Washington re-appeared and said he had looked everywhere, and so had Mrs. Sellers and the servants, but in vain; and went on to say he wished he could get his eye on a certain man about this time—no need to hunt up that pocket-book then. The Colonel's interest was awake at once.

"What man?"

"One-armed Pete they call him out there—out in the Cherokee country I mean. Robbed the bank in Tahlequah."

"Do they have banks in Tahlequah?"

"Yes—*a* bank, anyway. He was suspected of robbing it. Whoever did it got away with more than twenty thousand dollars. They offered a reward of five thousand. I believe I saw that very man, on my way east."

"No—is that so?"

"I certainly saw a man on the train, the first day I struck the railroad, that answered the description pretty exactly—at least as to clothes and a lacking arm."

"Why didn't you get him arrested and claim the reward?"

"I couldn't. I had to get a requisition, of course. But I meant to stay by him till I got my chance."

"Well?"

"Well, he left the train during the night some time."

"Oh, hang it, that's too bad."

"Not so very bad, either."

"Why?"

"Because he came down to Baltimore in the very train I was in, though I didn't know it in time. As we moved out of the station I saw him going toward the iron gate with a satchel in his hand."

"Good; we'll catch him. Let's lay a plan."

"Send description to the Baltimore police?"

"Why, what are you talking about? No. Do you want them to get the reward?"

"What shall we do, then?"

The Colonel reflected.

"I'll tell you. Put a personal in the Baltimore *Sun*. Word it like this:

A. DROP ME A LINE, PETE–

–"Hold on. Which arm has he lost?"

"The right."

"Good. Now then–

A. DROP ME A LINE, PETE, EVEN IF YOU HAVE TO WRITE with your left hand. Address X. Y. Z., General Postoffice, Washington. From YOU KNOW WHO.

"There–that'll fetch him."

"But he *won't* know who–will he?"

"No, but he'll want to know, won't he?"

"Why, certainly–I didn't think of that. What made you think of it?"

"Knowledge of human curiosity. Strong trait, very strong trait."

"Now I'll go to my room and write it out and enclose a dollar and tell them to print it to the worth of that."

CHAPTER 4

The day wore itself out. After dinner the two friends put in a long and harassing evening trying to decide what to do with the five thousand dollars reward which they were going to get when they should find One-Armed Pete, and catch him, and prove him to be the right person, and extradite him, and ship him to Tahlequah in the Indian Territory. But there were so many dazzling openings for ready cash that they found it impossible to make up their minds and keep them made up. Finally, Mrs. Sellers grew very weary of it all, and said:

"What is the sense in cooking a rabbit before it's caught?"

Then the matter was dropped, for the time being, and all went to bed. Next morning, being persuaded by Hawkins, the colonel made drawings and specifications and went down and applied for a patent for his toy puzzle, and Hawkins took the toy itself and started out to see what chance there might be to do something with it commercially. He did not have to go far. In a small old wooden shanty which had once been occupied as a dwelling by some humble negro family he found a keen-eyed Yankee engaged in repairing cheap chairs and other second-hand furniture. This man examined the toy indifferently; attempted to do the puzzle; found it not so easy as he had expected; grew more interested, and finally emphatically so; achieved a success at last, and asked—

"Is it patented?"

"Patent applied for."

"That will answer. What do you want for it?"

"What will it retail for?"

"Well, twenty-five cents, I should think."

"What will you give for the exclusive right?"

"I couldn't give twenty dollars, if I had to pay cash down; but I'll tell you what I'll do. I'll make it and market it, and pay you five cents royalty on each one."

Washington sighed. Another dream disappeared; no money in the thing. So he said—

"All right, take it at that. Draw me a paper."

He went his way with the paper, and dropped the matter out of his mind—dropped it out to make room for further attempts to think out the most promising way to invest his half of the reward, in case a partnership investment satisfactory to both beneficiaries could not be hit upon.

He had not been very long at home when Sellers arrived sodden with grief and booming with glad excitement—working both these emotions successfully, sometimes separately, sometimes together. He fell on Hawkins's neck sobbing, and said—

"Oh, mourn with me my friend, mourn for my desolate house: death has smitten my last kinsman and I am Earl of Rossmore—congratulate me!"

He turned to his wife, who had entered while this was going on, put his arms about her and said—"You will bear up, for my sake, my lady—it had to happen, it was decreed."

She bore up very well, and said—

"It's no great loss. Simon Lathers was a poor well-meaning useless thing and no account, and his brother never was worth shucks."

The rightful earl continued—

"I am too much prostrated by these conflicting griefs and joys to be able to concentrate my mind upon affairs; I will ask our good friend here to break the news by wire or post to the Lady Gwendolen and instruct her to—"

"*What* Lady Gwendolen?"

"Our poor daughter, who, alas!—"

"Sally Sellers? Mulberry Sellers, are you losing your mind?"

"There—please do not forget who you are, and who I am; remember your own dignity, be considerate also of mine. It were best to cease from using my family name, now, Lady Rossmore."

"Goodness gracious, well, I never! What *am* I to call you then?"

"In private, the ordinary terms of endearment will still be admissible, to some degree; but in public it will be more becoming if your ladyship will speak *to* me as my lord, or your lordship, and *of* me as Rossmore, or the Earl, or his Lordship, and—"

"Oh, scat! I can't ever do it, Berry."

"But indeed you must, my love—we must live up to our altered position and submit with what grace we may to its requirements."

"Well, all right, have it your own way; I've never set my wishes against your commands yet, Mul—my lord, and it's late to begin now, though to my mind it's the rottenest foolishness that ever was."

"Spoken like my own true wife! There, kiss and be friends again."

"But—Gwendolen! I don't know how I am ever going to stand that name. Why, a body wouldn't *know* Sally Sellers in it. It's too large for her; kind of like a cherub in an ulster, and it's a most outlandish sort of a name, anyway, to my mind."

"You'll not hear her find fault with it, my lady."

"That's a true word. She takes to any kind of romantic rubbish like she was born to it. She never got it from me, that's sure. And sending her to that silly college hasn't helped the matter any—just the other way."

"Now hear her, Hawkins! Rowena-Ivanhoe College is the selectest and most aristocratic seat of learning for young ladies in our country. Under no circumstances can a girl get in there unless she is either very rich and fashionable or can prove four generations of what may be called American nobility. Castellated college-buildings—towers and turrets and an imitation moat—and everything about the place named out of Sir Walter Scott's books and redolent of royalty and state and style; and all the richest girls keep phaetons, and coachmen in livery, and riding-horses, with English grooms in plug hats and tight-buttoned coats, and top-boots, and a whip-handle without any whip to it, to ride sixty-three feet behind them—"

"And they don't learn a blessed thing, Washington Hawkins, not a single blessed thing but showy rubbish and unamerican pretentiousness. But send for the Lady Gwendolen—do; for I reckon the peerage regulations require that she must come home and let on to go into seclusion and mourn for those Arkansas blatherskites she's lost."

"My darling! Blatherskites? Remember—*noblesse oblige*."

"There, there—talk to me in your own tongue, Ross—you don't know any other, and you only botch it when you try. Oh, don't stare—it was a slip, and no crime; customs of a life-time can't be dropped in a second. Ross*more*—there, now, be appeased, and go along with you and attend to Gwendolen. Are you going to write, Washington?—or telegraph?"

"He will telegraph, dear."

"I thought as much," my lady muttered, as she left the room. "Wants it so the address will have to appear on the envelop. It will just make a fool of that child. She'll get it, of course, for if there are any other Selterses there they'll not be able to claim it. And just leave her alone to show it around and make the most of it.———Well, maybe she's forgivable for that. She's so poor and they're so rich, of course she's had her share of snubs from the livery-flunkey sort, and I reckon it's only human to want to get even."

Uncle Dan'l was sent with the telegram; for although a conspicuous object in a corner of the drawing-room was a telephone hanging on a transmitter, Washington found all attempts to raise the central office vain. The Colonel grumbled something about its being "*always* out of order when you've got particular and especial use for it," but he didn't explain that one of the reasons for this was that the thing was only a dummy and hadn't any wire attached to it. And yet the Colonel often used it—when visitors were present—and seemed to get messages through it. Mourning paper and a seal were ordered, then the friends took a rest.

Next afternoon, while Hawkins, by request, draped Andrew Jackson's portrait with crape, the rightful earl wrote off the family bereavement to the usurper in England—a letter which we have already read. He also, by letter to the village authorities at Duffy's Corners, Arkansas, gave order that the remains of the late twins be embalmed by some St. Louis expert and shipped at once to the usurper—with bill. Then he drafted out the Rossmore arms and motto on a great sheet of brown paper, and he and Hawkins took it to Hawkins's Yankee furniture-mender and at the end of an hour came back with a couple of stunning hatchments, which they nailed up on the front of the house—attractions calculated to draw, and they did; for it was mainly an idle and shiftless negro neighborhood, with plenty of ragged children and indolent dogs to spare for a point of interest like that, and keep on sparing them for it, days and days together.

The new earl found—without surprise—this society item in the evening paper, and cut it out and scrapbooked it:

By a recent bereavement our esteemed fellow citizen, Colonel Mulberry Sellers, Perpetual Member-at-large of the Diplomatic Body, succeeds, as rightful lord, to the great earldom of Rossmore, third by order of precedence in the earldoms of Great Britain, and will take early measures, by suit in the House of Lords, to wrest the title and estates from the present usurping holder of them. Until the season of mourning is past, the usual Thursday evening receptions at Rossmore Towers will be discontinued.

Lady Rossmore's comment—to herself:

"Receptions! People who don't rightly know him may think he is commonplace, but to my mind he is one of the most unusual men I ever saw. As for suddenness and capacity in imagining things, his beat don't exist, I reckon. As like as not it wouldn't have occurred to anybody else to name this poor old rat-trap Rossmore Towers, but it just comes natural to him. Well, no doubt it's a blessed thing to have an imagination that can always make you satisfied, no matter how you are fixed. Uncle Dave Hopkins used to always say, 'Turn me into John Calvin, and I want to know which place I'm going to; turn me into Mulberry Sellers and I don't care.'"

The rightful earl's comment—to himself:

"It's a beautiful name, beautiful. Pity I didn't think of it before I wrote the usurper. But I'll be ready for him when he answers."

CHAPTER 5

No answer to that telegram; no arriving daughter. Yet nobody showed any uneasiness or seemed surprised; that is, nobody but Washington. After three days of waiting, he asked Lady Rossmore what she supposed the trouble was. She answered, tranquilly;

"Oh, it's some notion of hers, you never can tell. She's a Sellers, all through—at least in some of her ways; and a Sellers can't tell you beforehand what he's going to do, because he don't know himself till he's done it. *She's* all right; no occasion to worry about *her*. When she's ready she'll come or she'll write, and you can't tell which, till it's happened."

It turned out to be a letter. It was handed in at that moment, and was received by the mother without trembling hands or feverish eagerness, or any other of the manifestations common in the case of long delayed answers to imperative telegrams. She polished her glasses with tranquility and thoroughness, pleasantly gossiping along, the while, then opened the letter and began to read aloud:

KENILWORTH KEEP, REDGAUNTLET HALL,
ROWENA-IVANHOE COLLEGE, THURSDAY.

DEAR PRECIOUS MAMMA ROSSMORE:

Oh, the joy of it!—you can't think. They had always turned up their noses at our pretentions, you know; and I had fought back as well as I could by turning up mine at theirs. They always said it might be something great and fine to be rightful Shadow of an earldom, but to merely be shadow *of* a shadow, and two or three times removed at that—pooh-pooh! And I always retorted that not to be able to show four generations of American-Colonial-Dutch-Peddler-and-Salt-Cod-McAllister-Nobility might be endurable, but to *have* to confess such an origin—pfew-few! Well, the telegram, it was just a cyclone! The messenger came right into the great Rob Roy Hall of Audience, as excited as he could be, singing out, "Dispatch for Lady Gwendolen Sellers!" and you ought to have seen that simpering chattering assemblage of pinchbeck aristocrats turn to stone! I was off in the corner, of course, by myself—it's where Cinderella belongs. I took the telegram and read it, and tried to faint—and I could have done it if I had had any preparation, but it was all so sudden, you know—but no matter, I did the next best thing: I put my handkerchief to my eyes and fled sobbing to my room, dropping the telegram as I started. I released one corner of my eye a moment—just enough to see the herd swarm for the telegram—and then continued my broken-hearted flight just as happy as a bird.

Then the visits of condolence began, and I had to accept the loan of Miss Augusta-Templeton-Ashmore Hamilton's quarters because the press was so great and there isn't room for three and a cat in mine. And I've been holding a Lodge of Sorrow ever since and defending myself against people's attempts to claim kin. And do you know, the very first girl to fetch her tears and sympathy to my market was that foolish Skimperton girl who has always snubbed me so shamefully and claimed lordship and precedence of the whole college because some ancestor of hers, some time or other, was a McAllister. Why it was like the bottom bird in the menagerie putting on airs because its head ancestor was a pterodactyl.

But the ger-reatest triumph of all was—guess. But you'll never. This is it.

That little fool and two others have always been fussing and fretting over which was entitled to precedence—by rank, you know. They've nearly starved themselves at it; for each claimed the right to take precedence of all the college in leaving the table, and so neither of them ever finished her dinner, but broke off in the middle and tried to get out ahead of the others. Well, after my first day's grief and seclusion—I was fixing up a mourning dress you see—I appeared at the public table again, and then—what do you think? Those three fluffy goslings sat there contentedly, and squared up the long famine—lapped and lapped, munched and munched, ate and ate, till the gravy appeared in their eyes—humbly waiting for the Lady Gwendolen to take precedence and move out first, you see!

Oh, yes, I've been having a darling good time. And do you know, not one of these collegians has had the cruelty to ask me how I came by my new name. With some, this is due to charity, but with the others it isn't. They refrain, not from native kindness but from educated discretion. I educated them.

Well, as soon as I shall have settled up what's left of the old scores and snuffed up a few more of those pleasantly intoxicating clouds of incense, I shall pack and depart homeward. Tell papa I am as fond of him as I am of my new name. I couldn't put it stronger than that. What an inspiration it was! But inspirations come easy to him.

These, from your loving daughter,

GWENDOLEN

Hawkins reached for the letter and glanced over it.

"Good hand," he said, "and full of confidence and animation, and goes racing right along. She's bright—that's plain."

"Oh, they're all bright—the Sellerses. Anyway, they would be, if there were any. Even those poor Latherses would have been bright if they had been Sellerses; I mean full blood. Of course they had a Sellers strain in them—a big strain of it, too—but being a Bland dollar don't make it a *dollar* just the same."

The seventh day after the date of the telegram Washington came dreaming down to breakfast and was set wide awake by an electrical spasm of pleasure. Here was the most beautiful young creature he had ever seen in his life. It was Sally Sellers Lady Gwendolen; she had come in the night. And it seemed to him that her clothes were the prettiest and the daintiest he had ever looked upon, and the most exquisitely contrived and fashioned and combined, as to decorative trimmings, and fixings, and melting harmonies of color. It was only a morning dress, and inexpensive, but he confessed to himself, in the English common to Cherokee Strip, that it was a "corker." And now, as he perceived, the reason why the Sellers household poverties and sterilities had been made to blosson like the rose, and charm the eye and satisfy the spirit, stood explained; here was the magician; here in the midst of her works, and furnishing in her own person the proper accent and climaxing finish of the whole.

"My daughter, Major Hawkins—come home to mourn; flown home at the call of affliction to help the authors of her being bear the burden of bereavement. She was very fond of the late earl—idolized him, sir, idolized him—"

"Why, father, I've never seen him."

"True—she's right, I was thinking of another—er—of her mother—"

"*I* idolized that smoked haddock?—that sentimental, spiritless—"

"I was thinking of myself! Poor noble fellow, we were inseparable com—"

"Hear the man! Mulberry Sel—Mul—Rossmore!—hang the troublesome name I can never—if I've heard you say once, I've heard you say a thousand times that if that poor sheep—"

"I was thinking of—of—I don't know who I was thinking of, and it doesn't make any difference anyway; *some*body idolized him, I recollect it as if it were yesterday; and—"

"Father, I am going to shake hands with Major Hawkins, and let the introduction work along and catch up at its leisure. I remember you very well indeed, Major Hawkins, although I was a little child when I saw you last; and I am very, very glad indeed to see you again and have you in our house as one of us;" and beaming in his face she finished her cordial shake with the hope that he had not forgotten her.

He was prodigiously pleased by her outspoken heartiness, and wanted to repay her by assuring her that he remembered her, and not only that but better even than he remembered his own children, but the facts would not quite warrant this; still, he stumbled through a tangled sentence which answered just as well, since the purport of it was an awkward and unintentional confession that her extraordinary beauty had so stupefied him that he hadn't got back to his bearings, yet, and therefore couldn't be certain as to whether he remembered her at all or not. The speech made him her friend; it couldn't well help it.

In truth the beauty of this fair creature was of a rare type, and may well excuse a moment of our time spent in its consideration. It did not consist in the *fact* that she had eyes, nose, mouth, chin, hair, ears, it consisted in their arrangement. In true beauty, more depends upon right location and judicious distribution of feature than upon multiplicity of them. So also as regards color. The very combination of colors which in a volcanic irruption would add beauty to a landscape might detach it from a girl. Such was Gwendolen Sellers.

The family circle being completed by Gwendolen's arrival, it was decreed that the official mourning should now begin; that it should begin at six o'clock every evening, (the dinner hour,) and end with the dinner.

"It's a grand old line, major, a sublime old line, and deserves to be mourned for, almost royally; almost imperially, I may say. Er–Lady Gwendolen–but she's gone; never mind; I wanted my Peerage; I'll fetch it myself, presently, and show you a thing or two that will give you a realizing idea of what our house is. I've been glancing through Burke, and I find that of William the Conqueror's sixty-four natural ch–my dear, would you mind getting me that book? It's on the escritoire in our boudoir. Yes, as I was saying, there's only St. Albans, Buccleugh and Grafton ahead of us on the list–all the rest of the British nobility are in procession behind us. Ah, thanks, my lady. Now then, we turn to William, and we find–letter for XYZ? Oh, splendid–when'd you get it?"

"Last night; but I was asleep before you came, you were out so late; and when I came to breakfast Miss Gwendolen–well, she knocked everything out of me, you know–"

"Wonderful girl, wonderful; her great origin is detectable in her step, her carriage, her features–but what does he *say?* Come, this is exciting."

"I haven't read it–er–Rossm–Mr. Rossm–er–"

"M'lord! Just cut it short like that. It's the English way. I'll open it. Ah, now let's see."

A. TO YOU KNOW WHO. Think I know you. Wait ten days. Coming to Washington.

The excitement died out of both men's faces. There was a brooding silence for a while, then the younger one said with a sigh:

"Why, *we* can't wait ten days for the money."

"No–the man's unreasonable; we are down to the bed rock, financially speaking."

"If we could explain to him in some way, that we are so situated that time is of the utmost importance to us–"

"Yes-yes, that's it–and so if it would be as convenient for him to come at once it would be a great accommodation to us, and one which we–which we–"

–"which we–wh–"

—"well, which we should sincerely appreciate—"

"That's it—and most gladly reciprocate—"

"Certainly—that'll fetch him. Worded right, if he's a *man*—got any of the *feelings* of a man, *sympathies* and all that, he'll be here inside of twenty-four hours. Pen and paper—come, we'll get right at it."

Between them they framed twenty-two different advertisements, but none was satisfactory. A main fault in all of them was urgency. That feature was very troublesome: if made prominent, it was calculated to excite Pete's suspicion; if modified below the suspicion-point it was flat and meaningless. Finally the Colonel resigned, and said—

"I have noticed, in such literary experiences as I have had, that one of the most taking things to do is to conceal your meaning when you are *trying* to conceal it. Whereas, if you go at literature with a free conscience and nothing to conceal, you can turn out a book, every time, that the very elect can't understand. They all do."

Then Hawkins resigned also, and the two agreed that they must manage to wait the ten days some how or other. Next, they caught a ray of cheer: since they had something definite to go upon, now, they could probably borrow money on the reward—enough, at any rate, to tide them over till they got it; and meantime the materializing recipe would be perfected, and then good bye to trouble for good and all.

The next day, May the tenth, a couple of things happened—among others. The remains of the noble Arkansas twins left our shores for England, consigned to Lord Rossmore, and Lord Rossmore's son, Kirkcudbright Llanover Marjoribanks Sellers Viscount Berkeley, sailed from Liverpool for America to place the reversion of the earldom in the hands of the rightful peer, Mulberry Sellers, of Rossmore Towers in the District of Columbia, U. S. A.

These two impressive shipments would meet and part in mid-Atlantic, five days later, and give no sign.

CHAPTER 6

In the course of time the twins arrived and were delivered to their great kinsman. To try to describe the rage of that old man would profit nothing, the attempt would fall so far short of the purpose. However when he had worn himself out and got quiet again, he looked the matter over and decided that the twins had some moral rights, although they had no legal ones; they were of his blood, and it could not be decorous to treat them as common clay. So he laid them with their majestic kin in the Cholmondeley church, with imposing state and ceremony, and added the supreme touch by officiating as chief mourner himself. But he drew the line at hatchments.

Our friends in Washington watched the weary days go by, while they waited for Pete and covered his name with reproaches because of his calamitous procrastinations. Meantime, Sally Sellers, who was as practical and democratic as the Lady Gwendolen Sellers was romantic and aristocratic, was leading a life of intense interest and activity and getting the most she could out of her double personality. All day long in the privacy of her work-room, Sally Sellers earned bread for the Sellers family; and all the evening Lady Gwendolen Sellers supported the Rossmore dignity. All day she was American, practically, and proud of the work of her head and hands and its commercial result; all the evening she took holiday and dwelt in a rich shadow-land peopled with titled and coroneted fictions. By day, to her, the place was a plain, unaffected, ramshackle old trap—just that, and nothing more; by night it was Rossmore Towers. At college she had learned a trade without knowing it. The girls had found out that she was the designer of her own gowns. She had no idle moments after that, and wanted none; for the exercise of an extraordinary gift is the supremest pleasure in life, and it was manifest that Sally Sellers possessed a gift of that sort in the matter of costume-designing. Within three days after reaching home she had hunted up some work; before Pete was yet due in Washington, and before the twins were fairly asleep in English soil, she was already nearly swamped with work, and the sacrificing of the family chromos for debt had got an effective check.

"She's a brick," said Rossmore to the Major; "just her father all over: prompt to labor with head or hands, and not ashamed of it; capable, always capable, let the enterprise be what it may; successful by nature —don't know what defeat is; thus, intensely and practically American by inhaled nationalism, and at the same time intensely and aristocratically European by inherited nobility of blood. Just me, exactly: Mulberry Sellers in matter of finance and invention; after office hours, what do you find? The same clothes, yes, but what's in them? Rossmore of the peerage."

The two friends had haunted the general post-office daily. At last they had their reward. Toward evening the 20th of May, they got a letter for XYZ. It bore the Washington postmark; the note itself was not dated. It said:

"Ash barrel back of lamp post Black horse Alley. If you are playing square go and set on it to-morrow morning 21st 10.22 not sooner not later wait till I come."

The friends cogitated over the note profoundly. Presently the earl said:

"Don't you reckon he's afraid we are a sheriff with a requisition?"

"Why, m'lord?"

"Because that's no place for a séance. Nothing friendly, nothing sociable about it. And at the same time, a body that wanted to know who was roosting on that ash-barrel without exposing himself by going near it, or seeming to be interested in it, could just stand on the street corner and take a glance down the alley and satisfy himself, don't you see?"

"Yes, his idea is plain, now. He seems to be a man that can't *be* candid and straightforward. He acts as if he thought we—shucks, I wish he had come out like a man and told us what hotel he—"

"Now you've struck it! you've struck it sure, Washington; he has told us."

"Has he?"

"Yes, he has; but he didn't mean to. That alley is a lonesome little pocket that runs along one side of the New Gadsby. That's his hotel."

"What makes you think that?"

"Why, I just know it. He's got a room that's just across from that lamp post. He's going to sit there perfectly comfortable behind his shutters at 10.22 to-morrow, and when he sees us sitting on the ash-barrel, he'll say to himself, 'I saw *one* of those fellows on the train'—and then he'll pack his satchel in half a minute and ship for the ends of the earth."

Hawkins turned sick with disappointment:

"Oh, dear, it's all up, Colonel—it's exactly what he'll do."

"Indeed he won't!"

"Won't he? Why?"

"Because *you* won't be holding the ash barrel down, it'll be me. You'll be coming in with an officer and a requisition in plain clothes —the officer, I mean—the minute you see him arrive and open up a talk with me."

"Well, what a head you have got, Colonel Sellers! I never should have thought of that in the world."

"Neither would any earl of Rossmore, betwixt William's contribution and Mulberry—*as* earl; but it's office hours, now, you see, and the earl in me sleeps. Come—I'll show you his very room."

They reached the neighborhood of the New Gadsby about nine in the evening, and passed down the alley to the lamp post.

"There you are," said the colonel, triumphantly, with a wave of his hand which took in the whole side of the hotel. "There it is—what did I tell you?"

"Well, but—why, Colonel, it's six stories high. I don't quite make out which window you—"

"All the windows, all of them. Let him have his choice—I'm indifferent, now that I have located him. You go and stand on the corner and wait; I'll prospect the hotel."

The earl drifted here and there through the swarming lobby, and finally took a waiting position in the neighborhood of the elevator. During an hour crowds went up and crowds came down; and all complete as to limbs; but at last the watcher got a glimpse of a figure that was satisfactory—got a glimpse of the back of it, though he had missed his chance at the face through waning alertness. The glimpse revealed a cowboy hat, and below it a plaided sack of rather loud pattern, and an empty sleeve pinned up to the shoulder. Then the elevator snatched the vision aloft and the watcher fled away in joyful excitement, and rejoined the fellow-conspirator.

"We've got him, Major—got him sure! I've seen him—seen him good; and I don't care where or when that man approaches me backwards, I'll recognize him everytime. We're all right. Now for the requisition."

They got it, after the delays usual in such cases. By half past eleven they were at home and happy, and went to bed full of dreams of the morrow's great promise.

Among the elevator load which had the suspect for fellow-passenger was a young kinsman of Mulberry Sellers, but Mulberry was not aware of it and didn't see him. It was Viscount Berkeley.

CHAPTER 7

Arrived in his room Lord Berkeley made preparations for that first and last and all-the-time duty of the visiting Englishman—the jotting down in his diary of his "impressions" to date. His preparations consisted in ransacking his "box" for a pen. There was a plenty of steel pens on his table with the ink bottle, but he was English. The English people manufacture steel pens for nineteen-twentieths of the globe, but they never use any themselves. They use exclusively the prehistoric quill. My lord not only found a quill pen, but the best one he had seen in several years—and after writing diligently for some time, closed with the following entry:

But in one thing I have made an immense mistake. I ought to have sunk my title and changed my name before I started.

He sat admiring that pen a while, and then went on:

"All attempts to mingle with the common people and become permanently one of them are going to fail, unless I can get rid of it, disappear from it, and re-appear with the solid protection of a new name. I am astonished and pained to see how eager the most of these Americans are to get acquainted with a lord, and how diligent they are in pushing attentions upon him. They lack English servility, it is true—but they could acquire it, with practice. My quality travels ahead of me in the most mysterious way. I write my family name without additions, on the register of this hotel, and imagine that I am going to pass for an obscure and unknown wanderer, but the clerk promptly calls out, 'Front! show his lordship to four-eighty-two!' and before I can get to the lift there is a reporter trying to interview me, as they call it. This sort of thing shall cease at once. I will hunt up the American Claimant the first thing in the morning, accomplish my mission, then change my lodging and vanish from scrutiny under a fictitious name."

He left his diary on the table, where it would be handy in case any new "impressions" should wake him up in the night, then he went to bed and presently fell asleep. An hour or two passed, and then he came slowly to consciousness with a confusion of mysterious and augmenting sounds hammering at the gates of his brain for admission; the next moment he was sharply awake, and those sounds burst with the rush and roar and boom of an undammed freshet into his ears. Banging and slamming of shutters; smashing of windows and the ringing clash of falling glass; clatter of flying feet along the halls; shrieks, supplications, dumb moanings of despair, within, hoarse shouts of command outside; cracklings and snappings, and the windy roar of victorious flames!

Bang, bang, bang! on the door, and a cry—

"Turn out—the house is on fire!"

The cry passed on, and the banging. Lord Berkeley sprang out of bed and moved with all possible speed toward the clothes-press in the darkness and the gathering smoke, but fell over a chair and lost his bearings. He groped desperately about on his hands, and presently struck his head against the table and was deeply grateful, for it gave him his bearings again, since it stood close by the door. He seized his most precious possession, his journaled Impressions of America, and darted from the room.

He ran down the deserted hall toward the red lamp which he knew indicated the place of a fire-escape. The door of the room beside it was open. In the room the gas was burning full head; on a chair was a pile of clothing. He ran to the window, could not get it up, but smashed it with a chair, and stepped out on the landing of the fire-escape; below him was a crowd of men, with a sprinkling of women and youth, massed in a ruddy light. Must he go down in his spectral night dress? No—this side of the house was not yet on fire except at the further end; he would snatch on those clothes. Which he did. They fitted well enough, though a trifle loosely, and they were just a shade loud as to pattern. Also as to hat—which was of a new breed to him, Buffalo Bill not having been to England yet. One side of the coat went on, but the other side refused; one of its sleeves was turned up and stitched to the shoulder. He started down without waiting to get it loose, made the trip successfully, and was promptly hustled outside the limit-rope by the police.

The cowboy hat and the coat but half on made him too much of a centre of attraction for comfort, although nothing could be more profoundly respectful, not to say deferential, than was the manner of the crowd toward him. In his mind he framed a discouraged remark for early entry in his diary: "It is of no use; they know a lord through any disguise, and show awe of him—even something very like fear, indeed."

Presently one of the gaping and adoring half-circle of boys ventured a timid question. My lord answered it. The boys glanced wonderingly at each other and from somewhere fell the comment—

"*English* cowboy! Well, if that ain't curious."

Another mental note to be preserved for the diary: "Cowboy. Now what might a cowboy be? Perhaps—" But the viscount perceived that some more questions were about to be asked; so he worked his way out of the crowd, released the sleeve, put on the coat and wandered away to seek a humble and obscure lodging. He found it and went to bed and was soon asleep.

In the morning, he examined his clothes. They were rather assertive, it seemed to him, but they were new and clean, at any rate. There was considerable property in the pockets. Item, five one-hundred dollar bills. Item, near fifty dollars in small bills and silver. Plug of tobacco. Hymn-book, which refuses to open; found to contain whiskey. Memorandum book bearing no name. Scattering entries in it, recording in a sprawling, ignorant hand, appointments, bets, horse-trades, and so on, with people of strange, hyphenated name—Six-Fingered Jake, Young-Man-afraid-of-his-Shadow, and the like. No letters, no documents.

The young man muses—maps out his course. His letter of credit is burned; he will borrow the small bills and the silver in these pockets, apply part of it to advertising for the owner, and use the rest for sustenance while he seeks work. He sends out for the morning paper, next, and proceeds to read about the fire. The biggest line in the display-head announces his own death! The body of the account furnishes all the particulars; and tells how, with the inherited heroism of his caste, he went on saving women and children until escape for himself was impossible; then with the eyes of weeping multitudes upon him, he stood with folded arms and sternly awaited the approach of the devouring fiend; "and so standing, amid a tossing sea of flame and on-rushing billows of smoke, the noble young heir of the great house of Rossmore was caught up in a whirlwind of fiery glory, and disappeared forever from the vision of men."

The thing was so fine and generous and knightly that it brought the moisture to his eyes. Presently he said to himself: "What to do is as plain as day, now. My Lord Berkeley is dead—let him stay so. Died creditably, too; that will make the calamity the easier for my father. And I don't have to report to the American Claimant, now. Yes, nothing could be better than the way matters have turned out. I have only to furnish myself with a new name, and take my new start in life totally untrammeled. Now I breathe my first breath of real freedom; and how fresh and breezy and inspiring it is! At last I am a man! a man on equal terms with my neighbor; and by my manhood, and by it alone, I shall rise and be seen of the world, or I shall sink from sight and deserve it. This *is* the gladdest day, and the proudest, that ever poured its sun upon my head!"

CHAPTER 8

"God bless my soul, Hawkins!"

The morning paper dropped from the Colonel's nerveless grasp.

"What is it?"

"He's gone!—the bright, the young, the gifted, the noblest of his illustrious race—gone! gone up in flames and unimaginable glory!"

"Who?"

"My precious, precious young kinsman—Kirkcudbright Llanover Marjoribanks Sellers Viscount Berkeley, son and heir of usurping Rossmore."

"No!"

"It's true—too true."

"When?"

"Last night."

"Where?"

"Right here in Washington, where he arrived from England last night, the papers say."

"You don't say!"

"Hotel burned down."

"What hotel?"

"The New Gadsby!"

"Oh, my goodness! And have we lost *both* of them?"

"Both *who?*"

"One-Arm Pete."

"Oh, great guns, I forgot all about him. Oh, I hope not."

"Hope! Well, I should say! Oh, we *can't* spare *him!* We can better afford to lose a million viscounts than our only support and stay."

They searched the paper diligently, and were appalled to find that a one-armed man had been seen flying along one of the halls of the hotel in his underclothing and apparently out of his head with fright, and as he would listen to no one and persisted in making for a stairway which would carry him to certain death, his case was given over as a hopeless one.

"Poor fellow," sighed Hawkins; "and he had friends so near. I wish we hadn't come away from there—maybe we could have saved him."

The earl looked up and said calmly—

"His being dead doesn't matter. He was uncertain before. We've got him sure, this time."

"Got him? How?"

"I will materialize him."

"Rossmore, don't—don't trifle with me. Do you mean that? Can you do it?"

"I can do it, just as sure as you are sitting there. And I will."

"Give me your hand, and let me have the comfort of shaking it. I was perishing, and you have put new life into me. Get at it, oh, get at it right away."

"It will take a little time, Hawkins, but there's no hurry, none in the world—in the circumstances. And of course certain duties have devolved upon me now, which necessarily claim my first attention. This poor young nobleman—"

"Why, yes, I am sorry for my heartlessness, and you smitten with this new family affliction. Of course you must materialize him first —I quite understand that."

"I—I—well, I wasn't meaning just that, but,—why, what am I thinking of! Of course I must materialize him. Oh, Hawkins, selfishness is the bottom trait in human nature; I was only thinking that now, with the usurper's heir out of the way—— But you'll forgive that momentary weakness, and forget it. Don't ever remember it against me that Mulberry Sellers was once mean enough to think the thought that I was thinking. I'll materialize him—I will, on my honor—and I'd do it were he a thousand heirs jammed into one and stretching in a solid rank from here to the stolen estates of Rossmore, and barring the road forever to the rightful earl!"

"There spoke the real Sellers—the other had a false ring, old friend."

"Hawkins, my boy, it just occurs to me—a thing I keep forgetting to mention—a matter that we've got to be mighty careful about."

"What is that?"

"We must keep absolutely still about these materializations. Mind, not a hint of them must escape—not a hint. To say nothing of how my wife and daughter—high-strung, sensitive organizations—might feel about them, the negroes wouldn't stay on the place a minute."

"That's true, they wouldn't. It's well you spoke, for I'm not naturally discreet with my tongue when I'm not warned."

Sellers reached out and touched a bell-button in the wall; set his eye upon the rear door and waited; touched it again and waited; and just as Hawkins was remarking admiringly that the Colonel was the most progressive and most alert man he had ever seen, in the matter of impressing into his service every modern convenience the moment it was invented, and always keeping breast to breast with the drum major in the great work of material civilization, he forsook the button (which hadn't any wire attached to it,) rang a vast dinner bell which stood on the table, and remarked that he had tried that new-fangled dry battery, now, to his entire satisfaction, and had got enough of it; and added—

"Nothing would do Graham Bell but I must try it; said the mere *fact* of my trying it would secure public confidence, and get it a chance to show what it could do. I *told* him that in theory a dry battery was just a curled darling and no mistake, but when it come to *practice*, sho!—and here's the result. Was I right? What should *you* say, Washington Hawkins? You've seen me try that button twice. Was I right?—that's the idea. Did I know what I was talking about, or didn't I?"

"Well, you know how I feel about you, Colonel Sellers, and always have felt. It seems to me that you always know everything about *everything*. If that man had known you as I know you he would have taken your judgment at the start, and dropped his dry battery where it was."

"Did you ring, Marse Sellers?"

"No, Marse Sellers didn't."

"Den it was you, Marse Washington. I's heah, suh."

"No, it wasn't Marse Washington, either."

"De good lan'! who did ring her, den?"

"Lord Rossmore rang it!"

The old negro flung up his hands and exclaimed—

"Blame my skin if I hain't gone en forgit dat name agin! Come heah, Jinny—run heah, honey."

Jinny arrived.

"You take dish-yer order de lord gwine to give you. I's gwine down suller and study dat name tell I git it."

"I take de order! Who's yo' nigger las' year? De bell rung for *you*."

"Dat don't make no diffunce. When a bell ring for anybody, en old marster tell me to—"

"Clear out, and settle it in the kitchen!"

The noise of the quarreling presently sank to a murmur in the distance, and the earl added: "That's a trouble with old house servants that were your slaves once and have been your personal friends always."

"Yes, and members of the family."

"Members of the family is just what they become—*the* members of the family, in fact. And sometimes master and mistress of the household. These two are mighty good and loving and faithful and honest, but hang it, they do just about as they please, they chip into a conversation whenever they want to, and the plain fact is, they ought to be killed."

It was a random remark, but it gave him an idea—however, nothing could happen without that result.

"What I wanted, Hawkins, was to send for the family and break the news to them."

"O, never mind bothering with the servants, then. I will go and bring them down."

While he was gone, the earl worked his idea.

"Yes," he said to himself, "when I've got the materializing down to a certainty, I will get Hawkins to kill them, and after that they will be under better control. Without doubt a materialized negro could easily be hypnotized into a state resembling silence. And this could be made permanent—yes, and also modifiable, at will—sometimes *very* silent, sometimes turn on more talk, more action, more emotion, according to what you want. It's a prime good idea. Make it adjustable—with a screw or something."

The two ladies entered, now, with Hawkins, and the two negroes followed, uninvited, and fell to brushing and dusting around, for they perceived that there was matter of interest to the fore, and were willing to find out what it was.

Sellers broke the news with stateliness and ceremony, first warning the ladies, with gentle art, that a pang of peculiar sharpness was about to be inflicted upon their hearts—hearts still sore from a like hurt, still lamenting a like loss—then he took the paper, and with trembling lips and with tears in his voice he gave them that heroic death-picture.

The result was a very genuine outbreak of sorrow and sympathy from all the hearers. The elder lady cried, thinking how proud that great-hearted young hero's mother would be, if she were living, and how unappeasable her grief; and the two old servants cried with her, and spoke out their applauses and their pitying lamentations with the eloquent sincerity and simplicity native to their race. Gwendolen was touched, and the romantic side of her nature was strongly wrought upon. She said that such a nature as that young man's was rarely and truly noble, and nearly perfect; and that with nobility of birth added it was entirely perfect. For such a man she could endure all things, suffer all things, even to the sacrificing of her life. She wished she could have seen him; the slightest, the most momentary, contact with such a spirit would have ennobled her own character and made ignoble thoughts and ignoble acts thereafter impossible to her forever.

"Have they found the body, Rossmore?" asked the wife.

"Yes, that is, they've found several. It must be one of them, but none of them are recognizable."

"What are you going to do?"

"I am going down there and identify one of them and send it home to the stricken father."

"But papa, did you ever see the young man?"

"No, Gwendolen—why?"

"How will you identify it?"

"I—well, you know it says none of them are recognizable. I'll send his father one of them—there's probably no choice."

Gwendolen knew it was not worth while to argue the matter further, since her father's mind was made up and there was a chance for him to appear upon that sad scene down yonder in an authentic and official way. So she said no more—till he asked for a basket.

"A basket, papa? What for?"

"It might be ashes."

CHAPTER 9

The earl and Washington started on the sorrowful errand, talking as they walked.

"And as *usual!*"

"What, Colonel?"

"Seven of them in that hotel. Actresses. And all burnt out, of course."

"Any of them burnt *up?*"

"Oh, no they escaped; they always do; but there's never a one of them that knows enough to fetch out her jewelry with her."

"That's strange."

"Strange—it's the most unaccountable thing in the world. Experience teaches them nothing; they can't seem to learn anything except out of a book. In some cases there's manifestly a fatality about it. For instance, take What's-her-name, that plays those sensational thunder and lightning parts. She's got a perfectly immense reputation—draws like a dog-fight—and it all came from getting burnt out in hotels."

"Why, how could that give her a reputation as an actress?"

"It didn't—it only made her name familiar. People want to see her play because her name is familiar, but they don't know what made it familiar, because they don't remember. First, she was at the bottom of the ladder, and absolutely obscure—wages thirteen dollars a week and find her own pads."

"Pads?"

"Yes—things to fat up her spindles with so as to be plump and attractive. Well, she got burnt out in a hotel and lost $30,000 worth of diamonds——"

"She? Where'd she get them?"

"Goodness knows—given to her, no doubt, by spoony young flats and sappy old bald-heads in the front row. All the papers were full of it. She struck for higher pay and got it. Well, she got burnt out again and lost all her diamonds, and it gave her such a lift that she went starring."

"Well, if hotel fires are all she's got to depend on to keep up her name, it's a pretty precarious kind of a reputation I should think."

"Not with her. No, anything but that. Because she's so lucky; born lucky, I reckon. Every time there's a hotel fire she's in it. She's always there—and if she can't be there herself, her diamonds are. Now you can't make anything out of that but just sheer luck."

"I never heard of such a thing. She must have lost quarts of diamonds."

"Quarts, she's lost bushels of them. It's got so that the hotels are superstitious about her. They won't let her in. They think there will be a fire; and besides, if she's there it cancels the insurance. She's been waning a little lately, but this fire will set her up. She lost $60,000 worth last night."

"I think she's a fool. If I had $60,000 worth of diamonds I wouldn't trust them in a hotel."

"I wouldn't either; but you can't teach an actress that. This one's been burnt out thirty-five times. And yet if there's a hotel fire in San Francisco to-night she's got to bleed again, you mark my words. Perfect ass; they say she's got diamonds in every hotel in the country."

When they arrived at the scene of the fire the poor old earl took one glimpse at the melancholy morgue and turned away his face overcome by the spectacle. He said:

"It is too true, Hawkins—recognition is impossible, not one of the five could be identified by its nearest friend. You make the selection, I can't bear it."

"Which one had I better—"

"Oh, take any of them. Pick out the best one."

However, the officers assured the earl—for they knew him, everybody in Washington knew him—that the position in which these bodies were found made it impossible that any one of them could be that of his noble young kinsman. They pointed out the spot where, if the newspaper account was correct, he must have sunk down to destruction; and at a wide distance from this spot they showed him where the young man must have gone down in case he was suffocated in his room; and they showed him still a third place, quite remote, where he might possibly have found his death if perchance he tried to escape by the side exit toward the rear. The old Colonel brushed away a tear and said to Hawkins—

"As it turns out there was something prophetic in my fears. Yes, it's a matter of ashes. Will you kindly step to a grocery and fetch a couple more baskets?"

Reverently they got a basket of ashes from each of those now hallowed spots, and carried them home to consult as to the best manner of forwarding them to England, and also to give them an opportunity to "lie in state,"—a mark of respect which the colonel deemed obligatory, considering the high rank of the deceased.

They set the baskets on the table in what was formerly the library, drawingroom and workshop—now the Hall of Audience—and went up stairs to the lumber room to see if they could find a British flag to use as a part of the outfit proper to the lying in state. A moment later, Lady Rossmore came in from the street and caught sight of the baskets just as old Jinny crossed her field of vision. She quite lost her patience and said—

"Well, what will you do next? What in the world possessed you to clutter up the parlor table with these baskets of ashes?"

"Ashes?" And she came to look. She put up her hands in pathetic astonishment. "Well, I *never* see de like!"

"Didn't you do it?"

"Who, me? Clah to goodness it's de fust time I've sot eyes on 'em, Miss Polly. Dat's Dan'l. Dat ole moke is losin' his mine."

But it wasn't Dan'l, for he was called, and denied it.

"Dey ain't no way to 'splain dat. Wen hit's one er dese-yer common 'currences, a body kin reckon maybe de cat—"

"Oh!" and a shudder shook Lady Rossmore to her foundations. "I see it all. Keep away from them—they're *his*."

"*His*, m'lady?"

"Yes—your young Marse Sellers from England that's burnt up."

She was alone with the ashes—alone before she could take half a breath. Then she went after Mulberry Sellers, purposing to make short work with his program, whatever it might be; "for," said she, "when his sentimentals are up, he's a numskull, and there's no knowing what extravagance he'll contrive, if you let him alone." She found him. He had found the flag and was bringing it. When she heard that his idea was to have the remains "lie in state, and invite the government and the public," she broke it up. She said—

"Your intentions are all right—they always are—you want to do honour to the remains, and surely nobody can find any fault with that, for he was your kin; but you are going the wrong way about it, and you will see it yourself if you stop and think. You can't file around a basket of ashes trying to look sorry for it and make a sight that is really solemn, because the solemner it is, the more it isn't—anybody can see that. It would be so with one basket; it would be three times so with three. Well, it stands to reason that if it wouldn't be solemn with one mourner, it wouldn't be with a procession—and there would be five thousand people here. I don't know but it would be pretty near ridiculous; I think it would. No, Mulberry, they can't lie in state—it would be a mistake. Give that up and think of something else."

So he gave it up; and not reluctantly, when he had thought it over and realized how right her instinct was. He concluded to merely sit up with the remains—just himself and Hawkins. Even this seemed a doubtful attention, to his wife, but she offered no objection, for it was plain that he had a quite honest and simple-hearted desire to do the friendly and honourable thing by these forlorn poor relics which could command no hospitality in this far off land of strangers but his. He draped the flag about the baskets, put some crape on the door-knob, and said with satisfaction—

"There—he is as comfortable, now, as we can make him in the circumstances. Except—yes, we must strain a point there—one must do as one would wish to be done by—he must have it."

"Have what, dear?"

"Hatchment."

The wife felt that the house-front was standing about all it could well stand, in that way; the prospect of another stunning decoration of that nature distressed her, and she wished the thing had not occurred to him. She said, hesitatingly—

"But I thought such an honour as that wasn't allowed to any but very *very* near relations, who—"

"Right, you are quite right, my lady, perfectly right; but there aren't any nearer relatives than relatives by usurpation. We cannot avoid it; we are slaves of aristocratic custom and must submit."

The hatchments were unnecessarily generous, each being as large as a blanket, and they were unnecessarily volcanic, too, as to variety and violence of color, but they pleased the earl's barbaric eye, and they satisfied his taste for symmetry and completeness, too, for they left no waste room to speak of on the house-front.

Lady Rossmore and her daughter assisted at the sitting-up till near midnight, and helped the gentlemen to consider what ought to be done next with the remains. Rossmore thought they ought to be sent home—with a committee and resolutions,—at once. But the wife was doubtful. She said:

"Would you send all of the baskets?"

"Oh, yes, all."

"All at once?"

"To his father? Oh, no—by no means. Think of the shock. No—one at a time; break it to him by degrees."

"Would *that* have that effect, father?"

"Yes, my daughter. Remember, you are young and elastic, but he is old. To send him the whole at once might well be more than he could bear. But mitigated—one basket at a time, with restful intervals between, he would be used to it by the time he got all of him. And sending him in three ships is safer anyway. On account of wrecks and storms."

"I don't like the idea, father. If I were his father it would be dreadful to have him coming in that—in that—"

"On the installment plan," suggested Hawkins, gravely, and proud of being able to help.

"Yes—dreadful to have him coming in that incoherent way. There would be the strain of suspense upon me all the time. To have so depressing a thing as a funeral impending, delayed, waiting, unaccomplished—"

"Oh, no, my child," said the earl reassuringly, "there would be nothing of that kind; so old a gentleman could not endure a long-drawn suspense like that. There will be three funerals."

Lady Rossmore looked up surprised, and said—

"How is *that* going to make it easier for him? It's a total mistake, to my mind. He ought to be buried all at once; I'm sure of it."

"I should think so, too," said Hawkins.

"And certainly *I* should," said the daughter.

"You are all wrong," said the earl. "You will see it yourselves, if you think. Only one of these baskets has got him in it."

"Very well, then," said Lady Rossmore, "the thing is perfectly simple —bury *that* one."

"Certainly," said Lady Gwendolen.

"But it is *not* simple," said the earl, "because we do not know which basket he is in. We know he is in *one* of them, but that is all we *do* know. You see now, I reckon, that I was right; it takes three funerals, there is no other way."

"And three graves and three monuments and three inscriptions?" asked the daughter.

"Well—yes—to do it right. That is what I should do."

"It could not be done so, father. Each of the inscriptions would give the same name and the same facts and say he was under each and all of these monuments, and that would not answer at all."

The earl nestled uncomfortably in his chair.

"No," he said, "that *is* an objection. That is a serious objection. I see no way out."

There was a general silence for a while. Then Hawkins said—

"It seems to me that if we mixed the three ramifications together—"

The earl grasped him by the hand and shook it gratefully.

"It solves the whole problem," he said. "One ship, one funeral, one grave, one monument—it is admirably conceived. It does you honor, Major Hawkins, it has relieved me of a most painful embarrassment and distress, and it will save that poor stricken old father much suffering. Yes, he shall go over in one basket."

"When?" asked the wife.

"To-morrow—immediately, of course."

"I would wait, Mulberry."

"Wait? Why?"

"*You* don't want to break that childless old man's heart."

"God knows I don't!"

"Then wait till he sends for his son's remains. If you do that, you will never have to give him the last and sharpest pain a parent can know—I mean, the *certainty* that his son is dead. For he will never send."

"Why won't he?"

"Because to send—and find out the truth—would rob him of the one precious thing left him, the *uncertainty,* the dim hope that maybe, after all, his boy escaped, and he will see him again some day."

"Why Polly, he'll know by the *papers* that he was burnt up."

"He won't let himself *believe* the papers; he'll argue against anything and everything that proves his son is dead; and he will keep that up and live on it, and on nothing else till he dies. But if the *remains* should actually come, and be put before that poor old dim-hoping soul—"

"Oh, my God, they never shall! Polly, you've saved me from a crime, and I'll bless you for it always. *Now* we know what to do. We'll place them reverently away, and he shall never know."

CHAPTER 10

The young Lord Berkeley, with the fresh air of freedom in his nostrils, was feeling invincibly strong for his new career; and yet—and yet—if the fight should prove a very hard one at first, very discouraging, very taxing on untoughened moral sinews, he might in some weak moment want to retreat. Not likely, of course, but possibly that might happen. And so on the whole it might be pardonable caution to burn his bridges behind him. Oh, without doubt. He must not stop with advertising for the owner of that money, but must put it where he could not borrow from it himself, meantime, under stress of circumstances. So he went down town, and put in his advertisement, then went to a bank and handed in the $500 for deposit.

"What name?"

He hesitated and colored a little; he had forgotten to make a selection. He now brought out the first one that suggested itself—

"Howard Tracy."

When he was gone the clerks, marveling, said—

"The cowboy blushed."

The first step was accomplished. The money was still under his command and at his disposal, but the next step would dispose of that difficulty. He went to another bank and drew upon the first bank for the $500 by check. The money was collected and deposited a second time to the credit of Howard Tracy. He was asked to leave a few samples of his signature, which he did. Then he went away, once more proud and of perfect courage, saying—

"No help for me now, for henceforth I couldn't draw that money without identification, and that is become legally impossible. No resources to fall back on. It is work or starve from now to the end. I am ready—and not afraid!"

Then he sent this cablegram to his father:

"Escaped unhurt from burning hotel. Have taken fictitious name. Good-bye."

During the evening, while he was wandering about in one of the outlying districts of the city, he came across a small brick church, with a bill posted there with these words printed on it: "MECHANICS' CLUB DEBATE. ALL INVITED." He saw people, apparently mainly of the working class, entering the place, and he followed and took his seat. It was a humble little church, quite bare as to ornamentation. It had painted pews without cushions, and no pulpit, properly speaking, but it had a platform. On the platform sat the chairman, and by his side sat a man who held a manuscript in his hand and had the waiting look of one who is going to perform the principal part. The church was soon filled with a quiet and orderly congregation of decently dressed and modest people. This is what the chairman said:

"The essayist for this evening is an old member of our club whom you all know, Mr. Parker, assistant editor of the Daily Democrat. The subject of his essay is the American Press, and he will use as his text a couple of paragraphs taken from Mr. Matthew Arnold's new book. He asks me to read these texts for him. The first is as follows:

"'Goethe says somewhere that "the thrill of awe," that is to say, REVERENCE,' is the best thing humanity has."

"Mr. Arnold's other paragraph is as follows:

"'I should say that if one were searching for the best means to efface and kill in a whole nation the discipline of respect, one could not do better than take the American newspapers.'"

Mr. Parker rose and bowed, and was received with warm applause. He then began to read in a good round resonant voice, with clear enunciation and careful attention to his pauses and emphases. His points were received with approval as he went on.

The essayist took the position that the most important function of a public journal in any country was the propagating of national feeling and pride in the national name—the keeping the people "in love with *their* country and *its* institutions, and shielded from the allurements of alien and inimical systems." He sketched the manner in which the reverent Turkish or Russian journalist fulfilled this function—the one assisted by the prevalent "discipline of respect" for the bastinado, the other for Siberia. Continuing, he said—

The chief function of an English journal is that of all other journals the world over: it must keep the public eye fixed admiringly upon certain things, and keep it diligently diverted from certain others. For instance, it must keep the public eye fixed admiringly upon the glories of England, a processional splendor stretching its receding line down the hazy vistas of time, with the mellowed lights of a thousand years glinting from its banners; and it must keep it diligently diverted from the fact that all these glories were for the enrichment and aggrandizement of the petted and privileged few, at cost of the blood and sweat and poverty of the unconsidered masses who achieved them but might not enter in and partake of them. It must keep the public eye fixed in loving and awful reverence upon the throne as a sacred thing, and diligently divert it from the fact that no throne was ever set up by the unhampered vote of a majority of any nation; and that hence no throne exists that has a right to exist, and no symbol of it, flying from any flagstaff, is righteously entitled to wear any device but the skull and crossbones of that kindred industry which differs from royalty only business-wise—merely as retail differs from wholesale. It must keep the citizen's eye fixed in reverent docility upon that curious invention of machine politics, an Established Church, and upon that bald contradiction of common justice, a hereditary nobility; and diligently divert it from the fact that the one damns him if he doesn't wear its collar, and robs him under the gentle name of taxation whether he wears it or not, and the other gets all the honors while he does all the work.

The essayist thought that Mr. Arnold, with his trained eye and intelligent observation, ought to have perceived that the very quality which he so regretfully missed from our press—respectfulness, reverence—was exactly the thing which would make our press useless to us if it had it—rob it of the very thing which differentiates it from all other journalism in the world and makes it distinctively and preciously American, its frank and cheerful irreverence being by all odds the most valuable of all its qualities. "For its mission—overlooked by Mr. Arnold—is to stand guard over a nation's liberties, not its humbugs and shams." He thought that if during fifty years the institutions of the old world could be exposed to the fire of a flouting and scoffing press like ours, "monarchy and its attendant crimes would disappear from Christendom." Monarchists might doubt this; then "why not persuade the Czar to give it a trial in Russia?" Concluding, he said—

Well, the charge is, that our press has but little of that old world quality, reverence. Let us be candidly grateful that it is so. With its limited reverence it at least reveres the things which this nation reveres, as a rule, and that is sufficient: what other people revere is fairly and properly matter of light importance to us. Our press does not reverence kings, it does not reverence so called nobilities, it does not reverence established ecclesiastical slaveries, it does not reverence laws which rob a younger son to fatten an elder one, it does not reverence any fraud or sham or infamy, howsoever old or rotten or holy, which sets one citizen above his neighbor by accident of birth; it does not reverence any law or custom, howsoever old or decayed or sacred, which shuts against the best man in the land the best place in the land and the divine right to prove property and go up and occupy it. In the sense of the poet Goethe—that meek idolater of provincial three carat royalty and nobility—our press is certainly bankrupt in the "thrill of awe"—otherwise reverence; reverence for nickel plate and brummagem. Let us sincerely hope that this fact will remain a fact forever: for to my mind a discriminating irreverence is the creator and protector of human liberty—even as the other thing is the creator, nurse, and steadfast protector of all forms of human slavery, bodily and mental.

Tracy said to himself, almost shouted to himself, "I'm glad I came to this country. I was right. I was right to seek out a land where such healthy principles and theories are in men's hearts and minds. Think of the innumerable slaveries imposed by misplaced reverence! How well he brought that out, and how true it is. There's manifestly prodigious force in reverence. If you can get a man to reverence your ideals, he's your slave. Oh, yes, in all the ages the peoples of Europe have been diligently taught to avoid reasoning about the shams of monarchy and nobility, been taught to avoid examining them, been taught to reverence them; and now, as a natural result, to reverence them is second nature. In order to shock them it is sufficient to inject a thought of the opposite kind into their dull minds. For ages, any expression of so-called irreverence from their lips has been sin and crime. The sham and swindle of all this is apparent the moment one reflects that he is himself the only legitimately qualified judge of what *is* entitled to reverence and what is not. Come, I hadn't thought of that before, but it is true, absolutely true. What right has Goethe, what right has Arnold, what right has any dictionary, to define the word Irreverence for me? What their ideals are is nothing to me. So long as I reverence my own ideals my whole duty is done, and I commit no profanation if I laugh at theirs. I may scoff at other people's ideals as much as I want to. It is my right and my privilege. No man has any right to deny it."

Tracy was expecting to hear the essay debated, but this did not happen. The chairman said, by way of explanation—

"I would say, for the information of the strangers present here, that in accordance with our custom the subject of this meeting will be debated at the next meeting of the club. This is in order to enable our members to prepare what they may wish to say upon the subject with pen and paper, for we are mainly mechanics and unaccustomed to speaking. We are obliged to write down what we desire to say."

Many brief papers were now read, and several off-hand speeches made in discussion of the essay read at the last meeting of the club, which had been a laudation, by some visiting professor, of college culture, and the grand results flowing from it to the nation. One of the papers was read by a man approaching middle age, who said he hadn't had a college education, that he had got his education in a printing office, and had been graduated from there into the patent office, where he had been a clerk now for a great many years. Then he continued to this effect:

The essayist contrasted the America of to-day with the America of bygone times, and certainly the result is the exhibition of a mighty progress. But I think he a little overrated the college-culture share in the production of that result. It can no doubt be easily shown that the colleges have contributed the intellectual part of this progress, and that that part is vast; but that the material progress has been immeasurably vaster, I think you will concede. Now I have been looking over a list of inventors—the creators of this amazing material development—and I find that they were not college-bred men. Of course there are exceptions—like Professor Henry of Princeton, the inventor of Mr. Morse's system of telegraphy—but these exceptions are few. It is not overstatement to say that the imagination-stunning material development of this century, the only century worth living in since time itself was invented, is the creation of men not college-bred. We think we see what these inventors have done: no, we see only the visible vast frontage of their work; behind it is their far vaster work, and it is invisible to the careless glance. They have reconstructed this nation—made it over, that is—and metaphorically speaking, have multiplied its numbers almost beyond the power of figures to express. I will explain what I mean. What constitutes the population of a land? Merely the numberable packages of meat and bones in it called by courtesy men and women? Shall a million ounces of brass and a million ounces of gold be held to be of the same value? Take a truer standard: the measure of a man's contributing capacity to his time and his people—the work he can do—and then number the population of this country to-day, as multiplied by what a man can now do, more than his grandfather could do. By this standard of measurement, this nation, two or three generations ago, consisted of mere cripples, paralytics, dead men, as compared with the men of to-day. In 1840 our population was 17,000,000. By way of rude but striking illustration, let us consider, for argument's sake, that four of these millions consisted of aged people, little children, and other incapables, and that the remaining 13,000,000 were divided and employed as follows:

2,000,000 as ginners of cotton.
6,000,000 (women) as stocking-knitters.

2,000,000 (women) as thread-spinners.
500,000 as screw makers.
400,000 as reapers, binders, etc.
1,000,000 as corn shellers.
40,000 as weavers.
1,000 as stitchers of shoe soles.

Now the deductions which I am going to append to these figures may sound extravagant, but they are not. I take them from Miscellaneous Documents No. 50, second session 45th Congress, and they are official and trustworthy. To-day, the work of those 2,000,000 cotton-ginners is done by 2,000 men; that of the 6,000,000 stocking-knitters is done by 3,000 boys; that of the 2,000,000 thread-spinners is done by 1,000 girls; that of the 500,000 screw makers is done by 500 girls; that of the 400,000 reapers, binders, etc., is done by 4,000 boys; that of the 1,000,000 corn shellers is done by 7,500 men; that of the 40,000 weavers is done by 1,200 men; and that of the 1,000 stitchers of shoe soles is done by 6 men. To bunch the figures, 17,000 persons to-day do the above work, whereas fifty years ago it would have taken thirteen millions of persons to do it. Now then, how many of that ignorant race—our fathers and grandfathers—with their ignorant methods, would it take to do our work to-day? It would take forty thousand millions—a hundred times the swarming population of China—twenty times the present population of the globe. You look around you and you see a nation of sixty millions —apparently; but secreted in their hands and brains, and invisible to your eyes, is the true population of this Republic, and it numbers forty billions! It is the stupendous creation of those humble unlettered, un-college-bred inventors—all honor to their name.

"How grand that is!" said Tracy, as he wended homeward. "What a civilization it is, and what prodigious results these are! and brought about almost wholly by common men; not by Oxford-trained aristocrats, but men who stand shoulder to shoulder in the humble ranks of life and earn the bread that they eat. Again, I'm glad I came. I have found a country at last where one may start fair, and breast to breast with his fellow man, rise by his own efforts, and be something in the world and be proud of that something; not be something created by an ancestor three hundred years ago."

CHAPTER 11

During the first few days he kept the fact diligently before his mind that he was in a land where there was "work and bread for all." In fact, for convenience' sake he fitted it to a little tune and hummed it to himself; but as time wore on the fact itself began to take on a doubtful look, and next the tune got fatigued and presently ran down and stopped. His first effort was to get an upper clerkship in one of the departments, where his Oxford education could come into play and do him service. But he stood no chance whatever. There, competency was no recommendation; political backing, without competency, was worth six of it. He was glaringly English, and that was necessarily against him in the political centre of a nation where both parties prayed for the Irish cause on the house-top and blasphemed it in the cellar. By his dress he was a cowboy; that won him respect—when his back was not turned—but it couldn't get a clerkship for him. But he had said, in a rash moment, that he would wear those clothes till the owner or the owner's friends caught sight of them and asked for that money, and his conscience would not let him retire from that engagement now.

At the end of a week things were beginning to wear rather a startling look. He had hunted everywhere for work, descending gradually the scale of quality, until apparently he had sued for all the various kinds of work a man without a special calling might hope to be able to do, except ditching and the other coarse manual sorts—and had got neither work nor the promise of it.

He was mechanically turning over the leaves of his diary, meanwhile, and now his eye fell upon the first record made after he was burnt out:

"I myself did not doubt my stamina before, nobody could doubt it now, if they could see how I am housed, and realize that I feel absolutely no disgust with these quarters, but am as serenely content with them as any dog would be in a similar kennel. Terms, twenty-five dollars a week. I said I would start at the bottom. I have kept my word."

A shudder went quaking through him, and he exclaimed—

"What have I been thinking of! *This* the bottom! Mooning along a whole week, and these terrific expenses climbing and climbing all the time! I must end this folly straightway."

He settled up at once and went forth to find less sumptuous lodgings. He had to wander far and seek with diligence, but he succeeded. They made him pay in advance—four dollars and a half; this secured both bed and food for a week. The good-natured, hard-worked landlady took him up three flights of narrow, uncarpeted stairs and delivered him into his room. There were two double-bedsteads in it, and one single one. He would be allowed to sleep alone in one of the double beds until some new boarder should come, but he wouldn't be charged extra.

So he would presently be required to sleep with some stranger! The thought of it made him sick. Mrs. Marsh, the landlady, was very friendly and hoped he would like her house—they all liked it, she said.

"And they're a very nice set of boys. They carry on a good deal, but that's their fun. You see, this room opens right into this back one, and sometimes they're all in one and sometimes in the other; and hot nights they all sleep on the roof when it don't rain. They get out there the minute it's hot enough. The season's so early that they've already had a night or two up there. If you'd like to go up and pick out a place, you can. You'll find chalk in the side of the chimney where there's a brick wanting. You just take the chalk and—but of course you've done it before."

"Oh, no, I haven't."

"Why, of course you haven't—what am I thinking of? Plenty of room on the Plains without chalking, I'll be bound. Well, you just chalk out a place the size of a blanket anywhere on the tin that ain't already marked off, you know, and that's your property. You and your bed-mate take turn-about carrying up the blanket and pillows and fetching them down again; or one carries them up and the other fetches them down, you fix it the way you like, you know. You'll like the boys, they're everlasting sociable—except the printer. He's the one that sleeps in that single bed—the strangest creature; why, I don't believe you could get that man to sleep with another man, not if the house was afire. Mind you, I'm not just talking, I *know*. The boys tried him, to see. They took his bed out one night, and so when he got home about three in the morning—he was on a morning paper then, but he's on an evening one now—there wasn't any place for him but with the iron-moulder; and if you'll believe me, he just set up the rest of the night—he did, honest. They say he's cracked, but it ain't so, he's English—they're awful particular. You won't mind my saying that. You—you're English?"

"Yes."

"I thought so. I could tell it by the way you mispronounce the words that's got *a*'s in them, you know; such as saying loff when you mean laff—but you'll get over that. He's a right down good fellow, and a little sociable with the photographer's boy and the caulker and the blacksmith that work in the navy yard, but not so much with the others. The fact is, though it's private, and the others don't know it, he's a kind of an aristocrat, his father being a doctor, and *you* know what style *that* is—in England, I mean, because in this country a doctor ain't so *very* much, even it he's *that*. But over there of course it's different. So this chap had a falling out with his father, and was pretty high strung, and just cut for this country, and the first he knew he had to get to work or starve. Well, he'd been to college, you see, and so he judged *he* was all right—did you say anything?"

"No—I only sighed."

"And there's where he was mistaken. Why, he mighty near starved. And I reckon he would have starved sure enough, if some jour' printer or other hadn't took pity on him and got him a place as apprentice. So he learnt the trade, and then he was all right—but it was a close call. Once he thought he had *got* to haul in his pride and holler for his father and—why, you're sighing again. Is anything the matter with you?—does my clatter—"

"Oh, *dear*-no. Pray go on—I like it."

"Yes, you see, he's been over here ten years; he's twenty-eight, now, and he ain't pretty well satisfied in his mind, because he can't get reconciled to being a mechanic and associating with mechanics, he being, as he says to me, a *gentleman*, which is a pretty plain letting-on that the boys ain't, but of course I know enough not to let *that* cat out of the bag."

"Why—would there by any harm in it?"

"Harm in it? They'd lick him, wouldn't they? Wouldn't *you*? Of course you would. Don't you ever let a man say you ain't a gentleman in *this* country. But laws, what am I thinking about? I reckon a body would think twice before he said a cowboy wasn't a gentleman."

A trim, active, slender and very pretty girl of about eighteen walked into the room now, in the most satisfied and unembarrassed way. She was cheaply but smartly and gracefully dressed, and the mother's quick glance at the stranger's face as he rose, was of the kind which inquires what effect has been produced, and expects to find indications of surprise and admiration.

"This is my daughter Hattie—we call her Puss. It's the new boarder, Puss." This without rising.

The young Englishman made the awkward bow common to his nationality and time of life in circumstances of delicacy and difficulty, and these were of that sort; for, being taken by surprise, his natural, life-long self sprang to the front, and that self of course would not know just how to act when introduced to a chambermaid, or to the heiress of a mechanics' boarding house. His other self—the self which recognized the equality of all men—would have managed the thing better, if it hadn't been caught off guard and robbed of its chance. The young girl paid no attention to the bow, but put out her hand frankly and gave the stranger a friendly shake and said—

"How do you do?"

Then she marched to the one washstand in the room, tilted her head this way and that before the wreck of a cheap mirror that hung above it, dampened her fingers with her tongue, perfected the circle of a little lock of hair that was pasted against her forehead, then began to busy herself with the slops.

"Well, I must be going—it's getting towards supper time. Make yourself at home, Mr. Tracy, you'll hear the bell when it's ready."

The landlady took her tranquil departure, without commanding either of the young people to vacate the room. The young man wondered a little that a mother who seemed so honest and respectable should be so thoughtless, and was reaching for his hat, intending to disembarrass the girl of his presence; but she said—

"Where are you going?"

"Well—nowhere in particular, but as I am only in the way here—"

"Why, who said you were in the way? Sit down—I'll move you when you are in the way."

She was making the beds, now. He sat down and watched her deft and diligent performance.

"What gave you that notion? Do you reckon I need a whole room just to make up a bed or two in?"

"Well no, it wasn't that, exactly. We are away up here in an empty house, and your mother being gone—"

The girl interrupted him with an amused laugh, and said—

"Nobody to protect me? Bless you, I don't need it. I'm not afraid. I might be if I was alone, because I do hate ghosts, and I don't deny it. Not that I believe in them, for I don't. I'm only just afraid of them."

"How can you be afraid of them if you don't believe in them?"

"Oh, *I* don't know the *how* of it—that's too many for *me;* I only know it's *so*. It's the same with Maggie Lee."

"Who is that?"

"One of the boarders; young lady that works in the factry."

"She works in a factory?"

"Yes. Shoe factry."

"In a shoe factory; and you call her a young lady?"

"Why, she's only twenty-two; what should you call her?"

"I wasn't thinking of her age, I was thinking of the title. The fact is, I came away from England to get away from artificial forms—for artificial forms suit artificial people only—and here you've got them too. I'm sorry. I hoped you had only men and women; everybody equal; no differences in rank."

The girl stopped with a pillow in her teeth and the case spread open below it, contemplating him from under her brows with a slightly puzzled expression. She released the pillow and said—

"Why, they *are* all equal. Where's any difference in rank?"

"If you call a factory girl a young *lady,* what do you call the President's wife?"

"Call her an *old* one."

"Oh, you make age the only distinction?"

"There ain't any other to make as far as I can see."

"Then *all* women are ladies?"

"Certainly they are. All the respectable ones."

"Well, that puts a better face on it. Certainly there is no harm in a title when it is given to everybody. It is only an offense and a wrong when it is restricted to a favored few. But Miss—er—"

"Hattie."

"Miss Hattie, be frank; confess that that title *isn't* accorded by everybody to everybody. The rich American doesn't call her cook a lady—isn't that so?"

"Yes, it's so. What of it?"

He was surprised and a little disappointed, to see that his admirable shot had produced no perceptible effect.

"What *of* it?" he said. "Why this: equality is *not* conceded here, after all, and the Americans are no better off than the English. In fact there's no difference."

"Now *what* an idea. There's nothing in a title except what is *put* into it—you've said that yourself. Suppose the title is *clean,* instead of lady. You get that?"

"I believe so. Instead of speaking of a woman as a *lady,* you substitute clean and say she's a clean person."

"That's it. In England the swell folks don't speak of the working people as gentlemen and ladies?"

"Oh, no."

"And the working people don't call *themselves* gentlemen and ladies?"

"Certainly not."

"So if you used the other word there wouldn't be any change. The swell people wouldn't call anybody but themselves 'clean,' and those others would drop sort of meekly into their way of talking and *they* wouldn't call themselves clean. We don't do that way here. Everybody calls himself a lady or gentleman, and thinks he *is,* and don't care what anybody else thinks him, so long as he don't say it out loud. You think there's no difference. You *knuckle down* and we *don't.* Ain't that a difference?"

"It is a difference I hadn't thought of; I admit that. Still—*calling* one's self a lady doesn't—er—"

"I wouldn't go on if I were you."

Howard Tracy turned his head to see who it might be that had introduced this remark. It was a short man about forty years old, with sandy hair, no beard, and a pleasant face badly freckled but alive and intelligent, and he wore slop-shop clothing which was neat but showed wear. He had come from the front room beyond the hall, where he had left his hat, and he had a chipped and cracked white wash-bowl in his hand. The girl came and took the bowl.

"I'll get it for you. You go right ahead and *give* it to him, Mr. Barrow. He's the new boarder—Mr. Tracy—and I'd just got to where it was getting too deep for me."

"Much obliged if you will, Hattie. I was coming to borrow of the boys." He sat down at his ease on an old trunk, and said, "I've been listening and got interested; and as I was saying, I wouldn't go on, if I were you. You see where you are coming to, don't you? *Calling* yourself a lady doesn't elect you; that is what you were going to say; and you saw that if you said it you were going to run right up against another difference that you hadn't thought of: to-wit, Whose *right* is it to do the electing? Over there, twenty thousand people in a million elect themselves gentlemen and ladies, and the nine hundred and eighty thousand *accept* that decree and swallow the affront which it puts upon them. Why, if they didn't accept it, it wouldn't *be* an election, it would be a dead letter and have no force at all. Over here the twenty thousand would-be exclusives come up to the polls and vote themselves to be ladies and gentlemen. But the thing doesn't stop there. The nine hundred and eighty thousand come and vote themselves to be ladies and gentlemen *too,* and that elects the whole nation. Since the whole million vote themselves ladies and gentlemen, there is no question about that election. It *does* make absolute equality, and there is no fiction about it; while over yonder the *inequality,* (by decree of the infinitely feeble, and consent of the infinitely strong,) is also absolute—as real and absolute as our equality."

Tracy had shrunk promptly into his English shell when this speech began, notwithstanding he had now been in severe training several weeks for contact and intercourse with the common herd on the common herd's terms; but he lost no time in pulling himself out again, and so by the time the speech was finished his valves were open once more, and he was forcing himself to accept without resentment the common herd's frank fashion of dropping sociably into other people's conversations unembarrassed and uninvited. The process was not very difficult this time, for the man's smile and voice and manner were persuasive and winning. Tracy would even have liked him on the spot, but for the fact—fact which he was not really aware of—that the equality of men was not yet a reality to him, it was only a theory; the *mind* perceived, but the *man* failed to feel it. It was Hattie's ghost over again, merely turned around. Theoretically Barrow was his equal, but it was distinctly distasteful to see him exhibit it. He presently said:

"I hope in all sincerity that what you have said is true, as regards the Americans, for doubts have crept into my mind several times. It seemed that the equality must be ungenuine where the sign-names of castes were still in vogue; but those sign-names have certainly lost their offence and are wholly neutralized, nullified and harmless if they are the undisputed property of every individual in the nation. I think I realize that caste does not exist and cannot exist except by common consent of the masses outside of its limits. I thought caste created itself and perpetuated itself; but it seems quite true that it only creates itself, and is perpetuated by the people whom it despises, and who can dissolve it at any time by assuming its mere sign-names themselves."

"It's what I think. There isn't any power on earth that can prevent England's thirty millions from electing themselves dukes and duchesses to-morrow and calling themselves so. And within six months all the former dukes and duchesses would have retired from the business. I wish they'd try that. Royalty itself couldn't survive such a process. A handful of frowners against thirty million laughers in a state of irruption: Why, it's Herculaneum against Vesuvius; it would take another eighteen centuries to find that Herculaneum after the cataclysm. What's a Colonel in our South? He's a nobody; because they're all colonels down there. No, Tracy" (shudder from Tracy) "nobody in England would call you a gentleman and you wouldn't call yourself one; and I tell you it's a state of things that makes a man put himself into most unbecoming attitudes sometimes—the broad and general recognition and acceptance of caste *as* caste does, I mean. Makes him do it unconsciously—being bred in him, you see, and never thought over and reasoned out. You couldn't conceive of the Matterhorn being flattered by the notice of one of your comely little English hills, could you?"

"Why, no."

"Well, then, let a man in his right mind try to conceive of Darwin feeling flattered by the notice of a princess. It's so grotesque that it—well, it paralyzes the imagination. Yet that Memnon *was* flattered by the notice of that statuette; he *says* so—says so himself. The system that can make a god disown his godship and profane it—oh, well, it's all wrong, it's all wrong and ought to be abolished, I should say."

The mention of Darwin brought on a literary discussion, and this topic roused such enthusiasm in Barrow that he took off his coat and made himself the more free and comfortable for it, and detained him so long that he was still at it when the noisy proprietors of the room came shouting and skylarking in and began to romp, scuffle, wash, and otherwise entertain themselves. He lingered yet a little longer to offer the hospitalities of his room and his book shelf to Tracy and ask him a personal question or two:

"What is your trade?"

"They—well, they call me a cowboy, but that is a fancy; I'm not that. I haven't any trade."

"What do you work at for your living?"

"Oh, anything—I mean I *would* work at anything I could get to do, but thus far I haven't been able to find an occupation."

"Maybe I can help you; I'd like to try."

"I shall be very glad. I've tried, myself, to weariness."

"Well, of course where a man hasn't a regular trade he's pretty bad off in this world. What you needed, I reckon, was less book learning and more bread-and-butter learning. I don't know what your father could have been thinking of. You ought to have had a trade, you ought to have had a trade, by *all* means. But never mind about that; we'll stir up *something* to do, I guess. And don't you get homesick; that's a bad business. We'll talk the thing over and look around a little. You'll come out all right. Wait for me—I'll go down to supper with you."

By this time Tracy had achieved a very friendly feeling for Barrow and would have *called* him a friend, maybe, if not taken too suddenly on a straight-out requirement to realize on his theories. He was glad of his society, anyway, and was feeling lighter hearted than before. Also he was pretty curious to know what vocation it might be which had furnished Barrow such a large acquaintanceship with books and allowed him so much time to read.

CHAPTER 12

Presently the supper bell began to ring in the depths of the house, and the sound proceeded steadily upward, growing in intensity all the way up towards the upper floors. The higher it came the more maddening was the noise, until at last what it lacked of being absolutely deafening, was made up of the sudden crash and clatter of an avalanche of boarders down the uncarpeted stairway. The peerage did not go to meals in this fashion; Tracy's training had not fitted him to enjoy this hilarious zoölogical clamor and enthusiasm. He had to confess that there was something about this extraordinary outpouring of animal spirits which he would have to get inured to before he could accept it. No doubt in time he would prefer it; but he wished the process might be modified and made just a little more gradual, and not quite so pronounced and violent. Barrow and Tracy followed the avalanche down through an ever increasing and ever more and more aggressive stench of bygone cabbage and kindred smells; smells which are to be found nowhere but in a cheap private boarding house; smells which once encountered can never be forgotten; smells which encountered generations later are instantly recognizable, but never recognizable with pleasure. To Tracy these odors were suffocating, horrible, almost unendurable; but he held his peace and said nothing. Arrived in the basement, they entered a large dining-room where thirty-five or forty people sat at a long table. They took their places. The feast had already begun and the conversation was going on in the liveliest way from one end of the table to the other. The table cloth was of very coarse material and was liberally spotted with coffee stains and grease. The knives and forks were iron, with bone handles, the spoons appeared to be iron or sheet iron or something of the sort. The tea and coffee cups were of the commonest and heaviest and most durable stone ware. All the furniture of the table was of the commonest and cheapest sort. There was a single large thick slice of bread by each boarder's plate, and it was observable that he economized it as if he were not expecting it to be duplicated. Dishes of butter were distributed along the table within reach of people's arms, if they had long ones, but there were no private butter plates. The butter was perhaps good enough, and was quiet and well behaved; but it had more bouquet than was necessary, though nobody commented upon that fact or seemed in any way disturbed by it. The main feature of the feast was a piping hot Irish stew made of the potatoes and meat left over from a procession of previous meals. Everybody was liberally supplied with this dish. On the table were a couple of great dishes of sliced ham, and there were some other eatables of minor importance—preserves and New Orleans molasses and such things. There was also plenty of tea and coffee of an infernal sort, with brown sugar and condensed milk, but the milk and sugar supply was not left at the discretion of the boarders, but was rationed out at headquarters—one spoonful of sugar and one of condensed milk to each cup and no more. The table was waited upon by two stalwart negro women who raced back and forth from the bases of supplies with splendid dash and clatter and energy. Their labors were supplemented after a fashion by the young girl Puss. She carried coffee and tea back and forth among the boarders, but she made pleasure excursions rather than business ones in this way, to speak strictly. She made jokes with various people. She chaffed the young men pleasantly—and wittily, as she supposed, and as the rest also supposed, apparently, judging by the applause and laughter which she got by her efforts. Manifestly she was a favorite with most of the young fellows and sweetheart of the rest of them. Where she conferred notice she conferred happiness, as was seen by the face of the recipient; and at the same time she conferred unhappiness—one could see it fall and dim the faces of the other young fellows like a shadow. She never "Mistered" these friends of hers, but called them "Billy," "Tom," "John," and they called her "Puss" or "Hattie."

Mr. Marsh sat at the head of the table, his wife sat at the foot. Marsh was a man of sixty, and was an American; but if he had been born a month earlier he would have been a Spaniard. He was plenty good enough Spaniard as it was; his face was very dark, his hair very black, and his eyes were not only exceedingly black but were very intense, and there was something about them that indicated that they could burn with passion upon occasion. He was stoop-shouldered and lean-faced, and the general aspect of him was disagreeable; he was evidently not a very companionable person. If looks went for anything, he was the very opposite of his wife, who was all motherliness and charity, good will and good nature. All the young men and the women called her Aunt Rachael, which was another sign. Tracy's wandering and interested eye presently fell upon one boarder who had been overlooked in the distribution of the stew. He was very pale and looked as if he had but lately come out of a sick bed, and also as if he ought to get back into it again as soon as possible. His face was very melancholy. The waves of laughter and conversation broke upon it without affecting it any more than if it had been a rock in the sea and the words and the laughter veritable waters. He held his head down and looked ashamed. Some of the women cast glances of pity toward him from time to time in a furtive and half afraid way, and some of the youngest of the men plainly had compassion on the young fellow—a compassion exhibited in their faces but not in any more active or compromising way. But the great majority of the people present showed entire indifference to the youth and his sorrows. Marsh sat with his head down, but one could catch the malicious gleam of his eyes through his shaggy brows. He was watching that young fellow with evident relish. He had not neglected him through carelessness, and apparently the table understood that fact. The spectacle was making Mrs. Marsh very uncomfortable. She had the look of one who hopes against hope that the impossible may happen. But as the impossible did not happen, she finally ventured to speak up and remind her husband that Nat Brady hadn't been helped to the Irish stew.

Marsh lifted his head and gasped out with mock courtliness, "Oh, he hasn't, hasn't he? What a pity that is. I don't know how I came to overlook him. Ah, he must pardon me. You must indeed Mr—er—Baxter—Barker, you must pardon me. I—er—my attention was directed to some other matter, I don't know what. The thing that grieves me mainly is, that it happens every meal now. But you must try to overlook these little things, Mr. Bunker, these little neglects on my part. They're always likely to happen with me in any case, and they are especially likely to happen where a person has—er—well, where a person is, say, about three weeks in arrears for his board. You get my meaning?—you get my idea? Here is your Irish stew, and—er—it gives me the greatest pleasure to send it to you, and I hope that you will enjoy the charity as much as I enjoy conferring it."

A blush rose in Brady's white cheeks and flowed slowly backward to his ears and upward toward his forehead, but he said nothing and began to eat his food under the embarrassment of a general silence and the sense that all eyes were fastened upon him. Barrow whispered to Tracy:

"The old man's been waiting for that. He wouldn't have missed that chance for anything."

"It's a brutal business," said Tracy. Then he said to himself, purposing to set the thought down in his diary later:

"Well, here in this very house is a republic where all are free and equal, if men are free and equal anywhere in the earth, therefore I have arrived at the place I started to find, and I am a man among men, and on the strictest equality possible to men, no doubt. Yet here on the threshold I find an inequality. There are people at this table who are looked up to for some reason or another, and here is a poor devil of a boy who is looked down upon, treated with indifference, and shamed by humiliations, when he has committed no crime but that common one of being poor. Equality ought to make men noble-minded. In fact I had supposed it did do that."

After supper, Barrow proposed a walk, and they started. Barrow had a purpose. He wanted Tracy to get rid of that cowboy hat. He didn't see his way to finding mechanical or manual employment for a person rigged in that fashion. Barrow presently said—

"As I understand it, you're not a cowboy."

"No, I'm not."

"Well, now if you will not think me too curious, how did you come to mount that hat? Where'd you get it?"

Tracy didn't know quite how to reply to this, but presently said,—

"Well, without going into particulars, I exchanged clothes with a stranger under stress of weather, and I would like to find him and re-exchange."

"Well, why don't you find him? Where is he?"

"I don't know. I supposed the best way to find him would be to continue to wear his clothes, which are conspicuous enough to attract his attention if I should meet him on the street."

"Oh, very well," said Barrow, "the rest of the outfit is well enough, and while it's not too conspicuous, it isn't quite like the clothes that anybody else wears. Suppress the hat. When you meet your man he'll recognize the rest of his suit. That's a mighty embarrassing hat, you know, in a centre of civilization like this. I don't believe an angel could get employment in Washington in a halo like that."

Tracy agreed to replace the hat with something of a modester form, and they stepped aboard a crowded car and stood with others on the rear platform. Presently, as the car moved swiftly along the rails, two men crossing the street caught sight of the backs of Barrow and Tracy, and both exclaimed at once, "There he is!" It was Sellers and Hawkins. Both were so paralyzed with joy that before they could pull themselves together and make an effort to stop the car, it was gone too far, and they decided to wait for the next one. They waited a while; then it occurred to Washington that there could be no use in chasing one horse-car with another, and he wanted to hunt up a hack. But the Colonel said:

"When you come to think of it, there's no occasion for that at all. Now that I've got him materialized, I can command his motions. I'll have him at the house by the time we get there."

Then they hurried off home in a state of great and joyful excitement.

The hat exchange accomplished, the two new friends started to walk back leisurely to the boarding house. Barrow's mind was full of curiosity about this young fellow. He said,—

"You've never been to the Rocky Mountains?"

"No."

"You've never been out on the plains?"

"No."

"How long have you been in this country?"

"Only a few days."

"You've never been in America before?"

"No."

Then Barrow communed with himself. "Now what odd shapes the notions of romantic people take. Here's a young fellow who's read in England about cowboys and adventures on the plains. He comes here and buys a cowboy's suit. Thinks he can play himself on folks for a cowboy, all inexperienced as he is. Now the minute he's caught in this poor little game, he's ashamed of it and ready to retire from it. It is that exchange that he has put up as an explanation. It's rather thin, too thin altogether. Well, he's young, never been anywhere, knows nothing about the world, sentimental, no doubt. Perhaps it was the natural thing for him to do, but it was a most singular choice, curious freak, altogether."

Both men were busy with their thoughts for a time, then Tracy heaved a sigh and said,—

"Mr. Barrow, the case of that young fellow troubles me."

"You mean Nat Brady?"

"Yes, Brady, or Baxter, or whatever it was. The old landlord called him by several different names."

"Oh, yes, he has been very liberal with names for Brady, since Brady fell into arrears for his board. Well, that's one of his sarcasms—the old man thinks he's great on sarcasm."

"Well, what is Brady's difficulty? What is Brady—who is he?"

"Brady is a tinner. He's a young journeyman tinner who was getting along all right till he fell sick and lost his job. He was very popular before he lost his job; everybody in the house liked Brady. The old man was rather especially fond of him, but you know that when a man loses his job and loses his ability to support himself and to pay his way as he goes, it makes a great difference in the way people look at him and feel about him."

"Is that so! *Is* it so?"

Barrow looked at Tracy in a puzzled way. "Why of course it's so. Wouldn't you know that, naturally. Don't you know that the wounded deer is always attacked and killed by its companions and friends?"

Tracy said to himself, while a chilly and boding discomfort spread itself through his system, "In a republic of deer and men where all are free and equal, misfortune is a crime, and the prosperous gore the unfortunate to death." Then he said aloud, "Here in the boarding house, if one would have friends and be popular instead of having the cold shoulder turned upon him, he must be prosperous."

"Yes," Barrow said, "that is so. It's their human nature. They do turn against Brady, now that he's unfortunate, and they don't like him as well as they did before; but it isn't because of any lack in Brady—he's just as he was before, has the same nature and the same impulses, but they—well, Brady is a thorn in their consciences, you see. They know they ought to help him and they're too stingy to do it, and they're ashamed of themselves for that, and they ought also to hate themselves on that account, but instead of that they hate Brady because he makes them ashamed of themselves. I say that's human nature; that occurs everywhere; this boarding house is merely the world in little, it's the case all over—they're all alike. In prosperity we are popular; popularity comes easy in that case, but when the other thing comes our friends are pretty likely to turn against us."

Tracy's noble theories and high purposes were beginning to feel pretty damp and clammy. He wondered if by any possibility he had made a mistake in throwing his own prosperity to the winds and taking up the cross of other people's unprosperity. But he wouldn't listen to that sort of thing; he cast it out of his mind and resolved to go ahead resolutely along the course he had mapped out for himself.

Extracts from his diary:

Have now spent several days in this singular hive. I don't know quite what to make out of these people. They have merits and virtues, but they have some other qualities, and some ways that are hard to get along with. I can't enjoy them. The moment I appeared in a hat of the period, I noticed a change. The respect which had been paid me before, passed suddenly away, and the people became friendly—more than that—they became familiar, and I'm not used to familiarity, and can't take to it right off; I find that out. These people's familiarity amounts to impudence, sometimes. I suppose it's all right; no doubt I can get used to it, but it's not a satisfactory process at all. I have accomplished my dearest wish, I am a man among men, on an equal footing with Tom, Dick and Harry, and yet it isn't just exactly what I thought it was going to be. I—I miss home. Am obliged to say I am homesick. Another thing—and this is a confession—a reluctant one, but I will make it: The thing I miss most and most severely, is the respect, the deference, with which I was treated all my life in England, and which seems to be somehow necessary to me. I get along very well without the luxury and the wealth and the sort of society I've been accustomed to, but I do miss the respect and can't seem to get reconciled to the absence of it. There is respect, there is deference here, but it doesn't fall to my share. It is lavished on two men. One of them is a portly man of middle age who is a retired plumber. Everybody is pleased to have that man's notice. He's full of pomp and circumstance and self complacency and bad grammar, and at table he is Sir Oracle and when he opens his mouth not any dog in the kennel barks. The other person is a policeman at the capitol-building. He represents the government. The deference paid to these two men is not so very far short of that which is paid to an earl in England, though the method of it differs. Not so much courtliness, but the deference is all there.

Yes, and there is obsequiousness, too.

It does rather look as if in a republic where all are free and equal, prosperity and position constitute *rank.*

CHAPTER 13

The days drifted by, and they grew ever more dreary. For Barrow's efforts to find work for Tracy were unavailing. Always the first question asked was, "What Union do you belong to?"

Tracy was obliged to reply that he didn't belong to any trade-union.

"Very well, then, it's impossible to employ you. My men wouldn't stay with me if I should employ a 'scab,' or 'rat,'" or whatever the phrase was.

Finally, Tracy had a happy thought. He said, "Why the thing for me to do, of course, is to *join* a trade-union."

"Yes," Barrow said, "that is the thing for you to do—if you can."

"If I *can*? Is it difficult?"

"Well, yes," Barrow said, "it's sometimes difficult—in fact, very difficult. But you can try, and of course it will be best to try."

Therefore Tracy tried; but he did not succeed. He was refused admission with a good deal of promptness, and was advised to go back home, where he belonged, not come here taking honest men's bread out of their mouths. Tracy began to realize that the situation was desperate, and the thought made him cold to the marrow. He said to himself, "So there is an aristocracy of position here, and an aristocracy of prosperity, and apparently there is also an aristocracy of the ins as opposed to the outs, and I am with the outs. So the ranks grow daily, here. Plainly there are all kinds of castes here and only one that I belong to, the outcasts." But he couldn't even smile at his small joke, although he was obliged to confess that he had a rather good opinion of it. He was feeling so defeated and miserable by this time that he could no longer look with philosophical complacency on the horseplay of the young fellows in the upper rooms at night. At first it had been pleasant to see them unbend and have a good time after having so well earned it by the labors of the day, but now it all rasped upon his feelings and his dignity. He lost patience with the spectacle. When they were feeling good, they shouted, they scuffled, they sang songs, they romped about the place like cattle, and they generally wound up with a pillow fight, in which they banged each other over the head, and threw the pillows in all directions, and every now and then he got a buffet himself; and they were always inviting him to join in. They called him "Johnny Bull," and invited him with excessive familiarity to take a hand. At first he had endured all this with good nature, but latterly he had shown by his manner that it was distinctly distasteful to him, and very soon he saw a change in the manner of these young people toward him. They were souring on him as they would have expressed it in their language. He had never been what might be called popular. That was hardly the phrase for it; he had merely been liked, but now dislike for him was growing. His case was not helped by the fact that he was out of luck, couldn't get work, didn't belong to a union, and couldn't gain admission to one. He got a good many slights of that small ill-defined sort that you can't quite put your finger on, and it was manifest that there was only one thing which protected him from open insult, and that was his muscle. These young people had seen him exercising, mornings, after his cold sponge bath, and they had perceived by his performance and the build of his body, that he was athletic, and also versed in boxing. He felt pretty naked now, recognizing that he was shorn of all respect except respect for his fists. One night when he entered his room he found about a dozen of the young fellows there carrying on a very lively conversation punctuated with horse-laughter. The talking ceased instantly, and the frank affront of a dead silence followed. He said,

"Good evening gentlemen," and sat down.

There was no response. He flushed to the temples but forced himself to maintain silence. He sat there in this uncomfortable stillness some time, then got up and went out.

The moment he had disappeared he heard a prodigious shout of laughter break forth. He saw that their plain purpose had been to insult him. He ascended to the flat roof, hoping to be able to cool down his spirit there and get back his tranquility. He found the young tinner up there, alone and brooding, and entered into conversation with him. They were pretty fairly matched, now, in unpopularity and general ill-luck and misery, and they had no trouble in meeting upon this common ground with advantage and something of comfort to both. But Tracy's movements had been watched, and in a few minutes the tormentors came straggling one after another to the roof, where they began to stroll up and down in an apparently purposeless way. But presently they fell to dropping remarks that were evidently aimed at Tracy, and some of them at the tinner. The ringleader of this little mob was a short-haired bully and amateur prize-fighter named Allen, who was accustomed to lording it over the upper floor, and had more than once shown a disposition to make trouble with Tracy. Now there was an occasional cat-call, and hootings, and whistlings, and finally the diversion of an exchange of connected remarks was introduced:

"How many does it take to make a pair?"

"Well, two generally makes a pair, but sometimes there ain't stuff enough in them to make a whole pair." General laugh.

"What were you saying about the English a while ago?"

"Oh, nothing, the English are all right, only—I—"

"What was it you *said* about them?"

"Oh, I only said they swallow well."

"Swallow better than other people?"

"Oh, yes, the English swallow a good deal better than other people."

"What is it they swallow best?"

"Oh, insults." Another general laugh.

"Pretty hard to make 'em fight, ain't it?"

"No, tain't hard to make 'em fight."

"Ain't it, really?"

"No, tain't hard. It's impossible." Another laugh.

"This one's kind of spiritless, that's certain."

"*Couldn't* be the other way—in his case."

"Why?"

"Don't you know the secret of his birth?"

"No! has *he* got a secret of his birth?"

"You bet he has."

"What is it?"

"His father was a wax-figger."

Allen came strolling by where the pair were sitting; stopped, and said to the tinner;

"How are you off for friends, these days?"

"Well enough off."

"Got a good many?"

"Well, as many as I need."

"A friend is valuable, sometimes—as a protector, you know. What do you reckon would happen if I was to snatch your cap off and slap you in the face with it?"

"Please don't trouble me, Mr. Allen, I ain't doing anything to you."

"You answer me! What do you reckon would happen?"

"Well, I don't know."

Tracy spoke up with a good deal of deliberation and said,

"Don't trouble the young fellow, I can tell you what would happen."

"Oh, you can, can you? Boys, Johnny Bull can tell us what would happen if I was to snatch this chump's cap off and slap him in the face with it. Now you'll see."

He snatched the cap and struck the youth in the face, and before he could inquire what was going to happen, it had already happened, and he was warming the tin with the broad of his back. Instantly there was a rush, and shouts of "A ring, a ring, make a ring! Fair play all round! Johnny's grit; give him a chance."

The ring was quickly chalked on the tin, and Tracy found himself as eager to begin as he could have been if his antagonist had been a prince instead of a mechanic. At bottom he was a little surprised at this, because although his theories had been all in that direction for some time, he was not prepared to find himself actually eager to measure strength with quite so common a man as this ruffian. In a moment all the windows in the neighborhood were filled with people, and the roofs also. The men squared off, and the fight began. But Allen stood no chance whatever, against the young Englishman. Neither in muscle nor in science was he his equal. He measured his length on the tin time and again; in fact, as fast as he could get up he went down again, and the applause was kept up in liberal fashion from all the neighborhood around. Finally, Allen had to be helped up. Then Tracy declined to punish him further and the fight was at an end. Allen was carried off by some of his friends in a very much humbled condition, his face black and blue and bleeding, and Tracy was at once surrounded by the young fellows, who congratulated him, and told him that he had done the whole house a service, and that from this out Mr. Allen would be a little more particular about how he handled slights and insults and maltreatment around amongst the boarders.

Tracy was a hero now, and exceedingly popular. Perhaps nobody had ever been quite so popular on that upper floor before. But if being discountenanced by these young fellows had been hard to bear, their lavish commendations and approval and hero-worship was harder still to endure. He felt degraded, but he did not allow himself to analyze the reasons why, too closely. He was content to satisfy himself with the suggestion that he looked upon himself as degraded by the public spectacle which he had made of himself, fighting on a tin roof, for the delectation of everybody a block or two around. But he wasn't entirely satisfied with that explanation of it. Once he went a little too far and wrote in his diary that his case was worse than that of the prodigal son. He said the prodigal son merely fed swine, he didn't have to chum with them. But he struck that out, and said "All men are equal. I will not disown my principles. These men are as good as I am."

Tracy was become popular on the lower floors also. Everybody was grateful for Allen's reduction to the ranks, and for his transformation from a doer of outrages to a mere threatener of them. The young girls, of whom there were half a dozen, showed many attentions to Tracy, particularly that boarding house pet Hattie, the landlady's daughter. She said to him, very sweetly,—

"I think you're ever so nice." And when he said, "I'm glad you think so, Miss Hattie," she said, still more sweetly,—

"Don't call me Miss Hattie—call me Puss."

Ah, here was promotion! He had struck the summit. There were no higher heights to climb in that boarding house. His popularity was complete.

In the presence of people, Tracy showed a tranquil outside, but his heart was being eaten out of him by distress and despair.

In a little while he should be out of money, and then what should he do? He wished, now, that he had borrowed a little more liberally from that stranger's store. He found it impossible to sleep. A single torturing, terrifying thought went racking round and round in his head, wearing a groove in his brain: What should he do—What was to become of him? And along with it began to intrude a something presently which was very like a wish that he had not joined the great and noble ranks of martyrdom, but had stayed at home and been content to be merely an earl and nothing better, with nothing more to do in this world of a useful sort than an earl finds to do. But he smothered that part of his thought as well as he could; he made every effort to drive it away, and with fair success, but he couldn't keep it from intruding a little now and then, and when it intruded it came suddenly and nipped him like a bite, a sting, a burn. He recognized that thought by the peculiar sharpness of its pang. The others were painful enough, but that one cut to the quick when it came. Night after night he lay tossing to the music of the hideous snoring of the honest bread-winners until two and three o'clock in the morning, then got up and took refuge on the roof, where he sometimes got a nap and sometimes failed entirely. His appetite was leaving him and the zest of life was going along with it. Finally, one day, being near the imminent verge of total discouragement, he said to himself—and took occasion to blush privately when he said it, "If my father knew what my American name is,—he—well, my duty to my father rather *requires* that I furnish him my name. I have no right to make his days and nights unhappy, I can do enough unhappiness for the family all by myself. Really he ought to know what my American name is." He thought over it a while and framed a cablegram in his mind to this effect:

"My American name is Howard Tracy."

That wouldn't be suggesting anything. His father could understand that as he chose, and doubtless he would understand it as it was meant, as a dutiful and affectionate desire on the part of a son to make his old father happy for a moment. Continuing his train of thought, Tracy said to himself, "Ah, but if he should cable me to come home! I—I—couldn't do that—I *mustn't* do that. I've started out on a mission, and I mustn't turn my back on it in cowardice. No, no, I couldn't go home, at—at—least I shouldn't want to go home." After a reflective pause: "Well, maybe—perhaps—it would be my *duty* to go in the circumstances; he's very old and he does need me by him to stay his footsteps down the long hill that inclines westward toward the sunset of his life. Well, I'll think about that. Yes, of course it wouldn't be right to stay here. I—if I—well, perhaps I could just drop him a line and put it off a little while and satisfy him in that way. It would be—well, it would mar everything to have him require me to come instantly." Another reflective pause—then: "And yet if he should do that I don't know but—oh, dear me—*home!* how good it sounds! and a body is excusable for wanting to see his home again, now and then, anyway."

He went to one of the telegraph offices in the avenue and got the first end of what Barrow called the "usual Washington courtesy," where "they treat you as a tramp until they find out you're a congressman, and then they slobber all over you." There was a boy of seventeen on duty there, tying his shoe. He had his foot on a chair and his back turned towards the wicket. He glanced over his shoulder, took Tracy's measure, turned back, and went on tying his shoe. Tracy finished writing his telegram and waited, still waited, and still waited, for that performance to finish, but there didn't seem to be any finish to it; so finally Tracy said:

"Can't you take my telegram?"

The youth looked over his shoulder and said, by his manner, not his words:

"Don't you think you could wait a minute, if you tried?"

However, he got the shoe tied at last, and came and took the telegram, glanced over it, then looked up surprised, at Tracy. There was something in his look that bordered upon respect, almost reverence, it seemed to Tracy, although he had been so long without anything of this kind he was not sure that he knew the signs of it.

The boy read the address aloud, with pleased expression in face and voice.

"The Earl of Rossmore! Cracky! Do you know him?"

"Yes."

"Is that so! Does he know you?"

"Well—yes."

"Well, I swear! Will he answer you?"

"I think he will."

"Will he though? Where'll you have it sent?"

"Oh, nowhere. I'll call here and get it. When shall I call?"

"Oh, I don't know—I'll send it to you. Where shall I send it? Give me your address; I'll send it to you soon's it comes."

But Tracy didn't propose to do this. He had acquired the boy's admiration and deferential respect, and he wasn't willing to throw these precious things away, a result sure to follow if he should give the address of that boarding house. So he said again that he would call and get the telegram, and went his way.

He idled along, reflecting. He said to himself, "There *is* something pleasant about being respected. I have acquired the respect of Mr. Allen and some of those others, and almost the deference of some of them on pure merit, for having thrashed Allen. While their respect and their deference—if it is deference—is pleasant, a deference based upon a sham, a shadow, does really seem pleasanter still. It's no real merit to be in correspondence with an earl, and yet after all, that boy makes me feel as if there was."

The cablegram was actually gone home! the thought of it gave him an immense uplift. He walked with a lighter tread. His heart was full of happiness. He threw aside all hesitances and confessed to himself that he was glad through and through that he was going to give up this experiment and go back to his home again. His eagerness to get his father's answer began to grow, now, and it grew with marvelous celerity, after it began. He waited an hour, walking about, putting in his time as well as he could, but interested in nothing that came under his eye, and at last he presented himself at the office again and asked if any answer had come yet. The boy said,

"No, no answer yet," then glanced at the clock and added, "I don't think it's likely you'll get one to-day."

"Why not?"

"Well, you see it's getting pretty late. You can't always tell where 'bouts a man is when he's on the other side, and you can't always find him just the minute you want him, and you see it's getting about six o'clock now, and over there it's pretty late at night."

"Why yes," said Tracy, "I hadn't thought of that."

"Yes, pretty late, now, half past ten or eleven. Oh yes, you probably won't get any answer to-night."

CHAPTER 14

So Tracy went home to supper. The odors in that supper room seemed more strenuous and more horrible than ever before, and he was happy in the thought that he was so soon to be free from them again. When the supper was over he hardly knew whether he had eaten any of it or not, and he certainly hadn't heard any of the conversation. His heart had been dancing all the time, his thoughts had been far away from these things, and in the visions of his mind the sumptuous appointments of his father's castle had risen before him without rebuke. Even the plushed flunkey, that walking symbol of a sham inequality, had not been unpleasant to his dreaming view. After the meal Barrow said,—

"Come with me. I'll give you a jolly evening."

"Very good. Where are you going?"

"To my club."

"What club is that?"

"Mechanics' Debating Club."

Tracy shuddered, slightly. He didn't say anything about having visited that place himself. Somehow he didn't quite relish the memory of that time. The sentiments which had made his former visit there so enjoyable, and filled him with such enthusiasm, had undergone a gradual change, and they had rotted away to such a degree that he couldn't contemplate another visit there with anything strongly resembling delight. In fact he was a little ashamed to go; he didn't want to go there and find out by the rude impact of the thought of those people upon his reorganized condition of mind, how sharp the change had been. He would have preferred to stay away. He expected that now he should hear nothing except sentiments which would be a reproach to him in his changed mental attitude, and he rather wished he might be excused. And yet he didn't quite want to say that, he didn't want to show how he did feel, or show any disinclination to go, and so he forced himself to go along with Barrow, privately purposing to take an early opportunity to get away.

After the essayist of the evening had read his paper, the chairman announced that the debate would now be upon the subject of the previous meeting, "The American Press." It saddened the back-sliding disciple to hear this announcement. It brought up too many reminiscences. He wished he had happened upon some other subject. But the debate began, and he sat still and listened.

In the course of the discussion one of the speakers—a blacksmith named Tompkins—arraigned all monarchs and all lords in the earth for their cold selfishness in retaining their unearned dignities. He said that no monarch and no son of a monarch, no lord and no son of a lord ought to be able to look his fellow man in the face without shame. Shame for consenting to keep his unearned titles, property, and privileges at the expense of other people; shame for consenting to remain, on any terms, in dishonourable possession of these things, which represented bygone robberies and wrongs inflicted upon the general people of the nation. He said, "if there were a lord or the son of a lord here, I would like to reason with him, and try to show him how unfair and how selfish his position is. I would try to persuade him to relinquish it, take his place among men on equal terms, earn the bread he eats, and hold of slight value all deference paid him because of artificial position, all reverence not the just due of his own personal merits."

Tracy seemed to be listening to utterances of his own made in talks with his radical friends in England. It was as if some eavesdropping phonograph had treasured up his words and brought them across the

Atlantic to accuse him with them in the hour of his defection and retreat. Every word spoken by this stranger seemed to leave a blister on Tracy's conscience, and by the time the speech was finished he felt that he was all conscience and one blister. This man's deep compassion for the enslaved and oppressed millions in Europe who had to bear with the contempt of that small class above them, throned upon shining heights whose paths were shut against them, was the very thing he had often uttered himself. The pity in this man's voice and words was the very twin of the pity that used to reside in his own heart and come from his own lips when he thought of these oppressed peoples.

The homeward tramp was accomplished in brooding silence. It was a silence most grateful to Tracy's feelings. He wouldn't have broken it for anything; for he was ashamed of himself all the way through to his spine. He kept saying to himself:

"How unanswerable it all is—how absolutely unanswerable! It *is* basely, degradingly selfish to keep those unearned honors, and—and—oh, hang it, nobody but a cur—"

"What an idiotic damned speech that Tompkins made!"

This outburst was from Barrow. It flooded Tracy's demoralized soul with waters of refreshment. These were the darlingest words the poor vacillating young apostate had ever heard—for they whitewashed his shame for him, and that is a good service to have when you can't get the best of all verdicts, self-acquittal.

"Come up to my room and smoke a pipe, Tracy."

Tracy had been expecting this invitation, and had had his declination all ready: but he was glad enough to accept, now. Was it possible that a reasonable argument could be made against that man's desolating speech? He was burning to hear Barrow try it. He knew how to start him, and keep him going: it was to seem to combat his positions—a process effective with most people.

"What is it you object to in Tompkins's speech, Barrow?"

"Oh, the leaving out of the factor of human nature; requiring another man to do what you wouldn't do yourself."

"Do you mean—"

"Why here's what I mean; it's very simple. Tompkins is a blacksmith; has a family; works for wages; and hard, too—fooling around won't furnish the bread. Suppose it should turn out that by the death of somebody in England he is suddenly an earl—income, half a million dollars a year. What would he do?"

"Well, I—I suppose he would have to decline to—"

"Man, he would grab it in a second!"

"Do you really think he would?"

"Think?—I don't think anything about it, I know it."

"Why?"

"Why? Because he's not a fool."

"So you think that if he were a fool, he—"

"No, I don't. Fool or *no* fool, he would grab it. Anybody would. Anybody that's alive. And I've seen dead people that would get up and go for it. I would myself."

This was balm, this was healing, this was rest and peace and comfort.

"But I thought you were opposed to nobilities."

"Transmissible ones, yes. But that's nothing. I'm opposed to millionaires, but it would be dangerous to offer me the position."

"You'd take it?"

"I would leave the funeral of my dearest enemy to go and assume its burdens and responsibilities."

Tracy thought a while, then said—

"I don't know that I quite get the bearings of your position. You say you are opposed to hereditary nobilities, and yet if you had the chance you would—"

"Take one? In a minute I would. And there isn't a mechanic in that entire club that wouldn't. There isn't a lawyer, doctor, editor, author, tinker, loafer, railroad president, saint—land, there isn't a human *being* in the United States that wouldn't jump at the chance!"

"Except me," said Tracy softly.

"Except you!" Barrow could hardly get the words out, his scorn so choked him. And he couldn't get any further than that form of words; it seemed to dam his flow, utterly. He got up and came and glared upon Tracy in a kind of outraged and unappeasable way, and said again, "Except *you!*" He walked around him—inspecting him from one point of view and then another, and relieving his soul now and then by exploding that formula at him; "Except *you!*" Finally he slumped down into his chair with the air of one who gives it up, and said—

"He's straining his viscera and he's breaking his heart trying to get some low-down job that a good dog wouldn't have, and yet wants to let on that if he had a chance to scoop an earldom he wouldn't do it. Tracy, don't put this kind of a strain on me. Lately I'm not as strong as I was."

"Well, I wasn't meaning to put a strain on you, Barrow, I was only meaning to intimate that if an earldom ever does fall in my way—"

"There—I wouldn't give myself any worry about *that,* if I was you. And besides, I can settle what you would do. Are you any different from me?"

"Well—no."

"Are you any better than me?"

"O,—er—why, certainly not."

"Are you as *good?* Come!"

"Indeed, I—the fact is you take me so suddenly,—"

"Suddenly? What is there sudden about it? It isn't a difficult question is it? Or doubtful? Just measure us on the only fair lines—the lines of merit—and of course you'll admit that a journeyman chair-maker that earns his twenty dollars a week, and has had the good and genuine culture of contact with men, and care, and hardship, and failure, and success, and downs and ups and ups and downs, is just a trifle the superior of a young fellow like you, who doesn't know how to do anything that's valuable, can't earn his living in any secure and steady way, hasn't had any experience of life and its seriousness, hasn't any culture but the artificial culture of books, which adorns but doesn't really educate—come! if *I* wouldn't scorn an earldom, what the devil right have *you* to do it!"

Tracy dissembled his joy, though he wanted to thank the chair-maker for that last remark. Presently a thought struck him, and he spoke up briskly and said:

"But look here, I really can't quite get the hang of your notions—your principles, if they are principles. You are inconsistent. You are opposed to aristocracies, yet you'd take an earldom if you could. Am I to understand that you don't blame an earl for being and remaining an earl?"

"I certainly don't."

"And you wouldn't blame Tompkins, or yourself, or me, or anybody, for accepting an earldom if it was offered?"

"Indeed I wouldn't."

"Well, then, who *would* you blame?"

"The whole nation—any bulk and mass of population anywhere, in any country, that will put up with the infamy, the outrage, the insult of a hereditary aristocracy which *they* can't enter—and on absolutely free and equal terms."

"Come, aren't you beclouding yourself with distinctions that are not differences?"

"Indeed I am not. I am entirely clear-headed about this thing. If I could extirpate an aristocratic system by declining its honors, *then* I should be a rascal to accept them. And if enough of the mass would join me to make the extirpation possible, *then* I should be a rascal to do otherwise than help in the attempt."

"I believe I understand—yes, I think I get the idea. You have no blame for the lucky few who naturally decline to vacate the pleasant nest they were born into, you only despise the all-powerful and stupid mass of the nation for allowing the nest to exist."

"That's it, that's it! You *can* get a simple thing through your head if you work at it long enough."

"Thanks."

"Don't mention it. And I'll give you some sound advice: when you go back, if you find your nation up and ready to abolish that hoary affront, lend a hand; but if that isn't the state of things and you get a chance at an earldom, don't you be a fool—you take it."

Tracy responded with earnestness and enthusiasm—

"As I live, I'll do it!"

Barrow laughed.

"I never saw such a fellow. I begin to think you've got a good deal of imagination. With you, the idlest fancy freezes into a reality at a breath. Why, you looked, then, as if it wouldn't astonish you if you did tumble into an earldom." Tracy blushed. Barrow added: "Earldom! Oh, yes, take it, if it offers; but meantime we'll go on looking around, in a modest way, and if you get a chance to superintend a sausage-stuffer at six or eight dollars a week, you just trade off the earldom for a last year's almanac and stick to the sausage-stuffing."

CHAPTER 15

Tracy went to bed happy once more, at rest in his mind once more. He had started out on a high emprise—that was to his credit, he argued; he had fought the best fight he could, considering the odds against him—that was to his credit; he had been defeated—certainly there was nothing discreditable in that. Being defeated, he had a right to retire with the honors of war and go back without prejudice to the position in the world's society to which he had been born. Why not? even the rabid republican chair-maker would do that. Yes, his conscience was comfortable once more.

He woke refreshed, happy, and eager for his cablegram. He had been born an aristocrat, he had been a democrat for a time, he was now an aristocrat again. He marveled to find that this final change was not merely intellectual, it had invaded his feeling; and he also marveled to note that this feeling seemed a good deal less artificial than any he had entertained in his system for a long time. He could also have noted, if he had thought of it, that his bearing had stiffened, over night, and that his chin had lifted itself a shade. Arrived in the basement, he was about to enter the breakfast room when he saw old Marsh in the dim light of a corner of the hall, beckoning him with his finger to approach. The blood welled slowly up in Tracy's cheek, and he said with a grade of injured dignity almost ducal—

"Is that for me?"

"Yes."

"What is the purpose of it?"

"I want to speak to you—in private."

"This spot is private enough for me."

Marsh was surprised; and not particularly pleased. He approached and said—

"Oh, in public, then, if you prefer. Though it hasn't been my way."

The boarders gathered to the spot, interested.

"Speak out," said Tracy. "What is it you want?"

"Well, haven't you—er—forgot something?"

"I? I'm not aware of it."

"Oh, you're not? Now you stop and think, a minute."

"I refuse to stop and think. It doesn't interest me. If it interests you, speak out."

"Well, then," said Marsh, raising his voice to a slightly angry pitch, "You forgot to pay your board yesterday—if you're *bound* to have it public."

Oh, yes, this heir to an annual million or so had been dreaming and soaring, and had forgotten that pitiful three or four dollars. For penalty he must have it coarsely flung in his face in the presence of these people—people in whose countenances was already beginning to dawn an uncharitable enjoyment of the situation.

"Is *that* all! Take your money and give your terrors a rest."

Tracy's hand went down into his pocket with angry decision. But—it didn't come out. The color began to ebb out of his face. The countenances about him showed a growing interest; and some of them a heightened satisfaction. There was an uncomfortable pause—then he forced out, with difficulty, the words—

"I've—been robbed!"

Old Marsh's eyes flamed up with Spanish fire, and he exclaimed—

"Robbed, is it? *That's* your tune? It's too old—been played in this house too often; everybody plays it that can't get work when he wants it, and won't work when he can get it. Trot out Mr. Allen, somebody, and let *him* take a toot at it. It's *his* turn next, *he* forgot, too, last night. I'm laying for him."

One of the negro women came scrambling down stairs as pale as a sorrel horse with consternation and excitement:

"Misto Marsh, Misto Allen's skipped out!"

"What!"

"Yes-sah, and cleaned out his room *clean;* tuck bofe towels en de soap!"

"You lie, you hussy!"

"It's jes' so, jes' as I tells you—en Misto Sumner's socks is gone, en Misto Naylor's yuther shirt."

Mr. Marsh was at boiling point by this time. He turned upon Tracy—

"Answer up now—when are you going to settle?"

"To-day—since you seem to be in a hurry."

"*To-day* is it? Sunday—and you out of work? I like that. Come—where are you going to get the money?"

Tracy's spirit was rising again. He proposed to impress these people:

"I am expecting a cablegram from home."

Old Marsh was caught out, with the surprise of it. The idea was so immense, so extravagant, that he couldn't get his breath at first. When he did get it, it came rancid with sarcasm.

"A *cablegram*—think of it, ladies and gents, he's expecting a cablegram! *He's* expecting a cablegram—this duffer, this scrub, this bilk! From his father—eh? Yes—without a doubt. A dollar or two a word—oh, that's nothing—*they* don't mind a little thing like that—*this* kind's fathers don't. Now his father is—er—well, I reckon his father—"

"My father is an English earl!"

The crowd fell back aghast—aghast at the sublimity of the young loafer's "cheek." Then they burst into a laugh that made the windows rattle. Tracy was too angry to realize that he had done a foolish thing. He said—

"Stand aside, please. I—"

"Wait a minute, your lordship," said Marsh, bowing low, "where is your lordship going?"

"For the cablegram. Let me pass."

"Excuse me, your lordship, you'll stay right where you are."

"What do you mean by that?"

"I mean that I didn't begin to keep boarding-house yesterday. It means that I am not the kind that can be taken in by every hack-driver's son that comes loafing over here because he can't bum a living at home. It means that you can't skip out on any such—"

Tracy made a step toward the old man, but Mrs. Marsh sprang between, and said—

"Don't, Mr. Tracy, please." She turned to her husband and said, "*Do* bridle your tongue. What has he done to be treated so? Can't you *see* he has lost his mind, with trouble and distress? He's not responsible."

"Thank your kind heart, madam, but I've not lost my mind; and if I can have the mere privilege of stepping to the telegraph office—"

"Well, you can't," cried Marsh.

"—or sending—"

"Sending! That beats everything. If there's anybody that's fool enough to go on such a chuckleheaded errand—"

"Here comes Mr. Barrow—he will go for me. Barrow—"

A brisk fire of exclamations broke out—

"Say, Barrow, he's expecting a cablegram!"

"Cablegram from his father, you know!"

"Yes—cablegram from the wax-figger!"

"And say, Barrow, this fellow's an earl—take off your hat, pull down your vest!"

"Yes, he's come off and forgot his crown, that he wears Sundays. He's cabled over to his pappy to send it."

"You step out and get that cablegram, Barrow; his majesty's a little lame to-day."

"Oh stop," cried Barrow; "give the man a chance." He turned, and said with some severity, "Tracy, what's the matter with you? What kind of foolishness is this you've been talking. You ought to have more sense."

"I've not been talking foolishness; and if you'll go to the telegraph office—"

"Oh, don't talk so. I'm your friend in trouble and out of it, before your face and behind your back, for anything in *reason;* but you've lost your head, you see, and this moonshine about a cablegram—"

"*I'll* go there and ask for it!"

"Thank you from the bottom of my heart, Brady. Here, I'll give you a written order for it. Fly, now, and fetch it. We'll soon see!"

Brady flew. Immediately the sort of quiet began to steal over the crowd which means dawning doubt, misgiving; and might be translated into the words, "Maybe he *is* expecting a cablegram—maybe he *has* got a father somewhere—maybe we've been just a little too fresh, just a shade too 'previous'!" Loud talk ceased; then the mutterings and low murmurings and whisperings died out. The crowd began to crumble apart. By ones and twos the fragments drifted to the breakfast table. Barrow tried to bring Tracy in; but he said—

"Not yet, Barrow—presently."

Mrs. Marsh and Hattie tried, offering gentle and kindly persuasions; but he said;

"I would rather wait—till he comes."

Even old Marsh began to have suspicions that maybe he had been a trifle too "brash," as he called it in the privacy of his soul, and he pulled himself together and started toward Tracy with invitation in his eyes; but Tracy warned him off with a gesture which was quite positive and eloquent. Then followed the stillest quarter of an hour which had ever been known in that house at that time of day. It was so still, and so solemn withal, that when somebody's cup slipped from his fingers and landed in his plate the shock made people start, and the sharp sound seemed as indecorous there and as out of place as if a coffin and mourners were imminent and being waited for. And at last when Brady's feet came clattering down the stairs the sacrilege seemed unbearable. Everybody rose softly and turned toward the door, where stood Tracy; then with a common impulse, moved a step or two in that direction, and stopped. While they gazed, young Brady arrived, panting, and put into Tracy's hand,—sure enough—an envelope. Tracy fastened a bland victorious eye upon the gazers, and kept it there till one by one they dropped their eyes, vanquished and embarrassed. Then he tore open the telegram and glanced at its message. The yellow paper fell from his fingers and fluttered to the floor, and his face turned white. There was nothing there but one word—

"*Thanks.*"

The humorist of the house, the tall, raw-boned Billy Nash, caulker from the navy yard, was standing in the rear of the crowd. In the midst of the pathetic silence that was now brooding over the place and moving some few hearts there toward compassion, he began to whimper, then he put his handkerchief to his eyes and buried his face in the neck of the bashfulest young fellow in the company, a navy-yard blacksmith, shrieked "Oh, pappy, how *could* you!" and began to bawl like a teething baby, if one may imagine a baby with the energy and the devastating voice of a jackass.

So perfect was the imitation of a child's cry, and so vast the scale of it, and so ridiculous the aspect of the performer, that all gravity was swept from the place as if by a hurricane, and almost everybody there joined in the crash of laughter provoked by the exhibition. Then the small mob began to take its revenge—revenge for the discomfort and apprehension it had brought upon itself by its own too rash freshness of a little while before. It guyed its poor victim, baited him, worried him, as dogs do with a cornered cat. The victim answered back with defiances and challenges which included everybody, and which only gave the sport new spirit and variety; but when he changed his tactics and began to single out individuals and invite them by name, the fun lost its funniness and the interest of the show died out, along with the noise.

Finally Marsh was about to take an innings, but Barrow said—

"Never mind, now—leave him alone. You've no account with him but a money account. I'll take care of that myself."

The distressed and worried landlady gave Barrow a fervently grateful look for his championship of the abused stranger; and the pet of the house, a very prism in her cheap but ravishing Sunday rig, blew him a kiss from the tips of her fingers and said, with the darlingest smile and a sweet little toss of her head—

"You're the only man here, and I'm going to set my cap for you, you dear old thing!"

"For shame, Puss! How you talk! I *never* saw such a child!"

It took a good deal of argument and persuasion—that is to say, petting, under these disguises—to get Tracy to entertain the idea of breakfast. He at first said he would never eat again in that house; and added that he had enough firmness of character, he trusted, to enable him to starve like a man when the alternative was to eat insult with his bread.

When he had finished his breakfast, Barrow took him to his room, furnished him a pipe, and said cheerily—

"*Now,* old fellow, take in your battle-flag out of the wet, you're not in the hostile camp any more. You're a little upset by your troubles, and that's natural enough, but don't let your mind run on them any more than you can help; drag your thoughts away from your troubles—by the ears, by the heels, or any other way, so you manage it; it's the healthiest thing a body can do; dwelling on troubles is deadly, just deadly—and that's the softest name there is for it. You must keep your mind amused—you must, indeed."

"Oh, miserable me!"

"*Don't!* There's just pure heart-break in that tone. It's just as I say;

you've got to get right down to it and amuse your mind, as if it was salvation."

"They're easy words to say, Barrow, but how am I going to amuse, entertain, divert a mind that finds itself suddenly assaulted and overwhelmed by disasters of a sort not dreamed of and not provided for? No-no, the bare idea of amusement is repulsive to my feelings. Let us talk of death and funerals."

"No–not yet. That would be giving up the ship. We'll not give up the ship yet. I'm going to amuse you; I sent Brady out for the wherewithal before you finished breakfast."

"You did? What is it?"

"Come, this is a good sign–curiosity. Oh, there's hope for you yet."

CHAPTER 16

Brady arrived with a box, and departed, after saying–

"They're finishing one up, but they'll be along as soon as it's done."

Barrow took a frameless oil portrait a foot square from the box, set it up in a good light, without comment, and reached for another, taking a furtive glance at Tracy, meantime. The stony solemnity in Tracy's face remained as it was, and gave out no sign of interest. Barrow placed the second portrait beside the first, and stole another glance while reaching for a third. The stone image softened, a shade. No. 3 forced the ghost of a smile, No. 4 swept indifference wholly away, and No. 5 started a laugh which was still in good and hearty condition when No. 14 took its place in the row.

"Oh, *you're* all right, yet," said Barrow. "You see you're not past amusement."

The pictures were fearful, as to color, and atrocious as to drawing and expression; but the feature which squelched animosity and made them funny was a feature which could not achieve its full force in a single picture, but required the wonder-working assistance of repetition. One loudly dressed mechanic in stately attitude, with his hand on a cannon, ashore, and a ship riding at anchor in the offing,–this is merely odd; but when one sees the same cannon and the same ship in fourteen pictures in a row, and a different mechanic standing watch in each, the thing gets to be funny.

"Explain–explain these aberrations," said Tracy.

"Well, they are not the achievement of a single intellect, a single talent—it takes two to do these miracles. They are collaborations; the one artist does the figure, the other the accessories. The figure-artist is a German shoemaker with an untaught passion for art, the other is a simple hearted old Yankee sailor-man whose possibilities are strictly limited to his ship, his cannon and his patch of petrified sea. They work these things up from twenty-five-cent tintypes; they get six dollars apiece for them, and they can grind out a couple a day when they strike what they call a boost—that is, an inspiration."

"People actually pay money for these calumnies?"

"They actually do—and quite willingly, too. And these abortionists could double their trade and work the women in, if Capt. Saltmarsh could whirl a horse in, or a piano, or a guitar, in place of his cannon. The fact is, he fatigues the market with that cannon. Even the male market, I mean. These fourteen in the procession are not all satisfied. One is an old "independent" fireman, and he wants an engine in place of the cannon; another is a mate of a tug, and wants a tug in place of the ship—and so on, and so on. But the captain can't make a tug that is deceptive, and a fire engine is many flights beyond his power."

"This *is* a most extraordinary form of robbery, I never have heard of anything like it. It's interesting."

"Yes, and so are the artists. They are perfectly honest men, and sincere. And the old sailor-man is full of sound religion, and is as devoted a student of the Bible and misquoter of it as you can find anywhere. I don't know a better man or kinder hearted old soul than Saltmarsh, although he does swear a little, sometimes."

"He seems to be perfect. I want to know him, Barrow."

"You'll have the chance. I guess I hear them coming, now. We'll draw them out on their art, if you like."

The artists arrived and shook hands with great heartiness. The German was forty and a little fleshy, with a shiny bald head and a kindly face and deferential manner. Capt. Saltmarsh was sixty, tall, erect, powerfully built, with coal-black hair and whiskers, and he had a well tanned complexion, and a gait and countenance that were full of command, confidence and decision. His horny hands and wrists were covered with tattoo-marks, and when his lips parted, his teeth showed up white and blemishless. His voice was the effortless deep bass of a church organ, and would disturb the tranquility of a gas flame fifty yards away.

"They're wonderful pictures," said Barrow. "We've been examining them."

"It is very bleasant dot you like dem," said Handel, the German, greatly pleased. "Und you, Herr Tracy, you haf peen bleased mit dem too, alretty?"

"I can honestly say I have never seen anything just like them before."

"Schön!" cried the German, delighted. "You hear, Captain? Here is a chentleman, yes, vot abbreciate unser aart."

The captain was charmed, and said:

"Well, sir, we're thankful for a compliment yet, though they're not as scarce now as they used to be before we made a reputation."

"Getting the reputation is the up-hill time in most things, captain."

"It's so. It ain't enough to know how to reef a gasket, you got to make the mate know you know it. That's reputation. The good word, said at the right time, that's the word that makes us; and evil be to him that evil thinks, as Isaiah says."

"It's very relevant, and hits the point exactly," said Tracy.

"Where did you study art, Captain?"

"I haven't studied; it's a natural gift."

"He is born mit dose cannon in him. He tondt haf to do noding, his chenius do all de vork. Of he is asleep, und take a pencil in his hand, out come a cannon. Py crashus, of he could do a clavier, of he could do a guitar, of he could do a vashtub, it is a fortune, heiliger Yohanniss it is yoost a fortune!"

"Well, it is an immense pity that the business is hindered and limited in this unfortunate way."

The captain grew a trifle excited, himself, now—

"You've said it, Mr. Tracy! Hindered? well, I should say so. Why, look here. This fellow here, No. 11, he's a hackman,—a flourishing hackman, I may say. He wants his hack in this picture. Wants it where the cannon is. I got around that difficulty, by telling him the cannon's our trademark, so to speak—proves that the picture's our work, and I was afraid if we left it out people wouldn't know for certain if it *was* a Saltmarsh-Handel—now you wouldn't yourself—"

"What, Captain? You wrong yourself, indeed you do. Anyone who has once seen a genuine Saltmarsh-Handel is safe from imposture forever. Strip it, flay it, skin it out of every detail but the bare color and expression, and that man will still recognize it, still stop to worship—"

"Oh, how it makes me feel to hear dose oxpressions!—"

—"still say to himself again as he had said a hundred times before, the art of the Saltmarsh-Handel is an art apart, there is nothing in the heavens above or in the earth beneath that resembles it,—"

"Py chiminy, nur hören Sie einmal! In my lifeday haf I never heard so brecious worts."

"So I talked him out of the hack, Mr. Tracy, and he let up on that, and said put in a hearse, then—because he's chief mate of a hearse but don't own it—stands a watch for wages, you know. But I can't do a hearse any more than I can a hack; so here we are—becalmed, you see. And it's the same with women and such. They come and they want a little johnry picture—"

"It's the accessories that make it a *genre*?"

"Yes—cannon, or cat, or any little thing like that, that you heave in to whoop up the effect. We could do a prodigious trade with the women if we could foreground the things they like, but they don't give a damn for artillery. Mine's the lack," continued the captain with a sigh, "Andy's end of the business is all right—I tell you *he's* an artist from wayback!"

"Yoost hear dot old man! He always talk 'poud me like dot," purred the pleased German.

"Look at his work yourself! Fourteen portraits in a row. And no two of them alike."

"Now that you speak of it, it is true; I hadn't noticed it before. It is very remarkable. Unique, I suppose."

"I should say so. That's the very *thing* about Andy—he *discriminates*. Discrimination's the thief of time—forty-ninth Psalm; but that ain't any matter, it's the honest thing, and it pays in the end."

"Yes, he certainly is great in that feature, one is obliged to admit it; but—now mind, I'm not really criticising—don't you think he is just a trifle overstrong in technique?"

The captain's face was knocked expressionless by this remark. It remained quite vacant while he muttered to himself—"Technique—technique—poly-technique—pyro-technique; that's it, likely—fireworks—too much color." Then he spoke up with serenity and confidence, and said—

"Well, yes, he does pile it on pretty loud; but they all like it, you know—fact is, it's the life of the business. Take that No. 9, there, Evans the butcher. He drops into the stoodio as sober-colored as anything you ever see: *now* look at him. You can't tell him from scarlet fever. Well, it pleases that butcher to death. I'm making a study of a sausage-wreath to hang on the cannon, and I don't really reckon I can do it right, but if I can, we can break the butcher."

"Unquestionably your confederate—I mean your—your fellow craftsman—is a great colorist—"

"Oh, danke schön!—"

—"in fact a quite extraordinary colorist; a colorist, I make bold to say, without imitator here or abroad—and with a most bold and effective touch, a touch like a battering ram; and a manner so peculiar and romantic, and extraneous, and ad libitum, and heart-searching, that—that—he—he is an impressionist, I presume?"

"No," said the captain simply, "he is a Presbyterian."

"It accounts for it all—all—there's something divine about his art,—soulful, unsatisfactory, yearning, dim-hearkening on the void horizon, vague-murmuring to the spirit out of ultra-marine distances and far-sounding cataclysms of uncreated space—oh, if he—if he—has he ever tried distemper?"

The captain answered up with energy—

"Not if he knows himself! But his dog has, and—"

"Oh, no, it vas not *my* dog."

"Why, you *said* it was your dog."

"Oh, no, gaptain, I—"

"It was a white dog, wasn't it, with his tail docked, and one ear gone, and—"

"Dot's him, dot's him!—der fery dog. Wy, py Chorge, dot dog he vould eat baint yoost de same like—"

"Well, never mind that, now—'vast heaving—I never saw such a man. You start him on that dog and he'll dispute a year. Blamed if I haven't *seen* him keep it up a level two hours and a half."

"Why captain!" said Barrow. "I guess that must be hearsay."

"No, sir, no hearsay about it—he disputed with me."

"I don't see how you stood it."

"Oh, you've got to—if you run with Andy. But it's the only fault he's got."

"Ain't you afraid of acquiring it?"

"Oh, no," said the captain, tranquilly, "no danger of that, I reckon."

The artists presently took their leave. Then Barrow put his hands on Tracy's shoulders and said—

"Look me in the eye, my boy. Steady, steady. There—it's just as I thought—hoped, anyway; *you're* all right, thank goodness. Nothing the matter with your mind. But don't do that again—even for fun. It isn't wise. They wouldn't have believed you if you'd *been* an earl's son. Why, they *couldn't*—don't you know that? What ever possessed you to take such a freak? But never mind about that; let's not talk of it. It was a mistake; you see that yourself."

"Yes—it *was* a mistake."

"Well, just drop it out of your mind; it's no harm; we all make them. Pull your courage together, and don't brood, and don't give up. I'm at your back, and we'll pull through, don't you be afraid."

When he was gone, Barrow walked the floor a good while, uneasy in his mind. He said to himself, "I'm troubled about him. He never would have made a break like that if he hadn't been a little off his balance. But I know what being out of work and no prospect ahead can do for a man. First it knocks the pluck out of him and drags his pride in the dirt; worry does the rest, and his mind gets shaky. I must talk to these people. No—if there's any humanity in them—and there is, at bottom—they'll be easier on him if they think his troubles have disturbed his reason. But I've *got* to find him some work; work's the only medicine for his disease. Poor devil! away off here, and not a friend."

CHAPTER 17

The moment Tracy was alone his spirits vanished away, and all the misery of his situation was manifest to him. To be moneyless and an object of the chair-maker's charity—this was bad enough, but his folly in proclaiming himself an earl's son to that scoffing and unbelieving crew, and, on top of that, the humiliating result—the recollection of these things was a sharper torture still. He made up his mind that he would never play earl's son again before a doubtful audience.

His father's answer was a blow he could not understand. At times he thought his father imagined he could get work to do in America without any trouble, and was minded to let him try it and cure himself of his radicalism by hard, cold, disenchanting experience. That seemed the most plausible theory, yet he could not content himself with it. A theory that pleased him better was, that this cablegram would be followed by another, of a gentler sort, requiring him to come home. Should he write and strike his flag, and ask for a ticket home? Oh, no, that he couldn't *ever* do. At least, not yet. That cablegram would come, it certainly would. So he went from one telegraph office to another every day for nearly a week, and asked if there was a cablegram for Howard Tracy. No, there wasn't any. So they answered him at first. Later, they said it before he had a chance to ask. Later still they merely shook their heads impatiently as soon as he came in sight. After that he was ashamed to go any more.

He was down in the lowest depths of despair, now; for the harder

Barrow tried to find work for him the more hopeless the possibilities seemed to grow. At last he said to Barrow—

"Look here. I want to make a confession. I have got down, now, to where I am not only willing to acknowledge to myself that I am a shabby creature and full of false pride, but am willing to acknowledge it to you. Well, I've been allowing you to wear yourself out hunting for work for me when there's been a chance open to me all the time. Forgive my pride—what was left of it. It is all gone, now, and I've come to confess that if those ghastly artists want another confederate, I'm their man—for at last I am dead to shame."

"No? Really, can you paint?"

"Not as badly as *they*. No, I don't claim that, for I am not a genius; in fact, I am a very indifferent amateur, a slouchy dabster, a mere artistic sarcasm; but drunk or asleep I can beat *those* buccaneers."

"Shake! I want to shout! Oh, I tell you, I am immensely delighted and relieved. Oh, just to work—that is life! No matter what the work is —that's of no consequence. Just work itself is bliss when a man's been starving for it. I've *been* there! Come right along, we'll hunt the old boys up. Don't you feel good? I tell you *I* do."

The freebooters were not at home. But their "works" were,—displayed in profusion all about the little ratty studio. Cannon to the right of them, cannon to the left of them, cannon in front—it was Balaclava come again.

"Here's the uncontented hackman, Tracy. Buckle to—deepen the sea-green to turf, turn the ship into a hearse. Let the boys have a taste of your quality."

The artists arrived just as the last touch was put on. They stood transfixed with admiration.

"My souls but she's a stunner, that hearse! The hackman will just go all to pieces when he sees that—won't he Andy?"

"Oh, it is sphlennid, sphlennid! Herr Tracy, why haf you not said you vas a so sublime aartist? Lob' Gott, of you had lif'd in Paris you would be a Pree de Rome, dot's vot's de matter!"

The arrangements were soon made. Tracy was taken into full and equal partnership, and he went straight to work, with dash and energy, to reconstructing gems of art whose accessories had failed to satisfy. Under his hand, on that and succeeding days, artillery disappeared and the emblems of peace and commerce took its place—cats, hacks, sausages, tugs, fire engines, pianos, guitars, rocks, gardens, flower-pots, landscapes—whatever was wanted, he flung it in; and the more out of place and absurd the required object was, the more joy he got out of fabricating it. The pirates were delighted, the customers applauded, the sex began to flock in, great was the prosperity of the firm. Tracy was obliged to confess to himself that there was something about work,—even such grotesque and humble work as this—which most pleasantly satisfied a something in his nature which had never been satisfied before, and also gave him a strange new dignity in his own private view of himself.

The Unqualified Member from Cherokee Strip was in a state of deep dejection. For a good while, now, he had been leading a sort of life which was calculated to kill; for it had consisted in regularly alternating days of brilliant hope and black disappointment. The brilliant hopes were created by the magician Sellers, and they always promised that *now* he had got the trick, sure, and would effectively influence that materialized cowboy to call at the Towers before night. The black disappointments consisted in the persistent and monotonous failure of these prophecies.

At the date which this history has now reached, Sellers was appalled to find that the usual remedy was inoperative, and that Hawkins's low spirits refused absolutely to lift. Something must be done, he reflected; it was heart-breaking, this woe, this smileless misery, this dull despair that looked out from his poor friend's face. Yes, he must be cheered up. He mused a while, then he saw his way. He said in his most conspicuously casual vein—

"Er-uh—by the way, Hawkins, we are feeling disappointed about this thing—the way the materializee is acting, I mean—we are disappointed; you concede that?"

"Concede it? Why, yes, if you like the term."

"Very well; so far, so good. Now for the *basis* of the feeling. It is not that your heart, your affections are concerned; that is to say, it is not that you *want* the materializee *Itself*. You concede that?"

"Yes, I concede that, too—cordially."

"Very well, again; we are making progress. To sum up: The feeling, it is conceded, is not engendered by the mere conduct of the materializee; it is conceded that it does not arise from any pang which the *personality* of the materializee could assuage. Now then," said the earl, with the light of triumph in his eye, "the inexorable logic of the situation narrows us down to this: our feeling has its source in the *money*-loss involved. Come—isn't that so?"

"Goodness knows I concede that, with all my heart."

"Very well. When you've found out the source of a disease, you've also found out what remedy is required—just as in this case. In this case money is required. And *only* money."

The old, old seduction was in that airy, confident tone and those significant words—usually called pregnant words in books. The old answering signs of faith and hope showed up in Hawkins's countenance, and he said—

"*Only* money? Do you mean that you know a way to—"

"Washington, have you the impression that I have no resources but those I allow the public and my intimate friends to know about?"

"Well, I—er—"

"Is it *likely*, do you think, that a man moved by nature and taught by experience to keep his affairs to himself and a cautious and reluctant tongue in his head, wouldn't be thoughtful enough to keep a few resources in reserve for a rainy day, when he's got as many as I have to select from?"

"Oh, you make me feel so much better already, Colonel!"

"Have you ever been in my laboratory?"

"Why, no."

"That's it. You see you didn't even know that I had one. Come along. I've got a little trick there that I want to show you. I've kept it perfectly quiet, not fifty people know anything about it. But that's my way, always been my way. Wait till you're *ready*, that's the idea; and *when* you're ready, *zzip!*—let her go!"

"Well, Colonel, I've never seen a man that I've had such unbounded confidence in as you. When you say a thing right out, I always feel as if that ends it; as if that is evidence, and proof, and everything else."

The old earl was profoundly pleased and touched.

"I'm glad *you* believe in me, Washington; not everybody is so just."

"I always have believed in you; and I always shall as long as I live."

"Thank you, my boy. You shan't repent it. And you *can't*." Arrived in the "laboratory," the earl continued, "Now, cast your eye around this room—what do you see? *Apparently* a junk-shop; *apparently* a hospital connected with a patent office—in *reality*, the mines of Golconda in disguise! Look at that thing there. Now what would you take that thing to be?"

"I don't believe I could ever imagine."

"Of course you couldn't. It's my grand adaptation of the phonograph to the marine service. You store up profanity in it for use at sea. You know that sailors don't fly around worth a cent unless you swear at them—so the mate that can do the best job of swearing is the most valuable man. In great emergencies his talent saves the ship. But a ship is a large thing, and he can't be everywhere at once; so there have been times when one mate has lost a ship which could have been saved if they had had a hundred. Prodigious storms, you know. Well, a ship can't afford a hundred mates; but she can afford a hundred Cursing Phonographs, and distribute them all over the vessel—and there, you see, she's armed at every point. Imagine a big storm, and a hundred of my machines all cursing away at once—splendid spectacle, splendid!—you couldn't hear yourself think. Ship goes through that storm perfectly serene—she's just as safe as she'd be on shore."

"It's a wonderful idea. How do you prepare the thing?"

"Load it—simply load it."

"How?"

"Why you just stand over it and swear into it."

"That loads it, does it?"

"Yes—because every word it collars, it *keeps*—keeps it forever. Never wears out. Any time you turn the crank, out it'll come. In times of great peril, you can reverse it, and it'll swear backwards. *That* makes a sailor hump himself!"

"O, I see. Who loads them?—the mate?"

"Yes, if he chooses. Or I'll furnish them already loaded. I can hire an expert for $75 a month who will load a hundred and fifty phonographs in 150 hours, and do it *easy*. And an expert can furnish a stronger article, of course, than the mere average uncultivated mate could. Then you see, all the ships of the world will buy them ready loaded—for I shall have them loaded in any language a customer wants. Hawkins, it will work the grandest moral reform of the 19th century. Five years from now, *all* the swearing will be done by machinery—you won't ever hear a profane word come from human lips on a ship. Millions of dollars have been spent by the churches, in the effort to abolish profanity in the commercial marine. Think of it—my name will live forever in the affections of good men as the man, who, solitary and alone, accomplished this noble and elevating reform."

"O, it *is* grand and beneficent and beautiful. How *did* you ever come to think of it? You have a wonderful mind. How did you say you loaded the machine?"

"O, it's no trouble—perfectly simple. If you want to load it up loud and strong, you stand right over it and shout. But if you leave it open and all set, it'll *eavesdrop*, so to speak—that is to say, it will load itself up with any sounds that are made within six feet of it. Now I'll show you how it works. I had an expert come and load this one up yesterday. Hello, it's been left open—it's too bad—still I reckon it hasn't had much chance to collect irrelevant stuff. All you do is to press this button in the floor—so."

The phonograph began to sing in a plaintive voice:

> There is a boarding-house, far far away,
> Where they have ham and eggs, 3 times a day.

"Hang it, *that* ain't it. Somebody's been singing around here."

The plaintive song began again, mingled with a low, gradually rising wails of cats slowly warming up toward a fight;

> O, *how* the boarders yell,
> When they hear that dinner bell—
> They give that landlord—

(momentary outburst of terrific catfight which drowns out one word.)

> Three times a day.

(Renewal of furious catfight for a moment. The plaintive voice on a high fierce key, "*Scat,* you devils"—and a racket as of flying missiles.)

"Well, never mind—let it go. I've got some sailor-profanity down in there somewhere, if I could get to it. But it isn't any matter; you see how the machine works."

Hawkins responded with enthusiasm—

"O, it works admirably! I know there's a hundred fortunes in it."

"And mind, the Hawkins family get their share, Washington."

"O, thanks, thanks; you are just as generous as ever. Ah, it's the grandest invention of the age!"

"Ah, well, we live in wonderful times. The elements are crowded *full* of beneficent forces—always *have* been—and ours is the first generation to turn them to account and make them work for us. Why Hawkins, *everything* is useful—*nothing* ought ever to be wasted. Now look at sewer gas, for instance. Sewer gas has always been wasted, heretofore; nobody tried to save up sewer-gas—you can't name me a man. Ain't that so? *you* know perfectly well it's so."

"Yes it is so—but I never—er—I don't quite see why a body—"

"Should *want* to save it up? Well, I'll tell you. Do you see this little invention here?—it's a decomposer—I call it a decomposer. I give you my word of honor that if you show me a house that produces a given quantity of sewer-gas in a day, I'll engage to set up my decomposer there and make that house produce a hundred times that quantity of sewer-gas in less than half an hour."

"Dear me, but why should you want to?"

"*Want* to? Listen, and you'll see. My boy, for illuminating purposes and economy combined, there's nothing in the world that begins with sewer-gas. And really, it don't cost a cent. You put in a good inferior article of plumbing,—such as you find everywhere—and add my decomposer, and there you are. Just use the ordinary gas pipes—and there your expense ends. Think of it. Why, Major, in five years from now you won't see a house lighted with anything but sewer-gas. Every physician I talk to, recommends it; and every plumber."

"But isn't it dangerous?"

"O, yes, more or less, but everything is—coal gas, candles, electricity—there isn't anything that ain't."

"It lights up well, does it?"

"O, magnificently."

"Have you given it a good trial?"

"Well, no, not a first rate one. Polly's prejudiced, and she won't let me put it in here; but I'm playing my cards to get it adopted in the President's house, and *then* it'll go—don't you doubt it. I shall not need this one for the present, Washington; you may take it down to some boarding-house and give it a trial if you like."

CHAPTER 18

Washington shuddered slightly at the suggestion, then his face took on a dreamy look and he dropped into a trance of thought. After a little, Sellers asked him what he was grinding in his mental mill.

"Well, this. Have you got some secret project in your head which requires a Bank of England back of it to make it succeed?"

The Colonel showed lively astonishment, and said—

"Why, Hawkins, are you a mind-reader?"

"I? I never thought of a such a thing."

"Well, then how did you happen to drop onto that idea in this curious fashion? It's just mind-reading,—that's what it is, though you may not know it. Because I *have* got a private project that requires a Bank of England at its back. How could you divine that? What was the process? This is interesting."

"There wasn't any process. A thought like this happened to slip through my head by accident: How much would make you or me comfortable? A hundred thousand. Yet you are expecting two or three of these inventions of yours to turn out some billions of money—and you are *wanting* them to do that. If you wanted ten millions, I could understand that—it's inside the human limits. But billions! That's clear outside the limits. There must be a definite project back of that somewhere."

The earl's interest and surprise augmented with every word, and when Hawkins finished, he said with strong admiration—

"It's wonderfully reasoned out, Washington, it certainly is. It shows what I think is quite extraordinary penetration. For you've hit it; you've driven the centre, you've plugged the bulls-eye of my dream. Now I'll tell you the whole thing, and you'll understand it. I don't need to ask you to keep it to yourself, because you'll see that the project will prosper all the better for being kept in the background till the right time. Have you noticed how many pamphlets and books I've got lying around relating to Russia?"

"Yes, I think most anybody would notice that—anybody who wasn't dead."

"Well, I've been posting myself a good while. That's a great and splendid nation, and deserves to be set free." He paused, then added in a quite matter-of-fact way, "When I get this money I'm going to set it free."

"Great guns!"

"Why, what makes you jump like that?"

"Dear me, when you are going to drop a remark under a man's chair that is likely to blow him out through the roof, why don't you put some expression, some force, some noise into it that will prepare him? You shouldn't flip out such a gigantic thing as this in that colorless kind of a way. You do jolt a person up, so. Go on, now, I'm all right again. Tell me all about it. I'm all interest—yes, and sympathy, too."

"Well, I've looked the ground over, and concluded that the methods of the Russian patriots, while good enough considering the way the boys are hampered, are not the best; at least not the quickest. They are trying to revolutionize Russia from *within;* that's pretty slow, you know, and liable to interruption all the time, and is full of perils for the workers. Do you know how Peter the Great started his army? He didn't start it on the family premises under the noses of the Strelitzes; no, he started it away off yonder, privately,—only just one regiment, you know, and he built to *that*. The first thing the Strelitzes knew, the regiment was an *army*, their position was turned, and they had to take a walk. Just that little idea *made* the biggest and worst of all the despotisms the world has seen. The same idea can *un*make it. I'm going to prove it. I'm going to get out to one side and work my scheme the way Peter did."

"This is mighty interesting, Rossmore. What is it you are going to do?"

"I am going to buy Siberia and start a republic."

"There,—bang you go again, without giving any notice! Going to *buy* it?"

"Yes, as soon as I get the money. I don't care what the price is, I shall take it. I can afford it, and I will. Now then, consider this—and you've never thought of it, I'll warrant. Where is the place where there is twenty-five times more manhood, pluck, true heroism, unselfishness, devotion to high and noble ideals, adoration of liberty, wide education, and *brains,* per thousand of population, than any other domain in the whole world can show?"

"Siberia!"

"Right."

"It is true; it certainly is true, but I never thought of it before."

"Nobody ever thinks of it. But it's so, just the same. In those mines and prisons are gathered together the very finest and noblest and capablest multitude of human beings that God is able to create. Now if you had that kind of a population to sell, would you offer it to a despotism? No, the despotism has no use for it; you would lose money. A despotism has no use for anything but human cattle. But suppose you want to start a republic?"

"Yes, I see. It's just the material for it."

"Well, I should say so! There's Siberia with just the very finest and choicest material on the globe for a republic, and more coming—more coming all the time, don't you see! It is being daily, weekly, monthly recruited by the most perfectly devised system that has ever been invented, perhaps. By this system the whole of the hundred millions of Russia are being constantly and patiently sifted, sifted, sifted, by myriads of trained experts, spies appointed by the Emperor personally; and whenever they catch a man, woman or child that has got any brains or education or character, they ship that person straight to Siberia. It is admirable, it is wonderful. It is so searching and so effective that it keeps the general level of Russian intellect and education down to that of the Czar."

"Come, that sounds like exaggeration."

"Well, it's what they say anyway. But I think, myself, it's a lie. And it doesn't seem right to slander a whole nation that way, anyhow. Now, then, you see what the material is, there in Siberia, for a republic." He paused, and his breast began to heave and his eye to burn, under the impulse of strong emotion. Then his words began to stream forth, with constantly increasing energy and fire, and he rose to his feet as if to give himself larger freedom. "The minute I organize that republic, the light of liberty, intelligence, justice, humanity, bursting from it, flooding from it, flaming from it, will concentrate the gaze of the whole astonished world as upon the miracle of a new sun; Russia's countless multitudes of slaves will rise up and march, march!—eastward, with that great light transfiguring their faces as they come, and far back of them you will see—what will you see?—a vacant throne in an empty land! It can be done, and by God I will do it!"

He stood a moment bereft of earthly consciousness by his exaltation; then consciousness returned, bringing him a slight shock, and he said, with grave earnestness—

"I must ask you to pardon me, Major Hawkins. I have never used that expression before, and I beg you will forgive it this time."

Hawkins was quite willing.

"You see, Washington, it is an error which I am by nature not liable to. Only excitable people, impulsive people, are exposed to it. But the circumstances of the present case—I being a democrat by birth and preference, and an aristocrat by inheritance and relish—"

The earl stopped suddenly, his frame stiffened, and he began to stare speechless through the curtainless window. Then he pointed, and gasped out a single rapturous word—

"Look!"

"What *is* it, Colonel?"

"*It!*"

"No!"

"Sure as you're born. Keep perfectly still. I'll apply the influence—I'll turn on all my force. I've brought It thus far—I'll fetch It right into the house. You'll see."

He was making all sorts of passes in the air with his hands.

"There! Look at that. I've made It smile! See?"

Quite true. Tracy, out for an afternoon stroll, had come unexpectantly upon his family arms displayed upon this shabby house-front. The hatchments made him smile; which was nothing, they had made the neighborhood cats do that.

"Look, Hawkins, look! I'm drawing It over!"

"You're drawing it sure, Rossmore. If I ever had any doubts about materialization, they're gone, now, and gone for good. Oh, this is a joyful day!"

Tracy was sauntering over to read the door-plate. Before he was half way over he was saying to himself, "Why, manifestly these are the American Claimant's quarters."

"It's coming—coming right along. I'll slide down and pull It in. You follow after me."

Sellers, pale and a good deal agitated, opened the door and confronted Tracy. The old man could not at once get his voice: then he pumped out a scattering and hardly coherent salutation, and followed it with—

"Walk in, walk right in, Mr.—er—"

"Tracy—Howard Tracy."

—"Tracy—thanks—walk right in, you're expected."

Tracy entered, considerably puzzled, and said—

"Expected? I think there must be some mistake."

"Oh, I judge not," said Sellers, who noticing that Hawkins had arrived, gave him a sidewise glance intended to call his close attention to a dramatic effect which he was proposing to produce by his next remark. Then he said, slowly and impressively—"I am—*You Know Who.*"

To the astonishment of both conspirators the remark produced no dramatic effect at all; for the new comer responded with a quite innocent and unembarrassed air—

"No, pardon me. I don't *know* who you are. I only suppose—but no doubt correctly—that you are the gentleman whose title is on the doorplate."

"Right, quite right—sit down, pray sit down." The earl was rattled, thrown off his bearings, his head was in a whirl. Then he noticed Hawkins standing apart and staring idiotically at what to him was the apparition of a defunct man, and a new idea was born to him. He said to Tracy briskly—

"But a thousand pardons, dear sir, I am forgetting courtesies due to a guest and stranger. Let me introduce my friend General Hawkins—General Hawkins, our new Senator—Senator from the latest and grandest addition to the radiant galaxy of sovereign States, Cherokee Strip" —(to himself, "that name will shrivel him up!"—but it didn't, in the least, and the Colonel resumed the introduction piteously disheartened and amazed),—"Senator Hawkins, Mr. Howard Tracy, of—er—"

"England."

"England!—Why that's im—"

"England, yes, native of England."

"Recently from there?"

"Yes, quite recently."

Said the Colonel to himself, "This phantom lies like an expert. Purifying this kind by fire don't work. I'll sound him a little further, give him another chance or two to work his gift." Then aloud—with deep irony—

"Visiting our great country for recreation and amusement, no doubt. I suppose you find that traveling in the majestic expanses of our Far West is—"

"I haven't been West, and haven't been devoting myself to amusement with any sort of exclusiveness, I assure you. In fact, to merely live, an artist has got to work, not play."

"Artist!" said Hawkins to himself, thinking of the rifled bank; "that *is* a name for it!"

"Are *you* an artist?" asked the colonel; and added to himself, "*now* I'm going to catch him."

"In a humble way, yes."

"What line?" pursued the sly veteran.

"Oils."

"I've got him!" said Sellers to himself. Then aloud, "This is fortunate. Could I engage you to restore some of my paintings that need that attention?"

"I shall be very glad. Pray let me see them."

No shuffling, no evasion, no embarrassment, even under this crucial test. The Colonel was nonplussed. He led Tracy to a chromo which had suffered damage in a former owner's hands through being used as a lamp mat, and said, with a flourish of his hand toward the picture—

"This del Sarto—"

"Is *that* a del Sarto?"

The colonel bent a look of reproach upon Tracy, allowed it to sink home, then resumed as if there had been no interruption—

"This del Sarto is perhaps the only original of that sublime master in our country. You see, yourself, that the work is of such exceeding delicacy that the risk—could—er—would you mind giving me a little example of what you can do before we—"

"Cheerfully, cheerfully. I will copy one of these marvels."

Water-color materials—relics of Miss Sally's college life—were brought. Tracy said he was better in oils, but would take a chance with these. So he was left alone. He began his work, but the attractions of the place were too strong for him, and he got up and went drifting about, fascinated; also amazed.

CHAPTER 19

Meantime the earl and Hawkins were holding a troubled and anxious private consultation. The earl said—

"The mystery that bothers me, is, where did It get its other arm?"

"Yes—it worries me, too. And another thing troubles me—the apparition is English. How do you account for that, Colonel?"

"Honestly, I don't know, Hawkins, I don't really know. It is very confusing and awful."

"Don't you think maybe we've waked up the wrong one?"

"The wrong one? How do you account for the clothes?"

"The clothes *are* right, there's no getting around it. What are we going to do? We can't collect, as I see. The reward is for a one-armed American. This is a two-armed Englishman."

"Well, it may be that that is not objectionable. You see it isn't *less* than is called for, it is *more*, and so,—"

But he saw that this argument was weak, and dropped it. The friends sat brooding over their perplexities some time in silence. Finally the earl's face began to glow with an inspiration, and he said, impressively:

"Hawkins, this materialization is a grander and nobler science than we have dreamed of. We have little imagined what a solemn and stupendous thing we have done. The whole secret is perfectly clear to me, now, clear as day. *Every man is made up of heredities,* long-descended atoms and particles of his ancestors. This present materialization is incomplete. We have only brought it down to perhaps the beginning of this century."

"What do you mean, Colonel!" cried Hawkins, filled with vague alarms by the old man's awe-compelling words and manner.

"This. We've materialized this burglar's ancestor!"

"Oh, don't—don't say that. It's hideous."

"But it's true, Hawkins, I *know* it. Look at the facts. This apparition is distinctly English—note that. It uses good grammar—note that. It is an Artist—note that. It has the manners and carriage of a gentleman —note that. Where's your cow-boy? Answer me that."

"Rossmore, this is dreadful—it's too dreadful to think of!"

"Never resurrected a rag of that burglar but the clothes, not a solitary rag of him but the clothes."

"Colonel, do you really mean—"

The Colonel brought his fist down with emphasis and said—

"I mean exactly this. The materialization was immature, the burglar has evaded us, this is nothing but a damned ancestor!"

He rose and walked the floor in great excitement. Hawkins said plaintively—

"It's a bitter disappointment—bitter."

"I know it. I know it, Senator; I feel it as deeply as anybody could. But we've got to submit—on moral grounds. I need money, but God knows I am not poor enough or shabby enough to be an accessory to the punishing of a man's ancestor for crimes committed by that ancestor's posterity."

"But Colonel!" implored Hawkins; "stop and think; don't be rash; you know it's the *only* chance we've got to get the money; and besides, the Bible itself says posterity to the fourth generation shall be punished for the sins and crimes committed by ancestors four generations back that hadn't anything to do with them; and so it's only fair to turn the rule around and make it work both ways."

The Colonel was struck with the strong logic of this position. He strode up and down, and thought it painfully over. Finally he said:

"There's reason in it; yes, there's reason in it. And so, although it seems a piteous thing to sweat this poor ancient devil for a burglary he hadn't the least hand in, still if duty commands I suppose we must give him up to the authorities."

"*I* would," said Hawkins, cheered and relieved, "I'd give him up if he was a thousand ancestors compacted into one."

"Lord bless me, that's just what he is," said Sellers, with something like a groan, "it's exactly what he is; there's a contribution in him from every ancestor he ever had. In him there's atoms of priests, soldiers, crusaders, poets, and sweet and gracious women—all kinds and conditions of folk who trod this earth in old, old centuries, and vanished out of it ages ago, and now by act of ours they are summoned from their holy peace to answer for gutting a one-horse bank away out on the borders of Cherokee Strip, and it's just a howling outrage!"

"Oh, don't talk like that, Colonel; it takes the heart all out of me, and makes me ashamed of the part I am proposing to—"

"Wait—I've got it!"

"A saving hope? Shout it out, I am perishing."

"It's perfectly simple; a child would have thought of it. He is all right, not a flaw in him, as far as I have carried the work. If I've been able to bring him as far as the beginning of this century, what's to stop me now? I'll go on and materialize him down to date."

"Land, I never thought of that!" said Hawkins all ablaze with joy again. "It's the very thing. What a brain you have got! And will he shed the superfluous arm?"

"He will."

"And lose his English accent?"

"It will wholly disappear. He will speak Cherokee Strip—and other forms of profanity."

"Colonel, maybe he'll confess!"

"Confess? Merely that bank robbery?"

"Merely? Yes, but why 'merely'?"

The Colonel said in his most impressive manner:

"Hawkins, he will be wholly under my command. I will make him confess every crime he ever committed. There must be a thousand. Do you get the idea?"

"Well—not quite."

"The rewards will come to us."

"Prodigious conception! I *never* saw such a head for seeing with a lightning glance all the outlying ramifications and possibilities of a central idea."

"It is nothing; it comes natural to me. When his time is out in one jail he goes to the next and the next, and we shall have nothing to do but collect the rewards as he goes along. It is a perfectly steady income as long as we live, Hawkins. And much better than other kinds of investments, because he is indestructible."

"It looks—it really does look the way you say; it does indeed."

"Look?—why it *is*. It will not be denied that I have had a pretty wide and comprehensive financial experience, and I do not hesitate to say that I consider this one of the most valuable properties I have ever controlled."

"Do you really think so?"

"I do, indeed."

"O, Colonel, the wasting grind and grief of poverty! If we could realize immediately. I don't mean sell it all, but sell part—enough, you know, to—"

"See how you tremble with excitement. That comes of lack of experience. My boy, when you have been familiar with vast operations as long as I have, you'll be different. Look at me; is my eye dilated? do you notice a quiver anywhere? Feel my pulse: plunk—plunk—plunk—same as if I were asleep. And yet, what is passing through my calm cold mind? A procession of figures which would make a financial novice drunk—just the sight of them. Now it is by keeping cool, and looking at a thing all around, that a man sees what's really in it, and saves himself from the novice's unfailing mistake—the one you've just suggested—eagerness to *realize*. Listen to me. Your idea is to sell a part of him for ready cash. Now mine is—guess."

"I haven't an idea. What is it?"

"Stock him—of course."

"Well, I should never have thought of that."

"Because you are not a financier. Say he has committed a thousand crimes. Certainly that's a low estimate. By the look of him, even in his unfinished condition, he has committed all of a million. But call it only a thousand to be perfectly safe; five thousand reward, multiplied by a thousand, gives us a dead sure cash basis of—what? Five million dollars!"

"Wait—let me get my breath."

"And the property indestructible. Perpetually fruitful—perpetually; for a property with his disposition will go on committing crimes and winning rewards."

"You daze me, you make my head whirl!"

"Let it whirl, it won't do it any harm. Now that matter is all fixed—leave it alone. I'll get up the company and issue the stock, all in good time. Just leave it in my hands. I judge you don't doubt my ability to work it up for all it is worth."

"Indeed I don't. I can say that with truth."

"All right, then. That's disposed of. Everything in its turn. We old operators go by order and system—no helter-skelter business with us. What's the next thing on the docket? The carrying on of the materialization—the bringing it down to date. I will begin on that at once. I think—"

"Look here, Rossmore. You didn't lock It in. A hundred to one it has escaped!"

"Calm yourself, as to that; don't give yourself any uneasiness."

"But why shouldn't it escape?"

"Let it, if it wants to? What of it?"

"Well, *I* should consider it a pretty serious calamity."

"Why, my dear boy, once in my power, always in my power. It may go and come freely. I can produce it here whenever I want it, just by the exercise of my will."

"Well, I am truly glad to hear that, I do assure you."

"Yes, I shall give it all the painting it wants to do, and we and the family will make it as comfortable and contented as we can. No occasion to restrain its movements. I hope to persuade it to remain pretty quiet, though, because a materialization which is in a state of arrested development must of necessity be pretty soft and flabby and substanceless, and—er—by the way, I wonder where It comes from?"

"How? What do you mean?"

The earl pointed significantly—and interrogatively—toward the sky. Hawkins started; then settled into deep reflection; finally shook his head sorrowfully and pointed downwards.

"What makes you think so, Washington?"

"Well, I hardly know, but really you can see, yourself, that he doesn't seem to be pining for his last place."

"It's well thought! Soundly deduced. We've done that Thing a favor. But I believe I will pump it a little, in a quiet way, and find out if we are right."

"How long is it going to take to finish him off and fetch him down to date, Colonel?"

"I wish I knew, but I don't. I am clear knocked out by this new detail—this unforeseen necessity of working a subject down gradually from his condition of ancestor to his ultimate result as posterity. But I'll make him hump himself, anyway."

"Rossmore!"

"Yes, dear. We're in the laboratory. Come—Hawkins is here. Mind, now Hawkins—he's a sound, living, *human being* to all the family—*don't* forget that. Here she comes."

"Keep your seats, I'm not coming in. I just wanted to ask, who is it that's painting down there?"

"That? Oh, that's a young artist; young Englishman, named Tracy; very promising—favorite pupil of Hans Christian Andersen or one of the other old masters—Andersen I'm pretty sure it is; he's going to half-sole some of our old Italian masterpieces. Been talking to him?"

"Well, only a word. I stumbled right in on him without expecting anybody was there. I tried to be polite to him; offered him a snack" —(Sellers delivered a large wink to Hawkins from behind his hand), "but he declined, and said he wasn't hungry" (another sarcastic wink); "so I brought some apples" (double wink), "and he ate a couple of—"

"What!" and the colonel sprang some yards toward the ceiling and came down quaking with astonishment.

Lady Rossmore was smitten dumb with amazement. She gazed at the sheepish relic of Cherokee Strip, then at her husband, and then at the guest again. Finally she said—

"What is the matter with you, Mulberry?"

He did not answer immediately. His back was turned; he was bending over his chair, feeling the seat of it. But he answered next moment, and said—

"Ah, there it is; it was a tack."

The lady contemplated him doubtfully a moment, then said, pretty snappishly—

"All that for a tack! Praise goodness it wasn't a shingle nail, it would have landed you in the Milky Way. I do hate to have my nerves shook up so." And she turned on her heel and went her way.

As soon as she was safely out, the Colonel said, in a suppressed voice—

"Come—we must see for ourselves. It *must* be a mistake."

They hurried softly down and peeped in. Sellers whispered, in a sort of despair—

"It *is* eating! What a grisly spectacle! Hawkins it's horrible! Take me away—I can't stand it."

They tottered back to the laboratory.

CHAPTER 20

Tracy made slow progress with his work, for his mind wandered a good deal. Many things were puzzling him. Finally a light burst upon him all of a sudden—seemed to, at any rate—and he said to himself, "I've got the clew at last—this man's mind is off its balance; I don't know how much, but it's off a point or two, sure; off enough to explain this mess of perplexities, anyway. These dreadful chromos—which he takes for old masters; these villainous portraits—which to his frantic mind represent Rossmores; the hatchments; the pompous name of this ramshackle old crib—Rossmore Towers; and that odd assertion of his, that I was expected. How could I be expected? that is, Lord Berkeley. He knows by the papers that that person was burned up in the New Gadsby. Why, hang it, he really doesn't know *who* he was expecting; for his talk showed that he was not expecting an Englishman, or yet an artist, yet I answer his requirements notwithstanding. He seems sufficiently satisfied with me. Yes, he is a little off; in fact I am afraid he is a good deal off, poor old gentleman. But he's interesting—all people in about his condition are, I suppose. I hope he'll like my work; I would like to come every day and study him. And when I write my father—ah, that hurts! I mustn't get on that subject; it isn't good for my spirits. Somebody coming—I must get to work. It's the old gentleman again. He looks bothered. Maybe my clothes are suspicious; and they are—for an artist. If my conscience would allow me to make a change,—but that is out of the question. I wonder what he's making those passes in the air for, with his hands. I seem to be the object of them. Can he be trying to mesmerize me? I don't quite like it. There's something uncanny about it."

The colonel muttered to himself, "It has an effect on him, I can see it myself. That's enough for one time, I reckon. He's not very solid, yet, I suppose, and I might disintegrate him. I'll just put a sly question or two at him, now, and see if I can find out what his condition is, and where he's from."

He approached and said affably—

"Don't let me disturb you, Mr. Tracy; I only want to take a little glimpse of your work. Ah, that's fine—that's very fine indeed. You are doing it elegantly. My daughter will be charmed with this. May I sit down by you?"

"Oh, do; I shall be glad."

"It won't disturb you? I mean, won't dissipate your inspirations?"

Tracy laughed and said they were not ethereal enough to be very easily discommoded.

The colonel asked a number of cautious and well-considered questions—questions which seemed pretty odd and flighty to Tracy—but the answers conveyed the information desired, apparently, for the colonel said to himself, with mixed pride and gratification—

"It's a good job as far as I've got with it. He's solid. Solid and going to last; solid as the real thing. It's wonderful—wonderful. I believe I could petrify him."

After a little he asked, warily:

"Do you prefer being here, or—or there?"

"There? Where?"

"Why—er—where you've been?"

Tracy's thought flew to his boarding-house, and he answered with decision—

"Oh, *here*, much!"

The colonel was startled, and said to himself, "There's no uncertain ring about that. It indicates where *he's* been to, poor fellow. Well, I am satisfied, now. I'm glad I got him out."

He sat thinking, and thinking, and watching the brush go. At length he said to himself, "Yes, it certainly seems to account for the failure of my endeavors in poor Berkeley's case. *He* went in the other direction. Well, it's all right. He's better off."

Sally Sellers entered from the street, now, looking her divinest, and the artist was introduced to her. It was a violent case of mutual love at first sight, though neither party was entirely aware of the fact, perhaps. The Englishman made this irrelevant remark to himself, "Perhaps he is not insane, after all." Sally sat down, and showed an interest in Tracy's work which greatly pleased him, and a benevolent forgiveness of it which convinced him that the girl's nature was cast in a large mould. Sellers was anxious to report his discoveries to Hawkins; so he took his leave, saying that if the two "young devotees of the colored Muse" thought they could manage without him, he would go and look after his affairs. The artist said to himself, "I think he *is* a little eccentric, perhaps, but that is all." He reproached himself for having injuriously judged a man without giving him any fair chance to show what he really was.

Of course the stranger was very soon at his ease and chatting along comfortably. The average American girl possesses the valuable qualities of naturalness, honesty, and inoffensive straightforwardness; she is nearly barren of troublesome conventions and artificialities, consequently her presence and her ways are unembarrassing, and one is acquainted with her and on the pleasantest terms with her before he knows how it came about. This new acquaintanceship—friendship, indeed—progressed swiftly; and the unusual swiftness of it, and the thoroughness of it are sufficiently evidenced and established by one noteworthy fact—that within the first half hour both parties had ceased to be conscious of Tracy's clothes. Later this consciousness was re-awakened; it was then apparent to Gwendolen that she was almost reconciled to them, and it was apparent to Tracy that he wasn't. The re-awakening was brought about by Gwendolen's inviting the artist to stay to dinner. He had to decline, because he wanted to live, now—that is, now that there was something to live for—and he could not survive in those clothes at a gentleman's table. He thought he knew that. But he went away happy, for he saw that Gwendolen was disappointed.

And whither did he go? He went straight to a slop-shop and bought as neat and reasonably well-fitting a suit of clothes as an Englishman could be persuaded to wear. He said—*to* himself, but *at* his conscience—"I know it's wrong; but it would be wrong *not* to do it; and two wrongs do not make a right."

This satisfied him, and made his heart light. Perhaps it will also satisfy the reader—if he can make out what it means.

The old people were troubled about Gwendolen at dinner, because she was so distraught and silent. If they had noticed, they would have found that she was sufficiently alert and interested whenever the talk stumbled upon the artist and his work; but they didn't notice, and so the chat would swap around to some other subject, and then somebody would presently be privately worrying about Gwendolen again, and wondering if she were not well, or if something had gone wrong in the millinery line. Her mother offered her various reputable patent medicines, and tonics with iron and other hardware in them, and her father even proposed to send out for wine, relentless prohibitionist and head of the order in the District of Columbia as he was, but these kindnesses were all declined—thankfully, but with decision. At bedtime, when the family were breaking up for the night, she privately looted one of the brushes, saying to herself, "It's the one he has used the most."

The next morning Tracy went forth wearing his new suit, and equipped with a pink in his button-hole—a daily attention from Puss. His whole soul was full of Gwendolen Sellers, and this condition was an inspiration, art-wise. All the morning his brush pawed nimbly away at the canvases, almost without his awarity—awarity, in this sense being the sense of being aware, though disputed by some authorities—turning out marvel upon marvel, in the way of decorative accessories to the portraits, with a felicity and celerity which amazed the veterans of the firm and fetched out of them continuous explosions of applause.

Meantime Gwendolen was losing her morning, and many dollars. She supposed Tracy was coming in the forenoon—a conclusion which she had jumped to without outside help. So she tripped down stairs every little while from her work-parlor to arrange the brushes and things over again, and see if he had arrived. And when she was in her work-parlor it was not profitable, but just the other way—as she found out to her sorrow. She had put in her idle moments during the last little while back, in designing a particularly rare and capable gown for herself, and this morning she set about making it up; but she was absent minded, and made an irremediable botch of it. When she saw what she had done, she knew the reason of it and the meaning of it; and she put her work away from her and said she would accept the sign. And from that time forth she came no more away from the Audience Chamber, but remained there and waited. After luncheon she waited again. A whole hour. Then a great joy welled up in her heart, for she saw him coming. So she flew back up stairs thankful, and could hardly wait for him to miss the principal brush, which she had mislaid down there, but knew where she had mislaid it. However, all in good time the others were called in and couldn't find the brush, and then she was sent for, and she couldn't find it herself for some little time; but then she found it when the others had gone away to hunt in the kitchen and down cellar and in the woodshed, and all those other places where people look for things whose ways they are not familiar with. So she gave him the brush, and remarked that she ought to have seen that everything was ready for him, but it hadn't seemed necessary, because it was so early that she wasn't expecting—but she stopped there, surprised at herself for what she was saying; and he felt caught and ashamed, and said to himself, "I knew my impatience would drag me here before I was expected, and betray me, and that is just what it has done; she sees straight through me—and is laughing at me, inside, of course."

Gwendolen was very much pleased, on one account, and a little the other way in another; pleased with the new clothes and the improvement which they had achieved; less pleased by the pink in the button-hole. Yesterday's pink had hardly interested her; this one was just like it, but somehow it had got her immediate attention, and kept it. She wished she could think of some way of getting at its history in a properly colorless and indifferent way. Presently she made a venture. She said—

"Whatever a man's age may be, he can reduce it several years by putting a bright-colored flower in his button-hole. I have often noticed that. Is that your sex's reason for wearing a boutonnière?"

"I fancy not, but certainly that reason would be a sufficient one. I've never heard of the idea before."

"You seem to prefer pinks. Is it on account of the color, or the form?"

"Oh no," he said, simply, "they are given to me. I don't think I have any preference."

"They are given to him," she said to herself, and she felt a coldness toward that pink. "I wonder who it is, and what she is like." The flower began to take up a good deal of room; it obtruded itself everywhere, it intercepted all views, and marred them; it was becoming exceedingly annoying and conspicuous for a little thing. "I wonder if he cares for her." That thought gave her a quite definite pain.

CHAPTER 21

She had made everything comfortable for the artist; there was no further pretext for staying. So she said she would go, now, and asked him to summon the servants in case he should need anything. She went away unhappy; and she left unhappiness behind her; for she carried away all the sunshine. The time dragged heavily for both, now. He couldn't paint for thinking of her; she couldn't design or millinerize with any heart, for thinking of him. Never before had painting seemed so empty to him, never before had millinerizing seemed so void of interest to her. She had gone without repeating that dinner-invitation—an almost unendurable disappointment to him. On her part—well, she was suffering, too; for she had found she *couldn't* invite him. It was not hard yesterday, but it was impossible to-day. A thousand innocent privileges seemed to have been filched from her unawares in the past twenty-four hours. To-day she felt strangely hampered, restrained of her liberty. To-day she couldn't propose to herself to do anything or say anything concerning this young man without being instantly paralyzed into non-action by the fear that he might "suspect." Invite him to dinner *to-day?* It made her shiver to think of it.

And so her afternoon was one long fret. Broken at intervals. Three times she had to go down stairs on errands—that is, she thought she had to go down stairs on errands. Thus, going and coming, she had six glimpses of him, in the aggregate, without seeming to look in his direction; and she tried to endure these electric ecstasies without showing any sign, but they fluttered her up a good deal, and she felt that the naturalness she was putting on was overdone and quite too frantically sober and hysterically calm to deceive.

The painter had his share of the rapture; he had his six glimpses, and they smote him with waves of pleasure that assaulted him, beat upon him, washed over him deliciously, and drowned out all consciousness of what he was doing with his brush. So there were six places in his canvas which had to be done over again.

At last Gwendolen got some peace of mind by sending word to the Thompsons, in the neighborhood, that she was coming there to dinner. She wouldn't be reminded, at *that* table, that there was an absentee who ought to be a presentee—a word which she meant to look out in the dictionary at a calmer time.

About this time the old earl dropped in for a chat with the artist, and invited him to stay to dinner. Tracy cramped down his joy and gratitude by a sudden and powerful exercise of all his forces; and he felt that now that he was going to be close to Gwendolen, and hear her voice and watch her face during several precious hours, earth had nothing valuable to add to his life for the present.

The earl said to himself, "This spectre can eat apples, apparently. We shall find out, now, if that is a specialty. I think, myself, it's a specialty. Apples, without doubt, constitute the spectral limit. It was the case with our first parents. No, I am wrong—at least only partly right. The line *was* drawn at apples, just as in the present case, but it was from the other direction." The new clothes gave him a thrill of pleasure and pride. He said to himself, "I've got part of him down to date, anyway."

Sellers said he was pleased with Tracy's work; and he went on and engaged him to restore his old masters, and said he should also want him to paint his portrait and his wife's and possibly his daughter's. The tide of the artist's happiness was at flood, now. The chat flowed pleasantly along while Tracy painted and Sellers carefully unpacked a picture which he had brought with him. It was a chromo; a new one, just out. It was the smirking, self-satisfied portrait of a man who was inundating the Union with advertisements inviting everybody to buy his specialty, which was a three-dollar shoe or a dress-suit or something of that kind. The old gentleman rested the chromo flat upon his lap and gazed down tenderly upon it, and became silent and meditative. Presently Tracy noticed that he was dripping tears on it. This touched the young fellow's sympathetic nature, and at the same time gave him the painful sense of being an intruder upon a sacred privacy, an observer of emotions which a stranger ought not to witness. But his pity rose superior to other considerations, and compelled him to try to comfort the old mourner with kindly words and a show of friendly interest. He said—

"I am very sorry—is it a friend whom—"

"Ah, more than that, far more than that—a relative, the dearest I had on earth, although I was never permitted to see him. Yes, it is young Lord Berkeley, who perished so heroically in the awful confla—why, what is the matter?"

"Oh, nothing, nothing. It was a little startling to be so suddenly brought face to face, so to speak, with a person one has heard so much talk about. Is it a good likeness?"

"Without doubt, yes. I never saw him, but you can easily see the resemblance to his father," said Sellers, holding up the chromo and glancing from it to the chromo misrepresenting the Usurping Earl and back again with an approving eye.

"Well, no—I am not sure that I make out the likeness. It is plain that the Usurping Earl there has a great deal of character and a long face like a horse's, whereas his heir here is smirky, moon-faced and characterless."

"We are all that way in the beginning—all the line," said Sellers, undisturbed. "We all start as moon-faced fools, then later we tadpole along into horse-faced marvels of intellect and character. It is by that sign and by that fact that I detect the resemblance here and know this portrait to be genuine and perfect. Yes, all our family are fools at first."

"This young man seems to meet the hereditary requirement, certainly."

"Yes, yes, he was a fool, without any doubt. Examine the face, the shape of the head, the expression. It's all fool, fool, fool, straight through."

"Thanks," said Tracy, involuntarily.

"Thanks?"

"I mean for explaining it to me. Go on, please."

"As I was saying, fool is printed all over the face. A body can even read the *de*tails."

"What do they say?"

"Well, added up, he is a wobbler."

"A which?"

"Wobbler. A person that's always taking a firm stand about something or other—kind of a Gibraltar stand, *he* thinks, for unshakable fidelity and everlastingness—and then, inside of a little while, he begins to wobble; no more Gibraltar there; no, sir, a mighty ordinary commonplace weakling wobbling around on stilts. That's Lord Berkeley to a dot, you can *see* it—*look* at that sheep! But,—why are you blushing like sunset! Dear sir, have I unwittingly offended in some way?"

"Oh, no indeed, no indeed. Far from it. But it always makes me blush to hear a man revile his own blood." He said to himself, "How strangely his vagrant and unguided fancies have hit upon the truth. By accident, he has described me. I am that contemptible thing. When I left England I thought I knew myself; I thought I was a very Frederick the Great for resolution and staying capacity; whereas in truth I am just a Wobbler, simply a Wobbler. Well—after all, it is at least creditable to *have* high ideals and give birth to lofty resolutions; I will allow myself that comfort." Then he said, aloud, "Could this sheep, as you call him, breed a great and self-sacrificing idea in his head, do you think? Could he meditate such a thing, for instance, as the renunciation of the earldom and its wealth and its glories, and voluntary retirement to the ranks of the commonalty, there to rise by his own merit or remain forever poor and obscure?"

"*Could* he? Why, look at him—look at this simpering self-righteous mug! There is your answer. It's the very thing he would think of. And he would start in to do it, too."

"And then?"

"He'd wobble."

"And back down?"

"Every time."

"Is that to happen with *all* my—I mean would that happen to *all* his high resolutions?"

"Oh certainly—certainly. It's the Rossmore of it."

"Then this creature was fortunate to die! Suppose, for argument's sake, that I was a Rossmore, and—"

"It can't be done."

"Why?"

"Because it's not a supposable case. To be a Rossmore at your age, you'd have to be a fool, and you're not a fool. And you'd have to be a Wobbler, whereas anybody that is an expert in reading character can see at a glance that when you set your foot down once, it's there to stay; an earthquake can't wobble it." He added to himself, "That's enough to say to him, but it isn't half strong enough for the facts. The more I observe him, now, the more remarkable I find him. It is the strongest face I have ever examined. There is almost superhuman firmness here, immovable purpose, iron steadfastness of will. A most extraordinary young man."

He presently said, aloud—

"Some time I want to ask your advice about a little matter, Mr. Tracy. You see, I've got that young lord's remains—my goodness, how you jump!"

"Oh, it's nothing, pray go on. You've got his remains?"

"Yes."

"Are you sure they are his, and not somebody else's?"

"Oh, perfectly sure. Samples, I mean. Not all of him."

"Samples?"

"Yes—in baskets. Some time you will be going home; and if you wouldn't mind taking them along—"

"Who? I?"

"Yes—certainly. I don't mean *now;* but after a while; after—but look here, would you like to see them?"

"No! Most certainly not. I don't want to see them."

"O, very well. I only thought—heyo, where are you going, dear?"

"Out to dinner, papa."

Tracy was aghast. The colonel said, in a disappointed voice—

"Well, I'm sorry. Sho, I didn't know she was going out, Mr. Tracy." Gwendolen's face began to take on a sort of apprehensive What-have-I-done expression. "Three old people to one young one—well, it *isn't* a good team, that's a fact." Gwendolen's face betrayed a dawning hopefulness and she said—with a tone of reluctance which hadn't the hallmark on it—

"If you prefer, I will send words to the Thompsons that I—"

"Oh, is it the Thompsons? That simplifies it—sets everything right. We can fix it without spoiling your arrangements, my child. You've got your heart set on—"

"But papa, I'd *just* as soon go there some other—"

"No—I won't have it. You are a good hard-working darling child, and your father is not the man to disappoint you when you—"

"But papa, I—"

"Go along, I won't hear a word. We'll get along, dear."

Gwendolen was ready to cry with vexation. But there was nothing to do but start; which she was about to do when her father hit upon an idea which filled him with delight because it so deftly covered all the difficulties of the situation and made things smooth and satisfactory:

"I've got it, my love, so that you won't be robbed of your holiday and at the same time we'll be pretty satisfactorily fixed for a good time here. You send Belle Thompson here—perfectly beautiful creature, Tracy, per-fectly beautiful; I want you to see that girl; why, you'll just go mad; you'll go mad inside of a minute; yes, you send her right along, Gwendolen, and tell her—why, she's gone!" He turned—she was already passing out at the gate. He muttered, "I wonder what's the matter; I don't know what her mouth's doing, but I think her shoulders are swearing. Well," said Sellers blithely to Tracy, "I shall miss her—parents always miss the children as soon as they're out of sight, it's only a natural and wisely ordained partiality—but you'll be all right, because Miss Belle will supply the youthful element for you and to your entire content; and we old people will do our best, too. We shall have a good enough time. And you'll have a chance to get better acquainted with Admiral Hawkins. That's a rare character, Mr. Tracy—

one of the rarest and most engaging characters the world has produced. You'll find him worth studying. I've studied him ever since he was a child and have always found him developing. I really consider that one of the main things that has enabled me to master the difficult science of character-reading was the livid interest I always felt in that boy and the baffling inscrutabilities of his ways and inspirations."

Tracy was not hearing a word. His spirits were gone, he was desolate.

"Yes, a most wonderful character. Concealment—that's the basis of it. Always the first thing you want to do is to find the keystone a man's character is built on—then you've got it. No misleading and apparently inconsistent peculiarities can fool you then. What do you read on the Senator's surface? Simplicity; a kind of rank and protuberant simplicity; whereas, in fact, that's one of the deepest minds in the world. A perfectly honest man—an absolutely honest and honorable man—and yet without doubt the profoundest master of dissimulation the world has ever seen."

"O, it's devilish!" This was wrung from the unlistening Tracy by the anguished thought of what might have been if only the dinner arrangements hadn't got mixed.

"No, I shouldn't call it that," said Sellers, who was now placidly walking up and down the room with his hands under his coat-tails and listening to himself talk. "One could quite properly call it devilish in another man, but not in the Senator. Your *term* is right—perfectly right—I grant that—but the application is wrong. It makes a great difference. Yes, he is a marvelous character. I do not suppose that any other statesman ever had such a colossal sense of humor, combined with the ability to totally conceal it. I may except George Washington and Cromwell, and perhaps Robespierre, but I draw the line there. A person not an expert might be in Judge Hawkins's company a lifetime and never find out he had any more sense of humor than a cemetery."

A deep-drawn yard-long sigh from the distraught and dreaming artist, followed by a murmured "Miserable, oh, miserable!"

"Well, no, I shouldn't say *that* about it, quite. On the contrary, I admire his ability to conceal his humor even more if possible than I admire the gift itself, stupendous as it is. Another thing—General Hawkins is a thinker; a keen, logical, exhaustive, analytical thinker—perhaps the ablest of modern times. That is, of course, upon themes suited to his size, like the glacial period, and the correlation of forces, and the evolution of the Christian from the caterpillar—any of those things; give him a subject according to his size, and just stand back and watch him think! Why you can see the place rock! Ah, yes, you must know him; you must get on the inside of him. Perhaps the most extraordinary mind since Aristotle."

Dinner was kept waiting for a while for Miss Thompson, but as Gwendolen had not delivered the invitation to her the waiting did no good, and the household presently went to the meal without her. Poor old Sellers tried everything his hospitable soul could devise to make the occasion an enjoyable one for the guest, and the guest tried his honest best to be cheery and chatty and happy for the old gentleman's sake; in fact all hands worked hard in the interest of a mutual good time, but the thing was a failure from the start; Tracy's heart was lead in his bosom, there seemed to be only one prominent feature in the landscape and that was a vacant chair, he couldn't drag his mind away from Gwendolen and his hard luck; consequently his distractions allowed deadly pauses to slip in every now and then when it was his turn to say something, and of course this disease spread to the rest of the conversation—wherefore, instead of having a breezy sail in sunny waters, as anticipated, everybody was bailing out and praying for land. What *could* the matter be? Tracy alone could have told, the others couldn't even invent a theory.

Meanwhile they were having a similarly dismal time at the Thompson house; in fact a twin experience. Gwendolen was ashamed of herself for allowing her disappointment to so depress her spirits and make her so strangely and profoundly miserable; but feeling ashamed of herself didn't improve the matter any; it only seemed to aggravate the suffering. She explained that she was not feeling very well, and everybody could see that this was true; so she got sincere sympathy and commiseration; but that didn't help the case. Nothing helps that kind of a case. It is best to just stand off and let it fester. The moment the dinner was over the girl excused herself, and she hurried home feeling unspeakably grateful to get away from that house and that intolerable captivity and suffering.

Will he be gone? The thought arose in her brain, but took effect in her heels. She slipped into the house, threw off her things and made straight for the dining room. She stopped and listened. Her father's voice—with no life in it; presently her mother's—no life in that; a considerable vacancy, then a sterile remark from Washington Hawkins. Another silence; then, not Tracy's but her father's voice again.

"He's gone," she said to herself despairingly, and listlessly opened the door and stepped within.

"Why, my child," cried the mother, "how white you are! Are you—has anything—"

"White?" exclaimed Sellers. "It's gone like a flash; 'twasn't serious. Already she's as red as the soul of a watermelon! Sit down, dear, sit down—goodness knows you're welcome. Did you have a good time? We've had great times here—immense. Why didn't Miss Belle come? Mr. Tracy is not feeling well, and she'd have made him forget it."

She was content now; and out from her happy eyes there went a light that told a secret to another pair of eyes there and got a secret in return. In just that infinitely small fraction of a second those two great confessions were made, received, and perfectly understood. All anxiety, apprehension, uncertainty, vanished out of these young people's hearts and left them filled with a great peace.

Sellers had had the most confident faith that with the new reinforcement victory would be at this last moment snatched from the jaws of defeat, but it was an error. The talk was a stubbornly disjointed as ever. He was proud of Gwendolen, and liked to show her off, even against Miss Belle Thompson, and here had been a great opportunity, and what had she made of it? He felt a good deal put out. It vexed him to think that this Englishman, with the traveling Briton's everlasting disposition to generalize whole mountain ranges from single sample-grains of sand, would jump to the conclusion that American girls were as dumb as himself—generalizing the whole tribe from this single sample and she at her poorest, there being nothing at that table to inspire her, give her a start, keep her from going to sleep. He made up his mind that for the honor of the country he would bring these two together again over the social board before long. There would be a different result another time, he judged. He said to himself, with a deep sense of injury, "He'll put in his diary—they all keep diaries—he'll put in his diary that she was miraculously uninteresting—dear, dear, but *wasn't* she!—I never saw the like—and yet looking as beautiful as Satan, too—and couldn't seem to do anything but paw bread crumbs, and pick flowers to pieces, and look fidgety. And it isn't any better here in the Hall of Audience. I've had enough; I'll haul down my flag; the others may fight it out if they want to."

He shook hands all around and went off to do some work which he said was pressing. The idolaters were the width of the room apart, and apparently unconscious of each other's presence. The distance got shortened a little, now. Very soon the mother withdrew. The distance narrowed again. Tracy stood before a chromo of some Ohio politician which had been retouched and chain-mailed for a crusading Rossmore, and Gwendolen was sitting on the sofa not far from his elbow artificially absorbed in examining a photograph album that hadn't any photographs in it.

The "Senator" still lingered. He was sorry for the young people; it had been a dull evening for them. In the goodness of his heart he tried to make it pleasant for them now; tried to remove the ill impression necessarily left by the general defeat; tried to be chatty, even tried to be gay. But the responses were sickly, there was no starting any enthusiasm; he would give it up and quit—it was a day specially picked out and consecrated to failures.

But when Gwendolen rose up promptly and smiled a glad smile and said with thankfulness and blessing—"*Must* you go?" it seemed cruel to desert, and he sat down again.

He was about to begin a remark when—when he didn't. We have all been there. He didn't know how he knew his concluding to stay longer had been a mistake, he merely knew it; and knew it for dead certain, too. And so he bade goodnight, and went mooning out, wondering what he could have done that changed the atmosphere that way. As the door closed behind him those two were standing side by side, looking at that door—looking at it in a waiting, second-counting, but deeply grateful kind of way. And the instant it closed they flung their arms about each other's necks, and there, heart to heart and lip to lip—

"Oh, my God, she's kissing it!"

Nobody heard this remark, because Hawkins, who bred it, only thought it, he didn't utter it. He had turned, the moment he had closed the door, and had pushed it open a little, intending to re-enter and ask what ill-advised thing he had done or said, and apologize for it. But he didn't re-enter; he staggered off stunned, terrified, distressed.

CHAPTER 22

Five minutes later he was sitting in his room, with his head bowed within the circle of his arms, on the table—final attitude of grief and despair. His tears were flowing fast, and now and then a sob broke upon the stillness. Presently he said—

"I knew her when she was a little child and used to climb about my knees; I love her as I love my own, and now—oh, poor thing, poor thing, I cannot bear it!—she's gone and lost her heart to this mangy materializee! Why *didn't* we see that that might happen? But how could we? Nobody could; nobody could ever have dreamed of such a thing. You couldn't expect a person would fall in love with a wax-work. And this one doesn't even amount to that."

He went on grieving to himself, and now and then giving voice to his lamentations.

"It's done, oh, it's done, and there's no help for it, no undoing the miserable business. If I had the nerve, I would kill it. But that wouldn't do any good. *She* loves it; she thinks it's genuine and authentic. If she lost it she would grieve for it just as she would for a real person. And who's to break it to the family! Not I—I'll die first. Sellers is the best human being I ever knew and I wouldn't any more think of—oh, dear, why it'll break his heart when he finds it out. And Polly's too. *This* comes of meddling with such infernal matters! But for this, the creature would still be roasting in Sheol where it belongs. How is it that these people don't smell the brimstone? Sometimes I can't come into the same room with him without nearly suffocating."

After a while he broke out again:

"Well, there's *one* thing, sure. The materializing has got to stop right where it is. If she's got to marry a spectre, let her marry a decent one out of the Middle Ages, like this one—not a cowboy and a thief such as this protoplasmic tadpole's going to turn into if Sellers keeps on fussing at it. It costs five thousand dollars cash and shuts down on the incorporated company to stop the works at this point, but Sally Sellers's happiness is worth more than that."

He heard Sellers coming, and got himself to rights. Sellers took a seat, and said—

"Well, I've got to confess I'm a good deal puzzled. It did certainly eat, there's no getting around it. Not eat, exactly, either, but it nibbled; nibbled in an appetiteless way, but still it nibbled; and that's just a marvel. Now the question is, what does it do with those nibblings? That's it—what does it do with them? My idea is that we don't begin to know all there is to this stupendous discovery yet. But time will show —time and science—give us a chance, and don't get impatient."

But he couldn't get Hawkins interested; couldn't make him talk to amount to anything; couldn't drag him out of his depression. But at last he took a turn that arrested Hawkins's attention.

"I'm coming to like him, Hawkins. He is a person of stupendous character—absolutely gigantic. Under that placid exterior is concealed the most dare-devil spirit that was ever put into a man—he's just a Clive over again. Yes, I'm all admiration for him, on account of his character, and liking naturally follows admiration, you know. I'm coming to like him immensely. Do you know, I haven't the heart to degrade such a character as that down to the burglar estate for money or for anything else; and I've come to ask if you are willing to let the reward go, and leave this poor fellow—"

"Where he is?"

"Yes—not bring him down to date."

"Oh, there's my hand; and my heart's in it, too!"

"I'll never forget you for this, Hawkins," said the old gentleman in a voice which he found it hard to control. "You are making a great sacrifice for me, and one which you can ill afford, but I'll never forget your generosity, and if I live you shall not suffer for it, be sure of that."

Sally Sellers immediately and vividly realized that she was become a new being; a being of a far higher and worthier sort than she had been such a little while before; an earnest being, in place of a dreamer; and supplied with a reason for her presence in the world, where merely a wistful and troubled curiosity about it had existed before. So great and so comprehensive was the change which had been wrought, that she seemed to herself to be a real person who had lately been a shadow; a something which had lately been a nothing; a purpose, which had lately been a fancy; a finished temple, with the altar-fires lit and the voice of worship ascending, where before had been but an architect's confusion of arid working plans, unintelligible to the passing eye and prophesying nothing.

"Lady" Gwendolen! The pleasantness of that sound was all gone; it was an offense to her ear now. She said—

"There—that sham belongs to the past; I will not be called by it any more."

"I may call you simply Gwendolen? You will allow me to drop the formalities straightway and name you by your dear first name without additions?"

She was dethroning the pink and replacing it with a rosebud.

"There—that is better. I hate pinks—some pinks. Indeed yes, you are to call me by my first name without additions—that is,—well, I don't mean without additions *entirely*, but—"

It was as far as she could get. There was a pause; his intellect was struggling to comprehend; presently it did manage to catch the idea in time to save embarrassment all around, and he said gratefully—

"*Dear* Gwendolen! I may say that?"

"Yes—part of it. But—don't kiss me when I am talking, it makes me forget what I was going to say. You can call me by part of that form, but not the last part. Gwendolen is not my name."

"Not your name?" This in a tone of wonder and surprise.

The girl's soul was suddenly invaded by a creepy apprehension, a quite definite sense of suspicion and alarm. She put his arms away from her, looked him searchingly in the eye, and said—

"Answer me truly, on your honor. You are not seeking to marry me on account of my *rank?*"

The shot almost knocked him through the wall, he was so little prepared for it. There was something so finely grotesque about the question and its parent suspicion, that he stopped to wonder and admire, and thus was he saved from laughing. Then, without wasting precious time, he set about the task of convincing her that he had been lured by herself alone, and had fallen in love with her only, not her title and position; that he loved her with all his heart, and could not love her more if she were a duchess, or less if she were without home, name or family. She watched his face wistfully, eagerly, hopefully, translating his words by its expression; and when he had finished there was gladness in her heart—a tumultuous gladness, indeed, though outwardly she was calm, tranquil, even judicially austere. She prepared a surprise for him, now, calculated to put a heavy strain upon those disinterested protestations of his; and thus she delivered it, burning it away word by word as the fuse burns down to a bombshell, and watching to see how far the explosion would lift him:

"Listen—and do not doubt me, for I shall speak the exact truth. Howard Tracy, I am no more an earl's child than you are!"

To her joy—and secret surprise, also—it never phased him. He was ready, this time, and saw his chance. He cried out with enthusiasm, "Thank heaven for that!" and gathered her to his arms.

To express her happiness was almost beyond her gift of speech.

"You make me the proudest girl in all the earth," she said, with her head pillowed on his shoulder. "I thought it only natural that you should be dazzled by the title—maybe even unconsciously, you being English—and that you might be deceiving yourself in thinking you loved only me, and find you didn't love me when the deception was swept away; so it makes me proud that the revelation stands for nothing and that you *do* love just me, only me—oh, prouder than any words can tell!"

"It is only you, sweetheart, I never gave one envying glance toward your father's earldom. That is utterly true, dear Gwendolen."

"There—you mustn't call me that. I hate that false name. I told you it wasn't mine. My name is Sally Sellers—or Sarah, if you like. From this time I banish dreams, visions, imaginings, and will no more of them. I am going to be myself—my genuine self, my honest self, my natural self, clear and clean of sham and folly and fraud, and worthy of you. There is no grain of social inequality between us; I, like you, am poor; I, like you, am without position or distinction; you are a struggling artist, I am that, too, in my humbler way. Our bread is honest bread, we work for our living. Hand in hand we will walk hence to the grave, helping each other in all ways, living for each other, being and remaining one in heart and purpose, one in hope and aspiration, inseparable to the end. And though our place is low, judged by the world's eye, we will make it as high as the highest in the great essentials of honest work for what we eat and wear, and conduct above reproach. We live in a land, let us be thankful, where this is all-sufficient, and no man is better than his neighbor by the grace of God, but only by his own merit."

Tracy tried to break in, but she stopped him and kept the floor herself.

"I am not through, yet. I am going to purge myself of the last vestiges of artificiality and pretence, and then start fair on your own honest level and be worthy mate to you thenceforth. My father honestly thinks he is an earl. Well, leave him his dream, it pleases him and does no one any harm. It was the dream of his ancestors before him. It has made fools of the house of Sellers for generations, and it made something of a fool of me, but took no deep root. I am done with it now, and for good. Forty-eight hours ago I was privately proud of being the daughter of a pinchbeck earl, and thought the proper mate for me must be a man of like degree; but to-day—oh, how grateful I am for your love which has healed my sick brain and restored my sanity!—I could make oath that no earl's son in all the world—"

"Oh,—well, but—but—"

"Why, you look like a person in a panic. What is it? What is the matter?"

"Matter? Oh, nothing—nothing. I was only going to say"—but in his flurry nothing occurred to him to say, for a moment; then by a lucky inspiration he thought of something entirely sufficient for the occasion, and brought it out with eloquent force: "Oh, how beautiful you are! You take my breath away when you look like that."

It was well conceived, well timed, and cordially delivered—and it got its reward.

"Let me see. Where was I? Yes, my father's earldom is pure moonshine. Look at those dreadful things on the wall. You have of course supposed them to be portraits of his ancestors, earls of Rossmore. Well, they are not. They are chromos of distinguished Americans—all moderns; but he has carried them back a thousand years by re-labeling them. Andrew Jackson there, is doing what he can to be the late American earl; and the newest treasure in the collection is supposed to be the young English heir—I mean the idiot with the crape; but in truth it's a shoemaker, and not Lord Berkeley at all."

"Are you sure?"

"Why of course I am. He wouldn't look like that."

"Why?"

"Because his conduct in his last moments, when the fire was sweeping around him shows that he was a man. It shows that he was a fine, high-souled young creature."

Tracy was strongly moved by these compliments, and it seemed to him that the girl's lovely lips took on a new loveliness when they were delivering them. He said, softly—

"It is a pity he could not know what a gracious impression his behavior was going to leave with the dearest and sweetest stranger in the land of—"

"Oh, I almost loved him! Why, I think of him every day. He is always floating about in my mind."

Tracy felt that this was a little more than was necessary. He was conscious of the sting of jealousy. He said—

"It is quite right to think of him—at least now and then—that is, at intervals—in perhaps an admiring way—but it seems to me that—"

"Howard Tracy, are you jealous of that dead man?"

He was ashamed—and at the same time not ashamed. He was jealous—and at the same time he was not jealous. In a sense the dead man was himself; in that case compliments and affection lavished upon that corpse went into his own till and were clear profit. But in another sense the dead man was not himself; and in that case all compliments and affection lavished there were wasted, and a sufficient basis for jealousy. A tiff was the result of the dispute between the two. Then they made it up, and were more loving than ever. As an affectionate clincher of the reconciliation, Sally declared that she had now banished Lord Berkeley from her mind; and added, "And in order to make sure that he shall never make trouble between us again, I will teach myself to detest that name and all that have ever borne it or ever shall bear it."

This inflicted another pang, and Tracy was minded to ask her to modify that a little—just on general principles, and as practice in not overdoing a good thing—perhaps he might better leave things as they were and not risk bringing on another tiff. He got away from that particular, and sought less tender ground for conversation.

"I suppose you disapprove wholly of aristocracies and nobilities, now that you have renounced your title and your father's earldom."

"*Real* ones? Oh, dear no—but I've thrown aside our sham one for good."

This answer fell just at the right time and just in the right place, to save the poor unstable young man from changing his political complexion once more. He had been on the point of beginning to totter again, but this prop shored him up and kept him from floundering back into democracy and re-renouncing aristocracy. So he went home glad that he had asked the fortunate question. The girl would accept a little thing like a genuine earldom, she was merely prejudiced against the brummagem article. Yes, he could have his girl and have his earldom, too: that question was a fortunate stroke.

Sally went to bed happy, too; and remained happy, deliriously happy, for nearly two hours; but at last, just as she was sinking into a contented and luxurious unconsciousness, the shady devil who lives and lurks and hides and watches inside of human beings and is always waiting for a chance to do the proprietor a malicious damage, whispered to her soul and said, "That question had a harmless look, but what was *back* of it?—what was the secret motive of it?—what suggested it?"

The shady devil had knifed her, and could retire, now, and take a rest; the wound would attend to business for him. And it did.

Why should Howard Tracy ask that question? If he was not trying to marry her for the sake of her rank, what should suggest that question to him? Didn't he plainly look gratified when she said her objections to aristocracy had their limitations? Ah, he is after that earldom, that gilded sham—it isn't poor me he wants.

So she argued, in anguish and tears. Then she argued the opposite theory, but made a weak, poor business of it, and lost the case. She kept the arguing up, one side and then the other, the rest of the night, and at last fell asleep at dawn; fell in the fire at dawn, one may say; for that kind of sleep resembles fire, and one comes out of it with his brain baked and his physical forces fried out of him.

CHAPTER 23

Tracy wrote his father before he sought his bed. He wrote a letter which he believed would get better treatment than his cablegram received, for it contained what ought to be welcome news; namely, that he had tried equality and working for a living; had made a fight which he could find no reason to be ashamed of, and in the matter of earning a living had proved that he was able to do it; but that on the whole he had arrived at the conclusion that he could not reform the world single-handed, and was willing to retire from the conflict with the fair degree of honor which he had gained, and was also willing to return home and resume his position and be content with it and thankful for it for the future, leaving further experiment of a missionary sort to other young people needing the chastening and quelling persuasions of experience, the only logic sure to convince a diseased imagination and restore it to rugged health. Then he approached the subject of marriage with the daughter of the American Claimant with a good deal of caution and much painstaking art. He said praiseful and appreciative things about the girl, but didn't dwell upon that detail or make it prominent. The thing which he made prominent was the opportunity now so happily afforded, to reconcile York and Lancaster, graft the warring roses upon one stem, and end forever a crying injustice which had already lasted far too long. One could infer that he had thought this thing all out and chosen this way of making all things fair and right because it was sufficiently fair and considerably wiser than the renunciation-scheme which he had brought with him from England. One could infer that, but he didn't say it. In fact the more he read his letter over, the more he got to inferring it himself.

When the old earl received that letter, the first part of it filled him with a grim and snarly satisfaction; but the rest of it brought a snort or two out of him that could be translated differently. He wasted no ink in this emergency, either in cablegrams or letters; he promptly took ship for America to look into the matter himself. He had staunchly held his grip all this long time, and given no sign of the hunger at his heart to see his son; hoping for the cure of his insane dream, and resolute that the process should go through all the necessary stages without assuaging telegrams or other nonsense from home, and here was victory at last. Victory, but stupidly marred by this idiotic marriage project. Yes, he would step over and take a hand in this matter himself.

During the first ten days following the mailing of the letter Tracy's spirits had no idle time; they were always climbing up into the clouds or sliding down into the earth as deep as the law of gravitation reached. He was intensely happy or intensely miserable by turns, according to Miss Sally's moods. He never could tell when the mood was going to change, and when it changed he couldn't tell what it was that had changed it. Sometimes she was so in love with him that her love was tropical, torrid, and she could find no language fervent enough for its expression; then suddenly, and without warning or any apparent reason, the weather would change, and the victim would find himself adrift among the icebergs and feeling as lonesome and friendless as the north pole. It sometimes seemed to him that a man might better be dead than exposed to these devastating varieties of climate.

The case was simple. Sally *wanted* to believe that Tracy's preference was disinterested; so she was always applying little tests of one sort or another, hoping and expecting that they would bring out evidence which would confirm or fortify her belief. Poor Tracy did not know that these experiments were being made upon him, consequently he walked promptly into all the traps the girl set for him. These traps consisted in apparently casual references to social distinction, aristocratic title and privilege, and such things. Often Tracy responded to these references heedlessly and not much caring what he said provided it kept the talk going and prolonged the séance. He didn't suspect that the girl was watching his face and listening for his words as one who watches the judge's face and listens for the words which will restore him to home and friends and freedom or shut him away from the sun and human companionship forever. He didn't suspect that his careless words were being weighed, and so he often delivered sentence of death when it would have been just as handy and all the same to him to pronounce acquittal. Daily he broke the girl's heart, nightly he sent her to the rack for sleep. He couldn't understand it.

Some people would have put this and that together and perceived that the weather never changed until one particular subject was introduced, and that then it *always* changed. And they would have looked further, and perceived that that subject was always introduced by the one party, never the other. They would have argued, then, that this was done for a purpose. If they could not find out what that purpose was in any simpler or easier way, they would *ask*.

But Tracy was not deep enough or suspicious enough to think of these things. He noticed only one particular; that the weather was always sunny when a visit *began*. No matter how much it might cloud up later, it always began with a clear sky. He couldn't explain this curious fact to himself, he merely knew it to be a fact. The truth of the matter was, that by the time Tracy had been out of Sally's sight six hours she was so famishing for a sight of him that her doubts and suspicions were all consumed away in the fire of that longing, and so always she came into his presence as surprisingly radiant and joyous as she wasn't when she went out of it.

In circumstances like these a growing portrait runs a good many risks. The portrait of Sellers, by Tracy, was fighting along, day by day, through this mixed weather, and daily adding to itself ineradicable signs of the checkered life it was leading. It was the happiest portrait, in spots, that was ever seen; but in other spots a damned soul looked out from it; a soul that was suffering all the different kinds of distress there are, from stomach ache to rabies. But Sellers liked it. He said it was just himself all over—a portrait that sweated moods from every pore, and no two moods alike. He said he had as many different kinds of emotions in him as a jug.

It was a kind of a deadly work of art, maybe, but it was a starchy picture for show; for it was life size, full length, and represented the American earl in a peer's scarlet robe, with the three ermine bars indicative of an earl's rank, and on the gray head an earl's coronet, tilted just a wee bit to one side in a most gallus and winsome way. When Sally's weather was sunny the portrait made Tracy chuckle, but when her weather was overcast it disordered his mind and stopped the circulation of his blood.

Late one night when the sweethearts had been having a flawless visit together, Sally's interior devil began to work his specialty, and soon the conversation was drifting toward the customary rock. Presently, in the midst of Tracy's serene flow of talk, he felt a shudder which he knew was not his shudder, but exterior to his breast although immediately against it. After the shudder came sobs; Sally was crying.

"Oh, my darling, what have I done—what have I said? It has happened again! What *have* I done to wound you?"

She disengaged herself from his arms and gave him a look of deep reproach.

"What have you done? I will tell you what you have done. You have unwittingly revealed—oh, for the twentieth time, though I *could* not believe it, *would* not believe it!—that it is not me you love, but that foolish sham my father's imitation earldom; and you have broken my heart!"

"Oh, my child, what are you saying! I never dreamed of such a thing."

"Oh, Howard, Howard, the things you have uttered when you were forgetting to guard your tongue, have betrayed you."

"Things I have uttered when I was *forgetting* to guard my tongue? These are hard words. When have I *remembered* to guard it? Never in one instance. It has no office but to speak the truth. It needs no guarding for that."

"Howard, I have noted your words and weighed them, when you were not thinking of their significance—and they have told me more than you meant they should."

"Do you mean to say you have answered the trust I had in you by using it as an ambuscade from which you could set snares for my unsuspecting tongue and be safe from detection while you did it? You have not done this—surely you have not done this thing. Oh, one's enemy could not do it."

This was an aspect of the girl's conduct which she had not clearly perceived before. Was it treachery? Had she abused a trust? The thought crimsoned her cheeks with shame and remorse.

"Oh, forgive me," she said, "I did not know what I was doing. I have been so tortured—you *will* forgive me, you *must;* I have suffered so much, and I am so sorry and so humble; you *do* forgive me, *don't* you? —don't turn away, don't refuse me; it is only my love that is at fault, and you *know* I love you, love you with all my heart; I couldn't bear to—oh, dear, dear, I am so miserable, and I *never* meant any harm, and I didn't see where this insanity was carrying me, and how it was wronging and abusing the dearest heart in all the world to me—and —and—oh, take me in your arms again, I have no other refuge, no other home and hope!"

There was reconciliation again—immediate, perfect, all-embracing—and with it utter happiness. This would have been a good time to adjourn. But no, now that the cloud-breeder was revealed at last; now that it was manifest that all the sour weather had come from this girl's dread that Tracy was lured by her rank and not herself, he resolved to lay that ghost immediately and permanently by furnishing the best possible proof that he *couldn't* have had back of him at any time the suspected motive. So he said—

"Let me whisper a little secret in your ear—a secret which I have kept shut up in my breast all this time. Your rank *couldn't* ever have been an enticement. I am son and heir to an English earl!"

The girl stared at him—one, two, three moments, maybe a dozen—then her lips parted—

"You?" she said, and moved away from him, still gazing at him in a kind of blank amazement.

"Why—why, certainly I am. Why do you act like this? What have I done *now?*"

"What have you done? You have certainly made a most strange statement. You must see that yourself."

"Well," with a timid little laugh, "it may be a strange enough statement; but of what consequence is that, if it is true?"

"*If* it is true. You are already retiring from it."

"Oh, not for a moment! You should not say that. I have not deserved it. I have spoken the truth; why do you doubt it?"

Her reply was prompt.

"Simply because you didn't speak it earlier!"

"Oh!" It wasn't a groan, exactly, but it was an intelligible enough expression of the fact that he saw the point and recognized that there was reason in it.

"You have seemed to conceal nothing from me that I ought to know concerning yourself, and you were not privileged to keep back such a thing as this from me a moment after—after—well, after you had determined to pay your court to me."

"It's true, it's true, I know it! But there were circumstances—in—in the way—circumstances which—"

She waved the circumstances aside.

"Well, you see," he said, pleadingly, "you seemed so bent on our traveling the proud path of honest labor and honorable poverty, that I was terrified—that is, I was afraid—of—of—well, *you* know how you talked."

"Yes, I know how I talked. And I also know that before the talk was finished you inquired how I stood as regards aristocracies, and my answer was calculated to relieve your fears."

He was silent a while. Then he said, in a discouraged way—

"I don't see any way out of it. It was a mistake. That is in truth all it was, just a mistake. No harm was meant, no harm in the world. I didn't see how it might some time look. It is my way. I don't seem to see far."

The girl was almost disarmed, for a moment. Then she flared up again.

"An Earl's son! Do earls' sons go about working in lowly callings for their bread and butter?"

"God knows they don't! I have wished they did."

"Do earls' sons sink their degree in a country like this, and come sober and decent to sue for the hand of a born child of poverty when they can go drunk, profane, and steeped in dishonorable debt and buy the pick and choice of the millionaires' daughters of America? *You* an earl's son! Show me the signs."

"I thank God I am not able—if those are the signs. But yet I am an earl's son and heir. It is all I can say. I wish you would believe me, but you will not. I know no way to persuade you."

She was about to soften again, but his closing remark made her bring her foot down with smart vexation, and she cried out—

"Oh, you drive all patience out of me! Would you have one believe that you haven't your proofs at hand, and yet are what you say you are? You do not put your hand in your pocket *now*—for you have nothing there. You make a claim like this, and then venture to travel without credentials. These are simply incredibilities. Don't you see that, yourself?"

He cast about in his mind for a defence of some kind or other—hesitated a little, and then said, with difficulty and diffidence—

"I will tell you just the truth, foolish as it will seem to you—to anybody, I suppose—but it *is* the truth. I had an ideal—call it a dream, a folly, if you will—but I wanted to renounce the privileges and unfair advantages enjoyed by the nobility and wrung from the nation by force and fraud, and purge myself of my share of those crimes against right and reason, by thenceforth comrading with the poor and humble on equal terms, earning with my own hands the bread I ate, and rising by my own merit if I rose at all."

The young girl scanned his face narrowly while he spoke; and there was something about his simplicity of manner and statement which touched her—touched her almost to the danger point; but she set her grip on the yielding spirit and choked it to quiescence; it could not be wise to surrender to compassion or any kind of sentiment, yet; she must ask one or two more questions. Tracy was reading her face; and what he read there lifted his drooping hopes a little.

"An earl's son to do that! Why, he were a man! A man to love!—oh, more, a man to worship!"

"Why, I—"

"But he never lived! He is not born, he will not be born. The self-abnegation that could do that—even in utter folly, and hopeless of conveying benefit to any, beyond the mere example—could be mistaken for greatness; why, it would *be* greatness in this cold age of sordid ideals! A moment—wait—let me finish; I have one question more. Your father is earl of what?"

"Rossmore—and I am Viscount Berkeley!"

The fat was in the fire again. The girl felt so outraged that it was difficult for her to speak.

"How *can* you venture such a brazen thing! You know that he is dead, and you know that I know it. Oh, to rob the living of name and honors for a selfish and temporary advantage is crime enough, but to rob the defenceless dead—why it is more than crime, it *degrades* crime!"

"Oh, listen to me—just a word—don't turn away like that. Don't go—don't leave me, so—stay one moment. On my honor—"

"Oh, on your honor!"

"On my honor I am what I say! And I will prove it, and you will believe, I know you will. I will bring you a message—a cablegram—"

"When?"

"To-morrow—next day—"

"Signed 'Rossmore'?"

"Yes—signed Rossmore."

"What will that prove?"

"What will it prove? What *should* it prove?"

"If you force me to say it—possibly the presence of a confederate somewhere."

This was a hard blow, and staggered him. He said, dejectedly—

"It is true. I did not think of it. Oh, my God, I do not know any way to do; I do everything wrong. You are going?—and you won't say even good-night—or good-bye? Ah, we have not parted like this before."

"Oh, I *want* to run and—no, go, now." A pause—then she said, "You may bring the message when it comes."

"Oh, may I? God bless you."

He was gone; and none too soon; her lips were already quivering, and now she broke down. Through her sobbings her words broke from time to time.

"Oh, he is gone. I have lost him, I shall never see him any more. And he didn't kiss me good-bye; never even offered to force a kiss from me, and he *knowing* it was the very, very last, and I expecting he would, and never *dreaming* he would treat me so after all we have been to each other. Oh, oh, oh, oh, what shall I do, what *shall* I do! He is a dear, poor, miserable, good-hearted, transparent liar and humbug, but oh, I *do* love him so!" After a little she broke into speech again. "How dear he is! and I shall miss him so, I shall miss him so! Why *won't* he ever think to *forge* a message and fetch it?—but no, he never will, he never thinks of anything; he's so honest and simple it wouldn't ever occur to him. Oh, what *did* possess him to think he could succeed as a fraud—and he hasn't the first requisite except duplicity that I can see. Oh, dear, I'll go to bed and give it all up. Oh, I *wish* I had told him to come and tell me whenever he didn't get any telegram—and now it's all my own fault if I never see him again. How my eyes must look!"

CHAPTER 24

Next day, sure enough, the cablegram didn't come. This was an immense disaster; for Tracy couldn't go into the presence without that ticket, although it wasn't going to possess any value as evidence. But if the failure of the cablegram on that first day may be called an immense disaster, where is the dictionary that can turn out a phrase sizeable enough to describe the tenth day's failure? Of course every day that the cablegram didn't come made Tracy all of twenty-four hours' more ashamed of himself than he was the day before, and made Sally fully twenty-four hours more certain than ever that he not only hadn't any father anywhere, but hadn't even a confederate—and so it followed that he was a double-dyed humbug and couldn't be otherwise.

These were hard days for Barrow and the art firm. All these had their hands full, trying to comfort Tracy. Barrow's task was particularly hard, because he was made a confidant in full, and therefore had to humor Tracy's delusion that he had a father, and that the father was an earl, and that he was going to send a cablegram. Barrow early gave up the idea of trying to convince Tracy that he hadn't any father, because this had such a bad effect on the patient, and worked up his temper to such an alarming degree. He had tried, as an experiment, letting Tracy think he had a father; the result was so good that he went further, with proper caution, and tried letting him think his father was an earl; this wrought so well, that he grew bold, and tried letting him think he had two fathers, if he wanted to, but he didn't want to, so Barrow withdrew one of them and substituted letting him think he was going to get a cablegram—which Barrow judged he wouldn't, and was right; but Barrow worked the cablegram daily for all it was worth, and it was the one thing that kept Tracy alive; that was Barrow's opinion.

And these were bitter hard days for poor Sally, and mainly delivered up to private crying. She kept her furniture pretty damp, and so caught cold, and the dampness and the cold and the sorrow together undermined her appetite, and she was a pitiful enough object, poor thing. Her state was bad enough, as per statement of it above quoted; but all the forces of nature and circumstance seemed conspiring to make it worse—and succeeding. For instance, the morning after her dismissal of Tracy, Hawkins and Sellers read in the associated press dispatches that a toy puzzle called Pigs in the Clover, had come into sudden favor within the past few weeks, and that from the Atlantic to the Pacific all the populations of all the States had knocked off work to play with it, and that the business of the country had now come to a standstill by consequence; that judges, lawyers, burglars, parsons, thieves, merchants, mechanics, murderers, women, children, babies—everybody, indeed, could be seen from morning till midnight, absorbed in one deep project and purpose, and only one—to pen those pigs, work out that puzzle successfully; that all gayety, all cheerfulness had departed from the nation, and in its place care, preoccupation and anxiety sat upon every countenance, and all faces were drawn, distressed, and furrowed with the signs of age and trouble, and marked with the still sadder signs of mental decay and incipient madness; that factories were at work night and day in eight cities, and yet to supply the demand for the puzzle was thus far impossible. Hawkins was wild with joy, but Sellers was calm. Small matters could not disturb his serenity. He said—

"That's just the way things go. A man invents a thing which could revolutionize the arts, produce mountains of money, and bless the earth, and who will bother with it or show any interest in it?—and so you are just as poor as you were before. But you invent some worthless thing to amuse yourself with, and would throw it away if let alone, and all of a sudden the whole world makes a snatch for it and out crops a fortune. Hunt up that Yankee and collect, Hawkins—half is yours, you know. Leave me to potter at my lecture."

This was a temperance lecture. Sellers was head chief in the Temperance camp, and had lectured, now and then in that interest, but had been dissatisfied with his efforts; wherefore he was now about to try a new plan. After much thought he had concluded that a main reason why his lectures lacked fire or something, was, that they were too transparently amateurish; that is to say, it was probably too plainly perceptible that the lecturer was trying to tell people about the horrid effects of liquor when he didn't really know anything about those effects except from hearsay, since he had hardly ever tasted an intoxicant in his life. His scheme, now, was to prepare himself to speak from bitter experience. Hawkins was to stand by with the bottle, calculate the doses, watch the effects, make notes of results, and otherwise assist in the preparation. Time was short, for the ladies would be along about noon—that is to say, the temperance organization called the Daughters of Siloam—and Sellers must be ready to head the procession.

The time kept slipping along—Hawkins did not return—Sellers could not venture to wait longer; so he attacked the bottle himself, and proceeded to note the effects. Hawkins got back at last; took one comprehensive glance at the lecturer, and went down and headed off the procession. The ladies were grieved to hear that the champion had been taken suddenly ill and violently so, but glad to hear that it was hoped he would be out again in a few days.

As it turned out, the old gentleman didn't turn over or show any signs of life worth speaking of for twenty-four hours. Then he asked after the procession, and learned what had happened about it. He was sorry; said he had been "fixed" for it. He remained abed several days, and his wife and daughter took turns in sitting with him and ministering to his wants. Often he patted Sally's head and tried to comfort her.

"Don't cry, my child, don't cry so; *you* know your old father did it by mistake and didn't mean a bit of harm; you know he wouldn't intentionally do anything to make you ashamed for the world; you know he was trying to do good and only made the mistake through ignorance, not knowing the right doses and Washington not there to help. Don't cry so, dear, it breaks my old heart to see you, and think I've brought this humiliation on you and you so dear to me and so good. I won't ever do it again, indeed I won't; now be comforted, honey, that's a good child."

But when she wasn't on duty at the bedside the crying went on just the same; then the mother would try to comfort her, and say—

"Don't cry, dear, *he* never meant any harm; it was all one of those happens that you can't guard against when you are trying experiments, that way. You see *I* don't cry. It's because I know him so well. I could never look anybody in the face again if he had got into such an amazing condition as that a-purpose; but bless you his intention was pure and high, and that makes the *act* pure, though it was higher than was necessary. We're not humiliated, dear, he did it under a noble impulse and we don't need to be ashamed. There, don't cry any more, honey."

Thus, the old gentleman was useful to Sally, during several days, as an explanation of her tearfulness. She felt thankful to him for the shelter he was affording her, but often said to herself, "It's a shame to let him see in my cryings a reproach—as if he could ever do anything that could make me reproach him! But I can't confess; I've got to go on using him for a pretext, he's the only one I've got in the world, and I do need one so much."

As soon as Sellers was out again, and found that stacks of money had been placed in bank for him and Hawkins by the Yankee, he said, "*Now* we'll soon see who's the Claimant and who's the Authentic. I'll just go over there and warm up that House of Lords." During the next few days he and his wife were so busy with preparations for the voyage that Sally had all the privacy she needed, and all the chance to cry that was good for her. Then the old pair left for New York—and England.

Sally had also had a chance to do another thing. That was, to make up her mind that life was not worth living upon the present terms. If she *must* give up her impostor and die, doubtless she must submit; but might she not lay her whole case before some disinterested person, first, and see if there wasn't perhaps some saving way out of the matter? She turned this idea over in her mind a good deal. In her first visit with Hawkins after her parents were gone, the talk fell upon Tracy, and she was impelled to set her case before the statesman and take his counsel. So she poured out her heart, and he listened with painful solicitude. She concluded, pleadingly, with—

"*Don't* tell me he is an impostor. I suppose he is, but doesn't it look to you as if he isn't? You are cool, you know, and outside; and so, maybe it can look to you as if he isn't one, when it can't to me. *Doesn't* it look to you as if he isn't? Couldn't you—*can't* it look to you that way—for—for my sake?"

The poor man was troubled, but he felt obliged to keep in the neighborhood of the truth. He fought around the present detail a little while, then gave it up and said he couldn't really see his way to clearing Tracy.

"No," he said, "the truth is, he's an impostor."

"That is, you—you feel a little certain, but not entirely—oh, not *entirely*, Mr. Hawkins!"

"It's a pity to have to say it—I do hate to say it,—but I don't think anything about it, I *know* he's an impostor."

"Oh, now, Mr. Hawkins, you *can't* go that far. A body *can't* really know it, you know. It isn't *proved* that he's not what he says he is."

Should he come out and make a clean breast of the whole wretched business? Yes—at least the most of it—it ought to be done. So he set his teeth and went at the matter with determination, but purposing to spare the girl one pain—that of knowing that Tracy was a criminal.

"Now I am going to tell you a plain tale; one not pleasant for me to tell or for you to hear, but we've got to stand it. I know all about that fellow; and I *know* he is no earl's son."

The girl's eyes flashed, and she said:

"I don't care a snap for that—go on!"

This was so wholly unexpected that it at once obstructed the narrative; Hawkins was not even sure that he had heard aright. He said—

"I don't know that I quite understand. Do you mean to say that if he was all right and proper otherwise you'd be indifferent about the earl part of the business?"

"Absolutely."

"You'd be entirely satisfied with him and wouldn't *care* for his not being an earl's son,—that *being* an earl's son wouldn't add any value to him?"

"Not the least value that I would care for. Why, Mr. Hawkins, I've gotten over all that day-dreaming about earldoms and aristocracies and all such nonsense and am become just a plain ordinary nobody and content with it; and it is to *him* I owe my cure. And as to anything being able to add a value to him, nothing can do that. He is the whole world to me, just as he is; he comprehends *all* the values there are—then how can you *add* one?"

"She's pretty far gone." He said that to himself. He continued, still to himself, "I must change my plan again; I can't seem to strike one that will stand the requirements of this most variegated emergency five minutes on a stretch. Without making this fellow a criminal, I believe I will invent a name and a character for him calculated to disenchant her. If it fails to do it, then I'll know that the next rightest thing to do will be to help her to her fate, poor thing, not hinder her." Then he said aloud:

"Well, Gwendolen—"

"I want to be called Sally."

"I'm glad of it; I like it better, myself. Well, then, I'll tell you about this man Snodgrass."

"Snodgrass! Is *that* his name?"

"Yes—Snodgrass. The other's his nom de plume."

"It's hideous!"

"I know it is, but we can't help our names."

"And that is truly his real name—and not Howard Tracy?"

Hawkins answered, regretfully—

"Yes, it seems a pity."

The girl sampled the name musingly, once or twice—

"Snodgrass. Snodgrass. No, I could not endure that. I could not get used to it. No, I should call him by his first name. What is his first name?"

"His—er—his initials are S. M."

"His initials? I don't care anything about his initials. I can't call him by his initials. What do they *stand* for?"

"Well, you see, his father was a physician, and he—he—well he was an idolater of his profession, and he—well, he was a very eccentric man, and—"

"What do they *stand* for! What are you shuffling about?"

"They—well they stand for Spinal Meningitis. His father being a phy—"

"I never heard such an infamous name! Nobody can ever call a person *that*—a person they love. I wouldn't call an enemy by such a name. It sounds like an epithet." After a moment, she added with a kind of consternation, "Why, it would be *my* name! Letters would come with it on."

"Yes—Mrs. Spinal Meningitis Snodgrass."

"Don't repeat it—don't; I can't bear it. Was the father a lunatic?"

"No, that is not charged."

"I am glad of that, because that is transmissible. What do you think *was* the matter with him, then?"

"Well, I don't really know. The family used to run a good deal to idiots, and so, maybe—"

"Oh, there isn't any maybe about it. This one was an idiot."

"Well, yes—he could have been. He was suspected."

"Suspected!" said Sally, with irritation. "Would one *suspect* there was going to be a dark time if he saw the constellations fall out of the sky? But that is enough about the idiot, I don't take any interest in idiots; tell me about the son."

"Very well, then, this one was the eldest, but not the favorite. His brother, Zylobalsamum—"

"Wait—give me a chance to realize that. It is perfectly stupefying. Zylo—what did you call it?"

"Zylobalsamum."

"I never heard such a name. It sounds like a disease. Is it a disease?"

"No, I don't think it's a disease. It's either Scriptural or—"

"Well, it's not Scriptural."

"Then it's anatomical. I knew it was one or the other. Yes, I remember, now, it *is* anatomical. It's a ganglion—a nerve centre—it is what is called the zylobalsamum process."

"Well, go on; and if you come to any more of them, omit the names; they make one feel so uncomfortable."

"Very well, then. As I said, this one was not a favorite in the family, and so he was neglected in every way, never sent to school, always allowed to associate with the worst and coarsest characters, and so of course he has grown up a rude, vulgar, ignorant, dissipated ruffian, and—"

"He? It's no such thing! You ought to be more generous than to make such a statement as that about a poor young stranger who—who —why, he is the very opposite of that! He is considerate, courteous, obliging, modest, gentle, refined, cultivated—*oh,* for shame! how can you say such things about him?"

"I don't blame you, Sally—indeed I haven't a word of blame for you for being blinded by your affection—blinded to these minor defects which are so manifest to others who—"

"Minor defects? Do you call these minor defects? What are murder and arson, pray?"

"It is a difficult question to answer straight off—and of course estimates of such things vary with environment. With us, out our way, they would not necessarily attract as much attention as with you, yet they are often regarded with disapproval—"

"Murder and arson are regarded with disapproval?"

"Oh, frequently."

"With disapproval. Who *are* those Puritans you are talking about? But wait—how did you come to know so much about this family? Where did you get all this hearsay evidence?"

"Sally, it isn't hearsay evidence. That is the serious part of it. I *knew* that family—personally."

This was a surprise.

"You? You actually knew them?"

"Knew Zylo, as we used to call him, and knew his father, Dr. Snodgrass. I didn't know your own Snodgrass, but have had glimpses of him from time to time, and I heard about him all the time. He was the common talk, you see, on account of his—"

"On account of his not being a house-burner or an assassin, I suppose. That would have made him commonplace. Where did you know these people?"

"In Cherokee Strip."

"Oh, how preposterous! There are not enough people in Cherokee

Strip to *give* anybody a reputation, good or bad. There isn't a quorum. Why the whole population consists of a couple of wagon loads of horse thieves."

Hawkins answered placidly—

"Our friend was one of those wagon loads."

Sally's eyes burned and her breath came quick and fast, but she kept a fairly good grip on her anger and did not let it get the advantage of her tongue. The statesman sat still and waited for developments. He was content with his work. It was as handsome a piece of diplomatic art as he had ever turned out, he thought; and now, let the girl make her own choice. He judged she would let her spectre go; he hadn't a doubt of it in fact; but anyway, let the choice be made, and he was ready to ratify it and offer no further hindrance.

Meantime Sally had thought her case out and made up her mind. To the major's disappointment the verdict was against him. Sally said:

"He has no friend but me, and I will not desert him now. I will not marry him if his moral character is bad; but if he can prove that it isn't, I will—and he shall have the chance. To me he seems utterly good and dear; I've never seen anything about him that looked otherwise—except, of course, his calling himself an earl's son. Maybe that is only vanity, and no real harm, when you get to the bottom of it. I do *not* believe he is any such person as you have painted him. I want to see him. I want you to find him and send him to me. I will implore him to be honest with me, and tell me the whole truth, and not be afraid."

"Very well; if that is your decision I will do it. But Sally, you know, he's poor, and—"

"Oh, *I* don't care anything about that. That's neither here nor there. Will you bring him to me?"

"I'll do it. When?"

"Oh, dear, it's getting toward dark, now, and so you'll have to put it off till morning. But you *will* find him in the morning, *won't* you? Promise."

"I'll have him here by daylight."

"Oh, *now* you're your own old self again—and lovelier than ever!"

"I couldn't ask fairer than that. Good-bye, dear."

Sally mused a moment alone, then said earnestly, "I love him in *spite* of his name!" and went about her affairs with a light heart.

CHAPTER 25

Hawkins went straight to the telegraph office and disburdened his conscience. He said to himself, "She's not going to give this galvanized cadaver up, that's plain. Wild horses can't pull her away from him. I've done my share; it's for Sellers to take an innings, now." So he sent this message to New York:

"Come back. Hire special train. She's going to marry the materializee."

Meantime a note came to Rossmore Towers to say that the Earl of Rossmore had just arrived from England, and would do himself the pleasure of calling in the evening. Sally said to herself, "It is a pity he didn't stop in New York; but it's no matter; he can go up to-morrow and see my father. He has come over here to tomahawk papa, very likely—or buy out his claim. This thing would have excited me, a while back; but it has only one interest for me now, and only one value. I can say to—to—Spine, Spiny, Spinal—I don't like any *form* of that name!—I can say to him to-morrow, '*Don't* try to keep it up any more, or I shall have to tell you whom I have been talking with last night, and then you will be embarrassed.'"

Tracy couldn't know he was to be invited for the morrow, or he might have waited. As it was, he was too miserable to wait any longer; for his last hope—a letter—had failed him. It was fully due to-day; it had not come. Had his father really flung him away? It looked so. It was not like his father, but it surely looked so. His father was a rather tough nut, in truth, but had never been so with his son—still, this implacable silence had a calamitous look. Anyway, Tracy would go to the Towers and—then what? He didn't know; his head was tired out with thinking—he wouldn't think about what he must do or say—let it all take care of itself. So that he saw Sally once more, he would be satisfied, happen what might; he wouldn't care.

He hardly knew how he got to the Towers, or when. He knew and cared for only one thing—he was alone with Sally. She was kind, she was gentle, there was moisture in her eyes, and a yearning something in her face and manner which she could not wholly hide—but she kept her distance. They talked. Bye and bye she said—watching his downcast countenance out of the corner of her eye—

"It's so lonesome—with papa and mamma gone. I try to read, but I can't seem to get interested in any book. I try the newspapers, but they do put such rubbish in them. You take up a paper and start to read something you think's interesting, and it goes on and on and on about how somebody—well, Dr. Snodgrass, for instance—"

Not a movement from Tracy, not the quiver of a muscle. Sally was amazed—what command of himself he must have! Being disconcerted, she paused so long that Tracy presently looked up wearily and said—

"Well?"

"Oh, I thought you were not listening. Yes, it goes on and on about this Doctor Snodgrass, till you are *so* tired, and then about his younger son—*the favorite son*—Zylobalsamum Snodgrass—"

Not a sign from Tracy, whose head was drooping again. What supernatural self-possession! Sally fixed her eye on him and began again, resolved to blast him out of his serenity this time if she knew how to apply the dynamite that is concealed in certain forms of words when those words are properly loaded with unexpected meanings.

"And next it goes on and on and on about the eldest son—*not* the favorite, this one—and how he is neglected in his poor barren boyhood, and allowed to grow up unschooled, ignorant, coarse, vulgar, the comrade of the community's scum, and become in his completed manhood a rude, profane, dissipated ruffian—"

That head still drooped! Sally rose, moved softly and solemnly a step or two, and stood before Tracy—his head came slowly up, his meek eyes met her intense ones—then she finished with deep impressiveness—

"—named Spinal Meningitis Snodgrass!"

Tracy merely exhibited signs of increased fatigue. The girl was outraged by this iron indifference and callousness, and cried out—

"What *are* you made of?"

"I? Why?"

"Haven't you *any* sensitiveness? Don't these things touch any poor *remnant* of delicate feeling in you?"

"N-no," he said wonderingly, "they don't seem to. Why should they?"

"O, dear me, *how* can you look so innocent, and foolish, and good, and empty, and gentle, and all that, right in the hearing of such things as those! Look me in the eye—straight in the eye. There, now then, answer me without a flinch. Isn't Doctor Snodgrass your father, and isn't Zylobalsamum your brother," [here Hawkins was about to enter the room, but changed his mind upon hearing these words, and elected for a walk down town, and so glided swiftly away], "and isn't your name Spinal Meningitis, and isn't your father a doctor and an idiot, like all the family for generations, and doesn't he name all his children after poisons and pestilences and abnormal anatomical eccentricities of the human body? Answer me, some way or somehow—and quick. *Why* do you sit there looking like an envelope without any address on it and see me going mad before your face with suspense!"

"Oh, I wish I could do—do—I wish I could do something, *anything* that would give you peace again and make you happy; but I know of nothing—I know of no way. I have never heard of these awful people before."

"What? Say it again!"

"I have never—never in my life till now."

"Oh, you *do* look so honest when you say that! It *must* be true—surely you *couldn't* look that way, you *wouldn't* look that way if it were not true—*would* you?"

"I couldn't and wouldn't. It *is* true. Oh, let us end this suffering—take me back into your heart and confidence—"

"Wait—one more thing. Tell me you told that falsehood out of mere vanity and are sorry for it; that you're *not* expecting to ever wear the coronet of an earl—"

"Truly I am cured—cured this very day—I am *not* expecting it!"

"O, now you *are* mine! I've got you back in the beauty and glory of your unsmirched poverty and your honorable obscurity, and nobody shall ever take you from me again but the grave! And if—"

"De earl of Rossmore, fum Englan'!"

"My father!" The young man released the girl and hung his head.

The old gentleman stood surveying the couple—the one with a strongly complimentary right eye, the other with a mixed expression done with the left. This is difficult, and not often resorted to. Presently his face relaxed into a kind of constructive gentleness, and he said to his son—

"Don't you think you could embrace me, too?"

The young man did it with alacrity.

"Then you *are* the son of an earl, after all," said Sally, reproachfully.

"Yes, I—"

"Then I won't have you!"

"O, but you know—"

"No, I will not. You've told me another fib."

"She's right. Go away and leave us. I want to talk with her."

Berkeley was obliged to go. But he did not go far. He remained on the premises. At midnight the conference between the old gentleman and the young girl was still going blithely on, but it presently drew to a close, and the former said—

"I came all the way over here to inspect you, my dear, with the general idea of breaking off this match if there were *two* fools of you, but as there's only one, you can have him if you'll take him."

"Indeed I will, then! May I kiss you?"

"You may. Thank you. Now you shall have that privilege whenever you are good."

Meantime Hawkins had long ago returned and slipped up into the laboratory. He was rather disconcerted to find his late invention, Snodgrass, there. The news was told him: that the English Rossmore was come, "and I'm his son, Viscount Berkeley, not Howard Tracy any more."

Hawkins was aghast. He said—

"Good gracious, then you're dead!"

"Dead?"

"Yes, you are—we've got your ashes."

"Hang those ashes, I'm tired of them; I'll give them to my father."

Slowly and painfully the statesman worked the truth into his head that this was really a flesh and blood young man, and not the insubstantial resurrection he and Sellers had so long supposed him to be. Then he said with feeling—

"I'm so glad; so glad on Sally's account, poor thing. We took you for a departed materialized bank thief from Tahlequah. This will be a heavy blow to Sellers." Then he explained the whole matter to Berkeley, who said—

"Well, the Claimant must manage to stand the blow, severe as it is. But he'll get over the disappointment."

"Who—the colonel? He'll get over it the minute he invents a new miracle to take its place. And he's already at it by this time. But look here—what do you suppose became of the man you've been *representing* all this time?"

"I don't know. I saved his clothes—it was all I could do. I am afraid he lost his life."

"Well, you must have found twenty or thirty thousand dollars in those clothes, in money or certificates of deposit."

"No, I found only five hundred and a trifle. I borrowed the trifle and banked the five hundred."

"What'll we do about it?"

"Return it to the owner."

"It's easy said, but not easy to manage. Let's leave it alone till we get Sellers's advice. And that reminds me. I've got to run and meet Sellers and explain who you are *not* and who you *are*, or he'll come thundering in here to stop his daughter from marrying a phantom. But—suppose your father came over here to break off the match?"

"Well, isn't he down stairs getting acquainted with Sally? That's all safe."

So Hawkins departed to meet and prepare the Sellerses.

Rossmore Towers saw great times and late hours during the succeeding week. The two earls were such opposites in nature that they fraternized at once. Sellers said privately that Rossmore was the most extraordinary character he had ever met—a man just made out of the condensed milk of human kindness, yet with the ability to totally hide the fact from any but the most practised character-reader; a man whose whole being was sweetness, patience and charity, yet with a cunning so profound, an ability so marvelous in the acting of a double part, that many a person of considerable intelligence might live with him for centuries and never suspect the presence in him of these characteristics.

Finally there was a quiet wedding at the Towers, instead of a big one at the British embassy, with the militia and the fire brigades and the temperance organizations on hand in torchlight procession, as at first proposed by one of the earls. The art-firm and Barrow were present at the wedding, and the tinner and Puss had been invited, but the tinner was ill and Puss was nursing him—for they were engaged.

The Sellerses were to go to England with their new allies for a brief visit, but when it was time to take the train from Washington, the colonel was missing. Hawkins was going as far as New York with the party, and said he would explain the matter on the road. The explanation was in a letter left by the colonel in Hawkins's hands. In it he promised to join Mrs. Sellers later, in England, and then went on to say:

The truth is, my dear Hawkins, a mighty idea has been born to me within the hour, and I must not even stop to say goodbye to my dear ones. A man's highest duty takes precedence of all minor ones, and must be attended to with his best promptness and energy, at whatsoever cost to his affections or his convenience. And first of all a man's duties is his duty to his own honor—he must keep that spotless. Mine is threatened. When I was feeling sure of my imminent future solidity, I forwarded to the Czar of Russia—perhaps prematurely—an offer for the purchase of Siberia, naming a vast sum. Since then an episode has warned me that the method by which I was expecting to acquire this money—materialization upon a scale of limitless magnitude—is marred by a taint of temporary uncertainty. His imperial majesty may accept my offer at any moment. If this should occur now, I should find myself painfully embarrassed, in fact financially inadequate. I could not take Siberia. This would become known, and my credit would suffer.

Recently my private hours have been dark indeed, but the sun shines again, now; I see my way; I shall be able to meet my obligation, and without having to ask an extension of the stipulated time, I think. This grand new idea of mine—the sublimest I have ever conceived, will save me whole, I am sure. I am leaving for San Francisco this moment, to test it, by the help of the great Lick telescope. Like all of my more notable discoveries and inventions, it is based upon hard, practical scientific laws; all other bases are unsound and hence untrustworthy.

In brief, then, I have conceived the stupendous idea of reorganizing the climates of the earth according to the desire of the populations interested. That is to say, I will furnish climates to order, for cash or negotiable paper, taking the old climates in part payment, of course, at a fair discount, where they are in condition to be repaired at small cost and let out for hire to poor and remote communities not able to afford a good climate and not caring for an expensive one for mere display. My studies have convinced me that the regulation of climates and the breeding of new varieties at will from the old stock is a feasible thing. Indeed I am convinced that it has been done before; done in prehistoric times by now forgotten and unrecorded civilizations. Everywhere I find hoary evidences of artificial manipulation of climates in bygone times. Take the glacial period. Was that produced by accident? Not at all; it was done for money. I have a thousand proofs of it, and will some day reveal them.

I will confide to you an outline of my idea. It is to utilize the spots on the sun—get control of them, you understand, and apply the stupendous energies which they wield to beneficent purposes in the reorganizing of our climates. At present they merely make trouble and do harm in the evoking of cyclones and other kinds of electric storms; but once under humane and intelligent control this will cease and they will become a boon to man.

I have my plan all mapped out, whereby I hope and expect to acquire complete and perfect control of the sun-spots, also details of the method whereby I shall employ the same commercially; but I will not venture to go into particulars before the patents shall have been issued. I shall hope and expect to sell shop-rights to the minor countries at a reasonable figure and supply a good business article of climate to the great empires at special rates, together with fancy brands for coronations, battles and other great and particular occasions. There are billions of money in this enterprise, no expensive plant is required, and I shall begin to realize in a few days—in a few weeks at furthest. I shall stand ready to pay cash for Siberia the moment it is delivered, and thus save my honor and my credit. I am confident of this.

I would like you to provide a proper outfit and start north as soon as I telegraph you, be it night or be it day. I wish you to take up all the country stretching away from the north pole on all sides for many degrees south, and buy Greenland and Iceland at the best figure you can get now while they are cheap. It is my intention to move one of the tropics up there and transfer the frigid zone to the equator. I will have the entire Arctic Circle in the market as a summer resort next year, and will use the surplusage of the old climate, over and above what can be utilized on the equator, to reduce the temperature of opposition resorts. But I have said enough to give you an idea of the prodigious nature of my scheme and the feasible and enormously profitable character of it. I shall join all you happy people in England as soon as I shall have sold out some of my principal climates and arranged with the Czar about Siberia.

Meantime, watch for a sign from me. Eight days from now, we shall be wide asunder; for I shall be on the border of the Pacific, and you far out on the Atlantic, approaching England. That day, if I am alive and my sublime discovery is proved and established, I will send you greeting, and my messenger shall deliver it where you are, in the solitudes of the sea; for I will waft a vast sun-spot across the disk like drifting smoke, and you will know it for my love-sign, and will say "Mulberry Sellers throws us a kiss across the universe."

FINIS

APPENDIX

WEATHER FOR USE IN THIS BOOK

Selected from the Best Authorities

A brief though violent thunderstorm which had raged over the city was passing away; but still, though the rain had ceased more than an hour before, wild piles of dark and coppery clouds, in which a fierce and rayless glow was laboring, gigantically overhung the grotesque and huddled vista of dwarf houses, while in the distance, sheeting high over the low, misty confusion of gables and chimneys, spread a pall of dead, leprous blue, suffused with blotches of dull, glistening yellow, and with black plague-spots of vapor floating and faint lightnings crinkling on its surface. Thunder, still muttering in the close and sultry air, kept the scared dwellers in the street within, behind their closed shutters; and all deserted, cowed, dejected, squalid, like poor, stupid, top-heavy things that had felt the wrath of the summer tempest, stood the drenched structures on either side of the narrow and crooked way, ghastly and picturesque under the giant canopy. Rain dripped wretchedly in slow drops of melancholy sound from their projecting eaves upon the broken flagging, lay there in pools or trickled into the swollen drains, where the fallen torrent sullenly gurgled on its way to the river.—*"The Brazen Android."—W. D. O'Connor.*

The fiery mid-March sun a moment hung
Above the bleak Judean wilderness;
Then darkness swept upon us, and 't was night.
—*"Easter-Eve at Kerak-Moab."—Clinton Scollard.*

The quick-coming winter twilight was already at hand. Snow was again falling, sifting delicately down, incidentally as it were.—*"Felicia."—Fanny N. D. Murfree.*

Merciful heavens! The whole west, from right to left, blazes up with a fierce light, and next instant the earth reels and quivers with the awful shock of ten thousand batteries of artillery. It is the signal for the Fury to spring—for a thousand demons to scream and shriek—for innumerable serpents of fire to writhe and light up the blackness.

Now the rain falls—now the wind is let loose with a terrible shriek—now the lightning is so constant that the eyes burn, and the thunder-claps merge into an awful roar, as did the 800 cannon at Gettysburg. Crash! Crash! Crash! It is the cottonwood trees falling to earth. Shriek! Shriek! Shriek! It is the Demon racing along the plain and uprooting even the blades of grass. Shock! Shock! Shock! It is the Fury flinging his fiery bolts into the bosom of the earth.—*"The Demon and the Fury."*—*M. Quad.*

Away up the gorge all diurnal fancies trooped into the wide liberties of endless luminous vistas of azure sunlit mountains beneath the shining azure heavens. The sky, looking down in deep blue placidities, only here and there smote the water to azure emulations of its tint.—*"In the Stranger's Country."* —*Charles Egbert Craddock.*

There was every indication of a dust-storm, though the sun still shone brilliantly. The hot wind had become wild and rampant. It was whipping up the sandy coating of the plain in every direction. High in the air were seen whirling spires and cones of sand—a curious effect against the deep-blue sky. Below, puffs of sand were breaking out of the plain in every direction, as though the plain were alive with invisible horsemen. These sandy cloudlets were instantly dissipated by the wind; it was the larger clouds that were lifted whole into the air, and the larger clouds of sand were becoming more and more the rule.

Alfred's eye, quickly scanning the horizon, descried the roof of the boundary-rider's hut still gleaming in the sunlight. He remembered the hut well. It could not be farther than four miles, if as much as that, from this point of the track. He also knew these dust-storms of old; Bindarra was notorious for them. Without thinking twice, Alfred put spurs to his horse and headed for the hut. Before he had ridden half the distance the detached clouds of sand banded together in one dense whirlwind, and it was only owing to his horse's instinct that he did not ride wide of the hut altogether; for during the last half-mile he never saw the hut, until its outline loomed suddenly over his horse's ears; and by then the sun was invisible.—*"A Bride from the Bush."*

It rained forty days and forty nights.—*Genesis.*

Tom Sawyer Abroad

By HUCK FINN

Edited by MARK TWAIN

CONTENTS

CHAPTER 1

TOM SEEKS NEW ADVENTURES

Do you reckon Tom Sawyer was satisfied after all them adventures? I mean the adventures we had down the river, and the time we set the darky Jim free and Tom got shot in the leg. No, he wasn't. It only just p'isoned him for more. That was all the effect it had. You see, when we three came back up the river in glory, as you may say, from that long travel, and the village received us with a torchlight procession and speeches, and everybody hurrah'd and shouted, it made us heroes, and that was what Tom Sawyer had always been hankering to be.

For a while he *was* satisfied. Everybody made much of him, and he tilted up his nose and stepped around the town as though he owned it. Some called him Tom Sawyer the Traveler, and that just swelled him up fit to bust. You see he laid over me and Jim considerable, because we only went down the river on a raft and came back by the steamboat, but Tom went by the steamboat both ways. The boys envied me and Jim a good deal, but land! they just knuckled to the dirt before TOM.

Well, I don't know; maybe he might have been satisfied if it hadn't been for old Nat Parsons, which was postmaster, and powerful long and slim, and kind o' good-hearted and silly, and bald-headed, on account of his age, and about the talkiest old cretur I ever see. For as much as thirty years he'd been the only man in the village that had a reputation—I mean a reputation for being a traveler, and of course he was mortal proud of it, and it was reckoned that in the course of that thirty years he had told about that journey over a million times and enjoyed it every time. And now comes along a boy not quite fifteen, and sets everybody admiring and gawking over *his* travels, and it just give the poor old man the high strikes. It made him sick to listen to Tom, and to hear the people say "My land!" "Did you ever!" "My goodness sakes alive!" and all such things; but he couldn't pull away from it, any more than a fly that's got its hind leg fast in the molasses. And always when Tom come to a rest, the poor old cretur would chip in on *his* same old travels and work them for all they were worth, but they were pretty faded, and didn't go for much, and it was pitiful to see. And then Tom would take another innings, and then the old man again—and so on, and so on, for an hour and more, each trying to beat out the other.

You see, Parsons' travels happened like this: When he first got to be postmaster and was green in the business, there come a letter for somebody he didn't know, and there wasn't any such person in the village. Well, he didn't know what to do, nor how to act, and there the letter stayed and stayed, week in and week out, till the bare sight of it give him a conniption. The postage wasn't paid on it, and that was another thing to worry about. There wasn't any way to collect that ten cents, and he reckon'd the Gov'ment would hold him responsible for it and maybe turn him out besides, when they found he hadn't collected it. Well, at last he couldn't stand it any longer. He couldn't sleep nights, he couldn't eat, he was thinned down to a shadder, yet he da'sn't ask anybody's advice, for the very person he asked for advice might go back on him and let the Gov'ment know about the letter. He had the letter buried under the floor, but that did no good; if he happened to see a person standing over the place it'd give him the cold shivers, and loaded him up with suspicions, and he would sit up that night till the town was as still and dark, and then he would sneak there and get it out and bury it in another place. Of course people got to avoiding him and shaking their heads and whispering, because, the way he was looking and acting, they judged he had killed somebody or done something terrible, they didn't know what, and if he had been a stranger they would've lynched him.

Well, as I was saying, it got so he couldn't stand it any longer; so he made up his mind to pull out for Washington, and just go to the President of the United States and make a clean breast of the whole thing, not keeping back an atom, and then fetch the letter out and lay it before the whole Gov'ment, and say, "Now, there she is—do with me what you're a mind to; though as heaven is my judge I am an innocent man and not deserving of the full penalties of the law and leaving behind me a family that must starve and yet hadn't had a thing to do with it, which is the whole truth and I can swear to it."

So he did it. He had a little wee bit of steamboating, and some stagecoaching, but all the rest of the way was horseback, and it took him three weeks to get to Washington. He saw lots of land and lots of villages and four cities. He was gone 'most eight weeks, and there never was such a proud man in the village as when he got back. His travels made him the greatest man in all that region, and the most talked about; and people come from as much as thirty miles back in the country, and from over in the Illinois bottoms, too, just to look at him—and there they'd stand and gawk, and he'd gabble. You never see anything like it.

Well, there wasn't any way, now, to settle which was the greatest traveler; some said it was Nat, some said it was Tom. Everybody allowed that Nat had seen the most longitude, but they had to give in that whatever Tom was short in longitude he had made up in latitude and climate. It was about a stand-off; so both of them had to whoop up their dangerous adventures, and try to get ahead *that* way. That bullet-wound in Tom's leg was a tough thing for Nat Parsons to buck against, but he bucked the best he could; and at a disadvantage, too, for Tom didn't set still as he'd orter done, to be fair, but always got up and sauntered around and worked his limp while Nat was painting up the adventure that *he* had in Washington; for Tom never let go that limp when his leg got well, but practised it nights at home, and kept it good as new right along.

Nat's adventure was like this; I don't know how true it is; maybe he got it out of a paper, or somewhere, but I will say this for him, that he *did* know how to tell it. He could make anybody's flesh crawl, and he'd turn pale and hold his breath when he told it, and sometimes women and girls got so faint they couldn't stick it out. Well, it was this way, as near as I can remember:

He come a-loping into Washington, and put up his horse and shoved out to the President's house with his letter, and they told him the President was up to the Capitol, and just going to start for Philadelphia—not a minute to lose if he wanted to catch him. Nat 'most dropped, it made him so sick. His horse was put up, and he didn't know what *to* do. But just then along comes a darky driving an old ramshackly hack, and he sees his chance. He rushes out and shouts: "A half a dollar if you git me to the Capitol in half an hour, and a quarter extra if you do it in twenty minutes!"

"Done!" says the darky.

Nat he jumped in and slammed the door, and away they went a-ripping and a-tearing over the roughest road a body ever see, and the racket of it was something awful. Nat passed his arms through the loops and hung on for life and death, but pretty soon the hack hit a rock and flew up in the air, and the bottom fell out, and when it come down Nat's feet was on the ground, and he see he was in the most desperate danger if he couldn't keep up with the hack. He was horrible scared, but he laid into his work for all he was worth, and hung tight to the arm-loops and made his legs fairly fly. He yelled and shouted to the driver to stop, and so did the crowds along the street, for they could see his legs spinning along under the coach, and his head and shoulders bobbing inside, through the windows, and he was in awful danger; but the more they all shouted the more the nigger whooped and yelled and lashed the horses and shouted, "Don't you fret, I's gwine to git you dah in time, boss; I's gwine to do it, sho'!" for you see he thought they were all hurrying him up, and of course he couldn't hear anything for the racket he was making. And so they went ripping along, and everybody just petrified to see it; and when they got to the Capitol at last it was the quickest trip that ever was made, and everybody said so. The horses laid down, and Nat dropped, all tuckered out, and he was all dust and rags and barefooted; but he was in time and just in time, and caught the President and give him the letter, and everything was all right, and the President give him a free pardon on the spot, and Nat give the nigger two extra quarters instead of one because he could see that if he hadn't had the hack he wouldn't 'a' got there in time, nor anywhere near it.

It *was* a powerful good adventure, and Tom Sawyer had to work his bullet-wound mighty lively to hold his own against it.

Well, by and by Tom's glory got to paling down gradu'ly, on account of other things turning up for the people to talk about—first a horserace, and on top of that a house afire, and on top of that the circus, and on top of that the eclipse; and that started a revival, same as it always does, and by that time there wasn't any more talk about Tom, so to speak, and you never see a person so sick and disgusted.

Pretty soon he got to worrying and fretting right along day in and day out, and when I asked him what *was* he in such a state about, he said it 'most broke his heart to think how time was slipping away, and him getting older and older, and no wars breaking out and no way of making a name for himself that he could see. Now that is the way boys is always thinking, but he was the first one I ever heard come out and say it.

So then he set to work to get up a plan to make him celebrated; and pretty soon he struck it, and offered to take me and Jim in. Tom Sawyer was always free and generous that way. There's a plenty of boys that's mighty good and friendly when *you*'ve got a good thing, but when a good thing happens to come their way they don't say a word to you, and try to hog it all. That warn't ever Tom Sawyer's way, I can say that for him. There's plenty of boys that will come hankering and groveling around you when you've got an apple, and beg the core off of you; but when they've got one, and you beg for the core and remind them how you give them a core one time, they say thank you 'most to death, but there ain't a-going to be no core. But I notice they always git come up with; all you got to do is to wait.

Well, we went out in the woods on the hill, and Tom told us what it was. It was a crusade.

"What's a crusade?" I says.

He looked scornful the way he's always done when he was ashamed of a person, and says—

"Huck Finn, do you mean to tell me you don't know what a crusade is?"

"No," says I, "I don't. And I don't care to, nuther. I've lived till now and done without it, and had my health, too. But as soon as you tell me, I'll know, and that's soon enough. I don't see any use in finding out things and clogging up my head with them when I mayn't ever have any occasion to use 'em. There was Lance Williams, he learned how to talk Choctaw here till one come and dug his grave for him. Now, then, what's a crusade? But I can tell you one thing before you begin; if it's a patent-right, there's no money in it. Bill Thompson he—"

"Patent-right!" says he. "I never see such an idiot. Why, a crusade is a kind of war."

I thought he must be losing his mind. But no, he was in real earnest, and went right on, perfectly ca'm:

"A crusade is a war to recover the Holy Land from the paynim."

"Which Holy Land?"

"Why, *the* Holy Land—there ain't but one."

"What do *we* want of it?"

"Why, can't you understand? It's in the hands of the paynim, and it's our duty to take it away from them."

"How did we come to let them git hold of it?"

"We didn't come to let them git hold of it. They always had it."

"Why, Tom, then it must belong to them, don't it?"

"Why of course it does. Who said it didn't?"

I studied over it, but couldn't seem to git at the right of it, no way. I says:

"It's too many for me, Tom Sawyer. If I had a farm and it was mine, and another person wanted it, would it be right for him to—"

"Oh, shucks! you don't know enough to come in when it rains, Huck Finn. It ain't a farm, it's entirely different. You see, it's like this. They own the land, just the mere land, and that's all they *do* own; but it was our folks, our Jews and Christians, that made it holy, and so they haven't any business to be there defiling it. It's a shame, and we ought not to stand it a minute. We ought to march against them and take it away from them."

"Why, it does seem to me it's the most mixed-up thing I ever see! Now if I had a farm and another person—"

"Don't I tell you it hasn't got anything to do with farming? Farming is business, just common low-down business; that's all it is, it's all you can say for it; but this is higher, this is religious, and totally different."

"Religious to go and take the land away from people that owns it?"

"Certainly; it's always been considered so."

Jim he shook his head, and says:

"Mars Tom, I reckon dey's a mistake about it somers—dey mos' sholy is. I's religious myself, en I knows plenty religious people, but I hain't run across none dat acts like dat."

It made Tom hot, and he says:

"Well, it's enough to make a body sick, such mullet-headed ignorance! If either of you'd read anything about history, you'd know that Richard Cur de Loon, and the Pope, and Godfrey de Bulleyn, and lots more of the most noble-hearted and pious people in the world, hacked and hammered at the paynims for more than two hundred years trying to take their land away from them, and swum neck-deep in blood the whole time—and yet here's a couple of sap-headed country yahoos out in the backwoods of Missouri, setting themselves up to know more about the rights and wrongs of it than they did! Talk about cheek!"

Well, of course, that put a more different light on it, and me and Jim felt pretty cheap and ignorant, and wished we hadn't been quite so chipper. I couldn't say nothing, and Jim he couldn't for a while; then he says:

"Well, den, I reckon it's all right; beca'se ef dey didn't know, dey ain't no use for po' ignorant folks like us to be trying to know; en so, ef it's our duty, we got to go en tackle it en do de bes' we can. Same time, I feel as sorry for dem paynims as Mars Tom. De hard part gwine to be to kill folks dat a body hain't been 'quainted wid and dat hain't done him no harm. Dat's it, you see. Ef we wuz to go 'mongst 'em, jist we three, en say we's hungry, en ast 'em for a bite to eat, why, maybe dey's jist like yuther people. Don't you reckon dey is? Why, *dey*'d give it, I know dey would, en den—"

"Then what?"

"Well, Mars Tom, my idea is like dis. It ain't no use, we *can't* kill dem po' strangers dat ain't doin' us no harm, till we've had practice—I knows it perfectly well, Mars Tom—'deed I knows it perfectly well.

But ef we takes a' ax or two, jist you en me en Huck, en slips acrost de river to-night arter de moon's gone down, en kills dat sick fam'ly dat's over on the Sny, en burns dey house down, en—"

"Oh, you make me tired!" says Tom. "I don't want to argue any more with people like you and Huck Finn, that's always wandering from the subject, and ain't got any more sense than to try to reason out a thing that's pure theology by the laws that protect real estate!"

Now that's just where Tom Sawyer warn't fair. Jim didn't mean no harm, and I didn't mean no harm. We knowed well enough that he was right and we was wrong, and all we was after was to get at the *how* of it, and that was all; and the only reason he couldn't explain it so we could understand it was because we was ignorant—yes, and pretty dull, too, I ain't denying that; but, land! that ain't no crime, I should think.

But he wouldn't hear no more about it—just said if we had tackled the thing in the proper spirit, he would 'a' raised a couple of thousand knights and put them in steel armor from head to heel, and made me a lieutenant and Jim a sutler, and took the command himself and brushed the whole paynim outfit into the sea like flies and come back across the world in a glory like sunset. But he said we didn't know enough to take the chance when we had it, and he wouldn't ever offer it again. And he didn't. When he once got set, you couldn't budge him.

But I didn't care much. I am peaceable, and don't get up rows with people that ain't doing nothing to me. I allowed if the paynim was satisfied I was, and we would let it stand at that.

Now Tom he got all that notion out of Walter Scott's book, which he was always reading. And it *was* a wild notion, because in my opinion he never could've raised the men, and if he did, as like as not he would've got licked. I took the books and read all about it, and as near as I could make it out, most of the folks that shook farming to go crusading had a mighty rocky time of it.

CHAPTER 2

THE BALLOON ASCENSION

Well, Tom got up one thing after another, but they all had tender spots about 'em somewheres, and he had to shove 'em aside. So at last he was about in despair. Then the St. Louis papers begun to talk a good deal about the balloon that was going to sail to Europe, and Tom sort of thought he wanted to go down and see what it looked like, but couldn't make up his mind. But the papers went on talking, and so he allowed that maybe if he didn't go he mightn't ever have another chance to see a balloon; and next, he found out that Nat Parsons was going down to see it, and that decided him, of course. He wasn't going to have Nat Parsons coming back bragging about seeing the balloon, and him having to listen to it and keep quiet. So he wanted me and Jim to go too, and we went.

It was a noble big balloon, and had wings and fans and all sorts of things, and wasn't like any balloon you see in pictures. It was away out toward the edge of town, in a vacant lot, corner of Twelfth street; and there was a big crowd around it, making fun of it, and making fun of the man,—a lean pale feller with that soft kind of moonlight in his eyes, you know,—and they kept saying it wouldn't go. It made him hot to hear them, and he would turn on them and shake his fist and say they was animals and blind, but some day they would find they had stood face to face with one of the men that lifts up nations and makes civilizations, and was too dull to know it; and right here on this spot their own children and grandchildren would build a monument to him that would outlast a thousand years, but his name would outlast the monument. And then the crowd would burst out in a laugh again, and yell at him, and ask him what was his name before he was married, and what he would take to not do it, and what was his sister's cat's grandmother's name, and all the things that a crowd says when they've got hold of a feller that they see they can plague. Well, some things they said *was* funny,—yes, and mighty witty too, I ain't denying that,—but all the same it warn't fair nor brave, all them people pitching on one, and they so glib and sharp, and him without any gift of talk to answer back with. But, good land! what did he want to sass back for? You see, it couldn't do him no good, and it was just nuts for them. They *had* him, you know. But that was his way. I reckon he couldn't help it; he was made so, I judge. He was a good-enough sort of cretur, and hadn't no harm in him, and was just a genius, as the papers said, which wasn't his fault. We can't all be sound: we've got to be the way we're made. As near as I can make out, geniuses think they know it all, and so they won't take people's advice, but always go their own way, which makes everybody forsake them and despise them, and that is perfectly natural. If they was humbler, and listened and tried to learn, it would be better for them.

The part the professor was in was like a boat, and was big and roomy, and had water-tight lockers around the inside to keep all sorts of things in, and a body could sit on them, and make beds on them, too. We went aboard, and there was twenty people there, snooping around and examining, and old Nat Parsons was there, too. The professor kept fussing around, getting ready, and the people went ashore, drifting out one at a time, and old Nat he was the last. Of course it wouldn't do to let him go out behind *us*. We mustn't budge till he was gone, so we could be last ourselves.

But he was gone now, so it was time for us to follow. I heard a big shout, and turned around—the city was dropping from under us like a shot! It made me sick all through, I was so scared. Jim turned gray and couldn't say a word, and Tom didn't say nothing, but looked excited. The city went on dropping down, and down, and down; but we didn't seem to be doing nothing but just hang in the air and stand still. The houses got smaller and smaller, and the city pulled itself together, closer and closer, and the men and wagons got to looking like ants and bugs crawling around, and the streets like threads and cracks; and then it all kind of melted together, and there wasn't any city any more: it was only a big scar on the earth, and it seemed to me a body could see up the river and down the river about a thousand miles, though of course it wasn't so much. By and by the earth was a ball—just a round ball, of a dull color, with shiny stripes wriggling and winding around over it, which was rivers. The Widder Douglas always told me the earth was round like a ball, but I never took any stock in a lot of them superstitions o' hers, and of course I paid no attention to that one, because I could see myself that the world was the shape of a plate, and flat. I used to go up on the hill, and take a look around and prove it for myself, because I reckon the best way to get a sure thing on a fact is to go and examine for yourself, and not take anybody's say-so. But I had to give in, now, that the widder was right. That is, she was right as to the rest of the world, but she warn't right about the part our village is in; that part is the shape of a plate, and flat, I take my oath!

The professor had been quiet all this time, as if he was asleep; but he broke loose now, and he was mighty bitter. He says something like this:

"Idiots! They said it wouldn't go; and they wanted to examine it, and spy around and get the secret of it out of me. But I beat them. Nobody knows the secret but me. Nobody knows what makes it move but me; and it's a new power—a new power, and a thousand times the strongest in the earth! Steam's foolishness to it! They said I couldn't go to Europe. To Europe! Why, there's power aboard to last five years, and feed for three months. They are fools! What do they know about it? Yes, and they said my air-ship was flimsy. Why, she's good for fifty years! I can sail the skies all my life if I want to, and steer where I please, though they laughed at that, and said I couldn't. Couldn't steer! Come here, boy; we'll see. You press these buttons as I tell you."

He made Tom steer the ship all about and every which way, and learnt him the whole thing in nearly no time; and Tom said it was perfectly easy. He made him fetch the ship down 'most to the earth, and had him spin her along so close to the Illinois prairies that a body could talk to the farmers, and hear everything they said perfectly plain; and he flung out printed bills to them that told about the balloon, and said it was going to Europe. Tom got so he could steer straight for a tree till he got nearly to it, and then dart up and skin right along over the top of it. Yes, and he showed Tom how to land her; and he done it first-rate, too, and set her down in the prairies as soft as wool. But the minute we started to skip out the professor says, "No, you don't!" and shot her up in the air again. It was awful. I begun to beg, and so did Jim; but it only give his temper a rise, and he begun to rage around and look wild out of his eyes, and I was scared of him.

Well, then he got on to his troubles again, and mourned and grumbled about the way he was treated, and couldn't seem to git over it, and especially people's saying his ship was flimsy. He scoffed at that, and at their saying she warn't simple and would be always getting out of order. Get out of order! That graveled him; he said that she couldn't any more get out of order than the solar sister.

He got worse and worse, and I never see a person take on so. It give me the cold shivers to see him, and so it did Jim. By and by he got to yelling and screaming, and then he swore the world shouldn't ever have his secret at all now, it had treated him so mean. He said he would sail his balloon around the globe just to show what he could do, and then he would sink it in the sea, and sink us all along with it, too. Well, it was the awfullest fix to be in, and here was night coming on!

He give us something to eat, and made us go to the other end of the boat, and he laid down on a locker, where he could boss all the works, and put his old pepper-box revolver under his head, and said if anybody come fooling around there trying to land her, he would kill him.

We set scrunched up together, and thought considerable, but didn't say much—only just a word once in a while when a body had to say something or bust, we was *so* scared and worried. The night dragged along slow and lonesome. We was pretty low down, and the moonshine made everything soft and pretty, and the farmhouses looked snug and homeful, and we could hear the farm sounds, and wished we could be down there; but, laws! we just slipped along over them like a ghost, and never left a track.

Away in the night, when all the sounds was late sounds, and the air had a late feel, and a late smell, too,—about a two-o'clock feel, as near as I could make out,—Tom said the professor was so quiet this time he must be asleep, and we'd better—

"Better what?" I says in a whisper, and feeling sick all over, because I knowed what he was thinking about.

"Better slip back there and tie him, and land the ship," he says.

I says: "No, sir! Don't you budge, Tom Sawyer."

And Jim—well, Jim was kind o' gasping, he was so scared. He says: "Oh, Mars Tom, *don't!* Ef you teches him, we's gone—we's gone sho'! I ain't gwine anear him, not for nothin' in dis worl'. Mars Tom, he's plumb crazy."

Tom whispers and says: "That's *why* we've got to do something. If he wasn't crazy I wouldn't give shucks to be anywhere but here; you couldn't hire me to get out,—now that I've got used to this balloon and over the scare of being cut loose from the solid ground,—if he was in his right mind. But it's no good politics, sailing around like this with a person that's out of his head, and says he's going round the world and then drown us all. We've *got* to do something, I tell you, and do it before he wakes up, too, or we mayn't ever get another chance. Come!"

But it made us turn cold and creepy just to think of it, and we said we wouldn't budge. So Tom was for slipping back there by himself to see if he couldn't get at the steering-gear and land the ship. We begged and begged him not to, but it warn't no use; so he got down on his hands and knees, and begun to crawl an inch at a time, we a-holding our breath and watching. After he got to the middle of the boat he crept slower than ever, and it did seem like years to me. But at last we see him get to the professor's head, and sort of raise up soft and look a good spell in his face and listen. Then we see him begin to inch along again toward the professor's feet where the steering-buttons was. Well, he got there all safe, and was reaching slow and steady toward the buttons, but he knocked down something that made a noise, and we see him slump down flat an' soft in the bottom, and lay still. The professor stirred, and says, "What's that?" But everybody kept dead still and quiet, and he begun to mutter and mumble and nestle, like a person that's going to wake up, and I thought I was going to die, I was so worried and scared.

Then a cloud slid over the moon, and I 'most cried, I was so glad. She buried herself deeper and deeper into the cloud, and it got so dark we couldn't see Tom. Then it began to sprinkle rain, and we could hear the professor fussing at his ropes and things and abusing the weather. We was afraid every minute he would touch Tom, and then we would be goners, and no help; but Tom was already on his way back, and when we felt his hands on our knees my breath stopped sudden, and my heart fell down 'mongst my other works, because I couldn't tell in the dark but it might be the professor, which I thought it *was*.

Dear! I was so glad to have him back that I was just as near happy as a person could be that was up in the air that way with a deranged man. You can't land a balloon in the dark, and so I hoped it would keep on raining, for I didn't want Tom to go meddling any more and make us so awful uncomfortable. Well, I got my wish. It drizzled and drizzled along the rest of the night, which wasn't long, though it did seem so; and at daybreak it cleared, and the world looked mighty soft and gray and pretty, and the forests and fields so good to see again, and the horses and cattle standing sober and thinking. Next, the sun come a-blazing up gay and splendid, and then we began to feel rusty and stretchy, and first we knowed we was all asleep.

CHAPTER 3

TOM EXPLAINS

We went to sleep about four o'clock, and woke up about eight. The professor was setting back there at his end, looking glum. He pitched us some breakfast, but he told us not to come abaft the midship compass. That was about the middle of the boat. Well, when you are sharp-set, and you eat and satisfy yourself, everything looks pretty different from what it done before. It makes a body feel pretty near comfortable, even when he is up in a balloon with a genius. We got to talking together.

There was one thing that kept bothering me, and by and by I says:

"Tom, didn't we start east?"

"Yes."

"How fast have we been going?"

"Well, you heard what the professor said when he was raging round. Sometimes, he said, we was making fifty miles an hour, sometimes ninety, sometimes a hundred; said that with a gale to help he could make three hundred any time, and said if he wanted the gale, and wanted it blowing the right direction, he only had to go up higher or down lower to find it."

"Well, then, it's just as I reckoned. The professor lied."

"Why?"

"Because if we was going so fast we ought to be past Illinois, oughtn't we?"

"Certainly."

"Well, we ain't."

"What's the reason we ain't?"

"I know by the color. We're right over Illinois yet. And you can see for yourself that Indiana ain't in sight."

"I wonder what's the matter with you, Huck. You know by the *color?*"

"Yes, of course I do."

"What's the color got to do with it?"

"It's got everything to do with it. Illinois is green, Indiana is pink. You show me any pink down here, if you can. No, sir; it's green."

"Indiana *pink?* Why, what a lie?"

"It ain't no lie; I've seen it on the map, and it's pink."

You never see a person so aggravated and disgusted. He says:

"Well, if I was such a numskull as you, Huck Finn, I would jump over. Seen it on the map! Huck Finn, did you reckon the States was the same color out of doors as they are on the map?"

"Tom Sawyer, what's a map for? Ain't it to learn you facts?"

"Of course."

"Well, then, how's it going to do that if it tells lies? That's what I want to know."

"Shucks, you muggins! It don't tell lies."

"It don't, don't it?"

"No, it don't."

"All right, then; if it don't, there ain't no two States the same color. You git around *that,* if you can, Tom Sawyer."

He see I had him, and Jim see it too; and I tell you, I felt pretty good, for Tom Sawyer was always a hard person to git ahead of. Jim slapped his leg and says:

"I tell *you!* dat's smart, dat's right down smart. Ain't no use, Mars Tom; he got you *dis* time, sho!" He slapped his leg again, and says, "My *lan'*, but it was smart one!"

I never felt so good in my life; and yet *I* didn't know I was saying anything much till it was out. I was just mooning along, perfectly careless, and not expecting anything was going to happen, and never *thinking* of such a thing at all, when, all of a sudden, out it come. Why, it was just as much a surprise to me as it was to any of them. It was just the same way it is when a person is munching along on a hunk of cornpone, and not thinking about anything, and all of a sudden bites into a di'mond. Now all that *he* knows first off is that it's some kind of gravel he's bit into; but he don't find out it's a di'mond till he gits it out and brushes off the sand and crumbs and one thing or another, and has a look at it, and then he's surprised and glad—yes, and proud too; though when you come to look the thing straight in the eye, he ain't entitled to as much credit as he would 'a' been if he'd been *hunting* di'monds. You can see the difference easy if you think it over. You see, an accident, that way, ain't fairly as big a thing as a thing that's done a-purpose. Anybody could find that di'mond in that corn-pone; but mind you, it's got to be somebody that's got *that kind of a corn-pone.* That's where that feller's credit comes in, you see; and that's where mine comes in. I don't claim no great things,—I don't reckon I could 'a' done it again,—but I done it that time; that's all I claim. And I hadn't no more idea I could do such a thing, and warn't any more thinking about it or trying to, than you be this minute. Why, I was just as cam, a body couldn't be any cammer, and yet, all of a sudden, out it come. I've often thought of that time, and I can remember just the way everything looked, same as if it was only last week. I can see it all: beautiful rolling country with woods and fields and lakes for hundreds and hundreds of miles all around, and towns and villages scattered everywheres under us, here and there and yonder; and the professor mooning over a chart on his little table, and Tom's cap flopping in the rigging where it was hung up to dry. And one thing in particular was a bird right alongside, not ten foot off, going our way and trying to keep up, but losing ground all the time; and a railroad train doing the same thing down there, sliding among the trees and farms, and pouring out a long cloud of black smoke and now and then a little puff of white; and when the white was gone so long you had almost forgot it, you would hear a little faint toot, and that was the whistle. And we left the bird and the train both behind, *'way* behind, and done it easy too.

But Tom he was huffy, and said me and Jim was a couple of ignorant blatherskites, and then he says:

"Suppose there's a brown calf and a big brown dog, and an artist is making a picture of them. What is the *main* thing that that artist has got to do? He has got to paint them so you can tell them apart the minute you look at them, hain't he? Of course. Well, then, do you want him to go and paint *both* of them brown? Certainly you don't. He paints one of them blue, and then you can't make no mistake. It's just the same with the maps. That's why they make every State a different color; it ain't to deceive you, it's to keep you from deceiving yourself."

But I couldn't see no argument about that, and neither could Jim. Jim shook his head, and says:

"Why, Mars Tom, if you knowed what chuckle-heads dem painters is, you'd wait a long time before you'd fetch one er *dem* in to back up a fac'. I's gwine to tell you, den you kin see for youself. I see one of 'em a-paintin' away, one day, down in ole Hank Wilson's back lot, en I went down to see, en he was paintin' dat old brindle cow wid de near horn gone—you knows de one I means. En I ast him what he's paintin' her for, en he say when he git her painted, de picture's wuth a hundred dollars. Mars Tom, he could a got de cow fer fifteen, en I *tole* him so. Well, sah, if you'll b'lieve me, he jes' shuck his head, dat painter did, en went on a-dobbin'. Bless you, Mars Tom, *dey* don't know nothin'."

Tom he lost his temper. I notice a person 'most always does that's got laid out in an argument. He told us to shut up, and maybe we'd feel better. Then he see a town clock away off down yonder, and he took up the glass and looked at it, and then looked at his silver turnip, and then at the clock, and then at the turnip again, and says:

"That's funny! That clock's near about an hour fast."

So he put up his turnip. Then he see another clock, and took a look, and it was an hour fast too. That puzzled him.

"That's a mighty curious thing," he says. "I don't understand it."

Then he took the glass and hunted up another clock, and sure enough it was an hour fast too. Then his eyes began to spread and his breath to come out kinder gaspy like, and he says:

"Ger-reat Scott, it's the *longitude!*"

I says, considerably scared:

"Well, what's been and gone and happened now?"

"Why, the thing that's happened is that this old bladder has slid over Illinois and Indiana and Ohio like nothing, and this is the east end of Pennsylvania or New York, or somewheres around there."

"Tom Sawyer, you don't mean it!"

"Yes, I do, and it's dead sure. We've covered about fifteen degrees of longitude since we left St. Louis yesterday afternoon, and them clocks are *right*. We've come close on to eight hundred miles."

I didn't believe it, but it made the cold streaks trickle down my back just the same. In my experience I knowed it wouldn't take much short of two weeks to do it down the Mississippi on a raft.

Jim was working his mind and studying. Pretty soon he says:

"Mars Tom, did you say dem clocks uz right?"

"Yes, they're right."

"Ain't yo' watch right, too?"

"She's right for St. Louis, but she's an hour wrong for here."

"Mars Tom, is you tryin' to let on dat de time ain't de *same* everywheres?"

"No, it ain't the same everywheres, by a long shot."

Jim looked distressed, and says:

"It grieves me to hear you talk like dat, Mars Tom; I's right down ashamed to hear you talk like dat, arter de way you's been raised. Yassir, it'd break yo' Aunt Polly's heart to hear you."

Tom was astonished. He looked Jim over, wondering, and didn't say nothing, and Jim went on:

"Mars Tom, who put de people out yonder in St. Louis? De Lord done it. Who put de people here whar we is? De Lord done it. Ain' dey bofe his children? 'Cose dey is. *Well*, den! is he gwine to *scriminate* 'twixt 'em?"

"Scriminate! I never heard such ignorance. There ain't no discriminating about it. When he makes you and some more of his children black, and makes the rest of us white, what do you call that?"

Jim see the p'int. He was stuck. He couldn't answer. Tom says:

"He does discriminate, you see, when he wants to; but this case *here* ain't no discrimination of his, it's man's. The Lord made the day, and he made the night; but he didn't invent the hours, and he didn't distribute them around. Man did that."

"Mars Tom, is dat so? Man done it?"

"Certainly."

"Who tole him he could?"

"Nobody. He never asked."

Jim studied a minute, and says:

"Well, dat do beat me. I wouldn't 'a' tuck no sich resk. But some people ain't scared o' nothin'. Dey bangs right ahead; *dey* don't care what happens. So den dey's allays an hour's diff'unce everywhah, Mars Tom?"

"An hour? No! It's four minutes difference for every degree of longitude, you know. Fifteen of 'em's an hour, thirty of 'em's two hours, and so on. When it's one o'clock Tuesday morning in England, it's eight o'clock the night before in New York."

Jim moved a little way along the locker, and you could see he was insulted. He kept shaking his head and muttering, and so I slid along to him and patted him on the leg, and petted him up, and got him over the worst of his feelings, and then he says:

"Mars Tom talkin' sich talk as dat! Choosday in one place en Monday in t' other, bofe in the same day! Huck, dis ain't no place to joke —up here whah we is. Two days in one day! How you gwine to got two days inter one day? Can't git two hours inter one hour, kin you? Can't git two niggers inter one nigger skin, kin you? Can't git two gallons of whisky inter a one-gallon jug, kin you? No, sir, 't would strain de jug. Yes, en even den you couldn't, *I* don't believe. Why, looky here, Huck, s'posen de Choosday was New Year's—now den! is you gwine to tell me it's dis year in one place en las' year in t' other, bofe in de identical same minute? It's de beatenest rubbage! I can't stan' it—I can't stan' to hear tell 'bout it." Then he begun to shiver and turn gray, and Tom says:

"*Now* what's the matter? What's the trouble?"

Jim could hardly speak, but he says:

"Mars Tom, you ain't jokin', en it's *so*?"

"No I'm not, and it *is* so."

Jim shivered again, and says:

"Den dat Monday could be de las' day, en dey wouldn't be no las' day in England, en de dead wouldn't be called. We mustn't go over dah, Mars Tom. Please git him to turn back; I wants to be whah—"

All of a sudden we see something, and all jumped up, and forgot everything and begun to gaze. Tom says:

"Ain't that the—" He catched his breath, then says: "It *is*, sure as you live! It's the ocean!"

That made me and Jim catch our breath, too. Then we all stood petrified but happy, for none of us had ever seen an ocean, or ever expected to. Tom kept muttering:

"Atlantic Ocean—Atlantic. Land, don't it sound great! And that's *it* —and *we* are looking at it—we! Why, it's just too splendid to believe!"

Then we see a big bank of black smoke; and when we got nearer, it was a city—and a monster she was, too, with a thick fringe of ships around one edge; and we wondered if it was New York, and begun to jaw and dispute about it, and, first we knowed, it slid from under us and went flying behind, and here we was, out over the very ocean itself, and going like a cyclone. Then we woke up, I tell you!

We made a break aft and raised a wail, and begun to beg the professor to turn back and land us, but he jerked out his pistol and motioned us back, and we went, but nobody will ever know how bad we felt.

The land was gone, all but a little streak, like a snake, away off on the edge of the water, and down under us was just ocean, ocean, ocean—millions of miles of it, heaving and pitching and squirming, and white sprays blowing from the wave-tops, and only a few ships in sight, wallowing around and laying over, first on one side and then on t' other, and sticking their bows under and then their sterns; and before long there warn't no ships at all, and we had the sky and the whole ocean all to ourselves, and the roomiest place I ever see and the lonesomest.

CHAPTER 4

STORM

And it got lonesomer and lonesomer. There was the big sky up there, empty and awful deep; and the ocean down there without a thing on it but just the waves. All around us was a ring, where the sky and the water come together; yes, a monstrous big ring it was, and we right in the dead center of it—plumb in the center. We was racing along like a prairie fire, but it never made any difference, we couldn't seem to git past that center no way. I couldn't see that we ever gained an inch on that ring. It made a body feel creepy, it was so curious and unaccountable.

Well, everything was so awful still that we got to talking in a very low voice, and kept on getting creepier and lonesomer and less and less talky, till at last the talk ran dry altogether, and we just set there and "thunk," as Jim calls it, and never said a word the longest time.

The professor never stirred till the sun was overhead, then he stood up and put a kind of triangle to his eye, and Tom said it was a sextant and he was taking the sun to see whereabouts the balloon was. Then he ciphered a little and looked in a book, and then he begun to carry on again. He said lots of wild things, and amongst others he said he would keep up this hundred-mile gait till the middle of to-morrow afternoon, and then he'd land in London.

We said we would be humbly thankful.

He was turning away, but he whirled around when we said that, and give us a long look of his blackest kind—one of the maliciousest and suspiciousest looks I ever see. Then he says:

"You want to leave me. Don't try to deny it."

We didn't know what to say, so we held in and didn't say nothing at all.

He went aft and set down, but he couldn't seem to git that thing out of his mind. Every now and then he would rip out something about it, and try to make us answer him, but we dasn't.

It got lonesomer and lonesomer right along, and it did seem to me I couldn't stand it. It was still worse when night begun to come on. By and by Tom pinched me and whispers:

"Look!"

I took a glance aft, and see the professor taking a whet out of a bottle. I didn't like the looks of that. By and by he took another drink, and pretty soon he begun to sing. It was dark now, and getting black and stormy. He went on singing, wilder and wilder, and the thunder begun to mutter, and the wind to wheeze and moan amongst the ropes, and altogether it was awful. It got so black we couldn't see him any more, and wished we couldn't hear him, but we could. Then he got still; but he warn't still ten minutes till we got suspicious, and wished he would start up his noise again, so we could tell where he was. By and by there was a flash of lightning, and we see him start to get up, but he staggered and fell down. We heard him scream out in the dark:

"They don't want to go to England. All right, I'll change the course. They want to leave me. I know they do. Well, they shall—and *now!*"

I 'most died when he said that. Then he was still again,—still so long I couldn't bear it, and it did seem to me the lightning wouldn't *ever* come again. But at last there was a blessed flash, and there he was, on his hands and knees, crawling, and not four feet from us. My, but his eyes was terrible! He made a lunge for Tom, and says, "Overboard *you* go!" but it was already pitch-dark again, and I couldn't see whether he got him or not, and Tom didn't make a sound.

There was another long, horrible wait; then there was a flash, and I see Tom's head sink down outside the boat and disappear. He was on the rope-ladder that dangled down in the air from the gunnel. The professor let off a shout and jumped for him, and straight off it was pitch-dark again, and Jim groaned out, "Po' Mars Tom, he's a goner!" and made a jump for the professor, but the professor warn't there.

Then we heard a couple of terrible screams, and then another not so loud, and then another that was 'way below, and you could only *just* hear it; and I heard Jim say, "Po' Mars Tom!"

Then it was awful still, and I reckon a person could 'a' counted four thousand before the next flash come. When it come I see Jim on his knees, with his arms on the locker and his face buried in them, and he was crying. Before I could look over the edge it was all dark again, and I was glad, because I didn't want to see. But when the next flash come, I was watching, and down there I see somebody a-swinging in the wind on the ladder, and it was Tom!

"Come up!" I shouts; "come up, Tom!"

His voice was so weak, and the wind roared so, I couldn't make out what he said, but I thought he asked was the professor up there. I shouts:

"No, he's down in the ocean! Come up! Can we help you?"

Of course, all this in the dark.

"Huck, who is you hollerin' at?"

"I'm hollerin' at Tom."

"Oh, Huck, how kin you act so, when you know po' Mars Tom's—" Then he let off an awful scream, and flung his head and his arms back and let off another one, because there was a white glare just then, and he had raised up his face just in time to see Tom's, as white as snow, rise above the gunnel and look him right in the eye. He thought it was Tom's ghost, you see.

Tom clumb aboard, and when Jim found it *was* him, and not his ghost, he hugged him, and called him all sorts of loving names, and carried on like he was gone crazy, he was so glad. Says I:

"What did you wait for, Tom? Why didn't you come up at first?"

"I dasn't, Huck. I knowed somebody plunged down past me, but I didn't know who it was in the dark. It could 'a' been you, it could 'a' been Jim."

That was the way with Tom Sawyer—always sound. He warn't coming up till he knowed where the professor was.

The storm let go about this time with all its might; and it was dreadful the way the thunder boomed and tore, and the lightning glared out, and the wind sung and screamed in the rigging, and the rain come down. One second you couldn't see your hand before you, and the next you could count the threads in your coat-sleeve, and see a whole wide desert of waves pitching and tossing through a kind of veil of rain. A storm like that is the loveliest thing there is, but it ain't at its best when you are up in the sky and lost, and it's wet and lonesome, and there's just been a death in the family.

We set there huddled up in the bow, and talked low about the poor professor; and everybody was sorry for him, and sorry the world had made fun of him and treated him so harsh, when he was doing the best he could, and hadn't a friend nor nobody to encourage him and keep him from brooding his mind away and going deranged. There was plenty of clothes and blankets and everything at the other end, but we thought we'd ruther take the rain than go meddling back there.

CHAPTER 5

LAND

We tried to make some plans, but we couldn't come to no agreement. Me and Jim was for turning around and going back home, but Tom allowed that by the time daylight come, so we could see our way, we would be so far toward England that we might as well go there, and come back in a ship, and have the glory of saying we done it.

About midnight the storm quit and the moon come out and lit up the ocean, and we begun to feel comfortable and drowsy; so we stretched out on the lockers and went to sleep, and never woke up again till sun-up. The sea was sparkling like di'monds, and it was nice weather, and pretty soon our things was all dry again.

We went aft to find some breakfast, and the first thing we noticed was that there was a dim light burning in a compass back there under a hood. Then Tom was disturbed. He says:

"You know what that means, easy enough. It means that somebody has got to stay on watch and steer this thing the same as he would a ship, or she'll wander around and go wherever the wind wants her to."

"Well," I says, "what's she been doing since—er—since we had the accident?"

"Wandering," he says, kinder troubled—"wandering, without any doubt. She's in a wind, now, that's blowing her south of east. We don't know how long that's been going on, either."

So then he p'inted her east, and said he would hold her there till we rousted out the breakfast. The professor had laid in everything a body could want; he couldn't 'a' been better fixed. There wasn't no milk for the coffee, but there was water, and everything else you could want, and a charcoal stove and the fixings for it, and pipes and cigars and matches; and wine and liquor, which warn't in our line; and books, and maps, and charts, and an accordion; and furs, and blankets, and no end of rubbish, like brass beads and brass jewelry, which Tom said was a sure sign that he had an idea of visiting among savages. There was money, too. Yes, the professor was well enough fixed.

After breakfast Tom learned me and Jim how to steer, and divided us all up into four-hour watches, turn and turn about; and when his watch was out I took his place, and he got out the professor's papers and pens and wrote a letter home to his Aunt Polly, telling her everything that had happened to us, and dated it "*In the Welkin, approaching England,*" and folded it together and stuck it fast with a red wafer, and directed it, and wrote above the direction, in big writing, "*From Tom Sawyer, the Erronort,*" and said it would stump old Nat Parsons, the postmaster, when it come along in the mail. I says:

"Tom Sawyer, this ain't no welkin; it's a balloon."

"Well, now, who *said* it was a welkin, smarty?"

"You've wrote it on the letter, anyway."

"What of it? That don't mean that the balloon's the welkin."

"Oh, I thought it did. Well, then, what is a welkin?"

I see in a minute he was stuck. He raked and scraped around in his mind, but he couldn't find nothing, so he had to say:

"*I* don't know, and nobody don't know. It's just a word, and it's a mighty good word, too. There ain't many that lays over it. I don't believe there's *any* that does."

"Shucks!" I says. "But what does it *mean?*—that's the p'int."

"*I* don't know what it means, I tell you. It's a word that people uses for—for—well, it's ornamental. They don't put ruffles on a shirt to keep a person warm, do they?"

"Course they don't."

"But they put them *on,* don't they?"

"Yes."

"All right, then; that letter I wrote is a shirt, and the welkin's the ruffle on it."

I judged that that would gravel Jim, and it did.

"Now, Mars Tom, it ain't no use to talk like dat; en, moreover, it's sinful. You knows a letter ain't no shirt, en dey ain't no ruffles on it, nuther. Dey ain't no place to put 'em on; you can't put 'em on, and dey wouldn't stay ef you did."

"Oh, *do* shut up, and wait till something's started that you know something about."

"Why, Mars Tom, sholy you can't mean to say I don't know about shirts, when, goodness knows, I's toted home de washin' ever sence—"

"I tell you, this hasn't got anything to *do* with shirts. I only—"

"Why, Mars Tom, you said yo'self dat a letter—"

"Do you want to drive me crazy? Keep still. I only used it as a metaphor."

That word kinder bricked us up for a minute. Then Jim says—rather timid, because he see Tom was getting pretty tetchy:

"Mars Tom, what is a metaphor?"

"A metaphor's a—well, it's a—a—a metaphor's an illustration." He see *that* didn't git home, so he tried again. "When I say birds of a feather flocks together, it's a metaphorical way of saying—"

"But dey *don't*, Mars Tom. No, sir, 'deed dey don't. Dey ain't no feathers dat's more alike den a bluebird en a jaybird, but ef you waits till you catches *dem* birds together, you'll—"

"Oh, give us a rest! You can't get the simplest little thing through your thick skull. Now don't bother me any more."

Jim was satisfied to stop. He was dreadful pleased with himself for catching Tom out. The minute Tom begun to talk about birds I judged he was a goner, because Jim knowed more about birds than both of us put together. You see, he had killed hundreds and hundreds of them, and that's the way to find out about birds. That's the way people does that writes books about birds, and loves them so that they'll go hungry and tired and take any amount of trouble to find a new bird and kill it. Their name is ornithologers, and I could have been an ornithologer myself, because I always loved birds and creatures; and I started out to learn how to be one, and I see a bird setting on a limb of a high tree, singing with its head tilted back and its mouth open, and before I thought I fired, and his song stopped and he fell straight down from the limb, all limp like a rag, and I run and picked him up and he was dead, and his body was warm in my hand, and his head rolled about this way and that, like his neck was broke, and there was a little white skin over his eyes, and one little drop of blood on the side of his head; and, laws! I couldn't see nothing more for the tears; and I hain't never murdered no creature since that warn't doing me no harm, and I ain't going to.

But I was aggravated about that welkin. I wanted to know. I got the subject up again, and then Tom explained, the best he could. He said when a person made a big speech the newspapers said the shouts of the people made the welkin ring. He said they always said that, but none of them ever told what it was, so he allowed it just meant outdoors and up high. Well, that seemed sensible enough, so I was satisfied, and said so. That pleased Tom and put him in a good humor again, and he says:

"Well, it's all right, then; and we'll let bygones be bygones. I don't know for certain what a welkin is, but when we land in London we'll make it ring, anyway, and don't you forget it."

He said an erronort was a person who sailed around in balloons; and said it was a mighty sight finer to be Tom Sawyer the Erronort than to be Tom Sawyer the Traveler, and we would be heard of all round the world, if we pulled through all right, and so he wouldn't give shucks to be a traveler now.

Toward the middle of the afternoon we got everything ready to land, and we felt pretty good, too, and proud; and we kept watching with the glasses, like Columbus discovering America. But we couldn't see nothing but ocean. The afternoon wasted out and the sun shut down, and still there warn't no land anywheres. We wondered what was the matter, but reckoned it would come out all right, so we went on steering east, but went up on a higher level so we wouldn't hit any steeples or mountains in the dark.

It was my watch till midnight, and then it was Jim's; but Tom stayed up, because he said ship-captains done that when they was making the land, and didn't stand no regular watch.

Well, when daylight come, Jim give a shout, and we jumped up and looked over, and there was the land sure enough,—land all around, as far as you could see, and perfectly level and yaller. We didn't know how long we'd been over it. There warn't no trees, nor hills, nor rocks, nor towns, and Tom and Jim had took it for the sea. They took it for the sea in a dead cam; but we was so high up, anyway, that if it had been the sea and rough, it would 'a' looked smooth, all the same, in the night, that way.

We was all in a powerful excitement now, and grabbed the glasses and hunted everywheres for London, but couldn't find hair nor hide of it, nor any other settlement,—nor any sign of a lake or a river, either. Tom was clean beat. He said it warn't his notion of England; he thought England looked like America, and always had that idea. So he said we better have breakfast, and then drop down and inquire the quickest way to London. We cut the breakfast pretty short, we was so impatient. As we slanted along down, the weather began to moderate, and pretty soon we shed our furs. But it kept *on* moderating, and in a precious little while it was 'most too moderate. We was close down, now, and just blistering!

We settled down to within thirty foot of the land,—that is, it was land if sand is land; for this wasn't anything but pure sand. Tom and me clumb down the ladder and took a run to stretch our legs, and it felt amazing good,—that is, the stretching did, but the sand scorched our feet like hot embers. Next, we see somebody coming, and started to meet him; but we heard Jim shout, and looked around and he was fairly dancing, and making signs, and yelling. We couldn't make out what he said, but we was scared anyway, and begun to heel it back to the balloon. When we got close enough, we understood the words, and they made me sick:

"Run! Run fo' yo' life! Hit's a lion; I kin see him thoo de glass! Run, boys; do please heel it de bes' you kin. He's bu'sted outen de menagerie, en dey ain't nobody to stop him!"

It made Tom fly, but it took the stiffening all out of my legs. I could only just gasp along the way you do in a dream when there's a ghost gaining on you.

Tom got to the ladder and shinned up it a piece and waited for me; and as soon as I got a foothold on it he shouted to Jim to soar away. But Jim had clean lost his head, and said he had forgot how. So Tom shinned along up and told me to follow; but the lion was arriving, fetching a most ghastly roar with every lope, and my legs shook so I dasn't try to take one of them out of the rounds for fear the other one would give way under me.

But Tom was aboard by this time, and he started the balloon up a little, and stopped it again as soon as the end of the ladder was ten or twelve feet above ground. And there was the lion, a-ripping around under me, and roaring and springing up in the air at the ladder, and only missing it about a quarter of an inch, it seemed to me. It was delicious to be out of his reach, perfectly delicious, and made me feel good and thankful all up one side; but I was hanging there helpless and couldn't climb, and that made me feel perfectly wretched and miserable all down the other. It is most seldom that a person feels so mixed, like that; and it is not to be recommended, either.

Tom asked me what he'd better do, but I didn't know. He asked me if I could hold on whilst he sailed away to a safe place and left the lion behind. I said I could if he didn't go no higher than he was now;

but if he went higher I would lose my head and fall, sure. So he said, "Take a good grip," and he started.

"Don't go so fast," I shouted. "It makes my head swim."

He had started like a lightning express. He slowed down, and we glided over the sand slower, but still in a kind of sickening way; for it *is* uncomfortable to see things sliding and gliding under you like that, and not a sound.

But pretty soon there was plenty of sound, for the lion was catching up. His noise fetched others. You could see them coming on the lope from every direction, and pretty soon there was a couple of dozen of them under me, jumping up at the ladder and snarling and snapping at each other; and so we went skimming along over the sand, and these fellers doing what they could to help us to not forgit the occasion; and then some other beasts come, without an invite, and they started a regular riot down there.

We see this plan was a mistake. We couldn't ever git away from them at this gait, and I couldn't hold on forever. So Tom took a think, and struck another idea. That was, to kill a lion with the pepper-box revolver, and then sail away while the others stopped to fight over the carcass. So he stopped the balloon still, and done it, and then we sailed off while the fuss was going on, and come down a quarter of a mile off, and they helped me aboard; but by the time we was out of reach again, that gang was on hand once more. And when they see we was really gone and they couldn't get us, they sat down on their hams and looked up at us so kind of disappointed that it was as much as a person could do not to see *their* side of the matter.

CHAPTER 6

IT'S A CARAVAN

I was so weak that the only thing I wanted was a chance to lay down, so I made straight for my locker-bunk, and stretched myself out there. But a body couldn't get back his strength in no such oven as that, so Tom give the command to soar, and Jim started her aloft.

We had to go up a mile before we struck comfortable weather where it was breezy and pleasant and just right, and pretty soon I was all straight again. Tom had been setting quiet and thinking; but now he jumps up and says:

"I bet you a thousand to one *I* know where we are. We're in the Great Sahara, as sure as guns!"

He was so excited he couldn't hold still; but I wasn't. I says:

"Well, then, where's the Great Sahara? In England or in Scotland?"

" 'T ain't in either, it's in Africa."

Jim's eyes bugged out, and he begun to stare down with no end of interest, because that was where his originals come from; but I didn't more than half believe it. I couldn't, you know; it seemed too awful far away for us to have traveled.

But Tom was full of his discovery, as he called it, and said the lions and the sand meant the Great Desert, sure. He said he could 'a' found out, before we sighted land, that we was crowding the land somewheres, if he had thought of one thing; and when we asked him what, he said:

"These clocks. They're chronometers. You always read about them in sea voyages. One of them is keeping Grinnage time, and the other is keeping St. Louis time, like my watch. When we left St. Louis it was four in the afternoon by my watch and this clock, and it was ten at night by this Grinnage clock. Well, at this time of the year the sun sets about seven o'clock. Now I noticed the time yesterday evening when the sun went down, and it was half-past five o'clock by the Grinnage clock, and half-past eleven A. M. by my watch and the other clock. You see, the sun rose and set by my watch in St. Louis, and the Grinnage clock was six hours fast; but we've come so far east that it comes within less than half an hour of setting by the Grinnage clock, now, and I'm away out—more than four hours and a half out. You see, that meant that we was closing up on the longitude of Ireland, and would strike it before long if we was p'inted right—which we wasn't. No, sir, we've been a-wandering—wandering 'way down south of east, and it's my opinion we are in Africa. Look at this map. You see how the shoulder of Africa sticks out to the west. Think how fast we've traveled; if we had gone straight east we would be long past England by this time. You watch for noon, all of you, and we'll stand up, and when we can't cast a shadow we'll find that this Grinnage clock is coming mighty close to marking twelve. Yes, sir, *I* think we're in Africa; and it's just bully."

Jim was gazing down with the glass. He shook his head and says:

"Mars Tom, I reckon dey's a mistake som'er's. I hain't seen no niggers yit."

"That's nothing; they don't live in the desert. What is that, 'way off yonder? Gimme a glass."

He took a long look, and said it was like a black string stretched across the sand, but he couldn't guess what it was.

"Well," I says, "I reckon maybe you've got a chance, now, to find out whereabouts this balloon is, because as like as not that is one of these lines here, that's on the map, that you call meridians of longitude, and we can drop down and look at its number, and—"

"Oh, shucks, Huck Finn, I never see such a lunkhead as you. Did you s'pose there's meridians of longitude on the *earth*?"

"Tom Sawyer, they're set down on the map, and you know it perfectly well, and here they are, and you can see for yourself."

"Of course they're on the map, but that's nothing; there ain't any on the *ground*."

"Tom, do you know that to be so?"

"Certainly I do."

"Well, then, that map's a liar again. I never see such a liar as that map."

He fired up at that, and I was ready for him, and Jim was warming his opinion, too, and next minute we'd 'a' broke loose on another argument, if Tom hadn't dropped the glass and begun to clap his hands like a maniac and sing out—

"Camels!—Camels!"

So I grabbed a glass, and Jim, too, and took a look, but I was disappointed, and says—

"Camels your granny, they're spiders."

"Spiders in a desert, you shad? Spiders walking in a procession? You don't ever reflect, Huck Finn, and I reckon you really haven't got anything to reflect *with*. Don't you know we're as much as a mile up in the air, and that that string of crawlers is two or three miles away? Spiders, good land! Spiders as big as a cow? Perhaps you'd like to go down and milk one of 'em. But they're camels, just the same. It's a caravan, that's what it is, and it's a mile long."

"Well, then, le' 's go down and look at it. I don't believe in it, and ain't going to till I see it and know it."

"All right," he says, and give the command: "Lower away."

As we come slanting down into the hot weather, we could see that it was camels, sure enough, plodding along, an everlasting string of them, with bales strapped to them, and several hundred men in long white robes, and a thing like a shawl bound over their heads and hanging down with tassels and fringes; and some of the men had long guns and some hadn't, and some was riding and some was walking. And the weather—well, it was just roasting. And how slow they did creep along!

We swooped down, now, all of a sudden, and stopped about a hundred yards over their heads.

The men all set up a yell, and some of them fell flat on their stomachs, some begun to fire their guns at us, and the rest broke and scampered every which way, and so did the camels.

We see that we was making trouble, so we went up again about a mile, to the cool weather, and watched them from there. It took them an hour to get together and form the procession again; then they started along, but we could see by the glasses that they wasn't paying much attention to anything but us. We poked along, looking down at them with the glasses, and by and by we see a big sand mound, and something like people the other side of it, and there was something like a man laying on top of the mound, that raised his head up every now and then, and seemed to be watching the caravan or us, we didn't know which. As the caravan got nearer, he sneaked down on the other side and rushed to the other men and horses—for that is what they was —and we see them mount in a hurry; and next, here they come, like a house afire, some with lances and some with long guns, and all of them yelling the best they could.

They come a-tearing down onto the caravan, and the next minute both sides crashed together and was all mixed up, and there was such another popping of guns as you never heard, and the air got so full of smoke you could only catch glimpses of them struggling together. There must 'a' been six hundred men in that battle, and it was terrible to see. Then they broke up into gangs and groups, fighting tooth and nail, and scurrying and scampering around, and laying into each other like everything; and whenever the smoke cleared a little you could see dead and wounded people and camels scattered far and wide and all about, and camels racing off in every direction.

At last the robbers see they couldn't win, so their chief sounded a signal, and all that was left of them broke away and went scampering across the plain. The last man to go snatched up a child and carried it off in front of him on his horse, and a woman run screaming and begging after him, and followed him away off across the plain till she was separated a long ways from her people; but it warn't no use, and she had to give it up, and we see her sink down on the sand and cover her face with her hands. Then Tom took the hellum, and started for that yahoo, and we come a-whizzing down and made a swoop, and knocked him out of the saddle, child and all; and he was jarred considerable, but the child wasn't hurt, but laid there working its hands and legs in the air like a tumble-bug that's on its back and can't turn over. The man went staggering off to overtake his horse, and didn't know what had hit him, for we was three or four hundred yards up in the air by this time.

We judged the woman would go and get the child, now; but she didn't. We could see her, through the glass, still setting there, with her head bowed down on her knees; so of course she hadn't seen the performance, and thought her child was clean gone with the man. She was nearly a half a mile from her people, so we thought we might go down to the child, which was about a quarter of a mile beyond her, and snake it to her before the caravan people could git to us to do us any harm; and besides, we reckoned they had enough business on their hands for one while, anyway, with the wounded. We thought we'd chance it, and we did. We swooped down and stopped, and Jim shinned down the ladder and fetched up the kid, which was a nice fat little thing, and in a noble good humor, too, considering it was just out of a battle and been tumbled off of a horse; and then we started for the mother, and stopped back of her and tolerable near by, and Jim slipped down and crept up easy, and when he was close back of her the child goo-goo'd, the way a child does, and she heard it, and whirled and fetched a shriek of joy, and made a jump for the kid and snatched it and hugged it, and dropped it and hugged Jim, and then snatched off a gold chain and hung it around Jim's neck, and hugged him again, and jerked up the child again, a-sobbing and glorifying all the time; and Jim he shoved for the ladder and up it, and in a minute we was back up in the sky and the woman was staring up, with the back of her head between her shoulders and the child with its arms locked around her neck. And there she stood, as long as we was in sight a-sailing away in the sky.

CHAPTER 7

TOM RESPECTS THE FLEA

"Noon!" says Tom, and so it was. His shadder was just a blot around his feet. We looked, and the Grinnage clock was so close to twelve the difference didn't amount to nothing. So Tom said London was right north of us or right south of us, one or t'other, and he reckoned by the weather and the sand and the camels it was north; and a good many miles north, too; as many as from New York to the city of Mexico, he guessed.

Jim said he reckoned a balloon was a good deal the fastest thing in the world, unless it might be some kinds of birds—a wild pigeon, maybe, or a railroad.

But Tom said he had read about railroads in England going nearly a hundred miles an hour for a little ways, and there never was a bird in the world that could do that—except one, and that was a flea.

"A flea? Why, Mars Tom, in de fust place he ain't a bird, strickly speakin'—"

"He ain't a bird, eh? Well, then, what is he?"

"I don't rightly know, Mars Tom, but I speck he's only jist a' animal. No, I reckon dat won't do, nuther, he ain't big enough for a' animal. He mus' be a bug. Yassir, dat's what he is, he's a bug."

"I bet he ain't, but let it go. What's your second place?"

"Well, in de second place, birds is creturs dat goes a long ways, but a flea don't."

"He don't, don't he? Come, now, what *is* a long distance, if you know?"

"Why, it's miles, and lots of 'em—anybody knows dat."

"Can't a man walk miles?"

"Yassir, he kin."

"As many as a railroad?"

"Yassir, if you give him time."

"Can't a flea?"

"Well,—I s'pose so—ef you gives him heaps of time."

"Now you begin to see, don't you, that *distance* ain't the thing to judge by, at all; it's the time it takes to go the distance *in* that *counts,* ain't it?"

"Well, hit do look sorter so, but I wouldn't 'a' b'lieved it, Mars Tom."

"It's a matter of *proportion,* that's what it is; and when you come to gauge a thing's speed by its size, where's your bird and your man and your railroad, alongside of a flea? The fastest man can't run more than about ten miles in an hour—not much over ten thousand times his own length. But all the books says any common ordinary third-class flea can jump a hundred and fifty times his own length; yes, and he can make five jumps a second too,—seven hundred and fifty times his own length, in one little second—for he don't fool away any time stopping and starting—he does them both at the same time; you'll see, if you try to put your finger on him. Now that's a common, ordinary, third-class flea's gait; but you take an Eyetalian *first*-class, that's been the pet of the nobility all his life, and hasn't ever knowed what want or sickness or exposure was, and he can jump more than three hundred times his own length, and keep it up all day, five such jumps every second, which is fifteen hundred times his own length. Well, suppose a man could go fifteen hundred times his own length in a second–say, a mile and a half. It's ninety miles a minute; it's considerable more than five thousand miles an hour. Where's your man *now*?–yes, and your bird, and your railroad, and your balloon? Laws, they don't amount to shucks 'longside of a flea. A flea is just a comet b'iled down small."

Jim was a good deal astonished, and so was I. Jim said–

"Is dem figgers jist edjackly true, en no jokin' en no lies, Mars Tom?"

"Yes, they are; they're perfectly true."

"Well, den, honey, a body's got to respec' a flea. I ain't had no respec' for um befo', sca'sely, but dey ain't no gittin' roun' it, dey do deserve it, dat's certain."

"Well, I bet they do. They've got ever so much more sense, and brains, and brightness, in proportion to their size, than any other cretur in the world. A person can learn them 'most anything; and they learn it quicker than any other cretur, too. They've been learnt to haul little carriages in harness, and go this way and that way and t' other way according to their orders; yes, and to march and drill like soldiers, doing it as exact, according to orders, as soldiers does it. They've been learnt to do all sorts of hard and troublesome things. S'pose you could cultivate a flea up to the size of a man, and keep his natural smartness a-growing and a-growing right along up, bigger and bigger, and keener and keener, in the same proportion–where'd the human race be, do you reckon? That flea would be President of the United States, and you couldn't any more prevent it than you can prevent lightning."

"My lan', Mars Tom, I never knowed dey was so much *to* de beas'. No, sir, I never had no idea of it, and dat's de fac'."

"There's more to him, by a long sight, than there is to any other cretur, man or beast, in proportion to size. He's the interestingest of them all. People have so much to say about an ant's strength, and an elephant's, and a locomotive's. Shucks, they don't begin with a flea. He can lift two or three hundred times his own weight. And none of them can come anywhere near it. And moreover, he has got notions of his own, and is very particular, and you can't fool him; his instinct, or his judgment, or whatever it is, is perfectly sound and clear, and don't ever make a mistake. People think all humans are alike to a flea. It ain't so. There's folks that he won't go near, hungry or not hungry, and I'm one of them. I've never had one of them on me in my life."

"Mars Tom!"

"It's so; I ain't joking."

"Well, sah, I hain't ever heard de likes o' dat, befo'."

Jim couldn't believe it, and I couldn't; so we had to drop down to the sand and git a supply and see. Tom was right. They went for me and Jim by the thousand, but not a one of them lit on Tom. There warn't no explaining it, but there it was and there warn't no getting around it. He said it had always been just so, and he'd just as soon be where there was a million of them as not; they'd never touch him nor bother him.

We went up to the cold weather to freeze 'em out, and stayed a little spell, and then come back to the comfortable weather and went lazying along twenty or twenty-five miles an hour, the way we'd been doing for the last few hours. The reason was, that the longer we was in that solemn, peaceful desert, the more the hurry and fuss got kind of soothed down in us, and the more happier and contented and satisfied we got to feeling, and the more we got to liking the desert, and then loving it. So we had cramped the speed down, as I was saying, and was having a most noble good lazy time, sometimes watching through the glasses, sometimes stretched out on the lockers reading, sometimes taking a nap.

It didn't seem like we was the same lot that was in such a state to find land and git ashore, but it was. But we had got over that—clean over it. We was used to the balloon, now, and not afraid any more, and didn't want to be anywheres else. Why, it seemed just like home; it 'most seemed as if I had been born and raised in it, and Jim and Tom said the same. And always I had had hateful people around me, a-nagging at me, and pestering of me, and scolding, and finding fault, and fussing and bothering, and sticking to me, and keeping after me, and making me do this, and making me do that and t'other, and always selecting out the things I didn't want to do, and then giving me Sam Hill because I shirked and done something else, and just aggravating the life out of a body all the time; but up here in the sky it was so still and sunshiny and lovely, and plenty to eat, and plenty of sleep, and strange things to see, and no nagging and no pestering, and no good people, and just holiday all the time. Land, I warn't in no hurry to git out and buck at civilization again. Now, one of the worst things about civilization is, that anybody that gits a letter with trouble in it comes and tells you all about it and makes you feel bad, and the newspapers fetches you the troubles of everybody all over the world, and keeps you down-hearted and dismal 'most all the time, and it's such a heavy load for a person. I hate them newspapers; and I hate letters; and if I had my way I wouldn't allow nobody to load his troubles onto other folks he ain't acquainted with, on t'other side of the world, that way. Well, up in a balloon there ain't any of that, and it's the darlingest place there is.

We had supper, and that night was one of the prettiest nights I ever see. The moon made it just like daylight, only a heap softer; and once we see a lion standing all alone by himself, just all alone on the earth, it seemed like, and his shadder laid on the sand by him like a puddle of ink. That's the kind of moonlight to have.

Mainly we laid on our backs and talked; we didn't want to go to sleep. Tom said we was right in the midst of the Arabian Nights, now. He said it was right along here that one of the cutest things in that book happened; so we looked down and watched while he told about it, because there ain't anything that is so interesting to look at as a place that a book has talked about. It was a tale about a camel-driver that had lost his camel, and he come along in the desert and met a man, and says–

"Have you run across a stray camel to-day?"

And the man says–

"Was he blind in his left eye?"

"Yes."

"Had he lost an upper front tooth?"

"Yes."

"Was his off hind leg lame?"

"Yes."

"Was he loaded with millet-seed on one side and honey on the other?"

"Yes, but you needn't go into no more details–that's the one, and I'm in a hurry. Where did you see him?"

"I hain't seen him at all," the man says.

"Hain't seen him at all? How can you describe him so close, then?"

"Because when a person knows how to use his eyes, everything has got a meaning to it; but most people's eyes ain't any good to them. I knowed a camel had been along, because I seen his track. I knowed he was lame in his off hind leg because he had favored that foot and trod light on it, and his track showed it. I knowed he was blind on his left side because he only nibbled the grass on the right side of the trail. I knowed he had lost an upper front tooth because where he bit into the sod his teethprint showed it. The millet-seed sifted out on one side–

the ants told me that; the honey leaked out on the other—the flies told me that. I know all about your camel, but I hain't seen him."

Jim says—

"Go on, Mars Tom, hit's a mighty good tale, and powerful interestin'."

"That's all," Tom says.

"*All?*" says Jim, astonished. "What 'come o' de camel?"

"I don't know."

"Mars Tom, don't de tale say?"

"No."

Jim puzzled a minute, then he says—

"Well! Ef dat ain't de beatenes' tale ever *I* struck. Jist gits to de place whah de intrust is gittin' red-hot, en down she breaks. Why, Mars Tom, dey ain't no *sense* in a tale dat acts like dat. Hain't you got no *idea* whether de man got de camel back er not?"

"No, I haven't."

I see, myself, there warn't no sense in the tale, to chop square off, that way, before it come to anything, but I warn't going to say so, because I could see Tom was souring up pretty fast over the way it flatted out and the way Jim had popped onto the weak place in it, and I don't think it's fair for everybody to pile onto a feller when he's down. But Tom he whirls on me and says—

"What do *you* think of the tale?"

Of course, then, I had to come out and make a clean breast and say it did seem to me, too, same as it did to Jim, that as long as the tale stopped square in the middle and never got to no place, it really warn't worth the trouble of telling.

Tom's chin dropped on his breast, and 'stead of being mad, as I reckoned he'd be, to hear me scoff at his tale that way, he seemed to be only sad; and he says—

"Some people can see, and some can't—just as that man said. Let alone a camel, if a cyclone had gone by, *you* duffers wouldn't 'a' noticed the track."

I don't know what he meant by that, and he didn't say; it was just one of his irrulevances, I reckon—he was full of them, sometimes, when he was in a close place and couldn't see no other way out—but I didn't mind. We'd spotted the soft place in that tale sharp enough, he couldn't git away from that little fact. It graveled him like the nation, too, I reckon, much as he tried not to let on.

CHAPTER 8

THE DISAPPEARING LAKE

We had an early breakfast in the morning, and set looking down on the desert, and the weather was ever so bammy and lovely, although we warn't high up. You have to come down lower and lower after sundown, in the desert, because it cools off so fast; and so, by the time it is getting towards dawn you are skimming along only a little ways above the sand.

We was watching the shadder of the balloon slide along the ground, and now and then gazing off across the desert to see if anything was stirring, and then down at the shadder again, when all of a sudden almost right under us we see a lot of men and camels laying scattered about, perfectly quiet, like they was asleep.

We shut off the power, and backed up and stood over them, and then we see that they was all dead. It give us the cold shivers. And it made us hush down, too, and talk low, like people at a funeral. We dropped down slow, and stopped, and me and Tom clumb down and went amongst them. There was men, and women, and children. They was dried by the sun and dark and shriveled and leathery, like the pictures of mummies you see in books. And yet they looked just as human, you wouldn't 'a' believed it; just like they was asleep.

Some of the people and animals was partly covered with sand, but most of them not, for the sand was thin there, and the bed was gravel, and hard. Most of the clothes had rotted away; and when you took hold of a rag, it tore with a touch, like spider-web. Tom reckoned they had been laying there for years.

Some of the men had rusty guns by them, some had swords on and had shawl belts with long silver-mounted pistols stuck in them. All the camels had their loads on, yet, but the packs had busted or rotted and spilt the freight out on the ground. We didn't reckon the swords was any good to the dead people any more, so we took one apiece, and some pistols. We took a small box, too, because it was so handsome and inlaid so fine; and then we wanted to bury the people; but there warn't no way to do it that we could think of, and nothing to do it with but sand, and that would blow away again, of course.

Then we mounted high and sailed away, and pretty soon that black spot on the sand was out of sight and we wouldn't ever see them poor people again in this world. We wondered, and reasoned, and tried to guess how they come to be there, and how it all happened to them, but we couldn't make it out. First we thought maybe they got lost, and wandered around and about till their food and water give out and they starved to death; but Tom said no wild animals nor vultures hadn't meddled with them, and so that guess wouldn't do. So at last we give it up, and judged we wouldn't think about it no more, because it made us low-spirited.

Then we opened the box, and it had gems and jewels in it, quite a pile, and some little veils of the kind the dead women had on, with fringes made out of curious gold money that we warn't acquainted with. We wondered if we better go and try to find them again and give it back; but Tom thought it over and said no, it was a country that was full of robbers, and they would come and steal it, and then the sin would be on us for putting the temptation in their way. So we went on; but I wished we had took all they had, so there wouldn't 'a' been no temptation at all left.

We had had two hours of that blazing weather down there, and was dreadful thirsty when we got aboard again. We went straight for the water, but it was spoiled and bitter, besides being pretty near hot enough to scald your mouth. We couldn't drink it. It was Mississippi river water, the best in the world, and we stirred up the mud in it to see if that would help, but no, the mud wasn't any better than the water.

Well, we hadn't been so very, very thirsty before, whilst we was interested in the lost people, but we was, now, and as soon as we found we couldn't have a drink, we was more than thirty-five times as thirsty as we was a quarter of a minute before. Why, in a little while we wanted to hold our mouths open and pant like a dog.

Tom said to keep a sharp lookout, all around, everywheres, because we'd got to find an oasis or there warn't no telling what would happen. So we done it. We kept the glasses gliding around all the time, till our arms got so tired we couldn't hold them any more. Two hours—three hours—just gazing and gazing, and nothing but sand, sand, *sand,* and you could see the quivering heat-shimmer playing over it. Dear, dear, a body don't know what real misery is till he is thirsty all the way through and is certain he ain't ever going to come to any water any more. At last I couldn't stand it to look around on them baking plains; I laid down on the locker, and give it up.

But by and by Tom raised a whoop, and there she was! A lake, wide and shiny, with pam-trees leaning over it asleep, and their shadders in the water just as soft and delicate as ever you see. I never see anything look so good. It was a long ways off, but that warn't anything to us; we just slapped on a hundred-mile gait, and calculated to be there in seven minutes; but she stayed the same old distance away, all the time; we couldn't seem to gain on her; yes, sir, just as far, and shiny, and like a dream; but we couldn't get no nearer; and at last, all of a sudden, she was gone!

Tom's eyes took a spread, and he says—

"Boys, it was a *my*ridge!" Said it like he was glad. I didn't see nothing to be glad about. I says—

"May be. I don't care nothing about its name, the thing I want to know is, what's become of it?"

Jim was trembling all over, and so scared he couldn't speak, but he wanted to ask that question himself if he could 'a' done it. Tom says—

"What's *become* of it? Why, you see, yourself, it's gone."

"Yes, I know; but where's it gone *to*?"

He looked me over and says—

"Well, now, Huck Finn, where *would* it go to? Don't you know what a myridge is?"

"No, I don't. What is it?"

"It ain't anything but imagination. There ain't anything *to* it."

It warmed me up a little to hear him talk like that, and I says—

"What's the use you talking that kind of stuff, Tom Sawyer? Didn't I see the lake?"

"Yes—you think you did."

"I don't think nothing about it, I *did* see it."

"I tell you you *didn't* see it either—because it warn't there to see."

It astonished Jim to hear him talk so, and he broke in and says, kind of pleading and distressed—

"Mars Tom, *please* don't say sich things in sich an awful time as dis. You ain't only reskin' yo' own self, but you's reskin' us—same way like Anna Nias en' Siffira. De lake *wuz* dah—I seen it jis' as plain as I sees you en Huck dis minute."

I says—

"Why, he seen it himself! He was the very one that seen it first. *Now*, then!"

"Yes, Mars Tom, hit's so—you can't deny it. We all seen it, en dat *prove* it was dah."

"Proves it! *How* does it prove it?"

"Same way it does in de courts en everywheres, Mars Tom. One pusson might be drunk, or dreamy or suthin', en he could be mistaken;

en two might, maybe; but I tell you, sah, when three sees a thing, drunk er sober, it's *so.* Dey ain't no gittin' aroun' dat, en you knows it, Mars Tom."

"I don't know nothing of the kind. There used to be forty thousand million people that seen the sun move from one side of the sky to the other every day. Did that prove that the sun *done* it?"

"'Course it did. En besides, dey warn't no 'casion to prove it. A body 'at's got any sense ain't gwine to doubt it. Dah she is, now—a sailin' thoo de sky, like she allays done."

Tom turned on me, then, and says—

"What do *you* say—is the sun standing still?"

"Tom Sawyer, what's the use to ask such a jackass question? Anybody that ain't blind can see it don't stand still."

"Well," he says, "I'm lost in the sky with no company but a passel of low-down animals that don't know no more than the head boss of a university did three or four hundred years ago."

It warn't fair play, and I let him know it. I says—

"Throwin' mud ain't arguin', Tom Sawyer."

"Oh, my goodness, oh, my goodness gracious, dah's de lake ag'in!" yelled Jim, just then. "*Now,* Mars Tom, what you gwine to say?"

Yes, sir, there was the lake again, away yonder across the desert, perfectly plain, trees and all, just the same as it was before. I says—

"I reckon you're satisfied now, Tom Sawyer."

But he says, perfectly ca'm—

"Yes, satisfied there ain't no lake there."

Jim says—

"*Don't* talk so, Mars Tom—it sk'yers me to hear you. It's so hot, en you's so thirsty, dat you ain't in yo' right mine, Mars Tom. Oh, but don't she look good! 'clah I doan' know how I's gwine to wait tell we gits dah, I's *so* thirsty."

"Well, you'll have to wait; and it won't do you no good, either, because there ain't no lake there, I tell you."

I says—

"Jim, don't you take your eye off of it, and I won't, either."

"'Deed I won't; en bless you, honey, I couldn't ef I wanted to."

We went a-tearing along toward it, piling the miles behind us like nothing, but never gaining an inch on it—and all of a sudden it was gone again! Jim staggered, and 'most fell down. When he got his breath he says, gasping like a fish—

"Mars Tom, hit's a *ghos'*, dat's what it is, en I hopes to goodness we ain't gwine to see it no mo'. Dey's *been* a lake, en suthin's happened, en de lake's dead, en we's seen its ghos'; we's seen it twiste, en dat's proof. De desert's ha'nted, it's ha'nted, sho'; oh, Mars Tom, le's git outen it; I'd ruther die den have de night ketch us in it ag'in en de ghos' er dat lake come a-mournin' aroun' us en we asleep en doan' know de danger we's in."

"Ghost, you gander! It ain't anything but air and heat and thirstiness pasted together by a person's imagination. If I—gimme the glass!"

He grabbed it and begun to gaze off to the right.

"It's a flock of birds," he says. "It's getting toward sundown, and they're making a bee-line across our track for somewheres. They mean business—maybe they're going for food or water, or both. Let her go to starboard!—Port your hellum! Hard down! There—ease up—steady, as you go."

We shut down some of the power, so as not to outspeed them, and took out after them. We went skimming along a quarter of a mile behind them, and when we had followed them an hour and a half and was getting pretty discouraged, and was thirsty clean to unendurableness, Tom says—

"Take the glass, one of you, and see what that is, away ahead of the birds."

Jim got the first glimpse, and slumped down on the locker, sick. He was most crying, and says—

"She's dah ag'in Mars Tom, she's dah ag'in, en I knows I's gwine to die, 'case when a body sees a ghos' de third time, dat's what it means. I wisht I'd never come in dis balloon, dat I does."

He wouldn't look no more, and what he said made me afraid, too, because I knowed it was true, for that has always been the way with ghosts; so then I wouldn't look any more, either. Both of us begged Tom to turn off and go some other way, but he wouldn't, and said we was ignorant superstitious blatherskites. Yes, and he'll git come up with, one of these days, I says to myself, insulting ghosts that way. They'll stand it for a while, maybe, but they won't stand it always, for anybody that knows about ghosts knows how easy they are hurt, and how revengeful they are.

So we was all quiet and still, Jim and me being scared, and Tom busy. By and by Tom fetched the balloon to a standstill, and says—

"*Now* get up and look, you sapheads."

We done it, and there was the sure-enough water right under us!—clear, and blue, and cool, and deep, and wavy with the breeze, the loveliest sight that ever was. And all about it was grassy banks, and flowers, and shady groves of big trees, looped together with vines, and all looking so peaceful and comfortable, enough to make a body cry, it was so beautiful.

Jim *did* cry, and rip and dance and carry on, he was so thankful and out of his mind for joy. It was my watch, so I had to stay by the works, but Tom and Jim clumb down and drunk a barrel apiece, and fetched me up a lot, and I've tasted a many a good thing in my life, but nothing that ever begun with that water.

Then we went down and had a swim, and then Tom came up and spelled me, and me and Jim had a swim, and then Jim spelled Tom, and me and Tom had a foot-race and a boxing-mill, and I don't reckon I ever had such a good time in my life. It warn't so very hot, because it was close on to evening, and we hadn't any clothes on, anyway. Clothes is well enough in school, and in towns, and at balls, too, but there ain't no sense in them when there ain't no civilization nor other kinds of bothers and fussiness around.

"Lions a-comin'!—lions! Quick, Mars Tom, jump for yo' life, Huck!"

Oh, and didn't we! We never stopped for clothes, but waltzed up the ladder just so. Jim lost his head straight off—he always done it whenever he got excited and scared; and so now, 'stead of just easing the ladder up from the ground a little, so the animals couldn't reach it, he turned on a raft of power, and we went whizzing up and was dangling in the sky before he got his wits together and seen what a foolish thing he was doing. Then he stopped her, but he had clean forgot what to do next; so there we was, so high that the lions looked like pups, and we was drifting off on the wind.

But Tom he shinned up and went for the works and begun to slant her down, and back towards the lake, where the animals was gathering like a camp-meeting, and I judged he had lost *his* head, too; for he knowed I was too scared to climb, and did he want to dump me among the tigers and things?

But no, his head was level, he knowed what he was about. He swooped down to within thirty or forty feet of the lake, and stopped right over the centre, and sung out—

"Leggo, and drop!"

I done it, and shot down, feet first, and seemed to go about a mile toward the bottom; and when I come up, he says—

"Now lay on your back and float till you're rested and got your pluck back, then I'll dip the ladder in the water and you can climb aboard."

I done it. Now that was ever so smart in Tom, because if he had started off somewheres else to drop down on the sand, the menagerie would 'a' come along, too, and might 'a' kept us hunting a safe place till I got tuckered out and fell.

And all this time the lions and tigers was sorting out the clothes, and trying to divide them up so there would be some for all, but there was a misunderstanding about it somewheres, on accounts of some of them trying to hog more than their share; so there was another insurrection, and you never see anything like it in the world. There must 'a' been fifty of them, all mixed up together, snorting and roaring and snapping and biting and tearing, legs and tails in the air and you couldn't tell which was which, and the sand and fur a-flying. And when they got done, some was dead, and some was limping off crippled, and the rest was setting around on the battle-field, some of them licking their sore places and the others looking up at us and seemed to be kind of inviting us to come down and have some fun, but which we didn't want any.

As for the clothes, they warn't any, any more. Every last rag of them was inside of the animals; and not agreeing with them very well, I don't reckon, for there was considerable many brass buttons on them, and there was knives in the pockets, too, and smoking-tobacco, and nails and chalk and marbles and fish-hooks and things. But I wasn't caring. All that was bothering me was, that all we had, now, was the professor's clothes, a big enough assortment, but not suitable to go into company with, if we came across any, because the britches was as long as tunnels, and the coats and things according. Still, there was everything a tailor needed, and Jim was a kind of jack-legged tailor, and he allowed he could soon trim a suit or two down for us that would answer.

CHAPTER 9

TOM DISCOURSES ON THE DESERT

Still, we thought we would drop down there a minute, but on another errand. Most of the professor's cargo of food was put up in cans, in the new way that somebody had just invented, the rest was fresh. When you fetch Missouri beefsteak to the Great Sahara, you want to be particular and stay up in the coolish weather. So we reckoned we would drop down into the lion market and see how we could make out there.

We hauled in the ladder and dropped down till we was just above the reach of the animals, then we let down a rope with a slip-knot in it and hauled up a dead lion, a small tender one, then yanked up a cub tiger. We had to keep the congregation off with the revolver, or they would 'a' took a hand in the proceedings and helped.

We carved off a supply from both, and saved the skins, and hove the rest overboard. Then we baited some of the professor's hooks with the fresh meat and went a-fishing. We stood over the lake just a convenient distance above the water, and catched a lot of the nicest fish you ever see. It was a most amazing good supper we had; lion steak, tiger steak, fried fish and hot corn pone. I don't want nothing better than that.

We had some fruit to finish off with. We got it out of the top of a monstrous tall tree. It was a very slim tree that hadn't a branch on it from the bottom plumb to the top, and there it busted out like a feather-duster. It was a pam tree, of course; anybody knows a pam tree the minute he see it, by the pictures. We went for coconuts in this one, but there warn't none. There was only big loose bunches of things like over-sized grapes, and Tom allowed they was dates, because he said they answered the description in the Arabian Nights and the other books. Of course they mightn't be, and they might be pison; so we had to wait a spell, and watch and see if the birds et them. They done it; so we done it too, and they was most amazing good.

By this time monstrous big birds begun to come and settle on the dead animals. They was plucky creturs; they would tackle one end of a lion that was being gnawed at the other end by another lion. If the lion drove the bird away, it didn't do no good, he was back again the minute the lion was busy.

The big birds come out of every part of the sky—you could make them out with the glass whilst they was still so far away you couldn't see them with your naked eye. Tom said the birds didn't find out the meat was there by the smell, they had to find it out by seeing it. Oh, but ain't that an eye for you! Tom said at the distance of five mile a patch of dead lions couldn't look any bigger than a person's finger nail, and he couldn't imagine how the birds could notice such a little thing so far off.

It was strange and unnatural to see lion eat lion, and we thought maybe they warn't kin. But Jim said that didn't make no difference. He said a hog was fond of her own children, and so was a spider, and he reckoned maybe a lion was pretty near as unprincipled though maybe not quite. He thought likely a lion wouldn't eat his own father, if he knowed which was him, but reckoned he would eat his brother-in-law if he was uncommon hungry, and eat his mother-in-law any time. But *reckoning* don't settle nothing. You can reckon till the cows come home, but that don't fetch you to no decision. So we give it up and let it drop.

Generly it was very still in the Desert, nights, but this time there was music. A lot of other animals come to dinner; sneaking yelpers that Tom allowed was jackals, and roached-backed ones that he said was hyenas; and all the whole biling of them kept up a racket all the time. They made a picture in the moonlight that was more different than any picture I ever see. We had a line out and made fast to the top of a tree, and didn't stand no watch, but all turned in and slept, but I was up two or three times to look down at the animals and hear the music. It was like having a front seat at a menagerie for nothing, which I hadn't ever had before, and so it seemed foolish to sleep and not make the most of it, I mightn't ever have such a chance again.

We went a-fishing again in the early dawn, and then lazied around all day in the deep shade on an island, taking turn about to watch and see that none of the animals come a-snooping around there after erronorts for dinner. We was going to leave the next day, but couldn't, it was too lovely.

The day after, when we rose up toward the sky and sailed off eastward, we looked back and watched that place till it warn't nothing but just a speck in the Desert, and I tell you it was like saying good-by to a friend that you ain't ever going to see any more.

Jim was thinking to himself, and at last he says—

"Mars Tom, we's mos' to de end er de Desert now, I speck."

"Why?"

"Well, hit stan' to reason we is. You knows how long we's been a-skimmin' over it. Mus' be mos' out o' san'. Hit's a wonder to me dat it's hilt out as long as it has."

"Shucks, there's plenty sand, you needn't worry."

"Oh, I ain't a-worryin', Mars Tom, only wonderin', dat's all. De Lord's got plenty san' I ain't doubtin' dat, but nemmine, He ain' gwyne to *was'e* it jist on dat account; en I allows dat dis Desert's plenty big enough now, jist de way she is, en you can't spread her out no mo' 'dout was'in san'."

"Oh, go 'long! we ain't much more than fairly *started* across this Desert yet. The United States is a pretty big country, ain't it? Ain't it, Huck?"

"Yes," I says "there ain't no bigger one, I don't reckon."

"Well," he says, "this Desert is about the shape of the United States, and if you was to lay it down on top of the United States, it would cover the land of the free out of sight like a blanket. There'd be a little corner sticking out, up at Maine and away up northwest, and Florida sticking out like a turtle's tail, and that's all. We've took California away from the Mexicans two or three years ago, so that part of the Pacific coast is ours, now, and if you laid the Great Sahara down with her edge on the Pacific, she would cover the United States and stick out past New York six hundred miles into the Atlantic Ocean."

I says—

"Good land! have you got the documents for that, Tom Sawyer?"

"Yes, and they're right here, and I've been studying them. You can look for yourself. From New York to the Pacific is 2,600 miles. From one end of the Great Desert to the other is 3,200. The United States contains 3,600,000 square miles, the Desert contains 4,162,000. With the Desert's bulk you could cover up every last inch of the United States, and in under where the edges projected out, you could tuck England, Scotland, Ireland, France, Denmark, and all Germany. Yes, sir, you could hide the home of the brave and all of them countries clean out of sight under the Great Sahara, and you would still have 2,000 square miles of sand left."

"Well," I says, "it clean beats me. Why, Tom, it shows that the Lord took as much pains makin' this Desert as makin' the United States and all them other countries."

Jim says—"Huck, dat don' stan' to reason. I reckon dis Desert wa'n't made, at all. Now you take en look at it like dis—you look at it, and see ef I's right. What's a desert good for? 'T ain't good for nuthin'. Dey ain't no way to make it pay. Hain't dat so, Huck?"

"Yes, I reckon."

"Hain't it so, Mars Tom?"

"I guess so. Go on."

"Ef a thing ain't no good, it's made in vain, ain't it?"

"Yes."

"*Now*, den! Do de Lord make anything in vain? You answer me dat."

"Well—no, He don't."

"Den how come He make a desert?"

"Well, go on. How *did* He come to make it?"

"Mars Tom, *I* b'lieve it uz jes like when you's buildin' a house; dey's allays a lot o' truck en rubbish lef' over. What does you do wid it? Doan' you take en k'yart it off en dump it into a ole vacant back lot? 'Course.

Now, den, it's my opinion hit was jes like dat—dat de Great Sahara warn't made at all, she jes *happen'.*"

I said it was a real good argument, and I believed it was the best one Jim ever made. Tom he said the same, but said the trouble about arguments is, they ain't nothing but *theories,* after all, and theories don't prove nothing, they only give you a place to rest on, a spell, when you are tuckered out butting around and around trying to find out something there ain't no way *to* find out. And he says—

"There's another trouble about theories: there's always a hole in them somewheres, sure, if you look close enough. It's just so with this one of Jim's. Look what billions and billions of stars there is. How does it come that there was just exactly enough star-stuff, and none left over? How does it come there ain't no sandpile up there?"

But Jim was fixed for him and says—

"What's de Milky Way?—dat's what *I* wants to know. What's de Milky Way? Answer me dat!"

In my opinion it was just a sockdologer. It's only an opinion, it's only *my* opinion and others may think different; but I said it then and I stand to it now—it was a sockdologer. And moreover, besides, it landed Tom Sawyer. He couldn't say a word. He had that stunned look of a person that's been shot in the back with a kag of nails. All he said was, as for people like me and Jim, he'd just as soon have intellectual intercourse with a catfish. But anybody can say that—and I notice they always do, when somebody has fetched them a lifter. Tom Sawyer was tired of that end of the subject.

So we got back to talking about the size of the Desert again, and the more we compared it with this and that and t'other thing, the more nobler and bigger and grander it got to look, right along. And so, hunting amongst the figgers, Tom found, by and by, that it was just the same size as the Empire of China. Then he showed us the spread the Empire of China made on the map, and the room she took up in the world. Well, it was wonderful to think of, and I says—

"Why, I've heard talk about this Desert plenty of times, but *I* never knowed, before, how important she was."

Then Tom says—

"Important! Sahara important! That's just the way with some people. If a thing's big, it's important. That's all the sense they've got. All they can see is *size.* Why, look at England. It's the most important country in the world; and yet you could put it in China's vest pocket; and not only that, but you'd have the dickens's own time to find it again the next time you wanted it. And look at Russia. It spreads all around and everywhere, and yet ain't no more important in this world than Rhode Island is, and hasn't got half as much in it that's worth saving."

Away off, now, we see a little hill, a-standing up just on the edge of the world. Tom broke off his talk, and reached for a glass very much excited, and took a look, and says—

"That's it—it's the one I've been looking for, sure. If I'm right, it's the one the Dervish took the man into and showed him all the treasures."

So we begun to gaze, and he begun to tell about it out of the Arabian Nights.

CHAPTER 10

THE TREASURE-HILL

Tom said it happened like this.

A dervish was stumping it along through the desert, on foot, one blazing hot day, and he had come a thousand miles and was pretty poor, and hungry, and ornery and tired, and along about where we are now, he run across a camel driver with a hundred camels, and asked him for some ams. But the camel driver he asked to be excused. The dervish says—

"Don't you own these camels?"

"Yes, they're mine."

"Are you in debt?"

"Who—me? No."

"Well, a man that owns a hundred camels and ain't in debt, is rich—and not only rich, but very rich. Ain't it so?"

The camel driver owned up that it was so. Then the dervish says—

"God has made you rich, and He has made me poor. He has His reasons, and they are wise, blessed be His name. But He has willed that His rich shall help His poor, and you have turned away from me, your brother, in my need, and He will remember this, and you will lose by it."

That made the camel driver feel shaky, but all the same he was born hoggish after money and didn't like to let go a cent, so he begun to whine and explain, and said times was hard, and although he had took a full freight down to Balsora and got a fat rate for it, he couldn't git no return freight, and so he warn't making no great things out of his trip. So the dervish starts along again, and says—

"All right, if you want to take the risk, but I reckon you've made a mistake this time, and missed a chance."

Of course the camel driver wanted to know what kind of a chance he had missed, because maybe there was money in it; so he run after the dervish and begged him so hard and earnest to take pity on him and tell him, that at last the dervish give in, and says—

"Do you see that hill yonder? Well, in that hill is all the treasures of the earth, and I was looking around for a man with a particular good kind heart and a noble generous disposition, because if I could find just that man, I've got a kind of a salve I could put on his eyes and he could see the treasures and get them out."

So then the camel driver was in a sweat; and he cried, and begged, and took on, and went down on his knees, and said he was just that kind of a man, and said he could fetch a thousand people that would say he wasn't ever described so exact before.

"Well, then," says the dervish, "all right. If we load the hundred camels, can I have half of them?"

The driver was so glad he couldn't hardly hold in, and says—

"Now you're shouting."

So they shook hands on the bargain, and the dervish got out his box and rubbed the salve on the driver's right eye, and the hill opened and he went in, and there, sure enough, was piles and piles of gold and jewels sparkling like all the stars in heaven had fell down.

So him and the dervish laid into it and they loaded every camel till he couldn't carry no more, then they said good-by, and each of them started off with his fifty. But pretty soon the camel driver come a-running and overtook the dervish and says—

"You ain't in society, you know, and you don't really need all you've got. Won't you be good, and let me have ten of your camels?"

"Well," the dervish says, "I don't know but what you say is reasonable enough."

So he done it, and they separated and the dervish started off again with his forty. But pretty soon here comes the camel driver bawling after him again, and whines and slobbers around and begs another ten off of him, saying thirty camel loads of treasures was enough to see a dervish through, because they live very simple, you know, and don't keep house but board around and give their note.

But that warn't the end, yet. That ornery hound kept coming and coming till he had begged back all the camels and had the whole hundred. Then he was satisfied, and ever so grateful, and said he wouldn't ever forgit the dervish as long as he lived, and nobody hadn't ever been so good to him before, and liberal. So they shook hands good-by, and separated and started off again.

But do you know, it warn't ten minutes till the camel driver was unsatisfied again—he was the low-downest reptyle in seven counties—and he come a-running again. And this time the thing he wanted was to get the dervish to rub some of the salve on his other eye.

"Why?" said the dervish.

"Oh, you know," says the driver.

"Know what?"

"Well, you can't fool me," says the driver. "You're trying to keep back something from me, you know it mighty well. You know, I reckon, that if I had the salve on the other eye I could see a lot more things that's valuable. Come—please put it on."

The dervish says—

"I wasn't keeping anything back from you. I don't mind telling you what would happen if I put it on. You'd never see again. You'd be stone blind the rest of your days."

But do you know, that beat wouldn't believe him. No, he begged and begged, and whined and cried, till at last the dervish opened his box and told him to put it on, if he wanted to. So the man done it, and sure enough he was as blind as a bat, in a minute.

Then the dervish laughed at him and mocked at him and made fun of him; and says—

"Good-by—a man that's blind hain't got no use for jewelry."

And he cleared out with the hundred camels, and left that man to wander around poor and miserable and friendless the rest of his days in the desert.

Jim said he'd bet it was a lesson to him.

"Yes," Tom says, "and like a considerable many lessons a body gets. They ain't no account, because the thing don't ever happen the same way again—and can't. The time Hen Scovil fell down the chimbly and crippled his back for life, everybody said it would be a lesson to him. What kind of a lesson? How was he going to use it? He couldn't climb chimblies no more, and he hadn't no more backs to break."

"All de same, Mars Tom, dey *is* sich a thing as learnin' by expe'ence. De Good Book say de burnt chile shun de fire."

"Well, I ain't denying that a thing's a lesson if it's a thing that can happen twice just the same way. There's lots of such things, and *they* educate a person, that's what uncle Abner always said; but there's forty *million* lots of the other kind—the kind that don't happen the same way twice—and they ain't no real use, they ain't no more instructive than the small pox. When you've got it, it ain't no good to find out you ought to been vaccinated, and it ain't no good to get vaccinated afterwards, because the small-pox don't come but once. But on the other hand uncle Abner said that the person that had took a bull by the tail once had learnt sixty or seventy times as much as a person that hadn't, and said a person that started in to carry a cat home by the tail was gitting knowledge that was always going to be useful to him, and warn't ever going to grow dim or doubtful. But I can tell you, Jim, uncle Abner was down on them people that's all the time trying to dig a lesson out of everything that happens, no matter whether—"

But Jim was asleep. Tom looked kind of ashamed, because you know a person always feels bad when he is talking uncommon fine and thinks the other person is admiring, and that other person goes to sleep that way. Of course he oughtn't to go to sleep, because it's shabby; but the finer a person talks the certainer it is to make you sleep, and so when you come to look at it it ain't nobody's fault in particular, both of them's to blame.

Jim begun to snore—soft and blubbery, at first, then a long rasp, then a stronger one, then a half a dozen horrible ones like the last water sucking down the plug-hole of a bath-tub, then the same with more power to it, and some big coughs and snorts flung in, the way a cow does that is choking to death; and when the person has got to that point he is at his level best, and can wake up a man that is in the next block with a dipper full of loddanum in him, but can't wake himself up although all that awful noise of his'n ain't but three inches from his own ears. And that is the curiousest thing in the world, seems to me. But you rake a match to light the candle, and that little bit of a noise will fetch him. I wish I knowed what was the reason of that, but there don't seem to be no way to find out. Now there was Jim alarming the whole Desert, and yanking the animals out, for miles and miles around, to see what in the nation was going on up there; there warn't nobody nor nothing that was as close to the noise as *he* was, and yet he was the only cretur that wasn't disturbed by it. We yelled at him and whooped at him, it never done no good, but the first time there come a little wee noise that wasn't of a usual kind it woke him up. No, sir, I've thought it all over, and so has Tom, and there ain't no way to find out why a snorer can't hear himself snore.

Jim said he hadn't been asleep, he just shut his eyes so he could listen better.

Tom said nobody warn't accusing him.

That made him look like he wished he hadn't said anything. And he wanted to git away from the subject, I reckon, because he begun to abuse the camel driver, just the way a person does when he has got catched in something and wants to take it out of somebody else. He let into the camel driver the hardest he knowed how, and I had to agree with him; and he praised up the dervish the highest he could, and I had to agree with him there, too. But Tom says—

"I ain't so sure. You call that dervish so dreadful liberal and good and unselfish, but I don't quite see it. He didn't hunt up another poor dervish, did he? No, he didn't. If he was so unselfish, why didn't he go in there himself and take a pocket full of jewels and go along and be satisfied? No, sir, the person he was hunting for was a man with a hundred camels. He wanted to get away with all the treasure he could."

"Why, Mars Tom, he was willin' to divide, fair and square; he only struck for fifty camels."

"Because he knowed how he was going to get all of them by and by."

"Mars Tom, he *tole* de man de truck would make him bline."

"Yes, because he knowed the man's character. It was just the kind of a man he was hunting for—a man that never believes in anybody's word or anybody's honorableness, because he ain't got none of his own. I reckon there's lots of people like that dervish. They swindle, right and left, but they always make the other person *seem* to swindle himself. They keep inside of the letter of the law all the time, and there ain't no way to git hold of them. *They* don't put the salve on—oh, no, that would be sin; but they know how to fool *you* into putting it on, then it's you that blinds yourself. I reckon the dervish and the camel driver was just a pair—a fine, smart, brainy rascal, and a dull, coarse, ignorant one, but both of them rascals, just the same."

"Mars Tom, does you reckon dey's any o' dat kind o' salve in de worl' now?"

"Yes, uncle Abner says there is. He says they've got it in New York, and they put it on country people's eyes and show them all the railroads in the world, and they go in and git them, and then when they rub the salve on the other eye the other man bids them good-by and goes off with their railroads. Here's the treasure-hill, now. Lower away!"

We landed, but it warn't as interesting as I thought it was going to be, because we couldn't find the place where they went in to git the treasure. Still, it was plenty interesting enough, just to see the mere hill itself where such a wonderful thing happened. Jim said he wouldn't 'a' missed it for three dollars, and I felt the same way.

And to me and Jim, as wonderful a thing as any was the way Tom could come into a strange big country like this and go straight and find a little hump like that and tell it in a minute from a million other humps that was almost just like it, and nothing to help him but only his own learning and his own natural smartness. We talked and talked it over together, but couldn't make out how he done it. He had the best head on him I ever see; and all he lacked was age, to make a name for himself equal to Captain Kidd or George Washington. I bet you it would 'a' crowded either of *them* to find that hill, with all their gifts, but it warn't nothing to Tom Sawyer; he went across Sahara and put his finger on it as easy as you could pick a nigger out of a bunch of angels.

We found a pond of salt water close by and scraped up a raft of salt around the edges and loaded up the lion's skin and the tiger's so as they would keep till Jim could tan them.

CHAPTER 11

THE SAND-STORM

We went a-fooling along for a day or two, and then just as the full moon was touching the ground on the other side of the desert, we see a string of little black figgers moving across its big silver face. You could see them as plain as if they was painted on the moon with ink. It was another caravan. We cooled down our speed and tagged along after it, just to have company, though it warn't going our way. It was a rattler, that caravan, and a most bully sight to look at, next morning when the sun come a-streaming across the desert and flung the long shadders of the camels on the gold sand like a thousand grand-daddy-longlegses marching in procession. We never went very near it, because we knowed better, now, than to act like that and scare people's camels and break up their caravans. It was the gayest outfit you ever see, for rich clothes and nobby style. Some of the chiefs rode on dromedaries, the first we ever see, and very tall, and they go plunging along like they was on stilts, and they rock the man that is on them pretty violent and churn up his dinner considerable, I bet you, but they make noble good time and a camel ain't nowheres with them for speed.

The caravan camped, during the middle part of the day, and then started again about the middle of the afternoon. Before long the sun begun to look very curious. First it kind of turned to brass, and then to copper, and after that it begun to look like a blood-red ball, and the air got hot and close, and pretty soon all the sky in the west darkened up and looked thick and foggy, but fiery and dreadful like it looks through a piece of red glass, you know. We looked down and see a big confusion going on in the caravan and a rushing every which way like they was scared, and then they all flopped down flat in the sand and laid there perfectly still.

Pretty soon we see something coming that stood up like an amazing wide wall, and reached from the desert up into the sky and hid the sun, and it was coming like the nation, too. Then a little faint breeze struck us, and then it come harder, and grains of sand begun to sift against our faces and sting like fire, and Tom sung out—

"It's a sand-storm—turn your backs to it!"

We done it, and in another minute it was blowing a gale and the sand beat against us by the shovelfull and the air was so thick with it we couldn't see a thing. In five minutes the boat was level full and we was setting on the lockers buried up to the chin in sand and only our heads out and could hardly breathe.

Then the storm thinned, and we see that monstrous wall go a-sailing off across the desert, awful to look at, I tell you. We dug ourselves out and looked down, and where the caravan was before, there wasn't anything but just the sand ocean, now, and all still and quiet. All them people and camels was smothered and dead and buried—buried under ten foot of sand, we reckoned, and Tom allowed it might be years before the wind uncovered them, and all that time their friends wouldn't ever know what become of that caravan. Tom said—

"*Now* we know what it was that happened to the people we got the swords and pistols from."

Yes, sir, that was just it. It was as plain as day, now. They got buried in a sand-storm, and the wild animals couldn't get at them, and the wind never uncovered them again till they was dried to leather and warn't fit to eat. It seemed to me we had felt as sorry for them poor people as a person could for anybody, and as mournful, too, but we was mistaken; this last caravan's death went harder with us, a good deal harder. You see, the others was total strangers, and we never got to feeling acquainted with them at all, except, maybe, a little with the man that was watching the girl, but it was different with this last caravan. We was huvvering around them a whole night and 'most a whole day, and had got to feeling real friendly with them, and acquainted. I have found out that there ain't no surer way to find out whether you like people or hate them, than to travel with them. Just so with these. We kind of liked them from the start, and traveling with them put on the finisher. The longer we traveled with them, and the more we got used to their ways, the better and better we liked them and the gladder and gladder we was that we run across them. We had come to know some of them so well that we called them by name when we was talking about them, and soon got so familiar and sociable that we even dropped the Miss and the Mister and just used their plain names without any handle, and it did not seem unpolite, but just the right thing. Of course it wasn't their own names, but names we give them. There was Mr. Elexander Robinson and Miss Adaline Robinson, and Col. Jacob McDougal, and Miss Harryet McDougal, and Judge Jeremiah Butler and young Bushrod Butler, and these was big chiefs, mostly, that wore splendid great turbans and simmeters, and dressed like the Grand Mogul, and their families. But as soon as we come to know them good, and like them very much, it warn't Mister, nor Judge, nor nothing, any more, but only Elleck, and Addy, and Jake, and Hattie, and Jerry and Buck, and so on.

And you know, the more you join in with people in their joys and their sorrows, the more nearer and dearer they come to be to you. Now we warn't cold and indifferent, the way most travelers is, we was right down friendly and sociable, and took a chance in everything that was going, and the caravan could depend on us to be on hand every time, it didn't make no difference what it was.

When they camped, we camped right over them, ten or twelve hundred feet up in the air. When they et a meal, we et ourn, and it made it ever so much homeliker to have their company. When they had a wedding, that night, and Buck and Addy got married, we got ourselves up in the very starchiest of the professor's duds for the blow-out, and when they danced we jined in and shook a foot up there.

But it is sorrow and trouble that brings you the nearest, and it was a funeral that done it with us. It was next morning, just in the still dawn. We didn't know the diseased, and he warn't in our set, but that never made no difference, he belonged to the caravan, and that was enough, and there warn't no more sincerer tears shed over him than the ones we dripped on him from up there eleven hundred foot on high.

Yes, parting with this caravan was much more bitterer than it was to part with them others, which was comparative strangers, and been dead so long, anyway. We had knowed these in their lives, and was fond of them, too, and now to have death snatch them from right before our faces whilst we was looking, and leave us so lonesome and friendless in the middle of that big desert, it did hurt so, and we wished we mightn't ever make any more friends on that voyage if we was going to lose them again like that.

We couldn't keep from talking about them, and they was all the time coming up in our memory, and looking just the way they looked when we was all alive and happy together. We could see the line marching, and the shiny spearheads a-winking in the sun, we could see the dromedaries lumbering along, we could see the wedding and the funeral, and more oftener than anything else we could see them praying, because they don't allow nothing to prevent that; whenever the call come, several times a day, they would stop right there, and stand up and face to the east, and lift back their heads, and spread out their arms and begin, and four or five times they would go down on their knees, and then fall forwards and touch their forehead to the ground.

Well, it warn't good to go on talking about them, lovely as they was in their life, and dear to us in their life and death both, because it didn't do no good, and made us too downhearted. Jim allowed he was going to live as good a life as he could, so he could see them again in a better world; and Tom kept still and didn't tell him they was only Mohammedans, it warn't no use to disappoint him, he was feeling bad enough just as it was.

When we woke up next morning we was feeling a little cheerfuller, and had had a most powerful good sleep, because sand is the comfortablest bed there is, and I don't see why people that can afford it don't have it more. And it's terrible good ballast, too; I never see the balloon so steady before.

Tom allowed we had twenty tons of it, and wondered what we better do with it; it was good sand, and it didn't seem good sense to throw it away. Jim says—

"Mars Tom, can't we tote it back home en sell it? How long'll it take?"

"Depends on the way we go."

"Well, sah, she's wuth a quarter of a dollar a load, at home, en I reckon we's got as much as twenty loads, hain't we? How much would dat be?"

"Five dollars."

"By jings, Mars Tom, le's shove for home right on de spot! Hit's more'n a dollar en a half apiece, hain't it?"

"Yes."

"Well, ef dat ain't makin' money de easiest ever *I* struck! She jes' rained in—never cos' us a lick o' work. Le's mosey right along, Mars Tom."

But Tom was thinking and ciphering away so busy and excited he never heard him. Pretty soon he says—

"Five dollars—sho! Look here, this sand's worth—worth—why, it's worth no end of money."

"How is dat, Mars Tom? Go on, honey, go on!"

"Well, the minute people knows it's genuwyne sand from the genuwyne Desert of Sahara, they'll just be in a perfect state of mind to git hold of some of it to keep on the what-not in a vial with a label on it for a curiosity. All we got to do, is, to put it up in vials and float around all over the United States and peddle them out at ten cents apiece. We've got all of ten thousand dollars' worth of sand in this boat."

Me and Jim went all to pieces with joy, and begun to shout whoop-jamboreehoo, and Tom says—

"And we can keep on coming back and fetching sand, and coming back and fetching more sand, and just keep it a-going till we've carted this whole desert over there and sold it out; and there ain't ever going to be any opposition, either, because we'll take out a patent."

"My goodness," I says, "we'll be as rich as Creosote, won't we, Tom?"

"Yes—Creesus, you mean. Why, that dervish was hunting in that little hill for the treasures of the earth, and didn't know he was walking over the real ones for a thousand miles. He was blinder than he made the driver."

"Mars Tom, how much is we gwyne to be worth?"

"Well, I don't know, yet. It's got to be ciphered, and it ain't the easiest job to do, either, because it's over four million square miles of sand at ten cents a vial."

Jim was awful excited, but this faded it out considerable, and he shook his head and says—

"Mars Tom, we can't 'ford all dem vials—a king couldn't. We better not try to take de whole desert, Mars Tom, de vials gwyne to bust us, sho'."

Tom's excitement died out, too, now, and I reckoned it was on account of the vials, but it wasn't. He set there thinking, and got bluer and bluer, and at last he says—

42 "Boys, it won't work; we got to give it up."

"Why, Tom?"

"On account of the duties."

I couldn't make nothing out of that, neither could Jim. I says—

"What *is* our duty, Tom? Because if we can't git around it, why can't we just *do* it? People often has to."

But he says—

"Oh, it ain't that kind of duty. The kind I mean is a tax. Whenever you strike a frontier—that's the border of a country, you know—you find a custom house there, and the gov'ment officers comes and rummages amongst your things and charges a big tax, which they call a duty because it's their duty to bust you if they can, and if you don't pay the duty they'll hog your sand. They call it confiscating, but that don't deceive nobody, it's just hogging, and that's all it is. Now if we try to carry this sand home the way we're pointed now, we got to climb fences till we git tired—just frontier after frontier—Egypt, Arabia, Hindostan, and so on, and they'll all whack on a duty, and so you see, easy enough, we *can't* go *that* road."

"Why, Tom," I says, "we can sail right over their old frontiers; how are *they* going to stop us?"

He looked sorrowful at me, and says, very grave—

"Huck Finn, do you think that would be honest?"

I hate them kind of interruptions. I never said nothing, and he went on—

"Well, we're shut off the other way, too. If we go back the way we've come, there's the New York custom house, and that is worse than all of them others put together, on account of the kind of cargo we've got."

"Why?"

"Well, they can't raise Sahara sand in America, of course, and when they can't raise a thing there, the duty is fourteen hundred thousand per cent. on it if you try to fetch it in from where they do raise it."

"There ain't no sense in that, Tom Sawyer."

"Who said there *was*? What do you talk to me like that, for, Huck Finn? You wait till I say a thing's got sense in it before you go to accusing me of saying it."

"All right, consider me crying about it, and sorry. Go on."

Jim says—

"Mars Tom, do dey jam dat duty onto everything we can't raise in America, en don't make no 'stinction 'twix' anything?"

"Yes, that's what they do."

"Mars Tom, ain't de blessin' o' de Lord de mos' valuable thing dey is?"

"Yes, it is."

"Don't de preacher stan' up in de pulpit en call it down on de people?"

"Yes."

"Whah do it come from?"

"From heaven."

"Yassir! you's jes' right, 'deed you is, honey—it come from heaven, en dat's a foreign country. *Now* den! de dey put a tax on dat blessin'?"

"No, they don't."

"'Course dey don't; en so it stan' to reason dat you's mistaken, Mars Tom. Dey wouldn't put de tax on po' truck like san', dat everybody ain't 'bleeged to have, en leave it off'n, de bes' thing dey is, which nobody can't git along widout."

Tom Sawyer was stumped; he see Jim had got him where he couldn't budge. He tried to wiggle out by saying they had *forgot* to put on that tax, but they'd be sure to remember about it, next session of Congress, and then they'd put it on, but that was a poor lame come-off, and he knowed it. He said there warn't nothing foreign that warn't taxed but just that one, and so they couldn't be consistent without taxing it, and to be consistent was the first law of politics. So he stuck to it that they'd left it out unintentional and would be certain to do their best to fix it before they got caught and laughed at.

But I didn't feel no more interest in such things, as long as we couldn't git our sand through, and it made me low-spirited, and Jim the same. Tom he tried to cheer us up by saying he would think up another speculation for us that would be just as good as this one and better, but it didn't do no good, we didn't believe there was any as big as this. It was mighty hard; such a little while ago we was so rich, and could 'a' bought a country and started a kingdom and been celebrated and happy, and now we was so poor and ornery again, and had our sand left on our hands. The sand was looking so lovely, before, just like gold and dimonds, and the feel of it was so soft and so silky and nice, but now I couldn't bear the sight of it, it made me sick to look at it, and I knowed I wouldn't ever feel comfortable again till we got shut of it, and I didn't have it there no more to remind us of what we had been and what we had got degraded down to. The others was feeling the same way about it that I was. I knowed it, because they cheered up so, the minute I says le' 's throw this truck overboard.

Well, it was going to be work, you know, and pretty solid work, too; so Tom he divided it up according to fairness and strength. He said me and him would clear out a fifth apiece, of the sand, and Jim three fifths. Jim he didn't quite like that arrangement. He says—

" 'Course I's de stronges', en I's willin' to do a share accordin', but by jings you's kinder pilin' it onto ole Jim, Mars Tom, hain't you?"

"Well, I didn't think so, Jim, but you try your hand at fixing it, and let's see."

So Jim he reckoned it wouldn't be no more than fair if me and Tom done a *tenth* apiece. Tom he turned his back to git room and be private, and then he smole a smile that spread around and covered the whole Sahara to the westward, back to the Atlantic edge of it where we come from. Then he turned around again and said it was a good enough arrangement, and we was satisfied if Jim was. Jim said he was.

So then Tom measured off our two tenths in the bow and left the rest for Jim, and it surprised Jim a good deal to see how much difference there was and what a raging lot of sand his share come to, and said he was powerful glad, now, that he had spoke up in time and got the first arrangement altered, for he said that even the way it was now, there was more sand than enjoyment in his end of the contract, he believed.

Then we laid into it. It was mighty hot work, and tough; so hot we had to move up into cooler weather or we couldn't 'a' stood it. Me and Tom took turn about, and one worked while t'other rested, but there warn't nobody to spell poor old Jim, and he made all that part of Africa damp, he sweated so. We couldn't work good, we was so full of laugh, and Jim he kept fretting and wanting to know what tickled us so, and we had to keep making up things to account for it, and they was pretty poor inventions, but they done well enough, Jim didn't see through them. At last when we got done we was 'most dead, but not with work but with laughing. By and by Jim was 'most dead too, but it was with work; then we took turns and spelled him, and he was as thankful as he could be, and would set on the gunnel and swab the sweat, and heave and pant, and say how good we was to a poor old nigger, and he wouldn't ever forgit us. He was always the gratefulest nigger I ever see, for any little thing you done for him. He was only nigger outside; inside he was as white as you be.

CHAPTER 12

JIM STANDING SIEGE

The next few meals was pretty sandy, but that don't make no difference when you are hungry; and when you ain't it ain't no satisfaction to eat, anyway, and so a little grit in the meat ain't no particular drawback, as far as I can see.

Then we struck the east end of the desert at last, sailing on a northeast course. Away off on the edge of the sand, in a soft pinky light, we see three little sharp roofs like tents, and Tom says—

"It's the pyramids of Egypt."

It made my heart fairly jump. You see, I had seen a many and a many a picture of them, and heard tell about them a hundred times, and yet to come on them all of a sudden, that way, and find they was *real,* 'stead of imaginations 'most knocked the breath out of me with surprise. It's a curious thing, that the more you hear about a grand and big and bully thing or person, the more it kind of dreamies out, as you may say, and gets to be a big dim wavery figger made out of moonshine and nothing solid to it. It's just so with George Washington, and the same with them pyramids.

And moreover besides, the thing they always said about them seemed to me to be stretchers. There was a feller come to the Sunday-school, once, and had a picture of them, and made a speech, and said the biggest pyramid covered thirteen acres, and was most five hundred foot high, just a steep mountain, all built out of hunks of stone as big as a bureau, and laid up in perfectly regular layers, like stair-steps. Thirteen acres, you see, for just one building; it's a farm. If it hadn't been in Sunday-school, I would 'a' judged it was a lie; and outside I was certain of it. And he said there was a hole in the pyramid, and you could go in there with candles, and go ever so far up a long slanting tunnel, and come to a large room in the stomach of that stone mountain, and there you would find a big stone chest with a king in it, four thousand years old. I said to myself, then, if that ain't a lie I will eat that king if they will fetch him, for even Methusalem warn't that old, and nobody claims it.

As we come a little nearer we see the yaller sand come to an end in a long straight edge like a blanket, and onto it was joined, edge to edge, a wide country of bright green, with a snaky stripe crooking through it, and Tom said it was the Nile. It made my heart jump again, for the Nile was another thing that wasn't real to me. Now I can tell you one thing which is dead certain: if you will fool along over three thousand miles of yaller sand, all glimmering with heat so that it makes your eyes water to look at it, and you've been a considerable part of a week doing it, the green country will look so like home and heaven to you that it will make your eyes water *again.*

It was just so with me, and the same with Jim.

And when Jim got so he could believe it *was* the land of Egypt he was looking at, he wouldn't enter it standing up, but got down on his knees and took off his hat, because he said it wasn't fitten' for a humble poor nigger to come any other way where such men had been as Moses and Joseph and Pharaoh and the other prophets. He was a Presbyterian, and had a most deep respect for Moses which was a Presbyterian too, he said. He was all stirred up, and says—

"Hit's de lan' of Egypt, de lan' of Egypt, en I's 'lowed to look at it wid my own eyes! En dah's de river dat was turn' to blood, en I's looking at de very same groun' whah de plagues was, en de lice, en de frogs, en de locus', en de hail, en whah dey marked de door-pos', en de angel o' de Lord come by in de darkness o' de night en slew de fust-born in all de lan' o' Egypt. Ole Jim ain't worthy to see dis day!"

And then he just broke down and cried, he was so thankful. So between him and Tom there was talk enough, Jim being excited because the land was so full of history—Joseph and his brethren, Moses in the bulrushers, Jacob coming down into Egypt to buy corn, the silver cup in the sack, and all them interesting things, and Tom just as excited too, because the land was so full of history that was in *his* line, about Noureddin, and Bedreddin, and such like monstrous giants, that made Jim's wool rise, and a raft of other Arabian Nights folks, which the half of them never done the things they let on they done, I don't believe.

Then we struck a disappointment, for one of them early-morning fogs started up, and it warn't no use to sail over the top of it, because we would go by Egypt, sure, so we judged it was best to set her by compass straight for the place where the pyramids was gitting blurred and blotted out, and then drop low and skin along pretty close to the ground and keep a sharp lookout. Tom took the hellum, I stood by to let go the anchor, and Jim he straddled the bow to dig through the fog with his eyes and watch out for danger ahead. We went along a steady gait, but not very fast, and the fog got solider and solider, so solid that Jim looked dim and ragged and smoky through it. It was awful still, and we talked low and was anxious. Now and then Jim would say—

"Highst her a p'int, Mars Tom, highst her!" and up she would skip, a foot or two, and we would slide right over a flat-roofed mud cabin, with people that had been asleep on it just beginning to turn out and gap and stretch; and once when a feller was clear up on his hind legs so he could gap and stretch better, we took him a blip in the back and knocked him off. By and by, after about an hour, and everything dead still and we a-straining our ears for sounds and holding our breath, the fog thinned a little, very sudden, and Jim sung out in an awful scare—

"Oh, for de lan's sake, set her back, Mars Tom, here's de biggest giant outen de 'Rabian Nights a-comin' for us!" and he went over backwards in the boat.

Tom slammed on the back-action, and as we slowed to a standstill, a man's face as big as our house at home looked in over the gunnel, same as a house looks out of its windows, and I laid down and died. I must 'a' been clear dead and gone for as much as a minute or more; then I come to, and Tom had hitched a boat-hook onto the lower lip of the giant and was holding the balloon steady with it whilst he canted his head back and got a good long look up at that awful face.

Jim was on his knees with his hands clasped, gazing up at the thing in a begging way, and working his lips but not getting anything out. I took only just a glimpse, and was fading out again, but Tom says—

"He ain't alive, you fools, it's the Sphinx!"

I never see Tom look so little and like a fly; but that was because the giant's head was so big and awful. Awful, yes, so it was, but not dreadful, any more, because you could see it was a noble face, and kind of sad, and not thinking about you, but about other things and larger. It was stone, reddish stone, and its nose and ears battered, and that give it an abused look, and you felt sorrier for it, for that.

We stood off a piece, and sailed around it and over it, and it was just grand. It was a man's head, or maybe a woman's, on a tiger's body a hundred and twenty-five foot long, and there was a dear little temple between its front paws. All but the head used to be under the sand, for hundreds of years, maybe thousands, but they had just lately dug the sand away and found that little temple. It took a power of sand to bury that cretur; most as much as it would to bury a steamboat, I reckon.

We landed Jim on top of the head, with an American flag to protect him, it being a foreign land, then we sailed off to this and that and t'other distance, to git what Tom called effects and perspectives and proportions, and Jim he done the best he could, striking all the different kinds of attitudes and positions he could study up, but standing on his head and working his legs the way a frog does was the best. The further we got away, the littler Jim got, and the grander the Sphinx got, till at last it was only a clothes-pin on a dome, as you might say. That's the way perspective brings out the correct proportions, Tom said; he said Julus Cesar's niggers didn't know how big he was, they was too close to him.

Then we sailed off further and further, till we couldn't see Jim at all, any more, and then that great figger was at its noblest, a-gazing out over the Nile valley so still and solemn and lonesome, and all the little shabby huts and things that was scattered about it clean disappeared and gone, and nothing around it now but a soft wide spread of yaller velvet, which was the sand.

That was the right place to stop, and we done it. We set there a-looking and a-thinking for a half an hour, nobody a-saying anything, for it made us feel quiet and kind of solemn to remember it had been looking over that valley just that same way, and thinking its awful thoughts all to itself for thousands of years, and nobody can't find out what they are to this day.

At last I took up the glass and see some little black things a-capering around on that velvet carpet, and some more a-climbing up the cretur's back, and then I see two or three wee puffs of white smoke, and told Tom to look. He done it, and says—

"They're bugs. No—hold on; they—why, I believe they're men. Yes, it's men—men and horses, both. They're hauling a long ladder up onto the Sphinx's back—now ain't that odd? And now they're trying to lean it up a—there's some more puffs of smoke—it's guns! Huck, they're after Jim!"

We clapped on the power, and went for them a-biling. We was there in no time, and come a-whizzing down amongst them, and they broke and scattered every which way, and some that was climbing the ladder after Jim let go all holts and fell. We soared up and found him laying on top of the head panting and most tuckered out, partly from howling for help and partly from scare. He had been standing a siege a long time—a week, *he* said, but it warn't so, it only just seemed so to him because they was crowding him so. They had shot at him, and rained the bullets all around him, but he warn't hit, and when they found he wouldn't stand up and the bullets couldn't git at him when he was laying down, they went for the ladder, and then he knowed it was all up with him if we didn't come pretty quick. Tom was very indignant, and asked him why he didn't show the flag and command them to *git*, in the name of the United States. Jim said he done it, but they never paid no attention. Tom said he would have this thing looked into at Washington, and says—

"You'll see that they'll have to apologize for insulting the flag, and pay an indemnity, too, on top of it, even if they git off *that* easy."

Jim says—

"What's an indemnity, Mars Tom?"

"It's cash, that's what it is."

"Who gits it, Mars Tom?"

"Why, *we* do."

"En who gits de apology?"

"The United States. Or, we can take whichever we please. We can take the apology, if we want to, and let the gov'ment take the money."

"How much money will it be, Mars Tom?"

"Well, in an aggravated case like this one, it will be at least three dollars apiece, and I don't know but more."

"Well, den, we'll take de money, Mars Tom, blame de 'pology. Hain't dat yo' notion, too? En hain't it yourn, Huck?"

We talked it over a little and allowed that that was as good a way as any, so we agreed to take the money. It was a new business to me, and I asked Tom if countries always apologized when they had done wrong, and he says—

"Yes; the little ones does."

We was sailing around examining the pyramids, you know, and now we soared up and roosted on the flat top of the biggest one, and found it was just like what the man said in the Sunday-school. It was like four pairs of stairs that starts broad at the bottom and slants up and comes together in a point at the top, only these stair-steps couldn't be clumb the way you climb other stairs; no, for each step was as high as your chin, and you have to be boosted up from behind. The two other pyramids warn't far away, and the people moving about on the sand between looked like bugs crawling, we was so high above them.

Tom he couldn't hold himself he was so worked up with gladness and astonishment to be in such a celebrated place, and he just dripped history from every pore, seemed to me. He said he couldn't scarcely believe he was standing on the very identical spot the prince flew from on the Bronze Horse. It was in the Arabian Night times, he said. Somebody give the prince a bronze horse with a peg in its shoulder, and he could git on him and fly through the air like a bird, and go all over the world, and steer it by turning the peg, and fly high or low and land wherever he wanted to.

When he got done telling it there was one of them uncomfortable silences that comes, you know, when a person has been telling a whopper and you feel sorry for him and wish you could think of some way to change the subject and let him down easy, but git stuck and don't see no way, and before you can pull your mind together and *do* something, that silence has got in and spread itself and done the business. I was embarrassed, Jim he was embarrassed, and neither of us couldn't say a word. Well, Tom he glowered at me a minute, and says—

"Come, out with it. What do you think?"

I says—

"Tom Sawyer, *you* don't believe that, yourself."

"What's the reason I don't? What's to hender me?"

"There's one thing to hender you: it couldn't happen, that's all."

"What's the reason it couldn't happen?"

"You tell me the reason it *could* happen."

"This balloon is a good enough reason it could happen, I should reckon."

"*Why* is it?"

"*Why* is it? I never saw such an idiot. Ain't this balloon and the bronze horse the same thing under different names?"

"No, they're not. One is a balloon and the other's a horse. It's very different. Next you'll be saying a house and a cow is the same thing."

"By Jackson, Huck's got him ag'in! Dey ain't no wigglin' outer dat!"

"Shut your head, Jim; you don't know what you're talking about. And Huck don't. Look here, Huck, I'll make it plain to you, so you can understand. You see, it ain't the mere *form* that's got anything to do with their being similar or unsimilar, it's the *principle* involved; and the principle is the same in both. Don't you see, now?"

I turned it over in my mind, and says—

"Tom, it ain't no use. Principles is all very well, but they don't git around that one big fact, that the thing that a balloon can do ain't no sort of proof of what a horse can do."

"Shucks, Huck, you don't get the idea at all. Now look here a minute—it's perfectly plain. Don't we fly through the air?"

"Yes."

"Very well. Don't we fly high or fly low, just as we please?"

"Yes."

"Don't we steer whichever way we want to?"

"Yes."

"And don't we land when and where we please?"

"Yes."

"How do we move the balloon and steer it?"

"By touching the buttons."

"*Now* I reckon the thing is clear to you at last. In the other case the moving and steering was done by turning a peg. We touch a button, the prince turned a peg. There ain't an atom of difference, you see. I knowed I could git it through your head if I stuck to it long enough."

He felt so happy he begun to whistle. But me and Jim was silent, so he broke off surprised, and says–

"Looky here, Huck Finn, don't you see it *yet?*"

I says–

"Tom Sawyer, I want to ask you some questions."

"Go ahead," he says, and I see Jim chirk up to listen.

"As I understand it, the whole thing is in the buttons and the peg–the rest ain't of no consequence. A button is one shape, a peg is another shape, but that ain't any matter?"

"No, that ain't any matter, as long as they've both got the same power."

"All right, then. What is the power that's in a candle and in a match?"

"It's the fire."

"It's the same in both, then?"

"Yes, just the same in both."

"All right. Suppose I set fire to a carpenter shop with a match, what will happen to that carpenter shop?"

"She'll burn up."

"And suppose I set fire to this pyramid with a candle–will she burn up?"

"Of course she won't."

"All right. Now the fire's the same, both times. *Why* does the shop burn, and the pyramid don't?"

"Because the pyramid *can't* burn."

"Aha! and *a horse can't fly!*"

"My lan', ef Huck ain't got him ag'in! Huck's landed him high en dry dis time, *I* tell you! Hit's de smartes' trap I ever see a body walk inter–en ef I–"

But Jim was so full of laugh he got to strangling and couldn't go on, and Tom was that mad to see how neat I had floored him, and turned his own argument ag'in him and knocked him all to rags and flinders with it that all he could manage to say was that whenever he heard me and Jim try to argue it made him ashamed of the human race. I never said nothing, I was feeling pretty well satisfied. When I have got the best of a person that way, it ain't my way to go around crowing about it the way some people does, for I consider that if I was in his place I wouldn't wish him to crow over me. It's better to be generous, that's what I think.

CHAPTER 13

GOING FOR TOM'S PIPE

By and by we left Jim to float around up there in the neighborhood of the pyramids, and we clumb down to the hole where you go into the tunnel, and went in with some Arabs and candles, and away in there in the middle of the pyramid we found a room and a big stone box in it where they used to keep that king, just as the man in the Sunday-school said, but he was gone, now, somebody had got him. But I didn't take no interest in the place, because there could be ghosts there, of course; not fresh ones, but I don't like no kind.

So then we come out and got some little donkeys and rode a piece, and then went in a boat another piece, and then more donkeys, and got to Cairo; and all the way the road was as smooth and beautiful a road as ever I see, and had tall date pams on both sides, and naked children everywhere, and the men was as red as copper, and fine and strong and handsome. And the city was a curiosity. Such narrow streets—why, they were just lanes, and crowded with people with turbans, and women with veils, and everybody rigged out in blazing bright clothes and all sorts of colors, and you wondered how the camels and the people got by each other in such narrow little cracks, but they done it—a perfect jam, you see, and everybody noisy. The stores warn't big enough to turn around in, but you didn't have to go in; the storekeeper sat tailor fashion on his counter, smoking his snaky long pipe, and had his things where he could reach them to sell, and he was just as good as in the street, for the camel-loads brushed him as they went by.

Now and then a grand person flew by in a carriage with fancy dressed men running and yelling in front of it and whacking anybody with a long rod that didn't get out of the way. And by and by along comes the Sultan riding horseback at the head of a procession, and fairly took your breath away his clothes was so splendid; and everybody fell flat and laid on his stomach while he went by. I forgot, but a feller helped me remember. He was one that had a rod and run in front.

There was churches, but they don't know enough to keep Sunday, they keep Friday and break the Sabbath. You have to take off your shoes when you go in. There was crowds of men and boys in the church, setting in groups on the stone floor and making no end of noise—getting their lessons by heart, Tom said, out of the Koran, which they think is a Bible, and people that knows better knows enough to not let on. I never see such a big church in my life before, and most awful high, it was; it made you dizzy to look up; our village church at home ain't a circumstance to it; if you was to put it in there, people would think it was a dry-goods box.

What I wanted to see was a dervish, because I was interested in dervishes on accounts of the one that played the trick on the camel driver. So we found a lot in a kind of a church, and they called themselves Whirling Dervishes; and they did whirl, too, I never see anything like it. They had tall sugar-loaf hats on, and linen petticoats; and they spun and spun and spun, round and round like tops, and the petticoats stood out on a slant, and it was the prettiest thing I ever see, and made me drunk to look at it. They was all Moslems, Tom said, and when I asked him what a Moslem was, he said it was a person that wasn't a Presbyterian. So there is plenty of them in Missouri, though I didn't know it before.

We didn't see half there was to see in Cairo, because Tom was in such a sweat to hunt out places that was celebrated in history. We had a most tiresome time to find the granary where Joseph stored up the grain before the famine, and when we found it it warn't worth much to look at, being such an old tumble-down wreck, but Tom was satisfied, and made more fuss over it than I would make if I stuck a nail in my foot. How he ever found that place was too many for me. We passed as much as forty just like it before we came to it, and any of them would 'a' done for me, but none but just the right one would suit him; I never see anybody so particular as Tom Sawyer. The minute he struck the right one he reconnized it as easy as I would reconnize my other shirt if I had one, but how he done it he couldn't any more tell than he could fly; he said so himself.

Then we hunted a long time for the house where the boy lived that learned the cadi how to try the case of the old olives and the new ones, and said it was out of the Arabian Nights and he would tell me and Jim about it when he got time. Well, we hunted and hunted till I was ready to drop, and I wanted Tom to give it up and come next day and git somebody that knowed the town and could talk Missourian and could go straight to the place; but no, he wanted to find it himself, and nothing else would answer. So on we went. Then at last the remarkablest thing happened I ever see. The house was gone—gone hundreds of years ago—every last rag of it gone but just one mud brick. Now a person wouldn't ever believe that a backwoods Missouri boy that hadn't ever been in that town before could go and hunt that place over and find that brick, but Tom Sawyer done it. I know he done it, because I see him do it. I was right by his very side at the time, and see him see the brick and see him reconnize it. Well, I says to myself, how *does* he do it? is it knowledge, or is it instink?

Now there's the facts, just as they happened: let everybody explain it their own way. I've ciphered over it a good deal, and it's my opinion that some of it is knowledge but the main bulk of it is instink. The reason is this. Tom put the brick in his pocket to give to a museum with his name on it and the facts when he went home, and I slipped it out and put another brick considerable like it in its place, and he didn't know the difference—but there was a difference, you see. I think that settles it—it's mostly instink, not knowledge. Instink tells him where the exact *place* is for the brick to be in, and so he reconnizes it by the place it's in, not by the look of the brick. If it was knowledge, not instink, he would know the brick again by the look of it the next time he seen it—which he didn't. So it shows that for all the brag you hear about knowledge being such a wonderful thing, instink is worth forty of it for real unerringness. Jim says the same.

When we got back Jim dropped down and took us in, and there was a young man there with a red skull cap and tassel on and a beautiful blue silk jacket and baggy trousers with a shawl around his waist and pistols in it that could talk English and wanted to hire to us as guide and take us to Mecca and Medina and Central Africa and everywheres for a half a dollar a day and his keep, and we hired him and left, and piled on the power, and by the time we was through dinner we was over the place where the Israelites crossed the Red Sea when Pharaoh tried to overtake them and was caught by the waters. We stopped, then, and had a good look at the place, and it done Jim good to see it. He said he could see it all, now, just the way it happened; he could see the Israelites walking along between the walls of water, and the Egyptians coming, from away off yonder, hurrying all they could, and see them start in as the Israelites went out, and then, when they was all in, see the walls tumble together and drown the last man of them. Then we piled on the power again and rushed away and huvvered over Mount Sinai, and saw the place where Moses broke the tables of stone, and where the children of Israel camped in the plain and worshipped the golden calf, and it was all just as interesting as could be, and the guide knowed every place as well as I know the village at home.

But we had an accident, now, and it fetched all the plans to a standstill. Tom's old ornery corn-cob pipe had got so old and swelled and warped that she couldn't hold together any longer, notwithstanding the strings and bandages, but caved in and went to pieces. Tom he didn't know *what* to do. The professor's pipe wouldn't answer, it warn't anything but a mershum, and a person that's got used to a cob pipe knows it lays a long ways over all the other pipes in this world, and you can't git him to smoke any other. He wouldn't take mine, I couldn't persuade him. So there he was.

He thought it over, and said we must scour around and see if we could roust out one in Egypt or Arabia or around in some of these countries, but the guide said no, it warn't no use, they didn't have them. So Tom was pretty glum for a little while, then he chirked up and said he'd got the idea and knowed what to do. He says—

"I've got another corn-cob pipe, and it's a prime one, too, and nearly new. It's laying on the rafter that's right over the kitchen stove at home in the village. Jim, you and the guide will go and get it, and me and Huck will camp here on Mount Sinai till you come back."

"But Mars Tom, we couldn't ever find de village. I could find de pipe, 'caze I knows de kitchen, but my lan', *we* can't ever find de village, nur Sent Louis, nur none o' dem places. We don't know de way, Mars Tom."

That was a fact, and it stumped Tom for a minute. Then he said—

"Looky here, it can be done, sure; and I'll tell you how. You set your compass and sail west as straight as a dart, till you find the United States. It ain't any trouble, because it's the first land you'll strike the other side of the Atlantic. If it's daytime when you strike it, bulge right on, straight west from the upper part of the Florida coast, and in an hour and three quarters you'll hit the mouth of the Mississippi—at the speed that I'm going to send you. You'll be so high up in the air that the earth will be curved considerable—sorter like a washbowl turnd upside down—and you'll see a raft of rivers crawling around every which way, long before you get there, and you can pick out the Mississippi without any trouble. Then you can follow the river north nearly, an hour and three quarters, till you see the Ohio come in; then you want to look sharp, because you're getting near. Away up to your left you'll see another thread coming in—that's the Missouri and is a little above St. Louis. You'll come down low, then, so as you can examine the villages as you spin along. You'll pass about twenty-five in the next fifteen minutes, and you'll recognize ours when you see it—and if you don't, you can yell down and ask."

"Ef it's dat easy, Mars Tom, I reckon we kin do it—yassir, I knows we kin."

The guide was sure of it, too, and thought that he could learn to stand his watch in a little while.

"Jim can learn you the whole thing in a half an hour," Tom said. "This balloon's as easy to manage as a canoe."

Tom got out the chart and marked out the course and measured it, and says—

"To go back west is the shortest way, you see. It's only about seven thousand miles. If you went east, and so on around, it's over twice as far." Then he says to the guide, "I want you both to watch the tell-tale all through the watches, and whenever it don't mark three hundred miles an hour, you go higher or drop lower till you find a storm-current that's going your way. There's a hundred miles an hour in this old thing without any wind to help. There's two hundred-mile gales to be found, any time you want to hunt for them."

"We'll hunt for them, sir."

"See that you do. Sometimes you may have to go up a couple of miles, and it'll be p'ison cold, but most of the time you'll find your storm a

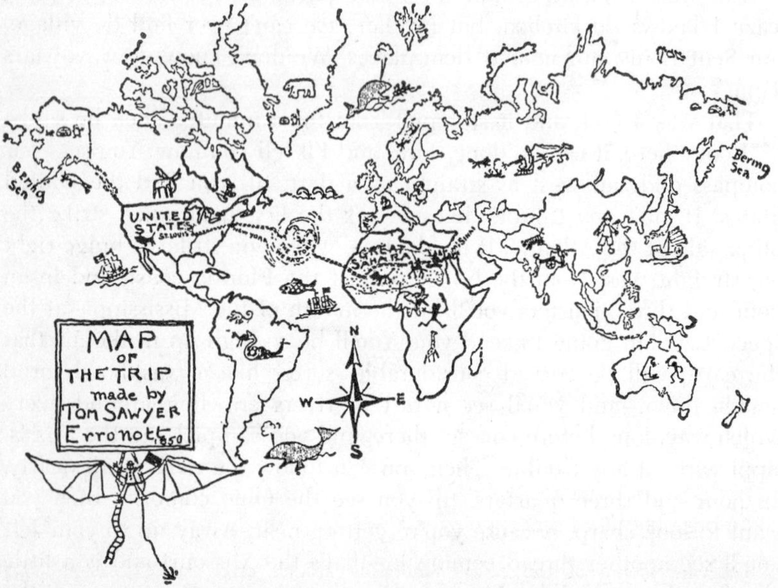

good deal lower. If you can only strike a cyclone—that's the ticket for you! You'll see by the professor's books that they travel west in these latitudes; and they travel low, too."

Then he ciphered on the time, and says—

"Seven thousand miles, three hundred miles an hour—you can make the trip in a day—twenty-four hours. This is Thursday; you'll be back here Saturday afternoon. Come, now, hustle out some blankets and food and books and things for me and Huck, and you can start right along. There ain't no occasion to fool around—I want a smoke, and the quicker you fetch that pipe the better."

All hands jumped for the things, and in eight minutes our things was out and the balloon was ready for America. So we shook hands good-bye, and Tom give his last orders:

"It's 10 minutes to 2 p. m., now, Mount Sinai time. In 24 hours you'll be home, and it'll be 6 to-morrow morning, village time. When you strike the village, land a little back of the top of the hill, in the woods, out of sight; then you rush down, Jim, and shove these letters in the postoffice, and if you see anybody stirring, pull your slouch down over your face so they won't know you. Then you go and slip in the back way, to the kitchen and git the pipe, and lay this piece of paper on the kitchen table and put something on it to hold it, and then slide out and git away and don't let Aunt Polly catch a sight of you, nor nobody else. Then you jump for the balloon and shove for Mount Sinai three hundred miles an hour. You won't have lost more than an hour. You'll start back at 7 or 8 a. m., village time, and be here in 24 hours, arriving at 2 or 3 p. m., Mount Sinai time."

Tom he read the piece of paper to us. He had wrote on it—

"THURSDAY AFTERNOON. *Tom Sawyer the Erronort sends his love to Aunt Polly from Mount Sinai where the Ark was, and so does Huck Finn, and she will get it to-morrow morning half past six.**

"TOM SAWYER THE ERRONORT."

"That'll make her eyes bulge out and the tears come," he says. Then he says—

"Stand by! One—two—three—away you go!"

And away she *did* go! Why, she seemed to whiz out of sight in a second.

Then we found a most comfortable cave that looked out over that whole big plain, and there we camped to wait for the pipe.

* This misplacing of the Ark is probably Huck's error, not Tom's.—M. T.

The balloon come back all right, and brung the pipe; but Aunt Polly had catched Jim when he was getting it, and anybody can guess what happened: she sent for Tom. So Jim he says—

"Mars Tom, she's out on de porch wid her eye sot on de sky a-layin' for you, en she say she ain't gwyne to budge from dah tell she gits hold of you. Dey's gwyne to be trouble, Mars Tom, 'deed dey is."

So then we shoved for home, and not feeling very gay, neither.

Pudd'nhead Wilson

A WHISPER TO THE READER

There is no character, howsoever good and fine, but it can be destroyed by ridicule, howsoever poor and witless. Observe the ass, for instance: his character is about perfect, he is the choicest spirit among all the humbler animals, yet see what ridicule has brought him to. Instead of feeling complimented when we are called an ass, we are left in doubt.

—Pudd'nhead Wilson's Calendar

A person who is ignorant of legal matters is always liable to make mistakes when he tries to photograph a court scene with his pen; and so I was not willing to let the law chapters in this book go to press without first subjecting them to rigid and exhausting revision and correction by a trained barrister—if that is what they are called. These chapters are right, now, in every detail, for they were rewritten under the immediate eye of William Hicks, who studied law part of a while in southwest Missouri thirty-five years ago and then came over here to Florence for his health and is still helping for exercise and board in Macaroni Vermicelli's horsefeed shed which is up the back alley as you turn around the corner out of the Piazza del Duomo just beyond the house where that stone that Dante used to sit on six hundred years ago is let into the wall when he let on to be watching them build Giotto's campanile and yet always got tired looking as soon as Beatrice passed along on her way to get a chunk of chestnut cake to defend herself with in case of a Ghibelline outbreak before she got to school, at the same old stand where they sell the same old cake to this day and it is just as light and good as it was then, too, and this is not flattery, far from it. He was a little rusty on his law, but he rubbed up for this book, and those two or three legal chapters are right and straight, now. He told me so himself.

Given under my hand this second day of January, 1893, at the Villa Viviani, village of Settignano, three miles back of Florence, on the hills—the same certainly affording the most charming view to be found on this planet, and with it the most dreamlike and enchanting sunsets to be found in any planet or even in any solar system—and given, too, in the swell room of the house, with the busts of Cerretani senators and other grandees of this line looking approvingly down upon me as they used to look down upon Dante, and mutely asking me to adopt them into my family, which I do with pleasure, for my remotest ancestors are but spring chickens compared with these robed and stately antiques, and it will be a great and satisfying lift for me, that six hundred years will.

MARK TWAIN

CHAPTER 1

Tell the truth or trump—but get the trick.

—*Pudd'nhead Wilson's Calendar*

The scene of this chronicle is the town of Dawson's Landing, on the Missouri side of the Mississippi, half a day's journey, per steamboat, below St. Louis.

In 1830 it was a snug little collection of modest one- and two-story frame dwellings whose whitewashed exteriors were almost concealed from sight by climbing tangles of rose-vines, honeysuckles and morning-glories. Each of these pretty homes had a garden in front fenced with white palings and opulently stocked with hollyhocks, marigolds, touch-me-nots, prince's-feathers and other old-fashioned flowers; while on the window-sills of the houses stood wooden boxes containing moss-rose plants and terra-cotta pots in which grew a breed of geranium whose spread of intensely red blossoms accented the prevailing pink tint of the rose-clad house-front like an explosion of flame. When there was room on the ledge outside of the pots and boxes for a cat, the cat was there—in sunny weather—stretched at full length, asleep and blissful, with her furry belly to the sun and a paw curved over her nose. Then that house was complete, and its contentment and peace were made manifest to the world by this symbol, whose testimony is infallible. A home without a cat—and a well-fed, well-petted and properly revered cat—may be a perfect home, perhaps, but how can it prove title?

All along the streets, on both sides, at the outer edge of the brick sidewalks, stood locust-trees with trunks protected by wooden boxing, and these furnished shade for summer and a sweet fragrance in spring when the clusters of buds came forth. The main street, one block back from the river, and running parallel with it, was the sole business street. It was six blocks long, and in each block two or three brick stores three stories high towered above interjected bunches of little frame shops. Swinging signs creaked in the wind, the street's whole length. The candy-striped pole which indicates nobility proud and ancient along the palace-bordered canals of Venice, indicated merely the humble barbershop along the main street of Dawson's Landing. On a chief corner stood a lofty unpainted pole wreathed from top to bottom with tin pots and pans and cups, the chief tinmonger's noisy notice to the world (when the wind blew) that his shop was on hand for business at that corner.

The hamlet's front was washed by the clear waters of the great river; its body stretched itself rearward up a gentle incline; its most rearward border fringed itself out and scattered its houses about the base-line of the hills; the hills rose high, inclosing the town in a half-moon curve, clothed with forests from foot to summit.

Steamboats passed up and down every hour or so. Those belonging to the little Cairo line and the little Memphis line always stopped; the big Orleans liners stopped for hails only, or to land passengers or freight; and this was the case also with the great flotilla of "transients." These latter came out of a dozen rivers—the Illinois, the Missouri, the Upper Mississippi, the Ohio, the Monongahela, the Tennessee, the Red River, the White River, and so on; and were bound every whither and stocked with every imaginable comfort or necessity which the Mississippi's communities could want, from the frosty Falls of St. Anthony down through nine climates to torrid New Orleans.

Dawson's Landing was a slaveholding town, with a rich slave-worked grain and pork country back of it. The town was sleepy and comfortable and contented. It was fifty years old, and was growing slowly—very slowly, in fact, but still it was growing.

The chief citizen was York Leicester Driscoll, about forty years old, judge of the county court. He was very proud of his old Virginian ancestry, and in his hospitalities and his rather formal and stately manners he kept up its traditions. He was fine and just and generous. To be a gentleman—a gentleman without stain or blemish—was his only religion, and to it he was always faithful. He was respected, esteemed and beloved by all the community. He was well off, and was gradually adding to his store. He and his wife were very nearly happy, but not quite, for they had no children. The longing for the treasure of a child had grown stronger and stronger as the years slipped away, but the blessing never came—and was never to come.

With this pair lived the Judge's widowed sister, Mrs. Rachel Pratt, and she also was childless—childless, and sorrowful for that reason, and not to be comforted. The women were good and commonplace people, and did their duty and had their reward in clear consciences and the community's approbation. They were Presbyterians, the Judge was a free-thinker.

Pembroke Howard, lawyer and bachelor, aged about forty, was another old Virginian grandee with proved descent from the First

Families. He was a fine, brave, majestic creature, a gentleman according to the nicest requirements of the Virginia rule, a devoted Presbyterian, an authority on the "code," and a man always courteously ready to stand up before you in the field if any act or word of his had seemed doubtful or suspicious to you, and explain it with any weapon you might prefer from brad-awls to artillery. He was very popular with the people, and was the Judge's dearest friend.

Then there was Colonel Cecil Burleigh Essex, another F. F. V. of formidable caliber—however, with him we have no concern.

Percy Northumberland Driscoll, brother to the Judge, and younger than he by five years, was a married man, and had had children around his hearthstone; but they were attacked in detail by measles, croup and scarlet fever, and this had given the doctor a chance with his effective antediluvian methods; so the cradles were empty. He was a prosperous man, with a good head for speculations, and his fortune was growing. On the 1st of February, 1830, two boy babes were born in his house: one to him, the other to one of his slave girls, Roxana by name. Roxana was twenty years old. She was up and around the same day, with her hands full, for she was tending both babies.

Mrs. Percy Driscoll died within the week. Roxy remained in charge of the children. She had her own way, for Mr. Driscoll soon absorbed himself in his speculations and left her to her own devices.

In that same month of February, Dawson's Landing gained a new citizen. This was Mr. David Wilson, a young fellow of Scotch parentage. He had wandered to this remote region from his birthplace in the interior of the State of New York, to seek his fortune. He was twenty-five years old, college-bred, and had finished a post-college course in an Eastern law school a couple of years before.

He was a homely, freckled, sandy-haired young fellow, with an intelligent blue eye that had frankness and comradeship in it and a covert twinkle of a pleasant sort. But for an unfortunate remark of his, he would no doubt have entered at once upon a successful career at Dawson's Landing. But he made his fatal remark the first day he spent in the village, and it "gaged" him. He had just made the acquaintance of a group of citizens when an invisible dog began to yelp and snarl and howl and make himself very comprehensively disagreeable, whereupon young Wilson said, much as one who is thinking aloud—

"I wish I owned half of that dog."

"Why?" somebody asked.

"Because I would kill my half."

The group searched his face with curiosity, with anxiety even, but found no light there, no expression that they could read. They fell away from him as from something uncanny, and went into privacy to discuss him. One said:

"'Pears to be a fool."

"'Pears?" said another. "*Is*, I reckon you better say."

"Said he wished he owned *half* of the dog, the idiot," said a third. "What did he reckon would become of the other half if he killed his half? Do you reckon he thought it would live?"

"Why, he must have thought it, unless he *is* the downrightest fool in the world; because if he hadn't thought it, he would have wanted to own the whole dog, knowing that if he killed his half and the other half died, he would be responsible for that half just the same as if he had killed that half instead of his own. Don't it look that way to you, gents?"

"Yes, it does. If he owned one half of the general dog, it would be so; if he owned one end of the dog and another person owned the other end, it would be so, just the same; particularly in the first case, because if you kill one half of a general dog, there ain't any man that can tell whose half it was, but if he owned one end of the dog, maybe he could kill his end of it and——"

"No, he couldn't either; he couldn't and not be responsible if the other end died, which it would. In my opinion the man ain't in his right mind."

"In my opinion he hain't *got* any mind."

No. 3 said: "Well, he's a lummox, anyway."

"That's what he is," said No. 4, "he's a labrick—just a Simon-pure labrick, if ever there was one."

"Yes, sir, he's a dam fool, that's the way I put him up," said No. 5. "Anybody can think different that wants to, but those are my sentiments."

"I'm with you, gentlemen," said No. 6. "Perfect jackass—yes, and it ain't going too far to say he is a pudd'nhead. If he ain't a pudd'nhead, I ain't no judge, that's all."

Mr. Wilson stood elected. The incident was told all over the town, and gravely discussed by everybody. Within a week he had lost his first name; Pudd'nhead took its place. In time he came to be liked, and well liked too; but by that time the nickname had got well stuck on, and it stayed. That first day's verdict made him a fool, and he was not able to get it set aside, or even modified. The nickname soon ceased to carry any harsh or unfriendly feeling with it, but it held its place, and was to continue to hold its place for twenty long years.

CHAPTER 2

Adam was but human—this explains it all. He did not want the apple for the apple's sake, he wanted it only because it was forbidden. The mistake was in not forbidding the serpent; then he would have eaten the serpent.

—*Pudd'nhead Wilson's Calendar*

Pudd'nhead Wilson had a trifle of money when he arrived, and he bought a small house on the extreme western verge of the town. Between it and Judge Driscoll's house there was only a grassy yard, with a paling fence dividing the properties in the middle. He hired a small office down in the town and hung out a tin sign with these words on it:

DAVID WILSON

ATTORNEY AND COUNSELOR-AT-LAW.

SURVEYING, CONVEYANCING, ETC.

But his deadly remark had ruined his chance—at least in the law. No clients came. He took down his sign, after a while, and put it up on his own house with the law features knocked out of it. It offered his services now in the humble capacities of land-surveyor and expert accountant. Now and then he got a job of surveying to do, and now and then a merchant got him to straighten out his books. With Scotch patience and pluck he resolved to live down his reputation and work his way into the legal field yet. Poor fellow, he could not foresee that it was going to take him such a weary long time to do it.

He had a rich abundance of idle time, but it never hung heavy on his hands, for he interested himself in every new thing that was born into the universe of ideas, and studied it and experimented upon it at his house. One of his pet fads was palmistry. To another one he gave no name, neither would he explain to anybody what its purpose was, but merely said it was an amusement. In fact he had found that his fads added to his reputation as a pudd'nhead; therefore he was growing chary of being too communicative about them. The fad without a name was one which dealt with people's finger-marks. He carried in his coat pocket a shallow box with grooves in it, and in the grooves strips of glass five inches long and three inches wide. Along the lower edge of each strip was pasted a slip of white paper. He asked people to pass their hands through their hair (thus collecting upon them a thin coating of the natural oil) and then make a thumb-mark on a glass strip, following it with the mark of the ball of each finger in succession. Under this row of faint grease-prints he would write a record on the strip of white paper—thus:

JOHN SMITH, *right hand*—

and add the day of the month and the year, then take Smith's left hand on another glass strip, and add name and date and the words "left hand." The strips were now returned to the grooved box, and took their place among what Wilson called his "records."

He often studied his records, examining and poring over them with absorbing interest until far into the night; but what he found there—if he found anything—he revealed to no one. Sometimes he copied on paper the involved and delicate pattern left by the ball of a finger, and then vastly enlarged it with a pantograph so that he could examine its web of curving lines with ease and convenience.

One sweltering afternoon—it was the first day of July, 1830—he was at work over a set of tangled account-books in his work-room, which looked westward over a stretch of vacant lots, when a conversation outside disturbed him. It was carried on in yells, which showed that the people engaged in it were not close together:

"Say, Roxy, how does yo' baby come on?" This from the distant voice.

"Fust-rate; how does *you* come on, Jasper?" This yell was from close by.

"Oh, I's middlin'; hain't got noth'n' to complain of. I's gwine to come a-court'n' you bimeby, Roxy."

"*You* is, you black mud-cat! Yah—yah—yah! I got somep'n' better to do den 'sociat'n' wid niggers as black as you is. Is ole Miss Cooper's Nancy done give you de mitten?" Roxy followed this sally with another discharge of care-free laughter.

"You's jealous, Roxy, dat's what's de matter wid *you,* you hussy—yah—yah—yah! Dat's de time I got you!"

"Oh, yes, *you* got me, hain't you. 'Clah to goodness if dat conceit o' yo'n strikes in, Jasper, it gwine to kill you sho'. If you b'longed to me I'd sell you down de river 'fo' you git too fur gone. Fust time I runs acrost yo' marster, I's gwine to tell him so."

This idle and aimless jabber went on and on, both parties enjoying the friendly duel and each well satisfied with his own share of the wit exchanged—for wit they considered it.

Wilson stepped to the window to observe the combatants; he could not work while their chatter continued. Over in the vacant lots was

Jasper, young, coal-black and of magnificent build, sitting on a wheelbarrow in the pelting sun—at work, supposably, whereas he was in fact only preparing for it by taking an hour's rest before beginning. In front of Wilson's porch stood Roxy, with a local hand-made baby-wagon, in which sat her two charges—one at each end and facing each other. From Roxy's manner of speech, a stranger would have expected her to be black, but she was not. Only one sixteenth of her was black, and that sixteenth did not show. She was of majestic form and stature, her attitudes were imposing and statuesque, and her gestures and movements distinguished by a noble and stately grace. Her complexion was very fair, with the rosy glow of vigorous health in the cheeks, her face was full of character and expression, her eyes were brown and liquid, and she had a heavy suit of fine soft hair which was also brown, but the fact was not apparent because her head was bound about with a checkered handkerchief and the hair was concealed under it. Her face was shapely, intelligent and comely—even beautiful. She had an easy, independent carriage—when she was among her own caste—and a high and "sassy" way, withal; but of course she was meek and humble enough where white people were.

To all intents and purposes Roxy was as white as anybody, but the one sixteenth of her which was black outvoted the other fifteen parts and made her a negro. She was a slave, and salable as such. Her child was thirty-one parts white, and he, too, was a slave, and by a fiction of law and custom a negro. He had blue eyes and flaxen curls like his white comrade, but even the father of the white child was able to tell the children apart—little as he had commerce with them—by their clothes: for the white babe wore ruffled soft muslin and a coral necklace, while the other wore merely a coarse tow-linen shirt which barely reached to its knees, and no jewelry.

The white child's name was Thomas à Becket Driscoll, the other's name was Valet de Chambre: no surname—slaves hadn't the privilege. Roxana had heard that phrase somewhere, the fine sound of it had pleased her ear, and as she had supposed it was a name, she loaded it on to her darling. It soon got shortened to "Chambers," of course.

Wilson knew Roxy by sight, and when the duel of wit began to play out, he stepped outside to gather in a record or two. Jasper went to work energetically, at once, perceiving that his leisure was observed. Wilson inspected the children and asked—

"How old are they, Roxy?"

"Bofe de same age, sir—five months. Bawn de fust o' Feb'uary."

"They're handsome little chaps. One's just as handsome as the other, too."

A delighted smile exposed the girl's white teeth, and she said:

"Bless yo' soul, Misto Wilson, it's pow'ful nice o' you to say dat, 'ca'se one of 'em ain't on'y a nigger. Mighty prime little nigger, *I* al'ays says, but dat's ca'se it's mine, o' course."

"How do you tell them apart, Roxy, when they haven't any clothes on?"

Roxy laughed a laugh proportioned to her size, and said:

"Oh, *I* kin tell 'em 'part, Misto Wilson, but I bet Marse Percy couldn't, not to save his life."

Wilson chatted along for awhile, and presently got Roxy's finger-prints for his collection—right hand and left—on a couple of his glass strips; then labeled and dated them, and took the "records" of both children, and labeled and dated them also.

Two months later, on the 3d of September, he took this trio of finger-marks again. He liked to have a "series," two or three "takings" at intervals during the period of childhood, these to be followed by others at intervals of several years.

The next day—that is to say, on the 4th of September—something occurred which profoundly impressed Roxana. Mr. Driscoll missed another small sum of money—which is a way of saying that this was not a new thing, but had happened before. In truth it had happened three times before. Driscoll's patience was exhausted. He was a fairly humane man toward slaves and other animals; he was an exceedingly humane man toward the erring of his own race Theft he could not abide, and plainly there was a thief in his house. Necessarily the thief must be one of his negroes. Sharp measures must be taken. He called his servants before him. There were three of these, besides Roxy: a man, a woman, and a boy twelve years old. They were not related. Mr. Driscoll said:

"You have all been warned before. It has done no good. This time I will teach you a lesson. I will sell the thief. Which of you is the guilty one?"

They all shuddered at the threat, for here they had a good home, and a new one was likely to be a change for the worse. The denial was general. None had stolen anything—not money, anyway—a little sugar, or cake, or honey, or something like that, that "Marse Percy wouldn't mind or miss," but not money—never a cent of money. They were eloquent in their protestations, but Mr. Driscoll was not moved by them. He answered each in turn with a stern "Name the thief!"

The truth was, all were guilty but Roxana; she suspected that the others were guilty, but she did not know them to be so. She was horrified to think how near she had come to being guilty herself; she had been saved in the nick of time by a revival in the colored Methodist Church, a fortnight before, at which time and place she "got religion." The very next day after that gracious experience, while her change of style was fresh upon her and she was vain of her purified condition, her master left a couple of dollars lying unprotected on his desk, and she happened upon that temptation when she was polishing around with a dust-rag. She looked at the money awhile with a steadily rising resentment, then she burst out with—

"Dad blame dat revival, I wisht it had 'a' be'n put off till to-morrow!"

Then she covered the tempter with a book, and another member of the kitchen cabinet got it. She made this sacrifice as a matter of religious etiquette; as a thing necessary just now, but by no means to be wrested into a precedent; no, a week or two would limber up her piety, then she would be rational again, and the next two dollars that got left out in the cold would find a comforter—and she could name the comforter.

Was she bad? Was she worse than the general run of her race? No. They had an unfair show in the battle of life, and they held it no sin to take military advantage of the enemy—in a small way; in a small way, but not in a large one. They would smouch provisions from the pantry whenever they got a chance; or a brass thimble, or a cake of wax, or an emery-bag, or a paper of needles, or a silver spoon, or a dollar bill, or small articles of clothing, or any other property of light value; and so far were they from considering such reprisals sinful, that they would go to church and shout and pray the loudest and sincerest with their plunder in their pockets. A farm smoke-house had to be kept heavily padlocked, for even the colored deacon himself could not resist a ham when Providence showed him in a dream, or otherwise, where such a thing hung lonesome and longed for some one to love. But with a hundred hanging before him the deacon would not take two—that is, on the same night. On frosty nights the humane negro prowler would warm the end of a plank and put it up under the cold claws of chickens roosting in a tree; a drowsy hen would step on to the comfortable board, softly clucking her gratitude, and the prowler would dump her into his bag, and later into his stomach, perfectly sure that in taking this trifle from the man who daily robbed him of an inestimable treasure—his liberty—he was not committing any sin that God would remember against him in the Last Great Day.

"Name the thief!"

For the fourth time Mr. Driscoll had said it, and always in the same hard tone. And now he added these words of awful import:

"I give you one minute"—he took out his watch. "If at the end of that time you have not confessed, I will not only sell all four of you, *but*—I will sell you DOWN THE RIVER!"

It was equivalent to condemning them to hell! No Missouri negro doubted this. Roxy reeled in her tracks and the color vanished out of her face; the others dropped to their knees as if they had been shot; tears gushed from their eyes, their supplicating hands went up, and three answers came in the one instant:

"I done it!"

"I done it!"

"I done it!—have mercy, marster—Lord have mercy on us po' niggers!"

"Very good," said the master, putting up his watch, "I will sell you *here* though you don't deserve it. You ought to be sold down the river."

The culprits flung themselves prone, in an ecstasy of gratitude, and kissed his feet, declaring that they would never forget his goodness and never cease to pray for him as long as they lived. They were sincere, for like a god he had stretched forth his mighty hand and closed the gates of hell against them. He knew, himself, that he had done a noble and gracious thing, and was privately well pleased with his magnanimity; and that night he set the incident down in his diary, so that his son might read it in after years, and be thereby moved to deeds of gentleness and humanity himself.

CHAPTER 3

Whoever has lived long enough to find out what life is, knows how deep a debt of gratitude we owe to Adam, the first great benefactor of our race. He brought death into the world.

—*Pudd'nhead Wilson's Calendar*

Percy Driscoll slept well the night he saved his house-minions from going down the river, but no wink of sleep visited Roxy's eyes. A profound terror had taken possession of her. Her child could grow up and be sold down the river! The thought crazed her with horror. If she dozed and lost herself for a moment, the next moment she was on her feet flying to her child's cradle to see if it was still there. Then she would gather it to her heart and pour out her love upon it in a frenzy of kisses, moaning, crying, and saying "Dey sha'n't, oh, dey *sha'n't!*—yo' po' mammy will kill you fust!"

Once, when she was tucking it back in its cradle again, the other child nestled in its sleep and attracted her attention. She went and stood over it a long time communing with herself:

"What has my po' baby done, dat he couldn't have yo' luck? He hain't done noth'n'. God was good to you; why warn't he good to him? Dey can't sell *you* down de river. I hates yo' pappy; he hain't got no heart—for niggers he hain't, anyways. I hates him, en I could kill him!" She paused awhile, thinking; then she burst into wild sobbings again, and turned away, saying, "Oh, I got to kill my chile, dey ain't no yuther way,—killin' *him* wouldn't save de chile fum goin' down de river. Oh, I got to do it, yo' po' mammy's got to kill you to save you, honey"—she gathered her baby to her bosom, now, and began to smother it with caresses—"Mammy's got to kill you—how *kin* I do it! But yo' mammy ain't gwine to desert you—no, no; *dah,* don't cry—she gwine 'wid you, she gwine to kill herself too. Come along, honey, come along wid mammy; we gwine to jump in de river, den de troubles o' dis worl' is all over—dey don't sell po' niggers down the river over *yonder.*"

She started toward the door, crooning to the child and hushing it; midway she stopped, suddenly. She had caught sight of her new Sunday gown—a cheap curtain-calico thing, a conflagration of gaudy colors and fantastic figures. She surveyed it wistfully, longingly.

"Hain't ever wore it yet," she said, "en it's jist lovely." Then she nodded her head in response to a pleasant idea, and added, "No, I ain't gwine to be fished out, wid everybody lookin' at me, in dis mis'able ole linsey-woolsey."

She put down the child and made the change. She looked in the glass and was astonished at her beauty. She resolved to make her death-toilet perfect. She took off her handkerchief-turban and dressed her glossy wealth of hair "like white folks"; she added some odds and ends of rather lurid ribbon and a spray of atrocious artificial flowers; finally she threw over her shoulders a fluffy thing called a "cloud" in that day, which was of a blazing red complexion. Then she was ready for the tomb.

She gathered up her baby once more; but when her eye fell upon its miserably short little gray tow-linen shirt and noted the contrast between its pauper shabbiness and her own volcanic irruption of infernal splendors, her mother-heart was touched, and she was ashamed.

"No, dolling, mammy ain't gwine to treat you so. De angels is gwine to 'mire you jist as much as dey does yo' mammy. Ain't gwine to have 'em putt'n' dey han's up 'fo' dey eyes en sayin' to David en Goliah en dem yuther prophets, 'Dat chile is dress' too indelicate fo' dis place.'"

By this time she had stripped off the shirt. Now she clothed the naked little creature in one of Thomas à Becket's snowy long baby-gowns, with its bright blue bows and dainty flummery of ruffles.

"Dah—now you's fixed." She propped the child in a chair and stood off to inspect it. Straightway her eyes began to widen with astonishment and admiration, and she clapped her hands and cried out, "Why, it do beat all!—I *never* knowed you was so lovely. Marse Tommy ain't a bit puttier—not a single bit."

She stepped over and glanced at the other infant; she flung a glance back at her own; then one more at the heir of the house. Now a strange light dawned in her eyes, and in a moment she was lost in thought. She seemed in a trance; when she came out of it she muttered, "When I 'uz a-washin' 'em in de tub, yistiddy, his own pappy asked me which of 'em was his'n."

She began to move about like one in a dream. She undressed Thomas à Becket, stripping him of everything, and put the tow-linen shirt on him. She put his coral necklace on her own child's neck. Then she placed the children side by side, and after earnest inspection she muttered—

"Now who would b'lieve clo'es could do de like o' dat? Dog my cats if it ain't all *I* kin do to tell t'other fum which, let alone his pappy."

She put her cub in Tommy's elegant cradle and said—

"You's young Marse *Tom* fum dis out, en I got to practise and git used to 'memberin' to call you dat, honey, or I's gwine to make a mistake some time en git us bofe into trouble. Dah—now you lay still en don't fret no mo', Marse Tom—oh, thank de good Lord in heaven, you's saved, you's saved!—dey ain't no man kin ever sell mammy's po' little honey down de river now!"

She put the heir of the house in her own child's unpainted pine cradle, and said, contemplating its slumbering form uneasily—

"I's sorry for you, honey; I's sorry, God knows I is,—but what *kin* I do, what *could* I do? Yo' pappy would sell him to somebody, some time, en den he'd go down de river, sho', en I couldn't, couldn't, *couldn't* stan' it."

She flung herself on her bed and began to think and toss, toss and think. By and by she sat suddenly upright, for a comforting thought had flown through her worried mind—

"'T ain't no sin—*white* folks has done it! It ain't no sin, glory to goodness it ain't no sin! *Dey's* done it—yes, en dey was de biggest quality in de whole bilin', too—*kings!*"

She began to muse; she was trying to gather out of her memory the dim particulars of some tale she had heard some time or other. At last she said—

"Now I's got it; now I 'member. It was dat ole nigger preacher dat tole it, de time he come over here fum Illinois en preached in de nigger church. He said dey ain't nobody kin save his own self—can't do it by faith, can't do it by works, can't do it no way at all. Free grace is de *on'y* way, en dat don't come fum nobody but jis' de Lord; en *he* kin give it to anybody he please, saint or sinner—*he* don't kyer. He do jis' as he's a mineter. He s'lect out anybody dat suit him, en put another one in his place, en make de fust one happy forever en leave t'other one to burn wid Satan. De preacher said it was jist like dey done in Englan' one time, long time ago. De queen she lef' her baby layin' aroun' one day, en went out callin'; en one o' de niggers roun'-'bout de place dat was 'mos' white, she come in en see de chile layin' aroun', en tuck en put her own chile's clo'es on de queen's chile, en put de queen's chile's clo'es on her own chile, en den lef' her own chile layin' aroun' en tuck en toted de queen's chile home to de nigger-quarter, en nobody ever foun' it out, en her chile was de king bimeby, en sole de queen's chile down de river one time when dey had to settle up de estate. Dah, now —de preacher said it his own self, en it ain't no sin, 'ca'se white folks done it. *Dey* done it—yes, *dey* done it; en not on'y jis' common white folks nuther, but de biggest quality dey is in de whole bilin'. Oh, I's *so* glad I 'member 'bout dat!"

She got up light-hearted and happy, and went to the cradles and spent what was left of the night "practising." She would give her own child a light pat and say humbly, "Lay still, Marse Tom," then give the real Tom a pat and say with severity, "Lay *still*, Chambers!—does you want me to take somep'n' *to* you?"

As she progressed with her practice, she was surprised to see how steadily and surely the awe which had kept her tongue reverent and her manner humble toward her young master was transferring itself to her speech and manner toward the usurper, and how similarly handy she was becoming in transferring her motherly curtness of speech and peremptoriness of manner to the unlucky heir of the ancient house of Driscoll.

She took occasional rests from practising, and absorbed herself in calculating her chances.

"Dey'll sell dese niggers to-day fo' stealin' de money, den dey'll buy some mo' dat don't know de chillen—so *dat's* all right. When I takes de chillen out to git de air, de minute I's roun' de corner I's gwine to gaum dey mouths all roun' wid jam, den dey can't *nobody* notice dey's changed. Yes, I gwineter do dat till I's safe, if it's a year.

"Dey ain't but one man dat I's afeard of, en dat's dat Pudd'nhead Wilson. Dey calls him a pudd'nhead, en says he's a fool. My lan', dat man ain't no mo' fool den I is! He's de smartes' man in dis town, less'n it's Jedge Driscoll or maybe Pem Howard. Blame dat man, he worries me wid dem ornery glasses o' hisn; *I* b'lieve he's a witch. But nemmine, I's gwine to happen aroun' dah one o' dese days en let on dat I reckon he wants to print de chillen's fingers ag'in; en if *he* don't notice dey's changed, I bound dey ain't nobody gwine to notice it, en den I's safe, sho'. But I reckon I'll tote along a hoss-shoe to keep off de witch-work."

The new negroes gave Roxy no trouble, of course. The master gave her none, for one of his speculations was in jeopardy, and his mind was so occupied that he hardly saw the children when he looked at them, and all Roxy had to do was to get them both into a gale of laughter when he came about; then their faces were mainly cavities exposing gums, and he was gone again before the spasm passed and the little creatures resumed a human aspect.

Within a few days the fate of the speculation became so dubious that Mr. Percy went away with his brother the Judge, to see what could be done with it. It was a land speculation as usual, and it had gotten complicated with a lawsuit. The men were gone seven weeks. Before they got back Roxy had paid her visit to Wilson, and was satisfied. Wilson took the finger-prints, labeled them with the names and with the date—October the first—put them carefully away and continued his chat with Roxy, who seemed very anxious that he should admire the great advance in flesh and beauty which the babies had made since he took their finger-prints a month before. He complimented their improvement to her contentment; and as they were without any disguise of jam or other stain, she trembled all the while and was miserably frightened lest at any moment he—

But he didn't. He discovered nothing; and she went home jubilant, and dropped all concern about the matter permanently out of her mind.

CHAPTER 4

Adam and Eve had many advantages, but the principal one was, that they escaped teething.

—Pudd'nhead Wilson's Calendar

There is this trouble about special providences—namely, there is so often a doubt as to which party was intended to be the beneficiary. In the case of the children, the bears and the prophet, the bears got more real satisfaction out of the episode than the prophet did, because they got the children.

—Pudd'nhead Wilson's Calendar

This history must henceforth accommodate itself to the change which Roxana has consummated, and call the real heir "Chambers" and the usurping little slave "Thomas à Becket"—shortening this latter name to "Tom," for daily use, as the people about him did.

"Tom" was a bad baby, from the very beginning of his usurpation. He would cry for nothing; he would burst into storms of devilish temper without notice, and let go scream after scream and squall after squall, then climax the thing with "holding his breath"—that frightful specialty of the teething nursling, in the throes of which the creature exhausts its lungs, then is convulsed with noiseless squirmings and twistings and kickings in the effort to get its breath, while the lips turn blue and the mouth stands wide and rigid, offering for inspection one wee tooth set in the lower rim of a hoop of red gums; and when the appalling stillness has endured until one is sure the lost breath will never return, a nurse comes flying, and dashes water in the child's face, and—presto! the lungs fill, and instantly discharge a shriek, or a yell, or a howl which bursts the listening ear and surprises the owner of it into saying words which would not go well with a halo if he had one. The baby Tom would claw anybody who came within reach of his nails, and pound anybody he could reach with his rattle. He would scream for water until he got it, and then throw cup and all on the floor and scream for more. He was indulged in all his caprices, howsoever troublesome and exasperating they might be; he was allowed to eat anything he wanted, particularly things that would give him the stomach-ache.

When he got to be old enough to begin to toddle about and say broken words and get an idea of what his hands were for, he was a more consummate pest than ever. Roxy got no rest while he was awake. He would call for anything and everything he saw, simply saying "Awnt it!" (want it), which was a command. When it was brought, he said in a frenzy, and motioning it away with his hands, "Don't awnt it! don't awnt it!" and the moment it was gone he set up frantic yells of "Awnt it! awnt it! awnt it!" and Roxy had to give wings to her heels to get that thing back to him again before he could get time to carry out his intention of going into convulsions about it.

What he preferred above all other things was the tongs. This was because his "father" had forbidden him to have them lest he break windows and furniture with them. The moment Roxy's back was turned he would toddle to the presence of the tongs and say "Like it!" and cock his eye to one side to see if Roxy was observing; then, "Awnt it!" and cock his eye again; then, "Hab it!" with another furtive glance; and finally, "Take it!"—and the prize was his. The next moment the heavy implement was raised aloft; the next, there was a crash and a squall, and the cat was off on three legs to meet an engagement; Roxy would arrive just as the lamp or a window went to irremediable smash.

Tom got all the petting, Chambers got none. Tom got all the delicacies, Chambers got mush and milk, and clabber without sugar. In consequence Tom was a sickly child and Chambers wasn't. Tom was "fractious," as Roxy called it, and overbearing; Chambers was meek and docile.

With all her splendid common sense and practical every-day ability, Roxy was a doting fool of a mother. She was this toward her child—and she was also more than this: by the fiction created by herself, he was become her master; the necessity of recognizing this relation outwardly and of perfecting herself in the forms required to express the recognition, had moved her to such diligence and faithfulness in practicing these forms that this exercise soon concreted itself into habit; it became automatic and unconscious; then a natural result followed: deceptions intended solely for others gradually grew practically into self-deceptions as well; the mock reverence became real reverence, the mock obsequiousness real obsequiousness, the mock homage real homage; the little counterfeit rift of separation between imitation-slave and imitation-master widened and widened, and became an abyss, and a very real one—and on one side of it stood Roxy, the dupe of her own deceptions, and on the other stood her child, no longer a usurper to her, but her accepted and recognized master. He was her darling, her master, and her deity all in one, and in her worship of him she forgot who she was and what he had been.

In babyhood Tom cuffed and banged and scratched Chambers unrebuked, and Chambers early learned that between meekly bearing it and resenting it, the advantage all lay with the former policy. The few times that his persecutions had moved him beyond control and made him fight back had cost him very dear at headquarters; not at the hands of Roxy, for if she ever went beyond scolding him sharply for "forgitt'n' who his young marster was," she at least never extended her punishment beyond a box on the ear. No, Percy Driscoll was the person. He told Chambers that under no provocation whatever was he privileged to lift his hand against his little master. Chambers overstepped the line three times, and got three such convincing canings from the man who was his father and didn't know it, that he took Tom's cruelties in all humility after that, and made no more experiments.

Outside of the house the two boys were together all through their boyhood. Chambers was strong beyond his years, and a good fighter; strong because he was coarsely fed and hard worked about the house, and a good fighter because Tom furnished him plenty of practice—on white boys whom he hated and was afraid of. Chambers was his constant body-guard, to and from school; he was present on the playground at recess to protect his charge. He fought himself into such a formidable reputation, by and by, that Tom could have changed clothes with him, and "ridden in peace," like Sir Kay in Launcelot's armor.

He was good at games of skill, too. Tom staked him with marbles to play "keeps" with, and then took all the winnings away from him. In the winter season Chambers was on hand, in Tom's worn-out clothes, with "holy" red mittens, and "holy" shoes, and pants "holy" at the knees and seat, to drag a sled up the hill for Tom, warmly clad, to ride down on; but he never got a ride himself. He built snow men and snow fortifications under Tom's directions. He was Tom's patient target when Tom wanted to do some snowballing, but the target couldn't fire back. Chambers carried Tom's skates to the river and strapped them on him, then trotted around after him on the ice, so as to be on hand when wanted; but he wasn't ever asked to try the skates himself.

In summer the pet pastime of the boys of Dawson's Landing was to steal apples, peaches, and melons from the farmers' fruitwagons,—mainly on account of the risk they ran of getting their heads laid open with the butt of the farmer's whip. Tom was a distinguished adept at these thefts—by proxy. Chambers did his stealing, and got the peach-stones, apple-cores, and melon-rinds for his share.

Tom always made Chambers go in swimming with him, and stay by him as a protection. When Tom had had enough, he would slip out and tie knots in Chambers's shirt, dip the knots in the water to make them hard to undo, then dress himself and sit by and laugh while the naked shiverer tugged at the stubborn knots with his teeth.

Tom did his humble comrade these various ill turns partly out of native viciousness, and partly because he hated him for his superiorities of physique and pluck, and for his manifold clevernesses. Tom couldn't dive, for it gave him splitting headaches. Chambers could dive without inconvenience, and was fond of doing it. He excited so much admiration, one day, among a crowd of white boys, by throwing back somersaults from the stern of a canoe, that it wearied Tom's spirit, and at last he shoved the canoe underneath Chambers while he was in the air—so he came down on his head in the canoe-bottom; and while he lay unconscious, several of Tom's ancient adversaries saw that their long-desired opportunity was come, and they gave the false heir such a drubbing that with Chambers's best help he was hardly able to drag himself home afterward.

When the boys were fifteen and upward, Tom was "showing off" in the river one day, when he was taken with a cramp, and shouted for help. It was a common trick with the boys—particularly if a stranger was present—to pretend a cramp and howl for help; then when the stranger came tearing hand over hand to the rescue, the howler would go on struggling and howling till he was close at hand, then replace the howl with a sarcastic smile and swim blandly away, while the town boys assailed the dupe with a volley of jeers and laughter. Tom had never tried this joke as yet, but was supposed to be trying it now, so the boys held warily back; but Chambers believed his master was in earnest, therefore he swam out, and arrived in time, unfortunately, and saved his life.

This was the last feather. Tom had managed to endure everything else, but to have to remain publicly and permanently under such an obligation as this to a nigger, and to this nigger of all niggers—this was too much. He heaped insults upon Chambers for "pretending" to think he was in earnest in calling for help, and said that anybody but a blockheaded nigger would have known he was funning and left him alone.

Tom's enemies were in strong force here, so they came out with their opinions quite freely. They laughed at him, and called him coward, liar, sneak, and other sorts of pet names, and told him they meant to call Chambers by a new name after this, and make it common in the town—"Tom Driscoll's niggerpappy,"—to signify that he had had a second birth into this life, and that Chambers was the author of his new being. Tom grew frantic under these taunts, and shouted—

"Knock their heads off, Chambers! knock their heads off! What do you stand there with your hands in your pockets for?"

Chambers expostulated, and said, "But, Marse Tom, dey's too many of 'em—dey's—"

"Do you hear me?"

"Please, Marse Tom, don't make me! Dey's so many of 'em dat——"

Tom sprang at him and drove his pocketknife into him two or three times before the boys could snatch him away and give the wounded lad a chance to escape. He was considerably hurt, but not seriously. If the blade had been a little longer his career would have ended there.

Tom had long ago taught Roxy "her place." It had been many a day now since she had ventured a caress or a fondling epithet in his quarter. Such things, from a "nigger," were repulsive to him, and she had been warned to keep her distance and remember who she was. She saw her darling gradually cease from being her son, she saw *that* detail perish utterly; all that was left was master—master, pure and simple, and it was not a gentle mastership, either. She saw herself sink from the sublime height of motherhood to the somber depths of unmodified slavery. The abyss of separation between her and her boy was complete. She was merely his chattel, now, his convenience, his dog, his cringing and helpless slave, the humble and unresisting victim of his capricious temper and vicious nature.

Sometimes she could not go to sleep, even when worn out with fatigue, because her rage boiled so high over the day's experiences with her boy. She would mumble and mutter to herself—

"He struck me, en I warn't no way to blame—struck me in de face, right before folks. En he's al'ays callin' me nigger-wench, en hussy, en all dem mean names, when I's doin' de very bes' I kin. Oh, Lord, I done so much for him—I lift' him away up to what he is—en dis is what I git for it."

Sometimes when some outrage of peculiar offensiveness stung her to the heart, she would plan schemes of vengeance and revel in the fancied spectacle of his exposure to the world as an impostor and a slave; but in the midst of these joys fear would strike her: she had made him too strong; she could prove nothing, and—heavens, she might get sold down the river for her pains! So her schemes always went for nothing, and she laid them aside in impotent rage against the fates, and against herself for playing the fool on that fatal September day in not providing herself with a witness for use in the day when such a thing might be needed for the appeasing of her vengeance-hungry heart.

And yet the moment Tom happened to be good to her, and kind,—and this occurred every now and then,—all her sore places were healed, and she was happy; happy and proud, for this was her son, her nigger son, lording it among the whites and securely avenging their crimes against her race.

There were two grand funerals in Dawson's Landing that fall—the fall of 1845. One was that of Colonel Cecil Burleigh Essex, the other that of Percy Driscoll.

On his death-bed Driscoll set Roxy free and delivered his idolized ostensible son solemnly into the keeping of his brother, the Judge and his wife. Those childless people were glad to get him. Childless people are not difficult to please.

Judge Driscoll had gone privately to his brother, a month before, and bought Chambers. He had heard that Tom had been trying to get his father to sell the boy down the river, and he wanted to prevent the scandal—for public sentiment did not approve of that way of treating family servants for light cause or for no cause.

Percy Driscoll had worn himself out in trying to save his great speculative landed estate, and had died without succeeding. He was hardly in his grave before the boom collapsed and left his hitherto envied young devil of an heir a pauper. But that was nothing; his uncle told him he should be his heir and have all his fortune when he died; so Tom was comforted.

Roxy had no home, now; so she resolved to go around and say good-by to her friends and then clear out and see the world—that is to say, she would go chambermaiding on a steamboat, the darling ambition of her race and sex.

Her last call was on the black giant, Jasper. She found him chopping Pudd'nhead Wilson's winter provision of wood.

Wilson was chatting with him when Roxy arrived. He asked her how she could bear to go off chambermaiding and leave her boys; and chaffingly offered to copy off a series of their finger-prints, reaching up to their twelfth year, for her to remember them by; but she sobered in a moment, wondering if he suspected anything; then she said she believed she didn't want them. Wilson said to himself, "The drop of black blood in her is superstitious; she thinks there's some devilry, some witch-business about my glass mystery somewhere; she used to come here with an old horseshoe in her hand; it could have been an accident, but I doubt it."

CHAPTER 5

Training is everything. The peach was once a bitter almond; cauliflower is nothing but cabbage with a college education.

—*Pudd'nhead Wilson's Calendar*

Remark of Dr. Baldwin's, concerning upstarts: We don't care to eat toadstools that think they are truffles.

—*Pudd'nhead Wilson's Calendar*

Mrs. York Driscoll enjoyed two years of bliss with that prize, Tom—bliss that was troubled a little at times, it is true, but bliss nevertheless; then she died, and her husband and his childless sister, Mrs. Pratt, continued the bliss-business at the old stand. Tom was petted and indulged and spoiled to his entire content—or nearly that. This went on till he was nineteen, then he was sent to Yale. He went handsomely equipped with "conditions," but otherwise he was not an object of distinction there. He remained at Yale two years, and then threw up the struggle. He came home with his manners a good deal improved; he had lost his surliness and brusqueness, and was rather pleasantly soft and smooth, now; he was furtively, and sometimes openly, ironical of speech, and given to gently touching people on the raw, but he did it with a good-natured semiconscious air that carried it off safely, and kept him from getting into trouble. He was as indolent as ever and showed no very strenuous desire to hunt up an occupation. People argued from this that he preferred to be supported by his uncle until his uncle's shoes should become vacant. He brought back one or two new habits with him, one of which he rather openly practised—tippling—but concealed another which was gambling. It would not do to gamble where his uncle could hear of it; he knew that quite well.

Tom's Eastern polish was not popular among the young people. They could have endured it, perhaps, if Tom had stopped there; but he wore gloves, and that they couldn't stand, and wouldn't; so he was mainly without society. He brought home with him a suit of clothes of such exquisite style and cut and fashion,—Eastern fashion, city fashion, —that it filled everybody with anguish and was regarded as a peculiarly wanton affront. He enjoyed the feeling which he was exciting, and paraded the town serene and happy all day; but the young fellows set a tailor to work that night, and when Tom started out on his parade next morning he found the old deformed negro bell-ringer straddling along in his wake tricked out in a flamboyant curtain-calico exaggeration of his finery, and imitating his fancy Eastern graces as well as he could.

Tom surrendered, and after that clothed himself in the local fashion. But the dull country town was tiresome to him, since his acquaintanceship with livelier regions, and it grew daily more and more so. He began to make little trips to St. Louis for refreshment. There he found companionship to suit him, and pleasures to his taste, along with more freedom, in some particulars, than he could have at home. So, during the next two years his visits to the city grew in frequency and his tarryings there grew steadily longer in duration.

He was getting into deep waters. He was taking chances, privately, which might get him into trouble some day—in fact, *did.*

Judge Driscoll had retired from the bench and from all business activities in 1850, and had now been comfortably idle three years. He was president of the Free-thinkers' Society, and Pudd'nhead Wilson was the other member. The society's weekly discussions were now the old lawyer's main interest in life. Pudd'nhead was still toiling in obscurity at the bottom of the ladder, under the blight of that unlucky remark which he had let fall twenty-three years before about the dog.

Judge Driscoll was his friend, and claimed that he had a mind above the average, but that was regarded as one of the Judge's whims, and it failed to modify the public opinion. Or rather, that was one of the reasons why it failed, but there was another and better one. If the Judge had stopped with bare assertion, it would have had a good deal of effect; but he made the mistake of trying to prove his position. For some years Wilson had been privately at work on a whimsical almanac, for his amusement—a calendar, with a little dab of ostensible philosophy, usually in ironical form, appended to each date; and the Judge thought that these quips and fancies of Wilson's were neatly turned and cute; so he carried a handful of them around, one day, and read them to some of the chief citizens. But irony was not for those people; their mental vision was not focussed for it. They read those playful trifles in the solidest earnest, and decided without hesitancy that if there had ever been any doubt that Dave Wilson was a pudd'nhead—which there hadn't—this revelation removed that doubt for good and all. That is just the way in this world; an enemy can partly ruin a man, but it takes a good-natured injudicious friend to complete the thing and make it perfect. After this the Judge felt tenderer than ever toward Wilson, and surer than ever that his calendar had merit.

Judge Driscoll could be a free-thinker and still hold his place in society because he was the person of most consequence in the community, and therefore could venture to go his own way and follow out his own notions. The other member of his pet organization was allowed the like liberty because he was a cipher in the estimation of the public, and nobody attached any importance to what he thought or did. He was liked, he was welcome enough all around, but he simply didn't count for anything.

The widow Cooper—affectionately called "aunt Patsy" by everybody—lived in a snug and comely cottage with her daughter Rowena, who was nineteen, romantic, amiable, and very pretty, but otherwise of no consequence. Rowena had a couple of young brothers—also of no consequence.

The widow had a large spare room which she let to a lodger, with board, when she could find one, but this room had been empty for a year now, to her sorrow. Her income was only sufficient for the family support, and she needed the lodging-money for trifling luxuries. But now, at last, on a flaming June day, she found herself happy; her tedious wait was ended; her year-worn advertisement had been answered; and not by a village applicant, oh, no!—this letter was from away off yonder in the dim great world to the North: it was from St. Louis. She sat on her porch gazing out with unseeing eyes upon the shining reaches of the mighty Mississippi, her thoughts steeped in her good fortune. Indeed it was specially good fortune, for she was to have two lodgers instead of one.

She had read the letter to the family, and Rowena had danced away to see to the cleaning and airing of the room by the slave woman Nancy, and the boys had rushed abroad in the town to spread the great news, for it was matter of public interest, and the public would wonder and not be pleased if not informed. Presently Rowena returned, all ablush with joyous excitement, and begged for a re-reading of the letter. It was framed thus:

HONORED MADAM: My brother and I have seen your advertisement, by chance, and beg leave to take the room you offer. We are twenty-four years of age and twins. We are Italians by birth, but have lived long in the various countries of Europe, and several years in the United States. Our names are Luigi and Angelo Capello. You desire but one guest; but dear Madam, if you will allow us to pay for two, we will not incommode you. We shall be down Thursday.

"Italians! How romantic! Just think, ma—there's never been one in this town, and everybody will be dying to see them, and they're all *ours!* Think of that!"

"Yes, I reckon they'll make a grand stir."

"Oh, indeed they will. The whole town will be on its head! Think—they've been in Europe and everywhere! There's never been a traveler in this town before. Ma, I shouldn't wonder if they've seen kings!"

"Well, a body can't tell; but they'll make stir enough, without that."

"Yes, that's of course. Luigi—Angelo. They're lovely names; and so grand and foreign—not like Jones and Robinson and such. Thursday they are coming, and this is only Tuesday; it's a cruel long time to wait. Here comes Judge Driscoll in at the gate. He's heard about it. I'll go and open the door."

The Judge was full of congratulations and curiosity. The letter was read and discussed. Soon Justice Robinson arrived with more congratulations, and there was a new reading and a new discussion. This was the beginning. Neighbor after neighbor, of both sexes, followed, and the procession drifted in and out all day and evening and all Wednesday and Thursday. The letter was read and re-read until it was nearly worn out; everybody admired its courtly and gracious tone, and smooth and practised style, everybody was sympathetic and excited, and the Coopers were steeped in happiness all the while.

The boats were very uncertain in low water, in these primitive times. This time the Thursday boat had not arrived at ten at night—so the people had waited at the landing all day for nothing; they were driven to their homes by a heavy storm without having had a view of the illustrious foreigners.

Eleven o'clock came; and the Cooper house was the only one in the town that still had lights burning. The rain and thunder were booming yet, and the anxious family were still waiting, still hoping. At last there was a knock at the door and the family jumped to open it. Two negro men entered, each carrying a trunk, and proceeded up-stairs toward the guest-room. Then entered the twins—the handsomest, the best dressed, the most distinguished-looking pair of young fellows the West had ever seen. One was a little fairer than the other, but otherwise they were exact duplicates.

CHAPTER 6

Let us endeavor so to live that when we come to die even the undertaker will be sorry.

—*Pudd'nhead Wilson's Calendar*

Habit is habit, and not to be flung out of the window by any man, but coaxed down-stairs a step at a time.

—*Pudd'nhead Wilson's Calendar*

At breakfast in the morning the twins' charm of manner and easy and polished bearing made speedy conquest of the family's good graces. All constraint and formality quickly disappeared, and the friendliest feeling succeeded. Aunt Patsy called them by their Christian names almost from the beginning. She was full of the keenest curiosity about them, and showed it; they responded by talking about themselves, which pleased her greatly. It presently appeared that in their early youth they had known poverty and hardship. As the talk wandered along the old lady watched for the right place to drop in a question or two concerning that matter, and when she found it she said to the blond twin who was now doing the biographies in his turn while the brunette one rested—

"If it ain't asking what I ought not to ask, Mr. Angelo, how did you come to be so friendless and in such trouble when you were little? Do you mind telling? But don't if you do."

"Oh, we don't mind it at all, madam; in our case it was merely misfortune, and nobody's fault. Our parents were well to do, there in Italy, and we were their only child. We were of the old Florentine nobility" —Rowena's heart gave a great bound, her nostrils expanded, and a fine light played in her eyes—"and when the war broke out my father was on the losing side and had to fly for his life. His estates were confiscated, his personal property seized, and there we were, in Germany, strangers, friendless, and in fact paupers. My brother and I were ten years old, and well educated for that age, very studious, very fond of our books, and well grounded in the German, French, Spanish, and English languages. Also, we were marvelous musical prodigies—if you will allow me to say it, it being only the truth.

"Our father survived his misfortunes only a month, our mother soon followed him, and we were alone in the world. Our parents could have made themselves comfortable by exhibiting us as a show, and they had many and large offers; but the thought revolted their pride, and they said they would starve and die first. But what they wouldn't consent to do we had to do without the formality of consent. We were seized for the debts occasioned by their illness and their funerals, and placed among the attractions of a cheap museum in Berlin to earn the liquidation money. It took us two years to get out of that slavery. We traveled all about Germany receiving no wages, and not even our keep. We had to be exhibited for nothing, and beg our bread.

"Well, madam, the rest is not of much consequence. When we escaped from that slavery at twelve years of age, we were in some respects men. Experience had taught us some valuable things; among others, how to take care of ourselves, how to avoid and defeat sharks and sharpers, and how to conduct our own business for our own profit and without other people's help. We traveled everywhere—years and years—picking up smatterings of strange tongues, familiarizing ourselves with strange sights and strange customs, accumulating an education of a wide and varied and curious sort. It was a pleasant life. We went to Venice—to London, Paris, Russia, India, China, Japan——"

At this point Nancy the slave woman thrust her head in at the door and exclaimed:

"Ole Missus, de house is plum' jam full o' people, en dey's jes a-spi'lin' to see de gen'lmen!" She indicated the twins with a nod of her head, and tucked it back out of sight again.

It was a proud occasion for the widow, and she promised herself high satisfaction in showing off her fine foreign birds before her neighbors and friends—simple folk who had hardly ever seen a foreigner of any kind, and never one of any distinction or style. Yet her feeling was moderate indeed when contrasted with Rowena's. Rowena was in the clouds, she walked on air; this was to be the greatest day, the most romantic episode, in the colorless history of that dull country town. She was to be familiarly near the source of its glory and feel the full flood of it pour over her and about her; the other girls could only gaze and envy, not partake.

The widow was ready, Rowena was ready, so also were the foreigners.

The party moved along the hall, the twins in advance, and entered the open parlor door, whence issued a low hum of conversation. The twins took a position near the door, the widow stood at Luigi's side, Rowena stood beside Angelo, and the march-past and the introductions began. The widow was all smiles and contentment. She received the procession and passed it on to Rowena.

"Good mornin', Sister Cooper"—hand-shake.

"Good morning, Brother Higgins—Count Luigi Capello, Mr. Higgins"—hand-shake, followed by a devouring stare and "I'm glad to see ye," on the part of Higgins, and a courteous inclination of the head and a pleasant "Most happy!" on the part of Count Luigi.

"Good mornin', Roweny"—hand-shake.

"Good morning, Mr. Higgins—present you to Count Angelo Capello." Hand-shake, admiring stare, "Glad to see ye,"—courteous nod, smily "Most happy!" and Higgins passes on.

None of these visitors was at ease, but, being honest people, they didn't pretend to be. None of them had ever seen a person bearing a title of nobility before, and none had been expecting to see one now, consequently the title came upon them as a kind of pile-driving surprise and caught them unprepared. A few tried to rise to the emergency, and got out an awkward "My lord," or "Your lordship," or something of that sort, but the great majority were overwhelmed by the unaccustomed word and its dim and awful associations with gilded courts and stately ceremony and anointed kingship, so they only fumbled through the hand-shake and passed on, speechless. Now and then, as happens at all receptions everywhere, a more than ordinarily friendly soul blocked the procession and kept it waiting while he inquired how the brothers liked the village, and how long they were going to stay, and if their families were well, and dragged in the weather, and hoped it would get cooler soon, and all that sort of thing, so as to be able to say, when they got home, "I had quite a long talk with them"; but nobody did or said anything of a regrettable kind, and so the great affair went through to the end in a creditable and satisfactory fashion.

General conversation followed, and the twins drifted about from group to group, talking easily and fluently and winning approval, compelling admiration and achieving favor from all. The widow followed their conquering march with a proud eye, and every now and then Rowena said to herself with deep satisfaction, "And to think they are ours—all ours!"

There were no idle moments for mother or daughter. Eager inquiries concerning the twins were pouring into their enchanted ears all the time; each was the constant center of a group of breathless listeners; each recognized that she knew now for the first time the real meaning of that great word Glory, and perceived the stupendous value of it, and understood why men in all ages had been willing to throw away meaner happinesses, treasure, life itself, to get a taste of its sublime and supreme joy. Napoleon and all his kind stood accounted for—and justified.

When Rowena had at last done all her duty by the people in the parlor, she went up-stairs to satisfy the longings of an overflow-meeting there, for the parlor was not big enough to hold all the comers. Again she was besieged by eager questioners and again she swam in sunset seas of glory. When the forenoon was nearly gone, she recognized with a pang that this most splendid episode of her life was almost over, that nothing could prolong it, that nothing quite its equal could ever fall to her fortune again. But never mind, it was sufficient unto itself, the grand occasion had moved on an ascending scale from the start, and was a noble and memorable success. If the twins could but do some crowning act, now, to climax it, something unusual, something startling, something to concentrate upon themselves the company's loftiest admiration, something in the nature of an electric surprise—

Here a prodigious slam-banging broke out below, and everybody rushed down to see. It was the twins knocking out a classic four-handed piece on the piano, in great style. Rowena was satisfied—satisfied down to the bottom of her heart.

The young strangers were kept long at the piano. The villagers were astonished and enchanted with the magnificence of their performance, and could not bear to have them stop. All the music that they had ever heard before seemed spiritless prentice-work and barren of grace or charm when compared with these intoxicating floods of melodious sound. They realized that for once in their lives they were hearing masters.

CHAPTER 7

One of the most striking differences between a cat and a lie is that a cat has only nine lives.

—Pudd'nhead Wilson's Calendar

The company broke up reluctantly, and drifted toward their several homes, chatting with vivacity, and all agreeing that it would be many a long day before Dawson's Landing would see the equal of this one again. The twins had accepted several invitations while the reception was in progress, and had also volunteered to play some duets at an amateur entertainment for the benefit of a local charity. Society was eager to receive them to its bosom. Judge Driscoll had the good fortune to secure them for an immediate drive, and to be the first to display them in public. They entered his buggy with him, and were paraded down the main street, everybody flocking to the windows and sidewalks to see.

The Judge showed the strangers the new graveyard, and the jail, and where the richest man lived, and the Freemasons' hall, and the Methodist church, and the Presbyterian church, and where the Baptist church was going to be when they got some money to build it with, and showed them the town hall and the slaughter-house, and got out the independent fire company in uniform and had them put out an imaginary fire; then he let them inspect the muskets of the militia company, and poured out an exhaustless stream of enthusiasm over all these splendors, and seemed very well satisfied with the responses he got, for the twins admired his admiration, and paid him back the best they could, though they could have done better if some fifteen or sixteen hundred thousand previous experiences of this sort in various countries had not already rubbed off a considerable part of the novelty of it.

The Judge laid himself out hospitably to make them have a good time, and if there was a defect anywhere it was not his fault. He told them a good many humorous anecdotes, and always forgot the nub, but they were always able to furnish it, for these yarns were of a pretty early vintage, and they had had many a rejuvenating pull at them before. And he told them all about his several dignities, and how he had held this and that and the other place of honor or profit, and had once been to the legislature, and was now president of the Society of Freethinkers. He said the society had been in existence four years, and already had two members, and was firmly established. He would call for the brothers in the evening if they would like to attend a meeting of it.

Accordingly he called for them, and on the way he told them all about Pudd'nhead Wilson, in order that they might get a favorable impression of him in advance and be prepared to like him. This scheme succeeded—the favorable impression was achieved. Later it was confirmed and solidified when Wilson proposed that out of courtesy to the strangers the usual topics be put aside and the hour be devoted to conversation upon ordinary subjects and the cultivation of friendly relations and good-fellowship,—a proposition which was put to vote and carried.

The hour passed quickly away in lively talk, and when it was ended the lonesome and neglected Wilson was richer by two friends than he had been when it began. He invited the twins to look in at his lodgings, presently, after disposing of an intervening engagement, and they accepted with pleasure.

Toward the middle of the evening they found themselves on the road to his house. Pudd'nhead was at home waiting for them and putting in his time puzzling over a thing which had come under his notice that morning. The matter was this: He happened to be up very early—at dawn, in fact; and he crossed the hall which divided his cottage through the center, and entered a room to get something there. The window of the room had no curtains, for that side of the house had long been unoccupied, and through this window he caught sight of something which surprised and interested him. It was a young woman—a young woman where properly no young woman belonged; for she was in Judge Driscoll's house, and in the bedroom over the Judge's private study or sitting-room. This was young Tom Driscoll's bedroom. He and the Judge, the Judge's widowed sister Mrs. Pratt and three negro servants were the only people who belonged in the house. Who, then, might this young lady be? The two houses were separated by an ordinary yard, with a low fence running back through its middle from the street in front to the lane in the rear. The distance was not great, and Wilson was able to see the girl very well, the window-shades of the room she was in being up, and the window also. The girl had on a neat and trim summer dress, patterned in broad stripes of pink and white, and her bonnet was equipped with a pink veil. She was practising steps, gaits and attitudes, apparently; she was doing the thing gracefully, and was very much absorbed in her work. Who could she be, and how came she to be in young Tom Driscoll's room?

Wilson had quickly chosen a position from which he could watch the girl without running much risk of being seen by her, and he remained there hoping she would raise her veil and betray her face. But she disappointed him. After a matter of twenty minutes she disappeared, and although he stayed at his post half an hour longer, she came no more.

Toward noon he dropped in at the Judge's and talked with Mrs. Pratt about the great event of the day, the levee of the distinguished foreigners at Aunt Patsy Cooper's. He asked after her nephew Tom, and she said he was on his way home, and that she was expecting him to arrive a little before night; and added that she and the Judge were gratified to gather from his letters that he was conducting himself very nicely and creditably—at which Wilson winked to himself privately.

Wilson did not ask if there was a newcomer in the house, but he asked questions that would have brought light-throwing answers as to that matter if Mrs. Pratt had had any light to throw; so he went away satisfied that he knew of things that were going on in her house of which she herself was not aware.

He was now waiting for the twins, and still puzzling over the problem of who that girl might be, and how she happened to be in that young fellow's room at daybreak in the morning.

CHAPTER 8

The holy passion of Friendship is of so sweet and steady and loyal and enduring a nature that it will last through a whole lifetime, if not asked to lend money.

—Pudd'nhead Wilson's Calendar

Consider well the proportions of things. It is better to be a young June-bug than an old bird of paradise.

—Pudd'nhead Wilson's Calendar

It is necessary now, to hunt up Roxy.

At the time she was set free and went away chambermaiding, she was thirty-five. She got a berth as second chambermaid on a Cincinnati boat in the New Orleans trade, the *Grand Mogul.* A couple of trips made her wonted and easy-going at the work, and infatuated her with the stir and adventure and independence of steamboat life. Then she was promoted and became head chambermaid. She was a favorite with the officers, and exceedingly proud of their joking and friendly ways with her.

During eight years she served three parts of the year on that boat, and the winters on a Vicksburg packet. But now for two months she had had rheumatism in her arms, and was obliged to let the wash-tub alone. So she resigned. But she was well fixed—rich, as she would have described it; for she had lived a steady life, and had banked four dollars every month in New Orleans as a provision for her old age. She said in the start that she had "put shoes on one bar' footed nigger to tromple on her with," and that one mistake like that was enough; she would be independent of the human race thenceforth forevermore if hard work and economy could accomplish it. When the boat touched the levee at New Orleans she bade good-by to her comrades on the *Grand Mogul* and moved her kit ashore.

But she was back in an hour. The bank had gone to smash and carried her four hundred dollars with it. She was a pauper, and homeless. Also disabled bodily, at least for the present. The officers were full of sympathy for her in her trouble, and made up a little purse for her. She resolved to go to her birthplace; she had friends there among the negroes, and the unfortunate always help the unfortunate, she was well aware of that; those lowly comrades of her youth would not let her starve.

She took the little local packet at Cairo, and now she was on the home-stretch. Time had worn away her bitterness against her son, and she was able to think of him with serenity. She put the vile side of him out of her mind, and dwelt only on recollections of his occasional acts of kindness to her. She gilded and otherwise decorated these, and made them very pleasant to contemplate. She began to long to see him. She would go and fawn upon him, slave-like—for this would have to be her attitude, of course—and maybe she would find that time had modified him, and that he would be glad to see his long-forgotten old nurse and treat her gently. That would be lovely; that would make her forget her woes and her poverty.

Her poverty! That thought inspired her to add another castle to her dream: maybe he would give her a trifle now and then—maybe a dollar, once a month, say; any little thing like that would help, oh, ever so much.

By the time she reached Dawson's Landing she was her old self again; her blues were gone, she was in high feather. She would get along, surely; there were many kitchens where the servants would share their meals with her, and also steal sugar and apples and other dainties for her to carry home—or give her a chance to pilfer them herself, which would answer just as well. And there was the church. She was a more rabid and devoted Methodist than ever, and her piety was no sham, but was strong and sincere. Yes, with plenty of creature comforts and her old place in the amen-corner in her possession again, she would be perfectly happy and at peace thenceforward to the end.

She went to Judge Driscoll's kitchen first of all. She was received there in great form and with vast enthusiasm. Her wonderful travels, and the strange countries she had seen and the adventures she had had, made her a marvel, and a heroine of romance. The negroes hung enchanted upon the great story of her experiences, interrupting her all along with eager questions, with laughter, exclamations of delight and expressions of applause; and she was obliged to confess to herself that if there was anything better in this world than steamboating, it was the glory to be got by telling about it. The audience loaded her stomach with their dinners, and then stole the pantry bare to load up her basket.

Tom was in St. Louis. The servants said he had spent the best part of his time there during the previous two years. Roxy came every day, and had many talks about the family and its affairs. Once she asked why Tom was away so much. The ostensible "Chambers" said:

"De fac' is, ole marster kin git along better when young marster's away den he kin when he's in de town; yes, en he love him better, too; so he gives him fifty dollahs a month——"

"No, is dat so? Chambers, you's a-jokin', ain't you?"

"'Clah to goodness I ain't, mammy; Marse Tom tole me so his own self. But nemmine, 't ain't enough."

"My lan', what de reason 't ain't enough?"

"Well, I's gwine to tell you, if you gimme a chanst, mammy. De reason it ain't enough is 'ca'se Marse Tom gambles."

Roxy threw up her hands in astonishment and Chambers went on—

"Ole marster found it out, 'ca'se he had to pay two hundred dollahs for Marse Tom's gamblin' debts, en dat's true, mammy, jes as dead certain as you's bawn."

"Two—hund'd—dollahs! Why, what is you talkin' 'bout? Two—hund'd —dollahs. Sakes alive, it's 'mos' enough to buy a tol'able good second-hand nigger wid. En you ain't lyin', honey?—you wouldn't lie to yo' ole mammy?"

"It's God's own truth, jes as I tell you—two hund'd dollahs—I wisht I may never stir outen my tracks if it ain't so. En, oh, my lan', ole Marse was jes a-hoppin'! he was b'ilin' mad, I tell you! He tuck 'n' dissenhurrit him."

He licked his chops with relish after that stately word. Roxy struggled with it a moment, then gave it up and said—

"Dissen*whiched* him?"

"Dissenhurrit him."

"What's dat? What do it mean?"

"Means he bu'sted de will."

"Bu's—ted de will! He wouldn't *ever* treat him so! Take it back, you mis'able imitation nigger dat I bore in sorrow en tribbilation."

Roxy's pet castle—an occasional dollar from Tom's pocket—was tumbling to ruin before her eyes. She could not abide such a disaster as that; she couldn't endure the thought of it. Her remark amused Chambers:

"Yah-yah-yah! jes listen to dat! If I's imitation, what is you? Bofe of us is imitation *white*—dat's what we is—en pow'ful good imitation, too—yah-yah-yah!—we don't 'mount to noth'n as imitation *niggers;* en as for——"

"Shet up yo' foolin', 'fo' I knock you side de head, en tell me 'bout de will. Tell me 't ain't bu'sted—do, honey, en I'll never forgit you."

"Well, *'tain't*—'ca'se dey's a new one made, en Marse Tom's all right ag'in. But what is you in sich a sweat 'bout it for, mammy? 'Tain't none o' your business I don't reckon."

"'Tain't none o' my business? Whose business is it den, I'd like to know? Wuz I his mother tell he was fifteen years old, or wusn't I?—you answer me dat. En you speck I could see him turned out po' en ornery on de worl' en never care noth'n' 'bout it? I reckon if you'd ever be'n a mother yo'self, Valet de Chambers, you wouldn't talk sich foolishness as dat."

"Well, den, ole Marse forgive him en fixed up de will ag'in—do dat satisfy you?"

Yes, she was satisfied now, and quite happy and sentimental over it. She kept coming daily, and at last she was told that Tom had come home. She began to tremble with emotion, and straightway sent to beg him to let his "po' ole nigger mammy have jes one sight of him en die for joy."

Tom was stretched at his lazy ease on a sofa when Chambers brought the petition. Time had not modified his ancient detestation of the humble drudge and protector of his boyhood; it was still bitter and uncompromising. He sat up and bent a severe gaze upon the fair face of the young fellow whose name he was unconsciously using and whose family rights he was enjoying. He maintained the gaze until the victim of it had become satisfactorily pallid with terror, then he said—

"What does the old rip want with me?"

The petition was meekly repeated.

"Who gave you permission to come and disturb me with the social attentions of niggers?"

Tom had risen. The other young man was trembling now, visibly. He saw what was coming, and bent his head sideways, and put up his left arm to shield it. Tom rained cuffs upon the head and its shield, saying no word: the victim received each blow with a beseeching "Please, Marse Tom!—oh, please, Marse Tom!" Seven blows—then Tom said, "Face the door—march!" He followed behind with one, two, three solid kicks. The last one helped the pure-white slave over the door-sill, and he limped away mopping his eyes with his old ragged sleeve. Tom shouted after him, "Send her in!"

Then he flung himself panting on the sofa again, and rasped out the remark, "He arrived just at the right moment; I was full to the brim with bitter thinkings, and nobody to take it out of. How refreshing it was! I feel better."

Tom's mother entered now, closing the door behind her, and approached her son with all the wheedling and supplicating servilities that fear and interest can impart to the words and attitudes of the born slave. She stopped a yard from her boy and made two or three admiring exclamations over his manly stature and general handsomeness, and Tom put an arm under his head and hoisted a leg over the sofa-back in order to look properly indifferent.

"My lan', how you is growed, honey! 'Clah to goodness, I wouldn't a-knowed you, Marse Tom! 'deed I wouldn't! Look at me good; does you 'member old Roxy?—does you know yo' old nigger mammy, honey? Well now, I kin lay down en die in peace, 'ca'se I 'se seed——"

"Cut it short, —— it, cut it short! What is it you want?"

"You heah dat? Jes de same old Marse Tom, al'ays so gay and funnin' wid de ole mammy. I 'uz jes as shore——"

"Cut it short, I tell you, and get along! What do you want."

This was a bitter disappointment. Roxy had for so many days nourished and fondled and petted her notion that Tom would be glad to see his old nurse, and would make her proud and happy to the marrow with a cordial word or two, that it took two rebuffs to convince her that he was not funning, and that her beautiful dream was a fond and foolish vanity, a shabby and pitiful mistake. She was hurt to the heart, and so ashamed that for a moment she did not quite know what to do or how to act. Then her breast began to heave, the tears came, and in her forlornness she was moved to try that other dream of hers—an appeal to her boy's charity; and so, upon the impulse, and without reflection, she offered her supplication:

"Oh, Marse Tom, de po' ole mammy is in sich hard luck dese days; en she's kinder crippled in de arms en can't work, en if you could gimme a dollah—on'y jes one little dol——"

Tom was on his feet so suddenly that the supplicant was startled into a jump herself.

"A dollar!—give you a dollar! I've a notion to strangle you! Is *that* your errand here? Clear out! and be quick about it!"

Roxy backed slowly toward the door. When she was half-way she stopped, and said mournfully:

"Marse Tom, I nussed you when you was a little baby, en I raised you all by myself tell you was 'most a young man; en now you is young en rich, en I is po' en gitt'n ole, en I come heah b'lievin' dat you would he'p de ole mammy 'long down de little road dat's lef' 'twix' her en de grave, en——"

Tom relished this tune less than any that had preceded it, for it began to wake up a sort of echo in his conscience; so he interrupted and said with decision, though without asperity, that he was not in a situation to help her, and wasn't going to do it.

"Ain't you ever gwine to he'p me, Marse Tom?"

"No! Now go away and don't bother me any more."

Roxy's head was down, in an attitude of humility. But now the fires of her old wrongs flamed up in her breast and began to burn fiercely. She raised her head slowly, till it was well up, and at the same time her great frame unconsciously assumed an erect and masterful attitude, with all the majesty and grace of her vanished youth in it. She raised her finger and punctuated with it:

"You has said de word. You has had yo' chance, en you has trompled it under yo' foot. When you git another one, you'll git down on yo' knees en *beg* for it!"

A cold chill went to Tom's heart, he didn't know why; for he did not reflect that such words, from such an incongruous source, and so solemnly delivered, could not easily fail of that effect. However, he did the natural thing: he replied with bluster and mockery:

"*You'll* give me a chance—*you!* Perhaps I'd better get down on my knees now! But in case I don't—just for argument's sake—what's going to happen, pray?"

"Dis is what is gwine to happen. I's gwine as straight to yo' uncle as I kin walk, en tell him every las' thing I knows 'bout you."

Tom's cheek blenched, and she saw it. Disturbing thoughts began to chase each other through his head. "How can she know? And yet she must have found out—she looks it. I've had the will back only three months, and am already deep in debt again, and moving heaven and earth to save myself from exposure and destruction, with a reasonably fair show of getting the thing covered up if I'm let alone, and now this fiend has gone and found me out somehow or other. I wonder how much she knows? Oh, oh, oh, it's enough to break a body's heart! But I've got to humor her—there's no other way."

Then he worked up a rather sickly sample of a gay laugh and a hollow chipperness of manner, and said:

"Well, well, Roxy dear, old friends like you and me mustn't quarrel. Here's your dollar—now tell me what you know."

He held out the wild-cat bill; she stood as she was, and made no movement. It was her turn to scorn persuasive foolery, now, and she did not waste it. She said, with a grim implacability in voice and manner which made Tom almost realize that even a former slave can remember for ten minutes insults and injuries returned for compliments and flatteries received, and can also enjoy taking revenge for them when the opportunity offers:

"What does I know? I'll tell you what I knows. I knows enough to bu'st dat will to flinders—en more, mind you, *more!*"

Tom was aghast.

"More?" he said. "What do you call more? Where's there any room for more?"

Roxy laughed a mocking laugh, and said scoffingly, with a toss of her head, and her hands on her hips—

"Yes!—oh, I reckon! *Co'se* you'd like to know—wid yo' po' little ole rag dollah. What you reckon I's gwine to tell *you* for?—you ain't got no money. I's gwine to tell yo' uncle—en I'll do it dis minute, too—he'll gimme *five* dollahs for de news, en mighty glad, too."

She swung herself around disdainfully, and started away. Tom was in a panic. He seized her skirts, and implored her to wait. She turned and said, loftily—

"Look-a-heah, what 'uz it I tole you?"

"You—you—I don't remember anything. What was it you told me?"

"I tole you dat de next time I give you a chance you'd git down on yo' knees en beg for it."

Tom was stupefied for a moment. He was panting with excitement. Then he said:

"Oh, Roxy, you wouldn't require your young master to do such a horrible thing. You can't mean it."

"I'll let you know mighty quick whether I means it or not! You call me names, en as good as spit on me when I comes here po' en ornery en 'umble, to praise you for bein' growed up so fine en handsome, en tell you how I used to nuss you en tend you en watch you when you 'uz sick en hadn't no mother but me in de whole worl', en beg you to give de po' ole nigger a dollah for to git her som'n' to eat, en you call me names—*names,* dad blame you! Yassir, I gives you jes one chance mo', and dat's *now,* en it las' on'y a half a second—you hear?"

Tom slumped to his knees and began to beg, saying—

"You see I'm begging, and it's honest begging, too! Now tell me, Roxy, tell me."

The heir of two centuries of unatoned insult and outrage looked down on him and seemed to drink in deep draughts of satisfaction. Then she said—

"Fine nice young white gen'l'man kneelin' down to a nigger-wench! I's wanted to see dat jes once befo' I's called. Now, Gabr'el, blow de hawn, I's ready . . . Git up!"

Tom did it. He said, humbly—

"Now, Roxy, don't punish me any more. I deserved what I've got, but be good and let me off with that. Don't go to uncle. Tell me—I'll give you the five dollars."

"Yes, I bet you will; en you won't stop dah, nuther. But I ain't gwine to tell you heah——"

"Good gracious, no!"

"Is you 'feared o' de ha'nted house?"

"N-no."

"Well, den, you come to de ha'nted house 'bout ten or 'leven to-night, en climb up de ladder, 'ca'se de sta'r-steps is broke down, en you'll find me. I's a-roostin' in de ha'nted house 'ca'se I can't 'ford to roos' nowhers' else." She started toward the door, but stopped and said, "Gimme de dollah bill!" He gave it to her. She examined it and said, "H'm—like enough de bank's bu'sted." She started again, but halted again. "Has you got any whisky?"

"Yes, a little."

"Fetch it!"

He ran to his room overhead and brought down a bottle which was two-thirds full. She tilted it up and took a drink. Her eyes sparkled with satisfaction, and she tucked the bottle under her shawl, saying, "It's prime. I'll take it along."

Tom humbly held the door for her, and she marched out as grim and erect as a grenadier.

CHAPTER 9

Why is it that we rejoice at a birth and grieve at a funeral? It is because we are not the person involved.

—*Pudd'nhead Wilson's Calendar*

It is easy to find fault, if one has that disposition. There was once a man who, not being able to find any other fault with his coal, complained that there were too many prehistoric toads in it.

—*Pudd'nhead Wilson's Calendar*

Tom flung himself on the sofa, and put his throbbing head in his hands, and rested his elbows on his knees. He rocked himself back and forth and moaned.

"I've knelt to a nigger wench!" he muttered. "I thought I had struck the deepest depths of degradation before, but oh, dear, it was nothing to this. . . . Well, there is one consolation, such as it is—I've struck bottom this time; there's nothing lower."

But that was a hasty conclusion.

At ten that night he climbed the ladder in the haunted house, pale, weak and wretched. Roxy was standing in the door of one of the rooms, waiting, for she had heard him.

This was a two-story log house which had acquired the reputation a few years before of being haunted, and that was the end of its usefulness. Nobody would live in it afterward, or go near it by night, and most people even gave it a wide berth in the daytime. As it had no competition, it was called *the* haunted house. It was getting crazy and ruinous, now, from long neglect. It stood three hundred yards beyond Pudd'nhead Wilson's house, with nothing between but vacancy. It was the last house in the town at that end.

Tom followed Roxy into the room. She had a pile of clean straw in the corner for a bed, some cheap but well-kept clothing was hanging on the wall, there was a tin lantern freckling the floor with little spots of light, and there were various soap-and-candle boxes scattered about, which served for chairs. The two sat down. Roxy said—

"Now den, I'll tell you straight off, en I'll begin to k'leck de money later on; I ain't in no hurry. What does you reckon I's gwine to tell you?"

"Well, you—you—oh, Roxy, don't make it too hard for me! Come right out and tell me you've found out somehow what a shape I'm in on account of dissipation and foolishness."

"Disposition en foolishness! *No* sir, dat ain't it. Dat jist ain't nothin' at all, 'longside o' what *I* knows."

Tom stared at her, and said—

"Why, Roxy, what do you mean?"

She rose, and gloomed above him like a Fate.

"I means dis—en it's de Lord's truth. You ain't no more kin to ole

Marse Driscoll den I is!—*dat's* what I means!" and her eyes flamed with triumph.

"What!"

"Yassir, en *dat* ain't all! You's a *nigger!—bawn* a nigger en a *slave!* —en you's a nigger en a slave dis minute; en if I opens my mouf ole Marse Driscoll'll sell you down de river befo' you is two days older den what you is now!"

"It's a thundering lie, you miserable old blatherskite!"

"It ain't no lie, nuther. It's jes de truth, en nothin' *but* de truth, so he'p me. Yassir—you's my *son*—"

"You devil!"

"En dat po' boy dat you's be'n a-kickin' en a-cuffin' to-day is Percy Driscoll's son en yo' *marster*——"

"You beast!"

"En *his* name's Tom Driscoll, en *yo'* name's Valet de Chambers, en you ain't *got* no fambly name, beca'se niggers don't *have* em!"

Tom sprang up and seized a billet of wood and raised it; but his mother only laughed at him, and said—

"Set down, you pup! Does you think you kin skyer me? It ain't in you, nor de likes of you. I reckon you'd shoot me in de back, maybe, if you got a chance, for dat's jist yo' style—*I* knows you, throo en throo —but I don't mind gitt'n killed beca'se all dis is down in writin' en it's in safe hands, too, en de man dat's got it knows whah to look for de right man when I gits killed. Oh, bless yo' soul, if you puts yo' mother up for as big a fool as *you* is, you's pow'ful mistaken, I kin tell you! Now den, you set still en behave yo'self; en don't you git up ag'in till I tell you!"

Tom fretted and chafed awhile in a whirlwind of disorganizing sensations and emotions, and finally said, with something like settled conviction—

"The whole thing is moonshine; now then, go ahead and do your worst; I'm done with you."

Roxy made no answer. She took the lantern and started toward the door. Tom was in a cold panic in a moment.

"Come back, come back!" he wailed. "I didn't mean it, Roxy; I take it all back, and I'll never say it again! Please come back, Roxy!"

The woman stood a moment, then she said gravely:

"Dat's one thing you's got to stop, Valet de Chambers. You can't call me *Roxy,* same as if you was my equal. Chillen don't speak to dey mammies like dat. You'll call me ma or mammy, dat's what you'll call me—leastways when dey ain't nobody aroun'. *Say* it!"

It cost Tom a struggle, but he got it out.

"Dat's all right. Don't you ever forgit it ag'in, if you knows what's good for you. Now den, you has said you wouldn't ever call it lies en moonshine ag'in. I'll tell you dis, for a warnin': if you ever does say it ag'in, it's de *las'* time you'll ever say it to me; I'll tramp as straight to de Judge as I kin walk, en tell him who you is, en *prove* it. Does you b'lieve me when I says dat?"

"Oh," groaned Tom, "I more than believe it; I *know* it."

Roxy knew her conquest was complete. She could have proved nothing to anybody, and her threat about the writings was a lie; but she knew the person she was dealing with, and had made both statements without any doubt as to the effect they would produce.

She went and sat down on her candle-box, and the pride and pomp of her victorious attitude made it a throne. She said—

"Now den, Chambers, we's gwine to talk business, en dey ain't gwine to be no mo' foolishness. In de fust place, you gits fifty dollahs a month; you's gwine to han' over half of it to yo' ma. Plank it out!"

But Tom had only six dollars in the world. He gave her that, and promised to start fair on next month's pension.

"Chambers, how much is you in debt?"

Tom shuddered, and said—

"Nearly three hundred dollars."

"How is you gwine to pay it?"

Tom groaned out— "Oh, I don't know; don't ask me such awful questions."

But she stuck to her point until she wearied a confession out of him: he had been prowling about in disguise, stealing small valuables from private houses; in fact, had made a good deal of a raid on his fellow-villagers a fortnight before, when he was supposed to be in St. Louis; but he doubted if he had sent away enough stuff to realize the required amount, and was afraid to make a further venture in the present excited state of the town. His mother approved of his conduct, and offered to help, but this frightened him. He tremblingly ventured to say that if she would retire from the town he should feel better and safer, and could hold his head higher—and was going on to make an argument, but she interrupted and surprised him pleasantly by saying she was ready; it didn't make any difference to where she stayed, so that she got her share of the pension regularly. She said she would not go far, and would call at the haunted house once a month for her money. Then she said—

"I don't hate you so much now, but I've hated you a many a year—

and anybody would. Didn't I change you off, en give you a good fambly en a good name, en made you a white gen'l'man en rich, wid store clothes on—en what did I git for it? You despised me all de time, en was al'ays sayin' mean hard things to me befo' folks, en wouldn't ever let me forgit I's a nigger—en—en——"

She fell to sobbing, and broke down. Tom said— "But you know I didn't know you were my mother; and besides——"

"Well, nemmine 'bout dat, now; let it go. I's gwine to fo'git it." Then she added fiercely, "En don't ever make me remember it ag'in, or you'll be sorry, *I* tell you."

When they were parting, Tom said, in the most persuasive way he could command—

"Ma, would you mind telling me who was my father?"

He had supposed he was asking an embarrassing question. He was mistaken. Roxy drew herself up with a proud toss of her head, and said—

"Does I mine tellin' you? No, dat I don't! You ain't got no 'casion to be shame' o' yo' father, *I* kin tell you. He wuz de highest quality in dis whole town—ole Virginny stock. Fust famblies, he wuz. Jes as good stock as de Driscolls en de Howards, de bes' day dey ever seed." She put on a little prouder air, if possible, and added impressively: "Does you 'member Cunnel Cecil Burleigh Essex, dat died de same year yo' young Marse Tom Driscoll's pappy died, en all de Masons en Odd Fellers en Churches turned out en give him de bigges' funeral dis town ever seed? Dat's de man."

Under the inspiration of her soaring complacency the departed graces of her earlier days returned to her, and her bearing took to itself a dignity and state that might have passed for queenly if her surroundings had been a little more in keeping with it.

"Dey ain't another nigger in dis town dat's as high-bawn as you is. Now den, go 'long! En jes you hold yo' head up as high as you want to —you has de right, en dat I kin swah."

CHAPTER 10

All say, "How hard it is that we have to die"—a strange complaint to come from the mouths of people who have had to live.

—*Pudd'nhead Wilson's Calendar*

When angry, count four; when very angry, swear.
—*Pudd'nhead Wilson's Calendar*

Every now and then, after Tom went to bed, he had sudden wakings out of his sleep, and his first thought was, "Oh, joy, it was all a dream!" Then he laid himself heavily down again, with a groan and the muttered words, "A nigger! I am a nigger! Oh, I wish I was dead!"

He woke at dawn with one more repetition of this horror, and then he resolved to meddle no more with that treacherous sleep. He began to think. Sufficiently bitter thinkings they were. They wandered along something after this fashion:

"Why were niggers *and* whites made? What crime did the uncreated first nigger commit that the curse of birth was decreed for him? And why is this awful difference made between white and black? . . . How hard the nigger's fate seems, this morning!—yet until last night such a thought never entered my head."

He sighed and groaned an hour or more away. Then "Chambers" came humbly in to say that breakfast was nearly ready. "Tom" blushed scarlet to see this aristocratic white youth cringe to him, a nigger, and call him "Young Marster." He said roughly—

"Get out of my sight!" and when the youth was gone, he muttered, "He has done me no harm, poor wretch, but he is an eyesore to me now, for he is Driscoll the young gentleman, and I am a—oh, I wish I was dead!"

A gigantic irruption, like that of Krakatoa a few years ago, with the accompanying earthquakes, tidal waves, and clouds of volcanic dust, changes the face of the surrounding landscape beyond recognition, bringing down the high lands, elevating the low, making fair lakes where deserts had been, and deserts where green prairies had smiled before. The tremendous catastrophe which had befallen Tom had changed his moral landscape in much the same way. Some of his low places he found lifted to ideals, some of his ideals had sunk to the valleys, and lay there with the sackcloth and ashes of pumice-stone and sulphur on their ruined heads.

For days he wandered in lonely places, thinking, thinking, thinking —trying to get his bearings. It was new work. If he met a friend, he found that the habit of a lifetime had in some mysterious way vanished—his arm hung limp, instead of involuntarily extending the hand for a shake. It was the "nigger" in him asserting its humility, and he blushed and was abashed. And the "nigger" in him was surprised when the white friend put out his hand for a shake with him. He found the "nigger" in him involuntarily giving the road, on the sidewalk, to the white rowdy and loafer. When Rowena, the dearest thing his heart knew, the idol of his secret worship, invited him in, the "nigger" in him made an embarrassed excuse and was afraid to enter and sit with the dread white folks on equal terms. The "nigger" in him went shrinking and skulking here and there and yonder, and fancying it saw suspicion and maybe detection in all faces, tones, and gestures. So strange and uncharacteristic was Tom's conduct that people noticed it, and turned to look after him when he passed on; and when he glanced back—as he could not help doing, in spite of his best resistance—and caught that puzzled expression in a person's face, it gave him a sick feeling, and he took himself out of view as quickly as he could. He presently came to have a hunted sense and a hunted look, and then he fled away to the hill-tops and the solitudes. He said to himself that the curse of Ham was upon him.

He dreaded his meals; the "nigger" in him was ashamed to sit at the white folks' table, and feared discovery all the time; and once when Judge Driscoll said, "What's the matter with you? You look as meek as a nigger," he felt as secret murderers are said to feel when the accuser says, "Thou art the man!" Tom said he was not well, and left the table.

His ostensible "aunt's" solicitudes and endearments were become a terror to him, and he avoided them.

And all the time, hatred of his ostensible "uncle" was steadily growing in his heart; for he said to himself, "He is white; and I am his chattel, his property, his goods, and he can sell me, just as he could his dog."

For as much as a week after this, Tom imagined that his character had undergone a pretty radical change. But that was because he did not know himself.

In several ways his opinions were totally changed, and would never go back to what they were before, but the main structure of his character was not changed, and could not be changed. One or two very important features of it were altered, and in time effects would result from this, if opportunity offered—effects of a quite serious nature, too. Under the influence of a great mental and moral upheaval his character and habits had taken on the appearance of complete change, but after a while with the subsidence of the storm both began to settle toward their former places. He dropped gradually back into his old frivolous and easy-going ways and conditions of feeling and manner of speech, and no familiar of his could have detected anything in him that differentiated him from the weak and careless Tom of other days.

The theft-raid which he had made upon the village turned out better than he had ventured to hope. It produced the sum necessary to pay his gaming-debts, and saved him from exposure to his uncle and another smashing of the will. He and his mother learned to like each other fairly well. She couldn't love him, as yet, because there "warn't nothing *to* him," as she expressed it, but her nature needed something or somebody to rule over, and he was better than nothing. Her strong character and aggressive and commanding ways compelled Tom's admiration in spite of the fact that he got more illustrations of them than he needed for his comfort. However, as a rule her conversation was made up of racy tattle about the privacies of the chief families of the town (for she went harvesting among their kitchens every time she came to the village), and Tom enjoyed this. It was just in his line. She always collected her half of his pension punctually, and he was always at the haunted house to have a chat with her on these occasions. Every now and then she paid him a visit there on between-days also.

Occasionally he would run up to St. Louis for a few weeks, and at last temptation caught him again. He won a lot of money, but lost it, and with it a deal more besides, which he promised to raise as soon as possible.

For this purpose he projected a new raid on his town. He never meddled with any other town, for he was afraid to venture into houses whose ins and outs he did not know and the habits of whose households he was not acquainted with. He arrived at the haunted house in disguise on the Wednesday before the advent of the twins—after writing his aunt Pratt that he would not arrive until two days after—and lay in hiding there with his mother until toward daylight Friday morning, when he went to his uncle's house and entered by the back way with his own key, and slipped up to his room, where he could have the use of mirror and toilet articles. He had a suit of girl's clothes with him in a bundle as a disguise for his raid, and was wearing a suit of his mother's clothing, with black gloves and veil. By dawn he was tricked out for his raid, but he caught a glimpse of Pudd'nhead Wilson through the window over the way, and knew that Pudd'nhead had caught a glimpse of him. So he entertained Wilson with some airs and graces and attitudes for a while, then stepped out of sight and resumed the other disguise, and by and by went down and out the back way and started down town to reconnoiter the scene of his intended labors.

But he was ill at ease. He had changed back to Roxy's dress, with the stoop of age added to the disguise, so that Wilson would not bother himself about a humble old woman leaving a neighbor's house by the back way in the early morning, in case he was still spying. But supposing Wilson had seen him leave, and had thought it suspicious, and had also followed him? The thought made Tom cold. He gave up the raid for the day, and hurried back to the haunted house by the obscurest route he knew. His mother was gone; but she came back, by and by, with the news of the grand reception at Patsy Cooper's, and soon persuaded him that the opportunity was like a special providence, it was so inviting and perfect. So he went raiding, after all, and made a nice success of it while everybody was gone to Patsy Cooper's. Success gave him nerve and even actual intrepidity; insomuch, indeed, that after he had conveyed his harvest to his mother in a back alley, he went to the reception himself, and added several of the valuables of that house to his takings.

After this long digression we have now arrived once more at the point where Pudd'nhead Wilson, while waiting for the arrival of the twins on that same Friday evening, sat puzzling over the strange apparition of that morning—a girl in young Tom Driscoll's bedroom; fretting, and guessing, and puzzling over it, and wondering who the shameless creature might be.

CHAPTER 11

There are three infallible ways of pleasing an author, and the three form a rising scale of compliment: 1, to tell him you have read one of his books; 2, to tell him you have read all of his books; 3, to ask him to let you read the manuscript of his forthcoming book. No. 1 admits you to his respect; No. 2 admits you to his admiration; No. 3 carries you clear into his heart.

—*Pudd'nhead Wilson's Calendar*

As to the Adjective: when in doubt, strike it out.

—*Pudd'nhead Wilson's Calendar*

The twins arrived presently, and talk began. It flowed along chattily and sociably, and under its influence the new friendship gathered ease and strength. Wilson got out his Calendar, by request, and read a passage or two from it, which the twins praised quite cordially. This pleased the author so much that he complied gladly when they asked him to lend them a batch of the work to read at home. In the course of their wide travels they had found out that there are three sure ways of pleasing an author; they were now working the best of the three.

There was an interruption, now. Young Tom Driscoll appeared, and joined the party. He pretended to be seeing the distinguished strangers for the first time when they rose to shake hands; but this was only a blind, as he had already had a glimpse of them, at the reception, while robbing the house. The twins made mental note that he was smooth-faced and rather handsome, and smooth and undulatory in his movements—graceful, in fact. Angelo thought he had a good eye; Luigi thought there was something veiled and sly about it. Angelo thought he had a pleasant free-and-easy way of talking; Luigi thought it was more so than was agreeable. Angelo thought he was a sufficiently nice young man; Luigi reserved his decision. Tom's first contribution to the conversation was a question which he had put to Wilson a hundred times before. It was always cheerily and good-naturedly put, and always inflicted a little pang, for it touched a secret sore; but this time the pang was sharp, since strangers were present.

"Well, how does the law come on? Had a case yet?"

Wilson bit his lip, but answered, "No—not yet," with as much indifference as he could assume. Judge Driscoll had generously left the law feature out of the Wilson biography which he had furnished to the twins. Young Tom laughed pleasantly, and said:

"Wilson's a lawyer, gentlemen, but he doesn't practise now."

The sarcasm bit, but Wilson kept himself under control, and said without passion:

"I don't practise, it is true. It is true that I have never had a case, and have had to earn a poor living for twenty years as an expert accountant in a town where I can't get hold of a set of books to untangle as often as I should like. But it is also true that I did fit myself well for the practice of the law. By the time I was your age, Tom, I had chosen a profession, and was soon competent to enter upon it." Tom winced. "I never got a chance to try my hand at it, and I may never get a chance; and yet if I ever do get it I shall be found ready, for I have kept up my law-studies all these years."

"That's it; that's good grit! I like to see it. I've a notion to throw all my business your way. My business and your law-practice ought to make a pretty gay team, Dave," and the young fellow laughed again.

"If you will throw—" Wilson had thought of the girl in Tom's bedroom, and was going to say, "If you will throw the surreptitious and disreputable part of your business my way, it may amount to something;" but thought better of it and said, "However, this matter doesn't fit well in a general conversation."

"All right, we'll change the subject; I guess you were about to give me another dig, anyway, so I'm willing to change. How's the Awful Mystery flourishing these days? Wilson's got a scheme for driving plain window-glass out of the market by decorating it with greasy finger-marks, and getting rich by selling it at famine prices to the crowned heads over in Europe to outfit their palaces with. Fetch it out, Dave."

Wilson brought three of his glass strips, and said—

"I get the subject to pass the fingers of his right hand through his hair, so as to get a little coating of the natural oil on them, and then press the balls of them on the glass. A fine and delicate print of the lines in the skin results, and is permanent, if it doesn't come in contact with something able to rub it off. You begin, Tom."

"Why, I think you took my finger-marks once or twice before."

"Yes; but you were a little boy the last time, only about twelve years old."

"That's so. Of course I've changed entirely since then, and variety is what the crowned heads want, I guess."

He passed his fingers through his crop of short hair, and pressed them one at a time on the glass. Angelo made a print of his fingers on another glass, and Luigi followed with the third. Wilson marked the glasses with names and date, and put them away. Tom gave one of his little laughs, and said—

"I thought I wouldn't say anything, but if variety is what you are after, you have wasted a piece of glass. The hand-print of one twin is the same as the hand-print of the fellow-twin."

"Well, it's done now, and I like to have them both, anyway," said Wilson, returning to his place.

"But look here, Dave," said Tom, "you used to tell people's fortunes, too, when you took their finger-marks. Dave's just an all-round genius—a genius of the first water, gentlemen; a great scientist running to seed here in this village, a prophet with the kind of honor that prophets generally get at home—for here they don't give shucks for his scientifics, and they call his skull a notion-factory—hey, Dave, ain't it so? But never mind; he'll make his mark some day—finger-mark, you know, he-he! But really, you want to let him take a shy at your palms once; it's worth twice the price of admission or your money's returned at the door. Why, he'll read your wrinkles as easy as a book, and not only tell you fifty or sixty things that's going to happen to you, but fifty or sixty thousand that ain't. Come, Dave, show the gentlemen what an inspired Jack-at-all-science we've got in this town, and don't know it."

Wilson winced under this nagging and not very courteous chaff, and the twins suffered with him and for him. They rightly judged, now, that the best way to relieve him would be to take the thing in earnest and treat it with respect, ignoring Tom's rather overdone raillery; so Luigi said—

"We have seen something of palmistry in our wanderings, and know very well what astonishing things it can do. If it isn't a science, and one of the greatest of them, too, I don't know what its other name ought to be. In the Orient——"

Tom looked surprised and incredulous. He said—

"That juggling a science? But really, you ain't serious, are you?"

"Yes, entirely so. Four years ago we had our hands read out to us as if our palms had been covered with print."

"Well, do you mean to say there was actually anything in it?" asked Tom, his incredulity beginning to weaken a little.

"There was this much in it," said Angelo: "what was told us of our characters was minutely exact—we could not have bettered it ourselves. Next, two or three memorable things that had happened to us were laid bare—things which no one present but ourselves could have known about."

"Why, it's rank sorcery!" exclaimed Tom, who was now becoming very much interested. "And how did they make out with what was going to happen to you in the future?"

"On the whole, quite fairly," said Luigi. "Two or three of the most striking things foretold have happened since; much the most striking one of all happened within that same year. Some of the minor prophecies have come true; some of the minor and some of the major ones have not been fulfilled yet, and of course may never be: still, I should be more surprised if they failed to arrive than if they didn't."

Tom was entirely sobered, and profoundly impressed. He said, apologetically—

"Dave, I wasn't meaning to belittle that science; I was only chaffing—chattering, I reckon I'd better say. I wish you would look at their palms. Come, won't you?"

"Why, certainly, if you want me to; but you know I've had no chance to become an expert, and don't claim to be one. When a past event is somewhat prominently recorded in the palm I can generally detect that, but minor ones often escape me,—not always, of course, but often,—but I haven't much confidence in myself when it comes to reading the future. I am talking as if palmistry was a daily study with me, but that is not so. I haven't examined half a dozen hands in the last half dozen years; you see, the people got to joking about it, and I stopped to let the talk die down. I'll tell you what we'll do, Count Luigi: I'll make a try at your past, and if I have any success there—no, on the whole, I'll let the future alone; that's really the affair of an expert."

He took Luigi's hand. Tom said—

"Wait—don't look yet, Dave! Count Luigi, here's paper and pencil. Set down that thing that you said was the most striking one that was foretold to you, and happened less than a year afterward, and give it to me so I can see if Dave finds it in your hand."

Luigi wrote a line privately, and folded up the piece of paper, and handed it to Tom, saying—

"I'll tell you when to look at it, if he finds it."

Wilson began to study Luigi's palm, tracing life lines, heart lines, head lines, and so on, and noting carefully their relations with the cobweb of finer and more delicate marks and lines that enmeshed them on all sides; he felt of the fleshy cushion at the base of the thumb, and noted its shape; he felt of the fleshy side of the hand between the wrist and the base of the little finger, and noted its shape also; he painstakingly examined the fingers, observing their form, proportions, and natural manner of disposing themselves when in repose. All this process was watched by the three spectators with absorbing interest, their heads bent together over Luigi's palm, and nobody disturbing the stillness with a word. Wilson now entered upon a close survey of the palm again, and his revelations began.

He mapped out Luigi's character and disposition, his tastes, aversions, proclivities, ambitions, and eccentricities in a way which sometimes made Luigi wince and the others laugh, but both twins declared that the chart was artistically drawn and was correct.

Next, Wilson took up Luigi's history. He proceeded cautiously and with hesitation, now, moving his finger slowly along the great lines of the palm, and now and then halting it at a "star" or some such landmark, and examining that neighborhood minutely. He proclaimed one or two past events, Luigi confirmed his correctness, and the search went on. Presently Wilson glanced up suddenly with a surprised expression—

"Here is record of an incident which you would perhaps not wish me to——"

"Bring it out," said Luigi, good-naturedly; "I promise you it sha'n't embarrass me."

But Wilson still hesitated, and did not seem quite to know what to do. Then he said—

"I think it is too delicate a matter to—to—I believe I would rather write it or whisper it to you, and let you decide for yourself whether you want it talked out or not."

"That will answer," said Luigi; "write it."

Wilson wrote something on a slip of paper and handed it to Luigi, who read it to himself and said to Tom—

"Unfold your slip and read it, Mr. Driscoll."

Tom read:

"*It was prophesied that I would kill a man. It came true before the year was out.*"

"Tom added, "Great Scott!"

Luigi handed Wilson's paper to Tom, and said—

"Now read this one."

Tom read:

"*You have killed some one, but whether man, woman or child, I do not make out.*"

"Cæsar's ghost!" commented Tom, with astonishment. "It beats anything that was ever heard of! Why, a man's own hand is his deadliest enemy! Just think of that—a man's own hand keeps a record of the deepest and fatalest secrets of his life, and is treacherously ready to expose him to any black-magic stranger that comes along. But what do you let a person look at your hand for, with that awful thing printed in it?"

"Oh," said Luigi, reposefully, "I don't mind it. I killed the man for good reasons, and I don't regret it."

"What were the reasons?"

"Well, he needed killing."

"I'll tell you why he did it, since he won't say himself," said Angelo, warmly. "He did it to save my life, that's what he did it for. So it was a noble act, and not a thing to be hid in the dark."

"So it was, so it was," said Wilson; "to do such a thing to save a brother's life is a great and fine action."

"Now come," said Luigi, "it is very pleasant to hear you say these things, but for unselfishness, or heroism, or magnanimity, the circumstances won't stand scrutiny. You overlook one detail; suppose I hadn't saved Angelo's life, what would have become of mine? If I had let the man kill him, wouldn't he have killed me, too? I saved my own life, you see."

"Yes; that is your way of talking," said Angelo, "but I know you—I don't believe you thought of yourself at all. I keep that weapon yet that Luigi killed the man with, and I'll show it to you sometime. That incident makes it interesting, and it had a history before it came into Luigi's hands which adds to its interest. It was given to Luigi by a great Indian prince, the Gaikowar of Baroda, and it had been in his family two or three centuries. It killed a good many disagreeable people who troubled that hearthstone at one time and another. It isn't much to look at, except that it isn't shaped like other knives, or dirks, or whatever it may be called—here, I'll draw it for you." He took a sheet of paper and made a rapid sketch. "There it is—a broad and murderous blade, with edges like a razor for sharpness. The devices engraved on it are the ciphers or names of its long line of possessors—I had Luigi's name added in Roman letters myself with our coat of arms, as you see. You notice what a curious handle the thing has. It is solid ivory, polished like a mirror, and is four or five inches long—round, and as thick as a large man's wrist, with the end squared off flat, for your thumb to rest on; for you grasp it, with your thumb resting on the blunt end—so—and lift it aloft and strike downward. The Gaikowar showed us how the thing was done when he gave it to Luigi, and before that night was ended Luigi had used the knife, and the Gaikowar was a man short by reason of it. The sheath is magnificently ornamented with gems of great value. You will find the sheath more worth looking at than the knife itself, of course."

Tom said to himself—

"It's lucky I came here. I would have sold that knife for a song; I supposed the jewels were glass."

"But go on; don't stop," said Wilson. "Our curiosity is up now, to hear about the homicide. Tell us about that."

"Well, briefly, the knife was to blame for that, all around. A native servant slipped into our room in the palace in the night, to kill us and steal the knife on account of the fortune incrusted on its sheath, without a doubt. Luigi had it under his pillow; we were in bed together. There was a dim night-light burning. I was asleep, but Luigi was awake, and he thought he detected a vague form nearing the bed. He slipped the knife out of the sheath and was ready, and unembarrassed by hampering bed-clothes, for the weather was hot and we hadn't any. Suddenly that native rose at the bedside, and bent over me with his right hand lifted and a dirk in it aimed at my throat; but Luigi grabbed his wrist, pulled him downward, and drove his own knife into the man's neck. That is the whole story."

Wilson and Tom drew deep breaths, and after some general chat about the tragedy, Pudd'nhead said, taking Tom's hand—

"Now, Tom, I've never had a look at your palms, as it happens; perhaps you've got some little questionable privacies that need—hel-lo!"

Tom had snatched away his hand, and was looking a good deal confused.

"Why, he's blushing!" said Luigi.

Tom darted an ugly look at him, and said sharply—

"Well, if I am, it ain't because I'm a murderer!" Luigi's dark face flushed, but before he could speak or move, Tom added with anxious haste: "Oh, I beg a thousand pardons. I didn't mean that; it was out before I thought, and I'm very, very sorry—you must forgive me!"

Wilson came to the rescue, and smoothed things down as well as he could; and in fact was entirely successful as far as the twins were concerned, for they felt sorrier for the affront put upon him by his guest's outburst of ill manners than for the insult offered to Luigi. But the success was not so pronounced with the offender. Tom tried to seem at his ease, and he went through the motions fairly well, but at bottom he felt resentful toward all the three witnesses of his exhibition; in fact, he felt so annoyed at them for having witnessed it and noticed it that he almost forgot to feel annoyed at himself for placing it before them. However, something presently happened which made him almost comfortable, and brought him nearly back to a state of charity and friendliness. This was a little spat between the twins; not much of a spat, but still a spat; and before they got far with it they were in a decided condition of irritation with each other. Tom was charmed; so pleased, indeed, that he cautiously did what he could to increase the irritation while pretending to be actuated by more respectable motives. By his help the fire got warmed up to the blazing-point, and he might have had the happiness of seeing the flames show up, in another moment, but for the interruption of a knock on the door—an interruption which fretted him as much as it gratified Wilson. Wilson opened the door.

The visitor was a good-natured, ignorant, energetic, middle-aged Irishman named John Buckstone, who was a great politician in a small way, and always took a large share in public matters of every sort. One of the town's chief excitements, just now, was over the matter of rum. There was a strong rum party and a strong anti-rum party. Buckstone was training with the rum party, and he had been sent to hunt up the twins and invite them to attend a mass-meeting of that faction. He delivered his errand, and said the clans were already gathering in the big hall over the market-house. Luigi accepted the invitation cordially, Angelo less cordially, since he disliked crowds, and did not drink the powerful intoxicants of America. In fact, he was even a tee-totaler sometimes—when it was judicious to be one.

The twins left with Buckstone, and Tom Driscoll joined company with them uninvited.

In the distance one could see a long wavering line of torches drifting down the main street, and could hear the throbbing of the bass drum, the clash of cymbals, the squeaking of a fife or two, and the faint roar of remote hurrahs. The tail-end of this procession was climbing the market-house stairs when the twins arrived in its neighborhood; when they reached the hall it was full of people, torches, smoke, noise and enthusiasm. They were conducted to the platform by Buckstone—Tom Driscoll still following—and were delivered to the chairman in the midst of a prodigious explosion of welcome. When the noise had moderated a little, the chair proposed that "our illustrious guests be at once elected, by complimentary acclamation, to membership in our ever-glorious organization, the paradise of the free and the perdition of the slave."

This eloquent discharge opened the flood-gates of enthusiasm again, and the election was carried with thundering unanimity. Then arose a storm of cries:

"Wet them down! Wet them down! Give them a drink!"

Glasses of whisky were handed to the twins. Luigi waved his aloft, then brought it to his lips; but Angelo set his down. There was another storm of cries:

"What's the matter with the other one?" "What is the blond one going back on us for?" "Explain! Explain!"

The chairman inquired, and then reported—

"We have made an unfortunate mistake, gentlemen. I find that the Count Angelo Cappello is opposed to our creed—is a teetotaler, in fact, and was not intending to apply for membership with us. He desires that we reconsider the vote by which he was elected. What is the pleasure of the house?"

There was a general burst of laughter, plentifully accented with whistlings and cat-calls, but the energetic use of the gavel presently restored something like order. Then a man spoke from the crowd, and said that while he was very sorry that the mistake had been made, it would not be possible to rectify it at the present meeting. According to the bylaws it must go over to the next regular meeting for action. He would not offer a motion, as none was required. He desired to apologize to the gentleman in the name of the house, and begged to assure him that as far as it might lie in the power of the Sons of Liberty, his temporary membership in the order would be made pleasant to him.

This speech was received with great applause, mixed with cries of—

"That's the talk!" "He's a good fellow, anyway, if he *is* a teetotaler!" "Drink his health!" "Give him a rouser, and no heeltaps!"

Glasses were handed around, and everybody on the platform drank Angelo's health, while the house bellowed forth in song:

For he's a jolly good fel-low,
For he's a jolly good fel-low,
For he's a jolly good fe-el-low,—
Which nobody can deny.

Tom Driscoll drank. It was his second glass, for he had drunk Angelo's the moment that Angelo had set it down. The two drinks made him very merry—almost idiotically so—and he began to take a most lively and prominent part in the proceedings, particularly in the music and cat-calls and side-remarks.

The chairman was still standing at the front, the twins at his side. The extraordinarily close resemblance of the brothers to each other suggested a witticism to Tom Driscoll, and just as the chairman began a speech he skipped forward and said with an air of tipsy confidence to the audience—

"Boys, I move that he keeps still and lets this human philopena snip you out a speech."

The descriptive aptness of the phrase caught the house, and a mighty burst of laughter followed.

Luigi's southern blood leaped to the boiling-point in a moment under the sharp humiliation of this insult delivered in the presence of four hundred strangers. It was not in the young man's nature to let the matter pass, or to delay the squaring of the account. He took a couple of strides and halted behind the unsuspecting joker. Then he drew back and delivered a kick of such titanic vigor that it lifted Tom clear over the footlights and landed him on the heads of the front row of the Sons of Liberty.

Even a sober person does not like to have a human being emptied on him when he is not doing any harm; a person who is not sober cannot endure such an attention at all. The nest of Sons of Liberty that Driscoll landed in had not a sober bird in it; in fact there was probably not an entirely sober one in the auditorium. Driscoll was promptly and indignantly flung on to the heads of Sons in the next row, and these Sons passed him on toward the rear, and then immediately began to pummel the front-row Sons who had passed him to them. This course was strictly followed by bench after bench as Driscoll traveled in his tumultuous and airy flight toward the door; so he left behind him an ever lengthening wake of raging and plunging and fighting and swearing humanity. Down went group after group of torches, and presently above the deafening clatter of the gavel, roar of angry voices, and crash of succumbing benches, rose the paralyzing cry of "FIRE!"

The fighting ceased instantly; the cursing ceased; for one distinctly defined moment there was a dead hush, a motionless calm, where the tempest had been; then with one impulse the multitude awoke to life and energy again, and went surging and struggling and swaying, this way and that, its outer edges melting away through windows and doors and gradually lessening the pressure and relieving the mass.

The fire-boys were never on hand so suddenly before; for there was no distance to go, this time, their quarters being in the rear end of the market-house. There was an engine company and a hook-and-ladder company. Half of each was composed of rummies and the other half of anti-rummies, after the moral and political share-and-share-alike fashion of the frontier town of the period. Enough anti-rummies were loafing in quarters to man the engine and the ladders. In two minutes they had their red shirts and helmets on—they never stirred officially in unofficial costume—and as the mass meeting overhead smashed through the long row of windows and poured out upon the roof of the arcade, the deliverers were ready for them with a powerful stream of water which washed some of them off the roof and nearly drowned the rest. But water was preferable to fire, and still the stampede from the windows continued, and still the pitiless drenchings assailed it until the building was empty; then the fire-boys mounted to the hall and flooded it with water enough to annihilate forty times as much fire as there was there; for a village fire-company does not often get a chance to show off, and so when it does get a chance it makes the most of it. Such citizens of that village as were of a thoughtful and judicious temperament did not insure against fire; they insured against the fire-company.

CHAPTER 12

Courage is resistance to fear, mastery of fear—not absence of fear. Except a creature be part coward it is not a compliment to say it is brave; it is merely a loose misapplication of the word. Consider the flea!—incomparably the bravest of all the creatures of God, if ignorance of fear were courage. Whether you are asleep or awake he will attack you, caring nothing for the fact that in bulk and strength you are to him as are the massed armies of the earth to a sucking child; he lives both day and night and all days and nights in the very lap of peril and the immediate presence of death, and yet is no more afraid than is the man who walks the streets of a city that was threatened by an earthquake ten centuries before. When we speak of Clive, Nelson, and Putnam as men who "didn't know what fear was," we ought always to add the flea—and put him at the head of the procession.

—Pudd'nhead Wilson's Calendar

Judge Driscoll was in bed and asleep by ten o'clock on Friday night, and he was up and gone a-fishing before daylight in the morning with his friend Pembroke Howard. These two had been boys together in Virginia when that State still ranked as the chief and most imposing member of the Union, and they still coupled the proud and affectionate adjective "old" with her name when they spoke of her. In Missouri a recognized superiority attached to any person who hailed from Old Virginia; and this superiority was exalted to supremacy when a person of such nativity could also prove descent from the First Families of that great commonwealth. The Howards and Driscolls were of this aristocracy. In their eyes it was a nobility. It had its unwritten laws, and they were as clearly defined and as strict as any that could be found among the printed statutes of the land. The F. F. V. was born a gentleman; his highest duty in life was to watch over that great inheritance and keep it unsmirched. He must keep his honor spotless. Those laws were his chart; his course was marked out on it; if he swerved from it by so much as half a point of the compass it meant shipwreck to his honor; that is to say, degradation from his rank as a gentleman. These laws required certain things of him which his religion might forbid: then his religion must yield—the laws could not be relaxed to accommodate religions or anything else. Honor stood first; and the laws defined what it was and wherein it differed in certain details from honor as defined by church creeds and by the social laws and customs of some of the minor divisions of the globe that had got crowded out when the sacred boundaries of Virginia were staked out.

If Judge Driscoll was the recognized first citizen of Dawson's Landing, Pembroke Howard was easily its recognized second citizen. He was called "the great lawyer"—an earned title. He and Driscoll were of the same age—a year or two past sixty.

Although Driscoll was a free-thinker and Howard a strong and determined Presbyterian, their warm intimacy suffered no impairment in consequence. They were men whose opinions were their own property and not subject to revision and amendment, suggestion or criticism, by anybody, even their friends.

The day's fishing finished, they came floating down stream in their skiff, talking national politics and other high matters, and presently met a skiff coming up from town, with a man in it who said:

"I reckon you know one of the new twins gave your nephew a kicking last night, Judge?"

"Did *what?*"

"Gave him a kicking."

The old Judge's lips paled, and his eyes began to flame. He choked with anger for a moment, then he got out what he was trying to say—

"Well—well—go on! give me the details."

The man did it. At the finish the Judge was silent a minute, turning over in his mind the shameful picture of Tom's flight over the footlights; then he said, as if musing aloud—"H'm—I don't understand it. I was asleep at home. He didn't wake me. Thought he was competent to manage his affair without my help, I reckon." His face lit up with pride and pleasure at that thought, and he said with a cheery complacency, "I like that—it's the true old blood—hey, Pembroke?"

Howard smiled an iron smile, and nodded his head approvingly. Then the news-bringer spoke again—

"But Tom beat the twin on the trial."

The Judge looked at the man wonderingly, and said—

"The trial? What trial?"

"Why, Tom had him up before Judge Robinson for assault and battery."

The old man shrank suddenly together like one who has received a death-stroke. Howard sprang for him as he sank forward in a swoon, and took him in his arms, and bedded him on his back in the boat. He sprinkled water in his face, and said to the startled visitor—

"Go, now—don't let him come to and find you here. You see what an effect your heedless speech has had; you ought to have been more considerate than to blurt out such a cruel piece of slander as that."

"I'm right down sorry I did it now, Mr. Howard, and I wouldn't have done it if I had thought: but it ain't slander; it's perfectly true, just as I told him."

He rowed away. Presently the old Judge came out of his faint and looked up piteously into the sympathetic face that was bent over him.

"Say it ain't true, Pembroke; tell me it ain't true!" he said in a weak voice.

There was nothing weak in the deep organ-tones that responded—

"You know it's a lie as well as I do, old friend. He is of the best blood of the Old Dominion."

"God bless you for saying it!" said the old gentleman, fervently. "Ah, Pembroke, it was such a blow!"

Howard stayed by his friend, and saw him home, and entered the house with him. It was dark, and past supper-time, but the Judge was not thinking of supper; he was eager to hear the slander refuted from headquarters, and as eager to have Howard hear it, too. Tom was sent for, and he came immediately. He was bruised and lame, and was not a happy-looking object. His uncle made him sit down, and said—

"We have been hearing about your adventure, Tom, with a handsome lie added to it for embellishment. Now pulverize that lie to dust! What measures have you taken? How does the thing stand?"

Tom answered guilelessly: "It don't stand at all; it's all over. I had him up in court and beat him. Pudd'nhead Wilson defended him—first case he ever had, and lost it. The judge fined the miserable hound five dollars for the assault."

Howard and the Judge sprang to their feet with the opening sentence—why, neither knew; then they stood gazing vacantly at each other. Howard stood a moment, then sat mournfully down without saying anything. The Judge's wrath began to kindle, and he burst out—

"You cur! You scum! You vermin! Do you mean to tell me that blood of my race has suffered a blow and crawled to a court of law about it? Answer me!"

Tom's head drooped, and he answered with an eloquent silence. His uncle stared at him with a mixed expression of amazement and shame and incredulity that was sorrowful to see. At last he said—

"Which of the twins was it?"

"Count Luigi."

"You have challenged him?"

"N—no," hesitated Tom, turning pale.

"You will challenge him to-night. Howard will carry it."

Tom began to turn sick, and to show it. He turned his hat round and round in his hand, his uncle glowering blacker and blacker upon him as the heavy seconds drifted by; then at last he began to stammer, and said piteously—

"Oh, please don't ask me to do it, uncle! He is a murderous devil—I never could—I—I'm afraid of him!"

Old Driscoll's mouth opened and closed three times before he could get it to perform its office; then he stormed out—

"A coward in my family! A Driscoll a coward! Oh, what have I done to deserve this infamy!" He tottered to his secretary in the corner repeating that lament again and again in heartbreaking tones, and got out of a drawer a paper, which he slowly tore to bits scattering the bits absently in his track as he walked up and down the room, still grieving and lamenting. At last he said—

"There it is, shreds and fragments once more—my will. Once more you have forced me to disinherit you, you base son of a most noble father! Leave my sight! Go—before I spit on you!"

The young man did not tarry. Then the Judge turned to Howard:

"You will be my second, old friend?"

"Of course."

"There is pen and paper. Draft the cartel, and lose no time."

"The Count shall have it in his hands in fifteen minutes," said Howard.

Tom was very heavy-hearted. His appetite was gone with his property and his self-respect. He went out the back way and wandered down the obscure lane grieving, and wondering if any course of future conduct, however discreet and carefully perfected and watched over, could win back his uncle's favor and persuade him to reconstruct once more that generous will which had just gone to ruin before his eyes. He finally concluded that it could. He said to himself that he had accomplished this sort of triumph once already, and that what had been done once could be done again. He would set about it. He would bend every energy to the task, and he would score that triumph once more, cost what it might to his convenience, limit as it might his frivolous and liberty-loving life.

"To begin," he said to himself, "I'll square up with the proceeds of my raid, and then gambling has got to be stopped—and stopped short off. It's the worst vice I've got—from my standpoint, anyway, because it's the one he can most easily find out, through the impatience of my creditors. He thought it expensive to have to pay two hundred dollars to them for me once. Expensive—*that!* Why, it cost me the whole of his fortune—but of course he never thought of that; some people can't think of any but their own side of a case. If he had known how deep I am in, now, the will would have gone to pot without waiting for a duel to help. Three hundred dollars! It's a pile! But he'll never hear of it, I'm thankful to say. The minute I've cleared it off, I'm safe; and I'll never touch a card again. Anyway, I won't while he lives, I make oath to that. I'm entering on my last reform—I know it—yes, and I'll win; but after that, if I ever slip again I'm gone."

CHAPTER 13

When I reflect upon the number of disagreeable people who I know have gone to a better world, I am moved to lead a different life.

—*Pudd'nhead Wilson's Calendar*

October. This is one of the peculiarly dangerous months to speculate in stocks in. The others are July, January, September, April, November, May, March, June, December, August, and February.

—*Pudd'nhead Wilson's Calendar*

Thus mournfully communing with himself Tom moped along the lane past Pudd'nhead Wilson's house, and still on and on between fences inclosing vacant country on each hand till he neared the haunted house, then he came moping back again, with many sighs and heavy with trouble. He sorely wanted cheerful company. Rowena! His heart gave a bound at the thought, but the next thought quieted it—the detested twins would be there.

He was on the inhabited side of Wilson's house, and now as he approached it he noticed that the sitting-room was lighted. This would do; others made him feel unwelcome sometimes, but Wilson never failed in courtesy toward him, and a kindly courtesy does at least save one's feelings, even if it is not professing to stand for a welcome. Wilson heard footsteps at his threshold, then the clearing of a throat.

"It's that fickle-tempered, dissipated young goose—poor devil, he finds friends pretty scarce to-day, likely, after the disgrace of carrying a personal-assault case into a lawcourt."

A dejected knock. "Come in!"

Tom entered, and drooped into a chair, without saying anything. Wilson said kindly—

"Why, my boy, you look desolate. Don't take it so hard. Try and forget you have been kicked."

"Oh, dear," said Tom, wretchedly, "it's not that, Pudd'nhead—it's not that. It's a thousand times worse than that—oh, yes, a million times worse."

"Why, Tom, what do you mean? Has Rowena—"

"Flung me? No, but the old man has."

Wilson said to himself, "Aha!" and thought of the mysterious girl in the bedroom. "The Driscolls have been making discoveries!" Then he said aloud, gravely:

"Tom, there are some kinds of dissipation which——"

"Oh, shucks, this hasn't got anything to do with dissipation. He wanted me to challenge that derned Italian savage, and I wouldn't do it."

"Yes, of course he would do that," said Wilson in a meditative matter-of-course way, "but the thing that puzzled me was, why he didn't look to that last night, for one thing, and why he let you carry such a matter into a court of law at all, either before the duel or after it. It's no place for it. It was not like him. I couldn't understand it. How did it happen?"

"It happened because he didn't know anything about it. He was asleep when I got home last night."

"And you didn't wake him? Tom, is that possible?"

Tom was not getting much comfort here. He fidgeted a moment, then said:

"I didn't choose to tell him—that's all. He was going a-fishing before dawn, with Pembroke Howard, and if I got the twins into the common calaboose—and I thought sure I could—I never dreamed of their slipping out on a paltry fine for such an outrageous offense—well, once in the calaboose they would be disgraced, and uncle wouldn't want any duels with that sort of characters, and wouldn't allow any."

"Tom, I am ashamed of you! I don't see how you could treat your good old uncle so. I am a better friend of his than you are; for if I had known the circumstances I would have kept that case out of court until I got word to him and let him have a gentleman's chance."

"You would?" exclaimed Tom, with lively surprise. "And it your first case! And you know perfectly well there never would have *been* any case if he had got that chance, don't you? And you'd have finished your days a pauper nobody, instead of being an actually launched and recognized lawyer to-day. And you would really have done that, would you?"

"Certainly."

Tom looked at him a moment or two, then shook his head sorrowfully and said—

"I believe you—upon my word I do. I don't know why I do, but I do. Pudd'nhead Wilson, I think you're the biggest fool I ever saw."

"Thank you."

"Don't mention it."

"Well, he has been requiring you to fight the Italian and you have refused. You degenerate remnant of an honorable line! I'm thoroughly ashamed of you, Tom!"

"Oh, that's nothing! I don't care for anything, now that the will's torn up again."

"Tom, tell me squarely—didn't he find any fault with you for anything but those two things—carrying the case into court and refusing to fight?"

He watched the young fellow's face narrowly, but it was entirely reposeful, and so also was the voice that answered:

"No, he didn't find any other fault with me. If he had had any to find, he would have begun yesterday, for he was just in the humor for it. He drove that jack-pair around town and showed them the sights, and when he came home he couldn't find his father's old silver watch that don't keep time and he thinks so much of, and couldn't remember what he did with it three or four days ago when he saw it last, and so when I arrived he was all in a sweat about it, and when I suggested that it probably wasn't lost but stolen, it put him in a regular passion and he said I was a fool—which convinced me, without any trouble, that that was just what he was afraid *had* happened, himself, but did not want to believe it, because lost things stand a better chance of being found again than stolen ones."

"Whe-ew!" whistled Wilson; "score another on the list."

"Another what?"

"Another theft!"

"Theft?"

"Yes, theft. That watch isn't lost, it's stolen. There's been another raid on the town—and just the same old mysterious sort of thing that has happened once before, as you remember."

"You don't mean it!"

"It's as sure as you are born! Have you missed anything yourself?"

"No. That is, I did miss a silver pencil-case that Aunt Mary Pratt gave me last birthday——"

"You'll find it stolen—that's what you'll find."

"No, I sha'n't; for when I suggested theft about the watch and got such a rap, I went and examined my room, and the pencil-case was missing, but it was only mislaid, and I found it again."

"You are sure you missed nothing else?"

"Well, nothing of consequence. I missed a small plain gold ring worth two or three dollars, but that will turn up. I'll look again."

"In my opinion you'll not find it. There's been a raid, I tell you, Come *in!*"

Mr. Justice Robinson entered, followed by Buckstone and the town-constable, Jim Blake. They sat down, and after some wandering and aimless weather-conversation Wilson said—

"By the way, we've just added another to the list of thefts, maybe two. Judge Driscoll's old silver watch is gone, and Tom here has missed a gold ring."

"Well, it is a bad business," said the Justice, "and gets worse the further it goes. The Hankses, the Dobsons, the Pilligrews, the Ortons, the Grangers, the Hales, the Fullers, the Holcombs, in fact everybody that lives around about Patsy Cooper's has been robbed of little things like trinkets and teaspoons and such-like small valuables that are easily carried off. It's perfectly plain that the thief took advantage of the reception at Patsy Cooper's when all the neighbors were in her house and all their niggers hanging around her fence for a look at the show, to raid the vacant houses undisturbed. Patsy is miserable about it; miserable on account of the neighbors, and particularly miserable on account of her foreigners, of course; so miserable on their account that she hasn't any room to worry about her own little losses."

"It's the same old raider," said Wilson. "I suppose there isn't any doubt about that."

"Constable Blake doesn't think so."

"No, you're wrong there," said Blake; "the other times it was a man; there was plenty of signs of that, as we know, in the profession, though we never got hands on him; but this time it's a woman."

Wilson thought of the mysterious girl straight off. She was always in his mind now. But she failed him again. Blake continued:

"She's a stoop-shouldered old woman with a covered basket on her arm, in a black veil, dressed in mourning. I saw her going aboard the ferry-boat yesterday. Lives in Illinois, I reckon; but I don't care where she lives, I'm going to get her—she can make herself sure of that."

"What makes you think she's the thief?"

"Well, there ain't any other, for one thing; and for another, some of the nigger draymen that happened to be driving along saw her coming out of or going into houses, and told me so—and it just happens that they was *robbed* houses, every time."

It was granted that this was plenty good enough circumstantial evidence. A pensive silence followed, which lasted some moments, then Wilson said—

"There's one good thing, anyway. She can't either pawn or sell Count Luigi's costly Indian dagger."

"My!" said Tom, "is *that* gone?"

"Yes."

"Well, that was a haul! But why can't she pawn it or sell it?"

"Because when the twins went home from the Sons of Liberty meeting last night, news of the raid was sifting in from everywhere, and Aunt Patsy was in distress to know if they had lost anything. They found that the dagger was gone, and they notified the police and pawnbrokers everywhere. It was a great haul, yes, but the old woman won't get anything out of it, because she'll get caught."

"Did they offer a reward?" asked Buckstone.

"Yes; five hundred dollars for the knife, and five hundred more for the thief."

"What a leather-headed idea!" exclaimed the constable. "The thief da'sn't go near them, nor send anybody. Whoever goes is going to get himself nabbed, for there ain't any pawnbroker that's going to lose the chance to——"

If anybody had noticed Tom's face at that time, the gray-green color of it might have provoked curiosity; but nobody did. He said to himself: "I'm gone! I never can square up; the rest of the plunder won't pawn or sell for half of the bill. Oh, I know it—I'm gone, I'm gone—and this time it's for good. Oh, this is awful—I don't know what to do, nor which way to turn!"

"Softly, softly," said Wilson to Blake. "I planned their scheme for them at midnight last night, and it was all finished up shipshape by two this morning. They'll get their dagger back, and then I'll explain to you how the thing was done."

There were strong signs of a general curiosity, and Buckstone said—

"Well, you have whetted us up pretty sharp, Wilson, and I'm free to say that if you don't mind telling us in confidence——"

"Oh, I'd as soon tell as not, Buckstone, but as long as the twins and I agreed to say nothing about it, we must let it stand so. But you can take my word for it you won't be kept waiting three days. Somebody will apply for that reward pretty promptly, and I'll show you the thief and the dagger both very soon afterward."

The constable was disappointed, and also perplexed. He said—

"It may all be—yes, and I hope it will, but I'm blamed if I can see my way through it. It's too many for yours truly."

The subject seemed about talked out. Nobody seemed to have anything further to offer. After a silence the justice of the peace informed Wilson that he and Buckstone and the constable had come as a committee, on the part of the Democratic party, to ask him to run for mayor—for the little town was about to become a city and the first charter election was approaching. It was the first attention which Wilson had ever received at the hands of any party; it was a sufficiently humble one, but it was a recognition of his début into the town's life and activities at last; it was a step upward, and he was deeply gratified. He accepted, and the committee departed, followed by young Tom.

CHAPTER 14

The true Southern watermelon is a boon apart, and not to be mentioned with commoner things. It is chief of this world's luxuries, king by the grace of God over all the fruits of the earth. When one has tasted it, he knows what the angels eat. It was not a Southern watermelon that Eve took: we know it because she repented.

—*Pudd'nhead Wilson's Calendar*

About the time that Wilson was bowing the committee out, Pembroke Howard was entering the next house to report. He found the old Judge sitting grim and straight in his chair, waiting.

"Well, Howard—the news?"

"The best in the world."

"Accepts, does he?" and the light of battle gleamed joyously in the Judge's eye.

"Accepts? Why, he jumped at it."

"Did, did he? Now that's fine—that's very fine. I like that. When is it to be?"

"Now! Straight off! To-night! An admirable fellow—admirable!"

"Admirable? He's a darling! Why, it's an honor as well as a pleasure to stand up before such a man. Come—off with you! Go and arrange everything—and give him my heartiest compliments. A rare fellow, indeed; an admirable fellow, as you have said!"

Howard hurried away, saying—

"I'll have him in the vacant stretch between Wilson's and the haunted house within the hour, and I'll bring my own pistols."

Judge Driscoll began to walk the floor in a state of pleased excitement; but presently he stopped, and began to think—began to think of Tom. Twice he moved toward the secretary, and twice he turned away again; but finally he said—

"This may be my last night in the world—I must not take the chance. He is worthless and unworthy, but it is largely my fault. He was intrusted to me by my brother on his dying bed, and I have indulged him to his hurt, instead of training him up severely, and making a man of him. I have violated my trust, and I must not add the sin of desertion to that. I have forgiven him once already, and would subject him to a long and hard trial before forgiving him again, if I could live; but I must not run that risk. No, I must restore the will. But if I survive the duel, I will hide it away, and he will not know, and I will not tell him until he reforms, and I see that his reformation is going to be permanent."

He re-drew the will, and his ostensible nephew was heir to a fortune again. As he was finishing his task, Tom, wearied with another brooding tramp, entered the house and went tiptoeing past the sitting-room door. He glanced in, and hurried on, for the sight of his uncle had nothing but terrors for him to-night. But his uncle was writing! That was unusual at this late hour. What could he be writing? A chill of anxiety settled down upon Tom's heart. Did that writing concern him? He was afraid so. He reflected that when ill luck begins, it does not come in sprinkles, but in showers. He said he would get a glimpse of that document or know the reason why. He heard some one coming, and stepped out of sight and hearing. It was Pembroke Howard. What could be hatching.

Howard said, with great satisfaction:

"Everything's right and ready. He's gone to the battle-ground with his second and the surgeon—also with his brother. I've arranged it all with Wilson—Wilson's his second. We are to have three shots apiece."

"Good! How is the moon?"

"Bright as day, nearly. Perfect, for the distance—fifteen yards. No wind—not a breath; hot and still."

"All good; all first-rate. Here, Pembroke, read this, and witness it."

Pembroke read and witnessed the will, then gave the old man's hand a hearty shake and said:

"Now that's right, York—but I knew you would do it. You couldn't leave that poor chap to fight along without means or profession, with certain defeat before him, and I knew you wouldn't, for his father's sake if not for his own."

"For his dead father's sake I couldn't, I know; for poor Percy—but you know what Percy was to me. But mind—Tom is not to know of this unless I fall to-night."

"I understand. I'll keep the secret."

The Judge put the will away, and the two started for the battle-ground. In another minute the will was in Tom's hands. His misery vanished, his feelings underwent a tremendous revulsion. He put the will carefully back in its place, and spread his mouth and swung his hat once, twice, three times around his head, in imitation of three rousing huzzas, no sound issuing from his lips. He fell to communing with himself excitedly and joyously, but every now and then he let off another volley of dumb hurrahs.

He said to himself: "I've got the fortune again, but I'll not let on that I know about it. And this time I'm going to hang on to it. I take no more risks. I'll gamble no more, I'll drink no more, because—well, because I'll not go where there is any of that sort of thing going on, again. It's the sure way, and the only sure way; I might have thought of that sooner—well, yes, if I had wanted to. But now—dear me, I've had a scare this time, and I'll take no more chances. Not a single chance more. Land! I persuaded myself this evening that I could fetch him around without any great amount of effort, but I've been getting more and more heavy-hearted and doubtful straight along, ever since. If he tells me about this thing, all right; but if he doesn't, I sha'n't, let on. I—well, I'd like to tell Pudd'nhead Wilson, but—no, I'll think about that; perhaps I won't." He whirled off another dead huzza, and said, "I'm reformed, and this time I'll stay so, sure!"

He was about to close with a final grand silent demonstration, when he suddenly recollected that Wilson had put it out of his power to pawn or sell the Indian knife, and that he was once more in awful peril of exposure by his creditors for that reason. His joy collapsed utterly, and he turned away and moped toward the door moaning and lamenting over the bitterness of his luck. He dragged himself up-stairs, and brooded in his room a long time disconsolate and forlorn, with Luigi's Indian knife for a text. At last he sighed and said:

"When I supposed these stones were glass and this ivory bone, the thing hadn't any interest for me because it hadn't any value, and couldn't help me out of my trouble. But now—why, now it is full of interest; yes, and of a sort to break a body's heart. It's a bag of gold that has turned to dirt and ashes in my hands. It could save me, and save me so easily, and yet I've got to go to ruin. It's like drowning with a life-preserver in my reach. All the hard luck comes to me, and all the good luck goes to other people—Pudd'nhead Wilson, for instance; even his career has got a sort of a little start at last, and what has he done to deserve it, I should like to know? Yes, he has opened his own road, but he isn't content with that, but must block mine. It's a sordid, selfish world, and I wish I was out of it." He allowed the light of the candle to play upon the jewels of the sheath, but the flashings and sparklings had no charm for his eye; they were only just so many pangs to his heart. "I must not say anything to Roxy about this thing," he said, "she is too daring. She would be for digging these stones out and selling them, and then—why, she would be arrested and the stones traced, and then—" The thought made him quake, and he hid the knife away, trembling all over and glancing furtively about, like a criminal who fancies that the accuser is already at hand.

Should he try to sleep? Oh, no, sleep was not for him; his trouble was too haunting, too afflicting for that. He must have somebody to mourn with. He would carry his despair to Roxy.

He had heard several distant gunshots, but that sort of thing was not uncommon, and they had made no impression upon him. He went out at the back door, and turned westward. He passed Wilson's house and proceeded along the lane, and presently saw several figures approaching Wilson's place through the vacant lots. These were the duelists returning from the fight; he thought he recognized them, but as he had no desire for white people's company, he stooped down behind the fence until they were out of his way.

Roxy was feeling fine. She said:

"Whah was you, child? Warn't you in it?"

"In what?"

"In de duel."

"Duel? Has there been a duel?"

"'Co'se dey has. De ole Jedge has be'n havin' a duel wid one o' dem twins."

"Great Scott!" Then he added to himself: "That's what made him re-make the will; he thought he might get killed, and it softened him toward me. And that's what he and Howard were so busy about. . . . Oh dear, if the twin had only killed him, I should be out of my——"

"What is you mumblin' bout, Chambers? Whah was you? Didn't you know dey was gwyne to be a duel?"

"No, I didn't. The old man tried to get me to fight one with Count

Luigi, but he didn't succeed, so I reckon he concluded to patch up the family honor himself."

He laughed at the idea, and went rambling on with a detailed account of his talk with the Judge, and how shocked and ashamed the Judge was to find that he had a coward in his family. He glanced up at last, and got a shock himself. Roxana's bosom was heaving with suppressed passion, and she was glowering down upon him with measureless contempt written in her face.

"En you refuse' to fight a man dat kicked you, 'stid o' jumpin' at de chance! En you ain't got no mo' feelin' den to come en tell me, dat fetched sich a po' low-down ornery rabbit into de worl'! Pah! it make me sick! It's de nigger in you, dat's what it is. Thirty-one parts o' you is white, en on'y one part nigger, en dat po' little one part is yo' *soul.* Tain't wuth savin'; tain't wuth totin' out on a shovel en throwin' in de gutter. You has disgraced yo' birth. What would yo' pa think o' you? It's enough to make him turn in his grave."

The last three sentences stung Tom into a fury, and he said to himself that if his father were only alive and in reach of assassination his mother would soon find that he had a very clear notion of the size of his indebtedness to that man, and was willing to pay it up in full, and would do it too, even at risk of his life; but he kept his thought to himself; that was safest in his mother's present state.

"Whatever has come o' yo' Essex blood? Dat's what I can't understan'. En it ain't on'y jist Essex blood dat's in you, not by a long sight—'deed it ain't! My great-great-great-gran'father en you' great-great-great-great-gran'father was Ole Cap'n John Smith, de highest blood dat Ole Virginny ever turned out, en *his* great-great-gran'mother or somers along back dah, was Pocahontas de Injun queen, en her husbun' was a nigger king outen Africa—en yit here you is, a slinkin' outen a duel en disgracin' our whole line like a ornery low-down hound! Yes, it's de nigger in you!"

She sat down on her candle-box and fell into a reverie. Tom did not disturb her; he sometimes lacked prudence, but it was not in circumstances of this kind. Roxana's storm went gradually down, but it died hard, and even when it seemed to be quite gone, it would now and then break out in a distant rumble, so to speak, in the form of muttered ejaculations. One of these was, "Ain't nigger enough in him to show in his finger-nails, en dat takes mighty little—yit dey's enough to paint his soul."

Presently she muttered. "Yassir, enough to paint a whole thimbleful of 'em." At last her ramblings ceased altogether, and her countenance began to clear—a welcome sign to Tom, who had learned her moods, and knew she was on the threshold of good-humor, now. He noticed that from time to time she unconsciously carried her finger to the end of her nose. He looked closer and said:

"Why, mammy, the end of your nose is skinned. How did that come?"

She sent out the sort of whole-hearted peal of laughter which God has vouchsafed in its perfection to none but the happy angels in heaven and the bruised and broken black slave on the earth, and said:

"Dad fetch dat duel, I be'n in it myself."

"Gracious! did a bullet do that?"

"Yassir, you bet it did!"

"Well, I declare! Why, how did that happen?"

"Happened dis-away. I 'uz a-sett'n' here kinder dozin' in de dark, en *che-bang!* goes a gun, right out dah. I skips along out towards t'other end o' de house to see what's gwyne on, en stops by de ole winder on de side to wards Pudd'nhead Wilson's house dat ain't got no sash in it,—but dey ain't none of 'em got any sashes, fur as dat's concerned,—en I stood dah in de dark en look out, en dar in de moonlight, right down under me 'uz one o' de twins a-cussin'—not much, but jist a-cussin' soft—it 'uz de brown one dat 'uz cussin', 'ca'se he 'uz hit in de shoulder. En Doctor Claypool he 'uz a-workin' at him, en Pudd'nhead Wilson he 'uz a-he'pin', en ole Jedge Driscoll en Pem Howard 'uz a-standin' out yonder a little piece waitin' for 'em to git ready agin. En treckly dey squared off en give de word, en *bang-bang* went de pistols, en de twin he say, 'Ouch!'—hit him on de han' dis time,—en I hear dat same bullet go *spat!* ag'in, de logs under de winder; en de nex' time dey shoot, de twin say, 'Ouch!' ag'in, en I done it too, 'ca'se de bullet glance' on his cheek-bone en skip up here en glance on de side o' de winder en whiz right acrost my face en tuck de hide off'n my nose—why, if I'd 'a be'n jist a inch or a inch en a half furder 'twould 'a' tuck de whole nose en disfiggered me. Here's de bullet; I hunted her up."

"Did you stand there all the time?"

"Dat's a question to ask, ain't it! What else would I do? Does I git a chance to see a duel every day?"

"Why, you were right in range! Weren't you afraid?"

The woman gave a sniff of scorn.

"'Fraid! De Smith-Pocahontases ain't 'fraid o' nothin', let alone bullets."

"They've got pluck enough, I suppose; what they lack is judgment. *I* wouldn't have stood there."

"Nobody's accusin' you!"

"Did anybody else get hurt?"

"Yes, we all got hit 'cep' de blon' twin en de doctor en de seconds. De Jedge didn't git hurt, but I hear Pudd'nhead say de bullet snip some o' his ha'r off."

" 'George!" said Tom to himself, "to come so near being out of my trouble, and miss it by an inch. Oh dear, dear, he will live to find me out and sell me to some nigger-trader yet—yes, and he would do it in a minute." Then he said aloud, in a grave tone—

"Mother, we are in an awful fix."

Roxana caught her breath with a spasm, and said—

"Chile! What you hit a body so sudden for, like dat? What's be'n en gone en happen'?"

"Well, there's one thing I didn't tell you. When I wouldn't fight, he tore up the will again, and—

Roxana's face turned a dead white, and she said—

"Now you's *done!*—done forever! Dat's de end. Bofe un us is gwyne to starve to—"

"Wait and hear me through, can't you! I reckon that when he resolved to fight, himself, he thought he might get killed and not have a chance to forgive me any more in this life, so he made the will again, and I've seen it, and it's all right. But——"

"Oh, thank goodness, den we's safe ag'in!—safe! en so what did you want to come here en talk sich dreadful——"

"Hold *on*, I tell you, and let me finish. The swag I gathered won't half square me up, and the first thing we know, my creditors—well, you know what'll happen."

Roxana dropped her chin, and told her son to leave her alone—she must think that matter out. Presently she said impressively:

"You got to go mighty keerful now, I tell you! En here's what you got to do. He didn't git killed, en if you gives him de least reason, he'll bust de will ag'in, en dat's de *las'* time, now you hear me! So—you's got to show him what you kin do in de nex' few days. You's got to be pison good, en let him see it; you got to do everything dat'll make him b'lieve in you, en you got to sweeten aroun' ole Aunt Pratt, too,—she's pow'ful strong wid de Jedge, en de bes' frien' you got. Nex', you'll go 'long away to Sent Louis, en dat'll *keep* him in yo' favor. Den you go en make a bargain wid dem people. You tell 'em he ain't gwyne to live long—en dat's de fac', too,—en tell 'em you'll pay 'em intrust, en big intrust, too,—ten per—what you call it?"

"Ten per cent. a month?"

"Dat's it. Den you take and sell yo' truck aroun', a little at a time, en pay de intrust. How long will it las'?"

"I think there's enough to pay the interest five or six months."

"Den you's all right. If he don't die in six months, dat don't make no diff'rence—Providence'll provide. You's gwyne to be safe—if you behaves." She bent an austere eye on him and added, "En you *is* gwyne to behave—does you know dat?"

He laughed and said he was going to try, anyway. She did not unbend. She said gravely:

"Tryin' ain't de thing. You's gwyne to *do* it. You ain't gwyne to steal a pin—'ca'se it ain't safe no mo'; en you ain't gwyne into no bad comp'ny—not even once, you understand; en you ain't gwyne to drink a drop—nary single drop; en you ain't gwyne to gamble one single gamble—not one! Dis ain't what you's gwyne to *try* to do, it's what you's gwyne to *do*. En I'll tell you how I knows it. Dis is how. I's gwyne to foller along to Sent Louis my own self; en you's gwyne to come to me every day o' yo' life, en I'll look you over; en if you fails in one single one o' dem things—jist *one*—I take my oath I'll come straight down to dis town en tell de Jedge you's a nigger en a slave—en *prove* it!" She paused to let her words sink home. Then she added, "Chambers, does you b'lieve me when I says dat?"

Tom was sober enough now. There was no levity in his voice when he answered:

"Yes, mother, I know, now, that I am reformed—and permanently. Permanently—and beyond the reach of any human temptation.

"Den g' long home en begin!"

CHAPTER 15

Nothing so needs reforming as other people's habits.

—*Pudd'nhead Wilson's Calendar*

Behold, the fool saith, "Put not all thine eggs in the one basket"—which is but a manner of saying, "Scatter your money and your attention;" but the wise man saith, "Put all your eggs in the one basket and—WATCH THAT BASKET."

—*Pudd'nhead Wilson's Calendar*

What a time of it Dawson's Landing was having! All its life it had been asleep, but now it hardly got a chance for a nod, so swiftly did big events and crashing surprises come along in one another's wake: Friday morning, first glimpse of Real Nobility, also grand reception at Aunt Patsy Cooper's, also great robber-raid; Friday evening, dramatic kicking of the heir of the chief citizen in presence of four hundred people; Saturday morning, emergence as practising lawyer of the long-submerged Pudd'nhead Wilson; Saturday night, duel between chief citizen and titled stranger.

The people took more pride in the duel than in all the other events put together, perhaps. It was a glory to their town to have such a thing happen there. In their eyes the principals had reached the summit of human honor. Everybody paid homage to their names; their praises were in all mouths. Even the duelists' subordinates came in for a handsome share of the public approbation: wherefore Pudd'nhead Wilson was suddenly become a man of consequence. When asked to run for the mayoralty Saturday night he was risking defeat, but Sunday morning found him a made man and his success assured.

The twins were prodigiously great, now; the town took them to its bosom with enthusiasm. Day after day, and night after night, they went dining and visiting from house to house, making friends, enlarging and solidifying their popularity, and charming and surprising all with their musical prodigies, and now and then heightening the effects with samples of what they could do in other directions, out of their stock of rare and curious accomplishments. They were so pleased that they gave the regulation thirty days' notice, the required preparation for citizenship, and resolved to finish their days in this pleasant place. That was the climax. The delighted community rose as one man and applauded; and when the twins were asked to stand for seats in the forthcoming aldermanic board, and consented, the public contentment was rounded and complete.

Tom Driscoll was not happy over these things; they sunk deep, and hurt all the way down. He hated the one twin for kicking him, and the other one for being the kicker's brother.

Now and then the people wondered why nothing was heard of the raider, or of the stolen knife or the other plunder, but nobody was able to throw any light on that matter. Nearly a week had drifted by, and still the thing remained a vexed mystery.

On Saturday Constable Blake and Pudd'nhead Wilson met on the street, and Tom Driscoll joined them in time to open their conversation for them. He said to Blake—"You are not looking well, Blake; you seem to be annoyed about something. Has anything gone wrong in the detective business? I believe you fairly and justifiably claim to have a pretty good reputation in that line, isn't it so?"—which made Blake feel good, and look it; but Tom added, "for a country detective"—which made Blake feel the other way, and not only look it, but betray it in his voice—

"Yes, sir, I *have* got a reputation; and it's as good as anybody's in the profession, too, country or no country."

"Oh, I beg pardon; I didn't mean any offense. What I started out to ask was only about the old woman that raided the town—the stoop-shouldered old woman, you know, that you said you were going to catch; and I knew you would, too, because you have the reputation of never boasting, and—well, you—you've caught the old woman?"

"D—— the old woman!"

"Why, sho! you don't mean to say you haven't caught her?"

"No; I haven't caught her. If anybody could have caught her, I could; but nobody couldn't, I don't care who he is."

"I am sorry, real sorry—for your sake; because, when it gets around that a detective has expressed himself so confidently, and then——"

"Don't you worry, that's all—don't you worry; and as for the town, the town needn't worry, either. She's my meat—make yourself easy about that. I'm on her track; I've got clues that——"

"That's good! Now if you could get an old veteran detective down from St. Louis to help you find out what the clues mean, and where they lead to, and then——"

"I'm plenty veteran enough myself, and I don't need anybody's help. I'll have her inside of a we—inside of a month. That I'll swear to!"

Tom said carelessly—

"I suppose that will answer—yes, that will answer. But I reckon she is pretty old, and old people don't often outlive the cautious pace of the professional detective when he has got his clues together and is out on his still-hunt."

Blake's dull face flushed under this gibe, but before he could set his retort in order Tom had turned to Wilson, and was saying, with placid indifference of manner and voice—

"Who got the reward, Pudd'nhead?"

Wilson winced slightly, and saw that his own turn was come.

"What reward?"

"Why, the reward for the thief, and the other one for the knife."

Wilson answered—and rather uncomfortably, to judge by his hesitating fashion of delivering himself—

"Well, the—well, in fact, nobody has claimed it yet."

Tom seemed surprised.

"Why, is that so?"

Wilson showed a trifle of irritation when he replied—

"Yes, it's so. And what of it?"

"Oh, nothing. Only I thought you had struck out a new idea, and invented a scheme that was going to revolutionize the time-worn and ineffectual methods of the——" He stopped, and turned to Blake, who was happy now that another had taken his place on the gridiron: "Blake, didn't you understand him to intimate that it wouldn't be necessary for you to hunt the old woman down?"

"B'George, he said he'd have thief and swag both inside of three days—he did, by hokey! and that's just about a week ago. Why, I said at the time that no thief and no thief's pal was going to try to pawn or sell a thing where he knowed the pawnbroker could get both rewards by taking *him* into camp *with* the swag. It was the blessedest idea that ever *I* struck!"

"You'd change your mind," said Wilson, with irritated bluntness, "if you knew the entire scheme instead of only part of it."

"Well," said the constable, pensively, "I had the idea that it wouldn't work, and up to now I'm right anyway."

"Very well, then, let it stand at that, and give it a further show. It has worked at least as well as your own methods, you perceive."

The constable hadn't anything handy to hit back with, so he discharged a discontented sniff, and said nothing.

After the night that Wilson had partly revealed his scheme at his house, Tom had tried for several days to guess out the secret of the rest of it, but had failed. Then it occurred to him to give Roxana's smarter head a chance at it. He made up a supposititious case, and laid it before her. She thought it over, and delivered her verdict upon it. Tom said to himself, "She's hit it, sure!" He thought he would test that verdict, now, and watch Wilson's face; so he said reflectively—

"Wilson, you're not a fool—a fact of recent discovery. Whatever your scheme was, it had sense in it, Blake's opinion to the contrary notwithstanding, I don't ask you to reveal it, but I will suppose a case—a case which will answer as a starting-point for the real thing I am going to come at, and that's all I want. You offered five hundred dollars for the knife, and five hundred for the thief. We will suppose, for argument's sake, that the first reward is *advertised* and the second offered by *private letter* to pawnbrokers and——"

Blake slapped his thigh, and cried out—

"By Jackson, he's got you, Puddn'head! Now why couldn't I or *any* fool have thought of that?"

Wilson said to himself, "Anybody with a reasonably good head would have thought of it. I am not surprised that Blake didn't detect it; I am only surprised that Tom did. There is more to him than I supposed." He said nothing aloud, and Tom went on:

"Very well. The thief would not suspect that there was a trap, and he would bring or send the knife, and say he bought it for a song, or found it in the road, or something like that, and try to collect the reward, and be arrested—wouldn't he?"

"Yes," said Wilson.

"I think so," said Tom. "There can't be any doubt of it. Have you ever seen that knife?"

"No."

"Has any friend of yours?"

"Not that I know of."

"Well, I begin to think I understand why your scheme failed."

"What do you mean, Tom? What are you driving at?" asked Wilson, with a dawning sense of discomfort.

"Why, that there *isn't* any such knife."

"Look here, Wilson," said Blake, "Tom Driscoll's right, for a thousand dollars—if I had it."

Wilson's blood warmed a little, and he wondered if he had been played upon by those strangers; it certainly had something of that look. But what could they gain by it? He threw out that suggestion. Tom replied:

"Gain? Oh, nothing that you would value, maybe. But they are strangers making their way in a new community. Is it nothing to them to appear as pets of an Oriental prince—at no expense? Is it nothing to them to be able to dazzle this poor little town with thousand-dollar rewards—at no expense? Wilson, there isn't any such knife, or your scheme would have fetched it to light. Or if there is any such knife, they've got it yet. I believe, myself, that they've seen such a knife, for Angelo pictured it out with his pencil too swiftly and handily for him to have been inventing it, and of course I can't swear that they've never had it; but this I'll go bail for—if they had it when they came to this town, they've got it yet."

Blake said—

"It looks mighty reasonable, the way Tom puts it; it most certainly does."

Tom responded, turning to leave—

"You find the old woman, Blake, and if she can't furnish the knife, go and search the twins!"

Tom sauntered away. Wilson felt a good deal depressed. He hardly knew what to think. He was loth to withdraw his faith from the twins, and was resolved not to do it on the present indecisive evidence; but —well, he would think, and then decide how to act.

"Blake, what do you think of this matter?"

"Well, Pudd'nhead, I'm bound to say I put it up the way Tom does. They hadn't the knife; or if they had it, they've got it yet."

The men parted. Wilson said to himself:

"I believe they had it; if it had been stolen, the scheme would have restored it, that is certain. And so I believe they've got it yet."

Tom had no purpose in his mind when he encountered those two men. When he began his talk he hoped to be able to gall them a little and get a trifle of malicious entertainment out of it. But when he left, he left in great spirits, for he perceived that just by pure luck and no troublesome labor he had accomplished several delightful things: he had touched both men on a raw spot and seen them squirm; he had modified Wilson's sweetness for the twins with one small bitter taste that he wouldn't be able to get out of his mouth right away; and, best of all, he had taken the hated twins down a peg with the community; for Blake would gossip around freely, after the manner of detectives, and within a week the town would be laughing at them in its sleeve for offering a gaudy reward for a bauble which they either never possessed or hadn't lost. Tom was very well satisfied with himself.

Tom's behavior at home had been perfect during the entire week. His uncle and aunt had seen nothing like it before. They could find no fault with him anywhere.

Saturday evening he said to the Judge—

"I've had something preying on my mind, uncle, and as I am going away, and might never see you again, I can't bear it any longer. I made you believe I was afraid to fight that Italian adventurer. I had to get out of it on some pretext or other, and maybe I chose badly, being taken unawares, but no honorable person could consent to meet him in the field, knowing what I knew about him."

"Indeed? What was that?"

"Count Luigi is a confessed assassin."

"Incredible!"

"It is perfectly true. Wilson detected it in his hand, by palmistry, and charged him with it, and cornered him up so close that he had to confess; but both twins begged us on their knees to keep the secret, and swore they would lead straight lives here; and it was all so pitiful that we gave our word of honor never to expose them while they kept that promise. You would have done it yourself, uncle."

"You are right, my boy; I would. A man's secret is still his own property, and sacred, when it has been surprised out of him like that. You did well, and I am proud of you." Then he added mournfully, "But I wish I could have been saved the shame of meeting an assassin on the field of honor."

"It couldn't be helped, uncle. If I had known you were going to challenge him I should have felt obliged to sacrifice my pledged word in order to stop it, but Wilson couldn't be expected to do otherwise than keep silent."

"Oh no; Wilson did right, and is in no way to blame. Tom, Tom, you have lifted a heavy load from my heart; I was stung to the very soul when I seemed to have discovered that I had a coward in my family."

"You may imagine what it cost *me* to assume such a part, uncle."

"Oh, I know it, poor boy, I know it. And I can understand how much it has cost you to remain under that unjust stigma to this time. But it is all right now, and no harm is done. You have restored my comfort of mind, and with it your own; and both of us had suffered enough."

The old man sat awhile plunged in thought; then he looked up with a satisfied light in his eye, and said: "That this assassin should have put the affront upon me of letting me meet him on the field of honor as if he were a gentleman is a matter which I will presently settle—but not now. I will not shoot him until after election. I see a way to ruin them both before; I will attend to that first. Neither of them shall be elected, that I promise. You are sure that the fact that he is an assassin has not got abroad?"

"Perfectly certain of it, sir."

"It will be a good card. I will fling a hint at it from the stump on the polling-day. It will sweep the ground from under both of them."

"There's not a doubt of it. It will finish them."

"That and outside work among the voters will, to a certainty. I want you to come down here by and by and work privately among the rag-tag and bobtail. You shall spend money among them; I will furnish it."

Another point scored against the detested twins! Really it was a great day for Tom. He was encouraged to chance a parting shot, now, at the same target, and did it.

"You know that wonderful Indian knife that the twins have been making such a to-do about? Well, there's no track or trace of it yet; so the town is beginning to sneer and gossip and laugh. Half the people believe they never had any such knife, the other half believe they had it and have got it still. I've heard twenty people talking like that to-day."

Yes, Tom's blemishless week had restored him to the favor of his aunt and uncle.

His mother was satisfied with him, too. Privately, she believed she was coming to love him, but she did not say so. She told him to go along to St. Louis, now, and she would get ready and follow. Then she smashed her whisky bottle and said—

"Dah now! I's a-gwyne to make you walk as straight as a string, Chambers, en so I's bown' you ain't gwyne to git no bad example out o' yo' mammy. I tole you you couldn't go into no bad comp'ny. Well, you's gwyne into my comp'ny, en I's gwyne to fill de bill. Now, den, trot along, trot along!"

Tom went aboard one of the big transient boats that night with his heavy satchel of miscellaneous plunder, and slept the sleep of the unjust, which is serener and sounder than the other kind, as we know by the hanging-eve history of a million rascals. But when he got up in the morning, luck was against him again: A brother-thief had robbed him while he slept, and gone ashore at some intermediate landing.

CHAPTER 16

If you pick up a starving dog and make him prosperous, he will not bite you. This is the principal difference between a dog and a man.

—*Pudd'nhead Wilson's Calendar*

We know all about the habits of the ant, we know all about the habits of the bee, but we know nothing at all about the habits of the oyster. It seems almost certain that we have been choosing the wrong time for studying the oyster.

—*Pudd'nhead Wilson's Calendar*

When Roxana arrived, she found her son in such despair and misery that her heart was touched and her motherhood rose up strong in her. He was ruined past hope, now; his destruction would be immediate and sure, and he would be an outcast and friendless. That was reason enough for a mother to love a child; so she loved him, and told him so. It made him wince, secretly—for she was a "nigger." That he was one himself was far from reconciling him to that despised race.

Roxana poured out endearments upon him, to which he responded uncomfortably, but as well as he could. And she tried to comfort him, but that was not possible. These intimacies quickly became horrible to him, and within the hour he began to try to get up courage enough to tell her so, and require that they be discontinued or very considerably modified. But he was afraid of her; and besides, there came a lull, now, for she had begun to think. She was trying to invent a saving plan. Finally she started up, and said she had found a way out. Tom was almost suffocated by the joy of this sudden good news. Roxana said:

"Here is de plan, en she'll win, sure. I's a nigger, en nobody ain't gwyne to doubt it dat hears me talk. I's wuth six hund'd dollahs. Take en sell me, en pay off dese gamblers."

Tom was dazed. He was not sure he had heard aright. He was dumb for a moment; then he said:

"Do you mean that you would be sold into slavery to save me?"

"Ain't you my chile? En does you know anything dat a mother won't do for her chile? Dey ain't nothin' a white mother won't do for her chile. Who made 'em so? De Lord done it. En who made de niggers? De Lord made 'em. In de inside, mothers is all de same. De good Lord he made 'em so. I's gwyne to be sole into slavery, en in a year you's gwyne to buy yo' ole mammy free ag'in. I'll show you how. Dat's de plan."

Tom's hopes began to rise, and his spirits along with them. He said—

"It's lovely of you, mammy—it's just—"

"Say it ag'in! En keep on sayin' it? It's all de pay a body kin want in dis worl', en it's mo' den enough. Laws bless you, honey, when I's slavin' aroun', en dey 'buses me, if I knows you's a-sayin' dat, 'way off yonder somers, it'll heal up all de sore places, en I kin stan' 'em."

"I *do* say it again, mammy, and I'll keep on saying it, too. But how am I going to sell you? You're free, you know."

"Much diff'rence dat make! White folks ain't partic'lar. De law kin sell me now if dey tell me to leave de State in six months en I don't go. You draw up a paper—bill o' sale—en put it 'way off yonder, down in de middle 'o Kaintuck somers, en sign some names to it, en say you'll sell me cheap 'ca'se you's hard up; you'll find you ain't gwyne to have no trouble. You take me up de country a piece, en sell me on a farm; dem people ain't gwyne to ask no questions if I's a bargain."

Tom forged a bill of sale and sold his mother to an Arkansas cotton-planter for a trifle over six hundred dollars. He did not want to commit this treachery, but luck threw the man in his way, and this saved him the necessity of going up country to hunt up a purchaser, with the added risk of having to answer a lot of questions, whereas this planter was so pleased with Roxy that he asked next to none at all. Besides, the planter insisted that Roxy wouldn't know where she was, at first, and that by the time she found out she would already have become contented. And Tom argued with himself that it was an immense advantage for Roxy to have a master who was so pleased with her, as this planter manifestly was. In almost no time his flowing reasonings carried him to the point of even half believing he was doing Roxy a splendid surreptitious service in selling her "down the river." And then he kept diligently saying to himself all the time: "It's for only a year. In a year I buy her free again; she'll keep that in mind, and it'll reconcile her." Yes; the little deception could do no harm, and everything would come out right and pleasant in the end, any way. By agreement, the conversation in Roxy's presence was all about the man's "upcountry" farm, and how pleasant a place it was, and how happy the slaves were there; so poor Roxy was entirely deceived; and easily, for she was not dreaming that her own son could be guilty of treason to a mother who, in voluntarily going into slavery—slavery of any kind, mild or severe, or of any duration, brief or long—was making a sacrifice for him compared with which death would have been a poor and commonplace one. She lavished tears and loving caresses upon him privately, and then went away with her owner—went away broken-hearted, and yet proud of what she was doing, and glad that it was in her power to do it.

Tom squared his accounts, and resolved to keep to the very letter of his reform, and never to put that will in jeopardy again. He had three hundred dollars left. According to his mother's plan, he was to put that safely away, and add her half of his pension to it monthly. In one year this fund would buy her free again.

For a whole week he was not able to sleep well, so much the villainy which he had played upon his trusting mother preyed upon his rag of a conscience; but after that he began to get comfortable again, and was presently able to sleep like any other miscreant.

The boat bore Roxy away from St. Louis at four in the afternoon, and she stood on the lower guard abaft the paddle-box and watched Tom through a blur of tears until he melted into the throng of people and disappeared; then she looked no more, but sat there on a coil of cable crying till far into the night. When she went to her foul steer-age-bunk at last, between the clashing engines, it was not to sleep, but only to wait for the morning, and, waiting, grieve.

It had been imagined that she "would not know," and would think she was traveling up stream. She! Why, she had been steamboating for years. At dawn she got up and went listlessly and sat down on the cable-coil again. She passed many a snag whose "break" could have told her a thing to break her heart, for it showed a current moving in the same direction that the boat was going; but her thoughts were elsewhere, and she did not notice. But at last the roar of a bigger and nearer break than usual brought her out of her torpor, and she looked up, and her practised eye fell upon that telltale rush of water. For one moment her petrified gaze fixed itself there. Then her head dropped upon her breast, and she said—

"Oh, de good Lord God have mercy on po' sinful me—*I's sole down de river!*"

CHAPTER 17

Even popularity can be overdone. In Rome, along at first, you are full of regrets that Michelangelo died; but by and by you only regret that you didn't see him do it.

—*Pudd'nhead Wilson's Calendar*

July 4. Statistics show that we lose more fools on this day than in all the other days of the year put together. This proves, by the number left in stock, that one Fourth of July per year is now inadequate, the country has grown so.

—*Pudd'nhead Wilson's Calendar*

The summer weeks dragged by, and then the political campaign opened—opened in pretty warm fashion, and waxed hotter and hotter daily. The twins threw themselves into it with their whole heart, for their self-love was engaged. Their popularity, so general at first, had suffered afterward; mainly because they had been *too* popular, and so a natural reaction had followed. Besides, it had been diligently whispered around that it was curious—indeed, *very* curious—that that wonderful knife of theirs did not turn up—*if* it was so valuable, or *if* it had ever existed. And with the whisperings went chucklings and nudgings and winks, and such things have an effect. The twins considered that success in the election would reinstate them, and that defeat would work them irreparable damage. Therefore they worked hard, but not harder than Judge Driscoll and Tom worked against them in the closing days of the canvass. Tom's conduct had remained so letter-perfect during two whole months, now, that his uncle not only trusted him with money with which to persuade voters, but trusted him to go and get it himself out of the safe in the private sitting-room.

The closing speech of the campaign was made by Judge Driscoll, and he made it against both of the foreigners. It was disastrously effective. He poured out rivers of ridicule upon them, and forced the big mass-meeting to laugh and applaud. He scoffed at them as adventurers, mountebanks, side-show riff-raff, dime museum freaks; he assailed their showy titles with measureless derision; he said they were back-alley barbers disguised as nobilities, peanut pedlers masquerading as gentlemen, organ-grinders bereft of their brother monkey. At last he stopped and stood still. He waited until the place had become absolutely silent and expectant, then he delivered his deadliest shot; delivered it with ice-cold seriousness and deliberation, with a significant emphasis upon the closing words: he said he believed that the reward offered for the lost knife was humbug and buncombe, and that its owner would know where to find it whenever he should have occasion *to assassinate somebody.*

Then he stepped from the stand, leaving a startled and impressive hush behind him instead of the customary explosion of cheers and party cries.

The strange remark flew far and wide over the town and made an extraordinary sensation. Everybody was asking, "What could he mean by that?" And everybody went on asking that question, but in vain; for the Judge only said he knew what he was talking about, and stopped there; Tom said he hadn't any idea what his uncle meant, and Wilson, whenever he was asked what he thought it meant, parried the question by asking the questioner what *he* thought it meant.

Wilson was elected, the twins were defeated—crushed, in fact, and left forlorn and substantially friendless. Tom went back to St. Louis happy.

Dawson's Landing had a week of repose, now, and it needed it. But it was in an expectant state, for the air was full of rumors of a new duel. Judge Driscoll's election labors had prostrated him, but it was said that as soon as he was well enough to entertain a challenge he would get one from Count Luigi.

The brothers withdrew entirely from society, and nursed their humiliation in privacy. They avoided the people, and went out for exercise only late at night, when the streets were deserted.

CHAPTER 18

Gratitude and treachery are merely the two extremities of the same procession. You have seen all of it that is worth staying for when the band and the gaudy officials have gone by.

–Pudd'nhead Wilson's Calendar

Thanksgiving Day. Let all give humble, hearty, and sincere thanks, now, but the turkeys. In the island of Fiji they do not use turkeys; they use plumbers. It does not become you and me to sneer at Fiji.

–Pudd'nhead Wilson's Calendar

The Friday after the election was a rainy one in St. Louis. It rained all day long, and rained hard, apparently trying its best to wash that soot-blackened town white, but of course not succeeding. Toward midnight Tom Driscoll arrived at his lodgings from the theatre in the heavy downpour, and closed his umbrella and let himself in; but when he would have shut the door, he found that there was another person entering—doubtless another lodger; this person closed the door and tramped up-stairs behind Tom. Tom found his door in the dark, and entered it and turned up the gas. When he faced about, lightly whistling, he saw the back of a man. The man was closing and locking his door for him. His whistle faded out and he felt uneasy. The man turned around, a wreck of shabby old clothes, sodden with rain and all a-drip, and showed a black face under an old slouch hat. Tom was frightened. He tried to order the man out, but the words refused to come, and the other man got the start. He said, in a low voice—

"Keep still—I's yo' mother!"

Tom sunk in a heap on a chair, and gasped out—

"It was mean of me, and base—I know it; but I meant it for the best, I did indeed—I can swear it."

Roxana stood awhile looking mutely down on him while he writhed in shame and went on incoherently babbling self-accusations mixed with pitiful attempts at explanation and palliation of his crime; then she seated herself and took off her hat, and her unkempt masses of long brown hair tumbled down about her shoulders.

"It ain't no fault o' yo'n dat dat ain't gray," she said sadly, noticing the hair.

"I know it, I know it! I'm a scoundrel. But I swear I meant it for the best. It was a mistake, of course, but I thought it was for the best, I truly did."

Roxy began to cry softly, and presently words began to find their way out between her sobs. They were uttered lamentingly, rather than angrily—

"Sell a pusson down de river—*down de river!*—for de bes'! I wouldn't treat a dog so! I is all broke down en wore out, now, en so I reckon it ain't in me to storm aroun' no mo', like I used to when I 'uz trompled on en 'bused. I don't know—but maybe it's so. Leastways, I's suffered so much dat mournin' seem to come mo' handy to me now den stormin'."

These words should have touched Tom Driscoll, but if they did, that effect was obliterated by a stronger one—one which removed the heavy weight of fear which lay upon him, and gave his crushed spirit a most grateful rebound, and filled all his small soul with a deep sense of relief. But he kept prudently still, and ventured no comment. There was a voiceless interval of some duration, now, in which no sounds were heard but the beating of the rain upon the panes, the sighing and complaining of the winds, and now and then a muffled sob from Roxana. The sobs became more and more infrequent, and at last ceased. Then the refugee began to talk again:

"Shet down dat light a little. More. More yit. A pusson dat is hunted don't like de light. Dah—dat'll do. I kin see whah you is, en dat's enough. I's gwine to tell you de tale, en cut it jes as short as I kin, en den I'll tell you what you's got to do. Dat man dat bought me ain't a bad man; he's good enough, as planters goes; en if he could 'a' had his way I'd 'a' be'n a house servant in his fambly en be'n comfortable: but his wife she was a Yank, en not right down good lookin', en she riz up agin me straight off; so den dey sent me out to de quarter 'mongst de common fiel' han's. Dat woman warn't satisfied even wid dat, but she worked up de overseer ag'in' me, she 'uz dat jealous en hateful; so de overseer he had me out befo' day in de mawnin's en worked me de whole long day as long as dey'uz any light to see by; en many's de lashin's I got 'ca'se I couldn't come up to de work o' de stronges'. Dat overseer wuz a Yank, too, outen New Englan', en anybody down South kin tell you what dat mean. *Dey* knows how to work a nigger to death, en day knows how to whale 'em, too—whale 'em till dey backs is welted like a washboard. 'Long at fust my marster say de good word for me to de overseer, but dat 'uz bad for me; for de mistis she fine it out, en arter dat I jist ketched it at every turn—dey warn't no mercy for me no mo'."

Tom's heart was fired—with fury against the planter's wife; and he said to himself, "But for that meddlesome fool, everything would have gone all right." He added a deep and bitter curse against her.

The expression of this sentiment was fiercely written in his face, and stood thus revealed to Roxana by a white glare of lightning which turned the somber dusk of the room into dazzling day at that moment. She was pleased—pleased and grateful; for did not that expression show that her child was capable of grieving for his mother's wrongs and of feeling resentment toward her persecutors?—a thing which she had been doubting. But her flash of happiness was only a flash, and went out again and left her spirit dark; for she said to herself, "He sole me down de river—he can't feel for a body long: dis'll pass en go." Then she took up her tale again.

"'Bout ten days ago I 'uz sayin' to myself dat I couldn't las' many mo' weeks I 'uz so wore out wid de awful work en de lashin's, en so downhearted en misable. En I didn't care no mo', nuther—life warn't wuth noth'n' to me, if I got to go on like dat. Well, when a body is in a frame o' mine like dat, what do a body care what a body do? Dey was a little sickly nigger wench 'bout ten year ole dat 'uz good to me, en hadn't no mammy, po' thing, en I loved her en she loved me; en she come out whah I 'uz workin' en she had a roasted tater, en tried to slip it to me,—robbin' herself, you see, 'ca'se she knowed de overseer didn't gimme enough to eat,—en he ketched her at it, en give her a lick acrost de back wid his stick, which 'uz as thick as a broom-handle, en she drop' screamin' on de groun', en squirmin' en wallerin' aroun' in de dust like a spider dat's got crippled. I couldn't stan' it. All de hell-fire dat 'uz ever in my heart flame' up, en I snatch de stick outen his han' en laid him flat. He laid dah moanin' en cussin', en all out of his head, you know, en de niggers 'uz plumb sk'yerd to death. Dey gathered roun' him to he'p him, en I jumped on his hoss en took out for de river as tight as I could go. I knowed what dey would do wid me. Soon as he got well he would start in en work me to death if marster let him; en if dey didn't do dat, they'd sell me furder down de river, en dat's de same thing. So I 'lowed to drown myself en git out o' my troubles. It 'uz gitt'n' towards dark. I 'uz at de river in two minutes. Den I see a canoe, en I says dey ain't no use to drown myself tell I got to; so I ties de hoss in de edge o' de timber en shove out down de river, keepin' in under de shelter o' de bluff bank en prayin' for de dark to shet down quick. I had a pow'ful good start, 'ca'se de big house 'uz three mile back f'om de river en on'y de work-mules to ride dah on, en on'y niggers to ride 'em, en *day* warn't gwine to hurry—dey'd gimme all de chance dey could. Befo' a body could go to de house en back it would be long pas' dark, en dey couldn't track de hoss en fine out which way I went tell mawnin', en de niggers would tell 'em all de lies dey could 'bout it.

"Well, de dark come, en I went on a-spinnin' down de river. I paddled mo'n two hours, den I warn't worried no mo', so I quit paddlin, en floated down de current, considerin' what I 'uz gwine to do if I didn't have to drown myself. I made up some plans, en floated along, turnin' 'em over in my mine. Well, when it 'uz a little pas' midnight, as I reckoned, en I had come fifteen or twenty mile, I see de lights o' a steamboat layin' at de bank, whah dey warn't no town en no woodyard, en putty soon I ketched de shape o' de chimbly-tops ag'in' de stars, en de good gracious me, I 'most jumped out o' my skin for joy! It 'uz de *Gran' Mogul*—I 'uz chambermaid on her for eight seasons in de Cincinnati en Orleans trade. I slid 'long pas'—don't see nobody stirrin' nowhah—hear 'em a-hammerin' away in de engine-room, den I knowed what de matter was—some o' de machinery's broke. I got asho' below de boat and turn' de canoe loose, den I goes 'long up, en dey 'uz jes one plank out, en I step' 'board de boat. It 'uz pow'ful hot, deckhan's en roustabouts 'uz sprawled aroun' asleep on de fo'cas'l', de second mate, Jim Bangs, he sot dah on de bitts wid his head down, asleep—'ca'se dat's de way de second mate stan' de cap'n's watch!—en de ole watchman, Billy Hatch, he 'uz a-noddin' on de companionway; —en I knowed 'em all; 'en, lan', but dey did look good! I says to myself, I wished old marster'd come along *now* en try to take me—bless yo' heart, I's 'mong frien's, I is. So I tromped right along 'mongst 'em, en went up on de b'iler deck en 'way back aft to de ladies' cabin guard, en sot down dah in de same cheer dat I'd sot in 'mos' a hund'd million times, I reckon; en it 'uz jist home ag'in, I tell you!

"In 'bout an hour I heard de ready-bell jingle, en den de racket begin. Putty soon I hear de gong strike. 'Set her back on de outside,' I says to myself—'I reckon I knows dat music!' I hear de gong ag'in. 'Come ahead on de inside,' I says. Gong ag'in. 'Stop de outside.' Gong ag'in. 'Come ahead on de outside—now we's pinted for Sent Louis, en I's outer de woods en ain't got to drown myself at all.' I knowed de *Mogul* 'uz in de Sent Louis trade now, you see. It 'uz jes fair daylight when we passed our plantation, en I seed a gang o' niggers en white folks huntin' up en down de sho', en troublin' deyselves a good deal 'bout me; but I warn't troublin' myself none 'bout dem.

"'Bout dat time Sally Jackson, dat used to be my second chambermaid en 'uz head chambermaid now, she come out on de guard, en 'uz pow'ful glad to see me, en so 'uz all de officers; en I tole 'em I'd got kidnapped en sole down de river, en dey made me up twenty dollahs en give it to me, en Sally she rigged me out wid good clo'es, en when I got here I went straight to whah you used to wuz, en den I come to dis house, en dey say you's away but 'spected back every day; so I didn't dast to go down de river to Dawson's, 'ca'se I might miss you.

"Well, las' Monday I 'uz pass'n' by one o' dem places in Fourth street whah deh sticks up runaway-nigger bills, en he'ps to ketch 'em, en I seed my marster! I 'mos' flopped down on de groun', I felt so gone. He had his back to me, en 'uz talkin' to de man en givin' him some bills —nigger-bills, I reckon, en I 'se de nigger. He's offerin' a reward—dat's it. Ain't I right, don't you reckon?"

Tom had been gradually sinking into a state of ghastly terror, and he said to himself, now: "I'm lost, no matter what turn things take! This man has said to me that he thinks there was something suspicious about that sale. He said he had a letter from a passenger on the *Grand Mogul* saying that Roxy came here on that boat and that everybody on board knew all about the case; so he says that her coming here instead of flying to a free State looks bad for me, and that if I don't find her for him, and that pretty soon, he will make trouble for me. I never believed that story; I couldn't believe she would be so dead to all motherly instincts as to come here, knowing the risk she would run of getting me into irremediable trouble. And after all, here she is! And I stupidly swore I would help him find her, thinking it was a perfectly safe thing to promise. If I venture to deliver her up, she—she—but how can I help myself? I've got to do that or pay the money, and where's the money to come from? I—I—well, I should think that if he would swear to treat her kindly hereafter—and she says, herself, that he is a good man—and if he would swear to never allow her to be overworked, or ill fed, or——"

A flash of lightning exposed Tom's pallid face, drawn and rigid with these worrying thoughts. Roxana spoke up sharply now, and there was apprehension in her voice—

"Turn up dat light! I want to see yo' face better. Dah now—lemme look at you. Chambers, you's as white as yo' shirt! Has you seen dat man? Has he be'n to see you?"

"Ye-s."

"When?"

"Monday noon."

"Monday noon! Was he on my track?"

"He—well, he thought he was. That is, he hoped he was. This is the bill you saw." He took it out of his pocket.

"Read it to me!"

She was panting with excitement, and there was a dusky glow in her eyes that Tom could not translate with certainty, but there seemed to be something threatening about it. The handbill had the usual rude woodcut of a turbaned negro woman running, with the customary bundle on a stick over her shoulder, and the heading in bold type, "$100 REWARD." Tom read the bill aloud—at least the part that described Roxana and named the master and his St. Louis address and the address of the Fourth-street agency; but he left out the item that applicants for the reward might also apply to Mr. Thomas Driscoll.

"Gimme de bill!"

Tom had folded it and was putting it in his pocket. He felt a chilly streak creeping down his back, but said as carelessly as he could—

"The bill? Why, it isn't any use to you; you can't read it. What do you want with it?"

"Gimme de bill!" Tom gave it to her, but with a reluctance which he could not entirely disguise. "Did you read it *all* to me?"

"Certainly I did."

"Hole up yo' han' en swah to it."

Tom did it. Roxana put the bill carefully away in her pocket, with her eyes fixed upon Tom's face all the while; then she said—

"Yo's lyin'!"

"What would I want to lie about it for?"

"I don't know—but you is. Dat's my opinion, anyways. But nemmine 'bout dat. When I seed dat man I 'uz dat sk'yerd dat I could sca'cely wobble home. Den I give a nigger man a dollar for dese clo'es, en I ain't be'n in a house sence, night ner day, till now. I blacked my face en laid hid in de cellar of a ole house dat's burnt down, daytimes, en robbed de sugar hogsheads en grain sacks on de wharf, nights, to git somethin' to eat, en never dast to try to buy noth'n', en I's 'mos' starved. En I never dast to come near dis place till dis rainy night, when dey ain't no people roun' sca'cely. But to-night I be'n a-stannin' in de dark alley ever sence night come, waitin' for you to go by. En here I is."

She fell to thinking. Presently she said—

"You seed dat man at noon, las' Monday?"

"Yes."

"I seed him de middle o' dat arternoon. He hunted you up, didn't he?"

"Yes."

"Did he give you de bill dat time?"

"No, he hadn't got it printed yet."

Roxana darted a suspicious glance at him.

"Did you he'p him fix up de bill?"

Tom cursed himself for making that stupid blunder, and tried to rectify it by saying he remembered, now, that it *was* at noon Monday that the man gave him the bill. Roxana said—

"You's lyin' ag'in, sho." Then she straightened up and raised her finger:

"Now den! I's gwine to ask you a question, en I wants to know how you's gwine to git aroun' it. You knowed he 'uz arter me; en if you run off, 'stid o' stayin' here to he'p him, he'd know dey 'uz somethin' wrong 'bout dis business, en den he would inquire 'bout you, en dat would take him to yo' uncle, en yo' uncle would read de bill en see dat you be'n sellin' a free nigger down de river, en you know *him,* I reckon! He'd t'ar up de will en kick you outen de house. Now, den, you answer me dis question: hain't you tole dat man dat I would be sho' to come here, en den you would fix it so he could set a trap en ketch me?"

Tom recognized that neither lies nor arguments could help him any longer—he was in a vise, with the screw turned on, and out of it there was no budging. His face began to take on an ugly look, and presently he said, with a snarl—

"Well, what could I do? You see, yourself, that I was in his grip and couldn't get out."

Roxy scorched him with a scornful gaze awhile, then she said—

"What could you do? You could be Judas to yo' own mother to save yo' wuthless hide! Would anybody b'lieve it? No—a dog couldn't! You is de low-downest orneriest hound dat was ever pup'd into dis worl'—en I's 'sponsible for it!"—and she spat on him.

He made no effort to resent this. Roxy reflected a moment, then she said—

"Now I'll tell you what you's gwine to do. You's gwine to give dat man de money dat you's got laid up, en make him wait till you kin go to de Jedge en git de res' en buy me free agin."

"Thunder! what are you thinking of? Go and ask him for three hundred dollars and odd? What would I tell him I want with it, pray?

Roxy's answer was delivered in a serene and level voice—

"You'll tell him you's sole me to pay yo' gamblin' debts en dat you lied to me en was a villain, en dat I 'quires you to git dat money en buy me back ag'in."

"Why, you've gone stark mad! He would tear the will to shreds in a minute—don't you know that?"

"Yes, I does."

"Then you don't believe I'm idiot enough to go to him, do you?"

"I don't b'lieve nothin' 'bout it—I *knows* you's a-goin'. I knows it 'ca'se you knows dat if you don't raise dat money I'll go to him myself, en den he'll sell *you* down de river, en you kin see how you like it!"

Tom rose, trembling and excited, and there was an evil light in his eye. He strode to the door and said he must get out of this suffocating place for a moment and clear his brain in the fresh air so that he could determine what to do. The door wouldn't open. Roxy smiled grimly, and said—

"I's got de key, honey—set down. You needn't cle'r up yo' brain none to fine out what you gwine to do—*I* knows what you's gwine to do." Tom sat down and began to pass his hands through his hair with a helpless and desperate air. Roxy said, "Is dat man in dis house?"

Tom glanced up with a surprised expression, and asked—

"What gave you such an idea?"

"You done it. Gwine out to cle'r yo' brain! In de fust place you ain't got none to cle'r, en in de second place yo' ornery eye tole on you. You's de low-downest hound dat ever—but I done tole you dat befo'. Now den, dis is Friday. You kin fix it up wid dat man, en tell him you's gwine away to git de res' o' de money, en dat you'll be back wid it nex' Tuesday, or maybe Wednesday. You understan'?"

Tom answered sullenly—

"Yes."

"En when you gits de new bill o' sale dat sells me to my own self, take en send it in de mail to Mr. Pudd'nhead Wilson, en write on de back dat he's to keep it tell I come. You understan'?"

"Yes."

"Dat's all den. Take yo' umbreller, en put on yo' hat."

"Why?"

"Beca'se you's gwine to see me home to de wharf. You see dis knife? I's toted it aroun' sence de day I seed dat man en bought dese clo'es en it. If he ketch me, I's gwine to kill myself wid it. Now start along, en go sof', en lead de way; en if you gives a sign in dis house, or if any-body comes up to you in de street, I's gwine to jam it right into you. Chambers, does you b'lieve me when I says dat?"

"It's no use to bother me with that question. I know your word's good."

"Yes, it's diff'rent from yo'n! Shet de light out en move along—here's de key."

They were not followed. Tom trembled every time a late straggler brushed by them on the street, and half expected to feel the cold steel in his back. Roxy was right at his heels and always in reach. After tramping a mile they reached a wide vacancy on the deserted wharves, and in this dark and rainy desert they parted.

As Tom trudged home his mind was full of dreary thoughts and wild plans; but at last he said to himself, wearily—

"There is but the one way out. I must follow her plan. But with a variation—I will not ask for the money and ruin myself; I will *rob* the old skinflint."

CHAPTER 19

Few things are harder to put up with than the annoyance of a good example.

—*Pudd'nhead Wilson's Calendar*

It were not best that we should all think alike; it is difference of opinion that makes horse-races.

—*Pudd'nhead Wilson's Calendar*

Dawson's Landing was comfortably finishing its season of dull repose and waiting patiently for the duel. Count Luigi was waiting, too; but not patiently, rumor said. Sunday came, and Luigi insisted on having his challenge conveyed. Wilson carried it. Judge Driscoll declined to fight with an assassin—"that is," he added significantly, "in the field of honor."

Elsewhere, of course, he would be ready. Wilson tried to convince him that if he had been present himself when Angelo told about the homicide committed by Luigi, he would not have considered the act discreditable to Luigi; but the obstinate old man was not to be moved.

Wilson went back to his principal and reported the failure of his mission. Luigi was incensed, and asked how it could be that the old gentleman, who was by no means dull-witted, held his trifling nephew's evidence and inferences to be of more value than Wilson's. But Wilson laughed, and said—

"That is quite simple; that is easily explicable. I am not his doll—his baby—his infatuation: his nephew is. The Judge and his late wife never had any children. The Judge and his wife were past middle age when this treasure fell into their lap. One must make allowances for a parental instinct that has been starving for twenty-five or thirty years. It is famished, it is crazed with hunger by that time, and will be entirely satisfied with anything that comes handy; its taste is atrophied, it can't tell mud-cat from shad. A devil born to a young couple is measurably recognizable by them as a devil before long, but a devil adopted by an old couple is an angel to them, and remains so, through thick and thin. Tom is this old man's angel; he is infatuated with him. Tom can persuade him into things which other people can't—not all things; I don't mean that, but a good many—particularly one class of things: the things that create or abolish personal partialities or prejudices in the old man's mind. The old man liked both of you. Tom conceived a hatred for you. That was enough; it turned the old man around at once. The oldest and strongest friendship must go to the ground when one of these late-adopted darlings throws a brick at it."

"It's a curious philosophy," said Luigi.

"It ain't a philosophy at all—it's a fact. And there is something pathetic and beautiful about it, too. I think there is nothing more pathetic than to see one of these poor old childless couples taking a menagerie of yelping little worthless dogs to their hearts; and then adding some cursing and squawking parrots and a jackass-voiced macaw; and next a couple of hundred screeching song-birds, and presently some fetid guinea-pigs and rabbits, and a howling colony of cats. It is all a groping and ignorant effort to construct out of base metal and brass filings, so to speak, something to take the place of that golden treasure denied them by Nature, a child. But this is a digression. The unwritten law of this region requires you to kill Judge Driscoll on sight, and he and the community will expect that attention at your hands—though of course your own death by his bullet will answer every purpose. Look out for him! Are you heeled—that is, fixed?"

"Yes; he shall have his opportunity. If he attacks me I will respond."

As Wilson was leaving, he said—

"The Judge is still a little used up by his campaign work, and will not get out for a day or so; but when he does get out, you want to be on the alert."

About eleven at night the twins went out for exercise, and started on a long stroll in the veiled moonlight.

Tom Driscoll had landed at Hackett's Store, two miles below Dawson's, just about half an hour earlier, the only passenger for that lonely spot, and had walked up the shore road and entered Judge

Driscoll's house without having encountered any one either on the road or under the roof.

He pulled down his window-blinds and lighted his candle. He laid off his coat and hat and began his preparations. He unlocked his trunk and got his suit of girl's clothes out from under the male attire in it, and laid it by. Then he blacked his face with burnt cork and put the cork in his pocket. His plan was, to slip down to his uncle's private sitting-room below, pass into the bedroom, steal the safe-key from the old gentleman's clothes, and then go back and rob the safe. He took up his candle to start. His courage and confidence were high, up to this point, but both began to waver a little, now. Suppose he should make a noise, by some accident, and get caught—say, in the act of opening the safe? Perhaps it would be well to go armed. He took the Indian knife from its hiding-place, and felt a pleasant return of his wandering courage. He slipped stealthily down the narrow stair, his hair rising and his pulses halting at the slightest creak. When he was half-way down, he was disturbed to perceive that the landing below was touched by a faint glow of light. What could that mean? Was his uncle still up? No, that was not likely; he must have left his night-taper there when he went to bed. Tom crept on down, pausing at every step to listen. He found the door standing open, and glanced in. What he saw pleased him beyond measure. His uncle was asleep on the sofa; on a small table at the head of the sofa a lamp was burning low, and by it stood the old man's small tin cash-box, closed. Near the box was a pile of bank-notes and a piece of paper covered with figures in pencil. The safe-door was not open. Evidently the sleeper had wearied himself with work upon his finances, and was taking a rest.

Tom set his candle on the stairs, and began to make his way toward the pile of notes, stooping low as he went. When he was passing his uncle, the old man stirred in his sleep, and Tom stopped instantly—stopped, and softly drew the knife from its sheath, with his heart thumping, and his eyes fastened upon his benefactor's face. After a moment or two he ventured forward again—one step—reached for his prize and seized it, dropping the knife-sheath. Then he felt the old man's strong grip upon him, and a wild cry of "Help! help!" rang in his ear. Without hesitation he drove the knife home—and was free. Some of the notes escaped from his left hand and fell in the blood on the floor. He dropped the knife and snatched them up and started to fly; transferred them to his left hand, and seized the knife again, in his fright and confusion, but remembered himself and flung it from him, as being a dangerous witness to carry away with him.

He jumped for the stair-foot, and closed the door behind him; and as he snatched his candle and fled upward, the stillness of the night was broken by the sound of urgent foot-steps approaching the house. In another moment he was in his room and the twins were standing aghast over the body of the murdered man!

Tom put on his coat, buttoned his hat under it, threw on his suit of girl's clothes, dropped the veil, blew out his light, locked the room door by which he had just entered, taking the key, passed through his other door into the back hall, locked that door and kept the key, then worked his way along in the dark and descended the back stairs. He was not expecting to meet anybody, for all interest was centered in the other part of the house, now; his calculation proved correct. By the time he was passing through the backyard, Mrs. Pratt, her servants, and a dozen half-dressed neighbors had joined the twins and the dead, and accessions were still arriving at the front door.

As Tom, quaking as with a palsy, passed out at the gate, three women came flying from the house on the opposite side of the lane. They rushed by him and in at the gate, asking him what the trouble was there, but not waiting for an answer. Tom said to himself, "Those old maids waited to dress—they did the same thing the night Stevens's house burned down next door." In a few minutes he was in the haunted house. He lighted a candle and took off his girl-clothes. There was blood on him all down his left side, and his right hand was red with the stains of the blood-soaked notes which he had crushed in it; but otherwise he was free from this sort of evidence. He cleansed his hand on the straw, and cleaned most of the smut from his face. Then he burned his male and female attire to ashes, scattered the ashes, and put on a disguise proper for a tramp. He blew out his light, went below, and was soon loafing down the river road with the intent to borrow and use one of Roxy's devices. He found a canoe and paddled off down-stream, setting the canoe adrift as dawn approached, and making his way by land to the next village, where he kept out of sight till a transient steamer came along, and then took deck passage for St. Louis. He was ill at ease until Dawson's Landing was behind him; then he said to himself, "All the detectives on earth couldn't trace me now; there's not a vestige of a clue left in the world; that homicide will take its place with the permanent mysteries, and people won't get done trying to guess out the secret of it for fifty years."

In St. Louis, next morning, he read this brief telegram in the papers —dated at Dawson's Landing:

Judge Driscoll, an old and respected citizen, was assassinated here about midnight by a profligate Italian nobleman or barber on account of a quarrel growing out of the recent election. The assassin will probably be lynched.

"One of the twins!" soliloquized Tom; "how lucky! It is the knife that has done him this grace. We never know when fortune is trying to favor us. I actually cursed Pudd'nhead Wilson in my heart for putting it out of my power to sell that knife. I take it back, now."

Tom was now rich and independent. He arranged with the planter, and mailed to Wilson the new bill of sale which sold Roxana to herself; then he telegraphed his Aunt Pratt:

Have seen the awful news in the papers and am almost prostrated with grief. Shall start by packet to-day. Try to bear up till I come.

When Wilson reached the house of mourning and had gathered such details as Mrs. Pratt and the rest of the crowd could tell him, he took command as mayor, and gave orders that nothing should be touched, but everything left as it was until Justice Robinson should arrive and take the proper measures as coroner. He cleared everybody out of the room but the twins and himself. The sheriff soon arrived and took the twins away to jail. Wilson told them to keep heart, and promised to do his best in their defense when the case should come to trial. Justice Robinson came presently, and with him Constable Blake. They examined the room thoroughly. They found the knife and the sheath. Wilson noticed that there were finger-prints on the knife-handle. That pleased him, for the twins had required the earliest comers to make a scrutiny of their hands and clothes, and neither these people nor Wilson himself had found any blood-stains upon them. Could there be a possibility that the twins had spoken the truth when they said they found the man dead when they ran into the house in answer to the cry for help? He thought of that mysterious girl at once. But this was not the sort of work for a girl to be engaged in. No matter; Tom Driscoll's room must be examined.

After the coroner's jury had viewed the body and its surroundings, Wilson suggested a search up-stairs, and he went along. The jury forced an entrance to Tom's room, but found nothing, of course.

The coroner's jury found that the homicide was committed by Luigi, and that Angelo was accessory to it.

The town was bitter against the unfortunates, and for the first few days after the murder they were in constant danger of being lynched. The grand jury presently indicted Luigi for murder in the first degree, and Angelo as accessory before the fact. The twins were transferred from the city jail to the county prison to await trial.

Wilson examined the finger-marks on the knife-handle and said to himself, "Neither of the twins made those marks." Then manifestly there was another person concerned, either in his own interest or as hired assassin.

But who could it be? That, he must try to find out. The safe was not open, the cash-box was closed, and had three thousand dollars in it. Then robbery was not the motive, and revenge was. Where had the murdered man an enemy except Luigi? There was but that one person in the world with a deep grudge against him.

The mysterious girl! The girl was a great trial to Wilson. If the motive had been robbery, the girl might answer; but there wasn't any girl that would want to take this old man's life for revenge. He had no quarrels with girls; he was a gentleman.

Wilson had perfect tracings of the finger-marks of the knife-handle; and among his glass-records he had a great array of the finger-prints of women and girls, collected during the last fifteen or eighteen years, but he scanned them in vain, they successfully withstood every test; among them were no duplicates of the prints on the knife.

The presence of the knife on the stage of the murder was a worrying circumstance for Wilson. A week previously he had as good as admitted to himself that he believed Luigi had possessed such a knife, and that he still possessed it notwithstanding his pretense that it had been stolen. And now here was the knife, and with it the twins. Half the town had said the twins were humbugging when they claimed that they had lost their knife, and now these people were joyful, and said, "I told you so!"

If their finger-prints had been on the handle—but it was useless to bother any further about that; the finger-prints on the handle were *not* theirs—that he knew perfectly.

Wilson refused to suspect Tom; for first, Tom couldn't murder anybody—he hadn't character enough; secondly, if he could murder a person he wouldn't select his doting benefactor and nearest relative; thirdly, self-interest was in the way; for while the uncle lived, Tom was sure of a free support and a chance to get the destroyed will revived again, but with the uncle gone, that chance was gone, too. It was true the will had really been revived, as was now discovered, but Tom could not have been aware of it, or he would have spoken of it, in his native talky, unsecretive way. Finally, Tom was in St. Louis when the murder was done, and got the news out of the morning journals, as was shown by his telegram to his aunt. These speculations were unemphasized sensations rather than articulated thoughts, for Wilson would have laughed at the idea of seriously connecting Tom with the murder.

Wilson regarded the case of the twins as desperate—in fact, about hopeless. For he argued that if a confederate was not found, an enlightened Missouri jury would hang them, sure; if a confederate was found, that would not improve the matter, but simply furnish one more person for the sheriff to hang. Nothing could save the twins but the discovery of a person who did the murder on his sole personal account—an undertaking which had all the aspect of the impossible. Still, the person who made the finger-prints must be sought. The twins might have no case *with* him, but they certainly would have none without him.

So Wilson mooned around, thinking, thinking, guessing, guessing, day and night, and arriving nowhere. Whenever he ran across a girl or a woman he was not acquainted with, he got her finger-prints, on one pretext or another; and they always cost him a sigh when he got home, for they never tallied with the finger-marks on the knife-handle.

As to the mysterious girl, Tom swore he knew no such girl, and did not remember ever seeing a girl wearing a dress like the one described by Wilson. He admitted that he did not always lock his room, and that sometimes the servants forgot to lock the house doors; still, in his opinion the girl must have made but few visits or she would have been discovered. When Wilson tried to connect her with the stealing-raid, and thought she might have been the old woman's confederate, if not the very thief herself disguised as an old woman, Tom seemed struck, and also much interested, and said he would keep a sharp eye out for this person or persons, although he was afraid that she or they would be too smart to venture again into a town where everybody would now be on the watch for a good while to come.

Everybody was pitying Tom, he looked so quiet and sorrowful, and seemed to feel his great loss so deeply. He was playing a part, but it was not all a part. The picture of his alleged uncle, as he had last seen him, was before him in the dark pretty frequently, when he was awake, and called again in his dreams, when he was asleep. He wouldn't go into the room where the tragedy had happened. This charmed the doting Mrs. Pratt, who realized now, "as she had never done before," she said, what a sensitive and delicate nature her darling had, and how he adored his poor uncle.

CHAPTER 20

Even the clearest and most perfect circumstantial evidence is likely to be at fault, after all, and therefore ought to be received with great caution. Take the case of any pencil, sharpened by any woman: if you have witnesses, you will find she did it with a knife; but if you take simply the aspect of the pencil, you will say she did it with her teeth.

—Pudd'nhead Wilson's Calendar

The weeks dragged along, no friend visiting the jailed twins but their counsel and Aunt Patsy Cooper, and the day of trial came at last —the heaviest day in Wilson's life; for with all his tireless diligence he had discovered no sign or trace of the missing confederate. "Confederate" was the term he had long ago privately accepted for that person— not as being unquestionably the right term, but as being at least possibly the right one, though he was never able to understand why the twins did not vanish and escape, as the confederate had done, instead of remaining by the murdered man and getting caught there.

The court-house was crowded, of course, and would remain so to the finish, for not only in the town itself, but in the country for miles around, the trial was the one topic of conversation among the people. Mrs. Pratt, in deep mourning, and Tom with a weed on his hat, had seats near Pembroke Howard, the public prosecutor, and back of them sat a great array of friends of the family. The twins had but one friend present to keep their counsel in countenance, their poor old sorrowing landlady. She sat near Wilson, and looked her friendliest. In the "nigger corner" sat Chambers; also Roxy, with good clothes on, and her bill of sale in her pocket. It was her most precious possession, and she never parted with it, day or night. Tom had allowed her thirty-five dollars a month ever since he came into his property, and had said that he and she ought to be grateful to the twins for making them rich; but had roused such a temper in her by this speech that he did not repeat the argument afterward. She said the old Judge had treated her child a thousand times better than he deserved, and had never done her an unkindness in his life; so she hated these outlandish devils for killing him, and shouldn't ever sleep satisfied till she saw them hanged for it. She was here to watch the trial, now, and was going to lift up just one "hooraw" over it if the County Judge put her in jail a year for it. She gave her turbaned head a toss and said, "When dat verdic' comes, I's gwine to lif' dat *roof*, now, I *tell* you."

Pembroke Howard briefly sketched the State's case. He said he would show by a chain of circumstantial evidence without break or fault in it anywhere, that the principal prisoner at the bar committed the murder; that the motive was partly revenge, and partly a desire to take his own life out of jeopardy, and that his brother, by his presence, was a consenting accessory to the crime; a crime which was the basest known to the calendar of human misdeeds—assassination; that it was conceived by the blackest of hearts and consummated by the cowardliest of hands; a crime which had broken a loving sister's heart, blighted the happiness of a young nephew who was as dear as a son, brought inconsolable grief to many friends, and sorrow and loss to the whole community. The utmost penalty of the outraged law would be exacted, and upon the accused, now present at the bar, that penalty would unquestionably be executed. He would reserve further remark until his closing speech.

He was strongly moved, and so also was the whole house; Mrs. Pratt and several other women were weeping when he sat down, and many an eye that was full of hate was riveted upon the unhappy prisoners.

Witness after witness was called by the State, and questioned at length; but the cross-questioning was brief. Wilson knew they could furnish nothing valuable for his side. People were sorry for Pudd'nhead; his budding career would get hurt by this trial.

Several witnesses swore they heard Judge Driscoll say in his public speech that the twins would be able to find their lost knife again when they needed it to assassinate somebody with. This was not news, but now it was seen to have been sorrowfully prophetic, and a profound sensation quivered through the hushed court-room when those dismal words were repeated.

The public prosecutor rose and said that it was within his knowledge, through a conversation held with Judge Driscoll on the last day of his life, that counsel for the defense had brought him a challenge from the person charged at this bar with murder; that he had refused to fight with a confessed assassin—"that is, on the field of honor," but had added significantly, that he would be ready for him elsewhere. Presumably the person here charged with murder was warned that he must kill or be killed the first time he should meet Judge Driscoll. If counsel for the defense chose to let the statement stand so, he would not call him to the witness stand. Mr. Wilson said he would offer no denial. [Murmurs in the house—"It is getting worse and worse for Wilson's case."]

Mrs. Pratt testified that she heard no outcry, and did not know what woke her up, unless it was the sound of rapid footsteps approaching the front door. She jumped and ran out in the hall just as she was, and heard the footsteps flying up the front steps and then following behind her as she ran to the sitting-room. There she found the accused standing over her murdered brother. [Here she broke down and sobbed. Sensation in the court.] Resuming, she said the persons entering behind her were Mr. Rogers and Mr. Buckstone.

Cross-examined by Wilson, she said the twins proclaimed their innocence; declared that they had been taking a walk, and had hurried to the house in response to a cry for help which was so loud and strong that they had heard it at a considerable distance; that they begged her and the gentlemen just mentioned to examine their hands and clothes —which was done, and no blood stains found.

Confirmatory evidence followed from Rogers and Buckstone.

The finding of the knife was verified, the advertisement minutely describing it and offering a reward for it was put in evidence, and its exact correspondence with that description proved. Then followed a few minor details, and the case for the State was closed.

Wilson said that he had three witnesses, the Misses Clarkson, who would testify that they met a veiled young woman leaving Judge Driscoll's premises by the back gate a few minutes after the cries for help were heard, and that their evidence, taken with certain circumstantial evidence which he would call the court's attention to, would in his opinion convince the court that there was still one person concerned in this crime who had not yet been found, and also that a stay of proceedings ought to be granted, in justice to his clients, until that person should be discovered. As it was late, he would ask leave to defer the examination of his three witnesses until the next morning.

The crowd poured out of the place and went flocking away in excited groups and couples, talking the events of the session over with vivacity and consuming interest, and everybody seemed to have had a satisfactory and enjoyable day except the accused, their counsel, and their old-lady friend. There was no cheer among these, and no substantial hope.

In parting with the twins Aunt Patsy did attempt a good-night with a gay pretense of hope and cheer in it, but broke down without finishing.

Absolutely secure as Tom considered himself to be, the opening solemnities of the trial had nevertheless oppressed him with a vague uneasiness, his being a nature sensitive to even the smallest alarms; but from the moment that the poverty and weakness of Wilson's case lay exposed to the court, he was comfortable once more, even jubilant. He left the court-room sarcastically sorry for Wilson. "The Clarksons met an unknown woman in the back lane," he said to himself—"*that* is his case! I'll give him a century to find her in—a couple of them if he likes. A woman who doesn't exist any longer, and the clothes that gave her her sex burnt up and the ashes thrown away—oh, certainly, he'll find *her* easy enough!" This reflection set him to admiring, for the hundredth time, the shrewd ingenuities by which he had insured himself against detection—more, against even suspicion.

"Nearly always in cases like this there is some little detail or other overlooked, some wee little track or trace left behind, and detection follows; but here there's not even the faintest suggestion of a trace left. No more than a bird leaves when it flies through the air—yes, through the night, you may say. The man that can track a bird through the air in the dark and find that bird is the man to track me out and find the Judge's assassin—no other need apply. And that is the job that has been laid out for poor Pudd'nhead Wilson, of all people in the world! Lord, it will be pathetically funny to see him grubbing and groping after that woman that don't exist, and the right person sitting under his very nose all the time!" The more he thought the situation over, the more the humor of it struck him. Finally he said, "I'll never let him hear the last of that woman. Every time I catch him in company, to his dying day, I'll ask him in the guileless affectionate way that used to gravel him so when I inquired how his unborn law-business was coming along, 'Got on her track yet—hey, Pudd'nhead?' " He wanted to laugh, but that would not have answered; there were people about, and he was mourning for his uncle. He made up his mind that it would be good entertainment to look in on Wilson that night and watch him worry over his barren law-case and goad him with an exasperating word or two of sympathy and commiseration now and then.

Wilson wanted no supper, he had no appetite. He got out all the finger-prints of girls and women in his collection of records and pored gloomily over them an hour or more, trying to convince himself that that troublesome girl's marks were there somewhere and had been overlooked. But it was not so. He drew back his chair, clasped his hands over his head, and gave himself up to dull and arid musings.

Tom Driscoll dropped in, an hour after dark, and said with a pleasant laugh as he took a seat—

"Hello, we've gone back to the amusements of our days of neglect and obscurity for consolation, have we?" and he took up one of the glass strips and held it against the light to inspect it. "Come, cheer up, old man; there's no use in losing your grip and going back to this child's-play merely because this big sunspot is drifting across your shiny new disk. It'll pass, and you'll be all right again,"—and he laid the glass down. "Did you think you could win always?"

"Oh, no," said Wilson, with a sigh, "I didn't expect that, but I can't believe Luigi killed your uncle, and I feel very sorry for him. It makes me blue. And you would feel as I do, Tom, if you were not prejudiced against those young fellows."

"I don't know about that," and Tom's countenance darkened, for his memory reverted to his kicking; "I owe them no good will, considering the brunette one's treatment of me that night. Prejudice or no prejudice, Pudd'nhead, I don't like them, and when they get their deserts you're not going to find me sitting on the mourner's bench."

He took up another strip of glass, and exclaimed—

"Why, here's old Roxy's label! Are you going to ornament the royal palaces with nigger paw-marks, too? By the date here, I was seven months old when this was done, and she was nursing me and her little nigger cub. There's a line straight across her thumb-print. How comes that?" and Tom held out the piece of glass to Wilson.

"That is common," said the bored man, wearily. "Scar of a cut or a scratch, usually"—and he took the strip of glass indifferently, and raised it toward the lamp.

All the blood sunk suddenly out of his face; his hand quaked, and he gazed at the polished surface before him with the glassy stare of a corpse.

"Great Heavens, what's the matter with you, Wilson? Are you going to faint?"

Tom sprang for a glass of water and offered it, but Wilson shrank shuddering from him and said—

"No, no!—take it away!" His breast was rising and falling, and he moved his head about in a dull and wandering way, like a person who has been stunned. Presently he said, "I shall feel better when I get to bed; I have been overwrought to-day; yes, and over worked for many days."

"Then I'll leave you and let you to get to your rest. Good-night, old man." But as Tom went out he couldn't deny himself a small parting gibe: "Don't take it so hard; a body can't win every time; you'll hang somebody yet."

Wilson muttered to himself, "It is no lie to say I am sorry I have to begin with you, miserable dog though you are!"

He braced himself up with a glass of cold whisky, and went to work again. He did not compare the new finger-marks unintentionally left by Tom a few minutes before on Roxy's glass with the tracings of the marks left on the knife-handle, there being no need of that (for his trained eye), but busied himself with another matter, muttering from time to time, "Idiot that I was!—Nothing but a *girl* would do me—a man in girl's clothes never occurred to me." First, he hunted out the plate containing the finger-prints made by Tom when he was twelve years old, and laid it by itself; then he brought forth the marks made by Tom's baby fingers when he was a suckling of seven months, and placed these two plates with the one containing this subject's newly (and unconsciously) made record.

"Now the series is complete," he said with satisfaction, and sat down to inspect these things and enjoy them.

But his enjoyment was brief. He stared a considerable time at the three strips, and seemed stupefied with astonishment. At last he put them down and said, "I can't make it out at all—hang it, the baby's don't tally with the others!"

He walked the floor for half an hour puzzling over his enigma, then he hunted out two other glass plates.

He sat down and puzzled over these things a good while, but kept muttering, "It's no use; I can't understand it. They don't tally right, and yet I'll swear the names and dates are right, and so of course they *ought* to tally. I never labeled one of these things carelessly in my life. There is a most extraordinary mystery here."

He was tired out, now, and his brains were beginning to clog. He said he would sleep himself fresh, and then see what he could do with this riddle. He slept through a troubled and unrestful hour, then unconsciousness began to shred away, and presently he rose drowsily to a sitting posture. "Now what was that dream?" he said, trying to recall it; "what was that dream?—it seemed to unravel that puz——"

He landed in the middle of the floor at a bound, without finishing the sentence, and ran and turned up his light and seized his "records." He took a single swift glance at them and cried out—

"It's so! Heavens, what a revelation! And for twenty-three years no man has ever suspected it!"

CHAPTER 21

He is useless on top of the ground; he ought to be under it, inspiring the cabbages.

—*Pudd'nhead Wilson's Calendar*

April 1. This is the day upon which we are reminded of what we are on the other three hundred and sixty-four.

—*Pudd'nhead Wilson's Calendar*

Wilson put on enough clothes for business purposes and went to work under a high pressure of steam. He was awake all over. All sense of weariness had been swept away by the invigorating refreshment of the great and hopeful discovery which he had made. He made fine and accurate reproductions of a number of his "records," and then enlarged them on a scale of ten to one with his pantograph. He did these pantograph enlargements on sheets of white cardboard, and made each individual line of the bewildering maze of whorls or curves or loops which constituted the "pattern," of a "record" stand out bold and black by reinforcing it with ink. To the untrained eye the collection of delicate originals made by the human finger on the glass plates looked about alike; but when enlarged ten times they resembled the markings of a block of wood that has been sawed across the grain, and the dullest eye could detect at a glance, and at a distance of many feet, that no two of the patterns were alike. When Wilson had at last finished his tedious and difficult work, he arranged its results according to a plan in which a progressive order and sequence was a principal feature; then he added to the batch several pantograph enlargements which he had made from time to time in bygone years.

The night was spent and the day well advanced, now. By the time he had snatched a trifle of breakfast it was nine o'clock, and the court was ready to begin its sitting. He was in his place twelve minutes later with his "records."

Tom Driscoll caught a slight glimpse of the records, and nudged his nearest friend and said, with a wink, "Pudd'nhead's got a rare eye to business—thinks that as long as he can't win his case it's at least a noble good chance to advertise his palace-window decorations without any expense." Wilson was informed that his witnesses had been delayed, but would arrive presently; but he rose and said he should probably not have occasion to make use of their testimony. [An amused murmur ran through the room—"It's a clean backdown! he gives up without hitting a lick!"] Wilson continued—"I have other testimony—and better. [This compelled interest, and evoked murmurs of surprise that had a detectible ingredient of disappointment in them.] If I seem to be springing this evidence upon the court, I offer as my justification for this, that I did not discover its existence until late last night, and have been engaged in examining and classifying it ever since, until half an hour ago. I shall offer it presently; but first I wish to say a few preliminary words.

"May it please the Court, the claim given the front place, the claim most persistently urged, the claim most strenuously and I may even say aggressively and defiantly insisted upon by the prosecution, is this—that the person whose hand left the blood-stained finger-prints upon the handle of the Indian knife is the person who committed the murder." Wilson paused, during several moments, to give impressiveness to what he was about to say, and then added tranquilly, "*We grant that claim.*"

It was an electrical surprise. No one was prepared for such an admission. A buzz of astonishment rose on all sides, and people were heard to intimate that the overworked lawyer had lost his mind. Even the veteran judge, accustomed as he was to legal ambushes and masked batteries in criminal procedure, was not sure that his ears were not deceiving him, and asked counsel what it was he had said. Howard's impassive face betrayed no sign, but his attitude and bearing lost something of their careless confidence for a moment. Wilson resumed:

"We not only grant that claim, but we welcome it and strongly endorse it. Leaving that matter for the present, we will now proceed to consider other points in the case which we propose to establish by evidence, and shall include that one in the chain in its proper place."

He had made up his mind to try a few hardy guesses, in mapping out his theory of the origin and motive of the murder—guesses designed to fill up gaps in it—guesses which could help if they hit, and would probably do no harm if they didn't.

"To my mind, certain circumstances of the case before the court seem to suggest a motive for the homicide quite different from the one insisted on by the State. It is my conviction that the motive was not revenge, but robbery. It has been urged that the presence of the accused brothers in that fatal room, just after notification that one of them must take the life of Judge Driscoll or lose his own the moment the parties should meet, clearly signifies that the natural instinct of self-preservation moved my clients to go there secretly and save Count Luigi by destroying his adversary.

"Then why did they stay there, after the deed was done? Mrs. Pratt had time, although she did not hear the cry for help, but woke up some moments later, to run to that room—and there she found these men standing and making no effort to escape. If they were guilty, they ought to have been running out of the house at the same time that she was running to that room. If they had had such a strong instinct toward self-preservation as to move them to kill that unarmed man, what had become of it now, when it should have been more alert than ever? Would any of us have remained there? Let us not slander our intelligence to that degree.

"Much stress has been laid upon the fact that the accused offered a very large reward for the knife with which this murder was done; that no thief came forward to claim that extraordinary reward; that the latter fact was good circumstantial evidence that the claim that the knife had been stolen was a vanity and a fraud; that these details taken in connection with the memorable and apparently prophetic speech of the deceased concerning that knife, and the final discovery of that very knife in the fatal room where no living person was found present with the slaughtered man but the owner of the knife and his brother, form an indestructible chain of evidence which fixes the crime upon those unfortunate strangers.

"But I shall presently ask to be sworn, and shall testify that there was a large reward offered for the *thief*, also; that it was offered secretly and not advertised; that this fact was indiscreetly mentioned—or at least tacitly admitted—in what was supposed to be safe circumstances, but may *not* have been. The thief may have been present himself. [Tom Driscoll had been looking at the speaker, but dropped his eyes at this point.] In that case he would retain the knife in his possession, not daring to offer it for sale, or for pledge in a pawn-shop. [There was a nodding of heads among the audience by way of admission that this was not a bad stroke.] I shall prove to the satisfaction of the jury that there *was* a person in Judge Driscoll's room several minutes before the accused entered it. [This produced a strong sensation; the last drowsy-head in the court-room roused up, now, and made preparation to listen.] If it shall seem necessary, I will prove by the Misses Clarkson that they met a veiled person—ostensibly a woman—coming out of the back gate a few minutes after the cry for help was heard. This person was not a woman, but a man dressed in woman's clothes." Another sensation. Wilson had his eye on Tom when he hazarded this guess, to see what effect it would produce. He was satisfied with the result, and said to himself, "It was a success—he's hit!"

"The object of that person in that house was robbery, not murder. It is true that the safe was not open, but there was an ordinary tin cash-box on the table, with three thousand dollars in it. It is easily supposable that the thief was concealed in the house; that he knew of this box, and of its owner's habit of counting its contents and arranging his accounts at night—if he had that habit, which I do not assert, of course;—that he tried to take the box while its owner slept, but made a noise and was seized, and had to use the knife to save himself from capture; and that he fled without his booty because he heard help coming.

"I have now done with my theory, and will proceed to the evidences by which I propose to try to prove its soundness." Wilson took up several of his strips of glass. When the audience recognized these familiar mementoes of Pudd'nhead's old-time childish "puttering" and folly, the tense and funereal interest vanished out of their faces, and the house burst into volleys of relieving and refreshing laughter, and Tom chirked up and joined in the fun himself; but Wilson was apparently not disturbed. He arranged his records on the table before him, and said—

"I beg the indulgence of the court while I make a few remarks in explanation of some evidence which I am about to introduce, and which I shall presently ask to be allowed to verify under oath on the witness stand. Every human being carries with him from his cradle to his grave certain physical marks which do not change their character, and by which he can always be identified—and that without shade of doubt or question. These marks are his signature, his physiological autograph, so to speak, and this autograph cannot be counterfeited, nor can he disguise it or hide it away, nor can it become illegible by the wear and mutations of time. This signature is not his face—age can change that beyond recognition; it is not his hair, for that can fall out; it is not his height, for duplicates of that exist; it is not his form, for duplicates of that exist also, whereas this signature is each man's very own—there is no duplicate of it among the swarming populations of the globe! [The audience were interested once more.]

"This autograph consists of the delicate lines or corrugations with which Nature marks the insides of the hands and the soles of the feet. If you will look at the balls of your fingers,—you that have very sharp eyesight,—you will observe that these dainty curving lines lie close together, like those that indicate the borders of oceans in maps, and that they form various clearly defined patterns, such as arches, circles, long curves, whorls, etc., and that these patterns differ on the different fingers. [Every man in the room had his hand up to the light, now, and his head canted to one side, and was minutely scrutinizing the balls of his fingers; there were whispered ejaculations of "Why, it's so—I never noticed that before!"] The patterns on the right hand are not the same as those on the left. [Ejaculations of "Why, that's so, too!"] Taken finger for finger, your patterns differ from your neighbor's. [Comparisons were made all over the house—even the judge and jury were absorbed in this curious work.] The patterns of a twin's right hand are not the same as those on his left. One twin's patterns are never the same as his fellow-twin's patterns—the jury will find that the patterns upon the finger-balls of the accused follow this rule. [An examination of the twins' hands was begun at once.] You have often heard of twins who were so exactly alike that when dressed alike their own parents could not tell them apart. Yet there was never a twin born into this world that did not carry from birth to death a sure identifier in this mysterious and marvelous natal autograph. That once known to you, his fellow-twin could never personate him and deceive you."

Wilson stopped and stood silent. Inattention dies a quick and sure death when a speaker does that. The stillness gives warning that something is coming. All palms and finger-balls went down, now, all slouching forms straightened, all heads came up, all eyes were fastened upon Wilson's face. He waited yet one, two, three moments, to let his pause complete and perfect its spell upon the house; then, when through the profound hush he could hear the ticking of the clock on the wall, he put out his hand and took the Indian knife by the blade and held it aloft where all could see the sinister spots upon its ivory handle; then he said in a level and passionless voice—

"Upon this haft stands the assassin's natal autograph, written in the blood of that helpless and unoffending old man who loved you and whom you all loved. There is but one man in the whole earth whose hand can duplicate that crimson sign,"—he paused and raised his eyes to the pendulum swinging back and forth,—"and please God we will produce that man in this room before the clock strikes noon!"

Stunned, distraught, unconscious of its own movement, the house half rose, as if expecting to see the murderer appear at the door, and a breeze of muttered ejaculations swept the place. "Order in the court! —sit down!" This from the sheriff. He was obeyed, and quiet reigned again. Wilson stole a glance at Tom, and said to himself, "He is flying signals of distress, now; even people who despise him are pitying him; they think this is a hard ordeal for a young fellow who has lost his benefactor by so cruel a stroke—and they are right." He resumed his speech:

"For more than twenty years I have amused my compulsory leisure with collecting these curious physical signatures in this town. At my house I have hundreds upon hundreds of them. Each and every one is labelled with name and date; not labelled the next day or even the next hour, but in the very minute that the impression was taken. When I go upon the witness stand I will repeat under oath the things which I am now saying. I have the finger-prints of the court, the sheriff, and every member of the jury. There is hardly a person in this room, white or black, whose natal signature I cannot produce, and not one of them can so disguise himself that I cannot pick him out from a multitude of his fellow-creatures and unerringly identify him by his hands. And if he and I should live to be a hundred I could still do it. [The interest of the audience was steadily deepening, now.]

"I have studied some of these signatures so much that I know them as well as the bank cashier knows the autograph of his oldest customer. While I turn my back now, I beg that several persons will be so good as to pass their fingers through their hair, and then press them upon one of the panes of the window near the jury, and that among them the accused may set *their* finger-marks. Also, I beg that these experimenters, or others, will set their finger-marks upon another pane, and add again the marks of the accused, but not placing them in the same order or relation to the other signatures as before—for, by one chance in a million, a person might happen upon the right marks by pure guess-work *once*, therefore I wish to be tested twice."

He turned his back, and the two panes were quickly covered with delicately-lined oval spots, but visible only to such persons as could get a dark background for them—the foliage of a tree, outside, for instance. Then, upon call, Wilson went to the window, made his examination, and said—

"This is Count Luigi's right hand; this one, three signatures below, is his left. Here is Count Angelo's right; down here is his left. Now for the other pane: here and here are Count Luigi's, here and here are his brother's." He faced about. "Am I right?"

A deafening explosion of applause was the answer. The Bench said—

"This certainly approaches the miraculous!"

Wilson turned to the window again and remarked, pointing with his finger—

"This is the signature of Mr. Justice Robinson. [Applause.] This, of Constable Blake. [Applause.] This, of John Mason, juryman. [Applause.] This, of the sheriff. [Applause.] I cannot name the others, but I have them all at home, named and dated, and could identify them all by my finger-print records."

He moved to his place through a storm of applause—which the sheriff stopped, and also made the people sit down, for they were all standing and struggling to see, of course. Court, jury, sheriff, and everybody had been too absorbed in observing Wilson's performance to attend to the audience earlier.

"Now, then," said Wilson, "I have here the natal autographs of two children—thrown up to ten times the natural size by the pantograph, so that any one who can see at all can tell the markings apart at a glance. We will call the children *A* and *B*. Here are *A's* finger-marks, taken at the age of five months. Here they are again, taken at seven months. [Tom started.] They are alike, you see. Here are *B's* at five months, and also at seven months. They, too, exactly copy each other, but the patterns are quite different from *A's*, you observe. I shall refer to these again presently, but we will turn them face down, now.

"Here, thrown up ten sizes, are the natal autographs of the two persons who are here before you accused of murdering Judge Driscoll. I made these pantograph copies last night, and will so swear when I go upon the witness stand. I ask the jury to compare them with the finger-marks of the accused upon the window panes, and tell the court if they are the same."

He passed a powerful magnifying-glass to the foreman.

One juryman after another took the cardboard and the glass and made the comparison. Then the foreman said to the judge—

"Your honor, we are all agreed that they are identical."

Wilson said to the foreman—

"Please turn that cardboard face down, and take this one, and compare it searchingly, by the magnifier, with the fatal signature upon the knife-handle, and report your finding to the court."

Again the jury made minute examinations, and again reported—

"We find them to be exactly identical, your honor."

Wilson turned toward the counsel for the prosecution, and there was a clearly recognizable note of warning in his voice when he said—

"May it please the court, the State has claimed, strenuously and persistently, that the blood-stained finger-prints upon that knife-handle were left there by the assassin of Judge Driscoll. You have heard us grant that claim, and welcome it." He turned to the jury: "Compare the finger-prints of the accused with the finger-prints left by the assassin —and report."

The comparison began. As it proceeded, all movement and all sound ceased, and the deep silence of an absorbed and waiting suspense settled upon the house; and when at last the words came—

"They do not even resemble," a thundercrash of applause followed and the house sprang to its feet, but was quickly repressed by official force and brought to order again. Tom was altering his position every few minutes, now, but none of his changes brought repose nor any small trifle of comfort. When the house's attention was become fixed once more, Wilson said gravely, indicating the twins with a gesture—

"These men are innocent—I have no further concern with them. [Another outbreak of applause began, but was promptly checked.] We will now proceed to find the guilty. [Tom's eyes were starting from their sockets—yes, it was a cruel day for the bereaved youth, everybody thought.] We will return to the infant autographs of *A* and *B*. I will ask the jury to take these large pantograph facsimiles of *A's* marked five months and seven months. Do they tally?"

The foreman responded—

"Perfectly."

"Now examine this pantograph, taken at eight months, and also marked *A*. Does it tally with the other two?"

The surprised response was—

"No—they differ widely!"

"You are quite right. Now take these two pantographs of *B's* autograph, marked five months and seven months. Do they tally with each other?"

"Yes—perfectly."

"Take this third pantograph marked *B*, eight months. Does it tally with *B's* other two?"

"By no means!"

"Do you know how to account for those strange discrepancies? I will tell you. For a purpose unknown to us, but probably a selfish one, somebody changed those children in the cradle."

This produced a vast sensation, naturally; Roxana was astonished at this admirable guess, but not disturbed by it. To guess the exchange was one thing, to guess who did it quite another. Pudd'nhead Wilson could do wonderful things, no doubt, but he couldn't do impossible ones. Safe? She was perfectly safe. She smiled privately.

"Between the ages of seven months and eight months those children were changed in the cradle"—he made one of his effect-collecting pauses, and added—"and the person who did it is in this house!"

Roxy's pulses stood still! The house was thrilled as with an electric shock, and the people half rose as if to seek a glimpse of the person who had made that exchange. Tom was growing limp; the life seemed oozing out of him. Wilson resumed:

"*A* was put into *B's* cradle in the nursery; *B* was transferred to the kitchen and became a negro and a slave, [Sensation—confusion of angry ejaculations]—but within a quarter of an hour he will stand before you white and free! [Burst of applause, checked by the officers.] From seven months onward until now, *A* has still been a usurper, and in my finger-record he bears *B's* name. Here is his pantograph at the age of twelve. Compare it with the assassin's signature upon the knife-handle. Do they tally?"

The foreman answered—

"*To the minutest detail!*"

Wilson said, solemnly—

"The murderer of your friend and mine—York Driscoll of the generous hand and the kindly spirit—sits in among you. Valet de Chambre, negro and slave,—falsely called Thomas à Becket Driscoll,—make upon the window the finger-prints that will hang you!"

Tom turned his ashen face imploringly toward the speaker, made some impotent movements with his white lips, then slid limp and lifeless to the floor.

Wilson broke the awed silence with the words—

"There is no need. He has confessed."

Roxy flung herself upon her knees, covered her face with her hands, and out through her sobs the words struggled—

"De Lord have mercy on me, po' misable sinner dat I is!"

The clock struck twelve.

The court rose; the new prisoner, hand-cuffed, was removed.

CONCLUSION

It is often the case that the man who can't tell a lie thinks he is the best judge of one.

—*Pudd'nhead Wilson's Calendar*

October 12, the Discovery. It was wonderful to find America, but it would have been more wonderful to miss it.

—*Pudd'nhead Wilson's Calendar*

The town sat up all night to discuss the amazing events of the day and swap guesses as to when Tom's trial would begin. Troop after troop of citizens came to serenade Wilson, and require a speech, and shout themselves hoarse over every sentence that fell from his lips—for all his sentences were golden, now, all were marvelous. His long fight against hard luck and prejudice was ended; he was a made man for good.

And as each of these roaring gangs of enthusiasts marched away, some remorseful member of it was quite sure to raise his voice and say—

"And this is the man the likes of us have called a pudd'nhead for more than twenty years. He has resigned from that position, friends."

"Yes, but it isn't vacant—we're elected."

The twins were heroes of romance, now, and with rehabilitated reputations. But they were weary of Western adventure, and straightway retired to Europe.

Roxy's heart was broken. The young fellow upon whom she had inflicted twenty-three years of slavery continued the false heir's pension of thirty-five dollars a month to her, but her hurts were too deep for money to heal; the spirit in her eye was quenched, her martial bearing departed with it, and the voice of her laughter ceased in the land. In her church and its affairs she found her only solace.

The real heir suddenly found himself rich and free, but in a most embarrassing situation. He could neither read nor write, and his speech was the basest dialect of the negro quarter. His gait, his attitudes, his gestures, his bearing, his laugh—all were vulgar and uncouth; his manners were the manners of a slave. Money and fine clothes could not mend these defects or cover them up; they only made them the more glaring and the more pathetic. The poor fellow could not endure the terrors of the white man's parlor, and felt at home and at peace nowhere but in the kitchen. The family pew was a misery to him, yet he could nevermore enter into the solacing refuge of the "nigger gallery"—that was closed to him for good and all. But we cannot follow his curious fate further—that it would be a long story.

The false heir made a full confession and was sentenced to imprisonment for life. But now a complication came up. The Percy Driscoll estate was in such a crippled shape when its owner died that it could pay only sixty per cent. of its great indebtedness, and was settled at that rate. But the creditors came forward, now, and complained that inasmuch as through an error for which *they* were in no way to blame the false heir was not inventoried at that time with the rest of the property, great wrong and loss had thereby been inflicted upon them.

They rightly claimed that "Tom" was lawfully their property and had been so for eight years; that they had already lost sufficiently in being deprived of his services during that long period, and ought not to be required to add anything to that loss; that if he had been delivered up to them in the first place, they would have sold him and he could not have murdered Judge Driscoll; therefore it was not he that had really committed the murder, the guilt lay with the erroneous inventory. Everybody saw that there was reason in this. Everybody granted that if "Tom" were white and free it would be unquestionably right to punish him—it would be no loss to anybody; but to shut up a valuable slave for life—that was quite another matter.

As soon as the Governor understood the case, he pardoned Tom at once, and the creditors sold him down the river.

FINIS

Those Extraordinary Twins

A man who is not born with the novel-writing gift has a troublesome time of it when he tries to build a novel. I know this from experience. He has no clear idea of his story; in fact he has no story. He merely has some people in his mind, and an incident or two, also a locality. He knows these people, he knows the selected locality, and he trusts that he can plunge those people into those incidents with interesting results. So he goes to work. To write a novel? No—that is a thought which comes later; in the beginning he is only proposing to tell a little tale; a very little tale; a six-page tale. But as it is a tale which he is not acquainted with, and can only find out what it is by listening as it goes along telling itself, it is more than apt to go on and on and on till it spreads itself into a book. I know about this, because it has happened to me so many times.

And I have noticed another thing: that as the short tale grows into the long tale, the original intention (or motif) is apt to get abolished and find itself superseded by a quite different one. It was so in the case of a magazine sketch which I once started to write—a funny and fantastic sketch about a prince and a pauper; it presently assumed a grave cast of its own accord, and in that new shape spread itself out into a book. Much the same thing happened with "Pudd'nhead Wilson." I had a sufficiently hard time with that tale, because it changed itself from a farce to a tragedy while I was going along with it,—a most embarrassing circumstance. But what was a great deal worse was, that it was not one story, but two stories tangled together; and they obstructed and interrupted each other at every turn and created no end of confusion and annoyance. I could not offer the book for publication, for I was afraid it would unseat the reader's reason, I did not know what was the matter with it, for I had not noticed, as yet, that it was two stories in one. It took me months to make that discovery. I carried the manuscript back and forth across the Atlantic two or three times, and read it and studied over it on shipboard; and at last I saw where the difficulty lay. I had no further trouble. I pulled one of the stories out by the roots, and left the other one—a kind of literary Cæsarean operation.

Would the reader care to know something about the story which I pulled out? He has been told many a time how the born-and-trained novelist works; won't he let me round and complete his knowledge by telling him how the jack-leg does it?

Originally the story was called "Those Extraordinary Twins." I meant to make it very short. I had seen a picture of a youthful Italian "freak"—or "freaks"—which was—or which were—on exhibition in our cities—a combination consisting of two heads and four arms joined to a single body and a single pair of legs—and I thought I would write an extravagantly fantastic little story with this freak of nature for hero—or heroes—a silly young Miss for heroine, and two old ladies and two boys for the minor parts. I lavishly elaborated these people and their doings, of course. But the tale kept spreading along and spreading along, and other people got to intruding themselves and taking up more and more room with their talk and their affairs. Among them came a stranger named Pudd'nhead Wilson, and a woman named Roxana; and presently the doings of these two pushed up into prominence a young fellow named Tom Driscoll, whose proper place was away in the obscure background. Before the book was half finished those three were taking things almost entirely into their own hands and working the whole tale as a private venture of their own—a tale which they had nothing at all to do with, by rights.

When the book was finished and I came to look around to see what had become of the team I had originally started out with—Aunt Patsy Cooper, Aunt Betsy Hale, the two boys, and Rowena the light-weight heroine—they were nowhere to be seen; they had disappeared from the story some time or other. I hunted about and found them—found them stranded, idle, forgotten, and permanently useless. It was very awkward. It was awkward all around, but more particularly in the case of Rowena, because there was a lovematch on, between her and one of the twins that constituted the freak, and I had worked it up to a blistering heat and thrown in a quite dramatic love-quarrel, wherein Rowena scathingly denounced her betrothed for getting drunk, and scoffed at his explanation of how it had happened, and wouldn't listen to it, and had driven him from her in the usual "forever" way; and now here she sat crying and broken-hearted; for she had found that he had spoken only the truth; that it was not he, but the other half of the freak that had drunk the liquor that made him drunk; that her half was a prohibitionist and had never drunk a drop in his life, and although tight as a brick three days in the week, was wholly innocent of blame; and indeed, when sober, was constantly doing all he could to reform his brother, the other half, who never got any satisfaction out of drinking, anyway, because liquor never affected him. Yes, here she was, stranded with that deep injustice of hers torturing her poor torn heart.

I didn't know what to do with her. I was as sorry for her as anybody could be, but the campaign was over, the book was finished, she was side-tracked, and there was no possible way of crowding her in, anywhere. I could not leave her there, of course; it would not do. After spreading her out so, and making such a to-do over her affairs, it would be absolutely necessary to account to the reader for her. I thought and thought and studied and studied; but I arrived at nothing. I finally saw plainly that there was really no way but one—I must simply give her the grand bounce. It grieved me to do it, for after associating with her so much I had come to kind of like her after a fashion, notwithstanding she was such an ass and said such stupid, irritating things and was so nauseatingly sentimental. Still it had to be done. So at the top of Chapter 17 I put a "Calendar" remark concerning July the Fourth, and began the chapter with this statistic:

"Rowena went out in the back yard after supper to see the fireworks and fell down the well and got drowned.

It seemed abrupt, but I thought maybe the reader wouldn't notice it, because I changed the subject right away to something else. Anyway it loosened up Rowena from where she was stuck and got her out of the way, and that was the main thing. It seemed a prompt good way of weeding out people that had got stalled, and a plenty good enough way for those others; so I hunted up the two boys and said "they went out back one night to stone the cat and fell down the well and got drowned." Next I searched around and found old Aunt Patsy Cooper and Aunt Betsy Hale where they were aground, and said "they went out back one night to visit the sick and fell down the well and got drowned." I was going to drown some of the others, but I gave up the idea, partly because I believed that if I kept that up it would arouse attention, and perhaps sympathy with those people, and partly because it was not a large well and would not hold any more anyway.

Still the story was unsatisfactory. Here was a set of new characters who were become inordinately prominent and who persisted in remaining so to the end; and back yonder was an older set who made a large noise and a great to-do for a little while and then suddenly played out utterly and fell down the well. There was a radical defect somewhere, and I must search it out and cure it.

The defect turned out to be the one already spoken of—two stories in one, a farce and a tragedy. So I pulled out the farce and left the tragedy. This left the original team in, but only as mere names, not as characters. Their prominence was wholly gone; they were not even worth drowning; so I removed that detail. Also I took those twins apart and made two separate men of them. They had no occasion to have foreign names now, but it was too much trouble to remove them all through, so I left them christened as they were and made no explanation.

THE SUPPRESSED FARCE

CHAPTER 1

The conglomerate twins were brought on the stage in Chapter 1 of the original extravaganza. Aunt Patsy Cooper has received their letter applying for board and lodging, and Rowena, her daughter, insane with joy, is begging for a hearing of it:

"Well, set down then, and be quiet a minute and don't fly around so; it fairly makes me tired to see you. It starts off so: 'HONORED MADAM—'"

"I like that, ma, don't you? It shows they're high-bred."

"Yes, I noticed that when I first read it. 'My brother and I have seen your advertisement, by chance, in a copy of your local journal——'"

"It's so beautiful and smooth, ma—don't you think so?"

"Yes, seems so to me—'and beg leave to take the room you offer. We are twenty-four years of age, and twins——'"

"Twins! How sweet! I do hope they are handsome, and I just know they are! Don't you hope they are, ma?"

"Land, I ain't particular. 'We are Italians by birth——'"

"It's so romantic! Just think—there's never been one in this town, and everybody will want to see them, and they're all *ours!* Think of that!"

"—'but have lived long in the various countries of Europe, and several years in the United States.'"

"Oh, just think what wonders they've seen, ma! Won't it be good to hear them talk?"

"I reckon so; yes, I reckon so. 'Our names are Luigi and Angelo Capello——'"

"Beautiful, perfectly beautiful! Not like Jones and Robinson and those horrible names."

"'You desire but one guest, but dear madam, if you will allow us to pay for two we will not discommode you. We will sleep together in the same bed. We have always been used to this, and prefer it.' And then he goes on to say they will be down Thursday."

"And this is Tuesday—I don't know how I'm ever going to wait, ma!

The time does drag along so, and I'm so dying to see them! Which of them do you reckon is the tallest, ma?"

"How do you s'pose I can tell, child? Mostly they are the same size—twins are."

"Well then, which do you reckon is the best looking?"

"Goodness knows—I don't."

"I think Angelo is; it's the prettiest name, anyway. Don't you think it's a sweet name, ma?"

"Yes, it's well enough. I'd like both of them better if I knew the way to pronounce them—the Eyetalian way, I mean. The Missouri way and the Eyetalian way is different I judge."

"Maybe—yes. It's Luigi that writes the letter. What do you reckon is the reason Angelo didn't write it?"

"Why, how can I tell? What's the difference who writes it, so long as it's done?"

"Oh, I hope it wasn't because he is sick! You don't think he is sick, do you, ma?"

"Sick your granny; what's to make him sick?"

"Oh, there's never any telling. These foreigners with that kind of names are so delicate, and of course that kind of names are not suited to our climate—you wouldn't expect it."

[And so-on and so-on, no end. The time drags along; Thursday comes; the boat arrives in a pouring storm toward midnight.]

At last there was a knock at the door and the anxious family jumped to open it. Two negro men entered, each carrying a trunk, and proceeded up-stairs toward the guest-room. Then followed a stupefying apparition—a double-headed human creature with four arms, one body, and a single pair of legs!

It—or they, as you please—bowed with elaborate foreign formality, but the Coopers could not respond immediately; they were paralyzed. At this moment there came from the rear of the group a fervent ejaculation—"My lan'!"—followed by a crash of crockery, and the slave-wench Nancy stood petrified and staring, with a tray of wrecked tea-things at her feet. The incident broke the spell, and brought the family to consciousness. The beautiful heads of the new-comer bowed again, and one of them said with easy grace and dignity:

"I crave the honor, madam and miss, to introduce to you my brother, Count Luigi Capello," (the other head bowed) "and myself—Count Angelo; and at the same time offer sincere apologies for the lateness of our coming, which was unavoidable," and both heads bowed again.

The poor old lady was in a whirl of amazement and confusion, but she managed to stammer out:

"I'm sure I'm glad to make your acquaintance, sir—I mean, gentlemen. As for the delay, it is nothing, don't mention it. This is my daughter Rowena, sir—gentlemen. Please step into the parlor and sit down and have a bite and sup; you are dreadful wet and must be uncomfortable—both of you, I mean."

But to the old lady's relief they courteously excused themselves, saying it would be wrong to keep the family out of their beds longer; then each head bowed in turn and uttered a friendly good-night, and the singular figure moved away in the wake of Rowena's small brothers, who bore candles, and disappeared up the stairs.

The widow tottered into the parlor and sank into a chair with a gasp, and Rowena followed, tongue-tied and dazed. The two sat silent in the throbbing summer heat unconscious of the million-voiced music of the mosquitoes, unconscious of the roaring gale, the lashing and thrashing of the rain along the windows and the roof, the white glare of the lightning, the tumultuous booming and bellowing of the thunder; conscious of nothing but that prodigy, that uncanny apparition that had come and gone so suddenly—that weird strange thing that was so soft-spoken and so gentle of manner and yet had shaken them up like an earthquake with the shock of its gruesome aspect. At last a cold little shudder quivered along down the widow's meager frame and she said in a weak voice:

"Ugh, it was awful—just the mere look of that phillipene!"

Rowena did not answer. Her faculties were still caked, she had not yet found her voice. Presently the widow said, a little resentfully:

"Always been *used* to sleeping together—in fact, *prefer* it. And I was thinking it was to accommodate me. I thought it was very good of them, whereas a person situated as that young man is——"

"Ma, you oughtn't to begin by getting up a prejudice against him. I'm sure he is good-hearted and means well. Both of his faces show it."

"I'm not so certain about that. The one on the left—I mean the one on *its* left—hasn't near as good a face, in my opinion, as its brother."

"That's Luigi."

"Yes, Luigi; anyway it's the dark-skinned one; the one that was west of his brother when they stood in the door. Up to all kinds of mischief and disobedience when he was a boy, I'll be bound. I lay his mother had trouble to lay her hand on him when she wanted him. But the one on the right is as good as gold, I can see that."

"That's Angelo."

"Yes, Angelo, I reckon, though I can't tell t'other from which by their names, yet awhile. But it's the right-hand one—the blonde one. He has such kind blue eyes, and curly copper hair and fresh complexion——"

"And such a noble face!—oh, it *is* a noble face, ma, just royal, you may say! And beautiful—deary me, how beautiful! But both are that; the dark one's as beautiful as a picture. There's no such wonderful faces and handsome heads in this town—none that even begin. And such hands—especially Angelo's—so shapely and——"

"Stuff, how could you tell which they belonged to?—they had gloves on."

"Why, didn't I see them take off their hats?"

"That don't signify. They might have taken off each other's hats. Nobody could tell. There was just a wormy squirming of arms in the air—seemed to be a couple of dozen of them, all writhing at once, and it just made me dizzy to see them go."

"Why, ma, I hadn't any difficulty. There's two arms on each shoulder——"

"There, now. One arm on each shoulder belongs to each of the creatures, don't it? For a person to have two arms on one shoulder wouldn't do him any good, would it? Of course not. Each has an arm on each shoulder. Now then, you tell me which of them belongs to which, if you can. *They* don't know, themselves—they just work whichever arm comes handy. Of course they do; especially if they are in a hurry and can't stop to think which belongs to which."

The mother seemed to have the rights of the argument, so the daughter abandoned the struggle. Presently the widow rose with a yawn and said:

"Poor thing, I hope it won't catch cold; it was powerful wet, just drenched, you may say. I hope it has left its boots outside, so they can be dried." Then she gave a little start, and looked perplexed. "Now I remember I heard one of them ask Joe to call him at half after seven —I think it was the one on the left—no, it was the one to the east of the other one—but I didn't hear the other one say anything. I wonder if he wants to be called too. Do you reckon it's too late to ask?"

"Why, ma, it's not necessary. Calling one is calling both. If one gets up, the other's *got* to."

"Sho, of course; I never thought of that. Well, come along, maybe we can get some sleep, but I don't know, I'm so shook up with what we've been through."

The stranger had made an impression on the boys, too. They had a word of talk as they were getting to bed. Henry, the gentle, the humane, said:

"I feel ever so sorry for it, don't you, Joe?"

But Joe was a boy of this world, active, enterprising, and had a theatrical side to him:

"Sorry? Why, how you talk! It can't stir a step without attracting attention. It's just grand!"

Henry said, reproachfully:

"Instead of pitying it, Joe, you talk as if——"

"Talk as if *what*? I know one thing mighty certain: if you can fix me so I can eat for two and only have to stub toes for one, I ain't going to fool away no such chance just for sentiment."

The twins were wet and tired, and they proceeded to undress without any preliminary remarks. The abundance of sleeves made the partnership-coat hard to get off, for it was like skinning a tarantula; but it came at last, after much tugging and perspiring. The mutual vest followed. Then the brothers stood up before the glass, and each took off his own cravat and collar. The collars were of the standing kind, and came high up under the ears, like the sides of a wheelbarrow, as required by the fashion of the day. The cravats were as broad as a bank bill, with fringed ends which stood far out to right and left like the wings of a dragon-fly, and this also was strictly in accordance with the fashion of the time. Each cravat, as to color, was in perfect taste, so far as its owner's complexion was concerned—a delicate pink, in the case of the blonde brother, a violent scarlet in the case of the brunette—but as a combination they broke all the laws of taste known to civilization. Nothing more fiendish and irreconcilable than those shrieking and blaspheming colors could have been contrived. The wet boots gave no end of trouble—to Luigi. When they were off at last, Angelo said, with bitterness:

"I wish you wouldn't wear such tight boots, they hurt my feet."

Luigi answered with indifference:

"My friend, when I am in command of our body, I choose my apparel according to my own convenience, as I have remarked more than several times already. When you are in command, I beg you will do as you please."

Angelo was hurt, and the tears came into his eyes. There was gentle reproach in his voice, but not anger, when he replied:

"Luigi, I often consult your wishes, but you never consult mine. When I am in command I treat you as a guest; I try to make you feel at home; when you are in command you treat me as an intruder, you make me feel unwelcome. It embarrasses me cruelly in company, for I can see that people notice it and comment on it."

"Oh, damn the people," responded the brother languidly, and with the air of one who is tired of the subject.

A slight shudder shook the frame of Angelo, but he said nothing and the conversation ceased. Each buttoned his own share of the nightshirt in silence; then Luigi, with Paine's "Age of Reason" in his hand, sat down in one chair and put his feet in another and lit his pipe, while Angelo took his "Whole Duty of Man," and both began to read. Angelo presently began to cough; his coughing increased and became mixed with gaspings for breath, and he was finally obliged to make an appeal to his brother's humanity:

"Luigi, if you would only smoke a little milder tobacco, I am sure I could learn not to mind it in time, but this is so strong, and the pipe is so rank that——"

"Angelo, I wouldn't be such a baby! I have learned to smoke in a week, and the trouble is already over with me; if you would try, you could learn too, and then you would stop spoiling my comfort with your everlasting complaints."

"Ah, brother, that is a strong word—everlasting—and isn't quite fair. I only complain when I suffocate; you know I don't complain when we are in the open air."

"Well, anyway, you could learn to smoke yourself."

"But my *principles*, Luigi, you forget my principles. You would not have me do a thing which I regard as a sin?"

"Oh, bosh!"

The conversation ceased again, for Angelo was sick and discouraged and strangling; but after some time he closed his book and asked Luigi to sing "From Greenland's Icy Mountains" with him, but he would not, and when he tried to sing by himself Luigi did his best to drown his plaintive tenor with a rude and rollicking song delivered in a thundering bass.

After the singing there was silence, and neither brother was happy. Before blowing the light out Luigi swallowed half a tumbler of whiskey, and Angelo, whose sensitive organization could not endure intoxicants of any kind, took a pill to keep it from giving him the headache.

CHAPTER 2

The family sat in the breakfast-room waiting for the twins to come down. The widow was quiet, the daughter was all alive with happy excitement. She said:

"Ah, they're a boon, ma, just a boon! don't you think so?"

"Laws, I hope so, I don't know."

"Why, ma, yes you do. They're so fine and handsome, and high-bred and polite, so every way superior to our gawks here in this village; why, they'll make life different from what it was—so humdrum and commonplace, you know—oh, you may be sure they're full of accomplishments, and knowledge of the world, and all that, that will be an immense advantage to society here. Don't you think so, ma?"

"Mercy on me, how should I know, and I've hardly set eyes on them yet." After a pause she added, "They made considerable noise after they went up."

"Noise? Why, ma, they were singing! And it was beautiful, too."

"Oh, it was well enough, but too mixed-up, seemed to me."

"Now, ma, honor bright, did you ever hear 'Greenland's Icy Mountains' sung sweeter—now did you?"

"If it had been sung by itself, it would have been uncommon sweet, I don't deny it; but what they wanted to mix it up with 'Old Bob Ridley' for, I can't make out. Why, they don't go together, at all. They are not of the same nature. 'Bob Ridley' is a common rackety slambang secular song, one of the rippingest and rantingest and noisiest there is. I am no judge of music, and I don't claim it, but in my opinion nobody can make those two songs go together right."

"Why, ma, I thought——"

"It don't make any difference what you thought, it can't be done. They tried it, and to my mind it was a failure. I never heard such a crazy uproar; seemed to me, sometimes, the roof would come off; and as for the cats—well, I've lived a many a year, and seen cats aggravated in more ways than one, but I've never seen cats take on the way they took on last night."

"Well, I don't think that that goes for anything, ma, because it is the nature of cats that any sound that is unusual——"

"Unusual! You may well call it so. Now if they are going to sing duets every night, I do hope they will both sing the same tune at the same time, for in my opinion a duet that is made up of two different tunes is a mistake; especially when the tunes ain't any kin to one another, that way."

"But, ma, I think it must be a foreign custom; and it must be right too, and the best way, because they have had every opportunity to know what is right, and it don't stand to reason that with their education they would do anything but what the highest musical authorities have sanctioned. You can't help but admit that, ma."

The argument was formidably strong; the old lady could not find any way around it; so, after thinking it over a while she gave in with a sigh of discontent, and admitted that the daughter's position was probably correct. Being vanquished, she had no mind to continue the topic at that disadvantage, and was about to seek a change when a change came of itself. A footstep was heard on the stairs, and she said:

"There—he's coming!"

"*They*, ma—you ought to say *they*—it's nearer right."

The new lodger, rather shoutingly dressed but looking superbly handsome, stepped with courtly carriage into the trim little breakfast-room and put out all his cordial arms at once, like one of those pocket-knives with a multiplicity of blades, and shook hands with the whole family simultaneously. He was so easy and pleasant and hearty that all embarrassment presently thawed away and disappeared, and a cheery feeling of friendliness and comradeship took its place. He—or preferably they—were asked to occupy the seat of honor at the foot of the table. They consented with thanks, and carved the beefsteak with one set of their hands while they distributed it at the same time with the other set.

"Will you have coffee, gentlemen, or tea?"

"Coffee for Luigi, if you please, madam, tea for me."

"Cream and sugar?"

"For me, yes, madam; Luigi takes his coffee black. Our natures differ a good deal from each other, and our tastes also."

The first time the negro girl Nancy appeared in the door and saw the two heads turned in opposite directions and both talking at once, then saw the commingling arms feed potatoes into one mouth and coffee into the other at the same time, she had to pause and pull herself out of a faintness that came over her; but after that she held her grip and was able to wait on the table with fair courage.

Conversation fell naturally into the customary grooves. It was a little jerky, at first, because none of the family could get smoothly through a sentence without a wobble in it here and a break there, caused by some new surprise in the way of attitude or gesture on the part of the twins. The weather suffered the most. The weather was all finished up and disposed of, as a subject, before the simple Missourians had gotten sufficiently wonted to the spectacle of one body feeding two heads to feel composed and reconciled in the presence of so bizarre a miracle. And even after everybody's mind became tranquilized there was still one slight distraction left: the hand that picked up a biscuit carried it to the wrong head, as often as any other way, and the wrong mouth devoured it. This was a puzzling thing, and marred the talk a little. It bothered the widow to such a degree that she presently dropped out of the conversation without knowing it, and fell to watching and guessing and talking to herself:

"Now that hand is going to take that coffee to—no, it's gone to the other mouth; I can't understand it; and now, here is the dark complected hand with a potato on its fork, I'll see what goes with it —there, the light complected head's got it, as sure as I live!" Finally Rowena said:

"Ma, what is the matter with you? Are you dreaming about something?"

The old lady came to herself and blushed; then she explained with the first random thing that came into her mind: "I saw Mr. Angelo take up Mr. Luigi's coffee, and I thought maybe he—sha'n't I give *you* a cup, Mr. Angelo?"

"Oh no, madam, I am very much obliged, but I never drink coffee, much as I would like to. You did see me take up Luigi's cup, it is true, but if you noticed, I didn't carry it to my mouth, but to his."

"Y—es, I thought you did. Did you mean to?"

"How?"

The widow was a little embarrassed again. She said:

"I don't know but what I'm foolish, and you mustn't mind; but you see, he got the coffee I was expecting to see you drink, and you got a potato that I thought he was going to get. So I thought it might be a mistake all around, and everybody getting what wasn't intended for him."

Both twins laughed and Luigi said:

"Dear madam, there wasn't any mistake. We are always helping each other that way. It is a great economy for us both; it saves time and labor. We have a system of signs which nobody can notice or understand but ourselves. If I am using both my hands and want some coffee, I make the sign and Angelo furnishes it to me; and you saw that when he needed a potato I delivered it."

"How convenient!"

"Yes, and often of the extremest value. Take the Mississippi boats, for instance. They are always over-crowded. There is table-room for only half of the passengers, therefore they have to set a second table for the second half. The stewards rush both parties, they give them no time to eat a satisfying meal, both divisions leave the table hungry. It isn't so with us. Angelo books himself for the one table, I book myself for the other. Neither of us eats anything at the other's table, but just simply works—works. Thus, you see there are four hands to feed Angelo, and the same four to feed me. Each of us eats two meals."

The old lady was dazed with admiration, and kept saying, "It is *per*fectly wonderful, perfectly wonderful!" and the boy Joe licked his chops enviously, but said nothing—at least aloud.

"Yes," continued Luigi, "our construction may have its disadvantages—in fact, *has*—but it also has its compensations, of one sort and another. Take travel, for instance. Travel is enormously expensive, in all countries; we have been obliged to do a vast deal of it—come, Angelo, don't put any more sugar in your tea, I'm just over one indigestion and don't want another right away—been obliged to do a deal of it, as I was saying. Well, we always travel as one person, since we occupy but one seat; so we save half the fare."

"How romantic!" interjected Rowena, with effusion.

"Yes, my dear young lady, and how practical too, and economical. In Europe, beds in the hotels are not charged with the board, but separately—another saving, for we stood to our rights and paid for the one bed only. The landlords often insisted that as both of us occupied the bed we ought——"

"No, they didn't," said Angelo. "They did it only twice, and in both cases it was a double bed—a rare thing in Europe—and the double bed gave them some excuse. Be fair to the landlords; twice doesn't constitute 'often.'"

"Well, that depends—that depends. I knew a man who fell down a well twice. He said he didn't mind the first time, but he thought the second time was once too often. Have I misused that word, Mrs. Cooper?"

"To tell the truth, I was afraid you had, but it seems to look, now, like you hadn't." She stopped, and was evidently struggling with the difficult problem a moment, then she added in the tone of one who is convinced without being converted, "It seems so, but I can't somehow tell why."

Rowena thought Luigi's retort was wonderfully quick and bright, and she remarked to herself with satisfaction that there wasn't any young native of Dawson's Landing that could have risen to the occasion like that. Luigi detected the applause in her face, and expressed his pleasure and his thanks with his eyes; and so eloquently withal, that the girl was proud and pleased, and hung out the delicate sign of it on her cheeks.

Luigi went on, with animation:

"Both of us get a bath for one ticket, theater seat for one ticket, pew-rent is on the same basis, but at peep-shows we pay double."

"We have much to be thankful for," said Angelo, impressively, with a reverent light in his eye and a reminiscent tone in his voice, "we have been greatly blessed. As a rule, what one of us has lacked, the other, by the bounty of Providence, has been able to supply. My brother is hardy, I am not; he is very masculine, assertive, aggressive; I am much less so. I am subject to illness, he is never ill. I cannot abide medicines, and cannot take them, but he has no prejudice against them, and——"

"Why, goodness gracious," interrupted the widow, "when you are sick, does he take the medicine for you?"

"Always, madam."

"Why, I never heard such a thing in my life! I think it's beautiful of you."

"Oh, madam, it's nothing, don't mention it, it's really nothing at all."

"But I say it's beautiful, and I stick to it!" cried the widow, with a speaking moisture in her eye. "A well brother to take the medicine for his poor sick brother—I wish I had such a son," and she glanced reproachfully at her boys. "I declare I'll never rest till I've shook you by the hand," and she scrambled out of her chair in a fever of generous enthusiasm, and made for the twins, blind with her tears, and began to shake. The boy Joe corrected her:

"You're shaking the wrong one, ma."

This flurried her, but she made a swift change and went on shaking.

"Got the wrong one again ma," said the boy.

"Oh, shut up, can't you!" said the widow, embarrassed and irritated. "Give me *all* your hands, I want to shake them all; for I know you are both just as good as you can be."

It was a victorious thought, a master-stroke of diplomacy, though, that never occurred to her and she cared nothing for diplomacy. She shook the four hands in turn cordially, and went back to her place in a state of high and fine exaltation that made her look young and handsome.

"Indeed I owe everything to Luigi," said Angelo, affectionately. "But for him I could not have survived our boyhood days, when we were friendless and poor—ah, so poor! We lived from hand to mouth—lived on the coarse fare of unwilling charity, and for weeks and weeks together not a morsel of food passed my lips, for its character revolted me and I could not eat it. But for Luigi I should have died. He ate for us both."

"How noble!" sighed Rowena.

"Do you hear that?" said the widow, severely, to her boys. "Let it be an example to you—I mean you, Joe."

Joe gave his head a barely perceptible disparaging toss and said: "Et for both. It ain't anything—I'd a done it."

"Hush, if you haven't got any better manners than that. You don't see the point at all. It wasn't good food."

"I don't care—it was food, and I'd 'a et it if it was rotten."

"Shame! Such language! Can't you understand? They were starving—actually starving—and he ate for both, and——"

"Shucks! you gimme a chance and I'll—"

"There, now—close your head! and don't you open it again till you're asked."

[Angelo goes on and tells how his parents the Count and Countess had to fly from Florence for political reasons, and died poor in Berlin bereft of their great property by confiscation; and how he and Luigi had to travel with a freak-show during two years and suffer semi-starvation.]

"That hateful black-bread! but I seldom ate anything during that time; that was poor Luigi's affair——"

"I'll never *Mister* him again!" cried the widow, with strong emotion, "he's Luigi to me, from this out!"

"Thank you a thousand times, madam, a thousand times! though in truth I don't deserve it."

"Ah, Luigi is always the fortunate one when honors are showering," said Angelo, plaintively, "now what have I done, Mrs. Cooper, that you leave me out? Come, you must strain a point in my favor."

"Call you Angelo? Why, certainly I will; what are you thinking of! In the case of twins, why——"

"But, ma, you're breaking up the story—do let him go on."

"You keep still, Rowena Cooper, and he can go on all the better, I reckon. One interruption don't hurt, it's two that makes the trouble."

"But you've added one, now, and that is three."

"Rowena! I will not allow you to talk back at me when you have got nothing rational to say."

CHAPTER 3

[After breakfast the whole village crowded in, and there was a grand reception in honor of the twins; and at the close of it the gifted "freak" captured everybody's admiration by sitting down at the piano and knocking out a classic four-handed piece in great style. Then the Judge took it—or them—driving in his buggy and showed off his village.]

All along the streets the people crowded the windows and stared at the amazing twins. Troops of small boys flocked after the buggy, excited and yelling. At first the dogs showed no interest. They thought they merely saw three men in a buggy—a matter of no consequence; but when they found out the facts of the case, they altered their opinion pretty radically, and joined the boys, expressing their minds as they came. Other dogs got interested; indeed all the dogs. It was a spirited sight to see them come leaping fences, tearing around corners, swarming out of every by-street and alley. The noise they made was something beyond belief—or praise. They did not seem to be moved by malice but only by prejudice, the common human prejudice against lack of conformity. If the twins turned their heads, they broke and fled in every direction, but stopped at a safe distance and faced about; and then formed and came on again as soon as the strangers showed them their back. Negroes and farmers' wives took to the woods when the buggy came upon them suddenly, and altogether the drive was pleasant and animated, and a refreshment all around.

[It was a long and lively drive. Angelo was a Methodist, Luigi was a Freethinker. The Judge was very proud of his Freethinker Society, which was flourishing along in a most prosperous way and already had two members—himself and the obscure and neglected Pudd'nhead Wilson. It was to meet that evening, and he invited Luigi to join; a thing which Luigi was glad to do, partly because it would please himself, and partly because it would gravel Angelo.]

They had now arrived at the widow's gate, and the excursion was ended. The twins politely expressed their obligations for the pleasant outing which had been afforded them; to which the Judge bowed his thanks, and then said he would now go and arrange for the Freethinkers' meeting, and would call for Count Luigi in the evening.

"For you also, dear sir," he added hastily, turning to Angelo and bowing. "In addressing myself particularly to your brother, I was not meaning to leave you out. It was an unintentional rudeness, I assure you, and due wholly to accident—accident and preoccupation. I beg you to forgive me."

His quick eye had seen the sensitive blood mount into Angelo's face, betraying the wound that had been inflicted. The sting of the slight had gone deep, but the apology was so prompt, and so evidently sincere, that the hurt was almost immediately healed, and a forgiving smile testified to the kindly Judge that all was well again.

Concealed behind Angelo's modest and unassuming exterior, and unsuspected by any but his intimates, was a lofty pride, a pride of almost abnormal proportions indeed, and this rendered him ever the prey of slights; and although they were almost always imaginary ones, they hurt none the less on that account. By ill fortune Judge Driscoll had happened to touch his sorest point, *i. e.*, his conviction that his brother's presence was welcomer everywhere than his own; that he was often invited, out of mere courtesy, where only his brother was wanted, and that in a majority of cases he would not be included in an invitation if he could be left out without offence. A sensitive nature like this is necessarily subject to moods; moods which traverse the whole gamut of feeling; moods which know all the climes of emotion, from the sunny heights of joy to the black abysses of despair. At times, in his seasons of deepest depression, Angelo almost wished that he and his brother might become segregated from each other and be separate individuals, like other men. But of course as soon as his mind cleared and these diseased imaginings passed away, he shuddered at the repulsive thought, and earnestly prayed that it might visit him no more. To be separate, and as other men are! How awkward it would seem; how unendurable. What would he do with his hands, his arms? How would his legs feel? How odd, and strange, and grotesque every action, attitude, movement, gesture would be. To sleep by himself, eat by himself, walk by himself—how lonely, how unspeakably lonely! No, no, any fate but that. In every way and from every point, the idea was revolting.

This was of course natural; to have felt otherwise would have been unnatural. He had known no life but a combined one; he had been familiar with it from his birth; he was not able to conceive of any other as being agreeable, or even bearable. To him, in the privacy of his secret thoughts, all other men were monsters, deformities; and during three-fourths of his life their aspect had filled him with what promised to be an unconquerable aversion. But at eighteen his eye began to take note of female beauty; and little by little, undefined longings grew up in his heart, under whose softening influences the old stubborn aversion gradually diminished, and finally disappeared. Men were still monstrosities to him, still deformities, and in his sober moments he had no desire to be like them, but their strange and unsocial and uncanny construction was no longer offensive to him.

This had been a hard day for him, physically and mentally. He had been called in the morning before he had quite slept off the effects of the liquor which Luigi had drunk; and so, for the first half hour had had the seedy feeling, and languor, the brooding depression, the cobwebby mouth and druggy taste that come of dissipation and are so ill a preparation for bodily or intellectual activities; the long violent strain of the reception had followed; and this had been followed, in turn, by the dreary sight-seeing, the Judge's wearying explanations and laudations of the sights, and the stupefying clamor of the dogs. As a congruous conclusion, a fitting end, his feelings had been hurt, a slight had been put upon him. He would have been glad to forego dinner and betake himself to rest and sleep, but he held his peace and said no word, for he knew his brother, Luigi, was fresh, unweary, full of life, spirit, energy; he would have scoffed at the idea of wasting valuable time on a bed or a sofa, and would have refused permission.

CHAPTER 4

Rowena was dining out, Joe and Harry were belated at play, there were but three chairs and four persons that noon at the home dinner-table—the twins, the widow, and her chum, Aunt Betsy Hale. The widow soon perceived that Angelo's spirits were as low as Luigi's were high, and also that he had a jaded look. Her motherly solicitude was aroused, and she tried to get him interested in the talk and win him to a happier frame of mind, but the cloud of sadness remained on his countenance. Luigi lent his help, too. He used a form and a phrase which he was always accustomed to employ in these circumstances. He gave his brother an affectionate slap on the shoulder and said, encouragingly:

"Cheer up, the worst is yet to come!"

But this did no good. It never did. If anything it made the matter worse, as a rule, because it irritated Angelo. This made it a favorite with Luigi. By and by the widow said:

"Angelo, you are tired, you've overdone yourself; you go right to bed, after dinner, and get a good nap and a rest, then you'll be all right."

"Indeed I would give anything if I could do that, madam."

"And what's to hender, I'd like to know? Land, the room's yours to do what you please with! The idea that you can't do what you like with your own!"

"But you see, there's one prime essential—an essential of the very first importance—which isn't my own."

"What is that?"

"My body."

The old ladies looked puzzled, and Aunt Betsy Hale said:

"Why bless your heart, how is that?"

"It's my brother's."

"Your brother's! I don't quite understand. I supposed it belonged to both of you."

"So it does. But not to both at the same time."

"That is mighty curious; I don't see how it can be. I shouldn't think it could be managed that way."

"Oh, it's a good enough arrangement, and goes very well; in fact it wouldn't do to have it otherwise. I find that the teetotalers and the anti-teetotalers hire the use of the same hall for their meetings. Both parties don't use it at the same time, do they?"

"You bet they don't!" said both old ladies in a breath.

"And moreover," said Aunt Betsy, "the Freethinkers and the Baptist Bible-class use the same room over the Market-house, but you can take my word for it they don't mush up together and use it at the same time."

"Very well," said Angelo, "you understand it now. And it stands to reason that the arrangement couldn't be improved. I'll prove it to you. If our legs tried to obey two wills, how could we ever get anywhere? I would start one way, Luigi would start another, at the same moment—the result would be a standstill, wouldn't it?"

"As sure as you are born! Now ain't that wonderful! A body would never have thought of it."

"We should always be arguing and fussing and disputing over the merest trifles. We should lose worlds of time, for we couldn't go downstairs or up, couldn't go to bed, couldn't rise, couldn't wash, couldn't dress, couldn't stand up, couldn't sit down, couldn't even cross our legs, without calling a meeting first and explaining the case and passing resolutions, and getting consent. It wouldn't ever do—now would it?"

"Do? Why, it would wear a person out in a week! Did you ever hear anything like it, Patsy Cooper?"

"Oh, you'll find there's more than one thing about them that ain't commonplace," said the widow, with the complacent air of a person with a property-right in a novelty that is under admiring scrutiny.

"Well now, how ever do you manage it? I don't mind saying I'm suffering to know."

"He who made us," said Angelo reverently, "and with us this difficulty, also provided a way out of it. By a mysterious law of our being, each of us has utter and indisputable command of our body a week at a time, turn and turn about."

"Well, I never! Now ain't that beautiful!"

"Yes, it is beautiful and infinitely wise and just. The week ends every Saturday at midnight to the minute, to the second, to the last shade of a fraction of a second, infallibly, unerringly, and in that instant the one brother's power over the body vanishes and the other brother takes possession, asleep or awake."

"How marvelous are His ways, and past finding out!"

Luigi said: "So exactly to the instant does the change come, that during our stay in many of the great cities of the world, the public clocks were regulated by it; and as hundreds of thousands of private clocks and watches were set and corrected in accordance with the public clocks, we really furnished the standard time for the entire city."

"Don't tell me that He don't do miracles any more! Blowing down the walls of Jericho with rams' horns wa'n't as difficult, in my opinion."

"And that is not all," said Angelo. "A thing that is even more marvelous, perhaps, is the fact that the change takes note of longitude and fits itself to the meridian we are on. Luigi is in command this week. Now, if on Saturday night at a moment before midnight we could fly in an instant to a point fifteen degrees west of here, he would hold possession of the power another hour, for the change observes *local* time and no other."

Betsy Hale was deeply impressed, and said with solemnity:

"Patsy Cooper, for *de*tail it lays over the Passage of the Red Sea."

"Now, I shouldn't go as far as that," said Aunt Patsy, "but if you've a mind to say Sodom and Gomorrah, I am with you, Betsy Hale."

"I am agreeable, then, though I do think I was right, and I believe Parson Maltby would say the same. Well now, there's another thing. Suppose one of you wants to borrow the legs a minute from the one that's got them, could he let him?"

"Yes, but we hardly ever do that. There were disagreeable results, several times, and so we very seldom ask or grant the privilege, nowdays, and we never even think of such a thing unless the case is extremely urgent. Besides, a week's possession at a time seems so little that we can't bear to spare a minute of it. People who have the use of their legs all the time never think of what a blessing it is, of course. It never occurs to them; it's just their natural ordinary condition, and so it does not excite them at all. But when I wake up, on Sunday morning, and it's my week and I feel the power all through me, oh, such a wave of exultation and thanksgiving goes surging over me, and I want to shout 'I can walk! I can walk!' Madam, do you ever, at your uprising want to shout 'I can walk! I can walk'?"

"No, you poor unfortunate cretur', but I'll never get out of my bed again without *doing* it! Laws, to think I've had this unspeakable blessing all my long life and never had the grace to thank the good Lord that gave it to me!"

Tears stood in the eyes of both the old ladies and the widow said, softly:

"Betsy Hale, we have learned something, you and me."

The conversation now drifted wide, but by and by floated back once more to that admired detail, the rigid and beautiful impartiality with which the possession of power had been distributed between the twins. Aunt Betsy saw in it a far finer justice than human law exhibits in related cases. She said:

"In my opinion it ain't right now, and never has been right, the way a twin born a quarter of a minute sooner than the other one gets all the land and grandeurs and nobilities in the old countries and his brother has to go bare and be a nobody. Which of you was born first?"

Angelo's head was resting against Luigi's; weariness had overcome him, and for the past five minutes he had been peacefully sleeping. The old ladies had dropped their voices to a lulling drone, to help him steal the rest his brother wouldn't take him up-stairs to get. Luigi listened a moment to Angelo's regular breathing, then said in a voice barely audible:

"We were both born at the same time, but I am six months older than he is."

"For the land's sake!"

"'Sh! don't wake him up; he wouldn't like my telling this. It has always been kept secret till now."

"But how in the world can it be? If you were both born at the same time, how can one of you be older than the other?"

"It is very simple, and I assure you it is true. I was born with a full crop of hair, he was as bald as an egg for six months. I could walk six months before he could make a step. I finished teething six months ahead of him. I began to take solids six months before he left the breast. I began to talk six months before he could say a word. Last, and absolutely unassailable proof, *the sutures in my skull closed six months ahead of his.* Always just that six months difference to a day. Was that accident? Nobody is going to claim that, I'm sure. It was ordained—it was law—it had its meaning, and we know what that meaning was. Now what does this overwhelming body of evidence establish? It establishes just one thing, and that thing it establishes beyond any peradventure whatever. Friends, we would not have it known for the world, and I must beg you to keep it strictly to yourselves, but the truth is, *we are no more twins than you are.*"

The two old ladies were stunned, paralyzed—petrified, one may almost say—and could only sit and gaze vacantly at each other for some moments; then Aunt Betsy Hale said impressively:

"There's no getting around proof like that. I do believe it's the most amazing thing I ever heard of." She sat silent a moment or two and breathing hard with excitement, then she looked up and surveyed the strangers steadfastly a little while, and added: "Well, it does beat me, but I would have took you for twins anywhere."

"So would I, so would I," said Aunt Patsy with the emphasis of a certainty that is not impaired by any shade of doubt.

"*Any*body would—anybody in the world, I don't care who he is," said Aunt Betsy with decision.

"You won't tell," said Luigi, appealingly.

"Oh, dear no!" answered both ladies promptly, "you can trust us, don't you be afraid."

"That is good of you, and kind. Never let on; treat us always as if we were twins."

"You can depend on us," said Aunt Betsy, "but it won't be easy, because now that I know you ain't, you don't *seem* so."

Luigi muttered to himself with satisfaction: "That swindle has gone through without change of cars."

It was not very kind of him to load the poor things up with a secret like that, which would be always flying to their tongues' ends every time they heard any one speak of the strangers as twins, and would become harder and harder to hang on to with every recurrence of the temptation to tell it, while the torture of retaining it would increase with every new strain that was applied; but he never thought of that, and probably would not have worried much about it if he had.

A visitor was announced—some one to see the twins. They withdrew to the parlor, and the two old ladies began to discuss with interest the strange things which they had been listening to. When they had finished the matter to their satisfaction, and Aunt Betsy rose to go, she stopped to ask a question:

"How does things come on between Roweny and Tom Driscoll?"

"Well, about the same. He writes tolerable often, and she answers tolerable seldom."

"Where is he?"

"In St. Louis, I believe, though he's such a gad-about that a body can't be very certain of him, I reckon."

"Don't Roweny know?"

"Oh, yes, like enough. I haven't asked her lately."

"Do you know how him and the Judge are getting along now?"

"First-rate, I believe. Mrs. Pratt says so; and being right in the house, and sister to the one and aunt to t'other, of course she ought to know. She says the Judge is real fond of him when he's away, but frets when he's around and is vexed with his ways, and not sorry to have him go again. He has been gone three weeks this time—a pleasant thing for both of them, I reckon."

"Tom's ruther harum-scarum, but there ain't anything bad in him, I guess."

"Oh no, he's just young, that's all. Still, twenty-three is old, in one way. A young man ought to be earning his living by that time. If Tom were doing that, or was even trying to do it, the Judge would be a heap better satisfied with him. Tom's always going to begin, but somehow he can't seem to find just the opening he likes."

"Well now, it's partly the Judge's own fault. Promising the boy his property wasn't the way to set him to earning a fortune of his own. But what do you think—is Roweny beginning to lean any towards him, or ain't she?"

Aunt Patsy had a secret in her bosom; she wanted to keep it there, but nature was too strong for her. She drew Aunt Betsy aside, and said in her most confidential and mysterious manner:

"Don't you breathe a syllable to a soul—I'm going to tell you something. In my opinion Tom Driscoll's chances were considerable better yesterday than they are to-day."

"Patsy Cooper, what *do* you mean?"

"It's so, as sure as you're born. I wish you could 'a' been at breakfast and seen for yourself."

"You don't mean it!"

"Well, if I'm any judge, there's a leaning—there's a leaning, sure."

"My land! Which one of 'em is it?"

"I can't say for certain, but I think it's the youngest one—Anjy."

Then there were handshakings, and congratulations, and hopes, and so on, and the old ladies parted, perfectly happy—the one in knowing something which the rest of the town didn't, and the other in having been the sole person able to furnish that knowledge.

The visitor who had called to see the twins was the Rev. Mr. Hotchkiss, pastor of the Baptist church. At the reception Angelo had told him he had lately experienced a change in his religious views, and was now desirous of becoming a Baptist, and would immediately join Mr. Hotchkiss's church. There was no time to say more, and the brief talk ended at that point. The minister was much gratified, and had dropped in for a moment, now, to invite the twins to attend his Bible-class at eight that evening. Angelo accepted, and was expecting Luigi to decline, but he did not, because he knew that the Bible-class and the Freethinkers met in the same room, and he wanted to treat his brother to the embarrassment of being caught in freethinking company.

CHAPTER 5

[A long and vigorous quarrel follows, between the twins. And there is plenty to quarrel about, for Angelo was always seeking truth, and this obliged him to change and improve his religion with frequency, which wearied Luigi, and annoyed him too; for he had to be present at each new enlistment—which placed him in the false position of seeming to indorse and approve his brother's fickleness; moreover, he had to go to Angelo's prohibition meetings, and he hated them. On the other hand, when it was *his* week to command the legs he gave Angelo just cause of complaint, for he took him to circuses and horse-races and fandangoes, exposing him to all sorts of censure and criticism; and he drank, too; and whatever he drank went to Angelo's head instead of his own and made him act disgracefully. When the evening was come, the two attended the Freethinkers' meeting, where Angelo was sad and silent; then came the Bible-class and looked upon him coldly, finding him in such company. Then they went to Wilson's house, and Chapter 11 of "Pudd'nhead Wilson" follows, which tells of the girl seen in Tom Driscoll's room; and closes with the kicking of Tom by Luigi at the anti-temperance mass meeting of the Sons of Liberty; with the addition of some account of Roxy's adventures as a chambermaid on a Mississippi boat. Her exchange of the children had been flippantly and farcically described in an earlier chapter.]

Next morning all the town was a-buzz with great news; Pudd'nhead Wilson had a lawcase! The public astonishment was so great and the public curiosity so intense, that when the justice of the peace opened his court, the place was packed with people, and even the windows were full. Everybody was flushed and perspiring, the summer heat was almost unendurable.

Tom Driscoll had brought a charge of assault and battery against the twins. Robert Allen was retained by Driscoll, David Wilson by the defense. Tom, his native cheerfulness unannihilated by his back-breaking and bone-bruising passage across the massed heads of the Sons of Liberty the previous night, laughed his little customary laugh, and said to Wilson:

"I've kept my promise, you see: I'm throwing my business your way. Sooner than I was expecting, too."

"It's very good of you—particularly if you mean to keep it up."

"Well, I can't tell about that, yet. But we'll see. If I find you deserve it I'll take you under my protection and make your fame and fortune for you."

"I'll try to deserve it, Tom."

A jury was sworn in; the Mr. Allen said:

"We will detain your honor but a moment with this case. It is not one where any doubt of the fact of the assault can enter in. These gentlemen—the accused—kicked my client at the Market Hall last night; they kicked him with violence; with extraordinary violence; with even unprecedented violence, I may say; insomuch that he was lifted entirely off his feet and discharged into the midst of the audience. We can prove this by four hundred witnesses—we shall call but three. Mr. Harkness will take the stand."

Mr. Harkness being sworn, testified that he was chairman upon the occasion mentioned; that he was close at hand and saw the defendants in this action kick the plaintiff into the air and saw him descend among the audience.

"Take the witness," said Allen.

"Mr. Harkness," said Wilson, "you say you saw these gentlemen, my clients, kick the plaintiff. Are you sure—and please remember that you are on oath—are you perfectly sure that you saw *both* of them kick him, or only one? Now be careful."

A bewildered look began to spread itself over the witness's face. He hesitated, stammered, but got out nothing. His eyes wandered to the twins and fixed themselves there with a vacant gaze.

"Please answer, Mr. Harkness, you are keeping the court waiting. It is a very simple question."

Counsel for the prosecution broke in with impatience:

"Your honor, the question is an irrelevant triviality. Necessarily they both kicked him, for they have but the one pair of legs, and both are responsible for them."

Wilson said, sarcastically:

"Will your honor permit this new witness to be sworn? He seems to possess knowledge which can be of the utmost value just at this moment—knowledge which would at once dispose of what every one must see is a very difficult question in this case. Brother Allen, will you take the stand?"

"Go on with your case!" said Allen, petulantly. The audience laughed, and got a warning from the court.

"Now, Mr. Harkness," said Wilson, insinuatingly, "we shall have to insist upon an answer to that question."

"I—er—well, of course I do not absolutely *know,* but in my opinion——"

"Never mind your opinion, sir—answer the question."

"I—why, I *can't* answer it."

"That will do, Mr. Harkness. Stand down."

The audience tittered, and the discomfited witness retired in a state of great embarrassment.

Mr. Wakeman took the stand and swore that he saw the twins kick the plaintiff off the platform. The defence took the witness.

"Mr. Wakeman, you have sworn that you saw these gentlemen kick the plaintiff. Do I understand you to swear that you saw them *both* do it?"

"Yes, sir,"—with decision.

"How do you know that both did it?"

"Because I *saw* them do it."

The audience laughed, and got another warning from the court.

"But by what means do you know that both, and not one, did it?"

"Well, in the first place, the insult was given to both of them equally, for they were called a pair of scissors. Of course they would both want to resent it, and so——"

"Wait! You are theorizing now. Stick to facts—counsel will attend to the arguments. Go on."

"Well, they both went over there—*that* I saw."

"Very good. Go on."

"And they both kicked him—I swear to it."

"Mr. Wakeman, was Count Luigi, here, willing to join the Sons of Liberty last night?"

"Yes, sir, he was. He did join, too, and drank a glass or two of whisky, like a man."

"Was his brother willing to join?"

"No, sir, he wasn't. He is a teetotaler, and was elected through a mistake."

"Was he given a glass of whisky?"

"Yes, sir, but of course that was another mistake, and not intentional. He wouldn't drink it. He set it down." A slight pause, then he added, casually and quite simply: "The plaintiff reached for it and hogged it."

There was a fine outburst of laughter, but as the justice was caught out himself, his reprimand was not very vigorous.

Mr. Allen jumped up and exclaimed: "I protest against these foolish irrelevancies. What have they to do with the case?"

Wilson said: "Calm yourself, brother, it was only an experiment. Now, Mr. Wakeman, if one of these gentlemen chooses to join an association and the other doesn't; and if one of them enjoys whisky and the other doesn't, but sets it aside and leaves it unprotected" (titter from the audience), "it seems to show that they have independent minds and tastes and preferences, and that one of them is able to approve of a thing at the very moment that the other is heartily disapproving of it. Doesn't it seem so to you?"

"Certainly it does. It's perfectly plain."

"Now then, it might be—I only say it might be—that one of these brothers wanted to kick the plaintiff last night, and that the other didn't want that humiliating punishment inflicted upon him in that public way and before all those people. Isn't that possible?"

"Of course it is. It's more than possible. I don't believe the blonde one would kick anybody. It was the other one that——"

"Silence!" shouted the plaintiff's counsel, and went on with an angry sentence which was lost in the wave of laughter that swept the house.

"That will do, Mr. Wakeman," said Wilson, "you may stand down."

The third witness was called. He had seen the twins kick the plaintiff. Mr. Wilson took the witness.

"Mr. Rogers, you say you saw these accused gentlemen kick the plaintiff?"

"Yes, sir."

"Both of them?"

"Yes, sir."

"Which of them kicked him first?"

"Why—they—they both kicked him at the same time."

"Are you perfectly sure of that?"

"Yes, sir."

"What makes you sure of it?"

"Why, I stood right behind them, and *saw* them do it."

"How many kicks were delivered?"

"Only one."

"If two men kick, the result should be two kicks, shouldn't it?"

"Why—why—yes, as a rule."

"Then what do you think went with the other kick?"

"I—well—the fact is, I wasn't thinking of two being necessary, this time."

"What do you think now?"

"Well, I—I'm sure I don't quite know what to think, but I reckon that one of them did half of the kick and the other one did the other half."

Somebody in the crowd sung out: "It's the first sane thing that any of them has said."

The audience applauded. The judge said: "Silence! or I will clear the court."

Mr. Allen looked pleased, but Wilson did not seem disturbed. He said:

"Mr. Rogers, you have favored us with what you think and what you reckon, but as thinking and reckoning are not evidence, I will now give you a chance to come out with something positive, one way or the other, and shall require you to produce it. I will ask the accused to stand up and repeat the phenomenal kick of last night." The twins stood up. "Now, Mr. Rogers, please stand behind them."

A Voice: "No, stand in front!" (Laughter. Silenced by the court.) Another Voice: "No, give Tommy another highst!" (Laughter. Sharply rebuked by the court.)

"Now then, Mr. Rogers, two kicks shall be delivered, one after the other, and I give you my word that at least one of the two shall be delivered by one of the twins alone, without the slightest assistance from his brother. Watch sharply, for you have got to render a decision without any if's and and's in it." Rogers bent himself behind the twins with his palms just above his knees, in the modern attitude of the catcher at a base-ball match, and riveted his eyes on the pair of legs in front of him. "Are you ready, Mr. Rogers?"

"Ready, sir."

"Kick!"

The kick was launched.

"Have you got that one classified, Mr. Rogers?"

"Let me study a minute, sir."

"Take as much time as you please. Let me know when you are ready."

For as much as a minute Rogers pondered, with all eyes and a breathless interest fastened upon him. Then he gave the word: "Ready, sir."

"Kick!"

The kick that followed was an exact duplicate of the first one.

"Now then, Mr. Rogers, one of those kicks was an individual kick, not a mutual one. You will now state positively which was the mutual one."

The witness said, with a crestfallen look:

"I've got to give it up. There ain't any man in the world that could tell t'other from which, sir."

"Do you still assert that last night's kick was a mutual kick?"

"Indeed I don't, sir."

"That will do, Mr. Rogers. If my brother Allen desires to address the court, your honor, very well; but as far as I am concerned I am ready to let the case be at once delivered into the hands of this intelligent jury without comment."

Mr. Justice Robinson had been in office only two months, and in that short time had not had many cases to try, of course. He had no knowledge of laws and courts except what he had picked up since he came into office. He was a sore trouble to the lawyers, for his rulings were pretty eccentric sometimes, and he stood by them with Roman simplicity and fortitude; but the people were well satisfied with him, for they saw that his intentions were always right, that he was entirely impartial, and that he usually made up in good sense what he lacked in technique, so to speak. He now perceived that there was likely to be a miscarriage of justice here, and he rose to the occasion.

"Wait a moment, gentlemen," he said, "it is plain that an assault has been committed—it is plain to anybody; but the way things are going, the guilty will certainly escape conviction. I cannot allow this. Now——"

"But, your honor!" said Wilson, interrupting him, earnestly but respectfully, "you are deciding the case yourself, whereas the jury——"

"Never mind the jury, Mr. Wilson; the jury will have a chance when there is a reasonable doubt for them to take hold of—which there isn't, so far. There is no doubt whatever that an assault has been committed. The attempt to show that both of the accused committed it has failed. Are they both to escape justice on that account? Not in this court, if I can prevent it. It appears to have been a mistake to bring the charge against them as a corporation; each should have been charged in his capacity as an individual, and——"

"But your honor!" said Wilson, "in fairness to my clients I must insist that inasmuch as the prosecution did not separate the——"

"No wrong will be done your clients, sir—they will be protected; also the public and the offended laws. Mr. Allen, you will amend your pleadings, and put one of the accused on trial at a time."

Wilson broke in: "But your honor! this is wholly unprecedented! To imperil an accused person by arbitrarily altering and widening the charge against him in order to compass his conviction when the charge as originally brought promises to fail to convict, is a thing unheard of before."

"Unheard of *where?*"

"In the courts of this or any other State."

The judge said with dignity: "I am not acquainted with the customs of other courts, and am not concerned to know what they are. I am responsible for this court, and I cannot conscientiously allow my judgment to be warped and my judicial liberty hampered by trying to conform to the caprices of other courts, be they——"

"But, your honor, the oldest and highest courts in Europe——"

"This court is not run on the European plan, Mr. Wilson; it is not run on any plan but its own. It has a plan of its own; and that plan is, to find justice for both State and accused, no matter what happens to be practice and custom in Europe or anywhere else." (Great applause.) "Silence! It has not been the custom of this court to imitate other courts; it has not been the custom of this court to take shelter behind the decisions of other courts, and we will not begin now. We will do the best we can by the light that God has given us, and while this court continues to have His approval, it will remain indifferent to what other organizations may think of it." (Applause.) "Gentlemen, I *must* have order!—quiet yourselves! Mr. Allen, you will now proceed against the prisoners one at a time. Go on with the case."

Allen was not at his ease. However, after whispering a moment with his client and with one or two other people, he rose and said:

"Your honor, I find it to be reported and believed that the accused are able to act independently in many ways, but that this independence does not extend to their legs, authority over their legs being vested exclusively in the one brother during a specific term of days, and then passing to the other brother for a like term, and so on, by regular alternation. I could call witnesses who would prove that the accused had revealed to them the existence of this extraordinary fact, and had also made known which of them was in possession of the legs yesterday—and this would of course indicate where the guilt of the assault belongs—but as this would be mere hearsay evidence, these revelations not having been made under oath——"

"Never mind about that, Mr. Allen. It may not all be hearsay. We shall see. It may at least help to put us on the right track. Call the witnesses."

"Then I will call Mr. John Buckstone, who is now present, and I beg that Mrs. Patsy Cooper may be sent for. Take the stand, Mr. Buckstone."

Buckstone took the oath, and then testified that on the previous evening the Count Angelo Capello had protested against going to the hall, and had called all present to witness that he was going by compulsion and would not go if he could help himself. Also, that the Count Luigi had replied sharply that he would *go*, just the same, and that he, Count Luigi, would see to that, himself. Also, that upon Count Angelo's complaining about being kept on his legs so long, Count Luigi retorted with apparent surprise, '*Your* legs!—I like your impudence!'"

"*Now* we are getting at the kernel of the thing," observed the judge, with grave and earnest satisfaction. "It looks as if the Count Luigi was in possession of the battery at the time of the assault."

Nothing further was elicited from Mr. Buckstone on direct examination. Mr. Wilson took the witness.

"Mr. Buckstone, about what time was it that that conversation took place?"

"Toward nine yesterday evening, sir."

"Did you then proceed directly to the hall?"

"Yes, sir."

"How long did it take you to go there?"

"Well, we walked; and as it was from the extreme edge of the town, and there was no hurry, I judge it took us about twenty minutes, maybe a trifle more."

"About what hour was the kick delivered?"

"At thirteen minutes and a half to ten."

"Admirable! You are a pattern witness, Mr. Buckstone. How did you happen to look at your watch at that particular moment?"

"I always do it when I see an assault. It's likely I shall be called as a witness, and it's a good point to have."

"It would be well if others were as thoughtful. Was anything said, between the conversation at my house and the assault, upon the detail which we are now examining into?"

"No, sir."

"If power over the mutual legs was in the possession of one brother at nine, and passed into the possession of the other one during the next thirty or forty minutes, do you think you could have detected the change?"

"By no means!"

"That is all, Mr. Buckstone."

Mrs. Patsy Cooper was called. The crowd made way for her, and she came smiling and bowing through the narrow human lane, with Betsy Hale, as escort and support, smiling and bowing in her wake, the audience breaking into welcoming cheers as the old favorites filed along. The judge did not check this kindly demonstration of homage and affection, but let it run its course unrebuked.

The old ladies stopped and shook hands with the twins with effusion, then gave the judge a friendly nod, and bustled into the seats provided for them. They immediately began to deliver a volley of eager questions at the friends around them: "What is this thing for?" "What is that thing for?" "Who is that young man that's writing at the desk? Why, I declare, it's Jack Bunce! I thought he was sick." "Which is the jury? Why, is *that* the jury? Billy Price and Job Turner, and Jack Lounsbury, and—well, I never!" "Now who would ever a' thought——"

But they were gently called to order at this point, and asked not to talk in court. Their tongues fell silent, but the radiant interest in their faces remained, and their gratitude for the blessing of a new sensation and a novel experience still beamed undimmed from their eyes. Aunt Patsy stood up and took the oath, and Mr. Allen explained the point in issue, and asked her to go on, now, in her own way, and throw as much light upon it as she could. She toyed with her reticule a moment or two, as if considering where to begin, then she said:

"Well, the way of it is this. They are Luigi's legs a week at a time, and then they are Angelo's, and he can do whatever he wants to with them."

"You are making a mistake, Aunt Patsy Cooper," said the judge. "You shouldn't state that as a *fact*, because you don't know it to *be* a fact."

"What's the reason I don't?" said Aunt Patsy, bridling a little.

"What is the reason that you do know it?"

"The best in the world—because they told me."

"That isn't a reason."

"Well, for the land's sake! Betsy Hale, do you hear that?"

"*Hear* it? I should think so," said Aunt Betsy, rising and facing the court. "Why, Judge, I was there and heard it myself. Luigi says to Angelo—no, it was Angelo said it to——"

"Come, come, Mrs. Hale, pray sit down, and——"

"Certainly it's all right, I'm going to sit down presently, but not until I've——"

"But you *must* sit down!"

"*Must!* Well, upon my word if things ain't getting to a pretty pass when——"

The house broke into laughter, but was promptly brought to order, and meantime Mr. Allen persuaded the old lady to take her seat. Aunt Patsy continued:

"Yes, they told me that, and I know it's true. They're Luigi's legs this week, but—"

"Ah, *they* told you that, did they?" said the justice, with interest.

"Well no, I don't know that *they* told me, but that's neither here nor there. I know, without that, that at dinner yesterday, Angelo was as tired as a dog, and yet Luigi wouldn't lend him the legs to go up-stairs and take a nap with."

"Did he ask for them?"

"Let me see—it seems to me somehow, that—that—Aunt Betsy, do you remember whether he——"

"Never mind about what Aunt Betsy remembers—she is not a witness; we only want to know what you remember, yourself," said the judge.

"Well, it does seem to me that you are most cantankerously particular about a little thing, Sim Robinson. Why, when I can't remember a thing myself, I always——"

"Ah, *please* go on!"

"Now how *can* she when you keep fussing at her all the time?" said Aunt Betsy. "Why, with a person pecking at *me* that way, I should get that fuzzled and fuddled that——"

She was on her feet again, but Allen coaxed her into her seat once more, while the court squelched the mirth of the house. Then the judge said:

"Madam, do you know——do you absolutely *know*, independently of anything these gentlemen have told you—that the power over their legs passes from the one to the other regularly every week?"

"Regularly? Bless your heart, regularly ain't any name for the exactness of it! All the big cities in Europe used to set the clocks by it." (Laughter, *suppressed by the court.*)

"How do you *know*? That is the question. Please answer it plainly and squarely."

"Don't you talk to me like that, Sim Robinson—I won't have it. How do I know, indeed! How do *you* know what you know? Because somebody told you. You didn't invent it out of your own head, did you? Why, these twins are the truthfulest people in the world; and I don't think it becomes you to sit up there and throw slurs at them when they haven't been doing anything to you. And they are orphans besides—both of them. All——"

But Aunt Betsy was up again, now, and both old ladies were talking at once and with all their might; but as the house was weltering in a storm of laughter, and the judge was hammering his desk with an iron paper-weight, one could only see them talk, not hear them. At last, when quiet was restored, the court said:

"Let the ladies retire."

"But, your honor, I have the right, in the interest of my clients, to cross-exam——"

"You'll not need to exercise it, Mr. Wilson—the evidence is thrown out."

"Thrown out!" said Aunt Patsy, ruffled; "and what's it thrown out for, I'd like to know."

"And so would I, Patsy Cooper. It seems to me that if we can save these poor persecuted strangers, it is our bounden duty to stand up here and talk for them till——"

"There, there, there, *do* sit down!"

It cost some trouble and a good deal of coaxing, but they were got into their seats at last. The trial was soon ended, now. The twins themselves became witnesses in their own defense. They established the fact, upon oath, that the leg-power passed from one to the other every Saturday night at twelve o'clock, sharp. But on cross-examination their counsel would not allow them to tell whose week of power the current week was. The judge insisted upon their answering, and proposed to compel them; but even the prosecution took fright and came to the rescue then, and helped stay the sturdy jurist's revolutionary hand. So the case had to go to the jury with that important point hanging in the air. They were out an hour, and brought in this verdict:

"We the jury do find: 1, that an assault was committed, as charged; 2, that it was committed by one of the persons accused, he having been seen to do it by several credible witnesses; 3, but that his identity is so merged in his brother's that we have not been able to tell which was him. We cannot convict both, for only one is guilty. We cannot acquit both, for only one is innocent. Our verdict is that justice has been defeated by the dispensation of God, and ask to be discharged from further duty."

This was read aloud in court and brought out a burst of hearty applause. The old ladies made a spring at the twins, to shake and congratulate, but were gently disengaged by Mr. Wilson and softly crowded back into their places.

The Judge rose in his little tribune, laid aside his silver-bowed spectacles, roached his gray hair up with his fingers, and said, with dignity and solemnity, and even with a certain pathos:

"In all my experience on the bench, I have not seen Justice bow her head in shame in this court until this day. You little realize what far-reaching harm has just been wrought here under the fickle forms of law. Imitation is the bane of courts—I thank God that this one is free from the contamination of that vice—and in no long time you will see the fatal work of this hour seized upon by profligate so-called guardians of justice in all the wide circumstance of this planet and perpetuated in their pernicious decisions. I wash my hands of this iniquity. I would have compelled these culprits to expose their guilt, but support failed me where I had most right to expect aid and encouragement. And I was confronted by a law made in the interest of crime, which protects the criminal from testifying against himself. Yet I had precedents of my own whereby I had set aside that law on two different occasions and thus succeeded in convicting criminals to whose crimes there were no witnesses but themselves. What have you accomplished this day? Do you realize it? You have set adrift, unadmonished, in this community, two men endowed with an awful and mysterious gift, a hidden and grisly power for evil—a power by which each in his turn may commit crime after crime of the most heinous character, and no man be able to tell which is the guilty or which the innocent party in any case of them all. Look to your homes—look to your property—look to your lives—for you have need!

"Prisoners at the bar, stand up. Through suppression of evidence, a jury of your—our—countrymen have been obliged to deliver a verdict concerning your case which stinks to heaven with the rankness of its injustice. By its terms you, the guilty one, go free with the innocent. Depart in peace, and come no more! The costs devolve upon the outraged plaintiff—another iniquity. The Court stands dissolved."

Almost everybody crowded forward to overwhelm the twins and

their counsel with congratulations; but presently the two old aunties dug the duplicates out and bore them away in triumph through the hurrahing crowd, while lots of new friends carried Pudd'nhead Wilson off tavern-wards to feast him and "wet down" his great and victorious entry into the legal arena. To Wilson, so long familiar with neglect and depreciation, this strange new incense of popularity and admiration was as a fragrance blown from the fields of paradise. A happy man was Wilson.

CHAPTER 6

A deputation came in the evening and conferred upon Wilson the welcome honor of a nomination for mayor; for the village has just been converted into a city by charter. Tom skulks out of challenging the twins. Judge Driscoll thereupon challenges Angelo, (accused by Tom of doing the kicking;) he declines, but Luigi accepts in his place against Angelo's timid protest.

It was late Saturday night—nearing eleven.

The Judge and his second found the rest of the war party at the further end of the vacant ground, near the haunted house. Pudd'nhead Wilson advanced to meet them, and said anxiously—

"I must say a word in behalf of my principal's proxy, Count Luigi, to whom you have kindly granted the privilege of fighting my principal's battle for him. It is growing late, and Count Luigi is in great trouble lest midnight shall strike before the finish."

"It is another testimony," said Howard, approvingly. "That young man is fine all through. He wishes to save his brother the sorrow of fighting on the Sabbath, and he is right; it is the right and manly feeling and does him credit. We will make all possible haste."

Wilson said—

"There is also another reason—a consideration, in fact, which deeply concerns Count Luigi himself. These twins have command of their mutual legs turn about. Count Luigi is in command, now; but at midnight, possession will pass to my principal, Count Angelo, and——well, you can foresee what will happen. He will march straight off the field, and carry Luigi with him."

"Why! sure enough!" cried the Judge, "we have heard something about that extraordinary law of their being, already—nothing very definite, it is true, as regards dates and durations of the power, but I see it is definite enough as regards to-night. Of course we must give Luigi every chance. Omit all the ceremonial possible, gentlemen, and place us in position."

The seconds at once tossed up a coin; Howard won the choice. He placed the Judge sixty feet from the haunted house and facing it; Wilson placed the twins within fifteen feet of the house and facing the Judge—necessarily. The pistol-case was opened and the long slim tubes taken out; when the moonlight glinted from them a shiver went through Angelo. The doctor was a fool, but a thoroughly well-meaning one, with a kind heart and a sincere disposition to oblige, but along with it an absence of tact which often hurt its effectiveness. He brought his box of lint and bandages, and asked Angelo to feel and see how soft and comfortable they were. Angelo's head fell over against Luigi's in a faint, and precious time was lost in bringing him to; which provoked Luigi into expressing his mind to the doctor with a good deal of vigor and frankness. After Angelo came to he was still so weak that Luigi was obliged to drink a stiff horn of brandy to brace him up.

The seconds now stepped at once to their posts, half way between the combatants, one of them on each side of the line of fire. Wilson was to count, very deliberately, "One—two—three—fire!—stop!" and the duelists could bang away at any time they chose during that recitation, but not after the last word. Angelo grew very nervous when he saw Wilson's hand rising slowly into the air as a sign to make ready, and he leaned his head against Luigi's and said—

"O, please take me away from here, I can't stay, I know I can't!"

"What in the world are you doing? Straighten up! What's the matter with you?—*you're* in no danger—nobody's going to shoot at you. Straighten up, I tell you!"

Angelo obeyed, just in time to hear—

"One—!"

"Bang!" Just one report, and a little tuft of white hair floated slowly to the Judge's feet in the moonlight. The Judge did not swerve; he still stood erect and motionless, like a statue, with his pistol-arm hanging straight down at his side. He was reserving his fire.

"Two—!"

"Three—!"

"Fire—!"

Up came the pistol-arm instantly—Angelo dodged with the report. He said "Ouch!" and fainted again.

The doctor examined and bandaged the wound. It was of no consequence, he said—bullet through fleshy part of arm—no bones broken—the gentleman was still able to fight—let the duel proceed.

Next time Angelo jumped just as Luigi fired, which disordered his aim and caused him to cut a chip out of Howard's ear. The Judge took his time again, and when he fired Angelo jumped and got a knuckle skinned. The doctor inspected and dressed the wounds. Angelo now spoke out and said he was content with the satisfaction he had got, and if the Judge—but Luigi shut him roughly up, and asked him not to make an ass of himself; adding—

"And I want you to stop dodging. You take a great deal too prominent a part in this thing for a person who has got nothing to do with it. You should remember that you are here only by courtesy, and are without official recognition; officially you are not here at all; officially you do not even exist. To all intents and purposes you are absent from this place, and you ought for your own modesty's sake to reflect that it cannot become a person who is not present here to be taking this sort of public and indecent prominence in a matter in which he is not in the slightest degree concerned. Now, don't dodge again; the bullets are not for you, they are for me; if I want them dodged I will attend to it myself. I never saw a person act so."

Angelo saw the reasonableness of what his brother had said, and he did try to reform, but it was of no use; both pistols went off at the same instant, and he jumped once more; he got a sharp scrape along his cheek from the Judge's bullet, and so deflected Luigi's aim that his ball went wide and chipped a flake of skin from Pudd'nhead Wilson's chin. The doctor attended to the wounded.

By the terms, the duel was over. But Luigi was entirely out of patience, and begged for one more exchange of shots, insisting that he had had no fair chance, on account of his brother's indelicate behavior. Howard was opposed to granting so unusual a privilege, but the Judge took Luigi's part, and added that indeed he himself might fairly be considered entitled to another trial, because although the proxy on the other side was in no way to blame for his (the Judge's) humiliatingly resultless work, the gentleman with whom he was fighting this duel was to blame for it, since if he had played no advantages and had held his head still, his proxy would have been disposed of early. He added—

"Count Luigi's request for another exchange is another proof that he is a brave and chivalrous gentleman, and I beg that the courtesy he asks may be accorded him."

"I thank you most sincerely for this generosity, Judge Driscoll," said

Luigi, with a polite bow, and moving to his place. Then he added—to Angelo, "Now hold your grip, hold your *grip*, I tell you, and I'll land him, sure!"

The men stood erect, their pistol-arms at their sides, the two seconds stood at their official posts, the doctor stood five paces in Wilson's rear with his instruments and bandages in his hands. The deep stillness, the peaceful moonlight, the motionless figures, made an impressive picture and the impending fatal possibilities augmented this impressiveness to solemnity. Wilson's hand began to rise—slowly—slowly—higher—still higher—in another moment—

"*Boom!*"—the first stroke of midnight swung up out of the distance: Angelo was off like a deer!

"Oh, you unspeakable traitor!" wailed his brother, as they went soaring over the fence.

The others stood astonished and gazing; and so stood, watching that strange spectacle until distance dissolved it and swept it from their view. Then they rubbed their eyes like people waking out of a dream.

"Well, I've never seen anything like that before!" said the Judge. "Wilson, I am going to confess, now, that I wasn't quite able to believe in that leg-business, and had a suspicion that it was a put-up convenience between those twins; and when Count Angelo fainted I thought I saw the whole scheme—thought it was pretext No. 1, and would be followed by others till twelve o'clock should arrive and Luigi would get off with all the credit of seeming to want to fight and yet not have to fight, after all. But I was mistaken. His pluck proved it. He's a brave fellow and did want to fight."

"There isn't any doubt about that," said Howard, and added in a grieved tone, "but what an unworthy sort of Christian that Angelo is—I hope and believe there are not many like him. It is not right to engage in a duel on the Sabbath—I could not approve of that myself; but to finish one that has been begun—that is a duty, let the day be what it may."

They strolled along, still wondering, still talking.

"It is a curious circumstance," remarked the surgeon, halting Wilson a moment to paste some more court plaster on his chin, which had gone to leaking blood again, "that in this duel neither of the parties who handled the pistols lost blood, while nearly all the persons present in the mere capacity of guests got hit. I have not heard of such a thing before. Don't you think it unusual?"

"Yes," said the Judge, "it has struck me as peculiar. Peculiar and unfortunate. I was annoyed at it, all the time. In the case of Angelo it made no great difference, because he was in a measure concerned, though not officially; but it troubled me to see the seconds compromised, and yet I knew no way to mend the matter."

"There was no way to mend it," said Howard, whose ear was being readjusted now by the doctor; "the code fixes our place, and it would not have been lawful to change it. If we could have stood at your side, or behind you, or in front of you, it—but it would not have been legitimate and the other parties would have had a just right to complain of our trying to protect ourselves from danger; infractions of the code are certainly not permissible in any case whatever."

Wilson offered no remarks. It seemed to him that there was very little place here for so much solemnity, but he judged that if a duel where nobody was in danger or got crippled but the seconds and the outsiders had nothing ridiculous about for these gentlemen, his pointing out that feature would probably not help them to see it.

He invited them in to take a nightcap, and Howard and the Judge accepted, but the doctor said he would have to go and see how Angelo's principal wound was getting on.

[It was now Sunday, and in the afternoon Angelo was to be received into the Baptist communion by immersion—a doubtful prospect, the doctor feared.]

CHAPTER 7

When the doctor arrived at Aunt Patsy Cooper's house, he found the lights going and everybody up and dressed and in a great state of solicitude and excitement. The twins were stretched on a sofa in the sitting-room, Aunt Patsy was fussing at Angelo's arm, Nancy was flying around under her commands, the two young boys were trying to keep out of the way and always getting in it, in order to see and wonder, Rowena stood apart, helpless with apprehension and emotion, and Luigi was growling in unappeasable fury over Angelo's shameful flight.

As has been reported before, the doctor was a fool—a kindhearted and well-meaning one, but with no tact; and as he was by long odds the most learned physician in the town, and was quite well aware of it, and could talk his learning with ease and precision, and liked to show off when he had an audience, he was sometimes tempted into revealing more of a case than was good for the patient.

He examined Angelo's wound, and was really minded to say nothing for once; but Aunt Patsy was so anxious and so pressing that he allowed his caution to be overcome, and proceeded to empty himself as follows, with scientific relish—

"Without going too much into detail, madam—for you would probably not understand it anyway—I concede that great care is going to be necessary here; otherwise exudation of the aesophagus is nearly sure to ensue, and this will be followed by ossification and extradition of the maxillaris superioris, which must decompose the granular surfaces of the great infusorial ganglionic system, thus obstructing the action of the posterior varioloid arteries, and precipitating compound strangulated sorosis of the valvular tissues, and ending unavoidably in the dispersion and combustion of the marsupial fluxes and the consequent embrocation of the bicuspid populo redax referendum rotulorum."

A miserable silence followed. Aunt Patsy's heart sank, the pallor of despair invaded her face, she was not able to speak; poor Rowena wrung her hands in privacy and silence, and said to herself in the bitterness of her young grief, "There is no hope—it is plain there is no hope;" the good-hearted negro wench, Nancy, paled to chocolate, then to orange, then to amber, and thought to herself with yearning sympathy and sorrow, "Po' thing, he ain' gwyne to las' throo de half o' dat;" small Henry choked up, and turned his head away to hide his rising tears, and his brother Joe said to himself, with a sense of loss, "The baptizing's busted, that's sure." Luigi was the only person who had any heart to speak. He said, a little bit sharply, to the doctor—

"Well, well, there's nothing to be gained by wasting precious time: give him a barrel of pills—I'll take them for him."

"You?" asked the doctor.

"Yes. Did you suppose he was going to take them himself?"

"Why, of course."

"Well, it's a mistake. He never took a dose of medicine in his life. He can't."

"Well, upon my word, it's the most extraordinary thing I ever heard of!"

"Oh," said Aunt Patsy, as pleased as a mother whose child is being admired and wondered at, "you'll find that there's more about them that's wonderful than their just being made in the image of God like the rest of His creatures, now you can depend on that, *I* tell you," and she wagged her complacent head like one who could reveal marvelous things if she chose.

The boy Joe began—

"Why, ma, they *ain't* made in the im——"

"You shut up, and wait till you're asked, Joe. I'll let you know when I want help. Are you looking for something, Doctor?"

The doctor asked for a few sheets of paper and a pen, and said he would write a prescription; which he did. It was one of Galen's; in fact, it was Galen's favorite, and had been slaying people for sixteen thousand years. Galen used it for everything, applied it to everything, said it would remove everything, from warts all the way through to lungs—and it generally did. Galen was still the only medical authority recognized in Missouri; his practice was the only practice known to the Missouri doctors, and his prescriptions were the only ammunition they carried when they went out for game. By and by Dr. Claypool laid down his pen and read the result of his labors aloud, carefully and deliberately, for this battery must be constructed on the premises by the family, and mistakes could occur; for he wrote a doctor's hand—the hand which from the beginning of time has been so disastrous to the apothecary and so profitable to the undertaker:

"Take of afarabocca, henbane, corpobalsamum, each two drams and a half; of cloves, opium, myrrh, cyperus, each two drams; of opobalsamum, Indian leaf, cinnamon, zedoary, ginger, coftus, coral, cassia, euphorbium, gum tragacanth, frankincense, styrax calamita, celtic, nard, spignel, hartwort, mustard, saxifrage, dill, anise, each one dram; of xylaloes, rheum ponticum, alipta moschata, castor, spikenard, galangals, opoponax, anacardium, mastich, brimstone, peony, eringo, pulp of dates, red and white hermodactyls, roses, thyme, acorns, pennyroyal, gentian, the bark of the root of mandrake, germander, valerian, bishop's weed, bay-berries, long and white pepper, xylobalsamum, carnabadium, macedonian, parsley-seeds, lovage, the seeds of rue, and sinon, of each a dram and a half; of pure gold, pure silver, pearls not perforated, the blatta byzantina, the bone of the stag's heart, of each the quantity of fourteen grains of wheat; of sapphire, emerald and jasper stones, each one dram; of hazel-nut, two drams; of pellitory of Spain, shavings of ivory, calamus odoratus, each the quantity of twenty-nine grains of wheat; of honey or sugar a sufficient quantity. Boil down and skim off."

"There," he said, "that will fix the patient; give his brother a dipperful every three-quarters of an hour——"

—"while he survives," muttered Luigi—

—"and see that the room is kept wholesomely hot, and the doors and windows closed tight. Keep Count Angelo nicely covered up with six or seven blankets, and when he is thirsty—which will be frequently—moisten a rag in the vapor of the tea-kettle and let his brother suck it. When he is hungry—which will also be frequently—he must not be humored oftener than every seven or eight hours; then toast part of a cracker until it begins to brown, and give it to his brother."

"That is all very well, as far as Angelo is concerned," said Luigi, "but what am I to eat?"

"I do not see that there is anything the matter with you," the doctor answered, "you may of course eat what you please."

"And also drink what I please, I suppose?"

"Oh, certainly—at present. When the violent and continuous perspiring has reduced your strength, I shall have to reduce your diet, of course, and also bleed you, but there is no occasion for that yet awhile." He turned to Aunt Patsy and said: "He must be put to bed, and sat up with, and tended with the greatest care, and not allowed to stir for several days and nights."

"For one, I'm sacredly thankful for that," said Luigi, "it postpones the funeral—I'm not to be drowned to-day, anyhow."

Angelo said quietly to the doctor:

"I will cheerfully submit to all your requirements, sir, up to two o'clock this afternoon, and will resume them after three, but cannot be confined to the house during that intermediate hour."

"Why, may I ask?"

"Because I have entered the Baptist communion, and by appointment am to be baptized in the river at that hour."

"Oh, insanity!—it cannot be allowed!"

Angelo answered with placid firmness—

"Nothing shall prevent it, if I am alive."

"Why, consider, my dear sir, in your condition it might prove fatal."

A tender and ecstatic smile beamed from Angelo's eyes, and he broke forth in a tone of joyous fervency—

"Ah, how blessed it would be to die for such a cause—it would be martyrdom!"

"But your brother—consider your brother; you would be risking his life, too."

"He risked mine an hour ago," responded Angelo, gloomily; "did he consider me?" A thought swept through his mind that made him shudder. "If I had not run, I might have been killed in a duel on the Sabbath day, and my soul would have been lost—lost."

"Oh, don't fret, it wasn't in any danger," said Luigi, irritably; "they wouldn't waste it for a little thing like that; there's a glass case all ready for it in the heavenly museum, and a pin to stick it up with."

Aunt Patsy was shocked, and said—

"Looy, Looy!—don't talk so, dear!"

Rowena's soft heart was pierced by Luigi's unfeeling words, and she murmured to herself, "Oh, if I but had the dear privilege of protecting and defending him with my weak voice!—but alas, this sweet boon is denied me by the cruel conventions of social intercourse."

"Get their bed ready," said Aunt Patsy to Nancy, "and shut up the windows and doors, and light their candles, and see that you drive all the mosquitoes out of their bar, and make up a good fire in their stove, and carry up some bags of hot ashes to lay to his feet——"

—"and a shovel of fire for his head, and a mustard plaster for his neck, and some gum shoes for his ears," Luigi interrupted, with temper; and added, to himself, "Damnation, I'm going to be roasted alive, I just know it!"

"Why, Looy! Do be quiet; I never saw such a fractious thing. A body would think you didn't care for your brother."

"I don't—to *that* extent, Aunt Patsy. I was glad the drowning was postponed a minute ago, but I'm not, now. No, that is all gone by: I want to be drowned."

"You'll bring a judgment on yourself just as sure as you live, if you go on like that. Why, I never heard the beat of it. Now, there,—there! you've said enough. Not another word out of you,—I won't have it!"

"But, Aunt Patsy——"

"Luigi! Didn't you hear what I told you?"

"But, Aunt Patsy, I—why, I'm not going to set my heart and lungs afloat in that pail of sewage which this criminal here has been prescri——"

"Yes, you are, too. You are going to be good, and do everything I tell you, like a dear," and she tapped his cheek affectionately with her finger. "Rowena, take the prescription and go in the kitchen and hunt up the things and lay them out for me. I'll sit up with my patient the rest of the night, Doctor; I can't trust Nancy, she couldn't make Luigi take the medicine. Of course you'll drop in again during the day. Have you got any more directions?"

"No, I believe not, Aunt Patsy. If I don't get in earlier, I'll be along by early candlelight, anyway. Meantime, don't allow him to get out of his bed."

Angelo said, with calm determination—

"I shall be baptized at two o'clock. Nothing but death shall prevent me."

The doctor said nothing aloud, but to himself he said:

"Why, this chap's got a manly side, after all! Physically he's a coward, but morally he's a lion. I'll go and tell the others about this; it will raise him a good deal in their estimation—and the public will follow their lead, of course."

Privately, Aunt Patsy applauded too, and was proud of Angelo's courage in the moral field as she was of Luigi's in the field of honor.

The boy Henry was troubled, but the boy Joe said, inaudibly, and gratefully, "We're all hunky, after all; and no postponement on account of the weather."

CHAPTER 8

By nine o'clock the town was humming with the news of the midnight duel, and there were but two opinions about it: one, that Luigi's pluck in the field was most praiseworthy and Angelo's flight most scandalous; the other, that Angelo's courage in flying the field for conscience' sake was as fine and creditable as was Luigi's in holding the field in the face of the bullets. The one opinion was held by half of the town, the other one was maintained by the other half. The division was clean and exact, and it made two parties, an Angelo party and a Luigi party. The twins had suddenly become popular idols along with Pudd'nhead Wilson, and haloed with a glory as intense as his. The children talked the duel all the way to Sunday-school, their elders talked it all the way to church, the choir discussed it behind their red curtain, it usurped the place of pious thought in the "nigger gallery."

By noon the doctor had added the news, and spread it, that Count Angelo, in spite of his wound and all warnings and supplications, was resolute in his determination to be baptized at the hour appointed. This swept the town like wildfire, and mightily reinforced the enthusiasm of the Angelo faction, who said, "If any doubted that it was moral courage that took him from the field, what have they to say now!"

Still the excitement grew. All the morning it was traveling country-wards, toward all points of the compass; so, whereas before only the farmers and their wives were intending to come and witness the remarkable baptism, a general holiday was now proclaimed and the children and negroes admitted to the privileges of the occasion. All the farms for ten miles around were vacated, all the converging roads emptied long processions of wagons, horses and yeomanry into the town. The pack and cram of people vastly exceeded any that had ever been seen in that sleepy region before. The only thing that had ever even approached it, was the time long gone by, but never forgotten, nor even referred to without wonder and pride, when two circuses and a Fourth of July fell together. But the glory of that occasion was extinguished, now, for good. It was but a freshet to this deluge.

The great invasion massed itself on the river bank and waited hungrily for the immense event. Waited, and wondered if it would really happen, or if the twin who was not a "professor" would stand out and prevent it.

But they were not to be disappointed. Angelo was as good as his word. He came attended by an escort of honor composed of several hundred of the best citizens, all of the Angelo party; and when the immersion was finished they escorted him back home; and would even have carried him on their shoulders, but that people might think they were carrying Luigi.

Far into the night the citizens continued to discuss and wonder over the strangely-mated pair of incidents that had distinguished and exalted the past twenty-four hours above any other twenty-four in the history of their town for picturesqueness and splendid interest; and long before the lights were out and burghers asleep it had been decided on all hands that in capturing these twins Dawson's Landing had drawn a prize in the great lottery of municipal fortune.

At midnight Angelo was sleeping peacefully. His immersion had not harmed him, it had merely made him wholesomely drowsy, and he had been dead asleep many hours now. It had made Luigi drowsy, too, but he had got only brief naps, on account of his having to take the medicine every three-quarters of an hour—and Aunt Betsy Hale was there to see that he did it. When he complained and resisted, she was quietly firm with him, and said in a low voice:

"No—no, that won't do; you mustn't talk, and you mustn't retch and gag that way, either—you'll wake up your poor brother."

"Well, what of it, Aunt Betsy, he——"

"'Sh-h! Don't make a noise, dear. You mustn't forget that your poor brother is sick and——"

"Sick, is he? Well, I wish I——"

"Sh-h-h! Will you be quiet, Luigi! Here, now, take the rest of it—

don't keep me holding the dipper all night. I declare if you haven't left a good fourth of it in the bottom! Come—that's a good boy."

"Aunt Betsy, don't make me! I feel like I've swallowed a cemetery; I do, indeed. Do let me rest a little—just a little; I can't take any more of the devilish stuff, now."

"Luigi! Using such language here, and him just baptized! Do you want the roof to fall on you?"

"I wish to goodness it would!"

"Why, you dreadful thing! I've a good notion to—let that blanket alone; do you want your brother to catch his death?"

"Aunt Betsy, I've *got* to have it off, I'm being roasted alive; nobody could stand it—you couldn't, yourself."

"Now, then, you're sneezing again—I just expected it."

"Because I've caught a cold in my head. I always do, when I go in the water with my clothes on. And it takes me weeks to get over it, too. I think it was a shame to serve me so."

"Luigi, you are unreasonable; you know very well they couldn't baptize him dry. I should think you would be willing to undergo a little inconvenience for your brother's sake."

"Inconvenience! Now how you talk, Aunt Betsy. I came as near as anything to getting drowned—you saw that, yourself; and do you call this inconvenience?—the room shut up as tight as a drum, and so hot the mosquitoes are trying to get out; and a cold in the head, and dying for sleep and no chance to get any on account of this infamous medicine that that assassin prescri——"

"There, you're sneezing again. I'm going down and mix some more of this truck for you, dear."

CHAPTER 9

During Monday, Tuesday and Wednesday the twins grew steadily worse; but then the doctor was summoned south to attend his mother's funeral and they got well in forty-eight hours. They appeared on the street on Friday, and were welcomed with enthusiasm by the new-born parties, the Luigi and Angelo factions. The Luigi faction carried its strength into the Democratic party, the Angelo faction entered into a combination with the Whigs. The Democrats nominated Luigi for alderman under the new city government, and the Whigs put up Angelo against him. The Democrats nominated Pudd'nhead Wilson for mayor, and he was left alone in this glory, for the Whigs had no man who was willing to enter the lists against such a formidable opponent. No politician had scored such a compliment as this before in the history of the Mississippi Valley.

The political campaign in Dawson's Landing opened in a pretty warm fashion, and waxed hotter every week. Luigi's whole heart was in it, and even Angelo developed a surprising amount of interest—which was natural, because he was not merely representing Whigism, a matter of no consequence to him, but he was representing something immensely finer and greater—to wit, Reform. In him was centred the hopes of the whole reform element of the town; he was the chosen and admired champion of every clique that had a pet reform of any sort or kind at heart. He was president of the great Teetotaller's Union, its chiefest prophet and mouthpiece.

But as the canvass went on, troubles began to spring up all around—troubles for the twins, and through them for all the parties and segments and fractions of parties. Whenever Luigi had possession of the legs, he carried Angelo to balls, rum shops, Sons of Liberty parades, horse races, campaign riots, and everywhere else that could damage him with his party and the church; and when it was Angelo's week he carried Luigi diligently to all manner of moral and religious gatherings, doing his best to regain the ground he had lost before. As a result of these double performances, there was a storm blowing all the time, an ever rising storm, too—a storm of frantic criticism of the twins, and rage over their extravagant, incomprehensible conduct.

Luigi had the final chance. The legs were his for the closing week of the canvass. He led his brother a fearful dance.

But he saved his best card for the very eve of the election. There was to be a grand turn-out of the Teetotaller's Union that day, and Angelo was to march at the head of the procession and deliver a great oration afterward. Luigi drank a couple of glasses of whiskey—which steadied his nerves and clarified his mind, but made Angelo drunk. Everybody who saw the march, saw that the Champion of the Teetotallers was half seas over, and noted also that his brother, who made no hypocritical protensions to extra temperance virtues, was dignified and sober. This eloquent fact could not be unfruitful at the end of a hot political canvass. At the mass meeting Angelo tried to make his great temperance oration but was so discommoded by hiccoughs and thickness of tongue that he had to give it up; then drowsiness overtook him and his head drooped against Luigi's and he went to sleep. Luigi apologized for him, and was going on to improve his opportunity with an appeal for a moderation of what he called "the prevailing teetotal madness," but persons in the audience began to howl and throw things at him, and then the meeting rose in wrath and chased him home.

This episode was a crusher for Angelo in another way. It destroyed his chances with Rowena. Those chances had been growing, right along, for two months. Rowena had partly confessed that she loved him, but wanted time to consider. Now the tender dream was ended, and she told him so, the moment he was sober enough to understand. She said she would never marry a man who drank.

"But I don't drink," he pleaded.

"That is nothing to the point," she said, coldly, "you get drunk, and that is worse."

[There was a long and sufficiently idiotic discussion here, which ended as reported in a previous note.]

CHAPTER 10

Dawson's Landing had a week of repose, after the election, and it needed it, for the frantic and variegated nightmare which had tormented it all through the preceding week had left it limp, haggard and exhausted at the end. It got the week of repose because Angelo had the legs, and was in too subdued a condition to want to go out and mingle with an irritated community that had come to distrust and detest him because there was such a lack of harmony between his morals, which were confessedly excellent, and his methods of illustrating them, which were distinctly damnable.

The new city officers were sworn in on the following Monday—at least all but Luigi. There was a complication in his case. His election was conceded, but he could not sit in the board of aldermen without his brother, and his brother could not sit there because he was not a member. There seemed to be no way out of the difficulty but to carry the matter into the courts, so this was resolved upon. The case was set for the Monday fortnight. In due course the time arrived. In the meantime the city government had been at a stand-still, because without Luigi there was a tie in the board of aldermen, whereas with him the liquor interest—the richest in the political field—would have one majority. But the court decided that Angelo could not sit in the board with him, either in public or executive sessions, and at the same time forbade the board to deny admission to Luigi, a fairly and legally chosen alderman. The case was carried up and up from court to court, yet still the same old original decision was confirmed every time. As a result, the city government not only stood still, with its hands tied, but everything it was created to protect and care for went a steady gait toward rack and ruin. There was no way to levy a tax, so the minor officials had to resign or starve; therefore they resigned. There being no city money, the enormous legal expenses on both sides had to be defrayed by private subscription. But at last the people came to their senses, and said—

"Pudd'nhead was right, at the start—we ought to have hired the official half of that human phillipene to resign; but it's too late, now; some of us haven't got anything left to hire him with."

"Yes, we have," said another citizen, "we've got this"—and he produced a halter.

Many shouted, "That's the ticket." But others said, "No—Count Angelo is innocent; we mustn't hang him."

"Who said anything about hanging him? We are only going to hang the other one."

"Then that is all right—there is no objection to that."

So they hanged Luigi. And so ends the history of "Those Extraordinary Twins."

FINAL REMARKS

As you see, it was an extravagant sort of a tale, and had no purpose but to exhibit that monstrous "freak" in all sorts of grotesque lights. But when Roxy wandered into the tale she had to be furnished with something to do; so she changed the children in the cradle: this necessitated the invention of a reason for it; this in turn resulted in making the children prominent personages—nothing could prevent it, of course. Their career began to take a tragic aspect, and some one had to be brought in to help work the machinery; so Pudd'nhead Wilson was introduced and taken on trial. By this time the whole show was being run by the new people and in their interest, and the original show was become side-tracked and forgotten; the twin-monster and the heroine and the lads and the old ladies had dwindled to inconsequentialities and were merely in the way. Their story was one story, the new people's story was another story, and there was no connection between them, no interdependence, no kinship. It is not practicable or rational to try to tell two stories at the same time; so I dug out the farce and left the tragedy.

The reader already knew how the expert works; he knows now how the other kind do it.

MARK TWAIN

Personal Recollections of Joan of Arc

BY

THE SIEUR LOUIS DE CONTE
(HER PAGE AND SECRETARY)

FREELY TRANSLATED
OUT OF THE ANCIENT FRENCH INTO MODERN ENGLISH
FROM THE ORIGINAL UNPUBLISHED MANUSCRIPT
IN THE NATIONAL ARCHIVES OF FRANCE

BY

JEAN FRANÇOIS ALDEN

Consider this unique and imposing distinction. Since the writing of human history began, Joan of Arc is the only person, of either sex, who has ever held supreme command of the military forces of a nation *at the age of seventeen.*

—LOUIS KOSSUTH

1870–1895

TO MY WIFE

OLIVIA LANGDON CLEMENS

THIS BOOK

is tendered on our wedding anniversary in grateful recognition of her twenty-five years of valued service as my literary adviser and editor

THE AUTHOR

TRANSLATOR'S PREFACE

To arrive at a just estimate of a renowned man's character one must judge it by the standards of his time, not ours. Judged by the standards of one century, the noblest characters of an earlier one lose much of their lustre; judged by the standards of to-day, there is probably no illustrious man of four or five centuries ago whose character could meet the test at all points. But the character of Joan of Arc is unique. It can be measured by the standards of all times without misgiving or apprehension as to the result. Judged by any of them, judged by all of them, it is still flawless, it is still ideally perfect; it still occupies the loftiest place possible to human attainment, a loftier one than has been reached by any other mere mortal.

When we reflect that her century was the brutalest, the wickedest, the rottenest in history since the darkest ages, we are lost in wonder at the miracle of such a product from such a soil. The contrast between her and her century is the contrast between day and night. She was truthful when lying was the common speech of men; she was honest when honesty was become a lost virtue; she was a keeper of promises when the keeping of a promise was expected of no one; she gave her great mind to great thoughts and great purposes when other great minds wasted themselves upon pretty fancies or upon poor ambitions; she was modest and fine and delicate when to be loud and coarse might be said to be universal; she was full of pity when a merciless cruelty was the rule; she was steadfast when stability was unknown, and honorable in an age which had forgotten what honor was; she was a rock of convictions in a time when men believed in nothing and scoffed at all things; she was unfailingly true in an age that was false to the core; she maintained her personal dignity unimpaired in an age of fawnings and servilities; she was of a dauntless courage when hope and courage had perished in the hearts of her nation; she was spotlessly pure in mind and body when society in the highest places was foul in both—she was all these things in an age when crime was the common business of lords and princes, and when the highest personages in Christendom were able to astonish even that infamous era and make it stand aghast at the spectacle of their atrocious lives black with unimaginable treacheries, butcheries, and bestialities.

She was perhaps the only entirely unselfish person whose name has a place in profane history. No vestige or suggestion of self-seeking can be found in any word or deed of hers. When she had rescued her King from his vagabondage, and set his crown upon his head, she was offered rewards and honors, but she refused them all, and would take nothing. All she would take for herself—if the King would grant it—was leave to go back to her village home, and tend her sheep again, and feel her mother's arms about her, and be her housemaid and helper. The selfishness of this unspoiled general of victorious armies, companion of princes, and idol of an applauding and grateful nation, reached but that far and no farther.

The work wrought by Joan of Arc may fairly be regarded as ranking any recorded in history, when one considers the conditions under which it was undertaken, the obstacles in the way, and the means at her disposal. Cæsar carried conquest far, but he did it with the trained and confident veterans of Rome, and was a trained soldier himself; and Napoleon swept away the disciplined armies of Europe, but he also was a trained soldier, and he began his work with patriot battalions inflamed and inspired by the miracle-working new breath of Liberty breathed upon them by the Revolution—eager young apprentices to the splendid trade of war, not old and broken men-at-arms, despairing survivors of an age-long accumulation of monotonous defeats; but Joan of Arc, a mere child in years, ignorant, unlettered, a poor village girl unknown and without influence, found a great nation lying in chains, helpless and hopeless under an alien domination, its treasury bankrupt, its soldiers disheartened and dispersed, all spirit torpid, all courage dead in the hearts of the people through long years of foreign and domestic outrage and oppression, their King cowed, resigned to its fate, and preparing to fly the country; and she laid her hand upon this nation, this corpse, and it rose and followed her. She led it from victory to victory, she turned back the tide of the Hundred Years' War, she fatally crippled the English power, and died with the earned title of DELIVERER OF FRANCE, *which she bears to this day.*

And for all reward, the French King whom she had crowned stood supine and indifferent while French priests took the noble child, the most innocent, the most lovely, the most adorable the ages have produced, and burned her alive at the stake.

A PECULIARITY OF JOAN OF ARC'S HISTORY

The details of the life of Joan of Arc form a biography which is unique among the world's biographies in one respect: *It is the only story of a human life which comes to us under oath,* the only one which comes to us from the witness-stand. The official records of the Great Trial of 1431, and of the Process of Rehabilitation of a quarter of a century later, are still preserved in the National Archives of France, and they furnish with remarkable fulness the facts of her life. The history of no other life of that remote time is known with either the certainty or the comprehensiveness that attaches to hers.

The Sieur Louis de Conte is faithful to her official history in his Personal Recollections, and thus far his trustworthiness is unimpeachable; but his mass of added particulars must depend for credit upon his own word alone.

THE TRANSLATOR

Authorities examined in verification of the truthfulness of this narrative:

J. E. J. Quicherat, *Condamnation et Réhabilitation de Jeanne d'Arc.*
J. Fabre, *Procès de Condamnation de Jeanne d'Arc.*
H. A. Wallon, *Jeanne d'Arc.*
M. Sepet, *Jeanne d'Arc.*
J. Michelet, *Jeanne d'Arc.*
Berriat de Saint-Prix, *La Famille de Jeanne d'Arc.*
La Comtesse A. de Chabannes, *La Vierge Lorraine.*
Monseigneur Ricard, *Jeanne d'Arc la Vénérable.*
Lord Ronald Gower, F.S.A., *Joan of Arc.*
John O'Hagan, *Joan of Arc.*
Janet Tuckey, *Joan of Arc the Maid.*

CONTENTS

THE SIEUR LOUIS DE CONTE TO HIS GREAT-GREAT-GRAND NEPHEWS AND NIECES

This is the year 1492. I am eighty-two years of age. The things I am going to tell you are things which I saw myself as a child and as a youth.

In all the tales and songs and histories of Joan of Arc which you and the rest of the world read and sing and study in the books wrought in the late invented art of printing, mention is made of me, the Sieur Louis de Conte—I was her page and secretary. I was with her from the beginning until the end.

I was reared in the same village with her. I played with her every day, when we were little children together, just as you play with your mates. Now that we perceive how great she was; now that her name fills the whole world, it seems strange that what I am saying is true; for it is as if a perishable paltry candle should speak of the eternal sun riding in the heavens and say, "He was gossip and housemate to me when we were candles together." And yet it is true, just as I say. I was her playmate, and I fought at her side in the wars; to this day I carry in my mind, fine and clear, the picture of that dear little figure, with breast bent to the flying horse's neck, charging at the head of the armies of France, her hair streaming back, her silver mail ploughing steadily deeper and deeper into the thick of the battle, sometimes nearly drowned from sight by tossing heads of horses, uplifted sword-arms, wind-blown plumes, and intercepting shields. I was with her to the end; and when that black day came whose accusing shadow will lie always upon the memory of the mitred French slaves of England who were her assassins, and upon France who stood idle and essayed no rescue, my hand was the last she touched in life.

As the years and the decades drifted by, and the spectacle of the marvellous child's meteor-flight across the war-firmament of France and its extinction in the smoke-clouds of the stake receded deeper and deeper into the past and grew ever more strange and wonderful and divine and pathetic, I came to comprehend and recognize her at last for what she was—the most noble life that was ever born into this world save only One.

Book I

IN DOMREMY

CHAPTER 1

I, the Sieur Louis de Conte, was born in Neufchâteau, the 6th of January, 1410; that is to say, exactly two years before Joan of Arc was born in Domremy. My family had fled to those distant regions from the neighborhood of Paris in the first years of the century. In politics they were Armagnacs—patriots: they were for our own French King, crazy and impotent as he was. The Burgundian party, who were for the English, had stripped them, and done it well. They took everything but my father's small nobility, and when he reached Neufchâteau he reached it in poverty and with a broken spirit. But the political atmosphere there was the sort he liked, and that was something. He came to a region of comparative quiet; he left behind him a region peopled with furies, madmen, devils, where slaughter was a daily pastime and no man's life safe for a moment. In Paris, mobs roared through the streets nightly, sacking, burning, killing, unmolested, uninterrupted. The sun rose upon wrecked and smoking buildings, and upon mutilated corpses lying here, there, and yonder about the streets, just as they fell, and stripped naked by thieves, the unholy gleaners after the mob. None had the courage to gather these dead for burial; they were left there to rot and create plagues.

And plagues they did create. Epidemics swept away the people like flies, and the burials were conducted secretly and by night; for public funerals were not allowed, lest the revelation of the magnitude of the plague's work unman the people and plunge them into despair. Then came, finally, the bitterest winter which had visited France in five hundred years. Famine, pestilence, slaughter, ice, snow—Paris had all these at once. The dead lay in heaps about the streets, and *wolves entered the city in daylight and devoured them.*

Ah, France had fallen low—so low! For more than three quarters of a century the English fangs had been bedded in her flesh, and so cowed had her armies become by ceaseless rout and defeat that it was said and accepted that the mere sight of an English army was sufficient to put a French one to flight.

When I was five years old the prodigious disaster of Agincourt fell upon France; and although the English king went home to enjoy his glory, he left the country prostrate and a prey to roving bands of Free Companions in the service of the Burgundian party, and one of these bands came raiding through Neufchâteau one night, and by the light of our burning roof-thatch I saw all that were dear to me in this world (save an elder brother, your ancestor, left behind with the Court) butchered while they begged for mercy, and heard the butchers laugh at their prayers and mimic their pleadings. I was overlooked, and escaped without hurt. When the savages were gone I crept out and cried the night away watching the burning houses; and I was all alone, except for the company of the dead and the wounded, for the rest had taken flight and hidden themselves.

I was sent to Domremy, to the priest, whose house-keeper became a loving mother to me. The priest in the course of time taught me to read and write, and he and I were the only persons in the village who possessed this learning.

At the time that the house of this good priest, Guillaume Fronte, became my home, I was six years old. We lived close by the village church, and the small garden of Joan's parents was behind the church. As to that family, there were Jacques d'Arc the father, his wife Isabel Romée; three sons—Jacques, ten years old, Pierre, eight, and Jean, seven; Joan, four, and her baby sister Catherine, about a year old. I had these children for playmates from the beginning. I had some other playmates besides—particularly four boys: Pierre Morel, Étienne Roze, Noël Rainguesson, and Edmond Aubrey, whose father was maire at that time; also two girls, about Joan's age, who by-and-by became her favorites; one was named Haumette, the other was called Little Mengette. These girls were common peasant children, like Joan herself. When they grew up, both married common laborers. Their estate was lowly enough, you see; yet a time came, many years after, when no passing stranger, howsoever great he might be, failed to go and pay his reverence to those two humble old women who had been honored in their youth by the friendship of Joan of Arc.

These were all good children, just of the ordinary peasant type; not bright, of course—you would not expect that—but good-hearted and companionable, obedient to their parents and the priest; and as they grew up they became properly stocked with narrownesses and prejudices got at second hand from their elders, and adopted without reserve; and without examination also—which goes without saying. Their religion was inherited, their politics the same. John Huss and his sort might find fault with the Church, in Domremy it disturbed nobody's faith; and when the split came, when I was fourteen, and we had three Popes at once, nobody in Domremy was worried about how to choose among them—the Pope of Rome was the right one, a Pope outside of Rome was no Pope at all. Every human creature in the village was an Armagnac—a patriot—and if we children hotly hated nothing else in the world, we did certainly hate the English and Burgundian name and polity in that way.

CHAPTER 2

Our Domremy was like any other humble little hamlet of that remote time and region. It was a maze of crooked, narrow lanes and alleys shaded and sheltered by the overhanging thatch roofs of the barn-like houses. The houses were dimly lighted by wooden-shuttered windows—that is, holes in the walls which served for windows. The floors were of dirt, and there was very little furniture. Sheep and cattle grazing was the main industry; all the young folks tended flocks.

The situation was beautiful. From one edge of the village a flowery plain extended in a wide sweep to the river—the Meuse; from the rear edge of the village a grassy slope rose gradually, and at the top was the great oak forest—a forest that was deep and gloomy and dense, and full of interest for us children, for many murders had been done in it by outlaws in old times, and in still earlier times prodigious dragons that spouted fire and poisonous vapors from their nostrils had their homes in there. In fact, one was still living in there in our own time. It was as long as a tree, and had a body as big around as a tierce, and scales like overlapping great tiles, and deep ruby eyes as large as a cavalier's hat, and an anchor-fluke on its tail as big as I don't know what, but very big, even unusually so for a dragon, as everybody said who knew about dragons. It was thought that this dragon was of a brilliant blue color, with gold mottlings, but no one had ever seen it, therefore this was not known to be so, it was only an opinion. It was not my opinion; I think there is no sense in forming an opinion when there is no evidence to form it on. If you build a person without any bones in him he may look fair enough to the eye, but he will be limber and cannot stand up; and I consider that *evidence* is the bones of an opinion. But I will take up this matter more at large at another time, and try to make the justness of my position appear. As to that dragon,

I always held the belief that its color was gold and without blue, for that has always been the color of dragons. That this dragon lay but a little way within the wood at one time is shown by the fact that Pierre Morel was in there one day and smelt it, and recognized it by the smell. It gives one a horrid idea of how near to us the deadliest danger can be and we not suspect it.

In the earliest times a hundred knights from many remote places in the earth would have gone in there one after another, to kill the dragon and get the reward, but in our time that method had gone out, and the priest had become the one that abolished dragons. Père Guillaume Fronte did it in this case. He had a procession, with candles and incense and banners, and marched around the edge of the wood and exorcised the dragon, and it was never heard of again, although it was the opinion of many that the smell never wholly passed away. Not that any had ever smelt the smell again, for none had; it was only an opinion, like that other—and lacked bones, you see. I know that the creature was there before the exorcism, but whether it was there afterwards or not is a thing which I cannot be so positive about.

In a noble open space carpeted with grass on the high ground towards Vaucouleurs stood a most majestic beech-tree with wide-reaching arms and a grand spread of shade, and by it a limpid spring of cold water; and on summer days the children went there—oh, every summer for more than five hundred years—went there and sang and danced around the tree for hours together, refreshing themselves at the spring from time to time, and it was most lovely and enjoyable. Also they made wreaths of flowers and hung them upon the tree and about the spring to please the fairies that lived there; for they liked that, being idle innocent little creatures, as all fairies are, and fond of anything delicate and pretty like wild flowers put together in that way. And in return for this attention the fairies did any friendly thing they could for the children, such as keeping the spring always full and clear and cold, and driving away serpents and insects that sting; and so there was never any unkindness between the fairies and the children during more than five hundred years—tradition said a thousand—but only the warmest affection and the most perfect trust and confidence; and whenever a child died the fairies mourned just as that child's playmates did, and the sign of it was there to see: for before the dawn on the day of the funeral they hung a little immortelle over the place where that child was used to sit under the tree. I know this to be true by my own eyes, it is not hearsay. And the reason it was known that the fairies did it was this—that it was made all of black flowers of a sort not known in France anywhere.

Now from time immemorial all children reared in Domremy were called the Children of the Tree; and they loved that name, for it carried with it a mystic privilege not granted to any others of the children of this world. Which was this: whenever one of these came to die, then beyond the vague and formless images drifting through his darkening mind rose soft and rich and fair a vision of the Tree—if all was well with his soul. That was what some said. Others said the vision came in two ways: once as a warning, one or two years in advance of death, when the soul was the captive of sin, and then the Tree appeared in its desolate winter aspect—then that soul was smitten with an awful fear. If repentance came, and purity of life, the vision came again, this time summer-clad and beautiful; but if it were otherwise with that soul the vision was withheld, and it passed from life knowing its doom. Still others said that the vision came but once, and then only to the sinless dying forlorn in distant lands and pitifully longing for some last dear reminder of their home. And what reminder of it could go to their hearts like the picture of the Tree that was the darling of their love and the comrade of their joys and comforter of their small griefs all through the divine days of their vanished youth?

Now the several traditions were as I have said, some believing one and some another. One of them I knew to be the truth, and that was the last one. I do not say anything against the others; I think they were true, but I only *know* that the last one was; and it is my thought that if one keep to the things he knows, and not trouble about the things which he cannot be sure about, he will have the steadier mind for it—and there is profit in that. I know that when the Children of the Tree die in a far land, then—if they be at peace with God—they turn their longing eyes toward home, and there, far-shining, as through a rift in a cloud that curtains heaven, they see the soft picture of the Fairy Tree, clothed in a dream of golden light; and they see the bloomy mead sloping away to the river, and to their perishing nostrils is blown faint and sweet the fragrance of the flowers of home. And then the vision fades and passes—but *they* know, *they* know! and by their transfigured faces you know also, you who stand looking on; yes, you know the message that has come, and that it has come from heaven.

Joan and I believed alike about this matter. But Pierre Morel, and Jacques d'Arc, and many others believed that the vision appeared twice—to a sinner. In fact they and many others said they *knew* it. Probably because their fathers had known it and had told them; for one gets most things at second hand in this world.

Now one thing that does make it quite likely that there were really two apparitions of the Tree is this fact: From the most ancient times if one saw a villager of ours with his face ash-white and rigid with a ghastly fright, it was common for every one to whisper to his neighbor, "Ah, he is in sin, and has got his warning." And the neighbor would shudder at the thought and whisper back, "Yes, poor soul, he has seen the Tree."

Such evidences as these have their weight; they are not to be put aside with a wave of the hand. A thing that is backed by the cumulative experience of centuries naturally gets nearer and nearer to being proof all the time; and if this continue and continue, it will some day become authority—and authority is a bedded rock, and will abide.

In my long life I have seen several cases where the Tree appeared announcing a death which was still far away; but in none of these was the person in a state of sin. No; the apparition was in these cases only a special grace; in place of deferring the tidings of that soul's redemption till the day of death, the apparition brought them long before, and with them peace—peace that might no more be disturbed—the eternal peace of God. I myself, old and broken, wait with serenity; for I have seen the vision of the Tree. I have seen it, and am content.

Always, from the remotest times, when the children joined hands and danced around the Fairy Tree they sang a song which was the Tree's Song, the Song of *L'Arbre Fée de Bourlemont*. They sang it to a quaint sweet air—a solacing sweet air which has gone murmuring through my dreaming spirit all my life when I was weary and troubled, resting me and carrying me through night and distance home again. No stranger can know or feel what that song has been, through the drifting centuries, to exiled Children of the Tree, homeless and heavy of heart in countries foreign to their speech and ways. You will think it a simple thing, that song, and poor perchance; but if you will remember what it was to us, and what it brought before our eyes when it floated through our memories, then you will respect it. And you will understand how the water wells up in our eyes and makes all things dim, and our voices break and we cannot sing the last lines:

"And when in exile wand'ring we
Shall fainting yearn for glimpse of thee,
O rise upon our sight!"

And you will remember that Joan of Arc sang this song with us around the Tree when she was a little child, and always loved it. And that hallows it, yes, you will grant that:

L'ARBRE FÉE DE BOURLEMONT

SONG OF THE CHILDREN

Now what has kept your leaves so green,
  Arbre Fée de Bourlemont?
The children's tears! They brought each grief,
  And you did comfort them and cheer
  Their bruisèd hearts, and steal a tear
    That healèd rose a leaf.

And what has built you up so strong,
  Arbre Fée de Bourlemont?
The children's love! They've loved you long:
  Ten hundred years, in sooth,
They've nourished you with praise and song,
And warmed your heart and kept it young—
  A thousand years of youth!

Bide alway green in our young hearts,
  Arbre Fée de Bourlemont!
And we shall alway youthful be,
  Not heeding Time his flight;
And when in exile wand'ring we
Shall fainting yearn for glimpse of thee,
  O rise upon our sight!

The fairies were still there when we were children, but we never saw them; because, a hundred years before that, the priest of Domremy had held a religious function under the tree and denounced them as being blood kin of the Fiend and barred out from redemption; and then he warned them never to show themselves again, nor hang any more immortelles, on pain of perpetual banishment from that parish.

All the children pleaded for the fairies, and said they were their good friends and dear to them and never did them any harm, but the priest would not listen, and said it was sin and shame to have such friends. The children mourned and could not be comforted; and they made an agreement among themselves that they would always continue to hang flower-wreaths on the tree as a perpetual sign to the fairies that they were still loved and remembered, though lost to sight.

But late one night a great misfortune befell. Edmond Aubrey's mother passed by the Tree, and the fairies were stealing a dance, not thinking anybody was by; and they were so busy, and so intoxicated with the wild happiness of it, and with the bumpers of dew sharpened up with honey which they had been drinking, that they noticed nothing; so Dame Aubrey stood there astonished and admiring, and saw the little fantastic atoms holding hands, as many as three hundred of them, tearing around in a great ring half as big as an ordinary bedroom, and leaning away back and spreading their mouths with laughter and song, which she could hear quite distinctly, and kicking their legs up as much as three inches from the ground in perfect abandon and hilarity—oh, the very maddest and witchingest dance the woman ever saw.

But in about a minute or two minutes the poor little ruined creatures discovered her. They burst out in one heart-breaking squeak of grief and terror and fled every which way, with their wee hazel-nut fists in their eyes and crying; and so disappeared.

The heartless woman—no, the foolish woman; she was not heartless, but only thoughtless—went straight home and told the neighbors all about it, whilst we, the small friends of the fairies, were asleep and not witting the calamity that was come upon us, and all unconscious that we ought to be up and trying to stop these fatal tongues. In the morning everybody knew, and the disaster was complete, for where everybody knows a thing the priest knows it, of course. We all flocked to Père Fronte, crying and begging—and he had to cry, too, seeing our sorrow, for he had a most kind and gentle nature; and he did not want to banish the fairies, and said so; but said he had no choice, for it had been decreed that if they ever revealed themselves to man again, they must go. This all happened at the worst time possible, for Joan of Arc was ill of a fever and out of her head, and what could we do who had not her gifts of reasoning and persuasion? We flew in a swarm to her bed and cried out, "Joan, wake! Wake, there is no moment to lose! Come and plead for the fairies—come and save them; only you can do it."

But her mind was wandering, she did not know what we said nor what we meant; so we went away knowing all was lost. Yes, all was lost, forever lost; the faithful friends of the children for five hundred years must go, and never come back any more.

It was a bitter day for us, that day that Père Fronte held the function under the tree and banished the fairies. We could not wear mourning that any could have noticed, it would not have been allowed; so we had to be content with some poor small rag of black tied upon our garments where it made no show; but in our hearts we wore mourning big and noble and occupying all the room, for our *hearts* were ours; they could not get at them to prevent that.

The great tree—*l'Arbre Fée de Bourlemont* was its beautiful name—was never afterward quite as much to us as it had been before, but it was always dear; is dear to me yet when I go there, now, once a year in my old age, to sit under it and bring back the lost playmates of my youth and group them about me and look upon their faces through my tears and break my heart, oh, my God! No, the place was not quite the same afterwards. In one or two ways it could not be; for, the fairies' protection being gone, the spring lost much of its freshness and coldness, and more than two-thirds of its volume, and the banished serpents and stinging insects returned, and multiplied, and became a torment and have remained so to this day.

When that wise little child, Joan, got well, we realized how much her illness had cost us; for we found that we had been right in believing she could save the fairies. She burst into a great storm of anger, for so little a creature, and went straight to Père Fronte, and stood up before him where he sat, and made reverence and said:

"The fairies were to go if they showed themselves to people again, is it not so?"

"Yes, that was it, dear."

"If a man comes prying into a person's room at midnight when that person is half naked, will you be so unjust as to say that that person is showing himself to that man?"

"Well—no." The good priest looked a little troubled and uneasy when he said it.

"Is a sin a sin anyway, even if one did not intend to commit it?"

Père Fronte threw up his hands and cried out—

"Oh, my poor little child, I see all my fault," and he drew her to his side and put his arm around her and tried to make his peace with her, but her temper was up so high that she could not get it down right away, but buried her head against his breast and broke out crying and said:

"Then the fairies committed no sin, for there was no intention to commit one, they not knowing that any one was by; and because they were little creatures and could not speak for themselves and say the law was against the intention, not against the innocent act, and because they had no friend to think that simple thing for them and say it, they have been sent away from their home forever, and it was wrong, *wrong* to do it!"

The good father hugged her yet closer to his side and said:

"Oh, out of the mouths of babes and sucklings the heedless and unthinking are condemned: would God I could bring the little creatures back, for your sake. And mine, yes, and mine; for I have been unjust. There, there, don't cry—nobody could be sorrier than your poor old friend—don't cry, dear."

"But I can't stop right away, I've *got* to. And it is no little matter, this thing that you have done. Is being sorry penance enough for such an act?"

Père Fronte turned away his face, for it would have hurt her to see him laugh, and said:

"Oh, thou remorseless but most just accuser, no, it is not. I will put on sackcloth and ashes; there—are you satisfied?"

Joan's sobs began to diminish, and she presently looked up at the old man through her tears, and said, in her simple way:

"Yes, that will do—if it will clear you."

Père Fronte would have been moved to laugh again, perhaps, if he had not remembered in time that he had made a contract, and not a very agreeable one. It must be fulfilled. So he got up and went to the fireplace, Joan watching him with deep interest, and took a shovelful of cold ashes, and was going to empty them on his old gray head when a better idea came to him, and he said:

"Would you mind helping me, dear?"

"How, father?"

He got down on his knees and bent his head low, and said:

"Take the ashes and put them on my head for me."

The matter ended there, of course. The victory was with the priest. One can imagine how the idea of such a profanation would strike Joan or any other child in the village. She ran and dropped upon her knees by his side and said:

"Oh, it is dreadful. I didn't know that that was what one meant by sackcloth and ashes—do please get up, father."

"But I can't until I am forgiven. Do you forgive me?"

"I? Oh, you have done nothing to me, father; it is *yourself* that must forgive yourself for wronging those poor things. Please get up, father, won't you?"

"But I am worse off now than I was before. I thought I was earning *your* forgiveness, but if it is my own, I can't be lenient; it would not become me. Now what can I do? Find me some way out of this with your wise little head."

The Père would not stir, for all Joan's pleadings. She was about to cry again; then she had an idea, and seized the shovel and deluged her own head with the ashes, stammering out through her chokings and suffocations—

"There—now it is done. Oh, please get up, father."

The old man, both touched and amused, gathered her to his breast and said—

"Oh, you incomparable child! It's a humble martyrdom, and not of a sort presentable in a picture, but the right and true spirit is in it; that I testify."

Then he brushed the ashes out of her hair, and helped her scour her face and neck and properly tidy herself up. He was in fine spirits now, and ready for further argument, so he took his seat and drew Joan to his side again, and said:

"Joan, you were used to make wreaths there at the Fairy Tree with the other children; is it not so?"

That was the way he always started out when he was going to corner me up and catch me in something—just that gentle, indifferent way that fools a person so, and leads him into the trap, he never noticing which way he is travelling until he is in and the door shut on him. He enjoyed that. I knew he was going to drop corn along in front of Joan now. Joan answered:

"Yes, father."

"Did you hang them on the tree?"

"No, father."

"Didn't hang them there?"

"No."

"Why didn't you?"

"I—well, I didn't wish to."

"Didn't wish to?"

"No, father."

"What did you do with them?"

"I hung them in the church."

"Why didn't you want to hang them in the tree?"

"Because it was said that the fairies were of kin to the Fiend, and that it was sinful to show them honor."

"Did you believe it was wrong to honor them so?"

"Yes. I thought it must be wrong."

"Then if it was wrong to honor them in that way, and if they were of kin to the Fiend, they could be dangerous company for you and the other children, couldn't they?"

"I suppose so—yes, I think so."

He studied a minute, and I judged he was going to spring his trap, and he did. He said:

"Then the matter stands like this. They were banned creatures, of fearful origin; they could be dangerous company for the children. Now give me a rational reason, dear, if you can think of any, why you call it a wrong to drive them into banishment, and why you would have saved them from it. In a word, what loss have you suffered by it?"

How stupid of him to go and throw his case away like that! I could have boxed his ears for vexation if he had been a boy. He was going along all right until he ruined everything by winding up in that foolish and fatal way. What had *she* lost by it! Was he never going to find out what kind of a child Joan of Arc was? Was he never going to learn that things which merely concerned her own gain or loss she cared nothing about? Could he never get the simple fact into his head that the sure way and the only way to rouse her up and set her on fire was to show her where some *other* person was going to suffer wrong or hurt or loss? Why, he had gone and set a trap for himself—that was all he had accomplished.

The minute those words were out of his mouth her temper was up, the indignant tears rose in her eyes, and she burst out on him with an energy and passion which astonished him, but didn't astonish me, for I knew he had fired a mine when he touched off his ill-chosen climax.

"Oh, father, how can you talk like that? Who owns France?"

"God and the King."

"Not Satan?"

"Satan, my child? This is the footstool of the Most High—Satan owns no handful of its soil."

"Then who gave those poor creatures their home? God. Who protected them in it all those centuries? God. Who allowed them to dance and play there all those centuries and found no fault with it? God. Who disapproved of God's approval and put a threat upon them? A man. Who caught them again in harmless sports that God allowed and a man forbade, and carried out that threat, and drove the poor things away from the home the good God gave them in His mercy and His pity, and sent down His rain and dew and sunshine upon it five hundred years in token of His peace? It was *their* home—theirs, by the grace of God and His good heart, and no man had a right to rob them of it. And they were the gentlest, truest friends that children ever had, and did them sweet and loving service all these five long centuries, and never any hurt or harm; and the children loved them, and now they mourn for them, and there is no healing for their grief. And what had the children done that they should suffer this cruel stroke? The poor fairies *could* have been dangerous company for the children? Yes, but never had been; and *could* is no argument. Kinsmen of the Fiend? What of it? Kinsmen of the Fiend have *rights,* and these had; and children have rights, and these had; and if I had been here I would have spoken—I would have begged for the children and the fiends, and stayed your hand and saved them all. But now—oh, now, all is lost; everything is lost, and there is no help more!"

Then she finished with a blast at that idea that fairy kinsmen of the Fiend ought to be shunned and denied human sympathy and friendship because salvation was barred against them. She said that for that very *reason* people ought to pity them, and do every humane and loving thing they could to make them forget the hard fate that had been put upon them by accident of birth and no fault of their own. "Poor little creatures!" she said. "What can a person's heart be made of that can pity a Christian's child and yet can't pity a devil's child, that a thousand times more *needs* it!"

She had torn loose from Père Fronte, and was crying, with her knuckles in her eyes, and stamping her small feet in a fury; and now she burst out of the place and was gone before we could gather our senses together out of this storm of words and this whirlwind of passion.

The Père had got upon his feet, toward the last, and now he stood there passing his hand back and forth across his forehead like a person who is dazed and troubled; then he turned and wandered toward the door of his little workroom, and as he passed through it I heard him murmur sorrowfully:

"Ah me, poor children, poor fiends, they *have* rights, and she said true—I never thought of that. God forgive me, I am to blame."

When I heard that, I knew I was right in the thought that he had set a trap for himself. It was so, and he had walked into it, you see. I seemed to feel encouraged, and wondered if mayhap I might get him into one; but upon reflection my heart went down, for this was not my gift.

CHAPTER 3

Speaking of this matter reminds me of many incidents, many things that I could tell, but I think I will not try to do it now. It will be more to my present humor to call back a little glimpse of the simple and colorless good times we used to have in our village homes in those peaceful days—especially in the winter. In the summer we children were out on the breezy uplands with the flocks from dawn till night, and then there was noisy frolicking and all that; but winter was the cosey time, winter was the snug time. Often we gathered in old Jacques d'Arc's big dirt-floored apartment, with a great fire going, and played games, and sang songs, and told fortunes, and listened to the old villagers tell tales and histories and lies and one thing and another till twelve o'clock at night.

One winter's night we were gathered there—it was the winter that for years afterward they called the hard winter—and that particular night was a sharp one. It blew a gale outside, and the screaming of the wind was a stirring sound, and I think I may say it was beautiful, for I think it *is* great and fine and beautiful to hear the wind rage and storm and blow its clarions like that, when you are inside and comfortable. And we were. We had a roaring fire, and the pleasant *spit-spit* of the snow and sleet falling in it down the chimney, and the yarning and laughing and singing went on at a noble rate till about ten o'clock, and then we had a supper of hot porridge and beans, and meal cakes with butter, and appetites to match.

Little Joan sat on a box apart, and had her bowl and bread on another one, and her pets around her, helping. She had more than was usual of them or economical, because all the outcast cats came and took up with her, and homeless or unlovable animals of other kinds heard about it and came, and these spread the matter to the other creatures, and they came also; and as the birds and the other timid wild things of the woods were not afraid of her, but always had an idea she was a friend when they came across her, and generally struck up an acquaintance with her to get invited to the house, she always had samples of those breeds in stock. She was hospitable to them all, for an animal was an animal to her, and dear by mere reason of being an animal, no matter about its sort or social station; and as she would allow of no cages, no collars, no fetters, but left the creatures free to come and go as they liked, that contented them, and they came; but they didn't go, to any extent, and so they were a marvellous nuisance, and made Jacques d'Arc swear a good deal; but his wife said God gave the child the instinct, and knew what He was doing when He did it, therefore it must have its course; it would be no sound prudence to meddle with His affairs when no invitation had been extended. So the pets were left in peace, and here they were, as I have said, rabbits, birds, squirrels, cats, and other reptiles, all around the child, and full of interest in her supper, and helping what they could. There was a very small squirrel on her shoulder, sitting up, as those creatures do, and turning a rocky fragment of prehistoric chestnut-cake over and over in its knotty hands, and hunting for the less indurated places, and giving its elevated bushy tail a flirt and its pointed ears a toss when it found one—signifying thankfulness and surprise—and then it filed that place off with those two slender front teeth which a squirrel carries for that purpose and not for ornament, for ornamental they never could be, as any will admit that have noticed them.

Everything was going fine and breezy and hilarious, but then there came an interruption, for somebody hammered on the door. It was one of those ragged road-stragglers—the eternal wars kept the country full of them. He came in, all over snow, and stamped his feet and shook and brushed himself, and shut the door, and took off his limp ruin of a hat and slapped it once or twice against his leg to knock off its fleece of snow, and then glanced around on the company with a pleased look upon his thin face, and a most yearning and famished one in his eye when it fell upon the victuals, and then he gave us a humble and conciliatory salutation, and said it was a blessed thing to have a fire like that on such a night, and a roof overhead like this, and that rich food to eat, and loving friends to talk with—ah, yes, this was true, and God help the homeless, and such as must trudge the roads in this weather.

Nobody said anything. The embarrassed poor creature stood there and appealed to one face after the other with his eyes, and found no welcome in any, the smile on his own face flickering and fading and perishing, meanwhile; then he dropped his gaze, the muscles of his face began to twitch, and he put up his hand to cover this womanish sign of weakness.

"Sit down!"

This thunder-blast was from old Jacques d'Arc, and Joan was the object of it. The stranger was startled, and took his hand away, and there was Joan standing before him offering him her bowl of porridge. The man said,

"God Almighty bless you, my darling!" and then the tears came, and ran down his cheeks, but he was afraid to take the bowl.

"Do you hear me? Sit down, I say!"

There could not be a child more easy to persuade than Joan, but this was not the way. Her father had not the art; neither could he learn it. Joan said,

"Father, he is hungry; I can see it."

"Let him go work for food, then. We are being eaten out of house and home by his like, and I have said I would endure it no more, and will keep my word. He has the face of a rascal anyhow, and a villain. Sit *down,* I tell you!"

"I know not if he is a rascal or no, but he is hungry, father, and shall have my porridge—I do not need it."

"If you don't obey me I'll— Rascals are not entitled to help from honest people, and no bite nor sup shall they have in this house. *Joan!*"

She set her bowl down on the box and came over and stood before her scowling father, and said:

"Father, if you will not let me, then it must be as you say; but I would that you would think—then you would see that it is not right to punish one part of him for what the other part has done; for it is that poor stranger's head that does the evil things, but it is not his head that is hungry, it is his stomach, and it has done no harm to anybody, but is without blame, and innocent, not having any *way* to do a wrong, even if it was minded to it. Please let—"

"What an idea! It is the most idiotic speech I ever heard."

But Aubrey, the maire, broke in, he being fond of an argument, and having a pretty gift in that regard, as all acknowledged. Rising in his place and leaning his knuckles upon the table and looking about him with easy dignity, after the manner of such as be orators, he began, smooth and persuasive:

"I will differ with you there, gossip, and will undertake to show the company"—here he looked around upon us and nodded his head in a confident way—"that there is a grain of sense in what the child has said; for look you, it is of a certainty most true and demonstrable that it is a man's head that is master and supreme ruler over his whole body. Is that granted? Will any deny it?" He glanced around again; everybody indicated assent. "Very well, then; that being the case, no part of the body is responsible for the result when it carries out an order delivered to it by the head; ergo, the head is alone responsible for crimes done by a man's hands or feet or stomach—do you get the idea? am I right thus far?" Everybody said yes, and said it with enthusiasm, and some said, one to another, that the maire was in great form to-night and at his very best—which pleased the maire exceedingly and made his eyes sparkle with pleasure, for he overheard these things; so he went on in the same fertile and brilliant way. "Now, then, we will consider what the term responsibility means, and how it affects the case in point. Responsibility makes a man responsible for only those things for which he is properly responsible"—and he waved his spoon around in a wide sweep to indicate the comprehensive nature of that class of responsibilities which render people responsible, and several exclaimed, admiringly, "He is right!—he has put that whole tangled thing into a nutshell—it is wonderful!" After a little pause to give the interest opportunity to gather and grow, he went on: "Very good. Let us suppose the case of a pair of tongs that falls upon a man's foot, causing a cruel hurt. Will you claim that the tongs are punishable for that? The question is answered: I see by your faces that you would call such a claim absurd. Now, why is it absurd? It is absurd because, there being no reasoning faculty—that is to say, no faculty of personal command—in a pair of tongs, personal responsibility for the acts of the tongs is wholly absent from the tongs; and therefore, responsibility being absent, punishment cannot ensue. Am I right?" A hearty burst of applause was his answer. "Now, then, we arrive at a man's stomach. Consider how exactly, how marvellously, indeed, its situation corresponds to that of a pair of tongs. Listen—and take careful note, I beg you. Can a man's stomach plan a murder? No. Can it plan a theft? No. Can it plan an incendiary fire? No. Now answer me—*can a pair of tongs?*" (There were admiring shouts of "No!" and "The cases are just exact!" and "Don't he do it splendid!") "Now, then, friends and neighbors, a stomach which cannot plan a crime cannot be a principal in the commission of it—that is plain, as you see. The matter is narrowed down by that much; we will narrow it further. Can a stomach, of its own motion, assist at a crime? The answer is no, because command is absent, the reasoning faculty is absent, volition is absent—as in the case of the tongs. We perceive, now, do we not, that the stomach is totally irresponsible for crimes committed, either in whole or in part, by it?" He got a rousing cheer for response. "Then what do we arrive at as our verdict? Clearly this: that there is no such thing in this world as a guilty stomach; that in the body of the veriest rascal resides a pure and innocent stomach; that, whatever its owner may do, *it* at least should be sacred in our eyes; and that while God gives us minds to think just and charitable and honorable thoughts, it should be and *is* our privilege, as well as our duty, not only to feed the hungry stomach that resides in a rascal, having pity for its sorrow and its need, but to do it gladly, gratefully, in recognition of its sturdy and loyal maintenance of its purity and innocence in the midst of temptation and in company so repugnant to its better feelings. I am done."

Well, you never saw such an effect! They rose—the whole house rose—and clapped, and cheered, and praised him to the skies; and one after another, still clapping and shouting, they crowded forward, some with moisture in their eyes, and wrung his hands, and said such glorious things to him that he was clear overcome with pride and happiness, and couldn't say a word, for his voice would have broken, sure. It was splendid to see; and everybody said he had never come up to that speech in his life before, and never could do it again. Eloquence *is* a power, there is no question of that. Even old Jacques d'Arc was carried away, for once in his life, and shouted out—

"It's all right, Joan—give him the porridge!"

She was embarrassed, and did not seem to know what to say, and so didn't say anything. It was because she had given the man the porridge long ago, and he had already eaten it all up. When she was asked why she had not waited until a decision was arrived at, she said the man's stomach was very hungry, and it would not have been wise to wait, since she could not tell what the decision would be. Now that was a good and thoughtful idea for a child.

The man was not a rascal at all. He was a very good fellow, only he was out of luck, and surely that was no crime at that time in France. Now that his stomach was proved to be innocent, it was allowed to make itself at home; and as soon as it was well filled and needed nothing more, the man unwound his tongue and turned it loose, and it was really a noble one to go. He had been in the wars for years, and the things he told, and the way he told them, fired everybody's patriotism away up high, and set all hearts to thumping and all pulses to leaping; then, before anybody rightly knew how the change was made, he was leading us a sublime march through the ancient glories of France, and in fancy we saw the titanic forms of the twelve paladins rise out of the mists of the past and face their fate; we heard the tread of the innumerable hosts sweeping down to shut them in; we saw this human tide flow and ebb, ebb and flow, and waste away before that little band of heroes; we saw each detail pass before us of that most stupendous, most disastrous, yet most adored and glorious day in French legendary history; here and there and yonder, across that vast field of the dead and dying, we saw this and that and the other paladin dealing his prodigious blows with weary arm and failing strength, and one by one we saw them fall, till only one remained—he that was without peer, he whose name gives name to the Song of Songs, the song which no Frenchman can hear and keep his feelings down and his pride of country cool; then, grandest and pitifulest scene of all, we saw his own pathetic death; and our stillness, as we sat with parted lips and breathless, hanging upon this man's words, gave us a sense of the awful stillness that reigned in that field of slaughter when that last surviving soul had passed.

And now, in this solemn hush, the stranger gave Joan a pat or two on the head and said:

"Little maid—whom God keep!—you have brought me from death to life this night; now listen: here is your reward," and at that supreme time for such a heart-melting, soul-rousing surprise, without another word he lifted up the most noble and pathetic voice that was ever heard, and began to pour out the great Song of Roland!

Think of that, with a French audience all stirred up and ready. Oh, where was your spoken eloquence now! what was it to this! How fine he looked, how stately, how inspired, as he stood there with that mighty chant welling from his lips and his heart, his whole body transfigured, and his rags along with it.

Everybody rose and stood, while he sang, and their faces glowed and their eyes burned; and the tears came and flowed down their cheeks, and their forms began to sway unconsciously to the swing of the song, and their bosoms to heave and pant; and moanings broke out, and deep ejaculations; and when the last verse was reached, and Roland lay dying, all alone, with his face to the field and to his slain, lying there in heaps and winrows, and took off and held up his gauntlet to God with his failing hand, and breathed his beautiful prayer with his paling lips, all burst out in sobs and wailings. But when the final great note died out and the song was done, they all flung themselves in a body at the singer, stark mad with love of him and love of France and pride in her great deeds and old renown, and smothered him with their embracings; but Joan was there first, hugged close to his breast, and covering his face with idolatrous kisses.

The storm raged on outside, but that was no matter; this was the stranger's home now, for as long as he might please.

CHAPTER 4

All children have nicknames, and we had ours. We got one apiece early, and they stuck to us; but Joan was richer in this matter, for as time went on she earned a second, and then a third, and so on, and we gave them to her. First and last she had as many as half a dozen. Several of these she never lost. Peasant girls are bashful naturally; but she surpassed the rule so far, and colored so easily, and was so easily embarrassed in the presence of strangers, that we nicknamed her the Bashful. We were all patriots, but she was called *the* Patriot, because our warmest feeling for our country was cold beside hers. Also she was called the Beautiful; and this was not merely because of the extraordinary beauty of her face and form, but because of the loveliness of her character. These names she kept, and one other—the Brave.

We grew along up, in that plodding and peaceful region, and got to be good-sized boys and girls—big enough, in fact, to begin to know as much about the wars raging perpetually to the west and north of us as our elders, and also to feel as stirred up over the occasional news from those red fields as they did. I remember certain of these days very clearly. One Tuesday a crowd of us were romping and singing around the Fairy Tree, and hanging garlands on it in memory of our lost little fairy friends, when little Mengette cried out:

"Look! What is that?"

When one exclaims like that, in a way that shows astonishment and apprehension, he gets attention. All the panting breasts and flushed faces flocked together, and all the eager eyes were turned in one direction—down the slope, toward the village.

"It's a black flag."

"A black flag! No—is it?"

"You can see for yourself that it is nothing else."

"It *is* a black flag, sure! Now, has any ever seen the like of that before?"

"What can it mean?"

"Mean? It means something dreadful—what else?"

"That is nothing to the point; anybody knows that without the telling. But *what*?—that is the question."

"It is a chance that he that bears it can answer as well as any that are here, if you can contain yourself till he come."

"He runs well. Who is it?"

Some named one, some another; but presently all saw that it was Étienne Roze, called the Sunflower, because he had yellow hair and a round, pock-marked face. His ancestors had been Germans some centuries ago. He came straining up the slope, now and then projecting his flag-stick aloft and giving his black symbol of woe a wave in the air, whilst all eyes watched him, all tongues discussed him, and every heart beat faster and faster with impatience to know his news. At last he sprang among us, and struck his flag-stick into the ground, saying:

"There! Stand there and represent France while I get my breath. She needs no other flag, now."

All the giddy chatter stopped. It was as if one had announced a death. In that chilly hush there was no sound audible but the panting of the breath-blown boy. When he was presently able to speak, he said:

"Black news is come. A treaty has been made at Troyes between France and the English and Burgundians. By it France is betrayed and delivered over, tied hand and foot, to the enemy. It is the work of the Duke of Burgundy and that she-devil the Queen of France. It marries Henry of England to Catharine of France—"

"Is not this a lie? Marries the daughter of France to the Butcher of Agincourt? It is not to be believed. You have not heard aright."

"If you cannot believe that, Jacques d'Arc, then you have a difficult task indeed before you, for worse is to come. Any child that is born of that marriage—if even a girl—is to inherit the thrones of both England and France, and this double ownership is to remain with its posterity forever!"

"Now *that* is certainly a lie, for it runs counter to our Salic law, and so is not legal and cannot have effect," said Edmond Aubrey, called the Paladin, because of the armies he was always going to eat up some day. He would have said more, but he was drowned out by the clamors of the others, who all burst into a fury over this feature of the treaty, all talking at once and nobody hearing anybody, until presently Haumette persuaded them to be still, saying:

"It is not fair to break him up so in his tale; pray let him go on. You find fault with his history because it seems to be lies. That were reason for satisfaction—*that* kind of lies—not discontent. Tell the rest, Étienne."

"There is but this to tell: Our King, Charles VI., is to reign until he dies, then Henry V. of England is to be Regent of France until a child of his shall be old enough to—"

"*That* man is to reign over us—the Butcher? It is lies! all lies!" cried the Paladin. "Besides, look you—what becomes of our Dauphin? What says the treaty about him?"

"Nothing. It takes away his throne and makes him an outcast."

Then everybody shouted at once and said the news was a lie; and all began to get cheerful again, saying, "Our King would have to sign the treaty to make it good; and that he would not do, seeing how it serves his own son."

But the Sunflower said: "I will ask you this: Would the *Queen* sign a treaty disinheriting her son?"

"That viper? Certainly. Nobody is talking of her. Nobody expects better of her. There is no villany she will stick at, if it feed her spite; and she hates her son. Her signing it is of no consequence. The King must sign."

"I will ask you another thing. What is the King's condition? Mad, isn't he?"

"Yes, and his people love him all the more for it. It brings him near to them by his sufferings; and pitying him makes them love him."

"You say right, Jacques d'Arc. Well, what would you of one that is mad? Does he know what he does? No. Does he do what others make him do? Yes. Now, then, I tell you he has signed the treaty."

"Who made him do it?"

"You know, without my telling. The Queen."

Then there was another uproar—everybody talking at once, and all heaping execrations upon the Queen's head. Finally Jacques d'Arc said:

"But many reports come that are not true. Nothing so shameful as this has ever come before, nothing that cuts so deep, nothing that has dragged France so low; therefore there is hope that this tale is but another idle rumor. Where did you get it?"

The color went out of his sister Joan's face. She dreaded the answer; and her instinct was right.

"The curé of Maxey brought it."

There was a general gasp. We knew him, you see, for a trusty man.

"Did he believe it?"

The hearts almost stopped beating. Then came the answer:

"He did. And that is not all. He said he *knew* it to be true."

Some of the girls began to sob; the boys were struck silent. The distress in Joan's face was like that which one sees in the face of a dumb animal that has received a mortal hurt. The animal bears it, making no complaint; she bore it also, saying no word. Her brother Jacques put his hand on her head and caressed her hair to indicate his sympathy, and she gathered the hand to her lips and kissed it for thanks, not saying anything. Presently the reaction came, and the boys began to talk. Noël Rainguesson said:

"Oh, are we never going to be men! We do grow along so slowly, and France never needed soldiers as she needs them now, to wipe out this black insult."

"I hate youth!" said Pierre Morel, called the Dragon-fly because his eyes stuck out so. "You've always got to wait, and wait, and wait—and here are the great wars wasting away for a hundred years, and you never get a chance. If I could only be a soldier now!"

"As for me, I'm not going to wait much longer," said the Paladin; "and when I do start you'll hear from me, I promise you that. There are some who, in storming a castle, prefer to be in the rear; but as for me, give me the front or none; I will have none in front of me but the officers."

Even the girls got the war spirit, and Marie Dupont said—

"I would I were a man; I would start this minute!" and looked very proud of herself, and glanced about for applause.

"So would I," said Cécile Letellier, sniffing the air like a war-horse that smells the battle; "I warrant you I would not turn back from the field though all England were in front of me."

"Pooh!" said the Paladin; "girls can brag, but that's all they are good for. Let a thousand of them come face to face with a handful of soldiers once, if you want to see what running is like. Here's little Joan—next *she'll* be threatening to go for a soldier!"

The idea was so funny, and got such a good laugh, that the Paladin gave it another trial, and said: "Why, you can just see her!—see her plunge into battle like any old veteran. Yes, indeed; and not a poor shabby common soldier like us, but an officer—an officer, mind you, with armor on, and the bars of a steel helmet to blush behind and hide her embarrassment when she finds an army in front of her that she hasn't been introduced to. An officer? Why, she'll be a captain! A captain, I tell you, with a hundred men at her back—or maybe girls. Oh, no common-soldier business for her! And, dear me, when she starts for that other army, you'll think there's a hurricane blowing it away!"

Well, he kept it up like that till he made their sides ache with laughing; which was quite natural, for certainly it was a very funny idea—at that time—I mean, the idea of that gentle little creature, that wouldn't hurt a fly, and couldn't bear the sight of blood, and was so girlish and shrinking in all ways, rushing into battle with a gang of soldiers at her back. Poor thing, she sat there confused and ashamed to be so laughed at; and yet at that very minute there was something about to happen which would change the aspect of things, and make those young people see that when it comes to laughing, the person that laughs last has the best chance. For just then a face which we all knew and all feared projected itself from behind the Fairy Tree, and the thought that shot through us all was, crazy Benoist has gotten loose from his cage, and we are as good as dead! This ragged and hairy and horrible creature glided out from behind the tree, and raised an axe as he came. We all broke and fled, this way and that, the girls screaming and crying. No, not all; all but Joan. She stood up and faced the man, and remained so. As we reached the wood that borders the grassy clearing and jumped into its shelter, two or three of us glanced back to see if Benoist was gaining on us, and that is what we saw—Joan standing, and the maniac gliding stealthily toward her with his axe lifted. The sight was sickening. We stood where we were, trembling and not able to move. I did not want to see the murder done, and yet I could not take my eyes away. Now I saw Joan step forward to meet the man, though I believed my eyes must be deceiving me. Then I saw him stop. He threatened her with his axe, as if to warn her not to come further, but she paid no heed, but went steadily on, until she was right in front of him—right under his axe. Then she stopped, and seemed to begin to talk with him. It made me sick, yes, giddy, and everything swam around me, and I could not see anything for a time—whether long or brief I do not know. When this passed and I looked again, Joan was walking by the man's side toward the village, holding him by his hand. The axe was in her other hand.

One by one the boys and girls crept out, and we stood there gazing, open-mouthed, till those two entered the village and were hid from sight. It was then that we named her the Brave.

We left the black flag there to continue its mournful office, for we had other matter to think of now. We started for the village on a run, to give warning, and get Joan out of her peril; though for one, after seeing what I had seen, it seemed to me that while Joan had the axe the man's chance was not the best of the two. When we arrived the danger was past, the madman was in custody. All the people were flocking to the little square in front of the church to talk and exclaim and wonder over the event, and it even made the town forget the black news of the treaty for two or three hours.

All the women kept hugging and kissing Joan, and praising her, and crying, and the men patted her on the head and said they wished she was a man, they would send her to the wars and never doubt but that she would strike some blows that would be heard of. She had to tear herself away and go and hide, this glory was so trying to her diffidence.

Of course the people began to ask us for the particulars. I was so ashamed that I made an excuse to the first comer, and got privately away and went back to the Fairy Tree, to get relief from the embarrassment of those questionings. There I found Joan, but she was there to get relief from the embarrassment of glory. One by one the others shirked the inquirers and joined us in our refuge. Then we gathered around Joan, and asked her how she had dared to do that thing. She was very modest about it, and said:

"You make a great thing of it, but you mistake; it was not a great matter. It was not as if I had been a stranger to the man. I know him, and have known him long; and he knows me, and likes me. I have fed him through the bars of his cage many times; and last December when they chopped off two of his fingers to remind him to stop seizing and wounding people passing by, I dressed his hand every day till it was well again."

"That is all well enough," said Little Mengette, "but he is a madman, dear, and so his likings and his gratitude and friendliness go for nothing when his rage is up. You did a perilous thing."

"Of course you did," said the Sunflower. "Didn't he threaten to kill you with the axe?"

"Yes."

"Didn't he threaten you more than once?"

"Yes."

"Didn't you feel afraid?"

"No—at least not much—very little."

"Why didn't you?"

She thought a moment, then said, quite simply—

"I don't know."

It made everybody laugh. Then the Sunflower said it was like a lamb trying to think out how it had come to eat a wolf, but had to give it up.

Cécile Letellier asked, "Why didn't you run when we did?"

"Because it was necessary to get him to his cage; else he would kill some one. Then he would come to the like harm himself."

It is noticeable that this remark, which implies that Joan was entirely forgetful of herself and her own danger, and had thought and wrought for the preservation of other people alone, was not challenged, or criticised, or commented upon by anybody there, but was taken by all as matter of course and true. It shows how clearly her character was defined, and how well it was known and established.

There was silence for a time, and perhaps we were all thinking of the same thing—namely, what a poor figure we had cut in that adventure as contrasted with Joan's performance. I tried to think up some good way of explaining why I had run away and left a little girl at the mercy of a maniac armed with an axe, but all of the explanations that offered themselves to me seemed so cheap and shabby that I gave the matter up and remained still. But others were less wise. Noël Rainguesson fidgeted a while, then broke out with a remark which showed what his mind had been running on:

"The fact is, I was taken by surprise. That is the reason. If I had had a moment to think, I would no more have thought of running than I would think of running from a baby. For, after all, what is Théophile Benoist, that I should seem to be afraid of him? Pooh! the idea of being afraid of that poor thing! I only wish he would come along now—I'd show you!"

"So do I!" cried Pierre Morel. "If I wouldn't make him climb this tree quicker than—well, you'd see what I would do! Taking a person by surprise, that way—why, I never meant to run; not in earnest, I mean. I never thought of running in earnest; I only wanted to have some fun, and when I saw Joan standing there, and him threatening her, it was all I could do to restrain myself from going there and just tearing the livers and lights out of him. I *wanted* to do it bad enough, and if it was to do over again, I *would!* If ever he comes fooling around me again, I'll—"

"Oh, hush!" said the Paladin, breaking in with an air of disdain; "the way you people talk, a person would think there's something heroic about standing up and facing down that poor remnant of a man. Why, it's nothing! There's small glory to be got in facing *him* down, I should say. Why, I wouldn't want any better fun than to face down a hundred like him. If he was to come along here now, I would walk up to him just as I am now—I wouldn't care if he had a thousand axes—and say—"

And so he went on and on, telling the brave things he would say and the wonders he would do; and the others put in a word from time to time, describing over again the gory marvels they would do if ever that madman ventured to cross their path again, for next time they would be ready for him, and would soon teach him that if he thought he could surprise them twice because he had surprised them once, he would find himself very seriously mistaken, that's all.

And so, in the end, they all got back their self-respect; yes, and even added somewhat to it; indeed, when the sitting broke up they had a finer opinion of themselves than they had ever had before.

CHAPTER 5

They were peaceful and pleasant, those young and smoothly flowing days of ours; that is, that was the case as a rule, we being remote from the seat of war, but at intervals roving bands approached near enough for us to see the flush in the sky at night which marked where they were burning some farmstead or village, and we all knew, or at least felt, that some day they would come yet nearer, and we should have our turn. This dull dread lay upon our spirits like a physical weight. It was greatly augmented a couple of years after the Treaty of Troyes.

It was truly a dismal year for France. One day we had been over to have one of our occasional pitched battles with those hated Burgundian boys of the village of Maxey, and had been whipped, and were arriving on our side of the river after dark, bruised and weary, when we heard the bell ringing the tocsin. We ran all the way, and when we got to the square we found it crowded with the excited villagers, and weirdly lighted by smoking and flaring torches.

On the steps of the church stood a stranger, a Burgundian priest, who was telling the people news which made them weep, and rave, and rage, and curse, by turns. He said our old mad King was dead, and that now we and France and the crown were the property of an English baby lying in his cradle in London. And he urged us to give that child our allegiance, and be its faithful servants and well-wishers; and said we should now have a strong and stable government at last, and that in a little time the English armies would start on their last march, and it would be a brief one, for all that it would need to do would be to conquer what odds and ends of our country yet remained under that rare and almost forgotten rag, the banner of France.

The people stormed and raged at him, and you could see dozens of them stretch their fists above the sea of torch-lighted faces and shake them at him; and it was all a wild picture, and stirring to look at; and the priest was a first-rate part of it, too, for he stood there in the strong glare and looked down on those angry people in the blandest and most indifferent way, so that while you wanted to burn him at the stake, you still admired the aggravating coolness of him. And his winding up was the coolest thing of all. For he told them how, at the funeral of our old King, the French King-at-Arms had broken his staff of office over the coffin of "Charles VI. and his dynasty," at the same time saying, in a loud voice, "God grant long life to Henry, King of France and England, our sovereign lord!" and then he asked them to join him in a hearty Amen to *that!*

The people were white with wrath, and it tied their tongues for the moment, and they could not speak. But Joan was standing close by, and she looked up in his face, and said in her sober, earnest way—"I would I might see thy head struck from thy body!"—then, after a pause, and crossing herself—"if it were the will of God."

This is worth remembering, and I will tell you why: it is the only harsh speech Joan ever uttered in her life. When I shall have revealed to you the storms she went through, and the wrongs and persecutions, then you will see that it was wonderful that she said but one bitter thing while she lived.

From the day that that dreary news came we had one scare after another, the marauders coming almost to our doors every now and then; so that we lived in ever-increasing apprehension, and yet were somehow mercifully spared from actual attack. But at last our turn did really come. This was in the spring of '28. The Burgundians swarmed in with a great noise, in the middle of a dark night, and we had to jump up and fly for our lives. We took the road to Neufchâteau, and rushed along in the wildest disorder, everybody trying to get ahead, and thus the movements of all were impeded; but Joan had a cool head—the only cool head there—and she took command and brought order out of that chaos. She did her work quickly and with decision and despatch, and soon turned the panic flight into a quite steady-going march. You will grant that for so young a person, and a girl at that, this was a good piece of work.

She was sixteen now, shapely and graceful, and of a beauty so extraordinary that I might allow myself any extravagance of language in describing it and yet have no fear of going beyond the truth. There was in her face a sweetness and serenity and purity that justly reflected her spiritual nature. She was deeply religious, and this is a thing which sometimes gives a melancholy cast to a person's countenance, but it was not so in her case. Her religion made her inwardly content and joyous; and if she was troubled at times, and showed the pain of it in her face and bearing, it came of distress for her country; no part of it was chargeable to her religion.

A considerable part of our village was destroyed, and when it became safe for us to venture back there we realized what other people had been suffering in all the various quarters of France for many years—yes, decades of years. For the first time we saw wrecked and smoke-blackened homes, and in the lanes and alleys carcasses of dumb creatures that had been slaughtered in pure wantonness—among them calves and lambs that had been pets of the children; and it was pity to see the children lament over them.

And then, the taxes, the taxes! Everybody thought of that. That burden would fall heavy, now, in the commune's crippled condition, and all faces grew long with the thought of it. Joan said—

"Paying taxes with naught to pay them with is what the rest of

France has been doing these many years, but we never knew the bitterness of that before. We shall know it now."

And so she went on talking about it and growing more and more troubled about it, until one could see that it was filling all her mind.

At last we came upon a dreadful object. It was the madman—hacked and stabbed to death in his iron cage in the corner of the square. It was a bloody and dreadful sight. Hardly any of us young people had ever seen a man before who had lost his life by violence; so this cadaver had an awful fascination for us; we could not take our eyes from it. I mean, it had that sort of fascination for all of us but one. That one was Joan. She turned away in horror, and could not be persuaded to go near it again. There—it is a striking reminder that we are but creatures of use and custom; yes, and it is a reminder, too, of how harshly and unfairly fate deals with us sometimes. For it was so ordered that the very ones among us who were most fascinated with mutilated and bloody death were to live their lives in peace, while that other, who had a native and deep horror of it, must presently go forth and have it as a familiar spectacle every day on the field of battle.

You may well believe that we had plenty of matter for talk, now, since the raiding of our village seemed by long odds the greatest event that had really ever occurred in the world; for although these dull peasants may have *thought* they recognized the bigness of some of the previous occurrences that had filtered from the world's history dimly into their minds, the truth is that they hadn't. One biting little fact, visible to their eyes of flesh and felt in their own personal vitals, became at once more prodigious to them than the grandest remote episode in the world's history which they had got at second-hand and by hearsay. It amuses me now when I recall how our elders talked then. They fumed and fretted in a fine fashion.

"Ah yes," said old Jacques d'Arc, "things are come to a pretty pass indeed! The King must be informed of this. It is time that he cease from idleness and dreaming, and get at his proper business." He meant our young disinherited King, the hunted refugee, Charles VII.

"You say well," said the maire. "He should be informed, and that at once. It is an outrage that such things should be permitted. Why, we are not safe in our beds, and he taking his ease yonder. It shall be made known, indeed it shall—all France shall hear of it!"

To hear them talk, one would have imagined that all the previous ten thousand sackings and burnings in France had been but fables, and this one the only fact. It is always the way: words will answer as long as it is only a person's neighbor who is in trouble, but when that person gets into trouble himself, it is time that the King rise up and *do* something.

The big event filled us young people with talk, too. We let it flow in a steady stream while we tended the flocks. We were beginning to feel pretty important, now, for I was eighteen and the other youths were from one to four years older—young men, in fact. One day the Paladin was arrogantly criticising the patriot generals of France and said—

"Look at Dunois, Bastard of Orleans—call *him* a general! Just put me in his place once—never mind what I would do, it is not for me to say, I have no stomach for talk, my way is to *act* and let others do the talking—but just put me in his place once, that's all! And look at Saintrailles—pooh! and that blustering La Hire, now what a general *that* is!"

It shocked everybody to hear these great names so flippantly handled, for to us these renowned soldiers were almost gods. In their far-off splendor they rose upon our imaginations dim and huge, shadowy and awful, and it was a fearful thing to hear them spoken of as if they were mere men, and their acts open to comment and criticism. The color rose in Joan's face, and she said—

"I know not how any can be so hardy as to use such words regarding these sublime men, who are the very pillars of the French State, supporting it with their strength and preserving it at daily cost of their blood. As for me, I could count myself honored past all deserving if I might be allowed but the privilege of looking upon them once—at a distance, I mean, for it would not become one of my degree to approach them too near."

The Paladin was disconcerted for a moment, seeing by the faces around him that Joan had put into words what the others felt, then he pulled his complacency together and fell to fault-finding again. Joan's brother Jean said—

"If you don't like what our generals do, why don't you go to the great wars yourself and better their work? You are always talking about going to the wars, but you don't go."

"Look you," said the Paladin, "it is easy to say that. Now I will tell you why I remain chafing here in a bloodless tranquillity which my reputation teaches you is repulsive to my nature. I do not go because I am not a gentleman. That is the whole reason. What can one private soldier do in a contest like this? Nothing. He is not permitted to rise from the ranks. If I were a gentleman would I remain here? Not one moment. I can save France—ah, you may laugh, but I know what is in me, I know what is hid under this peasant cap. I can save France, and I stand ready to do it, but not under these present conditions. If they want me, let them send for me; otherwise, let them take the consequences; I shall not budge but as an officer."

"Alas, poor France—France is lost!" said Pierre d'Arc.

"Since you sniff so at others, why don't you go to the wars yourself, Pierre d'Arc?"

"Oh, I haven't been sent for, either. I am no more a gentleman than you. Yet I will go; I promise to go. I promise to go as a private under your orders—when you are sent for."

They all laughed, and the Dragon-fly said—

"So soon? Then you need to begin to get ready; you might be called for in five years—who knows? Yes, in my opinion you'll march for the wars in five years."

"He will go sooner," said Joan. She said it in a low voice and musingly, but several heard it.

"How do you know that, Joan?" said the Dragon-fly, with a surprised look. But Jean d'Arc broke in and said—

"I want to go myself, but as I am rather young yet, I also will wait, and march when the Paladin is sent for."

"No," said Joan, "he will go with Pierre."

She said it as one who talks to himself aloud without knowing it, and none heard it but me. I glanced at her and saw that her knitting-needles were idle in her hands, and that her face had a dreamy and absent look in it. There were fleeting movements of her lips as if she might be occasionally saying parts of sentences to herself. But there was no sound, for I was the nearest person to her and I heard nothing. But I set my ears open, for those two speeches had affected me uncannily, I being superstitious and easily troubled by any little thing of a strange and unusual sort.

Noël Rainguesson said—

"There is one way to let France have a chance for her salvation. We've got *one* gentleman in the commune, at any rate. Why can't the Scholar change name and condition with the Paladin? Then he can be an officer. France will send for him then, and he will sweep these English and Burgundian armies into the sea like flies."

I was the Scholar. That was my nickname, because I could read and write. There was a chorus of approval, and the Sunflower said—

"That is the very thing—it settles every difficulty. The Sieur de Conte will easily agree to that. Yes, he will march at the back of Captain Paladin and die early, covered with common-soldier glory."

"He will march with Jean and Pierre, and live till these wars are forgotten," Joan muttered; "and at the eleventh hour Noël and the Paladin will join these, but not of their own desire." The voice was so low that I was not perfectly sure that these were the words, but they seemed to be. It makes one feel creepy to hear such things.

"Come, now," Noël continued, "it's all arranged; there's nothing to do but organize under the Paladin's banner and go forth and rescue France. You'll all join?"

All said yes, except Jacques d'Arc, who said—

"I'll ask you to excuse me. It is pleasant to talk war, and I am with you there, and I've always thought I should go soldiering about this time, but the look of our wrecked village and that carved-up and bloody madman have taught me that I am not made for such work and such sights. I could never be at home in that trade. Face swords and the big guns and death? It isn't in me. No, no; count me out. And besides, I'm the eldest son, and deputy prop and protector of the family. Since you are going to carry Jean and Pierre to the wars, somebody must be left behind to take care of our Joan and her sister. I shall stay at home, and grow old in peace and tranquillity."

"He will stay at home, but not grow old," murmured Joan.

The talk rattled on in the gay and careless fashion privileged to youth, and we got the Paladin to map out his campaigns and fight his battles and win his victories and extinguish the English and put our King upon his throne and set his crown upon his head. Then we asked him what he was going to answer when the King should require him to name his reward. The Paladin had it all arranged in his head, and brought it out promptly:

"He shall give me a dukedom, name me premier peer, and make me Hereditary Lord High Constable of France."

"And marry you to a princess—you're not going to leave that out, are you?"

The Paladin colored a trifle, and said, brusquely—

"He may keep his princesses—I can marry more to my taste."

Meaning Joan, though nobody suspected it at that time. If any had, the Paladin would have been finely ridiculed for his vanity. There was no fit mate in that village for Joan of Arc. Every one would have said that.

In turn, each person present was required to say what reward he would demand of the King if he could change places with the Paladin and do the wonders the Paladin was going to do. The answers were given in fun, and each of us tried to outdo his predecessors in the extravagance of the reward he would claim; but when it came to Joan's turn and they rallied her out of her dreams and asked her to testify, they had to explain to her what the question was, for her thought had been absent, and she had heard none of this latter part of our talk. She supposed they wanted a serious answer, and she gave it. She sat considering some moments, then she said—

"If the Dauphin out of his grace and nobleness should say to me, 'Now that I am rich and am come to my own again, choose and have,' I should kneel and ask him to give command that our village should nevermore be taxed."

It was so simple and out of her heart that it touched us and we did not laugh, but fell to thinking. We did not laugh; but there came a day when we remembered that speech with a mournful pride, and were glad that we had not laughed, perceiving then how honest her words had been, and seeing how faithfully she made them good when the time came, asking just that boon of the King and refusing to take even any least thing for herself.

CHAPTER 6

All through her childhood and up to the middle of her fourteenth year, Joan had been the most light-hearted creature and the merriest in the village, with a hop-skip-and-jump gait and a happy and catching laugh; and this disposition, supplemented by her warm and sympathetic nature and frank and winning ways, had made her everybody's pet. She had been a hot patriot all this time, and sometimes the war news had sobered her spirits and wrung her heart and made her acquainted with tears, but always when these interruptions had run their course her spirits rose and she was her old self again.

But now for a whole year and a half she had been mainly grave; not melancholy, but given to thought, abstraction, dreams. She was carrying France upon her heart, and she found the burden not light. I knew that this was her trouble, but others attributed her abstraction to religious ecstasy, for she did not share her thinkings with the village at large, yet gave me glimpses of them, and so I knew, better than the rest, what was absorbing her interest. Many a time the idea crossed my mind that she had a secret—a secret which she was keeping wholly to herself, as well from me as from the others. This idea had come to me because several times she had cut a sentence in two and changed the subject when apparently she was on the verge of a revelation of some sort. I was to find this secret out, but not just yet.

The day after the conversation which I have been reporting we were together in the pastures and fell to talking about France, as usual. For her sake I had always talked hopefully before, but that was mere lying, for really there was not anything to hang a rag of hope for France upon. Now it was such a pain to lie to her, and cost me such shame to offer this treachery to one so snow-pure from lying and treachery, and even from suspicion of such basenesses in others, as she was, that I was resolved to face about, now, and begin over again, and never insult her more with deception. I started on the new policy by saying—still opening up with a small lie, of course, for habit is habit, and not to be flung out of the window by any man, but coaxed down-stairs a step at a time—

"Joan, I have been thinking the thing all over, last night, and have concluded that we have been in the wrong all this time; that the case of France is desperate; that it has been desperate ever since Agincourt; and that to-day it is more than desperate, it is hopeless."

I did not look her in the face while I was saying it; it could not be expected of a person. To break her heart, to crush her hope with a so frankly brutal speech as that, without one charitable soft place in it—it seemed a shameful thing, and it was. But when it was out, the weight gone, and my conscience rising to the surface, I glanced at her face to see the result.

There was none to see. At least none that I was expecting. There was a barely perceptible suggestion of wonder in her serious eyes, but that was all; and she said, in her simple and placid way—

"The case of France hopeless? Why should you think that? Tell me."

It is a most pleasant thing to find that what you thought would inflict a hurt upon one whom you honor, has not done it. I was relieved, now, and could say all my say without any furtivenesses and without embarrassment. So I began:

"Let us put sentiment and patriotic illusions aside, and look the facts in the face. What do they say? They speak as plainly as the figures in a merchant's account-book. One has only to add the two columns up to see that the French house is bankrupt, that one-half of its property is already in the English sheriff's hands and the other half in nobody's—except those of irresponsible raiders and robbers confessing allegiance to nobody. Our King is shut up with his favorites and fools in inglorious idleness and poverty in a narrow little patch of the kingdom—a sort of back lot, as one may say—and has no authority there or anywhere else, hasn't a farthing to his name, nor a regiment of soldiers; he is not fighting, he is not intending to fight, he means to make no further resistance; in truth there is but one thing that he is intending to do—give the whole thing up, pitch his crown into the sewer, and run away to Scotland. There are the facts. Are they correct?"

"Yes, they are correct."

"Then it is as I have said: one needs but to add them together in order to realize what they mean."

She asked, in an ordinary, level tone—

"What—that the case of France is hopeless?"

"Necessarily. In face of these facts, doubt of it is impossible."

"How can you say that? How can you *feel* like that?"

"How can I? How could I think or feel in any other way, in the circumstances? Joan, with these fatal figures before you, have you really any hope for France—really and actually?"

"Hope—oh, more than that! France will win her freedom and keep it. Do not doubt it."

It seemed to me that her clear intellect must surely be clouded to-day. It must be so, or she would see that those figures *could* mean only the one thing. Perhaps if I marshalled them again she would see. So I said:

"Joan, your heart, which worships France, is beguiling your head. You are not perceiving the importance of these figures. Here—I want to make a picture of them, here on the ground with a stick. Now, this rough outline is France. Through its middle, east and west, I draw a river."

"Yes; the Loire."

"Now, then, this whole northern half of the country is in the tight grip of the English."

"Yes."

"And this whole southern half is really in nobody's hands at all—as our King confesses by meditating desertion and flight to a foreign land. England has armies here; opposition is dead; she can assume full possession whenever she may choose. In very truth, *all* France is gone, France is already lost, France has ceased to exist. What was France is now but a British province. Is this true?"

Her voice was low, and just touched with emotion, but distinct:

"Yes, it is true."

"Very well. Now add this clinching fact, and surely the sum is complete: When have French soldiers won a victory? Scotch soldiers, under the French flag, have won a barren fight or two a few years back, but

I am speaking of French ones. Since eight thousand Englishmen nearly annihilated sixty thousand Frenchmen a dozen years ago at Agincourt, French courage has been paralyzed. And so it is a common saying, to-day, that if you confront fifty French soldiers with five English ones, the French will run."

"It is a pity, but even these things are true."

"Then certainly the day for hoping is *past*."

I believed the case would be clear to her now. I thought it could not fail to be clear to her, and that she would say, herself, that there was no longer any ground for hope. But I was mistaken; and disappointed also. She said, without any doubt in her tone:

"France will rise again. You shall see."

"Rise?—with this burden of English armies on her back!"

"She will cast it off; she will trample it under foot!" This with spirit.

"Without soldiers to fight with?"

"The drums will summon them. They will answer, and they will march."

"March to the rear, as usual?"

"No; to the front—ever to the front—always to the front! You shall see."

"And the pauper King?"

"He will mount his throne—he will wear his crown."

"Well, of a truth this makes one's head dizzy. Why, if I could believe that in thirty years from now the English domination would be broken and the French monarch's head find itself hooped with a real crown of sovereignty—"

"Both will have happened before two years are sped."

"Indeed? and who is going to perform all these sublime impossibilities?"

"God."

It was a reverent low note, but it rang clear.

What could have put those strange ideas in her head? This question kept running in my mind during two or three days. It was inevitable that I should think of madness. What other way was there to account for such things? Grieving and brooding over the woes of France had weakened that strong mind, and filled it with fantastic phantoms—yes, that must be it.

But I watched her, and tested her, and it was not so. Her eye was clear and sane, her ways were natural, her speech direct and to the point. No, there was nothing the matter with her mind; it was still the soundest in the village and the best. She went on thinking for others, planning for others, sacrificing herself for others, just as always before. She went on ministering to her sick and to her poor, and still stood ready to give the wayfarer her bed and content herself with the floor. There was a secret somewhere, but madness was not the key to it. This was plain.

Now the key did presently come into my hands, and the way that it happened was this. You have heard all the world talk of this matter which I am about to speak of, but you have not heard an eye-witness talk of it before.

I was coming from over the ridge, one day—it was the 15th of May, '28—and when I got to the edge of the oak forest and was about to step out of it upon the turfy open space in which the haunted beech-tree stood, I happened to cast a glance from cover, first—then I took a step backward, and stood in the shelter and concealment of the foliage. For I had caught sight of Joan, and thought I would devise some sort of playful surprise for her. Think of it—that trivial conceit was neighbor, with but a scarcely measurable interval of time between, to an event destined to endure forever in histories and songs.

The day was overcast, and all that grassy space wherein the Tree stood lay in a soft rich shadow. Joan sat on a natural seat formed by gnarled great roots of the Tree. Her hands lay loosely, one reposing in the other, in her lap. Her head was bent a little toward the ground, and her air was that of one who is lost in thought, steeped in dreams, and not conscious of herself or of the world. And now I saw a most strange thing, for I saw a *white* shadow come slowly gliding along the grass toward the Tree. It was of grand proportions—a robed form, with wings—and the whiteness of this shadow was not like any other whiteness that we know of, except it be the whiteness of the lightnings, but even the lightnings are not so intense as it was, for one can look at them without hurt, whereas this brilliancy was so blinding that it pained my eyes and brought the water into them. I uncovered my head, perceiving that I was in the presence of something not of this world. My breath grew faint and difficult, because of the terror and the awe that possessed me.

Another strange thing. The wood had been silent—smitten with that deep stillness which comes when a storm-cloud darkens a forest, and the wild creatures lose heart and are afraid; but now all the birds burst forth in song, and the joy, the rapture, the ecstasy of it was beyond belief; and was so eloquent and so moving, withal, that it was plain it was an act of worship. With the first note of those birds Joan cast herself upon her knees, and bent her head low and crossed her hands upon her breast.

She had not seen the shadow yet. Had the song of the birds told her it was coming? It had that look to me. Then the like of this must have happened before. Yes, there might be no doubt of that.

The shadow approached Joan slowly; the extremity of it reached her, flowed over her, clothed her in its awful splendor. In that immortal light her face, only humanly beautiful before, became divine; flooded with that transforming glory her mean peasant habit was become like to the raiment of the sun-clothed children of God as we see them thronging the terraces of the Throne in our dreams and imaginings.

Presently she rose and stood, with her head still bowed a little, and with her arms down and the ends of her fingers lightly laced together in front of her; and standing so, all drenched with that wonderful light, and yet apparently not knowing it, she seemed to listen—but I heard nothing. After a little she raised her head, and looked up as one might look up toward the face of a giant, and then clasped her hands and lifted them high, imploringly, and began to plead. I heard some of the words. I heard her say—

"But I am so young! oh, so young to leave my mother and my home, and go out into the strange world to undertake a thing so great! Ah, how can I talk with men, be comrade with men?—soldiers! It would give me over to insult, and rude usage, and contempt. How can I go to the great wars, and lead armies?—I a girl, and ignorant of such things, knowing nothing of arms, nor how to mount a horse, nor ride it. . . . Yet—if it is commanded—"

Her voice sank a little, and was broken by sobs, and I made out no more of her words. Then I came to myself. I reflected that I had been intruding upon a mystery of God—and what might my punishment be? I was afraid, and went deeper into the wood. Then I carved a mark in the bark of a tree, saying to myself, it may be that I am dreaming and have not seen this vision at all. I will come again, when I know that I am awake and not dreaming, and see if this mark is still here; then I shall know.

CHAPTER 7

I heard my name called. It was Joan's voice. It startled me, for how could she know I was there? I said to myself, it is part of the dream; it is all dream—voice, vision and all; the fairies have done this. So I crossed myself and pronounced the name of God, to break the enchantment. I knew I was awake now and free from the spell, for no spell can withstand this exorcism. Then I heard my name called again, and I stepped at once from under cover, and there indeed was Joan, but not looking as she had looked in the dream. For she was not crying, now, but was looking as she had used to look a year and a half before, when her heart was light and her spirits high. Her old-time energy and fire were back, and a something like exaltation showed itself in her face and bearing. It was almost as if she had been in a trance all that time and had come awake again. Really, it was just as if she had been away and lost, and was come back to us at last; and I was so glad that I felt like running to call everybody and have them flock around her and give her welcome. I ran to her excited, and said—

"Ah, Joan, I've got such a wonderful thing to tell you about! You would never imagine it. I've had a dream, and in the dream I saw you right here where you are standing now, and—"

But she put up her hand and said—

"It was not a dream."

It gave me a shock, and I began to feel afraid again.

"Not a dream?" I said, "how can you know about it, Joan?"

"Are you dreaming now?"

"I—I suppose not. I think I am not."

"Indeed you are not. I know you are not. And you were not dreaming when you cut the mark in the tree."

I felt myself turning cold with fright, for now I knew of a certainty that I had not been dreaming, but had really been in the presence of a dread something not of this world. Then I remembered that my sinful feet were upon holy ground—the ground where that celestial shadow had rested. I moved quickly away, smitten to the bones with fear. Joan followed, and said—

"Do not be afraid; indeed there is no need. Come with me. We will sit by the spring and I will tell you all my secret."

When she was ready to begin, I checked her and said—

"First tell me this. You could not see me in the wood; how did you know I cut a mark in the tree?"

"Wait a little; I will soon come to that; then you will see."

"But tell me one thing now; what was that awful shadow that I saw?"

"I will tell you, but do not be disturbed; you are not in danger. It was the shadow of an archangel—Michael, the chief and lord of the armies of heaven."

I could but cross myself and tremble for having polluted that ground with my feet.

"You were not afraid, Joan? Did you see his face—did you see his form?"

"Yes; I was not afraid, because this was not the first time. I was afraid the first time."

"When was that, Joan?"

"It is nearly three years ago, now."

"So long? Have you seen him many times?"

"Yes, many times."

"It is this, then, that has changed you; it was this that made you thoughtful and not as you were before. I see it now. Why did you not tell us about it?"

"It was not permitted. It is permitted now, and soon I shall tell all. But only you, now. It must remain a secret a few days still."

"Has none seen that white shadow before but me?"

"No one. It has fallen upon me before when you and others were present, but none could see it. To-day it has been otherwise, and I was told why; but it will not be visible again to any."

"It was a sign to me, then—and a sign with a meaning of some kind?"

"Yes, but I may not speak of that."

"Strange—that that dazzling light could rest upon an object before one's eyes and not be visible."

"With it comes speech, also. Several saints come, attended by myriads of angels, and they speak to me; I hear their voices, but others do not. They are very dear to me—my Voices; that is what I call them to myself."

"Joan, what do they tell you?"

"All manner of things—about France I mean."

"What things have they been used to tell you?"

She sighed, and said—

"Disasters—only disasters, and misfortunes, and humiliations. There was naught else to foretell."

"They spoke of them to you *beforehand*?"

"Yes. So that I knew what was going to happen before it happened. It made me grave—as you saw. It could not be otherwise. But always there was a word of hope, too. More than that: France was to be rescued, and made great and free again. But how and by whom—that was not told. Not until to-day." As she said those last words a sudden deep glow shone in her eyes, which I was to see there many times in after-days when the bugles sounded the charge and learn to call it the battle-light. Her breast heaved, and the color rose in her face. "But to-day I know. God has chosen the meanest of His creatures for this work; and by His command, and in His protection, and by His strength, not mine, I am to lead His armies, and win back France, and set the crown upon the head of His servant that is Dauphin and shall be King."

I was amazed, and said—

"You, Joan? You, a child, lead armies?"

"Yes. For one little moment or two the thought crushed me; for it is as you say—I am only a child; a child and ignorant—ignorant of everything that pertains to war, and not fitted for the rough life of camps and the companionship of soldiers. But those weak moments passed; they will not come again. I am enlisted, I will not turn back, God helping me, till the English grip is loosed from the throat of France. My Voices have never told me lies, they have not lied to-day. They say I am to go to Robert de Baudricourt, governor of Vaucouleurs, and he will give me men-at-arms for escort and send me to the King. A year from now a blow will be struck which will be the beginning of the end, and the end will follow swiftly."

"Where will it be struck?"

"My Voices have not said; nor what will happen this present year, before it is struck. It is appointed me to strike it, that is all I know; and follow it with others, sharp and swift, undoing in ten weeks England's long years of costly labor, and setting the crown upon the Dauphin's head—for such is God's will; my Voices have said it, and shall I doubt it? No; it will be as they have said, for they say only that which is true."

These were tremendous sayings. They were impossibilities to my reason, but to my heart they rang true; and so, while my reason doubted, my heart believed—believed, and held fast to its belief from that day. Presently I said—

"Joan, I believe the things which you have said, and now I am glad that I am to march with you to the great wars—that is, if it is with you I am to march when I go."

She looked surprised, and said—

"It is true that you will be with me when I go to the wars, but how did you know?"

"I shall march with you, and so also will Jean and Pierre, but not Jacques."

"All true—it is so ordered, as was revealed to me lately, but I did not know until to-day that the marching would be with me, or that I should march at all. How did you know these things?"

I told her when it was that she had said them. But she did not remember about it. So then I knew that she had been asleep, or in a trance or an ecstasy of some kind, at that time. She bade me keep these and the other revelations to myself for the present, and I said I would, and kept the faith I promised.

None who met Joan that day failed to notice the change that had come over her. She moved and spoke with energy and decision; there was a strange new fire in her eye, and also a something wholly new and remarkable in her carriage and in the set of her head. This new light in the eye and this new bearing were born of the authority and leadership which had this day been vested in her by the decree of God, and they asserted that authority as plainly as speech could have done it, yet without ostentation or bravado. This calm consciousness of command, and calm unconscious outward expression of it, remained with her thenceforth until her mission was accomplished.

Like the other villagers, she had always accorded me the deference due my rank; but now, without word said on either side, she and I changed places: she gave orders, not suggestions, I received them with the deference due a superior, and obeyed them without comment. In the evening she said to me—

"I leave before dawn. No one will know it but you. I go to speak with the governor of Vaucouleurs as commanded, who will despise me and treat me rudely, and perhaps refuse my prayer at this time. I go first to Burey, to persuade my uncle Laxart to go with me, it not being meet that I go alone. I may need you in Vaucouleurs; for if the governor will not receive me I will dictate a letter to him, and so must have some one by me who knows the art of how to write and spell the words. You will go from here to-morrow in the afternoon, and remain in Vaucouleurs until I need you."

I said I would obey, and she went her way. You see how clear a head she had, and what a just and level judgment. She did not order me to go with her; no, she would not subject her good name to gossiping remark. She knew that the governor, being a noble, would grant me, another noble, audience; but no, you see, she would not have that, either. A poor peasant girl presenting a petition through a young nobleman—how would that look? She always protected her modesty from hurt; and so, for reward, she carried her good name unsmirched to the end. I knew what I must do, now, if I would have her approval: go to Vaucouleurs, keep out of her sight, and be ready when wanted.

I went the next afternoon, and took an obscure lodging; the next day

I called at the castle and paid my respects to the governor, who invited me to dine with him at noon of the following day. He was an ideal soldier of the time; tall, brawny, gray-headed, rough, full of strange oaths acquired here and there and yonder in the wars and treasured as if they were decorations. He had been used to the camp all his life, and to his notion war was God's best gift to man. He had his steel cuirass on, and wore boots that came above his knees, and was equipped with a huge sword; and when I looked at this martial figure, and heard the marvellous oaths, and guessed how little of poetry and sentiment might be looked for in this quarter, I hoped the little peasant girl would not get the privilege of confronting this battery, but would have to content herself with the dictated letter.

I came again to the castle the next day at noon, and was conducted to the great dining-hall and seated by the side of the governor at a small table which was raised a couple of steps higher than the general table. At the small table sat several other guests besides myself, and at the general table sat the chief officers of the garrison. At the entrance door stood a guard of halberdiers, in morion and breastplate.

As for talk, there was but one topic, of course—the desperate situation of France. There was a rumor, some one said, that Salisbury was making preparations to march against Orleans. It raised a turmoil of excited conversation, and opinions fell thick and fast. Some believed he would march at once, others that he could not accomplish the investment before fall, others that the siege would be long, and bravely contested; but upon one thing all voices agreed: that Orleans must eventually fall, and with it France. With that, the prolonged discussion ended, and there was silence. Every man seemed to sink himself in his own thoughts, and to forget where he was. This sudden and profound stillness where before had been so much animation, was impressive and solemn. Now came a servant and whispered something to the governor, who said—

"Would talk with *me?*"

"Yes, your Excellency."

"H'm! A strange idea, certainly. Bring them in."

It was Joan and her uncle Laxart. At the spectacle of the great people the courage oozed out of the poor old peasant and he stopped midway and would come no further, but remained there with his red nightcap crushed in his hands and bowing humbly here, there, and everywhere, stupefied with embarrassment and fear. But Joan came steadily forward, erect and self-possessed, and stood before the governor. She recognized me, but in no way indicated it. There was a buzz of admiration, even the governor contributing to it, for I heard him mutter, "By God's grace, it is a beautiful creature!" He inspected her critically a moment or two, then said—

"Well, what is your errand, my child?"

"My message is to you, Robert de Baudricourt, governor of Vaucouleurs, and it is this: that you will send and tell the Dauphin to wait and not give battle to his enemies, for God will presently send him help."

This strange speech amazed the company, and many murmured, "The poor young thing is demented." The governor scowled, and said—

"What nonsense is this? The King—or the Dauphin, as you call him—needs no message of *that* sort. He will wait, give yourself no uneasiness as to that. What further do you desire to say to me?"

"This. To beg that you will give me an escort of men-at-arms and send me to the Dauphin."

"What for?"

"That he may make me his general, for it is appointed that I shall drive the English out of France, and set the crown upon his head."

"What—you? Why, you are but a child!"

"Yet am I appointed to do it, nevertheless."

"Indeed? And when will all this happen?"

"Next year he will be crowned, and after will remain master of France."

There was a great and general burst of laughter, and when it had subsided the governor said—

"Who has sent you with these extravagant messages?"

"My Lord."

"What Lord?"

"The King of Heaven."

Many murmured, "Ah, poor thing, poor thing!" and others, "Ah, her mind is but a wreck!" The governor hailed Laxart, and said—

"Harkye!—take this mad child home and whip her soundly. That is the best cure for her ailment."

As Joan was moving away she turned and said, with simplicity—

"You refuse me the soldiers, I know not why, for it is my Lord that has commanded you. Yes, it is He that has made the command; therefore must I come again, and yet again; then I shall have the men-at-arms."

There was a great deal of wondering talk, after she was gone; and the guards and servants passed the talk to the town, the town passed it to the country; Domremy was already buzzing with it when we got back.

CHAPTER 8

Human nature is the same everywhere: it deifies success, it has nothing but scorn for defeat. The village considered that Joan had disgraced it with her grotesque performance and its ridiculous failure; so all the tongues were busy with the matter, and as bilious and bitter as they were busy; insomuch that if the tongues had been teeth she would not have survived her persecutions. Those persons who did not scold, did what was worse and harder to bear; for they ridiculed her, and mocked at her, and ceased neither day nor night from their witticisms and jeerings and laughter. Haumette and Little Mengette and I stood by her, but the storm was too strong for her other friends, and they avoided her, being ashamed to be seen with her because she was so unpopular, and because of the sting of the taunts that assailed them on her account. She shed tears in secret, but none in public. In public she carried herself with serenity, and showed no distress, nor any resentment—conduct which should have softened the feeling against her, but it did not. Her father was so incensed that he could not talk in measured terms about her wild project of going to the wars like a man. He had dreamed of her doing such a thing, some time before, and now he remembered that dream with apprehension and anger, and said that rather than see her unsex herself and go away with the armies, he would require her brothers to drown her; and that if they should refuse, he would do it with his own hands.

But none of these things shook her purpose in the least. Her parents kept a strict watch upon her to keep her from leaving the village, but she said her time was not yet; that when the time to go was come she should know it, and then the keepers would watch in vain.

The summer wasted along; and when it was seen that her purpose continued steadfast, the parents were glad of a chance which finally offered itself for bringing her projects to an end through marriage. The Paladin had the effrontery to pretend that she had engaged herself to him several years before, and now he claimed a ratification of the engagement.

She said his statement was not true, and refused to marry him. She was cited to appear before the ecclesiastical court at Toul to answer for her perversity; when she declined to have counsel, and elected to conduct her case herself, her parents and all her ill-wishers rejoiced, and looked upon her as already defeated. And that was natural enough; for who would expect that an ignorant peasant girl of sixteen would be otherwise than frightened and tongue-tied when standing for the first time in presence of the practised doctors of the law, and surrounded by the cold solemnities of a court? Yet all these people were mistaken. They flocked to Toul to see and enjoy this fright and embarrassment and defeat, and they had their trouble for their pains. She was modest, tranquil, and quite at her ease. She called no witnesses, saying she would content herself with examining the witnesses for the prosecution. When they had testified, she rose and reviewed their testimony in a few words, pronounced it vague, confused, and of no force, then she placed the Paladin again on the stand and began to search him. His previous testimony went rag by rag to ruin under her ingenious hands, until at last he stood bare, so to speak, he that had come so richly clothed in fraud and falsehood. His counsel began an argument, but the court declined to hear it, and threw out the case, adding a few words of grave compliment for Joan, and referring to her as "this marvellous child."

After this victory, with this high praise from so imposing a source added, the fickle village turned again, and gave Joan countenance, compliment, and peace. Her mother took her back to her heart, and even her father relented and said he was proud of her. But the time hung heavy on her hands, nevertheless, for the siege of Orleans was begun, the clouds lowered darker and darker over France, and still her Voices said wait, and gave her no direct commands. The winter set in, and wore tediously along; but at last there was a change.

Book II

IN COURT AND CAMP

CHAPTER 1

The 5th of January, 1429, Joan came to me with her uncle Laxart, and said—

"The time is come. My Voices are not vague, now, but clear, and they have told me what to do. In two months I shall be with the Dauphin."

Her spirits were high, and her bearing martial. I caught the infection and felt a great impulse stirring in me that was like what one feels when he hears the roll of the drums and the tramp of marching men.

"I believe it," I said.

"I also believe it," said Laxart. "If she had told me before, that she was commanded of God to rescue France, I should not have believed; I should have let her seek the governor by her own ways and held myself clear of meddling in the matter, not doubting she was mad. But I have seen her stand before those nobles and mighty men unafraid, and say her say; and she had not been able to do that but by the help of God. That, I know. Therefore with all humbleness I am at her command, to do with me as she will."

"My uncle is very good to me," Joan said. "I sent and asked him to come and persuade my mother to let him take me home with him to tend his wife, who is not well. It is arranged, and we go at dawn tomorrow. From his house I shall go soon to Vaucouleurs, and wait and strive until my prayer is granted. Who were the two cavaliers who sat to your left at the governor's table that day?"

"One was the Sieur Jean de Novelonpont de Metz, the other the Sieur Bertrand de Poulengy."

"Good metal—good metal, both. I marked them for men of mine. . . . What is it I see in your face? Doubt?"

I was teaching myself to speak the truth to her, not trimming it or polishing it; so I said—

"They considered you out of your head, and said so. It is true they pitied you for being in such misfortune, but still they held you to be mad."

This did not seem to trouble her in any way or wound her. She only said—

"The wise change their minds when they perceive that they have been in error. These will. They will march with me. I shall see them presently. . . . You seem to doubt again? Do you doubt?"

"N-no. Not now. I was remembering that it was a year ago, and that they did not belong there, but only chanced to stop a day on their journey."

"They will come again. But as to matters now in hand; I came to leave with you some instructions. You will follow me in a few days. Order your affairs, for you will be absent long."

"Will Jean and Pierre go with me?"

"No; they would refuse now, but presently they will come, and with them they will bring my parents' blessing, and likewise their consent that I take up my mission. I shall be stronger, then—stronger for that; for lack of it I am weak, now." She paused a little while, and the tears gathered in her eyes; then she went on: "I would say good-bye to Little Mengette. Bring her outside the village at dawn; she must go with me a little of the way—"

"And Haumette?"

She broke down and began to cry, saying—

"No, oh, no—she is too dear to me, I could not bear it, knowing I should never look upon her face again."

Next morning I brought Mengette, and we four walked along the road in the cold dawn till the village was far behind; then the two girls said their good-byes, clinging about each other's neck, and pouring out their grief in loving words and tears, a pitiful sight to see. And Joan took one long look back upon the distant village, and the Fairy Tree, and the oak forest, and the flowery plain, and the river, as if she was trying to print these scenes on her memory so that they would abide there always and not fade, for she knew she would not see them any more in this life; then she turned, and went from us, sobbing bitterly. It was her birthday and mine. She was seventeen years old.

CHAPTER 2

After a few days, Laxart took Joan to Vaucouleurs, and found lodging and guardianship for her with Catherine Royer, a wheelwright's wife, an honest and good woman. Joan went to mass regularly, she helped do the house-work, earning her keep in that way, and if any wished to talk with her about her mission—and many did—she talked freely, making no concealments regarding the matter now. I was soon housed near by, and witnessed the effects which followed. At once the tidings spread that a young girl was come who was appointed of God to save France. The common people flocked in crowds to look at her and speak with her, and her fair young loveliness won the half of their belief, and her deep earnestness and transparent sincerity won the other half. The well-to-do remained away and scoffed, but that is their way.

Next, a prophecy of Merlin's, more than eight hundred years old, was called to mind, which said that in a far future time France would be lost by a woman and restored by a woman. France was now, for the first time, lost—and by a woman, Isabel of Bavaria, her base Queen; doubtless this fair and pure young girl was commissioned of Heaven to complete the prophecy.

This gave the growing interest a new and powerful impulse; the excitement rose higher and higher, and hope and faith along with it; and so from Vaucouleurs wave after wave of this inspiring enthusiasm flowed out over the land, far and wide, invading all the villages and refreshing and revivifying the perishing children of France; and from these villages came people who wanted to see for themselves, hear for themselves; and they did see and hear, and believe. They filled the town; they more than filled it; inns and lodgings were packed, and yet half of the inflow had to go without shelter. And still they came, winter as it was, for when a man's soul is starving, what does he care for meat and roof so he can but get that nobler hunger fed? Day after day, and still day after day, the great tide rose. Domremy was dazed, amazed, stupefied, and said to itself, "Was this world-wonder in our familiar midst all these years and we too dull to see it?" Jean and Pierre went out from the village stared at and envied like the great and fortunate of the earth, and their progress to Vaucouleurs was like a triumph, all the country-side flocking to see and salute the brothers of one with whom angels had spoken face to face, and into whose hands by command of God they had delivered the destinies of France.

The brothers brought the parents' blessing and Godspeed to Joan, and their promise to bring it to her in person later; and so, with this culminating happiness in her heart and the high hope it inspired, she went and confronted the governor again. But he was no more tractable than he had been before. He refused to send her to the King. She was disappointed, but in no degree discouraged. She said—

"I must still come to you until I get the men-at-arms; for so it is commanded, and I may not disobey. I must go to the Dauphin, though I go on my knees."

I and the two brothers were with Joan daily, to see the people that came and hear what they said; and one day, sure enough, the Sieur Jean de Metz came. He talked with her in a petting and playful way, as one talks with children, and said—

"What are you doing here, my little maid? Will they drive the King out of France, and shall we all turn English?"

She answered him in her tranquil, serious way—

"I am come to bid Robert de Baudricourt take or send me to the King, but he does not heed my words."

"Ah, you have an admirable persistence, truly; a whole year has not turned you from your wish. I saw you when you came before."

Joan said, as tranquilly as before—

"It is not a wish, it is a purpose. He will grant it. I can wait."

"Ah, perhaps it will not be wise to make too sure of *that,* my child. These governors are stubborn people to deal with. In case he shall not grant your prayer—"

"He will grant it. He must. It is not matter of choice."

The gentleman's playful mood began to disappear—one could see that, by his face. Joan's earnestness was affecting him. It always happened that people who began in jest with her, ended by being in earnest. They soon began to perceive depths in her that they had not suspected; and then her manifest sincerity and the rocklike steadfastness of her convictions were forces which cowed levity, and it could not maintain its self-respect in their presence. The Sieur de Metz was thoughtful for a moment or two, then he began, quite soberly—

"Is it necessary that you go to the King soon?—that is, I mean—"

"Before Mid-Lent, even though I wear away my legs to the knees!"

She said it with that sort of repressed fieriness that means so much when a person's heart is in a thing. You could see the response in that nobleman's face; you could see his eye light up; there was sympathy there. He said, most earnestly—

"God knows I think you should have the men-at-arms, and that somewhat would come of it. What is it that you would do? What is your hope and purpose?"

"To rescue France. And it is appointed that I shall do it. For no one else in the world, neither kings, nor dukes, nor any other, can recover the kingdom of France, and there is no help but in me."

The words had a pleading and pathetic sound, and they touched that good nobleman. I saw it plainly. Joan dropped her voice a little, and said: "But indeed I would rather spin with my poor mother, for this is not my calling; but I must go and do it, for it is my Lord's will."

"Who is your Lord?"

"He is God."

Then the Sieur de Metz, following the impressive old feudal fashion, knelt and laid his hands within Joan's, in sign of fealty, and made oath that by God's help he himself would take her to the King.

The next day came the Sieur Bertrand de Poulengy, and he also pledged his oath and knightly honor to abide with her and follow whithersoever she might lead.

This day, too, toward evening, a great rumor went flying abroad through the town—namely, that the very governor himself was going to visit the young girl in her humble lodgings. So in the morning the streets and lanes were packed with people waiting to see if this strange thing would indeed happen. And happen it did. The governor rode in state, attended by his guards, and the news of it went everywhere, and made a great sensation, and modified the scoffings of the people of quality and raised Joan's credit higher than ever.

The governor had made up his mind to one thing: Joan was either a witch or a saint, and he meant to find out which it was. So he brought a priest with him to exorcise the devil that was in her in case there was one there. The priest performed his office, but found no devil. He merely hurt Joan's feelings and offended her piety without need, for he had already confessed her before this, and should have known, if he knew anything, that devils cannot abide the confessional, but utter cries of anguish and the most profane and furious cursings whenever they are confronted with that holy office.

The governor went away troubled and full of thought, and not knowing what to do. And while he pondered and studied, several days went by and the 14th of February was come. Then Joan went to the castle and said—

"In God's name, Robert de Baudricourt, you are too slow about sending me, and have caused damage thereby, for this day the Dauphin's cause has lost a battle near Orleans, and will suffer yet greater injury if you do not send me to him soon."

The governor was perplexed by this speech, and said—

"To-day, child, *to-day?* How can you know what has happened in that region to-day? It would take eight or ten days for the word to come."

"My Voices have brought the word to me, and it is true. A battle was lost to-day, and you are in fault to delay me so."

The governor walked the floor a while, talking within himself, but letting a great oath fall outside now and then; and finally he said—

"Harkye! go in peace, and wait. If it shall turn out as you say, I will give you the letter and send you to the King, and not otherwise."

Joan said with fervor—

"Now God be thanked, these waiting days are almost done. In nine days you will fetch me the letter."

Already the people of Vaucouleurs had given her a horse and had armed and equipped her as a soldier. She got no chance to try the horse and see if she could ride it, for her great first duty was to abide at her post and lift up the hopes and spirits of all who would come to talk with her, and prepare them to help in the rescue and regeneration of the kingdom. This occupied every waking moment she had. But it was no matter. There was nothing she could not learn—and in the briefest time, too. Her horse would find this out in the first hour. Meantime the brothers and I took the horse in turn and began to learn to ride. And we had teaching in the use of the sword and other arms, also.

On the 20th Joan called her small army together—the two knights and her two brothers and me—for a private council of war. No, it was not a council, that is not the right name, for she did not consult with us, she merely gave us orders. She mapped out the course she would travel toward the King, and did it like a person perfectly versed in geography; and this itinerary of daily marches was so arranged as to avoid here and there peculiarly dangerous regions by flank movements—which showed that she knew her political geography as intimately as she knew her physical geography; yet she had never had a day's schooling, of course, and was without education. I was astonished, but thought her Voices must have taught her. But upon reflection I saw that this was not so. By her references to what this and that and the other person had told her, I perceived that she had been diligently questioning those crowds of visiting strangers, and that out of them she had patiently dug all this mass of invaluable knowledge. The two knights were filled with wonder at her good sense and sagacity.

She commanded us to make preparations to travel by night and sleep by day in concealment, as almost the whole of our long journey would be through the enemy's country.

Also, she commanded that we should keep the date of our departure a secret, since she meant to get away unobserved. Otherwise we should be sent off with a grand demonstration which would advertise us to the enemy, and we should be ambushed and captured somewhere. Finally she said—

"Nothing remains, now, but that I confide to you the date of our departure, so that you may make all needful preparation in time, leaving nothing to be done in haste and badly at the last moment. We march the 23d, at eleven of the clock at night."

Then we were dismissed. The two knights were startled—yes, and troubled; and the Sieur Bertrand said—

"Even if the governor shall really furnish the letter and the escort, he still may not do it in time to meet the date she has chosen. Then how can she venture to name that date? It is a great risk—a great risk to select and decide upon the date, in this state of uncertainty."

I said—

"Since she has named the 23d, we may trust her. The Voices have told her, I think. We shall do best to obey."

We did obey. Joan's parents were notified to come before the 23d, but prudence forbade that they be told why this limit was named.

All day, the 23d, she glanced up wistfully whenever new bodies of strangers entered the house, but her parents did not appear. Still she was not discouraged, but hoped on. But when night fell, at last, her hopes perished, and the tears came; however, she dashed them away, and said—

"It was to be so, no doubt; no doubt it was so ordered; I must bear it, and will."

De Metz tried to comfort her by saying—

"The governor sends no word; it may be that they will come to-morrow, and—"

He got no further, for she interrupted him, saying—

"To what good end? We start at eleven to-night."

And it was so. At ten the governor came, with his guard and torch-bearers, and delivered to her a mounted escort of men-at-arms, with horses and equipments for me and for the brothers, and gave Joan a letter to the King. Then he took off his sword, and belted it about her waist with his own hands, and said—

"You said true, child. The battle *was* lost, on the day you said. So I have kept my word. Now go—come of it what may."

Joan gave him thanks, and he went his way.

The lost battle was the famous disaster that is called in history the Battle of the Herrings.

All the lights in the house were at once put out, and a little while after, when the streets had become dark and still, we crept stealthily through them and out at the western gate and rode away under whip and spur.

CHAPTER 3

We were twenty-five strong, and well equipped. We rode in double file, Joan and her brothers in the centre of the column, with Jean de Metz at the head of it and the Sieur Bertrand at its extreme rear. The knights were so placed to prevent desertions—for the present. In two or three hours we should be in the enemy's country, and then none would venture to desert. By-and-by we began to hear groans and sobs and execrations from different points along the line, and upon inquiry found that six of our men were peasants who had never ridden a horse before, and were finding it very difficult to stay in their saddles, and moreover were now beginning to suffer considerable bodily torture. They had been seized by the governor at the last moment and pressed into the service to make up the tale, and he had placed a veteran alongside of each with orders to help him stick to the saddle, and kill him if he tried to desert.

These poor devils had kept quiet as long as they could, but their physical miseries were become so sharp by this time that they were obliged to give them vent. But we were within the enemy's country now, so there was no help for them, they must continue the march, though Joan said that if they chose to take the risk they might depart. They preferred to stay with us. We modified our pace now, and moved cautiously, and the new men were warned to keep their sorrows to themselves and not get the command into danger with their curses and lamentations.

Toward dawn we rode deep into a forest, and soon all but the sentries were sound asleep in spite of the cold ground and the frosty air.

I woke at noon out of such a solid and stupefying sleep that at first my wits were all astray, and I did not know where I was nor what had been happening. Then my senses cleared, and I remembered. As I lay there thinking over the strange events of the past month or two the thought came into my mind, greatly surprising me, that one of Joan's prophecies had failed; for where were Noël and the Paladin, who were to join us at the eleventh hour? By this time, you see, I had gotten used to expecting everything Joan said to come true. So, being disturbed and troubled by these thoughts, I opened my eyes. Well, there stood the Paladin leaning against a tree and looking down on me! How often that happens: you think of a person, or speak of a person, and there he stands before you, and you not dreaming he is near. It looks as if his *being* near is really the thing that makes you think of him, and not just an accident, as people imagine. Well, be that as it may, there was the Paladin, anyway, looking down in my face and waiting for me to wake. I was ever so glad to see him, and jumped up and shook him by the hand, and led him a little way from the camp—he limping like a cripple—and told him to sit down, and said—

"Now, where have you dropped down from? And how did you happen to light in this place? And what do the soldier-clothes mean? Tell me all about it."

He answered—

"I marched with you last night."

"No!" (To myself I said, "The prophecy has not all failed—half of it has come true.")

"Yes, I did. I hurried up from Domremy to join, and was within a half a minute of being too late. In fact, I was too late, but I begged so hard that the governor was touched by my brave devotion to my country's cause—those are the words he used—and so he yielded, and allowed me to come."

I thought to myself, this is a lie, he is one of those six the governor recruited by force at the last moment; I know it, for Joan's prophecy said he would join at the eleventh hour, but not by his own desire. Then I said aloud—

"I am glad you came; it is a noble cause, and one should not sit at home in times like these."

"Sit at home! I could no more do it than the thunderstone could stay hid in the clouds when the storm calls it."

"That is the right talk. It sounds like you."

That pleased him.

"I'm glad you know me. Some don't. But they will, presently. They will know me well enough before I get done with this war."

"That is what I think. I believe that wherever danger confronts you you will make yourself conspicuous."

He was charmed with this speech, and it swelled him up like a bladder. He said—

"If I know myself—and I think I do—my performances in this campaign will give you occasion more than once to remember those words."

"I were a fool to doubt it. That, I know."

"I shall not be at my best, being but a common soldier; still, the country will hear of me. If I were where I belong; if I were in the place of La Hire, or Saintrailles, or the Bastard of Orleans—well, I say nothing, I am not of the talking kind, like Noël Rainguesson and his sort, I thank God. But it will be *something*, I take it—a novelty in this world, I should say—to raise the fame of a private soldier above theirs, and extinguish the glory of their names with its shadow."

"Why, look here, my friend," I said, "do you know that you have hit out a most remarkable idea there? Do you realize the gigantic proportions of it? For look you: to be a general of vast renown, what is that? Nothing—history is clogged and confused with them; one cannot keep their names in his memory, there are so many. But a common soldier of supreme renown—why, he would stand alone! He would be the one moon in a firmament of mustard-seed stars; his name would outlast the human race! My friend, who gave you that idea?"

He was ready to burst with happiness, but he suppressed betrayal of it as well as he could. He simply waved the compliment aside with his hand and said, with complacency—

"It is nothing. I have them often—ideas like that—and even greater ones. I do not consider this one much."

"You astonish me; you do indeed. So it is really your own?"

"Quite. And there is plenty more where it came from"—tapping his head with his finger, and taking occasion at the same time to cant his morion over his right ear, which gave him a very self-satisfied air—"I do not need to borrow my ideas, like Noël Rainguesson."

"Speaking of Noël, when did you see him last?"

"Half an hour ago. He is sleeping yonder like a corpse. Rode with us last night."

I felt a great upleap in my heart, and said to myself, now I am at rest and glad; I will never doubt her prophecies again. Then I said aloud—

"It gives me joy. It makes me proud of our village. There is no keeping our lion-hearts at home in these great times, I see that."

"Lion-heart! Who—that baby? Why, he begged like a dog to be let off. Cried, and said he wanted to go to his mother. Him a lion-heart! —that tumble-bug!"

"Dear me, why I supposed he volunteered, of course. Didn't he?"

"Oh yes, volunteered the way people do to the headsman. Why, when he found I was coming up from Domremy to volunteer, he asked me to let him come along in my protection, and see the crowds and the excitement. Well, we arrived and saw the torches filing out at the Castle, and ran there, and the governor had him seized, along with four more, and he begged to be let off, and I begged for his place, and at last the governor allowed me to join, but wouldn't let Noël off, because he was disgusted with him he was such a cry-baby. Yes, and much good *he'll* do the King's service: he'll eat for six and run for sixteen. I hate a pigmy with half a heart and nine stomachs!"

"Why, this is very surprising news to me, and I am sorry and disappointed to hear it. I thought he was a very manly fellow."

The Paladin gave me an outraged look, and said:

"I don't see how you can talk like that, I'm sure I don't. I don't see how you could have got such a notion. I don't dislike him, and I'm not saying these things out of prejudice, for I don't allow myself to have prejudices against people. I like him, and have always comraded with him from the cradle, but he must allow me to speak my mind about his faults, and I am willing he shall speak his about mine, if I have any. And true enough, maybe I have; but I reckon they'll bear inspection —I have that idea, anyway. A manly fellow! You should have heard him whine and wail and swear, last night, because the saddle hurt him. Why didn't the saddle hurt me? Pooh—I was as much at home in it as if I had been born there. And yet it was the first time I was ever on a horse. All those old soldiers admired my riding; they said they had never seen anything like it. But him—why, they had to hold him on, all the time."

An odor as of breakfast came stealing through the wood; the Paladin unconsciously inflated his nostrils in lustful response, and got up and limped painfully away, saying he must go and look to his horse.

At bottom he was all right and a good-hearted giant, without any harm in him, for it is no harm to bark, if one stops there and does not bite, and it is no harm to be an ass, if one is content to bray and not kick. If this vast structure of brawn and muscle and vanity and foolishness seemed to have a libellous tongue, what of it? There was no malice behind it; and besides, the defect was not of his own creation; it was the work of Noël Rainguesson, who had nurtured it, fostered it, built it up and perfected it, for the entertainment he got out of it. His careless light heart had to have somebody to nag and chaff and make fun of, the Paladin had only needed development in order to meet its requirements, consequently the development was taken in hand and diligently attended to and looked after, gnat-and-bull fashion, for years, to the neglect and damage of far more important concerns. The result was an unqualified success. Noël prized the society of the Paladin above everybody else's; the Paladin preferred anybody's to Noël's. The big fellow was often seen with the little fellow, but it was for the same reason that the bull is often seen with the gnat.

With the first opportunity, I had a talk with Noël. I welcomed him to our expedition, and said—

"It was fine and brave of you to volunteer, Noël."

His eye twinkled, and he answered—

"Yes, it was rather fine I think. Still, the credit doesn't all belong to me; I had help."

"Who helped you?"

"The governor."

"How?"

"Well, I'll tell you the whole thing. I came up from Domremy to see the crowds and the general show, for I hadn't ever had any experience of such things, of course, and this was a great opportunity; but I hadn't any mind to volunteer. I overtook the Paladin on the road and let him have my company the rest of the way, although he did not want it and said so; and while we were gawking and blinking in the glare of the governor's torches they seized us and four more and added us to the escort, and that is really how I came to volunteer. But after all, I wasn't sorry, remembering how dull life would have been in the village without the Paladin."

"How did he feel about it? Was he satisfied?"

"I think he was glad."

"Why?"

"Because he said he wasn't. He was taken by surprise, you see, and it is not likely that he could tell the truth without preparation. Not that he would have prepared, if he had had the chance, for I do not think he would. I am not charging him with that. In the same space of time that he could prepare to speak the truth, he could also prepare to lie; besides, his judgment would be cool then, and would warn him against fooling with new methods in an emergency. No, I am sure he was glad, because he said he wasn't."

"Do you think he was very glad?"

"Yes, I know he was. He begged like a slave, and bawled for his mother. He said his health was delicate, and he didn't know how to ride a horse, and knew he couldn't outlive the first march. But really he wasn't looking as delicate as he was feeling. There was a cask of wine there, a proper lift for four men. The governor's temper got afire, and he delivered an oath at him that knocked up the dust where it struck the ground, and told him to shoulder that cask or he would carve him to cutlets and send him home in a basket. The Paladin did it, and that secured his promotion to a privacy in the escort without any further debate."

"Yes, you seem to make it quite plain that he was glad to join—that is, if your premises are right that you start from. How did he stand the march last night?"

"About as I did. If he made the more noise, it was the privilege of his bulk. We stayed in our saddles because we had help. We are equally lame to-day, and if he likes to sit down, let him; I prefer to stand."

CHAPTER 4

We were called to quarters and subjected to a searching inspection by Joan. Then she made a short little talk in which she said that even the rude business of war could be conducted better without profanity and other brutalities of speech than with them, and that she should strictly require us to remember and apply this admonition. She ordered half an hour's horsemanship-drill for the novices then, and appointed one of the veterans to conduct it. It was a ridiculous exhibition, but we learned something, and Joan was satisfied and complimented us. She did not take any instruction herself or go through the evolutions and manœuvres, but merely sat her horse like a martial little statue and looked on. That was sufficient for her, you see. She would not miss or forget a detail of the lesson, she would take it all in with her eye and her mind, and apply it afterward with as much certainty and confidence as if she had already practised it.

We now made three night-marches of twelve or thirteen leagues each, riding in peace and undisturbed, being taken for a roving band of Free Companions. Country folk were glad to have that sort of people go by without stopping. Still, they were very wearing marches, and not comfortable, for the bridges were few and the streams many, and as we had to ford them we found the water dismally cold, and afterward had to bed ourselves, still wet, on the frosty or snowy ground, and get warm as we might and sleep if we could, for it would not have been prudent to build fires. Our energies languished under these hardships and deadly fatigues, but Joan's did not. Her step kept its spring and firmness and her eye its fire. We could only wonder at this, we could not explain it.

But if we had had hard times before, I know not what to call the five nights that now followed, for the marches were as fatiguing, the baths as cold, and we were ambuscaded seven times in addition, and lost two novices and three veterans in the resulting fights. The news had leaked out and gone abroad that the inspired Virgin of Vaucouleurs was making for the King with an escort, and all the roads were being watched now.

These five nights disheartened the command a good deal. This was aggravated by a discovery which Noël made, and which he promptly made known at headquarters. Some of the men had been trying to understand why Joan continued to be alert, vigorous, and confident while the strongest men in the company were fagged with the heavy marches and exposure and were become morose and irritable. There, it shows you how men can have eyes and yet not see. All their lives those men had seen their own womenfolks hitched up with a cow and dragging the plough in the fields while the men did the driving. They had also seen other evidences that women have far more endurance and patience and fortitude than men—but what good had their seeing these things been to them? None. It had taught them nothing. They were still surprised to see a girl of seventeen bear the fatigues of war better than trained veterans of the army. Moreover, they did not reflect that a great soul, with a great purpose, can make a weak body strong and keep it so; and here was the greatest soul in the universe; but how could they know that, those dumb creatures? No, they knew nothing, and their reasonings were of a piece with their ignorance. They argued and discussed among themselves, with Noël listening, and arrived at the decision that Joan was a witch, and had her strange pluck and strength from Satan; so they made a plan to watch for a safe opportunity and take her life.

To have secret plottings of this sort going on in our midst was a very serious business, of course, and the knights asked Joan's permission to hang the plotters, but she refused without hesitancy. She said:

"Neither these men nor any others can take my life before my mission is accomplished, therefore why should I have their blood upon my hands? I will inform them of this, and also admonish them. Call them before me."

When they came she made that statement to them in a plain matter-of-fact way, and just as if the thought never entered her mind that any one could doubt it after she had given her word that it was true. The men were evidently amazed and impressed to hear her say such a thing in such a sure and confident way, for prophecies boldly uttered never fall barren on superstitious ears. Yes, this speech certainly impressed them, but her closing remark impressed them still more. It was for the ringleader, and Joan said it sorrowfully—

"It is a pity that you should plot another's death when your own is so close at hand."

That man's horse stumbled and fell on him in the first ford which we crossed that night, and he was drowned before we could help him. We had no more conspiracies.

This night was harassed with ambuscades, but we got through without having any men killed. One more night would carry us over the hostile frontier if we had good luck, and we saw the night close down with a good deal of solicitude. Always before, we had been more or less reluctant to start out into the gloom and the silence to be frozen in the fords and persecuted by the enemy, but this time we were impatient to get under way and have it over, although there was promise of more and harder fighting than any of the previous nights had furnished. Moreover, in front of us about three leagues there was a deep stream with a frail wooden bridge over it, and as a cold rain mixed with snow had been falling steadily all day we were anxious to find out whether we were in a trap or not. If the swollen stream had washed away the bridge, we might properly consider ourselves trapped and cut off from escape.

As soon as it was dark we filed out from the depths of the forest where we had been hidden and began the march. From the time that we had begun to encounter ambushes Joan had ridden at the head of the column, and she took this post now. By the time we had gone a league the rain and snow had turned to sleet, and under the impulse of the storm-wind it lashed my face like whips, and I envied Joan and the knights, who could close their visors and shut up their heads in their helmets as in a box. Now, out of the pitchy darkness and close at hand, came the sharp command—

"Halt!"

We obeyed. I made out a dim mass in front of us which might be a body of horsemen, but one could not be sure. A man rode up and said to Joan in a tone of reproof—

"Well, you have taken your time, truly. And what have you found out? Is she still behind us, or in front?"

Joan answered in a level voice—

"She is still behind."

This news softened the stranger's tone. He said—

"If you know that to be true, you have not lost your time, Captain. But are you sure? How do you know?"

"Because I have seen her."

"Seen her! Seen the Virgin herself?"

"Yes, I have been in her camp."

"Is it possible! Captain Raymond, I ask you to pardon me for speaking in that tone just now. You have performed a daring and admirable service. Where was she camped?"

"In the forest, not more than a league from here."

"Good! I was afraid we might be still behind her, but now that we know she is behind us, everything is safe. She is our game. We will hang her. You shall hang her yourself. No one has so well earned the privilege of abolishing this pestilent limb of Satan."

"I do not know how to thank you sufficiently. If we catch her, I—"

"If! I will take care of that; give yourself no uneasiness. All I want is just a look at her, to see what the imp is like that has been able to make all this noise, then you and the halter may have her. How many men has she?"

"I counted but eighteen, but she may have had two or three pickets out."

"Is that all? It won't be a mouthful for my force. Is it true that she is only a girl?"

"Yes; she is not more than seventeen."

"It passes belief! Is she robust, or slender?"

"Slender."

The officer pondered a moment or two, then he said:

"Was she preparing to break camp?"

"Not when I had my last glimpse of her."

"What was she doing?"

"She was talking quietly with an officer."

"Quietly? Not giving orders?"

"No, talking as quietly as we are now."

"That is good. She is feeling a false security. She would have been restless and fussy else—it is the way of her sex when danger is about. As she was making no preparation to break camp,—"

"She certainly was not when I saw her last."

"—and was chatting quietly and at her ease, it means that this weather is not to her taste. Night-marching in sleet and wind is not for chits of seventeen. No; she will stay where she is. She has my thanks. We will camp, ourselves; here is as good a place as any. Let us get about it."

"If you command it—certainly. But she has two knights with her. They might force her to march, particularly if the weather should improve."

I was scared, and impatient to be getting out of this peril, and it distressed and worried me to have Joan apparently set herself to work to make delay and increase the danger—still, I thought she probably knew better than I what to do. The officer said—

"Well, in that case we are here to block the way."

"Yes, if they come this way. But if they should send out spies, and find out enough to make them want to try for the bridge through the woods? Is it best to allow the bridge to stand?"

It made me shiver to hear her.

The officer considered a while, then said:

"It might be well enough to send a force to destroy the bridge. I was intending to occupy it with the whole command, but that is not necessary now."

Joan said, tranquilly—

"With your permission, I will go and destroy it myself."

Ah, now I saw her idea, and was glad she had had the cleverness to invent it and the ability to keep her head cool and think of it in that tight place. The officer replied—

"You have it, Captain, and my thanks. With you to do it, it will be well done; I could send another in your place, but not a better."

They saluted, and we moved forward. I breathed freer. A dozen times I had imagined I heard the hoof-beats of the real Captain Raymond's troop arriving behind us, and had been sitting on pins and needles all the while that that conversation was dragging along. I breathed freer, but was still not comfortable, for Joan had given only the simple command, "Forward!" Consequently we moved in a walk. Moved in a dead walk past a dim and lengthening column of enemies at our side. The suspense was exhausting, yet it lasted but a short while, for when the enemy's bugles sang the "Dismount!" Joan gave the word to trot, and that was a great relief to me. She was always at herself, you see. Before the command to dismount had been given, somebody might have wanted the countersign somewhere along that line if we came flying by at speed, but now we seemed to be on our way to our allotted camping position, so we were allowed to pass unchallenged. The further we went the more formidable was the strength revealed by the hostile force. Perhaps it was only a hundred or two, but to me it seemed a thousand. When we passed the last of these people I was thankful, and the deeper we ploughed into the darkness beyond them the better I felt. I came nearer and nearer to feeling good, for an hour; then we found the bridge still standing, and I felt entirely good. We crossed it and destroyed it, and then I felt—but I cannot describe what I felt. One has to feel it himself in order to know what it is like.

We had expected to hear the rush of a pursuing force behind us, for we thought that the real Captain Raymond would arrive and suggest that perhaps the troop that had been mistaken for his belonged to the Virgin of Vaucouleurs; but he must have been delayed seriously, for when we resumed our march beyond the river there were no sounds behind us except those which the storm was furnishing.

I said that Joan had harvested a good many compliments intended for Captain Raymond, and that he would find nothing of a crop left but a dry stubble of reprimands when he got back, and a commander just in the humor to superintend the gathering of it in.

Joan said:

"It will be as you say, no doubt; for the commander took a troop for granted, in the night and unchallenged, and would have camped without sending a force to destroy the bridge if he had been left unadvised, and none are so ready to find fault with others as those who do things worthy of blame themselves."

The Sieur Bertrand was amused at Joan's naïve way of referring to her advice as if it had been a valuable present to a hostile leader who was saved by it from making a censurable blunder of omission, and then he went on to admire how ingeniously she had deceived that man and yet had not told him anything that was not the truth. This troubled Joan, and she said—

"I thought he was deceiving himself. I forbore to tell him lies, for that would have been wrong; but if my truths deceived him, perhaps that made them lies, and I am to blame. I would God I knew if I have done wrong."

She was assured that she had done right, and that in the perils and necessities of war deceptions that help one's own cause and hurt the enemy's were always permissible; but she was not quite satisfied with that, and thought that even when a great cause was in danger one ought to have the privilege of trying honorable ways first. Jean said—

"Joan, you told us yourself that you were going to Uncle Laxart's to nurse his wife, but you didn't say you were going further, yet you did go on to Vaucouleurs. There!"

"I see, now," said Joan, sorrowfully, "I told no lie, yet I deceived. I had tried all other ways first, but I could not get away, and I *had* to get away. My mission required it. I did wrong, I think, and am to blame."

She was silent a moment, turning the matter over in her mind, then she added, with quiet decision, "But the thing itself was right, and I would do it again."

It seemed an over-nice distinction, but nobody said anything. If we had known her as well as she knew herself, and as her later history revealed her to us, we should have perceived that she had a clear meaning there, and that her position was not identical with ours, as we were supposing, but occupied a higher plane. She would sacrifice herself—and her *best* self; that is, her truthfulness—to save her cause; but only that: she would not buy her *life* at that cost; whereas our war-ethics permitted the purchase of our lives, or any mere military advantage, small or great, by deception. Her saying seemed a commonplace at that time, the essence of its meaning escaping us; but one sees, now, that it contained a principle which lifted it above that and made it great and fine.

Presently the wind died down, the sleet stopped falling, and the cold was less severe. The road was become a bog, and the horses labored through it at a walk—they could do no better. As the heavy time wore on, exhaustion overcame us, and we slept in our saddles. Not even the dangers that threatened us could keep us awake.

This tenth night seemed longer than any of the others, and of course it was the hardest, because we had been accumulating fatigue from the beginning, and had more of it on hand now than at any previous time. But we were not molested again. When the dull dawn came at last we saw a river before us and we knew it was the Loire; we entered the town of Gien, and knew we were in a friendly land, with the hostiles all behind us. That was a glad morning for us.

We were a worn and bedraggled and shabby-looking troop; and still, as always, Joan was the freshest of us all, in both body and spirits. We had averaged above thirteen leagues a night, by tortuous and wretched roads. It was a remarkable march, and shows what men can do when they have a leader with a determined purpose and a resolution that never flags.

CHAPTER 5

We rested and otherwise refreshed ourselves two or three hours at Gien, but by that time the news was abroad that the young girl commissioned of God to deliver France was come; wherefore, such a press of people flocked to our quarters to get sight of her that it seemed best to seek a quieter place; so we pushed on and halted at a small village called Fierbois.

We were now within six leagues of the King, who was at the Castle of Chinon. Joan dictated a letter to him at once, and I wrote it. In it she said she had come a hundred and fifty leagues to bring him good news, and begged the privilege of delivering it in person. She added that although she had never seen him she would know him in any disguise and would point him out.

The two knights rode away at once with the letter. The troop slept all the afternoon, and after supper we felt pretty fresh and fine, especially our little group of young Domremians. We had the comfortable tap-room of the village inn to ourselves, and for the first time in ten unspeakably long days were exempt from bodings and terrors and hardships and fatiguing labors. The Paladin was suddenly become his ancient self again, and was swaggering up and down, a very monument of self-complacency. Noël Rainguesson said—

"I think it is wonderful, the way he has brought us through."

"Who?" asked Joan.

"Why, the Paladin."

The Paladin seemed not to hear.

"What had he to do with it?" asked Pierre d'Arc.

"Everything. It was nothing but Joan's confidence in his discretion that enabled her to keep up her heart. She could depend on us and on herself for valor, but discretion is the winning thing in war, after all; discretion is the rarest and loftiest of qualities, and he has got more of it than any other man in France—more of it, perhaps, than any other sixty men in France."

"Now you are getting ready to make a fool of yourself, Noël Rainguesson," said the Paladin, "and you want to coil some of that long tongue of yours around your neck and stick the end of it in your ear, then you'll be the less likely to get into trouble."

"I didn't know he had more discretion than other people," said Pierre, "for discretion argues brains, and he hasn't any more brains than the rest of us, in my opinion."

"No, you are wrong there. Discretion hasn't anything to do with brains; brains are an obstruction to it, for it does not reason, it feels. Perfect discretion means absence of brains. Discretion is a quality of the heart—solely a quality of the heart; it acts upon us through feeling. We know this because if it were an intellectual quality it would only perceive a danger, for instance, where a danger exists; whereas—"

"Hear him twaddle—the damned idiot!" muttered the Paladin.

"—whereas, it being purely a quality of the heart, and proceeding by feeling, not reason, its reach is correspondingly wider and sublimer, enabling it to perceive and avoid dangers that haven't any existence at all; as for instance that night in the fog, when the Paladin took his horse's ears for hostile lances and got off and climbed a tree—"

"It's a lie! a lie without shadow of foundation, and I call upon you all to beware how you give credence to the malicious inventions of this ramshackle slander-mill that has been doing its best to destroy my character for years, and will grind up your own reputations for you, next. I got off to tighten my saddle-girth—I wish I may die in my tracks if it isn't so—and whoever wants to believe it can, and whoever don't, can let it alone."

"There, that is the way with him, you see; he never can discuss a theme temperately, but always flies off the handle and becomes disagreeable. And you notice his defect of memory. He remembers getting off his horse, but forgets all the rest, even the tree. But that is natural; he would remember getting off the horse because he was so used to doing it. He always did it when there was an alarm and the clash of arms at the front."

"Why did he choose that time for it?" asked Jean.

"I don't know. To tighten up his girth, *he* thinks, to climb a tree, *I* think; I saw him climb nine trees in a single night."

"You saw nothing of the kind! A person that can lie like that deserves no one's respect. I ask you all to answer me. Do you believe what this reptile has said?"

All seemed embarrassed, and only Pierre replied. He said, hesitatingly—

"I—well, I hardly know what to say. It is a delicate situation. It seems offensive to refuse to believe a person when he makes so direct a statement, and yet I am obliged to say, rude as it may appear, that I am not able to believe the whole of it—no, I am not able to believe that you climbed nine trees."

"There!" cried the Paladin; "now what do you think of yourself, Noël Rainguesson? How many do you believe I climbed, Pierre?"

"Only eight."

The laughter that followed inflamed the Paladin's anger to white heat, and he said—

"I bide my time—I bide my time. I will reckon with you all, I promise you that!"

"Don't get him started," Noël pleaded; "he is a perfect lion when he gets started. I saw enough to teach me that, after the third skirmish. After it was over I saw him come out of the bushes and attack a dead man single-handed."

"It is another lie; and I give you fair warning that you are going too far. You will see me attack a live one if you are not careful."

"Meaning me, of course. This wounds me more than any number of injurious and unkind speeches could do. Ingratitude to one's benefactor—"

"Benefactor? What do I owe you, I should like to know?"

"You owe me your life. I stood between the trees and the foe, and kept hundreds and thousands of the enemy at bay when they were thirsting for your blood. And I did not do it to display my daring, I did it because I loved you and could not live without you."

"There—you have said enough! I will not stay here to listen to these infamies. I can endure your lies, but not your love. Keep that corruption for somebody with a stronger stomach than mine. And I want to say this, before I go. That you people's small performances might appear the better and win you the more glory, I hid my own deeds through all the march. I went always to the front, where the fighting was thickest, to be remote from you, in order that you might not see and be discouraged by the things I did to the enemy. It was my purpose to keep this a secret in my own breast, but you force me to reveal it. If you ask for my witnesses, yonder they lie, on the road we have come. I found that road mud, I paved it with corpses. I found that country sterile, I fertilized it with blood. Time and again I was urged to go to the rear because the command could not proceed on account of my dead. And yet you, you miscreant, accuse me of climbing trees! Pah!"

And he strode out, with a lofty air, for the recital of his imaginary deeds had already set him up again and made him feel good.

Next day we mounted and faced toward Chinon. Orleans was at our back, now, and close by, lying in the strangling grip of the English; soon, please God, we would face about and go to their relief. From Gien the news had spread to Orleans that the peasant Maid of Vaucouleurs was on her way, divinely commissioned to raise the siege. The news made a great excitement and raised a great hope—the first breath of hope those poor souls had breathed in five months. They sent commissioners at once to the King to beg him to consider this matter, and not throw this help lightly away. These commissioners were already at Chinon by this time.

When we were half-way to Chinon we happened upon yet one more squad of enemies. They burst suddenly out of the woods, and in considerable force, too; but we were not the apprentices we were ten or twelve days before; no, we were seasoned to this kind of adventure now; our hearts did not jump into our throats and our weapons tremble in our hands. We had learned to be always in battle array, always alert, and always ready to deal with any emergency that might turn up. We were no more dismayed by the sight of those people than our commander was. Before they could form, Joan had delivered the order, "Forward!" and we were down upon them with a rush. They stood no chance; they turned tail and scattered, we ploughing through them as if they had been men of straw. That was our last ambuscade, and it was probably laid for us by that treacherous rascal the King's own minister and favorite, De la Tremouille.

We housed ourselves in an inn, and soon the town came flocking to get a glimpse of the Maid.

Ah, the tedious King and his tedious people! Our two good knights came presently, their patience well wearied, and reported. They and we reverently stood—as becomes persons who are in the presence of Kings and the superiors of Kings—until Joan, troubled by this mark of homage and respect, and not content with it nor yet used to it, although we had not permitted ourselves to do otherwise since the day she prophesied that wretched traitor's death and he was straightway drowned, thus confirming many previous signs that she was indeed an ambassador commissioned of God, commanded us to sit; then the Sieur de Metz said to Joan:

"The King has got the letter, but they will not let us have speech with him."

"Who is it that forbids?"

"None forbids, but there be three or four that are nearest his person—schemers and traitors every one—that put obstructions in the way, and seek all ways, by lies and pretexts, to make delay. Chiefest of these are Georges de la Tremouille and that plotting fox the Archbishop of Rheims. While they keep the King idle and in bondage to his sports and follies, they are great and their importance grows; whereas if ever he assert himself and rise and strike for crown and country like a man, their reign is done. So they but thrive they care not if the crown go to destruction and the King with it."

"You have spoken with others besides these?"

"Not of the Court, no—the Court are the meek slaves of those reptiles, and watch their mouths and their actions, acting as they act, thinking as they think, saying as they say: wherefore they are cold to us, and turn aside and go another way when we appear. But we have spoken with the commissioners from Orleans. They said with heat: 'It is a marvel that any man in such desperate case as is the King can moon around in this torpid way, and see his all go to ruin without lifting a finger to stay the disaster. What a most strange spectacle it is! Here he is, shut up in this wee corner of the realm like a rat in a trap; his royal shelter this huge gloomy tomb of a castle, with wormy rags for upholstery and crippled furniture for use, a very house of desolation; in his treasury forty francs, and not a farthing more, God be witness! no army, nor any shadow of one; and by contrast with this hungry poverty you behold this crownless pauper and his shoals of fools and favorites tricked out in the gaudiest silks and velvets you shall find in any Court in Christendom. And look you, he knows that when our city falls—as fall it surely will except succor come swiftly—*France* falls; he knows that when that day comes he will be an outlaw and a fugitive, and that behind him the English flag will float unchallenged over every acre of his great heritage; he knows these things, he knows that our faithful city is fighting all solitary and alone against disease, starvation, and the sword to stay this awful calamity, yet he will not strike one blow to save her, he will not hear our prayers, he will not even look upon our faces.' That is what the commissioners said, and they are in despair."

Joan said, gently—

"It is pity, but they must not despair. The Dauphin will hear them presently. Tell them so."

She almost always called the King the Dauphin. To her mind he was not King yet, not being crowned.

"We will tell them so, and it will content them, for they believe you come from God. The Archbishop and his confederate have for backer that veteran soldier Raoul de Gaucourt, Grand Master of the Palace, a worthy man but simply a soldier, with no head for any greater matter. He cannot make out to see how a country girl, ignorant of war, can take a sword in her small hand and win victories where the trained generals of France have looked for defeats only, for fifty years—and always found them. And so he lifts his frosty mustache and scoffs."

"When God fights it is but small matter whether the hand that bears His sword is big or little. He will perceive this in time. Is there none in that Castle of Chinon who favors us?"

"Yes, the King's mother-in-law, Yolande, Queen of Sicily, who is wise and good. She spoke with the Sieur Bertrand."

"She favors us, and she hates those others, the King's beguilers," said Bertrand. "She was full of interest, and asked a thousand questions, all of which I answered according to my ability. Then she sat thinking over these replies until I thought she was lost in a dream and would wake no more. But it was not so. At last she said, slowly, and as if she were talking to herself: 'A child of seventeen—a girl—country bred—untaught—ignorant of war, the use of arms, and the conduct of battles—modest, gentle, shrinking—yet throws away her shepherd's crook and clothes herself in steel, and fights her way through a hundred and fifty leagues of hostile territory, never losing heart or hope and never showing fear, and comes—she to whom a king must be a dread and awful presence—and will stand up before such an one and say, Be not afraid, God has sent me to save you! Ah, whence could come a courage and conviction so sublime as this *but* from very God Himself!' She was silent again awhile, thinking, and making up her mind; then she said, 'And whether she comes of God or no, there is that in her heart that raises her above men—high above all men that breathe in France to-day—for in her is that mysterious something that puts heart into soldiers, and turns mobs of cowards into armies of fighters that forget what fear is when they are in that presence—fighters who go into battle with joy in their eyes and songs on their lips, and sweep over the field like a storm—that is the spirit that can save France, and that alone, come it whence it may! It is in her, I do truly believe, for what else could have borne up that child on that great march, and made her despise its dangers and fatigues? The King must see her face to face—and shall!' She dismissed me with those good words, and I know her promise will be kept. They will delay her all they can—those animals—but she will not fail, in the end."

"Would *she* were King!" said the other knight, fervently. "For there is little hope that the King himself can be stirred out of his lethargy. He is wholly without hope, and is only thinking of throwing away everything and flying to some foreign land. The commissioners say there is a spell upon him that makes him hopeless—yes, and that it is shut up in a mystery which they cannot fathom."

"I know the mystery," said Joan, with quiet confidence; "I know it, and he knows it, but no other but God. When I see him I will tell him a secret that will drive away his trouble, then he will hold up his head again."

I was miserable with curiosity to know what it was that she would tell him, but she did not say, and I did not expect she would. She was but a child, it is true; but she was not a chatterer to tell great matters and make herself important to little people; no, she was reserved, and kept things to herself, as the truly great always do.

The next day Queen Yolande got one victory over the King's keepers, for in spite of their protestations and obstructions she procured an audience for our two knights, and they made the most they could out of their opportunity. They told the King what a spotless and beautiful character Joan was, and how great and noble a spirit animated her, and they implored him to trust in her, believe in her, and have faith that she was sent to save France. They begged him to consent to see her. He was strongly moved to do this, and promised that he would not drop the matter out of his mind, but would consult with his council about it. This began to look encouraging. Two hours later there was a great stir below, and the inn-keeper came flying up to say a commission of illustrious ecclesiastics was come from the King—from the King his very self, understand!—think of this vast honor to his humble little hostelry!—and he was so overcome with the glory of it that he could hardly find breath enough in his excited body to put the facts into words. They were come from the King to speak with the Maid of Vaucouleurs. Then he flew down-stairs, and presently appeared again, backing into the room and bowing to the ground with every step, in front of four imposing and austere bishops and their train of servants.

Joan rose, and we all stood. The bishops took seats, and for a while no word was said, for it was their prerogative to speak first, and they were so astonished to see what a child it was that was making such a noise in the world and degrading personages of their dignity to the base function of ambassadors to her in her plebeian tavern, that they could not find any words to say, at first. Then presently their spokesman told Joan they were aware that she had a message for the King, wherefore she was now commanded to put it into words, briefly and without waste of time or embroideries of speech.

As for me, I could hardly contain my joy—our message was to reach the King at last! And there was the same joy and pride and exultation in the faces of our knights, too, and in those of Joan's brothers. And I knew that they were all praying—as I was—that the awe which we felt in the presence of these great dignitaries, and which would have tied our tongues and locked our jaws, would not affect her in the like degree, but that she would be enabled to word her message well, and with little stumbling, and so make a favorable impression here, where it would be so valuable and so important.

Ah dear, how little we were expecting what happened then! We were aghast to hear her say what she said. She was standing in a reverent attitude, with her head down and her hands clasped in front of her; for she was always reverent toward the consecrated servants of God. When the spokesman had finished, she raised her head and set her calm eye on those faces, not any more disturbed by their state and grandeur than a princess would have been, and said, with all her ordinary simplicity and modesty of voice and manner:

"Ye will forgive me, reverend sirs, but I have no message save for the King's ear alone."

Those surprised men were dumb for a moment, and their faces flushed darkly; then the spokesman said:

"Hark ye, do you fling the King's command in his face and refuse to deliver this message of yours to his servants appointed to receive it?"

"God has appointed one to receive it, and another's commandment may not take precedence of that. I pray you let me have speech of his grace the Dauphin."

"Forbear this folly, and come at your message! Deliver it, and waste no more time about it."

"You err indeed, most reverend fathers in God, and it is not well. I am not come hither to talk, but to deliver Orleans, and lead the Dauphin to his good city of Rheims, and set the crown upon his head."

"Is that the message you send to the King?"

But Joan only said, in the simple fashion which was her wont:

"Ye will pardon me for reminding you again—but I have no message to send to any one."

The King's messengers rose in deep anger and swept out of the place without further words, we and Joan kneeling as they passed.

Our countenances were vacant, our hearts full of a sense of disaster. Our precious opportunity was thrown away; we could not understand Joan's conduct, she who had been so wise until this fatal hour. At last the Sieur Bertrand found courage to ask her why she had let this great chance to get her message to the King go by.

"Who sent them here?" she asked.

"The King."

"Who moved the King to send them?" She waited for an answer; none came, for we began to see what was in her mind—so she answered herself: "The Dauphin's council moved him to it. Are they enemies to me and to the Dauphin's weal, or are they friends?"

"Enemies," answered the Sieur Bertrand.

"If one would have a message go sound and ungarbled, does one choose traitors and tricksters to send it by?"

I saw that we had been fools, and she wise. They saw it too, so none found anything to say. Then she went on:

"They had but small wit that contrived this trap. They thought to get my message and seem to deliver it straight, yet deftly twist it from its purpose. You know that one part of my message is but this—to move the Dauphin by argument and reasonings to give me men-at-arms and send me to the siege. If an enemy carried these in the right words, the exact words, and no word missing, yet left out the persuasions of gesture and supplicating tone and beseeching looks that inform the words and make them live, where were the value of that argument—whom could it convince? Be patient, the Dauphin will hear me presently; have no fear."

The Sieur de Metz nodded his head several times, and muttered as to himself:

"She was right and wise, and we are but dull fools, when all is said."

It was just my thought; I could have said it myself; and indeed it was the thought of all there present. A sort of awe crept over us, to think how that untaught girl, taken suddenly and unprepared, was yet able to penetrate the cunning devices of a King's trained advisers and defeat them. Marvelling over this, and astonished at it, we fell silent and spoke no more. We had come to know that she was great in courage, fortitude, endurance, patience, conviction, fidelity to all duties—in all things, indeed, that make a good and trusty soldier and perfect him for his post; now we were beginning to feel that maybe there were greatnesses in her brain that were even greater than these great qualities of the heart. It set us thinking.

What Joan did that day bore fruit the very day after. The King was obliged to respect the spirit of a young girl who could hold her own and stand her ground like that, and he asserted himself sufficiently to put his respect into an act instead of into polite and empty words. He moved Joan out of that poor inn, and housed her, with us her servants, in the Castle of Courdray, personally confiding her to the care of Madame de Bellier, wife of old Raoul de Gaucourt, Master of the Palace. Of course this royal attention had an immediate result: all the great lords and ladies of the Court began to flock there to see and listen to the wonderful girl-soldier that all the world was talking about, and who had answered the King's mandate with a bland refusal to obey. Joan charmed them every one with her sweetness and simplicity and unconscious eloquence, and all the best and capablest among them recognized that there was an indefinable something about her that testified that she was not made of common clay, that she was built on a grander plan than the mass of mankind, and moved on a loftier plane. These spread her fame. She always made friends and advocates that way; neither the high nor the low could come within the sound of her voice and the sight of her face and go out from her presence indifferent.

CHAPTER 6

Well, anything to make delay. The King's council advised him against arriving at a decision in our matter too precipitately. *He* arrive at a decision too precipitately! So they sent a committee of priests—always priests—into Lorraine to inquire into Joan's character and history—a matter which would consume several weeks, of course. You see how fastidious they were. It was as if people should come to put out the fire when a man's house was burning down, and they waited till they could send into another country to find out if he had always kept the Sabbath or not, before letting him try.

So the days poked along; dreary for us young people in some ways, but not in all, for we had one great anticipation in front of us; we had never seen a king, and now some day we should have that prodigious spectacle to see and to treasure in our memories all our lives; so we were on the lookout, and always eager and watching for the chance. The others were doomed to wait longer than I, as it turned out. One day great news came—the Orleans commissioners, with Yolande and our knights, had at last turned the council's position and persuaded the King to see Joan.

Joan received the immense news gratefully but without losing her head, but with us others it was otherwise; we could not eat or sleep or do any rational thing for the excitement and the glory of it. During two days our pair of noble knights were in distress and trepidation on Joan's account, for the audience was to be at night, and they were afraid that Joan would be so paralyzed by the glare of light from the long files of torches, the solemn pomps and ceremonies, the great concourse of renowned personages, the brilliant costumes, and the other splendors of the Court, that she, a simple country maid, and all unused to such things, would be overcome by these terrors and make a piteous failure.

No doubt I could have comforted them, but I was not free to speak. Would Joan be disturbed by this cheap spectacle, this tinsel show, with its small King and his butterfly dukelets?—she who had spoken face to face with the princes of heaven, the familiars of God, and seen their retinue of angels stretching back into the remoteness of the sky, myriads upon myriads, like a measureless fan of light, a glory like the glory of the sun streaming from each of those innumerable heads, the massed radiance filling the deeps of space with a blinding splendor? I thought not.

Queen Yolande wanted Joan to make the best possible impression upon the King and the Court, so she was strenuous to have her clothed in the richest stuffs, wrought upon the princeliest pattern, and set off with jewels; but in that she had to be disappointed, of course, Joan not being persuadable to it, but begging to be simply and sincerely dressed, as became a servant of God, and one sent upon a mission of a serious sort and grave political import. So then the gracious Queen imagined and contrived that simple and witching costume which I have described to you so many times, and which I cannot think of even now in my dull age without being moved just as rhythmical and exquisite music moves one; for *that* was music, that dress—that is what it was—music that one saw with the eyes and felt in the heart. Yes, she was a poem, she was a dream, she was a spirit when she was clothed in that.

She kept that raiment always, and wore it several times upon occasions of state, and it is preserved to this day in the Treasury of Orleans, with two of her swords, and her banner, and other things now sacred because they had belonged to her.

At the appointed time the Count of Vendôme, a great lord of the court, came richly clothed, with his train of servants and assistants, to conduct Joan to the King, and the two knights and I went with her, being entitled to this privilege by reason of our official positions near her person.

When we entered the great audience hall, there it all was, just as I have already painted it. Here were ranks of guards in shining armor and with polished halberds; two sides of the hall were like flower-gardens for variety of color and the magnificence of the costumes; light streamed upon these masses of color from two hundred and fifty flambeaux. There was a wide free space down the middle of the hall, and at the end of it was a throne royally canopied, and upon it sat a crowned and sceptred figure nobly clothed and blazing with jewels.

It is true that Joan had been hindered and put off a good while, but now that she was admitted to an audience at last, she was received with honors granted to only the greatest personages. At the entrance door stood four heralds in a row, in splendid tabards, with long slender silver trumpets at their mouths, with square silken banners depending from them embroidered with the arms of France. As Joan and the Count passed by, these trumpets gave forth in unison one long rich note, and as we moved down the hall under the pictured and gilded vaulting, this was repeated at every fifty feet of our progress—six times in all. It made our good knights proud and happy, and they held themselves erect, and stiffened their stride, and looked fine and soldierly. They were not expecting this beautiful and honorable tribute to our little country maid.

Joan walked two yards behind the Count, we three walked two yards behind Joan. Our solemn march ended when we were as yet some eight or ten steps from the throne. The Count made a deep obeisance, pronounced Joan's name, then bowed again and moved to his place among a group of officials near the throne. I was devouring the crowned personage with all my eyes, and my heart almost stood still with awe.

The eyes of all others were fixed upon Joan in a gaze of wonder which was half worship, and which seemed to say, "How sweet—how lovely—how divine!" All lips were parted and motionless, which was a sure sign that those people, who seldom forget themselves, had forgotten themselves now, and were not conscious of anything but the one object they were gazing upon. They had the look of people who are under the enchantment of a vision.

Then they presently began to come to life again, rousing themselves out of the spell and shaking it off as one drives away little by little a clinging drowsiness or intoxication. Now they fixed their attention upon Joan with a strong new interest of another sort; they were full of curiosity to see what she would do—they having a secret and particular reason for this curiosity. So they watched. This is what they saw:

She made no obeisance, nor even any slight inclination of her head, but stood looking toward the throne in silence. That was all there was to see, at present.

I glanced up at De Metz, and was shocked at the paleness of his face. I whispered and said—

"What is it man, what is it?"

His answering whisper was so weak I could hardly catch it—

"They have taken advantage of the hint in her letter to play a trick upon her! She will err, and they will laugh at her. That is not the King that sits there."

Then I glanced at Joan. She was still gazing steadfastly toward the throne, and I had the curious fancy that even her shoulders and the back of her head expressed bewilderment. Now she turned her head slowly, and her eye wandered along the lines of standing courtiers till it fell upon a young man who was very quietly dressed; then her face lighted joyously, and she ran and threw herself at his feet, and clasped his knees, exclaiming in that soft melodious voice which was her birthright and was now charged with deep and tender feeling—

"God of his grace give you long life, O dear and gentle Dauphin!"

In his astonishment and exultation De Metz cried out—

"By the shadow of God, it is an amazing thing!" Then he mashed all the bones of my hand in his grateful grip, and added, with a proud shake of his mane, "*Now,* what have these painted infidels to say!"

Meantime the young person in the plain clothes was saying to Joan—

"Ah, you mistake, my child, I am not the King. There he is," and he pointed to the throne.

The knight's face clouded, and he muttered in grief and indignation—

"Ah, it is a shame to use her so. But for this lie she had gone through safe. I will go and proclaim to all the house what—"

"Stay where you are!" whispered I and the Sieur Bertrand in a breath, and made him stop in his place.

Joan did not stir from her knees, but still lifted her happy face toward the King, and said—

"No, gracious liege, you are he, and none other."

De Metz's troubles vanished away, and he said—

"Verily, she was not guessing, she *knew.* Now, how could she know? It is a miracle. I am content, and will meddle no more, for I perceive that she is equal to her occasions, having that in her head that cannot profitably be helped by the vacancy that is in mine."

This interruption of his lost me a remark or two of the other talk; however, I caught the King's next question:

"But tell me who you are, and what would you?"

"I am called Joan the Maid, and am sent to say that the King of Heaven wills that you be crowned and consecrated in your good city of Rheims, and be thereafter Lieutenant of the Lord of Heaven, who is King of France. And He willeth also that you set me at my appointed work and give me men-at-arms." After a slight pause she added, her eye lighting at the sound of her words, "For then will I raise the siege of Orleans and break the English power!"

The young monarch's amused face sobered a little when this martial speech fell upon that sick air like a breath blown from embattled camps and fields of war, and his trifling smile presently faded wholly away and disappeared. He was grave, now, and thoughtful. After a little he waved his hand lightly and all the people fell away and left those two by themselves in a vacant space. The knights and I moved to the opposite side of the hall and stood there. We saw Joan rise at a sign, then she and the King talked privately together.

All that host had been consumed with curiosity to see what Joan would do. Well, they had seen, and now they were full of astonishment to see that she had really performed that strange miracle according to the promise in her letter; and they were fully as much astonished to find that she was not overcome by the pomps and splendors about her, but was even more tranquil and at her ease in holding speech with a monarch than ever they themselves had been, with all their practice and experience.

As for our two knights, they were inflated beyond measure with pride in Joan, but nearly dumb, as to speech, they not being able to think out any way to account for her managing to carry herself through this imposing ordeal without ever a mistake or an awkwardness of any kind to mar the grace and credit of her great performance.

The talk between Joan and the King was long and earnest, and held in low voices. We could not hear, but we had our eyes and could note effects; and presently we and all the house noted one effect which was memorable and striking, and has been set down in memoirs and histories and in testimony at the Process of Rehabilitation by some who witnessed it; for all knew it was big with meaning, though none knew what that meaning was at that time, of course. For suddenly we saw the King shake off his indolent attitude and straighten up like a man, and at the same time look immeasurably astonished. It was as if Joan had told him something almost too wonderful for belief, and yet of a most uplifting and welcome nature.

It was long before we found out the secret of this conversation, but we know it now, and all the world knows it. That part of the talk was like this—as one may read in all histories. The perplexed King asked Joan for a sign. He wanted to believe in her and her mission, and that her Voices were supernatural and endowed with knowledge hidden from mortals, but how could he do this unless these Voices could prove their claim in some absolutely unassailable way? It was then that Joan said—

"I will give you a sign, and you shall no more doubt. There is a secret trouble in your heart which you speak of to none—a doubt which wastes away your courage, and makes you dream of throwing all away and fleeing from your realm. Within this little while you have been praying, in your own breast, that God of his grace would resolve that doubt, even if the doing of it must show you that no kingly right is lodged in you."

It was that that amazed the King, for it was as she had said: his prayer was the secret of his own breast, and none but God could know about it. So he said:

"The sign is sufficient. I know, now, that these Voices are of God. They have said true in this matter; if they have said more, tell it me—I will believe."

"They have resolved that doubt, and I bring their very words, which are these: Thou art lawful heir to the King thy father, and true heir of France. God has spoken it. Now lift up thy head, and doubt no more, but give me men-at-arms and let me get about my work."

Telling him he was of lawful birth was what straightened him up and made a man of him for a moment, removing his doubts upon that head and convincing him of his royal right; and if any could have hanged his hindering and pestiferous council and set him free, he would have answered Joan's prayer and set her in the field. But no, those creatures were only checked, not checkmated; they could invent some more delays.

We had been made proud by the honors which had so distinguished Joan's entrance into that place—honors restricted to personages of very high rank and worth—but that pride was as nothing compared with the pride we had in the honor done her upon leaving it. For whereas those first honors were shown only to the great, these last, up to this time, had been shown only to the royal. The King himself led Joan by the hand down the great hall to the door, the glittering multitude standing and making reverence as they passed, and the silver trumpets sounding those rich notes of theirs. Then he dismissed her with gracious words, bending low over her hand and kissing it. Always—from all companies, high or low—she went forth richer in honor and esteem than when she came.

And the King did another handsome thing by Joan, for he sent us back to Courdray Castle torch-lighted and in state, under escort of his own troop—his guard of honor—the only soldiers he had; and finely equipped and bedizened they were, too, though they hadn't seen the color of their wages since they were children, as a body might say. The wonders which Joan had been performing before the King had been carried all around by this time, so the road was so packed with people who wanted to get a sight of her that we could hardly dig through; and as for talking together, we couldn't, all attempts at talk being drowned in the storm of shoutings and huzzas that broke out all along as we passed, and kept abreast of us like a wave the whole way.

CHAPTER 7

We were doomed to suffer tedious waits and delays, and we settled ourselves down to our fate and bore it with a dreary patience, counting the slow hours and the dull days and hoping for a turn when God should please to send it. The Paladin was the only exception—that is to say, he was the only one who was happy and had no heavy times. This was partly owing to the satisfaction he got out of his clothes. He bought them when he first arrived. He bought them at second hand—a Spanish cavalier's complete suit, wide-brimmed hat with flowing plumes, lace collar and cuffs, faded velvet doublet and trunks, short cloak hung from the shoulder, funnel-topped buskins, long rapier, and all that—a graceful and picturesque costume, and the Paladin's great frame was the right place to hang it for effect. He wore it when off duty; and when he swaggered by with one hand resting on the hilt of his rapier, and twirling his new mustache with the other, everybody stopped to look and admire; and well they might, for he was a fine and stately contrast to the small French gentleman of the day squeezed into the trivial French costume of the time.

He was king bee of the little village that snuggled under the shelter of the frowning towers and bastions of Courdray Castle, and acknowledged lord of the tap-room of the inn. When he opened his mouth there, he got a hearing. Those simple artisans and peasants listened with deep and wondering interest; for he was a traveller and had seen the world—all of it that lay between Chinon and Domremy, at any rate—and that was a wide stretch more of it than they might ever hope to see; and he had been in battle, and knew how to paint its shock and struggle, its perils and surprises, with an art that was all his own. He was cock of that walk, hero of that hostelry; he drew custom as honey draws flies; so he was the pet of the inn-keeper, and of his wife and daughter, and they were his obliged and willing servants.

Most people who have the narrative gift—that great and rare endowment—have with it the defect of telling their choice things over the same way every time, and this injures them and causes them to sound stale and wearisome after several repetitions; but it was not so with the Paladin, whose art was of a finer sort; it was more stirring and interesting to hear him tell about a battle the tenth time than it was the first time, because he did not tell it twice the same way, but always made a new battle of it and a better one, with more casualties on the enemy's side each time, and more general wreck and disaster all around, and more widows and orphans and suffering in the neighborhood where it happened. He could not tell his battles apart himself, except by their names; and by the time he had told one of them ten times he had to lay it aside and start a new one in its place, because it had grown so that there wasn't room enough in France for it any more, but was lapping over the edges. But up to that point the audience would not allow him to substitute a new battle, knowing that the old ones were the best, and sure to improve as long as France could hold them; and so, instead of saying to him as they would have said to another, "Give us something fresh, we are fatigued with that old thing," they would say, with one voice and with a strong interest, "Tell about the surprise at Beaulieu again—tell it three or four times!" That is a compliment which few narrative experts have heard in their lifetime.

At first when the Paladin heard us tell about the glories of the Royal Audience he was broken-hearted because he was not taken with us to it; next, his talk was full of what he would have done if he had been there; and within two days he was telling what he *did* do when he *was* there. His mill was fairly started, now, and could be trusted to take care of its affair. Within three nights afterwards all his battles were taking a rest, for already his worshippers in the tap-room were so infatuated with the great tale of the Royal Audience that they would have nothing else, and so besotted with it were they that they would have cried if they could not have gotten it.

Noël Rainguesson hid himself and heard it, and came and told me, and after that we went together to listen, bribing the inn hostess to let us have her little private parlor, where we could stand at the wickets in the door and see and hear.

The tap-room was large, yet had a snug and cosey look, with its inviting little tables and chairs scattered irregularly over its red brick floor, and its great fire flaming and crackling in the wide chimney. It was a comfortable place to be in on such chilly and blustering March nights as these, and a goodly company had taken shelter there, and were sipping their wine in contentment and gossiping one with another in a neighborly way while they waited for the historian. The host, the hostess, and their pretty daughter were flying here and there and yonder among the tables and doing their best to keep up with the orders. The room was about forty feet square, and a space or aisle down the centre of it had been kept vacant and reserved for the Paladin's needs. At the end of it was a platform ten or twelve feet wide, with a big chair and a small table on it, and three steps leading up to it.

Among the wine-sippers were many familiar faces: the cobbler, the farrier, the blacksmith, the wheelwright, the armorer, the maltster, the weaver, the baker, the miller's man with his dusty coat, and so on; and conspicuous and important, as a matter of course, was the barber-surgeon, for he is that in all villages. As he has to pull everybody's teeth, and purge and bleed all the grown people once a month to keep their health sound, he knows everybody, and by constant contact with all sorts of folk becomes a master of etiquette and manners and a conversationalist of large facility. There were plenty of carriers, drovers, and their sort, and journeymen artisans.

When the Paladin presently came sauntering indolently in, he was received with a cheer, and the barber bustled forward and greeted him with several low and most graceful and courtly bows, also taking his hand and touching his lips to it. Then he called in a loud voice for a stoup of wine for the Paladin, and when the host's daughter brought it up on to the platform and dropped her courtesy and departed, the barber called after her, and told her to add the wine to his score. This won him ejaculations of approval, which pleased him very much and made his little rat-eyes shine; and such applause is right and proper, for when we do a liberal and gallant thing it is but natural that we should wish to see notice taken of it.

The barber called upon the people to rise and drink the Paladin's health, and they did it with alacrity and affectionate heartiness, clashing their metal flagons together with a simultaneous crash, and heightening the effect with a resounding cheer. It was a fine thing to see how that young swashbuckler had made himself so popular in a strange land in so little a while, and without other helps to his advancement than just his tongue and the talent to use it given him by God—a talent which was but one talent in the beginning, but was now become ten through husbandry and the increment and usufruct that do naturally follow that and reward it as by a law.

The people sat down and began to hammer on the tables with their flagons and call for "the King's Audience!—the King's Audience!—the King's Audience!" The Paladin stood there in one of his best attitudes, with his plumed great hat tipped over to the left, the folds of his short cloak drooping from his shoulder, and the one hand resting upon the hilt of his rapier and the other lifting his beaker. As the noise died down he made a stately sort of a bow, which he had picked up somewhere, then fetched his beaker with a sweep to his lips and tilted his head back and drained it to the bottom. The barber jumped for it and set it upon the Paladin's table. Then the Paladin began to walk up and down his platform with a great deal of dignity and quite at his ease; and as he walked he talked, and every little while stopped and stood facing his house and so standing continued his talk.

We went three nights in succession. It was plain that there was a charm about the performance that was apart from the mere interest which attaches to lying. It was presently discoverable that this charm lay in the Paladin's sincerity. He was not lying consciously; he believed what he was saying. To him, his initial statements were facts, and whenever he enlarged a statement, the enlargement became a fact too. He put his heart into his extravagant narrative, just as a poet puts his heart into a heroic fiction, and his earnestness disarmed criticism—disarmed it as far as he himself was concerned. Nobody believed his narrative, but all believed that he believed it.

He made his enlargements without flourish, without emphasis, and so casually that often one failed to notice that a change had been made. He spoke of the governor of Vaucouleurs, the first night, simply as the governor of Vaucouleurs; he spoke of him the second night as his uncle the governor of Vaucouleurs; the third night he was his father. He did not seem to know that he was making these extraordinary changes; they dropped from his lips in a quite natural and effortless way. By his first night's account the governor merely attached him to the Maid's military escort in a general and unofficial way; the second night his uncle the governor sent him with the Maid as lieutenant of her rear guard; the third night his father the governor put the whole command, Maid and all, in his especial charge. The first night the governor spoke of him as a youth without name or ancestry, but "destined to achieve both"; the second night his uncle the governor spoke of him as the latest and worthiest lineal descendant of the chiefest and noblest of the Twelve Paladins of Charlemagne; the third night he spoke of him as the lineal descendant of the whole dozen. In three nights he promoted the Count of Vendôme from a fresh acquaintance to schoolmate, and then brother-in-law.

At the King's Audience everything grew, in the same way. First the four silver trumpets were twelve, then thirty-five, finally ninety-six; and by that time he had thrown in so many drums and cymbals that he had to lengthen the hall from five hundred feet to nine hundred to accommodate them. Under his hand the people present multiplied in the same large way.

The first two nights he contented himself with merely describing and exaggerating the chief dramatic incident of the Audience, but the third night he added illustration to description. He throned the barber in his own high chair to represent the sham King; then he told how the Court watched the Maid with intense interest and suppressed merriment, expecting to see her fooled by the deception and get herself swept permanently out of credit by the storm of scornful laughter which would follow. He worked this scene up till he got his house in a burning fever of excitement and anticipation, then came his climax. Turning to the barber, he said:

"But mark you what she did. She gazed steadfastly upon that sham's villain face as I now gaze upon yours—this being her noble and simple attitude, just as I stand now—then turned she—thus—to me, and stretching her arm out—so—and pointing with her finger, she said, in that firm, calm tone which she was used to use in directing the conduct of a battle, 'Pluck me this false knave from the throne!' I, striding forward as I do now, took him by the collar and lifted him out and held him aloft—thus—as if he had been but a child." (The house rose, shouting, stamping, and banging with their flagons, and went fairly mad over this magnificent exhibition of strength—and there was not the shadow of a laugh anywhere, though the spectacle of the limp but proud barber hanging there in the air like a puppy held by the scruff of its neck was a thing that had nothing of solemnity about it.) "Then I set him down upon his feet—thus—being minded to get him by a better hold and heave him out of the window, but she bid me forbear, so by that error he escaped with his life.

"Then she turned her about and viewed the throng with those eyes of hers, which are the clear-shining windows whence her immortal wisdom looketh out upon the world, resolving its falsities and coming at the kernel of truth that is hid within them, and presently they fell upon a young man modestly clothed, and him she proclaimed for what he truly was, saying, 'I am thy servant—thou art the King!' Then all were astonished, and a great shout went up, the whole six thousand joining in it, so that the walls rocked with the volume and the tumult of it."

He made a fine and picturesque thing of the march-out from the Audience, augmenting the glories of it to the last limit of the impossibilities; then he took from his finger and held up a brass nut from a bolt-head which the head-ostler at the castle had given him that morning, and made his conclusion—thus:

"Then the King dismissed the Maid most graciously—as indeed was her desert—and turning to me, said, 'Take this signet-ring, son of the Paladins, and command me with it in your day of need; and look you,' said he, touching my temple, 'preserve this brain, France has use for it; and look well to its casket also, for I foresee that it will be hooped with a ducal coronet one day.' I took the ring, and knelt and kissed his hand, saying, 'Sire, where glory calls, there will I be found; where danger and death are thickest, that is my native air; when France and the throne need help—well, I say nothing, for I am not of the talking sort—let my deeds speak for me, it is all I ask.'

"So ended that most fortunate and memorable episode, so big with future weal for the crown and the nation, and unto God be the thanks! Rise! Fill your flagons! Now—to France and the King—drink!"

They emptied them to the bottom, then burst into cheers and huzzas, and kept it up as much as two minutes, the Paladin standing at stately ease the while and smiling benignantly from his platform.

CHAPTER 8

When Joan told the King what that deep secret was that was torturing his heart, his doubts were cleared away; he believed she was sent of God, and if he had been let alone he would have set her upon her great mission at once. But he was not let alone. Tremouille and the holy fox of Rheims knew their man. All they needed to say was this—and they said it:

"Your Highness says her Voices have revealed to you, by her mouth, a secret known only to yourself and God. How can you know that her Voices are not of Satan, and she his mouthpiece?—for does not Satan know the secrets of men and use his knowledge for the destruction of their souls? It is a dangerous business, and your Highness will do well not to proceed in it without probing the matter to the bottom."

That was enough. It shrivelled up the King's little soul like a raisin, with terrors and apprehensions, and straightway he privately appointed a commission of bishops to visit and question Joan daily until they should find out whether her supernatural helps hailed from heaven or from hell.

The King's relative, the Duke of Alençon, three years prisoner of war to the English, was in these days released from captivity through promise of a great ransom; and the name and fame of the Maid having reached him—for the same filled all mouths now, and penetrated to all parts—he came to Chinon to see with his own eyes what manner of creature she might be. The King sent for Joan and introduced her to the Duke. She said, in her simple fashion:

"You are welcome; the more of the blood of France that is joined to this cause, the better for the cause and it."

Then the two talked together, and there was just the usual result: when they parted, the Duke was her friend and advocate.

Joan attended the King's mass the next day, and afterward dined with the King and the Duke. The King was learning to prize her company and value her conversation; and that might well be, for, like other Kings, he was used to getting nothing out of people's talk but guarded phrases, colorless and non-committal, or carefully tinted to tally with the color of what he said himself; and so this kind of conversation only vexes and bores, and is wearisome; but Joan's talk was fresh and free, sincere and honest, and unmarred by timorous self-watching and constraint. She said the very thing that was in her mind, and said it in a plain, straightforward way. One can believe that to the King this must have been like fresh cold water from the mountains to parched lips used to the water of the sun-baked puddles of the plain.

After dinner Joan so charmed the Duke with her horsemanship and lance-practice in the meadows by the Castle of Chinon, whither the King also had come to look on, that he made her a present of a great black war-steed.

Every day the commission of bishops came and questioned Joan about her Voices and her mission, and then went to the King with their report. These pryings accomplished but little. She told as much as she considered advisable, and kept the rest to herself. Both threats and trickeries were wasted upon her. She did not care for the threats, and the traps caught nothing. She was perfectly frank and childlike about these things. She knew the bishops were sent by the King, that their questions were the King's questions, and that by all law and custom a King's questions *must* be answered; yet she told the King in her naïve way at his own table one day that she answered only such of those questions as suited her.

The bishops finally concluded that they couldn't tell whether Joan was sent by God or not. They were cautious, you see. There were two powerful parties at Court; therefore to make a decision either way would infallibly embroil them with one of those parties; so it seemed to them wisest to roost on the fence and shift the burden to other shoulders. And that is what they did. They made final report that Joan's case was beyond their powers, and recommended that it be put into the hands of the learned and illustrious doctors of the University of Poitiers. Then they retired from the field, leaving behind them this little item of testimony, wrung from them by Joan's wise reticence: they said she was a "gentle and simple little shepherdess, very candid, *but not given to talking*."

It was quite true—in their case. But if they could have looked back and seen her with us in the happy pastures of Domremy, they would have perceived that she had a tongue that could go fast enough when no harm could come of her words.

So we travelled to Poitiers, to endure there three weeks of tedious delay while this poor child was being daily questioned and badgered before a great bench of—what? Military experts?—since what she had come to apply for was an army and the privilege of leading it to battle against the enemies of France. Oh no; it was a great bench of priests and monks—profoundly learned and astute casuists—renowned professors of theology! Instead of setting a military commission to find out if this valorous little soldier could win victories, they set a company of holy hair-splitters and phrase-mongers to work to find out if the soldier was sound in her piety and had no doctrinal leaks. The rats were devouring the house, but instead of examining the cat's teeth and claws, they only concerned themselves to find out if it was a holy cat. If it was a pious cat, a moral cat, all right, never mind about the other capacities, they were of no consequence.

Joan was as sweetly self-possessed and tranquil before this grim tribunal, with its robed celebrities, its solemn state and imposing ceremonials, as if she were but a spectator and not herself on trial. She sat there, solitary on her bench, untroubled, and disconcerted the science of the sages with her sublime ignorance—an ignorance which was a fortress; arts, wiles, the learning drawn from books, and all like missiles rebounded from its unconscious masonry and fell to the ground harmless; they could not dislodge the garrison which was within—Joan's serene great heart and spirit, the guards and keepers of her mission.

She answered all questions frankly, and she told all the story of her visions and of her experiences with the angels and what they said to her; and the manner of the telling was so unaffected, and so earnest and sincere, and made it all seem so life-like and real, that even that hard practical court forgot itself and sat motionless and mute, listening with a charmed and wondering interest to the end. And if you would have other testimony than mine, look in the histories and you will find where an eye-witness, giving sworn testimony in the Rehabilitation process, says that she told that tale "with a noble dignity and simplicity," and as to its effect, says in substance what I have said. Seventeen, she was—seventeen, and all alone on her bench by herself; yet was not afraid, but faced that great company of erudite doctors of law and theology, and by the help of no art learned in the schools, but using only the enchantments which were hers by nature, of youth, sincerity, a voice soft and musical, and an eloquence whose source was the heart, not the head, she laid that spell upon them. Now was not that a beautiful thing to see? If I could, I would put it before you just as I saw it; then I know what you would say.

As I have told you, she could not read. One day they harried and pestered her with arguments, reasonings, objections and other windy and wordy trivialities, gathered out of the works of this and that and the other great theological authority, until at last her patience vanished, and she turned upon them sharply and said—

"I don't know A from B; but I know this: that I am come by command of the Lord of Heaven to deliver Orleans from the English power and crown the King at Rheims, and the matters ye are puttering over are of no consequence!"

Necessarily those were trying days for her, and wearing for everybody that took part; but her share was the hardest, for she had no holidays, but must be always on hand and stay the long hours through, whereas this, that, and the other inquisitor could absent himself and rest up from his fatigues when he got worn out. And yet she showed no wear, no weariness, and but seldom let fly her temper. As a rule she put her day through calm, alert, patient, fencing with those veteran masters of scholarly sword-play and coming out always without a scratch.

One day a Dominican sprung upon her a question which made everybody cock up his ears with interest; as for me, I trembled, and said to myself she is caught this time, poor Joan, for there is no way of answering this. The sly Dominican began in this way—in a sort of indolent fashion, as if the thing he was about was a matter of no moment:

"You assert that God has willed to deliver France from this English bondage?"

"Yes, He has willed it."

"You wish for men-at-arms, so that you may go to the relief of Orleans, I believe?"

"Yes—and the sooner the better."

"God is all-powerful, and able to do whatsoever thing He wills to do, is it not so?"

"Most surely. None doubts it."

The Dominican lifted his head suddenly, and sprung that question I have spoken of, with exultation:

"Then answer me this. If He has willed to deliver France, and is able to do whatsoever He wills, where is the need for men-at-arms?"

There was a fine stir and commotion when he said that, and a sudden thrusting forward of heads and putting up of hands to ears to catch the answer; and the Dominican wagged his head with satisfaction, and looked about him collecting his applause, for it shone in every face. But Joan was not disturbed. There was no note of disquiet in her voice when she answered:

"He helps who help themselves. The sons of France will fight the battles, but *He* will give the victory!"

You could see a light of admiration sweep the house from face to face like a ray from the sun. Even the Dominican himself looked pleased, to see his master-stroke so neatly parried, and I heard a venerable bishop mutter, in the phrasing common to priest and people in that robust time, "By God, the child has said true. He willed that Goliath should be slain, and He sent a child like this to do it!"

Another day, when the inquisition had dragged along until everybody looked drowsy and tired but Joan, Brother Séguin, professor of theology in the University of Poitiers, who was a sour and sarcastic man, fell to plying Joan with all sorts of nagging questions in his bastard Limousin French—for he was from Limoges. Finally he said—

"How is it that you could understand those angels? What language did they speak?"

"French."

"In-deed! How pleasant to know that our language is so honored! Good French?"

"Yes—perfect."

"Perfect, eh? Well, certainly *you* ought to know. It was even better than your own, eh?"

"As to that, I—I believe I cannot say," said she, and was going on, but stopped. Then she added, almost as if she were saying it to herself, "Still, it was an improvement on yours!"

I knew there was a chuckle back of her eyes, for all their innocence. Everybody shouted. Brother Séguin was nettled, and asked brusquely—

"Do you believe in God?"

Joan answered with an irritating nonchalance—

"Oh, well, yes—better than you, it is likely."

Brother Séguin lost his patience, and heaped sarcasm after sarcasm upon her, and finally burst out in angry earnest, exclaiming—

"Very well, I can tell you this, you whose belief in God is so great: God has not willed that any shall believe in you without a sign. Where is your sign?—show it!"

This roused Joan, and she was on her feet in a moment, and flung out her retort with spirit:

"I have not come to Poitiers to show signs and do miracles. Send me to Orleans and you shall have signs enough. Give me men-at-arms—few or many—and let me go!"

The fire was leaping from her eyes—ah, the heroic little figure! can't you see her? There was a great burst of acclamations, and she sat down blushing, for it was not in her delicate nature to like being conspicuous.

This speech and that episode about the French language scored two points against Brother Séguin, while he scored nothing against Joan; yet, sour man as he was, he was a manly man, and honest, as you can see by the histories; for at the Rehabilitation he could have hidden those unlucky incidents if he had chosen, but he didn't do it, but spoke them right out in his evidence.

On one of the later days of that three weeks' session the gowned scholars and professors made one grand assault all along the line, fairly overwhelming Joan with objections and arguments culled from the writings of every ancient and illustrious authority of the Roman Church. She was well-nigh smothered; but at last she shook herself free and struck back, crying out:

"Listen! The Book of God is worth more than all these ye cite, and I stand upon *it*. And I tell ye there are things in that Book that not one among ye can read, with all your learning!"

From the first she was the guest, by invitation, of the dame De Rabateau, wife of a councillor of the Parliament of Poitiers; and to that house the great ladies of the city came nightly to see Joan and talk with her; and not these only, but the old lawyers, councillors, and scholars of the Parliament and the University. And these grave men, accustomed to weigh every strange and questionable thing, and cautiously consider it, and turn it about this way and that and still doubt it, came night after night, and night after night, falling ever deeper and deeper under the influence of that mysterious something, that spell, that elusive and unwordable fascination, which was the supremest endowment of Joan of Arc, that winning and persuasive and convincing something which high and low alike recognized and felt, but which neither high nor low could explain or describe; and one by one they all surrendered, saying, "This child is sent of God."

All day long Joan, in the great court and subject to its rigid rules of procedure, was at a disadvantage; her judges had things their own way; but at night she held court herself, and matters were reversed, she presiding, with her tongue free and her same judges there before her. There could be but one result: all the objections and hindrances they could build around her with their hard labors of the day she would charm away at night. In the end, she carried her judges with her in a mass, and got her great verdict without a dissenting voice.

The court was a sight to see when the president of it read it from his throne, for all the great people of the town were there who could get admission and find room. First there were some solemn ceremonies, proper and usual at such times; then, when there was silence again, the reading followed, penetrating the deep hush so that every word was heard in even the remotest parts of the house:

"It is found, and is hereby declared, that Joan of Arc, called the Maid, is a good Christian and good Catholic; that there is nothing in her person or her words contrary to the faith; and that the King may and ought to accept the succor she offers; for to repel it would be to offend the Holy Spirit, and render him unworthy of the aid of God."

The court rose, and then the storm of plaudits burst forth unrebuked, dying down and bursting forth again and again, and I lost sight of Joan, for she was swallowed up in a great tide of people who rushed to congratulate her and pour out benedictions upon her and upon the cause of France, now solemnly and irrevocably delivered into her little hands.

CHAPTER 9

It was indeed a great day, and a stirring thing to see.

She had won! It was a mistake of Tremouille and her other ill-wishers to let her hold court those nights.

The commission of priests sent to Lorraine ostensibly to inquire into Joan's character—in fact to weary her with delays and wear out her purpose and make her give it up—arrived back and reported her character perfect. Our affairs were in full career now, you see.

The verdict made a prodigious stir. Dead France woke suddenly to life, wherever the great news travelled. Whereas before, the spiritless and cowed people hung their heads and slunk away if one mentioned war to them, now they came clamoring to be enlisted under the banner of the Maid of Vaucouleurs, and the roaring of war-songs and the thundering of the drums filled all the air. I remembered now what she had said, that time there in our village when I proved by facts and statistics that France's case was hopeless, and nothing could ever rouse the people from their lethargy:

"They will hear the drums—and they will answer, they will march!"

It has been said that misfortunes never come one at a time, but in a body. In our case it was the same with good luck. Having got a start, it came flooding in, tide after tide. Our next wave of it was of this sort. There had been grave doubts among the priests as to whether the Church ought to permit a female soldier to dress like a man. But now came a verdict on that head. Two of the greatest scholars and theologians of the time—one of whom had been Chancellor of the University of Paris—rendered it. They decided that since Joan "must do the work of a man and a soldier, it is just and legitimate that her apparel should conform to the situation."

It was a great point gained, the Church's authority to dress as a man. Oh yes, wave on wave the good luck came sweeping in. Never mind about the smaller waves, let us come to the largest one of all, the wave that swept us small fry quite off our feet and almost drowned us with joy. The day of the great verdict, couriers had been despatched to the King with it, and the next morning bright and early the clear notes of a bugle came floating to us on the crisp air, and we pricked up our ears and began to count them. One—two—three; pause; one—two; pause; one—two—three, again—and out we skipped and went flying; for that formula was used only when the King's herald-at-arms would deliver a proclamation to the people. As we hurried along, people came racing out of every street and house and alley, men, women, and children, all flushed, excited, and throwing lacking articles of clothing on as they ran; still those clear notes pealed out, and still the rush of people increased till the whole town was abroad and streaming along the principal street. At last we reached the square, which was now packed with citizens, and there, high on the pedestal of the great cross, we saw the herald in his brilliant costume, with his servitors about him. The next moment he began his delivery in the powerful voice proper to his office:

"Know all men, and take heed therefore, that the most high, the most illustrious Charles, by the grace of God King of France, hath been pleased to confer upon his well-beloved servant Joan of Arc, called the Maid, the title, emoluments, authorities, and dignity of General-in-Chief of the Armies of France—"

Here a thousand caps flew into the air, and the multitude burst into a hurricane of cheers that raged and raged till it seemed as if it would never come to an end; but at last it did; then the herald went on and finished:

—"and hath appointed to be her lieutenant and chief of staff a prince of his royal house, his grace the Duke of Alençon!"

That was the end, and the hurricane began again, and was split up into innumerable strips by the blowers of it and wafted through all the lanes and streets of the town.

General of the Armies of France, with a prince of the blood for subordinate! Yesterday she was nothing—to-day she was this. Yesterday she was not even a sergeant, not even a corporal, not even a private—to-day, with one step, she was at the top. Yesterday she was less than nobody to the newest recruit—to-day her command was law to La Hire, Saintrailles, the Bastard of Orleans, and all those others, veterans of old renown, illustrious masters of the trade of war. These were the thoughts I was thinking; I was trying to realize this strange and wonderful thing that had happened, you see.

My mind went travelling back, and presently lighted upon a picture—a picture which was still so new and fresh in my memory that it seemed a matter of only yesterday—and indeed its date was no further back than the first days of January. This is what it was. A peasant girl in a far-off village, her seventeenth year not yet quite completed, and herself and her village as unknown as if they had been on the other side of the globe. She had picked up a friendless wanderer somewhere and brought it home—a small gray kitten in a forlorn and starving condition—and had fed it and comforted it and got its confidence and made it believe in her, and now it was curled up in her lap asleep, and she was knitting a coarse stocking and thinking—dreaming—about what, one may never know. And now—the kitten had hardly had time to become a cat, and yet already the girl is General of the Armies of France, with a prince of the blood to give orders to, and out of her village obscurity her name has climbed up like the sun and is visible from all corners of the land! It made me dizzy to think of these things, they were so out of the common order, and seemed so impossible.

CHAPTER 10

Joan's first official act was to dictate a letter to the English commanders at Orleans, summoning them to deliver up all strongholds in their possession and depart out of France. She must have been thinking it all out before and arranging it in her mind, it flowed from her lips so smoothly, and framed itself into such vivacious and forcible language. Still, it might not have been so; she always had a quick mind and a capable tongue, and her faculties were constantly developing in these latter weeks. This letter was to be forwarded presently from Blois. Men, provisions, and money were offering in plenty now, and Joan appointed Blois as a recruiting station and depot of supplies, and ordered up La Hire from the front to take charge.

The Great Bastard—him of the ducal house, and governor of Orleans—had been clamoring for weeks for Joan to be sent to him, and now came another messenger, old D'Aulon, a veteran officer, a trusty man and fine and honest. The King kept him, and gave him to Joan to be chief of her household, and commanded her to appoint the rest of her people herself, making their number and dignity accord with the greatness of her office; and at the same time he gave order that they should be properly equipped with arms, clothing, and horses.

Meantime the King was having a complete suit of armor made for her at Tours. It was of the finest steel, heavily plated with silver, richly ornamented with engraved designs, and polished like a mirror.

Joan's Voices had told her that there was an ancient sword hidden somewhere behind the altar of St. Catherine's at Fierbois, and she sent De Metz to get it. The priests knew of no such sword, but a search was made, and sure enough it was found in that place, buried a little way under the ground. It had no sheath and was very rusty, but the priests polished it up and sent it to Tours, whither we were now to come. They also had a sheath of crimson velvet made for it, and the people of Tours equipped it with another one, made of cloth of gold. But Joan meant to carry this sword always in battle; so she laid the showy sheaths away and got one made of leather. It was generally believed that this sword had belonged to Charlemagne, but that was only a matter of opinion. I wanted to sharpen that old blade, but she said it was not necessary, as she should never kill anybody, and should carry it only as a symbol of authority.

At Tours she designed her Standard, and a Scotch painter named

James Power made it. It was of the most delicate white *boucassin,* with fringes of silk. For device it bore the image of God the Father throned in the clouds and holding the world in His hand; two angels knelt at His feet, presenting lilies; inscription, JESUS, MARIA; on the reverse the crown of France supported by two angels.

She also caused a smaller standard or pennon to be made, whereon was represented an angel offering a lily to the Holy Virgin.

Everything was humming, there at Tours. Every now and then one heard the bray and crash of military music, every little while one heard the measured tramp of marching men—squads of recruits leaving for Blois; songs and shoutings and huzzas filled the air night and day, the town was full of strangers, the streets and inns were thronged, the bustle of preparation was everywhere, and everybody carried a glad and cheerful face. Around Joan's headquarters a crowd of people was always massed, hoping for a glimpse of the new General, and when they got it, they went wild; but they seldom got it, for she was busy planning her campaign, receiving reports, giving orders, despatching couriers, and giving what odd moments she could spare to the companies of great folk waiting in the drawing-rooms. As for us boys, we hardly saw her at all, she was so occupied.

We were in a mixed state of mind—sometimes hopeful, sometimes not; mostly not. She had not appointed her household yet—that was our trouble. We knew she was being overrun with applications for places in it, and that these applications were backed by great names and weighty influence, whereas we had nothing of the sort to recommend us. She could fill her humblest places with titled folk—folk whose relationships would be a bulwark for her and a valuable support at all times. In these circumstances would policy allow her to consider us? We were not as cheerful as the rest of the town, but were inclined to be depressed and worried. Sometimes we discussed our slim chances and gave them as good an appearance as we could. But the very mention of the subject was anguish to the Paladin; for whereas we had some little hope, he had none at all. As a rule, Noël Rainguesson was quite willing to let the dismal matter alone; but not when the Paladin was present. Once we were talking the thing over, when Noël said—

"Cheer up, Paladin; I had a dream last night, and you were the only one among us that got an appointment. It wasn't a high one, but it was an appointment, anyway—some kind of a lackey or body-servant, or something of that kind."

The Paladin roused up and looked almost cheerful; for he was a believer in dreams, and in anything and everything of a superstitious sort, in fact. He said, with a rising hopefulness—

"I wish it might come true. Do you think it will come true?"

"Certainly; I might almost say I know it will, for my dreams hardly ever fail."

"Noël, I could hug you if that dream could come true, I could indeed! To be servant to the first General of France and have all the world hear of it, and the news go back to the village and make those gawks stare that always said I wouldn't ever amount to anything—wouldn't it be great! Do you think it *will* come true, Noël? Don't you believe it will?"

"I do. There's my hand on it."

"Noël, if it comes true I'll never forget you—shake again! I should be dressed in a noble livery, and the news would go to the village, and those animals would say, '*Him*, lackey to the General-in-Chief, with the eyes of the whole world on him, admiring—well, he has shot up into the sky, now, hasn't he!'"

He began to walk the floor and pile castles in the air so fast and so high that we could hardly keep up with him. Then all of a sudden all the joy went out of his face and misery took its place, and he said:

"Oh dear, it is all a mistake, it will never come true. I forgot about that foolish business at Toul. I have kept out of her sight as much as I could, all these weeks, hoping she would forget that and forgive it—but I know she never will. She can't, of course. And after all, I wasn't to blame. I did say she promised to marry me, but they put me up to it and persuaded me, I swear they did!" The vast creature was almost crying. Then he pulled himself together and said, remorsefully, "It was the only lie I've ever told, and—"

He was drowned out with a chorus of groans and outraged exclamations; and before he could begin again, one of D'Aulon's liveried servants appeared and said we were required at headquarters. We rose, and Noël said—

"There—what did I tell you? I have a presentiment—the spirit of prophecy is upon me. She is going to appoint him, and we are to go there and do him homage. Come along!"

But the Paladin was afraid to go, so we left him.

When we presently stood in the presence, in front of a crowd of glittering officers of the army, Joan greeted us with a winning smile, and said she appointed all of us to places in her household, for she wanted her old friends by her. It was a beautiful surprise to have ourselves honored like this when she could have had people of birth and consequence instead, but we couldn't find our tongues to say so, she was become so great and so high above us now. One at a time we stepped forward and each received his warrant from the hand of our chief, D'Aulon. All of us had honorable places: the two knights stood highest; then Joan's two brothers; I was first page and secretary, a young gentleman named Raimond was second page; Noël was her messenger; she had two heralds, and also a chaplain and almoner, whose name was Jean Pasquerel. She had previously appointed a maître d'hôtel and a number of domestics. Now she looked around and said–

"But where is the Paladin?"

The Sieur Bertrand said–

"He thought he was not sent for, your Excellency."

"Now that is not well. Let him be called."

The Paladin entered humbly enough. He ventured no farther than just within the door. He stopped there, looking embarrassed and afraid. Then Joan spoke pleasantly, and said–

"I watched you on the road. You began badly, but improved. Of old you were a fantastic talker, but there is a man in you, and I will bring it out." It was fine to see the Paladin's face light up when she said that. "Will you follow where I lead?"

"Into the fire!" he said; and I said to myself, "By the ring of that, I think she has turned this braggart into a hero. It is another of her miracles, I make no doubt of it."

"I believe you," said Joan. "Here–take my banner. You will ride with me in every field, and when France is saved, you will give it me back."

He took the banner, which is now the most precious of the memorials that remain of Joan of Arc, and his voice was unsteady with emotion when he said–

"If I ever disgrace this trust, my comrades here will know how to do a friend's office upon my body, and this charge I lay upon them, as knowing they will not fail me."

CHAPTER 11

Noël and I went back together–silent at first, and impressed. Finally Noël came up out of his thinkings and said–

"The first shall be last and the last first–there's authority for this surprise. But at the same time *wasn't* it a lofty hoist for our big bull!"

"It truly was; I am not over being stunned yet. It was the greatest place in her gift."

"Yes, it was. There are many generals, and she can create more; but there is only one Standard-Bearer."

"True. It is the most conspicuous place in the army, after her own."

"And the most coveted and honorable. Sons of two dukes tried to get it, as we know. And of all people in the world, this majestic windmill carries it off. Well, isn't it a gigantic promotion, when you come to look at it!"

"There's no doubt about it. It's a kind of copy of Joan's own in miniature."

"I don't know how to account for it—do you?"

"Yes—without any trouble at all—that is, I think I do."

Noël was surprised at that, and glanced up quickly, as if to see if I was in earnest. He said—

"I thought you couldn't be in earnest, but I see you are. If you can make me understand this puzzle, do it. Tell me what the explanation is."

"I believe I can. You have noticed that our chief knight says a good many wise things and has a thoughtful head on his shoulders. One day, riding along, we were talking about Joan's great talents, and he said, 'But, greatest of all her gifts, she has the seeing eye.' I said, like an unthinking fool, 'The seeing eye?—I shouldn't count that for much—I suppose we all have it.' 'No,' he said; 'very few have it.' Then he explained, and made his meaning clear. He said the common eye sees only the outside of things, and judges by that, but the seeing eye pierces through and reads the heart and the soul, finding there capacities which the outside didn't indicate or promise, and which the other kind of eye couldn't detect. He said the mightiest military genius must fail and come to nothing if it have not the seeing eye—that is to say, if it cannot read men and select its subordinates with an infallible judgment. It sees as by intuition that this man is good for strategy, that one for dash and dare-devil assault, the other for patient bull-dog persistence, and it appoints each to his right place and wins, while the commander without the seeing eye would give to each the other's place and lose. He was right about Joan, and I saw it. When she was a child and the tramp came one night, her father and all of us took him for a rascal, but she saw the honest man through the rags. When I dined with the governor of Vaucouleurs so long ago, I saw nothing in our two knights, though I sat with them and talked with them two hours; Joan was there five minutes, and neither spoke with them nor heard them speak, yet she marked them for men of worth and fidelity, and they have confirmed her judgment. Whom has she sent for to take charge of this thundering rabble of new recruits at Blois, made up of old disbanded Armagnac raiders, unspeakable hellions, every one? Why, she has sent for Satan himself—that is to say, La Hire—that military hurricane, that godless swashbuckler, that lurid conflagration of blasphemy, that Vesuvius of profanity, forever in eruption. Does he know how to deal with that mob of roaring devils? Better than any man that lives; for he is the head devil of this world his own self, he is the match of the whole of them combined, and probably the father of most of them. She places him in temporary command until she can get to Blois herself—and then! Why, then she will certainly take them in hand personally, or I don't know her as well as I ought to, after all these years of intimacy. That will be a sight to see—that fair spirit in her white armor, delivering her will to that muck-heap, that rag-pile, that abandoned refuse of perdition."

"La Hire!" cried Noël, "our hero of all these years—I do want to see that man!"

"I too. His name stirs me just as it did when I was a little boy."

"I want to hear him swear."

"Of course. I would rather hear him swear than another man pray. He is the frankest man there is, and the naïvest. Once when he was rebuked for pillaging on his raids, he said it was nothing. Said he, 'If God the Father were a soldier, He would rob.' I judge he is the right man to take temporary charge there at Blois. Joan has cast the seeing eye upon him, you see."

"Which brings us back to where we started. I have an honest affection for the Paladin, and not merely because he is a good fellow, but because he is my child—I made him what he is, the windiest blusterer and most catholic liar in the kingdom. I'm glad of his luck, but I hadn't the seeing eye. I shouldn't have chosen him for the most dangerous post in the army, I should have placed him in the rear to kill the wounded and violate the dead."

"Well, we shall see. Joan probably knows what is in him better than we do. And I'll give you another idea. When a person in Joan of Arc's position tells a man he is brave, he *believes* it; and *believing* it is enough; in fact to believe yourself brave is to *be* brave; it is the one only essential thing."

"Now you've hit it!" cried Noël. "She's got the creating mouth as well as the seeing eye! Ah yes, that is the thing. France was cowed and a coward; Joan of Arc has spoken, and France is marching, with her head up!"

I was summoned now, to write a letter from Joan's dictation. During the next day and night our several uniforms were made by the tailors, and our new armor provided. We were beautiful to look upon now, whether clothed for peace or war. Clothed for peace, in costly stuffs and rich colors, the Paladin was a tower dyed with the glories of the sunset; plumed and sashed and iron-clad for war, he was a still statelier thing to look at.

Orders had been issued for the march towards Blois. It was a clear, sharp, beautiful morning. As our showy great company trotted out in column, riding two and two, Joan and the Duke of Alençon in the lead, D'Aulon and the big standard-bearer next, and so on, we made a handsome spectacle, as you may well imagine; and as we ploughed through the cheering crowds, with Joan bowing her plumed head to left and right and the sun glinting from her silver mail, the spectators realized that the curtain was rolling up before their eyes upon the first act of a prodigious drama, and their rising hopes were expressed in an enthusiasm that increased with each moment, until at last one seemed to even physically feel the concussion of the huzzas as well as hear them. Far down the street we heard the softened strains of wind-blown music, and saw a cloud of lancers moving, the sun glowing with a subdued light upon the massed armor but striking bright upon the soaring lance-heads—a vaguely luminous nebula, so to speak, with a constellation twinkling above it—and that was our guard of honor. It joined us, the procession was complete, the first war-march of Joan of Arc was begun, the curtain was up.

CHAPTER 12

We were at Blois three days. Oh, that camp, it is one of the treasures of my memory! Order? There was no more order among those brigands than there is among the wolves and the hyenas. They went roaring and drinking about, whooping, shouting, swearing, and entertaining themselves with all manner of rude and riotous horse-play; and the place was full of loud and lewd women, and they were no whit behind the men for romps and noise and fantastics.

It was in the midst of this wild mob that Noël and I had our first glimpse of La Hire. He answered to our dearest dreams. He was of great size and of martial bearing, he was cased in mail from head to heel, with a bushel of swishing plumes on his helmet, and at his side the vast sword of the time.

He was on his way to pay his respects in state to Joan, and as he passed through the camp he was restoring order, and proclaiming that the Maid was come, and he would have no such spectacle as this exposed to the head of the army. His way of creating order was his own, not borrowed. He did it with his great fists. As he moved along swearing and admonishing, he let drive this way, that way, and the other, and wherever his blow landed, a man went down.

"Damn you!" he said, "staggering and cursing around like this, and the Commander-in-Chief in the camp! Straighten up!" and he laid the man flat. What his idea of straightening up was, was his own secret.

We followed the veteran to headquarters, listening, observing, admiring—yes, devouring, you may say, the pet hero of the boys of France from our cradles up to that happy day, and their idol and ours. I called to mind how Joan had once rebuked the Paladin, there in the pastures of Domremy, for uttering lightly those mighty names, La Hire and the Bastard of Orleans, and how she said that if she could but be permitted to stand afar off and let her eyes rest once upon those great men, she would hold it a privilege. They were to her and the other girls just what they were to the boys. Well, here was one of them, at last—and what was his errand? It was hard to realize it, and yet it was true; he was coming to uncover his head before her and take her orders.

While he was quieting a considerable group of his brigands in his soothing way, near headquarters, we stepped on ahead and got a glimpse of Joan's military family, the great chiefs of the army, for they had all arrived now. There they were, six officers of wide renown, handsome men in beautiful armor, but the Lord High Admiral of France was the handsomest of them all and had the most gallant bearing.

When La Hire entered, one could see the surprise in his face at Joan's beauty and extreme youth, and one could see, too, by Joan's glad smile, that it made her happy to get sight of this hero of her childhood at last. La Hire bowed low, with his helmet in his gauntleted hand, and made a bluff but handsome little speech with hardly an oath in it, and one could see that those two took to each other on the spot.

The visit of ceremony was soon over, and the others went away; but La Hire stayed, and he and Joan sat there, and he sipped her wine, and they talked and laughed together like old friends. And presently she gave him some instructions, in his quality as master of the camp, which made his breath stand still. For, to begin with, she said that all those loose women must pack out of the place at once, she wouldn't allow one of them to remain. Next, the rough carousing must stop, drinking must be brought within proper and strictly defined limits, and discipline must take the place of disorder. And finally she climaxed the list of surprises with this—which nearly lifted him out of his armor:

"Every man who joins my standard must confess before the priest and absolve himself from sin; and all accepted recruits must be present at divine service twice a day."

La Hire could not say a word for a good part of a minute, then he said, in deep dejection:

"Oh, sweet child, they were littered in hell, these poor darlings of mine! Attend mass? Why, dear heart, they'll see us both damned first!"

And he went on, pouring out a most pathetic stream of arguments and blasphemy, which broke Joan all up, and made her laugh as she had not laughed since she played in the Domremy pastures. It was good to hear.

But she stuck to her point; so the soldier yielded, and said all right, if such were the orders he must obey, and would do the best that was in him; then he refreshed himself with a lurid explosion of oaths, and said that if any man in the camp refused to renounce sin and lead a pious life, he would knock his head off. That started Joan off again: she was really having a good time, you see. But she would not consent to that form of conversions. She said they must be voluntary.

La Hire said that that was all right, he wasn't going to kill the voluntary ones, but only the others.

No matter, none of them must be killed—Joan couldn't have it. She said that to give a man a chance to volunteer, on pain of death if he didn't, left him more or less trammelled, and she wanted him to be entirely free.

So the soldier sighed and said he would advertise the mass, but said he doubted if there was a man in camp that was any more likely to go to it than he was himself. Then there was another surprise for him, for Joan said—

"But dear man, *you* are going!"

"I? Impossible! Oh, this is lunacy!"

"Oh no, it isn't. You are going to the service—twice a day."

"Oh, am I dreaming? Am I drunk—or is my hearing playing me false? Why, I would rather go to—"

"Never mind where. In the morning you are going to begin, and after that it will come easy. Now *don't* look down-hearted like that. Soon you won't mind it."

La Hire tried to cheer up, but he was not able to do it. He sighed like a zephyr, and presently said—

"Well, I'll do it for you, but before I would do it for another, I swear I—"

"But don't swear. Break it off."

"Break it off? It is impossible. I beg you to—to—Why—oh, my General, it is my native speech!"

He begged so hard for grace for his impediment, that Joan left him one fragment of it; she said he might swear by his bâton, the symbol of his generalship.

He promised that he would swear only by his bâton when in her presence, and would try to modify himself elsewhere, but doubted if he could manage it, now that it was so old and stubborn a habit, and such a solace and support to his declining years.

That tough old lion went away from there a good deal tamed and civilized—not to say softened and sweetened, for perhaps those expressions would hardly fit him. Noël and I believed that when he was away from Joan's influence his old aversions would come up so strong in him that he could not master them, and so wouldn't go to mass. But we got up early in the morning to see.

Well, he really went. It was hardly believable, but there he was, striding along, holding himself grimly to his duty, and looking as pious as he could, but growling and cursing like a fiend. It was another instance of the same old thing: whoever listened to the voice and looked into the eyes of Joan of Arc fell under a spell, and was not his own man any more.

Satan was converted, you see. Well, the rest followed. Joan rode up and down that camp, and wherever that fair young form appeared in its shining armor, with that sweet face to grace the vision and perfect it, the rude host seemed to think they saw the god of war in person, descended out of the clouds; and first they wondered, then they worshipped. After that, she could do with them what she would.

In three days it was a clean camp and orderly, and those barbarians were herding to divine service twice a day like good children. The women were gone. La Hire was stunned by these marvels; he could not understand them. He went outside the camp when he wanted to swear. He was that sort of a man—sinful by nature and habit, but full of superstitious respect for holy places.

The enthusiasm of the reformed army for Joan, its devotion to her, and the hot desire she had aroused in it to be led against the enemy, exceeded any manifestations of this sort which La Hire had ever seen before in his long career. His admiration of it all, and his wonder over the mystery and miracle of it, were beyond his power to put into words. He had held this army cheap before, but his pride and confidence in it knew no limits now. He said—

"Two or three days ago it was afraid of a hen-roost; one could storm the gates of hell with it now."

Joan and he were inseparable, and a quaint and pleasant contrast they made. He was so big, she so little; he was so gray and so far along in his pilgrimage of life, she so youthful; his face was so bronzed and scarred, hers so fair and pink, so fresh and smooth; she was so gracious, and he so stern; she was so pure, so innocent, he such a cyclopædia of sin. In her eye was stored all charity and compassion, in his lightnings; when her glance fell upon you it seemed to bring benediction and the peace of God, but with his it was different, generally.

They rode through the camp a dozen times a day, visiting every corner of it, observing, inspecting, perfecting; and wherever they appeared the enthusiasm broke forth. They rode side by side, he a great figure of brawn and muscle, she a little master-work of roundness and grace; he a fortress of rusty iron, she a shining statuette of silver; and when the reformed raiders and bandits caught sight of them they spoke out with affection and welcome in their voices, and said—

"There they come—Satan and the Page of Christ!"

All the three days that we were in Blois, Joan worked earnestly and tirelessly to bring La Hire to God—to rescue him from the bondage of sin—to breathe into his stormy heart the serenity and peace of religion. She urged, she begged, she implored him to pray. He stood out, the three days of our stay, begging almost piteously to be let off—to be let off from just that one thing, that impossible thing; he would do anything else—anything—command, and he would obey—he would go through the fire for her if she said the word—but spare him this, only this, for he couldn't pray, had never prayed, he was ignorant of how to frame a prayer, he had no words to put it in.

And yet—can any believe it?—she carried even that point, she won that incredible victory. She made La Hire pray. It shows, I think, that nothing was impossible to Joan of Arc. Yes, he stood there before her and put up his mailed hands and made a prayer. And it was not borrowed, but was his very own; he had none to help him frame it, he made it out of his own head—saying:

"Fair Sir God, I pray you to do by La Hire as he would do by you if you were La Hire and he were God."*

Then he put on his helmet and marched out of Joan's tent as satisfied with himself as any one might be who has arranged a perplexed and difficult business to the content and admiration of all the parties concerned in the matter.

If I had known that he had been praying, I could have understood why he was feeling so superior, but of course I could not know that.

I was coming to the tent at that moment, and saw him come out, and saw him march away in that large fashion, and indeed it was fine and beautiful to see. But when I got to the tent door I stopped and stepped back, grieved and shocked, for I heard Joan crying, as I mistakenly thought—crying as if she could not contain nor endure the anguish of her soul, crying as if she would die. But it was not so, she was laughing—laughing at La Hire's prayer.

It was not until six-and-thirty years afterwards that I found that out, and then—oh, then I only cried when that picture of young care-free mirth rose before me out of the blur and mists of that long-vanished time; for there had come a day between, when God's good gift of laughter had gone out from me to come again no more in this life.

CHAPTER 13

We marched out in great strength and splendor, and took the road toward Orleans. The initial part of Joan's great dream was realizing itself at last. It was the first time that any of us youngsters had ever seen an army, and it was a most stately and imposing spectacle to us. It was indeed an inspiring sight, that interminable column, stretching away into the fading distances, and curving itself in and out of the crookedness of the road like a mighty serpent. Joan rode at the head of it with her personal staff; then came a body of priests singing the *Veni Creator*, the banner of the Cross rising out of their midst; after these the glinting forest of spears. The several divisions were commanded by the great Armagnac generals, La Hire, the Marshal de Boussac, the Sire de Retz, Florent d'Illiers, and Poton de Saintrailles.

* This prayer has been stolen many times and by many nations in the past four hundred and sixty years, but it originated with La Hire, and the fact is of official record in the National Archives of France. We have the authority of Michelet for this.—TRANSLATOR.

Each in his degree was tough, and there were three degrees—tough, tougher, toughest—and La Hire was the last by a shade, but only a shade. They were just illustrious official brigands, the whole party; and by long habits of lawlessness they had lost all acquaintanceship with obedience, if they had ever had any.

The King's strict orders to them had been, "Obey the General-in-Chief in everything; attempt nothing without her knowledge, do nothing without her command."

But what was the good of saying that? These independent birds knew no law. They seldom obeyed the King; they never obeyed him when it didn't suit them to do it. Would they obey the Maid? In the first place they wouldn't know *how* to obey her or anybody else, and in the second place it was of course not possible for them to take her military character seriously—that country girl of seventeen who had been trained for the complex and terrible business of war—how? By tending sheep.

They had no idea of obeying her except in cases where their veteran military knowledge and experience showed them that the thing she required was sound and right when gauged by the regular military standards. Were they to blame for this attitude? I should think not. Old war-worn captains are hard-headed, practical men. They do not easily believe in the ability of ignorant children to plan campaigns and command armies. No general that ever lived could have taken Joan seriously (militarily) before she raised the siege of Orleans and followed it with the great campaign of the Loire.

Did they consider Joan valueless? Far from it. They valued her as the fruitful earth values the sun—they fully believed she could produce the crop, but that it was in their line of business, not hers, to take it off. They had a deep and superstitious reverence for her as being endowed with a mysterious supernatural something that was able to do a mighty thing which they were powerless to do—blow the breath of life and valor into the dead corpses of cowed armies and turn them into heroes.

To their minds they were everything *with* her, but nothing without her. She could inspire the soldiers and fit them for battle—but fight the battle herself? Oh, nonsense—that was their function. They, the generals, would fight the battles, Joan would give the victory. That was their idea—an unconscious paraphrase of Joan's reply to the Dominican.

So they began by playing a deception upon her. She had a clear idea of how she meant to proceed. It was her purpose to march boldly upon

Orleans by the north bank of the Loire. She gave that order to her generals. They said to themselves, "The idea is insane—it is blunder No. 1; it is what might have been expected of this child who is ignorant of war." They privately sent the word to the Bastard of Orleans. He also recognized the insanity of it—at least he thought he did—and privately advised the generals to get around the order in some way.

They did it by deceiving Joan. She trusted those people, she was not expecting this sort of treatment, and was not on the lookout for it. It was a lesson to her; she saw to it that the game was not played a second time.

Why was Joan's idea insane, from the generals' point of view, but not from hers? Because her plan was to raise the siege immediately, by fighting, while theirs was to besiege the besiegers and starve them out by closing their communications—a plan which would require months in the consummation.

The English had built a fence of strong fortresses called bastilles around Orleans—fortresses which closed all the gates of the city but one. To the French generals the idea of trying to fight their way past those fortresses and lead the army into Orleans was preposterous; they believed that the result would be the army's destruction. One may not doubt that their opinion was militarily sound—no, *would* have been, but for one circumstance which they overlooked. That was this: the English soldiers were in a demoralized condition of superstitious terror; they had become satisfied that the Maid was in league with Satan. By reason of this a good deal of their courage had oozed out and vanished. On the other hand the Maid's soldiers were full of courage, enthusiasm, and zeal.

Joan could have marched by the English forts. However, it was not to be. She had been cheated out of her first chance to strike a heavy blow for her country.

In camp that night she slept in her armor on the ground. It was a cold night, and she was nearly as stiff as her armor itself when we resumed the march in the morning, for iron is not good material for a blanket. However, her joy in being now so far on her way to the theatre of her mission was fire enough to warm her, and it soon did it.

Her enthusiasm and impatience rose higher and higher with every mile of progress; but at last we reached Olivet, and down it went, and indignation took its place. For she saw the trick that had been played upon her—the river lay between us and Orleans.

She was for attacking one of the three bastilles that were on our side of the river and forcing access to the bridge which it guarded (a project which, if successful, would raise the siege instantly), but the long-ingrained fear of the English came upon her generals and they implored her not to make the attempt. The soldiers wanted to attack, but had to suffer disappointment. So we moved on and came to a halt at a point opposite Chécy, six miles above Orleans.

Dunois, Bastard of Orleans, with a body of knights and citizens, came up from the city to welcome Joan. Joan was still burning with resentment over the trick that had been put upon her, and was not in the mood for soft speeches, even to revered military idols of her childhood. She said—

"Are you the Bastard of Orleans?"

"Yes, I am he, and am right glad of your coming."

"And did you advise that I be brought by this side of the river instead of straight to Talbot and the English?"

Her high manner abashed him and he was not able to answer with anything like a confident promptness, but with many hesitations and partial excuses he managed to get out the confession that for what he and the council had regarded as imperative military reasons they had so advised.

"In God's name," said Joan, "my Lord's counsel is safer and wiser than yours. You thought to deceive me, but you have deceived yourselves, for I bring you the best help that ever knight or city had; for it is God's help, not sent for love of me, but by God's pleasure. At the prayer of St. Louis and St. Charlemagne He has had pity on Orleans, and will not suffer the enemy to have both the Duke of Orleans and his city. The provisions to save the starving people are here, the boats are below the city, the wind is contrary, they cannot come up hither. Now then tell me, in God's name, you who are so wise, what that council of yours was thinking about, to invent this foolish difficulty."

Dunois and the rest fumbled around the matter a moment, then gave in and conceded that a blunder had been made.

"Yes, a blunder has been made," said Joan, "and except God take your proper work upon Himself and change the wind and correct your blunder for you, there is none else that can devise a remedy."

Some of those people began to perceive that with all her technical ignorance she had practical good sense, and that with all her native sweetness and charm she was not the right kind of a person to play with.

Presently God did take the blunder in hand, and by His grace the wind did change. So the fleet of boats came up and went away loaded with provisions and cattle, and conveyed that welcome succor to the hungry city, managing the matter successfully under protection of a sortie from the walls against the bastille of St. Loup. Then Joan began on the Bastard again:

"You see here the army?"

"Yes."

"It is here on this side by advice of your council?"

"Yes."

"Now, in God's name, can that wise council explain why it is better to have it here than it would be to have it in the bottom of the sea?"

Dunois made some wandering attempts to explain the inexplicable and excuse the inexcusable, but Joan cut him short and said—

"Answer me this, good sir—has the army any value on this side of the river?"

The Bastard confessed that it hadn't—that is, in view of the plan of campaign which she had devised and decreed.

"And yet, knowing this, you had the hardihood to disobey my orders. Since the army's place is on the other side, will you explain to me how it is to get there?"

The whole size of the needless muddle was apparent. Evasions were of no use; therefore Dunois admitted that there was no way to correct the blunder but to send the army all the way back to Blois, and let it begin over again and come up on the other side this time, according to Joan's original plan.

Any other girl, after winning such a triumph as this over a veteran soldier of old renown, might have exulted a little and been excusable for it, but Joan showed no disposition of this sort. She dropped a word or two of grief over the precious time that must be lost, then began at once to issue commands for the march back. She sorrowed to see her army go; for she said its heart was great and its enthusiasm high, and that with it at her back she did not fear to face all the might of England.

All arrangements having been completed for the return of the main body of the army, she took the Bastard and La Hire and a thousand men and went down to Orleans, where all the town was in a fever of impatience to have sight of her face. It was eight in the evening when she and the troops rode in at the Burgundy gate, with the Paladin preceding her with her standard. She was riding a white horse, and she carried in her hand the sacred sword of Fierbois. You should have seen Orleans then. What a picture it was! Such black seas of people, such a starry firmament of torches, such roaring whirlwinds of welcome, such booming of bells and thundering of cannon! It was as if the world was come to an end. Everywhere in the glare of the torches one saw rank upon rank of upturned white faces, the mouths wide open, shouting, and the unchecked tears running down; Joan forged her slow way through the solid masses, her mailed form projecting above the pavement of heads like a silver statue. The people about her struggled along, gazing up at her through their tears with the rapt look of men and women who believe they are seeing one who is divine; and always her feet were being kissed by grateful folk, and such as failed of that privilege touched her horse and then kissed their fingers.

Nothing that Joan did escaped notice; everything she did was commented upon and applauded. You could hear the remarks going all the time.

"There—she's smiling—see!"

"Now she's taking her little plumed cap off to somebody—ah, it's fine and graceful!"

"She's patting that woman on the head with her gauntlet."

"Oh, she was born on a horse—see her turn in her saddle, and kiss the hilt of her sword to the ladies in the window that threw the flowers down."

"Now there's a poor woman lifting up a child—she's kissed it—oh, she's divine!"

"What a dainty little figure it is, and what a lovely face—and such color and animation!"

Joan's slender long banner streaming backward had an accident—the fringe caught fire from a torch. She leaned forward and crushed the flame in her hand.

"She's not afraid of fire nor anything!" they shouted, and delivered a storm of admiring applause that made everything quake.

She rode to the cathedral and gave thanks to God, and the people crammed the place and added their devotions to hers; then she took up her march again and picked her slow way through the crowds and the wilderness of torches to the house of Jacques Boucher, treasurer of the Duke of Orleans, where she was to be the guest of his wife as long as she stayed in the city, and have his young daughter for comrade and room-mate. The delirium of the people went on the rest of the night, and with it the clamor of the joy-bells and the welcoming cannon.

Joan of Arc had stepped upon her stage at last, and was ready to begin.

CHAPTER 14

She was ready, but must sit down and wait until there was an army to work with.

Next morning, Saturday, April 30, 1429, she set about inquiring after the messenger who carried her proclamation to the English from Blois—the one which she had dictated at Poitiers. Here is a copy of it. It is a remarkable document, for several reasons: for its matter-of-fact directness, for its high spirit and forcible diction, and for its naïve confidence in her ability to achieve the prodigious task which she had laid upon herself, or which had been laid upon her—which you please. All through it you seem to see the pomps of war and hear the rumbling of the drums. In it Joan's warrior soul is revealed, and for the moment the soft little shepherdess has disappeared from your view. This untaught country damsel, unused to dictating anything at all to anybody, much less documents of state to kings and generals, poured out this procession of vigorous sentences as fluently as if this sort of work had been her trade from childhood:

JESUS MARIA

King of England, and you Duke of Bedford who call yourself Regent of France; William de la Pole, Earl of Suffolk; and you Thomas Lord Scales, who style yourselves lieutenants of the said Bedford—do right to the King of Heaven. Render to the Maid who is sent by God the keys of all the good towns you have taken and violated in France. She is sent hither by God to restore the blood royal. She is very ready to make peace if you will do her right by giving up France and paying for what you have held. And you archers, companions of war, noble and otherwise, who are before the good city of Orleans, begone into your own land in God's name, or expect news from the Maid who will shortly go to see you to your very great hurt. King of England, if you do not so, I am chief of war, and wherever I shall find your people in France I will drive them out, willing or not willing; and if they do not obey I will slay them all, but if they obey, I will have them to mercy. I am come hither by God, the King of Heaven, body for body, to put you out of France, in spite of those who would work treason and mischief against the kingdom. Think not you shall ever hold the kingdom from the King of Heaven, the Son of the blessed Mary; King Charles shall hold it, for God wills it so, and has revealed it to him by the Maid. If you believe not the news sent by God through the Maid, wherever we shall meet you we will strike boldly and make such a noise as has not been in France these thousand years. Be sure that God can send more strength to the Maid than you can bring to any assault against her and her good men-at-arms; and then we shall see who has the better right, the King of Heaven, or you. Duke of Bedford, the Maid prays you not to bring about your own destruction. If you do her right, you may yet go in her company where the French shall do the finest deed that has ever been done in Christendom, and if you do not, you shall be reminded shortly of your great wrongs.

In that closing sentence she invites them to go on crusade with her to rescue the Holy Sepulchre.

No answer had been returned to this proclamation, and the messenger himself had not come back. So now she sent her two heralds with a new letter warning the English to raise the siege and requiring them to restore that missing messenger. The heralds came back without him. All they brought was notice from the English to Joan that they would presently catch her and burn her if she did not clear out now while she had a chance, and "go back to her proper trade of minding cows."

She held her peace, only saying it was a pity that the English would persist in inviting present disaster and eventual destruction when she was "doing all she could to get them out of the country with their lives still in their bodies."

Presently she thought of an arrangement that might be acceptable, and said to the heralds, "Go back and say to Lord Talbot this, from me: 'Come out of your bastilles with your host, and I will come with mine; if I beat you, go in peace out of France; if you beat me, burn me, according to your desire.' "

I did not hear this, but Dunois did, and spoke of it. The challenge was refused.

Sunday morning her Voices or some instinct gave her a warning, and she sent Dunois to Blois to take command of the army and hurry it to Orleans. It was a wise move, for he found Regnault de Chartres and some more of the King's pet rascals there trying their best to disperse the army, and crippling all the efforts of Joan's generals to head it for Orleans. They were a fine lot, those miscreants. They turned their attention to Dunois, now, but he had balked Joan once, with unpleasant results to himself, and was not minded to meddle in that way again. He soon had the army moving.

CHAPTER 15

We of the personal staff were in fairy-land, now, during the few days that we waited for the return of the army. We went into society. To our two knights this was not a novelty, but to us young villagers it was a new and wonderful life. Any position of any sort near the person of the Maid of Vaucouleurs conferred high distinction upon the holder and caused his society to be courted; and so the D'Arc brothers, and Noël, and the Paladin, humble peasants at home, were gentlemen here, personages of weight and influence. It was fine to see how soon their country diffidences and awkwardnesses melted away under this pleasant sun of deference and disappeared, and how lightly and easily they took to their new atmosphere. The Paladin was as happy as it was possible for any one in this earth to be. His tongue went all the time, and daily he got new delight out of hearing himself talk. He began to enlarge his ancestry and spread it out all around, and ennoble it right and left, and it was not long until it consisted almost entirely of Dukes. He worked up his old battles and tricked them out with fresh splendors; also with new terrors, for he added artillery now. We had seen cannon for the first time at Blois—a few pieces—here there was plenty of it, and now and then we had the impressive spectacle of a huge English bastille hidden from sight in a mountain of smoke from its own guns, with lances of red flame darting through it; and this grand picture, along with the quaking thunders pounding away in the heart of it, inflamed the Paladin's imagination and enabled him to dress out those ambuscade-skirmishes of ours with a sublimity which made it impossible for any to recognize them at all except people who had not been there.

You may suspect that there was a special inspiration for these great efforts of the Paladin's, and there was. It was the daughter of the house, Catherine Boucher, who was eighteen, and gentle and lovely in her ways, and very beautiful. I think she might have been as beautiful as Joan herself, if she had had Joan's eyes. But that could never be. There was never but that one pair, there will never be another. Joan's eyes were deep and rich and wonderful beyond anything merely earthly. They spoke all the languages—they had no need of words. They produced all effects—and just by a glance, just a single glance: a glance that could convict a liar of his lie and make him confess it; that could bring down a proud man's pride and make him humble; that could put courage into a coward and strike dead the courage of the bravest; that could appease resentments and real hatreds; that could speak peace to storms of passion and be obeyed; that could make the doubter believe and the hopeless hope again; that could purify the impure mind; that could persuade—ah, there it is—*persuasion!* that is the word; what or who is it that it couldn't persuade? The maniac of Domremy—the fairy-banishing priest—the reverend tribunal of Toul—the doubting and superstitious Laxart—the obstinate veteran of Vaucouleurs—the characterless heir of France—the sages and scholars of the Parliament and University of Poitiers—the darling of Satan, La Hire—the masterless Bastard of Orleans, accustomed to acknowledge no way as right and rational but his own—these were the trophies of that great gift that made her the wonder and mystery that she was.

We mingled companionably with the great folk who flocked to the big house to make Joan's acquaintance, and they made much of us and we lived in the clouds, so to speak. But what we preferred even to this happiness was the quieter occasions, when the formal guests were gone and the family and a few dozen of its familiar friends were gathered together for a social good time. It was then that we did our best, we five youngsters, with such fascinations as we had, and the chief object of them was Catherine. None of us had ever been in love before, and now we had the misfortune to all fall in love with the same person at the same time—which was the first moment we saw her. She was a merry heart, and full of life, and I still remember tenderly those few evenings that I was permitted to have my share of her dear society and of comradeship with that little company of charming people.

The Paladin made us all jealous the first night, for when he got fairly started on those battles of his he had everything to himself, and there was no use in anybody else's trying to get any attention. Those people had been living in the midst of real war for seven months; and to hear this windy giant lay out his imaginary campaigns and fairly swim in blood and spatter it all around, entertained them to the verge of the grave. Catherine was like to die, for pure enjoyment. She didn't laugh loud—we, of course, wished she would—but kept in the shelter of a fan, and shook until there was danger that she would unhitch her ribs from her spine. Then when the Paladin had got done with a battle and we began to feel thankful and hope for a change, she would speak up in a way that was so sweet and persuasive that it rankled in me, and ask him about some detail or other in the early part of his battle which she said had greatly interested her, and would he be so good as to describe that part again and with a little more particularity?—which of course precipitated the whole battle on us again, with a hundred lies added that had been overlooked before.

I do not know how to make you realize the pain I suffered. I had never been jealous before, and it seemed intolerable that this creature should have this good fortune which he was so ill entitled to, and I have to sit and see myself neglected when I was so longing for the least little attention out of the thousand that this beloved girl was lavishing upon him. I was near her, and tried two or three times to get started on some of the things that *I* had done in those battles—and I felt ashamed of myself, too, for stooping to such a business—but she cared for nothing but his battles, and could not be got to listen; and presently when one of my attempts caused her to lose some precious rag or other of his mendacities and she asked him to repeat, thus bringing on a new engagement of course and increasing the havoc and carnage tenfold, I felt so humiliated by this pitiful miscarriage of mine that I gave up and tried no more.

The others were as outraged by the Paladin's selfish conduct as I was—and by his grand luck, too, of course—perhaps, indeed, that was the main hurt. We talked our trouble over together, which was but natural, for rivals become brothers when a common affliction assails them and a common enemy bears off the victory.

Each of us could do things that would please and get notice if it were not for this person, who occupied all the time and gave others no chance. I had made a poem, taking a whole night to it—a poem in which I most happily and delicately celebrated that sweet girl's charms, without mentioning her name, but any one could see who was meant; for the bare title—"The Rose of Orleans" would reveal that, as it seemed to me. It pictured this pure and dainty white rose as growing up out of the rude soil of war and looking abroad out of its tender eyes upon the horrid machinery of death, and then—note this conceit—it blushes for the sinful nature of man, and *turns red* in a single night. Becomes a red rose, you see—a rose that was white before. The idea was my own, and quite new. Then it sent its sweet perfume out over the embattled city, and when the beleaguering forces smelt it they *laid down their arms and wept*. This was also my own idea, and new. That closed that part of the poem; then I put her into the similitude of the firmament—not the whole of it, but only part. That is to say, she was the moon, and all the constellations were following her about, their hearts in flames for love of her, but she would not halt, she would not listen, for 'twas thought she loved another. 'Twas thought she loved a poor unworthy suppliant who was upon the earth, facing danger, death, and possible mutilation in the bloody field, waging relentless war against a heartless foe to save her from an all too early grave, and her city from destruction. And when the sad pursuing constellations came to know and realize the bitter sorrow that was come upon them—note this idea—their hearts broke and their tears gushed forth, filling the vault of heaven with a fiery splendor, for those tears were *falling stars*. It was a rash idea, but beautiful; beautiful and pathetic; wonderfully pathetic, the way I had it, with the rhyme and all to help. At the end of each verse there was a two-line refrain pitying the poor earthly lover separated so far, and perhaps forever, from her he loved so well, and growing always paler and weaker and thinner in his agony as he neared the cruel grave—the most touching thing—even the boys themselves could hardly keep back their tears, the way Noël said those lines. There were eight four-line stanzas in the first end of the poem—the end about the rose, the horticultural end, as you may say, if that is not too large a name for such a little poem—and eight in the astronomical end—sixteen stanzas altogether, and I could have made it a hundred and fifty if I had wanted to, I was so inspired and so all swelled up with beautiful thoughts and fancies; but that would have been too many to sing or recite before a company, that way, whereas sixteen was just right, and could be done over again, if desired.

The boys were amazed that I could make such a poem as that out of my own head, and so was I, of course, it being as much a surprise to me as it could be to anybody, for I did not know that it was in me. If any had asked me a single day before if it was in me, I should have told them frankly no, it was not.

That is the way with us; we may go on half of our life not knowing such a thing is in us, when in reality it was there all the time, and all we needed was something to turn up that would call for it. Indeed, it was always so with our family. My grandfather had a cancer, and they never knew what was the matter with him till he died, and he didn't himself. It is wonderful how gifts and diseases can be concealed that way. All that was necessary in my case was for this lovely and inspiring girl to cross my path, and out came the poem, and no more trouble to me to word it and rhyme it and perfect it than it is to stone a dog. No, I should have said it was not in me; but it was.

The boys couldn't say enough about it, they were so charmed and astonished. The thing that pleased them the most was the way it would do the Paladin's business for him. They forgot everything in their anxiety to get him shelved and silenced. Noël Rainguesson was clear beside himself with admiration of the poem, and wished *he* could do such a thing, but it was out of his line and he couldn't, of course. He had it by heart in half an hour, and there was never anything so pathetic and beautiful as the way he recited it. For that was just his gift—that and mimicry. He could recite anything better than anybody in the world, and he could take off La Hire to the very life—or anybody else, for that matter. Now I never could recite worth a farthing; and when I tried with this poem the boys wouldn't let me finish; they would have nobody but Noël. So then, as I wanted the poem to make the best possible impression on Catherine and the company, I told Noël he might do the reciting. Never was anybody so delighted. He could hardly believe that I was in earnest, but I was. I said that to have them know that I was the author of it would be enough for me. The boys were full of exultation, and Noël said if he could just get one chance at those people it would be all he would ask; he would make them realize that there was something higher and finer than war-lies to be had here.

But how to get the opportunity—that was the difficulty. We invented several schemes that promised fairly, and at last we hit upon one that was sure. That was, to let the Paladin get a good start in a manufactured battle, and then send in a false call for him, and as soon as he was out of the room, have Noël take his place and finish the battle himself in the Paladin's own style, imitated to a shade. That would get great applause, and win the house's favor and put it in the right mood to hear the poem. The two triumphs together would finish the Standard-Bearer—modify him, anyway, to a certainty, and give the rest of us a chance for the future.

So the next night I kept out of the way until the Paladin had got his start and was sweeping down upon the enemy like a whirlwind at the head of his corps, then I stepped within the door in my official uniform and announced that a messenger from General La Hire's quarters desired speech with the Standard-Bearer. He left the room, and Noël took his place and said that the interruption was to be deplored, but that fortunately he was personally acquainted with the details of the battle himself, and if permitted would be glad to state them to the company. Then without waiting for the permission he turned himself into the Paladin—a dwarfed Paladin, of course—with manner, tones, gestures, attitudes, everything exact, and went right on with the battle, and it would be impossible to imagine a more perfectly and minutely ridiculous imitation than he furnished to those shrieking people. They went into spasms, convulsions, frenzies of laughter, and the tears flowed down their cheeks in rivulets. The more they laughed, the more inspired Noël grew with his theme and the greater the marvels he worked, till really the laughter was not properly laughing any more, but screaming. Blessedest feature of all, Catherine Boucher was dying with ecstasies, and presently there was little left of her but gasps and suffocations. Victory? It was a perfect Agincourt.

The Paladin was gone only a couple of minutes; he found out at once that a trick had been played on him, so he came back. When he approached the door he heard Noël ranting in there and recognized the state of the case; so he remained near the door but out of sight, and heard the performance through to the end. The applause Noël got when he finished was wonderful; and they kept it up and kept it up, clapping their hands like mad, and shouting to him to do it over again.

But Noël was clever. He knew the very best background for a poem of deep and refined sentiment and pathetic melancholy was one where great and satisfying merriment has prepared the spirit for the powerful contrast.

So he paused until all was quiet, then his face grew grave and assumed an impressive aspect, and at once all faces sobered in sympathy and took on a look of wondering and expectant interest. Now he began in a low but distinct voice the opening verses of The Rose. As he breathed the rhythmic measures forth, and one gracious line after another fell upon those enchanted ears in that deep hush, one could catch, on every hand, half-audible ejaculations of "How lovely—how beautiful—how exquisite."

By this time the Paladin, who had gone away for a moment with the opening of the poem, was back again, and had stepped within the door. He stood there, now, resting his great frame against the wall and gazing toward the reciter like one entranced. When Noël got to the second part, and that heart-breaking refrain began to melt and move all listeners, the Paladin began to wipe away tears with the back of first one hand and then the other. The next time the refrain was repeated he got to snuffling, and sort of half sobbing, and went to wiping his eyes with the sleeves of his doublet. He was so conspicuous that he embarrassed Noël a little, and also had an ill effect upon the audience. With the next repetition he broke quite down and began to cry like a calf, which ruined all the effect and started many in the audience to laughing. Then he went on from bad to worse, until I never saw such a spectacle; for he fetched out a towel from under his doublet and began to swab his eyes with it and let go the most infernal bellowings mixed up with sobbings and groanings and retchings and barkings and coughings and snortings and screamings and howlings—and he twisted himself about on his heels and squirmed this way and that, still pouring out that brutal clamor and flourishing his towel in the air and swabbing again and wringing it out. Hear? You couldn't hear yourself think. Noël was wholly drowned out and silenced, and those people were laughing the very lungs out of themselves. It was the most degrading sight that ever was. Now I heard the clankety-clank that plate-armor makes when the man that is in it is running, and then alongside my head there burst out the most inhuman explosion of laughter that ever rent the drum of a person's ear, and I looked, and it was La Hire; and he stood there with his gauntlets on his hips and his head tilted back and his jaws spread to that degree to let out his hurricanes and his thunders that it amounted to indecent exposure, for you could see everything that was in him. Only one thing more and worse could happen, and it happened: at the other door I saw the flurry and bustle and bowings and scrapings of officials and flunkeys which means that some great personage is coming—then Joan of Arc stepped in, and the house rose! Yes, and tried to shut its indecorous mouth and make itself grave and proper; but when it saw the Maid herself go to laughing, it thanked God for this mercy and the earthquake followed.

Such things make life a bitterness, and I do not wish to dwell upon them. The effect of the poem was spoiled.

CHAPTER 16

This episode disagreed with me and I was not able to leave my bed the next day. The others were in the same condition. But for this, one or another of us might have had the good luck that fell to the Paladin's share that day; but it is observable that God in His compassion sends the good luck to such as are ill equipped with gifts, as compensation for their defect, but requires such as are more fortunately endowed to get by labor and talent what those others get by chance. It was Noël who said this, and it seemed to me to be well and justly thought.

The Paladin, going about the town all the day in order to be followed and admired and overhear the people say in an awed voice, "Ssh!—look, it is the Standard-bearer of Joan of Arc!" had speech with all sorts and conditions of folk, and he learned from some boatmen that there was a stir of some kind going on in the bastilles on the other side of the river; and in the evening, seeking further, he found a deserter from the fortress called the "Augustins," who said that the English were going to send men over to strengthen the garrisons on our side during the darkness of the night, and were exulting greatly, for they meant to spring upon Dunois and the army when it was passing the bastilles and destroy it: a thing quite easy to do, since the "Witch" would not be there, and without her presence the army would do like the French armies of these many years past—drop their weapons and run when they saw an English face.

It was ten at night when the Paladin brought this news and asked leave to speak to Joan, and I was up and on duty then. It was a bitter stroke to me to see what a chance I had lost. Joan made searching inquiries, and satisfied herself that the word was true, then she made this annoying remark:

"You have done well, and you have my thanks. It may be that you have prevented a disaster. Your name and service shall receive official mention."

Then he bowed low, and when he rose he was eleven feet high. As he swelled out past me he covertly pulled down the corner of his eye with his finger and muttered part of that defiled refrain, "Oh tears, ah tears, oh sad sweet tears!—name in General Orders—personal mention to the King, you see!"

I wished Joan could have seen his conduct, but she was busy thinking what she would do. Then she had me fetch the knight Jean de Metz, and in a minute he was off for La Hire's quarters with orders for him and the Lord de Villars and Florent d'Iliers to report to her at five o'clock next morning with five hundred picked men well mounted. The histories say half-past four, but it is not true, I heard the order given.

We were on our way at five to the minute, and encountered the head of the arriving column between six and seven, a couple of leagues from the city. Dunois was pleased, for the army had begun to get restive and show uneasiness now that it was getting so near to the dreaded bastilles. But that all disappeared now, as the word ran down the line, with a huzzah that swept along the length of it like a wave, that the Maid was come. Dunois asked her to halt and let the column pass in review, so that the men could be sure that the report of her presence was not a ruse to revive their courage. So she took position at the side of the road with her staff, and the battalions swung by with a martial stride, huzzahing. Joan was armed, except her head. She was wearing the cunning little velvet cap with the mass of curved white ostrich plumes tumbling over its edges which the city of Orleans had given her the night she arrived—the one that is in the picture that hangs in the Hôtel de Ville at Rouen. She was looking about fifteen. The sight of soldiers always set her blood to leaping, and lit the fires in her eyes and brought the warm rich color to her cheeks; it was then that you saw that she was too beautiful to be of the earth, or at any rate that there was a subtle something somewhere about her beauty that differed it from the human types of your experience and exalted it above them.

In the train of wains laden with supplies a man lay on top of the goods. He was stretched out on his back, and his hands were tied together with ropes, and also his ankles. Joan signed to the officer in charge of that division of the train to come to her, and he rode up and saluted.

"What is he that is bound, there?" she asked.

"A prisoner, General."

"What is his offence?"

"He is a deserter."

"What is to be done with him?"

"He will be hanged, but it was not convenient on the march, and there was no hurry."

"Tell me about him."

"He is a good soldier, but he asked leave to go and see his wife who was dying, he said, but it could not be granted; so he went without leave. Meanwhile the march began, and he only overtook us yesterday evening."

"Overtook you? Did he come of his own will?"

"Yes, it was of his own will."

"*He* a deserter! Name of God! Bring him to me."

The officer rode forward and loosed the man's feet and brought him back with his hands still tied. What a figure he was—a good seven feet high, and built for business! He had a strong face; he had an unkempt shock of black hair which showed up in a striking way when the officer removed his morion for him; for weapon he had a big axe in his broad leathern belt. Standing by Joan's horse, he made Joan look littler than ever, for his head was about on a level with her own. His face was profoundly melancholy; all interest in life seemed to be dead in the man. Joan said—

"Hold up your hands."

The man's head was down. He lifted it when he heard that soft friendly voice, and there was a wistful something in his face which made one think that there had been music in it for him and that he would like to hear it again. When he raised his hands Joan laid her sword to his bonds, but the officer said with apprehension—

"Ah, madam—my General!"

"What is it?" she said.

"He is under sentence!"

"Yes, I know. I am responsible for him"; and she cut the bonds. They had lacerated his wrists, and they were bleeding. "Ah, pitiful!" she said; "blood—I do not like it"; and she shrank from the sight. But only for a moment. "Give me something, somebody, to bandage his wrists with."

The officer said—

"Ah, my General! it is not fitting. Let me bring another to do it."

"Another? De par le Dieu! You would seek far to find one that can do it better than I, for I learned it long ago among both men and beasts. And I can tie better than those that did this; if I had tied him the ropes had not cut his flesh."

The man looked on, silent, while he was being bandaged, stealing a furtive glance at Joan's face occasionally, such as an animal might that is receiving a kindness from an unexpected quarter and is gropingly trying to reconcile the act with its source. All the staff had forgotten the huzzahing army drifting by in its rolling clouds of dust, to crane their necks and watch the bandaging as if it was the most interesting and absorbing novelty that ever was. I have often seen people do like that—get entirely lost in the simplest trifle, when it is something that is out of their line. Now there in Poitiers, once, I saw two bishops and a dozen of those grave and famous scholars grouped together watching a man paint a sign on a shop; they didn't breathe, they were as good as dead; and when it began to sprinkle they didn't know it at first; then they noticed it, and each man hove a deep sigh, and glanced up with a surprised look as wondering to see the others there, and how he came to be there himself—but that is the way with people, as I have said. There is no way of accounting for people. You have to take them as they are.

"There," said Joan at last, pleased with her success; "another could have done it no better—not as well, I think. Tell me—what is it you did? Tell me all."

The giant said:

"It was this way, my angel. My mother died, then my three little children, one after the other, all in two years. It was the famine; others fared so—it was God's will. I saw them die; I had that grace; and I buried them. Then when my poor wife's fate was come, I begged for leave to go to her—she who was so dear to me—she who was all I had; I begged on my knees. But they would not let me. Could I let her die, friendless and alone? Could I let her die believing I would not come? Would she let *me* die and *she* not come—with her feet free to do it if she would, and no cost upon it but only her life? Ah, she would come—she would come through the fire! So I went. I saw her. She died in my arms. I buried her. Then the army was gone. I had trouble to overtake it, but my legs are long and there are many hours in a day; I overtook it last night."

Joan said, musingly, and as if she were thinking aloud—

"It sounds true. If true, it were no great harm to suspend the law this one time—any would say that. It may not be true, but if it *is* true—" She turned suddenly to the man and said, "I would see your eyes—look up!" The eyes of the two met, and Joan said to the officer, "The man is pardoned. Give you good-day; you may go." Then she said to the man, "Did you know it was death to come back to the army?"

"Yes," he said, "I knew it."

"Then why did you do it?"

The man said, quite simply—

"*Because* it was death. She was all I had. There was nothing left to love."

"Ah, yes, there was—France! The children of France have always their mother—*they* cannot be left with nothing to love. You shall live—and you shall serve France—"

"I will serve *you!*"

"—you shall fight for France—"

"I will fight for *you!*"

"You shall be France's soldier—"

"I will be *your* soldier!"

"—you shall give all your heart to France—"

"I will give all my heart to *you*—and all my soul, if I have one—and all my strength, which is great—for I was dead and am alive again; I had nothing to live for, but now I have! You are France for me. You are my France, and I will have no other."

Joan smiled, and was touched and pleased at the man's grave enthusiasm—solemn enthusiasm, one may call it, for the manner of it was deeper than mere gravity—and she said—

"Well, it shall be as you will. What are you called?"

The man answered with unsmiling simplicity—

"They call me the Dwarf, but I think it is more in jest than otherwise."

It made Joan laugh, and she said—

"It has something of that look, truly! What is the office of that vast axe?"

The soldier replied with the same gravity—which must have been born to him, it sat upon him so naturally—

"It is to persuade persons to respect France."

Joan laughed again, and said—

"Have you given many lessons?"

"Ah, indeed yes—many."

"The pupils behaved to suit you, afterwards?"

"Yes; it made them quiet—quite pleasant and quiet."

"I should think it would happen so. Would you like to be my man-at-arms?—orderly, sentinel, or something like that?"

"If I may!"

"Then you shall. You shall have proper armor, and shall go on teaching your art. Take one of those led horses there, and follow the staff when we move."

That is how we came by the Dwarf; and a good fellow he was. Joan picked him out on sight, but it wasn't a mistake; no one could be faithfuler than he was, and he was a devil and the son of a devil when he turned himself loose with his axe. He was so big that he made the Paladin look like an ordinary man. He liked to like people, therefore people liked him. He liked us boys from the start; and he liked the knights, and liked pretty much everybody he came across; but he thought more of a paring of Joan's finger-nail than he did of all the rest of the world put together.

Yes, that is where we got him—stretched on the wain, going to his death, poor chap, and nobody to say a good word for him. He was a good find. Why, the knights treated him almost like an equal—it is the honest truth; that is the sort of a man he was. They called him the Bastille, sometimes, and sometimes they called him Hellfire, which was on account of his warm and sumptuous style in battle, and you know they wouldn't have given him pet names if they hadn't had a good deal of affection for him.

To the Dwarf, Joan was France, the spirit of France made flesh—he never got away from that idea that he had started with; and God knows it was the true one. That was a humble eye to see so great a truth where some others failed. To me that seems quite remarkable. And yet, after all, it was, in a way, just what nations do. When they love a great and noble thing, they embody it—they want it so that they can see it with their eyes; like Liberty, for instance. They are not content with the cloudy abstract idea, they make a beautiful statue of it, and then their beloved idea is substantial and they can look at it and worship it. And so it is as I say; to the Dwarf, Joan was our country embodied, our country made visible flesh cast in a gracious form. When she stood before others, they saw Joan of Arc, but he saw France.

Sometimes he would speak of her by that name. It shows you how the idea was imbedded in his mind, and how real it was to him. The world has called our kings by it, but I know of none of them who has had so good a right as she to that sublime title.

When the march past was finished, Joan returned to the front and rode at the head of the column. When we began to file past those grim bastilles and could glimpse the men within, standing to their guns and ready to empty death into our ranks, such a faintness came over me and such a sickness that all things seemed to turn dim and swim before my eyes; and the other boys looked droopy too, I thought—including the Paladin, although I do not know this for certain, because he was ahead of me and I had to keep my eyes out toward the bastille side, because I could wince better when I saw what to wince at.

But Joan was at home—in Paradise, I might say. She sat up straight, and I could see that she was feeling different from me. The awfulest thing was the silence, there wasn't a sound but the screaking of the saddles, the measured tramplings, and the sneezing of the horses, afflicted by the smothering dust-clouds which they kicked up. I wanted to sneeze myself, but it seemed to me that I would rather go unsneezed, or suffer even a bitterer torture, if there is one, than attract attention to myself.

I was not of a rank to make suggestions, or I would have suggested that if we went faster we should get by sooner. It seemed to me that it was an ill-judged time to be taking a walk. Just as we were drifting in that suffocating stillness past a great cannon that stood just within a raised portcullis, with nothing between me and it but the moat, a most uncommon jackass in there split the world with his bray, and I fell out of the saddle. Sir Bertrand grabbed me as I went, which was well, for if I had gone to the ground in my armor I could not have gotten up again by myself. The English warders on the battlements laughed a coarse laugh, forgetting that every one must begin, and that there had been a time when they themselves would have fared no better when shot by a jackass.

The English never uttered a challenge nor fired a shot. It was said afterwards that when their men saw the Maid riding at the front and saw how lovely she was, their eager courage cooled down in many cases and vanished in the rest, they feeling certain that that creature was not mortal, but the very child of Satan, and so the officers were prudent and did not try to make them fight. It was said also that some of the officers were affected by the same superstitious fears. Well, in any case, they never offered to molest us, and we poked by all the grisly fortresses in peace. During the march I caught up on my devotions, which were in arrears; so it was not all loss and no profit for me, after all.

It was on this march that the histories say Dunois told Joan that the English were expecting reinforcements under the command of Sir John Falstaff, and that she turned upon him and said—

"Bastard, Bastard, in God's name I warn you to let me know of his coming as soon as you hear of it; for if he passes without my knowledge you shall lose your head!"

It may be so; I don't deny it; but I didn't hear it. If she really said it I think she only meant she would take off his official head—degrade him from his command. It was not like her to threaten a comrade's life. She did have her doubts of her generals, and was entitled to them, for she was all for storm and assault, and they were for holding still and tiring the English out. Since they did not believe in her way and were experienced old soldiers, it would be natural for them to prefer their own and try to get around carrying hers out.

But I did hear something that the histories didn't mention and don't know about. I heard Joan say that now that the garrisons on the other side had been weakened to strengthen those on our side, the most effective point of operations had shifted to the south shore; so she meant to go over there and storm the forts which held the bridge end, and that would open up communication with our own dominions and raise the siege. The generals began to balk, privately, right away, but they only baffled and delayed her, and that for only four days.

All Orleans met the army at the gate and huzzahed it through the bannered streets to its various quarters, but nobody had to rock it to sleep; it slumped down dog-tired, for Dunois had rushed it without mercy, and for the next twenty-four hours it would be quiet, all but the snoring.

CHAPTER 17

When we got home, breakfast for us minor fry was waiting in our mess-room and the family honored us by coming in to eat it with us. The nice old treasurer, and in fact all three were flatteringly eager to hear about our adventures. Nobody asked the Paladin to begin, but he did begin, because now that his specially ordained and peculiar military rank set him above everybody on the personal staff but old D'Aulon, who didn't eat with us, he didn't care a farthing for the knights' nobility nor mine, but took precedence in the talk whenever it suited him, which was all the time, because he was born that way. He said:

"God be thanked, we found the army in admirable condition. I think I have never seen a finer body of animals."

"Animals?" said Miss Catherine.

"I will explain to you what he means," said Noël. "He—"

"I will trouble you not to trouble yourself to explain anything for me," said the Paladin, loftily. "I have reason to think—"

"That is his way," said Noël; "always when he thinks he has reason to think, he thinks he does think, but this is an error. He didn't see the army. I noticed him, and he didn't see it. He was troubled by his old complaint."

"What is his old complaint?" Catherine asked.

"Prudence," I said, seeing my chance to help.

But it was not a fortunate remark, for the Paladin said:

"It probably isn't your turn to criticise people's prudence—you who fall out of the saddle when a donkey brays."

They all laughed, and I was ashamed of myself for my hasty smartness. I said:

"It isn't quite fair for you to say I fell out on account of the donkey's braying. It was emotion, just ordinary emotion."

"Very well, if you want to call it that, I am not objecting. What would you call it, Sir Bertrand?"

"Well, it—well, whatever it was, it was excusable, I think. All of you have learned how to behave in hot hand-to-hand engagements, and you don't need to be ashamed of your record in that matter; but to walk along in front of death, with one's hands idle, and no noise, no music, and nothing going on, is a very trying situation. If I were you, De Conte, I would name the emotion; it's nothing to be ashamed of."

It was as straight and sensible a speech as ever I heard, and I was grateful for the opening it gave me; so I came out and said:

"It was fear—and thank you for the honest idea, too."

"It was the cleanest and best way out," said the old treasurer; "you've done well, my lad."

That made me comfortable, and when Miss Catherine said, "It's what I think, too," I was grateful to myself for getting into that scrape.

Sir Jean de Metz said—

"We were all in a body together when the donkey brayed, and it was dismally still at the time. I don't see how any young campaigner could escape some little touch of that emotion."

He looked about him with a pleasant expression of inquiry on his good face, and as each pair of eyes in turn met his the head they were in nodded a confession. Even the Paladin delivered his nod. That surprised everybody, and saved the Standard-Bearer's credit. It was clever of him; nobody believed he could tell the truth that way without practice, or would tell that particular sort of a truth either with or without practice. I suppose he judged it would favorably impress the family. Then the old treasurer said—

"Passing the forts in that trying way required the same sort of nerve that a person must have when ghosts are about him in the dark, I should think. What does the Standard-Bearer think?"

"Well, I don't quite know about that, sir. I've often thought I would like to see a ghost if I—"

"Would you?" exclaimed the young lady. "We've got one! Would you try that one? Will you?"

She was so eager and pretty that the Paladin said straight out that he would; and then as none of the rest had bravery enough to expose the fear that was in him, one volunteered after the other with a prompt mouth and a sick heart till all were shipped for the voyage; then the girl clapped her hands in glee, and the parents were gratified too, saying that the ghosts of their house had been a dread and a misery to them and their forebears for generations, and nobody had ever been found yet who was willing to confront them and find out what their trouble was, so that the family could heal it and content the poor spectres and beguile them to tranquillity and peace.

CHAPTER 18

About noon I was chatting with Madame Boucher; nothing was going on, all was quiet, when Catherine Boucher suddenly entered in great excitement, and said—

"Fly, sir, fly! The Maid was dozing in her chair in my room, when she sprang up and cried out, 'French blood is flowing!—my arms, give me my arms!' Her giant was on guard at the door, and he brought D'Aulon, who began to arm her, and I and the giant have been warning the staff. Fly!—and stay by her; and if there really is a battle, keep her out of it—don't let her risk herself—there is no need—if the men know she is near and looking on, it is all that is necessary. Keep her out of the fight—don't fail of this!"

I started on a run, saying, sarcastically—for I was always fond of sarcasm, and it was said that I had a most neat gift that way—

"Oh yes, nothing easier than that—I'll attend to it!"

At the furthest end of the house I met Joan, fully armed, hurrying toward the door, and she said—

"Ah, French blood is being spilt, and you did not tell me."

"Indeed I did not know it," I said; "there are no sounds of war; everything is quiet, your Excellency."

"You will hear war-sounds enough in a moment," she said, and was gone.

It was true. Before one could count five there broke upon the stillness the swelling rush and tramp of an approaching multitude of men and horses, with hoarse cries of command; and then out of the distance came the muffled deep *boom!—boom-boom!—boom!* of cannon, and straightway that rushing multitude was roaring by the house like a hurricane.

Our knights and all our staff came flying, armed, but with no horses ready, and we burst out after Joan in a body, the Paladin in the lead with the banner. The surging crowd was made up half of citizens and half of soldiers, and had no recognized leader. When Joan was seen a huzzah went up, and she shouted—

"A horse—a horse!"

A dozen saddles were at her disposal in a moment. She mounted, a hundred people shouting—

"Way, there—way for the MAID OF ORLEANS!" The first time that that immortal name was ever uttered—and I, praise God, was there to hear it! The mass divided itself like the waters of the Red Sea, and down this lane Joan went skimming like a bird, crying "Forward, French hearts—follow me!" and we came winging in her wake on the rest of the borrowed horses, the holy standard streaming above us, and the lane closing together in our rear.

This was a different thing from the ghastly march past the dismal bastilles. No, we felt fine, now, and all a-whirl with enthusiasm. The explanation of this sudden uprising was this. The city and the little garrison, so long hopeless and afraid, had gone wild over Joan's coming, and could no longer restrain their desire to get at the enemy; so, without orders from anybody, a few hundred soldiers and citizens had plunged out at the Burgundy gate on a sudden impulse and made a charge on one of Lord Talbot's most formidable fortresses—St. Loup—and were getting the worst of it. The news of this had swept through the city and started this new crowd that we were with.

As we poured out at the gate we met a force bringing in the wounded from the front. The sight moved Joan, and she said—

"Ah, French blood; it makes my hair rise to see it!"

We were soon on the field, soon in the midst of the turmoil. Joan was seeing her first real battle, and so were we.

It was a battle in the open field; for the garrison of St. Loup had sallied confidently out to meet the attack, being used to victories when "witches" were not around. The sally had been re-enforced by troops from the "Paris" bastille, and when we approached the French were getting whipped and were falling back. But when Joan came charging through the disorder with her banner displayed, crying "Forward, men—follow me!" there was a change; the French turned about and surged forward like a solid wave of the sea, and swept the English before them, hacking and slashing, and being hacked and slashed, in a way that was terrible to see.

In the field the Dwarf had no assignment; that is to say, he was not under orders to occupy any particular place, therefore he chose his place for himself, and went ahead of Joan and made a road for her. It was horrible to see the iron helmets fly into fragments under his dreadful axe. He called it cracking nuts, and it looked like that. He made a good road, and paved it well with flesh and iron. Joan and the rest of us followed it so briskly that we outspeeded our forces and had the English behind us as well as before. The knights commanded us to face outwards around Joan, which we did, and then there was work done that was fine to see. One was obliged to respect the Paladin, now. Being right under Joan's exalting and transforming eye, he forgot his native prudence, he forgot his diffidence in the presence of danger, he forgot what fear was, and he never laid about him in his imaginary battles in a more tremendous way than he did in this real one; and wherever he struck there was an enemy the less.

We were in that close place only a few minutes; then our forces to the rear broke through with a great shout and joined us, and then the English fought a retreating fight, but in a fine and gallant way, and we drove them to their fortress foot by foot, they facing us all the time, and their reserves on the walls raining showers of arrows, cross-bow bolts, and stone cannon-balls upon us.

The bulk of the enemy got safely within the works and left us outside with piles of French and English dead and wounded for company—a sickening sight, an awful sight to us youngsters, for our little ambush fights in February had been in the night, and the blood and the mutilations and the dead faces were mercifully dim, whereas we saw these things now for the first time in all their naked ghastliness.

Now arrived Dunois from the city, and plunged through the battle on his foam-flecked horse and galloped up to Joan, saluting, and uttering handsome compliments as he came. He waved his hand toward the distant walls of the city, where a multitude of flags were flaunting gayly in the wind, and said the populace were up there observing her fortunate performance and rejoicing over it, and added that she and the forces would have a great reception now.

"*Now?* Hardly now, Bastard. Not yet!"

"Why not yet? Is there more to be done?"

"More, Bastard? We have but begun! We will take this fortress."

"Ah, you can't be serious! We can't take this place; let me urge you not to make the attempt; it is too desperate. Let me order the forces back."

Joan's heart was overflowing with the joys and enthusiasms of war, and it made her impatient to hear such talk. She cried out—

"Bastard, Bastard, will ye play *always* with these English? Now verily I tell you we will not budge until this place is ours. We will carry it by storm. Sound the charge!"

"Ah, my General—"

"Waste no more time, man—let the bugles sound the assault!" and we saw that strange deep light in her eye which we named the battle-light, and learned to know so well in later fields.

The martial notes pealed out, the troops answered with a yell, and down they came against that formidable work, whose outlines were lost in its own cannon smoke, and whose sides were spouting flame and thunder.

We suffered repulse after repulse, but Joan was here and there and everywhere encouraging the men, and she kept them to their work. During three hours the tide ebbed and flowed, flowed and ebbed; but at last La Hire, who was now come, made a final and resistless charge, and the bastille St. Loup was ours. We gutted it, taking all its stores and artillery, and then destroyed it.

When all our host was shouting itself hoarse with rejoicings, and there went up a cry for the General, for they wanted to praise her and glorify her and do her homage for her victory, we had trouble to find her; and when we did find her, she was off by herself, sitting among a ruck of corpses, with her face in her hands, crying—for she was a young girl, you know, and her hero-heart was a young girl's heart too, with the pity and the tenderness that are natural to it. She was thinking of the mothers of those dead friends and enemies.

Among the prisoners were a number of priests, and Joan took these under her protection and saved their lives. It was urged that they were most probably combatants in disguise, but she said—

"As to that, how can any tell? They wear the livery of God, and if even one of these wears it rightfully, surely it were better that all the guilty should escape than that we have upon our hands the blood of that innocent man. I will lodge them where I lodge, and feed them, and send them away in safety."

We marched back to the city with our crop of cannon and prisoners on view and our banners displayed. Here was the first substantial bit of war-work the imprisoned people had seen in the seven months that the siege had endured, the first chance they had had to rejoice over a French exploit. You may guess that they made good use of it. They and the bells went mad. Joan was their darling now, and the press of people struggling and shouldering each other to get a glimpse of her was so great that we could hardly push our way through the streets at all. Her new name had gone all about, and was on everybody's lips. The Holy Maid of Vaucouleurs was a forgotten title; the city had claimed her for its own, and she was the MAID OF ORLEANS now. It is a happiness to me to remember that I heard that name the first time it was ever uttered. Between that first utterance and the last time it will be uttered on this earth—ah, think how many mouldering ages will lie in that gap!

The Boucher family welcomed her back as if she had been a child of the house, and saved from death against all hope or probability.

They chided her for going into the battle and exposing herself to danger during all those hours. They could not realize that she had meant to carry her warriorship so far, and asked her if it had really been her purpose to go right into the turmoil of the fight, or hadn't she got swept into it by accident and the rush of the troops? They begged her to be more careful another time. It was good advice, maybe, but it fell upon pretty unfruitful soil.

CHAPTER 19

Being worn out with the long fight, we all slept the rest of the afternoon away and two or three hours into the night. Then we got up refreshed, and had supper. As for me, I could have been willing to let the matter of the ghost drop; and the others were of a like mind no doubt, for they talked diligently of the battle and said nothing of that other thing. And indeed it was fine and stirring to hear the Paladin rehearse his deeds and see him pile his dead, fifteen here, eighteen there, and thirty-five yonder; but this only postponed the trouble; it could not do more. He could not go on forever; when he had carried the bastille by assault and eaten up the garrison there was nothing for it but to stop, unless Catherine Boucher would give him a new start and have it all done over again—as we hoped she would, this time—but she was otherwise minded. As soon as there was a good opening and a fair chance, she brought up her unwelcome subject, and we faced it the best we could.

We followed her and her parents to the haunted room at eleven o'clock, with candles, and also with torches to place in the sockets on the walls. It was a big house, with very thick walls, and this room was in a remote part of it which had been left unoccupied for nobody knew how many years, because of its evil repute.

This was a large room, like a salon, and had a big table in it of enduring oak and well preserved; but the chairs were worm-eaten and the tapestry on the walls was rotten and discolored by age. The dusty cobwebs under the ceiling had the look of not having had any business for a century.

Catherine said—

"Tradition says that these ghosts have never been seen—they have merely been heard. It is plain that this room was once larger that it is now, and that the wall at this end was built in some bygone time to make and fence off a narrow room there. There is no communication anywhere with that narrow room, and if it exists—and of that there is no reasonable doubt—it has no light and no air, but is an absolute dungeon. Wait where you are, and take note of what happens."

That was all. Then she and her parents left us. When their footfalls had died out in the distance down the empty stone corridors an uncanny silence and solemnity ensued which was dismaller to me than the mute march past the bastilles. We sat looking vacantly at each other, and it was easy to see that no one there was comfortable. The longer we sat so, the more deadly still that stillness got to be; and when the wind began to moan around the house presently, it made me sick and miserable, and I wished I had been brave enough to be a coward this time, for indeed it is no proper shame to be afraid of ghosts, seeing how helpless the living are in their hands. And then these ghosts were invisible, which made the matter the worse, as it seemed to me. They might be in the room with us at that moment—we could not know. I felt airy touches on my shoulders and my hair, and I shrank from them and cringed, and was not ashamed to show this fear, for I saw the others doing the like, and knew that they were feeling those faint contacts too. As this went on—oh, eternities it seemed, the time dragged so drearily—all those faces became as wax, and I seemed sitting with a congress of the dead.

At last, faint and far and weird and slow, came a "boom!—boom!—boom!"—a distant bell tolling midnight. When the last stroke died, that depressing stillness followed again, and as before I was staring at those waxen faces and feeling those airy touches on my hair and my shoulders once more.

One minute—two minutes—three minutes of this, then we heard a long deep groan, and everybody sprang up and stood, with his legs quaking. It came from that little dungeon. There was a pause, then we heard muffled sobbings, mixed with pitiful ejaculations. Then there was a second voice, low and not distinct, and the one seemed trying to comfort the other; and so the two voices went on, with moanings, and soft sobbings, and, ah, the tones were so full of compassion and sorrow and despair! Indeed, it made one's heart sore to hear it.

But those sounds were so real and so human and so moving that the idea of ghosts passed straight out of our minds, and Sir Jean de Metz spoke out and said—

"Come! we will smash that wall and set those poor captives free. Here, with your axe!"

The Dwarf jumped forward, swinging his great axe with both hands, and others sprang for the torches and brought them. Bang!—whang! —slam!—smash went the ancient bricks, and there was a hole an ox could pass through. We plunged within and held up the torches.

Nothing there but vacancy! On the floor lay a rusty sword and a rotten fan.

Now you know all that I know. Take the pathetic relics, and weave about them the romance of the dungeon's long-vanished inmates as best you can.

CHAPTER 20

The next day Joan wanted to go against the enemy again, but it was the feast of the Ascension, and the holy council of bandit generals were too pious to be willing to profane it with bloodshed. But privately they profaned it with plottings, a sort of industry just in their line. They decided to do the only thing proper to do now in the new circumstances of the case—feign an attack on the most important bastille on the Orleans side, and then, if the English weakened the far more important fortresses on the other side of the river to come to its help, cross in force and capture those works. This would give them the bridge and free communication with the Sologne, which was French territory. They decided to keep this latter part of the programme secret from Joan.

Joan intruded and took them by surprise. She asked them what they were about and what they had resolved upon. They said they had resolved to attack the most important of the English bastilles on the Orleans side next morning—and there the spokesman stopped. Joan said—

"Well, go on."

"There is nothing more. That is all."

"Am I to believe this? That is to say, am I to believe that you have lost your wits?" She turned to Dunois, and said, "Bastard, you have sense, answer me this: if this attack is made and the bastille taken, how much better off would we be than we are now?"

The Bastard hesitated, and then began some rambling talk not quite germane to the question. Joan interrupted him and said—

"That will do, good Bastard, you have answered. Since the Bastard is not able to mention any advantage to be gained by taking that bastille and stopping there, it is not likely that any of you could better the matter. You waste much time here in inventing plans that lead to nothing, and making delays that are a damage. Are you concealing something from me? Bastard, this council has a general plan, I take it; without going into details, what is it?"

"It is the same it was in the beginning, seven months ago—to get provisions in for a long siege, and then sit down and tire the English out."

"In the name of God! As if seven months was not enough, you want to provide for a year of it. Now ye shall drop these pusillanimous dreams—the English shall go in three days!"

Several exclaimed—

"Ah, General, General, be prudent!"

"Be prudent and starve? Do ye call that war? I tell you this, if you do not already know it: The new circumstances have changed the face of matters. The true point of attack has shifted; it is on the other side of the river, now. One must take the fortifications that command the bridge. The English know that if we are not fools and cowards we will try to do that. They are grateful for your piety in wasting this day. They will re-enforce the bridge forts from this side to-night, knowing what ought to happen to-morrow. You have but lost a day and made our task harder, for we *will* cross and take the bridge forts. Bastard, tell me the truth—does not this council know that there is no other course for us than the one I am speaking of?"

Dunois conceded that the council did know it to be the most desirable, but considered it impracticable; and he excused the council as well as he could by saying that inasmuch as nothing was really and rationally to be hoped for but a long continuance of the siege and wearying out of the English, they were naturally a little afraid of Joan's impetuous notions. He said—

"You see, we are sure that the waiting game is the best, whereas you would carry everything by storm."

"That I would!—and moreover that I will! You have my orders—here and now. We will move upon the forts of the south bank to-morrow at dawn."

"And carry them by storm?"

"Yes, carry them by storm!"

La Hire came clanking in, and heard the last remark. He cried out—

"By *my baton*, that is the music I love to hear! Yes, that is the right tune and the beautiful words, my General—we will carry them by storm!"

He saluted in his large way and came up and shook Joan by the hand.

Some member of the council was heard to say—

"It follows, then, that we must begin with the bastille St. John, and that will give the English time to—"

Joan turned and said—

"Give yourselves no uneasiness about the bastille St. John. The English will know enough to retire from it and fall back on the bridge bastilles when they see us coming." She added, with a touch of sarcasm, "Even a war-council would know enough to do that, itself."

Then she took her leave. La Hire made this general remark to the council:

"She is a child, and that is all ye seem to see. Keep to that superstition if you must, but you perceive that this child understands this complex game of war as well as any of you; and if you want my opinion without the trouble of asking for it, here you have it without ruffles or embroidery—by God, I think she can teach the best of you how to *play* it!"

Joan had spoken truly; the sagacious English saw that the policy of the French had undergone a revolution; that the policy of paltering and dawdling was ended; that in place of taking blows, blows were to be struck, now; therefore they made ready for the new state of things by transferring heavy re-enforcements to the bastilles of the south bank from those of the north.

The city learned the great news that once more in French history, after all these humiliating years, France was going to take the offensive; that France, so used to retreating, was going to advance; that France, so long accustomed to skulking, was going to face about and strike. The joy of the people passed all bounds. The city walls were black with them to see the army march out in the morning in that strange new position—its front, not its tail, toward an English camp. You shall imagine for yourselves what the excitement was like and how it expressed itself, when Joan rode out at the head of the host with her banner floating above her.

We crossed the river in strong force, and a tedious long job it was, for the boats were small and not numerous. Our landing on the island of St. Aignan was not disputed. We threw a bridge of a few boats across the narrow channel thence to the south shore and took up our march in good order and unmolested; for although there was a fortress there—St. John—the English vacated and destroyed it and fell back on the bridge forts below as soon as our first boats were seen to leave the Orleans shore; which was what Joan had said would happen, when she was disputing with the council.

We moved down the shore and Joan planted her standard before the bastille of the Augustins, the first of the formidable works that protected the end of the bridge. The trumpets sounded the assault, and two charges followed in handsome style; but we were too weak, as yet, for our main body was still lagging behind. Before we could gather for a third assault the garrison of St. Privé were seen coming up to re-enforce the big bastille. They came on a run, and the Augustins sallied out, and both forces came against us with a rush, and sent our small army flying in a panic, and followed us, slashing and slaying, and shouting jeers and insults at us.

Joan was doing her best to rally the men, but their wits were gone, their hearts were dominated for the moment by the old-time dread of the English. Joan's temper flamed up, and she halted and commanded the trumpets to sound the advance. Then she wheeled about and cried out—

"If there is but a dozen of you that are not cowards, it is enough—follow me!"

Away she went, and after her a few dozen who had heard her words and been inspired by them. The pursuing force was astonished to see her sweeping down upon them with this handful of men, and it was their turn now to experience a grisly fright—surely this *is* a witch, this is a child of Satan! That was their thought—and without stopping to analyze the matter they turned and fled in a panic.

Our flying squadrons heard the bugle and turned to look; and when they saw the Maid's banner speeding in the other direction and the enemy scrambling ahead of it in disorder, their courage returned and they came scouring after us.

La Hire heard it and hurried his force forward and caught up with us just as we were planting our banner again before the ramparts of the Augustins. We were strong enough now. We had a long and tough piece of work before us, but we carried it through before night, Joan keeping us hard at it, and she and La Hire saying we were able to take that big bastille, and *must*. The English fought like—well, they fought like the English; when that is said, there is no more to say. We made assault after assault, through the smoke and flame and the deafening cannon-blasts, and at last as the sun was sinking we carried the place with a rush, and planted our standard on its walls.

The Augustins was ours. The Tourelles must be ours too, if we would free the bridge and raise the siege. We had achieved one great undertaking, Joan was determined to accomplish the other. We must lie on our arms where we were, hold fast to what we had got, and be ready for business in the morning. So Joan was not minded to let the men be demoralized by pillage and riot and carousings; she had the Augustins burned, with all its stores in it, excepting the artillery and ammunition.

Everybody was tired out with this long day's hard work, and of course this was the case with Joan; still, she wanted to stay with the army before the Tourelles, to be ready for the assault in the morning. The chiefs argued with her, and at last persuaded her to go home and prepare for the great work by taking proper rest, and also by having a leech look to a wound which she had received in her foot. So we crossed with them and went home.

Just as usual, we found the town in a fury of joy, all the bells clanging, everybody shouting, and several people drunk. We never went out or came in without furnishing good and sufficient reasons for one of these pleasant tempests, and so the tempest was always on hand. There had been a blank absence of reasons for this sort of upheavals for the past seven months, therefore the people took to the upheavals with all the more relish on that account.

CHAPTER 21

To get away from the usual crowd of visitors and have a rest, Joan went with Catherine straight to the apartment which the two occupied together, and there they took their supper and there the wound was dressed. But then, instead of going to bed, Joan, weary as she was, sent the Dwarf for me, in spite of Catherine's protests and persuasions. She said she had something on her mind, and must send a courier to Domremy with a letter for our old Père Fronte to read to her mother. I came, and she began to dictate. After some loving words and greetings to her mother and the family, came this:

"But the thing which moves me to write now, is to say that when you presently hear that I am wounded, you shall give yourself no concern about it, and refuse faith to any that shall try to make you believe it is serious."

She was going on, when Catherine spoke up and said:

"Ah, but it will fright her so to read these words. Strike them out, Joan, strike them out, and wait only one day—two days at most—then write and say your foot *was* wounded but is well again—for it will surely be well then, or very near it. Don't distress her, Joan; do as I say."

A laugh like the laugh of the old days, the impulsive free laugh of an untroubled spirit, a laugh like a chime of bells, was Joan's answer; then she said—

"My foot? Why should I write about such a scratch as that? I was not thinking of it, dear heart."

"Child, have you another wound and a worse, and have not spoken of it? What have you been dreaming about, that you—"

She had jumped up, full of vague fears, to have the leech called back at once, but Joan laid her hand upon her arm and made her sit down again, saying—

"There, now, be tranquil, there is no other wound, as yet; I am writing about one which I shall get when we storm that bastille tomorrow."

Catherine had the look of one who is trying to understand a puzzling proposition but cannot quite do it. She said, in a distraught fashion—

"A wound which you are *going* to get? But—but why grieve your mother when it—when it may not happen?"

"*May* not? Why, it *will*."

The puzzle was a puzzle still. Catherine said in that same abstracted way as before—

"*Will*. It is a strong word. I cannot seem to—my mind is not able to take hold of this. Oh, Joan, such a presentiment is a dreadful thing—it takes one's peace and courage all away. Cast it from you!—drive it out! It will make your whole night miserable, and to no good; for we will hope—"

"But it isn't a presentiment—it is a fact. And it will not make me miserable. It is uncertainties that do that, but this is not an uncertainty."

"Joan, do you *know* it is going to happen?"

"Yes, I know it. My Voices told me."

"Ah," said Catherine, resignedly, "if *they* told you— But are you sure it was they?—quite sure?"

"Yes, quite. It will happen—there is no doubt."

"It is dreadful! Since when have you known it?"

"Since—I think it is several weeks." Joan turned to me. "Louis, you will remember. How long is it?"

"Your Excellency spoke of it first to the King, in Chinon," I answered; "that was as much as seven weeks ago. You spoke of it again the 20th of April, and also the 22d, two weeks ago, as I see by my record here."

These marvels disturbed Catherine profoundly, but I had long ceased to be surprised at them. One can get used to anything in this world. Catherine said—

"And it is to happen to-morrow?—always to-morrow? Is it the same date always? There has been no mistake, and no confusion?"

"No," Joan said, "the 7th of May is the date—there is no other."

"Then you shall not go a step out of this house till that awful day is gone by! You will not dream of it, Joan, *will* you?—promise that you will stay with us."

But Joan was not persuaded. She said—

"It would not help the matter, dear good friend. The wound is to come, and come to-morrow. If I do not seek it, it will seek me. My duty calls me to that place to-morrow; I should have to go if my death were waiting for me there; shall I stay away for only a wound? Oh no, we must try to do better than that."

"Then you are determined to go?"

"Of a certainty, yes. There is only one thing that I can do for France —hearten her soldiers for battle and victory." She thought a moment, then added, "However, one should not be unreasonable, and I would do much to please you, who are so good to me. Do you love France?"

I wondered what she might be contriving now, but I saw no clew. Catherine said, reproachfully—

"Ah, what have I done to deserve this question?"

"Then you do love France. I had not doubted it, dear. Do not be hurt, but answer me—have you ever told a lie?"

"In my life I have not wilfully told a lie—fibs, but no lies."

"That is sufficient. You love France and do not tell lies; therefore I will trust you. I will go or I will stay, as you shall decide."

"Oh, I thank you from my heart, Joan! How good and dear it is of you to do this for me! Oh, you shall stay, and not go!"

In her delight she flung her arms about Joan's neck and squandered endearments upon her the least of which would have made me rich, but as it was, they only made me realize how poor I was—how miserably poor in what I would most have prized in this world. Joan said—

"Then you will send word to my headquarters that I am not going?"

"Oh, gladly. Leave that to me."

"It is good of you. And how will you word it?—for it must have proper official form. Shall I word it for you?"

"Oh, do—for you know about these solemn procedures and stately proprieties, and I have had no experience."

"Then word it like this: 'The chief of staff is commanded to make known to the King's forces in garrison and in the field, that the General-in-Chief of the Armies of France will not face the English on the morrow, she being afraid she may get hurt. Signed, JOAN OF ARC, by the hand of CATHERINE BOUCHER, who loves France.'"

There was a pause—a silence of the sort that tortures one into stealing a glance to see how the situation looks, and I did that. There was a loving smile on Joan's face, but the color was mounting in crimson waves into Catherine's, and her lips were quivering and the tears gathering; then she said—

"Oh, I am so ashamed of myself!—and you are so noble and brave and wise, and I am so paltry—so paltry and such a fool!" and she broke down and began to cry, and I did so want to take her in my arms and comfort her, but Joan did it, and of course I said nothing. Joan did it well, and most sweetly and tenderly, but I could have done it as well, though I knew it would be foolish and out of place to suggest such a thing, and might make an awkwardness too, and be embarrassing to us all, so I did not offer, and I hope I did right and for the best, though I could not know, and was many times tortured with doubts afterwards as having perhaps let a chance pass which might have changed all my life and made it happier and more beautiful than, alas, it turned out to be. For this reason I grieve yet, when I think of that scene, and do not like to call it up out of the deeps of my memory because of the pangs it brings.

Well, well, a good and wholesome thing is a little harmless fun in this world; it tones a body up and keeps him human and prevents him from souring. To set that little trap for Catherine was as good and effective a way as any to show her what a grotesque thing she was asking of Joan. It *was* a funny idea, now, wasn't it, when you look at it all around? Even Catherine dried up her tears and laughed when she thought of the English getting hold of the French Commander-in-Chief's reason for staying out of a battle. She granted that they could have a good time over a thing like that.

We got to work on the letter again, and of course did not have to strike out the passage about the wound. Joan was in fine spirits; but when she got to sending messages to this, that, and the other old playmate and friend, it brought our village and the Fairy Tree and the flowery plain and the browsing sheep and all the peaceful beauty of our old humble home-place back, and the familiar names began to tremble on her lips; and when she got to Haumette and Little Mengette it was no use, her voice broke and she couldn't go on. She waited a moment, then said—

"Give them my love—my warm love—my deep love—oh, out of my heart of hearts! I shall never see our home any more."

Now came Pasquerel, Joan's confessor, and introduced a gallant knight, the Sire de Rais, who had been sent with a message. He said he was instructed to say that the council had decided that enough had been done for the present; that it would be safest and best to be content with what God had already done; that the city was now well victualled and able to stand a long siege; that the wise course must necessarily be to withdraw the troops from the other side of the river and resume the defensive—therefore they had decided accordingly.

"The incurable cowards!" exclaimed Joan. "So it was to get me away from my men that they pretended so much solicitude about my fatigue. Take this message back, not to the council—I have no speeches for those disguised ladies' maids—but to the Bastard and La Hire, who are men. Tell them the army is to remain where it is, and I hold them responsible if this command miscarries. And say the offensive will be resumed in the morning. You may go, good sir."

Then she said to her priest—

"Rise early, and be by me all the day. There will be much work on my hands, and I shall be hurt between my neck and my shoulder."

CHAPTER 22

We were up at dawn, and after mass we started. In the hall we met the master of the house, who was grieved, good man, to see Joan going breakfastless to such a day's work, and begged her to wait and eat, but she couldn't afford the time—that is to say, she couldn't afford the patience, she being in such a blaze of anxiety to get at that last remaining bastille which stood between her and the completion of the first great step in the rescue and redemption of France. Boucher put in another plea:

"But think—we poor beleaguered citizens who have hardly known the flavor of fish for these many months, have spoil of that sort again, and we owe it to you. There's a noble shad for breakfast; wait—be persuaded."

Joan said—

"Oh, there's going to be fish in plenty; when this day's work is done the whole river-front will be yours to do as you please with."

"Ah, your Excellency will do well, *that* I know; but we don't require quite that much, even of you; you shall have a month for it in place of a day. Now be beguiled—wait and eat. There's a saying that he that would cross a river twice in the same day in a boat, will do well to eat fish for luck, lest he have an accident."

"That doesn't fit my case, for to-day I cross but once in a boat."

"Oh, don't say that. Aren't you coming back to us?"

"Yes, but not in a boat."

"How, then?"

"By the bridge."

"Listen to that—by the bridge! Now stop this jesting, dear General, and do as I would have you. It's a noble fish."

"Be good, then, and save me some for supper; and I will bring one of those Englishmen with me and he shall have his share."

"Ah, well, have your way if you must. But he that fasts must attempt but little and stop early. When shall you be back?"

"When I've raised the siege of Orleans. FORWARD!"

We were off. The streets were full of citizens and of groups and squads of soldiers, but the spectacle was melancholy. There was not a smile anywhere, but only universal gloom. It was as if some vast calamity had smitten all hope and cheer dead. We were not used to this, and were astonished. But when they saw the Maid, there was an immediate stir, and the eager question flew from mouth to mouth—

"Where is she going? Whither is she bound?"

Joan heard it, and called out—

"Whither would ye suppose? I am going to take the Tourelles."

It would not be possible for any to describe how those few words turned that mourning into joy—into exaltation—into frenzy; and how a storm of huzzahs burst out and swept down the streets in every direction and woke those corpse-like multitudes to vivid life and action and turmoil in a moment. The soldiers broke from the crowd and came flocking to our standard, and many of the citizens ran and got pikes and halberds and joined us. As we moved on, our numbers increased steadily, and the hurrahing continued—yes, we moved through a solid cloud of noise, as you may say, and all the windows on both sides contributed to it, for they were filled with excited people.

You see, the council had closed the Burgundy gate and placed a strong force there, under that stout soldier Raoul de Gaucourt, Bailly of Orleans, with orders to prevent Joan from getting out and resuming the attack on the Tourelles, and this shameful thing had plunged the city into sorrow and despair. But that feeling was gone now. They believed the Maid was a match for the council, and they were right.

When we reached the gate, Joan told Gaucourt to open it and let her pass.

He said it would be impossible to do this, for his orders were from the council and were strict. Joan said—

"There is no authority above mine but the King's. If you have an order from the King, produce it."

"I cannot claim to have an order from him, General."

"Then make way, or take the consequences!"

He began to argue the case, for he was like the rest of the tribe, always ready to fight with words, not acts; but in the midst of his gabble Joan interrupted with the terse order—

"Charge!"

We came with a rush, and brief work we made of that small job. It was good to see the Bailly's surprise. He was not used to this unsentimental promptness. He said afterwards that he was cut off in the midst of what he was saying—in the midst of an argument by which he could have proved that he could not let Joan pass—an argument which Joan could not have answered.

"Still, it appears she did answer it," said the person he was talking to.

We swung through the gate in great style, with a vast accession of noise, the most of which was laughter, and soon our van was over the river and moving down against the Tourelles.

First we must take a supporting work called a boulevard, and which was otherwise nameless, before we could assault the great bastille. Its rear communicated with the bastille by a drawbridge, under which ran a swift and deep strip of the Loire. The boulevard was strong, and Dunois doubted our ability to take it, but Joan had no such doubt. She pounded it with artillery all the forenoon, then about noon she ordered an assault and led it herself. We poured into the fosse through the smoke and a tempest of missiles, and Joan, shouting encouragements to her men, started to climb a scaling-ladder, when that misfortune happened which we knew was to happen—the iron bolt from an arbalest struck between her neck and her shoulder, and tore its way down through her armor. When she felt the sharp pain and saw her blood gushing over her breast, she was frightened, poor girl, and as she sank to the ground she began to cry, bitterly.

The English sent up a glad shout and came surging down in strong force to take her, and then for a few minutes the might of both adversaries was concentrated upon that spot. Over her and about her, English and French fought with desperation—for she stood for France, indeed she *was* France to both sides—whichever won her won France, *and could keep it forever.* Right there in that small spot, and in ten minutes by the clock, the fate of France, for all time, was to be decided, and *was* decided.

If the English had captured Joan then, Charles VII. would have flown the country, the Treaty of Troyes would have held good, and France, already English property, would have become, without further dispute, an English province, to so remain until the Judgment Day. A nationality and a kingdom were at stake there, and no more time to decide it in than it takes to hard-boil an egg. It was the most momentous ten minutes that the clock has ever ticked in France, or ever will. Whenever you read in histories about hours or days or weeks in which the fate of one or another nation hung in the balance, do not you fail to remember, nor your French hearts to beat the quicker for the remembrance, the ten minutes that France, called otherwise Joan of Arc, lay bleeding in the fosse that day, with two nations struggling over her for her possession.

And you will not forget the Dwarf. For he stood over her, and did the work of any six of the others. He swung his axe with both hands; whenever it came down, he said those two words, "For France!" and a splintered helmet flew like egg-shells, and the skull that carried it had learned its manners and would offend the French no more. He piled a bulwark of iron-clad dead in front of him and fought from behind it; and at last when the victory was ours we closed about him, shielding him, and he ran up a ladder with Joan as easily as another man would carry a child, and bore her out of the battle, a great crowd following and anxious, for she was drenched with blood to her feet, half of it her own and the other half English, for bodies had fallen across her as she lay and had poured their red life-streams over her. One couldn't see the white armor now, with that awful dressing over it.

The iron bolt was still in the wound—some say it projected out behind the shoulder. It may be—I did not wish to see, and did not try to. It was pulled out, and the pain made Joan cry again, poor thing. Some say she pulled it out herself because others refused, saying they could not bear to hurt her. As to this I do not know; I only know it was pulled out, and that the wound was treated with oil and properly dressed.

Joan lay on the grass, weak and suffering, hour after hour, but still insisting that the fight go on. Which it did, but not to much purpose, for it was only under her eye that men were heroes and not afraid.

They were like the Paladin; I think he was afraid of his shadow—I mean in the afternoon, when it was very big and long; but when he was under Joan's eye and the inspiration of her great spirit, what was he afraid of? Nothing in this world—and that is just the truth.

Toward night Dunois gave it up. Joan heard the bugles.

"What!" she cried. "Sounding the retreat!"

Her wound was forgotten in a moment. She countermanded the order, and sent another, to the officer in command of a battery, to stand ready to fire five shots in quick succession. This was a signal to a force on the Orleans side of the river under La Hire, who was not, as some of the histories say, with *us*. It was to be given whenever Joan should feel sure the boulevard was about to fall into her hands—then that force must make a counter-attack on the Tourelles by way of the bridge.

Joan mounted her horse, now, with her staff about her, and when our people saw us coming they raised a great shout, and were at once eager for another assault on the boulevard. Joan rode straight to the fosse where she had received her wound, and standing there in the rain of bolts and arrows, she ordered the Paladin to let her long standard blow free, and to note when its fringes should touch the fortress. Presently he said—

"It touches."

"Now, then," said Joan to the waiting battalions, "the place is yours—enter in! Bugles, sound the assault! Now, then—all together—*go!*"

And go it was. You never saw anything like it. We swarmed up the ladders and over the battlements like a wave—and the place was our property. Why, one might live a thousand years and never see so gorgeous a thing as that again. There, hand to hand, we fought like wild beasts, for there was no give-up to those English—there was no way to convince one of those people but to kill him, and even then he doubted. At least so it was thought, in those days, and maintained by many.

We were busy and never heard the five cannon-shots fired, but they *were* fired a moment after Joan had ordered the assault; and so, while we were hammering and being hammered in the smaller fortress, the reserve on the Orleans side poured across the bridge and attacked the Tourelles from that side. A fire-boat was brought down and moored under the drawbridge which connected the Tourelles with our boulevard; wherefore, when at last we drove our English ahead of us and they tried to cross that drawbridge and join their friends in the Tourelles, the burning timbers gave way under them and emptied them in a mass into the river in their heavy armor—and a pitiful sight it was to see brave men die such a death as that.

"Ah, God, pity them!" said Joan, and wept to see that sorrowful spectacle. She said those gentle words and wept those compassionate tears although one of those perishing men had grossly insulted her with a coarse name three days before, when she had sent him a message asking him to surrender. That was their leader, Sir William Glasdale, a most valorous knight. He was clothed all in steel; so he plunged under the water like a lance, and of course came up no more.

We soon patched a sort of bridge together and threw ourselves against the last stronghold of the English power that barred Orleans from friends and supplies. Before the sun was quite down, Joan's for-ever memorable day's work was finished, her banner floated from the fortress of the Tourelles, her promise was fulfilled, she had raised the siege of Orleans!

The seven months' beleaguerment was ended, the thing which the first generals of France had called impossible was accomplished; in spite of all that the King's ministers and war-councils could do to prevent it, this little country maid of seventeen had carried her immortal task through, and had done it in four days!

Good news travels fast, sometimes, as well as bad. By the time we were ready to start homewards by the bridge the whole city of Orleans was one red flame of bonfires, and the heavens blushed with satisfaction to see it; and the booming and bellowing of cannon and the banging of bells surpassed by great odds anything that even Orleans had attempted before in the way of noise.

When we arrived—well, there is no describing that. Why, those acres of people that we ploughed through shed tears enough to raise the river; there was not a face in the glare of those fires that hadn't tears streaming down it; and if Joan's feet had not been protected by iron they would have kissed them off of her. "Welcome! welcome to the Maid of Orleans!" That was the cry; I heard it a hundred thousand times. "Welcome to *our* Maid!" some of them worded it.

No other girl in all history has ever reached such a summit of glory as Joan of Arc reached that day. And do you think it turned her head, and that she sat up to enjoy that delicious music of homage and applause? No; another girl would have done that, but not this one. That was the greatest heart and the simplest that ever beat. She went straight to bed and to sleep, like any tired child; and when the people found she was wounded and would rest, they shut off all passage and traffic in that region and stood guard themselves the whole night through, to see that her slumbers were not disturbed. They said, "She has given us peace, she shall have peace herself."

All knew that that region would be empty of English next day, and all said that neither the present citizens nor their posterity would ever cease to hold that day sacred to the memory of Joan of Arc. That word has been true for more than sixty years; it will continue so always. Orleans will never forget the 8th of May, nor ever fail to celebrate it. It is Joan of Arc's day—and holy.*

CHAPTER 23

In the earliest dawn of the morning, Talbot and his English forces evacuated their bastilles and marched away, not stopping to burn, destroy, or carry off anything, but leaving their fortresses just as they were, provisioned, armed, and equipped for a long siege. It was difficult for the people to believe that this great thing had really happened; that they were actually free once more, and might go and come through any gate they pleased, with none to molest or forbid; that the terrible Talbot, that scourge of the French, that man whose mere name had been able to annul the effectiveness of French armies, was gone, vanquished, retreating—driven away by a girl.

The city emptied itself. Out of every gate the crowds poured. They swarmed about the English bastilles like an invasion of ants, but noisier than those creatures, and carried off the artillery and stores, then turned all those dozen fortresses into monster bonfires, imitation volcanoes whose lofty columns of thick smoke seemed supporting the arch of the sky.

The delight of the children took another form. To some of the younger ones seven months was a sort of lifetime. They had forgotten what grass was like, and the velvety green meadows seemed paradise to their surprised and happy eyes after the long habit of seeing nothing but dirty lanes and streets. It was a wonder to them—those spacious reaches of open country to run and dance and tumble and frolic in, after their dull and joyless captivity; so they scampered far and wide over the fair regions on both sides of the river, and came back at eventide weary, but laden with flowers and flushed with new health drawn from the fresh country air and the vigorous exercise.

* It is still celebrated every year with civic and military pomps and solemnities. —TRANSLATOR.

After the burnings, the grown folk followed Joan from church to church and put in the day in thanksgivings for the city's deliverance, and at night they fêted her and her generals and illuminated the town, and high and low gave themselves up to festivities and rejoicings. By the time the populace were fairly in bed, toward dawn, we were in the saddle and away toward Tours to report to the King.

That was a march which would have turned any one's head but Joan's. We moved between emotional ranks of grateful country people all the way. They crowded about Joan to touch her feet, her horse, her armor, and they even knelt in the road and kissed her horse's hoof-prints.

The land was full of her praises. The most illustrious chiefs of the Church wrote to the King extolling the Maid, comparing her to the saints and heroes of the Bible, and warning him not to let "unbelief, ingratitude, or other injustice" hinder or impair the divine help sent through her. One might think there was a touch of prophecy in that, and we will let it go at that; but to my mind it had its inspiration in those great men's accurate knowledge of the King's trivial and treacherous character.

The King had come to Tours to meet Joan. At the present day this poor thing is called Charles the Victorious, an account of victories which other people won for him, but in our time we had a private name for him which described him better, and was sanctified to him by personal deserving–Charles the Base. When we entered the presence he sat throned, with his tinselled snobs and dandies around him. He looked like a forked carrot, so tightly did his clothing fit him from his waist down; he wore shoes with a rope-like pliant toe a foot long that had to be hitched up to the knee to keep it out of the way; he had on a crimson velvet cape that came no lower than his elbows; on his head he had a tall felt thing like a thimble, with a feather in its jewelled band that stuck up like a pen from an inkhorn, and from under that thimble his bush of stiff hair stuck down to his shoulders, curving outwards at the bottom, so that the cap and the hair together made the head like a shuttlecock. All the materials of his dress were rich, and all the colors brilliant. In his lap he cuddled a miniature greyhound that snarled, lifting its lip and showing its white teeth whenever any slight movement disturbed it. The King's dandies were dressed in about the same fashion as himself, and when I remembered that Joan had called the war-council of Orleans "disguised ladies' maids," it reminded me of people who squander all their money on a trifle and then haven't anything to invest when they come across a better chance; that name ought to have been saved for these creatures.

Joan fell on her knees before the majesty of France, and the other frivolous animal in his lap—a sight which it pained me to see. What had that man done for his country or for anybody in it, that she or any other person should kneel to him? But she—she had just done the only great deed that had been done for France in fifty years, and had consecrated it with the libation of her blood. The positions should have been reversed.

However, to be fair, one must grant that Charles acquitted himself very well for the most part, on that occasion—very much better than he was in the habit of doing. He passed his pup to a courtier, and took off his cap to Joan as if she had been a queen. Then he stepped from his throne and raised her, and showed quite a spirited and manly joy and gratitude in welcoming her and thanking her for her extraordinary achievement in his service. My prejudices are of a later date than that. If he had continued as he was at that moment, I should not have acquired them.

He acted handsomely. He said—

"You shall not kneel to me, my matchless General; you have wrought royally, and royal courtesies are your due." Noticing that she was pale, he said, "But you must not stand; you have lost blood for France, and your wound is yet green—come." He led her to a seat and sat down by her. "Now, then, speak out frankly, as to one who owes you much and freely confesses it before all this courtly assemblage. What shall be your reward? Name it."

I was ashamed of him. And yet that was not fair, for how could he be expected to know this marvellous child in these few weeks, when we who thought we had known her all her life were daily seeing the clouds uncover some new altitudes of her character whose existence was not suspected by us before? But we are all that way: when *we* know a thing we have only scorn for other people who don't happen to know it. And I was ashamed of these courtiers, too, for the way they licked their chops, so to speak, as envying Joan her great chance, they not knowing her any better than the King did. A blush began to rise in Joan's cheeks at the thought that she was working for her country for pay, and she dropped her head and tried to hide her face, as girls always do when they find themselves blushing; no one knows why they do, but they do, and the more they blush the more they fail to get reconciled to it, and the more they can't bear to have people look at them when they are doing it. The King made it a great deal worse by calling attention to it, which is the unkindest thing a person can do when a girl is blushing; sometimes, when there is a big crowd of strangers, it is even likely to make her cry if she is as young as Joan was. God knows the reason for this, it is hidden from men. As for me, I would as soon blush as sneeze; in fact, I would rather. However, these meditations are not of consequence: I will go on with what I was saying. The King rallied her for blushing, and this brought up the rest of the blood and turned her face to fire. Then he was sorry, seeing what he had done, and tried to make her comfortable by saying the blush was exceedingly becoming to her and not to mind it—which caused even the dog to notice it now, so of course the red in Joan's face turned to purple, and the tears overflowed and ran down—I could have told anybody that that would happen. The King was distressed, and saw that the best thing to do would be to get away from this subject, so he began to say the finest kind of things about Joan's capture of the Tourelles, and presently when she was more composed he mentioned the reward again and pressed her to name it. Everybody listened with anxious interest to hear what her claim was going to be, but when her answer came their faces showed that the thing she asked for was not what they had been expecting.

"Oh, dear and gracious Dauphin, I have but one desire—only one. If—"

"Do not be afraid, my child—name it."

"That you will not delay a day. My army is strong and valiant, and eager to finish its work—march with me to Rheims and receive your crown."

You could see the indolent King shrink, in his butterfly clothes.

"To Rheims—oh, impossible, my General! *We* march through the heart of England's power?"

Could those be French faces there? Not one of them lighted in response to the girl's brave proposition, but all promptly showed satisfaction in the King's objection. Leave this silken idleness for the rude contact of war? None of these butterflies desired that. They passed their jewelled comfit-boxes one to another and whispered their content in the head butterfly's practical prudence. Joan pleaded with the King, saying—

"Ah, I pray you do not throw away this perfect opportunity. Everything is favorable—everything. It is as if the circumstances were specially made for it. The spirits of our army are exalted with victory, those of the English forces depressed by defeat. Delay will change this. Seeing us hesitate to follow up our advantage, our men will wonder, doubt, lose confidence, and the English will wonder, gather courage, and be bold again. Now is the time—prithee let us march!"

The King shook his head, and La Tremouille, being asked for an opinion, eagerly furnished it:

"Sire, all prudence is against it. Think of the English strongholds along the Loire; think of those that lie between us and Rheims!"

He was going on, but Joan cut him short, and said, turning to him—

"If we wait, they will all be strengthened, re-enforced. Will that advantage us?"

"Why—no."

"Then what is your suggestion?—what is it that you would propose to do?"

"My judgment is to wait."

"Wait for what?"

The minister was obliged to hesitate, for he knew of no explanation that would sound well. Moreover, he was not used to being catechised in this fashion, with the eyes of a crowd of people on him, so he was irritated, and said—

"Matters of state are not proper matters for public discussion."

Joan said, placidly—

"I have to beg your pardon. My trespass came of ignorance. I did not know that matters connected with your department of the government were matters of state."

The minister lifted his brows in amused surprise, and said, with a touch of sarcasm—

"I am the King's chief minister, and yet you had the impression that matters connected with my department are not matters of state? Pray how is that?"

Joan replied, indifferently—

"Because there is no state."

"No state!"

"No, sir, there is no state, and no use for a minister. France is shrunk to a couple of acres of ground; a sheriff's constable could take care of it; its affairs are not matters of state. The term is too large."

The King did not blush, but burst into a hearty, careless laugh, and the court laughed too, but prudently turned its head and did it silently. La Tremouille was angry, and opened his mouth to speak, but the King put up his hand, and said—

"There—I take her under the royal protection. She has spoken the truth, the ungilded truth—how seldom I hear it! With all this tinsel on me and all this tinsel about me, I am but a sheriff after all—a poor shabby two-acre sheriff—and you are but a constable," and he laughed his cordial laugh again. "Joan, my frank, honest General, *will* you name your reward? I would ennoble you. You shall quarter the crown and the lilies of France for blazon, and with them your victorious sword to defend them—speak the word."

It made an eager buzz of surprise and envy in the assemblage, but Joan shook her head and said—

"Ah, I cannot, dear and noble Dauphin. To be allowed to work for France, to spend one's self for France, is itself so supreme a reward that nothing can add to it—nothing. Give me the one reward I ask, the dearest of all rewards, the highest in your gift—march with me to Rheims and receive your crown. I will beg it on my knees."

But the King put his hand on her arm, and there was a really brave awakening in his voice and a manly fire in his eye when he said—

"No; sit. You have conquered me—it shall be as you—"

But a warning sign from his minister halted him, and he added, to the relief of the Court—

"Well, well, we will think of it, we will think it over and see. Does that content you, impulsive little soldier?"

The first part of the speech sent a glow of delight to Joan's face, but the end of it quenched it and she looked sad, and the tears gathered in her eyes. After a moment she spoke out with what seemed a sort of terrified impulse, and said—

"Oh, use me; I beseech you, use me—there is but little time!"

"But little time?"

"Only a year—I shall last only a year."

"Why, child, there are fifty good years in that compact little body yet."

"Oh, you err, indeed you do. In one little year the end will come. Ah, the time is so short, so short; the moments are flying, and so much to be done. Oh, use me, and quickly—it is life or death for France."

Even those insects were sobered by her impassioned words. The King looked very grave—grave, and strongly impressed. His eyes lit suddenly with an eloquent fire, and he rose and drew his sword and raised it aloft; then he brought it slowly down upon Joan's shoulder and said:

"Ah, thou art so simple, so true, so great, so noble—and by this accolade I join thee to the nobility of France, thy fitting place! And for thy sake I do hereby ennoble all thy family and all thy kin; and all their descendants born in wedlock, not only in the male but also in the female line. And more!—more! To distinguish thy house and honor it above all others, we add a privilege never accorded to any before in the history of these dominions: the females of thy line shall have and hold the right to ennoble their husbands when these shall be of inferior degree." [Astonishment and envy flared up in every countenance when the words were uttered which conferred this extraordinary grace. The King paused and looked around upon these signs with quite evident satisfaction.] "Rise, Joan of Arc, now and henceforth surnamed *Du Lis,* in grateful acknowledgment of the good blow which you have struck for the lilies of France; and they, and the royal crown, and your own victorious sword, fit and fair company for each other, shall be grouped in your escutcheon and be and remain the symbol of your high nobility forever."

As my lady Du Lis rose, the gilded children of privilege pressed forward to welcome her to their sacred ranks and call her by her new name; but she was troubled, and said these honors were not meet for one of her lowly birth and station, and by their kind grace she would remain simple Joan of Arc, nothing more—and so be called.

Nothing more! As if there *could* be anything more, anything higher, anything greater! My lady Du Lis—why, it was tinsel, petty, perishable. But—JOAN OF ARC! The mere sound of it sets one's pulses leaping.

CHAPTER 24

It was vexatious to see what a to-do the whole town, and next the whole country, made over the news. Joan of Arc ennobled by the King! People went dizzy with wonder and delight over it. You cannot imagine how she was gaped at, stared at, envied. Why, one would have supposed that some great and fortunate thing had happened to her. But *we* did not think any great things of it. To our minds no mere human hand could add a glory to Joan of Arc. To us she was the sun soaring in the heavens, and her new nobility a candle atop of it; to us it was swallowed up and lost in her own light. And she was as indifferent to it and as unconscious of it as the other sun would have been.

But it was different with her brothers. They were proud and happy in their new dignity, which was quite natural. And Joan was glad it had been conferred, when she saw how pleased they were. It was a clever thought in the King to outflank her scruples by marching on them under shelter of her love for her family and her kin.

Jean and Pierre sported their coat-of-arms right away; and their society was courted by everybody, the nobles and commons alike. The Standard-bearer said, with some touch of bitterness, that he could see that they just felt good to be alive, they were so soaked with the comfort of their glory; and didn't like to sleep at all, because when they were asleep they didn't know they were noble, and so sleep was a clean loss of time. And then he said—

"They can't take precedence of me in military functions and state ceremonies, but when it comes to civil ones and society affairs I judge they'll cuddle coolly in behind you and the knights, and Noël and I will have to walk behind *them*—hey?"

"Yes," I said, "I think you are right."

"I was just afraid of it—just afraid of it," said the Standard-bearer, with a sigh. "Afraid of it? I'm talking like a fool: of course I *knew* it. Yes, I was talking like a fool."

Noël Rainguesson said, musingly—

"Yes, I noticed something natural about the tone of it."

We others laughed.

"Oh, you did, did you? You think you are very clever, don't you? I'll take and wring your neck for you one of these days, Noël Rainguesson."

The Sieur de Metz said—

"Paladin, your fears haven't reached the top notch. They are away below the grand possibilities. Didn't it occur to you that in civil and society functions they will take precedence of *all* the rest of the personal staff—every individual of us?"

"Oh, come!"

"You'll find it's so. Look at their escutcheon. Its chiefest feature is the lilies of France. It's royal, man, royal—do you understand the size of that? The lilies are there by authority of the King—do you understand the size of *that*? Though not in detail and in entirety, they do nevertheless substantially *quarter the arms of France* in their coat. Imagine it! consider it! measure the magnitude of it! *We* walk in front of those boys? Bless you, we've done that for the last time. In my opinion there isn't a lay lord in this whole region that can walk in front of them, except the Duke d'Alençon, prince of the blood."

You could have knocked the Paladin down with a feather. He seemed to actually turn pale. He worked his lips a moment without getting anything out; then it came:

"*I* didn't know that, nor the half of it; how *could* I? I've been an idiot. I see it now—I've been an idiot. I met them this morning, and sung out *hello* to them just as I would to anybody. *I* didn't mean to be ill-mannered, but I didn't know the half of this that you've been telling. I've been an ass. Yes, that is all there is to it—I've been an ass."

Noël Rainguesson said, in a kind of weary way:

"Yes, that is likely enough; but I don't see why you should seem surprised at it."

"You don't, don't you? Well, *why* don't you?"

"Because I don't see any novelty about it. With some people it is a condition which is present all the time. Now you take a condition which is present all the time, and the results of that condition will be uniform; this uniformity of result will in time become monotonous; monotonousness, by the law of its being, is fatiguing. If you had manifested *fatigue* upon noticing that you had been an ass, that would have been logical, that would have been rational; whereas it seems to me that to manifest surprise was to be *again* an ass, because the condition of intellect that can enable a person to be surprised and stirred by inert monotonousness is a—"

"Now that is enough, Noël Rainguesson; stop where you are, before you get yourself into trouble. And don't bother me any more for some days or a week an it please you, for I cannot abide your clack."

"Come, I like that! *I* didn't want to talk. I tried to get out of talking. If you didn't want to hear my clack, what did you keep intruding your conversation on me for?"

"I? I never dreamed of such a thing."

"Well, you did it, anyway. And I have a right to feel hurt, and I do feel hurt, to have you treat me so. It seems to me that when a person goads, and crowds, and in a manner forces another person to talk, it is neither very fair nor very good-mannered to call what he says *clack*."

"Oh, snuffle—do! and break your heart, you poor thing. Somebody fetch this sick doll a sugar-rag. Look you, Sir Jean de Metz, do you feel absolutely certain about that thing?"

"What thing?"

"Why that Jean and Pierre are going to take precedence of all the lay noblesse hereabouts except the Duke d'Alençon?"

"I think there is not a doubt of it."

The Standard-bearer was deep in thoughts and dreams a few moments, then the silk-and-velvet expanse of his vast breast rose and fell with a sigh, and he said—

"Dear, dear, what a lift it is! It just shows what luck can do. Well, I don't care. I shouldn't care to be a painted accident—I shouldn't value it. I am prouder to have climbed up to where I am just by sheer natural merit than I would be to ride the very sun in the zenith and have to reflect that I was nothing but a poor little accident, and got shot up there out of somebody else's catapult. To me, merit is everything—in fact the only thing. All else is dross."

Just then the bugles blew the assembly, and that cut our talk short.

CHAPTER 25

The days began to waste away—and nothing decided, nothing done. The army was full of zeal, but it was also hungry. It got no pay, the treasury was getting empty, it was becoming impossible to feed it; under pressure of privation it began to fall apart and disperse—which pleased the trifling court exceedingly. Joan's distress was pitiful to see. She was obliged to stand helpless while her victorious army dissolved away until hardly the skeleton of it was left.

At last one day she went to the Castle of Loches, where the King was idling. She found him consulting with three of his councillors, Robert le Maçon, a former Chancellor of France, Christophe d'Harcourt, and Gerard Machet. The Bastard of Orleans was present also, and it is through him that we know what happened. Joan threw herself at the King's feet and embraced his knees, saying:

"Noble Dauphin, prithee hold no more of these long and numerous councils, but come, and come quickly, to Rheims and receive your crown."

Christophe d'Harcourt asked—

"Is it your Voices that command you to say that to the King?"

"Yes, and urgently."

"Then will you not tell us in the King's presence in what way the Voices communicate with you?"

It was another sly attempt to trap Joan into indiscreet admissions and dangerous pretensions. But nothing came of it. Joan's answer was simple and straightforward, and the smooth Bishop was not able to find any fault with it. She said that when she met with people who doubted the truth of her mission she went aside and prayed, complaining of the distrust of these, and then the comforting Voices were heard at her ear saying, soft and low, "Go forward, Daughter of God, and I will help thee." Then she added, "When I hear that, the joy in my heart, oh, it is insupportable!"

The Bastard said that when she said these words her face lit up as with a flame, and she was like one in an ecstasy.

Joan pleaded, persuaded, reasoned; gaining ground little by little, but opposed step by step by the council. She begged, she implored, leave to march. When they could answer nothing further, they granted that perhaps it had been a mistake to let the army waste away, but how could we help it now? how could we march without an army?

"Raise one!" said Joan.

"But it will take six weeks."

"No matter—begin! let us begin!"

"It is too late. Without doubt the Duke of Bedford has been gathering troops to push to the succor of his strongholds on the Loire."

"Yes, while we have been disbanding ours—and pity 'tis. But we must throw away no more time; we must bestir ourselves."

The King objected that he could not venture toward Rheims with those strong places on the Loire in his path. But Joan said:

"We will break them up. Then you can march."

With *that* plan the King was willing to venture assent. He could sit around out of danger while the road was being cleared.

Joan came back in great spirits. Straightway everything was stirring. Proclamations were issued calling for men, a recruiting camp was established at Selles in Berry, and the commons and the nobles began to flock to it with enthusiasm.

A deal of the month of May had been wasted; and yet by the 6th of June Joan had swept together a new army and was ready to march. She had eight thousand men. Think of that. Think of gathering together such a body as that in that little region. And these were veteran soldiers, too. In fact most of the men in France were soldiers, when you came to that; for the wars had lasted generations now. Yes, most Frenchmen were soldiers; and admirable runners, too, both by practice and inheritance; they had done next to nothing but run for near a century. But that was not their fault. They had had no fair and proper leadership—at least leaders with a fair and proper chance. Away back, King and Court got the habit of being treacherous to the leaders; then the leaders easily got the habit of disobeying the King and going their own way, each for himself and nobody for the lot. Nobody could win victories that way. Hence, running became the habit of the French troops, and no wonder. Yet all that those troops needed in order to be good fighters was a leader who would attend strictly to business—a leader with *all* authority in his hands in place of a tenth of it along with nine other generals equipped with an equal tenth apiece. They had a leader rightly clothed with authority now, and with a head and heart bent on war of the most intensely businesslike and earnest sort—and there would be *results*. No doubt of that. They had Joan of Arc; and under that leadership their legs would lose the art and mystery of running.

Yes, Joan was in great spirits. She was here and there and everywhere, all over the camp, by day and by night, pushing things. And wherever she came charging down the lines, reviewing the troops, it was good to hear them break out and cheer. And nobody could help cheering, she was such a vision of young bloom and beauty and grace, and such an incarnation of pluck and life and go! She was growing more and more ideally beautiful every day, as was plain to be seen—and these were days of development; for she was well past seventeen, now—in fact she was getting close upon seventeen and a half—indeed, just a little woman, as you may say.

The two young Counts de Laval arrived one day—fine young fellows allied to the greatest and most illustrious houses of France; and they could not rest till they had seen Joan of Arc. So the King sent for them and presented them to her, and you may believe she filled the bill of their expectations. When they heard that rich voice of hers they must have thought it was a flute; and when they saw her deep eyes and her face, and the soul that looked out of that face, you could see that the sight of her stirred them like a poem, like lofty eloquence, like martial music. One of them wrote home to his people, and in his letter he said, "It seemed something divine to see her and hear her." Ah, yes, and it was a true word. Truer word was never spoken.

He saw her when she was ready to begin her march and open the campaign, and this is what he said about it:

"She was clothed all in white armor save her head, and in her hand she carried a little battle-axe; and when she was ready to mount her great black horse he reared and plunged and would not let her. Then she said, 'Lead him to the cross.' This cross was in front of the church close by. So they led him there. Then she mounted, and he never budged, any more than if he had been tied. Then she turned toward the door of the church and said, in her soft womanly voice, 'You, priests and people of the Church, make processions and pray to God for us!' Then she spurred away, under her standard, with her little axe in her hand, crying 'Forward—march!' One of her brothers, who came eight days ago, departed with her; and he also was clad all in white armor."

I was there, and I saw it too; saw it all, just as he pictures it. And I see it yet—the little battle-axe, the dainty plumed cap, the white armor—all in the soft June afternoon; I see it just as if it were yesterday. And I rode with the staff—the personal staff—the staff of Joan of Arc.

That young Count was dying to go too, but the King held him back for the present. But Joan had made him a promise. In his letter he said:

"She told me that when the King starts for Rheims I shall go with him. But God grant I may not have to wait till then, but may have a part in the battles!"

She made him that promise when she was taking leave of my lady the Duchess d'Alençon. The Duchess was exacting a promise, so it seemed a proper time for others to do the like. The Duchess was troubled for her husband, for she foresaw desperate fighting; and she held Joan to her breast, and stroked her hair lovingly, and said:

"You must watch over him, dear, and take care of him, and send him back to me safe. I require it of you; I will not let you go till you promise."

Joan said:

"I give you the promise with all my heart; and it is not just words, it *is* a promise: you shall have him back without a hurt. Do you believe? And are you satisfied with me now?"

The Duchess could not speak, but she kissed Joan on the forehead; and so they parted.

We left on the 6th and stopped over at Romorantin; then on the 9th Joan entered Orleans in state, under triumphal arches, with the welcoming cannon thundering and seas of welcoming flags fluttering in the breeze. The Grand Staff rode with her, clothed in shining splendors of costume and decorations: the Duke d'Alençon; the Bastard of Orleans; the Sire de Boussac, Marshal of France; the Lord de Graville, Master of the Crossbowmen; the Sire de Culan, Admiral of France; Ambroise de Loré; Étienne de Vignoles, called La Hire; Gautier de Brusac, and other illustrious captains.

It was grand times: the usual shoutings, and packed multitudes, the usual crush to get sight of Joan; but at last we crowded through to our old lodgings, and I saw old Boucher and the wife and that dear Catherine gather Joan to their hearts and smother her with kisses—and my heart ached so! for I could have kissed Catherine better than anybody, and more and longer; yet was not thought of for that office, and I so famished for it. Ah, she was so beautiful, and oh, so sweet! I had loved her the first day I ever saw her, and from that day forth she was sacred to me. I have carried her image in my heart for sixty-three years —all lonely there, yes, solitary, for it never has had company—and I am grown so old, so old: but it, oh, it is as fresh and young and merry and mischievous and lovely and sweet and pure and witching and divine as it was when it crept in there, bringing benediction and peace to its habitation so long ago, so long ago—for it has not aged a day!

CHAPTER 26

This time, as before, the King's last command to the generals was this: *"See to it that you do nothing without the sanction of the Maid."* And this time the command was obeyed; and would continue to be obeyed all through the coming great days of the Loire campaign. That was a change! That was new! It broke the traditions. It shows you what sort of a reputation as a commander-in-chief the child had made for herself in ten days in the field. It was a conquering of men's doubts and suspicions and a capturing and solidifying of men's belief and confidence such as the grayest veteran on the Grand Staff had not been able to achieve in thirty years. Don't you remember that when at sixteen Joan conducted her own case in a grim court of law and won it, the old judge spoke of her as "this marvellous child?" It was the right name, you see.

These veterans were not going to branch out and do things without the sanction of the Maid—that is true; and it was a great gain. But at the same time there were some among them who still trembled at her new and dashing war-tactics and earnestly desired to modify them. And so, during the 10th, while Joan was slaving away at her plans and issuing order after order with tireless industry, the old-time consultations and arguings and speechifyings were going on among certain of the generals.

In the afternoon of that day they came in a body to hold one of these councils of war; and while they waited for Joan to join them they discussed the situation. Now this discussion is not set down in the histories; but I was there, and I will speak of it, as knowing you will trust me, I not being given to beguiling you with lies.

Gautier de Brusac was spokesman for the timid ones; Joan's side was resolutely upheld by D'Alençon, the Bastard, La Hire, the Admiral of France, the Marshal de Boussac, and all the other really important chiefs.

De Brusac argued that the situation was very grave; that Jargeau, the first point of attack, was formidably strong; its imposing walls bristling with artillery; with 7000 picked English veterans behind them, and at their head the great Earl of Suffolk and his two redoubtable brothers the De la Poles. It seemed to him that the proposal of Joan of Arc to try to take such a place by storm was a most rash and over-daring idea, and she ought to be persuaded to relinquish it in favor of the soberer and safer procedure of investment by regular siege. It seemed to him that this fiery and furious new fashion of hurling masses of men against impregnable walls of stone, in defiance of the established laws and usages of war, was—

But he got no further. La Hire gave his plumed helm an impatient toss and burst out with—

"By God she knows her trade, and none can teach it her!"

And before he could get out anything more, D'Alençon was on his feet, and the Bastard of Orleans, and half a dozen others, all thundering at once, and pouring out their indignant displeasure upon any and all that might hold, secretly or publicly, distrust of the wisdom of the Commander-in-Chief. And when they had said their say, La Hire took a chance again, and said:

"There are some that never know how to change. Circumstances may change, but those people are never able to see that *they* have got to change too, to meet those circumstances. All that they know is the one beaten track that their fathers and grandfathers have followed and that they themselves have followed in their turn. If an earthquake come and rip the land to chaos, and that beaten track now lead over precipices and into morasses, those people *can't* learn that they must strike out a new road—no; they will march stupidly along and follow the old one to death and perdition. Men, there's a new state of things; and a surpassing military genius has perceived it with her clear eye. And a new road is required, and that same clear eye has noted where it must go, and has marked it out for us. The man does not live, never has lived, never *will* live, that can improve upon it! The old state of things was defeat, defeat, defeat—and by consequence we had troops with no dash, no heart, no hope. Would you assault stone walls with such? No—there was but one way, with that kind: sit down before a place and wait, wait—starve it out, if you could. The new case is the very opposite; it is this: men all on fire with pluck and dash and vim and fury and energy—a restrained conflagration! What would you do with it? Hold it down and let it smoulder and perish and go out? What would Joan of Arc do with it? Turn it *loose*, by the Lord God of heaven and earth, and let it swallow up the foe in the whirlwind of its fires! Nothing shows the splendor and wisdom of her military genius like her instant comprehension of the size of the change which has come about, and her instant perception of the right and only right way to take advantage of it. With her is no sitting down and starving out; no dilly-dallying and fooling around; no lazying, loafing, and going to sleep; no, it is storm! storm! storm! and still storm! storm! storm! and forever storm! storm! storm! hunt the enemy to his hole, then turn her French hurricanes loose and carry him by storm! And that is *my* sort! Jargeau? What of Jargeau, with its battlements and towers, its devastating artillery, its seven thousand picked veterans? Joan of Arc is to the fore, and by the splendor of God its fate is sealed!"

Oh, he carried them. There was not another word said about persuading Joan to change her tactics. They sat talking comfortably enough after that.

By-and-by Joan entered, and they rose and saluted with their swords, and she asked what their pleasure might be. La Hire said:

"It is settled, my General. The matter concerned Jargeau. There were some who thought we could not take the place."

Joan laughed her pleasant laugh; her merry, care-free laugh; the laugh that rippled so buoyantly from her lips and made old people feel young again to hear it; and she said to the company—

"Have no fears—indeed there is no need nor any occasion for them. We will strike the English boldly by assault, and you will see." Then a far-away look came into her eyes, and I think that a picture of her home drifted across the vision of her mind; for she said very gently, and as one who muses, "But that I know God guides us and will give us success, I had liefer keep sheep than endure these perils."

We had a homelike farewell supper that evening—just the personal staff and the family. Joan had to miss it; for the city had given a banquet in her honor, and she had gone there in state with the Grand Staff, through a riot of joy-bells and a sparkling Milky Way of illuminations.

After supper some lively young folk whom we knew came in, and we presently forgot that we were soldiers, and only remembered that we were boys and girls and full of animal spirits and long-pent fun; and so there was dancing, and games, and romps, and screams of laughter—just as extravagant and innocent and noisy a good time as ever I had in my life. Dear, dear, how long ago it was!—and I was young then. And outside, all the while, was the measured tramp of marching battalions, belated odds and ends of the French power gathering for the morrow's tragedy on the grim stage of war. Yes, in those days we had those contrasts side by side. And as I passed along to bed there was another one: the big Dwarf, in brave new armor, sat sentry at Joan's door—the stern Spirit of War made flesh, as it were—and on his ample shoulder was curled a kitten asleep.

CHAPTER 27

We made a gallant show next day when we filed out through the frowning gates of Orleans, with banners flying and Joan and the Grand Staff in the van of the long column. Those two young De Lavals were come, now, and were joined to the Grand Staff. Which was well; war being their proper trade, for they were grandsons of that illustrious fighter Bertrand du Guesclin, Constable of France in earlier days. Louis de Bourbon, the Marshal de Rais, and the Vidame de Chartres were added also. We had a right to feel a little uneasy, for we knew that a force of five thousand men was on its way under Sir John Fastolfe to reinforce Jargeau, but I think we were not uneasy, nevertheless. In truth that force was not yet in our neighborhood. Sir John was loitering; for some reason or other he was not hurrying. He was losing precious time—four days at Étampes, and four more at Janville.

We reached Jargeau and began business at once. Joan sent forward a heavy force which hurled itself against the outworks in handsome style, and gained a footing and fought hard to keep it; but it presently began to fall back before a sortie from the city. Seeing this, Joan raised her battle-cry and led a new assault herself under a furious artillery fire. The Paladin was struck down at her side, wounded, but she snatched her standard from his failing hand and plunged on through the ruck of flying missiles, cheering her men with encouraging cries, and then for a good time one had turmoil, and clash of steel, and collision and confusion of struggling multitudes, and the hoarse bellowing of the guns; and then the hiding of it all under a rolling firmament of smoke; a firmament through which veiled vacancies appeared for a moment now and then, giving fitful dim glimpses of the wild tragedy enacting beyond; and always at these times one caught sight of that slight figure in white mail which was the centre and soul of our hope and trust, and whenever we saw that, with its back to us and its face to the fight, we knew that all was well. At last a great shout went up—a joyous roar of shoutings, in fact—and that was sign sufficient that the faubourgs were ours.

Yes, they were ours; the enemy had been driven back within the walls. On the ground which Joan had won, we camped; for night was coming on.

Joan sent a summons to the English, promising that if they surrendered she would allow them to go in peace and take their horses with them. Nobody knew that she could take that strong place, but she knew it—knew it well; yet she offered that grace—offered it in a time when such a thing was unknown in war; in a time when it was custom and usage to massacre the garrison and the inhabitants of captured cities without pity or compunction—yes, even to the harmless women and children sometimes. There are neighbors all about you who well remember the unspeakable atrocities which Charles the Bold inflicted upon the men and women and children of Dinant when he took that place some years ago. It was a unique and kindly grace which Joan offered that garrison; but that was her way, that was her loving and merciful nature—she always did her best to save her enemy's life and his soldierly pride when she had the mastery of him.

The English asked fifteen days' armistice to consider the proposal in. And Fastolfe coming with five thousand men! Joan said no. But she offered another grace: they might take both their horses and their side-arms—but they must go within the hour.

Well, those bronzed English veterans were pretty hardheaded folk. They declined again. Then Joan gave command that her army be made ready to move to the assault at nine in the morning. Considering the deal of marching and fighting which the men had done that day, D'Alençon thought the hour rather early; but Joan said it was best so, and so must be obeyed. Then she burst out with one of those enthusiasms which were always burning in her when battle was imminent, and said:

"Work! work! and God will work with us!"

Yes, one might say that her motto was "Work! stick to it; keep on working!" for in war she never knew what indolence was. And whoever will take that motto and live by it will be likely to succeed. There's many a way to win, in this world, but none of them is worth much without good hard work back of it.

I think we should have lost our big Standard-Bearer that day, if our bigger Dwarf had not been at hand to bring him out of the mêlée when he was wounded. He was unconscious, and would have been trampled to death by our own horse, if the Dwarf had not promptly rescued him and haled him to the rear and safety. He recovered, and was himself again after two or three hours; and then he was happy and proud, and made the most of his wound, and went swaggering around in his bandages showing off like an innocent big child—which was just what he was. He was prouder of being wounded than a really modest person would be of being killed. But there was no harm in his vanity, and nobody minded it. He said he was hit by a stone from a catapult—a stone the size of a man's head. But the stone grew, of course. Before he got through with it he was claiming that the enemy had flung a building at him.

"Let him alone," said Noël Rainguesson. "Don't interrupt his processes. To-morrow it will be a cathedral."

He said that privately. And, sure enough, to-morrow it *was* a cathedral. I never saw anybody with such an abandoned imagination.

Joan was abroad at the crack of dawn, galloping here and there and yonder, examining the situation minutely, and choosing what she considered the most effective positions for her artillery; and with such accurate judgment did she place her guns that her Lieutenant-General's admiration of it still survived in his memory when his testimony was taken at the Rehabilitation, a quarter of a century later.

In this testimony the Duke d'Alençon said that at Jargeau that morning of the 12th of June she made her dispositions not like a novice, but "with the sure and clear judgment of a trained general of twenty or thirty years' experience."

The veteran captains of the armies of France said she was great in war in all ways, but greatest of all in her genius for posting and handling artillery.

Who taught the shepherd girl to do these marvels—she who could not read, and had had no opportunity to study the complex arts of war? I do not know any way to solve such a baffling riddle as that, there being no precedent for it, nothing in history to compare it with and examine it by. For in history there is no great general, however gifted, who arrived at success otherwise than through able teaching and hard study and some experience. It is a riddle which will never be guessed. *I* think these vast powers and capacities were born in her, and that she applied them by an intuition which could not err.

At eight o'clock all movement ceased, and with it all sounds, all noise. A mute expectancy reigned. The stillness was something awful—because it meant so much. There was no air stirring. The flags on the towers and ramparts hung straight down like tassels. Wherever one saw a person, that person had stopped what he was doing, and was in a waiting attitude, a listening attitude. We were on a commanding spot, clustered around Joan. Not far from us, on every hand, were the lanes and humble dwellings of these outlying suburbs. Many people were visible—all were listening, not one was moving. A man had placed a nail; he was about to fasten something with it to the door-post of his shop—but he had stopped. There was his hand reaching up holding the nail; and there was his other hand in the act of striking with the hammer; but he had forgotten everything—his head was turned aside, listening. Even children unconsciously stopped in their play; I saw a little boy with his hoop-stick pointed slanting toward the ground in the act of steering the hoop around the corner; and so he had stopped and was listening—the hoop was rolling away, doing its own steering. I saw a young girl prettily framed in an open window, a watering-pot in her hand and window-boxes of red flowers under its spout—but the water had ceased to flow; the girl was listening. Everywhere were these impressive petrified forms; and everywhere was suspended movement and that awful stillness.

Joan of Arc raised her sword in the air. At the signal, the silence was torn to rags: cannon after cannon vomited flames and smoke and delivered its quaking thunders; and we saw answering tongues of fire dart from the towers and walls of the city, accompanied by answering deep thunders, and in a minute the walls and the towers disappeared, and in their place stood vast banks and pyramids of snowy smoke, motionless in the dead air. The startled girl dropped her watering-pot and clasped her hands together, and at that moment a stone cannon-ball crashed through her fair body.

The great artillery duel went on, each side hammering away with all its might; and it was splendid for smoke and noise, and most exalting to one's spirits. The poor little town around about us suffered cruelly. The cannon-balls tore through its slight buildings, wrecking them as if they had been built of cards; and every moment or two one would see a huge rock come curving through the upper air above the smoke clouds and go plunging down through the roofs. Fire broke out, and columns of flame and smoke rose toward the sky.

Presently the artillery concussions changed the weather. The sky became overcast, and a strong wind rose and blew away the smoke that hid the English fortresses.

Then the spectacle was fine: turreted gray walls and towers, and streaming bright flags, and jets of red fire and gushes of white smoke in long rows, all standing out with sharp vividness against the deep leaden background of the sky; and then the whizzing missiles began to knock up the dirt all around us, and I felt no more interest in the scenery. There was one English gun that was getting our position down finer and finer all the time. Presently Joan pointed to it and said:

"Fair Duke, step out of your tracks, or that machine will kill you."

The Duke d'Alençon did as he was bid; but Monsieur du Lude rashly took his place, and that cannon tore his head off in a moment.

Joan was watching all along for the right time to order the assault. At last, about nine o'clock, she cried out—

"Now—to the assault!" and the buglers blew the charge.

Instantly we saw the body of men that had been appointed to this service move forward toward a point where the concentrated fire of our guns had crumbled the upper half of a broad stretch of wall to ruins; we saw this force descend into the ditch and begin to plant the scaling-ladders. We were soon with them. The Lieutenant-General thought the assault premature. But Joan said:

"Ah, gentle Duke, are you afraid? Do you not know that I have promised to send you home safe?"

It was warm work in the ditches. The walls were crowded with men, and they poured avalanches of stones down upon us. There was one gigantic Englishman who did us more hurt than any dozen of his brethren. He always dominated the places easiest of assault, and flung down exceedingly troublesome big stones which smashed men and ladders both—then he would near burst himself with laughing over what he had done. But the Duke settled accounts with him. He went and found the famous cannoneer Jean le Lorrain, and said—

"Train your gun—kill me this demon."

He did it with the first shot. He hit the Englishman fair in the breast and knocked him backwards into the city.

The enemy's resistance was so effective and so stubborn that our people began to show signs of doubt and dismay. Seeing this, Joan raised her inspiring battle-cry and descended into the fosse herself, the Dwarf helping her and the Paladin sticking bravely at her side with the standard. She started up a scaling-ladder, but a great stone flung from above came crashing down upon her helmet and stretched her, wounded and stunned, upon the ground. But only for a moment. The Dwarf stood her upon her feet, and straightway she started up the ladder again, crying—

"To the assault, friends, to the assault—the English are ours! It is the appointed hour!"

There was a grand rush, and a fierce roar of war-cries, and we swarmed over the ramparts like ants. The garrison fled, we pursued; Jargeau was ours!

The Earl of Suffolk was hemmed in and surrounded, and the Duke d'Alençon and the Bastard of Orleans demanded that he surrender himself. But he was a proud nobleman and came of a proud race. He refused to yield his sword to subordinates, saying—

"I will die rather. I will surrender to the Maid of Orleans alone, and to no other."

And so he did; and was courteously and honorably used by her.

His two brothers retreated, fighting step by step, toward the bridge, we pressing their despairing forces and cutting them down by scores. Arrived on the bridge, the slaughter still continued. Alexander de la Pole was pushed overboard or fell over, and was drowned. Eleven hundred men had fallen; John de la Pole decided to give up the struggle. But he was nearly as proud and particular as his brother of Suffolk as to whom he would surrender to. The French officer nearest at hand was Guillaume Renault, who was pressing him closely. Sir John said to him—

"Are you a gentleman?"

"Yes."

"And a knight?"

"No."

Then Sir John knighted him himself, there on the bridge, giving him the accolade with English coolness and tranquillity in the midst of that storm of slaughter and mutilation; and then bowing with high courtesy took the sword by the blade and laid the hilt of it in the man's hand in token of surrender. Ah, yes, a proud tribe, those De la Poles.

It was a grand day, a memorable day, a most splendid victory. We had a crowd of prisoners, but Joan would not allow them to be hurt. We took them with us and marched into Orleans next day through the usual tempest of welcome and joy.

And this time there was a new tribute to our leader. From everywhere in the packed streets the new recruits squeezed their way to her side to touch the sword of Joan of Arc and draw from it somewhat of that mysterious quality which made it invincible.

CHAPTER 28

The troops must have a rest. Two days would be allowed for this.

The morning of the 14th I was writing from Joan's dictation in a small room which she sometimes used as a private office when she wanted to get away from officials and their interruptions. Catherine Boucher came in and sat down and said—

"Joan, dear, I want you to talk to me."

"Indeed I am not sorry for that, but glad. What is in your mind?"

"This. I scarcely slept, last night, for thinking of the dangers you are running. The Paladin told me how you made the Duke stand out of the way when the cannon-balls were flying all about, and so saved his life."

"Well, that was right, wasn't it?"

"Right? Yes; but you stayed there yourself. Why will you do like that? It seems such a wanton risk."

"Oh, no, it was not so. I was not in any danger."

"How can you say that, Joan, with those deadly things flying all about you?"

Joan laughed, and tried to turn the subject, but Catherine persisted. She said—

"It was horribly dangerous, and it could not be necessary to stay in such a place. And you led an assault again. Joan, it is tempting Providence. I want you to make me a promise. I want you to promise me that you will let others lead the assaults, if there *must* be assaults, and that you will take better care of yourself in those dreadful battles. Will you?"

But Joan fought away from the promise and did not give it. Catherine sat troubled and discontented awhile, then she said—

"Joan, are you going to be a soldier always? These wars are so long—so long. They last forever and ever and ever."

There was a glad flash in Joan's eye as she cried—

"This campaign will do all the really hard work that is in front of it in the next four days. The rest of it will be gentler—oh, far less bloody. Yes, in four days France will gather another trophy like the redemption of Orleans and make her second long step toward freedom!"

Catherine started (and so did I); then she gazed long at Joan like one in a trance, murmuring "four days—four days," as if to herself and unconsciously. Finally she asked, in a low voice that had something of awe in it:

"Joan, tell me—how is it that you know that? For you do know it, I think."

"Yes," said Joan, dreamily, "I know—I know. I shall strike—and strike again. And before the fourth day is finished I shall strike yet again." She became silent. We sat wondering and still. This was for a whole minute, she looking at the floor and her lips moving but uttering nothing. Then came these words, but hardly audible: "And in a thousand years the English power in France will not rise up from that blow."

It made my flesh creep. It was uncanny. She was in a trance again—I could see it—just as she was that day in the pastures of Domremy when she prophesied about us boys in the war and afterward did not know that she had done it. She was not conscious now; but Catherine did not know that, and so she said, in a happy voice—

"Oh, I believe it, I believe it, and I am so glad! Then you will come back and bide with us all your life long, and we will love you so, and so honor you!"

A scarcely perceptible spasm flitted across Joan's face, and the dreamy voice muttered—

"Before two years are sped I shall die a cruel death!"

I sprang forward with a warning hand up. That is why Catherine did not scream. She was going to do that—I saw it plainly. Then I whispered her to slip out of the place, and say nothing of what had happened. I said Joan was asleep—asleep and dreaming. Catherine whispered back, and said—

"Oh, I am so grateful that it is only a dream! It sounded like prophecy." And she was gone.

Like prophecy! I know it *was* prophecy; and I sat down crying, as knowing we should lose her. Soon she started, shivering slightly, and came to herself, and looked around and saw me crying there, and jumped out of her chair and ran to me all in a whirl of sympathy and compassion, and put her hand on my head, and said—

"My poor boy! What is it? Look up, and tell me."

I had to tell her a lie; I grieved to do it, but there was no other way. I picked up an old letter from my table, written by Heaven knows who, about some matter Heaven knows what, and told her I had just gotten it from Père Fronte, and that in it it said the children's Fairy Tree had been chopped down by some miscreant or other, and—

I got no further. She snatched the letter from my hand and searched it up and down and all over, turning it this way and that, and sobbing great sobs, and the tears flowing down her cheeks, and ejaculating all the time, "Oh, cruel, cruel! how could any be so heartless? Ah, poor Arbre Fée de Bourlemont gone—and we children loved it so! Show me the place where it says it!"

And I, still lying, showed her the pretended fatal words on the pretended fatal page, and she gazed at them through her tears, and said she could see, herself, that they were hateful, ugly words—they "had the very look of it."

Then we heard a strong voice down the corridor announcing—

"His Majesty's messenger—with despatches for her Excellency the Commander-in-Chief of the armies of France!"

CHAPTER 29

I knew she had seen the vision of the Tree. But when? I could not know. Doubtless before she had lately told the King to use her, for that she had but one year left to work in. It had not occurred to me at the time, but the conviction came upon me now that at that time she had already seen the Tree. It had brought her a welcome message; that was plain, otherwise she could not have been so joyous and light-hearted as she had been these latter days. The death-warning had nothing dismal about it for her; no, it was remission of exile, it was leave to come home.

Yes, she had seen the Tree. No one had taken the prophecy to heart which she made to the King; and for a good reason, no doubt: no one *wanted* to take it to heart; all wanted to banish it away and forget it. And all had succeeded, and would go on to the end placid and comfortable. All but me alone. I must carry my awful secret without any to help me. A heavy load, a bitter burden; and would cost me a daily heart-break. She was to die; and so soon. I had never dreamed of that. How could I, and she so strong and fresh and young, and every day earning a new right to a peaceful and honored old age? For at that time I thought old age valuable. I do not know why, but I thought so. All young people think it, I believe, they being ignorant and full of superstitions. She had seen the Tree. All that miserable night those ancient verses went floating back and forth through my brain:

"And when in exile wand'ring we
Shall fainting yearn for glimpse of thee,
O rise upon our sight!"

But at dawn the bugles and the drums burst through the dreamy hush of the morning, and it was turn out all! mount and ride. For there was red work to be done.

We marched to Meung without halting. There we carried the bridge by assault, and left a force to hold it, the rest of the army marching away next morning toward Beaugency, where the lion Talbot, the terror of the French, was in command. When we arrived at that place, the

English retired into the castle and we sat down in the abandoned town.

Talbot was not at the moment present in person, for he had gone away to watch for and welcome Fastolfe and his re-enforcement of five thousand men.

Joan placed her batteries and bombarded the castle till night. Then some news came: Richemont, Constable of France, this long time in disgrace with the King, largely because of the evil machinations of La Tremouille and his party, was approaching with a large body of men to offer his services to Joan—and very much she needed them, now that Fastolfe was so close by. Richemont had wanted to join us before, when we first marched on Orleans; but the foolish King, slave of those paltry advisers of his, warned him to keep his distance and refused all reconciliation with him.

I go into these details because they are important. Important because they lead up to the exhibition of a new gift in Joan's extraordinary mental make-up—statesmanship. It is a sufficiently strange thing to find that great quality in an ignorant country girl of seventeen and a half, but she had it.

Joan was for receiving Richemont cordially, and so was La Hire and the two young De Lavals and other chiefs, but the Lieutenant-General, D'Alençon, strenuously and stubbornly opposed it. He said he had absolute orders from the King to deny and defy Richemont, and that if they were overridden he would leave the army. This would have been a heavy disaster indeed. But Joan set herself the task of persuading him that the salvation of France took precedence of all minor things—even the commands of a sceptred ass; and she accomplished it. She persuaded him to disobey the King in the interest of the nation, and to be reconciled to Count Richemont and welcome him. That was statesmanship; and of the highest and soundest sort. Whatever thing men call great, look for it in Joan of Arc, and there you will find it.

In the early morning, June 17th, the scouts reported the approach of Talbot and Fastolfe with Fastolfe's succoring force. Then the drums beat to arms; and we set forth to meet the English, leaving Richemont and his troops behind to watch the castle of Beaugency and keep its garrison at home. By-and-by we came in sight of the enemy. Fastolfe had tried to convince Talbot that it would be wisest to retreat and not risk a battle with Joan at this time, but distribute the new levies among the English strongholds of the Loire, thus securing them against capture; then be patient and wait—wait for more levies from Paris; let Joan exhaust her army with fruitless daily skirmishing; then at the right time fall upon her in resistless mass and annihilate her. He was a wise old experienced general, was Fastolfe. But that fierce Talbot would hear of no delay. He was in a rage over the punishment which the Maid had inflicted upon him at Orleans and since, and he swore by God and Saint George that he would have it out with her if he had to fight her all alone. So Fastolfe yielded, though he said they were now risking the loss of everything which the English had gained by so many years' work and so many hard knocks.

The enemy had taken up a strong position, and were waiting, in order of battle, with their archers to the front and a stockade before them.

Night was coming on. A messenger came from the English with a rude defiance and an offer of battle. But Joan's dignity was not ruffled, her bearing was not discomposed. She said to the herald—

"Go back and say it is too late to meet to-night; but to-morrow, please God and our Lady, we will come to close quarters."

The night fell dark and rainy. It was that sort of light steady rain which falls so softly and brings to one's spirit such serenity and peace. About ten o'clock D'Alençon, the Bastard of Orleans, La Hire, Pothon of Saintrailles, and two or three other generals came to our head-quarters tent, and sat down to discuss matters with Joan. Some thought it was a pity that Joan had declined battle, some thought not. Then Pothon asked her why she had declined it. She said—

"There was more than one reason. These English are ours—they cannot get away from us. Wherefore there is no need to take risks, as at other times. The day was far spent. It is good to have much time and the fair light of day when one's force is in a weakened state—nine hundred of us yonder keeping the bridge of Meung under the Marshal de Rais, fifteen hundred with the Constable of France keeping the bridge and watching the castle of Beaugency."

Dunois said—

"I grieve for this depletion, Excellency, but it cannot be helped. And the case will be the same the morrow, as to that."

Joan was walking up and down, just then. She laughed her affectionate, comrady laugh, and stopping before that old war-tiger she put her small hand above his head and touched one of his plumes, saying—

"Now tell me, wise man, which feather is it that I touch?"

"In sooth, Excellency, that I cannot."

"Name of God, Bastard, Bastard! you cannot tell me this small thing, yet are bold to name a large one—telling us what is in the stomach of the unborn morrow: that we shall not have those men. Now it is my thought that they will be with us."

That made a stir. All wanted to know why she thought that. But La Hire took the word and said—

"Let be. If she thinks it, that is enough. It will happen."

Then Pothon of Saintrailles said—

"There were other reasons for declining battle, according to the saying of your Excellency?"

"Yes. One was that we being weak and the day far gone, the battle might not be decisive. When it is fought it *must* be decisive. And shall be."

"God grant it, and amen. There were still other reasons?"

"One other—yes." She hesitated a moment, then said: "This was not the day. To-morrow is the day. It is so written."

They were going to assail her with eager questionings, but she put up her hand and prevented them. Then she said—

"It will be the most noble and beneficent victory that God has vouchsafed to France at any time. I pray you question me not as to whence or how I know this thing, but be content that it is so."

There was pleasure in every face, and conviction and high confidence. A murmur of conversation broke out, but was interrupted by a messenger from the outposts who brought news—namely, that for an hour there had been stir and movement in the English camp of a sort unusual at such a time and with a resting army, he said. Spies had been sent under cover of the rain and darkness to inquire into it. They had just come back and reported that large bodies of men had been dimly made out who were slipping stealthily away in the direction of Meung.

The generals were very much surprised, as any might tell from their faces.

"It is a retreat," said Joan.

"It has that look," said D'Alençon.

"It certainly has," observed the Bastard and La Hire.

"It was not to be expected," said Louis de Bourbon, "but one can divine the purpose of it."

"Yes," responded Joan. "Talbot has reflected. His rash brain has cooled. He thinks to take the bridge of Meung and escape to the other side of the river. He knows that this leaves his garrison of Beaugency at the mercy of fortune, to escape our hands if it can; but there is no other course if he would avoid this battle, and that he also knows. But he shall not get the bridge. We will see to that."

"Yes," said D'Alençon, "we must follow him, and take care of that matter. What of Beaugency?"

"Leave Beaugency to me, gentle Duke; I will have it in two hours, and at no cost of blood."

"It is true, Excellency. You will but need to deliver this news there and receive the surrender."

"Yes. And I will be with you at Meung with the dawn, fetching the Constable and his fifteen hundred; and when Talbot knows that Beaugency has fallen it will have an effect upon him."

"By the mass, yes!" cried La Hire. "He will join his Meung garrison to his army and break for Paris. Then we shall have our bridge force with us again, along with our Beaugency-watchers, and be stronger for our great day's work by four-and-twenty hundred able soldiers, as was here promised within the hour. Verily this Englishman is doing our errands for us and saving us much blood and trouble. Orders, Excellency—give us our orders!"

"They are simple. Let the men rest three hours longer. At one o'clock the advance-guard will march, under your command, with Pothon of Saintrailles as second; the second division will follow at two under the Lieutenant-General. Keep well in the rear of the enemy, and see to it that you avoid an engagement. I will ride under guard to Beaugency and make so quick work there that I and the Constable of France will join you before dawn with his men."

She kept her word. Her guard mounted and we rode off through the puttering rain, taking with us a captured English officer to confirm Joan's news. We soon covered the journey and summoned the castle. Richard Guétin, Talbot's lieutenant, being convinced that he and his five hundred men were left helpless, conceded that it would be useless to try to hold out. He could not expect easy terms, yet Joan granted them nevertheless. His garrison could keep their horses and arms, and carry away property to the value of a silver mark per man. They could go whither they pleased, but must not take arms against France again under ten days.

Before dawn we were with our army again, and with us the Constable and nearly all his men, for we left only a small garrison in Beaugency castle. We heard the dull booming of cannon to the front, and knew that Talbot was beginning his attack on the bridge. But some time before it was yet light the sound ceased and we heard it no more.

Guétin had sent a messenger through our lines under a safe-conduct given by Joan, to tell Talbot of the surrender. Of course this poursuivant had arrived ahead of us. Talbot had held it wisdom to turn, now, and retreat upon Paris. When daylight came he had disappeared; and with him Lord Scales and the garrison of Meung.

What a harvest of English strongholds we had reaped in those three days!—strongholds which had defied France with quite cool confidence and plenty of it until we came.

CHAPTER 30

When the morning broke at last on that forever memorable 18th of June, there was no enemy discoverable anywhere, as I have said. But that did not trouble me. I knew we should find him, and that we should strike him; strike him the promised blow—the one from which the English power in France would not rise up in a thousand years, as Joan had said in her trance.

The enemy had plunged into the wide plains of La Beauce—a roadless waste covered with bushes, with here and there bodies of forest trees—a region where an army would be hidden from view in a very little while. We found the trail in the soft wet earth and followed it. It indicated an orderly march; no confusion, no panic.

But we had to be cautious. In such a piece of country we could walk into an ambush without any trouble. Therefore Joan sent bodies of cavalry ahead under La Hire, Pothon, and other captains, to feel the way. Some of the other officers began to show uneasiness; this sort of hide-and-go-seek business troubled them and made their confidence a little shaky. Joan divined their state of mind and cried out impetuously—

"Name of God, what would you? We must smite these English, and we will. They shall not escape us. Though they were hung to the clouds we would get them!"

By-and-by we were nearing Patay; it was about a league away. Now at this time our reconnaissance, feeling its way in the bush, frightened a deer, and it went bounding away and was out of sight in a moment. Then hardly a minute later a dull great shout went up in the distance toward Patay. It was the English soldiery. They had been shut up in garrison so long on mouldy food that they could not keep their delight to themselves when this fine fresh meat came springing into their midst. Poor creature, it had wrought damage to a nation which loved it well. For the French knew where the English were, now, whereas the English had no suspicion of where the French were.

La Hire halted where he was, and sent back the tidings. Joan was radiant with joy. The Duke d'Alençon said to her—

"Very well, we have found them; shall we fight them?"

"Have you good spurs, Prince?"

"Why? Will they make us run away?"

"Nenni, en nom de Dieu! These English are ours—they are lost. They will fly. Who overtakes them will need good spurs. Forward—close up!"

By the time we had come up with La Hire the English had discovered our presence. Talbot's force was marching in three bodies. First his advance-guard; then his artillery; then his battle corps a good way in the rear. He was now out of the bush and in a fair open country. He at once posted his artillery, his advance-guard, and five hundred picked archers along some hedges where the French would be obliged to pass, and hoped to hold this position till his battle corps could come up. Sir John Fastolfe urged the battle corps into a gallop. Joan saw her opportunity and ordered La Hire to advance—which La Hire promptly did, launching his wild riders like a storm-wind, his customary fashion.

The Duke and the Bastard wanted to follow, but Joan said—

"Not yet—wait."

So they waited—impatiently, and fidgeting in their saddles. But she was steady—gazing straight before her, measuring, weighing, calculating—by shades, minutes, fractions of minutes, seconds—with all her great soul present, in eye, and set of head, and noble pose of body—but patient, steady, master of herself—master of herself and of the situation.

And yonder, receding, receding, plumes lifting and falling, lifting and falling, streamed the thundering charge of La Hire's godless crew, La Hire's great figure dominating it and his sword stretched aloft like a flag-staff.

"O, Satan and his Hellions, see them go!" Somebody muttered it in deep admiration.

And now he was closing up—closing up on Fastolfe's rushing corps.

And now he struck it—struck it hard, and broke its order. It lifted the Duke and the Bastard in their saddles to see it; and they turned, trembling with excitement, to Joan, saying—

"*Now!*"

But she put up her hand, still gazing, weighing, calculating, and said again—

"Wait—not yet."

Fastolfe's hard-driven battle corps raged on like an avalanche toward the waiting advance-guard. Suddenly these conceived the idea that it was flying in panic before Joan; and so in that instant it broke and swarmed away in a mad panic itself, with Talbot storming and cursing after it.

Now was the golden time. Joan drove her spurs home and waved the advance with her sword. "Follow me!" she cried, and bent her head to her horse's neck and sped away like the wind!

We swept down into the confusion of that flying rout, and for three long hours we cut and hacked and stabbed. At last the bugles sang "Halt!"

The Battle of Patay was won.

Joan of Arc dismounted, and stood surveying that awful field, lost in thought. Presently she said—

"The praise is to God. He has smitten with a heavy hand this day." After a little she lifted her face, and looking afar off, said, with the manner of one who is thinking aloud, "In a thousand years—a thousand years—the English power in France will not rise up from this blow." She stood again a time, thinking, then she turned toward her grouped generals, and there was a glory in her face and a noble light in her eye; and she said—

"O, friends, friends, do you know?—do you comprehend? *France is on the way to be free!*"

"And had never been, but for Joan of Arc!" said La Hire, passing before her and bowing low, the others following and doing likewise; he muttering as he went, "I will say it though I be damned for it." Then battalion after battalion of our victorious army swung by, wildly cheering. And they shouted "Live forever, Maid of Orleans, live forever!" while Joan, smiling, stood at the salute with her sword.

This was not the last time I saw the Maid of Orleans on the red field of Patay. Toward the end of the day I came upon her where the dead and dying lay stretched all about in heaps and winrows; our men had mortally wounded an English prisoner who was too poor to pay a ransom, and from a distance she had seen that cruel thing done; and had galloped to the place and sent for a priest, and now she was holding the head of her dying enemy in her lap, and easing him to his death with comforting soft words, just as his sister might have done; and the womanly tears running down her face all the time.*

* Lord Ronald Gower (*Joan of Arc*, p. 82) says: "Michelet discovered this story in the deposition of Joan of Arc's page, Louis de Conte, who was probably an eyewitness of the scene." This is true. It was a part of the testimony of the author of these "Personal Recollections of Joan of Arc," given by him in the Rehabilitation proceedings of 1456.—TRANSLATOR.

CHAPTER 31

Joan had said true: France was on the way to be free.

The war called the Hundred Years' War was very sick to-day. Sick on its English side—for the very first time since its birth, ninety-one years gone by.

Shall we judge battles by the numbers killed and the ruin wrought? Or shall we not rather judge them by the results which flowed from them? Any one will say that a battle is only truly great or small according to its results. Yes, any one will grant that, for it is the truth.

Judged by results, Patay's place is with the few supremely great and imposing battles that have been fought since the peoples of the world first resorted to arms for the settlement of their quarrels. So judged, it is even possible that Patay has no peer among that few just mentioned, but stands alone, as the supremest of historic conflicts. For when it began France lay gasping out the remnant of an exhausted life, her case wholly hopeless in the view of all political physicians; when it ended, three hours later, she was convalescent. Convalescent, and nothing requisite but time and ordinary nursing to bring her back to perfect health. The dullest physician of them all could see this, and there was none to deny it.

Many death-sick nations have reached convalescence through a series of battles, a procession of battles, a weary tale of wasting conflicts stretching over years, but only one has reached it in a single day and by a single battle. That nation is France, and that battle Patay.

Remember it and be proud of it; for you are French, and it is the stateliest fact in the long annals of your country. There it stands, with its head in the clouds! And when you grow up you will go on pilgrimage to the field of Patay, and stand uncovered in the presence of—what? A monument with *its* head in the clouds? Yes. For all nations in all times have built monuments on their battle-fields to keep green the memory of the perishable deed that was wrought there and of the perishable name of him who wrought it; and will France neglect Patay and Joan of Arc? Not for long. And will she build a monument scaled to their rank as compared with the world's other fields and heroes? Perhaps—if there be room for it under the arch of the sky.

But let us look back a little, and consider certain strange and impressive facts. The Hundred Years' War began in 1337. It raged on and on, year after year and year after year; and at last England stretched France prone with that fearful blow at Crécy. But she rose and struggled on, year after year, and at last again she went down under another devastating blow—Poitiers. She gathered her crippled strength once more, and the war raged on, and on, and still on, year after year, decade after decade. Children were born, grew up, married, died—the war raged on; *their* children in turn grew up, married, died—the war raged on; *their* children, growing, saw France struck down again; this time under the incredible disaster of Agincourt—and still the war raged on, year after year, and in time *these* children married in their turn.

France was a wreck, a ruin, a desolation. The half of it belonged to England, with none to dispute or deny the truth; the other half belonged to nobody—in three months would be flying the English flag: the French King was making ready to throw away his crown and flee beyond the seas.

Now came the ignorant country maid out of her remote village and confronted this hoary war, this all-consuming conflagration that had swept the land for three generations. Then began the briefest and most amazing campaign that is recorded in history. In seven weeks it was finished. In seven weeks she hopelessly crippled that gigantic war that was ninety-one years old. At Orleans she struck it a staggering blow; on the field of Patay she broke its back.

Think of it. Yes, one can do that; but *understand* it? Ah, that is another matter; none will ever be able to comprehend that stupefying marvel.

Seven weeks—with here and there a little bloodshed. Perhaps the most of it, in any single fight, at Patay, where the English began six thousand strong and left two thousand dead upon the field. It is said and believed that in three battles alone—Crécy, Poitiers, and Agincourt—near a hundred thousand Frenchmen fell, without counting the thousand other fights of that long war. The dead of that war make a mournful long list—an interminable list. Of men slain in the field the count goes by tens of thousands; of innocent women and children slain by bitter hardship and hunger it goes by that appalling term, millions. It was an ogre, that war; an ogre that went about for near a hundred years, crunching men and dripping blood from his jaws. And with her little hand that child of seventeen struck him down; and yonder he lies stretched on the field of Patay, and will not get up any more while this old world lasts.

CHAPTER 32

The great news of Patay was carried over the whole of France in twenty hours, people said. I do not know as to that; but one thing is sure, anyway: the moment a man got it he flew shouting and glorifying God and told his neighbor; and that neighbor flew with it to the next homestead; and so on and so on without resting the word travelled; and when a man got it in the night, at what hour soever, he jumped out of his bed and bore the blessed message along. And the joy that went with it was like the light that flows across the land when an eclipse is receding from the face of the sun; and indeed you may say that France had lain in an eclipse this long time; yes, buried in a black gloom which these beneficent tidings were sweeping away, now, before the on-rush of their white splendor.

The news beat the flying enemy to Yeuville, and the town rose against its English masters and shut the gates against their brethren. It flew to Mont Pipeau, to Saint Simon, and to this, that, and the other English fortress; and straightway the garrison applied the torch and took to the fields and the woods. A detachment of our army occupied Meung and pillaged it.

When we reached Orleans that town was as much as fifty times insaner with joy than we had ever seen it before—which is saying much. Night had just fallen, and the illuminations were on so wonderful a scale that we seemed to plough through seas of fire; and as to the noise —the hoarse cheering of the multitude, the thundering of cannon, the clash of bells—indeed there was never anything like it. And everywhere rose a new cry that burst upon us like a storm when the column entered the gates, and nevermore ceased: "Welcome to Joan of Arc—way for the SAVIOR OF FRANCE!" And there was another cry: "Crécy is avenged! Poitiers is avenged! Agincourt is avenged!—Patay shall live forever!"

Mad? Why, you never could imagine it in the world. The prisoners were in the centre of the column. When that came along and the people caught sight of their masterful old enemy Talbot, that had made them dance so long to his grim war-music, you may imagine what the uproar was like if you can, for I cannot describe it. They were so glad to see him that presently they wanted to have him out and hang him; so Joan had him brought up to the front to ride in her protection. They made a striking pair.

CHAPTER 33

Yes, Orleans was in a delirium of felicity. She invited the King, and made sumptuous preparations to receive him, but—he didn't come. He was simply a serf at that time, and La Tremouille was his master. Master and serf were visiting together at the master's castle of Sully-sur-Loire.

At Beaugency Joan had engaged to bring about a reconciliation between the Constable Richemont and the King. She took Richemont to Sully-sur-Loire and made her promise good.

The great deeds of Joan of Arc are five:

1. The Raising of the Siege.
2. The Victory of Patay.
3. The Reconciliation at Sully-sur-Loire.
4. The Coronation of the King.
5. The Bloodless March.

We shall come to the Bloodless March presently; (and the Coronation). It was the victorious long march which Joan made through the enemy's country from Gien to Rheims, and thence to the gates of Paris, capturing every English town and fortress that barred the road, from the beginning of the journey to the end of it; and this by the mere force of her name, and without shedding a drop of blood—perhaps the most extraordinary campaign in this regard in history—this is the most glorious of her military exploits.

The Reconciliation was one of Joan's most important achievements. No one else could have accomplished it; and in fact no one else of high consequence had any disposition to try. In brains, in scientific warfare, and in statesmanship the Constable Richemont was the ablest man in France. His loyalty was sincere; his probity was above suspicion —(and it made him sufficiently conspicuous in that trivial and conscienceless Court).

In restoring Richemont to France, Joan made thoroughly secure the successful completion of the great work which she had begun. She had never seen Richemont until he came to her with his little army. Was it not wonderful that at a glance she should know him for the one man who could finish and perfect her work and establish it in perpetuity? How was it that that child was able to do this? It was because she had the "seeing eye," as one of our knights had once said. Yes, she had that great gift—almost the highest and rarest that has been granted to man. Nothing of an extraordinary sort was still to be done, yet the remaining work could not safely be left to the King's idiots; for it would require wise statesmanship and long and patient though desultory hammering of the enemy. Now and then, for a quarter of a century yet, there would be a little fighting to do, and a handy man could carry that on with small disturbance to the rest of the country; and little by little, and with progressive certainty, the English would disappear from France.

And that happened. Under the influence of Richemont the King became at a later time a man—a man, a king, a brave and capable and determined soldier. Within six years after Patay he was leading storming parties himself; fighting in fortress ditches up to his waist in water, and climbing scaling-ladders under a furious fire with a pluck that would have satisfied even Joan of Arc. In time he and Richemont cleared away all the English; even from regions where the people had been under their mastership for three hundred years. In such regions wise and careful work was necessary, for the English rule had been fair and kindly; and men who have been ruled in that way are not always anxious for a change.

Which of Joan's five chief deeds shall we call chiefest? It is my thought that each *in its turn* was that. This is saying that, taken as a whole, they *equalized* each other, and neither was then greater than its mate.

Do you perceive? Each was a stage in an ascent. To leave out one of them would defeat the journey; to achieve one of them at the wrong time and in the wrong place would have the same effect.

Consider the Coronation. As a masterpiece of diplomacy, where can you find its superior in our history? Did the King suspect its vast importance? No. Did his ministers? No. Did the astute Bedford, representative of the English crown? No. An advantage of incalculable importance was here under the eyes of the King and of Bedford; the King could get it by a bold stroke, Bedford could get it without an effort; but being ignorant of its value, neither of them put forth his hand. Of all the wise people in high office in France, only one knew the priceless worth of this neglected prize—the untaught child of seventeen, Joan of Arc—and she had known it from the beginning, had spoken of it from the beginning as an essential detail of her mission.

How did she know it? It is simple: she was a peasant. That tells the whole story. She was of the people and knew the people; those others moved in a loftier sphere and knew nothing much about them. We make little account of that vague, formless, inert mass, that mighty underlying force which we call "the people"—an epithet which carries contempt with it. It is a strange attitude; for at bottom we know that the throne which the people support, stands, and that when that support is removed, nothing in this world can save it.

Now, then, consider this fact, and observe its importance. Whatever the parish priest believes, his flock believes; they love him, they revere him; he is their unfailing friend, their dauntless protector, their comforter in sorrow, their helper in their day of need; he has their whole confidence; what he tells them to do, that they will do, with a blind and affectionate obedience, let it cost what it may. Add these facts thoughtfully together, and what is the sum? This: *The parish priest governs the nation.* What is the King, then, if the parish priest withdraw his support and deny his authority? Merely a shadow and no King; let him resign.

Do you get that idea? Then let us proceed. A priest is consecrated to his office by the awful hand of God, laid upon him by his appointed representative on earth. That consecration is final; nothing can undo it, nothing can remove it. Neither the Pope nor any other power can strip the priest of his office; God gave it, and it is forever sacred and secure. The dull parish knows all this. To priest and parish, whosoever is anointed of God bears an office whose authority can no longer be disputed or assailed. To the parish priest, and to his subjects the nation, an uncrowned king is a similitude of a person who has been named for holy orders but has not been consecrated; he has no office, he has not been ordained, another may be appointed in his place. In a word, an uncrowned king is a *doubtful* King; but if God appoint him and His servant the Bishop anoint him, the doubt is annihilated; the priest and the parish are his loyal subjects straightway, and while he lives they will recognize no king but him.

To Joan of Arc the peasant girl, Charles VII. was no King until he was crowned; to her he was only the *Dauphin;* that is to say, the *heir.* If I have ever made her call him King, it was a mistake; she called him the Dauphin, and nothing else until after the Coronation. It shows you as in a mirror—for Joan was a mirror in which the lowly hosts of France were clearly reflected—that to all that vast underlying force called "the people" he was no King but only Dauphin before his crowning, and was indisputably and irrevocably King *after* it.

Now you understand what a colossal move on the political chessboard the Coronation was. Bedford realized this by-and-by, and tried to patch up his mistake by crowning *his* King; but what good could that do? None in the world.

Speaking of chess, Joan's great acts may be likened to that game. Each move was made in its proper order, and it was great and effective because it *was* made in its proper order and not out of it. Each, at the time made, seemed the greatest move; but the final result made them all recognizable as equally essential and equally important. This is the game, as played:

1. Joan moves Orleans and Patay—*check.*
2. Then moves the Reconciliation—but does not proclaim check, it being a move for position, and to take effect later.
3. Next she moves the Coronation—*check.*
4. Next, the Bloodless March—*check.*
5. Final move (after her death) the reconciled Constable Richemont to the French King's elbow—*checkmate.*

CHAPTER 34

The Campaign of the Loire had as good as opened the road to Rheims. There was no sufficient reason now why the Coronation should not take place. The Coronation would complete the mission which Joan had received from heaven, and then she would be forever done with war, and would fly home to her mother and her sheep, and never stir from the hearthstone and happiness any more. That was her dream; and she could not rest, she was so impatient to see it fulfilled. She became so possessed with this matter that I began to lose faith in her two prophecies of her early death—and of course when I found that faith wavering I encouraged it to waver all the more.

The King was afraid to start to Rheims, because the road was mile-posted with English fortresses, so to speak. Joan held them in light esteem and not things to be afraid of in the existing modified condition of English confidence.

And she was right. As it turned out, the march to Rheims was nothing but a holiday excursion. Joan did not even take any artillery along, she was so sure it would not be necessary. We marched from Gien twelve thousand strong. This was the 29th of June. The Maid rode by the side of the King; on his other side was the Duke d'Alençon. After the Duke followed three other princes of the blood. After these followed the Bastard of Orleans, the Marshal de Boussac, and the

Admiral of France. After these came La Hire, Saintrailles, Tremouille, and a long procession of knights and nobles.

We rested three days before Auxerre. The city provisioned the army, and a deputation waited upon the King, but we did not enter the place.

Saint-Florentin opened its gates to the King.

On the 4th of July we reached Saint-Fal, and yonder lay Troyes before us—a town which had a burning interest for us boys; for we remembered how seven years before, in the pastures of Domremy, the Sunflower came with his black flag and brought us the shameful news of the Treaty of Troyes—that treaty which gave France to England, and a daughter of our royal line in marriage to the Butcher of Agincourt. That poor town was not to blame, of course; yet we flushed hot with that old memory, and hoped there would be a misunderstanding here, for we dearly wanted to storm the place and burn it. It was powerfully garrisoned by English and Burgundian soldiery, and was expecting re-enforcements from Paris. Before night we camped before its gates and made rough work with a sortie which marched out against us.

Joan summoned Troyes to surrender. Its commandant, seeing that she had no artillery, scoffed at the idea, and sent her a grossly insulting reply. Five days we consulted and negotiated. No result. The King was about to turn back now, and give up. He was afraid to go on, leaving this strong place in his rear. Then La Hire put in a word, with a slap in it for some of his Majesty's advisers:

"The Maid of Orleans undertook this expedition of her own motion; and it is my mind that it is her judgment that should be followed here, and not that of any other, let him be of whatsoever breed and standing he may."

There was wisdom and righteousness in that. So the King sent for the Maid, and asked her how she thought the prospect looked. She said, without any tone of doubt or question in her voice:

"In three days' time the place is ours."

The smug Chancellor put in a word now:

"If we were sure of it we would wait here six days."

"Six days, forsooth! Name of God, man, we will enter the gates tomorrow!"

Then she mounted, and rode her lines, crying out—

"Make preparation—to your work, friends, to your work! We assault at dawn!"

She worked hard that night; slaving away with her own hands like a common soldier. She ordered fascines and fagots to be prepared and thrown into the fosse, thereby to bridge it; and in this rough labor she took a man's share.

At dawn she took her place at the head of the storming force and the bugles blew the assault. At that moment a flag of truce was flung to the breeze from the walls, and Troyes surrendered without firing a shot.

The next day the King with Joan at his side and the Paladin bearing her banner entered the town in state at the head of the army. And a goodly army it was, now, for it had been growing ever bigger and bigger from the first.

And now a curious thing happened. By the terms of the treaty made with the town the garrison of English and Burgundian soldiery were to be allowed to carry away their "goods" with them. This was well, for otherwise how would they buy the wherewithal to live? Very well; these people were all to go out by the one gate, and at the time set for them to depart we young fellows went to that gate, along with the Dwarf, to see the march-out. Presently here they came in an interminable file, the foot-soldiers in the lead. As they approached one could see that each bore a burden of a bulk and weight to sorely tax his strength; and we said among ourselves, truly these folk are well off for poor common soldiers. When they were come nearer, what do you think? Every rascal of them had a French prisoner on his back! They were carrying away their "goods," you see—their property—strictly according to the permission granted by the treaty.

Now think how clever that was, how ingenious. What could a body say? what could a body do? For certainly these people were within their right. These prisoners were property; nobody could deny that. My dears, if those had been *English* captives, conceive of the richness of that booty! For English prisoners had been scarce and precious for a hundred years; whereas it was a different matter with French prisoners. They had been over-abundant for a century. The possessor of a French prisoner did not hold him long for ransom as a rule, but presently killed him to save the cost of his keep. This shows you how small was the value of such a possession in those times. When we took Troyes a calf was worth thirty francs, a sheep sixteen, a French prisoner eight. It was an enormous price for those other animals—a price which naturally seems incredible to you. It was the war, you see. It worked two ways: it made meat dear and prisoners cheap.

Well, here were these poor Frenchmen being carried off. What could we do? Very little of a permanent sort, but we did what we could. We sent a messenger flying to Joan, and we and the French guards halted the procession for a parley—to gain time, you see. A big Burgundian lost his temper and swore a great oath that none should stop *him;* he would go, and would take his prisoner with him. But we blocked him off, and he saw that he was mistaken about going—he couldn't do it. He exploded into the maddest cursings and revilings, then, and unlashing his prisoner from his back, stood him up, all bound and helpless; then drew his knife, and said to us with a light of sarcastic triumph in his eye—

"I may not carry him away, you say—yet he is mine, none will dispute it. Since I may not convey him hence, this property of mine, there is another way. Yes, I can kill him; not even the dullest among you will question *that* right. Ah, you had not thought of that—vermin!"

That poor starved fellow begged us with his piteous eyes to save him; then spoke, and said he had a wife and little children at home. Think how it wrung our heartstrings. But what could we do? The Burgundian was within his right. We could only beg and plead for the prisoner. Which we did. And the Burgundian enjoyed it. He stayed his hand to hear more of it, and laugh at it. That stung. Then the Dwarf said—

"Prithee, young sirs, let me beguile him; for when a matter requiring persuasion is to the fore, I have indeed a gift in that sort, as any will tell you that know me well. You smile; and that is punishment for my vanity, and fairly earned, I grant it you. Still, if I may toy a little, just a little—" saying which he stepped to the Burgundian and began a fair soft speech, all of goodly and gentle tenor; and in the midst he mentioned the Maid; and was going on to say how she out of her good heart would prize and praise this compassionate deed which he was about to—

It was as far as he got. The Burgundian burst into his smooth oration with an insult levelled at Joan of Arc. We sprang forward, but the Dwarf, his face all livid, brushed us aside and said, in a most grave and earnest way—

"I crave your patience. Am not I her guard of honor? This is my affair."

And saying this he suddenly shot his right hand out and gripped the great Burgundian by the throat, and so held him upright on his feet. "You have insulted the Maid," he said; "and the Maid is France. The tongue that does that earns a long furlough."

One heard the muffled cracking of bones. The Burgundian's eyes began to protrude from their sockets and stare with a leaden dulness at vacancy. The color deepened in his face and became an opaque purple. His hands hung down limp, his body collapsed with a shiver, every muscle relaxed its tension and ceased from its function. The Dwarf took away his hand and the column of inert mortality sank mushily to the ground.

We struck the bonds from the prisoner and told him he was free. His crawling humbleness changed to frantic joy in a moment, and his ghastly fear to a childish rage. He flew at that dead corpse and kicked it, spat in its face; danced upon it, crammed mud into its mouth, laughing, jeering, cursing and volleying forth indecencies and bestialities like a drunken fiend. It was a thing to be expected: soldiering makes few saints. Many of the on-lookers laughed, others were indifferent, none was surprised. But presently in his mad caperings the freed man capered within reach of the waiting file, and another Burgundian promptly slipped a knife through his neck, and down he went with a death-shriek, his brilliant artery-blood spurting ten feet as straight and bright as a ray of light. There was a great burst of jolly laughter all around from friend and foe alike; and thus closed one of the pleasantest incidents of my checkered military life.

And now came Joan hurrying, and deeply troubled. She considered the claim of the garrison, then said—

"You have right upon your side. It is plain. It was a careless word to put in the treaty, and covers too much. But ye may not take these poor men away. They are French, and I will not have it. The King shall ransom them, every one. Wait till I send you word from him; and hurt no hair of their heads; for I tell you, I who speak, that that would cost you very dear."

That settled it. The prisoners were safe for one while, anyway. Then she rode back eagerly and required that thing of the King, and would listen to no paltering and no excuses. So the King told her to have her way, and she rode straight back and bought the captives free in his name and let them go.

CHAPTER 35

It was here that we saw again the Grand Master of the King's Household, in whose castle Joan was guest when she tarried at Chinon in those first days of her coming out of her own country. She made him Bailiff of Troyes, now, by the King's permission.

And now we marched again; Châlons surrendered to us; and there by Châlons in a talk, Joan being asked if she had no fears for the future, said yes, one—treachery. Who could believe it? who could dream it? And yet in a sense it was prophecy. Truly man is a pitiful animal.

We marched, marched, kept on marching; and at last on the 16th of July we came in sight of our goal, and saw the great cathedral towers of Rheims rise out of the distance! Huzzah after huzzah swept the army from van to rear; and as for Joan of Arc, there where she sat her horse gazing, clothed all in white armor, dreamy, beautiful, and in her face a deep, deep joy, a joy not of earth, oh, she was not flesh, she was a spirit! Her sublime mission was closing—closing in flawless triumph. To-morrow she could say, "It is finished—let me go free."

We camped, and the hurry and rush and turmoil of the grand preparations began. The Archbishop and a great deputation arrived; and after these came flock after flock, crowd after crowd, of citizens and country folk hurrahing in, with banners and music, and flowed over the camp, one rejoicing inundation after another, everybody drunk with happiness. And all night long Rheims was hard at work, hammering away, decorating the town, building triumphal arches, and clothing the ancient cathedral within and without in a glory of opulent splendors.

We moved betimes in the morning: the coronation ceremonies would begin at nine and last five hours. We were aware that the garrison of English and Burgundian soldiers had given up all thought of resisting the Maid, and that we should find the gates standing hospitably open and the whole city ready to welcome us with enthusiasm.

It was a delicious morning, brilliant with sunshine but cool and fresh and inspiring. The army was in great form, and fine to see, as it uncoiled from its lair fold by fold, and stretched away on the final march of the peaceful Coronation Campaign.

Joan, on her black horse, with the Lieutenant-General and the personal staff grouped about her, took post for a final review and a good-bye; for she was not expecting to ever be a soldier again, or ever serve with these or any other soldiers any more after this day. The army knew this, and believed it was looking for the last time upon the girlish face of its invincible little Chief, its pet, its pride, its darling, whom it had ennobled in its private heart with nobilities of its own creation, calling her "Daughter of God," "Savior of France," "Victory's Sweetheart," "the Page of Christ," together with still softer titles which were simply naïf and frank endearments such as men are used to confer upon children whom they love. And so one saw a new thing now; a thing bred of the emotion that was present there on both sides. Always before, in the march-past, the battalions had gone swinging by in a storm of cheers, heads up and eyes flashing, the drums rolling, the bands braying pæans of victory; but now there was nothing of that. But for one impressive sound, one could have closed his eyes and imagined himself in a world of the dead. That one sound was all that visited the ear in the summer stillness—just that one sound—the muffled tread of the marching host. As the serried masses drifted by, the men put their right hands up to their temples, palms to the front, in military salute, turning their eyes upon Joan's face in mute God-bless-you and farewell, and keeping them there while they could. They still kept their hands up in reverent salute many steps after they had passed by. Every time Joan put her handkerchief to her eyes you could see a little quiver of emotion crinkle along the faces of the files.

The march-past after a victory is a thing to drive the heart mad with jubilation; but this one was a thing to break it.

We rode now to the King's lodging, which was the Archbishop's country palace; and he was presently ready, and we galloped off and took position at the head of the army. By this time the country people were arriving in multitudes from every direction and massing themselves on both sides of the road to get sight of Joan—just as had been done every day since our first day's march began. Our march now lay through the grassy plain, and those peasants made a dividing double border for that plain. They stretched right down through it, a broad belt of bright colors on each side of the road; for every peasant girl and woman in it had a white jacket on her body and a crimson skirt on the rest of her. Endless borders made of poppies and lilies stretching away in front of us—that is what it looked like. And that is the kind of lane we had been marching through all these days. Not a lane between multitudinous flowers standing upright on their stems—no, these flowers were always kneeling; kneeling, these human flowers, with their hands and faces lifted toward Joan of Arc, and the grateful tears streaming down. And all along, those closest to the road hugged her feet and kissed them and laid their wet cheeks fondly against them. I never, during all those days, saw any of either sex stand while she passed, nor any man keep his head covered. Afterwards in the Great Trial these touching scenes were used as a weapon against her. She had been made an object of adoration by the people, and this was proof that she was a heretic—so claimed that unjust court.

As we drew near the city the curving long sweep of ramparts and towers was gay with fluttering flags and black with masses of people; and all the air was vibrant with the crash of artillery and gloomed with drifting clouds of smoke. We entered the gates in state and moved in procession through the city, with all the guilds and industries in holiday costume marching in our rear with their banners; and all the route was hedged with a huzzahing crush of people, and all the windows were full and all the roofs; and from the balconies hung costly stuffs of rich colors; and the waving of handkerchiefs, seen in perspective through a long vista, was like a snow-storm.

Joan's name had been introduced into the prayers of the Church—an honor theretofore restricted to royalty. But she had a dearer honor and an honor more to be proud of, from a humbler source: the common people had had leaden medals struck which bore her effigy and her escutcheon, and these they wore as charms. One saw them everywhere.

From the Archbishop's Palace, where we halted, and where the King and Joan were to lodge, the King sent to the Abbey Church of St. Remi, which was over toward the gate by which we had entered the city, for the *Sainte Ampoule*, or flask of holy oil. This oil was not earthly oil; it was made in heaven; the flask also. The flask, with the oil in it, was brought down from heaven by a dove. It was sent down to St. Remi just as he was going to baptize King Clovis, who had become a Christian. I know this to be true. I had known it long before; for Père Fronte told me in Domremy. I cannot tell you how strange and awful it made me feel when I saw that flask and knew I was looking with my own eyes upon a thing which had actually been in heaven; a thing which had been seen by angels, perhaps; and by God Himself of a certainty, for He sent it. And I was looking upon it—I. At one time I could have touched it. But I was afraid; for I could not know but that God had touched it. It is most probable that He had.

From this flask Clovis had been anointed; and from it all the Kings of France had been anointed since. Yes, ever since the time of Clovis; and that was nine hundred years. And so, as I have said, that flask of holy oil was sent for, while we waited. A coronation without that would not have been a coronation at all, in my belief.

Now in order to get the flask, a most ancient ceremonial had to be gone through with; otherwise the Abbé of St. Remi, hereditary guardian in perpetuity of the oil, would not deliver it. So, in accordance with custom, the King deputed five great nobles to ride in solemn state and richly armed and accoutred, they and their steeds, to the Abbey Church as a guard of honor to the Archbishop of Rheims and his canons, who were to bear the King's demand for the oil. When the five great lords were ready to start, they knelt in a row and put up their mailed hands before their faces, palm joined to palm, and swore upon their lives to conduct the sacred vessel safely, and safely restore it again to the Church of St. Remi after the anointing of the King. The Archbishop and his subordinates, thus nobly escorted, took their way to St. Remi. The Archbishop was in grand costume, with his mitre on his head and his cross in his hand. At the door of St. Remi they halted and formed, to receive the holy phial. Soon one heard the deep tones of the organ and of chanting men; then one saw a long file of lights approaching through the dim church. And so came the Abbot, in his sacerdotal panoply, bearing the phial, with his people following after. He delivered it, with solemn ceremonies, to the Archbishop; then the march back began, and it was most impressive; for it moved, the whole way, between two multitudes of men and women who lay flat upon their faces and prayed in dumb silence and in dread while that awful thing went by that had been in heaven.

This august company arrived at the great west door of the cathedral; and as the Archbishop entered a noble anthem rose and filled the vast building. The cathedral was packed with people—people in thousands. Only a wide space down the centre had been kept free. Down this space walked the Archbishop and his canons, and after them followed those five stately figures in splendid harness, each bearing his feudal banner—and riding!

Oh, that was a magnificent thing to see. Riding down the cavernous vastness of the building through the rich lights streaming in long rays from the pictured windows—oh, there was never anything so grand!

They rode clear to the choir—as much as four hundred feet from the door, it was said. Then the Archbishop dismissed them, and they made deep obeisance till their plumes touched their horses' necks, then made those proud prancing and mincing and dancing creatures go backwards all the way to the door—which was pretty to see, and graceful; then they stood them on their hind-feet and spun them around and plunged away and disappeared.

For some minutes there was a deep hush, a waiting pause; a silence so profound that it was as if all those packed thousands there were steeped in dreamless slumber—why, you could even notice the faintest sounds, like the drowsy buzzing of insects; then came a mighty flood of rich strains from four hundred silver trumpets, and then, framed in the pointed archway of the great west door, appeared Joan and the King. They advanced slowly, side by side, through a tempest of welcome—explosion after explosion of cheers and cries, mingled with the deep thunders of the organ and rolling tides of triumphant song from chanting choirs. Behind Joan and the King came the Paladin with the Banner displayed; and a majestic figure he was, and most proud and lofty in his bearing, for he knew that the people were marking him and taking note of the gorgeous state dress which covered his armor.

At his side was the Sire d'Albret, proxy for the Constable of France, bearing the Sword of State.

After these, in order of rank, came a body royally attired representing the lay peers of France; it consisted of three princes of the blood, and La Tremouille and the young De Laval brothers.

These were followed by the representatives of the ecclesiastical peers—the Archbishop of Rheims, and the Bishops of Laon, Châlons, Orleans, and one other.

Behind these came the Grand Staff, all our great generals and famous names, and everybody was eager to get a sight of them. Through all the din one could hear shouts, all along, that told you where two of them were: "Live the Bastard of Orléans!" "Satan La Hire forever!"

The august procession reached its appointed place in time, and the solemnities of the Coronation began. They were long and imposing—with prayers, and anthems, and sermons, and everything that is right for such occasions; and Joan was at the King's side all these hours, with her Standard in her hand. But at last came the grand act: the King took the oath, he was anointed with the sacred oil; a splendid personage, followed by train-bearers and other attendants, approached, bearing the Crown of France upon a cushion, and kneeling offered it. The King seemed to hesitate—in fact *did* hesitate; for he put out his hand and then stopped with it there in the air over the crown, the fingers in the attitude of taking hold of it. But that was for only a moment—though a moment is a notable something when it stops the heart-beat of twenty thousand people and makes them catch their breath. Yes, only a moment; then he caught Joan's eye, and she gave him a look with all the joy of her thankful great soul in it, then he smiled, and took the Crown of France in his hand, and right finely and right royally lifted it up and set it upon his head.

Then what a crash there was! All about us cries and cheers, and the chanting of the choirs and groaning of the organ; and outside the clamoring of the bells and the booming of the cannon.

The fantastic dream, the incredible dream, the impossible dream of the peasant child stood fulfilled: the English power was broken, the Heir of France was crowned.

She was like one transfigured, so divine was the joy that shone in her face as she sank to her knees at the King's feet and looked up at him through her tears. Her lips were quivering, and her words came soft and low and broken:

"Now, oh gentle King, is the pleasure of God accomplished according to his command that you should come to Rheims and receive the crown that belongeth of right to you, and unto none other. My work which was given me to do is finished; give me your peace, and let me go back to my mother, who is poor and old, and has need of me."

The King raised her up, and there before all that host he praised her great deeds in most noble terms; and there he confirmed her nobility and titles, making her the equal of a count in rank, and also appointed a household and officers for her according to her dignity; and then he said:

"You have saved the crown. Speak—require—demand; and whatsoever grace you ask it shall be granted, though it make the kingdom poor to meet it."

Now that was fine, that was royal. Joan was on her knees again straightway, and said:

"Then, oh gentle King, if out of your compassion you will speak the word, I pray you give commandment that my village, poor and hard pressed by reason of the war, may have its taxes remitted."

"It is so commanded. Say on."

"That is all."

"All? Nothing but that?"

"It is all. I have no other desire."

"But that is nothing—less than nothing. Ask—do not be afraid."

"Indeed I cannot, gentle King. Do not press me. I will not have aught else, but only this alone."

The King seemed nonplussed, and stood still a moment, as if trying to comprehend and realize the full stature of this strange unselfishness. Then he raised his head and said:

"She has won a kingdom and crowned its King; and all she asks and all she will take is this poor grace—and even this is for others, not for herself. And it is well; her act being proportioned to the dignity of one who carries in her head and heart riches which outvalue any that any King could add, though he gave his all. She shall have her way. Now therefore it is decreed that from this day forth Domremy, natal village of Joan of Arc, Deliverer of France, called the Maid of Orleans, is freed from all taxation *forever.*" Whereat the silver horns blew a jubilant blast.

There, you see, she had had a vision of this very scene the time she was in a trance in the pastures of Domremy, and we asked her to name the boon she would demand of the King if he should ever chance to tell her she might claim one. But whether she had the vision or not, this act showed that after all the dizzy grandeurs that had come upon her, she was still the same simple unselfish creature that she was that day.

Yes, Charles VII. remitted those taxes "forever." Often the gratitude of kings and nations fades and their promises are forgotten or deliberately violated; but you, who are children of France, should remember with pride that France has kept this one faithfully. Sixty-three years have gone by since that day. The taxes of the region wherein Domremy lies have been collected sixty-three times since then, and all the villages of that region have paid except that one—Domremy. The tax-gatherer never visits Domremy. Domremy has long ago forgotten what that dreaded sorrow-sowing apparition is like. Sixty-three tax-books have been filled meantime, and they lie yonder with the other public records, and any may see them that desire it. At the top of every page in the sixty-three books stands the name of a village, and below that name its weary burden of taxation is figured out and displayed; in the case of all save one. It is true, just as I tell you. In each of the sixty-three books there is a page headed "Domremi," but under that name not a figure appears. Where the figures should be, there are three words written; and the same words have been written every year for all these years; yes, it is a blank page, with always those grateful words lettered across the face of it—a touching memorial. Thus:

DOMREMI

RIEN—LA PUCELLE

"NOTHING—THE MAID OF ORLEANS." How brief it is; yet how much it says! It is the nation speaking. You have the spectacle of that unsentimental thing, a Government, making reverence to that name and saying to its agent, "*Uncover, and pass on; it is France that commands.*" Yes, the promise has been kept; it will be kept always; "forever" was the King's word.*

* It was faithfully kept during three hundred and sixty years and more; then the over-confident octogenarian's prophecy failed. During the tumult of the French Revolution the promise was forgotten and the grace withdrawn. It has remained

At two o'clock in the afternoon the ceremonies of the Coronation came at last to an end; then the procession formed once more, with Joan and the King at its head, and took up its solemn march through the midst of the church, all instruments and all people making such clamor of rejoicing noises as was indeed a marvel to hear. And so ended the third of the great days of Joan's life. And how close together they stand—May 8th, June 18th, July 17th!

CHAPTER 36

We mounted and rode, a spectacle to remember, a most noble display of rich vestments and nodding plumes, and as we moved between the banked multitudes they sank down all along abreast of us as we advanced, like grain before the reaper, and kneeling hailed with a rousing welcome the consecrated King and his companion the Deliverer of France. But by-and-by when we had paraded about the chief parts of the city and were come near to the end of our course, we being now approaching the Archbishop's palace, one saw on the right, hard by the inn that is called the Zebra, a strange thing—two men not kneeling but *standing!* Standing in the front rank of the kneelers; unconscious, transfixed, staring. Yes, and clothed in the coarse garb of the peasantry, these two. Two halberdiers sprang at them in a fury to teach them better manners; but just as they seized them Joan cried out "Forbear!" and slid from her saddle and flung her arms about one of those peasants, calling him by all manner of endearing names, and sobbing. For it was her father; and the other was her uncle Laxart.

The news flew everywhere, and shouts of welcome were raised, and in just one little moment those two despised and unknown plebeians were become famous and popular and envied, and everybody was in a fever to get sight of them and be able to say, all their lives

---

in disuse ever since. Joan never asked to be remembered, but France has remembered her with an inextinguishable love and reverence; Joan never asked for a statue, but France has lavished them upon her; Joan never asked for a church for Domremy, but France is building one; Joan never asked for saintship, but even that is impending. Everything which Joan of Arc did not ask for has been given her, and with a noble profusion; but the one humble little thing which she did ask for and get, has been taken away from her. There is something infinitely pathetic about this. France owes Domremy a hundred years of taxes, and could hardly find a citizen within her borders who would vote against the payment of the debt.—NOTE BY THE TRANSLATOR

long, that they had seen the father of Joan of Arc and the brother of her mother. How easy it was for her to do miracles like to this! She was like the sun; on whatsoever dim and humble object her rays fell, that thing was straightway drowned in glory.

All graciously the King said:

"Bring them to me."

And she brought them; she radiant with happiness and affection, they trembling and scared, with their caps in their shaking hands; and there before all the world the King gave them his hand to kiss, while the people gazed in envy and admiration; and he said to old D'Arc—

"Give God thanks for that you are father to this child, this dispenser of immortalities. You who bear a name that will still live in the mouths of men when all the race of Kings has been forgotten, it is not meet that you bare your head before the fleeting fames and dignities of a day—cover yourself!" And truly he looked right fine and princely when he said that. Then he gave order that the Bailly of Rheims be brought; and when he was come, and stood bent low and bare, the King said to him, "These two are guests of France"; and bade him use them hospitably.

I may as well say now as later, that Papa D'Arc and Laxart were stopping in that little Zebra inn, and that there they remained. Finer quarters were offered them by the Bailly, also public distinctions and brave entertainment; but they were frightened at these projects, they being only humble and ignorant peasants: so they begged off, and had peace. They could not have enjoyed such things. Poor souls, they did not even know what to do with their hands, and it took all their attention to keep from treading on them. The Bailly did the best he could in the circumstances. He made the innkeeper place a whole floor at their disposal, and told him to provide everything they might desire, and charge all to the city. Also the Bailly gave them a horse apiece, and furnishings; which so overwhelmed them with pride and delight and astonishment that they couldn't speak a word; for in their lives they had never dreamed of wealth like this, and could not believe, at first, that the horses were real and would not dissolve to a mist and blow away. They could not unglue their minds from those grandeurs, and were always wrenching the conversation out of its groove and dragging the matter of animals into it, so that they could say "my horse" here, and "my horse" there and yonder and all around, and taste the words and lick their chops over them, and spread their legs and hitch their thumbs in their armpits, and feel as the good God feels when He looks out on His fleets of constellations ploughing the awful deeps of space and reflects with satisfaction that they are His—all His. Well, they *were* the happiest old children one ever saw, and the simplest.

The city gave a grand banquet to the King and Joan in mid-afternoon, and to the Court and the Grand Staff; and about the middle of it Père d'Arc and Laxart were sent for, but would not venture until it was promised that they might sit in a gallery and be all by themselves and see all that was to be seen and yet be unmolested. And so they sat there and looked down upon the splendid spectacle, and were moved till the tears ran down their cheeks to see the unbelievable honors that were paid to their small darling, and how naïvely serene and unafraid she sat there with those consuming glories beating upon her.

But at last her serenity was broken up. Yes, it stood the strain of the King's gracious speech; and of D'Alençon's praiseful words, and the Bastard's; and even La Hire's thunder-blast, which took the place by storm; but at last, as I have said, they brought a force to bear which was too strong for her. For at the close the King put up his hand to command silence, and so waited, with his hand up, till every sound was dead and it was as if one could almost *feel* the stillness, so profound it was. Then out of some remote corner of that vast place there rose a plaintive voice, and in tones most tender and sweet and rich came floating through that enchanted hush our poor old simple song "L'Arbre Fée de Bourlemont!" and then Joan broke down and put her face in her hands and cried. Yes, you see, all in a moment the pomps and grandeurs dissolved away and she was a little child again herding her sheep with the tranquil pastures stretched about her, and war and wounds and blood and death and the mad frenzy and turmoil of battle a dream. Ah, that shows you the power of music, that magician of magicians; who lifts his wand and says his mysterious word and all things real pass away and the phantoms of your mind walk before you clothed in flesh.

That was the King's invention, that sweet and dear surprise. Indeed, he had fine things hidden away in his nature, though one seldom got a glimpse of them, with that scheming Tremouille and those others always standing in the light, and he so indolently content to save himself fuss and argument and let them have their way.

At the fall of night we the Domremy contingent of the personal staff were with the father and uncle at the inn, in their private parlor, brewing generous drinks and breaking ground for a homely talk about Domremy and the neighbors, when a large parcel arrived from Joan to be kept till she came; and soon she came herself and sent her guard away, saying she would take one of her father's rooms and sleep under his roof, and so be at home again. We of the staff rose and stood, as was meet, until she made us sit. Then she turned and saw that the two old men had gotten up too, and were standing in an embarrassed and unmilitary way; which made her want to laugh, but she kept it in, as not wishing to hurt them; and got them to their seats and snuggled down between them, and took a hand of each of them upon her knees and nestled her own hands in them, and said—

"Now we will have no more ceremony, but be kin and playmates as in other times; for I am done with the great wars, now, and you two will take me home with you, and I shall see—" She stopped, and for a moment her happy face sobered, as if a doubt or a presentiment had flitted through her mind; then it cleared again, and she said, with a passionate yearning, "Oh, if the day were but come and we could start!"

The old father was surprised, and said—

"Why, child, are you in earnest? Would you leave doing these wonders that make you to be praised by everybody while there is still so much glory to be won; and would you go out from this grand comradeship with princes and generals to be a drudging villager again and a nobody? It is not rational."

"No," said the uncle, Laxart, "it is amazing to hear, and indeed not understandable. It is a stranger thing to hear her say she will stop the soldiering than it was to hear her say she would begin it; and I who speak to you can say in all truth that that was the strangest word that ever I had heard till this day and hour. I would it could be explained."

"It is not difficult," said Joan. "I was not ever fond of wounds and suffering, nor fitted by my nature to inflict them; and quarrellings did always distress me, and noise and tumult were against my liking, my disposition being toward peace and quietness, and love for all things that have life; and being made like this, how could I bear to think of wars and blood, and the pain that goes with them, and the sorrow and mourning that follow after? But by his angels God laid His great commands upon me, and could I disobey? I did as I was bid. Did he command me to do many things? No; only two: to raise the siege of Orleans, and crown the King at Rheims. The task is finished, and I am free. Has ever a poor soldier fallen in my sight, whether friend or foe, and I not felt his pain in my own body, and the grief of his home-mates in my own heart? No, not one; and, oh, it is such bliss to know that my release is won, and that I shall not any more see these cruel things or suffer these tortures of the mind again! Then why should I not go to my village and be as I was before? It is heaven! and ye wonder that I desire it. Ah, ye are men—just men! My mother would understand."

They didn't quite know what to say; so they sat still awhile, looking pretty vacant. Then old D'Arc said—

"Yes, your mother—that is true. I never saw such a woman. She worries, and worries, and worries; and wakes nights, and lies so, thinking—that is, worrying; worrying about you. And when the night-storms go raging along, she moans and says, 'Ah, God pity her, she is out in this with her poor wet soldiers.' And when the lightning glares and the thunder crashes she wrings her hands and trembles, saying, 'It is like the awful cannon and the flash, and yonder somewhere she is riding down upon the spouting guns and I not there to protect her.'"

"Ah, poor mother, it is pity, it is pity!"

"Yes, a most strange woman, as I have noticed a many times. When there is news of a victory and all the village goes mad with pride and joy, she rushes here and there in a maniacal frenzy till she finds out the one only thing she cares to know—that you are safe; then down she goes on her knees in the dirt and praises God as long as there is any breath left in her body; and all on your account, for she never mentions the battle once. And always she says, '*Now* it is over—*now* France is saved—*now* she will come home'—and always is disappointed and goes about mourning."

"Don't, father! it breaks my heart. I will be so good to her when I get home. I will do her work for her, and be her comfort, and she shall not suffer any more through me."

There was some more talk of this sort, then Uncle Laxart said—

"You have done the will of God, dear, and are quits; it is true, and none may deny it; but what of the King? You are his best soldier; what if he command you to stay?"

That was a crusher—and sudden! It took Joan a moment or two to recover from the shock of it; then she said, quite simply and resignedly:

"The King is my Lord; I am his servant." She was silent and thoughtful a little while, then she brightened up and said, cheerily, "But let us drive such thoughts away—this is no time for them. Tell me about home."

So the two old gossips talked and talked; talked about everything and everybody in the village; and it was good to hear. Joan out of her kindness tried to get *us* into the conversation, but that failed, of course.

She was the Commander-in-Chief, we were nobodies; her name was the mightiest in France, we were invisible atoms; she was the comrade of princes and heroes, we of the humble and obscure; she held rank above all Personages and all Puissances whatsoever in the whole earth, by right of bearing her commission direct from God. To put it in one word, she was JOAN OF ARC—and when that is said, all is said. To us she was divine. Between her and us lay the bridgeless abyss which that word implies. We could not be familiar with her. No, you can see yourselves that that would have been impossible.

And yet she was so human, too, and so good and kind and dear and loving and cheery and charming and unspoiled and unaffected! Those are all the words I think of now, but they are not enough; no, they are too few and colorless and meagre to tell it all, or tell the half. Those simple old men didn't realize her; they couldn't; they had never known any people but human beings, and so they had no other standard to measure her by. To them, after their first little shyness had worn off, she was just a girl—that was all. It was amazing. It made one shiver, sometimes, to see how calm and easy and comfortable they were in her presence, and hear them talk to her exactly as they would have talked to any other girl in France.

Why, that simple old Laxart sat up there and droned out the most tedious and empty tale one ever heard, and neither he nor Papa D'Arc ever gave a thought to the badness of the etiquette of it, or ever suspected that that foolish tale was anything but dignified and valuable history. There was not an atom of value in it; and whilst they thought it distressing and pathetic, it was in fact not pathetic at all, but actually ridiculous. At least it seemed so to me, and it seems so yet. Indeed I know it was, because it made Joan laugh; and the more sorrowful it got the more it made her laugh; and the Paladin said that he could have laughed himself if she had not been there, and Noël Rainguesson said the same. It was about old Laxart going to a funeral there at Domremy two or three weeks back. He had spots all over his face and hands, and he got Joan to rub some healing ointment on them, and while she was doing it, and comforting him, and trying to say pitying things to him, he told her how it happened. And first he asked her if she remembered that black bull calf that she left behind when she came away, and she said indeed she did, and he was a dear, and she loved him so, and was he well?—and just drowned him in questions about that creature. And he said it was a young bull now, and very frisky; and he was to bear a principal hand at a funeral; and she said, "The bull?" and he said "No, myself"; but said the bull *did* take a hand, but not because of his being invited, for he wasn't; but anyway he was away over beyond the Fairy Tree, and fell asleep on the grass with his Sunday funeral clothes on, and a long black rag on his hat and hanging down his back; and when he woke he saw by the sun how late it was, and not a moment to lose; and jumped up terribly worried, and saw the young bull grazing there, and thought maybe he could ride part way on him and gain time; so he tied a rope around the bull's body to hold on by, and put a halter on him to steer with, and jumped on and started; but it was all new to the bull, and he was discontented with it, and scurried around and bellowed and reared and pranced, and Uncle Laxart was satisfied, and wanted to get off and go by the next bull or some other way that was quieter, but he didn't dare try; and it was getting very warm for him, too, and disturbing and wearisome, and not proper for Sunday; but by-and-by the bull lost all his temper, and went tearing down the slope with his tail in the air and bellowing in the most awful way; and just in the edge of the village he knocked down some beehives, and the bees turned out and joined the excursion, and soared along in a black cloud that nearly hid those other two from sight, and prodded them both, and jabbed them and speared them and spiked them, and made them bellow and shriek, and shriek and bellow; and here they came roaring through the village like a hurricane, and took the funeral procession right in the centre, and sent that section of it sprawling, and galloped over it, and the rest scattered apart and fled screeching in every direction, every person with a layer of bees on him, and not a rag of that funeral left but the corpse; and finally the bull broke for the river and jumped in, and when they fished Uncle Laxart out he was nearly drowned, and his face looked like a pudding with raisins in it. And then he turned around, this old simpleton, and looked a long time in a dazed way at Joan where she had her face in a cushion, dying, apparently, and says—

"What do you reckon she is laughing at?"

And old D'Arc stood looking at her the same way, sort of absently scratching his head; but had to give it up, and said *he* didn't know—"must have been something that happened when we weren't noticing."

Yes, both of those old people thought that that tale was pathetic; whereas to my mind it was purely ridiculous, and not in any way valuable to any one. It seemed so to me then, and it seems so to me yet. And as for history, it does not resemble history, for the office of history is to furnish serious and important facts that *teach;* whereas this strange and useless event teaches nothing; nothing that I can see, except not to ride a bull to a funeral; and surely no reflecting person needs to be taught that.

CHAPTER 37

Now these were nobles, you know, by decree of the King!—these precious old infants. But they did not realize it; they could not be called conscious of it; it was an abstraction, a phantom; to them it had no substance; their minds could not take hold of it. No, they did not bother about their nobility; they lived in their horses. The horses were solid; they were visible facts, and would make a mighty stir in Domremy. Presently something was said about the Coronation, and old D'Arc said it was going to be a grand thing to be able to say, when they got home, that they were present in the very town itself when it happened. Joan looked troubled, and said—

"Ah, that reminds me. You were here and you didn't send me word. In the town, indeed! Why, you could have sat with the other nobles, and been welcome; and could have looked upon the crowning itself, and carried *that* home to tell. Ah, why did you use me so, and send me no word?"

The old father was embarrassed, now, quite visibly embarrassed, and had the air of one who does not quite know what to say. But Joan was looking up in his face, her hands upon his shoulders—waiting. He had to speak; so presently he drew her to his breast, which was heaving with emotion; and he said, getting out his words with difficulty—

"There, hide your face, child, and let your old father humble himself and make his confession. I—I—don't you see, don't you understand? —I could not know that these grandeurs would not turn your young head—it would be only natural. I might shame you before these great per—"

"Father!"

"And then I was afraid, as remembering that cruel thing I said once in my sinful anger. Oh, appointed of God to be a soldier, and the greatest in the land! and in my ignorant anger I said I would drown you with my own hands if you unsexed yourself and brought shame to your name and family. Ah, how could I ever have said it, and you so good and dear and innocent! I was afraid; for I was guilty. You understand it now, my child, and you forgive?"

Do you see? Even that poor groping old land-crab, with his skull full of pulp, had pride. Isn't it wonderful? And more—he had conscience; he had a sense of right and wrong, such as it was; he was able to feel remorse. It looks impossible, it looks incredible, but it is not. I believe that some day it will be found out that peasants are people. Yes, beings in a great many respects like ourselves. And I believe that some day *they* will find this out, too—and then! Well, then I think they will rise up and demand to be regarded as part of the race, and that by consequence there will be trouble. Whenever one sees in a book or in a king's proclamation those words "the nation," they bring before us the upper classes; only those; we know no other "nation"; for us and the kings no other "nation" exists. But from the day that I saw old D'Arc the peasant acting and feeling just as I should have acted and felt myself, I have carried the conviction in my heart that our peasants are not merely animals, beasts of burden put here by the good God to produce food and comfort for the "nation," but something more and better. You look incredulous. Well, that is your training; it is the training of everybody; but as for me, I thank that incident for giving me a better light, and I have never forgotten it.

Let me see—where was I? One's mind wanders around here and there and yonder, when one is old. I think I said Joan comforted him. Certainly, that is what she would do—there was no need to say that. She coaxed him and petted him and caressed him, and laid the memory of that old hard speech of his to rest. Laid it to rest until she should be dead. Then he would remember it again—yes, yes! Lord, how those things sting, and burn, and gnaw—the things which we did against the innocent dead! And we say in our anguish, "If they could only come back!" Which is all very well to say, but as far as I can see, it doesn't profit anything. In my opinion the best way is not to do the thing in the first place. And I am not alone in this; I have heard our two knights say the same thing; and a man there in Orleans—no, I believe it was at Beaugency, or one of those places—it seems more as if it was at Beaugency than the others—this man said the same thing exactly; almost the same words; a dark man with a cast in his eye and one leg shorter than the other. His name was—was—it is singular that I can't call that man's name; I had it in my mind only a moment ago, and I know it begins with—no, I don't remember what it begins with; but never mind, let it go; I will think of it presently, and then I will tell you.

Well, pretty soon the old father wanted to know how Joan felt when she was in the thick of a battle, with the bright blades hacking and flashing all around her, and the blows rapping and slatting on her shield, and blood gushing on her from the cloven ghastly face and broken teeth of the neighbor at her elbow, and the perilous sudden back surge of massed horses upon a person when the front ranks give way before a heavy rush of the enemy, and men tumble limp and groaning out of saddles all around, and battle-flags falling from dead hands wipe across one's face and hide the tossing turmoil a moment, and in the reeling and swaying and laboring jumble one's horse's hoofs sink into soft substances and shrieks of pain respond, and presently—panic! rush! swarm! flight! and death and hell following after! And the old fellow got ever so much excited; and strode up and down, his tongue going like a mill, asking question after question and never waiting for an answer; and finally he stood Joan up in the middle of the room and stepped off and scanned her critically, and said—

"No—I don't understand it. You are so little. So little and slender. When you had your armor on, to-day, it gave one a sort of notion of it; but in these pretty silks and velvets, you are only a dainty page, not a league-striding war-colossus, moving in clouds and darkness and breathing smoke and thunder. I would God I might see you at it and go tell your mother! *That* would help her sleep, poor thing! Here—teach me the arts of the soldier, that I may explain them to her."

And she did it. She gave him a pike, and put him through the manual of arms; and made him do the steps, too. His marching was incredibly awkward and slovenly, and so was his drill with the pike; but he didn't know it, and was wonderfully pleased with himself, and mightily excited and charmed with the ringing, crisp words of command. I am obliged to say that if looking proud and happy when one is marching were sufficient, he would have been the perfect soldier.

And he wanted a lesson in sword-play, and got it. But of course that was beyond him; he was too old. It was beautiful to see Joan handle the foils, but the old man was a bad failure. He was afraid of the things, and skipped and dodged and scrambled around like a woman who has lost her mind on account of the arrival of a bat. He was of no good as an exhibition. But if La Hire had only come in, that would have been another matter. Those two fenced often; I saw them many times. True, Joan was easily his master, but it made a good show for all that, for La Hire was a grand swordsman. What a swift creature Joan was! You would see her standing erect with her ankle-bones together and her foil arched over her head, the hilt in one hand and the button in the other—the old general opposite, bent forward, left hand reposing on his back, his foil advanced, slightly wiggling and squirming, his watching eye boring straight into hers—and all of a sudden she would give a spring forward, and back again; and there she was, with the foil arched over her head as before. La Hire had been hit, but all that the spectator saw of it was a something like a thin flash of light in the air, but nothing distinct, nothing definite.

We kept the drinkables moving, for that would please the Bailly and the landlord; and old Laxart and D'Arc got to feeling quite comfortable, but without being what you could call tipsy. They got out the presents which they had been buying to carry home—humble things and cheap, but they would be fine there, and welcome. And they gave to Joan a present from Père Fronte and one from her mother—the one a little leaden image of the Holy Virgin, the other half a yard of blue silk ribbon; and she was as pleased as a child; and touched, too, as one could see plainly enough. Yes, she kissed those poor things over and over again, as if they had been something costly and wonderful; and she pinned the Virgin on her doublet, and sent for her helmet and tied the ribbon on that; first one way, then another; then a new way, then another new way; and with each effort perching the helmet on her hand and holding it off this way and that, and canting her head to one side and then the other, examining the effect, as a bird does when it has got a new bug. And she said she could almost wish she was going to the wars again; for then she would fight with the better courage, as having always with her something which her mother's touch had blessed.

Old Laxart said he hoped she would go to the wars again, but home first, for that all the people there were cruel anxious to see her—and so he went on:

"They are proud of you, dear. Yes, prouder than any village ever was of anybody before. And indeed it is right and rational; for it is the first time a village has ever had anybody like you to be proud of and call its own. And it is strange and beautiful how they try to give your name to every creature that has a sex that is convenient. It is but half a year since you began to be spoken of and left us, and so it is surprising to see how many babies there are already in that region that are named for you. First it was just Joan; then it was Joan-Orleans; then Joan-Orleans-Beaugency-Patay; and now the next ones will have a lot of towns and the Coronation added, of course. Yes, and the animals the same. They know how you love animals, and so they try to do you honor and show their love for you by naming all those creatures after you; insomuch that if a body should step out and call 'Joan of Arc—come!' there would be a landslide of cats and all such things, each supposing it was the one wanted, and all willing to take the benefit of the doubt, anyway, for the sake of the food that might be on delivery. The kitten you left behind—the last estray you fetched home—bears your name, now, and belongs to Père Fronte, and is the pet and pride of the village; and people have come miles to look at it and pet it and stare at it and wonder over it because it was Joan of Arc's cat. Everybody will tell you that; and one day when a stranger threw a stone at it, not knowing it was your cat, the village rose against him as one man and hanged him! And but for Père Fronte—"

There was an interruption. It was a messenger from the King, bearing a note for Joan, which I read to her, saying he had reflected, and had consulted his other generals, and was obliged to ask her to remain at the head of the army and withdraw her resignation. Also, would she come immediately and attend a council of war? Straightway, at a little distance, military commands and the rumble of drums broke on the still night, and we knew that her guard was approaching.

Deep disappointment clouded her face for just one moment and no more—it passed, and with it the homesick girl, and she was Joan of Arc, Commander-in-Chief again, and ready for duty.

CHAPTER 38

In my double quality of page and secretary I followed Joan to the council. She entered that presence with the bearing of a grieved goddess. What was become of the volatile child that so lately was enchanted with a ribbon and suffocated with laughter over the distresses of a foolish peasant who had stormed a funeral on the back of a bee-stung bull? One may not guess. Simply it was gone, and had left no sign. She moved straight to the council-table, and stood. Her glance swept from face to face there, and where it fell, these it lit as with a torch, those it scorched as with a brand. She knew where to strike. She indicated the generals with a nod, and said—

"My business is not with you. You have not craved a council of war." Then she turned toward the King's privy council, and continued: "No; it is with you. A council of war! It is amazing. There is but one thing to do, and only one, and lo, ye call a council of war! Councils of war have no value but to decide between two or several doubtful courses. But a council of war when there is only *one* course? Conceive of a man in a boat and his family in the water, and he goes out among his friends to ask what he would better do? A council of war, name of God! To determine what?"

She stopped, and turned till her eyes rested upon the face of La Tremouille; and so she stood, silent, measuring him, the excitement in all faces burning steadily higher and higher, and all pulses beating faster and faster; then she said, with deliberation—

"Every sane man—whose loyalty to his King is not a show and a pretence—knows that there is but one rational thing before us—*the march upon Paris!*"

Down came the fist of La Hire with an approving crash upon the table. La Tremouille turned white with anger, but he pulled himself firmly together and held his peace. The King's lazy blood was stirred and his eye kindled finely, for the spirit of war was away down in him somewhere, and a frank bold speech always found it and made it tingle gladsomely. Joan waited to see if the chief minister might wish to defend his position; but he was experienced and wise, and not a man to waste his forces where the current was against him. He would wait; the King's private ear would be at his disposal by-and-by.

That pious fox the Chancellor of France took the word now. He washed his soft hands together, smiling persuasively, and said to Joan:

"Would it be courteous, your Excellency, to move abruptly from here without waiting for an answer from the Duke of Burgundy? You may not know that we are negotiating with his Highness, and that there is likely to be a fortnight's truce between us; and on his part a pledge to deliver Paris into our hands without cost of a blow or the fatigue of a march thither."

Joan turned to him and said, gravely—

"This is not a confessional, my lord. You were not obliged to expose that shame here."

The Chancellor's face reddened, and he retorted—

"Shame? What is there shameful about it?"

Joan answered in level, passionless tones—

"One may describe it without hunting far for words. I knew of this poor comedy, my lord, although it was not intended that I should know. It is to the credit of the devisers of it that they tried to conceal it—this comedy whose text and impulse are describable in two words."

The Chancellor spoke up with a fine irony in his manner:

"Indeed? And will your Excellency be good enough to utter them?"

"Cowardice and treachery!"

The fists of all the generals came down this time, and again the

King's eye sparkled with pleasure. The Chancellor sprang to his feet and appealed to his Majesty—

"Sire, I claim your protection."

But the King waved him to his seat again, saying—

"Peace. She had a right to be consulted before that thing was undertaken, since it concerned war as well as politics. It is but just that she be heard upon it now."

The Chancellor sat down trembling with indignation, and remarked to Joan—

"Out of charity I will consider that you did not know who devised this measure which you condemn in so candid language."

"Save your charity for another occasion, my lord," said Joan, as calmly as before. "Whenever anything is done to injure the interests and degrade the honor of France, all but the dead know how to name the two conspirators-in-chief."

"Sire, sire! this insinuation—"

"It is not an insinuation, my lord," said Joan, placidly, "it is a charge. I bring it against the King's chief minister and his Chancellor."

Both men were on their feet now, insisting that the King modify Joan's frankness; but he was not minded to do it. His ordinary councils were stale water—his spirit was drinking wine, now, and the taste of it was good. He said—

"Sit—and be patient. What is fair for one must in fairness be allowed the other. Consider—and be just. When have you two spared her? What dark charges and harsh names have you withheld when you spoke of her?" Then he added, with a veiled twinkle in his eye, "If these are offences I see no particular difference between them, except that she says her hard things to your faces, whereas you say yours behind her back."

He was pleased with that neat shot and the way it shrivelled those two people up, and made La Hire laugh out loud and the other generals softly quake and chuckle. Joan tranquilly resumed—

"From the first, we have been hindered by this policy of shilly-shally; this fashion of counselling and counselling and counselling where no counselling is needed, but only fighting. We took Orleans on the 8th of May, and could have cleared the region round about in three days and saved the slaughter of Patay. We could have been in Rheims six weeks ago, and in Paris now; and would see the last Englishman pass out of France in half a year. But we struck no blow after Orleans, but went off into the country—what for? Ostensibly to hold councils; really to give Bedford time to send re-enforcements to Talbot—which he did;

and Patay had to be fought. After Patay, more counselling, more waste of precious time. O my King, I would that you would be persuaded!" She began to warm up, now. "Once more we have our opportunity. If we rise and strike, all is well. Bid me march upon Paris. In twenty days it shall be yours, and in six months all France! Here is half a year's work before us; if this chance be wasted, I give you twenty years to do it in. Speak the word, O gentle King—speak but the one—"

"I cry you mercy!" interrupted the Chancellor, who saw a dangerous enthusiasm rising in the King's face. "March upon Paris? Does your Excellency forget that the way bristles with English strongholds?"

"*That* for your English strongholds!" and Joan snapped her fingers scornfully. "Whence have we marched in these last days? From Gien. And whither? To Rheims. What bristled between? English strongholds. What are they now? French ones—and they never cost a blow!" Here applause broke out from the group of generals, and Joan had to pause a moment to let it subside. "Yes, English strongholds bristled before us; now French ones bristle behind us. What is the argument? A child can read it. The strongholds between us and Paris are garrisoned by no new breed of English, but by the same breed as those others—with the same fears, the same questionings, the same weaknesses, the same disposition to see the heavy hand of God descending upon them. We have but to march!—on the instant—and they are ours, Paris is ours, France is ours! Give the word, O my King, command your servant to—"

"Stay!" cried the Chancellor. "It would be madness to put this affront upon his Highness the Duke of Burgundy. By the treaty which we have every hope to make with him—"

"O, the treaty which we hope to make with him! He has scorned you for years, and defied you. Is it your subtle persuasions that have softened his manners and beguiled him to listen to proposals? No; it was *blows!*—the blows which *we* gave him! That is the only teaching that that sturdy rebel can understand. What does he care for *wind?* The treaty which we hope to make with him—alack! *He* deliver Paris! There is no pauper in the land that is less able to do it. He deliver Paris! Ah, but that would make great Bedford smile! Oh, the pitiful pretext! the blind can see that this thin pourparler with its fifteen-day truce has no purpose but to give Bedford time to hurry forward his forces against us. More treachery—always treachery! We call a council of war—with nothing to counsel about; but Bedford calls no council to teach him what our one course is. He knows what he would do in our place. *He would hang his traitors and march upon Paris!* O gentle

King, rouse! The way is open, Paris beckons, France implores. Speak and we–"

"Sire, it is madness, sheer madness! Your Excellency, we cannot, we must not go back from what we have done; we have proposed to treat, we *must* treat with the Duke of Burgundy."

"And we *will!*" said Joan.

"Ah? How?"

"*At the point of the lance!*"

The house rose, to a man–all that had French hearts–and let go a crash of applause–and kept it up; and in the midst of it one heard La Hire growl out: "At the point of the lance! By God, that is the music!" The King was up, too, and drew his sword, and took it by the blade and strode to Joan and delivered the hilt of it into her hand, saying–

"There, the King surrenders. Carry it to Paris."

And so the applause burst out again, and the historical council of war that has bred so many legends was over.

CHAPTER 39

It was away past midnight, and had been a tremendous day in the matter of excitement and fatigue, but that was no matter to Joan when there was business on hand. She did not think of bed. The generals followed her to her official quarters, and she delivered her orders to them as fast as she could talk, and they sent them off to their different commands as fast as delivered; wherefore the messengers galloping hither and thither raised a world of clatter and racket in the still streets; and soon were added to this the music of distant bugles and the roll of drums–notes of preparation; for the vanguard would break camp at dawn.

The generals were soon dismissed, but I wasn't; nor Joan; for it was my turn to work, now. Joan walked the floor and dictated a summons to the Duke of Burgundy to lay down his arms and make peace and exchange pardons with the King; or, if he *must* fight, go fight the Saracens. "Pardonnez-vous l'un à l'autre de bon cœur, entièrement, ainsi que doivent faire loyaux chrétiens, et, s'il vous plait de guerroyer, allez contre les Sarrasins." It was long, but it was good, and had the sterling ring to it. It is my opinion that it was as fine and simple and straightforward and eloquent a state paper as she ever uttered.

It was delivered into the hands of a courier, and he galloped away with it. Then Joan dismissed me, and told me to go to the inn and stay; and in the morning give to her father the parcel which she had left there. It contained presents for the Domremy relatives and friends and a peasant dress which she had bought for herself. She said she would say good-bye to her father and uncle in the morning if it should still be their purpose to go, instead of tarrying awhile to see the city.

I didn't say anything, of course; but I could have said that wild horses couldn't keep those men in that town half a day. *They* waste the glory of being the first to carry the great news to Domremy—*the taxes remitted forever!*—and hear the bells clang and clatter, and the people cheer and shout? Oh, not they. Patay and Orleans and the Coronation were events which in a vague way these men understood to be colossal; but they were colossal mists, films, abstractions: *this* was a gigantic reality!

When I got there, do you suppose they were abed! Quite the reverse. They and the rest were as mellow as mellow could be; and the Paladin was doing his battles over in great style, and the old peasants were endangering the building with their applause. He was doing Patay now; and was bending his big frame forward and laying out the positions and movements with a rake here and a rake there of his formidable sword on the floor, and the peasants were stooped over with their hands on their spread knees observing with excited eyes and ripping out ejaculations of wonder and admiration all along:

"Yes, here we were, waiting—waiting for the word; our horses fidgeting and snorting and dancing to get away, we lying back on the bridles till our bodies fairly slanted to the rear; the word rang out at last—'*Go!*' and we went!

"Went? There was nothing like it ever seen! Where we swept by squads of scampering English, the mere wind of our passage laid them flat in piles and rows! Then we plunged into the ruck of Fastolfe's frantic battle-corps and tore through it like a hurricane, leaving a causeway of the dead stretching far behind; no tarrying, no slacking rein, but on! on! on! far yonder in the distance lay *our* prey—Talbot and his host looming vast and dark like a storm-cloud brooding on the sea! Down we swooped upon them, glooming all the air with a quivering pall of dead leaves flung up by the whirlwind of our flight. In another moment we should have struck them as world strikes world when disorbited constellations crash into the Milky Way, but by misfortune and the inscrutable dispensation of God I was recognized! Talbot turned white, and shouting, 'Save yourselves, it is the Standard-bearer of Joan of Arc!' drove his spurs home till they met in the middle of his horse's entrails, and fled the field with his billowing multitudes at his back! I could have cursed myself for not putting on a disguise. I saw reproach in the eyes of her Excellency, and was bitterly ashamed. I had caused what seemed an irreparable disaster. Another might have gone aside to grieve, as not seeing any way to mend it; but I thank God I am not of those. Great occasions only summon as with a trumpet-call the slumbering reserves of my intellect. I saw my opportunity in an instant—in the next I was away! Through the woods I vanished—*fst!* —like an extinguished light! Away around through the curtaining forest I sped, as if on wings, none knowing what was become of me, none suspecting my design. Minute after minute passed, on and on I flew; on, and still on; and at last with a great cheer I flung my Banner to the breeze and burst out in *front* of Talbot! Oh, it was a mighty thought! That weltering chaos of distracted men whirled and surged backward like a tidal wave which has struck a continent, and the day was ours! Poor helpless creatures, they were in a trap; they were surrounded; they could not escape to the rear, for there was our army; they could not escape to the front, for there was I. Their hearts shrivelled in their bodies, their hands fell listless at their sides. They stood still, and at our leisure we slaughtered them to a man; all except Talbot and Fastolfe, whom I saved and brought away, one under each arm."

Well, there is no denying it, the Paladin was in great form that night. Such style! such noble grace of gesture, such grandeur of attitude, such energy when he got going! such steady rise, on such sure wing, such nicely graduated expenditures of voice according to weight of matter, such skilfully calculated approaches to his surprises and explosions, such belief-compelling sincerity of tone and manner, such a climaxing peal from his brazen lungs, and such a lightning-vivid picture of his mailed form and flaunting banner when he burst out before that despairing army! And oh, the gentle art of the last half of his last sentence —delivered in the careless and indolent tone of one who has finished his real story, and only adds a colorless and inconsequential detail because it has happened to occur to him in a lazy way.

It was a marvel to see those innocent peasants. Why, they went all to pieces with enthusiasm, and roared out applauses fit to raise the roof and wake the dead. When they had cooled down at last and there was silence but for their heaving and panting, old Laxart said, admiringly—

"As it seems to me, you are an army in your single person."

"Yes, that is what he is," said Noël Rainguesson, convincingly. "He is a terror; and not just in *this* vicinity. His mere name carries a shudder with it to distant lands—just his mere name; and when he frowns, the shadow of it falls as far as Rome, and the chickens go to roost an hour before schedule time. Yes; and some say—"

"Noël Rainguesson, you are preparing yourself for trouble. I will say just one word to you, and it will be to your advantage to—"

I saw that the usual thing had got a start. No man could prophesy when it would end. So I delivered Joan's message and went off to bed.

Joan made her good-byes to those old fellows in the morning, with loving embraces and many tears, and with a packed multitude for sympathizers, and they rode proudly away on their precious horses to carry their great news home. I had seen better riders, I will say that; for horsemanship was a new art to them.

The vanguard moved out at dawn and took the road, with bands braying and banners flying; the second division followed at eight. Then came the Burgundian ambassadors, and lost us the rest of that day and the whole of the next. But Joan was on hand, and so they had their journey for their pains. The rest of us took the road at dawn, next morning, July 20th. And got how far? Six leagues. Tremouille was getting in his sly work with the vacillating King, you see. The King stopped at St. Marcoul and prayed three days. Precious time lost—for us; precious time gained for Bedford. He would know how to use it.

We could not go on without the King; that would be to leave him in the conspirators' camp. Joan argued, reasoned, implored; and at last we got under way again.

Joan's prediction was verified. It was not a campaign, it was only another holiday excursion. English strongholds lined our route; they surrendered without a blow; we garrisoned them with Frenchmen and passed on. Bedford was on the march against us with his new army by this time, and on the 25th of July the hostile forces faced each other and made preparation for battle; but Bedford's good judgment prevailed, and he turned and retreated toward Paris. Now was our chance. Our men were in great spirits.

Will you believe it? Our poor stick of a King allowed his worthless advisers to persuade him to start back for Gien, whence we had set out when we first marched for Rheims and the Coronation! And we actually did start back. The fifteen-day truce had just been concluded with the Duke of Burgundy, and we would go and tarry at Gien until he should deliver Paris to us without a fight.

We marched to Bray; then the King changed his mind once more, and with it his face toward Paris. Joan dictated a letter to the citizens of Rheims to encourage them to keep heart in spite of the truce, and promising to stand by them. She furnished them the news herself that the King had made this truce; and in speaking of it she was her usual frank self. She said she was not satisfied with it, and didn't know whether she would keep it or not; that if she kept it, it would be solely out of tenderness for the King's honor. All French children know those famous words. How naïve they are! "De cette trève qui a été faite, je ne suis pas contente, et je ne sais si je la tiendrai. Si je la tiens, ce sera seulement pour garder l'honneur du roi." But in any case, she said, she would not allow the blood royal to be abused, and would keep the army in good order and ready for work at the end of the truce.

Poor child, to have to fight England, Burgundy, and a French conspiracy all at the same time—it was too bad. She was a match for the others, but a conspiracy—ah, nobody is a match for that, when the victim that is to be injured is weak and willing. It grieved her, these troubled days, to be so hindered and delayed and baffled, and at times she was sad and the tears lay near the surface. Once, talking with her good old faithful friend and servant the Bastard of Orleans, she said—

"Ah, if it might but please God to let me put off this steel raiment and go back to my father and my mother, and tend my sheep again with my sister and my brothers, who would be so glad to see me!"

By the 12th of August we were camped near Dampmartin. Later we had a brush with Bedford's rear-guard, and had hopes of a big battle on the morrow, but Bedford and all his force got away in the night and went on toward Paris.

Charles sent heralds and received the submission of Beauvais. The Bishop Pierre Cauchon, that faithful friend and slave of the English, was not able to prevent it, though he did his best. He was obscure then, but his name was to travel round the globe presently, and live forever in the curses of France! Bear with me now, while I spit in fancy upon his grave.

Compiègne surrendered, and hauled down the English flag. On the 14th we camped two leagues from Senlis. Bedford turned and approached, and took up a strong position. We went against him, but all our efforts to beguile him out from his intrenchments failed, though he had promised us a duel in the open field. Night shut down. Let him look out for the morning! But in the morning he was gone again.

We entered Compiègne the 18th of August, turning out the English garrison and hoisting our own flag.

On the 23d Joan gave command to move upon Paris. The King and the clique were not satisfied with this, and retired sulking to Senlis, which had just surrendered. Within a few days many strong places submitted—Creil, Pont-Saint-Maxence, Choisy, Gournay-sur-Aronde, Remy, La Neufville-en-Hez, Moguay, Chantilly, Saintines. The English power was tumbling, crash after crash! And still the King sulked and disapproved, and was afraid of our movement against the capital.

On the 26th of August, 1429, Joan camped at Saint Denis; in effect, under the walls of Paris.

And still the King hung back and was afraid. If we could but have had him there to back us with his authority! Bedford had lost heart and decided to waive resistance and go and concentrate his strength in the best and loyalest province remaining to him—Normandy. Ah, if we could only have persuaded the King to come and countenance us with his presence and approval at this supreme moment!

CHAPTER 40

Courier after courier was despatched to the King, and he promised to come, but didn't. The Duke d'Alençon went to him and got his promise again, which he broke again. Nine days were lost thus; then he came, arriving at St. Denis September 7th.

Meantime the enemy had begun to take heart: the spiritless conduct of the King could have no other result. Preparations had now been made to defend the city. Joan's chances had been diminished, but she and her generals considered them plenty good enough yet. Joan ordered the attack for eight o'clock next morning, and at that hour it began.

Joan placed her artillery and began to pound a strong work which protected the gate St. Honoré. When it was sufficiently crippled the assault was sounded at noon, and it was carried by storm. Then we moved forward to storm the gate itself, and hurled ourselves against it again and again, Joan in the lead with her standard at her side, the smoke enveloping us in choking clouds, and the missiles flying over us and through us as thick as hail.

In the midst of our last assault, which would have carried the gate sure and given us Paris and in effect France, Joan was struck down by a crossbow bolt, and our men fell back instantly and almost in a panic—for what were they without her? *She* was the army, herself.

Although disabled, she refused to retire, and begged that a new assault be made, saying it *must* win; and adding, with the battle-light rising in her eyes, "I will take Paris now or die!" She had to be carried away by force, and this was done by Gaucourt and the Duke d'Alençon.

But her spirits were at the very top notch, now. She was brimming with enthusiasm. She said she would be carried before the gate in the morning, and in half an hour Paris would be ours without any question. She could have kept her word. About this there is no doubt. But she forgot one factor—the King, shadow of that substance named La Tremouille. The King forbade the attempt!

You see, a new Embassy had just come from the Duke of Burgundy, and another sham private trade of some sort was on foot.

You would know, without my telling you, that Joan's heart was nearly broken. Because of the pain of her wound and the pain at her heart she slept little that night. Several times the watchers heard muffled sobs from the dark room where she lay at St. Denis, and many times the grieving words "It could have been taken!—it could have been taken!" which were the only ones she said.

She dragged herself out of bed a day later with a new hope. D'Alençon had thrown a bridge across the Seine near St. Denis. Might she not cross by that and assault Paris at another point? But the King got wind of it and broke the bridge down! And more—he declared the campaign ended! And more still—he had made a new truce and a long one, in which he had agreed to leave Paris unthreatened and unmolested, and go back to the Loire whence he had come!

Joan of Arc, who had never been defeated by the enemy, was defeated by her own King. She had said once that all she feared for her cause was treachery. It had struck its first blow now. She hung up her white armor in the royal basilica of St. Denis, and went and asked the King to relieve her of her functions and let her go home. As usual, she was wise. Grand combinations, far-reaching great military moves were at an end, now; for the future, when the truce should end, the war would be merely a war of random and idle skirmishes, apparently; work suitable for subalterns, and not requiring the supervision of a sublime military genius. But the King would not let her go. The truce did not embrace all France; there were French strongholds to be watched and preserved; he would need her. Really, you see, Tremouille wanted to keep her where he could balk and hinder her.

Now came her Voices again. They said, *"Remain at St. Denis."* There was no explanation. They did not say why. That was the voice of God; it took precedence of the command of the King; Joan resolved to stay. But that filled La Tremouille with dread. She was too tremendous a force to be left to herself; she would surely defeat all his plans. He beguiled the King to use compulsion. Joan had to submit—because she was wounded and helpless. In the Great Trial she said she was carried away against her will; and that if she had not been wounded it could not have been accomplished. Ah, she had a spirit, that slender girl! a spirit to brave all earthly powers and defy them. We shall never know why the Voices ordered her to stay. We only know this: that if she could have obeyed, the history of France would not be as it now stands written in the books. Yes, well we know that.

On the 13th of September the army, sad and spiritless, turned its face toward the Loire, and marched—without music! Yes, one noted that detail. It was a funeral march; that is what it was. A long, dreary funeral march, with never a shout or a cheer; friends looking on in tears, all the way, enemies laughing. We reached Gien at last—that place whence we had set out on our splendid march toward Rheims less than three months before, with flags flying, bands playing, the victory-flush of Patay glowing in our faces, and the massed multitudes shouting and praising and giving us God-speed. There was a dull rain falling now, the day was dark, the heavens mourned, the spectators were few, we had no welcome but the welcome of silence, and pity, and tears.

Then the King disbanded that noble army of heroes; it furled its flags, it stored its arms: the disgrace of France was complete. La Tremouille wore the victor's crown; Joan of Arc, the unconquerable, was conquered.

CHAPTER 41

Yes, it was as I have said: Joan had Paris and France in her grip, and the Hundred Years' War under her heel, and the King made her open her fist and take away her foot.

Now followed about eight months of drifting about with the King and his council, and his gay and showy and dancing and flirting and hawking and frolicking and serenading and dissipating court—drifting from town to town and from castle to castle—a life which was pleasant to us of the personal staff, but not to Joan. However, she only *saw* it, she didn't live it. The King did his sincerest best to make her happy, and showed a most kind and constant anxiety in this matter. All others had to go loaded with the chains of an exacting court etiquette, but she was free, she was privileged. So that she paid her duty to the King once a day and passed the pleasant word, nothing further was required of her. Naturally, then, she made herself a hermit, and grieved the weary days through in her own apartments, with her thoughts and devotions for company, and the planning of now forever unrealizable military combinations for entertainment. In fancy she moved bodies of men from this and that and the other point, so calculating the distances to be covered, the time required for each body, and the nature of the country to be traversed, as to have them appear in sight of each other on a given day or at a given hour and concentrate for battle. It was her only game, her only relief from her burden of sorrow and inaction. She played it hour after hour, as others play chess; and lost herself in it, and so got repose for her mind and healing for her heart.

She never complained, of course. It was not her way. She was the sort that endure in silence. But—she was a caged eagle just the same, and pined for the free air and the alpine heights and the fierce joys of the storm.

France was full of rovers—disbanded soldiers ready for anything that might turn up. Several times, at intervals, when Joan's dull captivity grew too heavy to bear, she was allowed to gather a troop of cavalry and make a health-restoring dash against the enemy. These things were like a bath to her spirits.

It was like old times, there at Saint-Pierre-le-Moutier, to see her lead assault after assault, be driven back again and again, but always rally and charge anew, all in a blaze of eagerness and delight; till at last the tempest of missiles rained so intolerably thick that old D'Aulon, who was wounded, sounded the retreat (for the King had charged him on his head to let no harm come to Joan); and away everybody rushed after him—as he supposed; but when he turned and looked, there were we of the staff still hammering away; wherefore he rode back and urged her to come, saying she was mad to stay there with only a dozen men. Her eye danced merrily, and she turned upon him crying out—

"A dozen men! name of God, I have fifty thousand, and will never budge till this place is taken! Sound the charge!"

Which he did, and over the walls we went, and the fortress was ours. Old D'Aulon thought her mind was wandering; but all she meant was, that she felt the might of fifty thousand men surging in her heart. It was a fanciful expression; but, to my thinking, truer word was never said.

Then there was the affair near Lagny, where we charged the intrenched Burgundians through the open field four times, the last time victoriously; the best prize of it Franquet d'Arras, the freebooter and pitiless scourge of the region roundabout.

Now and then other such affairs; and at last, away toward the end of May, 1430, we were in the neighborhood of Compiègne, and Joan resolved to go to the help of that place, which was being besieged by the Duke of Burgundy.

I had been wounded lately, and was not able to ride without help; but the good Dwarf took me on behind him, and I held on to him and was safe enough. We started at midnight, in a sullen downpour of warm rain, and went slowly and softly and in dead silence, for we had to slip through the enemy's lines. We were challenged only once; we made no answer, but held our breath and crept steadily and stealthily along, and got through without any accident. About three or half past we reached Compiègne, just as the gray dawn was breaking in the east.

Joan set to work at once, and concerted a plan with Guillaume de Flavy, captain of the city—a plan for a sortie toward evening against the enemy, who was posted in three bodies on the other side of the Oise, in the level plain. From our side one of the city gates communicated with a bridge. The end of this bridge was defended on the other side of the river by one of those fortresses called a boulevard; and this boulevard also commanded a raised road, which stretched from its front across the plain to the village of Marguy. A force of Burgundians occupied Marguy; another was camped at Clairoix, a couple of miles *above* the raised road; and a body of English was holding Venette, a mile and a half *below* it. A kind of bow-and-arrow arrangement, you see: the causeway the arrow, the boulevard at the feather-end of it, Marguy at the barb, Venette at one end of the bow, Clairoix at the other.

Joan's plan was to go straight per causeway against Marguy, carry it by assault, then turn swiftly upon Clairoix, up to the right, and capture that camp in the same way, then face to the rear and be ready for heavy work, for the Duke of Burgundy lay behind Clairoix with a reserve. Flavy's lieutenant, with archers and the artillery of the boulevard, was to keep the English troops from coming up from below and seizing the causeway and cutting off Joan's retreat in case she should have to make one. Also, a fleet of covered boats was to be stationed near the boulevard as an additional help in case a retreat should become necessary.

It was the 24th of May. At four in the afternoon Joan moved out at the head of six hundred cavalry—on her last march in this life!

It breaks my heart. I had got myself helped up on to the walls, and from there I saw much that happened, the rest was told me long afterwards by our two knights and other eye-witnesses. Joan crossed the bridge, and soon left the boulevard behind her and went skimming away over the raised road with her horsemen clattering at her heels. She had on a brilliant silver-gilt cape over her armor, and I could see it flap and flare and rise and fall like a little patch of white flame.

It was a bright day, and one could see far and wide over that plain. Soon we saw the English force advancing, swiftly and in handsome order, the sunlight flashing from its arms.

Joan crashed into the Burgundians at Marguy and was repulsed. Then we saw the other Burgundians moving down from Clairoix. Joan rallied her men and charged again, and was again rolled back. Two assaults occupy a good deal of time—and time was precious here. The English were approaching the road, now, from Venette, but the boulevard opened fire on them and they were checked. Joan heartened her men with inspiring words and led them to the charge again in great style. This time she carried Marguy with a hurrah. Then she turned at once to the right and plunged into the plain and struck the Clairoix force, which was just arriving; then there was heavy work, and plenty of it, the two armies hurling each other backward turn about and about, and victory inclining first to the one, then to the other. Now all of a sudden there was a panic on our side. Some say one thing caused it, some another. Some say the cannonade made our front ranks think retreat was being cut off by the English, some say the rear ranks got the idea that Joan was killed. Anyway our men broke, and went flying in a wild rout for the causeway. Joan tried to rally them and face them around, crying to them that victory was sure, but it did no good, they divided and swept by her like a wave. Old D'Aulon begged her to retreat while there was yet a chance for safety, but she refused; so he seized her horse's bridle and bore her along with the wreck and ruin in spite of herself. And so along the causeway they came swarming, that wild confusion of frenzied men and horses—and the artillery had to stop firing, of course; consequently the English and Burgundians closed in in safety, the former in front, the latter behind their prey. Clear to the boulevard the French were washed in this enveloping inundation; and there, cornered in an angle formed by the flank of the boulevard and the slope of the causeway, they bravely fought a hopeless fight, and sank down one by one.

Flavy, watching from the city wall, ordered the gate to be closed and the drawbridge raised. This shut Joan out.

The little personal guard around her thinned swiftly. Both of our good knights went down, disabled; Joan's two brothers fell wounded; then Noël Rainguesson—all wounded while loyally sheltering Joan from blows aimed at her. When only the Dwarf and the Paladin were left, they would not give up, but stood their ground stoutly, a pair of steel towers streaked and splashed with blood; and where the axe of the one fell, and the sword of the other, an enemy gasped and died. And so fighting, and loyal to their duty to the last, good simple souls, they came to their honorable end. Peace to their memories! they were very dear to me.

Then there was a cheer and a rush, and Joan, still defiant, still laying about her with her sword, was seized by her cape and dragged from her horse. She was borne away a prisoner to the Duke of Burgundy's camp, and after her followed the victorious army roaring its joy.

The awful news started instantly on its round; from lip to lip it flew; and wherever it came it struck the people as with a sort of paralysis; and they murmured over and over again, as if they were talking to themselves, or in their sleep, "The Maid of Orleans taken! . . . Joan of Arc a prisoner! . . . the Savior of France lost to us!"—and would keep saying that over, as if they couldn't understand how it could be, or how God could permit it, poor creatures!

You know what a city is like when it is hung from eaves to pavement with rustling black? Then you know what Tours was like, and some other cities. But can any man tell you what the mourning in the hearts of the peasantry of France was like? No, nobody can tell you that; and, poor dumb things, they could not have told you themselves; but it was there—indeed yes. Why, it was the spirit of a whole nation hung with crape!

The 24th of May. We will draw down the curtain, now, upon the most strange, and pathetic, and wonderful military drama that has been played upon the stage of the world. Joan of Arc will march no more.

Book III

TRIAL AND MARTYRDOM

CHAPTER 1

I cannot bear to dwell at great length upon the shameful history of the summer and winter following the capture. For a while I was not much troubled, for I was expecting every day to hear that Joan had been put to ransom, and that the King—no, not the King, but grateful France—had come eagerly forward to pay it. By the laws of war she could not be denied the privilege of ransom. She was not a rebel; she was a legitimately constituted soldier, head of the armies of France by her King's appointment, and guilty of no crime known to military law; therefore she could not be detained upon any pretext, if ransom were proffered.

But day after day dragged by and no ransom was offered! It seems incredible, but it is true. Was that reptile Tremouille busy at the King's ear? All we know is, that the King was silent, and made no offer and no effort in behalf of this poor girl who had done so much for him.

But unhappily there was alacrity enough in another quarter. The news of the capture reached Paris the day after it happened, and the glad English and Burgundians deafened the world all the day and all the night with the clamor of their joy-bells and the thankful thunder of their artillery; and the next day the Vicar General of the Inquisition sent a message to the Duke of Burgundy requiring the delivery of the prisoner into the hands of the Church to be tried as an idolater.

The English had seen their opportunity, and it was the English power that was really acting, not the Church. The Church was being used as a blind, a disguise; and for a forcible reason: the Church was not only able to take the life of Joan of Arc, but to blight her influence and the valor-breeding inspiration of her name, whereas the English power could but kill her body; that would not diminish or destroy the influence of her name; it would magnify it and make it permanent. Joan of Arc was the only power in France that the English did not despise, the only power in France that they considered formidable. If the Church could be brought to take her life, or to proclaim her an idolater, a heretic, a witch, sent from Satan, not from heaven, it was believed that the English supremacy could be at once reinstated.

The Duke of Burgundy listened—but waited. He could not doubt that the French King or the French people would come forward presently and pay a higher price than the English. He kept Joan a close prisoner in a strong fortress, and continued to wait, week after week. He was a French Prince, and was at heart ashamed to sell her to the English. Yet with all his waiting no offer came to him from the French side.

One day Joan played a cunning trick on her jailer, and not only slipped out of her prison, but locked him up in it. But as she fled away she was seen by a sentinel, and was caught and brought back.

Then she was sent to Beaurevoir, a stronger castle. This was early in August, and she had been in captivity more than two months, now. Here she was shut up in the top of a tower which was sixty feet high. She ate her heart there for another long stretch—about three months and a half. And she was aware, all these weary five months of captivity, that the English, under cover of the Church, were dickering for her as one would dicker for a horse or a slave, and that France was silent, the King silent, all her friends the same. Yes, it was pitiful.

And yet when she heard at last that Compiègne was being closely besieged and likely to be captured, and that the enemy had declared that no inhabitant of it should escape massacre, not even children of seven years of age, she was in a fever at once to fly to our rescue. So she tore her bedclothes to strips and tied them together and descended this frail rope in the night, and it broke and she fell and was badly bruised, and remained three days insensible, meantime neither eating nor drinking.

And now came relief to us, led by the Count of Vendôme, and Compiègne was saved and the siege raised. This was a disaster to the Duke of Burgundy. He had to have money, now. It was a good time for a new bid to be made for Joan of Arc. The English at once sent a French Bishop—that forever infamous Pierre Cauchon of Beauvais. He was partly promised the Archbishopric of Rouen, which was vacant, if he should succeed. He claimed the right to preside over Joan's ecclesiastical trial because the battle-ground where she was taken was within his diocese.

By the military usage of the time the ransom of a royal Prince was 10,000 livres of gold, which is 61,125 francs—a fixed sum, you see. It must be accepted, when offered; it could not be refused.

Cauchon brought the offer of this very sum from the English—a royal Prince's ransom for the poor little peasant girl of Domremy. It shows in a striking way the English idea of her formidable importance. It was accepted. For that sum Joan of Arc the Savior of France was sold; sold to her enemies; to the enemies of her country; enemies who had lashed and thrashed and thumped and trounced France for a century and made holiday sport of it; enemies who had forgotten, years and years ago, what a Frenchman's face was like, so used were they to seeing nothing but his back; enemies whom she had whipped, whom she had cowed, whom she had taught to respect French valor, new-born in her nation by the breath of her spirit; enemies who hungered for her life as being the only puissance able to stand between English triumph and French degradation. Sold to a French priest by a French Prince, with the French King and the French nation standing thankless by and saying nothing.

And she—what did she say? Nothing. Not a reproach passed her lips. She was too great for that—she was Joan of Arc; and when that is said, all is said.

As a soldier, her record was spotless. She could not be called to account for anything under that head. A subterfuge must be found, and, as we have seen, was found. She must be tried by priests for crimes against religion. If none could be discovered, some must be invented. Let the miscreant Cauchon alone to contrive those.

Rouen was chosen as the scene of the trial. It was in the heart of the English power; its population had been under English dominion so many generations that they were hardly French now, save in language. The place was strongly garrisoned. Joan was taken there near the end of December, 1430, and flung into a dungeon. Yes, and clothed in chains, that free spirit!

Still France made no move. How do I account for this? I think there is only one way. You will remember that whenever Joan was not at the front, the French held back and ventured nothing; that whenever she led, they swept everything before them, so long as they could see her white armor or her banner; that every time she fell wounded or was reported killed—as at Compiègne—they broke in panic and fled like sheep. I argue from this that they had undergone no real transformation as yet; that at bottom they were still under the spell of a timorousness born of generations of unsuccess, and a lack of confidence in each other and in their leaders born of old and bitter experience in the way of treacheries of all sorts—for their kings had been treacherous to their great vassals and to their generals, and these in turn were treacherous to the head of the state and to each other. The soldiery found that they could depend utterly on Joan, and upon her alone. With her gone, everything was gone. She was the sun that melted the frozen torrents and set them boiling; with that sun removed, they froze again, and the army and all France became what they had been before, mere dead corpses—that and nothing more; incapable of thought, hope, ambition, or motion.

CHAPTER 2

My wound gave me a great deal of trouble clear into the first part of October; then the fresher weather renewed my life and strength. All this time there were reports drifting about that the King was going to ransom Joan. I believed these, for I was young and had not yet found out the littleness and meanness of our poor human race, which brags about itself so much, and thinks it is better and higher than the other animals.

In October I was well enough to go out with two sorties, and in the second one, on the 23d, I was wounded again. My luck had turned, you see. On the night of the 25th the besiegers decamped, and in the disorder and confusion one of their prisoners escaped and got safe into Compiègne, and hobbled into my room as pallid and pathetic an object as you would wish to see.

"What? Alive? Noël Rainguesson!"

It was indeed he. It was a most joyful meeting, that you will easily know; and also as sad as it was joyful. We could not speak Joan's name. One's voice would have broken down. We knew who was meant when she was mentioned; we could say "she" and "her," but we could not speak the name.

We talked of the personal staff. Old D'Aulon, wounded and a prisoner, was still with Joan and serving her, by permission of the Duke of Burgundy. Joan was being treated with the respect due to her rank and to her character as a prisoner of war taken in honorable conflict. And this was continued—as we learned later—until she fell into the hands of that bastard of Satan, Pierre Cauchon, Bishop of Beauvais.

Noël was full of noble and affectionate praises and appreciations of our old boastful big Standard-bearer, now gone silent forever, his real and imaginary battles all fought, his work done, his life honorably closed and completed.

"And think of his luck!" burst out Noël, with his eyes full of tears.

"Always the pet child of luck! See how it followed him and stayed by him, from his first step all through, in the field or out of it; always a splendid figure in the public eye, courted and envied everywhere; always having a chance to do fine things and always doing them; in the beginning called the Paladin in joke, and called it afterwards in earnest because he magnificently made the title good; and at last—supremest luck of all—died in the field! died with his harness on; died faithful to his charge, the Standard in his hand; died—oh, think of it—with the approving eye of Joan of Arc upon him! He drained the cup of glory to the last drop, and went jubilant to his peace, blessedly spared all part in the disaster which was to follow. What luck, what luck! And we? What was our sin that we are still here, we who have also earned our place with the happy dead?"

And presently he said:

"They tore the sacred Standard from his dead hand and carried it away, their most precious prize after its captured owner. But they haven't it now. A month ago we put our lives upon the risk—our two good knights, my fellow-prisoners, and I—and stole it, and got it smuggled by trusty hands to Orleans, and there it is now, safe for all time in the Treasury."

I was glad and grateful to learn that. I have seen it often since, when I have gone to Orleans on the 8th of May to be the petted old guest of the city and hold the first place of honor at the banquets and in the processions—I mean since Joan's brothers passed from this life. It will still be there, sacredly guarded by French love, a thousand years from now—yes, as long as any shred of it hangs together.*

Two or three weeks after this talk came the tremendous news like a thunder-clap, and we were aghast—Joan of Arc sold to the English!

Not for a moment had we ever dreamed of such a thing. We were young, you see, and did not know the human race, as I have said before. We had been so proud of our country, so sure of her nobleness,

* It remained there three hundred and sixty years, and then was destroyed in a public bonfire, together with two swords, a plumed cap, several suits of state apparel, and other relics of the Maid, by a mob in the time of the Revolution. Nothing which the hand of Joan of Arc is known to have touched now remains in existence except a few preciously guarded military and state papers which she signed, her pen being guided by a clerk or her secretary Louis de Conte. A bowlder exists from which she is known to have mounted her horse when she was once setting out upon a campaign. Up to a quarter of a century ago there was a single hair from her head still in existence. It was drawn through the wax of a seal attached to the parchment of a state document. It was surreptitiously snipped out, seal and all, by some vandal relic-hunter, and carried off. Doubtless it still exists, but only the thief knows where.—TRANSLATOR.

her magnanimity, her gratitude. We had expected little of the King, but of France we had expected everything. Everybody knew that in various towns patriot priests had been marching in procession urging the people to sacrifice money, property, everything, and buy the freedom of their heaven-sent deliverer. That the money would be raised we had not thought of doubting.

But it was all over, now, all over. It was a bitter time for us. The heavens seemed hung with black; all cheer went out from our hearts. Was this comrade here at my bedside really Noël Rainguesson, that light-hearted creature whose whole life was but one long joke, and who used up more breath in laughter than in keeping his body alive? No, no; *that* Noël I was to see no more. This one's heart was broken. He moved grieving about, and absently, like one in a dream; the stream of his laughter was dried at its source.

Well, that was best. It was my own mood. We were company for each other. He nursed me patiently through the dull long weeks, and at last, in January, I was strong enough to go about again. Then he said:

"Shall we go, now?"

"Yes."

There was no need to explain. Our hearts were in Rouen, we would carry our bodies there. All that we cared for in this life was shut up in that fortress. We could not help her, but it would be some solace to us to be near her, to breathe the air that she breathed, and look daily upon the stone walls that hid her. What if we should be made prisoners there? Well, we could but do our best, and let luck and fate decide what should happen.

And so we started. We could not realize the change which had come upon the country. We seemed able to choose our own route and go wherever we pleased, unchallenged and unmolested. When Joan of Arc was in the field, there was a sort of panic of fear everywhere; but now that she was out of the way, fear had vanished. Nobody was troubled about you or afraid of you, nobody was curious about you or your business, everybody was indifferent.

We presently saw that we could take to the Seine, and not weary ourselves out with land travel. So we did it, and were carried in a boat to within a league of Rouen. Then we got ashore; not on the hilly side, but on the other, where it is as level as a floor. Nobody could enter or leave the city without explaining himself. It was because they feared attempts at a rescue of Joan.

We had no trouble. We stopped in the plain with a family of peasants and stayed a week, helping them with their work for board and lodging, and making friends of them. We got clothes like theirs, and wore them. When we had worked our way through their reserves and gotten their confidence, we found that they secretly harbored French hearts in their bodies. Then we came out frankly and told them everything, and found them ready to do anything they could to help us. Our plan was soon made, and was quite simple. It was to help them drive a flock of sheep to the market of the city. One morning early we made the venture in a melancholy drizzle of rain, and passed through the frowning gates unmolested. Our friends had friends living over a humble wine-shop in a quaint tall building situated in one of the narrow lanes that run down from the cathedral to the river, and with these they bestowed us; and the next day they smuggled our own proper clothing and other belongings to us. The family that lodged us—the Pierrons—were French in sympathy, and we needed to have no secrets from them.

CHAPTER 3

It was necessary for me to have some way to gain bread for Noël and myself; and when the Pierrons found that I knew how to write, they applied to their confessor in my behalf, and he got a place for me with a good priest named Manchon, who was to be the chief recorder in the Great Trial of Joan of Arc now approaching. It was a strange position for me—clerk to the recorder—and dangerous if my sympathies and late employment should be found out. But there was not much danger. Manchon was at bottom friendly to Joan and would not betray me; and my name would not, for I had discarded my surname and retained only my given one, like a person of low degree.

I attended Manchon constantly straight along, out of January and into February, and was often in the citadel with him—in the very fortress where Joan was imprisoned, though not in the dungeon where she was confined, and so did not see her, of course.

Manchon told me everything that had been happening before my coming. Ever since the purchase of Joan, Cauchon had been busy packing his jury for the destruction of the Maid—weeks and weeks he had spent in this bad industry. The University of Paris had sent him a number of learned and able and trusty ecclesiastics of the stripe he wanted; and he had scraped together a clergyman of like stripe and great fame here and there and yonder, until he was able to construct a formidable court numbering half a hundred distinguished names. French names they were, but their interests and sympathies were English.

A great officer of the Inquisition was also sent from Paris, for the accused must be tried by the forms of the Inquisition; but this was a brave and righteous man, and he said squarely that this court had no power to try the case, wherefore he refused to act; and the same honest talk was uttered by two or three others.

The Inquisitor was right. The case as here resurrected against Joan had already been tried long ago at Poitiers, and decided in her favor. Yes, and by a higher tribunal than this one, for at the head of it was an Archbishop—he of Rheims—Cauchon's own metropolitan. So here, you see, a lower court was impudently preparing to re-try and re-decide a cause which had already been decided by its superior, a court of higher authority. Imagine it! No, the case could not properly be tried again. Cauchon could not properly preside in this new court, for more than one reason: Rouen was not in his diocese; Joan had not been arrested in her domicile, which was still Domremy; and finally this proposed judge was the prisoner's outspoken enemy, and therefore he was incompetent to try her. Yet all these large difficulties were gotten rid of. The territorial Chapter of Rouen finally granted territorial letters to Cauchon—though only after a struggle and under compulsion. Force was also applied to the Inquisitor, and he was obliged to submit.

So, then, the little English King, by his representative, formally delivered Joan into the hands of the court, but with this reservation: *if the court failed to condemn her, he was to have her back again!*

Ah, dear, what chance was there for that forsaken and friendless child? Friendless indeed—it is the right word. For she was in a black dungeon, with half a dozen brutal common soldiers keeping guard night and day in the room where her cage was—for she was in a cage; an iron cage, and chained to her bed by neck and hands and feet. Never a person near her whom she had ever seen before; never a woman at all. Yes, this was indeed friendlessness.

Now it was a vassal of Jean de Luxembourg who captured Joan at Compiègne, and it was Jean who sold her to the Duke of Burgundy. Yet this very De Luxembourg was shameless enough to go and show his face to Joan in her cage. He came with two English earls, Warwick and Stafford. He was a poor reptile. He told her he would get her set free if she would promise not to fight the English any more. She had been in that cage a long time now, but not long enough to break her spirit. She retorted scornfully—

"Name of God, you but mock me. I know that you have neither the power nor the will to do it."

He insisted. Then the pride and dignity of the soldier rose in Joan, and she lifted her chained hands and let them fall with a clash, saying—

"See these! They know more than you, and can prophesy better. I know that the English are going to kill me, for they think that when I am dead they can get the Kingdom of France. It is not so. Though there were a hundred thousand of them they would never get it."

This defiance infuriated Stafford, and he—now think of it—he a free, strong man, she a chained and helpless girl—he drew his dagger and flung himself at her to stab her. But Warwick seized him and held him back. Warwick was wise. Take her life in that way? Send her to Heaven stainless and undisgraced? It would make her the idol of France, and the whole nation would rise and march to victory and emancipation under the inspiration of her spirit. No, she must be saved for another fate than that.

Well, the time was approaching for the Great Trial. For more than two months Cauchon had been raking and scraping everywhere for any odds and ends of evidence or suspicion or conjecture that might be made usable against Joan, and carefully suppressing all evidence that came to hand in her favor. He had limitless ways and means and powers at his disposal for preparing and strengthening the case for the prosecution, and he used them all.

But Joan had no one to prepare her case for her, and she was shut up in those stone walls and had no friend to appeal to for help. And as for witnesses, she could not call a single one in her defence; they were all far away, under the French flag, and this was an English court; they would have been seized and hanged if they had shown their faces at the gates of Rouen. No, the prisoner must be the *sole* witness—witness for the prosecution, witness for the defence; and with a verdict of death resolved upon before the doors were opened for the court's first sitting.

When she learned that the court was made up of ecclesiastics in the interest of the English, she begged that in fairness an equal number of priests of the French party should be added to these. Cauchon scoffed at her message, and would not even deign to answer it.

By the law of the Church—she being a minor under twenty-one—it was her right to have counsel to conduct her case, advise her how to answer when questioned, and protect her from falling into traps set by cunning devices of the prosecution. She probably did not know that this was her right, and that she could demand it and require it, for there was none to tell her that; but she begged for this help at any rate. Cauchon refused it. She urged and implored, pleading her youth and her ignorance of the complexities and intricacies of the law and of legal procedure. Cauchon refused again, and said she must get along with her case as best she might by herself. Ah, his heart was a stone.

Cauchon prepared the *proces verbal*. I will simplify that by calling it the Bill of Particulars. It was a detailed list of the charges against her, and formed the basis of the trial. Charges? It was a list of *suspicions and public rumors*—those were the words used. It was merely charged that she was suspected of having been guilty of heresies, witchcraft, and other such offences against religion.

Now by law of the Church, a trial of that sort could not be begun until a searching inquiry had been made into the history and character of the accused, and it was essential that the result of this inquiry be added to the *proces verbal* and form a part of it. You remember that that was the first thing they did before the trial at Poitiers. They did it again, now. An ecclesiastic was sent to Domremy. There and all about the neighborhood he made an exhaustive search into Joan's history and character, and came back with his verdict. It was very clear. The searcher reported that he found Joan's character to be in every way what he "would like his own sister's character to be." Just about the same report that was brought back to Poitiers, you see. Joan's was a character which could endure the minutest examination.

This verdict was a strong point for Joan, you will say. Yes, it *would* have been if it could have seen the light; but Cauchon was awake, and it disappeared from the *proces verbal* before the trial. People were prudent enough not to inquire what became of it.

One would imagine that Cauchon was ready to begin the trial by this time. But no, he devised one more scheme for poor Joan's destruction, and it promised to be a deadly one.

One of the great personages picked out and sent down by the University of Paris was an ecclesiastic named Nicolas Loyseleur. He was tall, handsome, grave, of smooth soft speech and courteous and winning manners. There was no seeming of treachery or hypocrisy about him, yet he was full of both. He was admitted to Joan's prison by night, disguised as a cobbler; he pretended to be from her own country; he professed to be secretly a patriot; he revealed the fact that he was a priest. She was filled with gladness to see one from the hills and plains that were so dear to her; happier still to look upon a priest and disburden her heart in confession, for the offices of the Church were the bread of life, the breath of her nostrils to her, and she had been long forced to pine for them in vain. She opened her whole innocent heart to this creature, and in return he gave her advice concerning her trial which could have destroyed her if her deep native wisdom had not protected her against following it.

You will ask, what value could this scheme have, since the secrets of the confessional are sacred and cannot be revealed? True—but suppose another person should overhear them? That person is not bound to keep the secret. Well, that is what happened. Cauchon had previously caused a hole to be bored through the wall; and he stood with his ear to that hole and heard all. It is pitiful to think of these things. One wonders how they could treat that poor child so. She had not done them any harm.

CHAPTER 4

On Tuesday the 20th of February, whilst I sat at my master's work in the evening, he came in, looking sad, and said it had been decided to begin the trial at eight o'clock the next morning, and I must get ready to assist him.

Of course I had been expecting such news every day for many days; but no matter, the shock of it almost took my breath away and set me trembling like a leaf. I suppose that without knowing it I had been half imagining that at the last moment something would happen, something that would stop this fatal trial: maybe that La Hire would burst in at the gates with his hellions at his back; maybe that God would have pity and stretch forth His mighty hand. But now—now there was no hope.

The trial was to begin in the chapel of the fortress and would be public. So I went sorrowing away and told Noël, so that he might be there early and secure a place. It would give him a chance to look again upon the face which we so revered and which was so precious to us. All the way, both going and coming, I ploughed through chattering and rejoicing multitudes of English soldiery and English-hearted French citizens. There was no talk but of the coming event. Many times I heard the remark, accompanied by a pitiless laugh—

"The fat Bishop has got things as he wants them at last, and says he will lead the vile witch a merry dance and a short one."

But here and there I glimpsed compassion and distress in a face, and it was not always a French one. English soldiers feared Joan, but they admired her for her great deeds and her unconquerable spirit.

In the morning Manchon and I went early, yet as we approached the vast fortress we found crowds of men already there and still others gathering. The chapel was already full and the way barred against further admissions of unofficial persons. We took our appointed places. Throned on high sat the president, Cauchon, Bishop of Beauvais, in his grand robes, and before him in rows sat his robed court—fifty distinguished ecclesiastics, men of high degree in the Church, of clear-cut intellectual faces, men of deep learning, veteran adepts in strategy and casuistry, practised setters of traps for ignorant minds and unwary feet. When I looked around upon this army of masters of legal fence, gathered here to find just one verdict and no other, and remembered that Joan must fight for her good name and her life single-handed against them, I asked myself what chance an ignorant poor country girl of nineteen could have in such an unequal conflict; and my heart sank down low, very low. When I looked again at that obese president, puffing and wheezing there, his great belly distending and receding with each breath, and noted his three chins, fold above fold, and his knobby and knotty face, and his purple and splotchy complexion, and his repulsive cauliflower nose, and his cold and malignant eyes—a brute, every detail of him—my heart sank lower still. And when I noted that all were afraid of this man, and shrank and fidgeted in their seats when his eye smote theirs, my last poor ray of hope dissolved away and wholly disappeared.

There was one unoccupied seat in this place, and only one. It was over against the wall, in view of everyone. It was a little wooden bench without a back, and it stood apart and solitary on a sort of dais. Tall men-at-arms in morion, breast-plate, and steel gauntlets stood as stiff as their own halberds on each side of this dais, but no other creature was near by it. A pathetic little bench to me it was, for I knew whom it was for; and the sight of it carried my mind back to the great court at Poitiers, where Joan sat upon one like it and calmly fought her cunning fight with the astonished doctors of the Church and Parliament, and rose from it victorious and applauded by all, and went forth to fill the world with the glory of her name.

What a dainty little figure she was, and how gentle and innocent, how winning and beautiful in the fresh bloom of her seventeen years!

Those were grand days. And so recent—for she was but just nineteen now—and how much she had seen since, and what wonders she had accomplished!

But now—oh, all was changed, now. She had been languishing in dungeons, away from light and air and the cheer of friendly faces, for nearly three-quarters of a year—she, born child of the sun, natural comrade of the birds and of all happy free creatures. She would be weary, now, and worn with this long captivity, her forces impaired; despondent, perhaps, as knowing there was no hope. Yes, all was changed.

All this time there had been a muffled hum of conversation, and rustling of robes and scraping of feet on the floor, a combination of dull noises which filled all the place. Suddenly—

"Produce the accused!"

It made me catch my breath. My heart began to thump like a hammer. But there was silence, now—silence absolute. All those noises ceased, and it was as if they had never been. Not a sound; the stillness grew oppressive; it was like a weight upon one. All faces were turned towards the door; and one could properly expect that, for most of the people there suddenly realized, no doubt, that they were about to see, in actual flesh and blood, what had been to them before only an embodied prodigy, a word, a phrase, a world-girdling Name.

The stillness continued. Then, far down the stone-paved corridors, one heard a vague slow sound approaching: *clank* . . . . . . clink . . clank—Joan of Arc, Deliverer of France, in chains!

My head swam; all things whirled and spun about me. Ah, *I* was realizing, too.

CHAPTER 5

I give you my honor, now, that I am not going to distort or discolor the facts of this miserable trial. No, I will give them to you honestly, detail by detail, just as Manchon and I set them down daily in the official record of the court, and just as one may read them in the printed histories. There will be only this difference: that in talking familiarly with you I shall use my right to comment upon the proceedings and explain them as I go along, so that you can understand them better; also, I shall throw in trifles which came under our eyes and have a certain interest for you and me, but were not important enough to go into the official record.*

To take up my story, now, where I left off. We heard the clanking of Joan's chains down the corridors; she was approaching.

Presently she appeared; a thrill swept the house, and one heard deep breaths drawn. Two guardsmen followed her at a short distance to the rear. Her head was bowed a little, and she moved slowly, she being weak and her irons heavy. She had on men's attire—all black; a soft woollen stuff, intensely black, funereally black, not a speck of relieving color in it from her throat to the floor. A wide collar of this same black stuff lay in radiating folds upon her shoulders and breast; the sleeves of her doublet were full, down to the elbows, and tight thence to her manacled wrists; below the doublet, tight black hose down to the chains on her ankles.

Half-way to her bench she stopped, just where a wide shaft of light fell slanting from a window, and slowly lifted her face. Another thrill! —it was totally colorless, white as snow; a face of gleaming snow set in vivid contrast upon that slender statue of sombre unmitigated black. It was smooth and pure and girlish, beautiful beyond belief, infinitely sad and sweet. But, dear, dear! when the challenge of those untamed eyes fell upon that judge, and the droop vanished from her form and it straightened up soldierly and noble, my heart leaped for joy; and I said, all is well, all is well—they have not broken her, they have not conquered her, she is Joan or Arc still! Yes, it was plain to me, now, that there was one spirit there which this dreaded judge could not quell nor make afraid.

She moved to her place and mounted the dais and seated herself upon her bench, gathering her chains into her lap and nestling her little white hands there. Then she waited in tranquil dignity, the only person there who seemed unmoved and unexcited. A bronzed and brawny English soldier, standing at martial ease in the front rank of the citizen spectators, did now most gallantly and respectfully put up his great hand and give her the military salute; and she, smiling friendly, put up hers and returned it; whereat there was a sympathetic little break of applause, which the judge sternly silenced.

Now the memorable inquisition called in history the Great Trial began. Fifty experts against a novice, and no one to help the novice!

The judge summarized the circumstances of the case and the public reports and suspicions upon which it was based; then he required Joan

* He kept his word. His account of the Great Trial will be found to be in strict and detailed accordance with the sworn facts of history.—TRANSLATOR.

to kneel and make oath that she would answer with exact truthfulness to all questions asked her.

Joan's mind was not asleep. It suspected that dangerous possibilities might lie hidden under this apparently fair and reasonable demand. She answered with the simplicity which so often spoiled the enemy's best-laid plans in the trial at Poitiers, and said,

"No; for I do not know what you are going to ask me; you might ask of me things which I would not tell you."

This incensed the Court, and brought out a brisk flurry of angry exclamations. Joan was not disturbed. Cauchon raised his voice and began to speak in the midst of this noise, but he was so angry that he could hardly get his words out. He said—

"With the divine assistance of our Lord we require you to expedite these proceedings for the welfare of your conscience. Swear, with your hands upon the Gospels, that you will answer true to the questions which shall be asked you!" and he brought down his fat hand with a crash upon his official table.

Joan said, with composure—

"As concerning my father and mother, and the faith, and what things I have done since my coming into France, I will gladly answer; but as regards the revelations which I have received from God, my Voices have forbidden me to confide them to any save my King—"

Here there was another angry outburst of threats and expletives, and much movement and confusion; so she had to stop, and wait for the noise to subside; then her waxen face flushed a little and she straightened up and fixed her eye on the judge, and finished her sentence in a voice that had the old ring in it—

"—and I will never reveal these things though you cut my head off!"

Well, maybe you know what a deliberative body of Frenchmen is like. The judge and half the court were on their feet in a moment, and all shaking their fists at the prisoner and all storming and vituperating at once, so that you could hardly hear yourself think. They kept this up several minutes; and because Joan sat untroubled and indifferent, they grew madder and noisier all the time. Once she said, with a fleeting trace of the old-time mischief in her eye and manner—

"Prithee speak one at a time, fair lords, then I will answer all of you."

At the end of three whole hours of furious debating over the oath, the situation had not changed a jot. The Bishop was still requiring an unmodified oath, Joan was refusing for the twentieth time to take any except the one which she had herself proposed. There was a physical change apparent, but it was confined to court and judge; they were hoarse, droopy, exhausted by their long frenzy, and had a sort of haggard look in their faces, poor men, whereas Joan was still placid and reposeful and did not seem noticeably tired.

The noise quieted down; there was a waiting pause of some moments' duration. Then the judge surrendered to the prisoner, and with bitterness in his voice told her to take the oath after her own fashion. Joan sunk at once to her knees; and as she laid her hands upon the Gospels, that big English soldier set free his mind:

"By God if she were but English, she were not in this place another half a second!"

It was the soldier in him responding to the soldier in her. But what a stinging rebuke it was, what an arraignment of French character and French royalty! Would that he could have uttered just that one phrase in the hearing of Orleans! I know that that grateful city, that adoring city, would have risen, to the last man and the last woman, and marched upon Rouen. Some speeches—speeches that shame a man and humble him—burn themselves into the memory and remain there. That one is burnt into mine.

After Joan had made oath, Cauchon asked her her name, and where she was born, and some questions about her family; also what her age was. She answered these. Then he asked her how much education she had.

"I have learned from my mother the Pater Noster, the Ave Maria, and the Belief. All that I know was taught me by my mother."

Questions of this unessential sort dribbled on for a considerable time. Everybody was tired out by now, except Joan. The tribunal prepared to rise. At this point Cauchon forbade Joan to try to escape from prison, upon pain of being held guilty of the crime of heresy—singular logic! She answered simply—

"I am not bound by this prohibition. If I could escape I would not reproach myself, for I have given no promise, and I shall not."

Then she complained of the burden of her chains, and asked that they might be removed, for she was strongly guarded in that dungeon and there was no need of them. But the Bishop refused, and reminded her that she had broken out of prison twice before. Joan of Arc was too proud to insist. She only said, as she rose to go with the guard—

"It is true I have wanted to escape, and I do want to escape." Then she added, in a way that would touch the pity of anybody, I think, "It is the right of every prisoner."

And so she went from the place in the midst of an impressive stillness, which made the sharper and more distressful to me the clank of those pathetic chains.

What presence of mind she had! One could never surprise her out of it. She saw Noël and me there when she first took her seat on her bench; and we flushed to the forehead with excitement and emotion, but her face showed nothing, betrayed nothing. Her eyes sought us fifty times that day, but they passed on and there was never any ray of recognition in them. Another would have started upon seeing us, and then—why then there could have been trouble for us, of course.

We walked slowly home together, each busy with his own grief and saying not a word.

CHAPTER 6

That night Manchon told me that all through the day's proceedings Cauchon had had some clerks concealed in the embrasure of a window who were to make a special report garbling Joan's answers and twisting them from their right meaning. Ah, that was surely the cruelest man and the most shameless that has lived in this world. But his scheme failed. Those clerks had human hearts in them, and their base work revolted them, and they turned to and boldly made a straight report, whereupon Cauchon cursed them and ordered them out of his presence with a threat of drowning, which was his favorite and most frequent menace. The matter had gotten abroad and was making great and unpleasant talk, and Cauchon would not try to repeat this shabby game right away. It comforted me to hear that.

When we arrived at the citadel next morning, we found that a change had been made. The chapel had been found too small. The court had now removed to a noble chamber situated at the end of the great hall of the castle. The number of judges was increased to sixty-two—one ignorant girl against such odds, and none to help her.

The prisoner was brought in. She was as white as ever, but she was looking no whit worse than she looked when she had first appeared the day before. Isn't it a strange thing? Yesterday she had sat five hours on that backless bench with her chains in her lap, baited, badgered, persecuted by that unholy crew, without even the refreshment of a cup of water—for she was never offered anything, and if I have made you know her by this time you will know without my telling you that she was not a person likely to ask favors of those people. And she had spent the night caged in her wintry dungeon with her chains upon her; yet here she was, as I say, collected, unworn, and ready for the conflict; yes, and the only person there who showed no signs of the wear and worry of yesterday. And her eyes—ah, you should have seen them and broken your hearts. Have you seen that veiled deep glow, that pathetic hurt dignity, that unsubdued and unsubduable spirit that burns and smoulders in the eye of a caged eagle and makes you feel mean and shabby under the burden of its mute reproach? Her eyes were like that. How capable they were, and how wonderful! Yes, at all times and in all circumstances they could express as by print every shade of the wide range of her moods. In them were hidden floods of gay sunshine, the softest and peacefulest twilights, and devastating storms and lightnings. Not in this world have there been others that were comparable to them. Such is my opinion, and none that had the privilege to see them would say otherwise than this which I have said concerning them.

The seance began. And how did it begin, should you think? Exactly as it began before—with that same tedious thing which had been settled once, after so much wrangling. The Bishop opened thus:

"You are required, now, to take the oath pure and simple, to answer truly all questions asked you."

Joan replied placidly—

"I have made oath yesterday, my lord; let that suffice."

The Bishop insisted and insisted, with rising temper; Joan but shook her head and remained silent. At last she said—

"I made oath yesterday; it is sufficient." Then she sighed and said, "Of a truth, you do burden me too much."

The Bishop still insisted, still commanded, but he could not move her. At last he gave it up and turned her over for the day's inquest to an old hand at tricks and traps and deceptive plausibilities—Beaupere, a doctor of theology. Now notice the form of this sleek strategist's first remark—flung out in an easy, off-hand way that would have thrown any unwatchful person off his guard—

"Now, Joan, the matter is very simple; just speak up and frankly and truly answer the questions which I am going to ask you, as you have sworn to do."

It was a failure. Joan was not asleep. She saw the artifice. She said—

"No. You could ask me things which I could not tell you—and would not." Then, reflecting upon how profane and out of character it was for these ministers of God to be prying into matters which had proceeded from His hands under the awful seal of His secrecy, she added, with a warning note in her tone, "If you were well informed concerning me you would wish me out of your hands. I have done nothing but by revelation."

Beaupere changed his attack, and began an approach from another quarter. He would slip upon her, you see, under cover of innocent and unimportant questions.

"Did you learn any trade at home?"

"Yes, to sew and to spin." Then the invincible soldier, victor of Patay, conqueror of the lion Talbot, deliverer of Orleans, restorer of a king's crown, commander-in-chief of a nation's armies, straightened herself proudly up, gave her head a little toss, and said with naïve complacency, "And when it comes to that, I am not afraid to be matched against any woman in Rouen!"

The crowd of spectators broke out with applause—which pleased Joan—and there was many a friendly and petting smile to be seen. But Cauchon stormed at the people and warned them to keep still and mind their manners.

Beaupere asked other questions. Then—

"Had you other occupations at home?"

"Yes. I helped my mother in the household work and went to the pastures with the sheep and the cattle."

Her voice trembled a little, but one could hardly notice it. As for me, it brought those old enchanted days flooding back to me, and I could not see what I was writing for a little while.

Beaupere cautiously edged along up with other questions toward the forbidden ground, and finally repeated a question which she had refused to answer a little while back—as to whether she had received the Eucharist in those days at other festivals than that of Easter. Joan merely said—

"*Passez outre.*" Or, as one might say, "Pass on to matters which you are privileged to pry into."

I heard a member of the court say to a neighbor—

"As a rule, witnesses are but dull creatures, and an easy prey—yes, and easily embarrassed, easily frightened—but truly one can neither scare this child nor find her dozing."

Presently the house pricked up its ears and began to listen eagerly, for Beaupere began to touch upon Joan's Voices, a matter of consuming interest and curiosity to everybody. His purpose was, to trick her into heedless sayings that could indicate that the Voices had sometimes given her evil advice—hence that they had come from Satan, you see. To have dealings with the devil—well, that would send her to the stake in brief order, and that was the deliberate end and aim of this trial.

"When did you first hear these Voices?"

"I was thirteen when I first heard a Voice coming from God to help me to live well. I was frightened. It came at mid-day, in my father's garden in the summer."

"Had you been fasting?"

"Yes."

"The day before?"

"No."

"From what direction did it come?"

"From the right—from toward the church."

"Did it come with a bright light?"

"Oh, indeed yes. It was brilliant. When I came into France I often heard the Voices very loud."

"What did the Voice sound like?"

"It was a noble Voice, and I thought it was sent to me from God. The third time I heard it I recognized it as being an angel's."

"You could understand it?"

"Quite easily. It was always clear."

"What advice did it give you as to the salvation of your soul?"

"It told me to live rightly, and be regular in attendance upon the services of the Church. And it told me that I must go to France."

"In what species of form did the Voice appear?"

Joan looked suspiciously at the priest a moment, then said, tranquilly—

"As to that, I will not tell you."

"Did the Voice seek you often?"

"Yes. Twice or three times a week, saying, 'Leave your village and go to France.' "

"Did your father know about your departure?"

"No. The Voice said, 'Go to France'; therefore I could not abide at home any longer."

"What else did it say?"

"That I should raise the siege of Orleans."

"Was that all?"

"No, I was to go to Vaucouleurs, and Robert de Baudricourt would give me soldiers to go with me to France; and I answered, saying that I was a poor girl who did not know how to ride, neither how to fight."

Then she told how she was baulked and interrupted at Vaucouleurs, but finally got her soldiers, and began her march.

"How were you dressed?"

The court of Poitiers had distinctly decided and decreed that as God had appointed her to do a man's work, it was meet and no scandal to religion that she should dress as a man; but no matter, this court was ready to use any and all weapons against Joan, even broken and discredited ones, and much was going to be made of this one before this trial should end.

"I wore a man's dress, also a sword which Robert de Baudricourt gave me, but no other weapon."

"Who was it that advised you to wear the dress of a man?"

Joan was suspicious again. She would not answer.

The question was repeated.

She refused again.

"Answer. It is a command!"

"*Passez outre,*" was all she said.

So Beaupere gave up the matter for the present.

"What did Baudricourt say to you when you left?"

"He made them that were to go with me promise to take charge of me, and to me he said, 'Go, and let happen what may!'" (*Advienne que pourra!*)

After a good deal of questioning upon other matters she was asked again about her attire. She said it was necessary for her to dress as a man.

"Did your Voice advise it?"

Joan merely answered placidly—

"I believe my Voice gave me good advice."

It was all that could be got out of her, so the questions wandered to other matters, and finally to her first meeting with the King at Chinon. She said she chose out the King, who was unknown to her, by the revelation of her Voices. All that happened at that time was gone over. Finally—

"Do you still hear those Voices?"

"They come to me every day."

"What do you ask of them?"

"I have never asked of them any recompense but the salvation of my soul."

"Did the Voice always urge you to follow the army?"

He is creeping upon her again. She answered—

"It required me to remain behind at St. Denis. I would have obeyed if I had been free, but I was helpless by my wound, and the knights carried me away by force."

"When were you wounded?"

"I was wounded in the moat before Paris, in the assault."

The next question reveals what Beaupere had been leading up to—

"Was it a feast day?"

You see? The suggestion is that a voice coming from God would hardly advise or permit the violation, by war and bloodshed, of a sacred day.

Joan was troubled a moment, then she answered yes, it was a feast day.

"Now then, tell me this: did you hold it right to make the attack on such a day?"

This was a shot which might make the first breach in a wall which had suffered no damage thus far. There was immediate silence in the court and intense expectancy noticeable all about. But Joan disappointed the house. She merely made a slight little motion with her hand, as when one brushes away a fly, and said with reposeful indifference—

"*Passez outre.*"

Smiles danced for a moment in some of the sternest faces there, and several even laughed outright. The trap had been long and laboriously prepared; it fell, and was empty.

The court rose. It had sat for hours, and was cruelly fatigued. Most of the time had been taken up with apparently idle and purposeless inquiries about the Chinon events, the exiled Duke of Orleans, Joan's first proclamation, and so on, but all this seemingly random stuff had really been sown thick with hidden traps. But Joan had fortunately escaped them all, some by the protecting luck which attends upon ignorance and innocence, some by happy accident, the others by force of her best and surest helper, the clear vision and lightning intuitions of her extraordinary mind.

Now then, this daily baiting and badgering of this friendless girl, a captive in chains, was to continue a long, long time—dignified sport, a kennel of mastiffs and blood-hounds harassing a kitten!—and I may as well tell you, upon sworn testimony, what it was like from the first day to the last. When poor Joan had been in her grave a quarter of a century, the Pope called together that great court which was to re-examine her history, and whose just verdict cleared her illustrious name from every spot and stain, and laid upon the verdict and conduct of our Rouen tribunal the blight of its everlasting execrations. Manchon and several of the judges who had been members of our court were among the witnesses who appeared before that Tribunal of Rehabilitation.

Recalling these miserable proceedings which I have been telling you about, Manchon testified thus:—here you have it, all in fair print in the official history:

> When Joan spoke of her apparitions she was interrupted at almost every word. They wearied her with long and multiplied interrogatories upon all sorts of things. Almost every day the interrogatories of the morning lasted *three or four hours;* then from these morning-interrogatories they extracted the particularly difficult and subtle points, and these served as material for the afternoon-interrogatories, which lasted *two or three hours.* Moment by moment they skipped from one subject to another; yet in spite of this *she always responded with an astonishing wisdom and memory.* She often corrected the judges, saying, "But I have already answered that once before—ask the recorder," referring them to me.

And here is the testimony of one of Joan's judges. Remember, these witnesses are not talking about two or three days, they are talking about a tedious long *procession* of days:

> They asked her profound questions, but she extricated herself quite well. Sometimes the questioners changed suddenly and passed to another subject *to see if she would not contradict herself.* They burdened her with long interrogatories of two or three hours, from which *the judges themselves went forth fatigued.* From the snares with which she was beset *the expertest man in the world could not have extricated himself but with difficulty.* She gave her responses with great prudence; indeed to such a degree that during *three weeks I believed she was inspired.*

Ah, had she a mind such as I have described? You see what these priests say under oath—picked men, men chosen for their places in that terrible court on account of their learning, their experience, their keen and practised intellects and their strong bias against the prisoner. They make that poor young country girl out the match, and more than the match, of the sixty-two trained adepts. Isn't it so? They from the University of Paris, she from the sheepfold and the cow-stable! Ah yes, she was great, she was wonderful. It took six thousand years to produce her; her like will not be seen in the earth again in fifty thousand. Such is my opinion.

CHAPTER 7

The third meeting of the court was in that same spacious chamber, next day, 24th of February.

How did it begin work? In just the same old way. When the preparations were ended, the robed sixty-two massed in their chairs and the guards and order-keepers distributed to their stations, Cauchon spoke from his throne and commanded Joan to lay her hands upon the Gospels and swear to tell the truth concerning everything asked her!

Joan's eyes kindled, and she rose; rose and stood, fine and noble, and faced toward the Bishop and said—

"Take care what you do, my Lord, you who are my judge, for you take a terrible responsibility on yourself and you presume too far."

It made a great stir, and Cauchon burst out upon her with an awful threat—the threat of instant condemnation unless she obeyed. That made the very bones in my body turn cold, and I saw cheeks about me blanch—for it meant fire and the stake! But Joan, still standing, answered him back, proud and undismayed—

"Not all the clergy in Paris and Rouen could condemn me, lacking the right!"

This made a great tumult, and part of it was applause from the spectators. Joan resumed her seat. The Bishop still insisted. Joan said—

"I have already made oath. It is enough."

The Bishop shouted—

"In refusing to swear, you place yourself under suspicion!"

"Let be. I have sworn already. It is enough."

The Bishop continued to insist. Joan answered that "she would tell what she knew—but not all that she knew."

The Bishop plagued her straight along, till at last she said, in a weary tone—

"I came from God; I have nothing more to do here. Return me to God, from whom I came."

It was piteous to hear; it was the same as saying, "You only want my life; take it and let me be at peace."

The Bishop stormed out again—

"Once more I command you to—"

Joan cut in with a nonchalant *"Passez outre,"* and Cauchon retired from the struggle; but he retired with some credit this time, for he offered a compromise, and Joan, always clear-headed, saw protection for herself in it and promptly and willingly accepted it. She was to swear to tell the truth "as touching the matters set down in the *proces verbal.*" They could not sail her outside of definite limits, now; her course was over a charted sea, henceforth. The Bishop had granted more than he had intended, and more than he would honestly try to abide by.

By command, Beaupere resumed his examination of the accused. It being Lent, there might be a chance to catch her neglecting some detail of her religious duties. I could have told him he would fail there. Why, religion was her life!

"Since when have you eaten or drunk?"

If the least thing had passed her lips in the nature of sustenance, neither her youth nor the fact that she was being half starved in her prison could save her from dangerous suspicion of contempt for the commandments of the Church.

"I have done neither since yesterday at noon."

The priest shifted to the Voices again.

"When have you heard your Voice?"

"Yesterday and to-day."

"At what time?"

"Yesterday it was in the morning."

"What were you doing, then?"

"I was asleep and it woke me."

"By touching your arm?"

"No; without touching me."

"Did you thank it? Did you kneel?"

He had Satan in his mind, you see; and was hoping, perhaps, that by-and-by it could be shown that she had rendered homage to the archenemy of God and man.

"Yes, I thanked it; and knelt in my bed where I was chained, and joined my hands and begged it to implore God's help for me so that I might have light and instruction as touching the answers I should give here."

"Then what did the Voice say?"

"It told me to answer boldly, and God would help me." Then she turned toward Cauchon and said, "You say that you are my judge; now I tell you again, take care what you do, for in truth I am sent of God and you are putting yourself in great danger."

Beaupere asked her if the Voice's counsels were not fickle and variable.

"No. It never contradicts itself. This very day it has told me again to answer boldly."

"Has it forbidden you to answer only part of what is asked you?"

"I will tell you nothing as to that. I have revelations touching the King my master, and those I will not tell you." Then she was stirred by a great emotion, and the tears sprang to her eyes and she spoke out as with strong conviction, saying—

"I believe wholly—as wholly as I believe the Christian faith and that God has redeemed us from the fires of hell, that God speaks to me by that Voice!"

Being questioned further concerning the Voice, she said she was not at liberty to tell all she knew.

"Do you think God would be displeased at your telling the whole truth?"

"The Voice has commanded me to tell the King certain things, and not you—and some very lately—even last night; things which I would he knew. He would be more easy at his dinner."

"Why doesn't the Voice speak to the King itself, as it did when you were with him? Would it not if you asked it?"

"I do not know if it be the wish of God." She was pensive, a moment or two, busy with her thoughts and far away, no doubt; then she added a remark in which Beaupere, always watchful, always alert, detected a possible opening—a chance to set a trap. Do you think he jumped at it instantly, betraying the joy he had in his find, as a young hand at craft and artifice would do? No, oh, no, you could not tell that he had noticed the remark at all. He slid indifferently away from it at once, and began to ask idle questions about other things, so as to slip around and spring on it from behind, so to speak: tedious and empty questions as to whether the Voice had told her she would escape from this prison; and if it had furnished answers to be used by her in to-day's seance; if it was accompanied with a glory of light; if it had eyes, etc. That risky remark of Joan's was this:

"Without the Grace of God I could do nothing."

The court saw the priest's game, and watched his play with a cruel eagerness. Poor Joan was grown dreamy and absent; possibly she was tired. Her life was in imminent danger, and she did not suspect it. The time was ripe now, and Beaupere quietly and stealthily sprung his trap:

"Are you in a state of Grace?"

Ah, we had two or three honorable brave men in that pack of judges;

and Jean Lefevre was one of them. He sprang to his feet and cried out—

"It is a terrible question! The accused is not obliged to answer it!"

Cauchon's face flushed black with anger to see this plank flung to the perishing child, and he shouted—

"Silence! and take your seat. The accused will answer the question!"

There was no hope, no way out of the dilemma; for whether she said yes or whether she said no, it would be all the same—a disastrous answer, for the Scriptures had said one *cannot know* this thing. Think what hard hearts they were to set this fatal snare for that ignorant young girl and be proud of such work and happy in it. It was a miserable moment for me while we waited; it seemed a year. All the house showed excitement; and mainly it was glad excitement. Joan looked out upon these hungering faces with innocent untroubled eyes, and then humbly and gently she brought out that immortal answer which brushed the formidable snare away as it had been but a cobweb:

"If I be not in a state of Grace, I pray God place me in it; if I be in it, I pray God keep me so."

Ah, you will never see an effect like that; no, not while you live. For a space there was the silence of the grave. Men looked wondering into each other's faces, and some were awed and crossed themselves; and I heard Lefevre mutter—

"It was beyond the wisdom of man to devise that answer. *Whence* come this child's amazing inspirations?"

Beaupere presently took up his work again, but the humiliation of his defeat weighed upon him, and he made but a rambling and dreary business of it, he not being able to put any heart in it.

He asked Joan a thousand questions about her childhood and about the oak wood, and the fairies, and the children's games and romps under our dear *Arbre Fée de Bourlemont,* and this stirring up of old memories broke her voice and made her cry a little, but she bore up as well as she could, and answered everything.

Then the priest finished by touching again upon the matter of her apparel—a matter which was never to be lost sight of in this still-hunt for this innocent creature's life, but kept always hanging over her, a menace charged with mournful possibilities:

"Would you like a woman's dress?"

"Indeed yes, if I may go out from this prison—but here, no."

CHAPTER 8

The court met next on Monday the 27th. Would you believe it? The Bishop ignored the contract limiting the examination to matters set down in the *proces verbal* and again commanded Joan to take the oath without reservations. She said—

"You should be content; I have sworn enough."

She stood her ground, and Cauchon had to yield.

The examination was resumed, concerning Joan's Voices.

"You have said that you recognized them as being the voices of angels the third time that you heard them. What angels were they?"

"St. Catherine and St. Marguerite."

"How did you know that it was those two saints? How could you tell the one from the other?"

"I know it was they; and I know how to distinguish them."

"By what sign?"

"By their manner of saluting me. I have been these seven years under their direction, and I knew who they were because they told me."

"Whose was the first Voice that came to you when you were thirteen years old?"

"It was the Voice of St. Michael. I saw him before my eyes; and he was not alone, but attended by a cloud of angels."

"Did you see the archangel and the attendant angels in the body, or in the spirit?"

"I saw them with the eyes of my body, just as I see you; and when they went away I cried because they did not take me with them."

It made me see that awful shadow again that fell dazzling white upon her that day under *l'Arbre Fée de Bourlemont*, and it made me shiver again, though it was so long ago. It was really not very long gone by, but it seemed so, because so much had happened since.

"In what shape and form did St. Michael appear?"

"As to that, I have not received permission to speak."

"What did the archangel say to you that first time?"

"I cannot answer you to-day."

Meaning, I think, that she would have to get permission of her Voices first.

Presently, after some more questions as to the revelations which had been conveyed through her to the King, she complained of the unnecessity of all this, and said—

"I will say again, as I have said before, many times in these sittings, that I answered all questions of this sort before the court at Poitiers, and I would that you would bring here the record of that court and read from that. Prithee send for that book."

There was no answer. It was a subject that had to be got around and put aside. That book had wisely been gotten out of the way, for it contained things which would be very awkward here. Among them was a decision that Joan's mission was from God, whereas it was the intention of this inferior court to show that it was from the devil; also a decision permitting Joan to wear male attire, whereas it was the purpose of this court to make the male attire do hurtful work against her.

"How was it that you were moved to come into France—by your own desire?"

"Yes; and by command of God. But that it was his will I would not have come. I would sooner have had my body torn in sunder by horses than come, lacking that."

Beaupere shifted once more to the matter of the male attire, now, and proceeded to make a solemn talk about it. That tried Joan's patience; and presently she interrupted and said—

"It is a trifling thing and of no consequence. And I did not put it on by counsel of any man, but by command of God."

"Robert de Baudricourt did not order you to wear it?"

"No."

"Do you think you did well in taking the dress of a man?"

"I did well to do whatsoever thing God commanded me to do."

"But in this particular case do you think you did well in taking the dress of a man?"

"I have done nothing but by command of God."

Beaupere made various attempts to lead her into contradictions of herself; also to put her words and acts in disaccord with the Scriptures. But it was lost time. He did not succeed. He returned to her visions, the light which shone about them, her relations with the King, and so on.

"Was there an angel above the King's head the first time you saw him?"

"By the Blessed Mary!—"

She forced her impatience down, and finished her sentence with tranquillity: "If there was one I did not see it."

"Was there light?"

"There were more than three hundred soldiers there, and five hundred torches, without taking account of spiritual light."

"What made the King believe in the revelations which you brought him?"

"He had signs; also the counsel of the clergy."

"What revelations were made to the King?"

"You will not get that out of me this year." Presently she added: "During three weeks I was questioned by the clergy at Chinon and Poitiers. The King had a sign before he would believe; and the clergy were of opinion that my acts were good and not evil."

The subject was dropped now for a while, and Beaupere took up the matter of the miraculous sword of Fierbois to see if he could not find a chance there to fix the crime of sorcery upon Joan.

"How did you know that there was an ancient sword buried in the ground under the rear of the altar of the church of St. Catherine of Fierbois?"

Joan had no concealments to make as to this;

"I knew the sword was there because my Voices told me so; and I sent to ask that it be given to me to carry in the wars. It seemed to me that it was not very deep in the ground. The clergy of the church caused it to be sought for and dug up; and they polished it, and the rust fell easily off from it."

"Were you wearing it when you were taken in battle at Compiègne?"

"No. But I wore it constantly until I left St. Denis after the attack upon Paris."

This sword, so mysteriously discovered and so long and so constantly victorious, was suspected of being under the protection of enchantment.

"Was that sword blest? What blessing had been invoked upon it?"

"None. I loved it because it was found in the church of St. Catherine, for I loved that church very dearly."

She loved it because it had been built in honor of one of her angels.

"Didn't you lay it upon the altar, to the end that it might be lucky?" (The altar of St. Denis.)

"No."

"Didn't you pray that it might be made lucky?"

"Truly it were no harm to wish that my harness might be fortunate."

"Then it was not that sword which you wore in the field of Compiègne? What sword did you wear there?"

"The sword of the Burgundian Franquet d'Arras, whom I took prisoner in the engagement at Lagny. I kept it because it was a good war-sword—good to lay on stout thumps and blows with."

She said that quite simply; and the contrast between her delicate little self and the grim soldier-words which she dropped with such easy familiarity from her lips made many spectators smile.

"What is become of the other sword? Where is it now?"

"Is that in the *proces verbal?*"

Beaupere did not answer.

"Which do you love best, your banner or your sword?"

Her eye lighted gladly at the mention of her banner, and she cried out—

"I love my banner best—oh, forty times more than the sword! Sometimes I carried it myself when I charged the enemy, to avoid killing any one." Then she added, naïvely, and with again that curious contrast between her girlish little personality and her subject, "I have never killed any one."

It made a great many smile; and no wonder, when you consider what a gentle and innocent little thing she looked. One could hardly believe she had ever even seen men slaughtered, she looked so little fitted for such things.

"In the final assault at Orleans did you tell your soldiers that the arrows shot by the enemy and the stones discharged from their catapults and cannon would not strike any one but you?"

"No. And the proof is, that more than a hundred of my men were struck. I told them to have no doubts and no fears; that they would raise the siege. I was wounded in the neck by an arrow in the assault upon the bastille that commanded the bridge, but St. Catherine comforted me and I was cured in fifteen days without having to quit the saddle and leave my work."

"Did you know that you were going to be wounded?"

"Yes; and I had told it to the King beforehand. I had it from my Voices."

"When you took Jargeau, why did you not put its commandant to ransom?"

"I offered him leave to go out unhurt from the place, with all his garrison; and if he would not I would take it by storm."

"And you did, I believe."

"Yes."

"Had your Voices counselled you to take it by storm?"

"As to that, I do not remember."

Thus closed a weary long sitting, without result. Every device that could be contrived to trap Joan into wrong thinking, wrong doing, or disloyalty to the Church, or sinfulness as a little child at home or later had been tried, and none of them had succeeded. She had come unscathed through the ordeal.

Was the court discouraged? No. Naturally it was very much surprised, very much astonished, to find its work baffling and difficult instead of simple and easy, but it had powerful allies in the shape of hunger, cold, fatigue, persecution, deception, and treachery; and opposed to this array nothing but a defenceless and ignorant girl who must some time or other surrender to bodily and mental exhaustion or get caught in one of the thousand traps set for her.

And had the court made no progress during these seemingly resultless sittings? Yes. It had been feeling its way, groping here, groping there, and had found one or two vague trails which might freshen by-and-by and lead to something. The male attire, for instance, and the visions and Voices. Of course no one doubted that she had seen supernatural beings and been spoken to and advised by them. And of course no one doubted that by supernatural help miracles had been done by Joan, such as choosing out the King in a crowd when she had never seen him before, and her discovery of the sword buried under the altar. It would have been foolish to doubt these things, for we all know that the air is full of devils and angels that are visible to traffickers in magic on the one hand and to the stainlessly holy on the other; but what many and perhaps most did doubt was, that Joan's visions, voices, and miracles came from God. It was hoped that in time they could be proven to have been of satanic origin. Therefore, as you see, the court's persistent fashion of coming back to that subject every little while and spooking around it and prying into it was not to pass the time—it had a strictly business end in view.

CHAPTER 9

The next sitting opened on Thursday the first of March. Fifty-eight judges present—the others resting.

As usual, Joan was required to take an oath without reservations. She showed no temper this time. She considered herself well buttressed by the *proces verbal* compromise which Cauchon was so anxious to repudiate and creep out of; so she merely refused, distinctly and decidedly; and added, in a spirit of fairness and candor—

"But as to matters set down in the *proces verbal,* I will freely tell the whole truth—yes, as freely and fully as if I were before the Pope."

Here was a chance! We had two or three Popes, then; only one of them could be the true Pope, of course. Everybody judiciously shirked the question of *which* was the true Pope and refrained from naming him, it being clearly dangerous to go into particulars in this matter. Here was an opportunity to trick an unadvised girl into bringing herself into peril, and the unfair judge lost no time in taking advantage of it. He asked, in a plausibly indolent and absent way—

"Which one do you consider to be the true Pope?"

The house took an attitude of deep attention, and so waited to hear the answer and see the prey walk into the trap. But when the answer came it covered the judge with confusion, and you could see many people covertly chuckling. For Joan asked in a voice and manner which almost deceived even me, so innocent it seemed—

"Are there two?"

One of the ablest priests in that body and one of the best swearers there, spoke right out so that half the house heard him, and said—

"By God it was a master stroke!"

As soon as the judge was better of his embarrassment he came back to the charge, but was prudent and passed by Joan's question—

"Is it true that you received a letter from the Count of Armagnac asking you which of the three Popes he ought to obey?"

"Yes, and answered it."

Copies of both letters were produced and read. Joan said that hers had not been quite strictly copied. She said she had received the Count's letter when she was just mounting her horse; and added—

"So, in dictating a word or two of reply I said I would try to answer him from Paris or somewhere where I could be at rest."

She was asked again which Pope she had considered the right one.

"I was not able to instruct the Count of Armagnac as to which one he ought to obey"; then she added, with a frank fearlessness which sounded fresh and wholesome in that den of trimmers and shufflers, "but as for me, I hold that we are bound to obey our Lord the Pope who is at Rome."

The matter was dropped. Then they produced and read a copy of Joan's first effort at dictating—her proclamation summoning the English to retire from the siege of Orleans and vacate France—truly a great and fine production for an unpractised girl of seventeen.

"Do you acknowledge as your own the document which has just been read?"

"Yes, except that there are errors in it—words which make me give myself too much importance." I saw what was coming; I was troubled and ashamed. "For instance, I did not say 'Deliver up to the Maid' (*rendez a la Pucelle*); I said 'Deliver up to the King' (*rendez au Roi*); and I did not call myself 'Commander-in-Chief' (*chef de guerre*). All those are words which my secretary substituted; or mayhap he misheard me or forgot what I said."

She did not look at me when she said it; she spared me that embarrassment. I hadn't misheard her at all, and hadn't forgotten. I changed her language purposely, for she *was* Commander-in-Chief and entitled to call herself so, and it was becoming and proper, too; and who was going to surrender anything to the King?—at that time a stick, a cipher? If any surrendering was done, it would be to the noble Maid of Vaucouleurs, already famed and formidable though she had not yet struck a blow.

Ah, there would have been a fine and disagreeable episode (for me) there, if that pitiless court had discovered that the very scribbler of that piece of dictation, secretary to Joan of Arc, was present—and not only present, but helping build the record; and not only that, but destined at a far distant day to testify against lies and perversions smuggled into it by Cauchon and deliver them over to eternal infamy!

"Do you acknowledge that you dictated this proclamation?"

"I do."

"Have you repented of it? Do you retract it?"

Ah, then she was indignant!

"No! Not even these chains"—and she shook them—"not even these chains can chill the hopes that I uttered there. And more!"—she rose, and stood a moment with a divine strange light kindling in her face, then her words burst forth as in a flood—"I warn you now that before seven years a disaster will smite the English, oh, many fold greater than the fall of Orleans! and—"

"Silence! Sit down!"

"—and then, soon after, they will lose all France!"

Now consider these things. The French armies no longer existed. The French cause was standing still, our King was standing still, there was no hint that by-and-by the Constable Richemont would come forward and take up the great work of Joan of Arc and finish it. In face of all this, Joan made that prophecy—made it with perfect confidence—*and it came true.*

For within five years Paris fell—1436—and our King marched into it flying the victor's flag. So the first part of the prophecy was then fulfilled—in fact, almost the entire prophecy; for, with Paris in our hands, the fulfilment of the rest of it was assured.

Twenty years later all France was ours excepting a single town—Calais.

Now that will remind you of an earlier prophecy of Joan's. At the time that she wanted to take Paris and could have done it with ease if our King had but consented, she said that that was the golden time; that with Paris ours, all France would be ours in six months. But if this golden opportunity to recover France was wasted, said she, "*I give you twenty years to do it in.*"

She was right. After Paris fell, in 1436, the rest of the work had to be done city by city, castle by castle, and it took twenty years to finish it.

Yes, it was the first day of March, 1431, there in the court, that she stood in the view of everybody and uttered that strange and incredible prediction. Now and then, in this world, somebody's prophecy turns up correct, but when you come to look into it there is sure to be considerable room for suspicion that the prophecy was made after the fact. But here the matter is different. There in that court Joan's prophecy was set down in the official record at the hour and moment of its utterance, years before the fulfilment, and there you may read it to this day. Twenty-five years after Joan's death the record was produced in the great Court of the Rehabilitation and verified under oath by Manchon and me, and surviving judges of our court confirmed the exactness of the record in their testimony.

Joan's startling utterance on that now so celebrated first of March stirred up a great turmoil, and it was some time before it quieted down again. Naturally everybody was troubled, for a prophecy is a grisly and awful thing, whether one thinks it ascends from hell or comes down from heaven. All that these people felt sure of was, that the inspiration back of it was genuine and puissant. They would have given their right hands to know the source of it.

At last the questions began again.

"How do you know that those things are going to happen?"

"I know it by revelation. And I know it as surely as I know that you sit here before me."

This sort of answer was not going to allay the spreading uneasiness. Therefore, after some further dallying the judge got the subject out of the way and took up one which he could enjoy more.

"What language do your Voices speak?"

"French."

"St. Marguerite, too?"

"Verily; why not? She is on our side, not on the English?"

Saints and angels who did not condescend to speak English! a grave affront. They could not be brought into court and punished for contempt, but the tribunal could take silent note of Joan's remark and remember it against her; which they did. It might be useful by-and-by.

"Do your saints and angels wear jewelry?—crowns, rings, ear-rings?"

To Joan, questions like this were profane frivolities and not worthy of serious notice; she answered indifferently. But the question brought to her mind another matter, and she turned upon Cauchon and said—

"I had two rings. They have been taken away from me during my captivity. You have one of them. It is the gift of my brother. Give it back to me. If not to me, then I pray that it be given to the Church."

The judges conceived the idea that maybe these rings were for the working of enchantments. Perhaps they could be made to do Joan a damage.

"Where is the other ring?"

"The Burgundians have it."

"Where did you get it?"

"My father and mother gave it to me."

"Describe it."

"It is plain and simple and has '*Jesus and Mary*' engraved upon it."

Everybody could see that that was not a valuable equipment to do devil's work with. So that trail was not worth following. Still, to make sure, one of the judges asked Joan if she had ever cured sick people by touching them with the ring. She said no.

"Now as concerning the fairies, that were used to abide near by Domremy whereof there are many reports and traditions. It is said that your godmother surprised these creatures on a summer's night dancing under the tree called *L'Arbre Fée de Bourlemont.* Is it not possible that your pretended saints and angels are but those fairies?"

"Is that in your *proces*?"

She made no other answer.

"Have you not conversed with St. Marguerite and St. Catherine under that tree?"

"I do not know."

"Or by the fountain near the tree?"

"Yes, sometimes."

"What promises did they make you?"

"None but such as they had God's warrant for."

"But what promises *did* they make?"

"That is not in your *proces;* yet I will say this much: they told me that the King would become master of his kingdom in spite of his enemies."

"And what else?"

There was a pause; then she said humbly—

"They promised to lead me to Paradise."

If faces do really betray what is passing in men's minds, a fear came upon many in that house, at this time, that maybe, after all, a chosen servant and herald of God was here being hunted to her death. The interest deepened. Movements and whisperings ceased: the stillness became almost painful.

Have you noticed that almost from the beginning the nature of the questions asked Joan showed that in some way or other the questioner very often already knew his fact before he asked his question? Have you noticed that somehow or other the questioners usually knew just how and where to search for Joan's secrets; that they really knew the bulk of her privacies—a fact not suspected by her—and that they had no task before them but to trick her into exposing those secrets?

Do you remember Loyseleur the hypocrite, the treacherous priest, tool of Cauchon? Do you remember that under the sacred seal of the confessional Joan freely and trustingly revealed to him everything concerning her history save only a few things regarding her supernatural revelations which her Voices had forbidden her to tell to any one—and that the unjust judge, Cauchon, was a hidden listener all the time?

Now you understand how the inquisitors were able to devise that long array of minutely prying questions; questions whose subtlety and ingenuity and penetration are astonishing until we come to remember Loyseleur's performance and recognize their source. Ah, Bishop of Beauvais, you are now lamenting this cruel iniquity these many years in hell! Yes verily, unless one has come to your help. There is but one among the redeemed that would do it; and it is futile to hope that that one has not already done it—Joan of Arc.

We will return to the court and the questionings.

"Did they make you still another promise?"

"Yes, but that is not in your *proces*. I will not tell it now, but before three months I will tell it you."

The judge seems to know the matter he is asking about, already; one gets this idea from his next question.

"Did your Voices tell you that you would be liberated before three months?"

Joan often showed a little flash of surprise at the good guessing of the judges, and she showed one this time. I was frequently in terror to find my mind (which *I* could not control) criticising the Voices and saying, "They counsel her to speak boldly—a thing which she would do without any suggestion from *them* or anybody else—but when it comes to telling her any useful thing, such as how these conspirators manage to guess their way so skilfully into her affairs, they are always off attending to some other business." I am reverent by nature; and when such thoughts swept through my head they made me cold with fear, and if there was a storm and thunder at the time, I was so ill that I could but with difficulty abide at my post and do my work.

Joan answered—

"That is not in your *proces*. I do not know when I shall be set free, but some who wish me out of this world will go from it before me."

It made some of them shiver.

"Have your Voices told you that you will be delivered from this prison?"

Without a doubt they had, and the judge knew it before he asked the question.

"Ask me again in three months and I will tell you."

She said it with such a happy look, the tired prisoner! And I? And Noël Rainguesson, drooping yonder?—why, the floods of joy went streaming through us from crown to sole! It was all that we could do to hold still and keep from making fatal exposure of our feelings.

She was to be set free in three months. That was what she meant; we saw it. The Voices had told her so, and told her true—true to the very day—May 30. But we know, now, that they had mercifully hidden from her *how* she was to be set free, but left her in ignorance. Home again! That was our understanding of it—Noël's and mine; that was our dream; and now we would count the days, the hours, the minutes. They would fly lightly along; they would soon be over. Yes, we would carry our idol home; and there, far from the pomps and tumults of the world, we would take up our happy life again and live it out as we had begun it, in the free air and the sunshine, with the friendly sheep and the friendly people for comrades, and the grace and charm of the meadows, the woods, and the river always before our eyes and their deep peace in our hearts. Yes, that was our dream, the dream that carried us bravely through that three months to an exact and awful fulfilment, the thought of which would have killed us, I think, if we had foreknown it and been obliged to bear the burden of it upon our hearts the half of those heavy days.

Our reading of the prophecy was this: We believed the King's soul was going to be smitten with remorse; and that he would privately plan a rescue with Joan's old lieutenants, D'Alençon and the Bastard and La Hire, and that this rescue would take place at the end of the three months. So we made up our minds to be ready and take a hand in it.

In the present and also in later sittings Joan was urged to name the exact day of her deliverance; but she could not do that. She had not the permission of her Voices. Moreover, the Voices themselves did not name the precise day. Ever since the fulfilment of the prophecy, I have believed that Joan had the idea that her deliverance was going to come in the form of death. But not *that* death! Divine as she was, dauntless as she was in battle, she was human also. She was not solely a saint, an angel, she was a clay-made girl also—as human a girl as any in the world, and full of a human girl's sensitivenesses and tendernesses and delicacies. And so, *that* death! No, she could not have lived the three months with that one before her, I think. You remember that the first time she was wounded she was frightened, and cried, just as any other girl of seventeen would have done, although she had known for eighteen days that she was going to be wounded on that very day. No, she was not afraid of any ordinary death, and an ordinary death was what she believed the prophecy of deliverance meant, I think, for her face showed happiness, not horror, when she uttered it.

Now I will explain why I think as I do. Five weeks before she was captured in the battle of Compiègne, her Voices told her what was coming. They did not tell her the day or the place, but said she would be taken prisoner and that it would be before the feast of St. John. She begged that death, certain and swift, should be her fate, and the captivity brief; for she was a free spirit, and dreaded the confinement. The Voices made no promise, but only told her to bear whatever came. Now as they did not *refuse* the swift death, a hopeful young thing like Joan would naturally cherish that fact and make the most of it, allowing it to grow and establish itself in her mind. And so now that she was told she was to be "delivered" in three months, I think she believed it meant that she would die in her bed in the prison, and that that was why she looked happy and content—the gates of Paradise standing open for her, the time so short, you see, her troubles so soon to be over, her reward so close at hand. Yes, that would make her look happy, that would make her patient and bold, and able to fight her fight out like a soldier. Save herself if she could, of course, and try her best, for that was the way she was made; but die with her face to the front if die she must.

Then later, when she charged Cauchon with trying to kill her with a poisoned fish, her notion that she was to be "delivered" by death in the prison—if she had it, and I believe she had—would naturally be greatly strengthened, you see.

But I am wandering from the trial. Joan was asked to definitely name the time that she would be delivered from prison.

"I have always said that I was not permitted to tell you everything. I am to be set free, and I desire to ask leave of my Voices to tell you the day. This is why I wish for delay."

"Do your Voices forbid you to tell the truth?"

"Is it that you wish to know matters concerning the King of France? I tell you again that he will regain his kingdom, and that I know it as well as I know that you sit here before me in this tribunal." She sighed and, after a little pause, added: "I should be dead but for this revelation, which comforts me always."

Some trivial questions were asked her about St. Michael's dress and appearance. She answered them with dignity, but one saw that they gave her pain. After a little she said—

"I have great joy in seeing him, for when I see him I have the feeling that I am not in mortal sin." She added, "Sometimes St. Marguerite and St. Catherine have allowed me to confess myself to them."

Here was a possible chance to set a successful snare for her innocence.

"When you confessed were you in mortal sin, do you think?"

But her reply did her no hurt. So the inquiry was shifted once more to the revelations made to the King—secrets which the court had tried again and again to force out of Joan, but without success.

"Now as to the sign given to the King—"

"I have already told you that I will tell you nothing about it."

"Do you know what the sign was?"

"As to that, you will not find out from me."

All this refers to Joan's secret interview with the King—held apart, though two or three others were present. It was known—through Loyseleur, of course—that this sign was a crown and was a pledge of the verity of Joan's mission. But that is all a mystery until this day—the nature of the crown, I mean—and will remain a mystery to the end of time. We can never know whether a real crown descended upon the King's head, or only a symbol, the mystic fabric of a vision.

"Did you see a crown upon the King's head when he received the revelation?"

"I cannot tell you as to that, without perjury."

"Did the King have that crown at Rheims?"

"I think the King put upon his head a crown which he found there; but a much richer one was brought him afterwards."

"Have you seen that one?"

"I cannot tell you, without perjury. But whether I have seen it or not, I have heard say that it was rich and magnificent."

They went on and pestered her to weariness about that mysterious crown, but they got nothing more out of her. The sitting closed. A long, hard day for all of us.

CHAPTER 10

The court rested a day, then took up work again on Saturday the third of March.

This was one of our stormiest sessions. The whole court was out of patience; and with good reason. These three-score distinguished churchmen, illustrious tacticians, veteran legal gladiators, had left important posts where their supervision was needed, to journey hither from various regions and accomplish a most simple and easy matter—condemn and send to death a country lass of nineteen who could neither read nor write, knew nothing of the wiles and perplexities of legal procedure, could call not a single witness in her defence, was allowed no advocate or adviser, and must conduct her case by herself against a hostile judge and a packed jury. In two hours she would be hopelessly entangled, routed, defeated, convicted. Nothing could be more certain than this—so they thought. But it was a mistake. The two hours had strung out into days; what promised to be a skirmish had expanded into a siege; the thing which had looked so easy had proven to be surprisingly difficult; the light victim who was to have been puffed away like a feather remained planted like a rock; and on top of all this, if anybody had a right to laugh it was the country lass and not the court.

She was not doing that, for that was not her spirit; but others were doing it. The whole town was laughing in its sleeve, and the court knew it, and its dignity was deeply hurt. The members could not hide their annoyance.

And so, as I have said, the session was stormy. It was easy to see that these men had made up their minds to force words from Joan today which should shorten up her case and bring it to a prompt conclusion. It shows that after all their experience with her they did not know her yet. They went into the battle with energy. They did not leave the questioning to a particular member; no, everybody helped. They volleyed questions at Joan from all over the house, and sometimes so many were talking at once that she had to ask them to deliver their fire one at a time and not by platoons. The beginning was as usual:

"You are once more required to take the oath pure and simple."

"I will answer to what is in the *proces verbal.* When I do more, I will choose the occasion for myself."

That old ground was debated and fought over inch by inch with great bitterness and many threats. But Joan remained steadfast, and the questionings had to shift to other matters. Half an hour was spent over Joan's apparitions—their dress, hair, general appearance, and so on—in the hope of fishing something of a damaging sort out of the replies; but with no result.

Next, the male attire was reverted to, of course. After many well-worn questions had been re-asked, one or two new ones were put forward.

"Did not the King or the Queen sometimes ask you to quit the male dress?"

"That is not in your *proces.*"

"Do you think you would have sinned if you had taken the dress of your sex?"

"I have done best to serve and obey my sovereign Lord and Master."

After a while the matter of Joan's Standard was taken up, in the hope of connecting magic and witchcraft with it.

"Did not your men copy your banner in their pennons?"

"The lancers of my guard did it. It was to distinguish them from the rest of the forces. It was their own idea."

"Were they often renewed?"

"Yes. When the lances were broken they were renewed."

The purpose of the questions unveils itself in the next one.

"Did you not say to your men that pennons made like your banner would be lucky?"

The soldier-spirit in Joan was offended at this puerility. She drew herself up, and said with dignity and fire: "What I said to them was, 'Ride these English down!' and I did it myself."

Whenever she flung out a scornful speech like that at these French menials in English livery it lashed them into a rage; and that is what happened this time. There were ten, twenty, sometimes even thirty of them on their feet at a time, storming at the prisoner minute after minute, but Joan was not disturbed.

By-and-by there was peace, and the inquiry was resumed.

It was now sought to turn against Joan the thousand loving honors which had been done her when she was raising France out of the dirt and shame of a century of slavery and castigation.

"Did you not cause paintings and images of yourself to be made?"

"No. At Arras I saw a painting of myself kneeling in armor before the King and delivering him a letter; but I caused no such things to be made."

"Were not masses and prayers said in your honor?"

"If it was done it was not by my command. But if any prayed for me I think it was no harm."

"Did the French people believe you were sent of God?"

"As to that, I know not: but whether they believed it or not, I was not the less sent of God."

"If they thought you were sent of God do you think it was well thought?"

"If they believed it, their trust was not abused."

"What impulse was it, think you, that moved the people to kiss your hands, your feet, and your vestments?"

"They were glad to see me, and so they did those things; and I could not have prevented them if I had had the heart. Those poor people came lovingly to me because I had not done them any hurt, but had done the best I could for them according to my strength."

See what modest little words she uses to describe that touching spectacle, her marches about France walled in on both sides by the adoring multitudes: "They were glad to see me." Glad? Why, they were transported with joy to see her. When they could not kiss her hands or her feet, they knelt in the mire and kissed the hoof-prints of her horse. They worshipped her; and that is what these priests were trying to prove. It was nothing to them that she was not to blame for what other people did. No, if she was worshipped, it was enough; she was guilty of mortal sin. Curious logic, one must say.

"Did you not stand sponsor for some children baptized at Rheims?"

"At Troyes I did, and at St. Denis; and I named the boys Charles, in honor of the King, and the girls I named Joan."

"Did not women touch their rings to those which you wore?"

"Yes, many did, but I did not know their reason for it."

"At Rheims was your Standard carried into the church? Did you stand at the altar with it in your hand at the Coronation?"

"Yes."

"In passing through the country did you confess yourself in the churches and receive the sacrament?"

"Yes."

"In the dress of a man?"

"Yes. But I do not remember that I was in armor."

It was almost a concession! almost a half-surrender of the permission granted her by the Church at Poitiers to dress as a man. The wily court shifted to another matter: to pursue this one at this time might call Joan's attention to her small mistake, and by her native cleverness she might recover her lost ground. The tempestuous session had worn her and drowsed her alertness.

"It is reported that you brought a dead child to life in the church at Lagny. Was that in answer to your prayers?"

"As to that, I have no knowledge. Other young girls were praying for the child, and I joined them and prayed also, doing no more than they."

"Continue."

"While we prayed it came to life, and cried. It had been dead three days, and was as black as my doublet. It was straightway baptized, then it passed from life again and was buried in holy ground."

"Why did you jump from the tower of Beaurevoir by night and try to escape?"

"I would go to the succor of Compiègne."

It was insinuated that this was an attempt to commit the deep crime of suicide to avoid falling into the hands of the English.

"Did you not say that you would rather die than be delivered into the power of the English?"

Joan answered frankly, without perceiving the trap—

"Yes; my words were, that I would rather that my soul be returned unto God than that I should fall into the hands of the English."

It was now insinuated that when she came to, after jumping from the tower, she was angry and blasphemed the name of God; and that she did it again when she heard of the defection of the Commandant of Soissons. She was hurt and indignant at this, and said—

"It is not true. I have never cursed. It is not my custom to swear."

CHAPTER 11

A halt was called. It was time. Cauchon was losing ground in the fight, Joan was gaining it. There were signs that here and there in the court a judge was being softened toward Joan by her courage, her presence of mind, her fortitude, her constancy, her piety, her simplicity and candor, her manifest purity, the nobility of her character, her fine intelligence, and the good brave fight she was making, all friendless and alone against unfair odds, and there was grave room for fear that this softening process would spread further and presently bring Cauchon's plans in danger.

Something must be done, and it was done. Cauchon was not distinguished for compassion, but he now gave proof that he had it in his character. He thought it pity to subject so many judges to the prostrating fatigues of this trial when it could be conducted plenty well enough by a handful of them. Oh, gentle Judge! But he did not remember to modify the fatigues for the little captive.

He would let all the judges but a handful go, but he would select the handful himself, and he did. He chose tigers. If a lamb or two got in, it was by oversight, not intention; and he knew what to do with lambs when discovered.

He called a small council, now, and during five days they sifted the huge bulk of answers thus far gathered from Joan. They winnowed it of all chaff, all useless matter—that is, all matter favorable to Joan; they saved up all matter which could be twisted to her hurt, and out of this they constructed a basis for a new trial which should have the semblance of a continuation of the old one. Another change. It was plain that the public trial had wrought damage: its proceedings had been discussed all over the town and had moved many to pity the abused prisoner. There should be no more of that. The sittings should be secret hereafter, and no spectators admitted. So Noël could come no more. I sent this news to him. I had not the heart to carry it myself. I would give the pain a chance to modify before I should see him in the evening.

On the tenth of March the secret trial began. A week had passed since I had seen Joan. Her appearance gave me a great shock. She looked tired and weak. She was listless and far away, and her answers showed that she was dazed and not able to keep perfect run of all that was done and said. Another court would not have taken advantage of her state, seeing that her life was at stake here, but would have adjourned and spared her. Did this one? No; it worried her for hours, and with a glad and eager ferocity, making all it could out of this great chance, the first one it had had.

She was tortured into confusing herself concerning the "sign" which had been given the King, and the next day this was continued hour after hour. As a result, she made partial revealments of particulars forbidden by her Voices; and seemed to me to state as facts things which were but allegories and visions mixed with facts.

The third day she was brighter, and looked less worn. She was almost her normal self again, and did her work well. Many attempts were made to beguile her into saying indiscreet things, but she saw the purpose in view and answered with tact and wisdom.

"Do you know if St. Catherine and St. Marguerite hate the English?"

"They love whom Our Lord loves, and hate whom He hates."

"Does God hate the English?"

"Of the love or the hatred of God toward the English I know nothing." Then she spoke up with the old martial ring in her voice and the old audacity in her words, and added, "But I know this—that God will send victory to the French, and that all the English will be flung out of France but the dead ones!"

"Was God on the side of the English when they were *prosperous* in France?"

"I do not know if God hates the French, but I think that he allowed them to be chastised for their sins."

It was a sufficiently naïve way to account for a chastisement which had now strung out for ninety-six years. But nobody found fault with it. There was nobody there who would not punish a sinner ninety-six years if he could, nor anybody there who would ever dream of such a thing as the Lord's being any shade less stringent than men.

"Have you ever embraced St. Marguerite and St. Catherine?"

"Yes, both of them."

The evil face of Cauchon betrayed satisfaction when she said that.

"When you hung garlands upon *L'Arbre Fée de Bourlemont,* did you do it in honor of your apparitions?"

"No."

Satisfaction again. No doubt Cauchon would take it for granted that she hung them there out of sinful love for the fairies.

"When the saints appeared to you did you bow, did you make reverence, did you kneel?"

"Yes; I did them the most honor and the most reverence that I could."

A good point for Cauchon if he could eventually make it appear that these were no saints to whom she had done reverence, but devils in disguise.

Now there was the matter of Joan's keeping her supernatural commerce a secret from her parents. Much might be made of that. In fact, particular emphasis had been given to it in a private remark written in the margin of the *proces: "She concealed her visions from her parents and from every one."* Possibly this disloyalty to her parents might itself be the sign of the satanic source of her mission.

"Do you think it was right to go away to the wars without getting your parents' leave? It is written one must honor his father and his mother."

"I have obeyed them in all things but that. And for that I have begged their forgiveness in a letter and gotten it."

"Ah, you asked their pardon? So you *knew* you were guilty of sin in going without their leave!"

Joan was stirred. Her eyes flashed, and she exclaimed—

"I was commanded of God, and it was right to go! If I had had a hundred fathers and mothers and been a king's daughter to boot I would have gone."

"Did you never ask your Voices if you might tell your parents?"

"They were willing that I should tell them, but I would not for anything have given my parents that pain."

To the minds of the questioners this headstrong conduct savored of pride. That sort of pride would move one to seek sacrilegious adorations.

"Did not your Voices call you Daughter of God?"

Joan answered with simplicity, and unsuspiciously—

"Yes; before the siege of Orleans and since, they have several times called me Daughter of God."

Further indications of pride and vanity were sought.

"What horse were you riding when you were captured? Who gave it you?"

"The King."

"You had other things—riches—of the King?"

"For myself I had horses and arms, and money to pay the service in my household."

"Had you not a treasury?"

"Yes. Ten or twelve thousand crowns." Then she said with naïveté, "It was not a great sum to carry on a war with."

"You have it yet?"

"No. It is the King's money. My brothers hold it for him."

"What were the arms which you left as an offering in the church of St. Denis?"

"My suit of silver mail and a sword."

"Did you put them there in order that they might be adored?"

"No. It was but an act of devotion. And it is the custom of men of war who have been wounded to make such offering there. I had been wounded before Paris."

Nothing appealed to those stony hearts, those dull imaginations—not even this pretty picture, so simply drawn, of the wounded girl-soldier hanging her toy harness there in curious companionship with the grim and dusty iron mail of the historic defenders of France. No, there was nothing in it for them; nothing, unless evil and injury for that innocent creature could be gotton out of it somehow.

"Which aided most—you the Standard, or the Standard you?"

"Whether it was the Standard or whether it was I, is nothing—the victories came from God."

"But did you base your hopes of victory in yourself or in your Standard?"

"In neither. In God, and not otherwhere."

"Was not your Standard waved around the King's head at the Coronation?"

"No. It was not."

"Why was it that *your* Standard had place at the crowning of the King in the Cathedral of Rheims, rather than those of the other captains?"

Then, soft and low, came that touching speech which will live as long as language lives, and pass into all tongues, and move all gentle hearts wheresoever it shall come, down to the latest day:

*"It had borne the burden, it had earned the honor."**

How simple it is, and how beautiful. And how it beggars the studied

* What she said has been many times translated, but never with success. There is a haunting pathos about the original which eludes all efforts to convey it into our tongue. It is as subtle as an odor, and escapes in the transmission. Her words were these:

"Il avait été a la peine, c'etait bien raison qu'il fut a l'honneur."

Monseigneur Ricard, Honorary Vicar-General to the Archbishop of Aix, finely speaks of it (*"Jeanne d'Arc la Vénérable,"* page 197) as "that sublime reply, enduring in the history of celebrated sayings like the cry of a French and Christian soul wounded unto death in its patriotism and its faith."—TRANSLATOR.

eloquence of the masters of oratory. Eloquence was a native gift of Joan of Arc; it came from her lips without effort and without preparation. Her words were as sublime as her deeds, as sublime as her character; they had their source in a great heart and were coined in a great brain.

CHAPTER 12

Now as a next move, this small secret court of holy assassins did a thing so base that even at this day, in my old age, it is hard to speak of it with patience.

In the beginning of her commerce with her Voices there at Domremy, the child Joan solemnly devoted her life to God, vowing her pure body and her pure soul to his service. You will remember that her parents tried to stop her from going to the wars by haling her to the court at Toul to compel her to make a marriage which she had never promised to make—a marriage with our poor, good, windy, big, hard-fighting and most dear and lamented comrade the Standard-bearer, who fell in honorable battle and sleeps in God these sixty years, peace to his ashes! And you will remember how Joan, sixteen years old, stood up in that venerable court and conducted her case all by herself, and tore the poor Paladin's case to rags and blew it away with a breath; and how the astonished old judge on the bench spoke of her as "this marvellous child."

You remember all that. Then think what I felt, to see these false priests here in the tribunal wherein Joan had fought a fourth lone fight in three years, deliberately twist that matter entirely around and try to make out that Joan haled the Paladin into court and pretended that he had promised to marry her, and was bent on making him do it.

Certainly there was no baseness that those people were ashamed to stoop to in their hunt for that friendless girl's life. What they wanted to show was this—that she had committed the sin of relapsing from her vow and trying to violate it.

Joan detailed the true history of the case, but lost her temper as she went along, and finished with some words for Cauchon which he remembers yet, whether he is fanning himself in the world he belongs in or has swindled his way into the other.

The rest of this day and part of the next the court labored upon the old theme—the male attire. It was shabby work for those grave men to be engaged in; for they well knew one of Joan's reasons for clinging to the male dress was, that soldiers of the guard were always present in her room whether she was asleep or awake, and that the male dress was a better protection for her modesty than the other.

The court knew that one of Joan's purposes had been the deliverance of the exiled Duke of Orleans, and they were curious to know how she had intended to manage it. Her plan was characteristically business-like, and her statement of it as characteristically simple and straightforward:

"I would have taken English prisoners enough in France for his ransom; and failing that, I would have invaded England and brought him out by force."

That was just her way. If a thing was to be done, it was love first, and hammer and tongs to follow; but no shilly-shallying between. She added with a little sigh—

"If I had had my freedom three years, I would have delivered him."

"Have you the permission of your Voices to break out of prison whenever you can?"

"I have asked their leave several times, but they have not given it."

I think it is as I have said, she expected the deliverance of death, and within the prison walls, before the three months should expire.

"Would you escape if you saw the doors open?"

She spoke up frankly and said—

"Yes—for I should see in that the permission of Our Lord. God helps who help themselves, the proverb says. But except I thought I had permission, I would not go."

Now, then, at this point, something occurred which convinces me, every time I think of it—and it struck me so at the time—that for a moment, at least, her hopes wandered to the King, and put into her mind the same notion about her deliverance which Noël and I had settled upon—a rescue by her old soldiers. I think the idea of the rescue did occur to her, but only as a passing thought, and that it quickly passed away.

Some remark of the Bishop of Beauvais moved her to remind him once more that he was an unfair judge, and had no right to preside there, and that he was putting himself in great danger.

"What danger?" he asked.

"I do not know. St. Catherine has promised me help, but I do not know the form of it. I do not know whether I am to be delivered from this prison or whether when you send me to the scaffold there will happen a trouble by which I shall be set free. Without much thought as to this matter, I am of the opinion that it may be one or the other." After a pause she added these words, memorable forever—words whose meaning she may have miscaught, misunderstood, as to that we can never know; words which she may have rightly understood; as to that also, we can never know; but words whose mystery fell away from them many a year ago and revealed their real meaning to all the world:

"But what my Voices have said clearest is, that I shall be delivered *by a great victory*." She paused, my heart was beating fast, for to me that great victory meant the sudden bursting in of our old soldiers with war-cry and clash of steel at the last moment and the carrying off of Joan of Arc in triumph. But oh, that thought had such a short life! For now she raised her head and finished, with those solemn words which men still so often quote and dwell upon—words which filled me with fear, they sounded so like a prediction. "And always they say 'Submit to whatever comes; *do not grieve for your martyrdom;* from it you will ascend into the Kingdom of Paradise.'"

Was she thinking of fire and the stake? I think not. I thought of it myself, but I believe she was only thinking of this slow and cruel martyrdom of chains and captivity and insult. Surely martyrdom was the right name for it.

It was Jean de la Fontaine who was asking the questions. He was willing to make the most he could out of what she had said:

"As the Voices have told you you are going to Paradise, you feel certain that that will happen and that you will not be damned in hell. Is that so?"

"I believe what they told me. I know that I shall be saved."

"It is a weighty answer."

"To me the knowledge that I shall be saved is a great treasure."

"Do you think that after that revelation you could be able to commit mortal sin?"

"As to that, I do not know. My hope for salvation is in holding fast to my oath to keep my body and my soul pure."

"Since you know you are to be saved do you think it necessary to go to confession?"

The snare was ingeniously devised, but Joan's simple and humble answer left it empty—

"One cannot keep his conscience too clean."

We were now arriving at the last day of this new trial. Joan had come through the ordeal well. It had been a long and wearisome struggle for all concerned. All ways had been tried to convict the accused, and all had failed, thus far. The inquisitors were thoroughly vexed and dissatisfied. However, they resolved to make one more effort, put in one more day's work. This was done—March 17th. Early in the sitting a notable trap was set for Joan:

"Will you submit to the determination of the Church all your words and deeds, whether good or bad?"

That was well planned. Joan was in imminent peril now. If she should heedlessly say yes, it would put her mission *itself* upon trial, and one would know how to decide its source and character promptly. If she should say no, she would render herself chargeable with the crime of heresy.

But she was equal to the occasion. She drew a distinct line of separation between the Church's authority over her as a subject member, and the matter of her *mission.* She said she loved the Church and was ready to support the Christian faith with all her strength; but as to the works done under her mission, those must be judged by God alone, who had commanded them to be done.

The judge still insisted that she submit them to the decision of the Church. She said—

"I will submit them to Our Lord who sent me. It would seem to me that He and His Church are one, and that there should be no difficulty about this matter." Then she turned upon the judge and said, "Why do you make a difficulty where there is no room for any?"

Then Jean de la Fontaine corrected her notion that there was but one Church. There were two—the Church Triumphant, which is God, the saints, the angels, and the redeemed, and has its seat in heaven; and the Church Militant, which is our Holy Father the Pope, Vicar of God, the prelates, the clergy and all good christians and catholics, the which Church has its seat in the earth, is governed by the Holy Spirit, and cannot err. "Will you not submit those matters to the Church Militant?"

"I am come to the King of France from the Church Triumphant on high by its commandant, and to that Church I will submit all those things which I have done. For the Church Militant I have no other answer now."

The court took note of this straightly worded refusal, and would hope to get profit out of it; but the matter was dropped for the present, and a long chase was then made over the old hunting-ground—the fairies, the visions, the male attire, and all that.

In the afternoon the satanic Bishop himself took the chair and presided over the closing scenes of the trial. Along toward the finish, this question was asked by one of the judges:

"You have said to my lord the Bishop that you would answer him as you would answer before our Holy Father the Pope, and yet there are several questions which you continually refuse to answer. Would you not answer the Pope more fully than you have answered before my lord of Beauvais? Would you not feel obliged to answer the Pope, who is the Vicar of God, more fully?"

Now fell a thunder-clap out of a clear sky—

"*Take me to the Pope.* I will answer to everything that I ought to."

It made the Bishop's purple face fairly blanch with consternation. If Joan had only known, if she had only known! She had lodged a mine under this black conspiracy able to blow the Bishop's schemes to the four winds of heaven, and she didn't know it. She had made that speech by mere instinct, not suspecting what tremendous forces were hidden in it, and there was none to tell her what she had done. I knew, and Manchon knew; and if she had known how to read writing we could have hoped to get the knowledge to her somehow; but speech was the only way, and none was allowed to approach her near enough for that. So there she sat, once more Joan of Arc the Victorious, but all unconscious of it. She was miserably worn and tired, by the long day's struggle and by illness, or she must have noticed the effect of that speech and divined the reason of it.

She had made many master-strokes, but this was *the* master-stroke. It was *an appeal to Rome*. It was her clear right; and if she had persisted in it Cauchon's plot would have tumbled about his ears like a house of cards, and he would have gone from that place the worst beaten man of the century. He was daring, but he was not daring enough to stand up against that demand if Joan had urged it. But no, she was ignorant, poor thing, and did not know what a blow she had struck for life and liberty.

France was not the Church. Rome had no interest in the destruction of this messenger of God. Rome would have given her a fair trial, and that was all that her cause needed. From that trial she would have gone forth free and honored and blest.

But it was not so fated. Cauchon at once diverted the questions to other matters and hurried the trial quickly to an end.

As Joan moved feebly away, dragging her chains, I felt stunned and dazed, and kept saying to myself, "Such a little while ago she said the saving word and could have gone free; and now, there she goes to her death; yes, it is to her death, I know it, I feel it. They will double the guards; they will never let any come near her now between this and her condemnation, lest she get a hint and speak that word again. This is the bitterest day that has come to me in all this miserable time."

CHAPTER 13

So the second trial in the prison was over. Over, and no definite result. The character of it I have described to you. It was baser in one particular than the previous one; for this time the charges had not been communicated to Joan, therefore she had been obliged to fight in the dark. There was no opportunity to do any thinking beforehand; there was no foreseeing what traps might be set, and no way to prepare for them. Truly it was a shabby advantage to take of a girl situated as this one was. One day, during the course of it, an able lawyer of Normandy, Maître Lohier, happened to be in Rouen, and I will give you his opinion of that trial, so that you may see that I have been honest with you, and that my partisanship has not made me deceive you as to its unfair and illegal character. Cauchon showed Lohier the *proces* and asked his opinion about the trial. Now this was the opinion which he gave to Cauchon. He said that the whole thing was null and void; for these reasons: 1, because the trial was secret, and full freedom of speech and action on the part of those present not possible; 2, because the trial touched the honor of the King of France, yet he was not summoned to defend himself, nor any one appointed to represent him; 3, because the charges against the prisoner were not communicated to her; 4, because the accused, although young and simple, had been forced to defend her cause without help of counsel, notwithstanding she had so much at stake.

Did that please Bishop Cauchon? It did not. He burst out upon Lohier with the most savage cursings, and swore he would have him drowned. Lohier escaped from Rouen and got out of France with all speed, and so saved his life.

Well, as I have said, the second trial was over, without definite result. But Cauchon did not give up. He could trump up another. And still another and another, if necessary. He had the half-promise of an enormous prize—the Archbishopric of Rouen—if he should succeed in burning the body and damning to hell the soul of this young girl who had never done him any harm; and such a prize as that, to a man like the Bishop of Beauvais, was worth the burning and damning of fifty harmless girls, let alone one.

So he set to work again straight off, next day; and with high confidence, too, intimating with brutal cheerfulness that he should succeed this time. It took him and the other scavengers nine days to dig matter enough out of Joan's testimony and their own inventions to build up the new mass of charges. And it was a formidable mass indeed, for it numbered sixty-six articles!

This huge document was carried to the castle the next day, March 27th; and there, before a dozen carefully selected judges, the new trial was begun.

Opinions were taken, and the tribunal decided that Joan should hear the articles read, this time. Maybe that was on account of Lohier's remark upon that head; or maybe it was hoped that the reading would kill the prisoner with fatigue—for, as it turned out, this reading occupied several days. It was also decided that Joan should be required to answer squarely to every article, and that if she refused she should be considered *convicted.* You see, Cauchon was managing to narrow her chances more and more all the time; he was drawing the toils closer and closer.

Joan was brought in, and the Bishop of Beauvais opened with a speech to her which ought to have made even himself blush, so laden it was with hypocrisy and lies. He said that this court was composed of holy and pious churchmen whose hearts were full of benevolence and compassion toward her, and that they had no wish to hurt her body, but only a desire to instruct her and lead her into the way of truth and salvation.

Why, this man was born a devil; now think of his describing himself and those hardened slaves of his in such language as that.

And yet, worse was to come. For now, having in mind another of Lohier's hints, he had the cold effrontery to make to Joan a proposition which I think will surprise you when you hear it. He said that this court, recognizing her untaught estate and her inability to deal with the complex and difficult matters which were about to be considered, had determined, out of their pity and their mercifulness, to allow her to choose one or more persons *out of their own number* to help her with counsel and advice!

Think of that—a court made up of Loyseleur and his breed of reptiles. It was granting leave to a lamb to ask help of a wolf. Joan looked up to see if he was serious, and perceiving that he was at least pretending to be, she declined, of course.

The Bishop was not expecting any other reply. He had made a show of fairness and could have it entered on the minutes, therefore he was satisfied.

Then he commanded Joan to answer straightly to every accusation; and threatened to cut her off from the Church if she failed to do that or delayed her answers beyond a given length of time. Yes, he was narrowing her chances down, step by step.

Thomas de Courcelles began the reading of that interminable document, article by article. Joan answered to each article in its turn; sometimes merely denying its truth, sometimes by saying her answer would be found in the records of the previous trials.

What a strange document that was, and what an exhibition and exposure of the heart of man, the one creature authorized to boast that he is made in the image of God. To know Joan of Arc was to know one who was wholly noble, pure, truthful, brave, compassionate, generous, pious, unselfish, modest, blameless as the very flowers in the fields—a nature fine and beautiful, a character supremely great. To know her from that document would be to know her as the exact reverse of all that. Nothing that she *was* appears in it, everything that she was *not* appears there in detail.

Consider some of the things it charges against her, and remember who it is it is speaking of. It calls her a sorceress, a false prophet, an invoker and companion of evil spirits, a dealer in magic, a person ignorant of the Catholic faith, a schismatic; she is sacrilegious, an idolater, an apostate, a blasphemer of God and his saints, scandalous, seditious, a disturber of the peace; she incites men to war, and to the spilling of human blood; she discards the decencies and proprieties of her sex, irreverently assuming the dress of a man and the vocation of a soldier; she beguiles both princes and people; she usurps divine honors, and has caused herself to be adored and venerated, offering her hands and her vestments to be kissed.

There it is—every fact of her life distorted, perverted, reversed. As a child she had loved the fairies, she had spoken a pitying word for them when they were banished from their home, she had played under their tree and around their fountain—hence she was a comrade of evil spirits. She had lifted France out of the mud and moved her to strike for freedom, and led her to victory after victory—hence she was a disturber of the peace—as indeed she was, and a provoker of war—as indeed she was again! and France will be proud of it and grateful for it for many a century to come. And she had been adored—as if she could help that, poor thing, or was in any way to blame for it. The cowed veteran and the wavering recruit had drunk the spirit of war from her eyes and touched her sword with theirs and moved forward invincible—hence she was a sorceress.

And so the document went on, detail by detail, turning these waters of life to poison, this gold to dross, these proofs of a noble and beautiful life to evidences of a foul and odious one.

Of course the sixty-six articles were just a rehash of the things which had come up in the course of the previous trials, so I will touch upon this new trial but lightly. In fact Joan went but little into detail herself, usually merely saying "That is not true—*passez outre*"; or, "I have answered that before—let the clerk read it in his record"; or saying some other brief thing.

She refused to have her mission examined and tried by the earthly Church. The refusal was taken note of.

She denied the accusation of idolatry and that she had sought men's homage. She said—

"If any kissed my hands and my vestments it was not by my desire, and I did what I could to prevent it."

She had the pluck to say to that deadly tribunal that she did not know the fairies to be evil beings. She knew it was a perilous thing to say, but it was not in her nature to speak anything but the truth when she spoke at all. Danger had no weight with her in such things. Note was taken of her remark.

She refused, as always before, when asked if she would put off the male attire if she were given permission to commune. And she added this:

"When one receives the sacrament, the manner of his dress is a small thing and of no value in the eyes of Our Lord."

She was charged with being so stubborn in clinging to her male dress that she would not lay it off even to get the blessed privilege of hearing mass. She spoke out with spirit and said:

"I would rather die than be untrue to my oath to God."

She was reproached with doing man's work in the wars and thus deserting the industries proper to her sex. She answered, with some little touch of soldierly disdain—

"As to the matter of women's work, there's plenty to do it."

It was always a comfort to me to see the soldier-spirit crop up in her. While that remained in her she would be Joan of Arc, and able to look trouble and fate in the face.

"It appears that this mission of yours which you claim you had from God, was to make war and pour out human blood."

Joan replied quite simply, contenting herself with explaining that war was not her first move, but her second:

"To begin with, I demanded that peace should be made. If it was refused, then I would fight."

The judge mixed the Burgundians and English together in speaking of the enemy which Joan had come to make war upon. But she showed that she made a distinction between them by act and word, the Burgundians being Frenchmen and therefore entitled to less brusque treatment than the English. She said:

"As to the Duke of Burgundy, I required of him, both by letters and by his ambassadors, that he make peace with the King. As to the English, the only peace for them was that they leave the country and go home."

Then she said that even with the English she had shown a pacific disposition, since she had warned them away by proclamation before attacking them.

"If they had listened to me," said she, "they would have done wisely." At this point she uttered her prophecy again, saying with emphasis, "Before seven years they will see it themselves."

Then they presently began to pester her again about her male costume, and tried to persuade her to voluntarily promise to discard it. I was never deep, so I think it no wonder that I was puzzled by their persistency in what seemed a thing of no consequence, and could not make out what their reason could be. But we all know, now. We all know now that it was another of their treacherous projects. Yes, if they could but succeed in getting her to formally discard it they could play a game upon her which would quickly destroy her. So they kept at their evil work until at last she broke out and said—

"Peace! Without the permission of God I will not lay it off though you cut off my head!"

At one point she corrected the *proces verbal*, saying—

"It makes me say that everything which I have done was done by the counsel of Our Lord. I did not say that. I said 'all which I have *well* done.'"

Doubt was cast upon the authenticity of her mission because of the ignorance and simplicity of the messenger chosen. Joan smiled at that. She could have reminded these people that Our Lord, who is no respecter of persons, had chosen the lowly for his high purposes even oftener than he had chosen bishops and cardinals; but she phrased her rebuke in simpler terms:

"It is the prerogative of Our Lord to choose His instruments where He will."

She was asked what form of prayer she used in invoking counsel from on high. She said the form was brief and simple; then she lifted her pallid face and repeated it, clasping her chained hands:

"Most dear God, in honor of your holy passion I beseech you, if you love me, that you will reveal to me what I am to answer to these churchmen. As concerns my dress, I know by what command I have put it on, but I know not in what manner I am to lay it off. I pray you tell me what to do."

She was charged with having dared, against the precepts of God and His saints, to assume empire over men and make herself Commander-in-Chief. That touched the soldier in her. She had a deep reverence for priests, but the soldier in her had but small reverence for a priest's opinions about war; so, in her answer to this charge she did not condescend to go into any explanations or excuses, but delivered herself with bland indifference and military brevity.

"If I was Commander-in-Chief, it was to thrash the English!"

Death was staring her in the face here, all the time, but no matter: she dearly loved to make these English-hearted Frenchmen squirm, and whenever they gave her an opening she was prompt to jab her sting into it. She got great refreshment out of these little episodes. Her days were a desert; these were the oases in it.

Her being in the wars with men was charged against her as an indelicacy. She said–

"I had a woman with me when I could–in towns and lodgings. In the field I always slept in my armor."

That she and her family had been ennobled by the King was charged against her as evidence that the source of her deeds was sordid self-seeking. She answered that she had not asked this grace of the King, it was his own act.

This third trial was ended at last. And once again there was no definite result.

Possibly a fourth trial might succeed in defeating this apparently unconquerable girl. So the malignant Bishop set himself to work to plan it.

He appointed a commission to reduce the substance of the sixty-six articles to twelve compact lies, as a basis for the new attempt. This was done. It took several days.

Meantime Cauchon went to Joan's cell one day, with Manchon and two of the judges, Isambard de la Pierre and Martin Ladvenue, to see if he could not manage somehow to beguile Joan into submitting her mission to the examination and decision of the church militant—that is to say, to that part of the church militant which was represented by himself and his creatures.

Joan once more positively refused. Isambard de la Pierre had a heart in his body, and he so pitied this persecuted poor girl that he ventured to do a very daring thing; for he asked her if she would be willing to have her case go before the Council of Basel, and said it contained as many priests of her party as of the English party.

Joan cried out that she would gladly go before so fairly constructed a tribunal as that; but before Isambard could say another word, Cauchon turned savagely upon him and exclaimed—

"Shut up, in the devil's name!"

Then Manchon ventured to do a brave thing, too, though he did it in great fear for his life. He asked Cauchon if he should enter Joan's submission to the Council of Basel upon the minutes.

"No! It is not necessary."

"Ah," said poor Joan, reproachfully, "you set down everything that is against me, but you will not set down what is for me."

It was piteous. It would have touched the heart of a brute. But Cauchon was more than that.

CHAPTER 14

We were now in the first days of April. Joan was ill. She had fallen ill the 29th of March, the day after the close of the third trial, and was growing worse when the scene which I have just described occurred in her cell. It was just like Cauchon to go there and try to get some advantage out of her weakened state.

Let us note some of the particulars in the new indictment—the Twelve Lies.

Part of the first one says Joan asserts that she has found her salvation. She never said anything of the kind. It also says she refuses to submit herself to the Church. Not true. She was willing to submit all her acts to this Rouen tribunal except those done by command of God in fulfilment of her mission. Those she reserved for the judgment of God. She refused to recognize Cauchon and his serfs as the Church, but was willing to go before the Pope or the Council of Basel.

A clause of another of the Twelve says she admits having threatened with death those who would not obey her. Distinctly false. Another clause says she declares that all she has done has been done by command of God. What she really said was, all that she had done *well*—a correction made by herself as you have already seen.

Another of the Twelve says she claims that she has never committed any sin. She never made any such claim.

Another makes the wearing of the male dress a sin. If it was, she had high Catholic authority for committing it—that of the Archbishop of Rheims and the tribunal of Poitiers.

The Tenth Article was resentful against her for "pretending" that St. Catherine and St. Marguerite spoke French and not English, and were French in their politics.

The Twelve were to be submitted first to the learned doctors of theology of the University of Paris for approval. They were copied out and ready by the night of April 4th. Then Manchon did another bold thing: he wrote in the margin that many of the Twelve put statements in Joan's mouth which were the exact opposite of what she had said. *That* fact would not be considered important by the University of Paris, and would not influence its decision or stir its humanity, in case it had any—which it hadn't when acting in a political capacity, as at present—but it was a brave thing for that good Manchon to do, all the same.

The Twelve were sent to Paris next day, April 5th. That afternoon there was a great tumult in Rouen, and excited crowds were flocking through all the chief streets, chattering and seeking for news; for a report had gone abroad that Joan of Arc was sick unto death. In truth these long seances had worn her out, and she was ill indeed. The heads of the English party were in a state of consternation; for if Joan should die uncondemned by the Church and go to the grave unsmirched, the pity and the love of the people would turn her wrongs and sufferings and death into a holy martyrdom, and she would be even a mightier power in France dead, than she had been when alive.

The Earl of Warwick and the English Cardinal (Winchester) hurried to the castle and sent messengers flying for physicians. Warwick was a hard man, a rude coarse man, a man without compassion. There lay the sick girl stretched in her chains in her iron cage—not an object to move man to ungentle speech, one would think; yet Warwick spoke right out in her hearing and said to the physicians—

"Mind you take good care of her. The King of England has no mind to have her die a natural death. She is dear to him, for he bought her dear, and he does not want her to die, save at the stake. Now then, mind you cure her."

The doctors asked Joan what had made her ill. She said the Bishop of Beauvais had sent her a fish and she thought it was that.

Then Jean d'Estivet burst out on her, and called her names and abused her. He understood Joan to be charging the Bishop with poisoning her, you see; and that was not pleasing to him, for he was one of Cauchon's most loving and conscienceless slaves, and it outraged him to have Joan injure his master in the eyes of these great English chiefs, these being men who could ruin Cauchon and would promptly do it if they got the conviction that he was capable of saving Joan from the stake by poisoning her and thus cheating the English out of all the real value gainable by her purchase from the Duke of Burgundy.

Joan had a high fever, and the doctors proposed to bleed her. Warwick said—

"Be careful about that; she is smart and is capable of killing herself."

He meant that to escape the stake she might undo the bandage and let herself bleed to death.

But the doctors bled her anyway, and then she was better.

Not for long, though. Jean d'Estivet could not hold still, he was so worried and angry about the suspicion of poisoning which Joan had hinted at; so he came back in the evening and stormed at her till he brought the fever all back again.

When Warwick heard of this he was in a fine temper, you may be sure, for here was his prey threatening to escape again, and all through the over-zeal of this meddling fool. Warwick gave D'Estivet a quite admirable cursing—admirable as to strength, I mean, for it was said by persons of culture that the art of it was not good—and after that the meddler kept still.

Joan remained ill more than two weeks; then she grew better. She was still very weak, but she could bear a little persecution now without much danger to her life. It seemed to Cauchon a good time to furnish it. So he called together some of his doctors of theology and went to her dungeon. Manchon and I went along to keep the record—that is, to set down what might be useful to Cauchon, and leave out the rest.

The sight of Joan gave me a shock. Why, she was but a shadow! It was difficult for me to realize that this frail little creature with the sad face and drooping form was the same Joan of Arc that I had so often seen, all fire and enthusiasm, charging through a hail of death and the lightning and thunder of the guns at the head of her battalions. It wrung my heart to see her looking like this.

But Cauchon was not touched. He made another of those conscienceless speeches of his, all dripping with hypocrisy and guile. He told Joan that among her answers had been some which had seemed to endanger religion; and as she was ignorant and without knowledge of the Scriptures, he had brought some good and wise men to instruct her, if she desired it. Said he, "We are churchmen, and disposed by our good will as well as by our vocation to procure for you the salvation of your soul and your body, in every way in our power, just as we would do the like for our nearest kin or for ourselves. In this we but follow the example of Holy Church, who never closes the refuge of her bosom against any that are willing to return."

Joan thanked him for these sayings and said:

"I seem to be in danger of death from this malady; if it be the pleasure of God that I die here, I beg that I may be heard in confession and also receive my Saviour; and that I may be buried in consecrated ground."

Cauchon thought he saw his opportunity at last; this weakened body had the fear of an unblessed death before it and the pains of hell to follow. This stubborn spirit would surrender now. So he spoke out and said—

"Then if you want the Sacraments, you must do as all good Catholics do, and submit to the Church."

He was eager for her answer; but when it came there was no surrender in it, she still stood to her guns. She turned her head away and said wearily—

"I have nothing more to say."

Cauchon's temper was stirred, and he raised his voice threateningly and said that the more she was in danger of death the more she ought to amend her life; and again he refused the things she begged for unless she would submit to the Church. Joan said—

"If I die in this prison I beg you to have me buried in holy ground; if you will not, I cast myself upon my Saviour."

There was some more conversation of the like sort, then Cauchon demanded again, and imperiously, that she submit herself and all her deeds to the Church. His threatening and storming went for nothing. That body was weak, but the spirit in it was the spirit of Joan of Arc; and out of that came the steadfast answer which these people were already so familiar with and detested so sincerely—

"Let come what may, I will neither do nor say any otherwise than I have said already in your tribunals."

Then the good theologians took turn about and worried her with reasonings and arguments and Scriptures; and always they held the lure of the Sacraments before her famishing soul, and tried to bribe her with them to surrender her mission to the Church's judgment—that is to *their* judgment—as if *they* were the Church! But it availed nothing. I could have told them that beforehand, if they had asked me. But they never asked me anything; I was too humble a creature for their notice.

Then the interview closed with a threat; a threat of fearful import; a threat calculated to make a Catholic Christian feel as if the ground were sinking from under him—

"The Church calls upon you to submit; disobey, and she will abandon you as if you were a pagan!"

Think of being abandoned by the Church!—that august Power in whose hands is lodged the fate of the human race; whose sceptre stretches beyond the furthest constellation that twinkles in the sky; whose authority is over the millions that live and over the billions that wait trembling in purgatory for ransom or doom; whose smile opens the gates of Heaven to you, whose frown delivers you to the fires of everlasting hell; a Power whose dominion overshadows and belittles earthly empire as earthly empire overshadows and belittles the pomps and shows of a village. To be abandoned by one's King—yes, that is death, and death is much; but to be abandoned by Rome, to be abandoned by the Church! Ah, death is nothing to that, for that is consignment to endless *life*—and such a life!

I could see the red waves tossing in that shoreless lake of fire, I could see the black myriads of the damned rise out of them and struggle and sink and rise again; and I knew that Joan was seeing what I saw, while she paused musing; and I believed that she must yield now, and in truth I hoped she would, for these men were able to make the threat good and deliver her over to eternal suffering, and I knew that it was in their natures to do it.

But I was foolish to think that thought and hope that hope. Joan of Arc was not made as others are made. Fidelity to principle, fidelity to truth, fidelity to her word, all these were in her bone and in her flesh—they were parts of her. She could not change, she could not cast them out. She was the very genius of Fidelity, she was Steadfastness incarnated. Where she had taken her stand and planted her foot, there she would abide; hell itself could not move her from that place.

Her Voices had not given her permission to make the sort of submission that was required, therefore she would stand fast. She would wait, in perfect obedience, let come what might.

My heart was like lead in my body when I went out from that dungeon; but she—she was serene, she was not troubled. She had done what she believed to be her duty, and that was sufficient; the consequences were not her affair. The last thing she said, that time, was full of this serenity, full of contented repose—

"I am a good Christian born and baptized, and a good Christian I will die."

CHAPTER 15

Two weeks went by; the second of May was come, the chill was departed out of the air, the wild flowers were springing in the glades and glens, the birds were piping in the woods, all nature was brilliant with sunshine, all spirits were renewed and refreshed, all hearts glad, the world was alive with hope and cheer, the plain beyond the Seine stretched away soft and rich and green, the river was limpid and lovely, the leafy islands were dainty to see, and flung still daintier reflections of themselves upon the shining water; and from the tall bluffs above the bridge Rouen was become again a delight to the eye, the most exquisite and satisfying picture of a town that nestles under the arch of heaven anywhere.

When I say that all hearts were glad and hopeful, I mean it in a general sense. There were exceptions—we who were the friends of Joan of Arc, also Joan of Arc herself, that poor girl shut up there in that frowning stretch of mighty walls and towers: brooding in darkness, so close to the flooding downpour of sunshine yet so impossibly far away from it; so longing for any little glimpse of it, yet so implacably denied it by those wolves in the black gowns who were plotting her death and the blackening of her good name.

Cauchon was ready to go on with his miserable work. He had a new scheme to try, now. He would see what persuasion could do—argument, eloquence, poured out upon the incorrigible captive from the mouth of a trained expert. That was his plan. But the reading of the Twelve Articles to her was not a part of it. No, even Cauchon was ashamed to lay that monstrosity before her; even he had a remnant of shame in him, away down deep, a million fathoms deep, and that remnant asserted itself now and prevailed.

On this fair second of May, then, the black company gathered itself together in the spacious chamber at the end of the great hall of the castle—the Bishop of Beauvais on his throne, and sixty-two minor judges massed before him, with the guards and recorders at their stations and the orator at his desk.

Then we heard the far clank of chains, and presently Joan entered with her keepers and took her seat upon her isolated bench. She was looking well, now, and most fair and beautiful after her fortnight's rest from wordy persecution.

She glanced about and noted the orator. Doubtless she divined the situation.

The orator had written his speech all out, and had it in his hand, though he held it back of him out of sight. It was so thick that it resembled a book. He began flowingly, but in the midst of a flowery period his memory failed him and he had to snatch a furtive glance at his manuscript—which much injured the effect. Again this happened, and then a third time. The poor man's face was red with embarrassment, the whole great house was pitying him, which made the matter worse; then Joan dropped in a remark which completed his trouble. She said:

"*Read your book*—and then I will answer you!"

Why, it was almost cruel the way those mouldy veterans laughed; and as for the orator, he looked so flustered and helpless that almost anybody would have pitied him, and I had difficulty to keep from doing it myself. Yes, Joan was feeling very well after her rest, and the native mischief that was in her lay near the surface. It did not show, when she made the remark, but I knew it was close in there back of the words.

When the orator had gotten back his composure he did a wise thing; for he followed Joan's advice: he made no more attempts at sham impromptu oratory, but read his speech straight from his "book." In the speech he compressed the Twelve Articles into six and made these his text.

Every now and then he stopped and asked questions, and Joan replied. The nature of the church militant was explained, and once more Joan was asked to submit herself to it.

She gave her usual answer.

Then she was asked—

"Do you believe the Church can err?"

"I believe it cannot err; but for those deeds and words of mine which were done and uttered by command of God, I will answer to him alone."

"Will you say that you have no judge upon earth? Is not our Holy Father the Pope your judge?"

"I will say nothing to you about it. I have a good Master who is our Lord and to Him I will submit all."

Then came these terrible words:

"If you do not submit to the Church you will be pronounced a heretic by these judges here present and burned at the stake!"

Ah, that would have smitten you or me dead with fright, but it only roused the lion heart of Joan of Arc, and in her answer rang that martial note which had used to stir her soldiers like a bugle-call—

"I will not say otherwise than I have said already; and if I saw the fire before me I would say it again!"

It was uplifting to hear her battle-voice once more and see the battle-light burn in her eye. Many there were stirred; every man that was a *man* was stirred, whether friend or foe; and Manchon risked his life again, good soul, for he wrote in the margin of the record in good plain letters these brave words: "*Superba responsio!*" and there they have remained these sixty years, and there you may read them to this day.

"*Superba responsio!*" Yes, it was just that. For this "superb answer" came from the lips of a girl of nineteen with death and hell staring her in the face.

Of course the matter of the male attire was gone over again; and as usual at wearisome length; also, as usual, the customary bribe was offered: if she would discard that dress voluntarily they would let her hear mass. But she answered as she had often answered before—

"I will go in a woman's robe to all services of the church if I may be permitted, but I will resume the other dress when I return to my cell."

They set several traps for her in a tentative form; that is to say, they placed supposititious propositions before her and cunningly tried to commit her to one end of the propositions without committing themselves to the other. But she always saw the game and spoiled it. The trap was in this form—

"Would you be willing to do so and so if we should give you leave?"

Her answer was always in this form or to this effect:

"When you give me leave, then you will know."

Yes, Joan was at her best, that second of May. She had all her wits about her, and they could not catch her anywhere. It was a long, long session, and all the old ground was fought over again, foot by foot, and the orator-expert worked all his persuasions, all his eloquence; but the result was the familiar one—a drawn battle, the sixty-two retiring upon their base, the solitary enemy holding her original position within her original lines.

CHAPTER 16

The brilliant weather, the heavenly weather, the bewitching weather made everybody's heart to sing, as I have told you; yes, Rouen was feeling light-hearted and gay, and most willing and ready to break out and laugh upon the least occasion; and so when the news went around that the young girl in the tower had scored another defeat against Bishop Cauchon there was abundant laughter—abundant laughter among the citizens of both parties, for they all hated the Bishop. It is true, the English-hearted majority of the people wanted Joan burned, but that did not keep them from laughing at the man they hated. It would have been perilous for anybody to laugh at the English chiefs or at the majority of Cauchon's assistant judges, but to laugh at Cauchon or D'Estivet and Loyseleur was safe—nobody would report it.

The difference between Cauchon and *cochon** was not noticeable in speech, and so there was plenty of opportunity for puns: the opportunities were not thrown away.

Some of the jokes got well worn in the course of two or three months, from repeated use; for every time Cauchon started a new trial the folk said "The sow has littered† again"; and every time the trial failed they said it over again, with its other meaning, "The hog has made a mess of it."

And so, on the third of May, Noël and I, drifting about the town, heard many a wide-mouthed lout let go his joke and his laugh, and then move to the next group, proud of his wit and happy, to work it off again—

" 'Ods blood, the sow has littered five times, and five times has made a mess of it!"

And now and then one was bold enough to say—but he said it softly—

* Hog, pig. [—M.T.]

† *Cochonner,* to litter, to farrow; also, "to make a mess of!" [—M.T.]

"Sixty-three and the might of England against a girl, and she camps on the field five times!"

Cauchon lived in the great palace of the Archbishop, and it was guarded by English soldiery; but no matter, there was never a dark night but the walls showed, next morning, that the rude joker had been there with his paint and brush. Yes, he had been there, and had smeared the sacred walls with pictures of hogs in all attitudes except flattering ones; hogs clothed in a Bishop's vestments and wearing a Bishop's mitre irreverently cocked on the side of their heads.

Cauchon raged and cursed over his defeats and his impotence during seven days, then he conceived a new scheme. You shall see what it was; for you have not cruel hearts, and you would never guess it.

On the ninth of May there was a summons, and Manchon and I got our materials together and started. But this time we were to go to one of the other towers—not the one which was Joan's prison. It was round and grim and massive, and built of the plainest and thickest and solidest masonry—a dismal and forbidding structure.*

We entered the circular room on the ground floor, and I saw what turned me sick—the instruments of torture and the executioners standing ready! Here you have the black heart of Cauchon at the blackest, here you have the proof that in his nature there was no such thing as pity. One wonders if he ever knew his mother or ever had a sister.

Cauchon was there, and the Vice-Inquisitor and the Abbot of St. Corneille; also six others, among them that false Loyseleur. The guards were in their places, the rack was there, and by it stood the executioner and his aids in their crimson hose and doublets, meet color for their bloody trade. The picture of Joan rose before me stretched upon the rack, her feet tied to one end of it, her wrists to the other, and those red giants turning the windlass and pulling her limbs out of their sockets. It seemed to me that I could hear the bones snap and the flesh tear apart, and I did not see how that body of anointed servants of the merciful Jesus could sit there and look so placid and indifferent.

After a little, Joan arrived and was brought in. She saw the rack, she saw its attendants, and the same picture which I had been seeing must have risen in her mind; but do you think she quailed, do you think she shuddered? No, there was no sign of that sort. She straightened herself up, and there was a slight curl of scorn about her lip; but as for fear, she showed not a vestige of it.

This was a memorable session, but it was the shortest one of all the

* The lower half of it remains to-day just as it was then; the upper half is of a later date.—TRANSLATOR.

list. When Joan had taken her seat a résumé of her "crimes" was read to her. Then Cauchon made a solemn speech. In it he said that in the course of her several trials Joan had refused to answer some of the questions and had answered others with lies, but that now he was going to have the truth out of her, and the whole of it.

His manner was full of confidence this time; he was sure he had found a way at last to break this child's stubborn spirit and make her beg and cry. He would score a victory this time and stop the mouths of the jokers of Rouen. You see, he was only just a man, after all, and couldn't stand ridicule any better than other people. He talked high, and his splotchy face lighted itself up with all the shifting tints and signs of evil pleasure and promised triumph—purple, yellow, red, green—they were all there, with sometimes the dull and spongy blue of a drowned man, the uncanniest of them all. And finally he burst out in a great passion and said—

"There is the rack, and there are its ministers! You will reveal all, now, or be put to the torture. Speak."

Then she made that great answer, which will live forever; made it without fuss or bravado, and yet how fine and noble was the sound of it—

"I will tell you nothing more than I have told you; no, not even if you tear the limbs from my body. And even if in my pain I *did* say something otherwise, I would always say afterwards that it was the torture that spoke and not I."

There was no crushing that spirit. You should have seen Cauchon. Defeated again, and he had not dreamed of such a thing. I heard it said next day, around the town, that he had a full confession, all written out, in his pocket and all ready for Joan to sign. I do not know that that was true, but it probably was, for her mark signed at the bottom of a confession would be the kind of evidence (for effect with the public) which Cauchon and his people would particularly value, you know.

No, there was no crushing that spirit, and no beclouding that clear mind. Consider the depth, the wisdom of that answer, coming from an ignorant girl. Why, there were not six men in the world who had ever reflected that words forced out of a person by horrible tortures were not necessarily words of verity and truth, yet this unlettered peasant girl put her finger upon that flaw with an unerring instinct. I had always supposed that torture brought out the truth—everybody supposed it; and when Joan came out with those simple common-sense words they seemed to flood the place with light. It was like a lightning-flash at midnight which suddenly reveals a fair valley sprinkled over with silver streams and gleaming villages and farmsteads where was only an impenetrable world of darkness before. Manchon stole a sidewise look at me, and his face was full of surprise; and there was the like to be seen in other faces there. Consider—they were old, and deeply cultured, yet here was a village maid able to teach them something which they had not known before. I heard one of them mutter—

"Verily it is a wonderful creature. She has laid her hand upon an accepted truth that is as old as the world, and it has crumbled to dust and rubbish under her touch. Now whence got she that marvellous insight?"

The judges laid their heads together and began to talk low. It was plain, from chance words which one caught now and then, that Cauchon and Loyseleur were insisting upon the application of the torture, and that most of the others were urgently objecting.

Finally Cauchon broke out with a good deal of asperity in his voice and ordered Joan back to her dungeon. That was a happy surprise for me. I was not expecting that the Bishop would yield.

When Manchon came home that night he said he had found out why the torture was not applied. There were two reasons. One was, a fear that Joan might die under the torture, which would not suit the English at all; the other was, that the torture would effect nothing if Joan was going to take back everything she said under its pains; and as to putting her mark to a confession, it was believed that not even the rack could ever make her do that.

So all Rouen laughed again, and kept it up for three days, saying—

"The sow has littered six times, and made six messes of it."

And the palace walls got a new decoration—a mitred hog carrying a discarded rack home on its shoulder, and Loyseleur weeping in its wake. Many rewards were offered for the capture of these painters, but nobody applied. Even the English guard feigned blindness and would not see the artists at work.

The Bishop's anger was very high now. He could not reconcile himself to the idea of giving up the torture. It was the pleasantest idea he had invented yet, and he would not cast it by. So he called in some of his satellites on the twelfth, and urged the torture again. But it was a failure. With some, Joan's speech had wrought an effect; others feared she might die under the torture; others did not believe that any amount of suffering could make her put her mark to a lying confession. There were fourteen men present, including the Bishop. Eleven of them voted dead against the torture, and stood their ground in spite of Cauchon's abuse. Two voted with the Bishop and insisted upon the torture. These two were Loyseleur and the orator—the man whom Joan had bidden to "read his book"—Thomas de Courcelles, the renowned pleader, and master of eloquence.

Age has taught me charity of speech; but it fails me when I think of those three names—Cauchon, Courcelles, Loyseleur.

CHAPTER 17

Another ten days' wait. The great theologians of that treasury of all valuable knowledge and all wisdom, the University of Paris, were still weighing and considering and discussing the Twelve Lies.

I had but little to do, these ten days, so I spent them mainly in walks about the town with Noël. But there was no pleasure in them, our spirits being so burdened with cares, and the outlook for Joan growing so steadily darker and darker all the time. And then we naturally contrasted our circumstances with hers: this freedom and sunshine, with her darkness and chains; our comradeship, with her lonely estate; our alleviations of one sort and another, with her destitution in all. She was used to liberty, but now she had none; she was an out-of-door creature by nature and habit, but now she was shut up day and night in a steel cage like an animal; she was used to the light, but now she was always in a gloom where all objects about her were dim and spectral; she was used to the thousand various sounds which are the cheer and music of a busy life, but now she heard only the monotonous footfall of the sentry pacing his watch; she had been fond of talking with her mates, but now there was no one to talk to; she had had an easy laugh, but it was gone dumb, now; she had been born for comradeship, and blithe and busy work, and all manner of joyous activities, but here were only dreariness, and leaden hours, and weary inaction, and brooding stillness, and thoughts that travel day and night and night and day round and round in the same circle, and wear the brain and break the heart with weariness. It was death in life; yes, death in life, that is what it must have been. And there was another hard thing about it all. A young girl in trouble needs the soothing solace and support and sympathy of persons of her own sex, and the delicate offices and gentle ministries which only these can furnish; yet in all these months of gloomy captivity in her dungeon Joan never saw the face of a girl or a woman. Think how her heart would have leaped to see such a face.

Consider. If you would realize how great Joan of Arc was, remember that it was out of such a place and such circumstances that she came week after week and month after month and confronted the master intellects of France singlehanded, and baffled their cunningest schemes, defeated their ablest plans, detected and avoided their secretest traps and pitfalls, broke their lines, repelled their assaults, and camped on the field after every engagement; steadfast always, true to her faith and her ideals; defying torture, defying the stake, and answering threats of eternal death and the pains of hell with a simple "Let come what may, here I take my stand and will abide."

Yes, if you would realize how great was the soul, how profound the wisdom, and how luminous the intellect of Joan of Arc, you must study her there, where she fought out that long fight all alone—and not merely against the subtlest brains and deepest learning of France, but against the ignoblest deceits, the meanest treacheries, and the hardest hearts to be found in any land, pagan or Christian.

She was great in battle—we all know that; great in foresight; great in loyalty and patriotism; great in persuading discontented chiefs and reconciling conflicting interests and passions, great in the ability to discover merit and genius wherever it lay hidden; great in picturesque and eloquent speech; supremely great in the gift of firing the hearts of hopeless men with noble enthusiasms, the gift of turning hares into heroes, slaves and skulkers into battalions that march to death with songs upon their lips. But all these are exalting activities; they keep hand and heart and brain keyed up to their work: there is the joy of achievement, the inspiration of stir and movement, the applause which hails success; the soul is overflowing with life and energy, the faculties are at white heat; weariness, despondency, inertia—these do not exist.

Yes, Joan of Arc was great always, great everywhere, but she was greatest in the Rouen trials. There she rose above the limitations and infirmities of our human nature, and accomplished under blighting and unnerving and hopeless conditions all that her splendid equipment of moral and intellectual forces could have accomplished if they had been supplemented by the mighty helps of hope and cheer and light, the presence of friendly faces, and a fair and equal fight, with the great world looking on and wondering.

CHAPTER 18

Toward the end of the ten-day interval the University of Paris rendered its decision concerning the Twelve Articles. By this finding, Joan was guilty upon all the counts: she must renounce her errors and make satisfaction, or be abandoned to the secular arm for punishment.

The University's mind was probably already made up before the Articles were laid before it; yet it took it from the fifth to the eighteenth to produce its verdict. I think the delay may have been caused by temporary difficulties concerning two points:

1, As to who the fiends were who were represented in Joan's Voices;

2, As to whether her saints spoke French only.

You understand, the University decided emphatically that it was fiends who spoke in those Voices; it would need to prove that, and it did. It found out who the fiends were, and named them in the verdict: Belial, Satan, and Behemoth. This has always seemed a doubtful thing to me, and not entitled to much credit. I think so for this reason: if the University had actually known it was those three, it would for very consistency's sake have told *how* it knew it, and not stopped with the mere assertion, since it had made Joan explain how she knew they were *not* fiends. Does not that seem reasonable? To my mind the University's position was weak, and I will tell you why. It had claimed that Joan's angels were devils in disguise, and we all know that devils do disguise themselves as angels; up to that point the University's position was strong; but you see yourself that it eats its own argument when it turns around and pretends that *it* can tell who such apparitions are, while denying the like ability to a person with as good a head on her shoulders as the best one the University could produce.

The doctors of the University had to see those creatures in order to know; and if Joan was deceived, it is argument that they in their turn could also be deceived, for their insight and judgment were surely not clearer than hers.

As to the other point which I have thought may have proved a difficulty and cost the University delay, I will touch but a moment upon that, and pass on. The University decided that it was blasphemy for Joan to say that her saints spoke French and not English, and were on the French side in political sympathies. I think that the thing which troubled the doctors of theology was this: they had decided that the three Voices were Satan and two other devils; but they had also decided that these Voices were *not* on the French side—thereby tacitly asserting that they were on the English side; and if on the English side, then they must be angels and not devils. Otherwise, the situation was embarrassing. You see, the University being the wisest and deepest and most erudite body in the world, it would like to be logical if it could, for the sake of its reputation; therefore it would study and study, days and days, trying to find some good common-sense reason for proving the Voices devils in Article No. 1 and proving them angels in Article No. 10. However, they had to give it up. They found no way out: and so, to this day the University's verdict remains just so—devils in No. 1, angels in No. 10; and no way to reconcile the discrepancy.

The envoys brought the verdict to Rouen, and with it a letter for Cauchon which was full of fervid praise. The University complimented him on his zeal in hunting down this woman "whose venom had infected the faithful of the whole West," and as recompense it as good as promised him "a crown of imperishable glory in heaven." Only *that!* —a crown in heaven; a promissory note and no indorser; always something away off yonder; not a word about the Archbishopric of Rouen, which was the thing Cauchon was destroying his soul for. A crown in heaven; it must have sounded like a sarcasm to him, after all his hard work. What should *he* do in heaven? he did not know anybody there.

On the nineteenth of May a court of fifty judges sat in the archiepiscopal palace to discuss Joan's fate. A few wanted her delivered over to the secular arm at once for punishment, but the rest insisted that she be once more "charitably admonished" first.

So the same court met in the castle on the twenty-third, and Joan was brought to the bar. Pierre Maurice, a canon of Rouen, made a speech to Joan in which he admonished her to save her life and her soul by renouncing her errors and surrendering to the Church. He finished with a stern threat: if she remained obstinate the damnation of her soul was certain, the destruction of her body probable. But Joan was immovable. She said—

"If I were under sentence, and saw the fire before me, and the executioner ready to light it—more, if I were in the fire itself, I would say none but the things which I have said in these trials; and I would abide by them till I died."

A deep silence followed, now, which endured some moments. It lay upon me like a weight. I knew it for an omen. Then Cauchon, grave and solemn, turned to Pierre Maurice—

"Have you anything further to say?"

The priest bowed low, and said—

"Nothing, my lord."

"Prisoner at the bar, have you anything further to say?"

"Nothing."

"Then the debate is closed. To-morrow, sentence will be pronounced. Remove the prisoner."

She seemed to go from the place erect and noble. But I do not know; my sight was dim with tears.

To-morrow—twenty-fourth of May! Exactly a year since I saw her go speeding across the plain at the head of her troops, her silver helmet shining, her silvery cape fluttering in the wind, her white plumes flowing, her sword held aloft; saw her charge the Burgundian camp three times, and carry it; saw her wheel to the right and spur for the Duke's reserves; saw her fling herself against it in the last assault she was ever to make. And now that fatal day was come again—and see what it was bringing!

CHAPTER 19

Joan had been adjudged guilty of heresy, sorcery, and all the other terrible crimes set forth in the Twelve Articles, and her life was in Cauchon's hands at last. He could send her to the stake at once. His work was finished now, you think? He was satisfied? Not at all. What would his Archbishopric be worth if the people should get the idea into their heads that this faction of interested priests, slaving under the English lash, had wrongly condemned and burned Joan of Arc, Deliverer of France? That would be to make of her a holy martyr. Then her spirit would rise from her body's ashes, a thousand-fold reinforced, and sweep the English domination into the sea, and Cauchon along with it. No, the victory was not complete yet. Joan's guilt must be established by evidence which would satisfy the people. Where was that evidence to be found? There was only one person in the world who could furnish it—*Joan of Arc herself*. She must condemn herself, and in public—at least she must *seem* to do it.

But how was this to be managed? Weeks had been spent already in trying to get her to surrender—time wholly wasted; what was to persuade her now? Torture had been threatened, the fire had been threatened; what was left? Illness, deadly fatigue, and the sight of the fire, the presence of the fire! That was left.

Now that was a shrewd thought. She was but a girl, after all, and, under illness and exhaustion, subject to a girl's weaknesses.

Yes, it was shrewdly thought. She had tacitly said, herself, that under the bitter pains of the rack they would be able to extort a false confession from her. It was a hint worth remembering, and it was remembered.

She had furnished another hint at the same time: that as soon as the pains were gone, she would retract the confession. That hint was also remembered.

She had herself taught them what to do, you see. First, they must wear out her strength, then frighten her with the fire. Second, while the fright was on her, she must be made to sign a paper.

But she would demand a reading of the paper. They could not venture to refuse this, with the public there to hear. Suppose that during the reading her courage should return? she would refuse to sign, then. Very well, even that difficulty could be got over. They could read a short paper of no importance, then slip a long and deadly one into its place and trick her into signing *that*.

Yet there was still one other difficulty. If they made her seem to abjure, that would free her from the death penalty. They could keep her in a prison of the Church, but they could not kill her. That would not answer; for only her death would content the English. Alive she was a terror, in a prison or out of it. She had escaped from two prisons already.

But even that difficulty could be managed. Cauchon would make promises to her; in return, she would promise to leave off the male dress. He would violate his promises, and that would so situate her that she would not be able to keep hers. Her lapse would condemn her to the stake, and the stake would be ready.

These were the several moves; there was nothing to do but to make them, each in its order, and the game was won. One might almost name the day that the betrayed girl, the most innocent creature in France, and the noblest, would go to her pitiful death.

And the time was favorable—cruelly favorable. Joan's spirit had as yet suffered no decay, it was as sublime and masterful as ever; but her body's forces had been steadily wasting away in those last ten days, and a strong mind needs a healthy body for its rightful support.

The world knows, now, that Cauchon's plan was as I have sketched it to you, but the world did not know it at that time. There are sufficient indications that Warwick and all the other English chiefs except the highest one—the Cardinal of Winchester—were not let into the secret; also, that only Loyseleur and Beaupere, on the French side, knew the scheme. Sometimes I have doubted if even Loyseleur and Beaupere knew the whole of it at first. However, if any did, it was these two.

It is usual to let the condemned pass their last night of life in peace, but this grace was denied to poor Joan, if one may credit the rumors of the time. Loyseleur was smuggled into her presence, and in the character of priest, friend, and secret partisan of France and hater of England, he spent some hours in beseeching her to do "the only right and righteous thing"—submit to the Church, as a good Christian should; and that then she would straightway get out of the clutches of the dreaded English and be transferred to the Church's prison, where she would be honorably used and have women about her for jailers. He knew where to touch her. He knew how odious to her was the presence of her rough and profane English guards; he knew that her Voices had vaguely promised something which she interpreted to be escape, rescue, release of some sort, and the chance to burst upon France once more and victoriously complete the great work which she had been commissioned of Heaven to do. Also there was that other thing: if her failing body could be further weakened by loss of rest and sleep, now, her tired mind would be dazed and drowsy on the morrow, and in ill condition to stand out against persuasions, threats, and the sight of the stake, and also be purblind to traps and snares which it would be swift to detect when in its normal estate.

I do not need to tell you that there was no rest for me that night. Nor for Noël. We went to the main gate of the city before nightfall, with a hope in our minds, based upon that vague prophecy of Joan's Voices which seemed to promise a rescue by force at the last moment. The immense news had flown swiftly far and wide that at last Joan of Arc was condemned, and would be sentenced and burned alive on the morrow; and so, crowds of people were flowing in at the gate, and other crowds were being refused admission by the soldiery; these being people who brought doubtful passes or none at all. We scanned these crowds eagerly, but there was nothing about them to indicate that they were our old war-comrades in disguise, and certainly there were no familiar faces among them. And so, when the gate was closed at last, we turned away grieved, and more disappointed than we cared to admit, either in speech or thought.

The streets were surging tides of excited men. It was difficult to make one's way. Toward midnight our aimless tramp brought us to the neighborhood of the beautiful church of St. Ouen, and there all was bustle and work. The square was a wilderness of torches and people; and through a guarded passage dividing the pack, laborers were carrying planks and timbers and disappearing with them through the gate of the churchyard. We asked what was going forward; the answer was—

"Scaffolds and the stake. Don't you know that the French witch is to be burnt in the morning?"

Then we went away. We had no heart for that place.

At dawn we were at the city gate again; this time with a hope which our wearied bodies and fevered minds magnified into a large probability. We had heard a report that the Abbot of Jumièges with all his monks was coming to witness the burning. Our desire, abetted by our imagination, turned those nine hundred monks into Joan's old campaigners, and their Abbot into La Hire or the Bastard or D'Alençon; and we watched them file in, unchallenged, the multitude respectfully dividing and uncovering while they passed, with our hearts in our throats and our eyes swimming with tears of joy and pride and exultation; and we tried to catch glimpses of the faces under the cowls, and were prepared to give signal to any recognized face that we were Joan's men and ready and eager to kill and be killed in the good cause. How foolish we were; but we were young, you know, and youth hopeth all things, believeth all things.

CHAPTER 20

In the morning I was at my official post. It was on a platform raised the height of a man, in the churchyard, under the eaves of St. Ouen. On this same platform was a crowd of priests and important citizens, and several lawyers. Abreast it, with a small space between, was another and larger platform, handsomely canopied against sun and rain, and richly carpeted; also it was furnished with comfortable chairs, and with two which were more sumptuous than the others, and raised above the general level. One of these two was occupied by a prince of the royal blood of England, his Eminence the Cardinal of Winchester; the other by Cauchon, Bishop of Beauvais. In the rest of the chairs sat three bishops, the Vice-Inquisitor, eight abbots, and the sixty-two friars and lawyers who had sat as Joan's judges in her late trials.

Twenty steps in front of the platforms was another—a table-topped pyramid of stone, built up in retreating courses, thus forming steps.

Out of this rose that grisly thing the stake; about the stake bundles of fagots and firewood were piled. On the ground at the base of the pyramid stood three crimson figures, the executioner and his assistants. At their feet lay what had been a goodly heap of brands, but was now a smokeless nest of ruddy coals; a foot or two from this was a supplemental supply of wood and fagots compacted into a pile shoulder-high and containing as much as six pack-horse loads. Think of that. We seem so delicately made, so destructible, so insubstantial; yet it is easier to reduce a granite statue to ashes than it is to do that with a man's body.

The sight of the stake sent physical pains tingling down the nerves of my body; and yet, turn as I would, my eyes would keep coming back to it, such fascination has the grewsome and the terrible for us.

The space occupied by the platforms and the stake was kept open by a wall of English soldiery, standing elbow to elbow, erect and stalwart figures, fine and sightly in their polished steel; while from behind them on every hand stretched far away a level plain of human heads; and there was no window and no housetop within our view, howsoever distant, but was black with patches and masses of people.

But there was no noise, no stir; it was as if the world was dead. The impressiveness of this silence and solemnity was deepened by a leaden twilight, for the sky was hidden by a pall of low-hanging storm-clouds; and above the remote horizon faint winkings of heat-lightning played, and now and then one caught the dull mutterings and complainings of distant thunder.

At last the stillness was broken. From beyond the square rose an indistinct sound, but familiar—curt, crisp phrases of command; next I saw the plain of heads dividing, and the steady swing of a marching host was glimpsed between. My heart leaped, for a moment. Was it La Hire and his hellions? No—that was not their gait. No, it was the prisoner and her escort; it was Joan of Arc, under guard, that was coming; my spirits sank as low as they had been before. Weak as she was, they made her walk; they would increase her weakness all they could. The distance was not great—it was but a few hundred yards—but short as it was it was a heavy tax upon one who had been lying chained in one spot for months, and whose feet had lost their powers from inaction. Yes, and for a year Joan had known only the cool damps of a dungeon, and now she was dragging herself through this sultry summer heat, this airless and suffocating void. As she entered the gate, drooping with exhaustion, there was that creature Loyseleur at her side with his head bent to her ear. We knew afterwards that he had been with her again this morning in the prison wearying her with his persuasions and enticing her with false promises, and that he was now still at the same work at the gate, imploring her to yield everything that would be required of her, and assuring her that if she would do this all would be well with her: she would be rid of the dreaded English and find safety in the powerful shelter and protection of the Church. A miserable man, a stony-hearted man!

The moment Joan was seated on the platform she closed her eyes and allowed her chin to fall; and so sat, with her hands nestling in her lap, indifferent to everything, caring for nothing but rest. And she was so white again; white as alabaster.

How the faces of that packed mass of humanity lighted up with interest, and with what intensity all eyes gazed upon this fragile girl! And how natural it was; for these people realized that at last they were looking upon that person whom they had so long hungered to see; a person whose name and fame filled all Europe, and made all other names and all other renowns insignificant by comparison: Joan of Arc, the wonder of the time, and destined to be the wonder of all times! And I could read as by print, in their marvelling countenances, the words that were drifting through their minds: "Can it be true; is it believable, that it is this little creature, this girl, this child with the good face, the sweet face, the beautiful face, the dear and bonny face, that has carried fortresses by storm, charged at the head of victorious armies, blown the might of England out of her path with a breath, and fought a long campaign, solitary and alone, against the massed brains and learning of France—and had won it if the fight had been fair!"

Evidently Cauchon had grown afraid of Manchon because of his pretty apparent leanings toward Joan, for another recorder was in the chief place, here, which left my master and me nothing to do but sit idle and look on.

Well, I supposed that everything had been done which could be thought of to tire Joan's body and mind, but it was a mistake; one more device had been invented. This was to preach a long sermon to her in that oppressive heat.

When the preacher began, she cast up one distressed and disappointed look, then dropped her head again. This preacher was Guillaume Erard, an oratorical celebrity. He got his text from the Twelve Lies. He emptied upon Joan all the calumnies, in detail, that had been bottled up in that mess of venom, and called her all the brutal names that the Twelve were labelled with, working himself into a whirlwind of fury as he went on; but his labors were wasted, she seemed lost in dreams, she made no sign, she did not seem to hear. At last he launched this apostrophe:

"O France, how hast thou been abused! Thou hast always been the home of Christianity; but now, Charles, who calls himself thy King and governor, indorses like the heretic and schismatic that he is, the words and deeds of a worthless and infamous woman!" Joan raised her head, and her eyes began to burn and flash. The preacher turned toward her: "It is to you, Joan, that I speak, and I tell you that your King is schismatic and a heretic!"

Ah, he might abuse *her* to his heart's content; she could endure that; but to her dying moment she could never hear in patience a word against that ingrate, that treacherous dog our King, whose proper place was here, at this moment, sword in hand, routing these reptiles and saving this most noble servant that ever King had in this world—and he *would* have been there if he had not been what I have called him. Joan's loyal soul was outraged, and she turned upon the preacher and flung out a few words with a spirit which the crowd recognized as being in accordance with the Joan of Arc traditions—

"By my faith, sir! I make bold to say and swear, on pain of death, that he is the most noble Christian of all Christians, and the best lover of the faith and the Church!"

There was an explosion of applause from the crowd—which angered the preacher, for he had been aching long to hear an expression like this, and now that it was come at last it had fallen to the wrong person: he had done all the work; the other had carried off all the spoil. He stamped his foot and shouted to the sheriff—

"Make her shut up!"

That made the crowd laugh.

A mob has small respect for a grown man who has to call on a sheriff to protect him from a sick girl.

Joan had damaged the preacher's cause more with one sentence than he had helped it with a hundred; so he was much put out, and had trouble to get a good start again. But he needn't have bothered; there was no occasion. It was mainly an English-feeling mob. It had but obeyed a law of our nature—an irresistible law—to enjoy and applaud a spirited and promptly delivered retort, no matter who makes it. The mob was with the preacher; it had been beguiled for a moment, but only that; it would soon return. It was there to see this girl burnt; so that it got that satisfaction—without too much delay—it would be content.

Presently the preacher formally summoned Joan to submit to the Church. He made the demand with confidence, for he had gotten the

idea from Loyseleur and Beaupere that she was worn to the bone, exhausted, and would not be able to put forth any more resistance; and indeed, to look at her it seemed that they must be right. Nevertheless, she made one more effort to hold her ground, and said, wearily—

"As to that matter, I have answered my judges before. I have told them to report all that I have said and done to our holy Father the Pope—to whom, and to God first, I appeal."

Again, out of her native wisdom, she had brought those words of tremendous import, but was ignorant of their value. But they could have availed her nothing in any case, now, with the stake there and these thousands of enemies about her. Yet they made every churchman there blench, and the preacher changed the subject with all haste. Well might those criminals blench, for Joan's appeal of her case to the Pope stripped Cauchon at once of jurisdiction over it, and annulled all that he and his judges had already done in the matter and all that they should do in it thenceforth.

Joan went on presently to reiterate, after some further talk, that she had acted by command of God in her deeds and utterances; then, when an attempt was made to implicate the King, and friends of hers and his, she stopped that. She said—

"I charge my deeds and words upon no one, neither upon my King nor any other. If there is any fault in them, I am responsible and no other."

She was asked if she would not recant those of her words and deeds which had been pronounced evil by her judges. Her answer made confusion and damage again:

"I submit them to God and the Pope."

The Pope once more! It was very embarrassing. Here was a person who was asked to submit her case to the Church, and who frankly consents—offers to submit it to the very head of it. What more could anyone require? How was one to answer such a formidably unanswerable answer as that?

The worried judges put their heads together and whispered and planned and discussed. Then they brought forth this sufficiently shambling conclusion—but it was the best they could do, in so close a place: they said the Pope was so far away; and it was not necessary to go to him, anyway, because these present judges had sufficient power and authority to deal with the present case, and were in effect "the Church" to that extent. At another time they could have smiled at this conceit, but not now; they were not comfortable enough, now.

The mob was getting impatient. It was beginning to put on a threatening aspect; it was tired standing, tired of the scorching heat; and

the thunder was coming nearer, the lightning was flashing brighter. It was necessary to hurry this matter to a close. Erard showed Joan a written form, which had been prepared and made all ready beforehand, and asked her to abjure.

"Abjure? What is abjure?"

She did not know the word. It was explained to her by Massieu. She tried to understand, but she was breaking, under exhaustion, and she could not gather the meaning. It was all a jumble and confusion of strange words. In her despair she sent out this beseeching cry—

"I appeal to the Church universal whether I ought to abjure or no!"

Erard exclaimed—

"You shall abjure instantly, or instantly be burnt!"

She glanced up, at those awful words, and for the first time she saw the stake and the mass of red coals—redder and angrier than ever, now, under the constantly deepening storm-gloom. She gasped and staggered up out of her seat muttering and mumbling incoherently, and gazed vacantly upon the people and the scene about her like one who is dazed, or thinks he dreams, and does not know where he is.

The priests crowded about her imploring her to sign the paper, there were many voices beseeching and urging her at once, there was great turmoil and shouting and excitement, amongst the populace and everywhere.

"Sign! sign!" from the priests; "sign—sign and be saved!" And Loyseleur was urging at her ear, "Do as I told you—do not destroy yourself!"

Joan said plaintively to these people—

"Ah, you do not do well to seduce me."

The judges joined their voices to the others. Yes, even the iron in *their* hearts melted, and they said—

"Oh, Joan, we pity you so! Take back what you have said, or we must deliver you up to punishment."

And now there was another voice—it was from the other platform—pealing solemnly above the din: Cauchon's—reading the sentence of death!

Joan's strength was all spent. She stood looking about her in a bewildered way a moment, then slowly she sank to her knees, and bowed her head and said—

"I submit."

They gave her no time to reconsider—they knew the peril of that. The moment the words were out of her mouth Massieu was reading to her the abjuration, and she was repeating the words after him mechanically, unconsciously—and *smiling;* for her wandering mind was far away in some happier world.

Then this short paper of six lines was slipped aside and a long one of many pages was smuggled into its place, and she, noting nothing, put her mark to it, saying, in pathetic apology, that she did not know how to write. But a secretary of the King of England was there to take care of that defect; he guided her hand with his own, and wrote her name—*Jehanne.*

The great crime was accomplished. She had signed—what? She did not know—but the others knew. She had signed a paper confessing herself a sorceress, a dealer with devils, a liar, a blasphemer of God and His angels, a lover of blood, a promoter of sedition, cruel, wicked, commissioned of Satan; and this signature of hers bound her to resume the dress of a woman. There were other promises, but that one would answer, without the others; that one could be made to destroy her.

Loyseleur pressed forward and praised her for having done "such a good day's work."

But she was still dreamy, she hardly heard.

Then Cauchon pronounced the words which dissolved the excommunication and restored her to her beloved Church, with all the dear privileges of worship. Ah, she heard that! You could see it in the deep gratitude that rose in her face and transfigured it with joy.

But how transient was that happiness! For Cauchon, without a tremor of pity in his voice, added these crushing words—

"And that she may repent of her crimes and repeat them no more, she is sentenced to perpetual imprisonment, with the bread of affliction and the water of anguish!"

Perpetual imprisonment! She had never dreamed of that—such a thing had never been hinted to her by Loyseleur or by any other. Loyseleur had distinctly said and promised that "all would be well with her." And the very last words spoken to her by Erard, on that very platform, when he was urging her to abjure, was a straight, unqualified promise—that if she would do it she should *go free from captivity.*

She stood stunned and speechless a moment; then she remembered, with such solacement as the thought could furnish, that by another clear promise—a promise made by Cauchon himself—she would at least be the Church's captive, and have women about her in place of a brutal foreign soldiery. So she turned to the body of priests and said, with a sad resignation—

"Now, you men of the Church, take me to your prison, and leave me no longer in the hands of the English"; and she gathered up her chains and prepared to move.

But alas, now came these shameful words from Cauchon—and with them a mocking laugh:

"Take her to the prison whence she came!"

Poor abused girl! She stood dumb, smitten, paralyzed. It was pitiful to see. She had been beguiled, lied to, betrayed; she saw it all, now.

The rumbling of a drum broke upon the stillness, and for just one moment she thought of the glorious deliverance promised by her Voices —I read it in the rapture that lit her face; then she saw what it was —her prison escort—and that light faded, never to revive again. And now her head began a piteous rocking motion, swaying slowly, this way and that, as is the way when one is suffering unwordable pain, or when one's heart is broken; then drearily she went from us, with her face in her hands, and sobbing bitterly.

CHAPTER 21

There is no certainty that any one in all Rouen was in the secret of the deep game which Cauchon was playing except the Cardinal of Winchester. Then you can imagine the astonishment and stupefaction of that vast mob gathered there and those crowds of churchmen assembled on the two platforms, when they saw Joan of Arc moving away, alive and whole—slipping out of their grip at last, after all this tedious waiting, all this tantalizing expectancy.

Nobody was able to stir or speak, for a while, so paralyzing was the universal astonishment, so unbelievable the fact that the stake was actually standing there unoccupied and its prey gone. Then suddenly everybody broke into a fury of rage; maledictions and charges of treachery began to fly freely; yes, and even stones: a stone came near killing the Cardinal of Winchester—it just missed his head. But the man who threw it was not to blame, for he was excited, and a person who is excited never can throw straight.

The tumult was very great indeed, for a while. In the midst of it a chaplain of the Cardinal even forgot the proprieties so far as to opprobriously assail the august Bishop of Beauvais himself, shaking his fist in his face and shouting:

"By God, you are a traitor!"

"You lie!" responded the Bishop.

He a traitor! Oh, far from it; he certainly was the last Frenchman that any Briton had a right to bring that charge against.

The Earl of Warwick lost his temper, too. He was a doughty soldier, but when it came to the intellectuals—when it came to delicate chicane, and scheming, and trickery—he couldn't see any further through a millstone than another. So he burst out in his frank warrior fashion, and swore that the King of England was being treacherously used, and that Joan of Arc was going to be allowed to cheat the stake. But they whispered comfort into his ear—

"Give yourself no uneasiness, my lord; we shall soon have her again."

Perhaps the like tidings found their way all around, for good news travels fast as well as bad. At any rate the ragings presently quieted down, and the huge concourse crumbled apart and disappeared. And thus we reached the noon of that fearful Thursday.

We two youths were happy; happier than any words can tell—for we were not in the secret any more than the rest. Joan's life was saved. We knew that, and that was enough. France would hear of this day's infamous work—and then! Why, then her gallant sons would flock to her standard by thousands and thousands, multitudes upon multitudes, and their wrath would be like the wrath of the ocean when the storm-winds sweep it; and they would hurl themselves against this doomed city and overwhelm it like the resistless tides of that ocean, and Joan of Arc would march again! In six days—seven days—one short week—noble France, grateful France, indignant France, would be thundering at these gates—let us count the hours, let us count the minutes, let us count the seconds! Oh happy day, oh day of ecstasy, how our hearts sang in our bosoms!

For we were young, then; yes, we were very young.

Do you think the exhausted prisoner was allowed to rest and sleep after she had spent the small remnant of her strength in dragging her tired body back to the dungeon?

No; there was no rest for her, with those sleuth-hounds on her track. Cauchon and some of his people followed her to her lair, straightway; they found her dazed and dull, her mental and physical forces in a state of prostration. They told her she had abjured; that she had made certain promises—among them, to resume the apparel of her sex; and that if she relapsed, the Church would cast her out for good and all. She heard the words, but they had no meaning to her. She was like a person who has taken a narcotic and is dying for sleep, dying for rest from nagging, dying to be let alone, and who mechanically does everything the persecutor asks, taking but dull note of the things done, and but dully recording them in the memory. And so Joan put on the gown which Cauchon and his people had brought; and would come to herself by-and-by, and have at first but a dim idea as to when and how the change had come about.

Cauchon went away happy and content. Joan had resumed woman's dress without protest; also she had been formally warned against relapsing. He had witnesses to these facts. How could matters be better?

But suppose she should *not* relapse?

Why, then she must be forced to do it.

Did Cauchon hint to the English guards that thenceforth if they chose to make their prisoner's captivity crueler and bitterer than ever, no official notice would be taken of it? Perhaps so; since the guards did begin that policy at once, and no official notice *was* taken of it. Yes, from that moment Joan's life in that dungeon was made almost unendurable. Do not ask me to enlarge upon it. I will not do it.

CHAPTER 22

Friday and Saturday were happy days for Noël and me. Our minds were full of our splendid dream of France aroused—France shaking her mane—France on the march—France at the gates—Rouen in ashes, and Joan free! Our imagination was on fire; we were delirious with pride and joy. For we were very young, as I have said.

We knew nothing about what had been happening in the dungeon the yester-afternoon. We supposed that as Joan had abjured and been taken back into the forgiving bosom of the Church, she was being gently used, now, and her captivity made as pleasant and comfortable for her as the circumstances would allow. So, in high contentment, we planned out our share in the great rescue, and fought our part of the fight over and over again during those two happy days—as happy days as ever I have known.

Sunday morning came. I was awake, enjoying the balmy, lazy weather, and thinking. Thinking of the rescue—what else? I had no other thought now. I was absorbed in that, drunk with the happiness of it.

I heard a voice shouting, far down the street, and soon it came nearer, and I caught the words—

"Joan of Arc has relapsed! The witch's time has come!"

It stopped my heart, it turned my blood to ice. That was more than sixty years ago, but that triumphant note rings as clear in my memory to-day as it rang in my ear that long-vanished summer morning. We are so strangely made; the memories that could make us happy pass away; it is the memories that break our hearts that abide.

Soon other voices took up that cry—tens, scores, hundreds of voices; all the world seemed filled with the brutal joy of it. And there were other clamors—the clatter of rushing feet, merry congratulations, bursts of coarse laughter, the rolling of drums, the boom and crash of distant bands profaning the sacred day with the music of victory and thanksgiving.

About the middle of the afternoon came a summons for Manchon and me to go to Joan's dungeon—a summons from Cauchon. But by that time distrust had already taken possession of the English and their soldiery again, and all Rouen was in an angry and threatening mood. We could see plenty evidences of this from our own windows—fist-shaking, black looks, tumultuous tides of furious men billowing by along the street.

And we learned that up at the castle things were going very badly indeed; that there was a great mob gathered there who considered the relapse a lie and a priestly trick, and among them many half-drunk English soldiers. Moreover, these people had gone beyond words. They had laid hands upon a number of churchmen who were trying to enter the castle, and it had been difficult work to rescue them and save their lives.

And so Manchon refused to go. He said he would not go a step without a safeguard from Warwick. So next morning Warwick sent an escort of soldiers, and then we went. Matters had not grown peacefuler meantime, but worse. The soldiers protected us from bodily damage, but as we passed through the great mob at the castle we were assailed with insults and shameful epithets. I bore it well enough, though, and said to myself, with secret satisfaction, "In three or four short days, my lads, you will be employing your tongues in a different sort from this—and I shall be there to hear."

To my mind these were as good as dead men. How many of them would still be alive after the rescue that was coming? Not more than enough to amuse the executioner a short half-hour, certainly.

It turned out that the report was true. Joan had relapsed. She was sitting there in her chains, clothed again in her male attire.

She accused nobody. That was her way. It was not in her character to hold a servant to account for what his master had made him do, and her mind had cleared, now, and she knew that the advantage which had been taken of her the previous morning had its origin, not in the subordinate, but in the master—Cauchon.

Here is what had happened. While Joan slept, in the early morning of Sunday, one of the guards stole her female apparel and put her male attire in its place. When she woke she asked for the other dress, but the guards refused to give it back. She protested, and said she was forbidden to wear the male dress. But they continued to refuse. She had to have clothing, for modesty's sake; moreover, she saw that she could not save her life if she must fight for it against treacheries like this; so she put on the forbidden garments, knowing what the end would be. She was weary of the struggle, poor thing.

We had followed in the wake of Cauchon, the Vice-Inquisitor, and the others—six or eight—and when I saw Joan sitting there, despondent, forlorn, and still in chains, when I was expecting to find her situation so different, I did not know what to make of it. The shock was very great. I had doubted the relapse, perhaps; possibly I had believed in it, but had not realized it.

Cauchon's victory was complete. He had had a harassed and irritated and disgusted look for a long time, but that was all gone now, and contentment and serenity had taken its place. His purple face was full of tranquil and malicious happiness. He went trailing his robes and stood grandly in front of Joan, with his legs apart, and remained so more than a minute, gloating over her and enjoying the sight of this poor ruined creature, who had won so lofty a place for him in the service of the meek and merciful Jesus, Saviour of the World, Lord of the Universe—in case England kept her promise to him, who kept no promises himself.

Presently the judges began to question Joan. One of them, named Marguerie, who was a man with more insight than prudence, remarked upon Joan's change of clothing, and said—

"There is something suspicious about this. How could it have come about without connivance on the part of others? Perhaps even something worse?"

"Thousand devils!" screamed Cauchon, in a fury. "Will you shut your mouth?"

"Armagnac! Traitor!" shouted the soldiers on guard, and made a rush for Marguerie with their lances levelled. It was with the greatest difficulty that he was saved from being run through the body. He made no more attempts to help the inquiry, poor man. The other judges proceeded with the questionings.

"Why have you resumed this male habit?"

I did not quite catch her answer, for just then a soldier's halberd slipped from his fingers and fell on the stone floor with a crash; but I thought I understood Joan to say that she had resumed it of her own motion.

"But you have promised and sworn that you would not go back to it."

I was full of anxiety to hear her answer to that question; and when it came it was just what I was expecting. She said—quite quietly—

"I have never intended and never understood myself to swear I would not resume it."

There—I had been sure, all along, that she did not know what she was doing and saying on the platform Thursday, and this answer of hers was proof that I had not been mistaken. Then she went on to add this—

"But I had a right to resume it, because the promises made to me have not been kept—promises that I should be allowed to go to mass, and receive the communion, and that I should be freed from the bondage of these chains—but they are still upon me, as you see."

"Nevertheless, you have abjured, and have especially promised to return no more to the dress of a man."

Then Joan held out her fettered hands sorrowfully toward these unfeeling men and said—

"I would rather die than continue so. But if they may be taken off, and if I may hear mass, and be removed to a penitential prison, and have a woman about me, I will be good, and will do what shall seem good to you that I do."

Cauchon sniffed scoffingly at that. Honor the compact which he and his had made with her? Fulfil its conditions? What need of that? Conditions had been a good thing to concede, temporarily, and for advantage; but they had served their turn—let something of a fresher sort and of more consequence be considered. The resumption of the male dress was sufficient for all practical purposes, but perhaps Joan could be led to add something to that fatal crime. So Cauchon asked her if her Voices had spoken to her since Thursday—and he reminded her of her abjuration.

"Yes," she answered; and then it came out that the Voices had talked with her about the abjuration—*told* her about it, I suppose. She guilelessly reasserted the heavenly origin of her mission, and did it with the untroubled mien of one who was not conscious that she had ever knowingly repudiated it. So I was convinced once more that she had had no notion of what she was doing that Thursday morning on the platform. Finally she said, "My Voices told me I did very wrong to confess that what I had done was not well." Then she sighed, and said with simplicity, "But it was the fear of the fire that made me do so."

That is, fear of the fire had made her sign a paper whose contents she had not understood then, but understood now by revelation of her Voices and by testimony of her persecutors.

She was sane now, and not exhausted; her courage had come back, and with it her inborn loyalty to the truth. She was bravely and serenely speaking it again, knowing that it would deliver her body up to that very fire which had such terrors for her.

That answer of hers was quite long, quite frank, wholly free from concealments or palliations. It made me shudder; I knew she was pronouncing sentence of death upon herself. So did poor Manchon. And he wrote in the margin abreast of it—

RESPONSIO MORTIFERA.

Fatal answer. Yes, all present knew that it was indeed a fatal answer. Then there fell a silence such as falls in a sickroom when the watchers by the dying draw a deep breath and say softly one to another, "All is over."

Here, likewise, all was over; but after some moments Cauchon, wishing to clinch this matter and make it final, put this question—

"Do you still believe that your Voices are St. Marguerite and St. Catherine?"

"Yes—and that they come from God."

"Yet you denied them on the scaffold?"

Then she made direct and clear affirmation that she had never had any intention to deny them; and that if—I noted the *if*—"if she had made some retractions and revocations on the scaffold it was from fear of the fire, and was a violation of the truth."

There it is again, you see. She certainly never knew what it was she had done on the scaffold until she was told of it afterwards by these people and by her Voices.

And now she closed this most painful scene with these words; and there was a weary note in them that was pathetic—

"I would rather do my penance all at once; let me die. I cannot endure captivity any longer."

The spirit born for sunshine and liberty so longed for release that it would take it in any form, even that.

Several among the company of judges went from the place troubled and sorrowful, the others in another mood. In the court of the castle we found the Earl of Warwick and fifty English waiting, impatient for news. As soon as Cauchon saw them he shouted—*laughing*—think of a man destroying a friendless poor girl and then having the heart to laugh at it:

"Make yourselves comfortable—it's all over with her!"

CHAPTER 23

The young can sink into abysses of despondency, and it was so with Noël and me, now; but the hopes of the young are quick to rise again, and it was so with ours. We called back that vague promise of the Voices, and said the one to the other that the glorious release was to happen at "the last moment"—"that other time was not the last moment, but this is; it will happen now; the King will come, La Hire will come, and with them our veterans, and behind them all France!" And so we were full of heart again, and could already hear, in fancy, that stirring music the clash of steel and the war-cries and the uproar of the onset, and in fancy see our prisoner free, her chains gone, her sword in her hand.

But this dream was to pass also, and come to nothing. Late at night, when Manchon came in, he said—

"I am come from the dungeon, and I have a message for you from that poor child."

A message to me! If he had been noticing I think he would have discovered me—discovered that my indifference concerning the prisoner was a pretence; for I was caught off my guard, and was so moved and so exalted to be so honored by her that I must have shown my feeling in my face and manner.

"A message for me, your reverence?"

"Yes. It is something she wishes done. She said she had noticed the young man who helps me, and that he had a good face; and did I think he would do a kindness for her? I said I knew you would, and asked her what it was, and she said a letter—would you write a letter to her mother? And I said you would. But I said I would do it myself, and gladly; but she said no, that my labors were heavy, and she thought the young man would not mind the doing of this service for one not able to do it for herself, she not knowing how to write. Then I would have sent for you, and at that the sadness vanished out of her face. Why, it was as if she was going to see a friend, poor friendless thing. But I was not permitted. I did my best, but the orders remain as strict as ever, the doors are closed against all but officials; as before, none but officials may speak to her. So I went back and told her, and she sighed, and was sad again. Now this is what she begs you to write to her mother. It is partly a strange message, and to me means nothing, but she said her mother would understand. You will 'convey her adoring love to her family and her village friends, and say there will be no rescue, for that this night—and it is the third time in the twelvemonth, and is final—she has seen The Vision of the Tree.'"

"How strange!"

"Yes, it *is* strange, but that is what she said; and said her parents would understand. And for a little time she was lost in dreams and thinkings, and her lips moved, and I caught in her mutterings these lines, which she said over two or three times, and they seemed to bring peace and contentment to her. I set them down, thinking they might have some connection with her letter and be useful; but it was not so; they were a mere memory, floating idly in a tired mind, and they have no meaning, at least no relevancy."

I took the piece of paper, and found what I knew I should find:

"And when in exile wand'ring we
Shall fainting yearn for glimpse of thee,
O rise upon our sight!"

There was no hope any more. I knew it now. I knew that Joan's letter was a message to Noël and me, as well as to her family, and that its object was to banish vain hopes from our minds and tell us from her own mouth of the blow that was going to fall upon us, so that we, being her soldiers, would know it for a command to bear it as became us and her, and so submit to the will of God; and in thus obeying, find assuagement of our grief. It was like her, for she was always thinking of others, not of herself. Yes, her heart was sore for us; she could find time to think of us, the humblest of her servants, and try to soften our pain, lighten the burden of our troubles,—she that was drinking of the bitter waters; she that was walking in the Valley of the Shadow of Death.

I wrote the letter. You will know what it cost me, without my telling you. I wrote it with the same wooden stylus which had put upon parchment the first words ever dictated by Joan of Arc—that high summons to the English to vacate France, two years past, when she was a lass of seventeen; it had now set down the last ones which she was ever to dictate. Then I broke it. For the pen that had served Joan of Arc could not serve any that would come after her in this earth without abasement.

The next day, May 29th, Cauchon summoned his serfs, and forty-two responded. It is charitable to believe that the other twenty were ashamed to come. The forty-two pronounced her a relapsed heretic, and condemned her to be delivered over to the secular arm. Cauchon thanked them. Then he sent orders that Joan be conveyed the next morning to the place known as the Old Market, and that she be then delivered to the civil judge, and by the civil judge to the executioner. That meant that she would be burnt.

All the afternoon and evening of Tuesday the 29th the news was flying, and the people of the country-side flocking to Rouen to see the tragedy—all, at least, who could prove their English sympathies and count upon admission. The press grew thicker and thicker in the streets, the excitement grew higher and higher. And now a thing was noticeable again which had been noticeable more than once before—that there was pity for Joan in the hearts of many of these people. Whenever she had been in great danger it had manifested itself, and now it was apparent again—manifest in a pathetic dumb sorrow which was visible in many faces.

Early the next morning, Wednesday, Martin Ladvenu and another friar were sent to Joan to prepare her for death; and Manchon and I went with them—a hard service for me. We tramped through the dim corridors, winding this way and that, and piercing ever deeper and deeper into that vast heart of stone, and at last we stood before Joan. But she did not know it. She sat with her hands in her lap and her head bowed, thinking, and her face was very sad. One might not know what she was thinking of. Of her home, and the peaceful pastures, and the friends she was no more to see? Of her wrongs, and her forsaken estate, and the cruelties which had been put upon her? Or was it of death—the death which she had longed for, and which was now so close? Or was it of the *kind* of death she must suffer? I hoped not; for she feared only one kind, and that one had for her unspeakable terrors. I believed she so feared that one that with her strong will she would shut the thought of it wholly out of her mind, and hope and believe that God would take pity on her and grant her an easier one; and so it might chance that the awful news which we were bringing might come as a surprise to her, at last.

We stood silent awhile, but she was still unconscious of us, still deep in her sad musings and far away. Then Martin Ladvenu said, softly—

"Joan."

She looked up then, with a little start, and a wan smile, and said—

"Speak. Have you a message for me?"

"Yes, my poor child. Try to bear it. Do you think you can bear it?"

"Yes"—very softly, and her head drooped again.

"I am come to prepare you for death."

A faint shiver trembled through her wasted body. There was a pause. In the stillness we could hear our breathings. Then she said, still in that low voice—

"When will it be?"

The muffled notes of a tolling bell floated to our ears out of the distance.

"Now. The time is at hand."

That slight shiver passed again.

"It is so soon—ah, it is so soon!"

There was a long silence. The distant throbbings of the bell pulsed through it, and we stood motionless and listening. But it was broken at last—

"What death is it?"

"By fire!"

"Oh, I knew it, I knew it!" She sprang wildly to her feet, and wound her hands in her hair, and began to writhe and sob, oh, so piteously, and mourn and grieve and lament, and turn to first one and then another of us, and search our faces beseechingly, as hoping she might find help and friendliness there, poor thing—she that had never denied these to any creature, even her wounded enemy on the battle-field.

"Oh, cruel, cruel, to treat me so! And must my body, that has never been defiled, be consumed to-day and turned to ashes? Ah, sooner would I that my head were cut off seven times than suffer this woful death. I had the promise of the Church's prison when I submitted, and if I had but been there, and not left here in the hands of my enemies, this miserable fate had not befallen me. Oh, I appeal to God the Great Judge, against the injustice which has been done me."

There was none there that could endure it. They turned away, with the tears running down their faces. In a moment I was on my knees at her feet. At once she thought only of my danger, and bent and whispered in my ear: "Up!—do not peril yourself, good heart. There—God bless you always!" and I felt the quick clasp of her hand. Mine was the last hand she touched with hers in life. None saw it; history does not know of it or tell of it, yet it is true, just as I have told it. The next moment she saw Cauchon coming, and she went and stood before him and reproached him, saying—

"Bishop, it is by you that I die!"

He was not shamed, not touched; but said, smoothly—

"Ah, be patient, Joan. You die because you have not kept your promise, but have returned to your sins."

"Alas," she said, "if you had put me in the Church's prison, and given me right and proper keepers, as you promised, this would not have happened. And for this I summon you to answer before God!"

Then Cauchon winced, and looked less placidly content than before, and he turned him about and went away.

Joan stood awhile musing. She grew calmer, but occasionally she wiped her eyes, and now and then sobs shook her body; but their violence was modifying now, and the intervals between them were growing longer. Finally she looked up and saw Pierre Maurice, who had come in with the Bishop, and she said to him—

"Master Peter, where shall I be this night?"

"Have you not good hope in God?"

"Yes—and by His grace I shall be in Paradise."

Now Martin Ladvenu heard her in confession; then she begged for the sacrament. But how grant the communion to one who had been publicly cut off from the Church, and was now no more entitled to its privileges than an unbaptized pagan? The brother could not do this, but he sent to Cauchon to inquire what he must do. All laws, human and divine, were alike to that man—he respected none of them. He sent back orders to grant Joan whatever she wished. Her last speech to him had reached his fears, perhaps: it could not reach his heart, for he had none.

The Eucharist was brought now to that poor soul that had yearned for it with such unutterable longing all these desolate months. It was a solemn moment. While we had been in the deeps of the prison, the public courts of the castle had been filling up with crowds of the humbler sort of men and women, who had learned what was going on in Joan's cell, and had come with softened hearts to do—they knew not what; to hear—they knew not what. We knew nothing of this, for they were out of our view. And there were other great crowds of the like caste gathered in masses outside the castle gates. And when the lights and the other accompaniments of the Sacrament passed by, coming to Joan in the prison, all those multitudes kneeled down and began to pray for her, and many wept; and when the solemn ceremony of the communion began in Joan's cell, out of the distance a moving sound was borne moaning to our ears—it was those invisible multitudes chanting the litany for a departing soul.

The fear of the fiery death was gone from Joan of Arc now, to come again no more, except for one fleeting instant—then it would pass, and serenity and courage would take its place and abide till the end.

CHAPTER 24

At nine o'clock the Maid of Orleans, Deliverer of France, went forth in the grace of her innocence and her youth to lay down her life for the country she loved with such devotion, and for the King that had abandoned her. She sat in the cart that is used only for felons. In one respect she was treated worse than a felon; for whereas she was on her way to be sentenced by the civil arm, she already bore her judgment inscribed in advance upon a mitre-shaped cap which she wore:

HERETIC, RELAPSED, APOSTATE, IDOLATER

In the cart with her sat the friar Martin Ladvenu and Maître Jean Massieu. She looked girlishly fair and sweet and saintly in her long white robe, and when a gush of sunlight flooded her as she emerged from the gloom of the prison and was yet for a moment still framed in the arch of the sombre gate, the massed multitudes of poor folk murmured "A vision! a vision!" and sank to their knees praying, and many of the women weeping; and the moving invocation for the dying rose again, and was taken up and borne along, a majestic wave of sound, which accompanied the doomed, solacing and blessing her, all the sorrowful way to the place of death. "Christ have pity! Saint Margaret have pity! Pray for her, all ye saints, archangels, and blessed martyrs, pray for her! Saints and angels intercede for her! From thy wrath, good Lord, deliver her! O Lord God, save her! Have mercy on her, we beseech Thee, good Lord!"

It is just and true, what one of the histories has said: "The poor and the helpless had nothing but their prayers to give Joan of Arc; but these we may believe were not unavailing. There are few more pathetic events recorded in history than this weeping, helpless, praying crowd, holding their lighted candles and kneeling on the pavement beneath the prison walls of the old fortress."

And it was so all the way: thousands upon thousands massed upon their knees and stretching far down the distances, thick-sown with the faint yellow candle-flames, like a field starred with golden flowers.

But there were some that did not kneel; these were the English soldiers. They stood elbow to elbow, on each side of Joan's road, and walled it in, all the way; and behind these living walls knelt the multitudes.

By-and-by a frantic man in priest's garb came wailing and lamenting, and tore through the crowd and the barrier of soldiers and flung himself on his knees by Joan's cart and put up his hands in supplication, crying out—

"O, forgive, forgive!"

It was Loyseleur!

And Joan forgave him; forgave him out of a heart that knew nothing but forgiveness, nothing but compassion, nothing but pity for all that suffer, let their offence be what it might. And she had no word of reproach for this poor wretch who had wrought day and night with deceits and treacheries and hypocrisies to betray her to her death.

The soldiers would have killed him, but the Earl of Warwick saved his life. What became of him is not known. He hid himself from the world somewhere, to endure his remorse as he might.

In the square of the Old Market stood the two platforms and the stake that had stood before in the church-yard of St. Ouen. The platforms were occupied as before, the one by Joan and her judges, the other by great dignitaries, the principal being Cauchon and the English Cardinal—Winchester. The square was packed with people, the windows and roofs of the blocks of buildings surrounding it were black with them.

When the preparations had been finished, all noise and movement gradually ceased, and a waiting stillness followed which was solemn and impressive.

And now, by order of Cauchon, an ecclesiastic named Nicholas Midi preached a sermon, wherein he explained that when a branch of the vine—which is the Church—becomes diseased and corrupt, it must be cut away or it will corrupt and destroy the whole vine. He made it appear that Joan, through her wickedness, was a menace and a peril to the Church's purity and holiness, and her death therefore necessary. When he was come to the end of his discourse he turned toward her and paused a moment, then he said—

"Joan, the Church can no longer protect you. Go in peace!"

Joan had been placed wholly apart and conspicuous, to signify the Church's abandonment of her, and she sat there in her loneliness, waiting in patience and resignation for the end. Cauchon addressed her now. He had been advised to read the form of her abjuration to her, and had brought it with him; but he changed his mind, fearing that she would proclaim the truth—that she had never knowingly abjured—and so bring shame upon him and eternal infamy. He contented himself with admonishing her to keep in mind her wickednesses, and repent of them, and think of her salvation. Then he solemnly pronounced her excommunicate and cut off from the body of the Church. With a final word he delivered her over to the secular arm for judgment and sentence.

Joan, weeping, knelt and began to pray. For whom? Herself? Oh no—for the King of France. Her voice rose sweet and clear, and penetrated all hearts with its passionate pathos. She never thought of his treacheries to her, she never thought of his desertion of her, she never remembered that it was because he was an ingrate that she was here to die a miserable death; she remembered only that he was her King, that she was his loyal and loving subject, and that his enemies had undermined his cause with evil reports and false charges, and he not by to defend himself. And so, in the very presence of death, she forgot her own troubles to implore all in her hearing to be just to him; to believe that he was good and noble and sincere, and not in any way to blame for any acts of hers, neither advising them nor urging them, but being wholly clear and free of all responsibility for them. Then, closing, she begged in humble and touching words that all here present would pray for her and would pardon her, both her enemies and such as might look friendly upon her and feel pity for her in their hearts.

There was hardly one heart there that was not touched—even the English, even the judges showed it, and there was many a lip that trembled and many an eye that was blurred with tears; yes, even the English Cardinal's—that man with a political heart of stone but a human heart of flesh.

The secular judge who should have delivered judgment and pronounced sentence was himself so disturbed that he forgot his duty, and Joan went to her death unsentenced—thus completing with an illegality what had begun illegally and had so continued to the end. He only said—to the guards—

"Take her"; and to the executioner, "Do your duty."

Joan asked for a cross. None was able to furnish one. But an English soldier broke a stick in two and crossed the pieces and tied them together, and this cross he gave her, moved to it by the good heart that was in him; and she kissed it and put it in her bosom. Then Isambard de la Pierre went to the church near by and brought her a consecrated one; and this one also she kissed, and pressed it to her bosom with rapture, and then kissed it again and again, covering it with tears and pouring out her gratitude to God and the saints.

And so, weeping, and with her cross to her lips, she climbed up the cruel steps to the face of the stake, with the friar Isambard at her side. Then she was helped up to the top of the pile of wood that was built around the lower third of the stake, and stood upon it with her back against the stake, and the world gazing up at her breathless. The executioner ascended to her side and wound chains about her slender body, and so fastened her to the stake. Then he descended to finish his dreadful office; and there she remained alone—she that had had so many friends in the days when she was free, and had been so loved and so dear.

All these things I saw, albeit dimly and blurred with tears; but I could bear no more. I continued in my place, but what I shall deliver to you now I got by others' eyes and others' mouths. Tragic sounds there were that pierced my ears and wounded my heart as I sat there, but it is as I tell you: the latest image recorded by my eyes in that desolating hour was Joan of Arc with the grace of her comely youth still unmarred; and that image, untouched by time or decay, has remained with me all my days. Now I will go on.

If any thought that now, in that solemn hour when all transgressors repent and confess, she would revoke her revocation and say her great deeds had been evil deeds and Satan and his fiends their source, they erred. No such thought was in her blameless mind. She was not thinking of herself and her troubles, but of others, and of woes that might befall them. And so, turning her grieving eyes about her, where rose the towers and spires of that fair city, she said—

"Oh, Rouen, Rouen, must I die here, and must you be my tomb? Ah, Rouen, Rouen, I have great fear that you will suffer for my death."

A whiff of smoke swept upward past her face, and for one moment terror seized her and she cried out, "Water! Give me holy water!" but the next moment her fears were gone, and they came no more to torture her.

She heard the flames crackling below her, and immediately distress for a fellow-creature who was in danger took possession of her. It was the friar Isambard. She had given him her cross and begged him to raise it toward her face and let her eyes rest in hope and consolation upon it till she was entered into the peace of God. She made him go out from the danger of the fire. Then she was satisfied, and said—

"Now keep it always in my sight until the end."

Not even yet could Cauchon, that man without shame, endure to let her die in peace, but went toward her, all black with crimes and sins as he was, and cried out—

"I am come, Joan, to exhort you for the last time to repent and seek the pardon of God."

"I die through you," she said, and these were the last words she spoke to any upon earth.

Then the pitchy smoke, shot through with red flashes of flame, rolled up in a thick volume and hid her from sight; and from the heart of this darkness her voice rose strong and eloquent in prayer, and when by moments the wind shredded somewhat of the smoke aside, there were veiled glimpses of an upturned face and moving lips. At last a mercifully swift tide of flame burst upward, and none saw that face any more nor that form, and the voice was still.

Yes, she was gone from us: JOAN OF ARC! What little words they are, to tell of a rich world made empty and poor!

CONCLUSION

Joan's brother Jacques died in Domremy during the Great Trial at Rouen. This was according to the prophecy which Joan made that day in the pastures the time that she said the rest of us would go to the great wars.

When her poor old father heard of the martyrdom it broke his heart and he died.

The mother was granted a pension by the City of Orleans, and upon this she lived out her days, which were many. Twenty-four years after her illustrious child's death she travelled all the way to Paris in the winter time and was present at the opening of the discussion in the Cathedral of Nôtre Dame which was the first step in the Rehabilitation. Paris was crowded with people, from all about France, who came to get sight of the venerable dame, and it was a touching spectacle when she moved through these reverend wet-eyed multitudes on her way to the grand honors awaiting her at the cathedral. With her were Jean and Pierre, no longer the light-hearted youths who marched with us from Vaucouleurs, but war-worn veterans with hair beginning to show frost.

After the martyrdom Noël and I went back to Domremy, but presently when the Constable Richemont superseded La Tremouille as the King's chief adviser and began the completion of Joan's great work, we put on our harness and returned to the field and fought for the King all through the wars and skirmishes until France was freed of the English. It was what Joan would have desired of us; and, dead or alive, her desire was law for us. All the survivors of the personal staff were faithful to her memory and fought for the King to the end. Mainly we were well scattered, but when Paris fell we happened to be together. It was a great day and a joyous; but it was a sad one at the same time, because Joan was not there to march into the captured capital with us.

Noël and I remained always together, and I was by his side when death claimed him. It was in the last great battle of the war. In that battle fell also Joan's sturdy old enemy, Talbot. He was eighty-five years old, and had spent his whole life in battle. A fine old lion he was, with his flowing white mane and his tameless spirit; yes, and his indestructible energy as well; for he fought as knightly and vigorous a fight that day as the best man there.

La Hire survived the martyrdom thirteen years; and always fighting, of course, for that was all he enjoyed in life. I did not see him in all that time, for we were far apart, but one was always hearing of him.

The Bastard of Orleans and D'Alençon and D'Aulon lived to see France free, and to testify with Jean and Pierre d'Arc and Pasquerel and me at the Rehabilitation. But they are all at rest now, these many years. I alone am left of those who fought at the side of Joan of Arc in the great wars. She said I would live until these wars were forgotten—a prophecy which failed. If I should live a thousand years it would still fail. For whatsoever had touch with Joan of Arc, that thing is immortal.

Members of Joan's family married, and they have left descendants. Their descendants are of the nobility, but their family name and blood bring them honors which no other nobles receive or may hope for. You have seen how everybody along the way uncovered when those children came yesterday to pay their duty to me. It was not because they are noble, it is because they are grandchildren of the brothers of Joan of Arc.

Now as to the Rehabilitation. Joan crowned the King at Rheims. For reward he allowed her to be hunted to her death without making one effort to save her. During the next twenty-three years he remained indifferent to her memory; indifferent to the fact that her good name was under a damning blot put there by the priests because of the deeds which she had done in saving him and his sceptre; indifferent to the fact that France was ashamed, and longed to have the Deliverer's fair fame restored. Indifferent all that time. Then he suddenly changed and was anxious to have justice for poor Joan, himself. Why? Had he become grateful at last? Had remorse attacked his hard heart? No, he had a better reason—a better one for his sort of man. This better reason was that, now that the English had been finally expelled from the country, they were beginning to call attention to the fact that this King had gotten his crown by the hands of a person proven by the priests to have been in league with Satan and burnt for it by them as a sorceress—therefore, of what value or authority was such a Kingship as that? Of no value at all; no nation could afford to allow such a king to remain on the throne.

It was high time to stir, now, and the King did it. That is how Charles VII. came to be smitten with anxiety to have justice done the memory of his benefactress.

He appealed to the Pope, and the Pope appointed a great commission of churchmen to examine into the facts of Joan's life and award judgment. The Commission sat at Paris, at Domremy, at Rouen, at Orleans, and at several other places, and continued its work during several months. It examined the records of Joan's trials, it examined the Bastard of Orleans, and the Duke d'Alençon, and D'Aulon, and Pasquerel, and Courcelles, and Isambard de la Pierre, and Manchon, and me, and many others whose names I have made familiar to you; also they examined more than a hundred witnesses whose names are less familiar to you—friends of Joan in Domremy, Vaucouleurs, Orleans, and other places, and a number of judges and other people who had assisted at the Rouen trials, the abjuration, and the martyrdom. And out of this exhaustive examination Joan's character and history came spotless and perfect, and this verdict was placed upon record, to remain forever.

I was present upon most of these occasions, and saw again many faces which I have not seen for a quarter of a century; among them some well-beloved faces—those of our generals and that of Catherine Boucher (married, alas!), and also among them certain other faces that filled me with bitterness—those of Beaupere and Courcelles and a number of their fellow-fiends. I saw Haumette and Little Mengette—edging along toward fifty, now, and mothers of many children. I saw Noël's father, and the parents of the Paladin and the Sunflower.

It was beautiful to hear the Duke d'Alençon praise Joan's splendid capacities as a general, and to hear the Bastard indorse these praises with his eloquent tongue and then go on and tell how sweet and good Joan was, and how full of pluck and fire and impetuosity, and mischief, and mirthfulness, and tenderness, and compassion, and everything that was pure and fine and noble and lovely. He made her live again before me, and wrung my heart.

I have finished my story of Joan of Arc, that wonderful child, that sublime personality, that spirit which in one regard has had no peer and will have none—this: its purity from all alloy of self-seeking, self-interest, personal ambition. In it no trace of these motives can be found, search as you may, and this cannot be said of any other person whose name appears in profane history.

With Joan of Arc love of country was more than a sentiment—it was a passion. She was the Genius of Patriotism—she was Patriotism embodied, concreted, made flesh, and palpable to the touch and visible to the eye.

Love, Mercy, Charity, Fortitude, War, Peace, Poetry, Music—these may be symbolized as any shall prefer: by figures of either sex and of any age; but a slender girl in her first young bloom, with the martyr's crown upon her head, and in her hand the sword that severed her country's bonds—shall not this, and no other, stand for PATRIOTISM through all the ages until time shall end?

Tom Sawyer, Detective*

CHAPTER 1

Well, it was the next spring after me and Tom Sawyer set our old nigger Jim free, the time he was chained up for a runaway slave down there on Tom's uncle Silas's farm in Arkansaw. The frost was working out of the ground, and out of the air too, and it was getting closer and closer onto barefoot time every day; and next it would be marble time, and next mumbletypeg, and next tops and hoops, and next kites, and then right away it would be summer and going in a-swimming. It just makes a boy homesick to look ahead like that and see how far off summer is. Yes, and it sets him to sighing and saddening around, and there's something the matter with him, he don't know what. But anyway, he gets out by himself and mopes and thinks; and mostly he hunts for a lonesome place high up on the hill in the edge of the woods, and sets there and looks away off on the big Mississippi down there a-reaching miles and miles around the points where the timber looks smoky and dim it's so far off and still, and everything's so solemn it seems like everybody you've loved is dead and gone, and you 'most wish you was dead and gone too, and done with it all.

Don't you know what that is? It's spring fever. That is what the name of it is. And when you've got it, you want—oh, you don't quite know what it is you *do* want, but it just fairly makes your heart ache, you want it so! It seems to you that mainly what you want is to get away; get away from the same old tedious things you're so used to seeing and so tired of, and see something new. That is the idea; you want to go and be a wanderer; you want to go wandering far away to strange countries where everything is mysterious and wonderful and

* Strange as the incidents of this story are, they are not inventions, but facts—even to the public confession of the accused. I take them from an old-time Swedish criminal trial, change the actors, and transfer the scene to America. I have added some details, but only a couple of them are important ones.—M.T.

romantic. And if you can't do that, you'll put up with considerable less; you'll go anywhere you *can* go, just so as to get away, and be thankful of the chance, too.

Well, me and Tom Sawyer had the spring fever, and had it bad, too; but it warn't any use to think about Tom trying to get away, because, as he said, his aunt Polly wouldn't let him quit school and go traipsing off somers wasting time; so we was pretty blue. We was setting on the front steps one day about sundown talking this way, when out comes his aunt Polly with a letter in her hand and says—

"Tom, I reckon you've got to pack up and go down to Arkansaw—your aunt Sally wants you."

I 'most jumped out of my skin for joy. I reckoned Tom would fly at his aunt and hug her head off; but if you believe me he set there like a rock, and never said a word. It made me fit to cry to see him act so foolish, with such a noble chance as this opening up. Why, we might lose it if he didn't speak up and show he was thankful and grateful. But he set there and studied and studied till I was that distressed I didn't know what to do; then he says, very ca'm, and I could a shot him for it:

"Well," he says, "I'm right down sorry, Aunt Polly, but I reckon I got to be excused—for the present."

His aunt Polly was knocked so stupid and so mad at the cold impudence of it that she couldn't say a word for as much as a half a minute, and this give me a chance to nudge Tom and whisper:

"Ain't you got any sense? Sp'iling such a noble chance as this and throwing it away?"

But he warn't disturbed. He mumbled back:

"Huck Finn, do you want me to let her *see* how bad I want to go? Why, she'd begin to doubt, right away, and imagine a lot of sicknesses and dangers and objections, and first you know she'd take it all back. You lemme alone; I reckon I know how to work her."

Now I never would 'a' thought of that. But he was right. Tom Sawyer was always right—the levelest head I ever see, and always *at* himself and ready for anything you might spring on him. By this time his aunt Polly was all straight again, and she left fly. She says:

"You'll be excused! *You* will! Well, I never heard the like of it in all my days! The idea of you talking like that to *me!* Now take yourself off and pack your traps; and if I hear another word out of you about what you'll be excused from and what you won't, I lay *I'll* excuse you—with a hickory!"

She hit his head a thump with her thimble as we dodged by, and he let on to be whimpering as we struck for the stairs. Up in his room he hugged me, he was so out of his head for gladness because he was going travelling. And he says:

"Before we get away she'll wish she hadn't let me go, but she won't know any way to get around it now. After what she's said, her pride won't let her take it back."

Tom was packed in ten minutes, all except what his aunt and Mary would finish up for him; then we waited ten more for her to get cooled down and sweet and gentle again; for Tom said it took her ten minutes to unruffle in times when half of her feathers was up, but twenty when they was all up, and this was one of the times when they was all up. Then we went down, being in a sweat to know what the letter said.

She was setting there in a brown study, with it laying in her lap. We set down, and she says:

"They're in considerable trouble down there, and they think you and Huck'll be a kind of a diversion for them—'comfort,' they say. Much of that they'll get out of you and Huck Finn, I reckon. There's a neighbor named Brace Dunlap that's been wanting to marry their Benny for three months, and at last they told him pine blank and once for all, he *couldn't;* so he has soured on them, and they're worried about it. I reckon he's somebody they think they better be on the good side of, for they've tried to please him by hiring his no-account brother to help on the farm when they can't hardly afford it, and don't want him around anyhow. Who are the Dunlaps?"

"They live about a mile from Uncle Silas's place, Aunt Polly—all the farmers live about a mile apart down there—and Brace Dunlap is a long sight richer than any of the others, and owns a whole grist of niggers. He's a widower, thirty-six years old, without any children, and is proud of his money and overbearing, and everybody is a little afraid of him. I judge he thought he could have any girl he wanted, just for the asking, and it must have set him back a good deal when he found he couldn't get Benny. Why, Benny's only half as old as he is, and just as sweet and lovely as—well, you've seen her. Poor old Uncle Silas—why, it's pitiful, him trying to curry favor that way—so hard pushed and poor, and yet hiring that useless Jubiter Dunlap to please his ornery brother."

"What a name—Jubiter! Where'd he get it?"

"It's only just a nickname. I reckon they've forgot his real name long before this. He's twenty-seven, now, and has had it ever since the first time he ever went in swimming. The school-teacher seen a round brown mole the size of a dime on his left leg above his knee, and four little bits of moles around it, when he was naked, and he said it minded him of Jubiter and his moons; and the children thought it was funny, and so they got to calling him Jubiter, and he's Jubiter yet. He's tall, and lazy, and sly, and sneaky, and ruther cowardly, too, but kind of good-natured, and wears long brown hair and no beard, and hasn't got a cent, and Brace boards him for nothing, and gives him his old clothes to wear, and despises him. Jubiter is a twin."

"What's t'other twin like?"

"Just exactly like Jubiter—so they say; used to was, anyway, but he hain't been seen for seven years. He got to robbing when he was nineteen or twenty, and they jailed him; but he broke jail and got away—up North here, somers. They used to hear about him robbing and burglaring now and then, but that was years ago. He's dead, now. At least that's what they say. They don't hear about him any more."

"What was his name?"

"Jake."

There wasn't anything more said for a considerable while; the old lady was thinking. At last she says:

"The thing that is mostly worrying your aunt Sally is the tempers that that man Jubiter gets your uncle into."

Tom was astonished, and so was I. Tom says:

"Tempers? Uncle Silas? Land, you must be joking! I didn't know he *had* any temper."

"Works him up into perfect rages, your aunt Sally says; says he acts as if he would really hit the man, sometimes."

"Aunt Polly, it beats anything I ever heard of. Why, he's just as gentle as mush."

"Well, she's worried, anyway. Says your uncle Silas is like a changed man, on account of all this quarrelling. And the neighbors talk about it, and lay all the blame on your uncle, of course, because he's a preacher and hain't got any business to quarrel. Your aunt Sally says he hates to go into the pulpit he's so ashamed; and the people have begun to cool toward him, and he ain't as popular now as he used to was."

"Well, ain't it strange? Why, Aunt Polly, he was always so good and kind and moony and absent-minded and chuckle-headed and lovable—why, he was just an angel! What *can* be the matter of him, do you reckon?"

CHAPTER 2

We had powerful good luck; because we got a chance in a stern-wheeler from away North which was bound for one of them bayous or one-horse rivers away down Louisiana way, and so we could go all the way down the Upper Mississippi and all the way down the Lower Mississippi to that farm in Arkansaw without having to change steam-boats at St. Louis: not so very much short of a thousand miles at one pull.

A pretty lonesome boat; there warn't but few passengers, and all old folks, that set around, wide apart, dozing, and was very quiet. We was four days getting out of the "upper river," because we got aground so much. But it warn't dull—couldn't be for boys that was travelling, of course.

From the very start me and Tom allowed that there was somebody sick in the state-room next to ourn, because the meals was always toted in there by the waiters. By-and-by we asked about it—Tom did—and the waiter said it was a man, but he didn't look sick.

"Well, but *ain't* he sick?"

"I don't know; maybe he is, but 'pears to me he's just letting on."

"What makes you think that?"

"Because if he was sick he would pull his clothes off *some* time or other—don't you reckon he would? Well, this one don't. At least he don't ever pull off his boots, anyway."

"The mischief he don't! Not even when he goes to bed?"

"No."

It was always nuts for Tom Sawyer—a mystery was. If you'd lay out a mystery and a pie before me and him, you wouldn't have to say take your choice; it was a thing that would regulate itself. Because in my nature I have always run to pie, whilst in his nature he has always run to mystery. People are made different. And it is the best way. Tom says to the waiter:

"What's the man's name?"

"Phillips."

"Where'd he come aboard?"

"I think he got aboard at Elexandria, up on the Iowa line."

"What do you reckon he's a-playing?"

"I hain't any notion—I never thought of it."

I says to myself, here's another one that runs to pie.

"Anything peculiar about him?—the way he acts or talks?"

"No—nothing, except he seems so scary, and keeps his doors locked night and day both, and when you knock he won't let you in till he opens the door a crack and sees who it is."

"By jimminy, it's int'resting! I'd like to get a look at him. Say—the next time you're going in there, don't you reckon you could spread the door and—"

"No, indeedy! He's always behind it. He would block that game."

Tom studied over it, and then he says:

"Looky here. You lend me your apern and let me take him his breakfast in the morning. I'll give you a quarter."

The boy was plenty willing enough, if the head steward wouldn't mind. Tom says that's all right, he reckoned he could fix it with the head steward; and he done it. He fixed it so as we could both go in with aperns on and toting vittles.

He didn't sleep much, he was in such a sweat to get in there and find out the mystery about Phillips; and moreover he done a lot of guessing about it all night, which warn't no use, for if you are going to find out the facts of a thing, what's the sense in guessing out what ain't the facts and wasting ammunition? I didn't lose no sleep. I wouldn't give a dern to know what's the matter of Phillips, I says to myself.

Well, in the morning we put on the aperns and got a couple of trays of truck, and Tom he knocked on the door. The man opened it a crack, and then he let us in and shut it quick. By Jackson, when we got a sight of him, we 'most dropped the trays! and Tom says:

"Why, Jubiter Dunlap, where'd *you* come from?"

Well, the man was astonished, of course; and first off he looked like he didn't know whether to be scared, or glad, or both, or which, but finally he settled down to being glad; and then his color come back, though at first his face had turned pretty white. So we got to talking together while he et his breakfast. And he says:

"But I ain't Jubiter Dunlap. I'd just as soon tell you who I am, though, if you'll swear to keep mum, for I ain't no Phillips, either."

Tom says:

"We'll keep mum, but there ain't any need to tell who you are if you ain't Jubiter Dunlap."

"Why?"

"Because if you ain't him you're t'other twin, Jake. You're the spit'n image of Jubiter."

"Well, I *am* Jake. But looky here, how do you come to know us Dunlaps?"

Tom told about the adventures we'd had down there at his uncle Silas's last summer, and when he see that there warn't anything about his folks—or him either, for that matter—that we didn't know, he opened out and talked perfectly free and candid. He never made any bones about his own case; said he'd been a hard lot, was a hard lot yet, and reckoned he'd *be* a hard lot plumb to the end. He said of course it was a dangerous life, and—

He give a kind of gasp, and set his head like a person that's listening. We didn't say anything, and so it was very still for a second or so, and there warn't no sounds but the screaking of the wood-work and the chug-chugging of the machinery down below.

Then we got him comfortable again, telling him about his people, and how Brace's wife had been dead three years, and Brace wanted to marry Benny and she shook him, and Jubiter was working for Uncle Silas, and him and Uncle Silas quarrelling all the time—and then he let go and laughed.

"Land!" he says, "it's like old times to hear all this tittle-tattle, and does me good. It's been seven years and more since I heard any. How do they talk about me these days?"

"Who?"

"The farmers—and the family."

"Why, they don't talk about you at all—at least only just a mention, once in a long time."

"The nation!" he says, surprised; "why is that?"

"Because they think you are dead long ago."

"No! Are you speaking true?—honor bright, now." He jumped up, excited.

"Honor bright. There ain't anybody thinks you are alive."

"Then I'm saved, I'm saved, sure! I'll go home. They'll hide me and save my life. You keep mum. Swear you'll keep mum—swear you'll never, never tell on me. Oh, boys, be good to a poor devil that's being hunted day and night, and dasn't show his face! I've never done you any harm; I'll never do you any, as God is in the heavens; swear you'll be good to me and help me save my life."

We'd a swore it if he'd been a dog; and so we done it. Well, he couldn't love us enough for it or be grateful enough, poor cuss; it was all he could do to keep from hugging us.

We talked along, and he got out a little hand-bag and begun to open it, and told us to turn our backs. We done it, and when he told us to turn again he was perfectly different to what he was before. He had on blue goggles and the naturalest-looking long brown whiskers and mustashes you ever see. His own mother wouldn't 'a' knowed him. He asked us if he looked like his brother Jubiter, now.

"No," Tom said; "there ain't anything left that's like him except the long hair."

"All right, I'll get that cropped close to my head before I get there; then him and Brace will keep my secret, and I'll live with them as being a stranger, and the neighbors won't ever guess me out. What do you think?"

Tom he studied a while, then he says:

"Well, of course me and Huck are going to keep mum there, but if you don't keep mum yourself there's going to be a little bit of a risk—it ain't much, maybe, but it's a little. I mean, if you talk, won't people notice that your voice is just like Jubiter's; and mightn't it make them think of the twin they reckoned was dead, but maybe after all was hid all this time under another name?"

"By George," he says, "you're a sharp one! You're perfectly right. I've got to play deef and dumb when there's a neighbor around. If I'd a struck for home and forgot that little detail— However, I wasn't striking for home. I was breaking for any place where I could get away from these fellows that are after me; then I was going to put on this disguise and get some different clothes, and—"

He jumped for the outside door and laid his ear against it and listened, pale and kind of panting. Presently he whispers:

"Sounded like cocking a gun! Lord, what a life to lead!"

Then he sunk down in a chair all limp and sick like, and wiped the sweat off of his face.

CHAPTER 3

From that time out, we was with him 'most all the time, and one or t'other of us slept in his upper berth. He said he had been so lonesome, and it was such a comfort to him to have company, and somebody to talk to in his troubles. We was in a sweat to find out what his secret was, but Tom said the best way was not to seem anxious, then likely he would drop into it himself in one of his talks, but if we got to asking questions he would get suspicious and shet up his shell. It turned out just so. It warn't no trouble to see that he *wanted* to talk about it, but always along at first he would scare away from it when he got on the very edge of it, and go to talking about something else. The way it come about was this: He got to asking us, kind of indifferent like, about the passengers down on deck. We told him about them. But he warn't satisfied; we warn't particular enough. He told us to describe them better. Tom done it. At last, when Tom was describing one of the roughest and raggedest ones, he gave a shiver and a gasp and says:

"Oh, lordy, that's one of them! They're aboard sure—I just knowed it. I sort of hoped I had got away, but I never believed it. Go on."

Presently when Tom was describing another mangy, rough deck passenger, he give that shiver again and says—

"That's him!—that's the other one. If it would only come a good black stormy night and I could get ashore. You see, they've got spies on me. They've got a right to come up and buy drinks at the bar yonder forrard, and they take that chance to bribe somebody to keep watch on me—porter or boots or somebody. If I was to slip ashore without anybody seeing me, they would know it inside of an hour."

So then he got to wandering along, and pretty soon, sure enough, he was telling! He was poking along through his ups and downs, and when he come to that place he went right along. He says:

"It was a confidence game. We played it on a julery-shop in St. Louis. What we was after was a couple of noble big di'monds as big as a hazel-nuts, which everybody was running to see. We was dressed up fine, and we played it on them in broad daylight. We ordered the di'monds sent to the hotel for us to see if we wanted to buy, and when we was examining them we had paste counterfeits all ready, and *them* was the things that went back to the shop when we said the water wasn't quite fine enough for twelve thousand dollars."

"Twelve—thousand—dollars!" Tom says. "Was they really worth all that money, do you reckon?"

"Every cent of it."

"And you fellows got away with them?"

"As easy as nothing. I don't reckon the julery people know they've been robbed yet. But it wouldn't be good sense to stay around St. Louis, of course, so we considered where we'd go. One was for going one way, one another, so we throwed up, heads or tails, and the Upper Mississippi won. We done up the di'monds in a paper and put our names on it and put it in the keep of the hotel clerk, and told him not to ever let either of us have it again without the others was on hand to see it done; then we went down town, each by his own self—because I reckon maybe we all had the same notion. I don't know for certain, but I reckon maybe we had."

"What notion?" Tom says.

"To rob the others."

"What—one take everything, after all of you had helped to get it?"

"Cert'nly."

It disgusted Tom Sawyer, and he said it was the orneriest, low-downest thing he ever heard of. But Jake Dunlap said it warn't unusual in the profession. Said when a person was in that line of business he'd got to look out for his own intrust, there warn't nobody else going to do it for him. And then he went on. He says:

"You see, the trouble was, you couldn't divide up two di'monds amongst three. If there'd been three— But never mind about that, there *warn't* three. I loafed along the back streets studying and studying. And I says to myself, I'll hog them di'monds the first chance I get, and I'll have a disguise all ready, and I'll give the boys the slip, and when I'm safe away I'll put it on, and then let them find me if they can. So I got the false whiskers and the goggles and this countrified suit of clothes, and fetched them along back in a hand-bag; and when I was passing a shop where they sell all sorts of things, I got a glimpse of one of my pals through the window. It was Bud Dixon. I was glad, you bet. I says to myself, I'll see what he buys. So I kept shady, and watched. Now what do you reckon it was he bought?"

"Whiskers?" said I.

"No."

"Goggles?"

"No."

"Oh, keep still, Huck Finn, can't you, you're only just hendering all you can. What *was* it he bought, Jake?"

"You'd never guess in the world. It was only just a screw-driver—just a wee little bit of a screw-driver."

"Well, I declare! What did he want with that?"

"That's what *I* thought. It was curious. It clean stumped me. I says to myself, what can he want with that thing? Well, when he come out I stood back out of sight, and then tracked him to a second-hand slop-shop and see him buy a red flannel shirt and some old ragged clothes—just the ones he's got on now, as you've described. Then I went down to the wharf and hid my things aboard the up-river boat that we had picked out, and then started back and had another streak of luck. I seen our other pal lay in *his* stock of old rusty second-handers. We got the di'monds and went aboard the boat.

"But now we was up a stump, for we couldn't go to bed. We had to set up and watch one another. Pity, that was; pity to put that kind of a strain on us, because there was bad blood between us from a couple of weeks back, and we was only friends in the way of business. Bad anyway, seeing there was only two di'monds betwixt three men. First we had supper, and then tramped up and down the deck together smoking till most midnight; then we went and set down in my state-room and locked the doors and looked in the piece of paper to see if the di'monds was all right, then laid it on the lower berth right in full sight; and there we set, and set, and by-and-by it got to be dreadful hard to keep awake. At last Bud Dixon he dropped off. As soon as he was snoring a good regular gait that was likely to last, and had his chin on his breast and looked permanent, Hal Clayton nodded towards the di'monds and then towards the outside door, and I understood. I reached and got the paper, and then we stood up and waited perfectly still; Bud never stirred; I turned the key of the outside door very soft and slow, then turned the knob the same way, and we went tiptoeing out onto the guard, and shut the door very soft and gentle.

"There warn't nobody stirring anywhere, and the boat was slipping along, swift and steady, through the big water in the smoky moonlight. We never said a word, but went straight up onto the hurricane-deck and plumb back aft, and set down on the end of the skylight. Both of us knowed what that meant, without having to explain to one another. Bud Dixon would wake up and miss the swag, and would come straight for us, for he ain't afeard of anything or anybody, that man ain't. He would come, and we would heave him overboard, or get killed trying. It made me shiver, because I ain't as brave as some people, but if I showed the white feather—well, I knowed better than do that. I kind of hoped the boat would land somers, and we could skip ashore and not have to run the risk of this row, I was so scared of Bud Dixon, but she was an upper-river tub and there warn't no real chance of that.

"Well, the time strung along and along, and that fellow never come! Why, it strung along till dawn begun to break, and still he never come. 'Thunder,' I says, 'what do you make out of this?—ain't it suspicious?' 'Land!' Hal says, 'do you reckon he's playing us?—open the paper!' I done it, and by gracious there warn't anything in it but a couple of little pieces of loaf-sugar! *That's* the reason he could set there and snooze all night so comfortable. Smart? Well, I reckon! He had had them two papers all fixed and ready, and he had put one of them in place of t'other right under our noses.

"We felt pretty cheap. But the thing to do, straight off, was to make a plan; and we done it. We would do up the paper again, just as it was, and slip in, very elaborate and soft, and lay it on the bunk again, and let on *we* didn't know about any trick, and hadn't any idea he was a-laughing at us behind them bogus snores of his'n; and we would stick by him, and the first night we was ashore we would get him drunk and search him, and get the di'monds; and *do* for him, too, if it warn't too risky. If we got the swag, we'd *got* to do for him, or he would hunt us down and do for us, sure. But I didn't have no real hope. I knowed we could get him drunk—he was always ready for that—but what's the good of it? You might search him a year and never find—

"Well, right there I catched my breath and broke off my thought! For an idea went ripping through my head that tore my brains to rags—and land, but I felt gay and good! You see, I had had my boots off, to unswell my feet, and just then I took up one of them to put it on, and I catched a glimpse of the heel-bottom, and it just took my breath away. You remember about that puzzlesome little screw-driver?"

"You bet I do," says Tom, all excited.

"Well, when I catched that glimpse of that boot heel, the idea that went smashing through my head was, *I* know where he's hid the di'monds! You look at this boot heel, now. See, it's bottomed with a steel plate, and the plate is fastened on with little screws. Now there wasn't a screw about that feller anywhere but in his boot heels; so, if he needed a screw-driver, I reckoned I knowed why."

"Huck, ain't it bully!" says Tom.

"Well, I got my boots on, and we went down and slipped in and laid the paper of sugar on the berth, and sat down soft and sheepish and went to listening to Bud Dixon snore. Hal Clayton dropped off pretty soon, but I didn't; I wasn't ever so wide-awake in my life. I was spying out from under the shade of my hat brim, searching the floor for leather. It took me a long time, and I begun to think maybe my guess was wrong, but at last I struck it. It laid over by the bulkhead, and was nearly the color of the carpet. It was a little round plug about as thick as the end of your little finger, and I says to myself there's a di'mond in the nest you've come from. Before long I spied out the plug's mate.

"Think of the smartness and coolness of that blatherskite! He put up that scheme on us and reasoned out what we would do, and we went ahead and done it perfectly exact, like a couple of pudd'n heads. He set there and took his own time to unscrew his heel-plates and cut out his plugs and stick in the di'monds and screw on his plates again. He allowed we would steal the bogus swag and wait all night for him to come up and get drownded, and by George it's just what we done! *I* think it was powerful smart."

"You bet your life it was!" says Tom, just full of admiration.

CHAPTER 4

"Well, all day we went through the humbug of watching one another, and it was pretty sickly business for two of us and hard to act out, I can tell you. About night we landed at one of them little Missouri towns high up toward Iowa, and had supper at the tavern, and got a room upstairs with a cot and a double bed in it, but I dumped my bag under a deal table in the dark hall whilst we was moving along it to bed, single file, me last, and the landlord in the lead with a tallow candle. We had up a lot of whiskey, and went to playing high-low-jack for dimes, and as soon as the whiskey begun to take hold of Bud we stopped drinking, but we didn't let him stop. We loaded him till he fell out of his chair and laid there snoring.

"We was ready for business now. I said we better pull our boots off, and his'n too, and not make any noise, then we could pull him and haul him around and ransack him without any trouble. So we done it. I set my boots and Bud's side by side, where they'd be handy. Then we stripped him and searched his seams and his pockets and his socks and the inside of his boots, and everything, and searched his bundle. Never found any di'monds. We found the screw-driver, and Hal says, 'What do you reckon he wanted with that?' I said I didn't know; but when he wasn't looking I hooked it. At last Hal he looked beat and discouraged, and said we'd got to give it up. That was what I was waiting for. I says:

" 'There's one place we hain't searched.'

" 'What place is that?' he says.

" 'His stomach.'

" 'By gracious, I never thought of that! *Now* we're on the homestretch, to a dead moral certainty. How'll we manage?'

" 'Well,' I says, 'just stay by him till I turn out and hunt up a drugstore, and I reckon I'll fetch something that'll make them di'monds tired of the company they're keeping.'

"He said that's the ticket, and with him looking straight at me I slid myself into Bud's boots instead of my own, and he never noticed. They was just a shade large for me, but that was considerable better than being too small. I got my bag as I went a-groping through the hall, and in about a minute I was out the back way and stretching up the river road at a five-mile gait.

"And not feeling so very bad, neither—walking on di'monds don't have no such effect. When I had gone fifteen minutes I says to myself, there's more'n a mile behind me, and everything quiet. Another five minutes and I says there's considerable more land behind me now, and there's a man back there that's begun to wonder what's the trouble. Another five and I says to myself he's getting real uneasy—he's walking the floor now. Another five, and I says to myself, there's two mile and a half behind me, and he's *awful* uneasy—beginning to cuss, I reckon. Pretty soon I says to myself, forty minutes gone—he *knows* there's something up! Fifty minutes—the truth's a-busting on him now! he is reckoning I found the di'monds whilst we was searching, and shoved them in my pocket and never let on—yes, and he's starting out to hunt for me. He'll hunt for new tracks in the dust, and they'll as likely send him down the river as up.

"Just then I see a man coming down on a mule, and before I thought I jumped into the bush. It was stupid! When he got abreast he stopped and waited a little for me to come out; then he rode on again. But I didn't feel gay any more. I says to myself I've botched my chances by that; I surely have, if he meets up with Hal Clayton.

"Well, about three in the morning I fetched Elexandria and see this stern-wheeler laying there, and was very glad, because I felt perfectly safe, now, you know. It was just daybreak. I went aboard and got this state-room and put on these clothes and went up in the pilot-house—to watch, though I didn't reckon there was any need of it. I set there and played with my di'monds and waited and waited for the boat to start, but she didn't. You see, they was mending her machinery, but I didn't know anything about it, not being very much used to steamboats.

"Well, to cut the tale short, we never left there till plumb noon; and long before that I was hid in this state-room; for before breakfast I see a man coming, away off, that had a gait like Hal Clayton's, and it made me just sick. I says to myself, if he finds out I'm aboard this boat, he's got me like a rat in a trap. All he's got to do is to have me watched, and wait—wait till I slip ashore, thinking he is a thousand miles away, then slip after me and dog me to a good place and make me give up the di'monds, and then he'll—oh, *I* know what he'll do! Ain't it awful—awful! And now to think the *other* one's aboard, too! Oh, ain't it hard luck, boys—ain't it hard! But you'll help save me, *won't* you?—oh, boys, be good to a poor devil that's being hunted to death, and save me—I'll worship the very ground you walk on!"

We turned in and soothed him down and told him we would plan for him and help him, and he needn't be so afeard; and so by-and-by he got to feeling kind of comfortable again, and unscrewed his heel-plates and held up his di'monds this way and that, admiring them and loving them; and when the light struck into them they *was* beautiful, sure; why, they seemed to kind of bust, and snap fire out all around. But all the same I judged he was a fool. If I had been him I would a handed the di'monds to them pals and got them to go ashore and leave me alone. But he was made different. He said it was a whole fortune and he couldn't bear the idea.

Twice we stopped to fix the machinery and laid a good while, once in the night; but it wasn't dark enough, and he was afeard to skip. But the third time we had to fix it there was a better chance. We laid up at a country woodyard about forty mile above Uncle Silas's place a little after one at night, and it was thickening up and going to storm. So Jake he laid for a chance to slide. We begun to take in wood. Pretty soon the rain come a-drenching down, and the wind blowed hard. Of course every boat-hand fixed a gunny sack and put it on like a bonnet, the way they do when they are toting wood, and we got one for Jake, and he slipped down aft with his hand-bag and come tramping forrard just like the rest, and walked ashore with them, and when we see him pass out of the light of the torch-basket and get swallowed up in the dark, we got our breath again and just felt grateful and splendid. But it wasn't for long. Somebody told, I reckon; for in about eight or ten minutes them two pals come tearing forrard as tight as they could jump and darted ashore and was gone. We waited plumb till dawn for them to come back, and kept hoping they would, but they never did. We was awful sorry and low-spirited. All the hope we had was that Jake had got such a start that they couldn't get on his track, and he would get to his brother's and hide there and be safe.

He was going to take the river road, and told us to find out if Brace and Jubiter was to home and no strangers there, and then slip out about sundown and tell him. Said he would wait for us in a little bunch of sycamores right back of Tom's uncle Silas's tobacker-field on the river road, a lonesome place.

We set and talked a long time about his chances, and Tom said he was all right if the pals struck up the river instead of down, but it wasn't likely, because maybe they knowed where he was from; more likely they would go right, and dog him all day, him not suspecting, and kill him when it come dark, and take the boots. So we was pretty sorrowful.

CHAPTER 5

We didn't get done tinkering the machinery till away late in the afternoon, and so it was so close to sundown when we got home that we never stopped on our road, but made a break for the sycamores as tight as we could go, to tell Jake what the delay was, and have him wait till we could go to Brace's and find out how things was there. It was getting pretty dim by the time we turned the corner of the woods, sweating and panting with that long run, and see the sycamores thirty yards ahead of us; and just then we see a couple of men run into the bunch and heard two or three terrible screams for help. "Poor Jake is killed, sure," we says. We was scared through and through, and broke for the tobacker-field and hid there, trembling so our clothes would hardly stay on; and just as we skipped in there, a couple of men went tearing by, and into the bunch they went, and in a second out jumps four men and took out up the road as tight as they could go, two chasing two.

We laid down, kind of weak and sick, and listened for more sounds, but didn't hear none for a good while but just our hearts. We was thinking of that awful thing laying yonder in the sycamores, and it seemed like being that close to a ghost, and it give me the cold shudders. The moon come a-swelling up out of the ground, now, powerful big and round and bright, behind a comb of trees, like a face looking through prison bars, and the black shadders and white places begun to creep around, and it was miserable quiet and still and night-breezy and graveyardy and scary. All of a sudden Tom whispers:

"Look!—what's that?"

"Don't!" I says. "Don't take a person by surprise that way. I'm 'most ready to die, anyway, without you doing that."

"Look, I tell you. It's something coming out of the sycamores."

"Don't, Tom!"

"It's terrible tall!"

"Oh, lordy-lordy! let's—"

"Keep still—it's a-coming this way."

He was so excited he could hardly get breath enough to whisper.

I had to look. I couldn't help it. So now we was both on our knees with our chins on a fence-rail and gazing—yes, and gasping, too. It was coming down the road—coming in the shadder of the trees, and you couldn't see it good; not till it was pretty close to us; then it stepped into a bright splotch of moonlight and we sunk right down in our tracks—it was Jake Dunlap's ghost! That was what we said to ourselves.

We couldn't stir for a minute or two; then it was gone. We talked about it in low voices. Tom says:

"They're mostly dim and smoky, or like they're made out of fog, but this one wasn't."

"No," I says; "I seen the goggles and the whiskers perfectly plain."

"Yes, and the very colors in them loud countrified Sunday clothes —plaid breeches, green and black—"

"Cotton-velvet westcot, fire-red and yaller squares—"

"Leather straps to the bottoms of the breeches legs and one of them hanging unbuttoned—"

"Yes, and that hat—"

"What a hat for a ghost to wear!"

You see it was the first season anybody wore that kind—a black stiff-brim stove-pipe, very high, and not smooth, with a round top —just like a sugar-loaf.

"Did you notice if its hair was the same, Huck?"

"No—seems to me I did, then again it seems to me I didn't."

"I didn't either; but it had its bag along, I noticed that."

"So did I. How can there be a ghost-bag, Tom?"

"Sho! I wouldn't be as ignorant as that if I was you, Huck Finn. Whatever a ghost has, turns to ghost-stuff. They've got to have their things, like anybody else. You see, yourself, that its clothes was turned to ghost-stuff. Well, then, what's to hender its bag from turning, too? Of course it done it."

That was reasonable. I couldn't find no fault with it. Bill Withers and his brother Jack come along by, talking, and Jack says:

"What do you reckon he was toting?"

"I dunno; but it was pretty heavy."

"Yes, all he could lug. Nigger stealing corn from old Parson Silas, I judged."

"So did I. And so I allowed I wouldn't let on to see him."

"That's me, too."

Then they both laughed, and went on out of hearing. It showed how unpopular old Uncle Silas had got to be, now. They wouldn't 'a' let a nigger steal anybody else's corn and never done anything to him.

We heard some more voices mumbling along towards us and getting louder, and sometimes a cackle of a laugh. It was Lem Beebe and Jim Lane. Jim Lane says:

"Who?—Jubiter Dunlap?"

"Yes."

"Oh, I don't know. I reckon so. I seen him spading up some ground along about an hour ago, just before sundown—him and the parson. Said he guessed he wouldn't go to-night, but we could have his dog if we wanted him."

"Too tired, I reckon."

"Yes—works so hard!"

"Oh, you bet!"

They cackled at that, and went on by. Tom said we better jump out and tag along after them, because they was going our way and it wouldn't be comfortable to run across the ghost all by ourselves. So we done it, and got home all right.

That night was the second of September—a Saturday. I sha'n't ever forget it. You'll see why, pretty soon.

CHAPTER 6

We tramped along behind Jim and Lem till we come to the back stile where old Jim's cabin was that he was captivated in, the time we set him free, and here come the dogs piling around us to say howdy, and there was the lights of the house, too; so we warn't afeard any more, and was going to climb over, but Tom says:

"Hold on; set down here a minute. By George!"

"What's the matter?" says I.

"Matter enough!" he says. "Wasn't you expecting we would be the first to tell the family who it is that's been killed yonder in the sycamores, and all about them rapscallions that done it, and about the di'monds they've smouched off of the corpse, and paint it up fine, and have the glory of being the ones that knows a lot more about it than anybody else?"

"Why, of course. It wouldn't be you, Tom Sawyer, if you was to let such a chance go by. I reckon it ain't going to suffer none for lack of paint," I says, "when you start in to scollop the facts."

"Well, now," he says, perfectly ca'm, "what would you say if I was to tell you I ain't going to start in at all?"

I was astonished to hear him talk so. I says:

"I'd say it's a lie. You ain't in earnest, Tom Sawyer."

"You'll soon see. Was the ghost barefooted?"

"No, it wasn't. What of it?"

"You wait—I'll show you what. Did it have its boots on?"

"Yes. I seen them plain."

"Swear it?"

"Yes, I swear it."

"So do I. Now do you know what that means?"

"No. What does it mean?"

"Means that them thieves *didn't get the di'monds.*"

"Jimminy! What makes you think that?"

"I don't only think it, I know it. Didn't the breeches and goggles and whiskers and hand-bag and every blessed thing turn to ghost-stuff? Everything it had on turned, didn't it? It shows that the reason its boots turned too was because it still had them on after it started to go ha'nting around, and if that ain't proof that them blatherskites didn't get the boots, I'd like to know what you'd *call* proof."

Think of that now. I never see such a head as that boy had. Why, *I* had eyes and I could see things, but they never meant nothing to me. But Tom Sawyer was different. When Tom Sawyer seen a thing it just got up on its hind legs and *talked* to him—told him everything it knowed. *I* never see such a head.

"Tom Sawyer," I says, "I'll say it again as I've said it a many a time before: I ain't fitten to black your boots. But that's all right—that's neither here nor there. God Almighty made us all, and some He gives eyes that's blind, and some He gives eyes that can see, and I reckon it ain't none of our lookout what He done it for; it's all right, or He'd 'a' fixed it some other way. Go on—I see plenty plain enough, now, that them thieves didn't get way with the di'monds. Why didn't they, do you reckon?"

"Because they got chased away by them other two men before they could pull the boots off of the corpse."

"That's so! I see it now. But looky here, Tom, why ain't we to go and tell about it?"

"Oh, shucks, Huck Finn, can't you see? Look at it. What's a-going to happen? There's going to be an inquest in the morning. Them two men will tell how they heard the yells and rushed there just in time to not save the stranger. Then the jury'll twaddle and twaddle and twaddle, and finally they'll fetch in a verdict that he got shot or stuck or busted over the head with something, and come to his death by the inspiration of God. And after they've buried him they'll auction off his things for to pay the expenses, and then's *our* chance."

"How, Tom?"

"Buy the boots for two dollars!"

Well, it 'most took my breath.

"My land! Why, Tom, *we'll* get the di'monds!"

"You bet. Some day there'll be a big reward offered for them—a thousand dollars, sure. That's our money! Now we'll trot in and see the folks. And mind you we don't know anything about any murder, or any di'monds, or any thieves—don't you forget that."

I had to sigh a little over the way he had got it fixed. *I'd 'a' sold* them di'monds—yes, sir—for twelve thousand dollars; but I didn't say anything. It wouldn't done any good. I says:

"But what are we going to tell your aunt Sally has made us so long getting down here from the village, Tom?"

"Oh, I'll leave that to you," he says. "I reckon you can explain it somehow."

He was always just that strict and delicate. He never would tell a lie himself.

We struck across the big yard, noticing this, that, and t'other thing that was so familiar, and we so glad to see it again, and when we got to the roofed big passageway betwixt the double log house and the kitchen part, there was everything hanging on the wall just as it used to was, even to Uncle Silas's old faded green baize working-gown with the hood to it, and raggedy white patch between the shoulders that always looked like somebody had hit him with a snowball; and then we lifted the latch and walked in. Aunt Sally she was just a-ripping and a-tearing around, and the children was huddled in one corner, and the old man he was huddled in the other and praying for help in time of need. She jumped for us with joy and tears running down her face and give us a whacking box on the ear, and then hugged us and kissed us and boxed us again, and just couldn't seem to get enough of it, she was so glad to see us; and she says:

"Where *have* you been a-loafing to, you good-for-nothing trash! I've been that worried about you I didn't know what to do. Your traps has been here *ever* so long, and I've had supper cooked fresh about four times so as to have it hot and good when you come, till at last my patience is just plumb wore out, and I declare I—I—why I could skin you alive! You must be starving, poor things!—set down, set down, everybody; don't lose no more time."

It was good to be there again behind all that noble corn-pone and spareribs, and everything that you could ever want in this world. Old Uncle Silas he peeled off one of his bulliest old-time blessings, with as many layers to it as an onion, and whilst the angels was hauling in the slack of it I was trying to study up what to say about what kept us so long. When our plates was all loadened and we'd got a-going, she asked me, and I says:

"Well, you see,—er—Mizzes—"

"Huck Finn! Since when am I Mizzes to you? Have I ever been stingy of cuffs or kisses for you since the day you stood in this room and I took you for Tom Sawyer and blessed God for sending you to me, though you told me four thousand lies and I believed every one of them like a simpleton? Call me Aunt Sally—like you always done."

So I done it. And I says:

"Well, me and Tom allowed we would come along afoot and take a smell of the woods, and we run across Lem Beebe and Jim Lane, and they asked us to go with them blackberrying to-night, and said they could borrow Jubiter Dunlap's dog, because he had told them just that minute—"

"Where did they see him?" says the old man; and when I looked up to see how *he* come to take an intrust in a little thing like that, his eyes was just burning into me, he was that eager. It surprised me so it kind of throwed me off, but I pulled myself together again and says:

"It was when he was spading up some ground along with you, towards sundown or along there."

He only said, "Um," in a kind of a disappointed way, and didn't take no more intrust. So I went on. I says:

"Well, then, as I was a-saying—"

"That'll do, you needn't go no furder." It was Aunt Sally. She was boring right into me with her eyes, and very indignant. "Huck Finn," she says, "how'd them men come to talk about going a-blackberrying in September—in *this* region?"

I see I had slipped up, and I couldn't say a word. She waited, still a-gazing at me, then she says:

"And how'd they come to strike that idiot idea of going a-blackberrying in the night?"

"Well, m'm, they—er—they told us they had a lantern, and—"

"Oh, *shet* up—do! Looky here; what was they going to do with a dog?—hunt blackberries with it?"

"I think, m'm, they—"

"Now, Tom Sawyer, what kind of a lie are you fixing *your* mouth to contribit to this mess of rubbage? Speak out—and I warn you before you begin, that I don't believe a word of it. You and Huck's been up to something you no business to—*I* know it perfectly well; *I* know you, *both* of you. Now you explain that dog, and them blackberries, and the lantern, and the rest of that rot—and mind you talk as straight as a string—do you hear?"

Tom he looked considerable hurt, and says, very dignified:

"It is a pity if Huck is to be talked to that away, just for making a little bit of a mistake that anybody could make."

"What mistake has he made?"

"Why, only the mistake of saying blackberries when of course he meant strawberries."

"Tom Sawyer, I lay if you aggravate me a little more, I'll—"

"Aunt Sally, without knowing it—and of course without intending it—you are in the wrong. If you'd 'a' studied natural history the way you ought, you would know that all over the world except just here in Arkansaw they *always* hunt strawberries with a dog—and a lantern—"

But she busted in on him there and just piled into him and snowed him under. She was so mad she couldn't get the words out fast enough, and she gushed them out in one everlasting freshet. That was what Tom Sawyer was after. He allowed to work her up and get her started and then leave her alone and let her burn herself out. Then she would be so aggravated with that subject that she wouldn't say another word about it, nor let anybody else. Well, it happened just so. When she was tuckered out and had to hold up, he says, quite ca'm:

"And yet, all the same, Aunt Sally—"

"Shet up!" she says, "I don't want to hear another word out of you."

So we was perfectly safe, then, and didn't have no more trouble about that delay. Tom done it elegant.

CHAPTER 7

Benny she was looking pretty sober, and she sighed some, now and then; but pretty soon she got to asking about Mary, and Sid, and Tom's aunt Polly, and then Aunt Sally's clouds cleared off and she got in a good humor and joined in on the questions and was her lovingest best self, and so the rest of the supper went along gay and pleasant. But the old man he didn't take any hand hardly, and was absent-minded and restless, and done a considerable amount of sighing; and it was kind of heart-breaking to see him so sad and troubled and worried.

By-and-by, a spell after supper, come a nigger and knocked on the door and put his head in with his old straw hat in his hand bowing and scraping, and said his Marse Brace was out at the stile and wanted his brother, and was getting tired waiting supper for him, and would Marse Silas please tell him where he was? I never see Uncle Silas speak up so sharp and fractious before. He says:

"Am *I* his brother's keeper?" And then he kind of wilted together, and looked like he wished he hadn't spoken so, and then he says, very gentle: "But you needn't say that, Billy; I was took sudden and irritable, and I ain't very well these days, and not hardly responsible. Tell him he ain't here."

And when the nigger was gone he got up and walked the floor, backwards and forwards, mumbling and muttering to himself and ploughing his hands through his hair. It was real pitiful to see him. Aunt Sally she whispered to us and told us not to take notice of him, it embarrassed him. She said he was always thinking and thinking, since these troubles come on, and she allowed he didn't more'n about half know what he was about when the thinking spells was on him; and she said he walked in his sleep considerable more now than he used to, and sometimes wandered around over the house and even outdoors in his sleep, and if we catched him at it we must let him alone and not disturb him. She said she reckoned it didn't do him no harm, and may be it done him good. She said Benny was the only one that was much help to him these days. Said Benny appeared to know just when to try to soothe him and when to leave him alone.

So he kept on tramping up and down the floor and muttering, till by-and-by he begun to look pretty tired; then Benny she went and snuggled up to his side and put one hand in his and one arm around his waist and walked with him; and he smiled down on her, and reached down and kissed her; and so, little by little the trouble went out of his face and she persuaded him off to his room. They had very petting ways together, and it was uncommon pretty to see.

Aunt Sally she was busy getting the children ready for bed; so by-and-by it got dull and tedious, and me and Tom took a turn in the moonlight, and fetched up in the watermelon-patch and et one, and had a good deal of talk. And Tom said he'd bet the quarrelling was all Jubiter's fault, and he was going to be on hand the first time he got a chance, and see; and if it was so, he was going to do his level best to get Uncle Silas to turn him off.

And so we talked and smoked and stuffed watermelon as much as two hours, and then it was pretty late, and when we got back the house was quiet and dark, and everybody gone to bed.

Tom he always seen everything, and now he see that the old green baize work-gown was gone, and said it wasn't gone when he went out; and so we allowed it was curious, and then we went up to bed.

We could hear Benny stirring around in her room, which was next to ourn, and judged she was worried a good deal about her father and couldn't sleep. We found we couldn't, neither. So we set up a long time, and smoked and talked in a low voice, and felt pretty dull and down-hearted. We talked the murder and the ghost over and over again, and got so creepy and crawly we couldn't get sleepy nohow and noway.

By-and-by, when it was away late in the night and all the sounds was late sounds and solemn, Tom nudged me and whispers to me to look, and I done it, and there we see a man poking around in the yard like he didn't know just what he wanted to do, but it was pretty dim and we couldn't see him good. Then he started for the stile, and as he went over it the moon came out strong, and he had a long-handled shovel over his shoulder, and we see the white patch on the old work-gown. So Tom says:

"He's a-walking in his sleep. I wish we was allowed to follow him and see where he's going to. There, he's turned down by the tobacker-field. Out of sight now. It's a dreadful pity he can't rest no better."

We waited a long time, but he didn't come back any more, or if he did he come around the other way; so at last we was tuckered out and went to sleep and had nightmares, a million of them. But before dawn we was awake again, because meantime a storm had come up and been raging, and the thunder and lightning was awful, and the wind was a-thrashing the trees around, and the rain was driving down in slanting sheets, and the gullies was running rivers. Tom says:

"Looky here, Huck, I'll tell you one thing that's mighty curious. Up to the time we went out, last night, the family hadn't heard about Jake Dunlap being murdered. Now the men that chased Hal Clayton and Bud Dixon away would spread the thing around in a half an hour, and every neighbor that heard it would shin out and fly around from one farm to t'other and try to be the first to tell the news. Land, they don't have such a big thing as that to tell twice in thirty year! Huck, it's mighty strange; I don't understand it."

So then he was in a fidget for the rain to let up, so we could turn out and run across some of the people and see if they would say anything about it to us. And he said if they did we must be horribly surprised and shocked.

We was out and gone the minute the rain stopped. It was just broad day, then. We loafed along up the road, and now and then met a person and stopped and said howdy, and told them when we come, and how we left the folks at home, and how long we was going to stay, and all that, but none of them said a word about that thing; which was just astonishing, and no mistake. Tom said he believed if we went to the sycamores we would find that body laying there solitary and alone, and not a soul around. Said he believed the men chased the thieves so far into the woods that the thieves prob'ly seen a good chance and turned on them at last, and maybe they all killed each other, and so there wasn't anybody left to tell.

First we knowed, gabbling along that away, we was right at the sycamores. The cold chills trickled down my back and I wouldn't budge another step, for all Tom's persuading. But he couldn't hold in; he'd *got* to see if the boots was safe on that body yet. So he crope in —and the next minute out he come again with his eyes bulging he was so excited, and says:

"Huck, it's gone!"

I *was* astonished! I says:

"Tom, you don't mean it."

"It's gone, sure. There ain't a sign of it. The ground is trampled some, but if there was any blood it's all washed away by the storm, for it's all puddles and slush in there."

At last I give in, and went and took a look myself; and it was just as Tom said—there wasn't a sign of a corpse.

"Dern it," I says, "the di'monds is gone. Don't you reckon the thieves slunk back and lugged him off, Tom?"

"Looks like it. It just does. Now where'd they hide him, do you reckon?"

"I don't know," I says, disgusted, "and what's more I don't care. They've got the boots, and that's all *I* cared about. He'll lay around these woods a long time before *I* hunt him up."

Tom didn't feel no more intrust in him neither, only curiosity to know what come of him; but he said we'd lay low and keep dark and it wouldn't be long till the dogs or somebody rousted him out.

We went back home to breakfast ever so bothered and put out and disappointed and swindled. I warn't ever so down on a corpse before.

CHAPTER 8

It warn't very cheerful at breakfast. Aunt Sally she looked old and tired and let the children snarl and fuss at one another and didn't seem to notice it was going on, which wasn't her usual style; me and Tom had a plenty to think about without talking; Benny she looked like she hadn't had much sleep, and whenever she'd lift her head a little and steal a look towards her father you could see there was tears in her eyes; and as for the old man, his things stayed on his plate and got cold without him knowing they was there, I reckon, for he was thinking and thinking all the time, and never said a word and never et a bite.

By-and-by when it was stillest, that nigger's head was poked in at the door again, and he said his Marse Brace was getting powerful uneasy about Marse Jubiter, which hadn't come home yet, and would Marse Silas please—

He was looking at Uncle Silas, and he stopped there, like the rest of his words was froze; for Uncle Silas he rose up shaky and steadied himself leaning his fingers on the table, and he was panting, and his eyes was set on the nigger, and he kept swallowing, and put his other hand up to his throat a couple of times, and at last he got his words started, and says:

"Does he—does he—think—*what* does he think! Tell him—tell him—" Then he sunk down in his chair limp and weak, and says, so as you could hardly hear him: "Go away—go away!"

The nigger looked scared, and cleared out, and we all felt—well, I don't know how we felt, but it was awful, with the old man panting there, and his eyes set and looking like a person that was dying. None of us could budge; but Benny she slid around soft, with her tears running down, and stood by his side, and nestled his old gray head up against her and begun to stroke it and pet it with her hands, and nodded to us to go away, and we done it, going out very quiet, like the dead was there.

Me and Tom struck out for the woods mighty solemn, and saying how different it was now to what it was last summer when we was here and everything was so peaceful and happy and everybody thought so much of Uncle Silas, and he was so cheerful and simple-hearted and pudd'nheaded and good—and now look at him. If he hadn't lost his mind he wasn't much short of it. That was what we allowed.

It was a most lovely day, now, and bright and sunshiny; and the further and further we went over the hill towards the prairie the lovelier and lovelier the trees and flowers got to be and the more it seemed strange and somehow wrong that there had to be trouble in such a world as this. And then all of a sudden I catched my breath and grabbed Tom's arm, and all my livers and lungs and things fell down into my legs.

"There it is!" I says. We jumped back behind a bush, shivering, and Tom says:

" 'Sh!—don't make a noise."

It was setting on a log right in the edge of the little prairie, thinking. I tried to get Tom to come away, but he wouldn't, and I dasn't budge by myself. He said we mightn't ever get another chance to see one, and he was going to look his fill at this one if he died for it. So I looked too, though it give me the fan-tods to do it. Tom he *had* to talk, but he talked low. He says:

"Poor Jakey, it's got all its things on, just as he said he would. *Now* you see what we wasn't certain about—its hair. It's not long, now, the way it was; it's got it cropped close to its head, the way he said he would. Huck, I never see anything look any more naturaler than what It does."

"Nor I neither," I says; "I'd recognize it anywheres."

"So would I. It looks perfectly solid and genuwyne, just the way it done before it died."

So we kept a-gazing. Pretty soon Tom says:

"Huck, there's something mighty curious about this one, don't you know? *It* oughtn't to be going around in the daytime."

"That's so, Tom—I never heard the like of it before."

"No, sir, they don't ever come out only at night—and then not till after twelve. There's something wrong about this one, now you mark my words. I don't believe it's got any right to be around in the daytime. But don't it look natural! Jake was going to play deef and dumb here, so the neighbors wouldn't know his voice. Do you reckon it would do that if we was to holler at it?"

"Lordy, Tom, don't talk so! If you was to holler at it I'd die in my tracks."

"Don't you worry, I ain't going to holler at it. Look, Huck, it's a-scratching its head—don't you see?"

"Well, what of it?"

"Why, this. What's the sense of it scratching its head? There ain't anything there to itch; its head is made out of fog or something like that, and *can't* itch. A fog can't itch; any fool knows that."

"Well, then, if it don't itch and can't itch, what in the nation is it scratching it for? Ain't it just habit, don't you reckon?"

"No, sir, I don't. I ain't a bit satisfied about the way this one acts. I've a blame good notion it's a bogus one—I have, as sure as I'm a-sitting here. Because, if it—Huck!"

"Well, what's the matter now?"

"*You can't see the bushes through it!*"

"Why, Tom, it's so, sure! It's as solid as a cow. I sort of begin to think—"

"Huck, it's biting off a chaw of tobacker! By George, *they* don't chaw—they hain't got anything to chaw *with*. Huck!"

"I'm a-listening."

"It ain't a ghost at all. It's Jake Dunlap his own self!"

"Oh, your granny!" I says.

"Huck Finn, did we find any corpse in the sycamores?"

"No."

"Or any sign of one?"

"No."

"Mighty good reason. Hadn't ever been any corpse there."

"Why, Tom, you know we heard—"

"Yes, we did—heard a howl or two. Does that prove anybody was killed? Course it don't. And we seen four men run, then this one come walking out and we took it for a ghost. No more ghost than you are. It was Jake Dunlap his own self, and it's Jake Dunlap now. He's been and got his hair cropped, the way he said he would, and he's playing himself for a stranger, just the same as he said he would. Ghost? Hum! —he's as sound as a nut."

Then I see it all, and how we had took too much for granted. I was powerful glad he didn't get killed, and so was Tom, and we wondered which he would like the best—for us to never let on to know him, or how? Tom reckoned the best way would be to go and ask him. So he started; but I kept a little behind, because I didn't know but it might be a ghost, after all. When Tom got to where he was, he says:

"Me and Huck's mighty glad to see you again, and you needn't be afeard we'll tell. And if you think it'll be safer for you if we don't let on to know you when we run across you, say the word and you'll see you can depend on us, and would ruther cut our hands off than get you into the least little bit of danger."

First off he looked surprised to see us, and not very glad, either; but as Tom went on he looked pleasanter, and when he was done he smiled, and nodded his head several times, and made signs with his hands, and says:

"Goo-goo—goo-goo," the way deef and dummies does.

Just then we see some of Steve Nickerson's people coming that lived t'other side of the prairie, so Tom says:

"You do it elegant; I never see anybody do it better. You're right; play it on us, too; play it on us same as the others; it'll keep you in practice and prevent you making blunders. We'll keep away from you and let on we don't know you, but any time we can be any help, you just let us know."

Then we loafed along past the Nickersons, and of course they asked if that was the new stranger yonder, and where'd he come from, and what was his name, and which communion was he, Babtis' or Methodis', and which politics, Whig or Democrat, and how long is he staying, and all them other questions that humans always asks when a stranger comes, and animals does too. But Tom said he warn't able to make anything out of deef and dumb signs, and the same with goo-gooing. Then we watched them go and bullyrag Jake; because we was pretty uneasy for him. Tom said it would take him days to get so he wouldn't forget he was a deef and dummy sometimes, and speak out before he thought. When we had watched long enough to see that Jake was getting along all right and working his signs very good, we loafed along again, allowing to strike the school-house about recess time, which was a three-mile tramp.

I was so disappointed not to hear Jake tell about the row in the sycamores, and how near he come to getting killed, that I couldn't seem to get over it, and Tom he felt the same, but said if we was in Jake's fix we would want to go careful and keep still and not take any chances.

The boys and girls was all glad to see us again, and we had a real good time all through recess. Coming to school the Henderson boys had come across the new deef and dummy and told the rest; so all the scholars was chuck full of him and couldn't talk about anything else, and was in a sweat to get a sight of him because they hadn't ever seen a deef and dummy in their lives, and it made a powerful excitement.

Tom said it was tough to have to keep mum now; said we would be heroes if we could come out and tell all we knowed; but after all, it was still more heroic to keep mum, there warn't two boys in a million could do it. That was Tom Sawyer's idea about it, and I reckoned there warn't anybody could better it.

CHAPTER 9

In the next two or three days Dummy he got to be powerful popular. He went associating around with the neighbors, and they made much of him, and was proud to have such a rattling curiosity amongst them. They had him to breakfast, they had him to dinner, they had him to supper; they kept him loaded up with hog and hominy, and warn't ever tired staring at him and wondering over him, and wishing they knowed more about him, he was so uncommon and romantic. His signs warn't no good; people couldn't understand them and he prob'ly couldn't himself, but he done a sight of goo-gooing, and so everybody was satisfied, and admired to hear him go it. He toted a piece of slate around, and a pencil; and people wrote questions on it and he wrote answers; but there warn't anybody could read his writing but Brace Dunlap. Brace said he couldn't read it very good, but he could manage to dig out the meaning most of the time. He said Dummy said he belonged away off somers and used to be well off, but got busted by swindlers which he had trusted, and was poor now, and hadn't any way to make a living.

Everybody praised Brace Dunlap for being so good to that stranger. He let him have a little log-cabin all to himself, and had his niggers take care of it, and fetch him all the vittles he wanted.

Dummy was at our house some, because old Uncle Silas was so afflicted himself, these days, that anybody else that was afflicted was a comfort to him. Me and Tom didn't let on that we had knowed him before, and he didn't let on that he had knowed us before. The family talked their troubles out before him the same as if he wasn't there, but we reckoned it wasn't any harm for him to hear what they said. Generly he didn't seem to notice, but sometimes he did.

Well, two or three days went along, and everybody got to getting uneasy about Jubiter Dunlap. Everybody was asking everybody if they had any idea what had become of him. No, they hadn't, they said; and they shook their heads and said there was something powerful strange about it. Another and another day went by; then there was a report got around that praps he was murdered. You bet it made a big stir! Everybody's tongue was clacking away after that. Saturday two or three gangs turned out and hunted the woods to see if they could run across his remainders. Me and Tom helped, and it was noble good times and exciting. Tom he was so brim full of it he couldn't eat nor rest. He said if we could find that corpse we would be celebrated, and more talked about than if we got drownded.

The others got tired and give it up; but not Tom Sawyer—that warn't his style. Saturday night he didn't sleep any, hardly, trying to think up a plan; and towards daylight in the morning he struck it. He snaked me out of bed and was all excited, and says—

"Quick, Huck, snatch on your clothes—I've got it! Blood-hound!"

In two minutes we was tearing up the river road in the dark towards the village. Old Jeff Hooker had a blood-hound, and Tom was going to borrow him. I says—

"The trail's too old, Tom—and, besides, it's rained, you know."

"It don't make any difference, Huck. If the body's hid in the woods anywhere around the hound will find it. If he's been murdered and buried, they wouldn't bury him deep, it ain't likely, and if the dog goes over the spot he'll scent him, sure. Huck, we're going to be celebrated, sure as you're born!"

He was just a-blazing; and whenever he got afire he was most likely to get afire all over. That was the way this time. In two minutes he had got it all ciphered out, and wasn't only just going to find the corpse—no, he was going to get on the track of that murderer and hunt *him* down, too; and not only that, but he was going to stick to him till—

"Well," I says, "you better find the corpse first; I reckon that's a-plenty for to-day. For all we know, there *ain't* any corpse and nobody hain't been murdered. That cuss could 'a' gone off somers and not been killed at all."

That gravelled him, and he says—

"Huck Finn, I never see such a person as you to want to spoil everything. As long as *you* can't see anything hopeful in a thing, you won't let anybody else. What good can it do you to throw cold water on that corpse and get up that selfish theory that there ain't been any murder? None in the world. I don't see how you can act so. I wouldn't treat you like that, and you know it. Here we've got a noble good opportunity to make a ruputation, and—"

"Oh, go ahead," I says; "I'm sorry, and I take it all back. I didn't mean nothing. Fix it any way you want it. *He* ain't any consequence to me. If he's killed, I'm as glad of it as you are; and if he—"

"I never said anything about being glad; I only—"

"Well, then, I'm as *sorry* as you are. Any way you druther have it, that is the way *I* druther have it. He—"

"There ain't any druthers *about* it, Huck Finn; nobody said anything about druthers. And as for—"

He forgot he was talking, and went tramping along, studying. He begun to get excited again, and pretty soon he says—

"Huck, it'll be the bulliest thing that ever happened if we find the body after everybody else has quit looking, and then go ahead and hunt up the murderer. It won't only be an honor to us, but it'll be an honor to Uncle Silas because it was us that done it. It'll set him up again, you see if it don't."

But old Jeff Hooker he throwed cold water on the whole business when we got to his blacksmith-shop and told him what we come for.

"You can take the dog," he says, "but you ain't a-going to find any corpse, because there ain't any corpse to find. Everybody's quit looking, and they're right. Soon as they come to think, they knowed there warn't no corpse. And I'll tell you for why. What does a person kill another person *for,* Tom Sawyer?—answer me that."

"Why, he—er—"

"Answer up! You ain't no fool. What does he kill him *for?*"

"Well, sometimes it's for revenge, and—"

"Wait. One thing at a time. Revenge, says you; and right you are. Now who ever had anything agin that poor trifling no-account? Who do you reckon would want to kill *him?*—that rabbit!"

Tom was stuck. I reckon he hadn't thought of a person having to have a *reason* for killing a person before, and now he sees it warn't likely anybody would have that much of a grudge against a lamb like Jubiter Dunlap. The blacksmith says, by-and-by—

"The revenge idea won't work, you see. Well, then, what's next? Robbery? B'gosh, that must 'a' been it, Tom! Yes, sirree, I reckon we've struck it this time. Some feller wanted his gallus-buckles, and so he—"

But it was so funny he busted out laughing, and just went *on* laughing and laughing and laughing till he was 'most dead, and Tom looked so put out and cheap that I knowed he was ashamed he had come, and he wished he hadn't. But old Hooker never let up on him. He raked up everything a person ever could want to kill another person about, and any fool could see they didn't any of them fit this case, and he just made no end of fun of the whole business and of the people that had been hunting the body; and he said—

"If they'd had any sense they'd 'a' knowed the lazy cuss slid out because he wanted a loafing spell after all this work. He'll come pottering back in a couple of weeks, and then how'll you fellers feel? But, laws bless you, take the dog, and go and hunt his remainders. Do, Tom."

Then he busted out, and had another of them forty-rod laughs of hisn. Tom couldn't back down after all this, so he said, "All right, unchain him;" and the blacksmith done it, and we started home and left that old man laughing yet.

It was a lovely dog. There ain't any dog that's got a lovelier disposition than a blood-hound, and this one knowed us and liked us. He capered and raced around ever so friendly, and powerful glad to be free and have a holiday; but Tom was so cut up he couldn't take any intrust in him, and said he wished he'd stopped and thought a minute before he ever started on such a fool errand. He said old Jeff Hooker would tell everybody, and we'd never hear the last of it.

So we loafed along home down the back lanes, feeling pretty glum and not talking. When we was passing the far corner of our tobacker-field we heard the dog set up a long howl in there, and we went to the place and he was scratching the ground with all his might, and every now and then canting up his head sideways and fetching another howl.

It was a long square, the shape of a grave; the rain had made it sink down and show the shape. The minute we come and stood there we looked at one another and never said a word. When the dog had dug down only a few inches he grabbed something and pulled it up, and it was an arm and a sleeve. Tom kind of gasped out, and says—

"Come away, Huck—it's found."

I just felt awful. We struck for the road and fetched the first men that come along. They got a spade at the crib and dug out the body, and you never see such an excitement. You couldn't make anything out of the face, but you didn't need to. Everybody said—

"Poor Jubiter; it's his clothes, to the last rag!"

Some rushed off to spread the news and tell the justice of the peace and have an inquest, and me and Tom lit out for the house. Tom was all afire and 'most out of breath when we come tearing in where Uncle Silas and Aunt Sally and Benny was. Tom sung out—

"Me and Huck's found Jubiter Dunlap's corpse all by ourselves with a blood-hound, after everybody else had quit hunting and given it up; and if it hadn't a been for us it never *would* 'a' been found; and he *was* murdered too—they done it with a club or something like that; and I'm going to start in and find the murderer, next, and I bet I'll do it!"

Aunt Sally and Benny sprung up pale and astonished, but Uncle Silas fell right forward out of his chair onto the floor and groans out—

"Oh, my God, you've found him *now!*"

CHAPTER 10

Them awful words froze us solid. We couldn't move hand or foot for as much as half a minute. Then we kind of come to, and lifted the old man up and got him into his chair, and Benny petted him and kissed him and tried to comfort him, and poor old Aunt Sally she done the same; but, poor things, they was so broke up and scared and knocked out of their right minds that they didn't hardly know what they was about. With Tom it was awful; it 'most petrified him to think maybe he had got his uncle into a thousand times more trouble than ever, and maybe it wouldn't ever happened if he hadn't been so ambitious to get celebrated, and let the corpse alone the way the others done. But pretty soon he sort of come to himself again and says–

"Uncle Silas, don't you say another word like that. It's dangerous, and there ain't a shadder of truth in it."

Aunt Sally and Benny was thankful to hear him say that, and they said the same; but the old man he wagged his head sorrowful and hopeless, and the tears run down his face, and he says–

"No–I done it; poor Jubiter, I done it!"

It was dreadful to hear him say it. Then he went on and told about it, and said it happened the day me and Tom come–along about sundown. He said Jubiter pestered him and aggravated him till he was so mad he just sort of lost his mind and grabbed up a stick and hit him over the head with all his might, and Jubiter dropped in his tracks. Then he was scared and sorry, and got down on his knees and lifted his head up, and begged him to speak and say he wasn't dead; and before long he come to, and when he see who it was holding his head, he jumped like he was 'most scared to death, and cleared the fence and tore into the woods, and was gone. So he hoped he wasn't hurt bad.

"But laws," he says, "it was only just fear that gave him that last little spurt of strength, and of course it soon played out and he laid down in the bush, and there wasn't anybody to help him, and he died."

Then the old man cried and grieved, and said he was a murderer and the mark of Cain was on him, and he had disgraced his family and was going to be found out and hung. But Tom said–

"No, you ain't going to be found out. You *didn't* kill him. *One* lick wouldn't kill him. Somebody else done it."

"Oh yes," he says, "I done it–nobody else. Who else had anything against him? Who else *could* have anything against him?"

He looked up kind of like he hoped some of us could mention somebody that could have a grudge against that harmless no-account, but of course it warn't no use—he *had* us; we couldn't say a word. He noticed that, and he saddened down again, and I never see a face so miserable and so pitiful to see. Tom had a sudden idea, and says—

"But hold on!—somebody *buried* him. Now who—"

He shut off sudden. I knowed the reason. It give me the cold shudders when he said them words, because right away I remembered about us seeing Uncle Silas prowling around with a long-handled shovel away in the night that night. And I knowed Benny seen him, too, because she was talking about it one day. The minute Tom shut off he changed the subject and went to begging Uncle Silas to keep mum, and the rest of us done the same, and said he *must,* and said it wasn't his business to tell on himself, and if he kept mum nobody would ever know; but if it was found out and any harm come to him it would break the family's hearts and kill them, and yet never do anybody any good. So at last he promised. We was all of us more comfortable, then, and went to work to cheer up the old man. We told him all he'd got to do was to keep still, and it wouldn't be long till the whole thing would blow over and be forgot. We all said there wouldn't anybody ever suspect Uncle Silas, nor ever dream of such a thing, he being so good and kind, and having such a good character; and Tom says, cordial and hearty, he says—

"Why, just look at it a minute; just consider. Here is Uncle Silas, all these years a preacher—at his own expense, all these years doing good with all his might and every way he can think of—at his own expense, all the time; always been loved by everybody, and respected; always been peaceable and minding his own business, the very last man in this whole deestrict to touch a person, and everybody knows it. Suspect *him?* Why, it ain't any more possible than—"

"By authority of the State of Arkansaw, I arrest you for the murder of Jubiter Dunlap!" shouts the sheriff at the door.

It was awful. Aunt Sally and Benny flung themselves at Uncle Silas, screaming and crying, and hugged him and hung to him, and Aunt Sally said go away, she wouldn't ever give him up, they shouldn't have him, and the niggers they come crowding and crying to the door and—well, I couldn't stand it; it was enough to break a person's heart; so I got out.

They took him up to the little one-horse jail in the village, and we all went along to tell him good-by; and Tom was feeling elegant, and says to me, "We'll have a most noble good time and heaps of danger some dark night getting him out of there, Huck, and it'll be talked about everywheres and we will be celebrated;" but the old man busted that scheme up the minute he whispered to him about it. He said no, it was his duty to stand whatever the law done to him, and he would stick to the jail plumb through to the end, even if there warn't no door to it. It disappointed Tom and gravelled him a good deal, but he had to put up with it.

But he felt responsible and bound to get his uncle Silas free; and he told Aunt Sally, the last thing, not to worry, because he was going to turn in and work night and day and beat this game and fetch Uncle Silas out innocent; and she was very loving to him and thanked him and said she knowed he would do his very best. And she told us to help Benny take care of the house and the children, and then we had a good-by cry all around and went back to the farm, and left her there to live with the jailer's wife a month till the trial in October.

CHAPTER 11

Well, that was a hard month on us all. Poor Benny, she kept up the best she could, and me and Tom tried to keep things cheerful there at the house, but it kind of went for nothing, as you may say. It was the same up at the jail. We went up every day to see the old people, but it was awful dreary, because the old man warn't sleeping much, and was walking in his sleep considerable, and so he got to looking fagged and miserable, and his mind got shaky, and we all got afraid his troubles would break him down and kill him. And whenever we tried to persuade him to feel cheerfuler, he only shook his head and said if we only knowed what it was to carry around a murderer's load on your heart we wouldn't talk that way. Tom and all of us kept telling him it *wasn't* murder, but just accidental killing, but it never made any difference—it was murder, and he wouldn't have it any other way. He actu'ly begun to come out plain and square towards trial-time and acknowledge that he *tried* to kill the man. Why, that was awful, you know. It made things seem fifty times as dreadful, and there warn't no more comfort for Aunt Sally and Benny. But he promised he wouldn't say a word about his murder when others was around, and we was glad of that.

Tom Sawyer racked the head off of himself all that month trying to plan some way out for Uncle Silas, and many's the night he kept me up 'most all night with this kind of tiresome work, but he couldn't seem to get on the right track no way. As for me, I reckoned a body might as well give it up, it all looked so blue and I was so downhearted; but he wouldn't. He stuck to the business right along, and went on planning and thinking and ransacking his head.

So at last the trial come on, towards the middle of October, and we was all in the court. The place was jammed of course. Poor old Uncle Silas, he looked more like a dead person than a live one, his eyes was so hollow and he looked so thin and so mournful. Benny she set on one side of him and Aunt Sally on the other, and they had veils on, and was full of trouble. But Tom he set by our lawyer, and had his finger in everywheres, of course. The lawyer let him, and the judge let him. He 'most took the business out of the lawyer's hands sometimes; which was well enough, because that was only a mud-turtle of a back-settlement lawyer and didn't know enough to come in when it rains, as the saying is.

They swore in the jury, and then the lawyer for the prostitution got up and begun. He made a terrible speech against the old man, that made him moan and groan, and made Benny and Aunt Sally cry. The way *he* told about the murder kind of knocked us all stupid it was so different from the old man's tale. He said he was going to prove that Uncle Silas was *seen* to kill Jubiter Dunlap by two good witnesses, and done it deliberate, and *said* he was going to kill him the very minute he hit him with the club; and they seen him hide Jubiter in the bushes, and they seen that Jubiter was stone-dead. And said Uncle Silas come later and lugged Jubiter down into the tobacker-field, and two men seen him do it. And said Uncle Silas turned out, away in the night, and buried Jubiter, and a man seen him at it.

I says to myself, poor old Uncle Silas has been lying about it because he reckoned nobody seen him and he couldn't bear to break Aunt Sally's heart and Benny's; and right he was: as for me, I would 'a' lied the same way, and so would anybody that had any feeling, to save them such misery and sorrow which *they* warn't no ways responsible for. Well, it made our lawyer look pretty sick; and it knocked Tom silly, too, for a little spell, but then he braced up and let on that he warn't worried—but I knowed he *was,* all the same. And the people—my, but it made a stir amongst them!

And when that lawyer was done telling the jury what he was going to prove, he set down and begun to work his witnesses.

First, he called a lot of them to show that there was bad blood betwixt Uncle Silas and the diseased; and they told how they had heard Uncle Silas threaten the diseased, at one time and another, and how it got worse and worse and everybody was talking about it, and how diseased got afraid of his life, and told two or three of them he was certain Uncle Silas would up and kill him some time or another.

Tom and our lawyer asked them some questions; but it warn't no use, they stuck to what they said.

Next, they called up Lem Beebe, and he took the stand. It come into my mind, then, how Lem and Jim Lane had come along talking, that time, about borrowing a dog or something from Jubiter Dunlap; and that brought up the blackberries and the lantern; and that brought up Bill and Jack Withers, and how *they* passed by, talking about a nigger stealing Uncle Silas's corn; and that fetched up our old ghost that come along about the same time and scared us so—and here *he* was too, and a privileged character, on accounts of his being deef and dumb and a stranger, and they had fixed him a chair inside the railing, where he could cross his legs and be comfortable, whilst the other people was all in a jam so they couldn't hardly breathe. So it all come back to me just the way it was that day; and it made me mournful to think how pleasant it was up to then, and how miserable ever since.

Lem Beebe, sworn, said: "I was a-coming along, that day, second of September, and Jim Lane was with me, and it was towards sundown, and we heard loud talk, like quarrelling, and we was very close, only the hazel bushes between (that's along the fence); and we heard a voice say, 'I've told you more'n once I'd kill you,' and knowed it was this prisoner's voice; and then we see a club come up above the bushes and down out of sight again, and heard a smashing thump and then a groan or two; and then we crope soft to where we could see, and there laid Jubiter Dunlap dead, and this prisoner standing over him with the club; and the next he hauled the dead man into a clump of bushes and hid him, and then we stooped low, to be out of sight, and got away."

Well, it was awful. It kind of froze everybody's blood to hear it, and the house was 'most as still whilst he was telling it as if there warn't nobody in it. And when he was done, you could hear them gasp and sigh, all over the house, and look at one another the same as to say, "Ain't it perfectly terrible—ain't it awful!"

Now happened a thing that astonished me. All the time the first witnesses was proving the bad blood and the threats and all that, Tom Sawyer was alive and laying for them; and the minute they was through, he went for them, and done his level best to catch them in lies and spile their testimony. But now, how different. When Lem first begun to talk, and never said anything about speaking to Jubiter or

trying to borrow a dog off of him, he was all alive and laying for Lem, and you could see he was getting ready to cross-question him to death pretty soon, and then I judged him and me would go on the stand by-and-by and tell what we heard him and Jim Lane say. But the next time I looked at Tom I got the cold shivers. Why, he was in the brownest study you ever see—miles and miles away. He warn't hearing a word Lem Beebe was saying; and when he got through he was still in that brown-study, just the same. Our lawyer joggled him, and then he looked up startled, and says, "Take the witness if you want him. Lemme alone—I want to think."

Well, that beat me. I couldn't understand it. And Benny and her mother—oh, they looked sick, they was so troubled. They shoved their veils to one side and tried to get his eye, but it warn't any use, and I couldn't get his eye either. So the mud-turtle he tackled the witness, but it didn't amount to nothing; and he made a mess of it.

Then they called up Jim Lane, and he told the very same story over again, exact. Tom never listened to this one at all, but set there thinking and thinking, miles and miles away. So the mud-turtle went in alone again and come out just as flat as he done before. The lawyer for the prostitution looked very comfortable, but the judge looked disgusted. You see, Tom was just the same as a regular lawyer, nearly, because it was Arkansaw law for a prisoner to choose anybody he wanted to help his lawyer, and Tom had had Uncle Silas shove him into the case, and now he was botching it and you could see the judge didn't like it much.

All that the mud-turtle got out of Lem and Jim was this: he asked them—

"Why didn't you go and tell what you saw?"

"We was afraid we would get mixed up in it ourselves. And we was just starting down the river a-hunting for all the week besides; but as soon as we come back we found out they'd been searching for the body, so then we went and told Brace Dunlap all about it."

"When was that?"

"Saturday night, September 9th."

The judge he spoke up and says—

"Mr. Sheriff, arrest these two witnesses on suspicions of being accessionary after the fact to the murder."

The lawyer for the prostitution jumps up all excited, and says—

"Your honor! I protest against this extraordi—"

"Set down!" says the judge, pulling his bowie and laying it on his pulpit. "I beg you to respect the Court."

So he done it. Then he called Bill Withers.

Bill Withers, sworn, said: "I was coming along about sundown, Saturday, September 2d, by the prisoner's field, and my brother Jack was with me, and we seen a man toting off something heavy on his back and allowed it was a nigger stealing corn; we couldn't see distinct; next we made out that it was one man carrying another; and the way it hung, so kind of limp, we judged it was somebody that was drunk; and by the man's walk we said it was Parson Silas, and we judged he had found Sam Cooper drunk in the road, which he was always trying to reform him, and was toting him out of danger."

It made the people shiver to think of poor old Uncle Silas toting off the diseased down to the place in his tobacker-field where the dog dug up the body, but there warn't much sympathy around amongst the faces, and I heard one cuss say, "'Tis the coldest-blooded work I ever struck, lugging a murdered man around like that, and going to bury him like a animal, and him a preacher at that."

Tom he went on thinking, and never took no notice; so our lawyer took the witness and done the best he could, and it was plenty poor enough.

Then Jack Withers he come on the stand and told the same tale, just like Bill done.

And after him comes Brace Dunlap, and he was looking very mournful, and most crying; and there was a rustle and a stir all around, and everybody got ready to listen, and lots of the women folks said, "Poor cretur, poor cretur," and you could see a many of them wiping their eyes.

Brace Dunlap, sworn, said: "I was in considerable trouble a long time about my poor brother, but I reckoned things warn't near so bad as he made out, and I couldn't make myself believe anybody would have the heart to hurt a poor harmless cretur like that"—[by jings, I was sure I seen Tom give a kind of a faint little start, and then look disappointed again]—"and you know I *couldn't* think a preacher would hurt him—it warn't natural to think such an onlikely thing—so I never paid much attention, and now I sha'n't ever, ever forgive myself; for if I had a done different, my poor brother would be with me this day, and not laying yonder murdered, and him so harmless." He kind of broke down there and choked up, and waited to get his voice; and people all around said the most pitiful things, and women cried; and it was very still in there, and solemn, and old Uncle Silas, poor thing, he give a groan right out so everybody heard him. Then Brace he went on, "Saturday, September 2d, he didn't come home to supper. By-

and-by I got a little uneasy, and one of my niggers went over to this prisoner's place, but come back and said he warn't there. So I got uneasier and uneasier, and couldn't rest. I went to bed, but I couldn't sleep; and turned out, away late in the night, and went wandering over to this prisoner's place and all around about there a good while, hoping I would run across my poor brother, and never knowing he was out of his troubles and gone to a better shore—" So he broke down and choked up again, and most all the women was crying now. Pretty soon he got another start and says: "But it warn't no use; so at last I went home and tried to get some sleep, but couldn't. Well, in a day or two everybody was uneasy, and they got to talking about this prisoner's threats, and took to the idea, which I didn't take no stock in, that my brother was murdered; so they hunted around and tried to find his body, but couldn't and give it up. And so I reckoned he was gone off somers to have a little peace, and would come back to us when his troubles was kind of healed. But late Saturday night, the 9th, Lem Beebe and Jim Lane come to my house and told me all—told me the whole awful 'sassination, and my heart was broke. And *then* I remembered something that hadn't took no hold of me at the time, because reports said this prisoner had took to walking in his sleep and doing all kind of things of no consequence, not knowing what he was about. I will tell you what that thing was that come back into my memory. Away late that awful Saturday night when I was wandering around about this prisoner's place, grieving and troubled, I was down by the corner of the tobacker-field and I heard a sound like digging in a gritty soil; and I crope nearer and peeped through the vines that hung on the rail fence and seen this prisoner *shovelling*—shovelling with a long-handled shovel—heaving earth into a big hole that was most filled up; his back was to me, but it was bright moonlight and I knowed him by his old green baize work-gown with a splattery white patch in the middle of the back like somebody had hit him with a snowball. *He was burying the man he'd murdered!*"

And he slumped down in his chair crying and sobbing, and 'most everybody in the house busted out wailing, and crying, and saying, "Oh, it's awful—awful—horrible!" and there was a most tremenduous excitement, and you couldn't hear yourself think; and right in the midst of it up jumps old Uncle Silas, white as a sheet, and sings out—

"It's true, every word—I murdered him in cold blood!"

By Jackson, it petrified them! People rose up wild all over the house, straining and staring for a better look at him, and the judge was hammering with his mallet and the sheriff yelling "Order—order in the court—order!"

And all the while the old man stood there a-quaking and his eyes a-burning, and not looking at his wife and daughter, which was clinging to him and begging him to keep still, but pawing them off with his hands and saying he *would* clear his black soul from crime, he *would* heave off this load that was more than he could bear, and he *wouldn't* bear it another hour! And then he raged right along with his awful tale, everybody a-staring and gasping, judge, jury, lawyers, and everybody, and Benny and Aunt Sally crying their hearts out. And by George, Tom Sawyer never looked at him once! Never once—just set there gazing with all his eyes at something else, I couldn't tell what. And so the old man raged right along, pouring his words out like a stream of fire:

"I killed him! I am guilty! But I never had the notion in my life to hurt him or harm him, spite of all them lies about my threatening him, till the very minute I raised the club—then my heart went cold!—then the pity all went out of it, and I struck to kill! In that one moment all my wrongs come into my mind; all the insults that that man and the scoundrel his brother, there, had put upon me, and how they laid in together to ruin me with the people, and take away my good name, and *drive* me to some deed that would destroy me and my family that hadn't ever done *them* no harm, so help me God! And they done it in a mean revenge—for why? Because my innocent pure girl here at my side wouldn't marry that rich, insolent, ignorant coward, Brace Dunlap, who's been snivelling here over a brother he never cared a brass farthing for"—[I see Tom give a jump and look glad *this* time, to a dead certainty]—"and in that moment I've told you about, I forgot my God and remembered only my heart's bitterness, God forgive me, and I struck to kill. In one second I was miserably sorry—oh, filled with remorse; but I thought of my poor family, and I *must* hide what I'd done for their sakes; and I did hide that corpse in the bushes; and presently I carried it to the tobacker-field; and in the deep night I went with my shovel and buried it where—"

Up jumps Tom and shouts—

"*Now*, I've got it!" and waves his hand, oh, ever so fine and starchy, towards the old man, and says—

"Set down! A murder *was* done, but you never had no hand in it!"

Well, sir, you could a heard a pin drop. And the old man he sunk down kind of bewildered in his seat and Aunt Sally and Benny didn't know it, because they was so astonished and staring at Tom with their mouths open and not knowing what they was about. And the whole house the same. *I* never seen people look so helpless and tangled up, and I hain't ever seen eyes bug out and gaze without a blink the way theirn did. Tom says, perfectly ca'm—

"Your honor, may I speak?"

"For God's sake, yes—go on!" says the judge, so astonished and mixed up he didn't know what he was about hardly.

Then Tom he stood there and waited a second or two—that was for to work up an "effect," as he calls it—then he started in just as ca'm as ever, and says:

For about two weeks, now, there's been a little bill sticking on the front of this court-house offering two thousand dollars reward for a couple of big di'monds—stole at St. Louis. Them di'monds is worth twelve thousand dollars. But never mind about that till I get to it. Now about this murder. I will tell you all about it—how it happened—who done it—every *de*tail."

You could see everybody nestle, now, and begin to listen for all they was worth.

"This man here, Brace Dunlap, that's been snivelling so about his dead brother that *you* know he never cared a straw for, wanted to marry that young girl there, and she wouldn't have him. So he told Uncle Silas he would make him sorry. Uncle Silas knowed how powerful he was, and how little chance he had against such a man, and he was scared and worried, and done everything he could think of to smooth him over and get him to be good to him: he even took his no-account brother Jubiter on the farm and give him wages and stinted his own family to pay them; and Jubiter done everything his brother could contrive to insult Uncle Silas, and fret and worry him, and try to drive Uncle Silas into doing him a hurt, so as to injure Uncle Silas with the people. And it done it. Everybody turned against him and said the meanest kind of things about him, and it graduly broke his heart—yes, and he was so worried and distressed that often he warn't hardly in his right mind.

"Well, on that Saturday that we've had so much trouble about, two of these witnesses here, Lem Beebe and Jim Lane, come along by where Uncle Silas and Jubiter Dunlap was at work—and that much of what they've said is true, the rest is lies. They didn't hear Uncle Silas say he would kill Jubiter; they didn't hear no blow struck; they didn't see no dead man, and they didn't see Uncle Silas hide anything in the bushes. Look at them now—how they set there, wishing they hadn't been so handy with their tongues; anyway, they'll wish it before I get done.

"That same Saturday evening Bill and Jack Withers *did* see one man lugging off another one. That much of what they said is true, and the rest is lies. First off they thought it was a nigger stealing Uncle Silas's corn—you notice it makes them look silly, now, to find out somebody overheard them say that. That's because they found out by-and-by who it was that was doing the lugging, and *they* know best why they swore here that they took it for Uncle Silas by the gait—which it *wasn't*, and they knowed it when they swore to that lie.

"A man out in the moonlight *did* see a murdered person put under ground in the tobacker-field—but it wasn't Uncle Silas that done the burying. He was in his bed at that very time.

"Now, then, before I go on, I want to ask you if you've ever noticed this: that people, when they're thinking deep, or when they're worried, are most always doing something with their hands, and they don't know it, and don't notice what it is their hands are doing. Some stroke their chins; some stroke their noses; some stroke up *under* their chin with their hand; some twirl a chain, some fumble a button, then there's some that draws a figure or a letter with their finger on their cheek, or under their chin or on their under lip. That's *my* way. When I'm restless, or worried, or thinking hard, I draw capital V's on my cheek or on my under lip or under my chin, and never anything *but* capital V's—and half the time I don't notice it and don't know I'm doing it."

That was odd. That is just what I do; only I make an O. And I could see people nodding to one another, same as they do when they mean "*that's* so."

"Now then, I'll go on. That same Saturday—no, it was the night before—there was a steamboat laying at Flagler's Landing, forty miles above here, and it was raining and storming like the nation. And there was a thief aboard, and he had them two big di'monds that's advertised out here on this court-house door; and he slipped ashore with his hand-bag and struck out into the dark and the storm, and he was a-hoping he could get to this town all right and be safe. But he had two pals aboard the boat, hiding, and he knowed they was going to kill him the first chance they got and take the di'monds; because all three stole them, and then this fellow he got hold of them and skipped.

"Well, he hadn't been gone more'n ten minutes before his pals found it out, and they jumped ashore and lit out after him. Prob'ly they burnt matches and found his tracks. Anyway, they dogged along after him all day Saturday and kept out of his sight; and towards sundown he come to the bunch of sycamores down by Uncle Silas's field, and he went in there to get a disguise out of his hand-bag and put it on before he showed himself here in the town—and mind you he done that just a little after the time that Uncle Silas was hitting Jubiter Dunlap over the head with a club—for he *did* hit him.

"But the minute the pals see that thief slide into the bunch of sycamores, they jumped out of the bushes and slid in after him.

"They fell on him and clubbed him to death.

"Yes, for all he screamed and howled so, they never had no mercy on him, but clubbed him to death. And two men that was running along the road heard him yelling that way, and they made a rush into the sycamore bunch—which was where they was bound for, anyway—and when the pals saw them they lit out and the two new men after them a-chasing them as tight as they could go. But only a minute or two —then these two new men slipped back very quiet into the sycamores.

"*Then* what did they do? I will tell you what they done. They found where the thief had got his disguise out of his carpet-sack to put on; so one of them strips and puts on that disguise."

Tom waited a little here, for some more "effect"—then he says, very deliberate—

"The man that put on that dead man's disguise was—*Jubiter Dunlap!*"

"Great Scott!" everybody shouted, all over the house, and old Uncle Silas he looked perfectly astonished.

"Yes, it was Jubiter Dunlap. Not dead, you see. Then they pulled off the dead man's boots and put Jubiter Dunlap's old ragged shoes on the corpse and put the corpse's boots on Jubiter Dunlap. Then Jubiter Dunlap stayed where he was, and the other man lugged the dead body off in the twilight; and after midnight he went to Uncle Silas's house, and took his old green work-robe off of the peg where it always hangs in the passage betwixt the house and the kitchen and put it on, and stole the long-handled shovel and went off down into the tobacker-field and buried the murdered man."

He stopped, and stood a half a minute. Then—

"And who do you reckon the murdered man *was*? It was—*Jake* Dunlap, the long-lost burglar!"

"Great Scott!"

"And the man that buried him was—*Brace* Dunlap, his brother!"

"Great Scott!"

"And who do you reckon is this mowing idiot here that's letting on all these weeks to be a deef and dumb stranger? It's—*Jubiter* Dunlap!"

My land, they all busted out in a howl, and you never see the like of that excitement since the day you was born. And Tom he made a jump for Jubiter and snaked off his goggles and his false whiskers, and there was the murdered man, sure enough, just as alive as anybody! And Aunt Sally and Benny they went to hugging and crying and kissing and smothering old Uncle Silas to that degree he was more muddled and confused and mushed up in his mind than he ever was before, and that is saying considerable. And next, people begun to yell—

"Tom Sawyer! Tom Sawyer! Shut up everybody, and let him go on! Go on, Tom Sawyer!"

Which made him feel uncommon bully, for it was nuts for Tom Sawyer to be a public character thataway, and a hero, as he calls it. So when it was all quiet, he says—

"There ain't much left, only this. When that man there, Brace Dunlap, had most worried the life and sense out of Uncle Silas till at last he plum lost his mind and hit this other blatherskite his brother with a club, I reckon he seen his chance. Jubiter broke for the woods to hide, and I reckon the game was for him to slide out, in the night, and leave the country. Then Brace would make everybody believe Uncle Silas killed him and hid his body somers; and that would ruin Uncle Silas and drive *him* out of the country—hang him, maybe; I dunno. But when they found their dead brother in the sycamores without knowing him, because he was so battered up, they see they had a better thing; disguise *both* and bury Jake and dig him up presently all dressed up in Jubiter's clothes, and hire Jim Lane and Bill Withers and the others to swear to some handy lies—which they done. And there they set, now, and I told them they would be looking sick before I got done, and that is the way they're looking now.

"Well, me and Huck Finn here, we come down on the boat with the thieves, and the dead one told us all about the di'monds, and said the others would murder him if they got the chance; and we was going to help him all we could. We was bound for the sycamores when we heard them killing him in there; but we was in there in the early morning after the storm and allowed nobody hadn't been killed, after all. And when we see Jubiter Dunlap here spreading around in the very same disguise Jake told us *he* was going to wear, we thought it was Jake his own self—and he was goo-gooing deef and dumb, and *that* was according to agreement.

"Well, me and Huck went on hunting for the corpse after the others quit, and we found it. And was proud, too; but Uncle Silas he knocked us crazy by telling us *he* killed the man. So we was mighty sorry we found the body, and was bound to save Uncle Silas's neck if we could; and it was going to be tough work, too, because he wouldn't let us break him out of prison the way we done with our old nigger Jim.

"I done everything I could the whole month to think up some way to save Uncle Silas, but I couldn't strike a thing. So when we come into court to-day I come empty, and couldn't see no chance anywheres. But by-and-by I had a glimpse of something that set me thinking—just a little wee glimpse—only that, and not enough to make sure; but it set me thinking hard—and *watching*, when I was only letting on to think; and by-and-by, sure enough, when Uncle Silas was piling out that stuff about *him* killing Jubiter Dunlap, I catched that glimpse again, and this time I jumped up and shut down the proceedings, because I *knowed* Jubiter Dunlap was a-setting here before me. I knowed him by a thing which I seen him do—and I remembered it. I'd seen him do it when I was here a year ago."

He stopped then, and studied a minute—laying for an "effect"—I knowed it perfectly well. Then he turned off like he was going to leave the platform, and says, kind of lazy and indifferent—

"Well, I believe that is all."

Why, you never heard such a howl!—and it come from the whole house:

"What *was* it you seen him do? Stay where you are, you little devil! You think you are going to work a body up till his mouth's a-watering and stop there? What *was* it he done?"

That was it, you see—he just done it to get an "effect"; you couldn't 'a' pulled him off of that platform with a yoke of oxen.

"Oh, it wasn't anything much," he says. "I seen him looking a little excited when he found Uncle Silas was actuly fixing to hang himself for a murder that warn't ever done; and he got more and more nervous and worried, I a-watching him sharp but not seeming to look at him —and all of a sudden his hands begun to work and fidget, and pretty soon his left crept up and *his finger drawed a cross on his cheek*, and then I *had* him!"

Well, then they ripped and howled and stomped and clapped their hands till Tom Sawyer was that proud and happy he didn't know what to do with himself. And then the judge he looked down over his pulpit and says—

"My boy, did you *see* all the various details of this strange conspiracy and tragedy that you've been describing?"

"No, your honor, I didn't see any of them."

"Didn't see any of them! Why, you've told the whole history straight through, just the same as if you'd seen it with your eyes. How did you manage that?"

Tom says, kind of easy and comfortable—

"Oh, just noticing the evidence and piecing this and that together, your honor; just an ordinary little bit of detective work; anybody could 'a' done it."

"Nothing of the kind! Not two in a million could 'a' done it. You are a very remarkable boy."

Then they let go and give Tom another smashing round, and he —well, he wouldn't 'a' sold out for a silver mine. Then the judge says—

"But are you certain you've got this curious history straight?"

Perfectly, your honor. Here is Brace Dunlap—let him deny his share of it if he wants to take the chance; I'll engage to make him wish he hadn't said anything. . . . Well, you see *he's* pretty quiet. And his brother's pretty quiet, and them four witnesses that lied so and got paid for it, they're pretty quiet. And as for Uncle Silas, it ain't any use for him to put in his oar, I wouldn't believe him under oath!"

Well, sir, that fairly made them shout; and even the judge he let go and laughed. Tom he was just feeling like a rainbow. When they was done laughing he looks up at the judge and says—

"Your honor, there's a thief in this house."

"A thief?"

"Yes, sir. And he's got them twelve-thousand-dollar di'monds on him."

By gracious, but it made a stir! Everybody went shouting—

"Which is him? which is him? p'int him out!"

And the judge says—

"Point him out, my lad. Sheriff, you will arrest him. Which one is it?"

Tom says—

"This late dead man here—Jubiter Dunlap."

Then there was another thundering let-go of astonishment and excitement; but Jubiter, which was astonished enough before, was just fairly putrefied with astonishment this time. And he spoke up, about half crying, and says—

"Now *that's* a lie! Your honor, it ain't fair; I'm plenty bad enough without that. I done the other things—Brace he put me up to it, and persuaded me, and promised he'd make me rich, some day, and I done it, and I'm sorry I done it, and I wisht I hadn't; but I hain't stole no di'monds, and I hain't *got* no di'monds; I wisht I may never stir if it ain't so. The sheriff can search me and see."

Tom says—

"Your honor, it wasn't right to call him a thief, and I'll let up on that a little. He did steal the di'monds, but he didn't know it. He stole them from his brother Jake when he was laying dead, after Jake had stole them from the other thieves; but Jubiter didn't know he was stealing them; and he's been swelling around here with them a month; yes, sir, twelve thousand dollars' worth of di'monds on him—all that riches, and going around here every day just like a poor man. Yes, your honor, he's got them on him now."

The judge spoke up and says—

"Search him, sheriff."

Well, sir, the sheriff he ransacked him high and low, and everywhere: searched his hat, socks, seams, boots, everything—and Tom he stood there quiet, laying for another of them effects of hisn. Finally the sheriff he give it up, and everybody looked disappointed, and Jubiter says—

"There, now! what'd I tell you?"

And the judge says—

"It appears you were mistaken this time, my boy."

Then Tom he took an attitude and let on to be studying with all his might, and scratching his head. Then all of a sudden he glanced up chipper, and says—

"Oh, now I've got it! I'd forgot."

Which was a lie, and I knowed it. Then he says—

"Will somebody be good enough to lend me a little small screw-driver? There was one in your brother's hand-bag that you smouched, Jubiter, but I reckon you didn't fetch it with you."

"No, I didn't. I didn't want it, and I give it away."

"That was because you didn't know what it was for."

Jubiter had his boots on again, by now, and when the thing Tom wanted was passed over the people's heads till it got to him, he says to Jubiter—

"Put up your foot on this chair." And he kneeled down and begun to unscrew the heel-plate, everybody watching; and when he got that big di'mond out of that boot-heel and held it up and let it flash and blaze and squirt sunlight ever which away, it just took everybody's breath; and Jubiter he looked so sick and sorry you never see the like of it. And when Tom held up the other di'mond he looked sorrier than ever. Land! he was thinking how he would 'a' skipped out and been rich and independent in a foreign land if he'd only had the luck to guess what the screw-driver was in the carpet-bag for.

Well, it was a most exciting time, take it all around, and Tom got cords of glory. The judge took the di'monds, and stood up in his pulpit, and cleared his throat, and shoved his spectacles back on his head, and says—

"I'll keep them and notify the owners; and when they send for them it will be a real pleasure to me to hand you the two thousand dollars, for you've earned the money—yes, and you've earned the deepest and most sincerest thanks of this community besides, for lifting a wronged and innocent family out of ruin and shame, and saving a good and honorable man from a felon's death, and for exposing to infamy and the punishment of the law a cruel and odious scoundrel and his miserable creatures!"

Well, sir, if there'd been a brass band to bust out some music, then, it would 'a' been just the perfectest thing I ever see, and Tom Sawyer he said the same.

Then the sheriff he nabbed Brace Dunlap and his crowd, and by-and-by next month the judge had them up for trial and jailed the whole lot. And everybody crowded back to Uncle Silas's little old church, and was ever so loving and kind to him and the family and couldn't do enough for them; and Uncle Silas he preached them the blamedest jumbledest idiotic sermons you ever struck, and would tangle you up so you couldn't find your way home in daylight; but the people never let on but what they thought it was the clearest and brightest and elegantest sermons that ever was; and they would set there and cry, for love and pity; but, by George, they give me the jim-jams and the fan-tods and caked up what brains I had, and turned them solid; but by-and-by they loved the old man's intellects back into him again and he was as sound in his skull as ever he was, which ain't no flattery, I reckon. And so the whole family was as happy as birds, and nobody could be gratefuler and lovinger than what they was to Tom Sawyer; and the same to me, though I hadn't done nothing. And when the two thousand dollars come, Tom give half of it to me, and never told anybody so, which didn't surprise me, because I knowed him.